Mike Ashley is a leading authority on horror, fantasy and science fiction. Since 1974 he has written and edited over thirty books, including *Weird Legacies*, *Souls in Metal*, *Mrs Gaskell's Tales of Mystery and Horror*, *Jewels of Wonder*, *Best of British SF* (2 vols.), *Who's Who in Horror and Fantasy Fiction*, *The Mammoth Book of Short Horror Novels*, *The Pendragon Chronicles* and *The Camelot Chronicles*.

He has also contributed widely to fantasy magazines and encyclopedias in Britain and America, including *Amazing Stories*, *Locus* and *Twilight Zone Magazine*. In 1993 he published the first "Chronicles of Crime", *The Mammoth Book of Historical Whodunnits*, which has proved tremendously popular.

# The Mammoth Book of
# HISTORICAL
# DETECTIVES

### Edited by
### Mike Ashley

**Carroll & Graf Publishers, Inc.**
New York

Carroll & Graf Publishers, Inc.
260 Fifth Avenue
New York
NY 10001

This collection first published in the UK by Robinson
Publishing 1995

First Carroll & Graf edition 1995

Collection and introduction copyright ©
Mike Ashley 1995

ISBN 0–7867–0214–1

Printed and bound in the EC

10 9 8 7 6 5 4 3 2

# Contents

# Sources and Acknowledgements

The compilation of this anthology and the publication of the previous volume (*The Mammoth Book of Historical Whodunnits*) seem to have encouraged much response. My thanks to all of those who responded to the previous volume with ideas and suggestions (all, I might add, of a positive nature), some of which have borne fruit in this book. My thanks to Robert Adey for once again loaning some rare volumes, to Jack Adrian for likewise providing some rare texts, to Lawrence Schimel for alerting me to Charles Ardai's story (I only wish Lawrence himself could be present in this volume), and finally to all of the authors who have been so receptive and encouraging to my ideas.

Acknowledgements are accorded to the following for the rights to publish the stories in this anthology. Every effort has been made to trace the owners of copyright material. The Editor would be pleased to hear from anyone if they believe there has been an inadvertent transgression of copyright.

"Death in the Dawntime", © 1995 by F. Gwynplaine MacIntyre. Original story, first published in this anthology. Printed by permission of the author.

"Death Wears a Mask", © 1992 by Steven Saylor. First published in *Ellery Queen's Mystery Magazine*, July 1992. Reprinted by permission of the author.

"The King of Sacrifices", © 1995 by John Maddox Roberts. Original story, first published in this anthology. Printed by permission of the author.

"The Three Travellers", © 1975 by Edward D. Hoch. First published in *Ellery Queen's Mystery Magazine*, January 1976. Reprinted by permission of the author.

"The Case of the Murdered Senator", © 1950 by Wallace Nichols. First published in *London Mystery Magazine*, October 1950. Unable to trace the author's representative.

"A Mithraic Mystery", © 1995 by Mary Reed and Eric Mayer. Original story, first published in this anthology. Printed by permission of the authors.

"Abbey Sinister", © 1995 by Peter Berresford Ellis. Original story, first published in this anthology. Printed by permission of the author and the author's agent, A. M. Heath & Co.

"The Two Beggars", © 1967 by Robert van Gulik. First published in *Judge Dee at Work* (London: William Heinemann, 1967). Reprinted by permission of Dr Thomas M. van Gulik.

"The Investigation of Things", © 1991 by Charles Ardai. First published in *Alfred Hitchcock's Mystery Magazine*, February 1991. Reprinted by permission of the author.

"The Midwife's Tale", © 1995 by Mary Pulver Kuhfeld and Gail Frazer. Original story, first published in this anthology. Printed by permission of the author.

"The Duchess and the Doll", © 1950 by Edith Pargeter. First published in *The Uncertain Element*, edited by Kay Dick (London: Jarrolds Publishers, 1950). Reprinted by permission of the author and the author's agent, Deborah Owen Literary Agency.

"Ordeal by Fire", © 1995 by Mary Pulver Kuhfeld. Original story, first published in this anthology. Printed by permission of the author.

"The Chapman and the Tree of Doom", © 1995 by Kate Sedley. Original story, first published in this anthology. Printed by permission of the author and the author's agent, David Grossman Literary Agency.

"The Murder of Innocence", © 1995 by Paul C. Doherty. Original story, first published in this anthology. Printed by permission of the author.

"Cassandra's Castle", © 1975 by J. F. Peirce. First published in *Ellery Queen's Mystery Magazine*, May 1975. Reprinted by permission of the author.

"Man's Inherited Death", by Keith Heller © 1987 by Davis Publications. First published in *Ellery Queen's Mystery Magazine*, March 1987. Reprinted by permission of the author.

"The Curse of the Connecticut Clock", © 1979 by S. S. Rafferty. First published in *Fatal Flourishes* (New York: Avon Books, 1979) and reprinted in *Cork of the Colonies* (New York: International Polygonics, 1984). Reprinted by permission of the author.

"The Scent of Murder", © 1958 by Theodore Mathieson. First published as "Captain Cook, Detective" in *Ellery Queen's Mystery Magazine*, October 1958, and reprinted in *The Great "Detectives"* (New York: Simon & Schuster, 1960). Reprinted by permission of the author.

"The Inn of the Black Crow" by William Hope Hodgson. First published in *The Red Magazine*, October 1, 1915. Copyright expired in December 1965. No record of copyright renewal.

"The Spirit of the '76", © 1976 by Lillian de la Torre. First published in *Ellery Queen's Mystery Magazine*, January 1977. Reprinted by permission of the author's agent, David Higham Associates (UK) and Harold Ober Associates (US).

"Deadly Will and Testament", © 1995 by Ron Burns. Original story, first published in this anthology. Printed by permission of the author and the author's agent, The Mitchell J. Hamilburg Agency.

"The God of the Hills" by Melville Davisson Post. First published in *Country Gentleman*, September 1927, and reprinted in *The Methods of Uncle Abner* (Boulder, Colorado: The Aspen Press, 1974) and *The Complete Uncle Abner* (San Diego, California: University of California, 1977). Copyright expired, December 1980. No record of copyright renewal.

"The Admiral's Lady", © 1995 by Joan Aiken Enterprises Ltd. Original story, first published in this anthology. Printed by permission of the author.

"The Eye of Shiva", © 1995 by Peter Berresford Ellis. Original story, first published in this anthology. Printed by permission of the author and the author's agent, A. M. Heath & Co.

"The Trail of the Bells", © 1985 by Edward D. Hoch. First published in *Ellery Queen's Mystery Magazine*, April 1985. Reprinted by permission of the author.

"Murdering Mr Boodle", © 1995 by Amy Myers. Original story, first published in this anthology. Printed by permission of the author and the author's agent, the Dorian Literary Agency.

"The Phantom Pistol", © 1989 by Jack Adrian. First published in *Felonious Assaults*, edited by Bill Pronzini and Martin H. Greenberg (New York: Ivy Books, 1989). Reprinted by permission of the author.

"The Adventure of the Frightened Governess", © 1995 by Basil Copper. This is a complete and unabridged version of the story originally published in an edited version in *Some Uncollected Cases of Solar Pons* (New York: Pinnacle Books, 1980). This version is printed by permission of the author.

# Introduction
# THE SECOND BOOK
# OF CHRONICLES

Here is a second helping of the chronicles of crime. The reaction to the first volume, *The Mammoth Book of Historical Whodunnits*, has been very favourable, and this volume allows us to explore and enjoy an even wider set of stories.

This time you will find not only stories set in ancient Rome, the Far East, medieval England and the American colonies, as in the first volume, but you'll also be taken as far afield as the Pacific Ocean on the voyages of Captain Cook and as far back as Australia in 35,000 B C, in what must be the earliest ever setting for a murder mystery. There is also a story by Edith Pargeter (Ellis Peters) that has been unreprinted for over forty years, and a long-forgotten story by William Hope Hodgson not reprinted for eighty years. And because some readers were surprised that I drew the cut-off point in the last anthology at 1900 (with one exception), I've extended the coverage to introduce at least one story set in the 1920s. This volume thus contains detective stories spread over 37,000 years! There are twenty-nine stories, of which twelve are new and were specially written for this anthology and a further seven have never been published in book form before.

One of the pleasures of researching for and compiling an anthology like this is the thrill of discovery. I was delighted at the feedback on the first volume where readers suggested new names to me. In addition, historical detective stories and novels are now starting to appear regularly with scarcely a month passing without some new series beginning.

Some of these discoveries are included in this anthology. Steven Saylor is a young American writer who has produced several stories and novels about his Roman detective, Gordianus the Finder, and one of those early stories is reprinted here. Kate Sedley, whose books about the fifteenth-century pedlar Roger the Chapman have been appearing since 1991, has contributed a brand new story about his adventures. Keith Heller, who produced three novels about parish watchman George Man, has also written a couple of short stories, one of which is reprinted here. And Amy Myers has contributed a totally new story featuring her master chef, Auguste Didier.

In addition to these I have made other discoveries, and although the following authors are not represented here, you may be interested to learn about their books. (Similarly, if you have made any discoveries that I haven't mentioned in either this book or the last one, then I would be very interested to hear from you, c/o the publisher.)

I was grateful to Mr R. F. Glayzer, who wrote to draw my attention to the works of Raymond Foxall, who wrote a series of novels about the Bow Street Runners, based on the real life of Harry Adkins, one of the cleverest of the runners and sometime spy. The books are set around the year 1800. They began with *The Little Ferret* (1968) and include *The Dark Forest* (1972) and *The Silver Goblet* (1974).

Edward Marston, whose books about Elizabethan investigator Nicholas Bracewell I listed in the previous volume, has now started a new series about the investigations of Ralph Delchard and Gervase Bret set during the compilation of the Domesday Book in the reign of William I. So far I have seen two books, *The Wolves of Savernake* (1993) and *The Ravens of Blackwater* (1994).

For those who like the mysteries of ancient Egypt there is *Murder in the Place of Anubis* (1994) by Lynda S. Robinson, set during the reign of Tutankhamun. And in the medieval era, there is a new series set in fourteenth-century York by Candace Robb. This began with *The Apothecary Rose* (1994) followed by *The Lady Chapel* (1994). Set just twenty years after those novels, at the time of Chaucer's *Canterbury Tales*, is *Death is a Pilgrim* (1993) by Gertrude and Joseph Clancy, which came from a Welsh publisher, Northgate Books, in Aberystwyth, so may easily have been missed. This brings us on to the Elizabethan period, with *A Famine of Horses* (1994) by P. F. Chisholm, set in the Scottish borders in 1592.

Finally, I was interested to acquire a further anthology of historical detective stories, *Once Upon a Crime* (1994), edited by Janet Hutchings. This reprints thirteen stories from the pages of *Ellery Queen's Mystery Magazine*, with their settings ranging from ancient Rome (Steven Saylor's "The Lemures") to 1937 New England ("The Problem of the Leather Man" by Edward D. Hoch). None of the stories is duplicated in either of my volumes.

Those then are some of my discoveries since the last book, in addition to others revealed within this anthology. It seems that the historical detective story is thriving, and long may it continue to do so.

So, let's roll back the mists of crime . . .

*Mike Ashley*

# PART I
# The Ancient World

# DEATH IN
# THE DAWNTIME
# F. Gwynplaine MacIntyre

*When I was compiling* The Mammoth Book of Historical Whodunnits *I was searching high and low for a detective story set in
pre-history. I knew I'd seen one somewhere in a turn-of-the-century
magazine, but no matter how I searched, I couldn't find it. I still
haven't. But while working on this volume, I mentioned the idea to F.
Gwynplaine MacIntyre. He instantly took up the challenge. In fact, he
did more than that. He set the story in the ancient aboriginal culture
of Australia, allowing a chance to explore the origins of some of their
language and thinking.*

*F. Gwynplaine MacIntyre (b. 1948), "Froggy" to his friends, was
born in Scotland but was raised in Australia, hence his knowledge of the
native culture. He has since lived in England and Wales but currently
resides in the United States. He has been appearing in the science-fiction
magazines since 1980, and drew upon his Australian background for
one of his first stories, "Martian Walkabout" (Isaac Asimov's SF
Magazine, March 1980), but "Death in the Dawntime" is his first
published mystery story. It's set around 35,000 BC and I'm sure that
makes it the earliest setting ever used for a detective story. Can anyone
prove me wrong?*

The screaming came at sunrise, three dawns after the wet.
Nightwish had been asleep at the outer edge of the *ngurupal*,
the portion of the campsite reserved for initiated males – not inside
it, for at twelvesummers age he had not yet undergone the *kurini*,
the ritual of manhood – but as close as he dared to the edge
of the privileged area. Now the screaming awakened him, and in
the wide outback dawn he got up and ran towards the sounds of
the agony.

The screams came from the redstone caves. Other males of the
Wuradjeri had heard the screams too, for as Nightwish ran towards

the caves he saw men – Speartouch and Dauber and Rainspeak – running ahead of him, towards the same destination. Even lame old Toegone, with his mangled foot, had got here ahead of Nightwish and was limping briskly towards the caves. Yet by now the screams were silent. The red-ochre clay was still damp here, from the long days of wet, and the mud splattered the men's naked feet and bare legs as they ran through a clutter of wombats' mounds amid the grass and hurried on towards the caves.

There were four redstone caves here; two reserved for ritual purposes, one empty. The fourth cave was sealed with a large round boulder; sealed imperfectly, with a thin vertical aperture remaining. The screams had come from within.

With the sharp end of his boomerang, Speartouch rapped the boulder. "*Ei! Lungah!* Anybody in there?"

The boulder gave no reply.

Other men from the *ngurupal* were here now, as well as several women from the she-ground. Speartouch tapped three of the strongest men. "*Duku.* Help me move this thing." Someone caught his attention: the young Nightwish, eager to help. "You too, boy. Push."

As they bent to their task, Nightwish sang thoughts in his head. This cave was Grabtake's. Five days ago, when the nomad people Wuradjeri first made camp at this site, Nightwish's clan-brother Grabtake had been content to sleep in the privileged *ngurupal* space with the other elder males. But two days later he had suddenly claimed this cave as his personal residence – the cave with the boulder inside that was larger than the mouth of the cave – and Grabtake had walled himself inside every night by pushing the boulder up against the cave's mouth. And now he . . .

The boulder suddenly gave way, rolling backwards and into the cave. Speartouch pushed past it, with Dauber and the eager Nightwish just behind him. Dauber held the tribe's picture-magic; it would be his task to make the picture showing whatever had happened here.

Grabtake was dead. He lay sprawled on his side, in the dust at the cave's rear. His eyes, unblinking, gazed lifelessly upward towards the realm of Baiami the Skygod. His dead hands were claw-shapes, clutching at something invisible.

Healchant fingered the body. "*Paraka!* Get up! Awaken!" If any clevering in the world could bring this corpse back to life, Healchant was the one member of the Wuradjeri who would surely find it. But now Healchant paused and shook his head. "*Warai.* He's dead."

Speartouch prodded the corpse with his boomerang so that

Grabtake fell over on to his back. "*There* is what killed him. *Ngana!*"
There was a spear through Grabtake's heart. The lower half of the
shaft had broken off and was missing. There were no other entrances
to the cave, and no niches or hollows inside the cave large enough to
make a hiding-place.

The dead man had been murdered in a cave that had been sealed
from the inside. And no one had come out; the men of the tribe would
have seen the murderer escaping in the first light of dawn as they ran
towards the cave.

"What do *you* want, boy?" asked Speartouch, annoyed, as
Nightwish pressed forward to look at the body. "*Minja wontu
ngana?* What are you looking at? A man is dead. There is nothing
to see."

"Oh?" Nightwish pointed at the dead man's hands. "LOOK!"

The dead man's fingertips were *changed*. Some unknown god-thing
had altered the flesh at the ends of his hands, turned it black with a
foam of white blisters.

Healchant went pale beneath his ritual body-paint. "Something
has . . . something has *bitten* his hands," was the only explanation he
could clever at the moment. Then, in an awed whisper: "A god-thing
has done this."

"I think," said Speartouch, "that we should call a council."

The council talked much and decided little, which was often the way
with councils. Old Toegone suggested that the dead man had been
slain by a *dzir* or a *buginja*; since they were invisible evil spirits, they
could easily pass through solid rock, kill a man, and escape without
being seen. Speartouch unclevered this by pointing out that the dead
man had been slain with a spear, a man-weapon. *Dzir* and *buginja* were
evil enough to kill men, aye, but everyone knew that they possessed
death-magic far more weaponous than spears.

This was no spirit-death: it was a murder. And the murder had
occurred only two quickspans before the men arrived, Speartouch
reminded his council-brothers. They had *heard* the dead man's
screams with their own ears, and then the men of the tribe had
reached the murder scene barely two quickspans later. But how
could any man kill another man inside a sealed cave, and then
escape unseen in such a brief fragment of time?

And how came it that Grabtake's fingertips had been *transformed*,
changed in some manner that no member of the Wuradjeri had ever
seen before? Healchant believed that Grabtake must have touched
a thing that was taboo, and the taboo had bitten his fingers. Could
this be why the murderer had slain him?

At the far edge of the *ngurupal*, Nightwish stood bursting with desire to speak. He had his own ideas for how to investigate the murder. But Nightwish had not yet done walkabout or undergone *kurini*; if he dared to speak, his words would fall dead and unheard at the border of the warrior-place.

A hand touched Nightwish's shoulder. "Have the beardfaces finished babbling yet?" whispered a soft voice in his ear.

Nightwish turned. Tinglesweet stood there behind him. She was a twelvesummers female, the same age as Nightwish, yet already her breasts had ripened and she had undergone the bloodflow that proved she was a full woman of the Wuradjeri people. Nightwish was attracted to her, and he had privately sung dreams of coupling with her . . . dreams that he dared not sing aloud, because his *jarajuwa* totem-beast was Maruwai the Red Kangaroo, while Tinglesweet's *jarajuwa* was Kuru the Bandicoot. Most incompatible. Now, seeing the ripe evidence of Tinglesweet's female adulthood, Nightwish hastily put one hand over his own genitals, hoping she had not noticed that he lacked the *burumalwu*, the ritual cord of emu's sinew that men of the Wuradjeri bound about their testicles to signify man-status.

Tinglesweet saw the gesture: she slapped the boy's hand aside from his naked genitals, and she laughed when she saw the proof of his immaturity. "So the boy is not a man yet! I had wondered why you stand outside the council-ground."

"D'you know about the murder?" Nightwish asked her.

Tinglesweet nodded at the council. "The beardfaces are babbling, while somewhere a murderer dances. *Kala*, why don't you and I go to the murder-place? We can hunt for cleverings that might sing to us the killer's name."

Nightwish glanced back at the *ngurupal*. Rainspeak was arguing with Dauber, and other men were shouting theories. Clearly, nothing would be settled here in any handful of time. Nightwish reached over, and shyly touched Tinglesweet's hair. "*Bilaka*. I will show you the death-place."

The dead man had not walked away. This was good, for it proved that the spirit Jaruta – who likes to dress himself in dead men's bodies and walk about in their flesh – had no desire to inhabit this particular corpse. After glimpsing the dead man, Tinglesweet flinched, and she looked away hastily. Nightwish felt secretly pleased, for surely Tinglesweet would be impressed that Nightwish could look upon the corpse without flinching.

The boulder that had blocked the entrance to the cave was too heavy for Nightwish to move by himself. With gestures, he showed Tinglesweet how it had been wedged tightly into the cave's mouth when he and the others arrived. "*Ngana tu?* D'you see?" Nightwish demonstrated, shouldering aside a phantom stone. "Inside the cave each night, Grabtake pushed the stone so that it blocked the cave's mouth. Then, in the morning, he pushed the stone to one side so that he could get out."

"Push to come, and push to go." Tinglesweet slapped at a sandfly, then studied the boulder. "Could a man *pull* that stone into position, behind himself, on his way out of the cave?" she asked.

Nightwish frowned, and then he tried to pull the stone. But the boulder was made of psammite, soft yellow sandstone; when he tried to get a solid grip, clumps of the boulder came away in his hands. Finally he gave up. "This stone can only be pushed, not pulled," he deduced. "And because of its position when the murderer screamed, the stone must have been pushed into place from the *inside*. By the dead man, before he was murdered. Or else by the killer."

Tinglesweet nodded. "So there are two eithers. Either a murderer *outside* the cave somehow sent a spear *inside* – through solid rock – or else a man *inside* the cave did the killing, and then he got *out* – through solid rock – without disturbing the boulder at the entrance. And in either case the killer got away unseen, even while men were running towards the cave."

Nightwish clevered his thoughts, hoping that one of them would sing the answer. Suddenly he remembered something: "*Tungani!* I saw it! The shape of the stone did not truly match the shape of the cave's mouth. There *was* an opening . . . but it was too small for a man to pass through." With his hands, Nightwish fashioned a vertical slit in mid-air: barely more than a spear's width.

"That's it, then," said Tinglesweet. She began a dance, taking the various roles. "The murder happened at dawn, yes? Because old Kapata-the-Moon does not give enough light for men to kill by." As she danced, Tinglesweet became the murderer: glancing up at Kapata-the-Moon, stumbling in the dark because there was not enough moonlight. Now she was Kapata, the moon in the sky, looking down at the murderer's vigil. "And the cave's entrance faces the sunrise, yes? So! The murderer waited outside until dawn . . ." – she was the murderer again now, dancing warily – ". . . and, as soon as he had light to do his dirty work, he flung a spear through that narrow crack between the boulder and the cave. *Whishshst!*" Now, with hands clasped over her head, Tinglesweet *became* the spear. She mimicked its flight, dancing through the cave and whizzing towards the dead man. "*There!* The spear found its prey, and killed this man."

"That is *warai*. Impossible," said Nightwish, glad to have a chance to impress Tinglesweet with his knowledge of weaponry. As a young male preparing to undergo *kurini*, he knew more about spears than any she-one could know. "The cave's opening was a narrow slit. No man could throw a spear through such a tiny hole . . . not *accurately*. See? You can place a spear against the hole, but then the arm must be drawn *back*, to have power to hurl the spear, and it must come forward again quickly, so quickly that there is no time to make sure that the spear meets the hole."

As Nightwish spoke, Tinglesweet glanced downward at his bare genitals, unadorned by the *burumalwu* man-cord, and then she swiftly glanced away again. Nightwish clevered what the female was thinking: since Nightwish had not yet undergone the male hunt-ritual of walkabout, Tinglesweet was unwilling to consider him an expert witness on the subject of spears. Quickly, he added the biggest clever to his argument: "Besides, the other men and I, we would have seen the killer running away."

Tinglesweet mocked his words: "The *other* men and you? One boy and some beardfaces, you mean. And the murderer *did* escape, while you were running towards the cave." She stood up, and brushed yellow sand from her brown thighs. "Let us hunt for cleverings. Something within this cave may sing the murderer's name."

The two younglings searched the cave for clues. This was difficult, since neither knew precisely what they were looking for. Suddenly Nightwish cried out: "*Ngai!*"

"You have found something?"

"I have found a thing that is not here," Nightwish said.

"Your words jump like a kangaroo," said Tinglesweet.

"I mean, a thing that *should* be here is missing, and its missingness sings a piece of the mystery," Nightwish explained.

"What is missing, then?" Tinglesweet was eager.

"Look." Nightwish pointed to the broken half-length of spear protruding from the dead man's chest. "The other half of the spear – the rear half, the part that a man holds when he aims – is not here. I saw that it was missing when we found the body, but I thought that it was somewhere in this cave. It is not."

"The murderer took it with him," decided Tinglesweet.

"*Warai*. Why would the murderer take half the murder weapon, and leave the other half?" Nightwish shook his head. "No. I am certain that *this* half of the spear – the front half – is all that was ever here. But how can a man aim *half* a spear through a narrow slit of rock? A broken spear is harder to aim than a whole spear."

"I have a more important question," said Tinglesweet. "*Why* did someone murder Grabtake? There had to be a reason."

Again, Nightwish felt that he should have more clevers than this girl had. Nightwish and Grabtake were both totem-born to Maruwai the Red Kangaroo, and had quartered together. Tinglesweet, born under the sponsorship of Kuru the Bandicoot, could not have known Grabtake very well. "Grabtake was disliked," said Nightwish, truthfully. "The elder males have told me that he always held back in the hunts, and did less than his share. At hunt's ending, when the day's meat was brought to the campsite, Grabtake always tried to get more than his fair claim, and he always tried to snatch the choicest portions."

"Hardly cause for murder," Tinglesweet observed.

Suddenly a thought sang loud in Nightwish's head. "I remember now! During the wet, Grabtake walked with all the other hunt-males and slept among them, in the *ngurupal*. When we reached our present campsite, he did the same. But three days ago, he suddenly awayed himself from the rest of us. That was when he started to sleep in the cave, shutting himself in at night." Another remembering sang in Nightwish's memory. "And during the last three days, Grabtake spent much time sucking his fingers, as if they were hurt."

Tinglesweet glanced at the corpse's peculiar blistered fingertips, and she shuddered. "Three days ago, you say? Then *that* must have been the day when . . . when the god-thing changed his hands. But that doesn't explain why someone murdered him."

Nightwish started to nod, then suddenly a great cleverness sang amid his thoughts. "I know! Grabtake must have *owned* something. Something the murderer wanted." Nightwish was certain of it now. "Three days ago, it must have begun: that was when Grabtake would no longer walk or sleep among us. He must have *made* a something, or *found* a something . . . a thing so special that he wanted it all for himself, and he would let no others of the Wuradjeri see it. But the murderer knew. He came into the cave while Grabtake slept, took the important thing, killed Grabtake, and ran away."

Tinglesweet sucked on a strand of her hair. "There's a hole in your clevering, boy. How did the murderer get out of a sealed cave? And how did he get away unseen while you and the men ran *towards* the cave?" She shook her head. "That's not the answer. Let us hunt for more cleverings, and hope that they will sing the killer's name."

They kept searching the cave. Nightwish sang a silent clevering: if *he* were Grabtake, and if he owned a thing so precious that other men would kill to own it, where would he keep it? He would keep it on his person every waking moment, and then place it nearby when he slept. *Look under the bed.* Quickly, Nightwish went to the gathered mound of dead grass and soft moss at the rear of the cave that must have been Grabtake's bedding-place. Beside it was . . .

"LOOK!"

Tinglesweet approached the corpse reluctantly, to see what Nightwish had found.

There was a thin vein of *kirapurai* – red-ochre clay – at the rear of the cave, in exactly the spot beside the bedding where a man would place his most precious possession, so that he could touch it in the middle of the night and assure himself it was still there. But the clay itself was not why Nightwish had cried out. Someone had pushed something *into* the clay, for safekeeping. Now the something was gone, but it had left its shape behind: an indentation in the clay. Tinglesweet saw it too, and she cried out in astonishment.

The indentation in the clay possessed a shape that the Wuradjeri people had no word for: *a perfect hemisphere*, absolutely round, its diameter about half of Nightwish's thumb. Some spherical object had been pressed into the soft clay. Now it was gone, but its circular image remained.

"A god-thing was here, and a god-thing was taken," Nightwish shuddered. His trembling finger traced the edges of the circle. "D'you see? All of its edge is the same distance from its heart."

"Only one other thing wears that shape," said Tinglesweet, with awe in her voice. "Kapata-the-Moon has that shape, but only for three nights out of every month. It is . . ." she tried to draw the moon-shape with her hands, and then – unable to describe the wondrous thing with all the clevers in her mouth – she made up a new clever that would sing its true nature: "It is . . . a *circle*."

Nightwish let out a long whistling note, as he clevered this new concept. "A circle. Grabtake owned the only circle, and someone killed him for it. The murderer stole the only circle in the world."

All the way back to the campsite, Nightwish sang circles and Tinglesweet danced circles. By the time they reached the broad white chant-stone in the middle of the Wuradjeri campground, the two younglings had clevered a way to *make* circles. Nightwish explained to the elders what they had discovered. "Grabtake owned a circle. Someone else wanted it. The one who wanted the circle murdered him, and stole the circle."

"Very interesting." Speartouch rubbed his jaw. "What is a circle?"

Quickly, Nightwish borrowed an emu-cord from Healchant and a spear from Rainspeak. It was a prize spear, for its tip was a barb from a stingray's tail that Rainspeak had obtained in barter from a warrior whose tribal land bordered the northern sea.

Now men and women of the Wuradjeri watched curiously as Nightwish knotted one end of Healchant's cord round the shaft of Rainspeak's spear, then fastened the cord's other end to a sharp fragment of *karul*, transparent crystal quartz. "These have a circle," he explained.

Old Toegone, perched on a stone with his mangled foot thrust out in front of him, spat in contempt. "I see no circle, whatever a circle may be."

"All things have circles inside them," said Nightwish, putting words to the clever as it formed in his thoughts. "All things contain hidden circles . . . but we can sing the circles out, so that they can be seen."

With a shout, Nightwish thrust the spear's barb into the soft ground, burying it to the depth of a man's hand. Now Tinglesweet, gripping the sharp quartz, stepped as far from the spear as she could . . . until the cord that bound spear to quartz became *taut*.

Tinglesweet danced, chanting the song of the circle as she circuited the spear. She danced widdershins, anti-clockwise, in the same path as Ngunipinga-the-Sun . . . the Sun who was herself shaped like a squashed circle, and who now perched herself dusk-wise above the outback's western horizon. Tinglesweet's sharpened *karul* quartz bit the ground as she moved in her dance . . . but always and ever the same distance from the spear, so that the cord remained *taut*. Meanwhile, Nightwish gripped the spear. As the emu-cord approached his ankles he whooped, and leapt over it, so that Tinglesweet could finish her circuit.

"*There!*" she shouted triumphantly. "*Kalanduku!* All of you! Behold the circle!"

The first circle ever scribed by humans lay in the soft turf of the campground, with Nightwish in its centre and Tinglesweet at its border. The men and women pressed forward, to see this new shape.

Rainspeak reclaimed his spear, and made certain that Nightwish had not blunted its barb. "So that is a circle," said Speartouch. "What good is it?"

"It is pretty to look at," said Tinglesweet.

"But not pretty enough to kill for," said Speartouch. He jabbed a finger at the circle's rim. "You would have us believe that Grabtake was murdered for *that*?"

Rainspeak stood up. "Let me see this thing, then. *Kurana!* Show me!"

Hooting, jeering, the elders of both sexes followed Nightwish and Tinglesweet back to the murder scene. Even old Toegone, shouting at the others to wait for him, limped along at the procession's rear. At the mouth of the cave several women hung back; the sandflies had discovered Grabtake's corpse, and in the outback heat his scent was most unpleasant. Nightwish vaulted into the cave, and pointed to the indentation in the red-ochre clay. "There it is."

Speartouch looked, and for the first time in his life beheld *a perfect hemisphere*. "It is a god-shape!" he exclaimed.

"What, that mark on the ground?" Rainspeak pushed forward contemptuously, with a frown that warned Nightwish of danger.

"*Wari muluk!*" the boy shouted. "Someone stop him!"

Rainspeak thrust the butt of his spear into the soft clay, smudging the hemispherical indentation. "I see no god-things here," he spoke. "I see a mark on the ground." As he said this, Rainspeak fumbled with the emu-cord binding his genitals; he undid it, and he urinated on the smudge. "And now I see a puddle on the ground." He laughed. "No man would kill another man, and tempt the wrath of Baiami, for the sake of a mark on the ground. Let us go."

Laughing and jeering, the men and women of the Wuradjeri walked away, leaving Nightwish alone. Someone touched his fingers gently and he turned. Tinglesweet was there.

"I have thought of a clever," she told him. "Grabtake touched a god-thing that bit his hands, yes? And a god-thing – a circle shaped like the Moon – was stolen from his cave by whoever killed him. Perhaps the taboo that bit him and the thing that the murderer stole are both *the same object*."

The very same clever that Tinglesweet heard was now singing to Nightwish. "I see what you mean!" the boy whooped. "The god-thing bit Grabtake's hands when he found it. Someone has killed him, and taken the god-thing. But the god-thing bites whoever touches it. We must find someone whose hands are bitten like the dead man's. He who wears the bites, he is the murderer."

Tinglesweet nodded. "Let us search our totem-people, you and I. I will look at the hands of my Bandicoot people; you seek the hands of your Red Kangaroo-folk."

Nightwish felt a rush of excitement. "Then, if we have not found the killer, we will look among the other two clans of the Wuradjeri. I will search the hands of the people totem-born to Kilpatsha, the Black Kangaroo; you look among the hands of those whose *jarajuwa* is Jungkai the Grass Hen. I will meet you *ngaku*, afterwards at the chant-stone. Let the wind guide your feet! Hurry!"

For the next many timelongs, Nightwish looked at hands. Hunters' hands, chanters' hands, potters' hands, weaver-hands, gather-hands. Men's and women's and children's hands he examined, hoping to find the strange fleck of white blisters and black markings that he had seen on Grabtake's fingers: *the bite of the god-thing.*

By the time of twilight, he had examined the hands of every man, woman, and child born to two totem-clans . . . but found no trace of the god-thing. Tinglesweet was waiting at the chant-stone; by the look on her face, Nightwish knew that she also had failed.

"Perhaps the killer is not of Wuradjeri," Tinglesweet suggested.

"No. I am certain that the murderer is among us," Nightwish said. "Yet something is wrong. A man found a god-thing, and it bit his hands. *Why?* Another man killed him, and stole the god-thing, yet the god-thing did not bite the murderer. Why *not?* This is a mystery, and all my clevers in a heap can sing no answer."

Nightfall came, and the darkness and stars, yet Nightwish did not sleep. He sat awake, and wished for cleverthoughts.

He thought of Kalwaka, the ancient time, the time of his ancestors' ancestors. And before Kalwaka there was Ngurukanbu, the Beginning-of-All . . . a time so ancient that men and women had not yet been sung by their totem-beasts. At the time of Beginning-of-All there were no secrets, because Baiami came down from the sky and sang to the beasts, giving them the answers to all the world's mysteries. But that was long ago, and *now* the world was much more complicated, with so many more mysteries in it.

Kapata-the-Moon came out from a cloud over Nightwish's head, mocking him. On this particular night, Kapata's shape was a perfect circle, like the mark in the clay had been. The red clay inside Grabtake's cave had witnessed the murder, but it could no longer sing the killer's name because Rainspeak had defiled the clay with his essence. The clay that . . .

Suddenly Nightwish remembered a clever. The clay inside the dead man's cave was *kirapurai*, red ochre. And the clay on the ground outside the dead man's cave was the identical red ochre. So the two clays were one, and they owned the same song. Which meant that the clay *outside* the cave could sing Nightwish the answer to what had happened *in* the cave, during the murder.

Softly, silently, so as to awaken no-one, Nightwish got up and ran towards the cave.

There was moonlight, enough to see by. A shrub of *wilga*-wood, black willow, stood in Nightwish's path. He seized a branch of the shrub, bent it aside so that his body could slip past. The *wilga* branch, under tension, slipped out of his hand and shot back to its former position with a whistling sound that Nightwish feared would awaken the others. Nobody roused. He ran on.

When Nightwish got to the cave, he saw the hole in his own cleverness. The clay outside the murder scene could not sing its true chant, for it had been defiled. He could see the splattered footprints of his own feet and the elder men's outside the dead man's cave. And among these were the footprints of the women. And blades of grass, amongst the footprints, everywhere.

It was interesting, Nightwish discovered, how each footprint had its own especial song. The women's footprints were narrower than the men's, and the footprints of the children were smaller and more uncertain than the prints of their elders. And over there – *ngai!* – there were the broken footprints of Toegone; the marks of his whole foot deeper than the prints of his maimed foot, because he put more weight upon the good one. And other men had left their footprints here as well. It ought to be possible, Nightwish decided, to match each footprint with its original maker, and . . .

Suddenly the moonlight sang the answer.

One set of footprints were different from all their brothers and their sisters, in an unexpected way. Nightwish saw it: Yes. The other footprints all sang truth, but one set of footprints sang lies.

Now Nightwish knew who had murdered Grabtake and stolen the god-thing.

But he didn't know *how*. And the council would want proof.

Nightwish went back to the campsite. The elder males were asleep within the *ngurupal*, which the boy Nightwish was forbidden to enter. He selected a bed-likely spot in a patch of mossed grass, at the warrior-ground's southern edge. As Nightwish lay down for the night, he surreptitiously extended his arms across the border of the *ngurupal*. He was not yet a man, but tonight his hands would sleep among the warriors and hunters; perhaps some of the men's hunt-magic might enter him through his fingers. In the morning, Nightwish would need to wear a hunter's hands. For he would be hunting a murderer.

Dawntime came, and the usual chores. Nightwish saw no sign of Tinglesweet; the elder women must have put her to work performing she-tasks. Nightwish had his own duties: as an apprentice warrior, he was supposed to spend the day gathering tree-gum. Older men of the Wuradjeri – males whose minds held hunt-knowledge but whose bodies were too old to join the hunt – were sitting cross-legged in the *ngurupal* and chipping flints into long pointed spearheads. Later, these flintmen would use the sticky tree-gum gathered by Nightwish, as well as sinew-cords reaped from dead emus and kangaroos, to bind the spearheads to shafts for the men of the hunt.

Nightwish disliked gum-harvesting, for the tree-gum was messy and smelt unpleasant. Sandflies were attracted to the stuff, and tended to trap themselves in it. Today Nightwish had no desire to trap flies. He was planning to trap a murderer.

Among the hunters of Nightwish's totem, any beast was fair game for their spears except their own *jarajuwa*: Maruwai, the red kangaroo. A black 'roo, or a grey, or any other beast at all was worthy prey. The men set out then, in groups and pairs, and there were three or four men of independent spirit each of whom preferred to hunt alone. Nightwish saw one of these men leave the campground, and then he followed him. This man was the murderer.

The lone hunter walked northwest, away from the campground and into a stand of *wilga* trees. Nightwish was pleased; here in the woods, with many trees to hide behind, he could easily stalk his quarry. He crept along behind the murderer.

As the forest deepened, Nightwish began to think that perhaps he had outclevered himself. The murderer carried a bundle of spears, and in his left hand he clutched a pouch of bandicoot-skin that might contain unknown weapons . . . perhaps it even contained the stolen god-thing itself. But Nightwish was unarmed. For a moment the boy considered turning back. No; if he turned away now, Baiami the Skygod would witness his cowardice, and Nightwish would be cursed forever. He kept stalking his prey, deeper into the woods.

The murderer walked on, beyond the forest, until he emerged into the bare outback desert. This was open ground, with few places to hide. There were a few red sandstone outcroppings, some shallow grass, and a single stand of leafy *koolibah*. If Nightwish confronted his quarry here, the murderer would see him coming from a distance and be ready for him.

Nightwish hung back, at the edge of the forest, while the murderer went on through the low grass towards the *koolibah* trees. In the shadows, Nightwish's hands tallied the murderer's footsteps: *Firstfinger, secondfinger, thirdfinger, fourthfinger, hand. A double hand, two double hands* . . . At last the murderer reached the stand of trees, and sat down: thirdfinger-many double hands plus one hand more of footsteps away; too far away for Nightwish to take him by surprise. Among the *wilga*, Nightwish watched as the murderer sat in the pale outback sand and rested his bundle of spears by his side. There was a log of dead eucalyptus nearby; the murderer placed this in front of himself. Then he fumbled with his bandicoot-leather, unwrapped it, and took out . . .

. . . the god-thing.

It must have come from the sky, from the place where Baiami the Skygod dwelt, for Nightwish sensed that no such thing could have been birthed here in the world of men. The god-thing glittered like Baiami's crystal wife, the goddess Kurikuta, who is made of living quartz. Yet this glittering god-thing was an alien colour such as Nightwish had never seen before. *Grass* was the nearest thing to it in colour, but the green of grass was very distant to the hue of this god-thing. And just as Nightwish had envisioned, this god-thing was the same shape as the moon. The god-thing slid out of the leather, and rolled into the murderer's hand.

Nightwish watched, but did not comprehend. The god-thing had bitten Grabtake's fingers when he touched it. How was it possible that the man who murdered Grabtake and stole the god-thing could now hold it without being harmed?

As Nightwish watched, the killer lifted the god-thing and raised it towards Ngunipinga-the-Sun. The god-thing glittered ever brighter, like a star. For a timelong, nothing happened. Then, suddenly, *another god-thing appeared*.

This thing too was an alien colour. Not quite yellow like the sun over-sky, nor red like the sunset at dusking. This was a colour between them. The god-thing danced across the eucalyptus wood, and as it danced it sang a song all coloured black. And as Nightwish watched, the dancing sun-bright god-thing's chant became so loud that he could hear the words although he could not understand them: "*Kricka tricka crack, cricka track . . .*"

And as it danced, the chanting god-thing grew. The killer, who at first had watched the dancing apparition quite calmly, seemed to grow more apprehensive as the thing grew larger. Now he took the first god-thing – the green sphere – and slipped it back into his leather bag. He scooped handfuls of sand and flung them at the second god-thing. The god-thing's black chant ended, and its dance became more subdued. The thing-like-the-sun shrank, as more and more sand overwhelmed it. Then suddenly the thing *vanished*.

Nightwish, watching from his hiding place, could feel the hairs prickling at the back of his neck. He had come here, unarmed, to catch a killer who was weaponed well with spears. Now it was clear that the killer also possessed two god-things . . . and could make them *obey* his commands. *My quarry has powerful weapons.* For a timelong, Nightwish thought of tiptoeing back to the campground. Then he realized: *No. I am here, I have watched, and the killer has not clevered my presence. He has a god's weapons . . . but not a god's eyes, or else he'd have seen me. Baiami the Skygod must be my protector, then. Yet if I turn back now, Baiami will abandon me.*

Among the people Wuradjeri, a male is a hunter . . . or else he is nothing. Nightwish, the boy on his man-brink – twelvesummers his age – had chosen his prey, and stalked his quarry to this place. Now he must prove himself a hunter, by catching this murderer. Or else he was nothing, forever. To catch a killer, or die trying: either path would bring honour and god-favour. To flee now would be to make himself nothing.

Nightwish took a deep breath. He stepped out from among the *wilga* trees, and advanced into the bare outback plain. The murderer saw him coming, and looked up but did not rise. He sat calmly, waiting, beneath the *koolibah*.

"You have murdered a man," Nightwish told him. "You have killed the man Grabtake, a brother of my totem-clan . . . and of *yours*, for you and I and the dead man shared a totem-dance. You have killed our clan-brother."

The man beneath the *koolibah* was Toegone. He sat calmly, with his crippled foot extended in front of him. He beckoned Nightwish to approach. "The boy speaks boldly to the man," said Toegone mockingly. "Have you forgotten, boy? When Grabtake was slain in his cave, I was in the campground nearby you. When his death-scream awoke us, you and I went, together, to the scene of the murder . . . you running, I limping. So! I could not have done the crime."

"That is what I thought at first," Nightwish nodded. "But now I remember: when I awoke and ran to the cave of the murder, you were *ahead* of me. How can a limping man outspeed a runner? There is only one answer: you were already awake, already there. You must have been at the dead man's cave before dawn, *before* Grabtake screamed. And then, when men came running, you pretended to be running also."

Toegone seemed amused as he reached for his bundle of spears. "Who clevered this for you, boy?"

"The clay told me," said Nightwish. "I saw your footprints in the clay outside the cave. The footprints sang lies, but the clay sang the truth." As he advanced towards the killer, Nightwish pointed over his shoulder to his own trail of footprints in the outback sand. "*Ngana tu!* Do you see? As I walk, my heels bite more deeply into the earth than my toes. And the blades of grass in my footprints bend forwards. But at the cave where death sang murder, Toegone, I found one set of footprints with toes that bit deeper than heels, and grass that bent backwards. *Your* footprints were else-made from all the others. I thought at first that your prints were different because you limped. No; your footprints were else-made because you walked away from the murder scene *backwards*."

"Very interesting." Toegone took a spear from his bundle, and examined its shaft. "Have the emus stolen your brain, boy? I could never have killed our clan-brother. The entrance to the dead man's cave was *sealed* by a boulder."

Nightwish stood his ground. "You killed Grabtake by sending a spear through the narrow opening between the boulder and the cave's wall. What I cannot clever is how you managed to aim a spear truly — *half* a spear, I mean, because the other half is missing — through such a small opening. But you killed, and then you walked away backwards so that no man or god would see your else-footprints — broken footprints, with a maimed foot — pointing *away* from the death scene."

Toegone lifted his spear in both hands, and squinted along down the length of its shaft, to be certain of its trueness. "You seem to have clevered it all, boy."

"Almost all." Nightwish nodded. "You killed a man who found a god-thing, and then you stole the god-thing. At first I wondered how the murderer could steal the god-thing from a sealed cave. Now I know: you killed Grabtake, and you left empty-handed. Afterward, when several of us were in the cave together and no man watched, then you took the god-thing from where it slept in the clay. Now I charge thee, murderer: by the law of Wuradjeri, you must return to the council-place with me. Come back to the *ngurupal*, and sing your crimes to the elders. They will judge your fate, and they will decide what to do with the god-thing that you stole from the dead man."

"The god-thing is *mine!*" Toegone sat bolt upright in outrage. "Grabtake and I hunted together, four days past, when we both saw the god-thing fall out of the sky. We ran to the spot where it fell . . . aye, but *he* arrived first, because I cannot run swiftly." Toegone ruefully eyed his maimed foot as he spoke. "Grabtake and I saw the god-thing fall into a river. And when it fell, *clouds* — white growing clouds that hissed like serpents — rose out of the water. Even the water itself seemed to dance, where the god-thing fell, as if bewitched. *Tungani*, I saw Grabtake wade into the river. He reached in with both hands, to snatch the god-thing. Then he screamed, for the god-thing had bitten him. I saw the blooding of his fingertips."

"Did the god-thing show its teeth?" Nightwish asked.

"No, but Grabtake whimpered that the green thing that fell from the sky was *hot*, like the desert at noon when the sun is over-sky. Worse than that: the thing was so hot that it bit Grabtake's fingers, and blistered his hands. After a timelong, when the water stopped dancing, and the hissing clouds no longer rose above the water, Grabtake tried again. This time he plucked the god-thing from the water, and it did not bite him with the heat of the sun."

Nightwish said nothing.

"The god-thing is mine!" said Toegone, clutching his pouch made of bandicoot-skin. "When Grabtake showed it to me, it was I who discovered that the god-thing contains a wondrous cleverness: it can steal a piece of the sun, and bring it *here*. But then Grabtake snatched back the god-thing, and would not share. He went into the cave, and sealed it so that none could share the new cleverness. So I killed him, and took what is mine by right."

Nightwish nodded. During Toegone's murder-chant the boy had gradually come closer to the murderer, so that now there were only a two hands' manyworth of footsteps between them. "You must come back with me, to the elders, and confess," Nightwish declared.

"*Kuriapu*." Toegone shook his head. "I would rather stay here, boy, so that I can do . . . THIS!"

Suddenly he flicked his spear. Nightwish dodged, just in time to prevent the spear from biting into his heart. But then he screamed, as he felt the sharpened flint impale his leg. Nightwish fell, and as he toppled he saw the hunter reaching for another spear. This one would find its prey . . .

Somehow Nightwish got up. He managed to run, with blood streaming from his wounded leg and the shaft of the spear still buried in his limb. The second spear whistled past him, and already his wounded leg betrayed him and he fell again.

"*Kalantu palu!*" The murderer's voice danced in Nightwish's ears. "You will die, boy! *Paraka!* Stand up and die like a man, then! *Kalantu palu!*"

Ahead of Nightwish was a crust of red sandstone, bulging up from the floor of the desert. And beside the sandstone outcropping, probably nourished by some underground spring, grew a small stand of black *wilga*-trees. Crawling, stumbling, desperately trying to escape, Nightwish managed to fling himself behind the temporary shelter of the sandstone. A tell-tale stream of blood from his wounded leg showed precisely where he had concealed himself.

"You cannot hide, boy! Get ready to die!"

Escape was impossible. Nightwish was in the middle of the desert, unable to run, barely able to walk. With this spear in his leg, he could not possibly outspeed the killer. Nightwish could hear Toegone's voice, taunting him, as the murderer came limping steadily closer: "I saw where you went, boy. Thank your god-luck that I cannot walk fast, or I would have caught you by now. When I reach the place where you hide, I will kill you."

A weapon! A weapon! Nightwish glanced upwards frantically, and saw that the uppermost ridge of the sandstone was *sharp*. Could he use this? Rising onto the knee of his good leg, Nightwish seized a piece of the ridge in both hands, and pulled. The brittle sandstone broke off easily . . . and then it *crumbled* into fragments in his hands. Useless! *Worse* than useless, because now there was a long vertical notch in the outcropping, showing Toegone precisely where Nightwish was hiding behind the notched sandstone.

"You will die, boy . . ." Through the notch, Nightwish saw Toegone lift another spear.

A weapon! *A weapon!* Nightwish's injured leg was throbbing. He looked down, and saw that the shaft of the spear was still embedded in the muscle of his leg. Already the sandflies were on him, licking at the blood, where . . .

No.

Only half the spear was in Nightwish's leg. The lower half had broken off, and was somewhere out there on the outback floor. With a grimace, Nightwish managed to pull the sharpened tip of the weapon out of his leg.

"*Paraka!* Stand up, then, and die!"

*Half* a spear. Could Nightwish use it as a weapon against the oncoming killer? No; the broken spear was too short to be aimed properly. Nightwish crawled backwards, felt the supple *wilga*-shafts bending as he thrust himself against the willow shrubs. Through the notch in the sandstone, he could see Toegone limping steadily closer. Any moment now, the time of Nightwish's death-chant would . . .

A cleverness, a cleverness sang loud inside his head.

The notch in the sandstone was the same width as the narrow opening in the mouth of Grabtake's sealed cave. The half-spear in Nightwish's hands was very nearly the same length as the half-spear that Toegone had used to murder Grabtake. Suddenly Nightwish knew the missing pieces of the clever.

"*Kalantu palu!* Now you die!"

Toegone was two hands' many footsteps away, and limping closer. Swiftly, Nightwish uprooted a supple shoot of willow. With the heel of his hand he flattened the butt of the half-spear, where it had broken off uncleanly.

"*Paraka!* Stand up!"

Quickly, Nightwish fitted the half-spear into the notch within the sandstone . . . the same way that Toegone must have fitted the murder weapon into the notch between the boulder and the wall of the cave while he had waited until dawn to murder Grabtake. The dawn had been a part of Toegone's murder scheme; he had needed the first light of Ngunipinga-the-Sun to show him his prey. Now, with his shortened spear fitted into the notched sandstone, Nightwish turned it towards his approaching enemy. It was unnecessary to *aim* the spear now; it was pointed towards its target, and the two sides of the notch would hold it steady just as the narrow slit between the boulder and the cave's wall had steadied the spear that murdered Grabtake. Gritting his teeth to ignore the pain in his throbbing leg, Nightwish fitted one end of the willow-shoot to the butt of the half-spear. Now he bent the *wilga* double in his hands, until the two ends of the willow bough touched each other. He could feel the tension of the willow, straining to unbend itself. If he released one end, the other end of his new invention would snap forward, and propel the spear to its target with far more force than Nightwish's own arm could summon.

"Now I kill you, boy!" The angry face of Toegone loomed above the sandstone ridge. He saw Nightwish, and the murderer grinned in triumph as he raised his spear to claim another soul. And now, at the very last possible moment, Nightwish discovered the flaw in his own improvised weapon: he would have to kill Toegone with the first shot, because there would never come a second chance . . .

The Horniman Museum, near the Lambeth district in southeastern London, is privately owned. Thus the objects within its glass cases are arranged according to the whimsies and moods of the museum's original owner. For example, one exhibit-case – in defiance of all biological order or taxonomy – contains the stuffed figures of a kangaroo, a cricket, and a frog . . . simply because all three creatures *jump*. Another exhibit places a porcupine and a sea-urchin alongside a thistle . . . because all three of them possess *stickles*. Any two objects beneath the same glass may be entirely unrelated, except in Mr Horniman's fancy.

On a rainy Sunday morning, after visiting the Horniman Museum's aquarium, I passed into a corridor that I had never noticed before, and here I discovered a glass case containing two peculiar objects. The one on the left was a long slat of carved wood, with a crude handle at one end and a notched device at the other. A brief inscription on a brass plate underneath explained its origin:

> The *woomera* functioned as a multi-purpose tool: as a chisel, as a blade to strip bark from trees, but especially as a spear-thrower. Used as an extension of the warrior's arm, the *woomera* increased the spear's range and speed, but made it more difficult to aim. The example here was made by aborigines of New South Wales, Australia.

The second object in the same exhibit-case was much smaller. It was a nearly perfect sphere, of bright greenbottle glass, about the size of a child's shooting-marble; what we Clydesiders used to call a *penker*. Again, a brass plate underneath explained:

> The *australite* (so named because they are found only in Australia) is a form of tektite, or glassy stone of high silicate content. Tektites originated in outer space and fell to Earth as meteorites. Most australites are spherical, but some take the form of spheroids, discs, and even teardrops. The specimen above was found in New South Wales, Australia. Its date of origin is approximately 35,000 B C.

It was afternoon when Nightwish managed to return to the encampment, hopping on his good leg and dragging his injured leg behind him. With a shout, Healchant rushed over and examined the boy's injury, so that he would know what medicinal paste to prepare. Waving onlookers away, Nightwish managed to reach the common-ground.

Tinglesweet was there. She and two of her clan-sisters sat cross-legged and holding ridged flints, which they were using to whittle the ends of willow-shoots into sharpened fish-spears. A small mound of wood shavings and curled bark had accumulated in front of the women. Tinglesweet saw Nightwish approach, and she nodded towards his injured leg: "A boy who went hunting caught more than he bargained for," she murmured.

"I have caught more than that." Nightwish fumbled within the bag of bandicoot-skin that he was carrying, and he brought out a small object. "Behold! I have brought you a god-thing!"

"*Ahhh* . . ." Women, children, and old men of the Wuradjeri gathered closer, to admire the bauble. Its perfect shape and its brilliant green colour were two qualities that they had never seen before. But the few warriors present, men back from their hunt, seemed unimpressed.

"A god-thing, you call this?" mocked Rainspeak, and beside him Speartouch laughed sardonically. "A pretty toy for babies, but otherwise useless. Only a toy god, a baby god would give such things. Never a warrior-god."

Nightwish ignored this. He held the bright god-thing aloft as he had seen Toegone do, and he let it catch the bountiful rays of Ngunipinga-the-Sun. The sphere of silicate glass, acting as a convex lens, caught and refracted the sunlight. Within the pile of shavings and bark near Nightwish's feet, a bright pinpoint of light appeared. The light brightened. Smoke uncurled from the wood. And then . . .

"*Ahhh!*" A new thing, a wondrous new thing now appeared. For the first time in their history, the people of the Wuradjeri witnessed fire.

"Do not touch this thing," Nightwish warned, "or it will bite . . . no, a new word is needed. It will *burn* you, as it burnt Grabtake's fingers. If we feed this new thing, it will grow. If we respect it, it will serve us." He put the bright green sphere back into its bag. He took a twig from the ground nearby and fed it to the flame. The fire grew; its black smoke rippled and danced, and now the crackling fire sang its chant: "*Kricka tricka crack, cricka track*."

"A mighty god-thing indeed!" said Tinglesweet, in utter awe.

Nightwish was pleased that he had finally impressed her. "It is a god-thing now," he said. "But when we tame it, and make it serve us, it will no longer be a god-thing. It will be *ours*." He fed another piece of wood to the hungering flame, and the miracle grew. Others of the Wuradjeri, seeing this, ran to gather more wood.

And all that night the dark was bright as day, around the fire, as all the people danced their praises of the greatest cleverness that had ever come among them since the time of Beginning-of-All.

# THE JUDGEMENT OF DANIEL

*In the first volume I reprinted a detective story recorded by Herodotus in around 440 BC and suggested it may have been the earliest written historical detective story. Needless to say such statements are always open to challenge, which is exciting. I was reminded of several mystery stories in the Bible, particularly in the Book of Daniel. Daniel, one of the most famous prophets in the Old Testament, lived from about 630–536 BC. He is usually accepted as the writer of the Book of Daniel and technically it means any incident that he recalls is contemporary with him and not a historical story. I'm not sure, though, when the following extract was written. It doesn't appear in the authorized version of the Bible, having been excluded from the Jewish texts around the first century AD because it was not written in Hebrew. It may therefore be a later apocryphal addition, included to show the wisdom of Daniel. I am grateful to Richard Lonsdale of the Sacred Heart Church in Maine, who drew my attention to this episode, which is taken from the New Jerusalem Bible.*

In Babylon there lived a man named Joakim. He was married to a woman called Susanna daughter of Hilkiah, a woman of great beauty; and she was God-fearing, for her parents were worthy people and had instructed their daughter in the Law of Moses. Joakim was a very rich man and had a garden by his house; he used to be visited by a considerable number of the Jews, since he was held in greater respect than any other man. Two elderly men had been selected from the people, that year, to act as judges. Of such the Lord had said, "Wickedness has come to Babylon through the elders and judges posing as guides to the people." These men were often at Joakim's house, and all who were engaged in litigation used to come to them. At midday, when the people had gone away, Susanna would take a walk in her husband's garden. The two elders, who used to watch her every day as she came in to take her walk, gradually began to desire her. They threw reason aside, making no effort to turn their eyes to Heaven, and forgetting the demands of virtue. Both were inflamed by passion for her, but they hid their desire from each other, for they were ashamed to admit the longing to sleep with her, but they made sure of watching her every day. One day, having parted with the words, "Let us go home, then, it is time for the midday meal," they went off in different directions, only to retrace their steps and find themselves face to face again. Obliged then to explain, they admitted their desire and agreed to look for an opportunity of surprising her alone. So they waited for a favourable moment; and one day Susanna came as usual, accompanied only by two young maidservants. The day was hot and she wanted to bathe in the garden. There was no one about except the two elders, spying on her from their hiding place. She said to the servants, "Bring me some oil and balsam and shut the garden door while I bathe." They did as they were told, shutting the garden door and going back to the house by a side entrance to fetch what she had asked for; they knew nothing about the elders, for they had concealed themselves.

Hardly were the maids gone than the two elders sprang up and rushed upon her. "Look," they said, "the garden door is shut, no one can see us. We want to have you, so give in and let us! Refuse, and we shall both give evidence that a young man was with you and that this was why you sent your maids away." Susanna sighed.

"I am trapped," she said, "whatever I do. If I agree, it means death for me: if I resist, I cannot get away from you. But I prefer to fall innocent into your power than to sin in the eyes of the Lord." She then cried out as loud as she could. The two elders began shouting too, putting the blame on her, and one of them ran to open the garden door. The household, hearing the shouting in the garden, rushed out by the side entrance to see what had happened to her. Once the elders had told their story, the servants were thoroughly taken aback, since nothing of this sort had ever been said of Susanna.

Next day a meeting was held at the house of her husband Joakim. The two elders arrived, full of their wicked plea against Susanna, to have her put to death. They addressed the company, "Summon Susanna daughter of Hilkiah and wife of Joakim." She was sent for, and came accompanied by her parents, her children and all her relations. Susanna was very graceful and beautiful to look at; she was veiled, so the wretches made her unveil in order to feast their eyes on her beauty. All her own people were weeping, and so were all the others who saw her. The two elders stood up, with all the people round them, and laid their hands on her head. Tearfully she turned her eyes to Heaven, her heart confident in God. The elders then spoke. "While we were walking by ourselves in the garden, this woman arrived with two maids. She shut the garden door and then dismissed the servants. A young man, who had been hiding, went over to her and they lay together. From the end of the garden where we were, we saw this crime taking place and hurried towards them. Though we saw them together, we were unable to catch the man: he was too strong for us; he opened the door and took to his heels. We did, however, catch this woman and ask her who the young man was. She refused to tell us. That is our evidence."

Since they were elders of the people and judges, the assembly accepted their word: Susanna was condemned to death. She cried out as loud as she could, "Eternal God, you know all secrets and everything before it happens; you know that they have given false evidence against me. And now I must die, innocent as I am of everything their malice has invented against me!"

The Lord heard her cry and, as she was being led away to die, he roused the holy spirit residing in a young boy called Daniel who began to shout, "I am innocent of this woman's death!"

At this all the people turned to him and asked, "What do you mean by that?"

Standing in the middle of the crowd, he replied, "Are you so stupid, children of Israel, as to condemn a daughter of Israel unheard, and without troubling to find out the truth? Go back to the scene of the trial: these men have given false evidence against her."

All the people hurried back, and the elders said to Daniel, "Come and sit with us and tell us what you mean, since God has given you the gifts that elders have."

Daniel said, "Keep the men well apart from each other, for I want to question them." When the men had been separated, Daniel had one of them brought to him. "You have grown old in wickedness," he said, "and now the sins of your earlier days have overtaken you, you with your unjust judgements, your condemnation of the innocent, your acquittal of the guilty, although the Lord has said, 'You must not put the innocent and upright to death.' Now then, since you saw her so clearly, tell me what sort of tree you saw them lying under."

He replied, "Under an acacia tree."

Daniel said, "Indeed! Your lie recoils on your own head: the angel of God has already received from him your sentence and will cut you in half." He dismissed the man, ordered the other to be brought and said to him, "Son of Canaan, not of Judah, beauty has seduced you, lust has led your heart astray! This is how you have been behaving with the daughters of Israel, and they have been too frightened to resist; but here is a daughter of Judah who could not stomach your wickedness! Now then, tell me what sort of tree you surprised them under."

He replied, "Under an aspen tree."

Daniel said, "Indeed! Your lie recoils on your own head: the angel of God is waiting with a sword to rend you in half, and destroy the pair of you."

Then the whole assembly shouted, blessing God, the Saviour of those who trust in him. And they turned on the two elders whom Daniel had convicted of false evidence out of their own mouths. As the Law of Moses prescribes, they were given the same punishment as they had schemed to inflict on their neighbour. They were put to death. And thus, that day, an innocent life was saved. Hilkiah and his wife gave thanks to God for their daughter Susanna, and so did her husband Joakim and all his relations, because she had been acquitted of anything dishonourable.

From that day onwards, Daniel's reputation stood high with the people.

# DEATH WEARS A MASK
## Steven Saylor

*One of my most welcome discoveries following the publication of* The
Mammoth Book of Historical Whodunnits *is the work of Steven
Saylor, whom I had somehow overlooked and had not listed in the
appendix. Edward Hoch first drew him to my attention. He is the
author of (at the last count) four novels and eight short stories about
Gordianus the Finder, set at the time of Cicero in the first century*
BC. *The novels run* Roman Blood *(1991),* Arms of Nemesis
*(1992),* Catilina's Riddle *(1993) and* The Venus Throw *(1995),
and they are an absolute delight. Gordianus is not a transplanted
twentieth-century investigator, but someone at home in the bizarre
world of ancient Rome. He has no connections to the ruling aristocracy
and must survive by his own wiles and cunning. Saylor was born
in Texas in 1956, and grew up near Cross Plains, where Robert
E. Howard lived and wrote his stories about Conan. He now lives
in California where he has worked as an editor and writer. His
first short story about Gordianus was "A Will is a Way" (Ellery
Queen's Mystery Magazine, March 1992). This following was the
second.*

"Eco," I said, "do you mean to tell me that you have never seen
a play?"

He looked up at me with his big brown eyes and shook his head.

"Never laughed at the slaves on stage who have a falling-out and
bludgeon each other with clubs made of cork? Never swooned to see
the young heroine abducted by pirates? *Never* thrilled at the discovery
that our hero is not the penniless vagabond we thought, but the secret
heir to a vast fortune?"

Eco's eyes grew even larger, and he shook his head more vigorously
from side to side.

"Then there must be a remedy, this very day!" I said.

It was the Ides of September, and a more beautiful autumn day
the gods had never fashioned. The sun shone warmly on the narrow
streets and gurgling fountains of Rome; a light breeze swept up from

the Tiber, cooling the seven hills; the sky above was a bowl of purest azure, without a single cloud. It was the twelfth day of the sixteen days set aside each year for the Roman Festival, the city's oldest public holiday. Perhaps Jupiter himself had decreed that the weather should be so perfect; the holiday was in his honor.

For Eco, the Festival had been an endless orgy of discoveries. He had seen his first chariot race in the Circus Maximus, had watched wrestlers and boxers in the public squares, had eaten his first calf's-brain-and-almond sausage from a street vendor. The race had thrilled him, mostly because he thought the horses so beautiful; the pugilists had bored him, since he had seen plenty of brawling in public before; the sausage had not agreed with him (or perhaps his problem was the spiced green apples he gorged himself on later).

It was four months since I had rescued Eco in an alley in the Subura, from a gang of boys pursuing him with sticks and cruel jeers. I knew a little of his history, having met him briefly in my investigations for Cicero that spring. Apparently his widowed mother had chosen to abandon little Eco in her desperation, leaving him to fend for himself. What else could I do but take him home with me?

He struck me as exceedingly clever for a boy of ten. I knew he was ten, because whenever I asked, he held up ten fingers. Eco could hear (and add) perfectly well, but his tongue was useless.

At first his muteness was a great handicap for us both. (A fever caused it – the same fever that claimed his father's life.) Eco is a skillful mime, to be sure, but gestures can convey only so much. Someone had taught him the letters – the widow Polia, perhaps, or the boy's father before he died – but he could read and write only the simplest words. I had begun to teach him myself, but the going was made harder by his speechlessness.

His practical knowledge of the streets of Rome was deep but narrow. He knew all the back entrances to all the shops in the Subura, knew where the fish and meat vendors down by the Tiber left their scraps at the end of the day. But he had never been to the Forum or the Circus Maximus or the hot springs at Tarentum, had never heard a politician declaim (lucky boy!) or witnessed the spectacle of the theater. I spent many hours showing him the city that summer, rediscovering its marvels through the wide eyes of a ten-year-old boy.

So it was that, on the twelfth day of the Roman Festival, when a crier came running through the streets announcing that the company of Quintus Roscius would be performing in an hour, I determined that we should not miss it.

"Ah, the company of Roscius the Comedian!" I said. "The

magistrates in charge of the Festival have spared no expense. There is no more famous actor today than Quintus Roscius, and no more renowned troupe of performers than his!"

We made our way from the Subura down to the Forum, where holiday crowds thronged the open squares. Between the Temple of Jupiter Stator and the Senian Baths, a makeshift theater had been erected. Rows of benches were set before a wooden stage that had been raised in the narrow space between the brick walls.

"Some day," I remarked, "a rabble-rousing politician will build the first permanent theater in Rome. Imagine that, a proper theater made of stone, as sturdy as a temple! The old-fashioned moralists will be scandalized, of course – they hate the theater because it comes from Greece, and they think that all things Greek must be decadent and dangerous. Ah, we're early – we shall have good seats."

The usher led us to an aisle seat on a bench five rows back from the stage. The first four rows had been partitioned by a rope of purple cloth, set aside for those of senatorial rank. Occasionally the usher tromped down the aisle, followed by some toga-clad magistrate and his party, and pulled aside the rope to allow them access to the benches.

While the theater slowly filled around us, I pointed out to Eco the details of the stage. Before the first row of benches there was a small open space, the orchestra, where the musicians would play; three steps at either side led up to the stage itself. Behind the stage and enclosing it on either side was a screen of wood with a folding door in the middle and other doors set into the left and right wings. Through these doors the actors would enter and exit. Out of sight, behind the stage, the musicians could be heard warming up their pipes, trilling snatches of familiar tunes.

"Gordianus!"

I turned to see a tall, thin figure looming over us.

"Statilius!" I cried. "It's good to see you."

"And you as well. But who is this?" He ruffled Eco's mop of brown hair with his long fingers.

"This is Eco," I said.

"A long-lost nephew?"

"Not exactly."

"Ah. An indiscretion from the past?" Statilius raised a suggestive eyebrow.

"Not that, either." My face turned hot. And yet, I suddenly wondered, how would it have felt to say: "Yes, this is my son." Not for the first time I considered the possibility of adopting Eco legally – and as quickly banished the thought from my mind. A man like myself, who often risks death, has no business becoming a father; so I told myself. If I truly wanted sons, I could have married a proper Roman wife long ago and had a houseful by now. I quickly changed the subject.

"But Statilius, where is your costume and mask? Why aren't you backstage, getting ready?" I had known Statilius since we both were boys; he had become an actor in his youth, joining first one company and then another, always seeking the training of established comedians. The great Roscius had taken him on a year before.

"Oh, I still have plenty of time to get ready."

"And how is life in the company of the greatest actor in Rome?"

"Wonderful, of course!"

I frowned at the note of false bravado in his voice.

"Ah, Gordianus, you always could see through me. Not wonderful, then – terrible! Roscius – what a monster! Brilliant, to be sure, but a beast! If I were a slave I'd be covered with bruises. Instead, he whips me with his tongue. What a taskmaster! The man is relentless, and never satisfied. He makes a man feel no better than a worm. The galleys or the mines could hardly be worse. Is it my fault that I've grown too old to play heroines and haven't yet the proper voice to be an old miser or a braggart soldier? Ah, perhaps Roscius is right. I'm useless – talentless – I bring the whole company into disrepute."

"Actors are all alike," I whispered to Eco. "They need more coddling than babies." Then to Statilius: "Nonsense! I saw you in the spring, at the Festival of the Great Mother, when Roscius put on *The Brothers Menaechmus*. You were brilliant playing the twins."

"Do you really think so?"

"I swear it. I laughed so hard I almost fell off the bench."

He brightened a bit, then frowned. "I wish that Roscius thought so. Today I was all set to play Euclio, the old miser – "

"Ah, then we're seeing *The Pot of Gold?*"

"Yes – "

"One of my favorite plays, Eco. Quite possibly Plautus's funniest comedy. Crude, yet satisfying . . ."

"I was to play Euclio," Statilius said rather sharply, drawing the conversation back to himself, "when suddenly, this morning, Roscius explodes into a rage and says that I have the role all wrong, and that he can't suffer the humiliation of seeing me bungle it in front of all Rome. Instead I'll be Megadorus, the next-door neighbor."

"Another fine role," I said, trying to remember it.

"Fah! And who gets the plum role of Euclio? That parasite Panurgus – a mere slave, with no more comic timing than a slug!" He abruptly stiffened. "Oh no, what's this?"

I followed his gaze to the outer aisle, where the usher was leading a burly, bearded man toward the front of the theater. A blond giant with a scar across his nose followed close behind – the bearded man's bodyguard; I know a hired ruffian from the Subura when I see one. The usher led them to the far end of our bench; they stepped into the gap and headed toward us to take the empty spot beside Eco.

Statilius bent low to hide himself and groaned into my ear. "As if I hadn't enough worries – it's that awful moneylender Flavius and one of his hired bullies. The only man in Rome who's more of a monster than Roscius."

"And just how much do you owe this Flavius?" I began to say, when suddenly, from backstage, a roaring voice rose above the discordant pipes.

"Fool! Incompetent! Don't come to me now saying you can't remember the lines!"

"Roscius," Statilius whispered, "screaming at Panurgus, I hope. The man's temper is terrible."

The central door on the stage flew open, revealing a short, stocky man already dressed for the stage, wearing a splendid cloak of rich white fabric. His lumpy, scowling face was the sort to send terror into an underling's soul, yet this was, by universal acclaim, the funniest man in Rome. His legendary squint made his eyes almost invisible, but when he looked in our direction, I felt as if a dagger had been thrown past my ear and into the heart of Statilius.

"And you!" he bellowed. "Where have you been? Backstage, immediately! No, don't bother to go the long way round – backstage, now!" He gave commands as if he were speaking to a dog.

Statilius hurried up the aisle, leaped onto the stage, and disappeared backstage, closing the door behind him – but not, I noticed, before casting a furtive glance at the newcomer who had just seated himself beside Eco. I turned and looked at Flavius the moneylender, who returned my curious gaze with a scowl. He did not look like a man in the proper mood for a comedy.

I cleared my throat. "Today you'll see *The Pot of Gold*," I said pleasantly, leaning toward the newcomers. Flavius gave a start and wrinkled his bushy brows. "One of Plautus's very best plays, don't you think?"

Flavius parted his lips and peered at me suspiciously. The blond bodyguard looked at me with an expression of supreme stupidity.

I shrugged and turned my attention elsewhere.

From the open square behind us the crier made his last announcement. The benches rapidly filled. Latecomers and slaves stood wherever they could, crowding together on tiptoe. Two musicians stepped onto the stage and descended to the orchestra, where they began to blow upon their long pipes.

A murmur of recognition passed through the crowd at the familiar strains of the miser Euclio's theme, the first indication of the play we were about to see. Meanwhile the usher and the crier moved up and down the aisles, playfully hushing the noisier members of the audience.

At length the overture was finished. The central door on the stage rattled open. Out stepped Roscius, wearing his sumptuous white cloak, his head obscured by a mask of grotesque, happy countenance. Through the holes I glimpsed his squinting eyes; his mellow voice resonated throughout the theater.

"In case you don't know who I am, let me briefly introduce myself," he said. "I am the Guardian Spirit of this house – Euclio's house. I have been in charge of this place now for a great many years . . ." He proceeded to deliver the prologue, giving the audience a starting point for the familiar story – how the grandfather of Euclio had hidden a pot of gold beneath the floorboards of the house; how Euclio had a daughter who was in love with the next-door neighbor's nephew, and needed only a dowry to be happily married; and how he, the Guardian Spirit, intended to guide the greedy Euclio to the pot of gold and so set events in motion.

I glanced at Eco, who stared up at the masked figure enraptured, hanging on every word. Beside him, the moneylender Flavius wore the same unhappy scowl as before. The blond bodyguard sat with his mouth open and occasionally reached up to pick at the scar across his nose.

A muffled commotion was heard from backstage. "Ah," said Roscius in a theatrical whisper, "there's old Euclio now, pitching a fit as usual. The greedy miser must have located the pot of gold by now, and he wants to count his fortune in secret, so he's turning the old housekeeper out of the house." He quietly withdrew through the door in the right wing.

Through the central door emerged a figure wearing an old man's mask and dressed in bright yellow, the traditional color for greed. This was Panurgus, the slave-actor, taking the plum leading role of the miser Euclio. Behind him he dragged another actor dressed as a lowly female slave, and flung him to the middle of the stage. "Get out!" he shouted. "Out! By Hades, out with you, you old snooping bag of bones!"

Statilius had been wrong to disparage Panurgus's comic gifts; already I heard guffaws and laughter around me.

"What have I done? What? What?" cried the other actor. His

grimacing feminine mask was surmounted by a hideous tangled wig. His gown was in tatters about his knobby knees. "Why are you beating a long-suffering old hag?"

"To give you something to be long-suffering about, that's why! And to make you suffer as much as I do, just looking at you!" Panurgus and his fellow actor scurried about the stage, to the uproarious amusement of the audience. Eco bounced up and down on the bench and clapped his hands. The moneylender and his bodyguard sat with their arms crossed, unimpressed.

> HOUSEKEEPER: *But why must you drive me out of the house?*
> EUCLIO: *Why? Since when do I have to give you a reason? You're asking for a fresh crop of bruises!*
> HOUSEKEEPER: *Let the gods send me jumping off a cliff if I'll put up with this sort of slavery any longer!*
> EUCLIO: *What's she muttering to herself? I've a good mind to poke your eyes out, you damned witch!*

At length the slavewoman disappeared and the miser went back into his house to count his money; the neighbor Megadorus and his sister Eunomia occupied the stage. From the voice, it seemed to me that the sister was played by the same actor who had performed the cringing slavewoman; no doubt he specialized in female characters. My friend Statilius, as Megadorus, performed adequately, I thought, but he was not in the same class with Roscius, or even with his rival Panurgus. His comic turns inspired polite guffaws, not raucous laughter.

> EUNOMIA: *Dear brother, I've asked you out of the house to have a little talk about your private affairs.*
> MEGADORUS: *How sweet! You are as thoughtful as you are beautiful. I kiss your hand.*
> EUNOMIA: *What? Are you talking to someone behind me?*
> MEGADORUS: *Of course not. You're the prettiest woman I know!*
> EUNOMIA: *Don't be absurd. Every woman is uglier than every other, in one way or another.*
> MEGADORUS: *Mmm, but of course, whatever you say.*
> EUNOMIA: *Now give me your attention. Brother dear, I should like to see you married —*
> MEGADORUS: *Help! Murder! Ruin!*
> EUNOMIA: *Oh, quiet down!*

Even this exchange, usually so pleasing to the crowd, evoked only lukewarm titters. My attention strayed to Statilius's costume, made of

sumptuous blue wool embroidered with yellow, and to his mask, with
its absurdly quizzical eyebrows. Alas, I thought, it is a bad sign when
a comedian's costume is of greater interest than his delivery. Poor
Statilius had found a place with the most respected acting troupe in
Rome, but he did not shine there. No wonder the demanding Roscius
was so intolerant of him!

Even Eco grew restless. Next to him, the moneylender Flavius
leaned over to whisper something in the ear of his blond bodyguard
– disparaging the talents of the actor who owed him money, I
thought.

At length, the sister exited; the miser returned to converse with his
neighbor. Seeing the two of them together on the stage – Statilius and
his rival Panurgus – the gulf between their talents was painfully clear.
Panurgus as Euclio stole the scene completely, and not just because
his lines were better.

EUCLIO: *So you wish to marry my daughter. Good enough – but you
must know I haven't so much as a copper to donate to her dowry.*

MEGADORUS: *I don't expect even half a copper. Her virtue and good
name are quite enough.*

EUCLIO: *I mean to say, it's not as if I'd just happened to have found
some, oh, buried treasure in my house . . . say, a pot of gold buried by
my grandfather, or . . .*

MEGADORUS: *Of course not – how ridiculous! Say no more. You'll
give your daughter to me, then?*

EUCLIO: *Agreed. But what's that? Oh no, I'm ruined!*

MEGADORUS: *Jupiter Almighty, what's wrong?*

EUCLIO: *I thought I heard a spade . . . someone digging . . .*

MEGADORUS: *Why, it's only a slave I've got digging up some roots in
my garden. Calm down, good neighbor . . .*

I inwardly groaned for my friend Statilius; but if his delivery was
flat, he had learned to follow the master's stage directions without
a misstep. Roscius was famous not only for embellishing the old
comedies with colorful costumes and masks to delight the eyes,
but for choreographing the movements of his actors. Statilius and
Panurgus were never static on the stage, like the actors in inferior
companies. They circled one another in a constant comic dance, a
swirl of blue and yellow.

Eco tugged at my sleeve. With a shrug of his shoulder he gestured to
the men beside him. Flavius was again whispering in the bodyguard's
ear; the big blond was wrinkling his eyebrows, perplexed. Then he
rose and lumbered toward the aisle. Eco drew up his feet, but I was

too slow. The monster stepped on my foot. I let out a howl. Others around me started doing the same, thinking I was badgering the actors. The blond giant made no apology at all.

Eco tugged at my sleeve. "Let it go, Eco," I said. "One must learn to live with rudeness in the theater."

He only rolled his eyes and crossed his arms in exasperation. I knew that gesture: if only he could speak!

On the stage, the two neighbors concluded their plans for Megadorus to wed the daughter of Euclio; with a shrilling of pipes and the tinkling of cymbals, they left the stage and the first act was done.

The pipe players introduced a new theme. After a moment, two new actors appeared on stage. These were the quarreling cooks, summoned to prepare the wedding feast. A Rcman audience delights in jokes about food and gluttony, the cruder the better. While I groaned at the awful puns, Eco laughed aloud, making a hoarse, barking sound.

In the midst of the gaiety, my blood turned cold. Above the laughter, I heard a scream.

It was not a woman's scream, but a man's. Not a scream of fear, but of pain.

I looked at Eco, who looked back at me. He had heard it, too. No one else in the audience seemed to have noticed, but the actors on stage must have heard something. They bungled their lines and turned uncertainly toward the door, stepping on one another's feet. The audience only laughed harder at their clumsiness.

The quarreling cooks came to the end of their scene and disappeared backstage.

The stage was empty. There was a pause that grew longer and longer. Strange, unaccountable noises came from backstage — muffled gasps, confused shuffling, a loud shout. The audience began to murmur and move about on the benches.

At last the door from the left wing soundlessly opened. Onto the stage stepped a figure wearing the mask of the miser Euclio. He was dressed in bright yellow, but not in the same cloak as before. He threw his hands in the air. "Disaster!" he cried. I felt a cold shiver down my spine.

"Disaster!" he said again. "A daughter's marriage is a disaster! How can any man afford it? I've just come back from the market, and you wouldn't believe what they're charging for lamb — an arm and a leg for an arm and a leg, that's what they want . . ."

The character was miserly Euclio, but the actor was no longer

Panurgus; it was Roscius behind the mask. The audience seemed not to notice the substitution, or at least not to mind it; they started laughing almost immediately at the spectacle of poor Euclio befuddled by his own stinginess.

Roscius delivered the lines flawlessly, with the practiced comic timing that comes from having played a role many times, but I thought I heard a strange quavering in his voice. When he turned so that I could glimpse his eyes within the mask, I saw no sign of his famous squint. His eyes were wide with alarm. Was this Roscius the actor, frightened of something very real – or Euclio, afraid that the squabbling cooks would find his treasure?

"What's that shouting from the kitchen?" he cried. "Oh no, they're calling for a bigger pot to put the chicken in! Oh, my pot of gold!" He ran through the door backstage, almost tripping over his yellow cloak. There followed a cacophony of crashing pots.

The central door was thrown open. One of the cooks emerged on stage, crying out in a panic, "Help, help, help!"

It was the voice of Statilius! I stiffened and started to stand, but the words were only part of the play. "It's a madhouse in there," he cried, straightening his mask. He jumped from the stage and ran into the audience. "The miser Euclio's gone mad! He's beating us over the head with pots and pans! Citizens, come to our rescue!" He whirled about the central aisle until he came to a halt beside me. He bent low and spoke through his teeth so that only I could hear.

"Gordianus! Come backstage, now!"

I gave a start. Through the mask I looked into Statilius's anxious eyes.

"Backstage!" he hissed. "Come quick! A dagger – blood – Panurgus – murder!"

From beyond the maze of screens and awnings and platforms I occasionally heard the playing of the pipes and actors' voices raised in argument, followed by the muffled roar of the audience laughing. Backstage, the company of Quintus Roscius ran about in a panic, changing costumes, fitting masks onto one another's heads, mumbling lines beneath their breath, sniping at each other or exchanging words of encouragement, and in every other way trying to act as if this were simply another hectic performance and that a corpse was not lying in their midst.

The body was that of the slave Panurgus. He lay on his back in a secluded little alcove in the alley that ran behind the Temple of Jupiter. The place was a public privy, one of many built in out-of-the-way nooks on the perimeter of the Forum. Screened by two walls, a sloping floor tilted to a hole that emptied into the Cloaca Maxima. Panurgus had apparently come here to relieve himself between scenes. Now he lay dead with a knife plunged squarely into his chest. Above his heart a large red circle stained his bright yellow costume. A sluggish stream of blood trickled across the tiles and ran down the drain.

He was older than I had thought, almost as old as his master, with grey in his hair and a wrinkled forehead. His mouth and eyes were open wide in shock; his eyes were green, and in death they glittered dully like uncut emeralds.

Eco gazed down at the body and reached up to grasp my hand. Statilius ran up beside us. He was dressed in blue again and held the mask of Megadorus in his hands. His face was ashen. "Madness," he whispered. "Bloody madness."

"Shouldn't the play be stopped?"

"Roscius refuses. Not for a slave, he says. And he doesn't dare tell the crowd. Imagine: a murder, backstage, in the middle of our performance, on a holiday consecrated to Jupiter himself, in the very shadow of the god's temple – what an omen! What magistrate would ever hire Roscius and the company again? No, the show goes on – even though we must somehow figure out how to fill nine roles with five actors instead of six. Oh dear, and I've never learned the nephew's lines . . ."

"Statilius!" It was Roscius, returning from the stage. He threw off the mask of Euclio. His own face was far more grotesque, contorted with fury. "What do you think you're doing, standing there mumbling? If I'm playing Euclio, you have to play the nephew!" He rubbed his squinting eyes, then slapped his forehead. "But no, that's impossible – Megadorus and the nephew must be on stage at the same time. What a disaster! Jupiter, why me?"

The actors circled one another like frenzied bees. The dressers hovered about them uncertainly, as useless as drones. All was chaos in the company of Quintus Roscius.

I looked down at the bloodless face of Panurgus, who was beyond caring. All men become the same in death, whether slave or citizen, Roman or Greek, genius or pretender.

At last the play was over. The old bachelor Megadorus had escaped the clutches of marriage; miserly Euclio had lost and then recovered his pot of gold; the honest slave who restored it to him had been set free; the quarreling cooks had been paid by Megadorus and sent on their way; and the young lovers had been joyously betrothed. How this was accomplished under the circumstances, I do not know. By some miracle of the theater, everything came off without a hitch. The cast assembled together on the stage to roaring applause, and then returned backstage, their exhilaration at once replaced by the grim reality of the death among them.

"Madness," Statilius said again, hovering over the corpse. Knowing how he felt about his rival, I had to wonder if he was not secretly gloating. He seemed genuinely shocked, but that, after all, could have been acting.

"And who is this?" barked Roscius, tearing off the yellow cloak he had assumed to play the miser.

"My name is Gordianus. Men call me the Finder."

Roscius raised an eyebrow and nodded. "Ah, yes, I've heard of you. Last spring – the case of Sextus Roscius; no relation to myself, I'm glad to say, or very distant, anyway. You earned yourself a name with parties on both sides of that affair."

Knowing Roscius was an intimate of the dictator Sulla, whom I had grossly offended, I only nodded.

"So what are you doing here?" Roscius demanded.

"It was I who told him," said Statilius helplessly. "I asked him to come backstage. It was the first thing I thought of."

"You invited an outsider to intrude on this tragedy, Statilius? Fool! What's to keep him from standing in the Forum and announcing the news to everyone who passes? The scandal will be disastrous."

"I assure you, I can be quite discreet – for a client," I said.

"Oh, I see," said Roscius, squinting at me shrewdly. "Perhaps that's not a bad idea, provided you could actually be of some help."

"I think I might," I said modestly, already calculating a fee. Roscius was, after all, the most highly paid actor in the world. Rumor claimed he made as much as half a million sesterces in a single year. He could afford to be generous.

He looked down at the corpse and shook his head bitterly. "One of my most promising pupils. Not just a gifted artist, but a valuable piece of property. But why should anyone murder the slave? Panurgus had no vices, no politics, no enemies."

"It's a rare man who has no enemies," I said. I could not help but glance at Statilius, who hurriedly looked away.

There was a commotion among the gathered actors and stage-hands. The crowd parted to admit a tall, cadaverous figure with a shock of red hair.

"Chaerea! Where have you been?" growled Roscius.

The newcomer looked down his long nose, first at the corpse, then at Roscius. "Drove down from my villa at Fidenae," he snapped tersely. "Axle on the chariot broke. Missed more than the play, it appears."

"Gaius Fannius Chaerea," whispered Statilius in my ear. "He was Panurgus's original owner. When he saw the slave had comic gifts he handed him over to Roscius to train him, as part-owner."

"They don't seem friendly," I whispered back.

"They've been feuding over how to calculate the profits from Panurgus's performances . . ."

"So. Quintus Roscius," sniffed Chaerea, tilting his nose even higher, "this is how you take care of our common property. Bad management, I say. Slave's worthless, now. I'll send you a bill for my share."

"What? You think I'm responsible for this?" Roscius squinted fiercely.

"Slave was in your care; now he's dead. Theater people! So irresponsible." Chaerea ran his bony fingers through his orange mane and shrugged haughtily before turning his back. "Expect my bill tomorrow," he said, stepping through the crowd to join a coterie of attendants waiting in the alley. "Or I'll see you in court."

"Outrageous!" said Roscius. "You!" He pointed a stubby finger at me. "This is your job! Find out who did this, and why. If it was a slave or a pauper, I'll have him torn apart. If it was a rich man, I'll sue him blind for destroying my property. I'll go to Hades before I give Chaerea the satisfaction of saying this was my fault!"

I accepted the job with a grave nod and tried not to smile. I could almost feel the rain of glittering silver on my head. Then I glimpsed the contorted face of the dead Panurgus, and felt the full gravity of my commission. For a dead slave in Rome, there is seldom any attempt to find justice. I would find the killer, I silently vowed, not for Roscius and his silver, but to honor the shade of an artist cruelly cut down in his prime.

"Very well, Roscius. I will need to ask some questions. See that no one in the company leaves until I am done with him. If I may, I would talk with you in private first. Perhaps a cup of wine would calm us both . . ."

Late that afternoon, I sat on a bench beneath the shade of an olive tree, on a quiet street not far from the Temple of Jupiter. Eco sat beside me, pensively studying the play of leafy shadows on the paving stones.

"So, Eco, what do you think? Have we learned anything of value?"

He shook his head gravely from side to side.

"You judge too quickly." I laughed. "Consider: we last saw

Panurgus alive during his scene with Statilius at the close of the first act. Then those two left the stage; the pipers played an interlude, and next the quarreling cooks came on. Then there was a scream. That must have been Panurgus, when he was stabbed. It caused a commotion backstage; Roscius checked into the matter and discovered the body in the privy. Word quickly spread among the others. Roscius put on the dead man's mask and a yellow cloak, the closest thing he had to match Panurgus's costume, and rushed on stage just in time to keep the play going. Statilius, meanwhile, put on a cook's costume so that he could jump into the audience and plead for my help.

"Therefore, we know at least one thing: the actors playing the cooks were innocent, as were the pipe players, because they were on stage when the murder occurred."

Eco made a face to show he was not impressed.

"Yes, this is all very elementary, but to build a wall we begin with the first row of bricks. Now, who was backstage at the time of the murder, has no one to account for his whereabouts at the moment of the scream, and might have wanted Panurgus dead?"

Eco bounded up from the bench, ready to play the game. He performed a pantomime, jabbering with his jaw and waving his arms at himself.

I smiled sadly; the unflattering portrait could only be my talkative and self-absorbed friend Statilius. "Yes, Statilius must be foremost among the suspects, though I regret to say it. We know he had cause to hate Panurgus; so long as the slave was alive, a man of inferior talent like Statilius would never be given the best roles. We also learned, from questioning the company, that when the scream was heard, no one could account for Statilius's whereabouts. This may be only a coincidence, given the ordinary chaos that seems to reign backstage during a performance. Statilius himself vows that he was busy in a corner adjusting his costume. In his favor, he seems to have been truly shocked at the slave's death – but he might only be pretending. I call the man my friend, but do I really know him?"

I pondered for a moment. "Who else, Eco?"

He hunched his shoulders, scowled, and squinted.

"Yes, Roscius was also backstage when Panurgus screamed, and no one seems to remember seeing him at that instant. It was he who found the corpse – or was he there when the knife descended? Roscius is a violent man; all his actors say so. We heard him shouting angrily at someone before the play began – do you remember? 'Fool! Incompetent! Why can't you remember your lines?' Roscius now claims he can't remember the incident at all, but others saw him and told me it was Panurgus he was shouting at. Did the slave's performance in the first act displease him so much that he flew into a rage, lost his head, and murdered him? It hardly seems likely: I thought Panurgus was doing quite well. And Roscius, like Statilius, seemed genuinely offended by the murder. But then, Roscius is an actor of great skill."

Eco put his hands on his hips and his nose in the air and began to strut haughtily.

"Ah, Chaerea; I was coming to him. He claims not to have arrived until after the play was over, and yet he hardly seemed taken aback when he saw the corpse. He seems almost *too* unflappable. He was the slave's original owner. In return for cultivating Panurgus's talents, Roscius acquired half-ownership, but Chaerea seems to have been thoroughly dissatisfied with the arrangement. Did he decide that the slave was worth more to him dead than alive? Chaerea holds Roscius culpable for the loss, and intends to coerce Roscius into paying him half the slave's worth in silver. In a Roman court, with the right advocate, Chaerea will likely prevail."

I leaned back against the olive tree, dissatisfied. "Still, I wish we had uncovered someone else in the company with as strong a motive, and the opportunity to have done the deed. Yet no one seems to have borne a grudge against Panurgus, and almost everyone could account for his whereabouts when the victim screamed.

"Of course, the murderer may be someone from outside the company: the privy where Panurgus was stabbed was accessible to anyone passing through the alley behind the temple. Yet Roscius tells us, and the others confirm, that Panurgus had almost no dealings with anyone outside the troupe – he did not gamble or frequent brothels; he borrowed neither money nor other men's wives. His craft alone consumed him; so everyone says. Even if Panurgus *had* offended someone, the aggrieved party would surely have taken up the matter not with Panurgus but with Roscius, since he was the slave's owner and the man legally responsible for his actions."

I sighed with frustration. "The knife left in his heart was a common dagger, with no distinguishing features. No footprints surrounded the body. No telltale blood was found on any of the costumes. There were no witnesses, or none we knew of. Alas!" The shower of silver in my imagination dried to a trickle; with nothing to show, I would be lucky to press Roscius into paying me a day's fee for my trouble. Even worse, I felt the shade of dead Panurgus watching me. I had vowed I would find his killer, and it seemed the vow was rashly made.

\* \* \*

That night I took my dinner in the ramshackle garden at the center of my house. The lamps burned low. Fireflies flitted among the columns of the peristyle. Sounds of distant revelry occasionally wafted up from the streets of the Subura at the foot of the hill.

"Bethesda, the meal was exquisite," I said, lying with my usual grace. Perhaps I could have been an actor, I thought.

But Bethesda was not fooled. She looked at me from beneath her long lashes and smiled with half her mouth. She combed one hand through the great unbound mass of her glossy black hair and shrugged an elegant shrug, then began to clear the table.

As she departed to the kitchen, I watched the sinuous play of her hips within her loose green stola. When I bought her long ago at the slave market in Alexandria, it had not been for her cooking. Her cooking had never improved, but in many other ways she was beyond perfection. I peered into the blackness of the long tresses that cascaded to her waist; I imagined the fireflies lost in those tresses, like twinkling stars in the blue-black firmament of the sky. Before Eco had come into my life, Bethesda and I had spent almost every night together, just the two of us, in the solitude of the garden . . .

I was startled from my reverie by a tiny hand pulling at the hem of my tunic.

"Yes, Eco, what is it?"

Eco, reclining on the couch next to mine, put his fists together and pulled them apart, up and down, as if unrolling a scroll.

"Ah, your reading lesson. We had no time for it today, did we? But my eyes are weary, Eco, and yours must be, too. And there are other matters on my mind . . ."

He frowned at me in mock-dejection until I relented. "Very well. Bring that lamp nearer. What would you like to read tonight?"

Eco pointed at himself and shook his head, then pointed at me. He cupped his hands behind his ears and closed his eyes. He preferred it (and secretly, so did I) when I did the reading, and he could enjoy the luxury of merely listening. All that summer, on lazy afternoons and long summer nights, the two of us had spent many such hours in the garden; while I read Piso's history of Hannibal, Eco would sit at my feet and watch elephants among the clouds, or he would lie on his back and study the moon while I declaimed the tale of the Sabine women. He understood Greek, strangely enough, though he knew none of the letters. Of late I had been reading to him from an old, tattered scroll of Plato, a cast-off gift from Cicero. Eco followed the subtleties of the philosopher's discourses with fascination, though occasionally in his big brown eyes I saw a glimmer of sorrow that he could never hope to engage in such debates himself.

"Shall I read more Plato, then? They say philosophy after dinner aids digestion."

Eco nodded and ran to fetch the scroll. He emerged from the shadows of the peristyle a moment later, gripping it carefully in his hands. Suddenly he stopped and stood statue-like with a strange expression on his face.

"Eco, what is it?" I thought for a moment that he was ill; Bethesda's fish dumplings and turnips in cumin sauce had been undistinguished, but hardly so bad as to make him sick. He stared straight ahead at nothing, and did not hear me.

"Eco? Are you all right?" He stood rigid, trembling; a look which might have been fear or ecstasy crossed his face. Then he sprang toward me, pressed the scroll under my nose, and pointed at it frantically.

"I've never known a boy to be so mad for learning." I laughed, but he was not playing a game. His expression was deadly serious. "But Eco, it's only the same volume of Plato that I've been reading to you off and on all summer. Why are you suddenly so excited?"

Eco stood back to perform his pantomime. A dagger thrust into his heart could only indicate the dead Panurgus.

"Panurgus and Plato – Eco, I see no connection."

Eco bit his lip and scrambled about, desperate to express himself. At last he ran into the house and back out again, clutching two objects. He dropped them onto my lap.

"Eco, be careful! This little vase is made of precious green glass, and came all the way from Alexandria. And why have you brought me a bit of red tile? This must have fallen from the roof . . ."

Eco pointed emphatically at each object in turn, but I could not see what he meant.

He disappeared again and came back with my wax tablet and stylus, upon which he wrote the words for *red* and *green*.

"Yes, Eco. I can see that the vase is green and the tile is red. Blood is red . . ." Eco shook his head and pointed to his eyes. "Panurgus had green eyes . . ." I saw them in my memory, staring lifeless at the sky.

Eco stamped his foot and shook his head to let me know that I was badly off-course. He took the vase and the bit of tile from my lap and began to juggle them from hand to hand.

"Eco, stop that! I told you, the vase is precious!"

He put them carelessly down and reached for the stylus again. He rubbed out the words *red* and *green* and in their place wrote *blue*. It seemed he wished to write another word, but could not think of how to spell it. He nibbled on the stylus and shook his head.

"Eco, I think you must have a fever. You make no sense at all."

He took the scroll from my lap and began to unroll it, scanning it hopelessly. Even if the text had been in Latin it would have been a tortuous job for him to decipher the words and find whatever he was searching for, but the letters were Greek and utterly foreign to him.

He threw down the scroll and began to pantomime again, but he was excited and clumsy; I could make no sense of his wild gesturing. I shrugged and shook my head in exasperation, and Eco suddenly began to weep with frustration. He seized the scroll again and pointed to his eyes. Did he mean that I should read the scroll, or did he point to his tears? I bit my lip and turned up my palms, unable to help him.

Eco threw the scroll in my lap and ran crying from the room. A hoarse, stifled braying issued from his throat, not the sound of normal weeping; it tore my heart to hear it. I should have been more patient, but how was I to understand him? Bethesda emerged from the kitchen and gazed at me accusingly, then followed the sound of Eco's weeping to the little room where he slept.

I looked down at the scroll in my lap. There were so many words on the parchment; which ones had keyed an idea in Eco's memory, and what could they have to do with dead Panurgus? *Red, green, blue* – I vaguely remembered reading a passage in which Plato discoursed on the nature of light and color, but I could scarcely remember it, not having understood much of it in the first place. Some scheme about overlapping cones projected from the eyes to an object, or from the object to the eyes, I couldn't remember which; was this what Eco recalled, and could it have made any sense to him?

I rolled through the scroll, looking for the reference, but was unable to find it. My eyes grew weary. The lamp began to sputter. The Greek letters all began to look alike. Normally Bethesda would have come to put me to bed, but it seemed she had chosen to stay with Eco instead. I fell asleep on my dining couch beneath the stars, thinking of a yellow cloak stained with red, and of green eyes gazing at an empty blue sky.

Eco was ill the next day, or feigned illness. Bethesda solemnly informed me that he did not wish to leave his bed. I stood in the doorway of the little room and spoke to him gently, reminding him that the Roman Festival continued, and that today there would be a wild-beast show in the Circus Maximus, and another play put on by another company. He turned his back to me and pulled the coverlet over his head.

"I suppose I should punish him," I whispered to myself, trying to think of what a normal Roman father would do.

"I suppose you should not," whispered Bethesda as she passed me. Her haughtiness left me properly humbled.

I took my morning stroll, alone – for the first time in many days, I realized, acutely aware that Eco was not beside me. The Subura seemed a rather dull place without ten-year-old eyes through which to see it. I had only my own eyes to serve me, and they had seen it a million times before.

I would buy him a gift, I decided; I would buy them each a gift, for it was always a good idea to placate Bethesda when she was haughty. For Eco I bought a red leather ball, such as boys use to play trigon, knocking it back and forth to each other using their elbows and knees. For Bethesda I wanted to find a veil woven of blue midnight shot through with fireflies, but I decided to settle for one made of linen. On the street of the cloth merchants I found the shop of my old acquaintance Ruso.

I asked to see a veil of dark blue. As if by magic he produced the very veil I had been imagining, a gossamer thing that seemed to be made of blue-black spiderwebs and silver. It was also the most expensive item in the shop. I chided him for taunting me with a luxury beyond my means.

Ruso shrugged good-naturedly. "One never knows; you might have just won a fortune on a toss of the tiles. Here, these are more affordable." He smiled, laying a selection before me.

"No," I said, seeing nothing I liked, "I've changed my mind."

"Then something in a lighter blue, perhaps? A bright blue, like the sky."

"No. I think not – "

"Ah, but see what I have to show you first. Felix . . . Felix! Fetch me one of the new veils that just arrived from Alexandria, the bright blue ones with yellow stitching."

The young slave bit his lip nervously and seemed to cringe. This struck me as odd, for I knew Ruso to be a temperate man and not a cruel master.

"Go on, then – what are you waiting for?" Ruso turned to me and shook his head. "This new slave – worse than useless! I don't think he's very smart, no matter what the slave merchant said. He keeps the books well enough, but here in the shop – look, he's done it again! Unbelievable! Felix, what is wrong with you? Do you do this just to spite me? Do you want a beating? I won't put up with this any longer, I tell you!"

The slave shrank back, looking confused and helpless. In his hand he held a yellow veil.

"All the time he does this!" wailed Ruso, clutching his head. "He wants to drive me mad! I ask for blue and he brings me yellow! I ask for yellow and he brings me blue! Have you ever heard of such stupidity? I shall beat you, Felix, I swear it!" And he ran after the poor slave, brandishing a measuring rod.

And then I understood.

My friend Statilius, as I had expected, was not at his lodgings in the Subura. When I questioned his landlord, the old man gave me the sly look of a confederate charged with throwing hounds off the scent, and told me that Statilius had left Rome for the countryside.

He was in none of the usual places where he might have been on a festival day. No tavern had served him and no brothel had admitted him. He would not even think of appearing in a gambling house, I told myself – and then knew that the exact opposite must be true.

Once I set to searching the gaming places in the Subura, I found him easily enough. In a crowded apartment on the third floor of an old tenement I discovered him in the midst of a crowd of well-dressed men, some of them even wearing their togas. Statilius was down on his elbows and knees, shaking a tiny box and muttering prayers to Fortune. He cast the tiles; the crowd contracted in a tight circle and then drew back, exclaiming. The tiles had come up two black, two white.

"Yes! Yes!" Statilius cried, and held out his palms. The others handed over their coins.

I grabbed him by the collar of his tunic and pulled him squawking into the hall.

"I should think you're deeply enough in debt already," I said.

"Quite the contrary!" he protested, smiling broadly. His face was flushed and his forehead beaded with sweat, like a man with a fever.

"Just how much *do* you owe Flavius the moneylender?"

"A hundred thousand sesterces."

"A hundred thousand!" My heart leaped into my throat.

"But not any longer. You see, I'll be able to pay him off now!" He held up the coins in his hands. "I have two bags full of silver in the other room, where my slave's looking after them. And – can you believe it? – a deed to a house on the Caelian Hill. I've won my way out of it, don't you see?"

"At the expense of another man's life."

His grin became sheepish. "So, you've figured that out. But who could have foreseen such a tragedy? Certainly not I. And when it happened, I didn't rejoice in Panurgus's death – you saw that. I didn't hate him, not really. My jealousy was purely professional. But if the Fates decided better him than me, who am I to argue?"

"You're a worm, Statilius. Why didn't you tell Roscius what you knew? Why didn't you tell me?"

"What did I know, really? Someone completely unknown might have killed poor Panurgus. I didn't witness the event."

"But you guessed the truth, all the same. That's why you wanted me backstage, wasn't it? You were afraid the assassin would come back for you. What was I, your bodyguard?"

"Perhaps. After all, he didn't come back, did he?"

"Statilius, you're a worm."

"You said that already." The smile dropped from his face like a discarded mask. He jerked his collar from my grasp.

"You hid the truth from me," I said, "but why from Roscius?"

"What, tell him I had run up an obscene gambling debt for which a notorious moneylender was threatening to kill me?"

"Perhaps he'd have loaned you the money."

"Never! You don't know Roscius. I was lucky to be in his troupe to begin with; he's not the type to hand out favors to an underling in the amount of a hundred thousand sesterces. And if he knew Panurgus had mistakenly been murdered instead of me – oh, Roscius would have loved that! One Panurgus is worth ten Statilii, that's his view. I *would* have been a dead man then, with Flavius on one side and Roscius on the other. The two of them would have torn me apart like a chicken bone!" He stepped back and straightened his tunic. The smile flickered and returned to his lips. "You're not going to tell anyone, are you?"

"Statilius, do you ever stop acting?" I averted my eyes to avoid his charm.

"Well?"

"Roscius is my client, not you."

"But I'm your friend, Gordianus."

"I made a promise to Panurgus."

"Panurgus didn't hear you."

"The gods did."

Finding the moneylender Flavius was a simpler matter – a few questions in the right ear, a few coins in the right hands. I learned that he owned a wine shop in a portico near the Circus Flaminius, where he sold inferior vintages imported from his native Tarquinii. But on a festival day, my informants told me, I would be more likely to find him at the house of questionable repute across the street.

The place had a low ceiling and the musty smell of spilled wine and crowded humanity. Across the room I saw Flavius, holding court with a group of his peers – businessmen of middle age with crude country manners, dressed in expensive tunics and cloaks of a quality that only emphasized their wearers' crudeness. Closer at hand, leaning against a wall (and looking strong enough to hold it up), was the moneylender's bully.

The blond giant was looking rather drunk, or else exceptionally stupid. He slowly blinked when I approached. A glimmer of recognition lit his bleary eyes and then faded.

"Festival days are good drinking days," I said, raising my cup of wine. He looked at me without expression for a moment, then shrugged and nodded.

"Tell me," I said, "do you know any of those spectacular beauties?" I gestured to a group of four women who loitered at the far corner of the room, near the foot of the stairs.

The giant shook his head glumly.

"Then you are a lucky man this day." I leaned close enough to smell the wine on his breath. "I was just talking to one of them. She tells me that she longs to meet you. It seems she has an appetite for men with sunny hair and big shoulders. She tells me that for a man such as you . . ." I whispered in his ear.

The veil of lust across his face made him look even stupider. He squinted drunkenly. "Which one?" he asked in a husky whisper.

"The one in the blue gown," I said.

"Ah . . ." He nodded and burped, then pushed past me and stumbled toward the stairs. As I expected, he ignored the woman in green, as well as the woman in coral and the one in brown. Instead he placed his hand squarely upon the hip of the woman in yellow, who turned and looked up at him with a startled but not unfriendly gaze.

"Quintus Roscius and his partner Chaerea were both duly impressed by my cleverness," I explained later that night to Bethesda. I was unable to resist the theatrical gesture of swinging the little bag of silver up in the air and onto the table, where it landed with a jingling thump. "Not a pot of gold, perhaps, but a fat enough fee to keep us all happy through the winter."

Her eyes became as round and glittering as little coins. They grew even larger when I produced the veil from Ruso's shop.

"Oh! But what is it made of?"

"Midnight and fireflies," I said. "Spiderwebs and silver." She tilted her head back and spread the translucent veil over her naked throat and arms. I blinked and swallowed hard, and decided that the purchase was well worth the price.

Eco stood uncertainly in the doorway of his little room, where he had watched me enter and had listened to my hurried tale of the day's events. He seemed to have recovered from his distemper of the morning, but his face was somber. I held out my hand, and he cautiously approached. He took the leather ball readily enough, but he still did not smile.

"Only a small gift, I know. But I have a greater one for you . . ."

"Still, I don't understand," protested Bethesda. "You've said the blond giant was stupid, but how can anyone be so stupid as not to be able to tell one color from another?"

"Eco knows," I said, smiling ruefully down at him. "He figured it out last night and tried to tell me, but he didn't know how. He remembered a passage from Plato that I read to him months ago; I had forgotten all about it. Here, I think I can find it now." I reached for the scroll, which still lay upon my sleeping couch.

"'One may observe,'" I read aloud, "'that not all men perceive the same colors. Although they are rare, there are those who confuse the colors red and green, and likewise those who cannot tell yellow from blue; still others appear to have no perception of the various shades of green.' He goes on to offer an explanation of this, but I cannot follow it."

"Then the bodyguard could not tell blue from yellow?" said Bethesda. "Even so . . ."

"Flavius came to the theater yesterday intending to make good on his threat to murder Statilius. No wonder he gave a start when I leaned over and said, 'Today you'll see *The Pot of Gold*' – for a moment he thought I meant the debt Statilius owed him! He sat in the audience long enough to see that Statilius was playing Megadorus, dressed in blue; no doubt he could recognize him by his voice. Then he sent the assassin backstage, knowing the alley behind the Temple of Jupiter would be virtually deserted, there to lie in wait for the actor *in the blue cloak*. Eco must have overheard snatches of his instructions, if only the word 'blue.' He thought that something was amiss and tried to tell me at the time, but there was too much confusion, with the giant stepping on my toes and the audience howling around us. Am I right?"

Eco nodded, and slapped a fist against his palm: exactly right.

"Unfortunately for poor Panurgus in his yellow cloak, the assassin is also uncommonly stupid. He needed more information than the color blue to make sure he murdered the right man, but he didn't bother to ask for it; or if he did, Flavius must only have sneered at him and rushed him along, unable to understand his confusion. Catching Panurgus alone and vulnerable in his yellow cloak, which might as well have been blue, the assassin did his job – and bungled it.

"Knowing Flavius was in the audience and out to kill him, learning that Panurgus had been stabbed, and seeing that the hired assassin was no longer in the audience, Statilius guessed the truth; no wonder he was so shaken by Panurgus's death, knowing that he was the intended victim."

"So another slave is murdered, and by accident! And nothing will be done," Bethesda said moodily.

"Not exactly. Panurgus was valuable property. The law allows his owners to sue the man responsible for his death for his full market value. I understand that Roscius and Chaerea are each demanding one hundred thousand sesterces from Flavius. If Flavius contests the action and loses, the amount will be double. Knowing his greed, I suspect he'll tacitly admit his guilt and settle for the smaller figure."

"Small justice for a meaningless murder."

I nodded. "And small recompense for the destruction of so much talent. But such is the only justice that Roman law allows, when a citizen kills a slave."

A heavy silence descended on the garden. His insight vindicated, Eco turned his attention to the leather ball. He tossed it in the air, caught it, and nodded thoughtfully, satisfied at the way it fit his hand.

"Ah, but Eco, as I was saying, there is another gift for you." He looked at me expectantly. "It's here." I patted the sack of silver. "No longer shall I teach you in my own stumbling way how to read and write. You shall have a proper tutor, who will come every morning to teach you both Latin and Greek. He will be stern, and you shall suffer, but when he is done you will read and write better than I do. A boy as clever as you deserves no less."

Eco's smile was radiant. I have never seen a boy toss a ball so high.

The story is almost done, except for one final outcome.

Much later that night, I lay in bed with Bethesda with nothing to separate us but a gossamer veil shot through with silver threads. For a few fleeting moments I was completely satisfied with life and the universe. In my relaxation, without meaning to, I mumbled what I was thinking. "Perhaps I *should* adopt the boy," I muttered.

"And why not?" Bethesda demanded, imperious even when half-asleep. "What more proof do you want from him? The boy could not be more like your son if he were made of your own flesh and blood."

And of course, she was right.

# THE KING
# OF SACRIFICES
# John Maddox Roberts

*A contemporary of Gordianus, is Decius Caecilius Metellus, the creation
of John Maddox Roberts. His adventures have appeared in the novels*
SPQR *(1990),* The Catiline Conspiracy *(1991),* The Sacrilege
*(1992),* The Temple of the Muses *(1992) and* Saturnalia *(1993).*
*Metellus has one advantage over Gordianus in that being a member of
a noble Roman family, and a Roman official, he has access to people
and places normally denied the plebians. That doesn't, of course, make
his life any safer, as the fate of many noble Romans will attest, but
it does mean Metellus can sail rather close to the wind at times.
The following story, specially written for this anthology, takes place
towards the end of Metellus's long life, in the early days of the reign
of Augustus Caesar.*
*Roberts (b. 1947), is probably better known in Britain for his novels
continuing the adventures of Conan the Barbarian, although he is the
author of nearly thirty sf, fantasy and mystery novels. His contemporary
mystery novel* A Typical American Town *was published in Britain
in 1994. Perhaps it will not be too long before his novels about Metellus
will also be available in Britain.*

The First Citizen rarely summons me. This may be because we
detest one another so deeply. He has never bothered to have
me killed because I am a relic of the old Republic he claims to
have restored. As the oldest living senator I have a certain prestige.
Besides, I am not that important. Once, my family controlled the
most powerful voting blocs in the Senate, the Plebeian Assembly and
the Centurionate Assembly. But that great generation of vigorous
political men died in the civil wars and the remnants are scarcely
worth my attention, much less his.

But I have certain talents that are unique, and there have been
times when the First Citizen has had need of them. At such times he

requests my presence, smiles his false smile, and seeks my aid. One such occasion occurred in my 73rd year.

I spent the morning dozing through a Senate meeting. As the power and importance of that august body dwindled, so did its speeches expand. One time-serving nobody after another got up to discourse windily upon trifles. My neighbors discreetly nudged me any time my snoring became obtrusive.

The session ended at noon, not a moment too early. I pushed myself to my feet with my walking stick and left the Curia. I didn't really need a stick, it just lent me an air of venerability. Once outside, I paused at the top of the steps to breathe the clean air and survey my City.

The sight was not altogether pleasing. There was still much in evidence that was ancient and familiar, but the spate of building that had been going on for more than twenty years had changed the City almost beyond recognition. Temples that had been simple, sober and dignified had become masterpieces of the confectioner's art, their facades tarted up with white marble and frothy carving and gilding. And some of the temples were new, erected not to honor the gods but to the glory of a single family.

There was, for instance, the temple of Venus Genetrix, the goddess from whom Caesar had claimed descent. A tenuous connection for the First Citizen, who was merely the grandson of Caesar's sister. And then there was the temple of Mars the Avenger. Mars had always had his shrines outside the City walls. Now he had been brought within, solely to remind everyone that the First Citizen had avenged (so he claimed) the murder of the great Caius Julius. Some of the new public buildings were begun by Caesar, but most bore the name of the First Citizen, or of his cronies: Agrippa and Maecenas. Somehow, the whole city had become his clientele.

I used to make fun of my father for indulging in this sort of good-old-days grumbling. Now that I am old I rather enjoy it.

My grumpy musings were interrupted by the arrival of my grandson, Decius the Youngest. He is nicknamed Paris for his exceptional looks. It is not good for one so young to be so handsome. It presages a life of trouble and a bad end. All the splendidly handsome men I have known came to a bad end: Milo, Marcus Antonius, Vercingetorix, they flourished briefly to great admiration and were gone. On the other hand, there is much to be said for dying young.

"Grandfather!" He ran up the steps, scattering senators and their hangers-on like chaff before a whirlwind. The boy had yet to dedicate his first beard and he possessed a commendable lack of respect for authority. He was breathing heavily and thrust a small scroll at me. "A letter from the Palace!"

I accepted it. "From Himself, I take it?" I said loudly, using the term his sycophants often used. Time was when only slaves used that term to refer to their master.

"How should I know?" he said, all innocence.

"Because you've read it, imp. The seal is broken."

He shrugged. "The messenger must have dropped it."

"What a liar. By the time I was your age I could lie far better than that. Let's see, now." I held the missive at arm's length and read loudly, as if I were hard of hearing:

"*From the First Citizen to the venerable Senator Decius Caecilius Metellus, greeting.*" Actually, here he employed the name which he illegally usurped from a better man and which I refuse to use. Recently, the Senate had voted him the title of Augustus. The Senate can give him any silly title it likes. He will always be sneaky little Caius Octavius to me.

"*The First Citizen requests the honor of your company in his home this afternoon, to confer upon a matter concerning the good of the Senate and People of Rome.*" I snorted. "Summoning me like some Oriental despot, is he? Well, that's just like him. Got himself into a tight spot again and needs me to get him out of it, no doubt!" All over the Curia steps, senators began sidling away from me, as if to clear a target range for Jove's thunderbolt. I love to see them do that.

"Father says you shouldn't talk like that," Paris said, quite unconcerned.

"Your father has grown disgustingly respectable these last few years. In his younger days there wasn't a professional criminal in Rome who could match him for villainy. Come along." I took him by the shoulder. "Let's go find something to eat and pay a visit to the baths and then we'll go see what the First Citizen wants."

On the waterfront near the Aemilian Bridge was a colorful little establishment called the Nemean Lion. That district of Rome is much devoted to Hercules and references to the demigod's legend are numerous. It was owned by a man named Ulpius who, in his youth, had been one of Milo's thugs. His daughter-in-law made the best pork sausage in Rome and each Saturnalia I gave them a nice present, so that they kept for me a reserve of fine, unwatered Falernian.

Since the day was fine we sat out front beneath the awning and watched the river traffic while Ulpius's granddaughters loaded the table with food and brought a flask of my private stock.

"Mother says you drink too early in the day," Paris said, lighting into the eatables. "She says you drink too much generally."

"She does, eh? Three generations of my relatives have said the same thing. I've presided at most of their funerals. I'm not going to face the First Citizen sober."

"Why do you hate him so much?" he mumbled around a mouthful of honeyed date cake.

"Because he destroyed the Republic and set up a monarchy and killed all the best men in Rome – all the true republicans."

"Then why didn't he kill you?" Precocious little bugger.

"By the time he got around to considering me, he'd decided to pose as the benevolent savior of the State. It's one of the political rules: Kill all your important enemies as soon as you seize power. The survivors will be so relieved that they'll forget all about it within a year. His great-uncle Julius Caesar neglected to kill his own enemies, and look what happened to him. Pretending respect and affection for me bolsters his image as the all-forgiving father of his country. It costs him nothing since I no longer count for anything, politically."

Truthfully, he didn't murder the Republic. It committed suicide. He just rearranged the carcass to suit him better. And most of the best men killed each other before Julian had a chance at them. No sense confusing the boy with political subtleties at so tender an age, though.

"So why are you willing to help him?"

"Why don't you finish your lunch?"

Thus fortified, and with the worst of my aches massaged from my bones at my favorite bathing establishment, I felt up to the long trudge up the Palatine and an interview with my least favorite Roman.

From the bottom of the steps we encountered guards. Caius Octavius makes a great show of being an ordinary citizen, living among his fellows without fear, and claimed that he never violated the ancient law against bringing armed soldiers into the City. The burly men who lounged around the residence wore togas, but they clinked as they moved and they studied me with an unsettling fixity.

A steward greeted me in the atrium and disappeared into the interior of the vast house to announce me. A few minutes later a splendidly handsome and stately woman appeared.

"Decius Caecilius, how good of you to come! And this must be the handsome grandson of whom I hear such brilliant reports!"

"I don't know who you listen to, Livia, but if you've heard that he's anything but a lazy troublemaker your spies should be crucified."

"But so many of them are your relatives."

"All the more reason to nail them up," I grumbled. Of all the many intriguing and dangerous women I have known in my long life, Livia was the most perilous, the subtlest, and the most intelligent by a tremendous margin, and I knew Cleopatra, who may have been the most powerful as well as the best educated woman who ever lived. I always accorded Livia the highest respect.

"Come along, my husband is in his study. I do hope you'll be able to help him. He has great confidence in you."

This should be good, I thought.

We found Octavius sitting at a desk attended by secretaries, apparently absorbed by weighty matters of state. At our arrival he stood and extended his hands.

"Ah, my old friend Decius Caecilius Metellus, I am so pleased that you've found time to visit me." With his spindly body and his large head with its unruly hair, he rather resembled a thistle.

"Always happy to be of assistance to the Senate and People," I said pointedly. The irony sailed right past him.

"As all good men should be. Please, sit down, Senator. And this would be the youngest to bear your ancient name? What a splendid example of Roman youth."

I was beginning to regret having brought Paris. The less these people noticed him, the better. I found myself falling into these lapses of judgement as I aged. Not that my discernment had ever been worthy of praise. I feigned creakiness as I lowered myself into a chair and sat with my hands resting atop my stick. A slave brought in a tray bearing a platter and cups.

"Please, take something, my friend. It's a long walk up the Palatine."

The platter held fresh figs. The cups held plain water. His pose of plainness and austerity had been concocted for him by Livia. Even his banquets were Stoic affairs, featuring only peasant food. I could easily picture him sneaking off afterward, to gorge in private upon imported delicacies and rare wines.

"Thank you, no. I must take a care for my digestion, you know." Paris kept a straight face. He showed real promise.

"I see." He nodded commiseratingly. "My own health is rather uncertain." He was famously cold and wore two tunics even in summer, three or even four in winter, all under a great blanket of a toga. I think his inability to get warm was the result of perpetual fear. Like all tyrants he lived in terror of plots and poison.

Livia hovered nearby, her eyes always fixed adoringly upon her husband. I wondered if she bothered to do that when there were no witnesses.

"My husband has worn himself out in service to the state and the people," she intoned.

To my credit, I did not gag. "It seems I am here to take some of that burden upon my own aged shoulders," I said. "What might be the nature of this difficulty?"

"Ah, yes, well – esteemed Senator, you are aware of my concern for the declining morals of the citizenry, are you not?"

I said nothing, just raised my eyebrows.

"Well," he went on, "things have reached a shocking state, Senator, just shocking. The Roman family is not what it was in the days of our ancestors and the strength of character that made Rome great throughout the world has reached such a state of degeneracy that the very best of our families are dying out – yes, dying out, because our young men prefer dissipation and foreign vices to marrying and starting families!"

"How could I fail to notice?" I said. "You made that speech to the Senate last month."

"Proving, if any proof were needed, the seriousness of the problem!" Pedantic little twit.

"I hope you will not think I am boasting," I said, "but my own life has not been one of perfect probity. In fact, the words 'scandalous,' 'licentious,' and even 'degenerate' have been bandied about in company where my name was mentioned."

"That was when you were younger, Decius," Livia said. "You have acquired the respectability of venerable years. The follies of youth are quickly forgotten." The woman's political acuity was astounding.

"I have not given up the habit of folly," I told her.

"Excellent," she said, smiling. I knew then that I had said the wrong thing.

"I am sure you are aware," Octavius told me, "that the position of *Rex Sacrorum* has been vacant for some time?"

"Naturally," I said. "It's been vacant for most of my lifetime." The King of Sacrifices is a very ancient office, tremendously honorable, but surrounded by as many taboos as that of the *Flamen Dialis*. Usually, the position went to some doddering senator too old to mind the restrictions on his behavior. Such a priest rarely lasted more than a few years and then the office was vacant again.

"I had a candidate, eminently qualified, together with the concurrence of the Senate and the pontifical colleges."

"So I heard. Some jumped-up new patrician of yours, isn't he? Scandalous thing, if you ask me; making new patricians for the first time since Romulus."

The First Citizen reddened. "Decius Caecilius, you are perfectly aware that this was a measure necessary to restore the State! By ancient law many offices and priesthoods require patricians, and there were no longer enough of them to go around! In the days of Camillus there were more than a hundred patrician families. By the time of my first consulship there were no more than fourteen. Something had to be done."

"You were yourself offered that honor," Livia put in, "and your descendants."

"The *gens* Caecilia Metella has been the greatest of the plebeian families for centuries," I said peevishly. "I would not change that status. It is no honor for me and it would shame my ancestors." He began to puff up like Aesop's bullfrog but just then a significant detail penetrated my age-and-wine-fogged mind. "Your pardon, First Citizen, but did you say you 'had' a candidate for *Rex Sacrorum*? I know that one as well trained in the arts of rhetoric as you are does not employ tenses haphazardly."

"The fellow's dead," Livia said.

"Ah, now we approach the heart of the matter." I leaned forward, chin atop my cane. "Am I safe in assuming this new-minted patrician did not choke to death on an olive stone?"

"He was murdered," Octavius said, seeming almost upset by it.

"No doubt you can find a replacement," I reassured him.

"Not as easy as you might think," he muttered, "even for me. However, replacing him is not the problem. It is the murder. It is going to cause a scandal!"

This raised my eyebrows. "Not only a murder, but a scandal, eh? I do hope none of your relatives are involved." I suppose it was rather unfair of me to refer, even obliquely, to his daughter's scandalous life, but when was he ever fair to anybody?

"No, for which I render the gods due thanks. But for years now I have bent my efforts toward restoring respect for the traditional Roman family, and now this!" He smote his fist upon his bony knee in vexation.

"And now what?" I prodded.

"We think it was somebody in his family who did him in," Livia said. "His wife, perhaps, maybe a daughter or one of the other relatives. There were things about him . . . we did not know when we chose him for the position." I did not miss the significance of the "we." Octavius made few decisions without consulting her and rumor had it that he never made a move without her permission.

At last this was getting interesting. "What sort of things?"

"I will not countenance slanderous hearsay," her husband said, primly. "Such rumors may be baseless and are no better than the anonymous denunciations during the proscriptions!" What a hypocrite.

"Senator," Livia said, "you are renowned for your expertise in these things. We want you to investigate this murder and report to us."

"I see. Has a praetor been assigned?"

"Not yet," Octavius said. "Should your investigation produce evidence sufficient for a trial before a praetor's court, I assure you that all the proper forms will be respected. I am, after all, First Citizen, not Dictator." Such piety.

I rose. "The name of the unfortunate gentleman?"

"Aulus Gratidius Tubero. He was discovered dead in his house this morning." His spoiled-brat mouth twisted at the sheer impertinence of this death.

"Then as a former praetor and many times a *iudex*," I said, "I will undertake this investigation." It was mealy-mouthed of me to pretend that I was duty-bound by constitutional tradition to do as he wished. I merely did not want to admit that I did Octavius's bidding like everyone else. One could not be long in his Senate without contracting this disease of pious political hypocrisy.

Livia saw me to the door, a fine-boned hand resting on my equally bony shoulder. "Decius, you know I would never seek to influence your investigation."

I was expecting this. "What do you want?"

"My husband and I would be *most* grateful if our family were to be kept out of this dreadful mess."

Uh-oh, I thought. "Not Julia again?" Between them, Livia and Octavius had a sizable brood. Most were turning out, strangely, to be fairly decent. Tiberius and Drusus, Livia's boys by a previous marriage, were making their names as excellent soldiers. Julia was another matter. Although only nineteen years old, she was already a widow, her husband and Octavius's designated heir, Marcellus, having died a year or two previously. She had a reputation for extravagance, overweening pride and a taste for liaisons with married men. This was a bit of an embarrassment, since Octavius, in his zeal to restore Roman family values, had declared adultery a crime; a laughable concept if ever there was one.

"I'm afraid so," Livia affirmed sadly. "I fear that someone has laid her under a curse."

More likely under every bush and ceiling in Rome, I thought, wisely refraining from chuckling at her unfortunate choice of words.

"However, she is now betrothed to Vipsanius Agrippa." Her lip curled only slightly. There was venom between Livia and her husband's loyal soldier-advisor.

"Agrippa? The man's near my own age!"

"Don't be ridiculous. He's the same age as my husband. She needs a mature man who can keep her on a tight rein. This marriage is important and we can't have her embroiled in some squalid scandal."

"I'll make no promises," I said. I did not fool her. It was why she put up with my show of insolence. She knew that I would not endanger my family to save my wounded Republican pride.

"Nor would I ask you to," she said, smiling. "Your first duty is to the Senate and People." My, how the woman did love to rub it in.

As we walked from the palace Paris said, "So that's the First Citizen. He's not much to look at, is he?"

"Neither is a dagger in the back," I told him. "But you'd be foolish to ignore either one."

The house of Aulus Gratidius Tubero was situated on a slope of the Aventine overlooking the Circus Maximus. In the riots following Caesar's assassination the area had burned to the ground and a number of fine houses were built on the very desirable sites thus provided. There was a splendid view of the beautiful temple of Diana to the north. In front of the gate stood a pair of the clinking men.

"No admittance by order of *Imperator* Augustus," one of them said. So he already had them using his new title. The effect was somewhat spoiled by the man's thick, German accent.

"I am here by order of that same person," I informed him.

"Who are you?" Clearly, Livia had not bothered to send a messenger ahead.

"I may be the man who killed your grandfather when Caesar was proconsul in Gaul. Let me pass, you Teutonic ox!"

The man reddened, but the other put a hand on his shoulder. "Don't you know a senator when you see one?" This one's accent was at least Italian, although certainly not from Rome. He gave me a perfunctory if reasonably obsequious smile. "Sorry, sir, but our orders were very strict. Are you the *iudex* assigned to investigate?"

"I am. I've come here straight from the palace, but if you want to explain to the First Citizen . . ." I made to go.

"Oh, I'm sure it's all right," the Italian said hastily. "Anyone can see that you are a most distinguished gentleman."

"I should think so," I said, passing between them. Behind me I heard the German grumble something. The other said, in a low voice: "How much trouble can one old winesack of a senator cause, anyway?" Nothing wrong with my hearing, although what I hear does not always please me.

The *janitor* was chained to the gatepost in the style affected by householders who espouse unwavering adherence to ancestral practices. I've never done it in my house. My *janitor* always has a hook on the end of his chain. He attaches it to the ring on the gatepost when visitors call. This one announced me and a plump, pleasant-featured woman appeared from within.

"Welcome, Senator Metellus," she said. "I wish your visit could have been at a happier time." She was remarkably composed for a widow of such recent bereavement, but Romans have never been inclined to the sort of extravagant mourning fashionable among barbarians. We have hired mourners for all the wailing and breast-beating. Still, a tear or two might have been appropriate.

"This is such a dreadful occurrence!" she said, actually sounding quite put out. "But I do believe that the First Citizen is being too severe. Those detestable guards out there won't even let the undertaker's men come in. I mean, really! There are rites to be observed, after all!"

This was sounding worse by the minute. If nothing else, Octavius was a stickler for the religious niceties. "So the body is still on the premises?" Since she wasn't grieving heavily, I saw no reason why I should not be blunt.

She shuddered, or pretended to. "Yes, in that disgusting . . ., well, you will see."

"Then please take me there. I wish to begin my investigation with its prime object." She led me through a courtyard where household slaves stood around looking confused but dry-eyed. When even slaves can't fake a few tears you know that the departed was not a beloved master.

"I was given to understand," I said in a low voice, "that a certain person of the First Citizen's household may be involved." With such circumlocutions did we avoid saying "royal family."

"Oh, that trollop!" she hissed. At least something could rouse her to a pitch of emotion. "She and my husband . . . The things they . . . Oh!" The woman had trouble completing sentences.

Somehow, I suspected that the two had been up to more than mere dalliance. I was right.

We approached a door at the rear of the house, an area usually given over to storage, pantries, slave quarters and the kitchen. This was an unusual door, double-leaved, of massive wood construction and strapped with bronze. One leaf was slightly ajar. The smell wafting from within was not agreeable, something like the sort of blood-and-incense aroma you get at a sacrifice, only not as fresh.

"I cannot accompany you within, Senator," the woman said, primly. "It is too ghastly."

I pushed the door open. It was too dark to see much. "I need light."

Hands folded modestly before her, she turned her head and bawled like a drunken market-woman: "Leonidas! Come here and bring lamps, you lazy wretch!" So much, I thought, for Octavius's new patricians. The menial thus addressed appeared, a few others in tow, bearing lamps.

"You go in first," I said to the slave with the brightest lamp. With a look of extreme distaste, the man passed within.

Illuminated, the room was about the size of a typical triclinium although decorated in a manner rarely encountered in dining rooms. First, there was the altar. Altars are common enough in Roman houses, usually dedicated to ancestors or the guardian genius. This one was not the usual sober, square block of white marble. It was in the shape of a huge, coiled serpent, black in color, and it stood before a statue of a crocodile-headed Egyptian deity. I recalled that his name was Sobek. Like so many of those addicted to foreign cults, Tubero liked to mix them promiscuously. In a wall-niche was a bronze hand from which sprung a small human figure as well as a number of tiny animals and other symbols. It is called, I believe, a Sabazios hand, and is emblematic of some disgusting foreign sect or other. There were many other such talismans: a deformed human skull, a mummified baboon, a basket full of colorful, polished stones. Beside a brazier, now cold, stood a bronze bowl heaped with frankincense. And, of course, there was the body.

The late Aulus Gratidius Tubero lay on his back amid the considerable disarray of his toga. Upon his features sat a perfectly corpselike expression, which is to say, no expression at all. There was a great deal of blood. The whole floor was sticky with it. Whatever wound had brought about such an effusion, it was not visible. I crouched by the body, pulling up my clothes a little to keep them out of the blood. Even above the smells of blood and incense I detected the sour reek of wine.

"Remove his toga," I ordered the slaves. They just rolled their eyes fearfully. They were afraid, like most of us, of the contamination that comes of touching the dead before the proper rites are performed. I rose on creaky knees and took a handful of the incense. "I am a pontifex," I said truthfully, "and I can carry out the lustrum," lying through my remaining teeth this time. I sprinkled the yellow crystals over the body while mumbling unintelligibly. "There," I said. "He is purified. Now do as I say."

Without further protest, one of the slaves lifted the toga, rolling the corpse over on his belly. The pale back was striped with furrows like that of a chastised slave. The stripes were nearly vertical, slanting very slightly from the right buttock to the left shoulder. They formed shallow gouges and lay atop older stripes. They were not sufficient to account for all the blood. I glanced at the toga. It was liberally smeared with blood, but not soaked.

"Turn him over," I ordered. They rolled him onto his back. "Ah, here's the fatal wound," I said as the slaves backed away in horror. Tubero's genitals were entirely missing.

The soles of my sandals made sticky sounds as I examined the room in greater detail. The statue of Sobek stood upon a circular base, but the base stood upon a square patch of floor that was free of blood. I ran a hand along the Egyptian god's arm and came away with a deposit of dust. A similar test of the coiled-snake altar proved it to be clean. I left the shrine and found the wife of Gratidius standing outside.

"You found him like this?" I asked her.

"Yes," she said. "That is, the slaves located him when he was not to be found in his bed this morning." She spoke as if this were not an uncommon occurrence.

"Why did you notify the First Citizen instead of one of the praetors?"

She looked uncomfortable. "Well, because that woman was with him last night. Julia, the First Citizen's daughter."

"I see. And this was not the first time?"

"I have heard gossip. They frequented the same licentious parties. But this was the first time he brought her into *my house*!" She packed a lot of venom into those last two words.

"When did she arrive and when did she leave?"

"She arrived a little after sunset. I did not see her. I kept to my own quarters for the whole evening. I did not want to set eyes on her. It is difficult to believe that she is the child of the savior of the Republic." I had grown so accustomed to this sort of twaddle that I no longer even winced at it.

"By the way," I said, "please accept my congratulations upon your new patrician status. I do not believe your husband's tragic demise will affect that."

"You are too gracious," she said, preening.

"It is unfortunate that he never got to be invested as *Rex Sacrorum*."

"Oh, yes. That would have been a wonderful privilege." She sounded utterly indifferent. This was a distinction she would not miss. As wife of the *Rex Sacrorum* she would have endured as many taboos as he. She would have become all but a prisoner in her own house, lest she glimpse some forbidden sight, like a black dog or a man working at his trade.

"I'll take my leave now, but I wish to speak with your steward."

The man was a Greek in his middle years and I knew at once I would get little from him. He had the look of one who knew how to keep the secrets of the household. I spoke with him as he accompanied me to the door.

"Did you admit the lady Julia yesterday evening?"

"I did, Senator. That is, the porter admitted the lady and the master."

"And when did she leave?"

"I did not see her leave. I questioned the porter but he must have been asleep. I shall have him flogged soundly." Like all good and trustworthy retainers he could lie with a perfectly straight face.

"As you will. I do urge you to search your memory, though. It may be that you and the rest of the staff shall be called to testify in court, and slaves can only testify under torture."

He shrugged. "One endures what one must."

I walked away, wondering why the worst masters always seemed to have the best slaves. I have always striven to be an exemplary master, and my slaves have always been lazy good-for-nothings.

My weary feet took me back to the house on the Palatine, where the clinking men conducted me to Livia.

"I need to speak with Julia," I informed her.

"Is it truly necessary?"

"Absolutely."

"Very well then, if you must." She guided me to a wing of the sprawling but ostentatiously austere mansion where the various children of the family had their quarters. Julia sat in a spacious room, carding wool by the light of the late afternoon sun. This is what Octavius expected Roman wives to do, however high their birth. Even Livia pretended to card, spin and weave wool. I suppose she might have directed her slaves at the work, when she could spare the time.

"Julia," Livia said. "I believe you know the distinguished Senator Decius Caecilius Metellus. He is *iudex* investigating the murder of Gratidius Tubero and needs to speak with you." With that, Livia took a chair and watched me with gorgonlike intensity.

"Have we your leave, Madame?" I asked. "I would prefer to confer in privacy."

"That would not be proper," Livia insisted. "Julia is a widow of a patrician family."

"I believe my venerable years constitute sufficient chaperone."

"Not if half of what is said about your past is true." Nonetheless, she rose. "I do, however, trust your well-demonstrated sense of self preservation." She left, her spine rigid with indignation.

"It's so refreshing," Julia said, "to see someone with the nerve to defy her."

"I am old," I said. "I won't live much longer whatever I do. You, on the other hand, infuriate her regularly. You are very young and have to live in the same house with her."

"It's not courage," she said. "It's desperation." I had to sympathize. I always rather liked Julia. She was a spirited, intelligent young woman forced to adopt the false Stoicism of the Julio-Claudian house and marry for the sake of political alliances.

"You may have carried your independence a little too far this time. Gratidius Tubero is dead and you seem to be the most likely suspect. I hope you can convince me otherwise."

"How did he die?" I told her and her fair skin turned even paler.

"How may I convince you?" she asked, greatly sobered.

"First tell me about the events of last night."

"I encountered Tubero at a dinner party given by the Parthian ambassador. I'd seen him a few times before, at similar occasions. We frequent the same circles."

"The high-living set. In my youth I was fond of the same milieu. In your position it is unwise."

She shrugged. "Exile or death from boredom. Which is worse. Anyway, by nightfall we were both the worse for the wine and he urged me to come to his home to see his collection of foreign cult objects. I've taken part in some of the Mysteries . . . only the lawful ones," she added hastily. "Anyway, it seemed fascinating at the time. But the trip from the embassy to his house was a long one, and by the time we arrived I was sober enough for second thoughts. In his atrium I begged off, pleading illness. He was still very drunk and wild-eyed. Besides, I could see a woman, probably his wife, spying on us from a side room.

"So I returned home and that was all until this morning, when I found myself under virtual arrest."

I stood. "Very well, I have noted your story."

"Don't you believe me?" I could hear the desperation in her voice.

"I will take your words into consideration." A good scare would do her a world of good.

"Well?" Livia said, when I left Julia's chamber.

"I must consult with some experts. I would like to meet with you and the First Citizen at Tubero's house this evening."

"But are you satisfied that Julia had nothing to do with this sorry business?" She was almost pleading. How I loved that.

"Not yet. Will you meet with me there?"

She fumed for a while. "We will." It was good to have the upper hand with these people for a change.

I left the mansion on the Palatine and went to the houses of two of my fellow pontifexes who were far more learned than I in religious matters.

It was already dark when I reached the house of Gratidius Tubero once again. Paris carried a torch before me, overjoyed at the prospect of messing about in a murder investigation.

I found a whole crowd of metallic-sounding men in togas before the door of the house, as well as a number of lictors shouldering their *fasces*.

"You stay out here," I ordered Paris. "This business is entirely too ugly for one as young as you."

"But you've always told me that when you were my age . . ."

"Enough. Times were different then. Besides, this looks like a dangerous enough crowd to suit even you."

I went inside and found the First Citizen seated by the pool in the courtyard, along with Livia and Octavius's right-hand man, the formidably competent Marcus Vipsanius Agrippa, whose future marriage into the house depended upon the result of my investigation. The widow Gratidius stood by, looking suitably awed by the presence of so many mighty persons. A chair was thrust under me and I sank into it gratefully. I was getting rather old for these long, active days.

"I have indulged you because I know you to be efficient at this sort of work," said the First Citizen. "I trust you have reached a satisfactory conclusion."

"By 'satisfactory' I take it you mean one that clears your family of scandal?" I enjoyed the sight of his reddening face for a while, then added, "If so, be at ease. Julia didn't do it."

"What do you mean?" blurted the widow.

"Silence, woman!" Octavius barked, a little of his real nature showing through. "Explain, Senator." Relief oozed from his pores.

"Will you accompany me into the room where the murder occurred?"

He raised a hand piously. "Senator, you know quite well that, as *pontifex maximus* of Rome I may not look upon human blood. Livia is under the same rule."

"Are we going to maintain that fiction?" I said, mightily vexed. "You attend the *munera* like everyone else. Gladiators bleed rather profusely."

"Those are funeral games and therefore are religious observances. It is different," he said.

"Oh, very well," I said. "Marcus Agrippa, will you bear witness on behalf of the First Citizen?"

"I will," he said. So the two of us went into the now extremely smelly shrine while the royal couple waited just outside the door. The body was quite stiff now. A number of lamps now illuminated the grotesque scene.

"You have all heard Julia's story and I find it to be true in all relevant details."

"I knew it!" Octavius said.

"Then who killed him?" Livia demanded.

"Bear with me. How did you ever settle on such a man to be *Rex Sacrorum*?"

"Senator," Octavius said, "have you any idea how difficult it is to get *anyone* to accept that office?"

"Just so. He must have been drunk when he accepted. It seems he was often in that state. In any case, while his wife was very pleased to be promoted to patrician status, she had no interest in being the wife of the *Rex Sacrorum*."

"Then a Roman wife has murdered her husband, with the collusion of the household slaves? Infamous!" A tragedian could not have done it better.

"No!" squawked the widow.

"Much as I hate to clear that woman of anything," I said, "I fear I must tell you that she didn't do it either. In fact, there was no murder."

"This should be a good one," Agrippa said. "What happened?"

"The silly bugger did it himself."

That raised Agrippa's eyebrows. "I've heard of opening your veins, but this . . ."

"You will notice the toga. It is smeared with half-dried blood. Had the man been wearing it when the wound was inflicted, it would be soaked. The wife and servants found him here, dead and quite naked, and they wrapped him in it to make the scene marginally less bizarre."

"The blood is as described," Agrippa reported to those outside the door.

"This statue," I indicated the crocodile-headed god, "is not the one that stood here last night. Its base is round and the blood was stopped in its sticky progress by a square pedestal."

"I can confirm that," Agrippa reported.

"Now this god has a fearsome aspect with his reptilian head, but he is actually a Nile fertility god and quite benevolent. I suspect he is left over from an earlier enthusiasm of the late Tubero, who had a taste for the exotic, not to mention the unwholesome. He has a coating of dust, whereas the altar is quite clean. If you will institute a search of the house, you should find a statue of Cybele, along with certain paraphernalia associated with the worship of that goddess: cymbals, a scourge studded with knucklebones, a sickle and so forth. You may even discover the . . . ah . . . items missing from the gentleman here."

"Find them!" Livia barked. There was a rustling and clinking from without.

"Why Cybele?" the First Citizen asked.

"Allow me to wax pedantic. Almost two hundred years ago, Hannibal was still romping about in Italy. Our ancestors were frightened by a shower of stones that fell from the heavens. The Sybilline Books were consulted and it was revealed that the danger would be averted by this Phrygian goddess. From King Attalus the Senate received certain cult objects and the goddess was installed in the temple built for her on the Palatine. Hannibal was duly driven out and her worship continues to this day, but only in a decorous and lawful form.

"However," I continued, relishing this part, "there is another side to her worship; an alien, oriental and wholly disreputable side. It has long been forbidden in Rome, but it enjoys a certain vogue among those bored by the decorum of the State religion. The *Corybantes*, the ecstatic followers of the goddess in her more daemonic aspect, are noted for practicing flagellation, hence the studded scourge. In their religious transports, candidates for priesthood castrate themselves and throw their severed members upon the altar."

"Barbarous!" Octavius muttered.

"Last night poor Tubero, spurned by Julia, solaced himself with a good session of holy flagellation. You notice the whip marks? They are almost vertical, quite unlike the horizontal and diagonal stripes one sees when a slave is whipped by a second party. This is because Tubero was lashing himself, slinging the thongs over his left shoulder."

"That's what it looks like," Agrippa affirmed.

"I suspect that Tubero was a man who liked these private games. He allowed fantasy to become reality. In any case, having drunk himself silly and then inflamed his senses with the dubious pleasures of self-flagellation, he performed the final rite. He probably intended merely to mime the actions. After all, the lack of an audience would deprive the ritual of half the fun. But he was not in a steady state of mind and he went too far. The expression on his face when he realized what he was holding must have been worth seeing. This was not a conventional orgy of Cybele, so no one was there to stanch the blood and he perished."

"Disgusting!" Octavius shouted. "And to implicate my family!" The widow was already bawling and begging for mercy. Nobody paid any attention.

"Actually," I said, "it was rather clever. Julia had conveniently placed herself on the scene, and everyone knows what a stickler you are for the purity of Roman family life. The woman did not want it to come out that her husband, the new-minted patrician, was an idiotic loon. She figured that, by implicating Julia, she would trick you into covering up the whole squalid mess."

"To suspect me of such perfidy! I'll search the law tables until I find a charge under which she can be executed!" The woman blubbered even more vociferously.

"That would mean a court trial," Livia pointed out. "You don't want your name associated with such a squalid mess. There was no murder and trying to put one over on you doesn't really constitute treason. You are *pontifex maximus*. Charge her with some sort of sacrilege – desecration of a corpse or something. Exile her to one of those dreadful little islands we keep for the ones we can't condemn to death."

"If you say so, my dear," Octavius grumbled. "It's better than the treacherous bitch deserves."

"You've never seen those islands," I told him.

We left the house amid much wailing, the formidable escort all around us. Octavius placed a hand on my shoulder. "I can't tell you how grateful I am, Decius Caecilius. You really must accept a promotion to the patricianship."

Another hand came to rest on my other shoulder. "Decius," Livia purred, "we *truly* need a new *Rex Sacrorum*."

I closed my eyes wearily. "I don't suppose you have another of those islands handy?"

These things happened in the year 734 of the city of Rome, during the unconstitutional dictatorship of Caius Octavius, surnamed Augustus.

# THE
# THREE TRAVELLERS
## R. L. Stevens

*It is not the best-kept secret that R. L. Stevens is a pen name of Edward Hoch (b. 1930), probably the most prolific writer of mystery short stories, of which he has published over seven hundred. Most of them fall into one of a number of series. The following story, though, is a neat one-off, set at one of the most auspicious moments in history. After all, if one of the Three Wise Men couldn't double as a detective, who could?*

N ow the three had journeyed several days when at last they came upon the Oasis of Ziza, and Gaspar who was the wisest of them said, "We will rest our horses here this night. It will be safe."

"Safe for horses and men," Melchior agreed. "But what of the gold?"

"Safe for the gold also. No one knows we carry it."

The sun was low in the western sky as they approached, and Gaspar held up a hand to shield his eyes. It would be night soon.

A young herdsman came out to meet them and take their horses. And he said, "Welcome to the Oasis of Ziza. Have you ridden far?"

"A full moon's journey," Gaspar replied, speaking in the nomadic tongue. "What is your name?"

And the herdsman answered, "They call me Ramoth, sire."

"Here is a gold coin for you, Ramoth. Feed and water our mounts for the journey and another will be yours on the morrow."

"Which way do you travel, sire?"

"Towards the west," Gaspar said, purposely vague.

When the young herdsman had departed with the horses, fat Balthazar said, "I am not pleased, Gaspar. You lead us, it is true, but the keeping of the gold is my responsibility. And travellers guided by the heavens would do well to journey by night."

"The desert is cold by night, my friend. Let us cease this bickering and settle ourselves here till the dawn."

Then Melchior and Balthazar went off to put up their tent, and Gaspar was much relieved. It had been a long journey, not yet ended, and he treasured these moments alone. Presently he set off to inspect the oasis where they would spend the night, and he came upon a stranger who wore a sword at his waist.

"Greetings, traveller," the man said. "I am Nevar, of the northern tribe. Do you journey this route often?"

"Not often, no. My name is Gaspar and I come with my two companions from the east."

Nevar nodded, and stroked his great growth of beard. "Later, when the sun is gone, there are games of chance – and women for those who have the gold to pay."

"That does not interest me," Gaspar said.

"You will find the companionship warming," Nevar said. "Come to the fire near the well. That is where we will be."

Gaspar went on, pausing to look at the beads and trinkets the nomad traders offered. When he reached the well at the far end of the oasis, he saw a woman lifting a great earthen jar to her shoulder. She was little more than a child, and as he watched, the jar slipped from her grasp and shattered against the stones, splashing her with water. She burst into tears.

"Come, child," Gaspar said, comforting her. "There is always another jar to be had."

And she turned her wide brown eyes to him, revealing a beauty he had not seen before. "My father will beat me," she said.

"Here is a gold coin for him. Tell him a stranger named Gaspar bumped you and made the jar break."

"That would not be true."

"But it is true that I am Gaspar. Who are you?"

"Thantia, daughter of Nevar."

"Yes, I have met your father. You are very lovely, my child."

But his words seemed to frighten her, and she ran from him.

Then he returned to the place where Melchior had erected their tent. They had learned from past encampments to leave nothing of value with the horses, and Gaspar immediately asked the location of the gold.

"It is safe," Balthazar told him. "Hidden in the bottom of this grain bag."

"Good. And the perfume?"

"With our regular supplies. No one would steal that."

Melchior chuckled. "If they did, we could smell out the culprits quickly enough!"

And then Balthazar said, "There is gaming tonight, near the well."

"I know," Gaspar replied. "But it is not for us."

The fat man held out his hands in a gesture of innocence. "We could but look," he said.

And Gaspar reluctantly agreed. "Very well."

Later, when the fire had been kindled and the people of Ziza came forth from their tents to mingle, the three travellers joined them. Almost at once Gaspar was sought out by a village elder, a man with wrinkled skin and rotting teeth. "I am Dibon," he said, choosing a seat next to Gaspar. "Do you come from the east?"

"Yes, from Persia."

"A long journey. What brings you this far?"

Gaspar did not wish to answer. Instead, he motioned towards a group of men with small smooth stones before them. "What manner of sport is this?"

"It is learned from the Egyptians, as are most things sinful." Then the old man leaned closer, and Gaspar could smell the foul odour of his breath. "Some say you are a magus."

"I have studied the teachings of Zoroaster, as have my companions. In truth some would consider me a magus."

"Then you journey in search of Mazda?"

"In search of truth," Gaspar replied.

Then he felt the presence of someone towering over him, and saw it was the figure of Nevar. His right hand rested on the sword at his waist. "I would have words with you, Gaspar."

"What troubles you?"

"My only daughter Thantia, a virgin not yet twenty, tells me you gave her a gold coin today."

"Only because I feared the broken water jug was my fault."

"No stranger approaches Thantia! You will leave Ziza this night!"

"We leave in the morning," Gaspar said quietly.

Nevar drew his sword, and Gaspar waited no longer. He flung himself at the big man and they tumbled towards the fire as the game-players scattered. Gaspar pulled Nevar's sword from his grip.

Then Thantia broke from the crowd, running to her father.

"This stranger did me no harm!" she cried out.

"Silence, daughter!" Nevar reached for a piece of burning firewood and hurled it at Gaspar, but it went wide of its mark and landed on a low straw roof nearby.

"The stable!" someone shouted, and Gaspar saw it was the herdsman Ramoth hurrying to rescue the horses. The others helped to quench the flames with water from the well, but not before a quantity of feed and supplies had been destroyed.

Then Gaspar and Melchior went in search of fat Balthazar, who had disappeared during the commotion. They found him behind the row of tents, playing the Egyptian stone game with a half dozen desert riders. He had a small pile of gold coins before him.

"This must cease!" Gaspar commanded.

The nomads ran at his words, and Balthazar struggled to his feet. "It was merely a game."

"Our task is far more important than mere gaming," Gaspar reminded him, and the fat man looked sheepish. "While you idled I was near killed by the swordsman Nevar."

"A trouble-maker," Balthazar agreed. "I will not rest easy until Ziza is behind us on our journey."

Then as they passed the burned stable on the way to their tent, old Dibon approached them saying, "This ruin is your fault, Gaspar. Yours and Nevar's."

"That is true, old man. We will stay here tomorrow and help rebuild the stable."

Dibon bowed his head. "A generous offer. We thank you."

But when they were alone, Balthazar complained, "This will delay us an entire day!"

"We will travel a distance by night, as you wished."

Now another surprise was waiting at their tent. As Melchior raised the flap to enter, there was a whimper from within. Gaspar pushed past his hesitating companion and lit the oil lamp. By its glow they saw the girl Thantia crouched behind a pile of robes.

"Please!" she gasped. "Please hide me. My father has beaten me and I fear for my life!"

"I fear for ours if he finds you here," Melchior said.

Gaspar held the oil lamp closer and saw the bruises on her face and arms. "We cannot send you back to him. Remain here with Melchior and Balthazar. I will return shortly."

Then he made his way to the place where old Dibon rested, and he told the elder what had happened. Dibon nodded and said, "My daughter and her husband will find room for Thantia until Nevar regains his senses. You were wise to come to me."

Gaspar and his companions delivered the girl to Dibon, and went with them to the dwelling place of Dibon's daughter. Later, in their tent, Balthazar grumbled again about the delayed departure. But they settled down at last to sleep, as the fires of the encampment burned low around them.

In the morning, by the first rays of the rising sun, Gaspar was awakened by Balthazar's panic-filled voice. "Wake quickly, Gaspar!" he pleaded, shaking him. "Someone has stolen our gold!"

Gaspar saw at once that the words were true.

The leather sack of grain contained only grain now. Though the tent showed no sign of forced entry, and though their regular supplies were untouched, the gold had vanished.

"I cannot believe it!" Melchior gasped. "How could a thief have entered while we slept?"

Gaspar agreed such a thing was impossible. "The gold was stolen before we retired last night," he reasoned. "We were away from the tent during the gaming and fire, and again while escorting Thantia. A thief could have entered at either time."

"What of the perfume and incense?" Melchior asked.

"Untouched," Balthazar said. "My special knot is still in place on the other bags."

"Only the gold," Gaspar mused.

"It is truly as if someone knew where to look."

"The girl!" Balthazar exclaimed. "We found her in here! She could have searched for the gold and found it."

"Possible," Gaspar admitted. "But I cannot bring myself to believe it."

"We cannot leave Ziza without the gold," Melchior said.

"Let us put our minds to the problem while we work at the stable," Gaspar said.

Now when they reached the stable Nevar was already there, toiling with the others. He paused in his labours when he saw the three, and shot an accusing finger at Gaspar. "You have stolen away my daughter. I will revenge myself!"

"Your daughter is safe, in the care of Dibon and his family."

His words quieted Nevar, but Melchior asked, "If he was so concerned, why did he not come after us in the night?"

Balthazar agreed. "Or did he come, and steal our gold away?"

Then presently old Dibon appeared, with the girl Thantia at his side. She cast not a glance in her father's direction, and he went about his work ignoring her. Gaspar laboured diligently through the morning, instructing Dibon and the others in Persian building techniques. He too ignored Nevar, not wanting more trouble.

Once, while Balthazar was off to the well for water, Melchior whispered, "Is it possible that our companion betrays us, Gaspar?

Might he have stolen the gold himself to cover his losses at the stone game?"

But Gaspar would hear none of it. "We must never doubt each other, Melchior. In my heart I know Balthazar is innocent, as I know you are innocent. And I remember the scene at the stone game. There were gold coins in front of him. He was winning, not losing."

"How will we recover the gold, Gaspar?"

"Through the power of our minds, Melchior. We are wise men, and we must use our minds to determine the thief's identity."

"But there is no clue to his identity!"

"Sometimes the lack of a clue can be one."

Balthazar returned with the water and they drank eagerly. Later as they ate of their supplies, Thantia came to them. "I thank you for helping me," she said. "The elders have spoken to my father and he has promised never again to beat me. I will return to him now.'

"We need no thanks," Gaspar assured her.

Then old Dibon came to join them. "How may we repay you for your work on the stable?"

"You may recover our stolen gold," Balthazar blurted out.

"Gold? Stolen gold?"

"It was stolen from our tent," Balthazar hurried on, before Gaspar could silence him.

"There are no thieves in Ziza!"

"There is one."

"I will summon the elders. We will search for your gold."

"No, no," said Gaspar. "We will recover it."

"But how?"

"By finding the thief. It is best to say nothing and catch him off guard."

Old Dibon bowed his head. "I will do as you suggest."

"One favour. Could you ask that our horses be brought to us? We must appear to be leaving."

Then, as they waited, Balthazar gathered their supplies. And Melchior said, "I have put my mind to the problem, Gaspar. But there are too many possibilities. The girl Thantia could be the thief, or her father Nevar. Or any of the game players."

"Or old Dibon himself," Balthazar added. "There are too many to suspect."

Gaspar nodded. "What is needed is an oracle."

"You mean to kill a beast as the Romans do?"

Gaspar shook his head. "My oracle will be a living animal." He

saw the herdsman Ramoth leading their horses. "My steed will tell
me who has our gold."

"Your horse?" fat Balthazar laughed. "Who learns anything from
a dumb animal?"

Gaspar held out some grain for the horse. "You see how he eats?
He is hungry."

"What does that tell us?" Melchior asked.

"That our gold was stolen by Ramoth!"

Then presently old Dibon appeared, with the girl Thantia at his
side. She cast not a glance in her father's direction, and he went
about his work ignoring her. Gaspar laboured diligently through
the morning, instructing Dibon and the others in Persian building
techniques. He too ignored Nevar, not wanting more trouble.

Once, while Balthazar was off to the well for water, Melchior
whispered, "Is it possible that our companion betrays us, Gaspar?
Might he have stolen the gold himself to cover his losses at the stone
game?"

But Gaspar would hear none of it. "We must never doubt each
other, Melchior. In my heart I know Balthazar is innocent, as I
know you are innocent. And I remember the scene at the stone
game. There were gold coins in front of him. He was winning, not
losing."

"How will we recover the gold, Gaspar?"

"Through the power of our minds, Melchior. We are wise men,
and we must use our minds to determine the thief's identity."

"But there is no clue to his identity!"

"Sometimes the lack of a clue can be one."

Balthazar returned with the water and they drank eagerly. Later
as they ate of their supplies, Thantia came to them. "I thank you for
helping me," she said. "The elders have spoken to my father and he
has promised never again to beat me. I will return to him now."

"We need no thanks," Gaspar assured her.

Then old Dibon came to join them. "How may we repay you for
your work on the stable?"

"You may recover our stolen gold," Balthazar blurted out.

"Gold? Stolen gold?"

"It was stolen from our tent," Balthazar hurried on, before Gaspar
could silence him.

"There are no thieves in Ziza!"

"There is one."

"I will summon the elders. We will search for your gold."

"No, no," said Gaspar. "We will recover it."

"But how?"

"By finding the thief. It is best to say nothing and catch him off guard."

Old Dibon bowed his head. "I will do as you suggest."

"One favour. Could you ask that our horses be brought to us? We must appear to be leaving."

Then, as they waited, Balthazar gathered their supplies. And Melchior said, "I have put my mind to the problem, Gaspar. But there are too many possibilities. The girl Thantia could be the thief, or her father Nevar. Or any of the game players."

"Or old Dibon himself," Balthazar added. "There are too many to suspect."

Gaspar nodded. "What is needed is an oracle."

"You mean to kill a beast as the Romans do?"

Gaspar shook his head. "My oracle will be a living animal." He saw the herdsman Ramoth leading their horses. "My steed will tell me who has our gold."

"Your horse?" fat Balthazar laughed. "Who learns anything from a dumb animal?"

Gaspar held out some grain for the horse. "You see how he eats? He is hungry."

"What does that tell us?" Melchior asked.

"That our gold was stolen by Ramoth!" It was after Dibon spoke to Ramoth that the young herdsman confessed his crime and begged forgiveness. When the missing gold had been returned to Gaspar's hands, the others questioned him.

"How did you know it was Ramoth?" Melchior asked. "We barely spoke to the youth."

"My horse told me, as I told you he would. The horse was hungry, so had not been fed. You see, the thief never touched our other supplies, never unfastened Balthazar's special knot. How could he have found the gold so easily, without searching for it? But the gold was hidden in a sack of grain, and after the fire destroyed the stable, Ramoth came in search of feed for our horses. He came while we were away, and looked in only one place – the grain bag. Feeling the weight of it, his fingers reached through the grain and came upon the gold. He stole it, but then could not take the grain lest we realize he was the thief. So the horses went hungry."

"You are a wise man, Gaspar," Balthazar conceded.

"As we all are. Come, let us mount."

"It will be dark soon," Melchior said.

Gaspar nodded. "We will get bearings from the star."

Dibon was by the well to wish them farewell. "Ramoth will be punished," he promised.

"Show mercy," Gaspar said.

"Do you ride west with your gold?"

"West with gifts for a King. Gold and frankincense and myrrh."

"Good journey," Dibon said.

He watched them for a long time, until the three vanished from sight over the desert wastes.

# THE CASE OF THE MURDERED SENATOR
## Wallace Nichols

*Wallace Nichols (1888–1967) is really the grandfather of the Roman
detective story. His series about Sollius, the Slave Detective, began
in the pages of the* London Mystery Magazine *in 1950 and
ran for over sixty stories. I reprinted the first two stories in the
last volume. For the current selection, I've jumped over one story
to present the fourth in the series, first published in the October
1950 issue.*

## I

Gaius Sempronius Platorius was a tribune in the Danubian army.
He had won promotion early in the frontier wars of the Empire, and
had the reputation of being a young man of valour and headstrong
character. He was a rake and a gambler – but all the Roman frontier
officers were gamblers: what else could they do with their spare time
in the wilds?

Now he was on a well-earned leave, and on his way to Rome. His
great friend, a fellow officer named Torquatus, had left camp two days
ahead of him, and they had promised themselves a festive meeting in
Rome. Platorius had been away for six years, and wondered how he
would be received in his father's house. He knew how he intended to
be received if it lay in his power or determination to secure his rightful
position there. He was a youth no longer, but a man of experience. The
legions respected him. The Emperor himself had spoken approvingly
of his service.

Would it be best, after all, to let bygones be bygones? He knew
that in the past he had been an unsatisfactory son – but that was no
reason why he should be ousted from his father's will by an adopted
stepson: though it might be legal, it was against nature, and, as the

son of his father's body, he stood for the rights of nature rather than for those of mere legality.

He did not feel forgiving towards his father, and certainly he felt enmity towards Quintus, the son of the second wife, and whom his father had made his heir. And to be heir to Sempronius the Senator was to be the heir to great wealth. Platorius was not reconciled to the loss of his patrimony; nevertheless, he was riding homeward with a certain sardonic pleasure in the situation, and as the milestones to Rome were notched off in his reckoning, he went over carefully in his mind what he intended to do.

Thus brooding and planning, he rode down Italy, and came one evening to the final resting-place before the last few miles to Rome. It was a ramshackle inn, but he had occupied worse quarters many a time during his military life, and he shrugged his shoulders with cynical indifference. He had ridden a certain distance beyond the usual posting-inn, a far superior hostelry in all respects, but this dark, lonely and lesser inn suited his requirements very well. It was some hours nearer to Rome.

He reached it at twilight, and saw to his horse's stabling the first thing.

"You have another traveller?" he asked, surprise in his tone, and pointing to a second horse in the stable, a riding-horse, and not the usual heavy farm-horse such as might have been expected there.

"No traveller," gruffly replied the innkeeper, "only his horse. He left it yesterday, and is visiting, I suppose," he added, with a leer, "some woman in a villa hereabouts. He will be back to claim it. 'Tis naught to me. I ha' been paid for stall and fodder – and if he never returns I have a horse that'll fetch a fine price anywhere. I know a good horse when I see it. I shall lose naught either way."

He tapped his nose with a fore-finger, and they returned indoors. Platorius ate a rough meal, and then pleaded fatigue, and was shown by the landlord to an uncomfortable bed. He was the only guest staying the night; the inn's other frequenters were but an itinerant thief and an old vagabond, and a few farm-slaves from the neighbourhood, and none of these remained for long after the full falling of the dark. It was not an inn of much evening custom, but rather a daylight halt for muleteers and country wagoners making to and from the Roman markets. Platorius congratulated himself.

He slept late – assuredly he had ridden far during the previous twelve hours – and had to be roused by the landlord. After a swift meal, he rode away. While saddling his horse he had noticed that the other horse was still in the stable. He had gone to its stall and patted its flank. He loved horses. It was a well-bred bay, and like an army horse.

He did not hurry himself on that last stage of his long journey. Perhaps he was a little uneasy, now that the time for his unexpected home-coming drew near – unexpected because he had deliberately sent no word of his intention. He had meant to surprise his father: in surprise should lie the best augury for success. He spun out his ride now rather than pressed it, and arrived at his father's great Roman house some little time after midday.

It was not at all the kind of home-coming that any man would ordinarily expect, for he found a crowd surging about the gates, and the house itself in a turmoil, with weeping slaves and a distraught step-mother. His father had been murdered during the night, and Quintus, the adopted son, had already been accused.

# II

"It is terrible, terrible, Valeria; I have no words for it," said Titius Sabinus. "Is there anything I can do?"

The widow of Sempronius, who was also Sabinus's cousin, hesitated, and stared at him with a hard, tearless gaze, and her face was white and drawn.

"Your slave Sollius . . ." she breathed. "I wondered, Titius, whether . . . I know that my son did not do it, but everyone is convinced that he did! Perhaps your clever Sollius could discover the murderer?"

"Of course, Valeria, of course," Sabinus fussily assured her, a little put out of his stride by having his own offer of his astute slave forestalled. "I will send for him, and you shall take him back with you."

And so it came about that Sollius found himself committed to investigating the murder of his master's fellow senator, Sempronius. He did not relish the task. He felt that he had no standing, and did not see how he, a slave, could interrogate with any kind of authority those whom he might wish to question. It had been different when he had been employed as an investigator by the Emperor; he had then possessed powers. But now he was nothing more than a slave lent by his own master to the household of the lady Valeria.

He found the house of the murdered man in the occupation of soldiers from one of the Urban Cohorts, with the City Prefect there in person, for Sempronius had been an important man.

It was a lucky chance that one of the soldiers at the door recognized him and knew of his reputation as a solver of mysteries. This soldier, who was named Gratianus, stepped forward and barred his entrance.

"This slave attends me," said Valeria haughtily.

"I am not forbidding him entrance, lady," answered the soldier. "I wish, with your leave, but a word with him."

"Come to me as soon as you are allowed," said Valeria, turning to Sollius and ignoring the other. "A domestic shall be in wait for you."

She passed in through the portico, a hard-eyed, silent Fury. Gratianus made a grimace, and then caught Sollius by the arm.

"Why are you here?" he whispered. "Is she employing you . . . to save young Quintus? I doubt if he is innocent. The evidence against him is very strong."

"My master has lent me to the lady Valeria," replied Sollius, shrugging his shoulders, "and I must do what I can. I must do even nothing – if nothing, as you hint, is all I can do! – with the proper diligence and energy."

He smiled disarmingly and took a step towards the portico, but the other still had a hand on his arm, and restrained him.

"Listen," said Gratianus in a low tone. "The Prefect in yonder is not too happy. Young Quintus is his son's friend. He would be glad if a flaw could be found in the evidence, and who would find it – if a flaw there is – better than you? Shall I tell him you are here? He will know of you, for did you not give evidence about those treasury thefts before him in the secret enquiry about it? I was there on duty, and heard you."

"I remember," answered Sollius, and rubbed his chin, and then he said: "I should be most grateful, Gratianus, if you would tell the Prefect of the City why I am here."

The soldier released him, clapped him on the back, and motioned him to go forward. Sollius entered the house with a feeling of relief. He would be able to ask his questions after all. But apparently it was no light task that had been forced upon him, and a touch of uneasy despair in his thoughts made his limp more than usually noticeable. A domestic, as had been promised, was waiting for him in the atrium, and led him at once into a lofty, ornate chamber where the lady Valeria was seated on a Greek couch, with a youngish man standing before her. Believing that this was her accused son, Sollius took good note of him. He saw a tall, rather hard-bitten man, who seemed older in experience than in years; he was dark, with a long face, a predatory nose, and thin, decisive lips, and he was clean-shaven. He stood, thought Sollius, like a soldier.

"This is my stepson," announced Valeria, "my husband's son. It is a sad beginning to his leave from the frontier."

"I arrived," said Platorius, "to find my father – murdered. I have not been home for over six years, and now it hardly seems a home-coming at all."

Sollius murmured his sympathy, and looked from one to the other in turn.

"I have told my stepson about your cleverness in solving mysterious happenings," said Valeria, "and that you have been lent to us by Titius Sabinus to help clear my son from the ridiculous accusation against him."

Sollius bowed, and looked at Platorius.

"My name," said the latter, "is Gaius Sempronius Platorius, and I am my father's true son; Quintus was not only his stepson, but his adopted son. It is as well to get these family relationships clear," he added with a smile.

"The more I am told at first," replied Sollius, deceptively meek in manner, "the better I can measure what I may learn afterwards. But I cannot do anything until you tell me the circumstances of the murder."

"I myself can tell you nothing," said Platorius. "All, alas, had happened before I arrived home. Had I been here," he added, a fierce note entering his voice, "I would have marked the villain with his own blood, by the gods!"

"Do you mean you would have marked the lord Quintus? Do you suspect the lord Quintus yourself?" asked Sollius.

Taken aback at the slave's uncompromising directness, Platorius answered that he had meant the murderer, whoever he was.

"I know nothing at all," he continued. "I have no evidence to give, and therefore can have no suspicions of anyone – and certainly I do not suspect Quintus. The accusation can only be some official blunder: it is entirely unbelievable!"

"What points to him?" asked Sollius, turning to Valeria.

"My husband, who was ever a poor sleeper," she narrated, "always rose very early, often before dawn, and would go either into his library, when he might summon a slave to read to him, or, if it was warm weather, into the garden. Last night – but it would have been to-day, and before sunrise," she interjected mournfully – "he left his bed as usual, but since I was myself still asleep I did not hear him go. I was only awakened, indeed, by the clamour when he was found. I was then fetched by Cleander, my husband's Greek reading-slave, and he told me . . ."

Sollius had no compunction about interrupting her.

"Could I speak with this Cleander?" he asked. "Evidence at second hand, lady, is less valuable than a man's own remembrance of what he saw and heard."

"My stepmother can be trusted to tell the truth," burst out Platorius.

"To tell the truth about what she herself witnessed," said Sollius quietly. "But Cleander may have deceived her as to what *he* witnessed. He may even have reported – in quite good faith – mistakenly. I can only judge his reliability by hearing him tell his own tale himself. Will you, lady, send for him?"

"What, slave, you would give orders here?" cried Platorius.

"Peace, Gaius," said his stepmother. "He is more here than just a slave. The Emperor himself has employed him to unravel such things. I will send for Cleander. Dorica!" she called.

A female slave ran swiftly and quietly in.

"Send Cleander hither!" commanded her mistress, speaking in Greek, and the slave-girl, who was little more than a child, ran out again as swiftly and quietly as she had entered.

("A little Ægean dove . . ." thought Sollius to himself.)

"Is your son under arrest?" he asked aloud.

"He is still being questioned," answered Valeria. "The Prefect of the City now has come himself: the first questioning was by a subordinate, and he accused my son to his face. But here is Cleander . . ."

The Greek's story was that his master had aroused him and bidden him come to the library to read aloud to him. As soon as he was dressed, he had gone to the library as instructed. That chamber opened on to a small pillared portico which led directly into the garden. Not finding his master seated in the usual place, he had crossed to this portico to see if he had stepped out into the garden, and in the dim light, for only a small lamp was burning in the chamber, he had stumbled over his master's body, lying across the two or three shallow marble steps that led down to a statued terrace. Over the body, drawing a legionary's short stabbing-sword from a deep wound in the side, was leaning the young lord Quintus, and not only was he drawing the sword from the gash, but he was also smeared with blood on the front of his tunic. He seemed overcome with horror, and Cleander, unable to obtain a coherent statement from him, had at once aroused the household. He knew no more.

Sollius put no questions, and Cleander was dismissed.

"Did your son, lady, give you an explanation of his being found in such suspicious circumstances?" the slave detective then asked.

"Only that he had himself found his father stabbed with the sword, and at the point of death."

"And the sword?" asked Sollius. "Was it your husband's sword, or your son's – or the weapon of some unknown person?"

"It was my son's own sword," murmured Valeria, white to the lips, but with her head high, nevertheless.

Before Sollius could answer her, one of the apparitors attending the Prefect of the City entered without ceremony and addressed himself to the slave:

"His Excellency wishes to see you," he said, "and has sent me for you."

Sollius bowed to the lady Valeria, and followed the apparitor to another part of the house and into the dead man's library. Three men stood there on the threshold of the portico leading into the air: the Prefect himself in full, gleaming military garb; a subordinate, also in soldier's uniform, and a young man, pale, distraught, whose fashionable attire was disordered and streaked with dried blood. The Prefect came forward at once to speak in low tones to Sollius.

"I cannot tell you," he said, "how relieved I am at this good fortune. I know your skill, slave, and never was it more needed to save the innocent. I have no other course than to arrest the young man, for everything points to his guilt – I say, points to it, but there is no proof, and I cannot believe that he did it. But unless it is proved that he did *not* do it, I must give him to the law and condemn him myself. By the godhead of Cæsar, it is horrible!"

"You have questioned the young man?" asked Sollius.

"Examined and cross-examined him, statement by statement, three times over. It is always the same tale – a damning tale unless we can see it in some other light, and so be led to another culprit, at present only too well hidden. Will you question him yourself?"

"I was hoping to be allowed to do so, Excellency."

The Prefect smiled briefly, and led the way back to the two whom he had left.

"Tell your tale again," he commanded, addressing the young man whom Sollius took to be the accused.

"It is no tale, Prefect!" replied Quintus, but his tone was weary and sullen rather than defiant.

"Your Excellency's pardon," put in Sollius, "but might I question him instead of listening to what will now, true or not, be already a set story?"

"As you will," answered the Prefect, a puzzled note in his voice, though whether from his being so curtly overruled, or from a genuine sense of surprise in the procedure, none of them there could tell.

The young man stared at the slave, and the slave at the young man.

"Who is this?" demanded Quintus.

"Your questioner," snapped the Prefect, re-establishing his personal authority over Quintus and Sollius alike.

Quintus turned haggard and bloodshot eyes upon the slave, and with a sigh of exasperated acquiescence, signed to him to begin.

"You were the first, lord, to find your stepfather's body?"

"I was."

"You had come from your chamber? So early?"

"I was entering the house – from outside."

"Through this portico?"

"I have entered the house this way many times. It was quite usual."

"Had you been out all night?"

Quintus hesitated a moment before replying, and then his reply was simply a curt nod.

"A love-affair?" asked Sollius.

He liked the young man, who was handsome, upstanding, and with crisply curling chestnut hair, and had smiled at him as he spoke.

"I am not a boy," cried Quintus, flushing angrily. "And what has my being out at night to do with my stepfather's murder?"

"It might be," suggested Sollius, "that your stepfather had caught you on your return, that a quarrel had arisen, and that in the heat of it you had struck him down."

"It was not so," replied Quintus hotly. "I found him already dying. He died, in fact, as I drew the sword from the wound," he added, and his face puckered with grief, and he turned away his head to conceal a sudden gush of tears.

Sollius could not logically have explained why he went on with his questioning more hopefully:

"I am told that it was your own sword which had been used. Can you account for that?"

"Yesterday," answered Quintus, "I was on duty at a parade before the Augustus, and on my return home my stepfather asked me to work with him over some accounts. He was impatient to begin at once. I flung my sword, my helmet and my cloak in the corner yonder: the cloak and helmet – see! – are there still. The sword was taken – and used . . . Perhaps my stepfather, disturbing a thief, caught it up, was disarmed – and slain by the very weapon which he had taken for his defence."

"You could still have used the same weapon – and in precisely that way – yourself," put in the Prefect.

Quintus sighed deeply, and spread out his hands.

"Excellency, I did not!" he reaffirmed, and his tone was deep and earnest, and again Sollius felt that he believed him.

"The killer," said Sollius, "could have gone but a short time before you arrived. Did you catch no glimpse of him – of one fleeing? Or hear any sound?"

Quintus shook his head.

"Has anything been stolen?"

"Nothing," answered the Prefect, "or so I am informed."

"It is true," said Quintus.

"Your innocence being, for the moment, assumed," went on Sollius, "have you any suspicion as to the murderer?"

"I am wholly bewildered," replied Quintus. "I know of no one who was his enemy. If it was some thief, he escaped. It is incredible that anyone of the household could be such a villain."

"Except yourself," commented Sollius dryly.

"I know myself better than my accusers do!" flung back Quintus. "Were I told that I had done it in sleepwalking, I should not believe it: even my unconscious spirit is incapable of injuring a single hair of his head! I loved him."

Sollius gave him a long look, and then intimated to the Prefect that he had no further questions to put.

"Take the prisoner away!" commanded the Prefect.

## III

"You see," began the Prefect when he and Sollius were alone, "everything – except his own character – points to his guilt, and there is no alternative suspicion. And yet I believe him innocent."

"Let us have open minds," said Sollius. "Let us attack the problem, not from the angle of our wishes – for I, too, I confess it, would like to see the young man cleared – but from that of how the murder was committed. With a sword, certainly; and with the young man's sword: he admits it. Let us suppose that it was as he said, and that the sword, as yonder still the military cloak and the helmet, lay in the room ready for the attacker. That argues one thing at least: that the murder was improvised, that the attacker had not come armed for the purpose, but took the first weapon that he found to his hand."

"Go on," encouraged the Prefect.

"The killing, then, would be after a quarrel, a killing in haste and on the spur of the moment."

"That is how I myself had argued," said the Prefect, "and it points once again to the young man: for who else, coming home late, and so dubiously, was more likely to be the recipient of angry reproaches?"

Sollius suddenly beat his hands against his brow.

"Dolt, dolt that I am!" he cried. "Of course, there was no quarrel: there was no time for a quarrel. Cleander would have interrupted it before there was time for it to blaze so high. No, no; there was no quarrel: the killer came to kill, and killed at first sight."

"If that were so," argued the Prefect, "why did he not come provided with his own sword?"

"Perhaps he did," breathed Sollius, "but seeing the other to his hand, preferred to use it – and to leave it as evidence against – the lord Quintus?"

The Prefect began pacing slowly about.

"It was no thief," he murmured, "unless Cleander disturbed him."

"Who has a grudge against the lord Quintus?" asked Sollius.

"Nobody, I should think," replied the Prefect. "He is the pleasantest young man you could meet. My son is devoted to him, a Damon to his Pytheas."

Sollius coughed.

"Are the two stepbrothers a Damon and a Pytheas?" he asked quietly.

The Prefect halted abruptly in his pacing about, and swung round.

"Do you know the position here between the two: the son by nature and the son by adoption?"

"My master explained it to me before I came," replied Sollius, and the two looked at one another.

"Gaius Platorius was not here," said the Prefect. "He arrived well after the discovery of the murder."

He began pacing about again.

"Sir, could his itinerary be checked?" whispered Sollius.

"It will have to be checked," the Prefect answered with a sigh. "You can leave that to me. When it is done, I will send for you. In the meantime," he added, laying a hand on the slave's shoulder, "learn what you can from the lady Valeria and from Cleander. I recommend the interrogation of Cleander particularly to you! You have authority to come and go and question as you will. I am grateful for your help: we must clear the lord Quintus if we can. Meanwhile I shall confine him to his own chamber with a strong guard. Farewell!"

## IV

Sollius returned to the apartment where the lady Valeria had received him, and found her still there with her stepson.

"What did the Prefect have to say to you?" she asked eagerly. "Is my son released?"

"The lord Quintus, lady, is under guard in his own chamber."

"Can I see him?"

"No, lady."

"Why not? What did the Prefect say?"

"He let me question the lord Quintus in his presence. At the moment, lady, there is nothing to do but to await the result of an enquiry to be made by the Prefect – an enquiry, lady, which should be in favour of your son."

"What enquiry is that?" asked Platorius in the tone of a Roman officer speaking to a Gallic or Pannonian auxiliary.

"Only the Prefect, sir, can answer you that," said Sollius.

"How, slave! You dispute my command?"

"Peace, Gaius," murmured Valeria.

"It is an impertinence!" cried Platorius. "How dare a slave speak to me like that?"

"This slave is different, Gaius," said Valeria. "I told you so."

"A slave is a slave!" answered Platorius, and disgustedly turned away; nevertheless, Sollius noticed, he seemed to listen with a fully attentive ear to what followed.

"Can you give me any hope?" asked Valeria. "I am in despair, Sollius: justice in Rome is so hard a procedure."

Sollius carefully considered his reply, and when finally he uttered it, he spoke in a voice that would in no way strain the hearing of the listening tribune from the Army of the Danube.

"I have certain ideas, lady, that I must ponder and test before committing to words, even to you. Yet I think," he added with a touch of solemnity which it amused him to assume deliberately, "a more likely murderer than the lord Quintus might be postulated without unreason. But," he hastened to continue, before her maternal anxiety could interrupt his statement, "I cannot name him – even to myself. The Prefect is permitting me to follow my own line in the investigation, and I must not say more until I have compared my activities with his official action. But be of good hope, lady: for what it is worth, I think your son is innocent."

"Oh, praised be the gods!" she cried, and the tears streamed down her face. "Do what you will in this house: I have already given orders that you are to be obeyed in anything you may demand."

To the mutter of a contemptuous oath from the tribune, he turned, and withdrew in search of Cleander, but half-way down the passage leading to the atrium he purposely slackened step. He knew that Platorius would follow him, and was not surprised at being overtaken.

"Slave, did you mean what you said?" demanded the tribune.

"That I believe the lord Quintus to be innocent? Yes, lord."

"I believe it, too," exclaimed the other, looking carefully round as he spoke, and then he murmured underbreath: "I like not eavesdroppers. I trust, by the gods," he went on in a clearer voice, "that you can prove it."

"I hope so, lord."

"You have found evidence pointing to another?" pursued Platorius, catching him by the arm.

"No, lord, nothing. There is no true evidence anywhere, only oblique evidence, and even that may be falsely laid – or even false in itself. Yet suspicions are not always based on evidence."

"And you have suspicions?" whispered Platorius, and his grip tightened.

Sollius hesitated. A trickle of icy dewdrops seemed to moisten his spine. How should he answer?

"I will not call them suspicions, lord," he said quietly. "But – I have a guess. Ah, here is Cleander, and it is Cleander whom I am seeking."

He blessed the unexpected appearance of the murdered Senator's reading-slave, and was able to break off his present conversation easily and without subterfuge.

## V

"I want to speak with you, Cleander. Where can we talk alone?"

Cleander considered for a moment, and then led the way to a small courtyard which contained a fountain.

"Well?" he asked.

Sollius did not feel that the other was antagonistic: but certainly he felt that he was cautious.

"Did you see anyone inside the house just before you went to join your master in his library? Think well before you answer."

"I saw nobody."

"Did you hear any unusual sound? Any sound of voices, for instance?"

"None."

"Not even your master's fall when stabbed?"

"I heard nothing," said Cleander, and his eyes, widely open, were honest.

"How long have you been a slave here?" asked Sollius, abruptly changing the attack. "Have you been in the household long enough to remember the quarrel between your master and his son, the lord Gaius?"

"It was only six years ago," said Cleander. "I remember it very well. But it was more a disagreement than a quarrel. I mean, there was no violence of words: only a cold silence, which ended in the lord Gaius leaving home for the wars on the frontier. It is true that he was disinherited."

"Then the disagreement," commented Sollius, "must have been very serious."

"It was. It was over the wild life which the young man led. My master was of the old school, always quoting Cato as the only proper example to all Romans, and the young man could not stomach it."

"I understand," murmured Sollius. "Has the lord Gaius been home since – on leave, for instance – or is this his first return after the break with his father?"

"The very first," replied Cleander, "and a terrible homecoming it is. His bowels will be filled with remorse. Why else did he come home without warning –?"

"Without warning?" interjected Sollius.

"We had no idea of his coming. He would not have come like that if he had not found that time and experience had developed in him his better, rather than his worse, qualities. His tragedy is double: he has lost both a father and the satisfaction of repentance. We all pity him."

Sollius remained silent for a moment. Then he asked:

"How long after the discovery of the murder did he arrive?"

"Many hours," replied Cleander. "The murder was discovered when it was barely light; the lord Gaius arrived after midday."

Sollius nodded.

"I saw him weep," pursued Cleander.

Sollius nodded again.

"And the lord Quintus?" he asked abruptly. "Did you see *him* weep?"

"He seemed too frozen and stunned for tears. All he did was to cry for vengeance."

"Of course," said Sollius with grave irony, "he was only the adopted son. Nature would not speak in him, but only gratitude."

## VI

It was four days before the Prefect summoned Sollius by the same Gratianus whom the slave already knew, and the meeting took place in the austere headquarters of the Urban Cohorts which had jurisdiction over the domestic peace of Rome.

"Platorius, at least, is guiltless," the Prefect announced as soon as the slave detective was admitted into his presence.

"Oh!" exclaimed Sollius blankly.

"You are disappointed, I can see," said the Prefect. "But there is no doubt about it: he was asleep at an inn too far off for him to be here in Rome at the time of his father's murder. That has been tested by my officers."

"If Platorius is cleared," replied Sollius, plucking at his underlip, "there is only the lord Quintus left – unless your Excellency," he added, looking up hopefully, "has been able to unearth another suspect."

The Prefect sighed, and shook his head.

"It must lie between the two of them. Both had, doubtless, motive, but only one of them opportunity."

"It cannot be accidentally," Sollius mused aloud, "that the lord Quintus has been made to appear guilty: to use his sword, if a ruse of the moment, was deliberate – a swift decision, certainly. That swiftness of decision," he went on, looking fixedly at the Prefect, "is the sign of a soldier."

"So you are not convinced of a certain soldier's innocence," said the Prefect with a wry smile, "in spite of my assurance that he lacked opportunity?"

Sollius flushed.

"Forgive me, Excellency. I was disrespectful. I should have remembered to whom I was speaking . . ."

"Sollius," broke in the Prefect seriously, "you are no ordinary man, and I am not treating you as a slave. The Emperor spoke to me about you last night. He is concerned over this case, and is pleased that I am using you as an assistant. You have full leave to make any investigation which you consider may help justice – and justice, by its own nature, will acquit young Quintus of this parricide. If, therefore, you need powers to pursue your course, take them. I grant them freely."

"May I first hear, Excellency," begged Sollius, "the steps that were taken to prove that Platorius was asleep at an inn too far away for him to be in Rome when his father was murdered?"

The Prefect frowned, and then, commanding himself, laughed.

"You are an obstinate fellow," he said, "but it is an obstinacy for a good purpose. Gratianus shall tell you: it was he who conducted the investigation. I can find no flaw in his conclusions. But he is your friend, and both as a friend and an official will speak easily and openly about it. You may even wish to go over the same ground. You have leave to do so."

Sollius thanked him, and was dismissed.

"What is this all about?" asked Gratianus as soon as they were alone together. "Do you think I have had no experience in these matters? I have tracked the movements of hundreds of men. I am trained to do it."

"I know, I know, Gratianus," said Sollius placatingly. "I am not doubting your skill. I am only wondering whether this Platorius has not deceived you with a peculiar cunning."

"It will have been a very peculiar cunning," muttered Gratianus, still unappeased.

"Well, let us go over it together. Two heads are always better than one, even if only to confirm what the first head came to think."

"Answer *me* this question yourself," said Gratianus earnestly. "Why do you suspect Platorius so strongly?"

"He has two motives," replied Sollius, "revenge and cupidity; then the manner of the murder had a soldier's touch; finally, I . . . *sensed* his uneasiness. It was a very curious feeling, a kind of feeling which I have had before – and have always found reliable. Indeed," he added seriously, "I have never disregarded it without being sorry afterwards."

"You talk like a woman, Sollius," derisively answered Gratianus. "I think otherwise, because I know otherwise. Will *this* satisfy you? Platorius spent the night – the innkeeper and other witnesses prove it – at an inn . . . He even hired a girl to be his companion, and I can produce the girl – and, besides, no horse could have borne him hither from that inn, back again to the inn, and then hither again, and be in the condition it was on his arrival to find his father already murdered. No, Sollius, it is quite impossible."

## VII

Leaving the headquarters of the Urban Cohorts, Sollius walked back through the narrow, crowded and eternally noisy Roman streets towards the house of Titius Sabinus, his master. Absorbed in his cogitations, he made way from time to time for wayfarers in a hurry, chariots and litters with their huge, running bearers, in a kind of dream, acting automatically for his own safety, yet completely unaware the while of the identity of any for whom he stepped aside.

But one of such, at least, recognized *him*, and a curt order brought a pair of litter-bearers to a jolting halt.

"Here, you! You there, slave!" cried out a deep, insolent voice which roused Sollius at once from his thoughts. "Come hither, slave!"

"Lord?" enquired Sollius, going to the litter and looking in upon two men lolling together on the cushions.

"I was told you were good at solving mysteries," went on the same deep, insolent voice. "My stepmother thinks so, or says she does. But what have you done about my father's murder? Nothing, I'll be bound! Slave, you are a fraud! I have seen many a sly face like yours. Haven't you, Torquatus, too? Sly with the pretence of a cleverness not possessed! I know your kind! Don't you, Torquatus, too?"

His friend laughed. Both men, thought Sollius, seemed very pleased with life. Clearly Platorius was anticipating the uses of the inheritance which he could expect to receive after the execution of Quintus, and his friend was sharing in the good fortune.

"Lord," replied Sollius with great outward respect, "I have but just now left his Excellency the City Prefect, and can report that the case of your father's murder is . . . nearing its close."

He knew that he had claimed more than he should, but Platorius's manner had nettled him, and he had not guarded his tongue. But when he saw the swift look which Torquatus flashed upon his friend, and the twin, smouldering, half-ruined stars which were the eyes of that friend himself, he no longer regretted his unwary boasting, but followed it up with a remark which now was deliberate in its lack of caution.

"It is all a question," he said, trying to appear as foolish and fatuous as he could, "of disproving what the murderer said he did."

He had partially closed his eyes while speaking, and now he opened them full, and stared upon Torquatus. But it was Platorius who answered:

"What, slave, you know the murderer? Then why is he not under arrest?"

"He will be arrested," replied Sollius turning to him, "as soon as I have proved one piece of evidence . . . concerning his whereabouts at a certain time."

"By the gods," exclaimed Torquatus, "you will be a clever fellow if you can prove that a man is here, or there, when he says the contrary."

Sollius again turned his gaze upon Platorius's companion. He saw a thick-necked, burly man with a rounded, jovial face and a very large nose, a man almost the exact opposite to his friend, who was lean, long-faced and sardonic.

"Is the Prefect making this enquiry himself?" demanded Platorius.

"The Prefect," answered Sollius deliberately, "does not know what *I* know. I shall take him the knowledge with the proof. That is my way," he added, appearing still more fatuous in his affectation of self-esteem.

"Get on, you lazy cattle!" cried Platorius to his bearers sharply, and he flung himself back on the cushions as the litter lurched forward and went on.

## VIII

Sollius was no horseman, and a two-horsed chariot had been provided for him, which Gratianus drove. Two mounted men of the Urban Cohort rode with them.

"How far is it to this inn?" Sollius asked when they were well on their way.

Gratianus told him.

"It is the first posting-inn out of Rome northwards," he added, a trifle surlily, for he had not welcomed the slave's suggestion that the investigation of the movements of Platorius should be done again, but the Prefect had agreed and ordered it, and Gratianus did not conceal that the fact rankled.

The day was dry and hot even when they set out in the early light, and by the time they reached the inn for which they were making the sky was brazen with noon. It was a busy and well-conducted place: Sollius could see that with the first glance; but his interest was not in the inn as an inn, nor even in the questions which his companion put to the innkeeper. The answers only confirmed what had already been elicited: that Platorius, an army officer on leave who gave that name, had stayed at the inn on the night in question. That being so, his presence in Rome at the time of the murder of Sempronius was impossible.

"Do you wish to interrogate the girl whom he hired?" asked Gratianus maliciously.

"That is a very good idea," gravely answered Sollius. "Will you send for her?"

Gratianus stared. He had not expected his jesting offer to be taken seriously.

The girl, when brought to them, was pretty enough, and too young to need as much paint as she thought it proper and needful to put on; but she was already hard in eye, and tiredly wary of the offers and promises of men. She came suspiciously, determined to give as good as she might get.

But with his first question Sollius disarmed her by the virtue of surprise. Gratianus, too, was jolted out of his surliness and momentary malice.

"Is your memory good?" Sollius had asked.

The girl tossed her head.

"I remember any man with money!" had been her answer.

"The man about whom I am asking," said Sollius, "had money to spend on you, and spent it."

"I have been asked about him before," replied the girl. "I remember that, at least. It was you who asked about him," she went on, turning to Gratianus. "I remember you, too. I can swear that he was here, and that his name was Gaius Sempronius Platorius. He told me that that was his name over and over again in his cups. He was quite drunk in the end, thank the gods!" she concluded reminiscently.

"Yes, yes," said Sollius with some irritation. "It was to impress that name upon your memory. But that is not what I want to know if you remember, but something else. And I hope, I do hope, that your memory is good. Verily, a young man's life hangs upon it."

She grew interested at that, and became more natural.

"What is that 'something else'?" she asked in a lower and less brittle tone.

"Do you," pursued Sollius in his gentlest voice, "remember what Gaius Sempronius Platorius was like?"

"I remember that very well," she answered with a laugh. "We girls have to take the fat with the thin – and he was one of the fat, with his red moon-face and his large nose."

Gratianus gasped.

"The truth," said Sollius, "lies there. You may go, girl!"


## IX


"There were two in it," stated Sollius as they drove away from the posting-inn, "Platorius and a friend. I have seen the friend, but do not know his name."

"I know *that*," answered a meeker Gratianus. "It is Torquatus."

"Torquatus, at least," went on Sollius, partly musing aloud, "was not the murderer. He was here – under the name of Platorius – and fortunately for himself he can prove it, or we can prove it for him, which is unfortunate for the other. I begin now to see the whole plot in orderly shape."

"Plot?" exclaimed Gratianus.

"It was a plot, and most cunningly undertaken," asserted Sollius. "I see it like this: Platorius was determined to win back his lost inheritance, and could do that by only two means, a reconcilation with his father, or his father's death. He must have had no hope of the former, or he would not have laid his plot."

"But to kill his father," expostulated Gratianus, "would only make the lord Quintus inherit, not himself."

"An executed man cannot inherit anything," said Sollius grimly.

"But it was only by chance that the lord Quintus's sword was there to be used," Gratianus obstinately pointed out.

"I know that. It was the soldier in Platorius which evolved a new tactical stroke on the instant. I have no doubt that he had some plan for fixing the murder upon Quintus. But he saw Chance, as he considered, favouring him, and followed his luck as a clever general does at the crisis of a battle."

"I begin to see," muttered Gratianus. "You are as sharp as they say, after all!"

"We now have to work out the itineraries of *both* of them," pursued Sollius, and his tone took on a new energy.

"How do we begin?" asked Gratianus.

"We need not trouble about Torquatus. You have already proved that he stayed the night here and left at a certain hour on the morning after. The only difference is that you thought it was Platorius. When Torquatus reached Rome does not matter in the least. He dropped out of events as soon as he had provided Platorius with a named personality at a particular place during certain hours. But what, during those same hours, was Platorius himself doing?"

"It is easy to ask!" muttered Gratianus.

"Let us begin to think," said Sollius. "Draw in the horses under that group of elms yonder."

They descended from the chariot and sat down in the only highway shade, as it seemed, for miles, for the dusty landscape was but sparsely furnished with trees of any kind. The two mounted men of the Urban Cohort took their rest, too, near at hand in the same shade, allowing their horses to graze disappointedly on the scanty wayside herbage.

"It seems clear," pursued Sollius, "that Platorius would have ridden beyond his friend Torquatus, and have reached Rome in the night, or towards dawn. He would remember his father's habit of early rising, and had determined to profit by circumstances. Probably he found his father stepping out of the portico into the garden and returned into the house with him. Then he noticed the sword, used it instead of his own, and immediately slipped away – perhaps on hearing the lord Quintus's approach, a stroke, as he would have thought it, of additional luck. His horse would have been tethered near by, and he would have ridden out of Rome, to return in the middle of the day as though arriving directly from his long journey. It is that ride out of Rome, Gratianus, which we must seek to follow. He would have had some place in which to linger out the time. If we can discover that . . ."

"No loiterer, certainly no horseman, was seen leaving the garden of Sempronius," said Gratianus. "I had every enquiry possible made as to that, hoping to find another suspect, but . . . well, it was barely dawn, and a cloudy morning at that, and nobody was about."

"Luck alone could have given us such evidence!" sighed Sollius gloomily.

The two were sunk in their thoughts for some while, savouring, as it were, both silence and shade. Then Sollius said:

"There will be – there *must* be – some inn, probably of low character and perhaps sequestered a little from the direct highway, somewhere between the posting-inn which we have just visited and the outskirts of the city. Torquatus, as Platorius, put up at the posting-inn, and rode on at his leisure the next morning; Platorius would not have halted at the posting-inn. He must have ridden considerably farther on, and have put up at some other inn from which he could reach Rome, and get back to the inn, quickly and with ease. He would have pretended to stay the night there, but have slipped away, murdered his father, returned to the inn as secretly as he had left it, and then, after lying late, have continued his open journey in time to arrive at his father's house by midday. But we can only prove all this by finding that second inn."

"It is all guesswork," complained Gratianus. "But the Prefect will only back you up, so we had better set to work to discover this inn – if it exists at all! We will search the whole district, in width as well as in depth, between here and Rome, and if your deductions, Sollius, have misled us, I'll souse you in Father Tiber myself!"

X

But Sollius was in no danger of an immersion in the yellow Tiber, for they found the ramshackle inn where Platorius had stabled his horse on the fatal night. The innkeeper, fearing worse discoveries, met their questions grovelling. Yes, a traveller on horseback certainly had put up at his inn on that night, and had ridden away the next morning. He scratched his head over the suggestion that the traveller might have left the inn during the night: he had not seen him leave, nor yet seen him return. His horse? But his horse next morning had been perfectly fresh. No, they were mistaken to think otherwise. He had seen the condition of the horse himself. Suddenly his eyes gleamed, his mouth opened, and he guffawed aloud.

"What are you remembering, rogue?" snapped Gratianus.

"But there was another horse. I had a good bargain with that other horse!" replied the innkeeper, rubbing his hands together with greedy satisfaction.

"What other horse?" asked Sollius eagerly.

"I will tell you," replied the innkeeper with a leer of ingratiation. "A traveller came and left a horse in my stable the day before, paid for its stalling and keep for a day, saying he was on a visit in the neighbourhood. I took it to be a visit of love," he explained, winking grotesquely. "I cared not, for I could sell the horse if he never came back – which he never did. And I did sell the horse," he added, "and for a good price. But I can tell you this, sirs," he went on in a lower tone, as if an eavesdropper might be about, "*that* horse had been out during the night. It was still in sweat when I saw it in the morning."

"Two horses," murmured Sollius, "one planted by Torquatus, and then ridden into Rome and back by Platorius in the night; and two men, a false and a true Platorius, one at the posting-inn and the other committing murder. They could afford to throw away a horse! Do you see it, my friend?"

"I see it now," growled Gratianus, flushing with annoyance that he had not seen it himself before. "But can we prove it?"

"We have good witnesses in two innkeepers and a girl," said Sollius, "and we could trace, no doubt, that second horse."

A sudden cry from outside broke into their talk, a cry that was followed by the clash of steel. Gratianus hurried out, while Sollius stared after him from the doorway. But dusk had already fallen, and all he could see was a lurid shadow cast from a flaring torch, itself out of sight, and the twigs and bushes near the gate a-drip with the same lurid glow. Whatever was happening was round the angle of the building. The innkeeper behind him began moaning and wringing his hands.

And now Gratianus, with a bleeding gash in his left arm, ran back indoors, and his own drawn sword was bloody down all its keen length.

"Bar the door, innkeeper!" he cried breathlessly, and sprang to

help the other lift the great wooden bar and thrust it through the
iron sockets of the doorposts.

"What is happening?" asked Sollius.

"Platorius and Torquatus, with some armed ruffians, have followed
us. With both of us slain, and the innkeeper here either slain, too, or
well bribed, they will be safe from detection for ever."

"Where are the two soldiers?"

"One is dead, stabbed in the back. I shouted to the other – who
was still in the saddle as the villains crept through the gate – to ride
for help, but we shall have our work cut out to keep them off until
it comes."

"I am no fighting man," said Sollius dismally.

Gratianus clicked impatiently with his tongue.

"This door will not last long," he muttered.

"Is there no way out at the back?" suggested Sollius. "There is
still the chariot . . ."

"A way out – and as good a way in," snapped Gratianus, "and they
have taken the horses from the chariot. We are here till relieved!"

"How many are there?" asked Sollius, more out of curiosity
than fear.

"Some three now, as well as Platorius and the other, for I killed
one. Too many for us, I can tell you! But we must hold them off for
over an hour. It is a fair distance to Rome and back."

"Platorius rode it," said Sollius grimly.

"Twice in a long night," growled Gratianus. "*We* have to abide a
danger that never touched *him*. I can already smell burning!"

Loud cries of terror from the innkeeper's wife and serving-girl now
came to them from the inn's back quarters.

The two women and an old stableman came running in.

"Curses on you!" cried the innkeeper furiously. "The whole back
o' the house is ablaze!"

"You there – stableman – and you, innkeeper, unbar the door,"
commanded Gratianus with a fine show of calm, Roman efficiency.
"Then take the bar, and use it as a ram. Sollius, take the one end
of it, and keep it level and straight. When you are ready, I'll open.
Rush out at once, ramming your way. You two women, follow close
behind. I'll protect the rear with my sword. We should reach that old
dovecot beside the gate. I saw it as I came in. They can't burn brick
– though they can try to smoke us out. But it will give us a measure
of time, and time is our sole riches!"

With their desperation to infect them with strength, they found
the sufficient courage to do his will. Smoke and the fierce crackle of
fire insistent behind them, they hauled out the heavy wooden bar,

swung it round to project before them like a battering-ram, and stood ready to burst forth; and then Gratianus, sword in hand, tore open the door.

In the glare of a raised, flame-dripping torch Platorius, Torquatus and three others stood awaiting them in a ring. Gratianus swore.

"I thought they'd be dispersed round about!" he muttered, and swore again.

"It is no use," laughed Platorius. "We are too many. And you look for help? With what hope? Your man broke his neck when his horse fell! This road won't take a gallop – as I know from experience, you pestilent slave!" he added, his face working. "Are you coming out? 'Tis all one to me: either we kill you here, or you stay where you are, and burn. By Jupiter, slave, but you, at least, are too clever to live!"

The innkeeper's wife shrieked, and fell in a swoon into her man's arms. The heavy bar dropped with a crash. The serving-girl sank to her knees, wailing, and calling upon what gods she could remember, and the stableman made a blind dash outside, turning off towards the stables, only to be checked and cut down by one of Platorius's hired ruffians. Gratianus lowered the point of his sword, and stood rigid: he had no further invention for the situation as it now was. Laughing again, Platorius turned down his thumbs.

"Mithras, Saviour of the World, accept my breath!" murmured Gratianus, staring in front of him.

Sollius, who had a certain predilection towards the worship of Isis, prayed to that goddess silently; but, on a sudden, as he prayed, began wondering if there might not be a better efficacy in the deity of the Christians: he had heard good things of the Christians' God. Then he shrugged his shoulders, and again prayed to Isis.

"Are you coming?" impatiently called out Platorius, "or must we come in ourselves and sweep you backward into the flames?"

"Is there nothing we can do?" besought Sollius.

"I, armed, can at least die fighting!" muttered Gratianus.

"The altar is ready, the knives are sharpened, victims!" cried Platorius in a jesting tone, and then they heard it: the tramp, tramp, tramp, tramp of feet in the unison of a march, and the gathering roar of a soldiers' chorus:

> "We do not fear the Dorians,
> The Britons or Isaurians,
> Nor yet the Hyperboreans,
> For we are the Prætorians,
> Disposers of the State!

> *War is where we tramp;*
> *Peace is where we camp;*
> *And what we do is Fate:*
> — *For we are the Prætorians,*
> *The greatest of the great!"*

Nearer and nearer they came, the tramping and the singing: a cohort of Prætorian Guards on a route-march. They would surely investigate the burning inn on their way!

"Are we saved, think you?" whispered Sollius.

"Unless these fellows rush us in revengeful desperation," answered Gratianus. "But one of 'em – perhaps two! – will die before I do, I promise you that," he added grimly.

The Prætorian cohort was swinging into view.

"Halt!" rang out a voice of command. "What goes on here?"

"Decius! Oh, Decius!" cried Sollius, half sobbing in his relief.

"Who calls me?" answered the voice. "Castor and Pollux, *you*, slave?"

And Decius the centurion, who once, at the Emperor's command, had acted as Sollius's bodyguard, ran up to the inn. At the same instant, Platorius, in the high Roman fashion – as befitted a tribune of the Danubian army – drove his sword into his own heart.

# A MITHRAIC MYSTERY
# Mary Reed and Eric Mayer

*In the last volume I introduced the character of John the Eunuch, who served as Lord Chamberlain to Justinian, the last of the great Roman emperors who ruled from Byzantium in the sixth century. Once again Eric Mayer's ideas and Mary Reed's writing have combined to bring us another mystery to solve, this one even more dangerous than the first. Mary has had several mystery stories published in* Ellery Queen's Mystery Magazine, *but the bulk of her writing has been non-fiction, including a book about fruits and nuts of which its spiritual ancestor finds its way into the following story. Eric has also been a frequent writer of non-fiction for such diverse publications as* Baby Talk, Festivals, *and* Running Times. *For the latter he went on a half marathon to write about his experiences, but he admits that collaborating on this story was considerably less painful.*

Although he spoke four languages fluently, John the Eunuch swore in Egyptian, at least on those public occasions when it was merited. Privately, however, was a different matter, and the Lord Chamberlain's language upon hearing the news brought to him by the Emperor's secretary Anatolius would have horrified most of the Byzantine Court, less for the quality of the profanity than for its theological basis.

"By Mithra's Seven Runged Ladder! By the great Bull! I can hardly believe it!" John's staccato oaths matched his angry strides up and down the long sitting room. The day had just begun. The sun, rising over the Bosphorus, sent shafts of light through the octagonal panes of the room's single, tall window, lying in bright fringes across the mosaic hunting scene beneath John's feet.

Anatolius nodded miserably. "I had it from the captain of the excubitors."

John paced furiously, treading upon garishly costumed hunters and fantastic prey alike. "I must see the body before it's moved. In the mithraeum itself, of all places!"

When John strode from the room, Anatolius followed without a word. As an Occult, he was awed not by John's lofty public position but rather by the fact that the sunburnt Greek, a fellow Mithran, had achieved the sixth rank, Runner of the Sun, and was thus only a step away from advancement to Father, the seventh and highest rung on the Mithraic ladder. The irony of this did not escape Anatolius, though he did not engage in coarse jests at John's expense as did some of the Palace drudges, devotees of the fleshpots of Venus and Ashtoreth.

The two men crossed the cobbled street outside John's residence. Gulls, gathered to feed on the refuse that accumulated even within the grounds of the Great Palace, scattered and screamed their displeasure like Green and Blue partisans at the Circus. The men passed the Daphne Palace, the Pantheon – the Empress's official residence – and the Church of St Stephen. An unobtrusive doorway, in the dim recesses of an armory behind a barracks, led to a series of damp, slippery stairs and subterranean corridors and, finally, hidden away at the back, the mithraeum.

Usually these musty catacombs were deserted, but this morning spear-wielding excubitors stood guard at each turn. They looked glum. John recognized most as followers of Mithra.

Otto, the captain of the excubitors, met John and Anatolius outside the entrance to the mithraeum.

"Mithra forgive me, I was ordered to secure the mithraeum by the Master of Offices himself," said Otto, naming John's immediate superior in the Palace administration.

"Who discovered the body?" asked John.

"The Master didn't say. An informer, like as not."

John entered the holy place. The sacred flame, burning as always on the altar at the end of the sunken nave, illuminated the marble bas relief of Mithra wrestling the Great Bull behind it, and, on the steps before the altar, the body of a man, naked except for a Phrygian cap, the same type of head covering worn by the God Himself.

John went down seven steps into the lower level without hesitation but Anatolius hung back. Occults were not privileged to partake in the Mysteries, but only observed, faces obscured by black veils, from the wooden benches overlooking the area.

The body felt cold beneath John's thin hand. It was a young man, slight but muscular, barely twenty. His eyes had been bandaged, his hands bound with chicken entrails, in the manner of a Mithraic initiation mystery; in this case the ritual murder had not been simulated. There was a bloody wound in his side and on the otherwise unmarked marble floor, next to the body, was written in blood "Thus perish all who hate the Lord of Light".

John's summons to the Empress Theodora's private residence came unexpectedly. Theodora, a bear-keeper's daughter, former whore and worse – if the rumors were to be believed – greeted him warmly. Dressed in gold-embroidered robes, her hair tied in coils at the sides of her head, thin lips abundantly rouged to contrast with the pallor of her face, she was a beautiful and desirable woman. Or so John had been told. When he reflected upon the number and frequency of Theodora's affairs, and her lovers' habit of leaving for Malaga or Philae or some other far corner of the Empire when they fell from favor, he was glad that Fate had seen fit to spin his life as She had.

"How good to see you, Lord Chamberlain," said the Empress, taking his arm as her slaves withdrew, closing the heavily gilded door softly behind them.

She was much shorter than John, himself a man of average height.

"I must congratulate you again on the arrangements for the Egyptian Envoy's banquet," she said. "A most satisfying event."

John recalled the Empress had drunk too much wine and spent most of the banquet trying to convince an exceptionally muscular Egyptian scion to take dwarf olives from her pursed lips. Afterwards, emboldened by the Empress's advances, the man had actually tried to bribe him. "It is my privilege to serve the Imperial family," John replied.

"Come and sit with me." She led John towards one of the many low couches scattered amidst carved teak tables, the seat scarcely visible beneath a riot of rainbow-hued cushions. The room was furnished with an eye toward luxury, if not ostentation, from purple silk wall hangings to rosy plum and azure blue Indian carpets. A man of austere tastes, John found the room both overwhelming and vulgar, rather like Theodora herself.

"You must come and talk more often," said the Empress, leaning forward so that John could feel her warm breath on his neck and smell her musky perfume. "I have so little opportunity to talk to men in an intelligent manner. They are all such beasts. But you and I might discuss epigrams or even theology."

"Surely you haven't asked me here to discuss theology."

"No, I haven't. Such a pity." The Empress drew a forefinger down John's cheek. "I like a smooth face," she confided.

John found himself looking into her eyes. They were, from a distance, narrow eyes. But up close he could see that her pupils were tiny pinpoints. It gave her a knowing, almost oracular look, as if her gaze were focused on some perfect, distant truth. John almost wished he might experience the madness that had led so many men to throw away their lives for the pleasures those eyes promised. Then he recalled that her fashionably contracted pupils were merely the result of applications of deadly belladonna, and his momentary curiosity evaporated.

The Empress apparently noticed. She drew away slightly. "I am afraid I have asked you here about an unpleasant matter," she said. There was disappointment in her voice, and perhaps a touch of anger as she continued. "One of the Emperor's bodyguards, and therefore a man under your own command, Lord Chamberlain, has been found brutally murdered. Apparently this was the result of some hellish secret rite."

She stared at him with those poisonous eyes. John was careful to suppress his surprise. Although they were technically under his jurisdiction, John did not directly command the Silentiaries who guarded the Emperor, at least ceremonially, and would be unlikely to have known the victim.

"Where did this information come from?" he asked.

"The Master of Offices. He tells me the victim was named Alexander, a low born Thracian, new to the city just last year."

"And the hellish rites?"

"Mithrans," said Theodora. "It has been rumored that they engage in human sacrifice, although, until now, they have managed to keep their abominations secret. Here, what do you think of these figs?" She gestured toward a filigreed silver bowl of fruit on a nearby table.

John took one of the figs, bit into it and chewed slowly while his mind raced. As an initiate in the Mysteries, he knew that contrary to common wisdom such rites had not been carried out for hundreds of years, if ever. But he could hardly reveal his knowledge to the Empress. Though Mithraism, like some other pagan religions, was tolerated, a high official in the Christian Byzantine court would hardly dare reveal allegiance to an officially outlawed cult.

"But why have you summoned me about this matter?" he asked at last.

"The victim was under your command, as the murderer might be. It has been said that the Emperor's bodyguard has become a breeding ground for these vipers. I want you to investigate – discreetly."

"And what of the Emperor?"

"Justinian will be conducting his own investigation. So you need not report to him."

"And what if he finds out about . . . me?"

Theodora gave a brief, guttural laugh. "He will have no suspicions where you are concerned."

"I understand," said John. His face remained an expressionless mask. "I will look into the matter, but I can promise nothing." He rose from the couch. "The figs, by the way, are excellent."

"I'm glad you find them so, Lord Chamberlain. I will be sure to have more, when you return to talk to me."

She stood. Gold flashed from the threads of her robe, the tied coils of her hair, the rings on her fingers, her earrings.

"They are grown on a special tree," she said. "Not far from Trebizond." Theodora's thin, scarlet lips curved into a scythe of a smile. "It is said the peasants must use a seven-runged ladder to harvest the choicest fruits."

Mithraism was a soldier's religion, exclusively male, valuing above all the military virtues of discipline, self sacrifice and chastity. Perhaps because chastity came too easily to John, the Lord Chamberlain was zealous in practicing the other virtues. So it was, when he went to the Baths of Zeuxippus, as he always did immediately upon leaving the Empress, he inevitably confined himself to the cold pool.

The shock of icy water against his naked skin dissipated the sickly fog that had seemed to follow him away from the Empress's rooms. He scrubbed his wiry arms and splashed his face until he had washed away the last traces of her musk.

Emerging from the circular pool onto the slick marble, he was pleased to find Anatolius. It was no surprise, since it was not uncommon for the higher classes to attend the baths two or even three times daily. Judging from his flushed face, and the way his black hair lay in ringlets against the side of his head, John's friend had just come from the steam bath.

"I have just been to see Theodora," said John, seating himself at the pool's edge. The pool, and the surrounding cubicles were deserted, so though his voice echoed off the friezes overhead, there was no one to overhear.

Anatolius tested the water with his foot and grimaced. "So your morning has been doubly distasteful," he observed.

"She wants me to investigate the murder. Secretly. The victim was apparently a Silentiary."

"His name was Alexander," said Anatolius. "He was a fellow Occult."

John allowed his face to register surprise.

Anatolius said, "After leaving the mithraeum I spoke to one of the excubitors on guard, another man of my own rank. He had seen the body and recognized it."

"This may be even more difficult than I thought," said John. "Theodora seems to think the murder was committed by Mithrans."

"We aren't murderers." Anatolius seated himself beside John. Now that the effects of the steam bath were wearing off, his skin appeared pale, in contrast to John's deep brown coloring. "Besides," he added, "only Lions are allowed to take the part of the sufferer. Alexander was two steps removed from that rank."

"But I can hardly explain that to the Empress."

"No, not in your position."

"And she referred to the seven-runged ladder. Do you suppose she suspects me?"

"Theodora has always had an unhealthy interest in the forbidden," replied Anatolius, "including proscribed religions. A young scribe I knew told me a story he had from a servant girl in the Empress's service. According to the girl, Theodora actually accompanied her to one of the rituals of an Ashtoreth cult. The reality of it disappointed her. No less than the servant girl disappointed my friend, I may say." He smiled.

"But why would she care, suddenly, to persecute Mithrans?" continued John.

"Maybe she doesn't want to persecute Mithrans. Maybe she simply wants to clear them out of the Emperor's bodyguard."

"Or undermine the guard," said John. "Introduce her own men."

"Your mind is almost as devious as hers," commented Anatolius. "No doubt she has multiple aims, every one unwholesome and ruinous. Isn't it common knowledge among a certain class that she and Justinian are twin demons sent to plague humanity? Hardly a week passes that some wretch doesn't flee the Palace, convinced he's seen faceless devils stalking the halls at night. Last week, in fact, two fled. If you don't stop thinking so hard you'll convince yourself to follow them."

"Maybe that is her aim," John mused.

Anatolius rose and waded out into the pool. In truth, the Empress's words and actions troubled him, but he saw no point in revealing this. Even under the best of circumstances John was given to brooding like the hero of a Greek Tragedy.

John remained by the side of the pool. The air against his skin felt pleasingly cool. There had been a time when it had shamed him to reveal himself in the public baths. Although he had long since mastered those feelings, he still appreciated that Anatolius did not make a point of too politely averting his gaze.

Watching him wash his slim, muscular limbs, John was reminded of elegant sculptures of Greek antiquity, but more so of a woman he had known once. Was that why he had befriended Anatolius?

"Anatolius," John called. "Could you look into a few things for me?"

The fetid odor of streets and harbor filled John's small kitchen. In a few months, when winter's cold would force him to close its one small window, and his cook lit the charcoal brazier, the room would smell of roast lamb and boiled duck. On this hot August afternoon, however, John endured the ripe stench of decay because the alternative seemed to be suffocation.

He had emptied the contents of a leather pouch out onto the scarred wooden table. Sitting hunched over the table, he examined the objects he had found on the floor of the mithraeum. It had been a laborious search, in the guttering light of the altar flame, and he was not certain he had found everything there might be to find, or that what he had found bore any relationship to the crime.

There was a pearl clasp from a cloak. A shrivelled apple core, discarded recently enough, he decided, that the rats had not yet chewed it. A delicate gold chain. A gold solidus, drastically clipped, showing on its obverse – ironically John thought – the crucifixion of the Christian's gentle god. And, finally, a lopsided die, which may have been ivory. All were objects men might have carried on their persons for one reason or another and small enough not to be missed if dropped during the rituals.

John wiped sweat from his gaunt cheeks. Outside children yelled and he heard the clackety-clack of a hoop being rolled along cobbles. The murderer certainly knew where the mithraeum was now, but had he known before the killing? Was he actually a Mithran, or had he followed the victim? But then, why should a killing occur in the mithraeum at all?

Even in his own kitchen John could feel the poisoned eyes of the Empress upon him. Although it was Alexander who was dead, John felt that it was he himself who was the prey.

In his state of mind, footsteps on the wooden stairs leading up from the courtyard startled him more than they should, but it was only Anatolius, returning from his inquiries.

"I don't think I'll invite myself for dinner tonight," said his friend, glancing at the objects on the table. "Still looking for plots?"

John smiled tiredly. "Anatolius, I owe my position in court to mere survival, and I owe my survival mostly to my ability not just to feel the eyes on my back but to sense who they belong to. What did you find out?"

As Secretary to the Emperor, Anatolius had free access to the Imperial residence, and indeed, more than once he had assisted John. The Lord Chamberlain was a friend, after all – not to mention one of the more influential officials in the Palace. "I found very little," said Anatolius. "The Master of Offices claims he never ordered Captain Otto to the mithraeum, that he heard of the murder first from the Captain."

John frowned and began to speak but Anatolius cut him off.

"That may mean nothing," he cautioned. "I also learned that the Master was so drunk last night that he didn't know what day it was when he woke up this morning. He admitted it himself. Begged me not to tell the Emperor."

"He also conveniently wouldn't remember who informed him about the body, if he really was drunk," observed John.

"He looked hungover to me," said Anatolius. "He was green as a month-old leg of mutton."

"I see. What else?"

"The usual gossip in the Empress's residence. Her favorite stallion has gone lame. The large Egyptian who has been hanging around the court lately is, on the other hand, rumored to be in fine mettle. Some wall hangings weren't dyed correctly. A new servant – a country bumpkin named Michael – fled last week. Needless to say this is believed connected with a silver rouge pot once owned by Pulcheria. The Imperial life is difficult."

"Indeed," said John. "And apparently dull and unfulfilling as well. Do you know, the Empress wants to talk to me about epigrams and theology."

"If I were you, I would be at the library," said Anatolius.

As John approached Captain Otto's office he heard a crash and was nearly knocked down by a huge Egyptian who burst through the doorway like a fury.

John stepped aside nimbly. "Dioscurus," he said, remembering the man who had tried to bribe him after the envoy's banquet. It was the man's size, rather than the bribe, which were common enough, which was memorable. Many tried to curry favor with the Master of Offices through the Lord Chamberlain.

"Lord Chamberlain," said Dioscurus in perfect Greek. His heavy lips curled. "I apologize for offending you the other night. I imagined I was observing the custom of your great city."

"Never mind," said John, "I'm sure you must find our civilization confusing."

"Next time I will know to offer more," Dioscurus replied curtly.

Watching the young Egyptian on his way out, John realized that he must be Theodora's new consort – the one Anatolius had mentioned. And to think that a few weeks ago he had aspired only to gaining the Master of Office's wrinkled old ear, and failed at that. What was he doing in Captain Otto's office, John wondered?

He found the Captain hunched grimly over his ivory-inlaid desk. Beside his chair, and scattered across the floor, were the remains of a porphyry vase.

"Otto," said John, feigning more friendliness than he felt, for Otto was commander of the excubitors, a militia stationed inside the Palace, and they had at times been at odds since John was head of the Emperor's largely ceremonial bodyguard, the Silentiaries. Still, they were both Mithrans, the German having attained the rank, appropriately, of Soldier.

Otto replied with a grunt.

"Did the Empress send her young man to ensure you're pursuing the murder investigation?" asked John.

"No. He came about – another matter."

"He seems to have been rather clumsy."

"I shouldn't have had the vase so near the corner of the desk." John noticed that the Captain, usually a blunt and straightforward man, refused to meet his eyes.

A knot of cold formed in the pit of John's stomach. Perhaps Theodora had sent her Egyptian on account of John. Was it really John she was pursuing, and not Mithrans? Or was he just too ready to see plots and counterplots, as Anatolius said?

"What is it you want, Lord Chamberlain?" asked Otto. Though he had been in Constantinople for a decade his accent remained barbaric.

"I am not here, strictly, as the Lord Chamberlain," said John. "I am here more as a follower."

"So, then. What is it?" The rugged face which had turned unflinchingly toward foes more threatening than the thin eunuch, if not more formidable, remained averted.

"You said you had been ordered to the mithraeum by the Master of Offices. I believe this is not true. I am told he was dead drunk last night."

Now Otto did look at John, his chin pushed forward. His face reddened. "I am not known as a liar."

"As another who is climbing the ladder, I will tell you that some highly placed persons may use this murder as a weapon against all of us. Or have you learned that from the Egyptian, already?"

"As I said, I was ordered by the Master to secure the mithraeum."

"I am not inquiring as your Lord Chamberlain but as one who will very soon hold the rank of Father," John said bluntly.

Otto shrugged his broad shoulders. "I can't say more. I am a military man. I obey my superiors."

John had a sudden thought. "How are the chariot races treating you?"

"My bets have been blessed lately," said Otto. "What does that have to do with this?"

"I'm not sure," replied John. "Nothing, perhaps."

John slept poorly that night. The heat and stench of the city lay against his face like a stifling shroud. In the least of his nightmares, of those he remembered clearly upon wakening, he ran through dark catacombs, pursued by roaring demons. In his darker dreams, unimaginable horrors gnawed at the underside of reality, as quietly as rats.

The miasma of nightmare still lingered in his mind, even after he had risen and washed. Now he stood looking out over the deceptively calm Bosphorus from the window of his sitting room. The lower classes, those who swore the Emperor was a demon, also whispered that Theodora practiced the black arts. Had she disturbed his sleep, plucking at his mind with talons of mist? Surely Mithra would protect him from the darkness. But the Lord of Light had not seen fit to protect Alexander. Why had the young excubitor been killed? Had he died merely because he was a Mithran?

And what of the murderer? Had he too been a Mithran? How else could he have discovered the mithraeum?

John wondered also about Otto? Had he lied about the Master ordering him to the well-hidden holy place? And if he had, why?

It was late afternoon by the time John left through the gate of the Palace grounds, making his way across the Augustaeum and past the Hippodrome. He had dressed simply, but the length of his brown tunic, his soft leather shoes and his bearing distinguished him from town people. Sellers of perfumes and melons and jewelry singled him out, calling raucously from their stalls, and passersby did not jostle him as they did each other but stepped politely aside to let him pass.

He waited for Anatolius at a bookseller's stall. Under the blank gaze of the antique statues in front of the Baths of Zeuxippus, he examined the seller's collection of ancient papyrus scrolls and more recent parchments.

He was admiring one of the new, bound, codexes – a life of the Saints – when his friend arrived. "Look at these illuminations," John said. "If only our artists could match these Christians. Certainly our subject matter is far more glorious and dramatic."

"The Christians do have an advantage, not having to work in secret," remarked Anatolius. "Here, this new collection of love epigrams by Agathias may be more interesting to you."

"Don't worry, I haven't forgotten about the Empress's desire to discuss literature. What about Alexander?" John had asked Anatolius to inquire about him, fearing that the dead man's fellow Silentiaries might not speak so truthfully to their ultimate commander.

"Apparently, he was nothing more than what he seemed," said Anatolius. "A young, rough fellow from Thrace who came to Constantinople to make his way at court. It's a common enough story."

"What about dangerous vices? Did he have a taste for gambling, or wine or quarrels? Was he a womanizer? Which faction did he support at the circus?"

"He was young. I suppose he indulged in all the common vices. But, from what I gathered, he was a good Mithran. He would probably have traded his Occult's veil for a Soldier's helmet before I did."

Anatolius was sorting through abandoned geometries and Latin grammars. As he spoke, he picked up a large parchment. "Fruit and Nuts in Symbolism and Celebration," he read. "This might serve you well in your official duties, John."

"Yes. But can't you tell me anything more?"

Anatolius sighed. "I'm afraid he was an exemplary young man. A friend of his told me that in June, when a contingent of the guard accompanied the Imperial family to their summer retreat in Asia Minor, most returned with stories that would make an actress blush. But Alexander refused to say a word. Said it wasn't his place to speak against his rulers. Some of the guards considered him a stick-in-the-mud. But I doubt that's grounds for murder."

John nodded. "And Michael, the servant who ran away? Could you find out anything about him?"

"I obtained the address of his lodgings," was the reply. "But I would suggest you take a guard, or let me accompany you."

"I won't come to any harm." John hoped he sounded more confident than he felt.

"Michael? You won't find him here. You can't hurt him any more. He's dead." The young woman clutched the wooden cross that hung from a chain around her neck, glaring defiantly at John. She looked haggard and old beyond her years. The points of her skinny shoulders showed through her dirty, poorly mended tunic.

"I'm sorry," said John. "I didn't intend to harm him."

"You're from the Palace, aren't you? I can smell it." The woman backed away slightly. In truth there was little space to back away in the bare box of a room. Michael had, before entering service at the Palace, occupied this cramped, bare space on the fourth floor of a wooden tenement. Through the open window John could hear the sound of hammering as workmen toiled on Justinian's newest project, the Church of the Holy Wisdom.

"How did it happen?"

"As if you don't know. His poor neck was slashed. It was the work of a beast. Or a devil. Some unnatural thing. Like you." The woman's eyes glittered in their dark sockets.

"Please help me," said John. "Another man has also been murdered, and it might be the doing of the same person."

"No person. Devils."

"Why do you say that?" asked John, uneasily. His nightmares had left behind a residue of irrational dread.

"Because that was what he found in the Palace. Devils. We came from the country. We had a good life, working the fields. But he wanted more. The City tempted him, like Satan tempted Christ. We'd have a house, he said. I could tie my hair back with gold chains and wear silk robes like the ladies of the court. And instead, he found devils."

She bowed her head, clasping the cruxifix in both hands as if she were praying. A tear ran down along the shadowed concavity of her cheek.

"What do you mean, he found devils?" asked John.

The woman blinked back her tears. "It was the Emperor himself, the very King of the Demons. That's what he told me when he got here, running all the way from the Palace. His heart was practically bursting. He said . . . he said he wouldn't stay another night in that hellish place. He'd seen it before, a figure – stalking the halls. There's always someone around the halls at night. Up to no good, I'll wager. And they say the Emperor barely sleeps. But one night he saw a figure making its way toward the Empress's bedchamber. He came upon it accidentally, surprised the thing . . . the Emperor. It turned and looked right at him in the candle light. And it had no face! Where a head should be was only darkness."

When John left the tenement, the sun had fallen behind the city's seven hills (how appropriate it was, he often mused). Constantinople's soaring columns were barely visible against a sky whose faint lavender glow was deeping to Imperial purple. As he walked briskly through the darkening streets he thought he heard a movement behind him. He stopped, looked back. There was no one. He looked up. He was standing at the base of the modest pillar of a stylite.

He could barely make out the shadowy form of the Christian Holy Man who sat atop the pillar, night and day, exposed to the elements, mortifying his flesh. John couldn't help wrinkling his nose at the stench drifting down to the street. He couldn't understand a God who would welcome such a gross insult to a body He had created in His own image.

Had the noise been the stylite shifting his weight? John listened but heard nothing. Nor could he detect any motion atop the pillar.

Something moved again, and quick as a shadow dodging a swinging torch, John stepped to one side. There was the ring of a metal blade hitting the base of the stylite's pillar.

Now he got a glimpse of his attacker. He was a huge man, wearing an excubitor's helmet. He saw the glint of the raised sword and threw himself onto the cobbles, rolling sideways. Again the blade cracked against the pillar.

The stylite shrieked.

It was a choked, monstrous shriek. The sound the Great Bull must have made when Mithra dragged him to the cave and slit his throat.

John heard voices. People came running towards him.

The excubitor fled into the darkness, and John, too, slipped away, from the wondering crowd which had gathered below the man who had remained publicly silent for so many years.

As the Mithran made his way carefully, and uneventfully back to his dwelling, he wondered if he now owed his life to the inscrutable Christian God.

Though he expected more fearful dreams, John slept soundly enough until he was awakened by a pounding on his door. It was an obviously agitated Anatolius.

"John, have you heard? Captain Otto is dead. He threw himself from the Column of Arcadius sometime during the night."

"I was attacked by someone wearing an excubitor's helmet last night," said John.

"Could it be that – do you think – the captain was the murderer? Although, Mithra knows why he would desecrate the holy place. And you'd just been to see him, too. No doubt he feared for his safety." He paused, pondering the puzzle. "Nobody actually reported the murder

to him – they wouldn't have had to . . . if he was the murderer."
Enlightenment spread over his face.

"I don't believe that," said John. "He was a follower."

"But why would he take his own life?"

"A good question. Do you know, there are 233 stairs leading to
the platform under the statue of Arcadius. I know because of a
commemorative ceremony we staged there long ago. Think about
that. 233 steps to the top. 233 chances to turn back, lose resolve,
rethink one's imminent death. What could be so terrible that a man
would decide to die 233 times?"

"I don't know," said Anatolius. "I would have thought death itself
was the most terrible thing – forgetting of course that we shall all be
reborn in Mithra."

John smiled wanly. "Anatolius, I consider you a friend. There is a
loose brick just to the right of my kitchen hearth. There are important
papers behind that brick. If it becomes necessary I would appreciate
you taking charge of those papers. Please excuse me now, I must
dress. I am going to see the Empress."

The Empress saw him immediately. "I am told the Mithran murderer
has taken his own life," she said, without preamble, glaring at John
through the black pinpoints of her poison-contracted pupils. "It is
said he was the one who murdered Alexander. Do they think they
can escape justice by offering yet another bloody sacrifice? I intend
to enforce the law. These pagan monsters will all be sent directly to
that hell at which they scoff."

She was dressed in a purple robe glittering with precious stones and
gold thread, a gem-studded tiara atop her coiled hair. She did, indeed,
look more an Empress than a bear-keeper's daughter, John thought
ruefully. Unfortunately, he had no choice but to oppose her.

"The murder was not committed by a Mithran," he said. "Nor
was it part of a Mithraic ceremony."

"And how does the Emperor's Lord Chamberlain come to know
the secrets of Mithra?"

Controlling the quaver that threatened to creep into his voice,
John replied, "I know about them because I have attended them,
just as you have."

"You condemn yourself doubly, by your own admission and by
your scurrilous slander."

"Do you really think not one man there recognized you, in your
flimsy disguise?"

"Of whom do you speak?"

Ignoring her question, John pulled a delicate golden chain from inside his cloak. "Do you recognize this chain? It is the sort of thing a woman uses to fasten her hair. And yet Mithraism is a man's religion. The mithraeum is forbidden to women."

"A man's religion?" Theodora laughed. A coarse, raucous sound, like the cry of a hungry gull. "I would have more right to attend than you! But why would I?"

"Curiosity. Haven't you attended the rites of Ashtoreth, among others? Besides, you had taken a Mithran lover."

John hoped the pitch of his voice was not being taken by the Empress as a sign of the fear he was trying to conceal. She could have him killed, instantly, if she wished, before he had a chance to explain what such an act might cost. She glared as he continued.

"You must have singled out young Alexander when he accompanied the excubitor guard that you took to your summer retreat earlier this year. He became your intimate. He entered your residence at night, his face obscured by the Occult's veil he wore during ceremonies, apparently, thinking nothing of the blasphemy of it. I suppose you thought it funny that your superstitious servants mistook him for the rumored King of the Demons.

"And when one of the servants who was frightened by the charade fled, you had him killed, just in case he talked too much."

Theodora's sharp stare seemed to bite into his soul. He continued, his words more measured. "You killed Otto too. Of course he couldn't tell me who had alerted him to the murder because it was you, and you'd commanded his silence. He could neither betray you nor his God. A quick death was preferable."

"But only after he failed to kill you last night."

"You have already heard of that? Do you think I would have survived an attack by a trained excubitor? Hardly. It was a large man. Your newest lover, the Egyptian Dioscurus."

For the first time the Empress looked surprised.

"A hot-headed young man," said John. "He lost his temper when he discovered you and Alexander together, in this house. So inconvenient, a murder in your own bed chamber. So you had Dioscurus carry the body to the mithraeum. It was nearby. You had been there. There was no blood under the body, in front of the altar. That was how I knew he was not killed there"

"I think your infirmity has finally driven you mad, Lord Chamberlain." Theodora moved toward John until he could smell her musk. "I won't have you killed," she said, a smile working at the corners of her red lips. "As a kindness I shall have your eyes put out, so you will not be tortured by more hallucinations, and have your tongue cut off, so you cannot disturb others with your insane delusions, and then

I shall have you transported to a rock in the Mediterranean where you may enjoy the rest of your existence. I understand persons of your type live a long time."

"And then all that I have related will become public knowledge."

Theodora laughed. "Do you think the Emperor imagines me to be some poor virginal creature? Does every person in the Palace not tremble at my approach, knowing I have murdered and will murder again?"

"Justinian may not feel the need to excuse the fact that his wife is a whore, but what about the fact that she has blasphemously worshipped in the temple of a forbidden God? How will he explain that to the Patriarch or to his political supporters?"

"Who will testify I was there? Some dirty soldiers and stinking peasants? Who will take their word against mine?"

"No one would. But what about the word of a great landowner, senators, one of the Empire's most respected generals? Did you recognize those powerful men behind their veils and masks, Empress?"

"Why would they reveal themselves now?"

"Because they are Mithrans and you have shaken your fist at our God."

"I don't believe that. They would have more to lose than I would."

"Is it worth the chance? Can you be certain how the Emperor will choose to calculate costs? Besides, you may be sure your Egyptian will tell his story. He is too important a man to be detained because of some religious misstep."

For a second John expected Theodora to spring at him, like a street girl. But she controlled herself. "Leave my sight," she said, in a husky whisper. "And never forget, Lord Chamberlain, that the wife of the Emperor wishes you to burn in hell."

"I suspect she enjoyed it, binding the hands of the corpse with entrails, covering its eyes, writing out the message in blood in front of the altar. The perversity would have appealed to her. And, after all, she was an actress once."

John paused, pouring more wine into his cup. He and Anatolius were seated at a table, in a cafe, not far from the Augustaeum. A cool breeze carried the salty smell of the Sea of Marmora to them.

"I still don't understand it all," his friend confessed.

"She did it on a whim. It was the first thing that came to her mind. And not a bad idea, really. The military is largely Mithran. By persecuting Mithraism she might have been able to fill its high posts with men under her power."

"But why ask you to investigate?"

"Sheer perversity, perhaps. Or because her lover had a grudge against me." John bit into the fig he had taken from the wooden bowl on the table. It tasted much better than the figs in Theodora's chambers. "Or maybe it was more a . . . contest. I must have seemed an interesting challenge to her, since so many of her usual weapons are rendered useless by my infallible self-control." A wry smile creased his thin face.

"Still," said Anatolius. "She did get away with murder, or at least with assisting in one."

"Well, this is the Empire. She is the Empress. We take what justice we can get."

"And what kind of justice do you suppose the Empress has in store for you?"

"You forget, Anatolius. The Grand Chamberlain is the Emperor's personal servant. I am one of his closest confidants. Even before they became advisors and officers of state, Grand Chamberlains wielded influence because they had the Emperor's ear every day, in a society where most citizens are lucky to catch a glimpse of his face during their lifetimes. I think I can depend on his protection – as much as anyone can."

"Which still leaves the real murderer, Dioscurus, free to return to Egypt."

"You mean you didn't hear?" John put down his cup.

Anatolius looked at him blankly.

"And you are usually the one bringing the news to me," said John. "Dioscurus is dead. It happened at a small dinner party in the Empress's residence last evening. Officially it is a heart attack, or maybe some bad shellfish." John took a long draught of wine. "The Palace physician, who is a follower, told me that in reality he was poisoned – with belladonna."

And with that, John the Eunuch, follower of Mithra, realizing he had made a bitter enemy in Theodora, set off for home.

# ABBEY SINISTER
# Peter Tremayne

*Since the publication of "The High King's Sword" in the previous volume, Peter Tremayne's stories featuring Sister Fidelma have been going from strength to strength. In addition to at least half-a-dozen short stories (probably more by the time this sees print), there have been two novels,* Absolution by Murder *(1994) and* Shroud for an Archbishop *(1995). She is an advocate of the Irish Brehon Court, and has been called a "Dark Age Perry Mason". Peter Tremayne (b. 1943) is an expert on Celtic history and the author of over fifty books, including many novels of fantasy and horror fiction. His knowledge of Dark Age Britain means he can throw some light on that mysterious past and show that, contrary to what we might have believed, there was still law and order in those days.*

The black guillemot, with its distinctive orange legs and mournful, warning cry, swooped and darted above the currach. It was an isolated traveller among a crowd of more hardy, sooty, white-rumped storm petrels and large, dark coloured cormorants, wheeling, diving and flitting against the soft blue May sky.

Sister Fidelma sat relaxed in the stern of the boat and let the tangy odour of the salt water spray gently caress her senses as the two oarsmen, seated facing her, bent their backs to their task. Their oars, dipping in unison, caused the light craft to dance over the waves of the great bay which seemed so deceptively calm. The clawing waters of the hungry Atlantic were not usually so good natured as now and often the islands, through which the currach was weaving, could be cut off for weeks or months at a time.

They had left the mainland, with its rocky terrain and scrawny vegetation, to cross the waters of the large estuary known as Roaring Water Bay, off the south-west coast of Ireland. Here the fabled Cairbre's "hundred islands" had been randomly tossed like lumps of earth and rock into the sea as if by some giant's hand. At the moment the day was soft, the waters passive and the sun producing some warmth, making the scene one of tranquil beauty.

As the oarsmen stroked the vessel through the numerous islands, the heads of inquisitive seals popped out of the water to stare briefly at them, surprised at their aquatic intrusion, before darting away.

Sister Fidelma was accompanied by a young novitiate, a frightened young girl, who huddled beside her in the stern seat of the currach. Fidelma had felt obliged to take the girl under her protection on the journey to the abbey of St Ciaran of Saigher, which stood on the island of Chléire, the farthest island of this extensive group. But the escort of the novitiate was purely incidental for Fidelma's main purpose was to carry letters from Ultan, the archbishop of Armagh, to the abbot at Chléire and also to the abbot of Inis Chloichreán, a tiny religious house on one of the remoter rocky islands within the group.

The lead rower, a man made old before his time by a lifetime exposed to the coastal weather, eased his oar. He smiled, a disjointed, gap-toothed smile at Fidelma. His sea-coloured eyes, set deep in his leather-brown face, gazed appreciatively at the tall young woman with the rebellious strands of red hair escaping from her head dress. He had seen few religieuses who had such feminine poise as this one; few who seemed to be so effortlessly in command.

"There's Inis Cloichreán to our right, sister." He thrust out a gnarled hand to indicate the direction, realizing that, as he was facing the religieuse, the island actually lay to her left. "We are twenty minutes from it. Do you wish to land there first or go on to Chléire?"

"I have no need to be long on Chloichreán," Fidelma replied after a moment of thought. "We'll land there first as it is on our way."

The rower grunted in acknowledgement and nodded to the second rower. As if at a signal, they dipped their oars together and the currach sped swiftly over the waves towards the island.

It was a hilly, rocky island. From the sea, it appeared that its shores were nothing more than steep, inaccessible cliffs whose grey granite was broken into coloured relief by sea pinks and honeysuckle chambers which filled the rocky outcrops.

Lorcán, the chief rower, expertly directed the currach through offshore jagged peaks of rock, thrusting from the sea. The boat danced this way and that in the foam waters that hissed and gurgled around the jagged points of granite, creating tiny but dangerous whirlpools. He carefully manoeuvred a zig-zag path into a small, sheltered cove where a natural harbour awaited them.

Fidelma was amazed at his skill.

"None but a person with knowledge could land in such a place," she observed.

Lorcán grinned appreciatively.

"I am one of the few who know exactly where to land on this island, sister."

"But the members of the abbey, surely they must have some seamanship among them to be here?"

"Abbey is a grandiose name for Selbach's settlement," grunted the second oarsman, speaking for the first time since they had left the mainland.

"Maenach is right," confirmed Lorcán. "Abbot Selbach came here two years ago with about twelve brothers; he called them his apostles. But they are no more than young boys, the youngest fourteen and the eldest scarcely nineteen. They chose this island because it was inaccessible and few knew how to land on it. It is true that they have a currach but they never use it. It is only for emergencies. Four or five times a year I land here with any supplies that they might want from the mainland."

"Ah, so it is a hermitage," Fidelma said. There were many of the religious in Ireland who had become solitary hermits or, taking a few followers, had found some out of the way place to set up a community where they could live together in isolated contemplation of the faith. Fidelma did not really trusts hermits, or isolated communities. It was not, in her estimation, the way to serve God by shutting oneself off from His greatest Creation – the society of men and women.

"A hermitage, indeed," agreed Maenach mournfully.

Fidelma gazed around curiously.

"It is not a large island. Surely one of the brothers must have seen our landing yet no one has come to greet us."

Lorcán had secured the currach to a rock by a rope and now bent forward to assist Fidelma out of the craft while Maenach used his balance to steady it.

"We'd better all get out," Fidelma said, more for the attention of the frightened young novitiate, Sister Sárnat, than Maenach. The young girl, no more than sixteen, dutifully scrambled after Fidelma, keeping close like a chick to a mother hen.

Maenach followed, pausing to stretch languidly once he stood on dry land.

Lorcán was pointing up some steps carved in the granite slope which led from the small cove up to the top of the cliff.

"If you take those steps, sister, you'll come to Selbach's community," he said. "We'll await you here."

Fidelma nodded, turning to Sister Sárnat.

"Will you wait here or do you want to come with me?"

The young sister shivered as if touched by a cold wind and looked unhappy.

"I'll come with you, sister," she sniffed anxiously.

Fidelma sighed softly. The girl was long past "the age of choice" yet she was more like a ten-year-old, frightened with life and clutching at the nearest adult to protect her from potential lurking terrors. The girl intrigued Fidelma. She wondered what had possessed her to join a religious house while so young, without experience of life or people.

"Very well, follow me then," she instructed.

Lorcán called softly after her.

"I'd advise you not to be long, sister." He pointed to the western sky. "There's a backing wind coming and we'll have a storm before nightfall. The sooner we reach Chléire, the sooner we shall be in shelter."

"I'll not be long," Fidelma assured him and began to lead the way up the steps with Sárnat following quickly behind.

"How can he know that there'll be a storm," the young novitiate demanded breathlessly as she stumbled to keep up with Fidelma. "It's such a lovely day."

Fidelma grimaced.

"A seaman will know these things, Sárnat. The signs are there to be read in the sky. Did you observe the moon last night?"

Sárnat looked puzzled.

"The moon was bright," she conceded.

"But if you had truly examined it then you would have seen a red glow to it. The air was still and comparatively dry. It is almost a guarantee of stormy winds from the west."

Fidelma suddenly paused and pointed to some plants growing along the edge of the pathway.

"Here's another sign. See the trefoil? Look at the way its stem is swollen. And those dandelions nearby, their petals are contracting and closing. Both those signs mean it will be raining soon."

"How do you know these things?" asked the girl wonderingly.

"By observation and listening to the old ones, those who are wise in the ancient knowledge."

They had climbed above the rocky cliffs and stood overlooking a sheltered depression in the centre of the island where a few gaunt, bent trees grew amidst several stone, beehive-shaped huts and a small oratory.

"So this is Abbot Selbach's community?" Fidelma mused. She stood frowning at the collection of buildings. She could see no movement nor signs of life. She raised her voice. "Hello there!"

The only answer that came back was an angry chorus of disturbed seabirds; of newly arrived auks seeking their summer nesting places who suddenly rose, black and white or dark brown with brilliantly coloured bills and webbed feet. The black guillemots, gulls and storm petrels followed, swirling around the island in an angry, chiding crowd.

Fidelma was puzzled. Someone must have heard her yet there was no response.

She made her way slowly down the grassy path into the shallow depression in which the collection of stone buildings stood. Sárnat trotted dutifully at her side.

Fidelma paused before the buildings and called again. And again there was no reply.

She moved on through the complex of buildings, turning round a corner into a quadrangle. The shriek came from Sister Sárnat.

There was a tree in the centre of the quadrangle; a small tree no more than twelve feet high, bent before the cold Atlantic winds, gaunt and gnarled. To the thin trunk of this tree, secured by the wrists with leather thongs, which prevented it from slumping to the ground, the body of a man was tied. Although the body was secured with its face towards the tree trunk, there was no need to ask if the man was dead.

Sister Sárnat stood shaking in terror at her side.

Fidelma ignored her and moved forward a pace to examine the body. It was clad in bloodstained robes, clearly the robes of a religious. The head was shaven at the front, back to a line stretching from ear to ear. At the back of his head, the hair was worn long. It was the tonsure of the Irish church, the *airbacc giunnae* which had been an inheritance from the Druids. The dead man was in his sixties; a thin, sharp featured individual with sallow skin and a pinched mouth. She noticed that, hanging from a thong round his neck, he wore a crucifix of some value; a carefully worked silver cross. The bloodstains covered the back of the robe which actually hung in ribbons from the body.

Fidelma saw that the shoulders of the robe were torn and bloodied and beneath it was lacerated flesh. There were several small stab wounds in the back but the numerous ripping wounds showed that the man had clearly been scourged by a whip before he had met his death.

Fidelma's eyes widened in surprise as she noticed a piece of wood fixed to the tree. There was some writing on it. It was in Greek; "As the whirlwind passes, so is the wicked no more . . ." She tried to remember why it sounded so familiar. Then she realized that it was out of the "Book of Proverbs".

It was obvious to her eye that the man had been beaten and killed while tied to the tree.

She became distracted by the moaning of the girl and turned, suppressing her annoyance.

"Sárnat, go back to the cove and fetch Lorcán here." And when the girl hesitated, she snapped "Now!"

Sárnat turned and scurried away.

Fidelma took another step towards the hanged religious and let her eyes wander over the body, seeking more information. She could gather nothing further other than that the man was elderly and a religious of rank, if the wealth of the crucifix was anything to go by. Then she stepped back and gazed around her. There was a small oratory, no larger than to accommodate half-a-dozen people at most behind its dry stone walls. It was placed in the centre of the six stone cells which served as accommodation for the community.

Fidelma crossed to the oratory and peered inside.

She thought, at first in the gloom, that it was a bundle of rags lying on the small altar. Then, as her eyes grew accustomed to the dim light, she saw that it was the body of a young religious. It was a boy not even reached manhood. She noticed that his robes were dank and sodden. The fair brown hair dried flat against his temples. The features were not calm in death's repose but contorted in an odd manner, as if the boy had died in pain. She was about to move forward to make a closer investigation, when she nearly tripped over what seemed to be another bundle.

Another religious lay stretched face downwards, arms outstretched, almost like a supplicant praying towards the altar. His hair was dark. He was clad in the robes of a brother. This religious was older than the youth.

She moved forward and knelt down, seeking a pulse in his neck with her two fingers. It was faint but it was there right enough but the body was unnaturally cold. She bent further to examine the face. The man was about forty. Even unconscious the features were placid and quite handsome. A pleasant face, Fidelma conceded. But dried blood caked one side of the broad forehead where it had congealed around a wound.

She shook the man by the shoulder but he was deeply unconscious.

Checking her exhalation of breath, Fidelma stood up and, moving swiftly, she went from stone cell to stone cell but each one told the same story. There was no one hiding from her within the buildings. The cells of the community were deserted.

Lorcán came running along the path from the cove.

"I left the girl behind with Maenach," he grunted as he came up to Fidelma. "She was upset. She says that someone is dead and . . ."

He paused and stared around him. From this position, the tree with its gruesome corpse was hidden to him.

"Where is everyone?"

"There is a man still alive here," Fidelma said, ignoring the question. "He needs our immediate attention."

She led the way to the small oratory, stooping down to enter and then standing to one side so that Lorcán could follow.

Lorcán gasped and genuflected as he saw the young boy.

"I know this boy. His name is Sacán from Inis Beag. Why, I brought him here to join the community only six months ago."

Fidelma pointed to the figure of the dark-haired man on the floor which Lorcán had not observed.

"Do you recognize that brother?" she asked.

"The saints defend us!" exclaimed the boatman as he bent down. "This is Brother Spelán."

Fidelma pursed her lips.

"Brother Spelán?" she repeated unnecessarily.

Lorcán nodded unhappily.

"He served as Abbot Selbach's *dominus*, the administrator of this community. Who did this deed? Where is everyone?"

"Questions can be answered later. We need to take him to a more comfortable place and restore him to consciousness. The boy—Sacán, you called him?—well, he is certainly beyond our help."

"Sister," replied Lorcán, "my friend Maenach knows a little of the physician's art. Let me summon him so that he might assist us with Spelán."

"It will take too long."

"It will take but a moment," Lorcán assured her, taking a conch shell from a rough leather pouch at his side. He went to the door and blew on it long and loudly. It was echoed by a tremendous chorus of frightened birds. Lorcán paused a moment before turning with a smile to Fidelma. "I see Maenach on the cliff top with the young sister. They are coming this way."

"Then help me carry this brother to one of the nearby cells so that we may put him on a better bed than this rough floor," instructed Fidelma.

As she knelt down to help lift the man she suddenly noticed a small wooden cup lying nearby. She reached forward and placed it in her *marsupium*, her large purse-like bag, slung from her waist. There would be time to examine it later.

Between them, they carried Brother Spelán, who was quite heavy, to the nearest cell and laid him on one of two wooden cots which were within.

Maenach came hurrying in with Sister Sárnat almost clutching at his sleeve. Lorcán pointed to the unconscious religious.

"Can you revive him?" he asked.

Maenach bent over the man, raising the unconscious man's eyelids and then testing his pulse.

"He is in a deep coma. Almost as if he is asleep." He examined the wound. "It is curious that he has been rendered so deeply unconscious from the blow that made this wound. The wound seems superficial enough. The brother's breathing is regular and untroubled. I am sure he will regain consciousness after a while."

"Then do what you can, Maenach," Fidelma said. "Sister Sárnat, you will help him," she instructed the pale, shivering young girl who still hovered uncertainly at the door of the cell.

She then took the boatman, Lorcán, by the arm and led him from the cell, turning him towards the quadrangle, and pointing silently to the figure bound to the tree.

Lorcán took a step forward and then let out a startled exhalation of breath. It was the first time he had observed the body.

"God look down upon us!" he said slowly as he genuflected. "Now there are two deaths among the religious of Selbach!"

"Do you know this person?" Fidelma asked.

"Know him?" Lorcán sounded startled at the question. "Of course. It is the Abbot Selbach!"

"Abbot Selbach?"

Fidelma pursed her lips with astonishment as she reexamined the body of the dead abbot. Then she gazed around her towards the empty landscape.

"And did you not say that Selbach had a community of twelve brothers here with him?"

Lorcán followed her gaze uncertainly.

"Yes. Yet the island seems deserted," he muttered. "What terrible mystery is here?"

"That is something we must discover," Fidelma replied confidently.

"We must leave for the mainland at once," Lorcán advised. "We must get back to Dún na Séad and inform The Ó hEidersceoil."

The Ó hEidersceoil was the chieftain of the territory.

Fidelma raised a hand to stay the man even as he was turning back to the cell where they had left Brother Spelán.

"Wait, Lorcán. I am a *dálaigh*, an advocate of the Law of the *Fenechus*, holding the degree of *anruth*. It is my task to stay and

discover how Abbot Selbach and little Sacán met their deaths and
why Brother Spelán was wounded. Also we must discover where the
rest of the community has disappeared to."

Lorcán gazed at the young religieuse in surprise.

"That same danger may yet attend us," he protested. "What
manner of magic is it that makes a community disappear and
leaves their abbot dead like a common criminal bound to a tree,
the boy dead and their *dominus* assaulted and unconscious?"

"Human magic, if magic you want to call it," Fidelma replied
irritably. "As an advocate of the law courts of the five kingdoms
of Ireland, I call upon you for assistance. I have this right by the
laws of the *Fenechus*, under the authority of the Chief Brehon. Do you
deny my right?"

Lorcán gazed at the religieuse a moment in surprise and then
slowly shook his head.

"You have that right, sister. But, look, Abbot Selbach is not long
dead. What if his killers are hiding nearby?"

Fidelma ignored his question and turned back to regard the
hanging body, her head to one side in reflection.

"What makes you say that he is not long dead, Lorcán?"

The sailor shrugged impatiently.

"The body is cold but not very stiff. Also it is untouched by the
scavengers . . ."

He gestured towards the wheeling birds. She followed his gaze and
could see among the seabirds, the large forms of black-backed gulls,
one of the most vicious of coastal scavengers. And here and there
she saw the jet black of carrion crows. It was the season when the
eggs of these harsh-voiced predators would be hatching along the
cliff top nests and the young birds would be demanding to be fed by
the omnivorous parents, feeding off eggs of other birds, even small
mammals and often rotting carcasses. She realized that the wheeling
gulls and crows would sooner or later descend on a corpse but there
was no sign that they had done so already.

"Excellently observed, Lorcán," she commented. "And presumably Brother Spelán could not have been unconscious long. But do
you observe any other peculiar thing about the abbot's body?"

The boatman frowned at her and glanced at the slumped corpse.
He stared a moment and shook his head.

"Selbach was flogged and then stabbed three times in the back. I
would imagine that the thrust of the knife was upwards, between the
ribs, so that he died instantly. What strange ritual would so punish
a man before killing him?"

Lorcán stared more closely and sighed deeply.

"I don't understand."

"Just observe for the moment," Fidelma replied. "I may need you later to be a witness to these facts. I think we may cut down the body and place it out of reach of the birds within the oratory."

Lorcán took his sharp sailor's knife and quickly severed the ropes. Then he dragged the body into the oratory at Fidelma's direction.

Fidelma now had time to make a more careful examination of the young boy's body.

"He has clearly been immersed for a while in the sea. Not very long but several hours at least," she observed. "There are no immediate causes of death. He has not been stabbed nor has he been hit by any blunt instrument."

She turned the body and gave a quick sudden intake of breath.

"But he has been scourged. See, Lorcán?"

The boatman saw that the upper part of the boy's robe had been torn revealing that his back was covered in old and new welts and scars made by a whip.

"I knew the boy's family well on Inis Beag," he whispered. "He was a happy, dutiful boy. His body was without blemish when I brought him here."

Fidelma made a search of the boy's sodden clothing, the salt water drying out was already making white lines and patches on it. Her eyes narrowed as she examined the prayer cord which fastened the habit. A small metal hook was hanging from it on which a tiny leather sheath was fastened containing a small knife, a knife typical of those used by some rural orders to cut their meat or help them in their daily tasks. Caught on the projecting metal hook was a torn piece of woollen cloth. Carefully, Fidelma removed it and held it up.

"What is it, sister?" asked Lorcán.

"I don't know. A piece of cloth caught on the hook." She made a quick examination. "It is not from the boy's clothing." She placed it in her *marsupium*, along with the wooden cup. Then she cast one final look at the youthful body before covering it. "Come, let us see what else we can find."

"But what, sister?" Lorcán asked. "What can we do? There is a storm coming soon and if it catches us here then here we shall have to remain until it passes."

"I am aware of the coming storm," she replied imperturbably. "But first we must be sure of one thing. You say there were twelve brothers here as well as Selbach? Then we have accounted for only two of them, Spelán and Sacán. Our next step is clear – we must search the island to assure ourselves that they are not hidden from us."

Lorcán bit his lip nervously.

"What if it were pirates who did this deed? I have heard tales of Saxon raiders with their longboats, devastating villages further along the coast."

"A possibility," agreed Fidelma. "But it is not a likely one."

"Why so?" demanded Lorcán. "The Saxons have raided along the coasts of Gaul, Britain and Ireland for many years, looting and killing . . ."

"Just so," Fidelma smiled grimly. "Looting and burning communities; driving off livestock and taking the people to be slaves."

She gestured to the deserted but tranquil buildings.

Lorcán suddenly realized what she was driving at. There was no sign of any destruction nor of any looting or violence enacted against the property. On the slope behind the oratory, three or four goats munched at the heather while a fat sow snorted and grunted among her piglets. And if that were not enough, he recalled that the silver crucifix still hung around the neck of the dead abbot. There had been no theft here. Clearly, then, there had been no pirate raid on the defenceless community. Lorcán was even more puzzled.

"Come with me, Lorcán, and we will examine the cells of the brothers," instructed Fidelma.

The stone cell next to the one in which they had left Spelán had words inscribed on the lintel.

*Ora et labora.* Work and pray. A laudable exhortation thought Fidelma and she passed underneath. The cell was almost bare and its few items of furniture were simple. On a beaten earthen floor, covered with rushes strewn as a mat, there were two wooden cots, a cupboard, a few leather *tiag leabhair* or book satchels, hung from hooks, containing several small gosepl books. A large ornately carved wooden cross hung on a wall.

There was another maxim inscribed on a wall to one side of this cell.

> *Animi indices sunt oculi.*
> The eyes are the betrayer of the mind.

Fidelma found it a curious adage to exhort a Christian community to faith. Then her eyes fell on a piece of written vellum by the side of one of the cots. She picked it up. It was a verse from one of the Psalms. "Break thou the arm of the wicked and the evil man; seek out his wickedness till thou find none . . ." She shivered slightly for this was not a dictum of a God of love.

Her eyes fell on a box at the foot of the bed. On the top of the box was an inscription in Greek.

*Pathémata mathémata.* Sufferings are lessons.

She bent forward and opened the box. Her eyes rounded in astonishment. Contained in the box were a set of scourges, of whips and canes. There were some words carved on the underside of the lid. They were in plain Irish.

> God give me a wall of tears
> my sins to hide;
> for I remain, while no tears fall,
> unsanctified.

She looked across to Lorcán in surprise.

"Do you know whose cell this was?" she demanded.

"Assuredly," came the prompt reply. "Selbach shared this cell with his *dominus* – Spelán. The cell we placed Spelán in, the one nearest the oratory, belongs to two other members of the community."

"Do you know what sort of man Selbach was? Was he a man who was authoritarian, who liked to inflict punishment? Was the Rule of his community a harsh one?"

Lorcán shrugged.

"That I would not know. I did not know the community that well."

"There is evidence of pain and punishment in this place," Fidelma sensed a cold tingle against her spine. "I do not understand it."

She paused, noticing a shelf on which stood several jars and bottles. She moved to them and began to examine the contents of each jar, sniffing its odours or wetting the tip of her finger from the concoctions before cautiously tasting it. Then she reached into her *marsupium* and took the wooden cup she had retrieved from the floor of the oratory. It had recently been used for the wood still showed the dampness of its contents. She sniffed at it. A curious mixture of pungent odours came to her nostrils. Then she turned back to the shelf and examined the jars and bottles of herbs again. She could identify the dried heads of red clover, dried horse-chestnut leaves and mullein among the jars of herbs.

Lorcán stood watching her impatiently.

"Spelán uses this as the community's apothecary," he said. "On one of my trips here I cut my hand and it was Spelán who gave me a poultice of herbs to heal it."

Fidelma sighed a little as she gave a final look around.

Finally she left the cell, followed by an unhappy Lorcán, and began to examine the other cells again but this time more carefully. There was evidence in one or two of them that some personal items and

articles of clothing had been hurriedly removed but not enough to
support the idea of the community being attacked and robbed by an
outside force.

Fidelma emerged into the quadrangle feeling confused.

Lorcán, at her side, was gazing up at the sky, a worried expression
on his face.

Fidelma knew that he was still concerned about the approaching
weather but it was no time to retreat from this mystery. Someone
had killed the abbot of the community and a young brother, knocked
the *dominus* unconscious and made ten further members of the
brotherhood disappear.

"Didn't you say that the community had their own boat?" she
asked abruptly.

Lorcán nodded unhappily.

"It was not in the cove when we landed," Fidelma pointed out.

"No, it wouldn't be," replied the boatman. "They kept their boat
further along the shore in a sheltered spot. There is a small shingled
strand around the headland where a boat can be beached."

"Show me," Fidelma instructed. "There is nothing else to do until
Spelán recovers consciousness and we may learn his story."

Somewhat reluctantly, with another glance at the western sky,
Lorcán led the way along the pathway towards the cove but then
broke away along another path which led down on the other side of
a great rocky outcrop which served as a headland separating them
from the cove in which they had landed.

Fidelma knew something was wrong when they reached a knoll
before the path twisted and turned through granite pillars towards
the distant pounding sea. Her eyes caught the flash of black in the
sky circling over something on the shore below.

They were black-backed gulls. Of all gulls, these were birds to
be respected. They frequently nested on rocky islands such as Inis
Chloichreán. It was a carrion eater, a fierce predator given to taking
mammals even as large as cats. They had obviously found something
down on the beach. Fidelma could see that even the crows could not
compete with their larger brethren. There were several pairs of crows
above the mêlée, circling and waiting their chance.

Fidelma compressed her lips firmly.

Lorcán continued to lead the way down between the rocks. The area
was full of nesting birds. May was a month in which the black-backed
gulls, along with many another species, laid their eggs. The rocky
cliffs of the island were ideal sites for birds. The females screamed
furiously as they entered the area but Lorcán ignored their threatening displays. Fidelma did not pretend that she was unconcerned.

"The brothers kept their boat just here . . ." began Lorcán, reaching a large platform of rocky land about twelve feet above a short pebbly beach. He halted and stared.

Fidelma saw the wooden trestles, on which the boat had apparently been set. There was no vessel resting on them now.

"They used to store the boat here," explained Lorcán, "placed upside down to protect it against the weather."

It was the gathering further down on the pebbly strand, an area of beach no more than three yards in width and perhaps ten yards long, that caused Fidelma to exclaim sharply. She realized what the confusion of birds was about. A dozen or more large gulls were gathered, screaming and fighting each other, while forming an outer circle were several other birds who seemed to be interested spectators to the affair. Here and there a jet black carrion crow perched, black eyes watching intently for its chance, while others circled overhead. They were clustering around something which lay on the pebbles. Fidelma suspected what it was.

"Come on!" she cried, and climbed hastily down to the pebbly strand. Then she halted and picked up several large pebbles and began to hurl them at the host of carrion eaters. The scavengers let forth screaming cries of anger and flapped their great wings. Lorcán joined her, picking up stones and throwing them with all his strength.

It was not long before the wheeling mass of birds had dispersed from the object over which they had been fighting. But Fidelma saw that they had not retreated far. They swirled high in the air above them or strutted nearby, beady eyes watching and waiting.

Nonetheless, she strode purposefully across the shingle.

The religious had been young, very young with fair hair.

He lay on his back, his robes in an unseemly mess of torn and frayed wool covered in blood.

Fidelma swallowed hard. The gulls had been allowed an hour or so of uninterrupted work. The face was pitted and bloody, an eye was missing. Part of the skull had been smashed, a pulpy mess of blood and bone. It was obvious that no bird had perpetrated that damage.

"Can you tell who this was, Lorcán?" Fidelma asked softly.

The boatman came over, one wary eye on the gulls. They were standing well back but with their eyes malignantly on the humans who had dared drive them from their unholy feasting. Lorcán glanced down. He pulled a face at the sight.

"I have seen him here in the community, sister. Alas, I do not know his name. Sister, I am fearful. This is the third dead member of the community."

Fidelma did not reply but steeled herself to bend beside the corpse. The leather *crumena* or purse was still fastened at his belt. She forced herself to avoid the lacerated features of the youth and his one remaining bright, accusing eye, and put her hand into the purse. It was empty.

She drew back and shook her head.

Then a thought occurred to her.

"Help me push the body over face down," she instructed.

Keeping his curiosity to himself, Lorcán did so.

The robe was almost torn from the youth's back by the ravages of the birds. Fidelma did not have to remove the material further to see a patch of scars, some old, some new, some which showed signs of recent bleeding, criss-cross over his back.

"What do you make of that, Lorcán?" Fidelma invited.

The boatman thrust out his lower lip and raised one shoulder before letting it fall in an exaggerated shrug.

"Only that the boy has been whipped. Not once either but many times over a long period."

Fidelma nodded in agreement.

"That's another fact I want you to witness, Lorcán."

She stood up, picking up a few stones as she did so and shying them at two or three large gulls who were slowly closing the distance between them. They screamed in annoyance but removed themselves to a safer position.

"How big was the community's currach?" she asked abruptly.

Lorcán understood what she meant.

"It was big enough to carry the rest of the brethren," he replied. "They must be long gone, by now. They could be anywhere on the islands or have even reached the mainland." He paused and looked at her. "But did they go willingly or were they forced to go? Who could have done this?"

Fidelma did not reply. She motioned Lorcán to help her return the body to its original position and stared at the crushed skull.

"That was done with a heavy and deliberate blow," she observed. "This young religious was murdered and left here on the strand."

Lorcán shook his head in utter bewilderment.

"There is much evil here, sister."

"With that I can agree," Fidelma replied. "Come, let us build a cairn over his body with stones so that the gulls do not feast further on him – whoever he was. We cannot carry him back to the settlement."

"Isn't it best to leave him here?"

"No. The evidence might be needed later."

When they arrived back at the community, having completed their task, Maenach greeted them in the quadrangle with a look of relief.

"Brother Spelán is coming round. The young sister is nursing him."

Fidelma answered with a grim smile.

"Now perhaps we may learn some answers to this mystery."

Inside the cell, the brother was lying against a pillow. He looked very drowsy and blinked several times as his dark, black eyes tried to focus on Fidelma.

She motioned Sister Sárnat to move aside and sat on the edge of the cot by Spelán.

"I have given him water only, sister," the girl said eagerly, as if expecting her approval. "The boatman," she gestured towards Maenach, who stood at the doorway with Lorcán, "bathed and dressed the wound."

Fidelma smiled encouragingly at the brother.

"Are you Brother Spelán?"

The man closed his eyes for a moment, his voice sounded weak.

"I am Spelán. Who are you and what are you doing here?"

"I am Fidelma of Kildare. I am come here to bring the Abbot Selbach a letter from Ultan of Armagh."

Spelán stared at her.

"A letter from Ultan?" He sounded confused.

"Yes. That is why we landed on the island. What has happened here? Who hit you on the head?"

Spelán groaned and raised a hand to his forehead.

"I recall." His voice grew strong and commanding. "The abbot is dead, sister. Return to Dún na Séad and ask that a Brehon be sent here for there has been a great crime committed."

"I will take charge of the matter, Spelán," Fidelma said confidently.

"You?" Spelán stared at her in bewilderment. "You don't understand. It is a Brehon that is needed."

"I am a *dálaigh* of the court qualified to the level of *anruth*."

Spelán's eyes widened a fraction for he realized that the qualification of *anruth* allowed the young religieuse to sit in judgement with kings and even with the High King himself.

"Tell me what took place here?" Fidelma prompted.

Spelán's dark eyes found Sister Sárnat and motioned for her to hand him the cup of water from which he took several swallows.

"There was evil here, sister. An evil which grew unnoticed by me until it burst forth and enveloped us all in its maw."

Fidelma waited without saying anything.

Spelán seemed to gather his thoughts for a moment or two.

"I will start from the beginning."

"Always a good place for starting a tale," Fidelma affirmed solemnly.

"Two years ago I met Selbach who persuaded me to join him here in order to build a community which would be dedicated to isolation and meditative contemplation of the works of the Creator. I was the apothecary at an abbey on the mainland which was a sinful place – pride, gluttony and other vices were freely practised there. In Selbach I believed that I had found a kindred spirit who shared my own views. We searched together for a while and eventually came across eleven young souls who wanted to devote themselves to our purpose."

"Why so young?" demanded Fidelma.

Spelán blinked.

"We needed youth to help our community flourish for in youth lies strength against the hardships of this place."

"Go on," pressed Fidelma when the man paused.

"With the blessing of Ultan of Armagh and the permission of the local chieftain, The Ó hEidersceoil, we came to this isolated place."

He paused to take another sip of water.

"And what of this evil that grew in your midst?" encouraged Fidelma.

"I am coming to that. There is a philosophy among some of the ascetics of the faith that physical pain, even as the Son of the Living God had to endure, pain such as the tortures of the flesh, is the way to man's redemption, a way to salvation. Mortification and suffering are seen as the paths to spiritual salvation."

Fidelma sniffed in disapproval.

"I have heard that there are such misguided fools among us."

Spelán blinked.

"Not fools, sister, not fools," he corrected softly. "Many of our blessed saints believed in the efficacy of mortification. They held genuine belief that they must emulate the pain of Christ if they, too, would seek eternal paradise. There are many who will still wear crowns of thorns, who flagellate themselves, drive nails into their hands or pierce their sides so that they might share the suffering of Christ. No, you are too harsh, sister. They are not fools; visionaries – yes; and, perhaps, misguided in their path."

"Very well. We will not argue the matter at this stage, Spelán. What is this to do with what has happened here."

"Do not mistake my meaning, sister," replied Selbach contritely. "I am not an advocate for the *gortaigid*, those who seek the infliction of such pain. I, too, condemn them as you do. But I accept that their desire to experience pain is a genuine desire to share the pain of the Messiah through which he sought man's redemption. I would not call them fools. However, let me continue. For a while we were a happy community. It did not cross my mind that one among us felt that pain was his path to salvation."

"There was a *gortaigid* among you?"

The *dominus* nodded.

"I will spare the events that led to it but will simply reveal that it was none other than the venerable Abbot Selbach himself. But Selbach was not of those who simply inflicted pain and punishment upon himself. He persuaded the youthful brothers we had gathered here to submit to scourgings and whippings in order to satiate his desire to inflict pain and injury so that, he argued, they might approach a sharing of Christ's great suffering. He practised these abominations in secret and swore others to keep that secret on pain of their immortal souls."

"When was this discovered?" demanded Fidelma, slightly horrified.

Spelán bit his lip a moment.

"For certain? Only this morning. I knew nothing. I swear it. It was early this morning that the body of our youngest neophyte, Sacán, was found. He was fourteen years old. The brothers found him and it was known that Selbach had taken him to a special place at the far end of the island last night to ritually scourge the boy. So fierce did he lash the youth that he died of shock and pain."

The *dominus* genuflected.

Fidelma's mouth tightened.

"Go on. How were you, the *dominus* of this community, unaware of the abbot's actions before this morning?"

"He was cunning," replied Spelán immediately. "He made the young brothers take oath each time not to reveal the ritual scourgings to anyone else. He took one young brother at a time to the far end of the island. A shroud of silence enveloped the community. I dwelt in blissful ignorance."

"Go on."

"Selbach had tried to hide his guilt by throwing the poor boy's body over the cliffs last night but the tide washed the body along the rocky barrier that is our shore. It washed ashore early this morning at a point where two of our brethren were fishing for our daily meal."

He paused and sought another sip of water.

Behind her Lorcán said quietly: "Indeed, the tide from the headland would wash the body along to the pebble beach."

"I was asleep when I heard the noise. When I left my cell the brothers' anger had erupted and they had seized Selbach and lashed him to the quadrangle tree. One of the brothers was flogging him with his own whip, tearing at his flesh . . ."

The *dominus* paused again before continuing.

"And did you attempt to stop them?" inquired Fidelma.

"Of course I tried to stop them," Spelán replied indignantly. "I tried to remonstrate, as did another young brother, Snagaide, who told them they could not take the law into their own hands nor punish Selbach. They must take their complaint to Dún na Séad and place it before the Brehon of The Ó hEidersceoil. But the young brothers were so enraged that they would not listen. Instead, they seized Snagaide and myself and held us, ignoring our pleas, while they flogged Selbach. Their rage was great. And then, before I knew it, someone had thrust his knife into the back of Selbach. I did not see who it was.

"I cried to them that not only a crime had been done but now great sacrilege. I demanded that they surrender themselves to me and to Brother Snagaide. I promised that I would take them to Dún na Séad where they must answer for their deed but I would speak on their behalf."

Spelán paused and touched the wound on the side of his head once more with a grimace of pain.

"They argued among themselves then but, God forgive them, they found a determined spokesman in a brother named Fogach who said that they should not be punished for doing what was right and just in the eyes of God. An eye for an eye, a tooth for a tooth, they argued. It was right for Selbach to have met his death in compensation for the death of young Brother Sacán. He demanded that I should swear an oath not to betray the events on the island, recording the deaths as accidents. If I protested then they would take the currach and seek a place where they could live in peace and freedom, leaving me and Snagaide on the island until visited by Lorcán or some other boatman from the mainland."

"Then what happened?" urged Fidelma after the *dominus* paused.

"Then? As you might expect, I could not make such an oath. Their anger spilt over while I remonstrated with them. More for the fear of the consequences than anger, I would say. One of their number knocked me on the head. I knew nothing else until I came to with the young sister and the boatman bending over me."

Fidelma was quiet for a while.

"Tell me, Spelán, what happened to your companion, Brother Snagaide?"

Spelán frowned, looking around as if he expected to find the brother in a corner of the cell.

"Snagaide? I do not know, sister. There was a great deal of shouting and arguing. Then everything went black for me."

"Was Brother Snagaide young?"

"Most of the brethren, apart from myself and Selbach, were but youths."

"Did he have fair hair?"

Spelán shook his head to her surprise. Then it was not Snagaide who lay dead on the strand.

"No," Spelán repeated. "He had black hair."

"One thing that still puzzles me, Spelán. This is a small island, with a small community. For two years you have lived here in close confines. Yet you say that you did not know about the sadistic tendencies of Abbot Selbach; that each night he took young members of the community to some remote part of the island and inflicted pain on them, yet you did not know? I find this strange."

Spelán grimaced dourly.

"Strange though it is, sister, it is the truth. The rest of the community were young. Selbach dominated them. They thought that pain brought them nearer salvation. Being sworn by the Holy Cross never to speak of the whipping given them by the abbot, they remained in silence. Probably they thought that I approved of the whippings. Ah, those poor boys, they suffered in silence until the death of gentle, little Sacán . . . poor boy, poor boy."

Tears welled in the *dominus'* eyes.

Sister Sárnat reached forward and handed him the cup of water.

Fidelma rose silently and left the cell.

Lorcán followed after her as she went to the quadrangle and stood for a moment in silent reflection.

"A terrible tale, and no mistake," he commented, his eyes raised absently to the sky. "The brother is better now, however, and we can leave as soon as you like."

Fidelma ignored him. Her hands were clasped before her and she was gazing at the ground without focusing on it.

"Sister?" prompted Lorcán.

Fidelma raised her head, suddenly becoming aware of him.

"Sorry, you were saying something?"

The boatman shrugged.

"Only that we should be on our way soon. The poor brother needs to be taken to Chléire as soon as we can do so."

Fidelma breathed out slowly.

"I think that the poor brother . . ." she paused and grimaced. "I think there is still a mystery here which needs to be resolved."

Lorcán stared at her.

"But the explanation of Brother Spelán . . .?"

Fidelma returned his gaze calmly.

"I will walk awhile in contemplation."

The boatman spread his hands in despair.

"But, sister, the coming weather . . ."

"If the storm comes then we will remain here until it passes." And, as Lorcán opened his mouth to protest, she added: "I state this as a *dálaigh* of the court and you will observe that authority."

Lorcán's mouth drooped and, with a shrug of resignation, he turned away.

Fidelma began to follow the path behind the community, among the rocks to the more remote area of the island. She realized that this would have been the path which, according to Spelán, Abbot Selbach took his victims. She felt a revulsion at what had been revealed by Spelán, although she had expected some such explanation from the evidence of the lacerated backs of the two young brothers she had seen. She felt loathing at the ascetics who called themselves *gortaigid*, those who sought salvation by bestowing pain on themselves and others. Abbots and bishops condemned them and they were usually driven out into isolated communities.

Here, it seemed, that one evil man had exerted his will on a bunch of youths scarcely out of boyhood who had sought the religious life and knew no better than submit to his will until one of their number died. Now those youths had fled the island, frightened, demoralized and probably lost to the truth of Christ's message of love and peace.

In spite of general condemnation she knew that in many abbeys and monasteries some abbots and abbesses ordered strict rules of intolerable numbers of genuflections, prostrations and fasts. She knew that Erc, the bishop of Slane, who had been patron of the blessed Brendan of Clonfert, would take his acolytes to cold mountain streams, summer and winter, to immerse themselves in the icy waters four times a day to say their prayers and psalms. There was the ascetic, Mac Tulchan, who bred fleas on his body and, so that his pain might be the greater, he never scratched himself. Didn't Finnian of Clonard purposely set out to catch a virulent disease from a dying child that he might obtain salvation through suffering?

Mortification and suffering. Ultan of Armagh was one of the school preaching moderation to those who were becoming indulgently masochistic, ascetics who were becoming fanatical torturers of the body, wrenching salvation through unnatural wants, strain or physical suffering.

She paused in her striding and sat down on a rock, her hands demurely folded in front of her, as she let her mind dwell on the evidence. It certainly appeared that everything fitted in with Spelán's explanation. Why did she feel that there was something wrong? She opened her *marsupium* and drew out the piece of cloth she had found ensnared on the belt hook of the youthful Sacán. It had obviously been torn away from something and not from the boy's habit. And there was the wooden cup, which had dried out now, which she had found on the floor of the oratory. It had obviously been used for an infusion of herbs.

She suddenly saw a movement out of the corner of her eye, among the rocks. She swung round very fast. For a moment her eyes locked into the dark eyes of a startled youth, the cowl of his habit drawn over his head. Then the youth darted away among the rocks.

"Stop!" Fidelma came to her feet, thrusting the cup and cloth into her *marsupium*. "Stop brother, I mean you no harm."

But the youth was gone, bounding away through the rocky terrain.

With an exasperated sigh, Fidelma began to follow, when the sound of her name being called halted her.

Sister Sárnat came panting along the path.

"I have been sent by Brother Spelán and Lorcán," she said. "Lorcán entreats you to have a care of the approaching storm, sister."

Fidelma was about to say something sarcastic about Lorcán's concern but Sárnat continued.

"Brother Spelán agrees we should leave the island immediately and report the events here to the abbot of Chléire. The brother is fully recovered now and he is taking charge of things. He says that he recalls your purpose here was to bring a letter from Ultan to the Abbot Selbach. Since Selbach is dead and he is *dominus* he asks that you give him the letter in case anything requires to be done about it before we leave the island."

Fidelma forgot about the youth she was about to pursue.

She stared hard at Sister Sárnat.

The young novitiate waited nervously, wondering what Fidelma was staring at.

"Sister . . ." she began nervously.

Fidelma sat down on the nearest rock abruptly.

"I have been a fool," she muttered, reaching into her *marsupium* and bringing out the letters she was carrying. She thrust back the letter addressed to the abbot of Chléire and tore open Ultan's letter to Selbach, to the astonished gaze of Sister Sárnat. Her eyes rapidly read the letter and her features broke into a grim smile.

"Go, sister," she said, arising and thrusting the letter back into the *marsupium.* "Return to Brother Spelán. Tell him and Lorcán that I will be along in a moment. I think we will be able to leave here before the storm develops."

Sárnat stared at her uncertainly.

"Very well, sister. But why not return with me?"

Fidelma smiled.

"I have to talk to someone first."

A short while later Fidelma strode into the cell where Spelán was sitting on the cot, with Lorcán and Maenach lounging nearby. Sister Sárnat was seated on a wooden bench by one wall. As Fidelma entered, Lorcán looked up in relief.

"Are you ready now, sister? We do not have long."

"A moment or two, if you please, Lorcán," she said, smiling gently.

Spelán was rising.

"I think we should leave immediately, sister. I have much to report to the abbot of Chléire. Also . . ."

"How did you come to tear your robe, Spelán?"

Fidelma asked the question with an innocent expression. Beneath that expression, her mind was racing for she had made her opening arrow-shot into the darkness. Spelán stared at her and then stared at his clothing. It was clear that he did not know whether his clothing was torn or not. But his eyes lighted upon a jagged tear in his right sleeve. He shrugged.

"I did not notice," he replied.

Fidelma took the piece of torn cloth from her *marsupium* and laid it on the table.

"Would you say that this cloth fitted the tear, Lorcán."

The boatman, frowning, picked it up and took it to place against Spelán's sleeve.

"It does, sister," he said quietly.

"Do you recall where I found it?"

"I do. It was snagged on the hook of the belt of the young boy, Sacán."

The colour drained from Spelán's face.

"It must have been caught there when I carried the body from the strand . . ." he began.

"*You* carried the body from the strand?" asked Fidelma with emphasis. "You told us that some of the young brothers fishing there saw it and brought it back and all this happened before you were awakened after they had tied Selbach to the tree and killed him."

Spelán's mouth worked for a moment without words coming.

"I will tell you what happened on this island," Fidelma said. "Indeed, you did have a *gortaigid* here. One who dedicated his life to the enjoyment of mortification and suffering but not from any pious ideal of religious attainment . . . merely from personal perversion. Where better to practise his disgusting sadism than a hermitage of youths whom he could dominate and devise tortures for by persuading them that only by that pain could they obtain true spirituality?"

Spelán was staring malignantly at her.

"In several essentials, your story was correct, Spelán. There was a conspiracy of secrecy among the youths. Their tormentor would take them one at a time, the youngest and most vulnerable, to a remote part of the island and inflict his punishment, assuring the boy it was the route to eternal glory. Then one day one of the youths, poor little Sacán, was beaten so severely that he died. In a panic the tormentor tried to dispose of his evil deed by throwing the body over the cliffs. As he did so, the hook on the boy's belt tore a piece of cloth from the man's robe. Then the next morning the body washed ashore."

"Utter nonsense. It was Selbach who . . ."

"It was Selbach who began to suspect that he had a *gortaigid* in his community."

Spelán frowned.

"All this is supposition," he sneered but there was a fear lurking in his dark eyes.

"Not quite," Fidelma replied without emotion. "You are a very clever man, Spelán. When Sacán's body was discovered, the youths who found him gathered on the shore around it. They did not realize that their abbot, Selbach, was really a kindly man who had only recently realized what was going on in his community and certainly did not condone it. As you said yourself, the conspiracy of silence was such that the youthful brothers thought that you were acting with Selbach's approval. They thought that mortification was a silent rule of the community. They decided to flee from the island there and then. Eight of them launched the currach and rowed away, escaping from what had become for them an accursed place . . ."

Lorcán, who had been following Fidelma's explanation with some astonishment, whistled softly.

"Where would they have gone, sister?"

"It depends. If they had sense they would have gone to report the matter to Chléire or even to Dún na Séad. But, perhaps, they thought their word would be of no weight against the abbot and *dominus* of this house. Perhaps these innocents still think that mortification is an accepted rule of the Faith."

"May I remind you that I was knocked unconscious by these same innocents?" sneered Spelán.

Maenach nodded emphatically.

"Indeed, sister, that is so. How do you explain that?"

"I will come to that in a moment. Let me tell you firstly what happened here. The eight young brothers left the island because they believed everyone else supported the rule of mortification. It was then that Brother Fogach came across the body and carried it to the oratory and alerted you, Spelán."

"Why would he do that?"

"Because Brother Fogach was not your enemy, nor was Brother Snagaide. They were your chosen acolytes who had actually helped you carry out your acts of sadism in the past. They were young and gullible enough to believe your instructions were the orders of the Faith and the Word of God. But inflicting punishment on their fellows was one thing, murder was another."

"You'll have a job to prove this," sneered Spelán.

"Perhaps," replied Fidelma. "At this stage Fogach and Snagaide were willing to help you. You realized that your time was running out. If those brothers reported matters then an official of the church, a *dálaigh*, would be sent to the island. You had to prepare your defence. An evil scheme came into your mind. It was still early. Selbach was still asleep. You persuaded Snagaide and Fogach that Selbach was responsible in the same way that you had persuaded their fellows that Selbach approved of this mortification. You told them that Selbach had flogged Sacán that night – not you – and now he must be ritually scourged in turn. Together you awoke Selbach and took him and tied him to that tree. You knew exactly what you were going to do but first you whipped that venerable old man.

"In his pain, the old man cried out and told your companions the truth. They listened, horrified at how they had been misled. Seeing this, you stabbed the abbot to stop him speaking. But the abbot's life would have been forfeit anyway. It was all part of your plan to hide all the evidence against you, to show that you were simply the dupe of Selbach.

"Snagaide and Fogach ran off. You now had to silence them. You caught up with Fogach and killed him, smashing his skull with a stone. But when you turned in search of Snagaide you suddenly observed a currach approaching. It was Lorcán's currach. But you thought it was coming in answer to the report of the eight brothers.

"You admitted that you were a trained apothecary. You hurried to your cell and mixed a potion of herbs, a powerful sleeping draught which would render you unconscious within a short time. First you picked up a stone and smote your temple hard enough to cause a nasty-looking wound. But Maenach, who knows something of a physician's art, told us that he would not have expected you to be unconscious from it. In fact, after you had delivered that blow, you drank your portion and stretched yourself in the oratory where I found you. You were not unconscious from the blow but merely in a deep sleep from your potion. You had already worked out the story that you would tell us. It would be your word against the poor, pitiful and confused youths."

Fidelma slowly took out the cup and placed it on the table.

"That was the cup I found lying near you in the oratory. It still smells of the herbs, like mullein and red clover tops, which would make up the powerful sleeping draught. You have jars of such ingredients in your cell."

"You still can't prove this absurd story," replied Spelán.

"I think I can. You see, not only did Abbot Selbach begin to suspect that there was a *gortaigid* at work within his community but he wrote to Ultan of Armagh outlining his suspicions."

She took out the letter from Ultan of Armagh.

Spelán's eyes narrowed. She noticed that tiny beads of sweat had begun to gather on his brow for the first time since she had begun to call his bluff. She held the letter tantalizingly in front of her.

"You see, Spelán, when you showed yourself anxious to get your hands on this letter, I realized that it was the piece of evidence I was looking for; indeed, that I was overlooking. The letter is remarkably informative, a reply to all Selbach's concerns about you."

Spelán's face was white. He stared aghast at the letter as she placed it on the table.

"Selbach named me to Ultan?"

Fidelma pointed to the letter.

"You may see for yourself."

With a cry of rage that stunned everyone into immobility, Spelán suddenly launched himself across the room towards Fidelma with his hands outstretched.

He had gone but a few paces when he was abruptly halted as if by a gigantic hand against his chest. He stood for a moment, his eyes bulging in astonishment, and then he slid to the ground without another word.

It was only then that they saw the hilt of the knife buried in Spelán's heart and the blood staining his robes.

There was a movement at the door. A young, dark-haired youth in the robes of a religious took a hesitant step in. Lorcán, the first to recover his senses, knelt by the side of Spelán and reached for a pulse. Then he raised his eyes and shook his head.

Fidelma turned to the trembling youth who had thrown the knife. She reached out a hand and laid it on his shaking arm.

"I had to do it," muttered the youth. "I had to."

"I know," she pacified.

"I do not care. I am ready to be punished." The youth drew himself up.

"In your suffering of mind, you have already punished yourself enough, Brother Snagaide. These here," she gestured towards Lorcán, Maenach and Sárnat, "are witnesses to Spelán's action which admitted of his guilt. Your case will be heard before the Brehon in Chléire and I shall be your advocate. Does not the ancient law say every person who places themselves beyond the law is without the protection of the law? You slew a violator of the law and therefore this killing is justified under the Law of the *Fenechus*."

She drew the youth outside. He was scarcely the age of credulous and unworldly Sister Sárnat. Fidelma sighed deeply. If she could one day present a law to the council of judges of Ireland she would make it a law that no one under the age of twenty-five could be thrust into the life of the religious. Youth needed to grow to adulthood and savour life and understand something of the world before they isolated themselves on islands or in cloisters away from it. Only in such sequestered states of innocence and fear of authority could evil men like Spelán thrive. She placed a comforting arm around the youth's shoulder as he fell to heart-retching sobbing.

"Come, Lorcán," Fidelma called across her shoulder. "Let's get down to the currach and reach Inis Chléire before your storm arrives."

Sister Sárnat emerged from the cell, holding the letter which Fidelma had laid on the table.

"Sister . . ." She seemed to find difficulty in speaking. "This letter from Ultan to Selbach . . . it does not refer to Spelán. Selbach didn't suspect Spelán at all. He thought that mortification was just a fashion among the youthful brothers."

Fidelma's face remained unchanged.

"Selbach could not bring himself to suspect his companion. It was a lucky thing that Spelán didn't realize that, wasn't it?"

# THE TWO BEGGARS
# Robert van Gulik

*Robert van Gulik (1910–67) was a Dutch ambassador to Japan. He became intrigued by the traditional Chinese stories about the seventh-century magistrate Judge Dee, and he translated these into English as* Dee Goong An *in 1949. Thereafter he continued the series with a long run of novels and stories which vividly recreated this fascinating character. The following story is set in the year 668 and takes place shortly after the events described in* The Chinese Bell Murders *(1958) and just before those in* The Red Pavilion *(1964).*

When the last visitor had left, Judge Dee leaned back in his chair with a sigh of relief. With tired eyes he looked out over his back garden where in the gathering dusk his three small sons were playing among the shrubbery. They were suspending lighted lanterns on the branches, painted with the images of the Eight Genii.

It was the fifteenth day of the first month, the Feast of Lanterns. People were hanging gaily painted lanterns of all shapes and sizes in and outside their houses, transforming the entire city into a riot of garish colours. From the other side of the garden wall the judge heard the laughter of people strolling in the park.

All through the afternoon the notables of Poo-yang, the prosperous district where Judge Dee had now been serving one year as magistrate, had been coming to his residence at the back of the tribunal compound to offer him their congratulations on this auspicious day. He pushed his winged judge's cap back from his forehead and passed his hand over his face. He was not accustomed to drinking so much wine in the daytime; he felt slightly sick. Leaning forward, he took a large white rose from the bowl on the tea-table, for its scent is supposed to counteract the effects of alcohol. Inhaling deeply the flower's fresh fragrance, the judge reflected that his last visitor, Ling, the master of the goldsmiths' guild, had really overstayed his welcome, had seemed glued to his chair. And Judge Dee had to change and refresh himself before going to his women's quarters, where his three wives were now supervising the preparations for the festive family dinner.

Excited children's voices rang out from the garden. The judge looked round and saw that his two eldest boys were struggling to get hold of a large coloured lantern.

"Better come inside now and have your bath!" Judge Dee called out over to them.

"Ah-kuei wants that nice lantern made by Big Sister and me all for himself!" his eldest son shouted indignantly.

The judge was going to repeat his command, but out of the corner of his eye he saw the door in the back of the hall open. Sergeant Hoong, his confidential adviser, came shuffling inside. Noticing how wan and tired the old man looked, Judge Dee said quickly, "Take a seat and have a cup of tea, Hoong! I am sorry I had to leave all the routine business of the tribunal to you today. I had to go over to the chancery and do some work after my guests had left, but Master Ling was more talkative than ever. He took his leave only a few moments ago."

"There was nothing of special importance, Your Honour," Sergeant Hoong said, as he poured the judge and himself a cup of tea. "My only difficulty was to keep the clerks with their noses to the grindstone. Today's festive spirit had got hold of them!"

Hoong sat down and sipped his tea, carefully holding up his ragged grey moustache with his left thumb.

"Well, the Feast of Lanterns is on," the judge said, putting the white rose back on the table. "As long as no urgent cases are reported, we can afford to be a little less strict for once."

Sergeant Hoong nodded. "The warden of the north quarter came to the chancery just before noon and reported an accident, sir. An old beggar fell into a deep drain, in a back street not far from Master Ling's residence. His head hit a sharp stone at the bottom, and he died. Our coroner performed the autopsy and signed the certificate of accidental death. The poor wretch was clad only in a tattered gown, he hadn't even a cap on his head, and his greying hair was hanging loose. He was a cripple. He must have stumbled into the drain going out at dawn for his morning rounds. Sheng Pa, the head of the beggars, couldn't identify him. Poor fellow must have come to the city from up-country expecting good earnings here during the feast. If nobody comes to claim the corpse, we'll have it burned tomorrow."

Judge Dee looked round at his eldest son, who was moving an armchair among the pillars that lined the open front of the hall. The judge snapped: "Stop fiddling around with that chair, and do as I told you! All three of you!"

"Yes, sir!" the three boys shouted in chorus.

While they were rushing away, Judge Dee said to Hoong: "Tell the warden to have the drain covered up properly, and give him a good talking to! Those fellows are supposed to see to it that the streets in their quarter are kept in good repair. By the way, we expect you to join our small family dinner tonight, Hoong!"

The old man bowed with a gratified smile.

"I'll go now to the chancery and lock up, sir! I'll present myself at Your Honour's residence again in half an hour."

After the sergeant had left, Judge Dee reflected that he ought to go too and change from his ceremonial robe of stiff green brocade into a comfortable house-gown. But he felt loath to leave the quiet atmosphere of the now empty hall, and thought he might as well have one more cup of tea. In the park outside it had grown quiet too; people had gone home for the evening rice. Later they would swarm out into the street again, to admire the display of lanterns and have drinking bouts in the roadside wine-houses. Putting his cup down, Judge Dee reflected that perhaps he shouldn't have given Ma Joong and his two other lieutenants the night off, for later in the evening there might be brawls in the brothel district. He must remember to tell the headman of the constables to double the night watch.

He stretched his hand out again for his teacup. Suddenly he checked himself. He stared fixedly at the shadows at the back of the hall. A tall old man had come in. He seemed to be clad in a tattered robe, his head with the long flowing hair was bare. Silently he limped across the hall, supporting himself on a crooked staff. He didn't seem to notice the judge, but went straight past with bent head.

Judge Dee was going to shout and ask what he meant by coming in unannounced, but the words were never spoken. The judge froze in sudden horror. The old man seemed to flit right through the large cupboard, then stepped down noiselessly into the garden.

The judge jumped up and ran to the garden steps. "Come back, you!" he shouted angrily.

There was no answer.

Judge Dee stepped down into the moonlit garden. Nobody was there. He quickly searched the low shrubbery along the wall, but found nothing. And the small garden gate to the park outside was securely locked and barred as usual.

The judge remained standing there. Shivering involuntarily, he pulled his robe closer to his body. He had seen the ghost of the dead beggar.

After a while he took hold of himself. He turned round abruptly, went back up to the hall and entered the dim corridor leading to the front of his private residence. He returned absent-mindedly the respectful greeting of his doorman, who was lighting two brightly coloured lanterns at the gate, then crossed the central courtyard of the tribunal compound and walked straight to the chancery.

The clerks had gone home already; only Sergeant Hoong was there, sorting out a pile of papers on his desk by the light of a single candle. He looked up astonished as he saw the judge come in.

"I thought that I might as well have a look at that dead beggar after all," Judge Dee said casually.

Hoong quickly lit a new candle. He led the judge through the dark, deserted corridors to the jail at the back of the courtroom. In the side hall a thin form was lying on a deal table, covered by a reed mat.

Judge Dee took the candle from Hoong, and motioned him to remove the mat. Raising the candle, the judge stared at the lifeless, haggard face. It was deeply lined, and the cheeks were hollow, but it lacked the coarse features one would expect in a beggar. He seemed about fifty; his long, tousled hair was streaked with grey. The thin lips under the short moustache were distorted in a repulsive death grimace. He wore no beard.

The judge pulled open the lower part of the tattered, patched gown. Pointing at the misshapen left leg, he remarked, "He must have broken his knee once, and it was badly set. He must have walked with a pronounced limp."

Sergeant Hoong picked up a long crooked staff standing in the corner and said, "Since he was quite tall, he supported himself on this crutch. It was found by his side, at the bottom of the drain."

Judge Dee nodded. He tried to raise the left arm of the corpse, but it was quite stiff. Stooping, he scrutinized the hand, then righting himself, he said, "Look at this, Hoong! These soft hands without any callouses, the long, well-tended fingernails! Turn the body over!"

When the sergeant had rolled the stiff corpse over on its face Judge Dee studied the gaping wound at the back of the skull. After a while he handed the candle to Hoong, and taking a paper handkerchief from his sleeve, he used it to carefully brush aside the matted grey hair, which was clotted with dried blood. He then examined the handkerchief under the candle. Showing it to Hoong, he said curtly: "Do you see this fine sand and white grit? You wouldn't expect to find that at the bottom of a drain, would you?"

Sergeant Hoong shook his head perplexedly. He replied slowly, "No, sir. Slime and mud rather, I'd say."

Judge Dee walked over to the other end of the table and looked at the bare feet. They were white, and the soles were soft. Turning to the sergeant, he said gravely, "I fear that our coroner's thoughts were on tonight's feast rather than on his duties when he performed the post-mortem. This man wasn't a beggar, and he didn't fall accidentally into the drain. He was thrown into it when he was dead already. By the person who murdered him."

Sergeant Hoong nodded, ruefully pulling at his short grey beard. "Yes, the murderer must have stripped him, and put him in that beggar's gown. It should have struck me at once that the man was naked under that tattered robe. Even a poor beggar would have been wearing something underneath; the evenings are still rather chilly." Looking again at the gaping wound, he asked: "Do you think the head was bashed in with a heavy club, sir?"

"Perhaps," Judge Dee replied. He smoothed down his long, black beard. "Has any person been reported missing recently?"

"Yes, Your Honour! Guildmaster Ling sent a note yesterday stating that Mr Wang, the private tutor of his children, had failed to come back from his weekly holiday two days ago."

"Strange that Ling didn't mention that when he came to visit me just now!" Judge Dee muttered. "Tell the headman to have my palankeen ready! And let my house steward inform my First Lady not to wait for me with dinner!"

After Hoong had left, the judge remained standing there, looking down at the dead man whose ghost he had seen passing through the hall.

The old guildmaster came rushing out into his front courtyard when the bearers deposited Judge Dee's large official palankeen. While assisting the judge to descend, Ling inquired boisterously, "Well, well, to what fortunate occurrence am I indebted for this unexpected honour?"

Evidently Ling had just left a festive family dinner, for he reeked of wine and his words were slightly slurred.

"Hardly fortunate, I fear," Judge Dee remarked, as Ling led him and Sergeant Hoong to the reception hall. "Could you give me a description of your house tutor, the one who has disappeared?"

"Heavens, I do hope the fellow didn't get himself into trouble! Well, he wasn't anything special to look at. A tall thin man, with a short moustache, no beard. Walked with a limp, left leg was badly deformed."

"He has met with a fatal accident," Judge Dee said evenly.

Ling gave him a quick look, then motioned his guest to sit in the place of honour at the central table under the huge lantern of coloured silk hung there for the feast. He himself sat down opposite the judge. Hoong remained standing behind his master's chair. While the steward was pouring the tea, Guildmaster Ling said slowly, "So that's why Wang didn't turn up two days ago, after his weekly day off!" The sudden news seemed to have sobered him up considerably.

"Where did he go to?" Judge Dee asked.

"Heaven knows! I am not a man who pries into the private affairs of his household staff. Wang had every Thursday off; he would leave here Wednesday night before dinner, and return Thursday evening, also at dinner time. That's all I know, and all I need to know, if I may say so, sir!"

"How long had he been with you?"

"About one year. Came from the capital with an introduction from a well-known goldsmith there. Since I needed a tutor to teach my grandsons, I engaged him. Found him a quiet, decent fellow. Quite competent too."

"Do you know why he chose to leave the capital and seek employment here in Poo-yang? Did he have any family here?"

"I don't know," Ling replied crossly. "It was not my habit to discuss with him anything except the progress of my grandchildren."

"Call your house steward!"

The guildmaster turned round in his chair and beckoned the steward who was hovering about in the back of the spacious hall.

When he had come up to the table and made his obeisance, Judge Dee said to him, "Mr Wang has met with an accident and the tribunal must inform the next of kin. You know the address of his relatives here, I suppose?"

The steward cast an uneasy glance at his master. He stammered, "He . . . as far as I know Mr Wang didn't have any relatives living here in Poo-yang, Your Honour."

"Where did he go then for his weekly holidays?"

"He never told me, sir. I suppose he went to see a friend or something." Seeing Judge Dee's sceptical expression, he quickly went on, "Mr Wang was a taciturn man, Your Honour, and he always evaded questions about his private affairs. He liked to be alone. He spent his spare hours in the small room he has in the back yard of this residence. His only recreation was brief walks in our garden."

"Didn't he receive or send any letters?"

"Not that I know of, sir." The steward hesitated a moment. "From some chance remarks of his about his former life in the capital I gathered that his wife had left him. It seemed that she was of a very jealous disposition." He gave his employer an anxious glance. As he saw that Ling was staring ahead and didn't seem to be listening, he went on with more self-assurance: "Mr Wang had no private means at all, sir, and he was very parsimonious. He hardly spent one cent of his salary, never even took a sedan chair when he went out on his day off. But he must have been a wealthy man once, I could tell that from some small mannerisms of his. I think that he was even an official once, for sometimes when caught off guard he would address me in rather an authoritative tone. I understand he lost everything, his money and his official position. Didn't seem to mind, though. Once he said to me: 'Money is of no use if you don't enjoy life spending it; and when your money is spent, official life has lost its glamour.' Rather a frivolous remark coming from such a learned gentleman, I thought, sir – if I may make so bold, sir."

Ling glared at him and said with a sneer, "You seem to find time hanging heavily on your hands in this household! Gossiping instead of supervising the servants!"

"Let the man speak!" the judge snapped at Ling. And to the steward: "Was there absolutely no clue as to where Mr Wang used to go on his days off? You must know; you saw him go in and out, didn't you?"

The steward frowned. Then he replied, "Well, it did strike me that Mr Wang always seemed happy when he went, but when he came back he was usually rather depressed. He had melancholy moods at times. Never interfered with his teaching, though, sir. He was always ready to answer difficult questions, the young miss said the other day."

"You stated that Wang only taught your grandchildren," the judge said sharply to Ling. "Now it appears that he also taught your daughter!"

The guildmaster gave his steward a furious look. He moistened his lips, then replied curtly, "He did. Until she was married, two months ago."

"I see." Judge Dee rose from his chair and told the steward: "Show me Mr Wang's room!" He motioned to Sergeant Hoong to follow him. As Ling made a move to join them, the judge said: "Your presence is not required."

The steward led the judge and Hoong through a maze of corridors to the back yard of the extensive compound. He unlocked a narrow door, lifted the candle and showed them a small, poorly furnished room. There was only a bamboo couch, a simple writing-desk with a straight-backed chair, a bamboo rack with a few books and a black-leather clothes-box. The walls were covered with long strips of paper, bearing ink-sketches of orchids, done with considerable skill. Following Judge Dee's glance, the steward said:

"That was Mr Wang's only hobby, sir. He loved orchids, knew everything about tending them."

"Didn't he have a few potted orchids about?" the judge asked.

"No, sir. I don't think he could afford to buy them – they are quite expensive, sir!"

Judge Dee nodded. He picked up a few of the dog-eared volumes from the book rack and glanced through them. It was romantic poetry, in cheap editions. Then he opened the clothes-box. It was stuffed with men's garments, worn threadbare, but of good quality. The cash box at the bottom of the box contained only some small change. The judge turned to the desk. The drawer had no lock. Inside were the usual writing materials, but no money and not a scrap of inscribed paper, not even a receipted bill. He slammed the drawer shut and angrily asked the steward, "Who has rifled this room during Mr Wang's absence?"

"Nobody has been here, Your Honour!" the frightened steward stammered. "Mr Wang always locked the door when he went out, and I have the only spare key."

"You yourself told me that Wang didn't spend a cent, didn't you? What has happened to his savings over the past year? There's only some small change here!"

The steward shook his head in bewilderment. "I really couldn't say, Your Honour! I am sure nobody came in here. And all the servants have been with us for years. There has never been any pilfering, I can assure you, sir!"

Judge Dee remained standing for a while by the desk. He stared at the paintings, slowly tugging at his moustache. Then he turned round and said: "Take us back to the hall!"

While the steward was conducting them again through the winding corridors, Judge Dee remarked casually, "This residence is situated in a nice, quiet neighbourhood."

"Oh yes, indeed, sir, very quiet and respectable!"

"It's exactly in such a nice, respectable neighbourhood that one finds the better houses of assignation," the judge remarked dryly. "Are there any near here?"

The steward seemed taken aback by this unexpected question. He cleared his throat and replied diffidently, "Only one, sir, two streets away. It's kept by a Mrs Kwang – very high class, visited by the best people only, sir. Never any brawls or other trouble there, sir."

"I am glad to hear that," Judge Dee said.

Back in the reception hall he told the guildmaster that he would have to accompany him to the tribunal to make the formal identification of the dead man. While they were being carried out there in Judge Dee's palankeen, the guildmaster observed a surly silence.

After Ling had stated that the dead body was indeed that of his house tutor and filled out the necessary documents, Judge Dee let him go. Then he said to Sergeant Hoong, "I'll now change into a more comfortable robe. In the meantime you tell our headman to stand by in the courtyard with two constables."

Sergeant Hoong found the judge in his private office. He had changed into a simple robe of dark-grey cotton with a broad black sash, and he had placed a small black skull-cap on his head.

Hoong wanted to ask him where they were going, but seeing Judge Dee's preoccupied mien, he thought better of it and silently followed him out into the courtyard.

The headman and two constables sprang to attention when they saw the judge.

"Do you know the address of a house of assignation in the north quarter, close by Guildmaster Ling's residence?" Judge Dee asked.

"Certainly, Your Honour!" the headman answered officiously. "That's Mrs Kwang's establishment. Properly licensed, and very high class, sir, only the best . . ."

"I know, I know!" the judge cut him short impatiently. "We'll walk out there. You lead the way with your men!"

Now the streets were crowded again with people. They were milling around under the garlands of coloured lanterns that spanned the streets and decorated the fronts of all the shops and restaurants. The headman and the two constables unceremoniously elbowed people aside, making way for the judge and Sergeant Hoong.

Even in the back street where Mrs Kwang lived there were many people about. When the headman had knocked and told the gatekeeper that the magistrate had arrived, the frightened old man quickly conducted the judge and Hoong to a luxuriously appointed waiting-room in the front court.

An elderly, sedately dressed maidservant placed a tea-set of exquisite antique porcelain on the table. Then a tall, handsome woman of about thirty came in, made a low bow and introduced herself as Mrs Kwang, a widow. She wore a straight, long-sleeved robe, simple in style but made of costly, dark-violet damask. She herself poured the tea for the judge, elegantly holding up with her left hand the trailing sleeve of the right. She remained standing in front of the judge, respectfully waiting for him to address her. Sergeant Hoong stood behind Judge Dee's chair, his arms folded in his wide sleeves.

Leisurely tasting the fragrant tea, Judge Dee noticed how quiet it was; all noise was kept out by the embroidered curtains and wall-hangings of heavy brocade. The faint scent of rare and very expensive incense floated in the air. All very high class indeed. He set down his cup and began, "I disapprove of your trade, Mrs Kwang. I recognize, however, that it is a necessary evil. As long as you keep everything orderly and treat the girls well, I won't make any trouble for you. Tell me, how many girls have you working here?"

"Eight, Your Honour. All purchased in the regular manner, of course, mostly directly from their parents. Every three months the ledgers with their earnings are sent to the tribunal, for the assessment of my taxes. I trust that . . ."

"No, I have no complaints about that. But I am informed that one of the girls was bought out recently by a wealthy patron. Who is the fortunate girl?"

Mrs Kwang looked politely astonished. "There must be some misunderstanding, Your Honour. All my girls here are still very young – the eldest is just nineteen – and haven't yet completed their training in music and dancing. They try hard to please, of course, but none of them has yet succeeded in captivating the favour of a wealthy patron so as to establish an ah . . . more permanent relationship." She paused, then added primly, "Although such a transaction means, of course, a very substantial monetary gain for me, I don't encourage it until a courtesan is well into her twenties, and in every respect worthy of attaining the crowning success of her career."

"I see," Judge Dee said. He thought ruefully that this information disposed effectively of his attractive theory. Now that his hunch had proved wrong, this case would necessitate a long investigation, beginning with the goldsmith in the capital who had introduced Wang to Guildmaster Ling. Suddenly another possibility flashed through his mind. Yes, he thought he could take the chance. Giving Mrs Kwang a stern look he said coldly:

"Don't prevaricate, Mrs Kwang! Besides the eight girls who are living here, you have established another in a house of her own. That's a serious offence, for your licence covers this house only."

Mrs Kwang put a lock straight in her elaborate coiffure. The gesture made her long sleeve slip back, revealing her white, rounded forearm. Then she replied calmly:

"That information is only partly correct, Your Honour. I suppose it refers to Miss Liang, who lives in the next street. She is an accomplished courtesan from the capital, about thirty years old – her professional name is Rosedew. Since she was very popular in elegant circles in the capital, she saved a great deal of money and bought herself free, without, however, handing in her licence. She wanted to settle down, and came here to Poo-yang for a period of rest, and to have a leisurely look around for a suitable marriage partner. She's a very intelligent woman, sir; she knows that all those elegant, flighty young men in the capital don't go for permanent arrangements, so she wanted a steady, elderly man of some means and position. Only occasionally did she receive such selected clients here in my house. Your Honour will find the pertaining entries in a separate ledger, also duly submitted regularly for inspection. Since Miss Liang has kept her licence, and since the taxes on her earnings are paid . ..."

She let her voice trail off. Judge Dee was secretly very pleased, for he knew now that he had been on the right track after all. But he assumed an angry mien, hit his fist on the table and barked, "So the man who is buying Rosedew out to marry her is being meanly deceived! For there is no redemption fee to be paid! Not one copper, neither to you nor to her former owner in the capital! Speak up! Weren't you and she going to share that fee, obtained from the unsuspecting patron under false pretences?"

At this Mrs Kwang lost her composure at last. She knelt down in front of Judge Dee's chair and repeatedly knocked her forehead on the floor. Looking up, she wailed, "Please forgive this ignorant person, Excellency! The money has not yet been handed over. Her patron is an exalted person, Excellency, a colleague of Your Excellency, in fact, the magistrate of a district in this same region. If he should hear about this, he . . ."

She burst into tears.

Judge Dee turned round and gave Sergeant Hoong a significant look. That could be no one else but his amorous colleague of Chin-hwa, Magistrate Lo! He barked at Mrs Kwang: "It was indeed Magistrate Lo who asked me to investigate. Tell me where Miss Liang lives; I shall interrogate her personally about this disgraceful affair!"

A short walk brought the judge and his men to the address in the next street that the tearful Mrs Kwang had given him.

Before knocking on the gate, the headman quickly looked up and down the street, then said, "If I am not greatly mistaken, sir, the drain that beggar fell into is located right at the back of this house."

"Good!" Judge Dee exclaimed. "Here, I'll knock myself. You and your two men keep close to the wall while I go inside with the sergeant. Wait here till I call you!"

After repeated knocking the peephole grate in the gate opened and a woman's voice asked, "Who is there?"

"I have a message from Magistrate Lo, for a Miss Rosedew," Judge Dee said politely.

The door opened at once. A small woman dressed in a thin

houserobe of white silk asked the two men to enter. As she preceded them to the open hall in the front court, the judge noticed that despite her frail build she had an excellent figure.

When they were inside she gave her two visitors a curious look, then bade them seat themselves on the couch of carved rosewood. She said somewhat diffidently: "I am indeed Rosedew. Who do I have the honour of . . ."

"We shan't take much of your time, Miss Liang," the judge interrupted quickly. He looked her over. She had a finely chiselled, mobile face, with expressive, almond-shaped eyes and a delicate small mouth – a woman of considerable intelligence and charm. Yet something didn't fit with his theory.

He surveyed the elegantly furnished hall. His eye fell on a high rack of polished bamboo in front of the side window. Each of its three superimposed shelves bore a row of orchid plants, potted in beautiful porcelain bowls. Their delicate fragrance pervaded the air. Pointing at the rack, he said: "Magistrate Lo told me about your fine collection of orchids, Miss Liang. I am a great lover of them myself. Look, what a pity! The second one on the top shelf has wilted, it needs special treatment, I think. Could you get it down and show it to me?"

She gave him a doubtful look, but apparently decided that it was better to humour this queer friend of Magistrate Lo. She took a bamboo step-ladder from the corner, placed it in front of the rack, and nimbly climbed up, modestly gathering the thin robe round her shapely legs. When she was about to take the pot, Judge Dee suddenly stepped up close to the ladder and remarked casually:

"Mr Wang used to call you Orchid, didn't he, Miss Liang? So much more apposite than Rosedew, surely!" When Miss Liang stood motionless, looking down at the judge with eyes that were suddenly wide with fear, he added sharply: "Mr Wang was standing exactly where I am standing now when you smashed the flower pot down on his head, wasn't he?"

She started to sway. Uttering a cry, she wildly groped for support. Judge Dee quickly steadied the ladder. Reaching up, he caught her round her waist and set her down on the floor. She clasped her hands to her heaving bosom and gasped: "I don't . . . Who are you?"

"I am the magistrate of Poo-yang," the judge replied coldly. "After you murdered Wang, you replaced the broken flower pot by a new one, and transplanted the orchid. That's why it's wilted, isn't it?"

"It's a lie!" she cried out. "Wicked slander. I shall . . ."

"I have proof!" Judge Dee cut her short. "A servant of the neighbours saw you dragging the dead body to the drain behind your house here. And I found in Wang's room a note of his, stating that he feared you would harm him, now that you had a wealthy patron who wanted to marry you."

"The treacherous dog!" she shouted. "He swore he didn't keep one scrap of paper relating to . . ." She suddenly stopped and angrily bit her red lips.

"I know everything," the judge said evenly. "Wang wanted more than his weekly visits. Thus he endangered your affair with Magistrate Lo, an affair that would not only bring in a lump sum of money for you and Mrs Kwang, but also set you up for life. Therefore you had to kill your lover."

"Lover?" she screamed. "Do you think I allowed that disgusting cripple ever to touch me here? It was bad enough to have to submit to his odious embraces before, when we were still in the capital!"

"Yet you allowed him to share your bed here," Judge Dee remarked with disdain.

"You know where he slept? In the kitchen! I wouldn't have allowed him to come at all, but he made himself useful by answering my love letters for me, and he paid for and tended those orchids there, so that I would have flowers to wear in my hair. He also acted as doorman and brought tea and refreshments when one of my lovers was here. What else do you think I allowed him to come here for?"

"Since he had spent his entire fortune on you I thought perhaps . . ." Judge Dee said dryly.

"The damnable fool!" she burst out again. "Even after I had told him that I was through with him, he kept on running after me, saying he couldn't live without seeing my face now and then – the cringing beggar! His ridiculous devotion spoilt my reputation. It was because of him that I had to leave the capital and bury myself in this dreary place. And I, fool that I was, trusted that simpering wretch! Leaving a note accusing me! He's ruined me, the dirty traitor!"

Her beautiful face had changed into an evil mask. She stamped her small foot on the floor in impotent rage.

"No," Judge Dee said in a tired voice, "Wang didn't accuse you. What I said just now about that note wasn't true. Beyond a few paintings of orchids which he did when thinking of you, there wasn't one clue to you in his room. The poor, misguided man remained loyal to you, to his very end!" He clapped his hands. When the headman and the two constables had come rushing inside, he ordered: "Put this woman in chains and lock her up in jail. She has confessed to a foul murder." As the two constables grabbed her arms and the headman started to chain her, the judge said: "Since there is not a single reason for clemency, you shall be beheaded on the execution ground."

He turned round and left, followed by Sergeant Hoong. The woman's frantic cries were drowned by the loud shouts and laughter of a happy group of youngsters who came surging through the street, waving brightly coloured lanterns.

When they were back in the tribunal, Judge Dee took Hoong straight to his own residence. While walking with him to the back hall, he said, "Let's just have one cup of tea before we go and join the dinner in my women's quarters."

The two men sat down at the round table. The large lantern hanging from the eaves, and those among the shrubs in the garden had been extinguished. But the full moon lit up the hall with its eerie light.

Judge Dee quickly emptied his cup, then he sat back in his chair and began without further preliminaries:

"Before we went to see Guildmaster Ling, I knew only that the beggar was no beggar, and that he had been murdered elsewhere by having the back of his skull bashed in, probably with a flower pot – as suggested by the fine sand and white grit. Then, during our interview with Ling, I suspected for a moment that the guildmaster was involved in this crime. He hadn't said a word about Wang's disappearance when he came to visit me, and I thought it strange that later he didn't inquire what exactly had happened to Wang. But I soon realized that Ling is that unpleasant kind of person who doesn't take the slightest interest in his personnel, and that he was cross because I had interrupted his family party. What the steward told me about Wang brought to light a fairly clear pattern. The steward said that Wang's family life had been broken up because he squandered his wealth, and his mentioning Mrs Wang's jealousy pointed to another woman being involved. Thus I deducted that Wang had become deeply infatuated with a famous courtesan."

"Why not with some decent girl or woman, or even with a common prostitute?" the sergeant objected.

"If it had been a decent woman, Wang would not have needed to spend his fortune on her; he could have divorced his wife and married his lady-love. And if she had been a common prostitute, he could have bought her out at a moderate price, and set her up in a small house of her own – all without sacrificing his wealth and his official position. No, I was certain that Wang's mistress must have been a famous courtesan in the capital, who could afford to squeeze a lover dry, then discard him and go on to the next. But I assumed that Wang refused to let himself be thrown away like a chewed-out piece of sugar cane, and that he made a nuisance of himself. That she fled from the capital and came to Poo-yang in order to start her game all over again. For it's well known that many wealthy merchants are living here in this district. I assumed that Wang had traced her here and had forced her to let him visit her regularly, threatening to expose her callous racket if she refused. Finally, that after she had caught my foolish colleague Lo, Wang began to blackmail her, and that therefore she had killed him." He sighed, then added: "We now know that it was quite different. Wang sacrificed everything he had for her, and even the pittance he received as tutor he spent on orchids for her. He was quite content to be allowed to see and talk to her every week, frustrating and humiliating as those few hours were. Sometimes, Hoong, a man's folly is engendered by such a deep and reckless passion that it lends him a kind of pathetic grandeur."

Sergeant Hoong pensively pulled at his ragged grey moustache. After a while he asked, "There are a great many courtesans here in Poo-yang. How did Your Honour know that Wang's mistress must belong to the house of Mrs Kwang? And why did it have to be his mistress who murdered him and not, for instance, another jealous lover?"

"Wang used to go there on foot. Since he was a cripple, this proved that she must live near to the guildmaster's house, and that led us to Mrs Kwang's establishment. I asked Mrs Kwang what courtesan had been recently bought out, because such an occurrence supplied the most plausible motive for the murder, namely that the courtesan had to get rid of an embarrassing former lover. Well, we know that Wang was indeed embarrassing her, but not by threatening to blackmail her or by any other wicked scheme. It was just his dog-like devotion that made her hate and despise him. As to the other possibilities you just mentioned, I had of course also reckoned with those. But if the murderer had been a man, he would have carried the body away to some distant spot, and he would also have been more thorough in his attempts at concealing his victim's identity. The fact that the attempt was confined to dressing the victim in a tattered beggar's gown, loosening his top-knot and mussing up his hair, pointed to a woman having done the deed. Women know that a different dress and hair-do can completely alter their own appearance. Miss Liang applied this method to a man – and that was a bad mistake."

Judge Dee took a sip from the cup the sergeant had refilled for him, then resumed, "As a matter of course it could also have been an elaborate scheme to inculpate Miss Liang. But I considered that a remote possibility. Miss Liang herself was our best chance. When the headman informed me that the dead beggar had been found at the back of her house, I knew that my theory must be correct.

However, when we had gone inside I saw that she was a rather small and frail woman, who could never have bashed in the head of her tall victim. Therefore I at once looked around for some death-trap, and found it in the potted orchids on the high shelf, where the wilted plant supplied the final clue. She must have climbed up the ladder, probably asking Wang to steady it for her. Then she made some remark or other that made him turn his head, and smashed the pot down on his skull. These and other details we'll learn tomorrow when I question Miss Liang in the tribunal. Now as regards the role played by Mrs Kwang, I don't think she did more than help Miss Liang to concoct the scheme of getting the fictitious redemption fee out of Lo. Our charming hostess draws the line at murder; hers is a high-class establishment, remember!"

Sergeant Hoong nodded. "Your Honour has not only uncovered a cruel murder, but at the same time saved Magistrate Lo from an alliance with a determined and evil woman!"

Judge Dee smiled faintly. "Next time I meet Lo," he said, "I'll tell him about this case – without mentioning, of course, that I know it was he who patronized Miss Liang. My gay friend must have been visiting my district incognito! This case will teach him a lesson – I hope!"

Hoong discreetly refrained from commenting further on one of his master's colleagues. He remarked with a satisfied smile: "So now all the points of this curious case have been cleared up!"

Judge Dee took a long draught from his tea. As he set the cup down he shook his head and said unhappily: "No, Hoong. Not all the points."

He thought he might as well tell the sergeant now about the ghostly apparition of the dead beggar, without which this murder would have been dismissed as an ordinary accident. But just as he was about to speak, his eldest son came rushing inside. Seeing his father's angry look, the boy said with a quick bow: "Mother said we might take that nice lantern to our bedroom, sir!"

As his father nodded, the small fellow pushed an armchair up to one of the pillars. He climbed on the high backrest, reached up and unhooked the large lantern of painted silk hanging down from the eaves. He jumped down, lit the candle inside with his tinderbox, and held up the lantern for his father to see.

"It took Big Sister and me two days to make this, sir!" he said proudly. "Therefore we didn't want Ah-kuei to spoil it. We like the Immortal Lee, he is such a pathetic, ugly old fellow!"

Pointing at the figure the children had painted on the lantern, the judge asked: "Do you know his story?" When the boy shook his head, his father continued: "Many, many years ago Lee was a very handsome young alchemist who had read all books and mastered all magic arts. He could detach his soul from his body and then float at will in the clouds, leaving his empty body behind, to resume it when he came down to earth again. One day, however, when Lee had carelessly left his body lying in a field, some farmers came upon it. They thought it was an abandoned corpse, and burned it. So when Lee came down, he found his own beautiful body gone. In despair he had to enter the corpse of a poor old crippled beggar which happened to be lying by the roadside, and Lee had to keep that ugly shape for ever. Although later he found the Elixir of Life, he could never undo that one mistake, and it was in that form that he entered the ranks of the Eight Immortals: Lee with the Crutch, the Immortal Beggar."

The boy put the lantern down. "I don't like him anymore!" he said with disdain. "I'll tell Big Sister that Lee was a fool who only got what he deserved!"

He knelt down, wished his father and Hoong good night, and scurried away.

Judge Dee looked after him with an indulgent smile. He took up the lantern to blow out the candle inside. But suddenly he checked himself. He stared at the tall figure of the Immortal Beggar projected on the plaster wall. Then he tentatively turned the lantern round, as it would turn in the draught. He saw the ghostly shadow of the crippled old man move slowly along the wall, then disappear into the garden.

With a deep sigh the judge blew the candle out and put the lantern back on the floor. He said gravely to Sergeant Hoong, "You were right after all, Hoong! All our doubts are solved – at least those about the mortal beggar. He was a fool. As to the Immortal Beggar – I am not too sure." He rose and added with a wan smile, "If we measure our knowledge not by what we know but by what we don't, we are just ignorant fools, Hoong, all of us! Let's go now and join my ladies."

# PART II
## The Middle Ages

# THE INVESTIGATION
## OF THINGS
## Charles Ardai

*We stay in ancient China for the next story, though we move on four hundred years. Charles Ardai (b. 1969) is a New York writer and editor who, in addition to his stories in* Ellery Queen's Mystery Magazine *and* Alfred Hitchcock's Mystery Magazine, *has edited several anthologies, including* Great Tales of Madness and the Macabre (1990) *and* Great Tales of Crime & Detection (1991). *He has also been the story consultant for several television series, including* The Hidden Room *and* The Hitchhiker. *It was while he was studying and lecturing on British Romantic Poetry at Columbia University that he began to research eleventh-century Chinese history. That was when he discovered the real-life characters of Ch'eng I and Ch'eng Hao who feature in this story. He also discovered the Judge Dee stories at that time. "The characters cried out to have a mystery written around them," Ardai told me, "and the van Gulik novels inspired me to experiment with a more mannered style than I normally employ." Here's the result. My thanks to writer Lawrence Schimel for alerting me to this story.*

*"The extension of knowledge lies in the investigation of things. For only when things are investigated is knowledge extended . . ."*

*Ta Hsueh, The Great Learning*

C h'eng I sat in the Grove of the Ninth Bamboo studying tea. He had twenty-four varieties on a great wooden palette, spread out before him like a portrait artist's paints. Each was labeled in meticulous calligraphy and kept in place with a bit of paste. Ch'eng I noted the subtle variations in the contours and textures of the leaves, labeling salient points directly on the wood with a fine-point brush.

Next to him, his brother, Ch'eng Hao, sipped from a teacup and watched in silence.

Ch'eng I selected a pouch from among the twenty-four at his feet. He pulled out a pinch of tea and spread it on his palette, separating the leaves with the end of his brush. "You see, brother," he said without looking up from his task, "the lung-ching is flat, like the edge of a fine sword, and slick, like wet hair."

"It tastes excellent," Ch'eng Hao said, tossing back the last of his tea, "not at all like wet hair. Beyond that I know nothing. What else matters about tea? How it tastes, whether it pleases one, that is all. You are not a tea farmer, to worry about the plant. You are not Lu Yu, to write another *Ch'a Ch'ing*. You ruin your eyes peering at tea when you should be drinking it."

Ch'eng I pulled a pinch from another pouch and spread it on his board. "Pi lo-chun dries in a spiral. It is the smallest of all the teas I have examined." He scratched a few more notes onto the wood, then laid the brush aside and looked up at his brother. "Please try not to be so selfish. Tea is not merely a flavor in your mouth. Tea exists even if your mouth does not. You must not understand tea in terms of yourself. You must understand yourself in terms of tea."

Ch'eng Hao shook his head. "You do not understand yourself. You do not understand tea. You spend your days picking things apart, but there will always be more things than there are days. Your tea, your pouch, your brush, your tunic – these are all tools. You shouldn't study them. You should use them: drink your tea, write with your brush, wear your tunic. When you sit down to think, you should think about *this*." Ch'eng Hao tapped a finger against his forehead.

Ch'eng I gathered his materials, wrapping the palette in its silk case and stringing the pouches along his belt. "No, brother, you are mistaken." He tapped his head. "This is the tool. You should use it to think about this – " He swept his free hand around him in an open gesture. "About this – " He lifted one of the pouches and let it fall to his side again. "And this – " He ran his hand along the trunk of a tree. "Grow until your mind is the size of the world. Do not try to compress the world to make it fit inside your mind."

"But there is more in the world than you can ever hope to know," Ch'eng Hao said.

"So you would argue that I shouldn't try to know anything?"

"I say only, as Chuang Tzu says, that 'To pursue that which is unlimited with that which is limited is to know sorrow.' The world is huge; we are small and have short lives."

"When did you become a Taoist," Ch'eng I said, "that you quote Chuang Tzu?"

"Not a Taoist, I, a realist." Ch'eng Hao tried to wave the whole discussion away. "You will have to learn this for yourself. It is at least possible for one to fully understand oneself. That is a finite task. Through this understanding, one can understand everything else in the world."

"No, brother. The *Great Learning* says that self-perfection must come from the Investigation of Things, not the Investigation of Self."

"All things can be found in the self," Ch'eng Hao said.

"Now," said Ch'eng I, "you sound like a Buddhist."

"If you weren't my brother," Ch'eng Hao said, "I would demand an apology."

"If I weren't your brother," Ch'eng I said, "I might give you one."

Ch'eng Hao was about to answer when a scuffle of footsteps arose and a messenger burst into the grove. The messenger bowed deeply. The two brothers returned the courtesy, their argument temporarily set aside.

"Forgive me, please, for intruding," the messenger said, "but you are the brothers Ch'eng, are you not? Hao and I?"

Ch'eng I nodded. "We are."

"Then you must come. The Seventh Patriarch has requested your presence."

The brothers exchanged surprised glances. The Seventh Patriarch was the leader of the district's Ch'an Buddhist temple, and rarely one to invite outsiders into his sanctuary. Especially Confucian outsiders.

"He wants to see us?" Ch'eng Hao said. "Why?"

The messenger tried to look Ch'eng Hao in the eye and failed. His eyes fell on the ground and remained there, his chin pressed against his chest.

"What is it, man?"

The messenger spoke quietly: "There has been a murder."

The Temple of the Seventh Patriarch rose out of the flat land it was built on like a needle piercing upwards through a piece of fabric. It was a tower five times the height of a man, roughly pointed at the top, with walls of packed earth supported by wooden beams. The structure looked unstable and precarious, yet Ch'eng Hao knew that it was older than he was.

The messenger, who had identified himself as Wu Han-Fei, led them to the entrance and then stepped aside. "I may not enter," he said, in answer to the unasked question.

Ch'eng Hao and Ch'eng I stepped inside cautiously.

A body lay on the ground, its feet toward them. It was clearly that of a Buddhist monk – there was no mistaking the coarse robe or the waxy pallor of the skin, so deathlike in life, how much more so in

death! Ch'eng I knelt beside the corpse to examine it more closely
while Ch'eng Hao looked around the inside of the room.

The neck of the monk's robe was soaked with a liquid Ch'eng I
knew to be blood – indeed, the entire front of the robe was. When
he opened the robe, Ch'eng I discovered a ragged hole in the man's
throat. He lifted the head and pulled off the hood. The monk's head
was neatly shaved, as Ch'eng I had known it would be. The wound
in his throat penetrated cleanly, ending in a round, puckered hole on
the other side. The ground beneath the body was coated with blood,
by now nearly dry, and the beams in the far wall were spattered with
brown spots. Ch'eng I laid the man's head back down and replaced
the hood.

Ch'eng Hao paced around the room's perimeter. It was not a
large room, though it took on a sense of space because of the high
roof. Other than the body and themselves, the room was completely
empty and devoid of decoration. There was no more mistaking a
Ch'an meditation room than there was a Ch'an monk. Only prisons
were this spare in the outside world . . . and graves.

Ch'eng I left the monk's body and walked over to the far wall,
where the spray of blood had struck. He examined it closely, inching
his way down from eye level until he stopped about two feet above the
floor. He pulled his drawing brush from his belt and knelt to his work,
using the handle to pry something out from a tiny hole in the wall.
Ch'eng I had to be careful not to break the brush, but he worked as
quickly as he dared. Ch'eng Hao stood behind him, watching.

"What have you found?" Ch'eng Hao asked.

"I do not know yet. I will have to investigate."

Ch'eng I scraped around the edges of the hole, coaxing out the
object that was lodged inside. Finally, it fell to the ground and
Ch'eng I picked it up. He tested it with a fingernail. "It is a piece
of soft metal," he said, holding it out on his palm for his brother to
see. It was a dark, flattened lump slightly larger than a cashew. Then
he held up his thumbnail. "Coated with blood, as you can see. This
little ball seems to have killed the unfortunate man at our feet."

"This ball?" Ch'eng Hao was incredulous. "How can that be?"

Ch'eng I stepped over to the open entryway. "Through here. It
came in, struck the monk in the throat, and killed him."

"But that is impossible!" Ch'eng Hao said. "Think of the force
required! Think how hard it would have had to have been thrown
in order to pierce the man's neck!"

Ch'eng I shook his head. "It is worse than that. The metal was
thrown with enough force to pierce the monk's neck and then continue
its flight to the opposite wall, where it lodged itself three finger-widths

deep. But you are wrong to say it is impossible. The evidence of our senses demonstrates that it has happened."

Ch'eng Hao looked at the bloody metal and at the corpse and said nothing.

Wu Han-Fei reappeared at the entrance. "The Seventh Patriarch will see you now," he said.

"Will he?" Ch'eng I took the murder weapon back from his brother and found an empty pouch for it on his belt. "How good of him." He left the temple. Ch'eng Hao followed.

Ch'eng I scanned the landscape more carefully than he had before. The temple was the only building in sight, surrounded at a distance of ten yards by a dense forest; it stood like an obelisk in the center of a flat and empty meadow. "Where will we find the Seventh Patriarch?" he asked.

"You will follow me," Wu Han-Fei said. He started off for the forest.

"Hold on," Ch'eng I shouted. Wu Han-Fei stopped and turned around. "I realize that we will follow you. What I asked is *where* we will find him, not *how* we will."

Wu Han-Fei was confused. "There." He pointed in the direction he had started to walk.

"In the forest?"

He shook his head. "In a clearing. Like this."

"How far?"

He shrugged uncomfortably. "Not far. You will see."

"Yes, I imagine I will see. But first – "

"Never mind," Ch'eng Hao interrupted. "There will be plenty of time for your questions later." Then to Wu Han-Fei: "You will have to forgive my brother. He wants to know everything there is to know."

This explanation apparently satisfied the messenger, who turned around again and continued into the forest.

"I will not interfere with your investigation," Ch'eng I said as they followed their guide, "and I will ask you kindly not to interfere with mine."

"Brother," Ch'eng Hao said, "if I hadn't interfered, you would still be badgering this poor man with your questions. You'd have kept at it until we all died of old age out there."

"Perhaps," Ch'eng I said. "Perhaps I would have found the truth sooner than that."

"The truth? You were asking him how far it was to where we are going! Of what possible consequence – "

"You think truth is limited to thought and reason and motive,"

Ch'eng I said calmly, "and that is a mistake. Truth is also distance, and size, and weight, and force. You can seek truth in your way. I will seek it in mine."

"Sirs," Wu Han-Fei interrupted. "We are here."

They had passed through about forty feet of dense forest and were now in another clearing. A dozen small buildings were clustered in the center. The messenger pointed to one of them. "You will find the Patriarch there."

"And you?" Ch'eng I looked closely at the man for the first time. This was no Buddhist – he had a fine head of long, black hair and a dark, earthy complexion; and if his robe was coarse it was due to poverty, not piety. Most telling, a respect for the public authority Ch'eng I and Ch'eng Hao represented was clear in the way he never met their eyes for more than a second; a devoted Buddhist would stare down the Emperor himself, even if it meant death. It was indeed as Hui-Yuan had written: "A monk does not bow down before a king."

"I will go no further," Wu Han-Fei said.

"What are you doing here?" Ch'eng Hao asked, suddenly curious. "You are not one of them."

"No," Wu Han-Fei said. "I am their link with the secular world."

"I thought they did not need one," Ch'eng Hao said.

"They thought so, too." Wu Han-Fei spread his hands before him. "Murder changes such things."

"Tell me again," Ch'eng Hao said, "exactly how you found Kung." He paced as he spoke and did not turn to face the Patriarch when the old man answered.

"Kung was meditating," the Patriarch said. He had a voice that rumbled softly like a running stream. Ch'eng Hao was not insensible to beauty; he appreciated the sound of a wise and serene voice. But he listened with a suspicious ear to hear the silences, the words that remained unspoken. "Kung had grave matters on his conscience. Very grave."

"What were these grave matters?" Ch'eng Hao asked.

"Kung would not say." The Patriarch looked genuinely saddened by his monk's death, but Hao was aware that such apparent sadness might be no more than a mask. Men conceal, as he had often told his brother, in a way that nature does not. Honesty is a path only infrequently followed, and even then not without straying.

"Why would he not?"

The Patriarch caught Hao's eye and held it. "Ssu-ma Ch'ien was offered suicide but chose castration. He felt an honorable death would impair his mission on earth. So he sacrificed personal honor for the greater good."

"And . . .?"

The Patriarch said nothing more.

"I want none of your *koans*," Ch'eng Hao said sharply. "Speak plainly or not at all."

"Silence is the sound of a man speaking plainly," the Patriarch said. And silence fell.

After the strained quiet had stretched out for a minute, Ch'eng I spoke. "It would be helpful if you would describe the circumstances under which Kung's body was discovered."

The Patriarch nodded. "Kung left for the temple early in the morning. Before an hour had passed, Lin-Yu came to see me. He told me that he had gone to the temple and found Kung's body, in the condition that you observed."

"Who might have killed him?" Ch'eng Hao asked.

"Any one of us," the Patriarch said, "myself included."

"Did you?"

The Patriarch favored Ch'eng Hao with a condescending smile. "I do not think so . . . do you?"

Hao shook his head. "No. Had you killed him you could easily have arranged to rid yourself of the body without any attention. The outside world is unaware of what goes on here – even apathetic. If I had an illustrious ancestor for every time someone has said to me, 'Let the monks starve to death, we do not care,' I would be the most favored man under heaven. You would have had no reason to ask us to investigate, for that could only call punishment down on your head. No, you did not kill Kung. But," and here Ch'eng Hao paused for a bit to let his words have their full effect, "I would be very surprised if you did not know why he was killed."

The old man shook his head. "Then I will have the pleasure of surprising you, Ch'eng Hao. For I know nothing of this matter beyond the fact that I was unfortunate enough not to be able to prevent it. One of my men killed another: a son has murdered a brother. I want to know who and I want to know why."

"And how." This from Ch'eng I.

The Patriarch nodded slowly. "'How' and 'why' are such similar questions, so fundamentally intertwined. You will not find one answer without the other."

"Then the investigation commences," Ch'eng I said. He stepped out of the room abruptly and headed toward the forest.

"If I might speak with the monks," Ch'eng Hao said, "all of them at once, it might give me the perspective necessary to understand the murderous act."

The Patriarch stood. "It shall be so."

Ch'eng I measured the distance from the edge of the forest to the temple using his own footsteps for a standard. Forty paces brought him from the nearest trees to the entrance.

It was extraordinary, he thought, that such a thing was possible. For surely the attacker had concealed himself in the forest – Kung had been facing his attacker when he had been hit in the throat after all, and he would not have stood still had he seen that an attack was imminent. But for a pellet of metal, even a small one, to be propelled forty paces through the air, then through a man's neck, then for this pellet to penetrate three finger-widths deep into a solid earthen wall . . . It was extraordinary indeed.

But more extraordinary things had happened in history. Had not the Yellow Emperor fought off an army single-handedly? Had not the Duke of Chou braved the fury of heaven and lived? A metal ball had been propelled with great force? So be it. It remained only to determine how it had been accomplished.

No arm could be strong enough, Ch'eng I decided quickly, or at least no *human* arm could. An inhuman arm was a possibility he did not care to contemplate. But murder, he knew, was not a tool of the spirits. Murder was an act of man against man.

This knowledge reassured Ch'eng I. If a man had done it, a man *could* do it, as impossible as it appeared to be. And if a man could do it, then Ch'eng I could figure out how. It was that simple.

The monks under the Seventh Patriarch's tutelage drew together in their largest building, one they normally used for the preparation and service of meals. Ch'eng Hao stood next to the Patriarch, who instructed the monks to answer all of the investigator's questions.

There appeared to be no resistance to this order; Ch'eng Hao had feared there might be. But then resistance, he knew, like dishonesty, does not always appear on a man's face when it burns in his heart. It remained to be seen whether the monks actually *would* answer his questions, or whether they would dance around him with elaborate riddles and pointless anecdotes as their Master had done.

"A man has been murdered," Ch'eng Hao said to the assembled monks. It was best to get the basic information out of the way immediately. "As most of you know, it was your fellow monk, Kung." It galled Ch'eng Hao to refer to the dead man only by his chosen name; the man had once had two names like everyone else, and neither had been "Kung." But Kung was the name he had taken when he had severed his ties with his earthly family, and Kung was the name by which his fellows knew him. Ch'eng Hao swallowed his contempt and went on. "Kung was killed in a most unusual manner. My esteemed brother, Ch'eng I, is investigating this aspect of his death. I am concerned with only one question. That question is, *Who killed Kung?*" Knowing the positive effect of a weighty pause, Ch'eng Hao paused.

"It was almost certainly someone in this room."

No one moved. It was unnerving, Ch'eng Hao thought, the stoicism with which they received this accusation. Any other roomful of people would have been fidgeting with anxiety and outrage. Not these men. They would not fidget if their own parents accused them of murdering their children. Of course, for that they would have had to have children, as most – shamefully enough – did not.

"I will speak with each of you in turn," Ch'eng Hao said. "If any of you know anything about Kung's death, I strongly suggest you divulge it without hesitation." Still no response. "You," he said, picking a fellow out of the front row at random. "You will be first."

Ch'eng I bent over the corpse and inhaled deeply. It was not only death he smelled, though that scent was powerful; there was an acrid edge to the still air in the temple, a smell of fire and ashes. Incense was Ch'eng I's first thought, but he found no sign that an incense burner had been in the temple: the ground was unbroken and the walls showed no smoke stains. Then, too, the smell lacked the pungent sweetness of incense. But something, he was convinced, had been burning.

He put that thought aside and began a meticulous study of Kung's body. Ch'eng I searched it inch by inch, making mental notes as he went. The monk had been relatively healthy, he saw – somewhat undernourished, perhaps, but then who these days was not?

The first curious observation Ch'eng I made was when he came to Kung's right hand. The fleshy pads of his fingers were singed – not so severely burned as to destroy the flesh, but burned all the same, as though Kung had taken hold of something burning and had not let go. This corroborated Ch'eng I's earlier suspicion, but beyond corroboration it offered little other than puzzlement.

The second curious observation was this: Kung's head was scarred in two places, at the base of his skull and under his chin. The scarring had evidently occurred many years before, appearing now only as raised, white scar tissue against the dark tan of the rest of Kung's head. But the scarring was clearly not the result of an accident, since the two scars were identical – the shape was that of the character *wang*, three short horizontal lines intersected by a vertical.

Ch'eng I considered this for some time, deciding eventually that it was most likely the result of early childhood scarification, a common enough practice among the families of the plains. Kung's father would have placed the mark on his son, as his father's father must have done before him, and his great-grandfather before that. Ch'eng I could not help but wonder if this brutal tradition had influenced the young Kung in his decision to abandon his family for the monastery.

This thought, too, Ch'eng I set aside for further consideration at another time. Soon the body would start to decompose in earnest and at that point no further study would be possible. Ch'eng I focused his attention on the wound. It was at this point that he made his third curious observation: the neck of Kung's robe had no hole in it.

"Would you say that Kung was a well-liked man?" Ch'eng Hao asked.

"I would say that Kung was a man." A heavyset monk named Tso sat across from Ch'eng Hao, looking and acting like a stone wall.

"Had Kung no enemies?"

"Is one who bears you ill will an enemy?"

"I would say so."

"Then evidently he had at least one enemy," Tso said.

"But you have no idea who that might be."

Tso said nothing. He was well trained, Ch'eng Hao thought. Half the art of Buddhism is appearing to have all the answers and the other half is being sure never to give them. Even the Patriarch had been more helpful than this.

"You may go," Ch'eng Hao said. Tso was difficult on purpose, but then so were all the other monks he had interviewed. He had no reason to believe that Tso knew anything about Kung's death.

On his way out, Tso sent the next man in.

Bo-Tze was the oldest of the monks, by at least ten years. If he was not quite as old as the Patriarch, it was only because *no one* else was that old. The Patriarch was four hundred and three, rumor said; and even if rumor exaggerated, the Patriarch had certainly seen the tail end of ninety and was moving up on the century mark. Bo-Tze, Ch'eng Hao guessed, was about sixty.

His face had the texture of a hide left too long out in the sun and his robe was more worn than the others Ch'eng Hao had seen. He looked well weathered, a point Ch'eng Hao knew Bo-Tze would have prided himself on if monks permitted themselves pride. Unlike the

other monks Ch'eng Hao had spoken to, Bo-Tze sat in front of him
without even a trace of nervousness.

"Mister Ch'eng," Bo-Tze said, stressing the family name with
disdain, "Kung was an undisciplined man. This was quite a serious
problem. Do you know anything about Ch'an Buddhism, Mister
Ch'eng? Ch'an is not what people in the world outside the monasteries
think it is. Ch'an means 'meditation,' and meditation is our practice.
Silent meditation: internal quiet, external harmony." The old monk
took a raspy breath. Ch'eng Hao waited for him to continue.

"Kung was a dreamer and a visionary. We do *not* have visions,
Mister Ch'eng. We are not the navel-staring mystics you think
we are."

"I think no such thing," Ch'eng Hao said. Then: "Kung had
visions?"

"Irrepressible visions," Bo-Tze said. "Or *irrepressed*, in any event.
All men pray, in their fashion; Kung thought that his prayers were
answered. When he meditated, he saw visions. He turned these
visions into art — into art and into artifice. Then Heaven saw fit
to strike him down. Surely this tells us something."

"What does it tell us?"

"That Kung's visions were not favored by . . ." Bo-Tze seemed to
be groping for a concept.

"By . . .?" Ch'eng Hao prodded.

"By a force powerful enough to do to him what was done to him."

"Which was?"

"I do not know, Mister Ch'eng." Bo-Tze kept up his placid facade,
but Ch'eng Hao sensed a vein of anger in his voice. "But it killed
him. I regret his death, of course — " of course, Ch'eng Hao thought
"— but only because he died unenlightened. He will return to plague
this world again and again until he achieves Nirvana, which he never
will if he keeps on like this. *Visions!*" Bo-Tze spat the word out like
a plum pit.

Vituperation aside, this was the most information Ch'eng Hao had
gotten about the dead man from anyone. Kung had had visions? At
last, a line of inquiry to pursue.

"Where is this 'art' you referred to," Ch'eng Hao asked, "in which
Kung recorded his visions?"

Bo-Tze waved the question away. "In his cell, I am sure. But you
do not understand. Kung was doing things he should not have been
doing. This is why he died."

"You mean it is why you killed him," Ch'eng Hao ventured.

Bo-Tze absorbed the remark with a slow blink of his eyelids. "I
did not kill Kung," he said. "A monk does not kill."

Monks *do* kill, Ch'eng Hao wanted to say, or at least one monk did, since a monk is now dead and it does not look as though suicide is a plausible explanation. But he said none of this. "You may go."

Bo-Tze rose calmly and exited. Only Lin-Yu remained for Ch'eng Hao to see.

A grotesque figure, Lin-Yu moved painfully and with great difficulty. His legs were withered almost to the point of uselessness, but somehow they just managed to keep his great bulk from collapsing. One sleeve of his robe flapped empty at his side and he was missing an eye. The empty socket stared at Ch'eng Hao. He looked aside.

"Bo-Tze tells me that Kung had visions," Ch'eng Hao said. "Do you know anything about this?"

"Bo-Tze is an old man. He talks too much and thinks too little." Lin-Yu's voice was soft, almost feminine. "Kung was a fortunate man, possessed of life's most generous curse: a creative soul. He created in a night's sleep works of greater ingenuity than most men create in a lifetime of waking hours. Kung was the best man here."

"What were the visions visions *of*?" Ch'eng Hao asked.

"Everything." Ch'eng Hao had expected this: a typically obscure Ch'an answer. But Lin-Yu explained, "Sometimes, merely images. Mandalas, with a thousand buddhas in the eye of the thousand-and-first. You can see some of these – the Patriarch keeps them in his cell. He appreciated Kung's talent."

"But surely there was more to it than mandalas – "

"Oh, of course!" Excitement lit Lin-Yu's face. "He dreamt machines and tools – why do you think we are able to farm on such poor land as we have? Kung created tools for us. The universal buddha nature spoke through him, gave him knowledge of the unknown . . . For instance – "

Lin-Yu stood and lifted the skirts of his robe. His withered legs were bound in metal-and-leather braces with fabric joints at the knees. "Kung made these for me. Mister Ch'eng, please understand, Kung was a genius and a compassionate soul. This is a very rare and special combination."

Ch'eng Hao noticed that when Lin-Yu said, "Mister Ch'eng" the words carried no tone of disapproval.

"I believe you," Ch'eng Hao said. "I only wish the others had been as open with me as you are."

"The others are performing for you, Mister Ch'eng," Lin-Yu said. "How often do they have the pleasure of an outsider's presence? They want to show each other how good they can be at the game. They have much to learn. But then, don't we all?"

Much to learn. Yes, Ch'eng Hao thought, we have much to learn.

I, for instance, have to learn who killed this compassionate, visionary monk – so far I have made little progress. "Thank you," Ch'eng Hao said. He hoped he sounded more appreciative than he knew he usually did. "You may go."

"One moment please!" Ch'eng I dashed into the room through the parted tapestry that hung over the entrance. He put a hand on Lin-Yu's shoulder. "There are questions *I* must ask, brother." Ch'eng Hao nodded his assent.

"What can I tell you?" Lin-Yu asked.

Ch'eng I helped Lin-Yu once more to a seated position. "Please describe for me the condition in which you found Kung's body."

"Kung was dead," Lin-Yu said. The words came haltingly and tears formed in Lin-Yu's single eye. "He had a wound in his throat. There was blood all over the ground."

"You say 'throat,'" Ch'eng I said. "Do you not mean 'neck'?"

Lin-Yu considered this. "I suppose 'neck' is as good. I said 'throat' because he was on his back."

"He was on his back," Ch'eng I repeated. "Fascinating. And he was not wearing his hood?"

"No," Lin-Yu said, "he was. His hood was on."

"Brother," Ch'eng Hao said, "have you gone mad? You know all this. This is how he was when *we* saw the body."

Ch'eng I turned to his brother. "You must be less cavalier with your accusations, Hao. I am not mad, merely curious. You see," here he turned back to Lin-Yu, "when we saw him, Kung *was* as you describe. But this is not how he was when he was killed."

Lin-Yu arched an eyebrow; it was the one above the empty socket and Ch'eng Hao had to look away again.

"I have spent a good deal of time examining Kung's body," Ch'eng I said. "He was hit with this." He pulled the lump of metal from its pouch and showed it to Lin-Yu. "But he was not hit in the throat. He was hit in the back of the neck. He did not fall backward; he fell forward. And he was not wearing his hood at the time."

"How do you know all this?" Ch'eng Hao asked, caught between admiration and disbelief.

"Simple." Ch'eng I ticked off points on his fingers. "The pellet penetrated Kung's neck and continued to the opposite wall. Yet there was no hole in Kung's hood. How can this be? Kung was not wearing his hood.

"Next: the front of Kung's robe was soaked with blood as well as the back. If the force of the attack had knocked him backwards, the front of his robe would have received very little blood. If, on the other hand, he fell forward, into his pooling blood, it

**180**  CHARLES ARDAI

would account for the condition of his robe. Therefore, he fell forward.

"Finally: the wound on the back of his neck was smaller and more contained than the wound in his throat. This suggests that the latter was the exit wound, not the entry wound. Therefore, he was hit in the back of the neck."

"Very well," Ch'eng Hao said. "I accept your analysis. But why then was Kung not on his chest with his hood off when Lin-Yu found him?"

"Someone changed the position of Kung's body," Ch'eng I said. "Turned him over and covered his head." Also, he said to himself, took away whatever had been burning in the temple and erased all signs of his presence. "Why someone would do this is a mystery. However, we do know now that there was someone with Kung when he died."

"Yes, the murderer," Ch'eng Hao said. "We already knew that."

"No," said Ch'eng I, "a third man. Because the murderer was at the edge of the forest directly across from the temple entrance – where I searched and found this." He undid the strings of the largest pouch on his belt and poured two objects out onto the floor: a small metal mallet and a flattened metal capsule not much larger than the murder weapon.

"What is this?" Lin-Yu asked. He picked up the mallet and turned it over in his hands. The head was remarkably heavy for a tool so small.

"It is part of the murderer's device," Ch'eng I said. "I am still trying to piece together just how the device operated. It would help if I had it in its entirety. However, these pieces give us a starting point. Smell the capsule."

Ch'eng Hao picked up the dented metal packet. "You mean this?" Ch'eng I nodded. Ch'eng Hao sniffed at it. "It smells like . . ." He hesitated. "I cannot place it. But I know I have smelled it before." He handed the capsule to Lin-Yu.

"Black powder," Lin-Yu said as soon as he put the piece to his nose. "We use it from time to time for certain ceremonies. In explosive pyrotechnics."

Ch'eng I nodded enthusiastically; his suspicions had been confirmed. "A bamboo tube," he recited, "packed with black powder. One end open, the other closed except for a tiny hole. A fuse is attached to the latter. An explosive projectile is placed in the tube above the powder. The fuse is lit. The ignition of the powder ejects the projectile, which in turn explodes in mid-air. Am I correct?"

"That is how the fireworks work, yes," Lin-Yu said, "although I cannot imagine how you found out. It is a secret among monks – "

"I have experimented on my own," Ch'eng I said abruptly. "The principles are readily apparent. What is not so clear is how they were adapted to destructive ends." He thought the problem through aloud. "A narrower tube to suit the smaller projectile, I imagine . . . and, of course, the tube would be aimed at a target rather than at the sky . . . and in place of a fuse, this capsule . . . the capsule containing a small amount of black powder, which when compressed by a blow from the mallet explodes, igniting the main load of powder in the tube . . . and finally, a tripod to steady the apparatus, to account for the three circular indentations in the soil where I found the mallet and the capsule." Ch'eng I folded his arms and waited for his brother's reaction.

"Fireworks as a weapon," Ch'eng Hao whispered. "Ingenious." Then he realized what he had said and he shot a glance at Lin-Yu, whose expression betrayed that he had had the same thought. Ch'eng Hao voiced it for both of them. "One of Kung's inventions."

"No one else could have invented it," Lin-Yu said.

Ch'eng I was taken back. "You think Kung invented the weapon that killed him? I find that unlikely – "

Ch'eng Hao silenced him. "I will tell you what *I* have learned while you were away," he said. "In the meantime, we should see Kung's cell. I will fill you in on the way."

The cells they passed on the way to Kung's were as bare as the temple. Wooden cots with no matting were the only furniture the brothers saw and the walls were unadorned. But Kung's cell was different. He, too, had the painful-looking cot – but every inch of his walls was covered with ink drawings and elaborate calligraphy.

As Lin-Yu had said, much of the art was religious. One entire wall, for instance, was devoted to images of the Buddha and his boddhisatvas in intricate interrelations. The painting was flat and monochromatic, but somehow deeply hypnotic.

It was the other walls that revealed Kung's true genius, however, for it was there that he had composed dozens of sketches for tools and devices of mind-boggling complexity. Lin-Yu's braces were on the wall, along with drawings of the special plows and wells Kung had designed for the monks – as well as plenty of drawings of objects at whose function the brothers could only guess. The one drawing that was conspicuously absent from the wall was that of the murder weapon. None of the sketches looked similar to the machine Ch'eng I had described.

"All of these," Lin-Yu said when Ch'eng Hao asked, "are devices that Kung actually finished and gave to us. Perhaps the weapon was not perfected yet."

"It certainly worked well enough," Ch'eng Hao said.

"We do *not* know that for certain," Ch'eng I corrected his brother. "We do not yet know what happened."

"If these are Kung's finished inventions," Ch'eng Hao asked Lin-Yu, "where did he sketch ideas for new projects?"

"On the floor," Lin-Yu said. He indicated a sharp stick leaning against the cot and then a particularly scarred portion of the dirt floor. It did look as though Kung had used the space for this purpose – Ch'eng I was able to make out a character here and there – but trying to "read" it would have been futile.

"Had he no more permanent record?" Ch'eng I asked.

Lin-Yu knelt in front of the cot and reached under it. After groping for a few seconds he pulled out a flat metal board. "He used this from time to time. When he wanted to show an idea to the Patriarch, for instance. He would stretch a piece of fabric over it and then draw on it." Lin-Yu pointed to four hook-shaped protrusions at the corners of the board. "He designed this, too."

"So there may be a fabric sketch of the weapon somewhere . . ." Ch'eng Hao began – but Ch'eng I was already out of the room.

Ch'eng Hao ran after him. Lin-Yu followed as quickly as he could. They caught up with him outside Bo-Tze's cell. Ch'eng I burst in before they could restrain him.

Bo-Tze was seated in the lotus position on his cot, his legs crossed tightly over one another, his hands outstretched on his knees. As Ch'eng I entered, Bo-Tze opened his eyes with a start and dropped his hands to his sides.

"You were contemptuous of your fellow monk," Ch'eng I said without preamble. Then, in answer to the confusion in the old man's eyes, "My brother told me what you said about Kung. That he had 'visions' – and that you hated him for it. That you feel the world looks down on *you* because of men like him. That on some level you were obsessively jealous of him."

"I was never jealous of that man," Bo-Tze snarled. In the heat of confrontation, he did not even try to hide his anger. "He was a disgrace to us."

"Why?" Lin-Yu asked. There was pain and loss in his voice. "Because of his imagination?"

"Yes," Bo-Tze said, "if you want to call it that. But that is not all. He was dealing with the outside world!"

Lin-Yu shook his head. "That is ludicrous."

"I agree," Bo-Tze said. "It is ludicrous. It is also a fact. Kung was not just creating things for our use. He was also selling his creations in the secular world. He was not a monk – he was a merchant!"

"No," Lin-Yu insisted. "You know he never left the grounds. How could he – "

"Are you *completely* blind now?" Bo-Tze shouted. "*Wu* sold Kung's goods for him."

"Wu Han-Fei?" Ch'eng Hao asked. "The messenger?"

"Our 'link to the secular world,'" Bo-Tze said sarcastically. "It was a mistake to employ him, as I predicted it would be. But who talked the Patriarch into it? Kung did! Do you not see? *Do none of you see?*"

"It is clear that you want desperately to prove yourself right," Ch'eng I said. "Is that why you went to the temple this morning when you knew Kung was there?"

Bo-Tze's guard went up at last. "I was nowhere near the temple," he said.

Ch'eng I reached out and grabbed Bo-Tze's right hand. Bo-Tze resisted but Ch'eng I was by far the stronger man. Slowly, Ch'eng I turned the monk's hand palm upwards. The pads of Bo-Tze's fingers were seared red. "Note the singed fingers," Ch'eng I said. "Compare them to the seared fingers of Kung's body. Identical."

Bo-Tze pulled his hand away. "Yes," he said, breaking down at last, "yes, I was there! I was there because it was my last chance to expose Kung to the lot of you!" Ch'eng Hao was surprised – it was hard to believe that this was the same man he had interrogated unsuccessfully so recently. Corner a lion in the field and it attacks, he reminded himself, but corner one in its den and it falls at your feet.

"I cornered Wu outside the dining hall," Bo-Tze said furiously. "He is a coward! I threatened to expose him, and he turned on Kung like this." Bo-Tze snapped his trembling fingers. "Wu said that Kung had gone to the temple to burn all the evidence of their dealings. I went there to get this evidence for myself. Sure enough, Kung was there. There was a sheet of cloth stretched out on that metal board of his and he had already set it on fire. I grabbed it; he grabbed it, too. We struggled over it – then, all of a sudden, there was a loud explosion and Kung fell forward with blood spurting all over his face and I ran out of there as quickly as I could . . ." Bo-Tze was crying and out of breath; his chest heaved and his head sank forward until it almost touched his ankles.

Ch'eng Hao pulled his brother and Lin-Yu out of the room. Bo-Tze was not the murderer they sought, Ch'eng Hao knew; and at an exposed moment like this even a Buddhist deserved his privacy.

The Patriarch's cell was no larger than any of the others. He slept on the same cot. But like Kung's, his walls were not bare. Also like Kung's, his walls were covered with Kung's art: complex ink drawings, passionate attempts to render the transcendent universe accessible to the human eye – Ch'eng Hao would have found it all very moving if he had been a Buddhist. As it was, he could only marvel at the artist's skill.

"We all have our failings," the Patriarch said. He was staring at Kung's largest image and his voice betrayed the rapture he felt. "Kung was an artist at heart, I a connoisseur. Neither is appropriate for a monk: a monk must lose all attachments to the things of this world, because such things, in their impermanence, can only produce suffering. The more beautiful a thing is, the more pain it will bring by its inevitable absence." The Patriarch sighed. "Yet if life is suffering, can we not take from it what little pleasure there is to be had? How could I tell Kung not to paint? That would have increased his suffering – surely our purpose is not *that*."

"There is more to this matter than the art," Ch'eng Hao said.

"Yes," the Patriarch said. "The tools. I should let my men starve rather than use the tools Kung devised? This is Bo-Tze's position, but he is a fool. If we cannot use Kung's tools, from the same argument we should not use any tools at all. We should dig in the dirt with our hands as our ancestors did. Perhaps we should not farm at all, since our oldest ancestors did not. Innovation is not evil; new tools are not worse than old. And heaven knows it is easier to meditate with a full belly than an empty one. Gautama himself said so – the Buddha himself! Starvation is not for Buddhists any more than decadence is."

"I understand," Ch'eng Hao said, "and I agree. But there remains the question of Kung's trade with the outside world."

For a long time, the Patriarch was silent.

"Bo-Tze says – "

"He is correct," the Patriarch whispered. "I looked the other way."

"You knew – "

"Ch'eng Hao, how could I not know?" At this moment the Patriarch looked very old and helpless. "I simply chose to tolerate it. Kung was too special a man, and too valuable to our lives, for me to risk losing him over such a minor point. So he sent his creations to people like yourself? There are graver sins. Perhaps it even made some Confucians think twice before cursing us. Surely it did no harm."

"No harm," Ch'eng Hao said, "but now Kung is dead."

"Yes," the Patriarch said. "That is so. And this is what comes of forming attachments to things of this world – now that we have lost him, we suffer."

Ch'eng Hao considered for a moment. "When we first spoke, you indicated that Kung had grave matters on his conscience. But if he knew that you tolerated his dealings with the outside world, surely he was not anxious about that?" The Patriarch shook his head. "What then?"

"I repeat what I told you before: I do not know."

Ch'eng Hao let this pass. "Just one more question," he said. "When Kung traded his goods through Wu Han-Fei, what did he get in return? Not money, obviously; he had no use for that."

The Patriarch shrugged. "It is a question I never considered." Ch'eng Hao could see from the Patriarch's face that he really *hadn't* considered it. "Perhaps he simply received the satisfaction of knowing his creations were being put to good use."

*To good use.* The phrase resonated for Ch'eng Hao. Yes, he thought, good use. But surely that was not all?

Lin-Yu directed Ch'eng I to a small building on the outskirts of the monastery complex. It was no more than a hut, really, but a solid and well-constructed one as huts went. Lin-Yu stood guard outside the door while Ch'eng I went inside.

A few minutes later, Ch'eng I emerged carrying a scorched square of fabric and a bamboo tube.

Ch'eng I steadied the tripod he had brought by pressing it down in the damp soil at the edge of the forest. The bamboo tube was clamped in place, the repaired capsule inserted in the tube's smaller hole. Lin-Yu had procured the necessary black powder and, what was equally important, the spare monk's robe that knelt, stuffed to overflowing with straw and twigs, just inside the temple entrance. Ch'eng Hao held back the small crowd of onlookers he had gathered: the Patriarch, Bo-Tze, Tso, and a handful of other monks. Wu Han-Fei was not among the group.

"I am ready," Ch'eng I announced.

Lin-Yu moved to join the others. They all turned to face the dummy Ch'eng I had erected.

Ch'eng I aimed the bamboo tube carefully, sighting along its length. Then he inserted the small white stone he had selected as a projectile and took several test swings with the mallet. He steadied himself with two deep breaths.

"Proceed," Ch'eng Hao said.

Ch'eng I swung the mallet again. This time it connected with a sharp crack, squeezing the capsule flat. This tiny explosion was followed by a much larger one, one that startled all the spectators. Even Bo-Tze, who knew what to expect, started at the noise.

But the dummy did not fall. After the cloud of smoke around him cleared, Ch'eng I inspected the tube. The projectile *had* been ejected. He ran to the temple and made a quick search of the far wall. The white stone he had chosen expressly for this reason stood out clearly against the brown of the packed earth in which it was now embedded.

"Come here," he said. The others crowded into the temple, pushing the dummy aside. They stared at the stone in the wall as though it was a religious relic and worthy of their rapt attention. Ch'eng I pushed his way back through the crowd until he was able to join his brother outside the temple.

"You missed," Ch'eng Hao said.

"Indeed. It was the strike of the mallet that ruined my aim. I had not taken it into account."

"Never mind," Ch'eng Hao said. "It is of no consequence. You will never need to use that cursed instrument again."

"I do not doubt that you are right," Ch'eng I said, "but I disagree that it is of no consequence. You see – "

But at that moment Bo-Tze and the Patriarch exited the temple and intruded on the brothers' conversation.

"So that is how the murder was accomplished," the Patriarch said, clapping a hand to the small of Ch'eng I's back.

"Wu used Kung's own machine against him when he thought Kung might expose him," Bo-Tze said, his voice once again thick with disdain. "In a thief's camp, no man sleeps with both eyes closed. Kung should have known Wu would silence him if it ever proved necessary."

"How and why the murder was committed," Ch'eng Hao agreed. "You now have your answers. And we must give full credit to Ch'eng I for the greater part of this investigation – his methods proved most fruitful."

"Esteemed brother," Ch'eng I said, holding up his hand for silence, "I do not deserve your praise, or indeed any man's, if I allow the investigation to end here."

"What do you mean?" the Patriarch said. "We have seen proof – or do you, of all people, think that this was not the murder weapon?" He gestured toward the distant tripod.

"It was the murder weapon," Ch'eng I agreed.

"And did you not find the weapon, together with other incriminating evidence, in the hut of Wu Han-Fei?" Bo-Tze added.

"I did," Ch'eng I said.

Even Ch'eng Hao was confused. "And did you not put Wu Han-Fei in restraints? Surely you would not have done that unless you were as convinced as we are that he is the murderer."

"I did and I am," Ch'eng I said, "but that is only the beginning of an answer to what went on here this morning. You wrongly indict a man if you credit him with motives he did not hold."

Ch'eng Hao put a hand on Ch'eng I's shoulder. "Brother, I bow to your expertise in matters scientific, but do me the courtesy of acknowledging my insight into human character. It has to be as I explained it to you.

"Kung distributed his creations as widely as he could out of sheer good will. Lin-Yu testifies to this. Wu Han-Fei, on the other hand, had a more concrete motive for getting involved with Kung: he sold Kung's inventions for personal profit." The word "profit" always wore a sneer the way Ch'eng Hao said it, and this time was no exception.

"Recently," Ch'eng Hao continued, "Kung dreamt up the extraordinary weapon you just demonstrated. In his initial enthusiasm he gave a working model to Wu. But Kung was a compassionate man, dedicated to the easing of life's sufferings – consider his other inventions: implements to improve farming, Lin-Yu's leg braces, and so forth. Now, for the first time, he had created a weapon. This horrible realization, combined with the fact that he had placed it in the hands of an unscrupulous man, preyed mightily on his conscience. This is why he went to the temple: to destroy the plans for this device. The murderer stole the plans from the scene of Kung's death – and are they not the very same half-burned plans you found in Wu Han-Fei's hut?

"There is nothing more to know about this murder."

"Nothing?" Ch'eng I directed this remark at all three men, but his next was reserved for his brother. "I am disappointed in you, Hao. If Wu Han-Fei planned Kung's murder, why did he send Bo-Tze to the temple to witness it? You might argue that Bo-Tze *forced* Wu Han-Fei to tell him where Kung was – but if this was the case, why didn't Wu delay the murder until a more propitious time? And how do you explain the change in the position of Kung's body after his death?"

Ch'eng Hao said nothing.

"There can be only one answer," Ch'eng I said. "Wu Han-Fei knew Bo-Tze wanted to expose Kung's dealings with him, so he lured Bo-Tze to the temple with a story about Kung's 'destroying evidence.' Then he hid in the forest, intending to use Kung's weapon to silence Bo-Tze." Bo-Tze drew a sharp breath. "Kung was not Wu Han-Fei's intended target. Bo-Tze was."

"I bow to your superior perception," Ch'eng Hao said, grasping Ch'eng I's reasoning. "So you would argue that Wu Han-Fei wanted to kill Bo-Tze – but that from a distance of forty paces, two men in brown robes looked too similar to tell apart and as a result he killed the wrong man."

"No," Ch'eng I said. "Trust your own eyes. Do you not see that Bo-Tze's robe is considerably more worn than Kung's and that his skin looks visibly older? You will recall that at least one man was not wearing his hood."

"Very likely neither man was," Ch'eng Hao said. "But one bald head looks much like another – "

Ch'eng I shook his head. "They look entirely different."

"But from a distance of forty paces – "

"Entirely different," Ch'eng I said firmly. "It is not only that Bo-Tze's head looked older – Kung's bore a highly visible mark. A prominent scar at the top of his neck. Am I correct?" This question was directed to the Patriarch.

"You are," the Patriarch said.

"A scar?" Ch'eng Hao asked.

"Not just any scar," Ch'eng I said, "a family brand. Clearly visible at forty paces, particularly if one is looking for it. As I believe Wu Han-Fei was. Consider this: suppose you were right that Wu Han-Fei could not tell the two men apart – do you think under those circumstances that he would have used the weapon?"

After a moment, Ch'eng Hao slowly shook his head. "Then how do you account for what happened?"

"The device was not perfected," Ch'eng I said gravely. "Wu Han-Fei knew which man he wanted to hit. *He simply missed.*"

They stood outside Wu Han-Fei's hut, Ch'eng I and Ch'eng Hao, Bo-Tze and the Seventh Patriarch. They stood outside because none of them wanted to enter.

"If what you have said is true," Bo-Tze said, "then we have been victims of an even greater deception than I feared."

"It cannot be," the Patriarch said.

"There is only one demonstration that will convince you," said Ch'eng I. He stepped into the hut.

The other men followed. Inside, Wu Han-Fei was in a seated position, his wrists and ankles bound behind him. The room was furnished better than the monks' cells: there were small windows with mullioned glass panes and swing shutters controlled from the inside; a mattress padded with layers of reed matting; and a stool whose top opened to reveal a bowl and a set of utensils. Ch'eng I pointed all this out while Wu Han-Fei watched in silence.

"This is the extent of Wu Han-Fei's personal profit," Ch'eng I said. "Things Kung created especially for him. If he did sell Kung's goods for money, he kept none of it. Perhaps it was all sent back to . . . his family."

Ch'eng I walked behind Wu Han-Fei and put his hand on the kneeling man's head. "A fine head of hair. He is not a Buddhist, so he can keep his hair – and can live here at a distance from the monks. A neat arrangement. When they need something from the outside world – such as men to investigate a murder – he brings it. Otherwise, he is left to himself.

"But why would a man who is not a Buddhist attach himself to a monastery in this way? It is the worst of lives, surely, caught with one leg in each of two worlds that despise one another. One must have a compelling reason to choose such a life. Why," Ch'eng I asked Wu Han-Fei, "did you?"

Wu Han-Fei said nothing.

"This was one of the questions that bothered me." Ch'eng I said. "Why would he live here? And: why would he kill to protect a monk? What was the worst the monks could do to him if his activities were exposed – send him away? Hardly a severe punishment for a man who has no ties to the monastic life anyway. No, the man they could punish was Kung – but why would a mercenary secularist care?

"A fine head of hair," Ch'eng I said again, running his fingers through Wu Han-Fei's black locks. "A lifetime of growth concealing a scalp that hasn't seen the sun in thirty years." He turned to Ch'eng Hao. "You know, when we first met Wu, I thought he lowered his eyes out of respect for us, or perhaps fear. But then I realized it was neither – it was for want of a beard."

He bent forward over Wu's shoulder. "Look up," he commanded.

Wu Han-Fei shot a sullen glance at the ceiling.

"No," Ch'eng I said, "turn your head up." Wu Han-Fei did not respond. "Your *head*, Mister Wu . . ." – Ch'eng I took a tight grip on the young man's hair and pulled his head back – ". . . or should I say Mister *Wang*?"

Bo-Tze stared at the character carved in white relief on the underside of Wu Han-Fei's chin. The Patriarch sat on the edge of the mattress and put his head in his hands. Ch'eng I released Wu Han-Fei's head. "What was Kung's real name," he asked, "his birth name?"

"Wang," the Patriarch said, nodding, his voice rumbling like the largest and saddest of gongs. "Wang Deng-Mo."

"Wang Deng-Mo," Ch'eng I repeated. "And this, we can assume, is *Wang*, not Wu, Han-Fei."

"I do not understand," the Patriarch said. "Why . . .?"

"Why?" Ch'eng I said. "Because family is a more powerful bond than you give it credit for being. Kung took on a new identity when he joined your monastery – and so did his . . . brother?"

Wang Han-Fei let a single word escape through his clenched teeth. "Yes."

"His brother," Ch'eng I said. "As I thought. To maintain the family tie despite all else; to send resources back home, to help the rest of the family survive; to live and die and kill for a brother *because* he is a brother – *this* is 'why.' "

"But brother," Ch'eng Hao said, his face red with chagrin, "how could you possibly have known? What started you thinking in this direction?"

"The question that was at once the simplest and the most complex," Ch'eng I said. "Why had Kung's body been moved? Bo-Tze would not have done it, not when it would have meant returning to the scene of the murder. Lin-Yu might have done it but he would not have concealed it from us if he had. This meant it had to have been the murderer who had done it. But why would the murderer have moved Kung's body? I asked myself this question again and again.

"Then all at once I understood. Kung's body had not merely been moved. You will recall that Bo-Tze said Kung's blood spurted all over his face when he was hit – yet when we found the body, Kung's face was clean; his hood was neatly arranged; and he was lying on his back in a dignified position. It is no way for a man to be found, lying face down in his own blood – but that a killer recognizes this is most unusual. That is how I knew that the killer had compassion for his victim. More than compassion, even – love, and more than love, a sense of duty."

Ch'eng Hao had more questions to ask, and he asked them; Ch'eng I answered them in more detail than was absolutely necessary; Bo-Tze and the Patriarch left as quickly as they could; and no one noticed when off in his corner, his head hung low, Wang Han-Fei began to weep.

Ch'eng Hao sipped from a cup of bone-stock soup that Ch'eng I had prepared. Was that the faint flavor of tea he tasted, whispering under the rich marrow? Perhaps it was. Ch'eng Hao knew his brother was wont to experiment in the oddest directions. He set the cup down. "I would not have released him," he said.

Ch'eng I paused at the fire then went on stirring. "Why, brother? Because he was a killer and killers should not go unpunished?"

"No," Ch'eng Hao said. "He killed his brother. That was punishment enough for both of them."

"Why, then?"

"Because you should have known he would kill himself."

Ch'eng I tipped the stock pot forward to fill his cup. The thick soup steamed and he held his hands in the steam to warm them. "Forcing him to live would have been the most cruel of punishments. He could not have escaped the voice of censure no matter where he fled under heaven. A man's greatest freedom," Ch'eng I said, "is the freedom to hoard or spend his life as he chooses."

Ch'eng Hao could not disagree. "The tragedy of it is that a man such as Kung had to lie to live as he chose, that his brother had to lie to be near him, and that these lies accumulated until a killing became inevitable. A pointless killing . . ." He turned to other thoughts, less troubling for being more abstract. "I still do not understand, brother, how you knew to investigate Wu – Wang – in the first place. Even granting that you suspected that the killer was a family member – why him?"

"You were investigating the monks and making no progress," Ch'eng I said. "I trusted that had there been progress to be made, you would have made it. So I operated on the assumption that you were looking in the wrong direction entirely. As you were."

"But my approach was the logical one – "

"Yes, it was," Ch'eng I said, "but not the correct one. Therein lies one of life's great mysteries."

Ch'eng Hao bent once more to his soup. November winds were beginning to roar on the plains and the small warmth was welcome. The chill in his soul was not to be so easily dispelled. "I," he said, "If it came to that, would you kill to defend me?"

Ch'eng I looked up from his task. "I am your brother," he said. He brought the cup to his lips. "Heaven grant me good aim."

# THE MIDWIFE'S TALE
## Margaret Frazer

*In the previous volume I introduced the first short story featuring Sister Frevisse, a nun at the abbey of St Frideswide in fifteenth-century Oxfordshire. The character has appeared in four novels,* The Novice's Tale *(1992),* The Servant's Tale *(1993), which was nominated for an Edgar award,* The Outlaw's Tale *(1994), and* The Bishop's Tale *(1994). The next in the series,* The Boy's Tale *should be published by the time this book appears.*

> O cursed synne of alle cursedness!
> O traytours homycide, O wikkednesse!
>
> *The Pardoner's Tale*

The light from the yet unrisen sun flowed softly gold and rose between the long blue shadows of the village houses and across the fields and hedgerows full of birdsong. Ada Bychurch, standing in the doorway of Martyn Fisher's low-eaved house, shivered a little in the morning's coolness and huddled her cloak around her, hoping for more warmth from its worn gray wool.

She wished she could as readily huddle away from the sorrow in the house behind her. She was village midwife and had done what she could but it had not been enough and now there was nothing left but the hope that after Father Clement's ministrations, Cisily's soul would go safe to whatever blessings she had earned in her short life. But despite her faith Ada could not help the feeling Cisily's mortal life had been too short. Far too short for the motherless newborn daughter and the grieving husband she was leaving behind her, however fortunate Cisily was to be soon free of the world's troubles.

Martyn Fisher's house was at the nunnery end of the village, just before the lane curved and the houses ended and the road ran on a quarter mile or so between fields to the nunnery gates. Cisily had often said how she loved the fact that there were no houses across the way from her, that she could see through a field gate to the countryside from her front doorstep. And she had been pleased,

too, that just leftward not so very far was the village green and all
the village busyness.

Priors Byfield was a fair-sized village, with all a village's interests
and pleasures. Ada looked toward the green where the last drift of
smoke from last night's Midsummer bonfire was a fading smudge
across the sunrise. The revelling had gone on nearly to dawn as
usual, and she doubted anyone would be out to the early plowing
and knew for certain that the bailiff would be hard put to bring folk
to the haying by late morning or maybe even afternoon despite the
fact it looked to be a second fine, fair day after a week of damp and
drizzle. It had been taken as a sign of God's favor when yesterday
had early cleared for the young folk to be off to the woods and ways
to gather Midsummer greenery and the older folk to build up the
bonfire for the evening's dancing and sport.

Father Clement had given his usual sharp sermon last Sunday
against what he felt were such unchristian ways, but the Midsummer
bonfire and other such revelling through the year were like the bone
in the village's body: no one could imagine doing without them. And
Ada doubted that even Father Clement would have grudged Cisily
Fisher her midsummer revels this year, if it could have replaced her
slow bleeding to death in childbed. Hardly a year married and now
this, and her husband still so in love with her he had dared, when
it was clear there was nothing else Ada as midwife could do, to go
to the nunnery and beg for their infirmarian's help. He must have
pleaded most pitiably because the infirmarian had not merely sent
some mix of medicines but come herself and was still here, though
there was no more hope for Cisily's life, only for a painless death and
nothing left for anyone to do except give comfort.

"I pray you, pardon me," someone said softly behind Ada's
shoulder. She looked around, then moved out of the doorway and
aside on the broad, flat stone that served as step beyond the low
doorsill, out of the way for the nun who had accompanied Dame
Claire, the infirmarian, from the priory.

With an acknowledging bow of her head, she stepped out, raised her
face to the lightening sky and drew a deep breath. Her face was almost
as pale as the white wimple that encircled it inside the black frame
of her veil, and Ada guessed that, like her, she had been unable to
endure the stifling, blood-tainted air inside the house any longer.

Ada thought she remembered her name and hazarded, "Dame
Frevisse, aren't you?"

The nun inclined her head again, politely, but said nothing. And
that was only right, Ada supposed. In cloister or out they were
supposed to be as silent as might be; and of course, being a

nun, she was far better born than Ada, was at least of gentle and maybe even noble blood. She was tall for a woman, with a strong-boned face and beautifully kept, long-fingered hands. Her gown was plain Benedictine black, just as it should be, but amply made from fine-woven wool, its color all even despite black being notoriously hard to dye, and there were uncountable small black buttons from wrist to nearly elbow of the black undergown's tight sleeves. Probably more buttons than any ten women of the village had all together, Ada guessed. But except for the gold ring on her left wedding finger and her belt-hung rosary of richly polished wood, she had no finery such as Ada had heard tell was all too common among some nuns. Nor did she seem arrogant, only tired and sad, and Ada liked her the better for it.

They stood silently side by side while the daylight broadened around them and birdsong rose from hedgerows as if joy were newly discovered in the world, until in the house, where there had been deep stillness for this while and a while past, people began to move, to talk low among themselves, some of them trying to comfort a man weeping. The wait was over and the task of dealing with the dead was come. It was a task that every village woman knew, and all did their best at it, knowing it was something that sooner or later would have to be done for each of them, when her time came.

The baby made a mewling cry and was quieted. She seemed healthy enough, was already baptized, and Johane living just down the way had already said she would suckle it with her own, she having milk enough for a calf, as she put it, so that was all right.

Ada knew she should go back in now, was bracing herself for it when someone came up behind her in the doorway. She and Dame Frevisse both shifted further aside to make way, Ada supposing it was Dame Claire, leaving now there was nothing more the nuns could do, but it was Elyn Browster, Cisily's neighbor from two houses farther along, right at the village's very end. Though barren herself, Elyn was at almost every child birthing and always took a loss like this to heart; and this one even more to heart than usual, it looked like. Normally a vigorous, wide-gesturing woman, she was gray-faced with weariness and grief and she would have gone between Ada and the nun without speaking except Ada said, "It's a sorry thing. Martyn is taking it hard, seems."

"There'll be those who'll comfort him," Elyn said and went on without pause or a look up from where her feet were trudging. It was the way she showed pain, Ada knew. She had feelings that cut deep, did Elyn, but kept them to herself as much as might be.

"Jenkyn to see to?" Ada asked at her back.

"Aye," Elyn said and went on, a swag-hipped woman on tired feet, along the verge of the lane still muddy from the past few days of rain.

"She's a good woman, is Elyn Browster," Ada said, not because she thought Dame Frevisse needed to know but simply to have something in her own mind besides thought of Cisily lying dead now. "Her husband Jenkyn, he's not much and would be less if it weren't for her. She's had to take the man's part around their holding more often than not because he won't. It's not what she wanted when she married him, I'd guess, but she's never faltered. She – "

Ada broke off as she found Dame Frevisse's gaze fixed on her with a disconcerting directness that made her realize she had been gossiping to someone who not only had no interest in such things, but should not be hearing them at all.

She was saved from deciding what to say next by Dame Claire, the infirmarian, coming out. She was a small woman and seemed smaller for being beside Dame Frevisse. She looked as sad and tired as Elyn Browster had and her surprisingly deep voice grated with weariness as she said, "I think maybe you should go in, Mistress Bychurch. Father Clement is beginning to comfort Martyn Fisher."

Knowing exactly what that meant, Ada dropped a deep curtsy to them both and hurried back into the house. Father Clement might be a good priest, but he was rigid and had no gift for solace. What Martyn needed was real comforting, a shoulder to cry on and someone saying how sorry they were, not a lecture on how priceless was the saved soul gone to God.

Just as Frevisse had, Dame Claire lifted her face to the clear, bright sky and drew a deep breath. The early light had thickened to a flow of molten gold now; the thick dew on the grass was sheened to silver.

"The baby looks likely to live," Dame Claire said.

"And the woman who's taking her to nurse seems clean and healthy." Frevisse offered that comfort as gently as she could. St Frideswide's Priory was small, with only eleven nuns, and set lonely in the Oxfordshire countryside, so that all of them had to have as many skills as they could. To that end, Frevisse had been set this past half year to assist Dame Claire in her duties as infirmarian and learn from her. Though not so apt as Dame Claire at herbs and healing, she had done well enough, able to do what she was told and to grasp Dame Claire's admonition, "You have to try to understand what's happening inwardly as well as outwardly to a body, and you have to think about what it means or you can never well tend to anyone's hurts or illness, only pretend to."

What Frevisse understood now was that Dame Claire was grieving

for the woman she had not known until a few hours ago and had not
been able to save. Unable to say anything to mend or comfort that
– assuredly nothing so useless as "You did what you could" – she
held silent, both of them gazing out at the morning, until in a while
Dame Claire sighed deeply, said, "Come then. We'd best be going,"
and stepped away from the door, bound for the nunnery.

Side by side as much as they could while keeping to what there
was of a grassy verge along the muddy road, they passed the last few
houses of the village, walking quickly, partly to warm themselves
against the morning's chill, partly in hope that though they were
surely late for the office of Prime and its dawn prayers, they might
be in time for breakfast and Mass.

They were beyond the last house, with only the dawn-bright road
and hedges ahead of them, their shoes and the hems of their black
gowns already soaked through with dew, when a woman behind
them called out, "Sisters! Pray you, come back, please!" desperate
and frightened enough that they swung around together.

Elyn Browster was standing in the muddy road outside the doorway
of the village's last house, her hands wrung in her skirt as she went
on saying, "Come, please. Hurry!" even as they came. "He's hurt.
He's . . ." The words she needed were not there. "He's . . ." She
pointed at her open doorway. "There. I can't . . . he won't . . . Oh,
please, my ladies!" Her finger shifted its vague, stunned pointing into
the house to the grassy patch beside the stone doorstep. There were
muddy footprints on the stone, but Elyn was asking them to wipe
their feet clean. Frevisse knew how one could cling to the familiar
to keep the frightening at bay, so she followed Dame Claire's lead
and wiped her soft-soled shoes on the grass before following Dame
Claire inside, Elyn behind them.

The shutters had been slid down from the windows, letting in the
morning light, but even so the room was dark to her eyes after the
brilliant outdoors. She and Dame Claire both paused, waiting to see
better, only gradually able to tell more about where they were. Like
most village houses, the front door was near the middle of one long
side. To their left was the living area, with hearth and a large, heavy
wooden table, two benches, a scattering of stools, a bed along the
farthest wall, a large chest at its foot. Rightward then should be
where the animals were kept but there was no smell of them, and
she realized that instead of stalls there was a board wall making a
second room of the house's other end.

"He's here," Elyn said at their backs. "Just over here. Come."

But she went no nearer herself, stayed where she was beside them,
pointing to the floor left of the door. No, not at the floor. Frevisse's

eyes had adjusted and now she could see the man lying in the shadows there, stretched stiffly out, flat on his back, arms rigid at his sides. Except that he was dressed for going out to work, even to the cloth coif closely covering his head, tied neatly under his chin, he was like a corpse laid out for burial.

But he was alive; even as she and Dame Claire crossed themselves, supposing the worst, he drew a hoarse, snoring breath.

"Oh, merciful God," Dame Claire said and went quickly forward to kneel beside him.

"He's drunk?" Frevisse asked.

"He never drinks that much!" Elyn said. "And there's naught in the house for him to be that drunk on."

"Did you lay him out like this?" Dame Claire asked. Her hands were briskly going over the man, feeling for what might be broken and for a pulse at throat and wrists.

"He was like that when I found him. Just like that." Elyn wrung her hands more tightly into her skirt. "He's a considerate man, is Jenkyn. Thoughtful. He . . . he's . . ." Her voice caught on a rising note of desperation. Without looking around from Jenkyn, Dame Claire said, "Take her outside."

Grasping the woman by one arm above the elbow, Frevisse guided her out the door. Elyn was nearly her height and as well-muscled as her life demanded of her but she came outside and sank weakly down on her doorstep and bent over as if in pain, her skirt huddled up to hide her face, muffling her voice as she said, "He's dying, isn't he?"

"Dame Claire will know soon." That was all the comfort Frevisse dared offer and saw with relief one of the women who had been at the Fishers' coming along the road to her own house next door.

But even as Frevisse raised a hand to beckon her, the woman saw something was amiss, turned her head to call to someone out of sight around the lane's curve, and then came on briskly past her own door to Elyn and Frevisse, asking as she came, "Elyn, what's toward with you? What is it?"

Her face still hidden as if her tears were something of which to be ashamed, Elyn said, "It's Jenkyn. He's hurt himself somehow."

"And it's bad?"

"I don't know. He's breathing all odd, and he won't wake up."

Two other women came hurrying to join them, one of them the firm-handed, kind-spoken midwife Frevisse remembered from the Fishers'.

"There now," Ada said when she understood how matters stood, her arm around Elyn's shoulders. "Dame Claire's with him and she'll do all that can be done. She's a good hand at this manner of thing."

The other women murmured agreement and reassurance, one of them patting Elyn on the knee comfortingly the while.

Frevisse had drawn back, knowing they would do more for Elyn than she could, and now turned toward the doorway with relief as Dame Claire appeared. Her relief faded as she saw the infirmarian's face was set in the particular way she had when calmness was an enforced choice. "I need you to come back in, please, Dame."

Elyn lifted her head and started to rise. Dame Claire gestured for her to stay. "Not yet. Soon." To the other women she said, even more quietly, "One of you had best run for Father Clement."

A cry escaped Elyn. The midwife's arm tightened around her, her head close to Elyn's as she murmured comforts.

Frevisse followed Dame Claire inside where nothing was changed except that the man's breathing was, if anything, louder and less steady. Standing over him, Dame Claire said bluntly, "His skull is broken."

"Badly?"

"I can feel the skull bone give at the back of his head. Smashed. And I'd guess that's where he hit it." She pointed to the wall above where he lay. A common enough wall of wattle and daub – clay over interlaced withies, a rough coat of white plaster over the clay. At about eye level a hand's breadth of the plastered clay was caved irregularly inward, and it looked lately done.

Frevisse looked around the neatly kept room and asked, "What could he have fallen over?" None of the sparse furnishings was near enough, not even one of the joint stools. "Was he drunk, do you think, despite what his wife says?"

"There's no smell of ale on him. It might have been a seizure maybe, but I don't know what kind it would be, to fling him so hard against the wall . . ."

Dame Claire trailed off, not going on to the next possibility. Frevisse, not wanting to either, said after a moment too full of Jenkyn's ugly breathing, "How long ago did it happen?"

"I can't tell. With something like this you can die on the instant or linger an hour or even a day. He can't have been lying here long, he's dressed to go out to work, and it's only just sunrise."

"But he won't live?"

"It would be a miracle if he did. When the skull is smashed like this . . ."

Frevisse heard a man's voice outside encouraging Elyn to be brave in the face of God's will and then Father Clement entered. He paused for the moment his eyes needed to adjust to the house's dimness, started forward toward Jenkyn, and pulled up short, startled at sight of him stretched out so rigidly on the rushes, with blue lips, nostrils flared, his breathing strange.

"God have mercy!" Father Clement turned his exclamation into blessing by drawing a hasty cross in the air over Jenkyn.

Frevisse and Dame Claire crossed themselves in echo, and Dame Claire said, "He needs to be shriven."

Elyn had followed Father Clement into the house. Now her despairing cry startled Father Clement out of his shock. Brisk with officious importance because what needed to be done only he could do, he said, "Then best you let me see to it. Ada, take Elyn over there. You others go with her too. Pray. A pater, an ave, a creed. And Dame Claire, Dame Frevisse, if you'll help me here."

The women urged Elyn to the far side of her hearth, sat her on a stool, and clustered around her with soothing sounds. She was crying almost silently, tears gleaming on her face as she looked past the women to the priest as he put down and opened his box of priestly things, brought with him from the Fishers', and took out the candles, the chrism, all the things needed to see Jenkyn's soul safe from his body into heaven. With the nuns' assistance, the matter was quickly seen to. And to clear effect, because as Father Clement folded his stole and put it away, Jenkyn drew a long, gargling breath and let it out in a forced gasp that brought the eyes of everyone in the room around to him.

He drew another, not quite so long but driven out of him with all the force of the first. And another after that, long and gargling and let out in a rush.

"What is it?" one of the women whispered.

Dame Claire opened her mouth to answer, but Father Clement said, "He's forcing the devils out of him that would have taken his soul to hell."

Another breath drove from Jenkyn's unconscious body. Elyn groaned and, shuddering, covered her ears. Everyone, Father Clement included, crossed themselves.

Ada Bychurch would not have thought there was that much evil in Jenkyn Browster to be driven out. He had always seemed a quiet, goodly man. But who but God could judge a man's heart?

Because it would be easier on everyone to be doing something, she said, "Can't he be moved now he's shriven? Won't it be better if he dies in his own bed?"

Dame Claire said, "He's past being harmed. Do it."

Ada could see Father Clement was annoyed at the nun for giving permission instead of leaving it to him in his greater authority. He had long since settled into complacency with himself and his place in

the village, and in return the village was used to him. He always had
the right words if never quite the right sympathy, and never cared to
be crossed in anything.

Now he looked around and demanded, "Where's Pers?" with the
clear thought that two men were better than one in lifting poor
Jenkyn even though Jenkyn by any description was nowhere near
a big man.

For the first time Ada wondered too where Pers was. He was
Jenkyn's nephew and heir and had come to live with his uncle and
aunt two years ago when his older brother had taken a new wife and
wanted that the house he and Pers had shared to himself and her. Pers
had taken it in good part, and the Browsters had welcomed him, a well
grown, happily disposed young man willing to put himself to whatever
work was to hand. And it had been the more convenient because a few
years before then Jenkyn, at Elyn's prompting, had asked the priory's
steward for the holding next to theirs when it fell vacant with no heir
to claim it. He had been given it, and Elyn had seen to turning its
house into a byre so there had been no longer need to keep their cow,
the sheep, and chickens in their own house, and she had had Jenkyn
build a wall to make that end of their house a separate room, used
for storage but given over to Pers when he came to live with them.

So where was he now when his uncle needed him for this final
kindness?

"He's not . . . here," Elyn choked out between sobs.

"Then where – ?" Father Clement began, but paused, maybe with
the same thought Ada had.

Yesternight had been Midsummer Eve, and Pers had likely been
out with all the other village young folk, gone to the woods for greenery
and dancing at the bonfire so, "Likely he's at Pollard's," Ada said.
"He's been working there of days when he wasn't needed here and
has his eye on Pollard's Kate."

"And she on him," Mary Cedd, one of the other women, put in.
"Aye, likely he's there. I'll go for him."

She left. Father Clement with Ada to help him lifted Jenkyn and
carried him to his bed along the far wall, Dame Claire steadying his
head. His breathing was shorter now, a gasping in and a gasping out.
The straw-stuffed mattress crackled under his slight weight as they
settled him onto it, and Dame Claire eased his head down onto the
pillow as gently as if maybe he would feel it.

With a final gasp, his breathing stopped.

Stillness filled the room, no one moving, staring at him, waiting
for it to begin again, longer and longer, until the waiting broke and
they realized it was over.

But then he drew a long, gargling suck of air deep into his lungs and drove it explosively out. And drew another after it. And another.

In too calm a voice, Dame Claire said, "I've seen a man die of a broken skull this way before. The breathing stops and then comes back, with the breaths shorter and shorter each time, until it finally stops altogether."

Elyn moaned and hid her face in her hands. Ada murmured something between a prayer and protective spell, crossing herself as she did, then with her arm around Elyn again said, "Come sit by him now."

Face still covered, Elyn shook her head, refusing.

Ada had seen this before – the idea that by not doing what was expected of you, you could keep the inevitable at bay. Before she could urge Elyn again to what would bring her greater comfort in the long run despite what she thought now, Father Clement said, "You have to trust in God's mercy, Elyn. For him and for yourself. And let us all see the lesson in it. That anyone can be taken to God's judgement on the instant and all unprepared. 'You do not know the day or the hour.' It comes by God's will and – "

"This may not be God's will," the taller of the two nuns said. Dame Frevisse. She had been so silent this while that Ada had thought she was deep in prayer for Jenkyn's soul, but now she was looking at the wall where Jenkyn had struck it.

Father Clement, not used to being interrupted, snapped, "What do you mean?"

Apparently not noticing his tone, she answered, "Look at the wall here. Jenkyn's not a tall man. Shorter than I am." That was true; Jenkyn was shorter than his wife, and she was a head shorter than Dame Frevisse. "But see where he hit." She pointed at the dent. "It's almost as high as where I would have struck, if I'd fallen against the wall. And if I'd fallen hard enough, over something or however, to break the wall like that, I'd have been falling very hard indeed and would have hit the wall much farther down, much lower than my head level, because I'd be falling. The dent in the wall should be *lower* than Jenkyn's head, not higher the way it is. He didn't fall against the wall."

"He didn't fall?" Father Clement repeated her ridiculous statement. "Then how did he hit the wall?"

"He might have been standing on something and fallen off it," Ada said promptly.

Too promptly, because she realized the problem with that even as Dame Frevisse asked, "Off what? Nothing is near the wall. Unless, Elyn, did you move anything when you first came in?"

Elyn was staring at her. "No," she said uncertainly. She thought a moment. "I came in and called to Jenkyn and when he didn't answer I thought he was gone to his work and went about opening the shutters for some light and didn't see him until I came to open the one beside where he was. I didn't move anything." She steadied to certainty. "No, not a thing."

"Then he didn't fall against the wall," Dame Frevisse said.

"But of course he did," said Father Clement. He was beginning to be overtly indignant. "There's the place where he hit it. That break wasn't there when I was here yesterday. How else could it have happened?"

"He could have been thrown."

The response to that was startled silence, until Father Clement declared, "Nonsense!"

But, "How else?" Dame Frevisse asked back.

"But there was no one here," Elyn protested. "He doesn't hold with Midsummer wandering. We stayed home and he was already to bed when I was called to Cisily."

"He's dressed now and with his coif on for going out," Dame Frevisse pointed out.

"Midsummer's come. He meant to be out early to cut the thistles in the far field."

Since thistles cut before Midsummer Day grew back threefold, sensible men waited until then to deal with them.

"But Jenkyn has been cut down instead of them," Father Clement said. "God's hand – "

"– did not throw him against the wall," interrupted Dame Frevisse. Father Clement's face darkened with displeasure. Ignoring that, she said, "There were a man's muddy footprints on the doorstep when we came in, side by side as if he had stood there and knocked."

"They could be Jenkyn's footprints," Father Clement shot back. "He could have stepped out to see how the morning did."

Even if he had, he'd not have been so dull as to muddy his shoes and Elyn's doorstep, Ada thought tartly, while Dame Frevisse met the priest's challenge with, "There's no mud on his shoes."

Elyn, rousing to something she understood, put in, "Those are his house shoes. He'd never muddy them. His outdoor shoes are kept by the back door always."

Ada looked toward the door that led into the garden behind the house. "They aren't there now."

Elyn pulled away from the women around her and took a few uncertain steps toward the door, staring at the place where Jenkyn always set his shoes. "Where are they?" she asked, bewildered.

"They're always there." Her expression opened with a thought and she exclaimed, "They've been taken! Someone's stolen them!"

Ada went to take hold of her again, less comforting now than trying to steady her. "They're only misplaced, likely. You know men. As like to put a shovel in the turnip bin as hang it where it's supposed to be. We'll look for them. They're here somewhere. Come you, sit down by Jenkyn now and say farewell to him."

But Elyn stayed standing where she was, insisting, "He wouldn't put them somewhere else. Where else would he put them? He always put them there. They're gone and I'm telling you so! Someone was here and took them!" Her face harshened with alarm. "Our money!" She ran to the hearth, knelt down heavily, and with knowing fingers pried up one of the stones around it.

Why do we think that's a clever place to hide things? wondered Ada. Everyone she knew did it, including herself, when they had any that didn't need to be spent at once. It was nobody's secret.

"No," Elyn said with naked relief, her hand on the bag that lay in the hole she had opened. "All's here still." She began to refit the stone, stopped, and said in a different voice, "But the stone's the wrong way around. Look, you can see!"

"Jenkyn, likely," Ada said.

"He'd never. He knew better." Elyn rose clumsily to her feet, looking desperately around the room. "There's been a thief here! He's taken Jenkyn's shoes and was after our money!"

"But he didn't take it," Father Clement said. "You have to calm yourself. No one's been here. A thief wouldn't have left the money."

Elyn turned wide, frightened eyes toward him. "I frightened him away ere he could take it! He'd hurt Jenkyn but when he heard me coming he ran away! He was here when I came home!"

"Of course!" exclaimed Ada, suddenly grasping what Elyn was saying. "And he went out the back way! When he heard you at the front, he went out the back!"

She started for the back door, the women and Father Clement with her, but Dame Frevisse was suddenly before them, stopping them with her arm across the doorway, saying, "Whatever happened, he's long gone by now and you'll trample over any tracks he's left if you all go out. I'll see what he's left."

What indignation Ada might have felt was lost at sight of Father Clement's face, surprise going to red-tinged indignation on it at realization that a woman – and a nun at that – had told him what he should do and she would do; and by the time he had his mouth working to object, Dame Frevisse was already gone. Ada pushed past him to crane her head out the door to see what she was about. On his dignity, Father Clement turned back to go on uncomforting Elyn.

Frevisse, with no compunction at all for thwarting Father Clement and careless of what the women thought, stood on the rear doorstep and overlooked the garden that ran from almost the back door to the woven withy fence that closed it off from the byre yard to one side, the neighboring garden to the other, and the field path and bean field to the back. It was long and narrow, like the house, and its only gate led into the byre yard. The path that ran from the back door to there between beds rich with the late June growth of peas and beans and greens was narrow and neatly surfaced with small, round river stones, showing no trace of footprints, muddy or otherwise. Frevisse walked it with her eyes down, hoping something had been dropped or a careless footprint somehow left, but she found nothing.

At its end, the gate was a new one, hung on leather thongs, with another thong to latch it closed and a flat stone laid under it to keep the way from wearing hollow. It was a little open, enough that someone turned sideways could have easily slid through. A narrow someone, for a spider's elaborate orb web was silver laced and sparkled with diamond dew across it now.

From the byre – it looked to have been a house not too long ago – a cow was lowing in complaint over her unmilked udder and chickens were softly cawing to be uncooped so they could be at their morning scratching. Frevisse stayed where she was inside the gate, studying the muddy yard before turning to go back into the house.

The two village women made no pretense they had not been watching her. They backed hastily inside as she approached, and she followed them in, to say to everyone – priest and the wife and Dame Claire, too, "There's nothing in the garden, but beyond the gate into the byre yard, there's a line of footprints – a man's by the size of them – through the mud, overlaying all the others and going straight across to the outer gate. The garden gate and that one are both open," she added with an inquiring look at Elyn, who promptly said, "We never leave those open. They're always closed. Always."

"Then surely he's gone that way!" the midwife declared. "Along the field path and probably toward the woods! We have to raise the hue and cry!"

If it could be shown a village had not pursued and done their best to seize a felon by hue and cry fresh after a crime, the village was liable to heavy fine for the failure. Because of that, and for the plain joy of hunting down a legal quarry, a hue and cry was rarely hard to raise. But this was early morning after Midsummer's Eve and there was surely more interest among the village men in being in their beds for as long as they could manage rather than haring across the countryside.

Frevisse was darkly amused to see that counted for nothing with the women or Father Clement. They had been up all the night and not at merrymaking for most of it. He and one of the women after quick talk and a nod from the midwife hasted out the door and shortly could be heard calling the hue and cry around the village green.

The midwife had turned back to Elyn by then, left standing alone by her hearth, and gone to put an arm around her. "At least come pray beside your man," Ada said. "There at the foot of the bed."

Head bowed, shoulders hunched, arms wrapped around herself, Elyn sank down on the nearest stool. "He's going to die," she muttered brokenly, "And Father Clement has done what be can be done. There's no use in my prayers then, is there?"

Ada had no answer to that that Elyn would find reasonable. Even the nuns held silent, pity on their faces, and the only sound in the room was Jenkyn's noisy, snoring breathing. After a moment Elyn closed her eyes and began to rock back and forth in silence, leaving Ada nothing to do but stand beside her, ready to give more comfort if it were wanted.

Dame Frevisse went to Dame Claire. Their heads close and voices low, they spoke together briefly, then Dame Frevisse went aside, to the room's other end, and beckoned for Ada to come to her. Since Elyn seemed to be noticing nothing beyond herself, Ada went, curious and a little wary as to why she was wanted.

But it was only for a bit of gossip, it seemed, which went to show nuns were not so different after all, because Dame Frevisse said low-voiced beyond Elyn's hearing, "Everything looks to have been going so well for them, it's a pity it's come to this. Were they happy together?"

Ada thought about that. Happy or unhappy did not much matter after a marriage had gone on long enough, just so the pair rubbed along as best they might. And Elyn and Jenkyn had done that well enough, she supposed. "Aye, they did well together," she said. With the desire to think of something other than Jenkyn's unnerving breathing, she went on, "And that's been mostly Elyn's doing. Jenkyn is – was – is – " The wording was so difficult, things being as they were. "– so easy-going a man he'd likely never have brought himself around to marrying at all except she took a liking to him fifteen years – " She paused to think about that. "Nay, closer to twelve maybe. Or thirteen."

"A while," Dame Frevisse suggested. "It was a while ago."

"Yes, it was surely that," Ada agreed. "Elyn took a liking to him, despite her father had doubts and her mother thought she could do better, but she knew what she wanted and managed him to the church door, just as she meant to. And they've done well. Mostly because of her, I'll have to say and so would anyone else who knows them, but Jenkyn's been a good husband to her." She was keeping an eye on Elyn, still sitting with her eyes closed and arms wrapped around herself. Ada lowered her voice even farther. "Except they've had no children and that's a pity, for Elyn sorely wanted them. It was when she still had hope of having them that she pushed Jenkyn into asking for the tumble-down holding next door when it came vacant, so she could keep the animals over there and have a better house with more room here. But the children never came, and she gave herself over to managing Jenkyn in their stead. He'd be content to have no better than a barn to sleep in and do naught more than he had to to eat, only she stirs him up, and they've both lived the better because of it. Though mind you, it's helped that Pers has come to live with them these past two years. There's only so much Elyn can do with a man who's not – was not – " This was annoyingly difficult. "– a big man or strong. Nor so young as he once was."

"Pers is the nephew, who's missing now?" Dame Frevisse asked.

"He's not missing, only at Pollard's courting their Kate." Ada smiled fondly over the thought. "That will be a match before long, and a good one, that's certain."

"But Pers won't inherit when Jenkyn dies, will he?" Dame Frevisse asked.

"No. All this goes to Elyn for her lifetime. Though likely Pers will stay on here to help at least until he marries. But since he's like to marry Pollard's Kate, he'll do well enough, she being Pollard's only child and everything to come to her eventually."

"But Pers has no inheritance of his own?"

"Not while Elyn lives, and she's a healthy woman, God bless her. Though we're all in his hands," she added conscientiously, seeing over Dame Frevisse's shoulder that Father Clement was giving them both a hard stare. She was gossiping, Ada had to admit, but felt no guilt at it. And closed up in that nunnery, the nun must have little enough of it in her life.

But before she could go on, the front door was pushed hard open and five men rushed in. Elyn, lost in her grieving until then, rose to her feet with a startled cry. Ada went hastily to hold her, saying angrily, "Will! Nab! The rest of you! There's a man dying here. Where's your sense?"

Abashed, the men crowded to a halt. Will muttered, "Sorry. We're right sorry. Only we were told to come, and – "

"Aye, aye," Dickon agreed. "It's hue and cry, my woman said, so which way do we go?"

"Out the back. There. Go on." Ada pointed them out the back door. "There's footprints through the byre yard. That's your trail."

"I'll bring the others round," Nab said and went back out the front where voices in the road told other men were coming. Will and the other three hastily crossed themselves as they went on past Jenkyn on his bed, their faces showing their dismay at the look and sound of him.

Father Clement followed them out to bless their mission. The room was left to Jenkyn's harsh breathing and the muffled tangle of men's voices, in the byre yard now, until a single hard rap at the front door brought in two more men, a barrel-chested older one and a youth tall enough he had to duck below the lintel as he entered.

"You're nigh too late, Tom Pollard," Ada said. "Haste out back, or they'll be gone."

"No need to push, Ada," Pollard rumbled. "My regrets, Elyn," he added to the widow-to-be; but his gaze swung around the room, speculative and assessing, and that was Tom Pollard to the core, Ada knew. A hand to the plow and plans for the harvest all at once. "You'd best stay here, Pers," he said. "For your uncle and to help your aunt. There's enough of the rest of us to see to what needs doing."

Pers' broad, pleasant face under its thatch of tow hair betrayed how much he did not want to stay, and Ada did not blame him. He was hardly seventeen yet, for all that he was so well grown. Too young yet to be easy around someone's dying. But he stayed and Pollard left, as outside the men's voices rose in a flurry, Father Clement's blessing done and the hue and cry begun in angry earnest.

Hesitantly, Pers looked around the room, then went uncertainly to his uncle's side.

"He's beyond us now," Dame Claire said kindly. "I doubt he's feeling anything."

Pers nodded without looking at her, his gaze fixed on his uncle, his expression grading from wariness to increasing horror as the dying man's breathing sank through its pattern, each indrawn breath shorter than the one before, each breath rasping harshly out . . . Dame Claire began to explain that the breathing was something that went with a broken skull, but Father Clement entered then and, seeing Pers, went to him to lay a hand on his arm and cut off what she was saying to offer his sympathy and add, "The men are off now. They'll do all that can be done to right this wrong."

Pers nodded dumbly, still watching his uncle. The breathing

stopped and they all waited, frozen in the silence, until Jenkyn's chest heaved upwards again, drawing in another hideous breath, and the pattern went on, perhaps more shallow now, more slow.

Elyn on her stool crouched more in on herself. Pers pulled out of Father Clement's hold and said in a strangling voice, "I'd best see to the animals. Clover needs milking sure by now. I'll be back."

Without waiting for any answer, he escaped out the back door. Frevisse waited until Father Clement had bowed his head to pray over Jenkyn, then drifted quietly after Pers.

The sun was above the hedgerows now, bold in a cloudless sky, the day perfect for haying but so early yet that dew still silvered wherever shadows lay. For all his haste to be away, Pers had gone no farther than the garden's end and stood there now, holding to the top of the gate, staring out. Moving slowly, careful to let him hear her coming, Frevisse joined him. He acknowledged her with a look and a low bow of his head, but when she did not speak, neither did he and they stood together looking out for a few moments, Frevisse noticing that the hue and cry had trampled out the earlier footprints with the myriad of their own, and left the outer gate wide open behind them. Someone had bothered to shove the garden gate almost closed, though, and the spider had begun to spin her web again. So far only a single strand across the gap, but she was already dropping another down from it. Watching her, Frevisse said, "I'm sorry about your uncle, that there was nothing we could do to help him."

"It's as she said, then? There's no hope?"

"None, I'm afraid."

Pers drew a deep, uneven breath and let it out in a ragged sigh. "He's always been good to me. He's a kind man."

"He's likely glad then you'll be here for your aunt, and have the holding after her, when the time comes."

"Oh, aye," Pers said as if the thought were new to him.

"But your aunt will have the rule here while she lives, no doubt of that."

"Aye, she will!" Pers was very clear on that.

"But you'll stay on to help her."

"Surely. That's the right way of it." His mind was still only half on her questions and his answers, and he showed where his thoughts more strongly were by saying suddenly, "I should have gone with the hunt despite what Pollard said. I want my hands on the cur who did this!"

"They'll bring him back here if he's taken."

"Aye, if he's taken. But it's none so far to the forest and if he's right away to there, they'll likely never have him then.

Some ditch-living bastard, clean away and my uncle dead!"
Remembering too late to whom he was talking, he added, "Beg
pardon, my lady."

Unoffended, Frevisse asked, "You think that's how it was? A
passing stranger taking a chance at theft and murder?"

He looked at her. "How else could it have been? There's no one
here would harm my uncle. He never quarreled with anyone nor
anyone with him."

"Not even his wife?"

"Aunt Elyn?" Pers scorned the notion. "She might quarrel with a
neighbor, but not him. He never gave her cause, always did what
she asked of him."

"And will you when you're living with her? Do what you're
told?"

A blush brightened under his tan. "For a while," he said uncomfortably. "But I'm marrying at Lammastide." Despite his effort to hold it
back, a shy but broadening smile tugged at his mouth. "We agreed on
it last night, Kate and me." He added hastily, as if worried that Frevisse
might be off to spread the word on the instant, "Only don't say so to
anyone! No one knows yet. We were going to tell her Da today. Well,
ask him if we could but he'll say yes to it and be glad, we know."

His happiness shone on him, burning for the moment even stronger
than his anger and grief. For him, just now, Death was a thing that
happened to other people, not something that should come near him
or his Kate. The thought crossed Frevisse's mind that a year ago it
must have seemed just so to Martyn Fisher, grieving now for his
dead young wife.

"I'll tell no one," she said and let her questioning fall aside for
a while.

But she did not leave him, only contented herself with watching
the spider at her web-weaving between the gate and gatepost. A
lovely spider, mottled light brown and gold, almost as big as her
thumbnail. The creature had nearly finished her web's frame. Then
would come the spiral outward from its center, and she was precise
but quick about her business because there was food to be caught
and no telling when forces beyond her spidery comprehension would
bring her work to naught again.

The cow lowed earnestly from the byre, and Pers reached to open
the gate, to go through. Frevisse put out her hand, stopping him.
"Go around," she said. "Or over the fence." He stared at her as if
in doubt of her senses, and she added, "I'm watching the spider."

Pers drew back. "Oh, aye," he agreed but plainly seeing no sense to
it. "But I have to see to the animals and this is the way through."

"Go over the fence."

"It's too high to jump, please you, my lady, and it'll crack if I climb it," he replied, carefully, as if beginning to think she were simple. But what he said was true enough. The fence was too high to jump and its withies would not hold much weight beyond a very small child's.

Patiently, Frevisse said, "Then go back through the house, out the front door and around. I'm watching the spider."

Pers louted her a bow and went, taking his perplexity with him, because after all half the village was owned by the nunnery, maybe even the Browster's considerable holding, and that gave Frevisse authority to tell him what to do, woman though she was. Authority like no woman in the village had over any man, unless she came to it the way Elyn Browster had, simply by being the stronger in her marriage, and even that was not so very much power in the long run.

But Elyn would have a prosperous widowhood; and maybe after her first grief eased, she would even enjoy it. Or would she, without someone over whom to wield her authority? Jenkyn would be gone and Pers would shortly go, and though she could likely find another husband if she chose, was she likely to find another as amenable to her will as Jenkyn had been?

Patiently – could it be called patience and a virtue when done simply out of a creature's blind nature? – the spider crept on around her strands, beginning her webbed spiral in the morning sunlight.

Ada would not have thought that Jenkyn could have gone on breathing for so long. The huge gasping lasted less long between the nerve-jerking silences but always it came back again. Father Clement stood at the foot of the bed, praying of course, but his hands clenched together as if holding himself there by force of will. More quietly, Dame Claire stood at Jenkyn's head. Neither Pers nor Dame Frevisse had returned; and Elyn still sat on the stool by the hearth, elbows on her knees, head in her hands, eyes fixed on her lap. Half a dozen other women had come after the men had gone, roused to Elyn's need, but she had taken no comfort from them. Though occasionally one or another patted her shoulder, whispered something kind to her, she seemed beyond noticing them.

It was a relief to hear the men's voices coming along the road out front. Though by the sound of them the hue and cry had had no luck, at least it was a change from their own miserable waiting. As Ada went quickly to open the front door to them, Dame Frevisse returned through the back. She went to stand beside Dame Claire. Pers came in almost immediately behind her, his feet unwiped from the byre so that he stopped just inside the back door as Ada opened the front.

Most of the men there were standing away, in the road, some of them already trailing on toward their homes. It was Pollard who came to the door and started, "We're back then but – "

"Come in with it, man," Father Clement called. "We all want to hear."

Pollard looked back at his fellows. They waved him on, willing to leave it to him, so he came in, glanced at the bed and immediately away, looked at Elyn for some notice he was there and when she gave none, went on with, "It wasn't any use. There was no trail to follow once we were out of the yard. And we were tired to start with and it's growing hot – " He was half-apologizing as well as explaining. "– and the bailiff expects us to the haying soon. We did what we could but there was no use to it, truly."

Father Clement said, "You did what you could. That will be enough for the sheriff and crowner." Enough to save the village a fine, anyway. "But we'd best send someone around to the near villages to warn them there's a murdering thief at large."

"There's no need for that," Dame Frevisse said quietly. "Whoever did this didn't run away."

Father Clement frowned at her. "We know that he did, dame."

"Ran out the back when he heard Elyn coming in," Pollard said. "Through the byre yard. We all saw his prints. They show clear what he did."

Dame Frevisse shook her head. "The footprints in the yard mud are a lie. No one went out that way at dawn today."

Sternly, letting his disapproval of her show, Father Clement said, "That's a foolish thought, dame. Leave this to those who know."

Ada listened amazed to such talk between nun and priest. Nuns were more bold than she had thought. Or at least this one was. And even now, faced with Father Clement's reproof, Dame Frevisse said, "There's more to know than that, I think." She turned from him to Dame Claire and asked, "May I lift Jenkyn's head? Will it cause him any harm?"

"Dame, this is hardly – " Father Clement began to protest.

Ignoring him, Dame Claire answered, "He's past more harm. May I help? What do you want?"

"To take off his coif."

Dame Claire carefully lifted Jenkyn's head and held it while Dame Frevisse carefully untied and took off his coif, laid it aside, and then felt at the back of his head with her long fingers.

"Yes," she murmured to herself. And to Father Clement, "Come here, if it please you, Father. And you." She included Ada; and Ada, more eagerly than the priest, went to her. As gently as if Jenkyn might feel it, Dame Frevisse took hold of his head from Dame Claire and turned it sideways so they could see the back of it. "You see there's blood here, matted in his hair."

Father Clement, managing not to look too closely at skull or blood, snapped, "As well there might be." Elyn moaned and covered her ears with her hands.

"But no blood on the coif," Dame Frevisse said. She set Jenkyn's head down on the pillow again and picked up the cloth hat. "See. There's blood in plenty dried into his hair but none on his coif."

"And there should be," said Ada, grasping what she meant.

"There should be," Dame Frevisse agreed. "Elyn, when did you leave your husband last night?"

"Last night?" Elyn repeated, lifting her head. She made an effort to gather her wits. "We went to the bonfire on the green and watched the dancing. He wouldn't dance, he hasn't for years, but we watched. And then we came home and he went to bed." The effort to think seemed to be steadying her; she became more certain. "He went to bed but I stayed up a little and was about to cover the fire when Ada came because of Cisily and I left him sleeping and went out with her."

Ada nodded readily. "That's right. I came for her when it began to look bad for Cisily and I didn't come in because Elyn feared I'd wake Jenkyn."

"But you didn't see him?"

"Well, no. Not from outside, would I?"

A little more roused, Elyn said, "He was sleeping when I left. He meant to be out at dawn to cut those thistles. He was in bed and when I came home at dawn I found him like that." Her eyes flinched toward the bed and away again. "On the floor and all dressed but like that." Her voice quavered toward tears.

Ada and the other women closed around her, Ada murmuring, "It's all right, love. It's all right."

It was Pollard who said indignantly, "A thief came in while he was readying to go out this morning, killed him, and then ran out the back way when he heard Elyn coming. That's plain."

"It isn't plain," Dame Frevisse snapped. "If it happened that way, there should be blood on the coif and there isn't. And when I first went into the garden, before anyone else did, there was a spider's web across the open garden gateway. An unbroken spider's web all hung with dew. No one went through that gateway this dawn."

"Then he went over the fence," Pollard said impatiently.

With a glance at Dame Frevisse and the air of someone accurately repeating a lesson, Pers put in, "The fence is too high to be jumped and too weak to be climbed." Then flushed as Pollard looked angrily at him.

"And aside from that," Dame Frevisse said, "the footprints show he went through the gateway, not over the fence."

"You just said he didn't go through the gateway!" Pollard quickly pointed out.

"Not at dawn," Dame Frevisse answered back. "Whoever did this to Jenkyn didn't run through that gate at dawn. He would have broken the spider's web, and it wasn't broken. This was done last night." To Father Clement she said, "Among the men Jenkyn knew, who had reason to want him dead? Or will have the most from his death?"

With a shock, Ada found that she had looked without thinking at Pers. And that so had everyone else in the room. He gaped back at them, speechless, but Elyn exclaimed, "No! He'd not harm a hair of Jenkyn's head! There'd be no point. Everything comes to me. Everyone knows that."

"But he'd be the man here," Dame Frevisse said. "Just you and he to run things and no Jenkyn in the way."

Elyn flushed a dark, shamed red at what was implied behind the words. Furiously indignant for both of them, Father Clement cut in. "Here now! No one's ever thought of any such thing!"

"There's nothing between us," Elyn whispered. "There's nothing and never has been."

More loudly and more definitely, Pers declared, "That's right!"

Pollard, more outraged than either of them, said, "He's to marry my girl!"

Ignoring their combined indignation, Dame Frevisse asked Pers, "Did you dance with Pollard's Kate at the bonfire last night?"

"Aye. Of course." Defiantly.

"And spent the night with her?"

Angrily Pollard put in, with an uneasy glance at Father Clement – fathers had to pay fines for girls who were wayward before their marriage – "That he did, but in my house with all the rest of us. So we know where he was all last night and he had no chance of doing anything to his uncle."

Dame Frevisse turned to Ada, and Ada found her direct, demanding gaze disconcerting even before she asked, "Did Elyn come out with you right away when you came last night? Or did you have to wait a while?"

"She said she had to cover the fire and I should go back to Cisily," Ada answered, trying to see why it mattered. This was all going too quickly for her. "She said she'd be there just after me and she was."

"A little after? Or longer?"

Beginning to understand but unwilling to, Ada answered slowly, "I was busy with Cisily. I don't know. A little while. Not much."

"Enough while that she could have put on Jenkyn's shoes and made those footprints on the doorstep and across the byre yard?"

Ada wanted to say, No, there hadn't been enough time for Elyn to have done all that; but as she started to, she looked at Elyn's white, frozen face and held silent.

From beside the bed Dame Frevisse said, "The footprints were like those of a child wearing shoes too big for him, deep in the heels and nothing in the toes. You've little feet, Elyn, for your size, and Jenkyn has a man's. Where did you hide the shoes so you could claim someone had stolen them?"

Elyn, staring at something in front of her that was not there for anyone else to see, did not answer. It was Pers, his voice raw with disbelief and hurt, who asked, "But why?"

Elyn did not answer nor her expression change. Surprisingly gently, Dame Frevisse said, "Why, Elyn? What was the reason?"

Where there had been nothing, feeling shimmered at last in Elyn's eyes. "Because I couldn't bear him. Not anymore."

"Jenkyn?" Ada asked, her disbelief an echo of Pers'. "You couldn't bear Jenkyn?"

Still staring in front of her, Elyn nodded and finally said, in a low voice, "He was so nothing. No matter what I did, he was nothing. And last night, at the bonfire, I was watching Pers." Her gaze slid up to him and then away to the floor in front of her feet. "I watched him dancing with his Kate. Both of them so beautiful. And happy. And then I had to come home with Jenkyn, because he wouldn't dance. It was too much trouble, he said. Nor he didn't like staying up at night nor Midsummer wandering. He didn't much like anything that cost him any effort."

Bitterness and scorn and the anger that must have been in her for a long time before last night tightened her voice. "I tried to talk with him when we were home, trying to make him see how things could be different, better between us. But everything was too much trouble for him. I always had to talk a week to make him do a day's work. He was forever dragging back on everything I asked him. He wouldn't . . ." Her hands, knotted in her lap, clenched and unclenched. "I suddenly couldn't bear him any longer. He stood up, saying he was going to bed, and I . . . I took him and threw him . . . he weighs hardly more than my big iron kettle . . . backwards against the wall. I'd wanted to do that to him . . . do something to him . . . hurt him . . . for so very long. I didn't know, I didn't mean . . ." She stopped, then said dully, "Or maybe I did. Maybe I did mean it to kill him. I don't know."

Gently but with the same remorseless searching, Dame Frevisse said, "So he was lying there, and you were trying to decide what to do when Ada came to say you were needed, and you thought maybe there was a way out of what you had done after all."

Elyn nodded into her hands. "The idea came to me all at once and I knew what I could do. Make it look like a thief came in, a stranger, and killed him. I made the footprints, just as you said. The shoes are in the midden by the byre. Then I went to Cisily. I thought he'd be dead when I came home. He wasn't and that was awful. And there was the blood but he wasn't bleeding anymore so I shifted the rushes, buried the bloody ones under clean ones, meaning to be rid of them later and no one the wiser, and put his coif on him to cover what was in his hair. I'd be the one to ready him for burial and no one would have to see and likely no one would have thought about it anyway." She raised sad, accusing eyes to the nun. "But you did. I should have waited until you'd gone before I came out crying about him. Then it would have been all right."

Stirred at last out of the silence holding them all, Father Clement said, "You've sinned, Elyn. And sinned worse in meaning to let him die unshriven, his soul likely bound straight for hell."

Ada shivered and was not the only one to cross herself at that. But Elyn only said bitterly, "He never sinned enough to go to hell. And purgatory wouldn't hurt him any worse than he's hurt me these years. Only – " Now she wrapped her arms around herself and looked toward the bed resentfully. "– only I hadn't thought he'd go on alive so long. And with that breathing. Isn't he ever going to stop it?"

He did, a little later. One last, faint rasping out of breath and, this time, nothing after it. The silence drawing out and out, until they knew he would not breathe again.

And afterwards, freed at last to go on home, matching her long stride to Dame Claire's shorter one as they walked again along the lane's grassy verge toward the priory, Frevisse tried to find a prayer that would answer, for her at least, some of the pain the past hours had held. And Dame Claire's mind, too, was behind them rather than ahead, because out of the quiet between them she suddenly asked, "Would you have paid so much heed to the footprints if it hadn't been for the spider's web?"

"No. I doubt it. I'd probably not have thought about them at all. Or wondered about the blood."

"So it wasn't the footprints or the blood that trapped her."

"No. Only the spider's web." And the fact that Frevisse had chosen to think about it.

A spider's web and a moment's thought. So small a pair of things to be so deadly.

As small as the break in a woman's heart between enduring and despair.

# THE DUCHESS AND THE DOLL
## Edith Pargeter
## (*Ellis Peters*)

*There is no doubt that it is the success of the Brother Cadfael novels
by Ellis Peters that has made the historical detective story so popular. Ellis Peters has written only three short stories about the wily
monk, all of which are included in the book* A Rare Benedictine
*(1988). It seemed unnecessary to reprint another when they are so
widely available. The success of these stories has, ironically, overshadowed Ellis Peters's earlier work, particularly her early short stories, mostly written under her own name of Edith Pargeter. One of
these, "The Duchess and the Doll", has remained unreprinted since
1950; it is not so much a detective story as a fascinating retelling
of a genuine case of witchcraft and heresy in the reign of Henry
VI.*

On Sunday, 23 July 1441, at Paul's Cross, at sermon-time of the
morning, this history begins.

A crowd had gathered about a high stage, reared to draw in all
eyes to a fellow-creature's penance. If an example be not as public
as the mind can devise, who will profit by the warning? And though
the sermon against witchcraft was eloquent as lengthy, and touched
a dark world every man knew to be close at his heels even in broad
daylight, yet words go by very lightly without some picture to stamp
home the lesson.

It was not at the priest they gazed, but at the penitent. He was a man
of middle age, wrapped in robes signed with mysterious and terrifying
signs, and seated in a chair from the corners of which projected four
swords, with small copper images impaled upon their points. In his
right hand was propped a sword, and in his left a sceptre that wavered
and recovered as he wearied in the July heat. His face was fixed as

a mask, and had the calm of a mask, but no less the suggestion of incalculable terrors behind. As yet he had only been questioned and brought to confession, and to this public abjuration of his art; trial was yet to come, verdict and sentence yet to break on him. He had but begun to draw upon the length of his endurance.

The instruments of his art, by which he had attempted to know and perhaps to alter the future, were disposed about him upon the scaffold, as terrible and mysterious as the signs upon his clothing; and among them, alone of instant significance to the layman's eye, stood a small image of wax, a roughly shaped doll. Those behind craned to see it better; those before passed back information concerning it. It was clearly made to represent a human being, they said; it was male, it had features, but who could say it resembled this man or that?

Likeness was not held to be necessary where not every practitioner had an artist at his elbow. Baptism could bestow the doubled personality more surely than any resemblance, and they whispered that if this mannikin wore no crown its name might none the less be Henry Plantagenet. This once said, the rest came rushing upon its heels. To what exact use had the doll been put? Had it been set to the fire? For the King had not ailed more gravely than at any other time. Yet the process might have been no more than begun when the information was laid which brought Roger Bolingbroke to Paul's Cross and penance.

The thing must be done slowly, a wasting away so gradual that the victim may be past help before he knows he needs the physicians. Perhaps the heat had never got beyond a glaze and a glisten on the little naked waxen body before the wizard and his accomplices had been taken into hold. His stars and all his instruments, and all the devils he could raise by their means, had never been long-sighted enough to show him the gallows, the bench or the block, but he surely saw them now clear enough before him without the aid of ink or glass.

Latecomers pressing in upon the skirts of the crowd asked eager questions.

"Who is he? What has he done?"

"Roger Bolingbroke, one of Duke Humphrey's chaplains, so they say. He knows astrology, and other arts beside. He has conjured; he confesses it."

"Has he renounced his art? What did he say?"

"He says he was seduced to it against his conscience."

"By whom?"

The answer was whispered, "By the Lady of Gloucester."

They would never give her her title if they could help it, but always used this name for her. Let her be what she might, the King's aunt by marriage, the first lady of England, yet they hated her. She knew it, and understood the reasons for it. They hated her because she was no better born than many a merchant's wife of London, and yet had made a capture of the great Duke of Gloucester, a prince and a Plantagenet, and had taken him from a princess, too, by right of conquest; and no less because she had been his mistress before she was his wife; but most of all because she had never stirred herself to court them from their bad opinion of her, and their most daring affronts had drawn from her only flashes of contempt. Now was come, it seemed, the time when this haughty lady should learn how far the high have to fall.

"Does he say she made the image?"

"He says it was she who would have it made."

"Then this is high treason she stands accused of?"

"The highest."

"Duke Humphrey was not enough for her, it seems!"

"Not enough as he stands. She would have him the taller by the height of a crown."

This and all the other white-hot gossip of the town came back in due course to Her Grace the Duchess of Gloucester, that handsome, imperious and unpopular woman. She heard all in silence, and a whole day bore her knowledge without sign. It was none of it new, for she had been hearing some such tidings in nightmares ever since the chaplain had vanished from his place; only it had drawn perceptibly nearer to her liberty and her life. Nor was the lance levelled only against her own breast. Man and wife are one flesh. The steel would lodge where they meant it should who were already behind the opportune thrust, in the heart of Humphrey Plantagenet, Duke of Gloucester. Not Cardinal Beaufort, not Suffolk, not Stafford, not the greatest nor the least of his enemies had forged the weapon to destroy Humphrey. They had recognized it, they would know how to use it, but it was she who had made it and put it into their hands.

And was that all she had done for him in the end? In more than ten years of marriage, and longer of love, was that all she had given him for a keepsake? No heir, no new lustre to his name, no land, no wealth, nothing but her body for a season of passion and this deathblow at the end of it. All her ambitions, all her pride, dropped to earth here, and her life after them. Much may be ventured against a duchess whose death will loose no war of vengeance against the land, whose fortune left behind will cause no factions to form about it across the grain of those far too many factions already in being.

For Jacqueline, graced and glittering with her regalia of half the

Netherlands, Hainault, Holland and Zeeland, swords might be drawn
and armies take the field, but for Eleanor Cobham of Sterborough,
dubious daughter of a minor English nobleman, there would never
be even a brush of men-at-arms in a London street. Let her be the
first woman of England while the sun shone on her, at the fall of the
first shadow she would be stripped naked to the cold of justice and
not a hand raised for her.

It was a long time since she had thought of Jacqueline, but now,
going restlessly about her house with her ears stretched for the
first strange hoofbeat upon the walk and her heart in her bosom
shrinking hard with fear, she remembered her very clearly. A fine
woman at her coming to England twenty years ago. Some had found
her person beautiful, some her three counties in the Low Countries
more beautiful yet, while some had sighed their hearts out for her
romantic wrongs, and her courage and fire in maintaining her cause
against all odds. Which aspect of her had first caught Humphrey
Plantagenet's eye he best knew, but with his bold breadth of vision
he had certainly missed none of the three in the end. Beauty and
estate were much to his mind, yet to do him right the challenge of
her exiled condition would have called him to her side as surely, if
not for chivalry's sake for pride's. For consider her story.

Widowed from her first weakly husband, the Dauphin John, she
had entered into all her father's lands just in time to marry them
innocently to a second as feeble, the Duke John of Brabant, the
cousin and pawn of Philip of Burgundy, and in less than two years
had suffered the humiliation of seeing this lord of hers separate her
from certain of her lands to Philip's profit.

She had foreseen in this first mild lopping the final loss of all, and
with indignation had taken her person out of the keeping of such a
husband to find asylum in England, where the Council had made her
godmother to the infant King, and given her a pension to keep her in
some shadow of her accustomed state. Humphrey's hand had been
in the matter even thus early, no doubt, for he took his hazards as fast
as they came, and more often than not leaped to meet them; for the
following year the Spanish anti-Pope, Benedict XIII, had declared
her Brabant marriage annulled, and by the autumn she had taken a
third husband. Doubtless in this Plantagenet, Lord Protector of the
realm of England and second in line of succession to the crown, she
had grasped at a powerful, willing and ambitious ally. Doubtless,
too, she had looked upon this man, thirty years of age, handsome
for all his excesses, lettered, learned, a patron of scholars, courtly of
manner, brilliant of bearing, and loved him.

Well, they had gone far to undo England's interests in France by the match. Burgundy was necessary to Bedford's designs there, and Burgundy was rudely estranged now by Gloucester's alliance with Brabant's dubiously-divorced wife and her titles. One bone between two dogs, snapped at fiercely by both, the Netherlands bade fair to cast English arms out of Europe.

And here began the ludicrous expedition which first threw Eleanor Cobham in the Duke's way. The French had seized eagerly upon the quarrel, and by means of forged letters had sought to prove that even Bedford himself, the regent of England in France, was joined with his impulsive brother in a plot against Burgundy's life. Bedford had made hurried efforts to mediate, calling Pope Martin V into the arena as peace-maker; and Humphrey had stopped his mouth as sharply by taking his wife and all her train of ladies, and leading an army into Hainault. There had been no resistance; he had been received submissively as Count. None the less, Jacqueline had lost all her hopes there upon a bloodless field.

Her ladies! There had been one among them who was handsomer than the rest, and readier to seize the passing chance of his notice when his wife grew tedious and her cause harassing. A woman of unobtrusive birth, questionably legitimate, but magnificently grasping when opportunity leaned to her. His match in arrogance and audacity, her high temper pleasing to him, her hot nature satisfying beyond Jacqueline's royal reach. Eleanor, daughter of Lord Cobham of Sterborough; her reputation as dubious as her birth, her aim as lofty as her looks. Remembering the first of it, when his eyes as yet barely lit and lingered upon her, she could still smile for a moment. Poor Jacqueline!

Where do they go, these passionate attachments, these banners and trumpets and laurels of love, when they suddenly and silently fold up their glories and pass from us? He, who had set out to win a kingdom for his bride, and thrown England into the scale to weigh it low enough for his hand, by what enchantment did he fall into this new sickness of indifference before the fanfares were well out of his ears?

Too confident of his royal privilege to assume a grace where he had lost it, Humphrey had not dissembled his weariness with his wife, and at the most had covered the nakedness of his new amour with no more than the cynical pretence of decency. Burgundy had helped him there, with his grandiloquent offer of single combat to settle the dispute; and gravely he had confided to Jacqueline that he must set England's affairs in order, no less than his own, before he took his life to the issue. He was well assured that Bedford would never suffer the duel to take place, but the pretext was good, and impotently she watched him go from her. Nor did he sail for England alone; his wife's household was the less by one lady-in-waiting that night. Within the month Jacqueline was a prisoner of Burgundy.

But who would have thought the new love would last longer than the old? The victor herself, had she gambled upon gaining more than a short summertime of favour? She remembered vividly that April voyage home, the insolent entry into London, the bewildered people almost too startled to shout for their "good Duke Humphrey" because the lady by his side was not the right lady. She remembered old Beaufort's thunderous face, and the way the words stuck in his throat as he welcomed his nephew home. Oh, they had hated her then and they hated her now, the noble and the simple alike. Yet none of them had ever dreamed how high she would rise. Even when the Pope had declared Humphrey's marriage with Jacqueline null and void they had not supposed he would dare to make his mistress royal, nor she to accept the honour and the challenge.

Those righteous London housewives who accosted the Lords on her account in 1428, protesting at the Lord Protector's abandonment of his wife to her distresses while he amused himself with a harlot like Eleanor – their very words, God damn them! – had they imagined she dared be so splendidly avenged? Even Jacqueline in Holland, surrendering at last her citadel of defiance, taking Philip for heir and co-regent of her lands and acquiescing bitterly in the annulment of that brief English marriage, had she foreseen that the harlot dared so superbly put on the duchess before the whole world? Yet he had married her. More, she had kept him. Double the years of Jacqueline's marriage she had kept him, a faithful lord no less for innumerable infidelities. She had him still, his heart and his mind. After weariness of all other women he came to her breast still.

Was it the philtres? She had never quite dared to suppose she had no more need of them, and ever and again he had drunk magic in his wine through those ten years. How if this must come to light now? Her heart raged at the thought of the smiles which would flash from lip to lip through London when it was known that after all no charms of hers had drawn him to her, but spells bought with money. Yet the philtres had been no more than a beginning. There was high treason now to answer, and more than mockery to fear. Bolingbroke had abjured his art, and named her for the instigator of his traitorous blasphemies; Margery Jourdemayne was taken, Hume taken, Southwell taken, all in prison but Eleanor Cobham, the patroness, the procuress of witchcraft.

What a fool she had been to go on beyond the philtres! Yet it had begun innocently and simply. The Duke of Bedford was six years dead in France, and the King in his teens a sickly, bookish boy not yet married. Surely it was right and meet that the wife of one now heir to the throne should spend some pains to make herself fit for her destiny? She had only sought to know her own future, that she might be ready to make faithful delivery of all that should be required of her. Was it treasonable that she should ask by divination: "Am I to be called to this last duty? Is this my fortune?"

But she knew, only too well, in what other and most sinister light they would regard it. "Shall I rise yet higher?" is a dangerous question from one already close to a throne; it may be only a step from the thought to the deed. And beyond the instruments of divination, beyond the Mass which had been said over them, there was the wax doll.

What had Bolingbroke said of it? If she but knew what tale he had told to account for it she might yet come off safely. Does a man under the question think fast and clearly? Had he had the wit to bestow another identity upon that miserable mannikin of wax? Surely, even to stave off torture, he had not fallen in with all they wished him to say, and agreed with them to call the thing King Henry VI of England? But if he had! How richly Jacqueline was avenged if he had!

Southwell had been their mistake, the chink by which discovery had come in to them. Bolingbroke would have a priest to say Mass over his tools, that the divination might be true and trenchant, and therefore they had taken to them the Canon of St Stephen's, an old, subtle and reverend man, but one with a houseful of servants long-eared and ready at keyholes. Who could say for sure if the Mass in Hornsey Park had not been spied on? At least they knew of it now, and Southwell was in the Tower, and never likely to come forth again but for sentence and the traitor's double death. There had been too many of them. First Southwell, then, because of her knowledge of the ingredients of low magic and the use of wax, Margery had been called from her philtres to a more dangerous service. Too many by far for so perilous a secret.

As one had already cast the burden upon her, so would they all. How better be rid of it? This hated woman, this upstart duchess, she shall carry all the guilt, for by this means at least we may get what countenance the favour of the commons can give us. There will be a hope at least, some shadow of a hope of pity and pardon for whoever throws Eleanor Cobham to the dogs. So they would reason, and rightly.

Bolingbroke had already shown the way, and Margery would not be slow to follow, for she had little title to leniency unless by this means. Once already, ten years ago now, but the memory of the law is as long as its arm, she had been taken up for a suspected witch and borne away from her prosperous little business of herbs and charms in the manor of Eye, to face a charge of sorcery at Windsor. Clerks were ever her natural companions. Friar Ashewell and John Virley then, Roger Bolingbroke and Canon Southwell now, she had but moved a step or two up in the world. But then for lack of hanging evidence they were all loosed, and went cautiously back to their old practices, and that was a thing which would not happen a second time. Certainly they would wish to take her with them to hell, or wherever else they were bent.

What, then, was to be done? She could do no more than hold fast her good sense, and go about as if no circumstance threatened her; and his name, his power, might still avail to frown them off from touching her.

She bore it until nightfall on Tuesday, and then could bear it no more. Panic fell on her with the darkness. Sick with waiting, she roused herself and fled into sanctuary at Westminster, and after her as at the snapping of a leash swooped all the haggards of fear. It had needed only this one false step to make her enemies content.

So it began. She was summoned forth to deliver herself from formal charges of necromancy, witchcraft, heresy and treason. You cannot for ever stay in sanctuary, nor can you ever hope to leave it unobserved; it is the last place where the wise take refuge. She knew these things too late, but she did what could be done to recover the ground she had thrown away. She had flown to hiding like a runaway servant, but she came forth like a duchess, and submitted herself with a stony calm to her first examination.

It was in St Stephen's Chapel at Westminster that she was called to appear, before two who hated her as well as any. The Cardinal Bishop of Winchester, who had fought a long battle for dominance with Humphrey and must now be seeing clearly his way to winning it at last, and his fellow, Archbishop Ayscough, like all of his cloth as loyal a Beaufortite as Beaufort himself: two such as these could hardly be expected to show any sorrow for an event which gave their faction the absolute power in England.

Yet they were grave, courteous and fatherly with her, as befitted the custodians of her soul. The old man, himself a Plantagenet by-blow of the house of John of Gaunt, had as much ambition in his venerable head as Humphrey could lay claim to, though his bend sinister had made him turn left-handed to the Church for his kingdom; the main difference was that he had lived longer and more warily, and grown more practised in seeming other than he was. He knew how to lean his head on his hand and look upon her with the sorrowing love of a father as he questioned her of heresies and treasons, hoping to have her heart out of her to hold before Humphrey's eyes when next they crossed. He, whose bullies had ruffled it in London streets with the Gloucester men-at-arms not long since, and fetched the harassed Bedford over from France to make peace between them! He, who felt cunningly in every move for a thumbhold over young Henry's manhood faster than any Humphrey had kept over his infancy! Well, it was not with that poor little half-monk, half-student he had to deal here, and so he should find.

Two grasping churchmen, one the King's great-uncle, the other the King's confessor: how could they justly judge? Was it possible they could empty their heads of the conviction that the waxen doll was certainly an image of Henry, named for him and designed to be his death? Yet Eleanor knew by then what path she must follow, and though it would mean careful walking she was prepared to accept the risk.

Some degree of confidence in the name of Gloucester had returned to her. Deny all at first, but in such general terms that you may admit later those items which must be admitted, without too abject an about-face. The doll cannot well be denied, for they have seen it and handled it; it can only be translated into something harmless. There may be other things as absolute, and these too may be painted in milder colours but not utterly painted out. So proceed, she thought; an inch at a time, and let them go before.

But old Henry Beaufort could be as subtle and delicate as any woman when he would, and had the advantage of her in this, that he was not afraid. The chill feel of death laid hold on her before she was out of his presence, though she kept her head and her resolve. She owned that she had been indiscreet, and had perhaps induced others to actions which could be misinterpreted. She had shown interest in astrology and other obscure arts, which were diabolical only to the ignorant, since God Himself had set the stars in their significant order and made herbs to grow upon the earth; but malice or treason she firmly denied.

Had she caused spirits to be raised to answer her questions? No. Had she procured that Mass should be said over the instruments of divination? It was the part of every devout enquirer, surely, to attempt nothing upon which God's blessing dared not be invoked.

No deed of hers had been or needed to be so hidden. The paper of figures with which some play had been made against Bolingbroke was no more than it seemed to be, a table of calculations concerned with the casting of her horoscope. The church had not forbidden this study. And the chaplain's confession? She kept fast hold of her courage here, for she did not know exactly what he had confessed. She said only that she had committed no treason, nor intended any. What a man in fear of his life will say to serve himself was not for her to guess, nor could she go aside from truth to confirm or combat it. She had never knowingly seduced him to do for her anything which was unlawful. She had desired to know her own future, but not to any other creature's detriment.

And the doll of wax? Was that also a part of her future? She answered yes, it was her dearest hope. She had been ten years married, and was still childless. The doll was a charm to represent the heir she most ardently desired to give to the Duke before her life was too far spent. It was designed to procure her a son, and for no other end. No fire had ever warmed it, but only her hands and her body while she kept it constantly about her. A desperate remedy for an ill she began to find desperate; perhaps an error of judgement and feeling; certainly no crime against any body or soul but her own. With what name then, they asked her, had the figure been baptized? She said firmly that it never had, for the child could have no name until it should be born.

To this she held, seeing no hope of a better front to put on. It was not deliverance, it might not be even life, but she could do no more. This was but the beginning; they would be in no haste to bring her to a trial which must either acquit or destroy her, when by delay and doubt they could drive Humphrey in harness whichever way they wished him to go. A long wait, Eleanor. She wondered where it would be spent.

It was to Leeds Castle in Kent they committed her, on the 11th day of August, there to remain until October, and longer, perhaps, if Humphrey had not gone about the raising of her case with all the energy left in him. Such word as reached her from him in this period was brief always, and devious often, for the ears of the Beauforts were everywhere.

It seemed to her that he had receded from her not merely by the inconsiderable miles separating her prison from London, but by the width of worlds. Often for days together she never thought of him, and ever oftener as time lengthened away from their last meeting she could spare no thought for anyone but herself.

But ever and again his image came back to her, not as he was, but as her fearful and lonely mind desired him to be; not an intelligent, dissolute and cynical man of fifty suddenly smitten into premature age by the shock of his wife's disgrace, but young Humphrey Plantagenet at his height, the great Duke, the Protector of England, levelling his truncheon in anger against his enemies and hers. Almost she persuaded herself he was about the business of raising forces to come and snatch her out of captivity; almost she believed he would indeed come, and listened for the first alarm of trumpets at the gate. That Italianate spirit of his, insatiable in curiosity, ambition and arrogance, should have manifested itself now in arms; his will should have flashed sword-like across the processes of law, and shaken after it echoings of swords.

But at this point he was as English as any of them. He did not come. He sent her no word but the measured and temperate counsel of his love, that she should keep a good heart, speak her defence moderately, and abide the movement of justice as he for his part must abide it.

His mind, which she had believed as lawless as her own, was at bottom a pattern of order. He had committed crimes against it, perhaps, but he had never denied it. Whatever he had done in that long and audacious pursuit of his princely interests, he had never quite lost his reverence for the law of the land, that image he had helped to maintain after his fashion even while he transgressed against it. He had kept the faith of the State as forcibly as he had kept the faith of the Church. He had burned heretics; the Lollards had withered before his fires. How then should he lift his voice for a relapsed witch, two heretical priests and their employer, though she was the very stuff of his own being?

Eleanor fell from this into sick rages, cursed him for a coward and a renegade because he had left her to the mercy of her enemies, wept passionately for her own griefs until she could not see his. Between waiting for him and despairing of him she divided her days most miserably. Jacqueline in Holland, watching in vain for the money and troops he had promised her, and seeing Philip's Burgundians close in upon her at leisure, must have suffered the same anguished alternations of hope and desperation. Jacqueline in the end must have let fall the last of hope out of her hands, and said farewell to the image of him as to a dead man. So at last did Eleanor. A part of that debt for old treason was paid. Her circumstances were comfortable enough, her state maintained; so had been Jacqueline's. She was, none the less, a close prisoner and abandoned by her lord; so had Jacqueline been imprisoned, so forsaken. There might have been less bitterness left in that old wound now, could she have known how exquisitely she was avenged.

By early October they were ready to proceed, the readier because they were assured by then that no armed attack would be made to release her. A special commission had been set up to examine the case against all the accused, and before this panel they were at last indicted of treason, Bolingbroke and Southwell as principals, Eleanor Cobham and Margery Jourdemayne as accessories.

Now at length the Duchess saw her creatures again, and wondered if she herself was so greatly changed. Southwell from old was grown very old in a few short weeks, whitened like a worm that lives underground, dim and peering of vision. A breath of wind must have swayed him, and a gust broken him. His face was so fallen dull with senility that it was not easy to know if he followed what passed with dread or indifference, or indeed if he followed it at all. She thought they would have to make haste if they wanted to hang him. Bolingbroke was not so. He had been a man of vigour and intellect, and without the means to exercise either had grown gaunt and wild and pining as an unflighted hawk. His face was a horn lantern of terror, hard and fixed without, flame within. She did not forget that it was he who had most surely betrayed her. Let him die, as hideously as they could devise, if she could but separate herself from him.

As for the wise woman of Eye, she had wept herself away to a swollen, blowsy distress from which Eleanor turned her eyes in loathing. She was growing old, was Margery, and had hoped to die in her bed; but even after the warning of Windsor she could not let herbs and philtres alone. It was powerful in the blood, this love of being more knowing than the neighbours; and even at some risk, a woman must live.

Their very looks, thought the Duchess, condemn them; but are they to be allowed to damn me also? Or is it possible that I bear myself as wretchedly and seem as guilty as they? I have wept a great deal; I am pale from confinement; but is my face so signed with fear as theirs? She looked about her wonderingly, meeting the eyes of many who had eaten at her table; they regarded her as if she had indeed changed out of recognition, warily, curiously, with an expectation in which she believed she saw pleasure.

The sun had passed from the Duchess of Gloucester now; it was not worth while to smile upon her. None of them had ever courted her for any other reason but to be in the sun, and they made haste to scamper away now she was in shadow, to a place from which they could enjoy her eclipse. Hers she thought it, until she turned her head to see where their sidelong glances travelled from her, and saw her husband seated apart.

Then she understood fully at last their satisfaction in her fall. It was not even for her own sake they most hated her, and delighted deepest to see her disgraced. She was no longer a woman in her own right, innocent or guilty; she was a knife to be slipped in his back and twisted until he died of it, first in reputation, then in very body.

And he was only fifty years old! Seeing him now for the first time in two months, she felt her heart turn in her at his ageing face. Was this her signature? He had lived, it was true, wildly and at the wind's speed since he was made knight at eight years old, and innumerable women before her had contributed their mite to undo him body and mind; yet she had never before remarked this dullness of eye in him, nor seen his forehead so seamed with the shadows of old age and great weariness. He had burned out with too much loving and hating the half of his more than ordinary energy, but she had put flame to the other half before the hour was ripe. He had spent sixty years' value of action and thought in much less of time, but the remaining riches of his life she had poured out for a wizard's fee and left him bankrupt. She looked upon him with anguish, for after her fashion, with all the tenacity and more than the greed of other women, she had loved him.

He went sumptuously, as ever, and bore himself proudly, for pride had been the habit of his body lifelong, and needed no motion of his mind or will to keep it in being. What remained of his beauty now was but colourless and cold, a shell of withered comeliness through which looked out at the eyes an old, sick, sad man prisoned in loneliness and silence from all his fellow-men. This she had made of him.

For a moment she lost her fear for herself and all her resentment of his quiescence in a passion of sorrow which was wholly for him. For a moment only. For this was her life; and happiness, his or hers, was but a secondary prize. Yet her eyes went back to him again and again even while the lords of the Commission questioned her, so that sometimes she answered astray, and had to be prompted a second time. And always she drew back her mind from this groping pursuit of him in renewed dread, almost in anger that he should still be able to trouble her when he no longer could or would help her. It was not in her experience that she should continue to love what had ceased to be profitable to her.

The Commission presented a very comprehensive array of the enemies of Gloucester, apart from a few of the judges, put there, she supposed, to lend credit to the enquiry. There was Huntingdon, there was Stafford, there was William de la Pole, Earl of Suffolk, looking grave and grim and satisfied like a cat sodden and sleepy with cream.

Not even a Beaufort could have hated Humphrey more than he did. What hope had she against such examiners as these? What hope was she meant to have? And there was the whole wretched story to

be dragged through and through again and again, to weariness, to
sickness, the first innocent enquiries after her horoscope, the deeper
questionings after, the Mass in Hornsey Park by night over the
instruments of divination, the wax doll. She must remember to
deny that the mannikin had ever been christened; had it been so
it must have represented either the King or some other living person
for harm, since unborn children bear no Christian names.

Whatever these others might swear against her, she must be
positive in this. If Southwell in extremity said he had baptized the
thing, she would contend they had already driven the old man past
the incalculable point where truth loses its meaning, after which he
would pour out confession after confession upon every crime they
thrust into his consciousness, from a conviction that only by so doing
could he hope ever to be left alone.

If Bolingbroke said it, he lied from malice against her, believing
her the source of his sufferings, and desiring to make her suffer no less
terribly. If Margery — But Margery was now so abject, so miserable
a creature that there was little to fear from her if the others could
be silenced. At the worst she must hold by her story though they all
combined against her. It was at least better to be Eleanor Cobham
than Margery Jourdemayne in this one thing, that they dared not
use the instruments to bring a duchess to confession.

She told over the same story, the credible story of her longing to
give Gloucester an heir. The future she had wished to know was
her future as the mother of a son. But when she looked again at
Humphrey she saw that he had leaned his head by the temple upon
his hand in order that his face might be in shadow even from her.
Rings upon his long fingers took the light. In his curled hair she saw
wastes of grey encroaching. He remained quiet; even the movement
to hide himself had been made with an unobtrusive grace. Of what
use was it to continue thus in dignity at all cost, when the dullest
there must know he was broken with grief past mending? Again she
thought, "Is this all I have done for him in the end?"

Once — she remembered it well — he had not been able to ride
through London without a crowd running at his stirrups, cheering
and shouting for their "good Duke Humphrey". He had every grace
the Cardinal Bishop of Winchester lacked, and could flourish the
people's adoration in the old man's face whenever he pleased, merely
by showing his own upon the streets. She remembered the rash
pageant of the embarkation for Flanders, when she had ridden in
Jacqueline's train admiring the casual grace of his back as he saluted
his people king-like along the way, tossing his smiles left and right for
largesse, the very pattern of his brother Harry, and adored for it by his

brother Harry's citizens. The puny little King had been nothing then, for here in the Protector's person rode royalty itself. He had laughed at the title they gave him, knowing himself no closer acquainted than most men with goodness, nor willing for expediency's sake to draw any nearer to so unprofitable a virtue; but he had kept the legend alive without an effort, and always that shouting had gone before him through the town.

All his life until then he had gone surrounded by clouds of witness. When had the tide begun to ebb? It was far out now, and would not turn again. When she had thought thus far she could not well keep out of her mind those London housewives, women of good repute and fair standing, who had felt so bitterly about her that they had gone to the Lords to protest against the Duke's abandonment of his wife to her distresses for the sake of a harlot. Was not this clear enough? For them the harlot had remained a harlot even after she had supplanted the wife, and never again could Humphrey's gracious manners make them forget or forgive the irregularities of his private life. He was to blame in this, that he had made that life a matter of public interest; but it was she who had made it a public scandal.

What had followed? The turbulent period of the quarrels with the Cardinal had helped to make London perhaps a little weary of both Beaufort and Plantagenet. The Council had so detested his rule that they had caused the King to be crowned in 1429, at eight years of age, and declared the protectorate to be at an end, the better to be rid of the stranglehold of Gloucester, and for all he had been supreme again while Henry was being crowned in France, Archbishop Kemp and others of Beaufort's party had seen to it that his power was narrower than before.

The commons had liked his strict dealings with heresy among the Lollards, and his championship of British rights in France, never observing that it was he himself who had made them impossible of maintenance; yet the reins had somehow slipped from his hands since he took her to wife. Of late no more public appointments, less shouting for him in the streets; and now at last the shadow of treason drawing so near him that his face was blackened. There he sat shading his eyes with his hand, an old man, with the ruins of all his titles, past and present, lying in invisible shards about him; Humphrey Plantagenet, Duke of Gloucester, Earl of Pembroke, veteran of Harfleur and Agincourt, Lord of the March of Llanstephan near Carmarthen, Warden of the Cinque Ports, Constable of Dover, Lord of the Isle of Wight and of Carisbrooke, and of God knew what lands beside. He had been a whole man until his wife had broken his life in pieces.

For her tears she scarcely saw the faces of her examiners as they gave judgement, and for the thunder of the outgoing tide of his fortune in her ears scarcely heard or understood what was said of herself. Afterwards they told her that she was committed to the ecclesiastical court with Margery Jourdemayne, but Southwell and Bolingbroke were in the hands of the secular justices. Nor was the waiting long. Of this she could be glad even in the stupor of her despair, as men under torture are glad to draw nearer to death.

She was now so exhausted with emotion that she sat her days through in a dead calm, which was never broken but for those rare moments when some word or message carried the memory of her husband again into her heart. No other news did more than ripple her indifference. When they told her that Canon Southwell was dead in the Tower she seemed only to grudge him his happiness. And again more gently she wished that Margery too might die before sentence, for she had dealt honestly in the matter of the philtres, and even purchased so his faithfulness had been no little nor light possession.

On the 21 October she came again to St Stephen's Chapel before a new Commission of bishops, and heard the full indictment against her, in all twenty-eight articles of treason, conspiracy, witchcraft and heresy. Once again she firmly denied every count of treason or heresy, but thought well to admit her unwisdom in certain minor counts.

It was now so familiar as to be wearisome, and her lips stiffened against the long stupidity and sorrow of speaking it again. Still they questioned, and still she must reply. It was not for her to collapse in incoherent weeping, half imbecile with terror, like poor Margery. Whatever witnesses were brought to testify against her she must keep her countenance and her calm. So much at least she owed to Humphrey. But if Southwell's damned servants had been more strictly watched, all this coil need never have begun. She dared not think of that now. It was enough to remember and repeat, in spite of her fatigue and disgust, the story of her design to gain a child by sympathetic means. That was the mainspring. She could do no more, and if this did not avail she would remain erect, at least, and utter no appeal. Having repeated in face of the testimony of witnesses her firm denials, she said only that she submitted herself to the correction of the bishops in the matter of her lesser errors; and so was silent.

They were found to be guilty both, as in her heart she had known they must be.

Sentence was not pronounced until her last appearance before the Commission, upon the 13th day of November. Margery, as a relapsed witch, was condemned to the fire at Smithfield, and for Eleanor there waited three days of public penance, and thereafter perpetual imprisonment. Sir Thomas Stanley was named as the warden of her captivity, and for her maintenance, because she was the consort of a prince, the sum of one hundred marks a year was set aside. Nevertheless this was a death, and the price the price of a funeral.

When she was again removed to her solitude she asked what was become of Bolingbroke, and learned that he was to suffer the traitor's death. Hume, long since pardoned, for what services she could well guess, would think himself happily delivered of this dolorous company. Perhaps he would be in the streets tomorrow when the crier belled for her, and the candle was set in her hand. She dared not think of Humphrey now. Let him forget for three days at least that he had ever taken a second wife. She now for the first time would have her own progress through London streets, shouting enough about her ears, and crowds to run beside her. This time they would be content with their duchess at last.

She performed her penance. For three days she was paraded through London upon a triple penitential pilgrimage, wrapped in the loose white garment of the returned sinner, bareheaded, barefooted, bearing a two-pound candle in her hand. Such a show was always worth seeing, whoever the victim might be; but for Eleanor Cobham they made full holiday.

Such things are not forgotten, because the mind receives from them not merely an impression, as though a hand had pressed deeply into a cushion, but a patterned corrosion which time may weather a little but never efface until the material itself perishes. Her penitent's sheet was no whiter than her face as she went upon her barefoot triumph.

She looked like an image of snow, or like her own waxen mannikin. Unborn child or recluse King, what did it matter now? If it had been meant to kill it had not failed of its effect, for three deaths had already been brought about by it, and who knew how many more might not follow? If it had been meant to bring to birth the ritual had somewhere gone terribly awry, for all it had engendered was pain, ruin and despair. Let it rest now. It was enough, surely, that she walked thus steadily with filed eyes and marble mouth, looking neither to left nor right for all the faces that crowded upon her, and all the voices that shrilled in her ears. It was enough that her soiled feet trod tenderly and slow, leaving smears of blood along the cobbles, and her outstretched hand wavered under the candle's weight, and her heart in her breast felt to her like a white-hot stone.

Three days in indignity and exhaustion she made her enforced devotions, setting her candle upon the altar out of a hand that shook violently at the relief from its weight, staring mutely into its flame as it settled into a steady burning, and turning from it upon her return journey without a look aside for fear she should somewhere see among the many faces the one face she dreaded most to see. And having so far discharged under guard the worst of her punishment, she lay all night sleepless, regarding her blank and bitter despair.

Before she was taken away to her prison at Chester Castle her husband was permitted to see her. They looked upon each other for what it seemed must be the last time.

There was little to say, now that they were given time and opportunity; it was too late by far for reproaches or for hopes. The case at law was dead ground, and her presumption and folly as far past as his abandonment of her to justice. There was little left to be said. Strange silences came down between them, during which they looked fixedly upon each other, as though the eyes had a more articulate language left them than had the tongue.

"I shall not cease," he said, "to intercede for you with the King until I obtain your pardon."

"The King will not let you into his presence," she replied. "You stand too close to me to be safe company for kings."

"I have stood in my time close to him also, and it has been to his profit. We are of the same blood; he will not forget that."

"And we are one flesh," she said, "and he will not forget that, either. Save yourself, for I am damned."

"What avails, then, my salvation, since we are one flesh? Yet do not doubt, my lady, that I shall reach him by one means or another. If I live, your cause shall be constantly before him until he relents towards you. This is all I can promise, and this I vow to you from my heart."

"Do not entertain any hope," she said, "for death has been let loose between us, and I doubt I shall never get by him to join hands with you honestly again." And suddenly she shook for the rising thoughts of Margery shrieking in the fire, and Bolingbroke's head shrivelling upon London Bridge and his dismembered body scattered among the cities of England.

At the end, when he was about to leave her, she looked up at him suddenly and said, "You do not call me innocent, nor ask me anything of what I have done."

"To what end?" he said. "Whether the answer be well or ill, I am yours no less. We have known each other too well to live upon virtue or faith. Birth, death — it is all one in the end."

"But you do not believe me guilty?" she said.

"Nor innocent either. My mind is quite gone by it."

It was in this fashion they parted. Long afterwards a woman who waited upon her asked in strictest confidence the question he had forborne to ask, "Madam, tell me truly, was the wax image indeed of the child you lacked, or was it to stand for the King?" And she smiled, for by then in a sombre fashion she could smile; but she made no answer.

She had been wise after her kind, for the summer of Gloucester was over. From that time the King, nervous of the very name, denied him his presence. It was safe for any man to lift the threat of impeachment against him, to allege this misconduct or that in the years of his protectorate, to hint at calling him to account for old sins. She in her solitude, at Chester first and then at Kenilworth, heard rumours of his usage, and knew at whose door it lay. Between them they had done infamous things; no worse, perhaps, than most creatures do into whose hands fortune drops the corruption of power, yet infamous things. But all came home in the end.

By the year 1447, when the last requital fell due, she was in Peel Castle in the Isle of Man, there to remain until her death; and there they brought her word of his.

Parliament met at Bury that year on 10 February, and certain of his enemies made great play with the fact that Humphrey was not there to the day. He was in Wales, they said, raising an armed revolt against the King; and they so worked upon the poor wretch – what could not his new spitfire of a wife do with him, all the more surely with William de la Pole to back her arguments? – that he sent out to meet the Duke at his late coming before he could enter the town, and ordered him directly to his lodging in the North Spital of St Saviour's, on the Thetford Road. There after dinner on the same night Buckingham and Beaumont and others came to him and put him under arrest at the King's orders, and after him most of his followers were also placed under guard. After that who could say what had happened? He was lost to sight of all but his keepers. They said he fell ill; it might well be true. On 23 February he died, so much was certain. Death is a very positive thing, however shy and irresolute its causes may be. He was dead, and they had buried him, on the north side of the shrine at St Albans, where he had once spent Christmas with Jacqueline of Hainault, and with her been admitted to the fraternity of the abbey. All comes home in the end. If her body was not laid with his, no doubt but she had left a morsel of her heart there to wait for him.

"Is it true," said Eleanor, pondering, "that he went to Bury under arms?"

"It is true, madam, that he had some force with him, but not a great force."

Enough, however, she thought, to intimidate Henry at a pinch. For he had sent her word he was determined to use this Parliament to get the King's ear, and give him no peace until he had granted her pardon. No peace, but perhaps a sword. His best special pleading had always been done with the sword. How could she know if his death was murder, or his deed treason? And did it matter that she must never know? It might well be that his arrogant heart, worn out with long misuse and vehement grief, had burst at this last indignity. But there were other possibilities. A pillow over the face in sleep! A little draught in the wine of a guarded man! These things have been known.

Whether so cold a wind had blown on it or whether it had guttered out of itself, the flame was extinguished now. Why should she question if he had not questioned? Every man, every woman, is alone at last with secrets. Let it rest, and let him rest. As for her, now that he was gone her function was ended, and no-one would trouble about her any more. She would not even die, but only dwindle away inchmeal from every mind which had known her, and in the end be forgotten of man, disappearing into the obscurity from which she had come. She was dead while she still lived.

So in his new grave on the north side of the shrine at St Albans, on the 4th day of March, 1447, his history and hers end together.

# ORDEAL BY FIRE
# Mary Monica Pulver

*We have already encountered Mary Pulver as one half of the writing team whose nom de plume is Margaret Frazer. Mary Pulver is an accomplished author in her own right, with a series of novels about mid-west police detective Peter Brichter. But she has also written a short series about Father Hugh, a fifteenth-century priest, who has some rather unorthodox methods of rooting out sin and solving crimes. The following is a new story, specially written for this anthology.*

F ather Hugh, mass priest of St Osburga's Abbey, invited his three visitors in and seated them in the main room of his little house outside the cloister wall. It was between Vespers and Compline, and the early evening air was further darkened by a light fog, but he had said it would be a brief meeting on a matter of some importance.

Because of the fog the air was chill, though it was May. Father Hugh offered each visitor a cup of mulled wine from a pot he was keeping warm before the fire. He sat on his little stool in front of the hearth, and the three men sat down to drink their wine.

"Robin, I want to thank you for braving the flames when Annie Bridges' house burnt three nights ago," Father Hugh began conversationally. "It was a blessing you happened by." He was a small man, barely more than child-sized, though his tonsure was less an artifice each year. "If you hadn't, poor Annie might have been burnt in her bed."

Robin Fitzralph bent his fair head and blushed to the tips of his ears. He was sitting on the room's second stool in the middle of the floor, unable to decide whether to sprawl and be comfortable, or keep his knees drawn up and so take up less space. "I wished I'd known about the piglets," he murmured. "I could've carried out two small piglets along with her, easy." He was seventeen, tall and very strong, the second son of a prosperous franklin, but for all that as shy as a girl.

"Nae the less, she's the better for the fire, now, be'nt she?"

demanded Pers Hawkins from his place on the bench against the wall. He thumped a work-marred hand on the table in front of him, an unconscious gesture of frustration. Pers was a prosperous villein, working hard to earn the money that would purchase his freedom. He had been elected reeve this year by his fellow villager, and was resentful of the burden this office laid on him. A gaunt man, he had a long, narrow face with a nose that stuck out like the blade of a hatchet.

"God works in mysterious ways," remarked the man sharing the bench. Father Clement, rector of St Mary's in the nearby village, was tall, with a square, strong face. He was not clever, and was made nervous by people trying to rise above themselves, a too-common ambition in this year of our Lord's grace, 1451.

Since her husband had died two years ago, Annie had often been at her wits' end to keep body and soul together. She had somewhere gotten two sickly piglets, and had hoped to save them by keeping them warm by her hearth. Though in the end Father Clement had comforted her as she stood weeping in the ashes of what had been her house, first he rebuked her for not properly banking her fire.

"'Tis greed for more than God wants you to have that brought you to this," he had said. "You were trying to keep those piglets alive, and let your fire burn after you went to bed instead of covering it. And see what happened? Sparks from it rose up and set your thatch alight."

Annie had denied it, of course; some folk, even caught redhanded in sin, were brought to contrition only with difficulty. It hadn't helped that the whole village rallied around to build her a new cottage that was sounder of roof and wall than her old one. Worse, it was like a slap to his rebuke when Robin brought her a fine young gelt to replace the sick piglets.

To her credit, Annie had said she didn't deserve a new pig. That set off a quarrel so loud half the village came to see what the noise was about. Mortified with shyness and embarrassment, Robin had explained that he'd failed to save her piglets, so this was not a gift but his way of setting things right. The onlookers found this backwards argument – he insisting she take a valuable pig, she trying to refuse it – amusing. It had become a joke for miles around. Both for saving her life and giving her the pig, the still foolish but now also brave Robin had become a kind of folk hero, which left him in a more or less permanent blush. And Annie, instead of suffering for her sin of greed, was rarely in want of friends or help any more.

"Yes, she's not in danger of losing her holding, is she?" said Father Hugh now, in reply to Pers' angry question. Annie Bridges had in right of her late husband only a single strip in each of the three great fields that sprawled around the village; and one, of course, must lie fallow each year. But the strips had produced just enough grain and peas to keep her going.

Then her old ox had died this past winter, so she could not add to the village plow team. Nor was she strong enough to help in some other way and so maintain her right to sow and reap in the fields. Pers' several strips lay alongside hers, as his big house sat beside her cottage in the village; and with three strong sons and four oxen, well able to add to his holding. It had seemed inevitable that he would be granted hers, and that she would become another of the beggars that came daily to the abbey gates seeking the meager remains of the nuns' dinners.

That would have been a harsh end for Annie, Pers agreed, but he felt he needed that holding. The King, pushed by his voracious wife, had overspent himself and Commons, in its supine way, had voted a rise in taxes to help him meet his needs. The tax collectors had been unusually thorough, and Pers' lord had passed along the pain, asking more of his peasants. Meanwhile the country was being overrun by government officials eager to sniff out treason. Last year, Pers' oldest son had sympathized with the Jack Cade rebellion, and Pers feared he might have to find the bribes it would take to deaden the official noses. He needed to expand in order just to stay even.

But it now appeared he couldn't volunteer to take on Annie's holding until she died, since the village was willing to exert itself to keep Annie, and the pig joke, going.

The rise in the village's good will and charity was so marvelous that Father Clement was ready to believe it was another of God's mysterious workings – if he could only be convinced the root cause of the whole event wasn't Annie's greed.

"Your horse must have eyes like a cat," said Father Hugh to Robin as he refilled his cup. "I hear you like to ride at night."

"No, he's just a plain old horse," replied Robin. "But in the dark he just barely lifts his feet off the ground, and so he doesn't stumble. It makes for a smoother ride than in daylight."

"I hope you give your horse a chance to rest during the day, to make up for your working him at night," said Father Hugh, who had a soft spot in his heart for animals.

"Er-hem," said Father Clement diffidently, but seeing the meek eyes of the young man turned to him, dared to ask, "What does your father say about your going out when good Christians are in bed?"

"Oh, nothing much." But as if replying to his father's "nothing much," the boy continued defensively, "I've nothing better to do, anyhow. My brother is the heir, he's the one who needs to rest from his labors. Besides, it was my going out that saved poor Annie's life, and that was a deed worth doing."

"Amen," said Father Hugh.

"I have a horse that would fall into a hole the size of a church in broad daylight," said Pers, partly in order to boast that he had a riding horse himself. "When I have to go out at night, I go on foot."

"Were you also out and about the night Annie's cottage burned?" asked Father Hugh.

Pers blinked at him. "No," he said.

"Someone set fire to Annie's cottage, you know," said Father Hugh.

"Here now, you don't mean it!" said Father Clement.

Robin rose from the low stool he had set in the center of the room. "Of course he doesn't," he said with a too-big gesture. "We all know the abbey priest is fond of jests. This one has come up lame, Father," he said, turning to the monk. "And so now perhaps you will tell us why you asked us here. You said you had a purpose."

"I do. I wish to discover who set Annie's house on fire." Father Hugh peered upward nearsightedly at Robin, who was gaping foolishly at him. The monk was gentle in mien and normally soft-spoken, but he was ruthlessly honest and he hated sin, in himself as much as others. With his common manners and his racy sermons, no one was quite sure how he had come to be mass priest for an abbey of gentle nuns, but few were surprised when he took a more than passing interest in the worldly affairs of the neighborhood.

Robin recovered enough to blush and sit down again. Robin's father had recently consulted Father Hugh about sending the boy to Oxford and making a priest of him. Though he had not put it so strongly, Father Hugh felt Master Fitzralph could sooner make a silk purse of a pig's ear. Robin was no scholar, and a boy of his size and strength would be welcome to take livery and maintenance in almost any lord's household. Father Hugh was sorry Robin's father had not taken his advice; becoming a liveried retainer might have knocked some of the foolishness out of the young man, and his parents would have been well rid of a hearty eater who had nothing better to do than teach his horse to ramble in the dark.

Pers asked in his gruffest voice, "What makes you think the fire was set?"

Father Hugh sipped his wine and said, "For one thing, it began on the outside of the cottage. Several people who came running to Robin's shout told me the whole thatch was alight when Robin staggered out with Annie in his arms. If it had begun inside and spread to the roof, Robin could not have gone in and lived."

"But a spark from an uncovered fire will go through the smoke hole —" began Father Clement.

"Annie's fire was banked," interrupted Father Hugh.

"So she says, but those piglets she somehow acquired — "

"— were not in front of the fire but in her bed with her."

"She never told me — "

"She was ashamed of it, of course. Sleeping with pigs, very like the prodigal son before he repented. But she was trying hard to save the creatures, as hard as if they'd been the children God never blessed her with, to her sorrow and shame."

There was a little silence. Children were an essential blessing. They grew up and cared for their parents as they had been cared for, even as they expected to be cared for by their own children in turn. It was the way of the world, and a good and proper way. Unless, like Annie, one had no children.

"Nab's barn fire started on the outside," said Pers. "Are you saying it was set as well? Perhaps you think all fires hereabouts lately were set!" With houses routinely thatched with reeds and straw, and every one of them containing an open fire, accidents were not uncommon. It was a wonder more people were not burnt in their beds.

"I believe at least three of them were. Nab's barn, Annie Bridges' cottage, and Robin's father's house."

"No, no," protested Robin, rising again to gesture largely. "'Twas the cook, leaving the pot of grease too near the fire while he went out to the jakes. It spilled and ran into the fire and the whole kitchen went up." Robin's eyes grew round with the memory. "I was coming to see how long before dinner, and I heard our servant Jennie screaming and I just ran in and pulled her out. Lost my eyebrows and burnt my hand." He rubbed the back of it reflectively. "She said she was scrubbing parsnips and didn't go near the fire nor the grease pot."

"Going in for her, that was very bravely done, Robin," said Father Clement warmly.

"Yes, people think very well of you for your courage, Robin," agreed Father Hugh.

"I ain't afraid of a bit o' fire," Robin murmured dismissively, but he grinned at the praise.

"Even a bonfire scares me," said Pers with a shudder. "Them sparks flying in every direction. I'd sooner die of cold or starvation than be burnt."

"'Man is born to trouble, as the sparks fly upward,' " said Father Hugh, not exactly pertinently. He was regarding Pers closely.

Robin said to Pers, "I don't like being burnt, either, but I happened to be near, and I couldn't just watch, could I? There's little to fear if you move quick. I wish I could be at every fire, to save people."

"God save your stout heart!" said Father Clement, raising a hand in blessing.

Robin tried to hide the return of his shy grin by turning away, but ran into Father Hugh's regard, which made him blush even deeper. But he lifted his chin and said, "As for someone setting the fires, I never saw anyone running away from my father's kitchen nor Annie's house."

"Were you looking for someone running away?"

"Well . . . no, I guess not." Made restless by Father Hugh's piercing look, Robin began a circuit of the room, seeking a new topic. But the small room was bare of anything more than a table and bench, two books on a shelf, and a pair of stools. "Here, what's this?" he said, pointing with his foot at a narrow length of black iron beside the hearth. It was rough surfaced, as if it had been long neglected until someone had rubbed the rust off.

"It's the ordeal iron from St Frideswide's in Oxford," said Father Hugh. "They were going to give it to the smith to make into horseshoes, but I wouldn't let them. It was famous in its time."

"Famous for what?"

"Back in the days when men trusted to the judgement of God," replied Father Hugh in a voice that suddenly held echoes of his high-pitched sermon cry, "if a man was suspected of a crime, they would accuse him before the altar, and if he still denied his guilt, they would lift that iron out of a brazier with pincers. Red hot, it was, and the accused had to take hold of it in his naked hand and walk ten paces before he dropped it. They would say a Mass and pray God would judge the case, and wrap the hand in a clean cloth and leave it three days. If it was healing clean when they unwrapped it, he was innocent. But if the burn mortified, he was guilty."

"Pah, that's but superstition," said Pers, who was something of a freethinker.

"I think God wants us to use our wits and our hearts when we seek the truth of evil doing," agreed Father Clement, but mildly, because he was willing to see the hand of God in everything. "I was taught that because our Lord Jesu said, 'Thou shalt not tempt the Lord thy God,' we don't do the ordeal any longer."

"What, am I the only man present who believes in miracles?" said Father Hugh.

"Nay, nay," said Robin, "God can do anything, we all know that. Why, Father Hugh, you know yourself my Aunt Elizabeth had a growth in her throat that melted away when she prayed that St John might ask our Lord Jesu to help her. She went on pilgrimage to Compostella in thanksgiving. You have said many a time that God watches over each of us."

"And so He does," said Father Clement.

"Why then the iron shouldn't burn the hand of the innocent at all, should it?" asked Pers, boldly arguing theology in the face of two priests. "God should put His own hand between the hot iron and the innocent flesh of the man being tested, leaving it whole."

"Pers, if I should heat this iron red hot in the forge in your village and ask you to walk ten paces with it, would you expect God to protect your hand?" asked Father Hugh.

Pers hesitated. "That's not fair," he said at last. "I am innocent of fire-setting, but I believe my hand would be burnt, same as any man's would be, even your own."

"But you did say when Annie's cottage burnt down that you should acquire her holding."

Pers was suddenly aware of the danger he was in. "But I didn't think it beforehand! I didn't ever say, *if* Annie's cottage should burn down, I would ask for her holding. It only come to me after that it should."

"That sounds like an honest reply. Still – Hand me the iron, Robin."

The young man stooped eagerly to pick it up. And immediately screamed and dropped it again, making everyone else start to his feet.

"Here, what's the matter?" asked Father Clement, coming to take Robin by the arm.

"My hand, it burnt my hand!" gasped the young man, gripping himself at the wrist. Father Clement turned it over to show the palm red and blistered.

"Well, why did you reach into the fire for it, then?" asked Pers.

"It wasn't in the fire." The boy was staring first at the iron, then his injured palm.

Father Hugh stooped and picked up the bar, ignoring a warning cry from Robin. "It doesn't feel warm to me." He tested its weight in his hand before dropping it with a loud clang. Father Clement gaped at him, but the little monk only came to peer at Robin's hand. "Oh yes, what an ugly blister! Come along, you need to have that seen to. Dame Agnes, our infirmarian, has a salve that soothes burns. Get the door, Pers."

But Pers was gaping, too, his eyes moving from Father Hugh to Robin and back again. "What nonsense is this?" he demanded.

"Does this look like nonsense?" cried Robin, holding out his hand. "See how it burnt me but not Father Hugh? We don't need any salve, there's no salve that will keep this hand from mortifying. This was the hand that set Nab's barn alight, and spilled the grease onto the kitchen hearth! This was the hand that kindled the thatch of Annie Bridges' cottage; God saw it and God has judged me!"

Pers crossed himself and Father Hugh said, "Speak ye true, Robert Fitzralph?" calling the young man by his Christian name.

"Aye, by my head, I do."

"This is God's doing!" proclaimed Father Clement. "How else to explain cold iron burning a guilty man's hand?"

"But – why?" asked Pers. "Did you have a quarrel with Annie Bridges?"

"Yes, tell us," said Father Hugh in a high-pitched voice. "Why did you burn the barn, and your father's kitchen, and Annie's cottage?"

"I have no quarrel with any man," said Robin. "It began as a prank. I was out riding at night, and saw the barn all alone in the field, no one around, and set it alight with my lantern. I had no reason, it was just for fun, and I hid behind a tree and watched it burn. But two servants ran in and saved some of the wool that was stored in it, and folks made heroes of them. I knew I could be as brave as any servant, if I had the chance. So then I spilled the grease into the fire, and when Jennie began screaming, I ran in and dragged her out. 'Twasn't much of a fire, but I never had such a round of shoulder clapping and praise before. My heart swelled in me, and I liked that. So I set Annie's house on fire, shouted so people would come to watch, then ran in and saved her. That was harder, but I did it. And everywhere I went, I was not pointed out as a fool like before but the man I truly am."

"Yes, we see now the kind of man you are," said Father Hugh in a strained voice. "But enough, come along. Take hold of him, Father Clement. Get the door, Pers. After we put something on that hand, Robin, we'll have to find a safe place to keep you until the crowner comes. Excuse me, I will go ahead to the cloister gate and ring the bell for our infirmarian to come at once."

Robin was treated and then locked in an empty larder. Father Clement rode off on Robin's horse to notify his family. The bell for Compline not yet having rung, Father Hugh was granted an audience with the abbess.

"I first suspected Pers, because he had a strong motive, and thinks his need is even greater than it is. Then I suspected Robin because he was seen riding out after dark, and is a great foolish gawp who too clearly enjoyed being a hero. And he too readily agreed to give Annie a pig after I talked with him."

"So you were sure Robin was the guilty one before he came to your house," guessed Abbess Margaret.

"No, not until I talked to both of them in my house. It was as we talked I became certain that Robin was guilty of all three fires. I was already reasonably sure he set the kitchen fire, for no one else was there besides Jennie, and she would not start a fire that would trap her in the kitchen with it. Pers had a better motive for Annie's house, but he's afraid of fire; he is the sort who would not dare stand under a thatch and light it lest its flames reach out and burn him to a crisp. And Robin's sudden fondness for riding at night bespeaks a man doing what he does not wish anyone to see. His description of his horse's stepping carefully fits that of a horse walking without the aid of a lantern."

Abbess Margaret asked shrewdly, "If God's truth disagreed with your reasoning and Robin's hand was not burnt, would you have handed the ordeal iron to Pers?"

"The ordeal iron would have burnt the hand of any man who grasped it, Domina."

"So it wasn't a miracle," said the abbess.

"No, I heated the iron all afternoon in my fireplace, and then let the talk go on until I could barely feel the heat from it with my foot before I asked the guilty man to pick it up. I wouldn't have minded letting a fire-setter's hand burn to the bone, but I knew to make him confess I would have to pick it up after him." Domina Margaret's eyebrows lifted and he hastened to explain, "A man cannot be a priest without working fingers, and I wasn't about to risk that. And never fear the false rumor of a miracle; I made sure Father Clement and Pers both saw Dame Agnes put her salve on my hand as well." When the bandage on his right hand was changed three days later, the burn was healing clean.

# THE CHAPMAN AND THE TREE OF DOOM
## Kate Sedley

*I only encountered the Roger the Chapman novels by Kate Sedley after I had finalized* The Mammoth Book of Historical Whodunnits. *The series has so far run to four novels, the first of which was* Death and the Chapman *(1991). The year is 1471, and we encounter Roger, a nineteen-year-old lapsed Benedictine novice who, having discovered that he is not suited to the monastic life, has set out on the road as a chapman, or pedlar. He soon finds himself trying to solve the mystery of not one but two disappearances. His adventures have followed in* The Plymouth Cloak *(1992),* The Hanged Man *(1993) and* The Holy Innocents *(1994), by which time we have only reached 1475, so there is clearly much more to tell of Roger's long and active life. The following is the first short story about Roger's travels and investigations and was written specially for this anthology.*

*Kate Sedley is the pen name of Brenda Clarke (b. 1926), the author of a dozen romantic novels and, under her maiden name of Brenda Honeyman, the author of a further sixteen historical novels, starting with* Richard by Grace of God *(1968). She is a native of Bristol, the setting of several of Roger the Chapman's adventures, and took to writing after a period in the Civil Service and a stint with the British Red Cross during the latter part of the war.*

Although the wind tasted salt in my mouth, the sea was not yet in sight. I was walking through a clinging September mist, and in the distance, I could hear the gentle sobbing of the waves.

My chapman's pack weighed heavily, for I had been on the move since early morning, with only a single halt at an alehouse, now some miles behind me. The landlord had done his best to dissuade me from travelling further.

"You could lose yer way easy in this weather, chapman," he advised, in his thick Devonshire burr. "And few enough people in those fishing hamlets to make it worth your while when you get there."

I shrugged. "There are women, I suppose, who need needles and thread and pins. And I've never met a female yet, however isolated her existence, who won't spend the odd coin on a ribbon or a piece of lace. I've walked the South Hams before, although not this particular stretch of them."

My host shrugged and left the matter there. I might have followed his advice and turned back inland, but for a temporary lightening of the sky which determined me to press on and reach my goal. I had only walked a few miles, however, when a mist descended, hampering my progress.

Now, however, it lifted abruptly, as it is apt to do in those parts, and in something less than the length of half a furrow, I had stepped from a grey pall into clear, if pallid sunshine. Ahead, I could see the edge of a line of cliffs, and in a few moments more, was looking down at the shining stretch of sand below me.

I was standing on a headland, a promontory which separated two bays, each with its own cluster of slate-roofed cottages. Fishing nets were laid outside to dry. A line of redshanks waded in the shallows, their black bills pecking hungrily at bits of flotsam, whilst a flock of gulls wheeled and screamed overhead, their bellies and underwings gleaming in the sunlight, turning them into the firebirds of ancient myth. Thin grasses crested the dunes, affording protection for upturned boats, and the rocks were veined with yellow seaweed.

But what really drew my attention was an island, some two or three hundred yards offshore, connected to the mainland by a causeway of hard-packed sand; a causeway plainly submerged at high tide, pitted and rutted as it was by the constant washing of the tide. On the summit of this rocky mound stood a chapel, part of the monastic building closer to the water's edge. Sheep grazed on the rising ground and the man who tended them wore the white habit of the Cistercians, indicating that this was a cell of either Buckfast or Buckland Abbey. There was also a small stone cottage like those of the fishermen, enclosed in a wattle paling. It was a peaceful scene.

I became aware of someone standing beside me, and glanced down to see a thin, barefoot girl, holding a basket of mushrooms.

"Want to buy some?" she asked. "They're fresh. I just picked 'em."

"It's forbidden to sell field mushrooms by law," I answered. "They resemble the death cap mushroom too closely."

The child snorted. "City law don't run 'ere, maister. We makes our own." She pointed to a solitary, wind-bitten tree which grew some few feet back from the edge of the cliff, sinister somehow in its isolation. "That's what we call the Tree of Doom, that is." She turned a sharp little face up to mine, the pale eyes glittering with a morbid excitement. "There'll be goings on there, this morning. They're goin' to 'ang the stranger and Colin Cantilupe from that tree. And then they'll burn Rowena." A nervous tongue shot out to lick the pretty lips. "That's what they do to women 'oo murder their 'usbands."

I turned the girl round to face me and I could feel the fragile bones beneath the skin.

"What do you mean?" I demanded suspiciously. "Who are 'they'? And what authority do they have to put people to death without trial?"

"Lemme go!" She wriggled furiously in an effort to free herself. "The elders, that's 'oo 'they' are. An' if you don' believe me, look down there!"

She pointed triumphantly at the shore below us, and I saw that the tranquillity of a few moments earlier had been banished by a procession which was now wending its way across the causeway from the island. Two men and a woman, frantically protesting, their arms tightly pinioned, were being dragged by a score or so of others towards the mainland. One of their captors carried a stout hempen rope coiled around his shoulder, while one of the white-robed monks trotted alongside, flapping ineffectual hands and making a half-hearted attempt to halt the procession's progress. The remaining Brothers watched from the safety and distance of the monastic enclosure.

I released the girl so suddenly that she toppled over, and her invective pursued me as I ran down the stony track which led from the cliff top to the sands. My pack thumped against my back, but I scarcely noticed it, so intent was I on preventing what was about to happen. I raced towards the grim procession, shouting, and the leaders gradually slowed to a halt, their mouths sagging open with surprise. I stopped in front of them, my arms widespread, and after a moment, a tall, grey-haired man with a weather-beaten face stepped out of the ruck and fixed me with a pair of piercing blue eyes.

"Who are you," he asked, "and what is your business here?"

I nodded at the prisoners. "Whatever crime you accuse these people of committing, you cannot execute them out of hand. The sheriff's officers must be sent for from Plymouth. They must be given a fair and proper hearing."

There was an angry murmur and several of the men made

threatening movements in my direction, but the older man raised an arm and at once there was silence.

"I ask again, who are you? And how dare you interfere in our affairs?"

I returned his gaze steadily, but was suddenly afraid. There was an air of menace about the little crowd, heightened by the loneliness of the spot and the grey, tossing, restless waves.

"I'm just a chapman," I answered, "come to see if your womenfolk have need of my wares. But I can't stand by and watch you take the lives of three people who haven't received the full benefit of law." I appealed to the monk, who stood miserably kneading his hands together. "Brother, you and the other members of your cell cannot possibly give your blessing to such proceedings."

"My son," he replied, "we have to live among these people and our protests are not heeded. It is wild and remote here, and they have their own ways of dealing with offenders. We are peaceful men."

And scared men, too, I thought. Too scared to inform your Abbot of what goes on in these parts for fear of what may happen to you. I knew that there were many communities like these fishermen, cut off from the life of the towns, subject to no laws but those of their own devising. Their retribution was usually harsh and swift.

I glanced at the three accused; at the extreme terror on the face of the half-fainting woman, at the wild-eyed ferocity of the younger man, and at the older's expression of mingled fear and resignation. I swung up my cudgel, grasping it in both hands and weighing it with slow deliberation.

"I am willing to offer myself as these people's champion," I said. "You may kill them without trial, but you will have to kill me first."

My heart beat even faster as I waited for someone to call my bluff. Would I really have laid down my life for three strangers, who, for all I knew at the time, might well have been guilty of the crime of which they were charged? I have often wondered, for I am a coward at heart, like most men. I was relying, as I had done so often in the past, on my height and girth to impress my audience. I raised my heels slightly so that I towered above them, even their leader, who was himself only a little short of six feet tall.

Taking advantage of their momentary hesitation, I continued, "At least tell me what your prisoners are accused of."

It was the woman captive who, gathering her scattered wits and buoyed up by a sudden, unexpected gleam of hope, answered my question.

"They say Colin and I paid this man here to kill my husband!"
Her voice rose hysterically. "But we didn't! We didn't!"

"Before God, we did not!" the younger man echoed. "Michael
Cantilupe was a good man and my uncle. I would never have had
him done to death."

A feminine voice shrilled, "But you didn't mind cuckoldin' 'im,
did you?"

There was a mutter of agreement from the rest of the crowd, and
once again the mood became threatening. The grey-haired man said,
"We are wasting time! Take the men to the cliff top and hang them!
Then gather wood for the fire."

The woman let out a howl of animal terror, and this time fainted
clean away. I swung my cudgel and stood my ground.

"Listen to me!" I shouted. "If you have no respect for man's law,
have respect for God's! Think of the peril to your immortal souls if
even one of these three is innocent of the charge laid against them.
Brother! Tell them that everyone here will be guilty of murder should
that prove to be so."

The Cistercian nodded vigorously, made bolder by the presence
of an ally. The group fell back a little, seized by doubt and looked
towards the older man for guidance. He, however, was not so easily
intimidated.

"Michael Cantilupe was my friend. I'll not see his murderers go
free." His eyes blazed defiance at me.

"Then send to Plymouth for the sheriff."

His lips curled angrily.

"We've no need of city justice! For generations, we've known
how to deal with our own." He turned to the others. "Take them
up!"

"Wait!" I pleaded desperately. "First listen to what I have to say.
Your prisoners may be guilty, but for the sake of Our Blessed Lady,
let us be certain. I have had some small success in solving mysteries
and ferreting out the truth of such things. It's a talent that the Good
Lord, in His wisdom, has bestowed upon me. Give me until noon
tomorrow to talk to people, to ask questions. If, at the end of that
time, I have nothing more to add to what you already know, I will
go on my way and make no trouble for you or yours. On that you
have my solemn promise."

The grey-haired man eyed me with hostility.

"You don't understand, chapman." He indicated the eldest of the
prisoners. "This man, who calls himself Baldwin Zouche, was caught
by Brother Anselm in the act of withdrawing his knife from Michael's
back, and he has since confessed that Rowena and Colin Cantilupe

paid him to do the deed. The money, six gold angels, was found upon his person."

"It's a lie!" Colin Cantilupe shrilled. "We didn't hire him to kill anyone. Where would I lay my hands on so much money?"

"Did I say that the coins were yours?" the older man asked grimly. "But Michael was a thrifty man who worked hard all his life and saved his money. Who would know better where he kept it than his wife?"

Mistress Cantilupe, who had recovered consciousness in time to hear this accusation, spat viciously.

"He never told me where he kept his precious hoard!"

I saw that she was not a woman who would win much sympathy. She had once been very pretty, but discontent had carved deep lines about her eyes and mouth. It was, like the younger man's, a weak face, and I judged that here were two unhappy people drawn together by a mutual bond of misery and dissatisfaction.

I switched my gaze to Baldwin Zouche, the only one of the three who had confessed to the murder. But why should he accuse the other two if they were innocent? I studied him carefully and noted that in spite of fear for his approaching end, there was a look of secret satisfaction in the slight smile that lifted the corners of his mouth. I had met people of his stamp before; people who gloried in making mischief. Even standing on the brink of eternity, they could derive a malignant pleasure from the thought of doing further evil.

And it was in that moment that I became convinced of Colin and Rowena Cantilupe's innocence. But who was Baldwin Zouche protecting by his lies? I turned again to the fishermen's leader.

"A day," I begged. "That's all I ask to try to discover the truth of this matter. A short enough time, I should have thought, to ensure the health of your immortal souls."

A little sigh ran through the assembled company, and there was a sudden slackening of intent. I could feel it and so could the grey-haired man. He hesitated a moment longer, but knew that he was being willed to agree. Grudgingly, he gave his assent.

"A day then, that's all. This time tomorrow, unless you can show us any reason to the contrary, the fire will be lit and the Tree of Doom receive its fruit." He turned once again to his followers and indicated the prisoners. "Take them back to Michael's cottage and lock them in, then set a guard about the place. No one but the chapman is to be allowed in or out, except one goodwife who will take them food." He swung back to me. "Very well, you have had your way. I am Jude Bonifant, the Chief Elder of this community." His hawk-like features relaxed a little. "Are you hungry?" And when I nodded, he added,

"In that case, you'd better come with me. My Goody will feed us, and while she does so, I'll tell you of Michael Cantilupe and what happened on the island last night."

While we drank a good fish soup and ate bread fresh from Goody Bonifant's oven, her husband told me the history of the murdered man.

"Michael Cantilupe was born here and christened for the Archangel Michael, patron saint of mariners, whose chapel you may see atop the island. Cantilupes, Shapwicks and Bonifants've lived along this shore and on the other side of the headland for as long as men can remember. Most of us stay here and are content to do so, but Michael, when he was a young man, got restless and vanished for a while. When he returned, some three or four summers later, he said he'd been soldiering in France." Jude Bonifant took a swig of ale. "Didn't talk much about it, though I recall him saying once that he'd fought under the Earl of Shrewsbury."

"Knew 'e'd made a mistake by going away," Goody Bonifant put in. "But 'e saw sense while 'e were still young and came back 'ome. 'E married Jane Shapwick, a lass as lovely to look at as 'e was 'andsome. They made as pretty a young couple as you'd see in many a long day."

Jude Bonifant ignored the interruption and continued, "Michael Cantilupe was a good man, a loyal friend, a skilled fisherman and a generous neighbour. You'll find no one on either side the headland who'll have a bad word to say of him. When he got older – and he'd seen more'n forty summers – "

"More like fifty," his wife amended.

"– he was appointed by the lord Abbot to aid the monks on the island. He was given the cottage next to the enclosure and it was his job to light the lamp in the chapel tower on stormy nights. He helped, too, with the sheep and tended the vegetables. His woman did the cooking for the Brothers."

"Until she died," Goody Bonifant snorted. "This one – " she spoke with venom "– this Rowena, she can't cook! Found 'er in Plymouth, 'e did, on one of 'is trips. Ensnared 'im, I reckon, in 'er witch's toils."

I thought of the tired, strained face of the woman I had seen and asked, "How long ago were she and Michael Cantilupe married?"

"Eight year or more. A summer and a winter after poor Jane died." Jude rubbed his chin, looking perplexed. "When that happened, we expected Michael would take another wife. A man can't live alone with no woman to care for him, but we thought he'd wed a cousin of mine, Anne Bonifant, a decent, sober body whose own man had been drowned the previous spring. She'd've had him, too, and pleased to do so, but no! He clapped eyes on Rowena during one of his visits to Plymouth and nothing would do but he must have her. It was the only time Michael and I fell out. 'No fool like an old fool,' I told him, but he was set on her, and there was no getting him to change his mind."

"Did Master Cantilupe go away often?"

"Now and then. He'd feel the need to be off, but only for a while, and he never again went further than Plymouth."

"Had he been there of late?"

Goody Bonifant felt that she had been silent long enough and cut in before her husband could reply.

"A week nor more 'e went last an' was away two nights. Told me 'e'd offered to take Rowena with 'im, but she wouldn't go." The Goody spat. "O' course she wouldn't go! Good chance, wasn't it, fer 'er to cuckold 'im with 'is nephew!"

"She and Colin Cantilupe, had they been lovers long?"

"A year, maybe more." Jude Bonifant wiped the last of his soup from the bowl and licked his fingers. "Several of us'd tried to warn Michael what was going on, but he wouldn't believe us. There'd been others afore Colin, I reckon. She was always a restless, discontented piece."

"It must have been lonely here for a young girl bred up in the town," I suggested, but I could see by their faces that such a thought was beyond their understanding. This life was all they knew, this wild, windswept shore their only horizon. I went on quickly, "Tell me about the events of last night."

Jude Bonifant shrugged. "There's little enough to tell. Just before dinnertime, when the sun was westering, I saw Michael walking across the causeway towards the island. Colin was with him and Michael had his arm about Colin's shoulders, for he'd never believe any ill of him, no more than he would of Rowena. It's my belief Colin had invited himself to dinner, knowing what was going to happen. The tide was rising. It comes from both directions until it meets in the middle of the causeway and cuts off the island from the shore. Because of the cross-currents, trying to return by boat, especially in the dark, would have been hazardous, even for the most skilled of oarsmen."

"So Colin would have had to stay the night?"

"He would that. And then, a bit later, when I went to haul in my nets, I saw the stranger walking across the causeway. By then it was almost flooded, but there was just enough sand left for a man to keep his feet dry if he were careful."

"How could you tell it was a stranger?"

Jude looked at me with mild astonishment.

"I know every man, woman and child in this community. I can recognize their shape and the way they walk at a greater distance than I was from that man yesterevening. Anyhow, I weren't the only one to remark him."

Goody Bonifant was quick with her support.

"I saw 'im, too, chapman. Jude called me outside. 'A stranger goin' to the island this time o' day,' he said. 'Now what can 'e want?'"

"And what did you decide?" I asked.

"That he were a messenger from the Abbot of Buckfast to the Brothers." Jude sucked the last remnants of fish from a broken tooth. "They come every now and again, and some of 'em are laymen."

"And then?" I prompted, as my host fell silent.

"A sudden squall o' wind blew up, about an hour later. We were thinking of going to bed, for the nights draw in early this time of year. We'd noticed the wind rising, but thought nothing of it until we heard shouting. We went outside and saw folk running to and fro along the sands. Then I saw that a boat out at sea was in trouble. Someone said it was Stephen Shapwick and his daughter, Marianne, rowing home round the headland after visiting his brother. The squall had blown 'em off course and they were in danger of being smashed against the rocks of the island."

"I saw one o' the Brothers run down to the water's edge," Goody Bonifant added as Jude paused for breath. "Then 'e ran back quick to Michael's cottage, shoutin' and flappin' 'is arms. After a few moments, Michael came out. You couldn't mistake 'im in that white frieze cloak 'e always wore. Never seen 'im wear anything else. Said 'e took it off a Frenchman. Said it'd last 'is lifetime." Tears welled up in her rheumy eyes. "'E never said a truer word."

"There, there, my girl." Her husband patted her hand. "He's gone straight to Heaven. You can be sure of that." His lips thinned to a vengeful line. "But we'll hang his killers and burn that murderess, never fear." He suddenly recollected my presence. "If they're guilty," he added. But it was easy to see that he had no doubts on that score.

"What happened after that?" I urged. "How was Master Cantilupe murdered?"

Jude waved his wife to silence and resumed the story.

"By that time, thanks to his own skill and the fact that the wind had dropped as suddenly as it had risen, Stephen Shapwick had brought his boat safely into the lee of the island and managed to make it fast. There's a stake driven hard into the sand between two rocks, and half of it stands clear of the water, even at high tide. Michael was scrambling down towards the boat, to help Stephen and his daughter climb ashore, when a figure comes rushing out of the darkness and stabs him in the back, clean through the heart. Brother Anselm and two of the other monks who had come out to give aid and succour were witness to everything."

The tide was at its lowest ebb and the causeway therefore at its widest. My boots left clear impressions in the firm, wet sand.

There were three or four stalwart fishermen standing guard outside Michael Cantilupe's cottage, and they eyed me with hostility as I climbed the short, steep path which led to its door. I did not immediately demand entrance, however. Instead, I turned aside to enter the monks' enclosure. One of the Brothers I could see up on the hill, tending the sheep, but the others were within, including Brother Anselm. Jude Bonifant had described him to me – "short and stout with at least three chins" – and I had no difficulty in recognizing my man. I requested some of his time and this he willingly granted as Vespers was some while off.

We went outside to talk, sitting on an outcrop of rock, staring over the water to the distant bays and inlets of the shore.

"A terrible business! A terrible business!" Brother Anselm declared, his chins quivering with horror. "What the lord Abbot would say, should he ever hear of it, I dare not think. A murder on church land is bad enough, but for the community to take punishment of the malefactors into its own hands is even worse."

"Can't you or one of the other Brothers dissuade the villagers from this course?" I asked.

The little monk shook his head sadly.

"What can we do? So few against so many. And it has always been their way in these parts. The Sheriff and his officers know full well what goes on, but prefer to feign ignorance. It saves the expense of a trial and transporting witnesses to Totnes or to Plymouth. They wouldn't thank anyone who drew the matter to their attention."

"We are too late to prevent the first murder," I said, "but let us try to avoid at least two more. Will you tell me what you know of this business?" And I recounted quickly what I had already learned from Jude Bonifant.

Brother Anselm spread small, plump hands. "Then you know almost as much as I do. After the other Brothers and I had wrestled this man to the ground, we dragged him into the cottage and bound him with a rope Michael had been carrying. Indeed, the villain offered little resistance and seemed resigned to his fate."

"And where were Mistress Cantilupe and the dead man's nephew while this was happening?"

"Colin Cantilupe assisted us in our endeavours. Mistress Cantilupe, when she realized what was toward, ran screaming out of doors, looking for her husband, and Brother Jerome followed to fetch her back, afraid that she might do herself a mischief. He's a strong lad, which is just as well, as he was forced to carry her. Master Cantilupe then went to comfort her, after which she sat on a stool in the corner, sobbing."

"Not the sort of behaviour you would expect of either if they had arranged the murder?" I suggested.

Brother Anselm regarded me with small, shrewd eyes, embedded in rolls of fat.

"Or precisely the sort of behaviour you would expect if they wished to avert suspicion."

I smiled acknowledgement of this thrust, but was ready with my parry.

"Doesn't it seem to you, Brother, a very clumsy way to murder an unwanted husband? With the sea so close at hand, a drowning 'accident' would have been much simpler. And where and when did either Rowena or Colin Cantilupe meet this Baldwin Zouche? When did they hand over the money which was found upon his person? And why would he agree to kill Michael Cantilupe for them?"

"My reply to your first question is that people are not always clever about these things. As for your second and third, I do not know the answers. And in response to your final query I would only say that, sadly, some men will do anything for money."

"But Baldwin Zouche was almost certain to be caught," I argued. "There was no chance that I can see for him to escape."

"As matters fell out, no," Brother Anselm agreed. "But the sudden storm was unexpected, as was the appearance of Stephen Shapwick."

I shook my head. "There is something in all this that makes no sense. But tell me about events before the murder. Was it you who first espied the boat?"

"It was indeed. I had gone out to satisfy myself that the sheep pen was safely fastened. The catch of the gate is broken, and I was afraid it might swing open in the wind. It was then I saw the boat and heard the cries of Stephen and his daughter. They were nearly on the rocks and I ran to Master Cantilupe's cottage."

"And what were he and his wife and nephew doing when you burst in upon them?"

Brother Anselm blinked. "I'm not sure. Just sitting, I think, and talking."

"And when you gave your news?"

"Michael grabbed his cloak and a length of rope and ran outside.
"Immediately?"

"Yes, of . . . course." The monk's voice had a dying fall, however, and I glanced at him sharply. He continued thoughtfully, "Well, now you ask, there was a momentary hesitation because I remember urging him to hurry. 'Master Shapwick and Marianne will be drowned!' I said. 'Come quickly!'"

"And then?"

"Oh, he leapt up at once and threw on his cloak. The rope he took from several coils lying in a corner."

"Did his nephew follow?"

"Not immediately. A minute or two later, perhaps. At the time I thought nothing of it, but now I suppose it was because he didn't want to witness his uncle's murder."

"Michael Cantilupe was dead then when Colin made his appearance?"

"He was struck down before he had time to reach the water's edge. I was a few paces behind, calling Brother Jerome and Brother Mark who had come out to see what had delayed me, when suddenly a shadow rushed out of the darkness and fell upon poor Michael. He went down with a great cry, sprawled across the rocks, and the man we now know to be Baldwin Zouche knelt beside him to withdraw his dagger.

"After that, all was confusion. The Brothers and I threw ourselves upon the attacker, and meanwhile, Master Shapwick had managed to make fast his boat to the mooring post and clamber ashore with Marianne. Colin had arrived by then, and he helped Brother Jerome to drag the assailant indoors, where we bound him with the rope Michael had been carrying. But I have told you this already. Brother Mark, who had remained with Michael, came briefly to the cottage door to say that he was dead, and it was then that Mistress Cantilupe ran out screaming."

"And what of Master Shapwick and his daughter?"

"They, naturally enough, were at first too shaken by their own brush with death to take in what had happened. Brother Mark conducted them indoors and assisted Jerome to make up the fire. Later, Mark and Jerome went to carry Michael's body up to the chapel."

"And what of Baldwin Zouche all this while?"

"He just sat silent in the corner where we had put him, watching

us with those strangely colourless eyes of his. Once, he asked to be
allowed to relieve himself and we unbound his legs so that he could
walk outside. Jerome and Mark went with him, although with his
arms pinioned and the tide still in, there was little chance, as you
pointed out just now, that he could have run away. But that was
all. There was nothing that any of us could do until the causeway
was once more passable."

"Baldwin did not immediately accuse Rowena and Colin Cantilupe
of hiring him to murder her husband?"

"No. It was not until the villagers were all assembled on the island
the following morning, and the elders were questioning him, that he
made his accusation."

"And they believed him?"

Brother Anselm rose stiffly from his rocky perch, rubbing his
buttocks tenderly. I also rose, glad to stretch my limbs.

"His word was accepted without question, partly, I suppose,
because it was what everyone wanted to believe. Michael Cantilupe
was a revered and well-liked man, who had recently been appointed to
the ranks of the village elders. It had been long suspected that Rowena
was betraying him with his nephew, and it was only Michael's refusal
to allow one word to be said against either of them that had prevented
an open accusation of adultery. So their protestations of innocence fell
on deaf ears. They were condemned out of hand along with Baldwin
Zouche, and were being dragged to their deaths when, by the grace
of God, you intervened."

"Do you think them guilty?"

"I should prefer them to stand trial," was the careful answer, but
further than that, Brother Anselm refused to be drawn.

Michael Cantilupe's dwelling was guarded by a ring of stout fishermen, all armed with staves and cudgels, and the three prisoners were
held within. I needed to see each one separately, however, so I asked
for Colin and Rowena Cantilupe and Baldwin Zouche to be brought
to me outside, one at a time.

But first, I walked around the cottage, mounting the higher ground
to the back of it, where the island sloped gently towards its summit.
At the cliff edge, I could see something snared on one of the rocks
below; a cloak, judging by its clasp, turned now to a black sodden
mess by the flying spume and last night's rain. I thought it likely
that it belonged to Stephen Shapwick.

I returned to the cottage and requested one of the fishermen to
have Baldwin Zouche brought out to the rock which I had shared
earlier with Brother Anselm. There was some reluctance on the part

of the two young men who accompanied the prisoner to leave him with me, until I pointed out that they could stand within sight of their charge, but out of earshot. Also, his arms were bound.

Baldwin Zouche was, I judged, well into his latter years, maybe between forty-five and fifty summers. He had a livid scar which ran from his left temple down to his chin, puckering the lined and weather-beaten skin of his cheek. His eyes were as Brother Anselm had described them, so pale a grey that they appeared almost devoid of colour. His clothes, which had seen better days, were roughly patched and there was a hole in the toe of one of his boots. His manner was civil, but cold, even sneering, and he glanced frequently towards the distant shore and the Tree of Doom perched high on its cliff top. He knew that he could not escape his grisly end, and had the courage to look upon death without flinching.

He confessed that he had been hired to kill Michael Cantilupe, but insisted that it was Colin who had done the hiring. The little, secret smile which accompanied this admission again persuaded me that he was lying, but to most of my other questions he remained mute, refusing to say where he had met Colin, or when and how they had struck their murderous bargain. On the subject of his past life he was equally reticent, except for a single unguarded reference to having recently been discharged from the ranks of the Duke of Brittany's mercenaries.

"After you reached the island," I persisted, "where did you conceal yourself?"

Again, he did not answer directly, but, with a jerk of his head, indicated a nearby outcropping of rock and a stunted tree.

I thought this improbable, but did not, for the moment, contest it.

"How were you sure, in all the rain and darkness, that it was Michael Cantilupe who had come out of the cottage?"

Zouche bared his teeth in a death's head grin.

"The white frieze cloak that he always wore had been described to me."

"But why did you choose to kill him then, when three of the Brothers were present as witnesses?"

"I didn't see them."

"You must have seen Brother Anselm enter the cottage, or at least heard him calling for help. By such a public knifing, you made escape for yourself impossible."

But Baldwin Zouche had said his last word, lowering his chin upon his breast and closing his eyes against a world which would soon have done with him forever. I signalled to the fishermen to remove him, but as they hustled him roughly away, I called out, "Master Zouche! Were you ever at Castillon, in southern France?"

He glanced back, startled, but again did not answer. All the same, I felt certain that the bow I had drawn at a venture had hit its mark.

I asked for Colin Cantilupe to be brought to me next. His guards had loosed him from his bonds, evidently fearing nothing from him. Indeed it was impossible to conceive of him making a bid for freedom, trembling as he was with terror and abject self-pity. It was several minutes before I could coax any sensible answers from him, but eventually I was able to persuade him to talk.

"You must . . . understand," he said, haltingly at first, then the words coming out in a rush, "that . . . Rowena and I have never betrayed my uncle. We love one another, yes, but we have never betrayed him! Never!" Tears sprang to his eyes and he raised a hand to dash them away. "I cannot believe that God will let us be punished for what was only in our hearts!"

I felt I could not answer for God, so I urged him gently, "Tell me about yesterday evening."

He sniffed and wiped his nose with his fingers.

"My uncle came to my cottage about three o'clock of the afternoon and asked me to dine with him and Rowena. He knew I had been sick these past few days and unable to go out fishing. My parents are both dead," Colin added by way of explanation, "and Michael is – was – closest to me in blood in the community."

"And you went with him."

"And glad to, and not just because it meant that I could see and be near Rowena. I respected my uncle and was thankful for some company other than my own for an hour or so. I had intended returning home after the meal."

"Why didn't you?"

"Dinner was delayed for one reason and another – at one point my uncle had to put on his cloak and go out to light the lamp in the church tower, because the wind was rising – and by the time we had finished eating, the sea had covered the causeway. Uncle wouldn't hear of me rowing myself home, for the cross-currents are very dangerous."

"So Master Bonifant told me. Go on! What happened later?"

"The three of us were sitting, talking, by the fire when Brother Anselm burst in, shouting that a boat was in trouble. My uncle seized his cloak and some rope and went rushing out of the cottage."

"He didn't hesitate?"

Colin looked vaguely surprised. "Well . . . only momentarily, perhaps, as a man may do when events catch him unawares."

"And you followed him?"

"Yes. I was delayed a moment or two because I couldn't find my cloak, and in the end I was forced to run out without it." Colin's voice caught in his throat. "But . . . by that time it . . . had happened. My uncle had been murdered. The man was there, kneeling beside his body, and then the three Brothers bore him to the ground."

The rest of Colin's story was much the same as Brother Anselm's, and when he had concluded, he again denied all responsibility for his uncle's death.

"I never saw this Baldwin Zouche in my life before," he whimpered.

Once more I made a sign to the two young fishermen who were watching intently from a distance, but before they reached us, I asked, "What is your cloak like? Of what material?"

Colin stared at me for a second, puzzled, before answering, "Of dark brown byrrhus."

"And have you found it?"

"No. But I haven't had another chance to look for it." His voice rose and he gave a high-pitched laugh which cracked in the middle. "It isn't important now, I suppose. I'm not going to need it."

His gaolers escorted him back to the cottage and brought out Rowena.

I could detect the remnants of beauty in a face that was now heavily lined and pitted by the merciless weather. There had probably been a time when that leathery skin was as soft and delicate as that of a peach. I did not question her concerning the events of the previous evening. Instead, I asked her how she had come to meet Michael Cantilupe.

"I lived in Plymouth with my father. Michael first saw me during one of his visits. His wife, he told us, was a dying woman and he was looking for another. My father was anxious to get rid of me and forced me into the marriage as soon as Michael's first wife had died. I had no mother to intervene on my behalf."

"I'm sorry," I murmured. "You didn't love your husband?"

Rowena grimaced. "He was too old. And demanding!" she added, suddenly vicious. "But then, who am I to complain? He had a husband's rights."

"A beautiful girl such as you must surely have had other suitors. Why did your father favour Master Cantilupe?"

Her tone was bitter.

"Because Michael offered him more gold for me than any of the others."

"Do you know how your husband came by this money?"

"He said he ransomed a prisoner when he was soldiering in France." Her lips curled. "Maybe. Or maybe he stole it from some wretched Frenchman. He thought I didn't know where he kept his precious hoard, but I did. It was buried under a stone in a corner of the chapel."

"This is the money which was found on Baldwin Zouche's person?"

"Yes." Realizing what she had said, Rowena turned large, scared eyes upon me. "But I didn't give it to him! I never touched it!"

I patted her hand. "No, I don't think you did. How did Master Cantilupe treat you?"

"Well enough to begin with. For the first few years he was kind and considerate, but for a long time now he's ignored me, except to demand his rights as a husband. I'm not pretty any more, as you can see."

"And are you and Colin Cantilupe lovers?"

"No!" Her tone was fierce. "He's a kind, gentle soul and we love one another, but he wouldn't betray his uncle."

It was the same answer that Colin had given me.

I had two more things to do before giving the village elders the benefit of my reasoning in the morning. I obtained from one of the fishermen on guard the location of Stephen Shapwick's cottage, then walked across the causeway, which was rapidly disappearing beneath the incoming tide. I knocked on the Shapwicks' door and waited for someone to open it.

My luck was in, for the person who answered could be none other than Stephen Shapwick's daughter. The girl's eyelids were red with weeping and her general appearance unkempt, but nothing could mar her youthful prettiness. She was about fifteen years of age with huge, dark eyes, softly curving, cherry-red lips and a mane of black curls which hung about her shoulders.

A voice from within called, "Who is it, Marianne?" and an older woman appeared in the open doorway. "And what might you want?" the goodwife demanded truculently. Without, however, giving me time to reply, she added briskly, "Be off with you! We want no strangers here. This is a house of mourning."

I did not argue. I had found out what I needed to know, and made my way along the cliffside path to the Bonifants' dwelling. Goody Bonifant was preparing their evening meal, and once again I was invited to share it. I was also offered a bed for the night, and gratefully accepted both food and lodging. I had not been looking forward to sharing the austerity of the Brothers' enclosure on the island.

"Well, what progress have you made, chapman?" Jude Bonifant inquired as I rid myself of my cloak and pack and propped my cudgel in a corner.

I drew up a stool and sat down with him at the table.

"Enough, I trust, to convince you and the rest of your community tomorrow morning that Colin and Rowena Cantilupe are innocent of this conspiracy." My host raised his eyebrows at that and I nodded. "Oh yes, I'm sure there was a conspiracy, but not of their making."

"Do you have proof?" he demanded bluntly.

"I hope to persuade Baldwin Zouche to confess the truth, and I hope too that I shall be given a fair hearing."

Master Bonifant regarded me with hard, bright eyes. "As long as Michael's murderer is brought to justice, we shall be satisfied. Is there anything more that I can tell you?"

"Yes, which is the reason why I'm here." I propped my elbows on the board and cupped my chin in my hands. "I need honest answers to two questions."

Jude Bonifant looked suddenly wary, but after a moment he answered reluctantly, "Very well. I'll do my best to help you."

We were all assembled, the prisoners, the Brothers, myself and every inhabitant from both sides of the headland. The wet foreshore, where we stood, gleamed corpse-like in the early morning light, while above us, on the cliff-top, the Tree of Doom spread its wind-bitten branches. Someone had already placed a rope around one of them and Baldwin Zouche passed his tongue over dry, cracked lips.

Jude Bonifant and his fellow elders stood gravely in a semi-circle, facing the rest of us. No boats had as yet put to sea, for everyone wanted to be present when Michael Cantilupe's murderers paid the penalty for their heinous crime. There was a hungry, predatory look on all their faces, one which I had seen huntsmen wear just before the chase. There was a general hum of anticipation.

Jude Bonifant held up his hand and the noise ceased immediately. He nodded in my direction.

"Chapman, you may begin."

I cleared my throat.

"My friends," I said, "you may not like what I am about to tell you, but I beg, in God's name and the cause of justice, that you will hear me out. I am not here to speak in defence of Baldwin Zouche. He killed Michael Cantilupe, of that there can be no possible doubt, but he killed the wrong man. He was meant to murder Colin. And his fellow conspirator was Michael himself."

There was a growl of disbelief and Mistress Shapwick, who had a comforting arm about her daughter's waist, shrilled, "That's a lie! Seize him! He's as bad as the others!"

I glanced at Master Bonifant who, though eyeing me askance, stepped forward and once again commanded silence.

"We will hear the pedlar out. Then we will judge him and his story. Continue, chapman."

I went on bravely, "Michael Cantilupe had a weakness, as I see it, for young and beautiful wives, but when they got older and began to lose their looks he no longer wanted them. His first, Jane Shapwick, so Elder Bonifant and his good lady informed me, was a very lovely girl, about the same age as her kinswoman is now, when Michael first married her. But Mistress Jane grew plainer with the passing years, as happens to us all.

"Now, Michael Cantilupe used to go twice a year to Plymouth, and it was on one of these visits that he saw Rowena, who at that time was as young and pretty as her predecessor had once been. Would anyone deny that? When he married her after the death of his first wife and brought this lady here, was she not beautiful?"

No one spoke. Indeed there was no sound at all except for the hushing of the sea as the little waves broke upon the sands. But I could almost feel their resistance to my argument, so strong was their desire to believe no ill of Michael Cantilupe, who had always been so revered amongst them. I lifted my chin defiantly.

"Now, however, Rowena has lost much of those youthful charms. It's a hard life you lead here, at the mercy of storm and wind. But Marianne Shapwick is not yet old enough to be touched by the inclemency of the weather. She is young and lovely, just blossoming into womanhood. Sooner or later, she was bound to catch Michael Cantilupe's eye." I raised my voice. "And before any of you attempt to deny it, Elder Bonifant himself told me last night that Michael has spent much time of late at the Shapwicks' cottage, certainly more than he used to do in days gone by."

Heads turned in the direction of Jude Bonifant who was looking a little shaken. But to his credit, he did not deny my words.

"Friends, kinsmen, it is true. I admit that until now I saw no deeper motive in the visits than an increased friendship on Michael's part with Stephen. But proceed, chapman. We've promised you a hearing."

I thanked him and continued with growing confidence.

"Elder Bonifant also told me last night that Jane Cantilupe's death was not a lingering one, as Michael had pretended to Rowena and her father. Instead, she died swiftly, through eating a poisonous mushroom. A simple enough accident, I grant you, and that is why the law condemns the picking of field mushrooms, which can so easily be mistaken for the white-gilled death cap; a law which, like so many others, you seem to ignore in these parts. And for that very reason no one queried Jane Cantilupe's death. You all thought it a tragic mistake. Suppose, however, that it wasn't. Suppose the death cap was given to her deliberately by her husband because he wanted her out of the way, so that he could marry his new love, Rowena?"

There was an outcry then, and Jude Bonifant demanded sternly, "Can you prove this?"

It was the question I had been dreading. I had to gamble everything now on Baldwin Zouche telling the truth. I turned towards him.

"Well?" I asked. "Didn't your old comrade-in-arms open his heart when he hired you to murder his nephew?"

"Comrade-in-arms?" another of the elders asked sharply. "Do you mean to say that this evil rogue was a friend of Michael?"

I forced myself to speak with authority, in order to convince my listeners that my guesses were in truth facts.

"They were soldiers together. Michael Cantilupe, again according to Elder Bonifant, fought in France, under the banner of the Earl of Shrewsbury. When I asked this man if he had ever been to Castillon, in southern France, he did not deny it. Shrewsbury met his death there. Moreover, Zouche has, on his own admission, recently been in the pay of the Duke of Brittany. Returning to England, where would he be most likely to disembark? Why, at Plymouth, where, a week or so ago, Michael Cantilupe met up with him again quite by chance. But that meeting suggested to him a way of disposing of both his wife and his nephew, without besmirching his own spotless reputation."

Elder Bonifant would have intervened at that moment, but I begged him to let me finish what I had to say before he questioned his prisoner.

"Several things," I went on, "puzzled me about the happenings of the night before last, as they were recounted to me. Firstly, according to Colin, his uncle went out during the evening to light the warning lamp in the chapel tower. He wore his white frieze cloak, which Baldwin Zouche claims had been described to him. So why did he not kill his quarry then, when no one else was about to witness the crime, and throw the body into the sea? Secondly, when news was brought of a boat being in trouble, Master Cantilupe did not immediately bestir himself. Is that not what you told me, Brother Anselm?"

"That . . . That is so, yes," the little monk conceded.

"But when you told him that it was Stephen Shapwick and his daughter in the boat, he ran out immediately?"

"Yes, yes. But what does that prove?"

"To me, Brother, it suggests that Master Cantilupe was loath to leave the cottage until he heard that Marianne Shapwick was in danger, when all other considerations were wiped from his mind. And the reason for his reluctance was that he knew Baldwin Zouche to be lying in wait for a man in a white frieze cloak."

Jude Bonifant took a hasty step forward. "What nonsense is this?" he demanded. "How could he possibly have known?"

I stood my ground.

"Because he was the one who had brought Baldwin to the island. Wait! Let me finish! Brother Anselm, when Colin ran out of the cottage, was he wearing a cloak?"

The monk thought for a moment, then he slowly shook his head.

"No. No, he wasn't."

"That was because he couldn't find it. Nor has he discovered its whereabouts since. But I know where it may be found. It is trapped on the rocks below the far side of the cottage. But who threw it there, and why? Only Michael went out of doors after his nephew's arrival; that nephew he had persuaded to stay for the night. He could easily have taken it without being noticed, while the other two were talking, and tossed it, as he thought, into the sea."

"But why?" The words were startled out of Colin Cantilupe himself.

I looked at him. "I am certain that you were to be persuaded, under some pretext or another, to leave the cottage later on that night, when the tide had begun to turn and the causeway was becoming passable. And when your cloak could not easily be found, your uncle would have offered you his. You would then have been despatched with a dagger between the shoulder-blades, and Baldwin Zouche sent on his way with his money."

Jude Bonifant spoke for all when he said, "I still do not understand."

"Baldwin had made no secret of his presence on the island. He had crossed the causeway while it was still light, not caring who might see him. It was part of the plan that he was known to be there. Michael Cantilupe's story would be that his wife and nephew had hired someone to murder him, but that the plot had miscarried because Colin was wearing his cloak. In fact the opposite of what actually happened. With the greatest show of reluctance and profoundest sorrow, he would have been forced to accept his wife's complicity in the conspiracy. There would have been nothing he could have done to save her from the rest of you when, as always, you took it upon yourselves to mete out punishment."

There was a moment's silence. Then Jude Bonifant exclaimed, "It's a farrago of nonsense! I don't believe a word of it. Chapman, you're out of your wits."

"Ask this man," I said, turning to Baldwin Zouche. "Baldwin, remember that you hold two innocent lives in your hands. Within the hour, you will go to meet your Maker. Think of your immortal soul! Admit the truth."

He did not answer at once and my heart sank, but suddenly he glanced up and shrugged.

"Very well . . . All you've said is as it happened. I met Michael in Plymouth a week or more ago and we recognized each other at once, even though we hadn't met for many years. Yes, we fought in France together." He sneered. "From our very first encounter, I'd known him to be a kindred spirit. The only difference between us was that while I didn't care who knew I was a villain, Michael always liked to keep his vices secret. Except with me. He knew I couldn't be fooled. During that meeting in Plymouth, at the sign of the Turk's Head, he told me everything; how he had murdered his first wife and no one any the wiser. And how he now wanted to be rid of his second, but dared not again use the death cap mushroom. So we devised the plot between us and fixed a day when high tide was early in the evening and his nephew could be persuaded to stop the night."

"But why," I asked, "did you kill the wrong man? You must have realized that it was much earlier than the time arranged for the murder and that there were other people about. And, more importantly, you must have recognized that the man in the white frieze cloak was Michael himself and not his nephew, Colin."

"I lost my temper. It's always been my downfall, and Michael had tried to cheat me over the money when he came to the chapel where I was hiding. I got to remembering all the times he had cheated me in the past; the girls he had lured away from me with lies and false promises, the punishments I'd received for misdeeds which were really his. And that cloak! It was mine. He must have stolen it the very day we parted company in France. It had been my father's and his father's before him. It was my talisman, and I've not had a day's good fortune since I lost it. I didn't know, until I met him in Plymouth, that he was the one who took it. But I should have guessed."

"And so you succumbed to a momentary desire for revenge and thereby encompassed your own doom. But why did you pretend that it was Rowena and Colin Cantilupe who had hired you?"

Once again, Baldwin gave his death's head grin.

"It amused me. I had no doubt that I was going straight to hell, so I might as well be hanged for a sheep as for a lamb. But now I swear to you, by Our Saviour's death upon the Cross, that they are as innocent of plotting Michael Cantilupe's death as he was guilty of planning theirs. And that is all I have to say."

I had saved the lives of Rowena and Colin Cantilupe, but there was nothing more that I could do for Baldwin Zouche. He would forfeit his life for his misdeeds, just as his desperate need for revenge, the need that now and then God stirs in all of us, had ensured that his co-conspirator and fellow murderer had paid the penalty with his.

I left him to his fate and went my way, glad to be free of that wild and desolate place. But as I reached the summit of the rising ground and glanced back over my shoulder, I saw that the Tree of Doom already bore its grisly fruit.

# PART III
# The Age of Discovery

# THE MURDER
# OF INNOCENCE
# P. C. Doherty

*Paul Doherty is currently the most prolific writer of historical detective novels with around twenty novels to his credit under both his own name and several pseudonyms. As Doherty, his best known character is Hugh Corbett, the thirteenth-century clerk to the King's Bench, who becomes a detective and spy for King Edward I. His adventures began in* Satan in St Mary's *(1986) and have continued through* Crown in Darkness *(1988),* Spy in Chancery *(1988),* The Angel of Death *(1989),* The Prince of Darkness *(1992),* Murder Wears a Cowl *(1992),* The Assassin in the Greenwood *(1993) and* The Song of a Dark Angel *(1994). Writing as Paul Harding he has created Brother Athelstan, a parish priest in fourteenth-century Southwark, who is assistant to the City of London coroner, Sir John Cranston. His adventures have appeared in* The Nightingale Gallery *(1991),* The House of the Red Slayer *(1992),* Murder Most Holy *(1992),* The Anger of God *(1993) and* By Murder's Bright Light *(1994). As Michael Clynes he has produced a series about Sir Roger Shallot, a rather Falstaffian rogue in the reign of Henry VII, whose investigations have been recorded in* The White Rose Murders *(1991),* The Poisoned Chalice *(1992),* The Grail Murders *(1993) and* A Brood of Vipers *(1994). Meanwhile, as C. L. Grace, he has created a new series featuring Kathryn Swinbrooke, a physician and chemist in fifteenth-century Canterbury. So far there has appeared* A Shrine of Murders *(1993) and* The Eye of God *(1994). And this is not all of Doherty's output!*

*When I asked Paul whether he would be able to contribute a story to this anthology he decided to create a new character, set in a slightly later period, in the early years of the reign of Elizabeth I. So, may I unveil the first extract from the true memoirs of Mary Frith ("Moll Flanders"), set early in her life, long before her tumultuous career in the Elizabethan Secret Service: the Office of the Night.*

Yesterday I hanged three men. As High Sheriffess of the county, I travelled by carriage to the crossroads where the scaffold stands. The prisoners, three Moon men, wanderers, had ambushed two bawdy baskets on a lonely, windswept trackway out on the moors. Having cruelly ravished and then killed the women, these reprobates buried their bodies in a ditch. Of course, as High Sheriffess, all I did was sit in my carriage and watch the three prisoners being pushed up the scaffold. When the ladder was turned, I glanced away. I felt no pity: evil men, they deserved their fate. Afterwards, as I journeyed back, the bright green fields became overcast: clouds swept in from the north, low, black and threatening. My escort begged me not to continue and so we stopped in a small village and I took chambers at the *Kestrel*; a pleasant hostelry where the chamber was swept, the bed was narrow but the sheets were clean and free of fleas.

One of my servants built up the fire; I sat as I often do, thinking about the past. Taverns bring back so many memories: when you sleep in your own bed, between your own sheets you are safe, like a baby nestling in a cot. You think your usual thoughts, your feet are set on the path you intend to tread. But a new bed turns the mind to fanciful matters and, when you are old, there is nothing new under the sun, so you journey back in time. The *Kestrel* reminded me of another tavern, the *Bishop's Mitre* in Smithfield where I and my Worshipful Guardian, Parson Snodgrass, Vicar of St Botolph's in Islip, Kent, stayed. Every year Parson Snodgrass travelled to London to meet the Dean of the Arches near St Paul's: he always stayed at the *Bishop's Mitre* in Smithfield. In that particular year, the time of the great sweating sickness when Elizabeth had been only two years on the throne, Parson Snodgrass took me with him. I, poor Molly Frith, foundling of the Parish who had been taken into the Parson's much trumpeted loving care.

Now Smithfield is a large open space between the great abbey church of St Bartholomew and the fleshing market of London. The houses round that great open expanse are crammed together, divided by dark, furtive alleyways. In my time a filthy, fetid place: chamber pots were emptied out of the windows and offal from the butchers' stalls oozed and slipped across the execution ground where men were hanged or women burnt to death, tied to a thick, blackened beam. Even the trees stank of death: the kites, busy after tearing at freshly severed heads, would build their nests amongst the branches with rags and pieces of offal. The *Bishop's Mitre* fronted all this, a spacious tavern with its own garden, yards and even a balcony: here, visitors could stand on execution day and have a good view of some hapless felon being choked to death in his hempen noose. We were on the second floor. Worshipful Guardian had a chamber, I and a tavern maid shared a narrow closet alongside. I forget the girl's name. She was rosy-cheeked and fresh-eyed and whispered stories about lusty grooms and their constant invitation to join them in the tavern hay loft.

Now, on the second morning of our stay there, Worshipful Guardian and I had gone down to break our fast on strips of roast duck and a basket of freshly cut bread. There were other guests present but Parson Snodgrass, strict in his ways, kept to himself and bade me do the same.

"You are too sharp, Moll," he would comment. "And your tongue clacks as fast as your wits." Then he would stroke my face with his thumb, the only time he ever touched or showed me any sign of affection.

I would force a smile and Worshipful Guardian's eyes would take on a wistful, dreamy look. He was a clever, subtle man with a deep knowledge of herbs and potions and always hoped for a grander living with a stately house and spacious gardens where he could dabble to his heart's content. Anyway, on that bright summer's day with the sunshine pouring through the open doorway, Murder announced itself. There was a shouting and clashing on the stairs and a young man, handsome faced, his blond hair curled, his beard neatly clipped, burst into the morning room shouting for the landlord.

"What is it, sir?" Worshipful Guardian rose, knocking over the goblet he had been sipping.

The young man, his face pale, eyes starting, scratched at his tufty beard then played with the buckle of the belt he carried. He had apparently not finished his dressing, he had one shoe on, the points of his breeches were not fully tied whilst the collar of his doublet was all awry.

"It's Uncle!" the young man cried.

He looked down at his stockinged foot and blushed with embarrassment. The landlord came bustling in; fresh from gibbeting some chicken, he wiped bloody fingers on his stained apron.

"Lackaday, lackaday, sir, what is the matter?" he cried.

"It's my uncle. Sir Nicholas Hopton."

I vaguely remembered the evening before. The young man was more serene then, sitting in a corner of the tavern at the table specially screened off by a wooden partition. His companion had been an older man, plump, red-faced with popping eyes and silver-white hair combed back to cover a bald patch, his voice deep and plummy. The young man had left and, when Worshipful Guardian and I were obliged to help the older man up to his chamber, he struck me as one who had drunk deeply of the wine of life and savoured every drop.

"I am a Parson," Worshipful Guardian intervened. "Though I am not of these parts." He grasped the young man by the shoulders. "What is wrong with your uncle?"

"I cannot wake him," the young man replied. "I hammered on his door but there was no reply."

"Master Charles," the taverner interrupted. "Your uncle, as ever, drank deep last night."

"Nonsense!" Charles Hopton replied, pleading with Worshipful Guardian. "Uncle was no toper and there's blood seeping out from under the door."

The landlord hurried off, quick as a whippet up the stairs, the fumbling young man trailing after him. Worshipful Guardian followed and, of course, so did I. The Hoptons had the chambers on the first gallery overlooking the sweet-smelling garden well away from the dirt and foul odours of Smithfield. The door of the young man's chamber was open. I noticed how the door was of thick, blackened oak reinforced with strips of metal and rows of iron studs. The second door was of similar quality, a pool of blood oozed out from beneath the rim forming a dark, accusing puddle on the polished wooden floor. Parson Snodgrass and the landlord pounded on the door but, of course, the dead cannot answer. Charles Hopton danced from foot to foot then hurried back to his chamber, so he told me, to find his other shoe.

"It's futile," Worshipful Guardian exclaimed, at mine host's pounding on the door.

The landlord, a sly cozen, fluttered his bloodied fingers and wailed disconsolately. Now many people regard me as a wild devil, a Winchester goose who made her fortune filching white money or spending my time at a vaulting house down on Southwark side. However, that was all in the future. I had not yet fallen into ruin and acted upon the stage or dressed in male swagger, or gone to the Tower to meet Lord Cecil and the other spies and dagger boys of the Office of the Night. To be sure, in my youth, I was a rumskuckle, a tomboy, but I had sharp eyes and keen wits and, watching that landlord flail his podgy hands and pick at his hairy nose, I smelt villainy.

"Take the door off!" Parson Snodgrass exclaimed.

"Impossible!" Hopton came back out to the gallery and the landlord chorused what he said. "For the Lord's sake, the doors are solid oak, the hinges are steel not leather!"

"True, true!" the landlord wailed. He crouched down and peered through the key-hole. "And the key's still in the lock, I cannot open it!"

"The chamber overlooks the garden?" Parson Snodgrass asked. "Then come, sirs."

We went downstairs out along the pebbled path, around the tavern and into a sweet-smelling fragrant garden. Beyond were the stable yards and, at my Worshipful Guardian's insistence, the landlord scurried off, bringing back a ladder. He placed this carefully against the wall.

"See." The landlord pointed up to a casement window, the mullion glass gleaming in the sunlight. "That's Sir Nicholas's chamber."

Young Hopton put one foot on the rung of the ladder, but Parson Snodgrass waved him away. He pointed down to his long leather boots.

"I'd be safer." He smiled and tousled my black, curly hair. "As young Mary will tell you, I am used to scaling the ladders of my belfry or mending my roof."

I nodded solemnly. Indeed, he was: Parson Snodgrass could climb as nimble as a squirrel.

"I'll go up," he declared gravely and waved away the ostlers and grooms who had now begun to gather.

"You'll need a chisel," the landlord shouted and sent a tapster to fetch one.

Worshipful Guardian grasped this then scampered up the ladder as skilfully as a monkey up a pole. At the top he pressed his face against the window.

"What can you see?" the landlord shouted.

"Nothing," Worshipful Guardian replied. "The shutters within are closed."

He drew back the chisel, told us to stand away and shattered one of the small panes of glass. He put his hand carefully inside and lifted the latch. Next we heard the sound of breaking wood as Worshipful Guardian battered against the inside shutters. These flew open and in he climbed. We waited for a while then Worshipful Guardian poked his head out of the window, his face all pallid.

"Your uncle . . .!" It was more of a strangled sob than a cry.

"Take the ladder away!" he urged. "Come round. I shall open the door!"

The landlord obeyed and we hurried back into the tavern and up the stairs. Just after we arrived, we heard the bolts drawn, the key turned and the door swung open. Inside was a scene the playwright Middleton or that roaring boy Dekker would have been proud of:

chaos, blood and gore! Despite the open window and flung back
shutters the place smelt foul. There was a close stool in the corner
over which fat, black flies buzzed like imps from hell. The sheets
on the four-poster bed were crumpled and disarrayed. A chest had
been knocked over but Sir Nicholas's corpse drew all eyes. He lay
sprawled on the rushes, his throat slashed from ear to ear. The blood
had poured out like that of a gutted pig, seeping amongst the rushes,
finding its way along the paving stones and under the door.

"God have mercy on us!" Worshipful Guardian breathed.

I stared at old Hopton's face, so surprised by death: the white
bristling moustache and beard, the sunken cheeks, the tongue curling
out like that of a snake: the eyes were terrifying: popping as if Sir
Nicholas had seen a vision of hell and all its fury before he died.
The floor was sticky underfoot and I had to seize my mouth, close
my eyes and pray that my stomach would not betray me. Young
Charles, all a-trembling, sat down on a stool.

"I came through the window," Worshipful Guardian explained.
"Sir Nicholas was just lying there." He smiled wanly. "I'm sorry for
any delay but," he glanced round fearfully, "I thought the assassin
was still here." He pointed to the door. "The key was still in the lock
and the windows all shuttered . . ."

"So how did it happen?" young Charles bleated.

The commotion began again and a search was made: the cup Sir
Nicholas had brought up from the taproom lay on the floor, the wine
all gone but the water in the bowl and jug on the great wooden
lavarium was still pure and unused. While they all babbled and
scampered about, I went across to the bed. I was always fascinated
by the way people had slept: how they lay and what did they do when
darkness fell. I ran my hand across the grimy sheet. The bed was
cold but then I espied it, a woman's stocking, blue and decorated
with yellow clocks. I pulled this out and held it up to admire it.

"Your uncle's?" I asked.

Hopton whirled round, his jaw fell: behind him the landlord's
hand went to his mouth.

"It seems my uncle was not alone last night. Here fellow," Hopton
turned back to the landlord. "Sir Nicholas was no dog. Help me lift
him onto the bed."

The landlord obeyed like some mute bereft of speech. Whilst
Hopton picked up his uncle's body under the armpits, the landlord
lifted the feet but his eyes never left that stocking still in my hand.

"He's so cold," Young Hopton whispered. "He must have been
dead for hours."

Worshipful Guardian came over and snatched the stocking out

of my hand and stared round the room: Sir Nicholas's own clothes hung on a peg on the wall, his boots beneath it.

"Is there anything missing?" Worshipful Guardian asked.

"Oh, Lord save us!" Hopton wailed.

He drew the sheet over his uncle's face then, like some Abraham man devoid of wit, he scampered round the room muttering to himself. Coffers and chests were flung open, clothes rummaged through. A pair of leather panniers unbuckled, their contents spilled onto the floor.

"What is it?" Worshipful Guardian asked.

"The money belt!" Hopton cried, running a hand through his hair. "Twice a year, two days after Lady's Day and then again after the feast of St Michael and All Angels, Uncle brought his gold to the merchants in Cheapside. He was to bank it today but now it's gone!"

The landlord, his face turning yellow like a lump of doughy paste, edged out of the room and disappeared down the gallery. Hopton slumped down on a stool at the foot of the bed.

"My uncle was murdered!" he exclaimed. "Someone came into his chamber last night." He pointed to the stocking. "Some whore took my uncle's money belt and slit his throat."

Worshipful Guardian, all christian concern, went over and patted him gently on the shoulder.

"You are sure of this?" he asked.

"Of course!" Hopton cried. "Uncle was fit and happy when I left him."

"And did you visit him again?"

The young man looked up sheepishly. "I went out," he stammered. "The pleasures of the town, sir. London is a far cry from the fields and woods of Sussex."

"And your uncle?"

"He was a ladies' man," Hopton confessed. "He was well known to the women of the town."

Oh, aye, I thought, a precious pair these two, uncle and nephew, full of the good things of life. They came up to town in their richly garbed clothes, bellies full of wine and pippin pie, then out to the nearest brothel to bestride some callet or fresh young pullet. Young Charles had to find his own, but a man like Sir Nicholas would demand such soft flesh be brought to him.

"Where's the landlord?" Hopton suddenly asked, rising to his feet. "Where is that jackanapes?"

He ran out of the room and down the gallery. Worshipful Guardian followed but I stayed. Even though of the gentler sex, I had a hard heart and a curious nose. The chamber was now deserted. I looked at the blood which had congealed upon the rushes thick and crusting: the overturned chests and coffers: the broken window and shattered shutters, the key in the lock. I tiptoed over to the bed and pulled back the sheet. Sir Nicholas lay, eyes open, beaky nose up in the air. I wondered idly where his soul was: to die after taking a whore, the imps might surely have it! I stared curiously at the cheeks, noticing the little veins streaked there, silent testimony to Sir Nicholas's love of claret and deep bowls of canary. Then, pushing my nose closer, I sniffed and caught the cheap perfume which still lingered on the straggling grey temples of hair and bloodstained night shirt.

"Mary!" Worshipful Guardian shouted over an ever-growing hubbub of noise. "Mary, where are you? Come down now!"

Of course, I disobeyed, lingering a few more minutes for this was the first time I'd been in a death chamber. I recalled the old stories of how the ghost loved to linger. Heigh nonny no, fifteen years of age, I was already wilful and set in my ways. Worshipful Guardian called again so I hurried down: the taproom seemed full of people, shouting and gesturing at each other. At the far end the landlord sat slumped on a stool. Now and again he would lift his head and howl like a dog before hiding his face in his hands; beside him stood the high constable, a brave burly boy with his staff of office and broad-brimmed hat: a man of importance who made sure everyone was fully aware that he was an officer of the law, the Queen's own man. On the other side of the landlord was a strapping lass with golden curls, the bodice of her bottle-green dress cut so low her breasts, ripe young pears, jutted out ready for the touch. However, her face was red with anger, her eyes flashing as she raved like some Bess o' Bedlam.

"Worshipful Guardian." I pulled my face into the most pious grimace. "What is happening?"

"Master Hopton and the Constable are questioning the maid." Parson Snodgrass bent down. "Apparently the stocking belonged to her."

"What's your name?" the Constable asked, his face only a few inches away from the girl's.

"Sarah," the girl replied all a-quiver: despite her defiance, Sarah had to clench the edge of the beer barrel to stop herself fainting.

"Sarah what?"

"Bartholomew. I was a foundling."

"What's this then?"

A young man came through the back door: he had greasy red hair and a dirt-smeared face. He took one look at quivering Sarah and would have launched himself on the Constable if the landlord had not intervened and pulled him back.

"Who's he?" Hopton stepped back, frightened of this angry young man with his snarling, gap-toothed mouth and flailing hands.

"He's my only son," the landlord wailed. "Simkin."

"And sweet on Sarah," I whispered to Worshipful Guardian.

The whole scene would have ended in fisticuffs and violence if Parson Snodgrass hadn't intervened. He plucked the Constable by his cloak and whispered in his ear, the fellow nodded portentously.

"No good will come of this," the Constable trumpeted. He waved to one of the tables. "I have to make my enquiries." He continued, "I can make them here or in the gatehouse at Newgate."

The prospect of a visit to that foul, pestilential place sent everyone hurrying round the table, Worshipful Guardian included, whilst I stood behind his chair and watched, open-mouthed. Nothing in my short but very boring life could equal that scene. Neither the mummers who visited our village nor even Widow Grayport's noisy tirade against Goodwoman Cuthbertson outside the parish church could rival the awful hangman drama in that tavern taproom so many years ago. The Constable, for all his pomposity, was a sharp man, and the sight of his cudgel on the table, which he raised now and again for silence, kept good order. Sarah, flustered, wept and, glancing fearfully at Simkin, blubberingly confessed.

"I was with the old gentleman," she wailed. "He offered me a silver piece."

"To do what?" the Constable asked.

I would have sniggered but I kept as still as a statue lest Worshipful Guardian should remember I was present.

"To accommodate him," Sarah muttered.

This was too much for Simkin who rocked backwards and forwards on a stool. I thought he was a fool. If Sarah with her dangling tits was his idea of chastity then never did a man so richly deserve a cuckold's horns.

"He gave me a coin," Sarah continued. "I slipped into the old man's chamber to, to . . ." she stammered. "To frolic for a while."

"And?" the Constable barked.

"The old man was fuddled, in his cups. I left him."

"Did he lock the door when you went?"

"Oh, yes, he did!"

Sarah leaned forward on the table, the Constable licked his lips before he remembered who he was and tried not to stare down into her bodice.

"Stay here!" the officer declared and, taking the landlord by the arm, dragged him away from the table.

There was a whispered conversation and the landlord led him off up the stairs, walking like a felon on his way up to meet Jack Ketch at Tyburn.

For a while we sat in silence. Sarah trembled, Simkin slouched, head in his hands, Hopton nervously drummed his fingers on the table. Worshipful Guardian looked over his shoulder and smiled at me.

"Master Charles," I gabbled, hoping to divert the Parson's attention. "How long do you intend to stay in the city?"

"Oh, another day," he replied off-handedly. "I was to stay here whilst Uncle went to Cheapside."

I was about to ask him where he had gone the previous evening when there was a crashing on the stairs. The Constable swept into the kitchen holding a blood-stained dagger triumphantly before him.

"I found it." He pointed at the quivering Sarah. "In your closet behind some clothes."

"And the money?" Young Hopton sprang to his feet.

The Constable shook his head. "No sign." He marched across and laid a hand on Sarah's shoulder. "Sarah Bartholomew," he intoned, "I arrest you in the name of the Queen for the horrible crimes of murder and robbery."

He dragged the young woman to her feet even as he blew on his whistle. Two bailiffs came in from outside, loathsome men with greasy spiked hair, beer-sodden faces and bleary eyes. One of them lashed the young girl's hands together behind her back even as the other took liberties with her body, grasping her around the breasts, chuckling to himself. The Constable raised his stick threateningly.

"She's the Queen's prisoner, not a sack of goods!" he warned.

And, without further ado, the Constable swept out of the tavern, the two bailiffs almost carrying the sobbing Sarah between them. I quickly looked round: the landlord for all his fear had a calculating look, and what I thought was a smirk. Simkin did not seem too contrite whilst Parson Snodgrass, my Worshipful Guardian, leaned his elbows on the arms of the chair, steepling his fingers as if in prayer.

"Truly," he muttered, "the love of riches is the root of all evil."

Hopton moved his stool across and stared at Worshipful Guardian. He narrowed his eyes. "Sir, I have seen you before?"

"Possibly," Parson Snodgrass replied. "I had a curacy in Sussex. Perhaps it was there."

Hopton blinked, muttering under his breath.

"And what will you do now, sir?" my Worshipful Guardian

asked, as the landlord and son shuffled to their feet, mumbling about work to be done. They scuttled into the kitchen to whisper amongst themselves. Hopton watched them go.

"I shall stay here for a while," he replied slowly. "Uncle's corpse has got to be dressed, embalmed and carted back to Tidmarsh before the weather becomes too warm."

"And the money?" I asked, slipping onto a stool beside my guardian.

"Oh, yes, the money. That, too, has to be found."

Parson Snodgrass shook his head mournfully. "The wench has hidden it away."

"I think she's innocent," I blurted out.

"Why, Mary, dearest," Parson Snodgrass looked at me in surprise. "Whatever makes you say that?"

"She's big and brawny," I replied. "But poor Sarah does not have the wit to carry out such a crime. Your uncle was a healthy man?"

Hopton nodded, watching us carefully.

"He was an old ram," I continued, ignoring my Worshipful Guardian's gasp of surprise. "Not a man to bare his throat to the slayer. There was no struggle, no sound was heard, yet we are to believe that she cut your uncle's throat, took the money belt and heigh-ho off to her own chamber. She was apparently bright enough to hide the money but not the dagger which will send her to the gallows." I paused. "Nor has anyone explained how she could have locked the door from inside."

"True," Worshipful Guardian added, "but she may have an accomplice."

Hopton pulled his stool closer. "What are you saying?"

I pointed to the scullery. "I think it's best if you had words with mine host and his son, Simkin."

My Worshipful Guardian, steepling his fingers before his mouth, stared at me for a while.

"Out of the mouths of babes and infants," he intoned. "Stay awhile, Master Hopton."

And, striding into the scullery, Parson Snodgrass shouted for mine host and Simkin and led them back into the deserted taproom. All the other drinkers and diners had long fled: even the drovers and butchers from Smithfield Market, like ancient priests of old, had divined the signs. A murder had been done at the *Bishop's Mitre*, a bloody corpse had been found and the Constable had arrived. Those who were close to such a death might be implicated in it. In a place like Smithfield I suppose everyone has something to hide.

The taverner and his son sat down at one end of the grease-covered table, Parson Snodgrass, Hopton and myself on the other. I had to stifle a smile; we looked like three justices on circuit whilst the landlord and his son, with their greasy faces and sly-eyed looks, would not have been out of place in any hanging cart.

"Do you think Sarah is guilty?" Parson Snodgrass began. "She is in your service."

"A mere foundling," mine host replied callously.

Oh, my heart went out to her. Nevertheless, I smiled beatifically, tossing back my ringlets; silently, I cursed this dirty tub of lard who would allow a girl to swing from the scaffold just because she was a foundling.

"And you, Simkin?" Hopton asked. "You were sweet on the girl?"

The young man opened his mouth in a fine display of yellow, rotting teeth.

"We had a tryst," he stammered. "I met her at St Bartholomew's Fair three years ago. My father gave her employment."

Aye, to warm your beds, I thought, but I kept my mouth shut.

"Last night," Parson Snodgrass continued, "what happened at the tavern?"

The landlord waved his dirty hands, his nails were thickly caked with muck. I quietly vowed I'd eat no more in this tavern.

"Sir, you know as much as we do," he replied. "Sir Nicholas and his nephew dined on lamb stew. You and your – "

"My ward," Worshipful Guardian supplied.

"Yes, yes, you saw them here."

"And then what happened?"

"Well, I left for the city," Hopton replied.

"And your uncle stayed down here for a while," the landlord said. "You remember him, sir?" he said, pointing at Worshipful Guardian.

"Aye, we had a few words with him," Parson Snodgrass replied. "But he was well in his cups."

"Parson Snodgrass and I helped him up to his chamber," I added.

"And young Sarah?" Worshipful Guardian asked.

Again the landlord stretched those filthy hands. "When the day is done," he replied, "and all duties are finished, who am I to say who goes where or does what?"

"Was Sarah in the habit of entertaining old men?" Hopton asked harshly.

"Old men, young men," mine host replied. "What does it matter? The girl had an eye for a silver piece."

"Did you send her to him?" I asked.

The landlord threw me a look of contempt whilst his son Simkin pulled a face.

"Well, did you?" Hopton asked. "Surely you must have missed her in the scullery or taproom?"

"What are you implying?" mine host demanded.

"We are implying nothing," Parson Snodgrass intervened smoothly. "We simply find it difficult to believe that Sarah had the strength to kill a man like Sir Nicholas. We also wondered at her foolishness in managing to hide away the money belt and yet not conceal the dagger. And where would she get such a knife, eh?"

"I was going to ask the same questions."

We spun round, the Constable stood in the doorway. He walked leisurely across and placed a leather sack on the table, opened the cord at the neck and let the long-bladed knife fall out. We all stared at it.

"Do you recognize it, sir?" the Constable asked, turning to the landlord.

"Of course," mine host stammered. He picked it up by the battered wooden handle: it winked in the light, blood still stained its evil-looking point. "It's one of our fleshing knives," the landlord declared. "There are at least a score of these in the kitchen. It would be easy for anyone to pick it up and smuggle it out."

The Constable's leathery face broke into a smile. "Truly spoken!" His grin widened as he sat down. "I see there's a Court of Inquiry in session here and I would like to join it. Poor Sarah's in Newgate. But that does not mean she's guilty." His words hung like a noose in the air. "As I walked up Giltspur Street," the Constable continued, "and watched poor Sarah being carried like a sack in the hands of those bailiffs, I wondered how such a girl could kill a wily old man like Sir Nicholas with so much stealth and silence." His smile faded. "And I am no fool. Why should I find the knife and not the money? So," he loosened his cloak and let it fall around him, "in the porter's lodge at Newgate I made Sarah an offer. Tell me where the money was and she'd have a pardon." He tapped his hand on the table like a man beating a drum. "Now any man or woman faced with a stay in a condemned hole, followed by a ride in the hell-cart to Tyburn, would seize such an offer with both hands." He paused his tapping. "She claimed to be innocent of any crime. Moreover," he continued, "there's a problem with the key, isn't there? It was in the lock: the old man must have turned it but he couldn't do that if his throat was slashed." He bowed mockingly at Worshipful Guardian. "Parson Snodgrass, you bravely broke into the room, how did you find it?"

"The shutters were closed," my Worshipful Guardian replied. "As was the window casement itself." He pulled a face. "The door was both bolted and locked, the key turned. Poor Sir Nicholas was lying on the floor, his throat all gutted."

"And the body was cold?" the Constable asked.

"Like ice," young Hopton replied. "It was ten o'clock in the morning when we burst in. Uncle must have been dead at least eight hours."

The Constable studied him closely. "And you, sir, were his beloved nephew and now his heir?"

"Yes," Hopton replied. He straightened his shoulders, puffing his chest out. "According to my uncle's will, I am heir to his manor and his estates. Why, sir?"

"Honi soit qui mal y pense," the Constable replied drily. "Evil to them who evil think."

"I left the *Bishop's Mitre* last night," Hopton snapped, looking flushed. "My uncle was here, in the tap room, slightly drunk but very much alive. I went up Giltspur Street to a molly house in Cock Lane. Ask the mistress there, Nan Twitchett."

"I know her very well," the Constable interrupted with a half-smile.

"I played a game of dice." Hopton bit his lip and closed his eyes. "Hazard. Then a young lady with hair as black as night and a face like a gipsy entertained me into the early hours. I came downstairs and broke my fast on light ale, bread, butter and some lovely jam."

"Quite so, quite so." The Constable grinned at me. "Mistress Twitchett's sweetmeats are well known. And when you came back, sir?"

"I went upstairs to my own room, washed and bathed. I then went to wake uncle and saw the blood. The rest you know."

"And you, sir?" The Constable turned to Worshipful Guardian.

"As I have told you," Parson Snodgrass replied, calm and serene as ever; at that moment my Worshipful Guardian had the face of a saint, like a Solomon come to judgement, his grey hair, neatly parted down the middle, falling down to his snow-white collar above his black gown. "Little Mary here and myself dined in the taproom. Sir Nicholas was much in his cups and we helped him up the stairs. Isn't that right, girl?"

I nodded.

"Sir Nicholas was in good spirits, a wine cup in one hand, full of mine host's claret. We steered him into his room. I never saw him again."

"Which leaves mine host," the Constable declared.

"We live and work here," the fellow replied. "And neither my son nor myself went anywhere near Sir Nicholas's chamber. Even if we did, how could we get in? The door was locked and bolted from the inside, the key in place, the windows were shuttered and, before you ask, there are no secret tunnels or passageways inside. You can search the room yourself," mine host sighed. "It was as you saw it, with one window and a door."

The Constable breathed out noisily. "So, we have Sir Nicholas who leaves the taproom. By the way, where was the money belt?"

"As always, strapped round his waist," Hopton replied. "He even went to bed with it. My uncle was not the most generous of men and most untrusting to human kind, which explains why the windows were closed and shuttered."

"So," the Constable replied. "He goes into his bedroom and changes. Earlier in the day he'd made an assignation with young Sarah who now comes tripping along to service him. She says he was much the worse for drink. There was a tussle on the bed which achieved very little. Out she went and he locks the door behind her. Now, Sir Nicholas may have had another visitor who cut his throat and took his money belt but, how could that happen, if the door remained bolted, the key turned in the lock and the window shuttered?" The Constable got to his feet. He threw his cloak over one arm and grasped his cane. "So, there's nothing for it but to visit young Sarah again."

"We should all go!" I exclaimed.

Worshipful Guardian turned, his eyes rounded in amazement.

"Child, child," he intoned. "The horrors of Newgate are not for you."

"She's a foundling," I replied. "And so am I. She's been wrongly accused and must be terrified." My wits grew sharper. "Surely, sir, we should go. Did not the good Lord tell us to visit those in prison?"

Parson Snodgrass smiled benignly. "I have business, child."

"I could take her," the Constable offered kindly.

I smiled back, feeling guilty at the hasty judgement I'd first made about him.

"But that's improper," Parson Snodgrass blustered.

"I'll go too," Hopton volunteered.

Worshipful Guardian steepled his fingers as if in prayer.

"Very well," he declared. "But be not too long. Give the poor girl all the comfort you can." He glanced at Hopton. "Surely you should look after your uncle's cadaver?"

"There is very little I can do now," the young man replied. "But

I can call in to see the vicar at St Sepulchre's and pay a fee to have it taken to the death house there."

Worshipful Guardian agreed. The Constable and I left the tavern. We stood outside the gate, just near the butchers' stalls whilst young Hopton went back to his room to prepare himself for the city. The Constable held my hand, leaning on his staff of office. He looked down at me and winked. I blushed with embarrassment and turned away. A butcher's apprentice came from behind a stall. He grasped the head of a sheep bleating in terror and, with one slash of his knife, cut the poor creature's throat: its legs buckled and it fell into its own pool of splashing hot blood. The gore burst out like water from a fountain. The Constable caught my gaze.

"It's a cruel world, child," he commented. "And you'll come to worse sights by and by." He patted me on my black mop of hair. "The poor creature's well gone: this is a wicked world and the devil tramples on every side. Ah well, here comes our rich, young heir."

Hopton came swaggering out, he had changed into a blue tabard jacket with a peascod belly and multi-coloured hose. He now wore his swordbelt and carried a silver-topped cane, walking with all the hauteur of a rich, young courtier.

"Quite the man about town," the Constable whispered out of the corner of his mouth. "And hardly the grieving nephew."

Hopton gave us a mocking bow and we all crossed Smithfield market. We pushed our way through the throng, past the stocks, the neck, the hand, the feet and the finger, all full to overflowing with the naps and foists. As the Constable passed, he was greeted by a raucous cheer from these miscreants whilst he lifted his hat in a sardonic salute.

At the entrance to Giltspur Street we had to pause for a while as two cat's-meat men, poles slung over their shoulders with pieces of offal hanging from them, fought over who should lead the motley collection of cats which now thronged hungrily about them.

"Why are they doing that?" I whispered.

"Whoever gets the cats," the Constable replied gruffly, "gets their skins."

"People wear catskin!" I exclaimed.

"Of course," the Constable replied. "Some people swear by it, especially when it rains."

We went up the street. I gazed round-eyed at all the sights: courtiers in their silks and taffetas strutting like peacocks; bare-arsed children begging for coins. An Abraham Man, naked except for a piece of cloth round his private parts, did a curious dance outside St Bartholomew's Hospital. Two whores, lashed back to back, their skirts raised to expose grimy thighs and knees, were dragged down to the stocks by a sweaty-faced bailiff. A doctor with a mask covering his face wandered by, a staff in his hand. The mask was like something out of a nightmare: his face and neck were fully covered, the eyelets of the hood covered by pieces of glass and it had a strange bird-like beak which, the Constable explained, was stuffed with perfumes to keep away the contagious air. At last the great, dark mass of Newgate, stone towers soaring above its iron-clad gates, came into view. I thought we would go there but the Constable stopped at the entrance to a narrow, dark street. On the corner was the *Ship* tavern and outside this stood a pretty young woman standing over a plate of charcoal, her skirts hoist. Hopton saw this and smirked.

"What is she doing?" I whispered.

"She's a whore. She's fumigating herself against the pox," the Constable replied. "Now you, my dear, just stay here with this gentleman."

The Constable bowed mockingly at Hopton. "This is Cock Lane, sir, and it won't take me long to see if Mistress Twitchett corroborates your story."

The Constable walked down the alleyway, swinging his staff of office, impervious to the shouts and catcalls which came out from the doors and windows as he passed. Hopton watched him go with a narrow-eyed look.

"A strange fellow," he drawled. He glanced sullenly down at me. "What are you looking at, cat eyes?"

"I don't know," I replied tartly. "The label's fallen off!"

He took a step threateningly towards me.

"I'll scream!" I warned.

Hopton's lips curled. "Well stay there, waiting for your Constable." He pointed to the spires of St Sepulchre's. "I cannot tarry here to wait for that base-born rogue to tell me I've been speaking the truth."

And, swinging his cane, he sauntered off. I wasn't afraid. My stomach tingled and, beneath the serge dress I always wore, my legs trembled but that's because I was free. No Worshipful Guardian, no ladies of the parish telling me how fortunate I was, none of their children sweeping past me, noses in the air. I, Mary Frith, or Moll as I liked to be called, was, for a short while, truly alone in a strange place.

I stood, open-mouthed, drinking in the sights. A journeyman wandered by, a tray slung round his neck. He winked at me as he shouted, "Elixirs, cures, come buy my plague water!" He tried to stop a young fop swaggering along with his codpiece out like a standard before him. "Have some unicorn's horn, rampant as a boar it will make you! Or you, my lady." He tried to grasp the sleeve of a woman passing by, a hood across her hair, a mask over her face. "Frogs' legs!" he called. "Give it to your husband and you'll have no need for a lover!"

He went on by. A young boy ran up, a small cage in his hand. He held it up before me. I looked at the sorry little linnet perched on a rod and turned away. Parson Snodgrass never gave me any coins. I felt a hand on my shoulder: an old man, his blue eyes watery and bleary, his face flushed, his breath heavy with ale, looked down at me. He ran his wet tongue round his lips.

"A pert little piece," he lisped. "A tumble for a shilling?"

His hand came down to squeeze one of my breasts. I could not move, but suddenly the Constable's cane blurred past my eyes and struck the fellow harshly on the back of his hand. The old man yelped like a dog and leapt back. The Constable pushed him further away, prodding his chest with the pointed end of his staff.

"Be gone you toper and leave the child alone!"

The old man stumbled against a whore coming out of Cock Lane, the woman a veritable harridan, turned screeching like a cat. The Constable, his hand still on my shoulder, led me off.

"Where's Hopton?" he growled.

I caught my breath. The Constable squeezed my shoulder gently.

"Don't worry about the old poltroon," he declared. "There are some who think everything in the city is for sale and," he added cautiously, "they might be right."

"Hopton's gone to St Sepulchre's," I replied.

"He shouldn't have left you!" The Constable took me into the sweet-smelling darkness of a baker's shop and bought me a slab of gingerbread.

"Mistress Twitchett?" I asked between mouthfuls.

"He was where he said he was," the Constable replied. He took me round to the front of St Sepulchre's and, lifting his staff, pointed to the door. "That's where she'll go," he explained. "Poor Sarah, after she has been condemned, will be taken across there and made to sit on her coffin whilst a parson lectures her before she's put into the death cart and heigh-ho to Tyburn."

"Do you think she'll hang?"

"Aye. A man has been killed and she has the knife."

He led me across the busy thoroughfare, dodging between carts and pack horses, and pulled at the bell-rope of Newgate prison. A side door swung open and the Constable led me, like Virgil did Dante, into a veritable hell-hole. Passageways and corridors where the stone walls were moist and dripping green with mossy slime. Dark as night it was, except for the tallow candles, their flames low and sullen as if oppressed by the stinking, fetid air. The Constable grasped my hand as I stumbled across the sour rushes, trying not to start or scream as dark furry bodies came darting out of every crevice and corner, eyes bright as beams, the rats of Newgate were foraging for food.

We passed cells from which a raucous din emerged: screams, shouted obscenities, the chanting of the deranged and sometimes the sheer howling of the forgotten and the desolate. The turnkey went before us, head pushed back into his shoulders. He was like some gruesome waddling toad; now and again he'd bang at the iron-grilled doors with his keys. At last he stopped before one cell, inserted a key in the lock and ushered us into the stinking pit of Newgate's condemned cell, a narrow room about eight foot high and three foot across. Sarah sat on a pile of wet rushes in the corner manacled at the wrists and ankles by metal gyves. All her prettiness was gone. She seemed to have aged in a matter of hours: her cheeks were hollow, shadows ringed her eyes. She looked fearfully at the Constable and tried to smile at me. I pushed the remaining gingerbread into her mouth. She chewed it greedily.

"If I could have some water?" she muttered.

"I'll arrange for it as I leave," the Constable replied. "We have come to ask you some questions."

"What's the use?" the girl replied. "I'll hang." She blinked and stared around. "I've done nothing wrong," she muttered. She lurched forward but her chains dragged her back. "I'm a good girl, sir. I . . ." She leaned back against the wall, tears streaming down her face. "I didn't kill the old man," she sobbed. "Nor rob his silver."

"Tell me," the Constable said, "last night when you were with Sir Nicholas, did he have the money belt round his waist?"

Sarah closed her eyes. "Yes, yes, he did. I remember it because it hurt me."

"And did you copulate?" the Constable asked bluntly.

"Oh no," she replied. "Though Sir Nicholas could be vigorous."

"Could be?" the Constable asked.

"Oh yes, he stayed at the *Bishop's Mitre* twice a year on the same dates.' She forced a laugh. "It wasn't the first time I'd visited him in his room. Always the same pattern. He in his cups. His young nephew off to savour the pleasures of the town. I and Sir Nicholas would bounce on the bed." She shrugged in a rattle of chains. "But that night was different. He was tired so I left. He locked the door behind me and I went back to my own chamber, a small garret at the top of that tavern."

"And in the morning?" the Constable asked.

"I was up early, going about my business." She wiped her dirty face and stared hard at the Constable. "You know that." She whispered hoarsely. "You drink many a tankard there."

"The landlord and Simkin will miss you," I added slyly.

Sarah flounced her head. "No, they won't. They are glad I'm gone."

"Why?"

"I told them I was pregnant," Sarah replied. "But I am not. I hoped Simkin would marry me." She put her face in her hands and began to sob. "I wish I was," she blurted out. "I wish I was, then I wouldn't hang." She raised her dirty, tear-streaked face. "The parson," she whispered, "Vicar Snodgrass, ask him to come and see me. He knows I am a good girl."

I leaned over and patted her hands. "Of course I will."

We left shortly afterwards. The Constable stopped to order a pannikin of fresh water and some victuals for poor Sarah. Then he took me back to the *Bishop's Mitre*, chucking me under the chin and telling me to be a good girl.

I wandered into the taproom. It was deserted, the sour rushes had been cleaned, the floor swept and mopped, giving it a fresh soapy smell. Simkin came staggering in, a pail of water in each hand. I asked if Worshipful Guardian had returned but he morosely shook his head. I went out and sat in the garden. It was one of those beautiful, sun-filled English afternoons: the air was fragrant with a flowery perfume, bees buzzed lazily, hunting for nectar and crickets sang in the long grass. It reminded me of the graveyard at Parson Snodgrass's church. I'd always gone there to hide from him and his sharp-tongued wife. Lord save me, I have seen more christianity in a toad than in that puffed-up bag of wind. No wonder Worshipful Guardian liked to visit London to see the Dean of the Arches. I stared at the herbs. Parson Snodgrass loved herbs and was skilled in making poultices and potions. I sat, my back against a wall, half-dozing, dreaming about what had happened: Parson Snodgrass climbing the ladder; Sarah desperate in prison; the Constable tall and protective; the sheep having its throat cut in Smithfield Market; the blood bubbling out; old Hopton's face. How had he been murdered? How could anyone enter that room with the key still in the lock?

"Mary?"

I turned. Worshipful Guardian was standing in the doorway. He was dressed in his best gown and fine Spanish leather shoes with their high-wedged heels.

"Mary, are you well?"

"Yes, Worshipful Guardian," I replied.

He smiled benignly and went back in. I remembered the blood splashing from that sheep's throat – that's what was wrong! I felt a tingle of excitement in my belly. I waited a while, re-entered the tavern and crept up the stairs to old Hopton's room. The door was unlocked, I creaked it open. It smelt sour and fetid. The grisly corpse still lay in the bed under a dirty sheet. I stepped inside the door and examined the blood on the floor, recalling where Sir Nicholas had lain. With the toe of my shoe I brushed the rushes aside. I then studied the blood stain which had seeped under the door now dried to a rusty red. I stood thinking, my heart stopped hammering. I left the chamber and returned to Parson Snodgrass: the room was empty so I grasped his boots and felt very carefully inside. My hand touched the sticky wetness, I could have screamed with relief. I was washing my hands in the bowl, watching the water turn a dullish red when I heard the footfall behind me.

"Why, child, what are you doing?"

Worshipful Guardian stood in the doorway.

"I know who murdered Sir Nicholas," I smiled, folding the napkin carefully, hoping he wouldn't notice it.

Parson Snodgrass walked towards me. I backed away so he sat on the bed, his face framed by lank, grey hair. He was all sanctimonious and serene with that benign smile which never reached those watchful, dark eyes. He sat, hands clasped in his lap, legs crossed at the ankles like some Brownist ready to declaim the Lord's praises.

"Young Sarah killed Sir Nicholas," he explained, slowly as if I was devoid of wit and understanding.

"Worshipful Guardian," I replied. "How could she? How could a young girl murder a man like Sir Nicholas and meet no resistance? She tumbled with him on the bed so where could she hide the knife she'd brought to kill him? And, if she cut his throat, why did he so obligingly get up to lock and bolt the door behind her?"

"What are you saying, dearest child?"

"You come to London quite often," I replied. "You stay here at the *Bishop's Mitre*. Young Hopton recalled you but couldn't place the time and whereabouts. You knew about Sir Nicholas and his heavy belt of gold. You knew his routine, his love of the deep-bowled cup and those lusts of the flesh which you always lecture us about every Sunday."

The smile faded from Parson Snodgrass's lips.

"You planned his murder," I continued defiantly. "You brought me here to be your catspaw. Who would ever suspect the saintly Snodgrass? The pious parson who, from the kindness of his heart, had taken a young girl into his care?"

"But you were there!" Worshipful Guardian exclaimed, head on one side as if I were the dimmest child in his Sunday School class. "You saw the blood seeping from under the doorway. You saw the key in the lock and how I climbed up and prised open the shutter. Are you a Bess of Bedlam, Moll? Has the visit to Newgate numbed your wits?"

"Last night we stayed in the taproom," I replied. "You and I helped Sir Nicholas up to bed during which you slipped some powder or potions into his bowl of claret. What was it, Worshipful Guardian? Some henbane, some hemlock or a little nightshade? Sir Nicholas becomes weak. Little Sarah trots along but she is then dismissed. Sir Nicholas locks the door behind her and, shortly afterwards, falls into a deep swoon and so into death."

"And?" Parson Snodgrass eased himself back on the bed.

I could tell from the paleness of his face and the sneer round those thin, prim lips that I'd hit my mark.

"Early this morning," I continued, "you brought up a small pouch of blood, bought in the market outside, and pushed it under the door. Once it was in place, you pierced it with a pin and the blood seeped out. You then hurried along up to little Sarah's garret: the fleshing knife, which you'd filched from the tavern and smeared with cattle blood the previous day, you hid in her closet. And the stage was set."

"For what?"

"Master Charles coming back and glimpsing the blood trickling underneath his Uncle's door. He raised the alarm, you made sure that we are in the taproom ready to intervene. I thought it was strange that you put your riding boots on. Why should a parson dressed in his best, ready to go down to St Paul's, put on his riding boots? Unless, of course, you were preparing to climb a ladder? Everyone would accept that: a man of God is 'used to climbing the ladders in his church steeple'," I smiled. "You'd prepared well: you knew how thick and heavy the doors of this tavern are. The only way to break into a chamber is through an outside window. And you were ready to do that. The landlord gives you a chisel and up you go. You force both the shutter and the window and climb in. Sir Nicholas is sprawled on the floor. You do three things whilst the rest of us are waiting. You slit Sir Nicholas's throat with the knife concealed in your boot. You take off the money belt and slip it round your waist and you pick up the remains of the small pouch of blood and push it into the stinking close stool where no one will think of looking. The poisoned wine you drain into the rushes. You clean your hands from the water jug, draw back the bolts, then unlock the door. Who would suspect? Everyone thought Sir Nicholas had his throat cut before you ever climbed that ladder. And, of course, because your potion had done its deadly work, his body is cold."

"But, dearest child, how could I possibly do all this, you were all outside?"

"You were prepared," I answered. "The knife in your boot, you climb into the room, Hopton's throat is slashed, the knife slipped back, the tattered, bloody pouch thrown into the close-stool, the cup drained, fingers washed, the water splashed on to the rushes, who'd notice? And, finally, Hopton's money pouch wrapped round your waist, carefully hidden beneath your jerkin and priestly gown."

"But it would take so long!"

"Nonsense!" I scoffed. "Worshipful Guardian, if I counted slowly to sixty, you could do all that I've described. Remember, how we waited for a while in the yard below before you came back to the window? How we had to come round and climb the stairs and then wait again? Oh, you had time enough!"

"And what further proof do you have, dear child?" Parson Snodgrass's lips were curled like a mastiff ready to attack.

"Oh, I went back to Sir Nicholas's room. I noticed how the blood from the old man's throat had trickled through the rushes on to the floor, but there's a gap, at least five to six inches, between that blood and the stain which seeped under the door. Now, why should that be, eh? Secondly, I was puzzled by you wearing your boots so I came up here and felt inside. There's a bloodstain still there where you hid the knife." I gazed round the chamber. "Somewhere here is Sir Nicholas's money belt, not to mention the stockings you later changed, before you left to meet the Dean of the Arches."

"Sharp, dear child!"

"Thank you, Worshipful Guardian."

"You have been thinking deeply, my child."

"As did you, Worshipful Guardian. Sir Nicholas was a creature of habit, mean, miserly and a toper. You studied him closely: how he drank deeply and entertained his doxy for a while. He'd always keep his window shut and, to keep his money belt safe, he made sure the visiting trollop did not stay the night. The potion you gave him would take hours to work: Sir Nicholas, however, could get little help from his dear nephew, who'd be off to Cock Lane as fast as a whippet after a bone."

"I was risking a great deal!" he snarled.

"No, Worshipful Guardian, you were not: the doors in this tavern are of solid oak and cannot be forced. All you had to risk was being the one to climb that ladder. Even if that opportunity slipped, you were stil protected. Who'd suspect? Once you were in the room, you were alone, to do what you wanted. And in the hubbub afterwards, who'd suspect you?"

Parson Snodgrass rose to his feet.

"If you come any closer," I whispered, smiling beatifically, "I shall scream." I picked up the bowl of water from the lavarium. "And throw this with such force through the window that everyone in Smithfield will know something is wrong."

Parson Snodgrass sat down. "So, what do you want, dear child?"

I stared at him even as my mind raced. I remembered the freedom I had enjoyed earlier in the day, the Constable's warm hand, the delightful sights and smells of the city compared to my grim days at the Parsonage.

"Some of the gold," I lisped.

"And?"

I pointed to the door. "I shall walk out of here and you'll never see me again."

"Stay in London all by yourself? That's dangerous!"

"Not as perilous," I replied, "as staying with a Parson who commits murder and robbery and who plans, in the near future, to leave his boring little parish and his sharp-tongued wife for pastures new."

Parson Snodgrass rose to his feet. "Those who ask shall receive," he intoned piously and, shifting the bed, he lifted a loose floor board and drew out Sir Nicholas's money belt, its fat purses bulging along the edge. "How much?" he asked.

"Three of the purses," I replied. "Place the money on the table," I demanded. "And, remember, I can still scream."

Parson Snodgrass obeyed. I made him go back and sit on the bed whilst I placed the coins in a napkin and tied my little bundle up. I glanced at Worshipful Guardian's face and saw the hatred blazing in his eyes.

"And what about poor Sarah?"

"Oh, she can hang!" I replied flippantly. "Now, Worshipful Guardian, please lie down on the bed."

Still clutching the money belt, he obeyed. I raced like a greyhound for the door. I took the key from the lock, slammed the door shut, locked it, ignoring Worshipful Guardian's cries, I skipped downstairs, the bundle in my hand, eager to get into the market place and seek the Constable's help.

# CASSANDRA'S CASTLE; or, The Devious Disappearances
## J. F. Peirce

*Elizabethan and Stuart England is a ripe setting for stories of international intrigue and mystery. Back in 1964, J. F. Peirce wrote a satire on Shakespearean scholarship called "The Great Shakespeare Mystery" (Ellery Queen's Mystery Magazine, May 1964), which revealed his extensive knowledge of the Great Bard, so it is not too surprising that a few years later he returned to Shakespeare as the central character in a series of detective stories. The series began with "The Double Death of Nell Quigley" (EQMM, December 1973), and he wrote four others of which "Cassandra's Castle" (EQMM, May 1975) was the last. Peirce (b. 1918) is emeritus professor of English at Texas A&M University where he taught for over thirty-seven years.*

"The reason I summoned you," Lord Burleigh said, addressing the young actor-playwright, Will Shakespeare, "is far different from the last, when I sought your assistance with respect to the increasing number of rogues and vagabonds in the city. This time the matter is of little consequence. It has to do with a scandal at Court – a conundrum that plagues our curiosity."

He paused and gestured to the three men seated with them in a conversational circle – William Davison, Queen Elizabeth's Scottish secretary; Sir Francis Walsingham, Her Majesty's Secretary of State; and Henry Herbert, the Earl of Pembroke and President of Wales.

"Frankly," the Lord High Treasurer continued, "I have bet these gentlemen a considerable sum that you can undo the tangled skeins of events that comprise this puzzle. If you do, half my winnings will be yours. But win or lose, I will pay all expenses."

"His Lordship has bragged mightily on you," Walsingham said. "We've been anxious to make your acquaintance."

Both Davison and the Earl nodded.

"First, let me give you the facts as we know them," Lord Burleigh said, pulling at his beard. "No doubt you've heard of the Countess of Chommondley, who is famous for her height, which is o'er six feet, and for her constant companion, an ugly little man, no larger than a child, who's called The Monkey."

Shakespeare nodded.

"He was a magician when they first met. In fact, he still entertains at the Countess's parties. Women are attracted rather than repulsed by his appearance – perhaps because he makes the ugliest of women *seem* attractive by comparison."

"Not that the Countess has any need for such comparison," the Earl said. "She's a damned attractive woman with a willowy figure." He coughed, then added, "That is, those who've seen her in *other* than a farthingale report so."

Lord Burleigh smiled and curled the ends of his moustache with the backs of his index fingers. "It's the curse of our age that women conceal their nether halves in such floor-length garments."

"I confess I agree, Your Lordship," Shakespeare said.

"Though The Monkey's had numerous chances to betray the Countess with younger, more attractive women," Burleigh continued, "he remained faithful to her till recently. Then a few months ago he met the courtesan, Cassandra – "

"The one they call The Giantess, Your Lordship?"

Burleigh nodded. "She's o'er six and a half feet tall, and by piling her hair high and wearing those damnable Italian *chopines*, she adds another half-foot or so to her height. You do know what *chopines* are?"

"Aye. Shoes with thick, cork platform-soles," the playwright said. "Boy actors who play women's parts wear them to increase their stature." He paused, then asked, "How came The Monkey to meet Cassandra, Your Lordship? I thought she ran a brothel in Southwark?"

"She does," Burleigh said, "and a most successful one." He frowned, then went on: "The Court attracts all kinds. Some, bored with their lives and their own kind, surround themselves with such courtesans and criminals to add zest to their existence. One such fool introduced Cassandra to the Court. And as she towers o'er the Countess and is statuesque, whereas the Countess is slender, The Monkey fell madly in love with her – and she with him. Since then he's spent most of his time with her to the dismay and displeasure of the Countess."

"Why does he not leave the Countess altogether, Your Lordship?"

"Because she's a woman of great wealth and his tastes are many and expensive."

"I should think that Mistress Cassandra would be equally wealthy, running as she does such a notorious brothel."

"Nay. Her wealth is as poverty compared with that of the Countess."

"Have you seen her brothel? – Cassandra's Castle, as 'tis called," Walsingham asked.

"Only from a distance, Sir Francis."

"Let me describe it for you, then. In effect it's an island, as 'tis surrounded by a moat. And it can be entered from but one side – by a drawbridge, which is guarded by a pander dressed in full armour and carrying a halberd. And its three-storey house has a studded door containing an espial wicket."

He paused, then continued. "I don't know about Lord Burleigh, but the rest of us have all been there for one reason or t'other. It's the fashionable place to go – to see and be seen. The island has a large formal garden for amorous strolling and an arbour for *al fresco* entertainment. One can obtain the finest of food and drink there, be entertained with music and the reading of plays and poetry, and see elaborate displays of fireworks at night."

"Fortunately it's located outside the city," Davison interjected. "Otherwise, our Puritan friend, the Lord Mayor, would have ordered it closed."

Lord Burleigh coughed, and Walsingham and Davison allowed the Lord High Treasurer to pursue his tale.

"As time passed," Burleigh said, "the Countess became increasingly distraught. And each time The Monkey went out, she set lackeys to following him. Last week, after a rather disagreeable argument between them, she decided to bring the matter to a head. She had twenty of her lackeys in disguise follow him. At first, he appeared unaware that he was being followed, for he made straight for Southwark.

"But once he had crossed London Bridge, he evidently realized that men were dogging his heels, for he tried to elude them – but without success. When he entered the castle, the men surrounded it as if laying siege. And a short time later the Countess arrived at the gallop in her carriage, like a general about to direct the course of battle."

Lord Burleigh paused and pushed up the ends of his moustache with the backs of his index fingers. "Seeing the Countess," he went on, "the guard notified Cassandra, who set about entertaining her 'guests' royally to take their minds off the fact that they were, in a sense, imprisoned. Food and wine were brought from the cellars. Strolling musicians played for their entertainment. There was much merriment and carousal. But amidst all this activity, no one caught even the briefest glimpse of The Monkey.

"The Countess, for her part, made arrangements for a house to be available to her nearby. She sent for food and water and more lackeys. And when they arrived, she stationed them about the moat with the others to watch the castle. At most no two of them were more than six yards apart.

"Darkness approached. The Countess ordered torches, and each sentry was given enough to last out the night. On the island, lanterns and flambeaux were lighted. There was dancing, and there were water displays and fireworks. Rockets spangled the night with coloured stars. A fire-drake winged its way across the sky. Reflected light danced upon the water."

The Lord High Treasurer paused again. "The revelry lasted throughout the night, and the Countess and her men maintained their ceaseless vigil. Then, with the first light of dawn, the drawbridge was lowered, and Cassandra in a red velvet farthingale swept majestically across it, like Drake's *Golden Hinde* under full sail swept before the wind. She was closely followed by her guard, walking stiff-legged in full armour.

"'What do you want?' Cassandra demanded rudely when she at last stood before the Countess.

"'My Monkey! My precious Monkey!' the haggard Countess replied.

"'Go home!' Cassandra commanded. 'You'll find him there.'

"'You lie, for he lies with you in the castle!'

"'Nay. I swear he's not under my roof, though he's under my protection. Go home! You'll find him there. He's at home where he is.'

"'Let me enter the castle and see for myself!' the Countess demanded.

"'Very well,' the courtesan replied and gestured towards the open doorway.

"Leaving half her men still surrounding the island, the Countess led the others across the drawbridge. They searched the house from cellar to rooftop and the garden and the arbour as well. But The Monkey had disappeared as the night with the coming day.

"At last convinced that he was not there, the Countess retreated in defeat across the bridge without looking at or speaking to the courtesan, who had remained with her guard on shore. Leaving some of her men still to watch the castle, the Countess returned home to discover The Monkey asleep in his room, a smile of satisfaction o'erspreading his features.

"At the sight of him, the Countess broke down and wept. And when her weeping awakened him, she begged his forgiveness, and while the rogue had her thus at his mercy, he made her agree to a villainous bargain – to allow him to divide his time between herself and Cassandra."

"Now our question is," the Earl said, leaning forwards, "how did The Monkey escape from the island?"

Shakespeare frowned. "Is there no chance that he escaped before the guards were posted, My Lord?"

"None. The men saw him enter the castle, and they had the island surrounded before he could escape."

"Did anyone leave the castle *after* he entered, My Lord?"

"No one. A short time after The Monkey entered, a boy entered with a sack o'er his shoulder, crossed the bridge *to* the castle, and once he was across, the drawbridge was raised."

Shakespeare frowned. "What would a boy be doing on the island, My Lord?"

"There are two boys who work there. They care for the garden, run errands for the girls, and do such-like."

"I see. Could any of the lackeys have been bribed to look elsewhere, My Lord, while The Monkey escaped?"

"I doubt it. Too many others would have seen him."

Shakespeare bent his brow in concentration, and the others waited in silence for him to speak.

"There are three ways of escape from the island," Shakespeare said at last. "By air, o'er the water, and across the bridge. Four if, by chance, there's a tunnel under the moat."

Lord Burleigh shook his head. "We've anticipated you on that score," he said. "The man who built the castle still lives, and he assures us there is no tunnel."

Shakespeare slitted his hooded eyelids and ran his thin fingers through his swept-back auburn hair. "I assume we can rule out that he flew through the air like the fire-drake. Can he swim? Perhaps he swam the moat and escaped when one of the lackeys had his attention momentarily distracted."

"He's an excellent swimmer," Burleigh said. "He's strong and wiry and has defeated much larger men in hand-to-hand combat who have made slighting remarks about his appearance and size. But the moat is guarded by two crocodiles, ten feet in length or longer. They're rumoured to be well fed, but I doubt he would care to test that rumour."

"Surely they aren't in the moat constantly, My Lord."

"No. There *are* ramps that they can climb and walkways on both sides of the moat for them to crawl about on and sun themselves. The walkways are guarded by spiked-iron fences, high enough so that the crocs cannot escape into the street or the garden. On occasion the beasts are pinned down with forked sticks and chained to one of the fences so that the girls and their guests can swim in the moat. But they weren't chained that night. Several of the guards reported seeing them floating in the water."

"Then he must have escaped across the drawbridge, Your Lordship."

"But how? It was kept raised till morning." He pulled at his beard thoughtfully. "Well, do you think you can solve this puzzle?"

"I can try, Your Lordship. How long do I have?"

"A week," Burleigh said, glancing at the others, who nodded.

"Could Cassandra be persuaded to let me put on a performance duplicating The Monkey's escape?" Shakespeare asked.

Lord Burleigh turned to the Earl.

"I think it can be arranged," the Earl said. "My secretary, Peregrine, is a frequent visitor to the castle. Cassandra's quite fond of him."

After learning the whereabouts of the Earl's secretary, Shakespeare rose and said, "Then I'll meet Your Lordship and these gentlemen at the castle at this time next week." And bowing, he departed.

The next morning, accompanied by Dick Burbage, the talented actor-artist, and Peregrine, the Earl's hawk-like secretary, Shakespeare went to Cassandra's Castle. The island was as it had been described. Two crocodiles floated lazily in the water. One opened its great mouth, revealing its sharp white teeth, and the playwright shuddered.

Overhead, a thin wire stretched from a triple window on the third floor of the castle to a double window on the second floor of a building on shore. The wire canted downwards at a 15-degree angle. It was obviously not strong enough, Shakespeare observed, to support the weight of a boy, not even of a small one.

A fire-drake, or fiery dragon, rode above the wire. The winged dragon, as the playwright knew from having helped make one as a boy, was constructed of thin strips of wood, bent and tied to form the shape of the dragon. This framework had been covered with paper scales and the scales had been painted.

Metal canisters containing a slow-burning gunpowder were located in the dragon's mouth and tail, so that when they were lighted, the dragon would appear to belch fire. A larger canister of gunpowder hung below the wire, counterbalancing the dragon and supplying its motive power. Neither the dragon nor the canister, Shakespeare noted, was large enough to conceal The Monkey, thus eliminating the dragon as a means of escape.

The pander on guard was dressed in armour made of thick, heavy leather, and as they approached, he raised his visor and smiled. Peregrine spoke to him familiarly, and they were permitted to cross the bridge and enter the brothel. Inside they were greeted by Cassandra, who towered over them. Shakespeare was both attracted to and repulsed by her.

After gaining her permission, Peregrine conducted the actor and the playwright on a tour of the castle. In Cassandra's quarters, while searching her wardrobe for a possible hidden passage, Shakespeare discovered two of The Monkey's suits, both bright orange, concealed amongst the courtesan's clothing, and he could not help smiling at the disparity in their sizes.

Later in the garden, Peregrine introduced Shakespeare and Burbage to Cassandra's girls. The courtesans were of different colours, shapes, and sizes, and Shakespeare was amazed at the variety.

Once the tour was completed, the playwright instructed his companions as to what he expected of each of them.

"That's too much to accomplish in but a week!" Burbage protested. "I doubt it's possible."

"Get Cuthbert and others to help you. Money's no problem – you'll be well rewarded."

"If you insist," the actor grumbled. "I'll try."

"Good lad! I know you can do it," the playwright said.

Burbage and Peregrine left the castle shortly thereafter, but Shakespeare remained a while longer to get the feel of the island and observe its life.

Later that morning Shakespeare appeared at the manor house of the Countess of Chommondley. A few pieces of silver to the cook gave him entrance to the kitchen and the answers to a number of questions. A few pieces more enabled him to search The Monkey's bedroom and wardrobe. At the sight of so many pastel-coloured suits, the playwright gave an involuntary whistle. He whistled again when The Monkey's manservant pointed out the suit The Monkey had worn the day he disappeared. The suit was bright orange and of a distinctive design.

After obtaining the name of The Monkey's tailor, Shakespeare
sought out one of the lackeys the Countess had had follow the
little man that day. And for a few pieces of silver, the lackey led
the playwright along the path The Monkey had taken.

He had made straight for Southwark; then, realizing that he was
being followed, he had taken a twisting-turning route down alleys
and sidestreets. But the last hundred yards were in the open. It would
have been impossible in daylight for his pursuers to have mistaken or
overlooked either the colour of his costume or its distinctive design.

Later that day at The Monkey's tailor, Shakespeare was not
surprised to learn that The Monkey was in the habit of ordering
several suits at a time. And as the tailor kept patterns for all of
them, he readily agreed to make six copies of The Monkey's bright
orange suit and at once set his apprentices to work on them.

The following week, as stipulated, Shakespeare met Lord Burleigh
and the others at the drawbridge of Cassandra's Castle. Accompanying the playwright were four boy actors whom Peregrine had recruited
for him from the Children of The Royal Chapel at Blackfriars. Each
of the boys wore a floppy orange hat, a bright orange suit, and
a monkey's tail and mask that Dick Burbage had made. The
youngsters were capricious and unruly, and Shakespeare had to
reprimand them often.

The group was joined moments later by the actor, Will Kemp,
who approached them from across the bridge. He was wearing
Cassandra's red velvet farthingale, and its skirt had been hastily
pinned up to keep it from dragging on the ground. For though Kemp
was a big man, he was half-a-foot shorter than the giant courtesan.

The four "monkeys" scampered about him, leaping and jumping.
They moved hunched over, their knuckles touching the ground, and
they chattered: "Chi! Chi! Chi!" in their high-pitched voices till
Shakespeare silenced them.

Once all was ready, Shakespeare sent Kemp back across the bridge
to the island and then had one of the boys remove his mask and tail,
so that he could be readily identified. The boy had a large strawberry
birthmark on his right cheek, and Shakespeare had Burleigh and the
others inspect it, so that they would know that it was real and not
make-up.

Then with Burleigh, Davison, Walsingham, the four monkeys, and
forty lackeys following him, Shakespeare led the way to the spot where
The Monkey had realized that he was being followed. At this point,
Shakespeare sent the boy with the strawberry birthmark on ahead
to play The Monkey's part, and the boy set off along the path The

Monkey had taken, followed closely by the rest. He was out of sight for brief moments when he turned corners suddenly, but at last he was in the open with no place to hide, and he made his way quickly across the drawbridge and into the castle.

Shakespeare then asked Walsingham to play the part of the Countess, and Walsingham gave the lackeys careful instructions, stationing them around the moat.

Shortly thereafter, a boy carrying a sack over his shoulder crossed the drawbridge and entered the castle. Shakespeare, followed by the three remaining monkeys, crossed the bridge also, and the bridge was at once raised.

Immediately a party began in the garden. But though Kemp, dressed as Cassandra, and Shakespeare were much in evidence, nothing was seen of the four orange-suited boy actors or the boy with the sack. Shakespeare appeared briefly at the third-floor window to check the fire-drake for the evening's performance, and later he was seen in the garden, drinking and flirting with some of the girls. Later still he was noticed walking about the edge of the moat, as if checking on the positions of the crocodiles.

The day wore on. Afternoon became evening. The watchers grew impatient. Burleigh sent for food and drink and a supply of torches. Though the liquid refreshments were plentiful and varied, the men did not drink heavily, wishing to keep their heads clear and their eyesight sharp.

Night fell. Rockets sent rainbows arching across the sky or burst in showers of falling stars. The fiery dragon winged its way over the moat in search of St George or a beautiful damsel. A water fountain became a liquid vase of fluid flowers. Those on the island caroused into the night, their revelry continuing till sunrise.

Then the drawbridge was lowered, and Kemp, dressed as Cassandra, clomped across the bridge, followed by the playwright and the stiff-legged guard in full armour. Kemp stumbled once and almost fell when he tripped on the hem of the farthingale, but Shakespeare fortunately caught him.

The big actor seemed to have grown in his part, for when he and Walsingham repeated the angry exchange between the Countess and Cassandra, his gestures were properly mincing and his voice convincingly falsetto.

Once the exchange between them was completed, Walsingham called twenty of his men to follow him and led them across the bridge. As before, the castle was searched from cellar to rooftop, and the garden and the arbour as well, but none of the four boy actors was found. And the boy who had carried the sack across the bridge was also missing. At last admitting defeat, Walsingham gathered together his men and returned to the shore.

"Well, are you satisfied, gentlemen?" Burleigh asked.

"Damn me, no!" the Earl exclaimed. "And I'll not be till I receive an explanation of their disappearance." He turned to the playwright. "My compliments, young man. I'm sure we all agree that his Lordship has most definitely understated your talents."

"I confess that I, too, am anxiously awaiting your explanation," Burleigh added.

"Instead, allow me to give you a demonstration if you will," Shakespeare said. He whistled and the four boy actors minus the floppy orange hats they had worn and the boy with the sack appeared out of a house nearby, and followed by Kemp and the visored guard, they scampered across the drawbridge, which was once again raised.

"You'll recall," Shakespeare said, "that I explained that there were three ways to escape from the island – by air, by water, and across the bridge. Four if there was a tunnel, which was eliminated on the builder's evidence and my own examination of the castle and island. Now let me demonstrate, first, how The Monkey *could* have escaped by air."

The playwright pointed to the third-floor window of the castle where one of the boys was attaching a fire-drake to the wire stretching from the island to the shore.

"Now," Shakespeare said, "see what happened under cover of darkness, while your attention was centred on the lewd carousal taking place in the garden before the fireworks began."

The playwright whistled, and the boy was joined at the window by Peregrine and Dick Burbage, who removed the fire-drake and began pulling on the wire, which was loosened by Cuthbert Burbage, who stood in the second-floor window of the house on shore.

To the end of the wire, as it issued from the house window, Cuthbert attached two ropes – one heavy, the other light. And once the heavy rope was secured inside the castle, Peregrine started pulling on the lighter rope, drawing a larger, sturdier fire-drake out of the window of the house on shore. When it reached the castle, its hinged top was thrown open, and the boy entered. The gunpowder was lighted, and the dragon flew down the rope and was caught by Cuthbert Burbage, who helped the boy out of its bowels.

"Marvellous!" Lord Burleigh exclaimed.

"It's like a *deus ex machina*, a machine in which the gods come down to earth to settle the affairs of mortals, as used in the masques at Court," Davison said.

Shakespeare nodded. "Now imagine that the aerial fireworks cease. The watchers' eyes are drawn by a sudden burst of activity to the people in the garden. But keep *your* eyes on the castle window and see what *could* have happened under the cover of night."

Shakespeare whistled. A second boy climbed out the window. Grasping the thick rope, he swung hand-over-hand down it, to disappear into the house on shore as the watchers applauded.

Immediately the rope was pulled back into the window, and the wire installed in its place.

"Now consider the possibility of escape by water. Pray look at the crocodile in the water," Shakespeare said. "Remember that it is night with only flick'ring torches to light it and shimm'ring reflections to confuse the eye."

The playwright whistled, and on cue the crocodile swam across the moat and crawled up the ramp to the walkway along the shore.

"Keep *your* eyes on the crocodile," Shakespeare said, "but imagine, if you will, a tremendous burst of rockets that would draw the eye of e'en the most dedicated watcher skyward."

Again the playwright whistled, and the crocodile reared upwards, revealing a shell-like framework that had concealed a third boy dressed in dark clothing, his face and hands blackened with burnt cork. Quickly the boy slid the crocodile shell into the water, then slipped over the fence and, keeping low, ran towards the house on shore.

"Where did he come from?" Burleigh demanded.

"He donned the shell and slid quietly into the water while you were engrossed in watching the fire-drake wing its way across the sky. Like the fire-drake, Your Lordship, the crocodile was designed by Dick Burbage and built under his direction. The real crocodiles are chained at the back of the garden."

Again he whistled. "It's daybreak," he said.

As he spoke, the drawbridge was lowered, and Kemp, followed by the stiff-legged guard, strode across it towards them. Reaching the shore, Kemp acted overly coquettish till Shakespeare frowned, causing him to assume a more decorous demeanour.

"Now let us examine the possibility of escape across the draw-bridge," Shakespeare said. "Imagine, if you will, the dialogue behind Cassandra and the Countess. Visualize her men moving across the bridge towards the castle. *Look!* Look at the open doorway!"

Though Burleigh and the others looked as directed, nothing happened – no one appeared. Then, turning back to the playwright, they gasped. For a fourth boy stood by his side.

"God's blood!" Burleigh exclaimed. "How did you perform *this* miracle?"

Stepping over to Kemp, Shakespeare lifted the skirt of his red velvet farthingale, revealing the *chopines* that added half-a-foot to his height. And at a nod, the boy actor slipped between Kemp's legs, and Shakespeare dropped the skirt as he would a curtain.

"So *this* is how The Monkey escaped the island!" Burleigh exclaimed. "Apollo gave the Trojan Cassandra the gift of prophecy, then placed a curse upon her when she would not lie with him, so that none would believe her. Like her namesake, Mistress Cassandra spoke the truth *and* the Countess did not believe her. 'He's not under my roof,' she said, 'though he's under my protection . . . He's at home where he is.' He *was* under her 'protection' – for he was under her dress which protected them both. And surely he *was* 'at home' between her legs."

"God's wound!" Walsingham exclaimed. "What a delightful way to disappear!"

"But *where* is the fifth boy?" Davison demanded.

Shakespeare turned to the guard, who lifted his visor, revealing himself to be the fifth boy.

"He's wearing short stilts 'neath his armour," Shakespeare said. "And his gauntlets are designed with false hands to make his arms appear longer."

"But where is the orange suit of the boy in black face?" Pembroke asked. "They all appeared white and were dressed alike when they returned to the island after their escape."

Shakespeare pointed to a sack beside him. "The boy who escaped betwixt Kemp's legs carried the orange suit," he said.

Burleigh frowned. "But by which of these means *did* The Monkey escape?" he demanded.

Shakespeare smiled and said, "By none of them, Your Lordship." He whistled, and the boy with the strawberry birthmark came out of the castle. "I sent him across the bridge to the castle with the others since, as you recall, the lad dressed as the guard did not remove his disguise during the first escape."

The viewers appeared dumbstruck.

"Your Lordship was right," Shakespeare continued, "in saying that, like her namesake, Cassandra spoke the literal truth. But you were mistaken in your interpretation. The Monkey *was* at home – at the Countess's manor. He both supped and slept there whilst the Countess spent a drear day and a sleepless night watching the castle."

"God's blood!" Burleigh said. "Keep us not in suspense! How did he manage it? How do you know?"

"I *know*," Shakespeare said, "because I questioned the Countess's cook and The Monkey's manservant — something no one else bothered to do. They told me that The Monkey provoked a quarrel with the Countess on the morning he 'disappeared,' that he goaded her into sending men to follow him by saying that if she caught him on the island, he would give up Cassandra, but that if she tried and failed, he'd give up *her*."

"Monstrous!" Burleigh said.

"Earlier I'd discovered two orange suits belonging to The Monkey hidden amongst Cassandra's clothing. Later I discovered a third orange suit in The Monkey's wardrobe. This, plus the fact that on his way to the castle he'd have been out of the view of his pursuers each time he turned a corner and could have escaped at these times, yet apparently he made no effort to — which aroused my suspicions."

Burleigh nodded.

"Then I remembered the lad with the sack o'er his shoulder and the strange fact that once he crossed o'er the bridge, it was raised as if on cue. 'What,' I asked myself, 'if The Monkey had hired the two boys who work at the castle to hide in doorways along his route dressed in identical floppy hats and suits of orange clothing — could he not have slipped into a doorway on turning a corner where one of the lads was hidden, and that lad then took The Monkey's place in the chase?'"

"But why *two* boys?" Pembroke asked.

"To make doubly sure of his escape, My Lord, because of the high stakes for which he was playing. If his pursuers were following too close when he reached the first lad's hiding place, he could increase his lead and change places with the second. Then, whichever lad was passed by could remove his orange suit, having his own clothes under it, put the suit in the sack, the sack o'er his shoulder, and return to the castle."

"But why would The Monkey concoct such a scheme?" Davison asked.

"To trick the Countess into agreeing to his dividing his time betwixt herself and Cassandra. In that way he would have the best of both of his worlds — love *and* money!"

Burleigh frowned. "What I cannot understand," he said, "is *why*, knowing The Monkey did not escape from the island, you still put on such an elaborate performance?"

"For two reasons, Your Lordship. For one, since you had such a sizeable bet with these gentlemen, I wished to give them the most for their money."

"And the other?"

"To be perfectly honest, Your Lordship, I wished to determine how *I* would have escaped had *I* been trapped on the island."

Walsingham laughed. "And which method would you have used?" he asked.

"Can there be any doubt in your mind as to that, Sir Francis?" the playwright countered.

Lord Burleigh smiled, and the others applauded.

# MAN'S
# INHERITED DEATH
## Keith Heller

*One of the earliest letters of comment I received on* The Mammoth
Book of Historical Whodunnits *was from Martin Edwards, who
drew my attention to the works of Keith Heller. One of the real pleasures
of producing books and hearing from readers is in making such new
discoveries. Heller (b. 1949) has written a series of novels about George
Man, a London parish watchman. The first book,* Man's Illegal Life
(1984), *was set in the year 1722, and brings London life at that time
vividly into focus. It also portrays Man, who was then aged 45, as
an honest, shrewd, conscientious and extremely painstaking watchman.
Two other novels appeared.* Man's Storm (1985) *is set in 1703, and*
Man's Loving Family (1986) *in 1727. I was delighted to discover
there had been two short stories featuring Man, and the first of them is
reprinted here.*

*Heller has also written two stories under the alias Allan Lloyd which
feature the Chinese magistrate Ti Jen-Chieh on whom Robert van Gulik
based Judge Dee, and more recently he has created a new series of
detective stories around that eighteenth-century painter and visionary,
William Blake.*

In the deeper half of January, 1729, in the short darkness of York
Street, one of the dingiest Covent Garden tributaries London had
to offer, George Man – fifty, hoarse, and wearied, a professional
watchman for most of his adult life – stood stiff and winded, with
his staff and lanthorn in his hands, and decided it was time for him
to quit.

He should not have come out at all tonight, should have stayed
snug and drinking in the watch-house with the other men. No one
needed him tonight, no one else had been foolish enough to brave
tonight's weather, not even the usual hard and screaming revelers
who nightly circulated about Covent Garden like clods in sludge. It

was two o'clock – he had just called it out to the deaf and inanimate
street – and he had met no more than a handful of people all night.
Like him, they had been too busy struggling for breath to bother
thinking of trouble, too intent upon finding or reaching some door
that they could close against the cold. And once inside, they probably
wanted nothing more than to fall into the kind of wrapping sleep a
January snowstorm can give.

Man was jealous of them, of their secured windows and their
mounded, heating blankets. He had fought long enough tonight
against the crazing wind and cutting snow. He had kneed his way
through enough cold and solid drifts for one night, grappled with
plenty of dizzying gusts; and now his boots were cracking, his nose
was pinched, and his eyelids were shriveled almost shut. He must
be a fool. Nothing could be happening tonight.

It was a wonder that he heard the window opening at all, what
with the storm and his wet ears. A crashing somewhere in the darkness
above him sounded across his shoulders and a sharp voice came down
to him, brittle and shrunken with the wind.

"Here, man! Help me! Here!"

The watchman hoisted his lanthorn higher and saw only whipped
snow. "The watch, the watch is here! Name yourself!" Man thought
his voice was too weak to rise, the wind was taking it too far
away.

"Wait," the man called. "I see your light. I'll be down, sir. To the
door, the door of the shop."

Reaching forward with his light, Man saw the barred door of a
shuttered house. The beaten signboard above it could be barely
read: *Edmund Cowley, Jeweller.* An etched depiction of a lion holding
a huge ring in his mouth, a rough border of loose stones. The sign
hung dangerously from a bending rod.

A bank of swept snow drifted up toward the door. Man saw a single,
vague set of bootprints, now all but filled, there was heard an inward
noise of bolts and latches, and then another lanthorn mirroring his
own. A shaking hand reached out.

"Will you come up, sir?" Man heard a normally strong voice
quaver. "It's my father. Upstairs. He is dead, I think."

The watchman was led through an unaired shop toward an
invisible flight of back stairs. He had doused his own candle and
now followed the host light through a succession of skimming visions
– murky shelves and cabinets, a forbidding counter crowned with
more than one pair of scales, low doors suggesting rarely unlocked
storerooms – all the trademarks of the shrewd and careful jeweller.
It was the kind of shop that, in a newer house and in a higher

neighborhood, might well invite some of the best society of London. Man sensed a stark economy surrounding him, but no poverty. It was rather as though all had been drawn in and tightened, sealed off from the outside, as if to make ready for the storms of avarice and envy that would always threaten.

The light showed the watchman a little of the man ahead of him. A man of about forty years, fastidiously dressed in a serviceable coat and inexpensive wig, a lean man, almost gaunt and hungry but with the enduring leanness of a cautiously whittled switch. His wrung face looked whiter than the yellowing candle alone should have made it. Man noticed in his movements a tension that could have been mere force of character, personal determination; yet right now it seemed more like painfully restrained excitement. Halfway up the steps and still climbing, his host was already upstairs, talking even faster than he had climbed.

"I came in late tonight, due to the heat of the storm. I thought I might not get back at all, such piles of snow turning me right out of the Strand. This day and night have made a most dreadful havoc among the trades."

They had reached the upstairs landing and come to a stop in a short hallway with three doors, all closed. The air about them was stale and very cold.

"I came up here to wish my father a good night before going to my own bed. There was no light, but I know he sleeps very little. And – he wanted to see me." The watchman listened to the man's voice, hearing the terror or joy or madness hidden in it. "I found him at his table – sleeping, I thought – but when I touched him – " The lanthorn shook the frail light. "I cannot quite believe it yet."

Man frowned at him, set down staff and lanthorn, and brushed past him into the unlocked room.

The room was small, a cramped marriage of business and rest. A low, curtained bed took up most of one wall. It was old and breaking, and it had not been slept in tonight. An unmatched pair of elbow-chairs stood with their backs to it, facing a ponderous walnut desk that was symmetrically bordered with piled ledgers and bound papers. A sloping stand for books rested on top, next to a bowed figure that looked as if it had been crumpled and twisted and thrown hurriedly aside. Man noticed first, ridiculously, the breathing rise and fall of white neck hairs in a secret draft. Then the quill pen discarded near one hand and the bare space on the desktop.

"Was he writing?"

The watchman's question distracted the other's examination of the business ledgers shelved on the wall behind the desk. He looked blankly at the still pen.

"What? Writing?"

Man glanced about him. "You have moved nothing? Removed nothing?"

"I assure you, sir, I have not."

Bending over the dead man, the watchman observed the uncomfortable grey nightgown, the old wrenched throat, the sparrow's face hardened first by life, then by death. The cheek was cold as new paper.

"This is your father, then?"

"It was, sir." The inflection stood alone in the dulled room. "He was Edmund Cowley, the jeweller. I am his son, Harold Cowley. His first son."

The watchman reached beneath his greatcoat for his pipe, to warm himself. He could hear the storm outside, jostling thickly the tired house.

He found a twist of straw in his pocket and with it lit his pipe from the lanthorn.

"You have a brother?"

"Christopher, yes."

"But he does not live here in his father's house?"

Harold Cowley was fingering some papers almost at his father's elbow. Man's question straightened him, stiffening.

"My brother is married, sir. He has his own family. In Rood Lane, next the shop where he works as a journeyman joiner. He has been there I should say almost ten years now. Living with his wife and son." A distant satisfaction. "Very poorly, I am afraid."

Man was smoking, slowly stalking the room. "Does no one else live here?"

"No one, sir."

"No servants, then?"

"My father could never abide them, nor their demands." He paused, added proudly: "I have always done for him myself, sir."

The watchman came to a stop behind the inert father. Very carefully, he took the pipe out of his mouth, read the dome of fine ash in the bowl, and stuffed it burning back into his pocket. He spoke gravely, officially, staring at nothing somewhere off to the younger man's left.

"Your father, sir, has had his life choked out of him this night, that much is clear. Now I am nothing beyond a simple watchman myself. I can do no more, say no more. We have no way of saying who has done this act: I have no felon here that I can lay hold of and carry to the nearest watch-house, which is all my work." He looked, explaining, directly at Harold Cowley, then away again. "You understand, sir, that we cannot alone take your father through the streets in this dark storm. Enough for us to find a way for ourselves through the high snow without."

"I must go with you, then?" The jeweller's first son sounded as if he wanted never to move again, though he obviously was not tired. "Where must we go?"

Man considered it.

"Constable Marlowe's house is hard by us here – in White Hart Yard, as I remember. We should be able to reach there in half an hour or less. Quicker than the watch-house in the Strand, at any rate. And he's a man of lively parts, never one to mind his being taken from his sleep. His dreams, he tells me, only weary him more than his waking."

Facet by facet, the watchman smoothly studied the room a last time. Then he delicately drifted the jeweller's son toward the door. "If the storm dies some, the coroner will want to sit here tomorrow to question the death formally," he said, opening the door. "Do you have a key?"

"Of course," Cowley assured him. "For this and for the other rooms. And the street."

Just as they were leaving the quiet of the room, Man had another thought.

"Is anything missing, do you think?"

The other's eyes searched, wondered, could not decide. "I've been looking all this while. I think not. But – " He strained for perfect honesty. "There's really not so very much here, you see, and I know it all so well. There's nothing taken, I think, nothing that should be here and is not. I'm certain. And yet – from the first tonight I've thought the room was different in some way. Some way changed. Everything is in its place, but there is something altered somewhere. I don't know." Harold Cowley faltered. "Perhaps it is only his death that has made the room seem new to me."

"Yes," Man agreed quietly. "Death can do that."

The next day – cold, but still and clear – found George Man sharing more than one cup of warmed wine in the house of Constable Marlowe. The watchman slept through most of most mornings, but today his wife, Sarah, had thrown him out with the corner dust. They were in the process of moving – no, Sarah was in the process of moving them – from their long-lived apartments in Ironmonger Row off Old Street north of the City to others somewhat smaller and less dear in Bow Street. Now was the worst season of the year, and the worst weather of the season, to move: how many times had Man told her? But once set in motion, Sarah could not be stalled. So now she was hectoring and frazzled, hip-deep in opened trunks and roped boxes. The few possessions they meant to keep had interbred overnight, hiding most of the floor. Man could have gone anywhere, but he was curious about last night's death, and he was always ready to trade cups and news with Constable Marlowe.

Humphry Marlowe was a bony, yellowish man, a drooping and dour cutler and razor-maker. His was not a happy face. The indentation in his upper lip had formed from a lifetime spent refining daily miseries, the dent in his forehead from a dread of contentment as deep-seated as most men's fear of paralysis. Marlowe distrusted joy, especially his own – he could never feel at ease with it. Now he had the unpaid and compulsory position of parish constable to add to his own continuing trade, to take him hourly away from his rightful work, to introduce him to the purest trouble the streets had to show. He hadn't felt this good in years.

The watchman was sitting with him at a scored table midway between a healthy fire and a window sparkling with cold sunlight. The granular falsetto of a grindstone reached between them from a back room, but the constable had learned long since to modulate his voice in harmony with it.

"Aye, George," he said, "Coroner Dicey is even now sitting in the jeweller's house in York Street, doubtless casting his legal dust about him and blinding every eye. He's a very complete man is that one!" Constable Marlowe made a rude noise in his tapered nose. "Have the fellow stripped and on his knee by this hour, say I."

"Was it not your business to attend?"

The constable looked even more hurt than usual.

"My business is here, sir, and it is failing me even as we speak. And I don't love Mr Dicey so much, I'll own it to any who will hear. Our coroner and I have found us a conflict between us, you see. Of minds," he added dryly. "I have one."

"What will be the upshot of it, do you know?" Man spoke with some care, knowing his own powerlessness in the parish and the constable's dissatisfied pride in not excelling in a job he did not want. "Will Mr Dicey determine it a killing theft?"

The thin cutler mulled a mouthful of wine and thoughtfully lifted his overgrown pipe off the table.

"Bring us a piece of fire, will you, George?"

Man stepped over to the fireplace and carried back a flaming straw. In a minute the two men were clouding the air over their heads blue and dimming at the window the light and silence of White Hart Yard.

"Well, there's little question of the end of last night's work, is there?" Constable Marlowe asked. "I know myself a small something of that shop in York Street and of the man that made it. Edmund Cowley was widowed with the two sons as quick as the second pulled his feet out of the mother. She was glad to go, I'd wager, before her man could think of some way to make her pay him for her passage to heaven. Aye, that was a pinching penny-father, was that one. One that would make the boys chew the same lump of bread twice, my thought. I heard it said that he never so much as slept the night for fear he might forget the day's count. Loved it, they say, as a right-minded man loves his smoke. And he taught his first son the same song, until he could sing it even better than his father."

"The business thrived, then?"

"Few better in this side of the town. The father made and sold stones to those whose names he'd never dare write out. He gave that work mainly to Harold – best said Harold took it for himself. That's where the boy was supposed last night, out carrying a pocketful of rings to a dame in Golden Square. Took him a long hour or more to fight his way home – if you believe his word."

Man squinted through his smoke at the constable's sour look.

"You think otherwise, Mr Marlowe?"

"I do. As does Coroner Dicey and most other men. 'Tis no great puzzler, is it?" Marlowe asked the watchman lightly. "Look you, the first son's a chip of the same block with the father, truth? He knows the trade even better, loves it more, the height of coin it can get him. He's the very image of him, a second Edmund. And for too long now he's been naught but the running link-boy of the shop, carrying the scraps from Westminster to Wapping, waiting for the sire to kick up long past his time. There's a turn, friend, will weary a man in a time. First-born and working day by day for the old man's shop, and then comes the last will and testament as the final and meanest cast to – "

"What will is this you speak of?" Man interrupted.

The cutler allowed himself to show a thin triumph.

"Well, the same the jeweller himself writ out this same week!"

"It has been found, then."

"Eh? Why, no, not quite now. But there's a lawman over in Gray's Inns who promises that Father Cowley made it. And – " Constable Marlowe breathed slyly "– he says the paper, every word on it, saves the shop and every stone and every penny for the second son – this Christopher that lives only to hammer his master's chairs and tables together. As if he wanted it, as if he knew what to do with it if he had it!"

"Nothing for the older brother? Nothing?"

"Not a shadow to sell a blind man!"

The watchman was surprised. "But why?"

The constable paused to stare disconsolately into his pipe bowl, then he rapped out the dead ash onto the floor. The distant grindstone slowed down, ground to a stop.

"As well as I can know it, the old man never loved the young woodworkman over-well, and never forgave him the running out from the family, the trade. I can see that – a man wants what he leaves behind him to be his still. And the boy's been as much help as a pair of Mahometan whiskers on a new bride's lip, carrying himself off to another street, showing his back to what his father made for him." He shook his head at such unmercantile ingratitude. "Still, seems the boy did, at hazard, at last gift the old fellow with what he'd all the time wanted more than anything – more even than his shop and all."

Man nodded.

"A grandson," he murmured.

His sudden insight keenly disappointed Constable Marlowe.

"As you say. A boy to keep the name living even longer than the trade – something the other son could most like never manage. And so the old man makes his plans to give all he's got to him that don't want it, until – " the voice crackled significantly "– until the son that's earned it learns who it's going to and spirits away father and paper at one single swoop. He knows it's his as first-born, so he picks a stormy night to murder the jeweller and – "

"And runs to the window to call me in as witness and invite himself at once to the gallow-tree at Tyburn. Yes, that is wise."

Suspicious and unhappy, the constable regarded Man with a long, unwinking stare and started to scrape his chair backward. "Wise enough at leastways to gull a simple watchman, eh? But not sharp enough to hoodwink the rest of them that know!"

Humphry Marlowe walked him to the door, but Man thought it closed a little more roughly than usual. Yet it could have been the cold, or even the fitful wind that was growing in the brisk street. There could be many explanations.

The fact was, the Mans had a favorite chair that needed mending badly. It had never sat level or well; and what better time to have it fixed than en route to Bow Street? Rood Lane lay out of his way, but the joiner's shop in it was said to do good work.

If the streets had been clear of snow, Man could have borrowed a wheelbarrow; by the time he got there, he had had enough of carrying it and his arms ached with cramp. As he tapped on the front door of the shop, his first thought was to wonder if the proprietor might not happen to own some kind of a cart, lying idle for the day.

The master joiner was nowhere to be found, but Man did not trouble himself greatly to look. A dusted workman led him and his chair into a long, low-ceilinged room that was a concentrate of hot sawdust, aromatic shavings, the grunting and noisiness of six or seven working men. There was nothing crowded or chaotic about the shop: each man seemed satisfied with his place and work, the floor was comfortably carpeted with fresh litter, the air was that of an open wood. It was the kind of place that Man had always liked best – a place of simple accomplishment and simple rest – and as he lowered his chair he felt that he was in no real hurry to question the young man coming forward gladly to greet him.

Christopher Cowley was a solid and healthy man of thirty or so, robust as apples, who looked as though he could never be unsettled or rushed. He wore a leather apron hung with dully glinting tools, a cloth of limpid green roped around his neck, and a tight cap; and the watchman thought he had two of the firmest hands to be seen anywhere in London.

The journeyman joiner greeted the chair first.

"She's standing a bit poorly, ain't she?"

Man explained the circumstances of his wife's preference for the chair and of their moving.

"Let's carry her over to the corner here so we can see after her quiet-like," the joiner said, cradling it.

In the corner, the watchman bent over Christopher Cowley, admiring his work. "May I say, sir," he said in a low voice, "that I can feel your present sorrow."

The joiner looked up, his clear face shadowed.

"You are Mr Christopher Cowley?"

"Kit, sir."

"Kit. I am George Man. I – know something of your family and its new – reverses."

He saw the joiner tense slightly, the working of his hands intensify.

The watchman, interested in both the man and his craft, crouched down beside him.

"It's a hard chance, Kit, that makes a man lose both father and brother at the one throw – the father murdered, the brother accused. I say nothing of shame, trust me," Man hurriedly reassured him. "No, this runs far deeper."

Kit Cowley hesitated, then turned to him.

"My brother, sir, cannot be guilty of this."

"Your forgiveness. Yet even now he lies chained in Newgate Prison. Few men are ever Newgated for nothing."

"He is innocent."

"Perhaps. Yet I fear – " Man began.

"That small hammer there, sir, if you please."

The joiner busied himself with what he knew best. The shop became a detached wash of energy around the two kneeling men, around their gentle probing of one another. Kit Cowley was shy, anxious, defensive; the watchman was caring and insistent. He shifted his weight, coming closer, and tried again.

"I may tell you," he lied softly, "that the Justice of Peace and I are close. It may be that a word to him – "

"You would do that for him, sir?"

"Do you wish your brother freed from this once and away?"

"Of course, of course." Troubled, the joiner seemed to distance himself from his work, trusting his hands to their mechanical experience. "My brother and I have never agreed – we might have been born and grown in different streets – yet he is my brother, and older, and I have always loved him as one. When I left our father's house ten years ago or more, he had a mouthful of hard words for me – harder even than my father's, and his were hard enough. Neither of them understood me, could know me deeply enough to understand. The business has ever been as nothing to me, no more than a sinking burden attached to the Cowley name. And the stones are cold, dead – only things to please the eye alone." The young man stroked a leg of the chair, felt its grain, followed a warm curve with his blunt fingers. "I found a craft for myself that I could follow with care and pride, making the wood grow and change as I willed it. It lives, it can be used to make another man's life easier and happier. And even before I turned away from the house, I had found another to share it with."

"Your wife?"

Cowley nodded. "They would not love her, they would not believe that she wanted to love them. My brother could never see her as more than one who was bent upon injuring the family. Perhaps it is his remembering our mother too well, too sorrowfully. He knew her."

Man gave him a moment, then asked him, "You have prospered?"

"I think I have, sir," he answered, smiling contentedly. "My good wife has given me one tall son and is now big with another child. I am blessed with greater treasures than most men, I think."

"I meant," Man corrected him gently, "in your trade."

The young man tugged uncomfortably at a joint in the chair.

"I think I do as well as I can. I have modest enough talents for the work; at times I find each one of my fingers turned a thumb."

What might have sounded false from another man became an honest complaint from Kit Cowley, the uneasiness of a man who can never trust himself to succeed.

Man watched him coaxing the chair back into shape and marveled at the precise efficiency of his gestures.

"No, Kit, I should call you as able a man as any other, perhaps more. I wonder that you do not make a shop of your own someday and become master of yourself."

The journeyman squatted back and dropped his voice. He spoke directly at his work, losing the watchman.

"A master? To lay me down at night with waking fears of the morrow and start the day in dread of losing all? To work with the ghost of failure and disgrace always at my side? To lower all my loved family into shadow so that they will not distract me from my love of gain?" He paused, seeming to contract himself into a smaller space. "No, sir. I have seen too much of the cold and misery that come with a fuller purse. They can kill a man against his will – his wife, his children, his life's happiness."

Man looked away, thinking he understood him now. He felt the active shop wrapping itself more snugly about them.

The chair stood firm and true now. Both men rose to their feet, clumsily avoiding each other's eyes. The wooden smells of the room were so clean and piercing that the watchman felt a moment's dizziness. He knew what he had to say.

"A man makes his own happiness, Kit. And a purse may be worn as easy heavily as no. You will have to learn that yourself, when the will is found."

The young man stumbled without moving.

"What will?"

"Your father's, of course. You knew of it." It was a statement, not a question. "Even more of it than your brother, am I right?"

"What? Harold? But he knew nothing of it!"

"Are you certain of this?" Man asked him closely.

"Yes – yes, I am. I learned of it only two or three days before our father's death, when I carried back the reading-desk I had mended. He meant to tell my brother sometime later."

The joiner ended weakly, adrift, but Man believed him. The old jeweller would have wanted his first-born son to wait this time.

"Can you save my brother?" Kit asked, grieving.

Man turned to him sharply. "I hope to do so. I do not wish his death. Neither of us does. Remember this, Kit," he insisted. "If he hangs, there is no way you can stop the shop from coming to you."

The young face blanched – it was seeing something the first time. Kit was a wild bird in a dark and narrowing cave.

"But what can be done?" he begged to know.

The shop was beginning to coast into its mid-day halt. A few workmen had already unwrapped their bread and cheese, uncorked their thick bottles of ale. A dusty quiet settled into the room, the elementary peacefulness of unthinking rest. One man, old and pitted with scars, was cutting his food into mouthfuls with his working saw. The master joiner had never appeared.

The watchman took it all in at once: the unchanging rhythm of the shop, the rooted steadiness of laboring men, the security, the anonymity, the worry and irresolution of the young journeyman joiner. Everything here, Man could now see, formed an enduring whole.

He set down his chair with a grateful sigh and bent slightly forward.

"I think you have nothing for it, Kit, but to own to be guilty of the murdering yourself."

The Mans were finally settled into their new rooms in Bow Street, and George Man at least approved. Their old home in Ironmonger Row had been somewhat bigger, certainly less stuffy, and constantly perfumed with the rising odors of the bake-shop downstairs; but the street, so far to the north and near to the fields, lay so much apart from the current of the city's life. Bow Street had more to offer, more shouting and trading by day and more arguing and fighting by night. Every class of people met and passed through Bow Street, not always peaceably, and that civic heartbeat was enough to make Man feel right at home.

Sarah Man felt the same, though she would never admit it. She grumbled about the want of space, the noise and danger outside, the little light. She missed the friendliness of the bake-shop and she was sure one of their new neighbors lived with a mistress. Yet the liveliness of the street had already worked on her almost as much as on her husband, and she sometimes spent as much time as he did leaning and nodding out the flung-open window.

Today Man was sitting near the window in his mended chair, appreciating its new and comforting sturdiness. He was enjoying, too, the sight of Sarah hovering over their tiny oven, baking the kind of home-raised bread he had missed when she used to depend upon the bake-shop.

The afternoon in the street outside was mild and grey, the sky low, and the air soft with random flakes. Sarah had just laid the bread out to cool, brown and crisp, when the knock Man had been expecting all day rattled the door.

Harold Cowley was a different man, profoundly altered, aged and overshadowed even since the last time Man had seen him. That had been only two days before, a heartbreakingly frozen day when they had both watched the shivering body of Christopher Cowley, narrowing and twisting slowly from the gallows at Tyburn. The faces of the brothers then had never looked more alike.

Now the jeweller sat across from Man at the window and accepted a cup of his brandy. The watchman wondered if he would ever lose the fine shaking in his hands.

"Constable Marlowe told me, Mr Man, that I have you to thank for my life." Cowley bowed his shoulders formally. "I thank you, sir."

Man accepted his gratitude with a grim nod.

"But I do not understand the deaths of my father, my brother – "

A shadow marred the window: a clod of snow falling from the roof.

"Your father was dying?" Man asked suddenly.

The jeweller had not expected this.

"He was, sir. He knew it. The doctors promised he would never finish the year. I had thought he was making himself ready to go."

"And he did. An old man who has worked and excelled all his days, with little thought of his end, finds much to hurry him as it finally comes nearer. He sees most things newly, he finds new losses he had never noticed before, he easily forgets old promises, spoken or not." Man looked kindly at the merchant across from him. "If your father thought to leave his work to your brother, it was no insult to your long help. It was only that he feared leaving nothing behind him but coins and stones. An old man pains sometimes for something more."

Sarah Man helped enclose the room with her homely bustling, the way she lovingly swaddled the bread in a clean cloth.

Harold Cowley began saying something about his father's illness, but Man was only half listening. He was remembering leading Kit Cowley out of the shop in Rood Lane. The young joiner had turned for a final look at the energetic room. He had seemed to be trying to memorize it all – the yellow air, the wooden clatter, the manual persistence of the workmen. He had left his apron and tools in a far corner, and at the door he had gazed back at them with a yearning that could be seen in his entire body. His last words to a fellow workman had been barely audible:

"Tell Mr Singleton, would you, that I'll not be needing my place tomorrow?"

Man poured another cup for Harold Cowley, politely avoiding the desperate questioning in his look.

"And so you knew nothing of your father's wish to write his will."

"I promise you, I did not. I knew he had been ailing especially of late – worse, the afternoon of that day – but I knew nothing of what he meant to do." The jeweller frowned uncertainly at a brown scar in the floor. "He must have felt very bad to call my brother out on such a night. And I was not with him."

Man gave him a long moment to recover, then explained: "He was afraid, I think, that he had waited too long, that he might not have enough time to write it out and give it, with his reasons, to your brother. So he sent for him, storm or no, to come to him at once. You should feel no pain, sir, for your actions that night. You were about your father's business."

"If I had only known that Kit had been there with him."

"You sensed it, in a fashion. Remember? Your feelings that something in that room had been changed or moved? It was your father's lectern, the reading-desk he used for his ledgers. A small enough matter, I grant you, but significant."

"But it was there on the desk that night when I took you in, sir – I remember!"

"Of course it was," Man said with some excitement. "But it should not have been there. Remember? Your brother had taken it to Rood Lane to mend. Do you recall his carrying it back?"

Cowley considered for a time. "I do not," he said finally.

"Because he brought it back on the night of your father's death. He must have done so. The truth is, you had grown so familiar with the sight of it in its place that you could not remark that it should still have been at the workshop. Nothing was missing from the room, but something had been added that night – by your brother."

"It must have been as you say. But how did you know it?"

"I did not," Man admitted grimly. "I supposed it. And then, sometime later in Rood Lane, I recognized Kit's workmanship." Unconsciously, he dropped his hand to stroke a jointure in the mended chair beneath him.

Mostly to himself, the other man groaned: "But how could our Kit have murdered him? It should have been myself, I think."

In his voice, Man heard the same brittle echo of private agony, hollow as regret, that he had heard in Kit Cowley's, locked in the solid dark of Newgate Prison and helpless to explain the knotted reasons for the murder.

"Many thought you did," Man said, willfully misunderstanding him. "But you, sir, are altogether too much your father; and what man in his right senses ever chooses to murder himself? Your brother, now, was someone else. He early left his family and home to make his own, he left riches for meanness, he found his happiness in being no one – in being one of a thousand common workmen in a thousand common streets, each of them content to live unknown, unremarked, invisible to all the world. He was never a man who could show himself, not even to raise himself higher in his chosen work, though he was able. Mr Singleton, the master joiner in Rood Lane, tells me that Kit could have many times made his own shop – more than one had promised him money to start. But he was afraid – do you understand? – he was afraid to be seen, or afraid that he might succeed too well and become his father."

Man looked into the clouded, distant eyes in front of him. "It must have made him mad that night to hear his father's plan to burden him with a life he could not live, to see him begin to write it out. I'm certain it was only accident that made him push his father back so hard from the paper. He told me his hands had ever been stronger than he knew. He remembered almost nothing."

Harold Cowley turned painfully away, breathing, "And I thank God for that."

Man walked the jeweller down to the street, comforting him with empty talk of the weather that had now begun to settle into blanketing flurries. It was not until he learned that Harold Cowley was going to visit for the first time his brother's family in Rood Lane that the watchman knew this work was done.

Death is never easy for any man, he reflected, as he stood rooted deep in the Bow Street drifts. For Kit Cowley, it must have been doubly bitter, dying as he had done before the hundreds of straining eyes in Tyburn's habitually craning crowd. There, and during the ride up Holborn in an open cart, his life's worst nightmare had kept him awake. For those few hours, he had been the most famous man in all London.

The watchman made his way back upstairs, looking nowhere. He was trying not to remember the young joiner's last moments, how he had finally turned away from the crowd's ogling to approach the gallows, how one broad hand had been stretched out to the scaffold as if for support. But then, trembling, the hand had moved in one slow and sensitive touch, the workman admiring the wood, the craftsman approving of the enduring workmanship.

Man only hoped it had helped.

# THE CURSE OF THE CONNECTICUT CLOCK
## S. S. Rafferty

*In the first volume I reprinted "The Christmas Masque", one of Rafferty's stories featuring administrator Captain Jeremy Cork who travels throughout colonial America solving his "social puzzles". The following is set eight years after "The Christmas Masque" and features one of my favourite ploys – the cryptogram.*

The fact that Captain Jeremy Cork, my employer, avoids profitable endeavors in favor of dabbling in the solution of social puzzles is my cross to bear, and I accept it and persevere in spite of him. However, the pawky methods he uses to resist my making him the richest man in the American colonies are downright frustrating, although admittedly ingenious.

No better example of his cleverness at resisting industry, while thoroughly enjoying a crime, exists than in the autumn of 1762, when we returned to the Oar and Eagle on the Connecticut coast. Cork considers this his home port, although we pass no more time there than anywhere else. The only reason for giving this snug inn *dominium* status is that it contains the only bed in the Americas that will accommodate his six-foot-six frame. That massive sleeping couch is part of the private rooms, fitted as a ship's cabin, that he rents on an annual basis. His apartment is on the ground floor, off the public rooms. Mine is above stairs, although I work at an accounts dais in his chambers during the daylight hours and take my meals there.

It was in the forenoon of a crisp October day when I decided to broach the subject of manufacturing his Apple Knock and shipping it about the colonies. It is a potent potable which has gained great favor with his friends, and it occurred to me that a good profit could be turned from the venture.

"I believe we would gain more if we barrel it by the percheon or pipe rather than by hogshead," I said, bringing a rather brilliant analysis to a close. "That would mean lower cost per gallon shipped and . . ."

"You would involve me in barter and score?" he roared. "*Sell* liquor? By Jerusalem, Wellman Oaks, you are without soul. TEDDERHORN!"

Bertram Tedderhorn is the innkeeper of the Oar and Eagle who believes Cork is the next best thing to the Divinity. Considering the rent and the lavish meals the Captain pays for, he may be right. He burst into the chamber within seconds of Cork's shout.

"Yes, Captain?" He was breathless because his corpulence is not given to quick movements.

"After this moment, we are now to use the winter formulation for the Knock." Cork took up a quill. Tedderhorn looked confused.

"But sir, it is only October 30. The solstice is weeks away."

"True, Tedderhorn," Cork said as he wrote on a piece of paper, "but we are victims of habit, and be wary that habit becomes ritual, and ritual breeds dogma, and that is not healthy for the mind *or* body. The receipt is as before with the addition of one new ingredient which I have written here and will be known only to you and me."

As he handed the innkeeper the paper, Tedderhorn gave me a sheepish look. As well he should, for I am Cork's confidential yeoman, and usually nothing is privy from me. Yet I held my tongue and bore no ill will for the innkeeper. He was merely a pawn in my employer's playful game.

It was what you can expect from Captain Jeremy Cork. All he had to say was "no" to the venture, but that wouldn't have been dramatic enough. A simple negative response would have robbed him of a chance to jape me.

Tedderhorn was leaving the room when he suddenly turned. "'Pon my word, I forgot, Captain. There's a man to see you. I was coming in to tell you when you called."

"Show him in, by all means." Cork went back to his book with a self-satisfied look on his face.

I am not a man to waste energy in hurt feelings. "I assure you I have no intention of skulduggering around to learn the new receipt," I told him. "It was only a suggestion."

"Your suggestions, Oaks, have a way of becoming burdensome realities. People who sell liquor are in the same class as people who sell love, and they share a common name. One may traffic with whores without becoming one. Hello, sir, come in, I think we have met before."

This last statement was to the man who had entered the room. My heart sank, for now, on the heels of my idea having been scuttled, was a person obviously distraught and in need of help. Before he even spoke, I knew it, for I have come to recognize the characteristics of a new puzzle looming into view.

"Yes, Captain, we met several years ago at the Widow Chandler's in Fairfield. My name is Gerret Hull."

"Of course. What can I do for you, Mr Hull?" Cork indicated a chair and Hull sat. He was a shortish man, clean shaven and dressed in a plain suit and obviously fresh linen for his visit.

"I have had a great tragedy in my life recently, and until today, I was convinced it was God's will, and humbly accepted it. Now . . ." he drew something from his coat which turned out to be a copybook. ". . . well, now I'm not sure that my fourteen-year-old son's death was accidentally caused by a schoolboy prank."

Cork requested details, and I sat there and listened to the father tell his sad story with but mild interest.

Gerret Hull went on. "I am not a wealthy man, gentlemen. Just a small farm and a fair sized cooperage. But if life had limited my horizons, I was bound that it would not be so for my oldest boy, Chad. It was hard on my purse, but I enrolled him at the Fenway School above New Haven in the hope that he would go on to Yale and then to a profession. He was not happy at Fenway during his first year, for he was a poor boy among the sons of wealthy families, which is not always an easy road. But Chad stuck to his books and returned to Fenway this September with high hopes. Then, last week, the awful news came. Chad had been killed while performing the foolish prank of scaling a belltower in the middle of the night. It is not uncommon for a boy to try to place a chamberpot or underdrawer on the spire for all to see in the morning."

"He fell?" I asked.

The father closed his eyes as if in the grip of some horrible mental picture. "No, Mr Oaks, he was stabbed to death by a jacamart."

For an instant I shared Hull's horrible picture. A jacamart is a life-sized statue, usually a knight in armor, that moves across the face of a tower clock to strike the hour bell with a sword or lance.

"The school officials told me that Chad must have reached the clockface platform at precisely one o'clock, and was impaled on the jacamart's sword as he stood there preparing to scale higher."

"How ghastly," I said, "and unfortunate that the poor boy was there just at the stroke of one." .

"Precisely as I felt, Mr Oaks. I saw it as fate. Although Chad was not a wild boy, I assumed he wanted to be one of the fellows, and fell victim to the accursed clock."

"But now you have reason to question the accidental aspects of the affair? What is the source of your suspicion?" Cork wanted to know.

"Suspicion is a strong word, Captain, for I wouldn't want to cast any shadows over Fenway's reputation. It's more a feeling that I do not have the whole story." He opened the copybook and withdrew a piece of notepaper. "I received this letter from Chad earlier this week. On the face of it, it is a dutiful son informing his father that he is trying his best." He handed the letter to Cork, who read it through and passed it to me. It was in a neat hand without the scholarly flourishes so common to academicians.

> Fenway School
> Derby, Connecticut
> 21 October 1762
>
> Father:
> All is much the same here, but I persevere. But take heart, for I have come onto something which may take the burden of my education from your shoulders. Be of good spirit, sir, and wish me well. My best to all.
>
> Your son,
> Chad
>
> P.S. I shall try my best to put my mind to the task.

"You see, gentlemen, Chad had previously mentioned that there was the possibility of receiving emoluments for good scholarship, and I assumed he was in competition for one. A student grant would obviously ease my financial load."

"That is certainly a reasonable interpretation," I said, giving him back the letter.

"I agree, Mr Oaks, but yesterday, I finally overcame my grief enough to go through the clothes and things I brought back home with Chad's remains. In this copybook, I came across some queer notations which puzzle me. I have heard of your reasoning powers, Captain Cork, and wondered if you could make something of it."

Cork took the book, and I leaned over his shoulder as he leafed through it. It appeared to be a typical lesson book, with each page containing daily lessons.

"The Fenway curricula seems to be well rounded," Cork remarked as he perused page after page of Latin translation, Ancient History, Mathematics, and Physics.

"To be sure, Captain, the school is the finest of its kind. The notations to which I refer are in the back of the copybook, where the boys are allowed to make their own scribblings and work out problems."

Cork turned to the back pages and finally found one bearing a very peculiar inscription. It read:

Blandersfield Program

Sept 19
  EF/FG/GA/AB/BC/CD/DE/EF?

Oct 10
  78−34=44=GB?
  78−32=46=GA?

Oct 20
  VI=EF!

The Captain furrowed his brows and studied the symbols for some minutes. "It's quite cryptic, of course," he said at last, "but schoolboys are often given to secret writings as a pastime, Mr Hull. What makes this suspicious in connection with your son's death?"

"The 'Blandersfield Program' overline, Captain. Blandersfield is what the boys at Fenway call the jacamart, 'Sir Jack Blandersfield'."

Rarely have I ever seen Cork shift from mild interest to intense occupation so rapidly. "Most interesting indeed. Tell me, on what date did Chad meet his death?"

"So you've noticed it then. October 21, the evening after the last notation, or really the morning of the 22nd, since he died at one o'clock in the morning. All I can make of it is that Chad had an interest in the jacamart beyond a prank."

"Yes, that seems patent," Cork agreed. "If he were merely trying to put a chamberpot atop a spire, why all the hocus-pocus with codes?"

"Perhaps he was trying to compute the proper time for the jacamart's movements," I put in.

Cork looked up at me with that smirk-a-mouth of his. "Hardly, Oaks. That could be done by a child of no education. These notations are a thought progression. The first, on September 19, obviously did not give him an answer since he ends it with an interrogation mark. Then, on the 10th of October, he has refined his thinking, but still we have an interrogation mark. But on the 20th of October, Chad discovered something in the VI=EF equation, for he ends it with an exclamative. And then he died in the process of putting his theory to a test."

"But what does the last entry mean, Captain?" Hull asked.

"Several notions present themselves, but to speak now would be to conjecture, based on a paucity of facts. It looks as if we shall be going to school again, Oaks."

"Then you believe there is foul play involved, Captain?" Hull was obviously agitated.

"No, sir, I venture no such idea, for the minds of young boys are labyrinths, full of twists and turns which can be confounding to the adult who ventures in there. This I *will* say, Mr Hull. Initially, it struck me as odd that Chad was on the clock face platform at the exact stroke of one. Now this Blandersfield enigma adds more to the mystery. Mind you, my inquiries may produce aspects of your son that you might not care to know. Will you chance it?"

Hull bowed his head as if in prayer; his voice was low as he piously intoned, "I swear by his soul that Chad was a good boy."

"To be sure. Tell me, sir, was the boy a musician of any kind?"

The father smiled, recalling an old thought. "No, sir, no ear for it at all. My wife has taught the children to sing, but poor Chad had a voice like a strangled bird."

"I see. Then it is done. Go about your business, sir, and try to balm your grief. I should have something for you in a few days."

When the farmer-cooper had left, I went back to my place at the accounts dais. Tedderhorn came in bearing a tray with two tankards on it and set them down, one before each of us. I sipped the Knock and said, "Do you think it could be murder?"

Cork shrugged and took a deep draft. "What I said about the minds of boys still holds. They can be a pack of scoundrels at times. Chad could have been put up to it by his school chums, but his letter to his father indicates that he expected to be in funds very soon."

"The emolument, of course."

"I think not. His lesson book shows an average mind, and certainly not one of high scholarship. No, if he was to soon be in funds to alleviate his father's burden, it had to come from another source."

"Blackmail, possibly?"

"Very perceptive, Oaks. It's a possibility. Boys have eyes and ears, and they sometimes use them effectively."

"But whom would he blackmail?"

"A schoolmaster? A classmate? The students are all wealthy."

"But the Blandersfield notations. They confuse it."

"No, Oaks, they put more raisins in the bun. These alphabetical notations are some sort of progression. Note the September 19 notation. The first two are EF, the second set repeats the last of the first and adds a new letter, becoming FG. In the third, the

'G' has become the initial letter, and 'A' is added. Actually, he is only dealing with the letters E,F,G,A,B,C, and D in a repeating pattern."

"Perhaps the letters, properly arranged, spell out a word."

"I think not, at least not a meaningful word. And that does not seem to have been Chad's thinking either, for, on October 10, he tries a completely different trick, using two sets of subtractions. But where did he get the numerals? No matter, for the moment. It is obvious that he took the two remainders, 44 and 46, and went back to his September 19 progression to count the fourth and eighth letters to arrive at 44=GB and 46=GA."

"And you feel that Chad wasn't a bright student, Captain? This certainly seems to indicate an inquring mind of some subtlety at work."

"An embrangled mind, Oaks. One that has mired itself in a complex approach to a solution. It is not limited to schoolboys. Too many times, seemingly intelligent people cannot find an answer when it lies in front of them. Obviously, Chad woke up to his error on October 20, for a new element, 'VI,' has jumped into his mind. The first two notations on September 19 and October 10 are mere exercises in garbled logic. I am sure the October 20 thought was a stroke of luck. He even matches it with an exclamative to prove the point, like someone stepping back and saying, 'My, my, there it is!' No, the boy was no genius, and indeed, may have been a fool. How is the Knock?"

I smacked my lips. "It tastes the same to me."

"That's the subtlety of it. Well, we shall be off for Fenway at dawn with a short stop off in New Haven."

"For lunch?"

"No, my old son, I think it is time we had your watch cleaned."

The trade of Jared Elliot was proclaimed by a wooden sign displaying a clockface fixed forever at twenty minutes after eight o'clock. The shop itself was a small bow-windowed establishment tucked into a commercial alley just off High Street. Its owner was a gnome-like, white-thatched man with thick spectacles and a scratchy voice. The interior of the place was filled with timepieces of all description, lantern clocks of brass and long case instruments of beautiful floral marquetry. One unique item was an elephant clock with the dial and bell in the howdah and the beast's eyes moving with every tick of each minute. Cork's attention was on the watchmaker as he opened the case of my pocketwatch and peered into the works through an optical glass.

"I see you travel a bit, Mr Oaks, for many ⸺ his hand to this piece."

I was fascinated by the elephant's eye mov⸺ agreed with a nod. Cork, on the other hand, sho⸺ in Jared Elliot's work, and enjoined him in conver⸺ questions to the old man, I could see the reason for⸺

"You seem to be a master at watches, sir, and ho⸺ you have any knowledge of tower clocks?"

"Great Clocks is the proper name," Elliot grumped. "⸺ don't build them. Too old."

"I hear there is one of great interest out at the Fenway School. Well worth seeing."

"That old monstrosity! Ha, it's something out of the fourteenth century, son."

"That old? It must have been brought over from the old country."

"It's only a score and some. Twenty-five's the more like it. Built by an old faker named deJoonge."

"Didn't know his business, I take it?"

"That's a mild way to put it, son. That clock has a foliot for a time controller, mind you, as if the man never heard of the pendulum. It's only been around since old Christian Huygen invented it in 1656."

"I'm sorry, but I've just gotten interested in clocks. What is a foliot?"

"The old makers used to employ them centuries ago. It's a swing bar that has an unpredictable period of swing or vibration. It's the pendulum that makes present day clocks accurate. Old deJoonge had some gall, passing himself off as an 'orologier,' he did. That monster has stone weights," he started to chuckle and shake his head to emphasize his incredulousness. "Never saw the like of it."

Cork continued to coax information from him. "I'm told the clock has an ingenious jacamart."

"Ingenious! Now that's a bold face concoction. It's not a true jacamart at all because it doesn't really strike the chimes. They are in the spire above the clock. All the jacamart does is come out of a guardhouse on the hour and cross the face of the clock where its sword fits into a slot in the far buttress. It's a fake, like deJoonge himself."

"Did this deJoonge move on after the Great Clock was built?"

"No, son, he stayed right out there at Fenway. Still there, six feet under. He died just after the clock was finished." Elliot closed the inner dome of my pocketwatch and snapped the outer silver back with a snap. "Just a bit of dust was all. Hardly worth the charge."

can remunerate you in another way. Would you rent
s back there on your shelf?"

The old watchmaker turned his head and looked at the two
volumes. "You must surely be interested in clocks and watches, sir.
*The Horologium* by Huygens is in Latin, and makes rough reading.
The other, *A Compendium of Watchmaking*, is easier going."

"Two pence for each, per day," Cork suggested.

"To be sure. But don't waste your time on that Fenway clock.
You'll learn nothing from it."

"Probably not." Cork gave him some coins. "I am told there was
some sort of misfortune out there recently."

"Could have been. I keep to myself and my clocks. They are more
reliable than people. What was the misfortune?"

"Some poor lad was accidentally killed by the jacamart," I
said.

His wizened old face grew dark and his eyes behind the spectacles
popped wide. "Killed by the jacamart! My Lord, that's just the way
old deJoonge died. Yes sir, the day after the clock was completed.
He was making an adjustment on the face when the jacamart broke
loose and ran him through." He gazed off in space for a moment and
then turned to us. "Maybe the stories are true that the clock is cursed.
My, my. But they do have a heart of their own, you know, and their
own logic. My, my."

Captain Cork has many skills, and one of them is the uncanny
ability to read while riding a horse. I tried it the once and got a
headache for my efforts. All the way to Fenway, he had his nose
buried in the books he had rented from the old clockmaker.

It was drawing near to four in the afternoon when we turned off
the King's Highway at a rude sign that indicated the school lay
to the northwest. All afternoon, during our silent ride, I had been
thinking about this mystery the Captain had created. It could be
nutmeg, or possibly cinnamon, but I was damned if I could taste it.
Now if he had changed the formulation for the summer Knock, the
new ingredient would have been more easily discernible, since the
summer version does not have a slab of butter and a fist of sugar to
mask any subtle additives.

"You amaze me, Oaks," I heard his voice say as we turned off to
the northwest. "Here we are, heading into what might be a most
tantalizing confrontation, and you waste your time toying with the
new Knock receipt."

I looked at him with some amazement. "You have learned to read
minds from these new books of yours?"

"No, but you have been moving your lips and tongue in a manner to suggest you were trying to remember the taste of something. When you are trying to discover a hidden substance or meaning, it is better to rely on facts, and not vague memory. Ho, there is our nemesis hoving into view in that vale."

We had come over a small rise, and there below in a gentle dip in the earth was a large quadrangle of field by a belltower that rose out of the main structure some forty feet into free air. The clock, I assumed, faced the inner courtyard, for the towerside in our view was solid stone; an ominous grey finger becoming hazy in the descending autumnal dusk. We were about to start into the vale when we heard the grim tolling of four o'clock from the tower top.

"Do you confirm it?" Cork asked me and I checked my newly cleaned timepiece.

"No, I show five minutes after the hour."

Cork smiled and put spurs to his horse. "Come, old son," he said as he galloped away, "I want to see this jacamart at work."

We clattered through the gate at Fenway seconds later in time to see the clock sentinel still poised at the far side of the clockface. Jack Blandersfield was garbed as a fourteenth-century knight with a coat of mail covering the upper torso and jambs and sollerets at the cuffs and feet. A two-edged sword held upright in the right gauntlet withdrew from a slot in the far buttress as the deadly knight moved slowly backward to its guardhouse. We were both looking up at this instrument of death when an elderly gatekeeper raced up to us, shouting, "Here, here, you men. What's this racing in here like a thunderstorm? You'll have Headmaster to answer to, my fine swift fellows."

He had been dealing with schoolboys for so long that he obviously treated everyone as a child. Cork slid from his saddle and his immense height seemed to prove he was no adolescent. The man was undismayed, however. "Fine thing, fine doings. You'll catch a switching for this, mind you, and I hope Mr Crisp lays it on, for he's the best at it."

"Mr Crisp is the headmaster then?" Cork asked.

"None of your devilment. All knows who the headmaster be. Now come away with me, you scuds, the Reverend will do for you."

The Reverend Obadiah Travistock, the headmaster of Fenway School, looked like a willow tree in winter. His limbs and trunk were thin and grey, but you detected a certain resilience in his very marrow, which is uncommon among men of the cloth in New England. Stern, to be sure, dedicated, no doubt, but long years of teaching boys to be men had mellowed him to a point of amused acceptance. His chambers were an admixture of religious simplicity and scholarly messiness. There were piles of paper everywhere.

"You will have to excuse Amos, gentlemen. He has been at his gate duties so long he has lost track of time. When I took over here from my late father, over fifteen years ago, it took him a long time to accept me. Well, you have an interest in old Great Clocks, you say."

"Yes," Cork said it with aplomb and without the hesitation of a man about to lie to a man of God. "I was considering doing a treatise on clocks in the colonies. Mr Oaks is aiding in the preparation."

"Admirable undertaking, Captain, but I must be honest and ask you to be judicious when writing about the Fenway clock."

Cork feigned a puzzled look and the headmaster smiled. "You see, the clock has a rather sordid history, and a more recent notoriety that could foul the school's reputation if broadcast about like seed. In fact, I had a mind to tear the cursed thing down, but the undermasters have dissuaded me. Perhaps they are right. Accidents will happen."

"Accidents?" Cork asked. "With the clock? Pray, Reverend Travistock, anything you tell me will be held in confidence."

The headmaster then related all that we already knew, with the addition of another student who had fallen from the tower twelve years ago when engaged in a midnight attempt to affix a pair of ladies' undergarments to the weathervane atop the spire.

"What was this latest boy . . . er, Hull, I think you said . . . what was the object he attempted to use in his prank?"

The headmaster looked a bit embarrassed. "A chamberpot, I'm sorry to say. It was found on the clockface platform where he dropped it when the jacamart struck."

"Tell me," Cork leaned forward in his chair. "Is there no way to get to the upper tower other than by scaling it?"

"Of course. There is a ladderway on the inside that leads up to the clockworks and a door opening onto the clockface, but the tower is locked at night, so the only way up is to scale the outside."

"And what of deJoonge? Did you know him?"

"I was just a child when he built the tower and the clock. A Dutchman who wandered by one day and offered to do the work for my father at cost and room and board. Then, just when it was done, he was killed. I'm still not sure the tower shouldn't be torn down." He looked up at a woman who had just entered the room carrying a tea service. "Ah, Manites, how good of you. Gentlemen, my sister, Manites Travistock."

Miss Travistock was a familial copy of her older brother, but her eyes were blacker and her bearing more erect. She nodded when we bowed and we all resumed our seats. I watched her as she poured and handed the cups to us. There was a flintiness in her speech that indicated a taciturn nature, and the darting movements of her black eyes could be taken for suspicion.

"I hope, Obadiah dear, that you have not been boring our guests with that talk about the clock," she said. "You must forgive my brother, good sirs, but there are times when he prattles on like one of his own students."

"Not at all, Miss Travistock," Cork sipped the tea without making a face. "How many boys do you have here at Fenway?"

"Forty-four, Captain," she said. "In four forms. All from the finest families, I might add."

"Now, Manites," the headmaster wagged a finger at her, "there is no such thing as quality in heaven, so let's not have it here on earth."

"I am merely stating that it is our duty to provide for those who know their station. These upstarts who have their souls above buttons have no place here. Next we'll have farriers' sons among us."

The headmaster was about to chastise her when the room was filled with the ringing of a loud gong. Miss Travistock reached for the watch attached to the chatelaine belt around her waist. She checked the time and muttered, "Seven minutes late now. Such a watch."

Confused, I took my own timepiece from my pocket. It was quarter past five, and yet the tower clock had rung only once.

"I see you are a bit dismayed by our queer clock, Mr Oaks," the headmaster chuckled. "Old deJoonge was a frugal Dutchman, and used a Roman strike in the tower clock instead of the conventional system."

"Roman strike?" I asked.

Cork nodded his head. "Of course, most ingenious, and very rare, Reverend. A Roman strike, Oaks, uses two bells, one low toned and another of a higher pitch. The low bell stands for five, and when struck twice, it means it is ten o'clock."

"Quite correct, Captain," Travistock beamed. "Thus, Mr Oaks, the hours one through four are struck on the high bell, one for each hour. Five o'clock is sounded just as you heard, once on the low bell."

"Ah," I said, "and eleven o'clock would be two low and one high bells."

"Let me see," Cork did a quick mental calculation. "Yes, frugal indeed. Instead of the regular seventy-eight strikes required to sound out individual hours, this Roman system needs only thirty-four blows to run through the hours."

The Reverend chuckled. "Oh, that's not correct, I'm afraid. You see, the clock doesn't strike at six o'clock at all, so there are only thirty-two blows in the Fenway run of hours, since six o'clock would be one low and one high bell."

"Was it always so?" Cork asked.

"Yes. It was one of those things left unfinished by deJoonge's death. And we are all quite used to it."

Cork turned to Miss Travistock. "But you said your watch was wrong, m'am."

"Always is, sir." She corrected the watch hands with the stem. "I will never understand how deJoonge could have made a tower clock that is always right, and a watch that is always wrong."

"Do tell. May I see it, please?"

She freed the timepiece from the chain and handed it to him. It was an elaborate thing in a beautifully tooled case that hung from a metal fob to which the winding key was attached.

"It is a lovely thing," the Captain handed it back, "but it is not strange that it is inferior, for clockmakers rarely make good watch mechanisitions. Do you have a music master on faculty, Reverend?"

"Music! Heavens no. It is difficult enough getting Latin and Greek and history and mathematics into their heads. However, my sister has taught the boys their scales for choir practice. Why do you ask? Are you interested in music, too, Captain?"

"Only of late. I take it that forty-four boys require a large staff."

"Oh, that it were possible." The headmaster looked rueful. "There is just myself, Mr Crisp for mathematics, Mr Goselow for languages, and young Biggard for everything else. Quite proud of Biggard we are. One of our own boys who went up to Yale from here and came back to his alma mater to teach. Always hoped he would be drawn to the ministry. Well, I see that darkness is upon us, and the boys will be at supper in a few minutes. We will take supper when they are finished. Of course, you won't be able to examine the tower clock now in the dark, so I offer you our humble hospitality for the evening. In the meantime, I have my evening meditations to attend to, and my sister must oversee the dining hall. Perhaps you would care to spend some time in our common room. The faculty uses it for lesson preparations and social talk. Come, I'll introduce you around."

The common room was a roomy hall with exposed beams. At its center was a long mahogany table where the staff obviously took their meals. In each of the four corners was an alcove with a writing table and chairs, which we learned was the working area for the undermasters and Miss Travistock. The walls of each alcove were lined with books, as was most of the main room. A fire blazed in the north wall fireplace, but its cheeriness did little to warm the greeting of the room's two inhabitants. Tom Biggard, we were told, was on proctor duty at the boys' mess in the far wing. Mr Moses Crisp and Mr Alonzo Goselow were hard at work on the boys' copybooks.

"Dolts, pure and simple," Mr Crisp said, handing a pile of the copybooks to his colleague. "I hope they did better with declensions than they have with my fluctions today, Goselow." Crisp was a heavy florid man of forty-odd years who had been at Fenway for the past six. Alonzo Goselow was decidedly Crisp's junior in age, but not in pedanticism.

"I haven't the heart to read them tonight," he said, "but I have a duty to the ancients. You are here to see the clock, Captain?"

"And just in time. I understand the Reverend is thinking of tearing it down since the unfortunate episode recently."

"The headmaster has become a bit over-excited," Goselow said with a prissy grin. He was no more than thirty, and thin and pale as a flounder's belly. "It's ludicrous, isn't it? Tear down a perfectly good clock because some jackanapes decides to play a prank and gets himself killed. Hull was a common boy – a mere farmer, and what he was doing here, I'll never . . ."

"For an education, Mr Goselow, which is not an exclusive preserve."

The speaker was a young blond fellow who had just entered the room.

"Ah," Goselow said, turning toward the new arrival, "enter the schoolboys' hero, our own Mr Biggard. Have your darlings been fed and bedded?"

Tom Biggard ignored Goselow and strode across the room toward us.

"You must be Captain Cork and Mr Oaks," he said, shaking our hands. "You'll have to forgive my colleagues, gentlemen. The dust of antiquity clouds their humanity."

"Schoolboys have no humanity," Crisp said, yawning. "When do we eat?"

There was a knock at the door and it opened without anyone having answered. Amos, the gatekeeper, shuffled in carrying a large keyring. "All's secured, Tommy," he said. "Tower, dorm, and main gate." He hung the ring on a hook to the left of the door. "Nighty to you, Tommy and all," he mumbled over his shoulder as he left.

"Why you allow that ignorant old fool to call you by your Christian name, I'll never know," Crisp said. "It's disgraceful."

"Amos knew me when I was here as a lad, Mr Crisp. I take no offense."

"Do I understand that the main gate is locked?" Cork got to his feet. "You see, Oaks and I must be leaving."

"I understood you were to spend the night here. Reverend Travistock just told me so."

"He offered, Mr Biggard, but I must apologize that we cannot accept. We have business to the north and will stop to see the clock on our way back. Tomorrow, or the next day at the latest. You will give our regards to the headmaster and his sister. No, don't bother, gentlemen, I see your supper has arrived. Just give me the key and I will give it to Amos to return to you when we have passed through."

"But it's after dark," Mr Crisp warned us.

"Things are more interesting by moonlight at times. Here, Oaks, we'll take some of these hot biscuits to tide us over on the ride."

I thought it quite rude of him when he took several rolls from the basket that a serving girl had placed on the table. He then took the keyring, and we were off like a gust of wind. Amos was locking the gate behind us when Cork steadied his mount and said, "Tell me, good fellow, is there a farrier in the neighborhood? Our horses are still summer shod, and there seems to be a heavy frost up."

"A mile north, ya night birds, ya. Don't go for unlocking and locking and unlocking all night, so you're out to stay and that's the end of it. Horseshoes at night. Bah. Look for the sign of the Inn of the Hanging Dog and you're there."

The moon was at the full when we reached the Inn of the Hanging Dog. It was a rude one-storied structure quite unlike the accommodations we were used to. The host was a morose fellow named Jobbot who was not happy to have tired and hungry guests at his doorsill. A few coins from Cork's purse rekindled any hospitality the scoundrel ever had. He told us that he had but one sleeping room, for the place was more a country tavern than a hostelry, and he sent his wife to prepare it.

The Captain and I took a table in the deserted public rooms where we were promised cold pork and beans. Sly dog that he is, Cork ordered straight rum lest he have to divulge his precious Knock's secret ingredient in front of me.

"Is there a blacksmith in these parts, innkeeper?" Cork asked when the plates were put down before us.

"Aye, Lemuel Stroud has a forge nearby."

When he had left us to our meal, I asked, "A smith? I thought you wanted a farrier to shoe the mounts, and while I'm at it, have we convinced ourselves that Chad Hull's death was an accident?"

"Our needing a blacksmith should answer your question." He

reached into his pocket and brought forth one of the biscuits he had taken from the table. He had torn it in two, and a curious imprint was sunk into the soft bread.

"The key, you made an impression of the key when we were on our way to the gate. But why? And if Chad was played foul, shouldn't we have stayed to see it through?"

"Best to allay any suspicions. I believe the boy was done in, but I do not yet know why. The rest is all in place, but the reason eludes me, damn it."

"The whole affair eludes me. How are you so sure he was killed . . . ouch . . ." he had poked me soundly in the ribs, and I dropped my mug of rum. "What the devil . . .?"

"Precisely the point, my old son. If you had a chamberpot in your hand, you would certainly have dropped it when a jacamart's sword pierced your back, and it would have been smashed to a million pieces. Chad would have dropped the pot off the platform and yet it was found laying next to his body."

"Possibly, but it could have happened."

"Also consider that the tower was locked, so he had to scale the outside of the edifice carrying the item. It's an impossible task, I feel."

"But if not out to make a prank, then why climb the tower in the first place?"

"Good Lord, man, use your memory. The boy sends a letter home implying that money will soon be his. His copybook contains a cryptic progression of thought that now makes sense."

He suddenly looked up at the innkeeper who was just leaving the tap with a tray of mugs. "So there we have it. I should have guessed."

"Guessed what, the meaning of the notations?"

"No, the reason why an innkeeper would be drawing four mugs of cider for the third time in an hour."

"It is an inn, is it not?"

"An empty inn, Oaks, and a one-storey inn at that. And yet, while we sit here talking, you can hear shuffling up in the eaves."

"Squirrels, no doubt."

"Well, a nest, at least. Come, Oaks, quickly."

I followed him out of the public room and stopped behind him in the shadows of the passageway. Suddenly the passage ceiling seemed to lower itself, and by the gods, it was a hidden ladderway that lowered on ropes. The innkeeper was descending, and we let him pass in the half light, and then Cork raced to stop the stairway from ascending to the ceiling again. We slowly made our way up the stairs; voices could be heard somewhere above. A chill went up my back as we listened to the voices chanting in unison:

"Find my measure
Find my treasure
Know no pleasure
Death, death, death"

"Now!" Cork cried, and we rushed up the last two steps and into one of the most bizarre rooms I have ever seen in my life.

The candlelight from atop a circular table cast eerie shadows about the walls and danced upon a life-sized painting. I gave a gasp, for the image was that of Blandersfield, the jacamart. The four figures around the table jumped up in startlement at our bounding in on them.

"Please be seated, gentlemen," Cork commanded. "I believe I have the pleasure of addressing the leading members of the Fenway School Fourth Form, do I not?"

What then ensued was a jumble of tumbled chairs, frightened faces, and much calming by the Captain. When he had convinced the lads that he meant them no harm, the students took their seats and introduced themselves and explained the ritual. As Cork surmised, they were all fourth form members: Lemfent Pieterse, Pardee Davis, Edmund Edwards, and Jonathan Lott. Pieterse was the eldest at sixteen, Lott the youngest at fourteen.

"We are doing no harm, Captain Cork," Pieterse said. "Blandersfield's Ba . . ." he stopped and looked at his cohorts.

"You are among men, Master Pieterse," Cork chuckled.

"Blandersfield's Bastards has been a school club for years. All our fathers belonged to it. It's just a spot of fun, sir."

"And what of the incantation?"

"Well, Captain," Pardee Davis spoke up, "it's just an old tale that's as old as the school."

The boy went on to tell the same story that had been handed down from member to member over the years. Hector deJoonge, so the legend went, was a Dutch pirate who used the Fenway School to hide from his fellow cutthroats from whom he had stolen a sack of jewels. Having been trained as a clockmaker in his youth, he posed as a benevolent man wanting to make a contribution to the school, and built the Great Clock. He had hidden his treasure somewhere in or near the tower and set Jack Blandersfield to guard it.

"All these years, no one has ever found it, but the club goes on just for fun," Pardee Davis concluded.

"Was Chad Hull a member?" Cork asked.

"Hull!" Jonathan Lott said. "That clod?"

"He was all right, Johno," Pieterse corrected him. "Just a bit awkward."

"But he could have known about the legend?"

"Oh, to be sure, Captain," Pieterse answered for all. "Most of the young 'uns have heard about it, but no one seriously believes about the treasure."

"I have a feeling that Chad Hull did, and it cost him his life, lads. How would you like to help me snare a killer?"

Their eyes went wide in wonder and the answer was a resounding yes.

"Good, now which is the best sneak here? No modesty, please, my lads."

"Johno, to be sure," Pieterse said with admiration, and all eyes turned to young Lott.

"The envy of your peers is a compliment indeed, Johno. Do you think you can slip into the common room tomorrow night and take the keyring?"

The boy's smile showed that the task was not a maiden voyage for him.

Cork returned the grin. "Excellent, now, tell me, are your copybooks turned in at the end of each day?"

"At three on the dot," Johno assured him.

"You have pen and paper there on the table. May I please? Tomorrow, Johno, you will copy what I write here exactly into the back of your book and turn it in as usual. Then, at night, just after the clock strikes ten o'clock, you will borrow the key from the common room and let yourself into the clock tower and climb to the clockface platform."

"Whatever for, Captain?"

"To meet Mr Oaks, who will be there waiting for you. Now this notation is done, and take care to copy it exactly."

I looked on as the boys read it:

BLANDERSFIELD PROGRAM 10/31

```
                    DO
                 TI
               LA
             SO
           FA
         ME
       RE
   DO
   V       I!
```

"Makes little sense to me," I said after the boys had left and we were in our room. "And how am I to get to the top of the tower . . . oh yes, I see, the key impression in the bread and your need for a blacksmith. And where might you be, may I ask?"

"Tripping my snare."

"One thing hasn't gotten past me. You asked at the school if the boys studied music, and tonight you wrote out the do-re-me's for Johno (what an appalling hypocorism) to copy. So we now know that Chad was after this mythical treasure and someone stopped him."

"Who said it was mythical?"

"But Captain, the boys implied that it was only an old tale perpetuated by a secret club."

"People are seldom murdered over myths, Oaks. Over the years, these true stories take on the trappings of myth, but some are true all the same." He took out his rented books and began to read again.

"And you think the treasure is hidden in the clock?"

"I *know* where the treasure is. I don't need a snare for that. Now why don't you get some sleep? You'll need it."

"Yes, of course. One thing, though. If the students are locked in every night, how the deuce did these four get out?"

He gave me that smirk-a-mouth again. "Wellman Oaks, I am now convinced that you came into this world a fully grown man with a ledger book under each arm. Man has dictated many a rule and many a circumscription, but these do not apply to boys, for boyhood is the epitome of cleverness. At least not on this night, man. The date, man, think. It is All Hallow's Eve."

I closed my eyes thinking there had been one extra boy at the meeting of the Blandersfield Bastards this night.

I woke the next morning to the chagrin that I had overslept, and to my surprise, Cork was gone. A note and a large iron key were at my bedside table:

Oaks:
Herewith your means of entry to gate and tower. Stay here till nine tonight and thence to Fenway. Enter the tower after the stroke of ten and await Johno on the clockface platform. I am about other business, but shall be there when needed. Mind, lock the tower and gate behind you.

                                                    Godspeed,
                                                    Cork

It was ten-ten by my timepiece as I stood huddled against the clockface. The wind had turned from west to nor'west, and the fingers of coming winter played upon me. The moon was slipping behind high clouds, leaving me with alternate light and sudden dark. To be sure, I was truly shaken. Here I had climbed a perilously long ladder inside the tower and fumbled in the darkness to find the opening to the outer platform. That was wearing enough, but now I stood on a platform of very small width looking down at the quad, which seemed miles away. On the right side of the clock platform was the ominous jacamart's guardhouse, its shadow standing in deadly stillness in the intermittent moonlight.

A fissure of panic started to crease my brain. If for some reason young Lott could not get the key, and perchance I miscalculated the time, I could well meet the same fate as Chad Hull. Suddenly, my ears harked. I could hear a muggled noise down below, and, minutes later, the creak of the ladder within the tower. My heart was a'bump and the creak came closer and closer.

"Mr Oaks," a voice whispered. "It's Johno, Mr Oaks."

"Out here, lad," I said. "Take care the edge now."

"Where is the Captain?" the boy asked when he reached me. "I thought he would be here too." His voice sounded more than disappointed. More excited or nervous. My Lord, the thought struck me, could this stripling be the murderer? Had Cork used me as the lure for his snare, and if so, where was he? "Don't stand too close, my boy," I told him gingerly, "this is a small platform indeed."

"I know, sir, I've been up here before."

"When?"

"Last . . . what's that? Someone's coming up the ladderway!"

Thank God, I told myself, Cork hadn't failed me. The two of us could handle this young murderer.

"Johno," a voice whispered, "you out there, lad?"

"Yes, who is it?"

"Where in the dome, Johno, my boy? Where is it? We could split the treasure, laddie."

"Split it!" my voice got away from me.

"Who's with you out there?" the man asked as he stepped out onto the platform. At that moment the moon slipped from behind a cloud, bathing the figure of Tom Biggard, a sword in his hand. He started out for us, his weapon held treacherously in front of him.

"So you're back, Mr Oaks. Well, that makes it all the better. It will be a simple case of you two killing each other over the loot."

He started for us and I grabbed the Lott boy and put him on the other side of me to protect him from the first thrust of the blade. He was at the center of the platform now, and ready to strike, when I saw it move. The jacamart came rushing forward and ran Biggard through with its steel.

"Well, don't stand there, Oaks," the jacamart said to me. "Hold this fiend up. I don't want him splattered all over the Reverend's quad."

Tom Biggard was badly wounded but alive when the Justice of the Peace came and had his men take him away. We were all in the common room, where Cork was holding forth with gusto in front of a slateboard.

"Oh, the shame of it," Reverend Travistock was saying. "One of our own graduates."

"And who else, sir? He had been a student here, he well knew the legend, and was probably once a member of a secret club which shall remain mercifully nameless."

"But I don't understand all this nonsense about Lott putting that do-re-me gibberish in his copybook," Crisp was yawning, but not bored.

"To fully appreciate the affair, let me say you were all suspects when I arrived here, and then the pieces began to fall in place. Let me put Chad Hull's September 19 notation on the slate." He wrote:

EF/FG/GA/AB/BC/CD/DE/EF?

"As a mathematics teacher, does that suggest anything to you, Mr Crisp?"

"It's a progression. The second letter of the first set becomes the first letter of the next set, and so on. But it doesn't make any sense to me."

"As well it shouldn't, unless you knew that Chad was attempting to find the jacamart's treasure. The letters in progression are the notes of the musical scale. I believe Chad felt the uniqueness of the Roman strike, and tried to find some clue in the notes of the scale, since he runs from E, a low note, to F, a high note. But he gets nowhere with it. He is truly embrangled. It is almost the same on October 10, but he starts to get closer to the mark in a small way.

"He shifts from the musical scale to the frugality of the Roman strike system." Cork wrote the October 10 notation on the board:

78−34=44=GB?
78−32=46=GA?

"Now, this is nothing more than finding the stroke differences between the regular strike system and the Roman strike system, and transferring the numbers into his progression scale of notes. Pure rot. But the second line of the notation shows us that a glimmer of light has come through, for Chad now calculates the difference between the regular strike and deJoonge's Roman system minus two strokes for the missing six o'clock sounding. Chad is still at sea, but at least he is thinking like old deJoonge. If a man were hiding a treasure, he would not mark a path for a confederate with such complexities. He would make it decidedly simple. I have reason to believe Chad had no real ear for music."

He knew very well, for so Chad's father had informed us. Miss Travistock, however, confirmed it again, thus protecting our previous association with the Hull family.

"Hark," Cork said, "the clock is striking eleven."

We all listened to the two low gongs and the one high. "What notes in the scale would you say those bell sounds are?"

She smiled. "I have known that since I was a girl. They are E and G, the first and third letters of the scale."

"And since the Reverend has told us that there are only two bells in the system, the scale notes are always the same in one E or G combination or another. So the missing six o'clock strike, VI, or one low and one high, would be EG. Of course, Chad Hull's tin ear at first saw it as EF, the first and second notes in the scale. But that would make the low and high rings almost indiscernible, and deJoonge widened the bell tone scale to EG, and thus told us where the treasure is by leaving six o'clock silent."

"I can't see where EG gets us," Crisp, the mathematics teacher, said.

"No, not as EG, but suppose they were sung in the so-fa syllables such as children do."

"Do and mi," Miss Travistock said.

"Or do and *me*, as it is often expressed in the tonic scale, so-fa."

"Do . . . me, dome," I said. "The dome of the clock is where the treasure is hidden. That's why you had young Lott put the do-re-me's into his notebook."

"Since all the instructors would see it and believe that Chad's work had been decoded, his killer would watch Lott like a hawk, and he did."

The Reverend looked dumbly at the slate. "You mean there really is a treasure up there in the tower? When I was a child, I remember some tough fellows showed up just after deJoonge died, looking for him. It was the only lie my father ever told. He informed them that the Dutchman had gone south to the Carolinas, and they left in pursuit.

My father never talked about it again, although I heard talk during my student days."

"A headmaster's son is hardly a schoolboy's confidant, Reverend."

I was overcome with glee. After all, if Cork had solved the riddle, then the treasure was rightly his. "Well, shall we start a thorough search of the dome?" I suggested.

"I'm afraid you would search in vain, Oaks."

"Then there is no treasure?"

"Oh yes, my old friend. I believe there is. But think, the tower does not have a dome. It has a spire. No, deJoonge was a sly old fox, but he gave himself away. You'll remember that our watchmaker in New Haven told us of the crudity of the Fenway clock. It doesn't even keep proper time. And yet, the same man constructs the beautiful piece of precision hanging now from Miss Travistock's chatelaine."

"This old thing?" she said holding it up. "I always correct it to match the tower clock."

"And thus fall for the Dutchman's deception. May I have it again, please? I'm afraid you weren't paying much attention, Oaks, when the New Haven man was cleaning your watch. He told you that your timepiece had been worked on by several people over the years. Do you know how he knew that? No, because you, like most people, are hesitant to open a precision instrument that you might harm." He put his thumbnail along the back of the catch and flipped the cover open.

"Do you see this inner cover? It's called a dome, is it not, and if we open that we find ... ah yes, an inscription in the same place watchmakers carve their initials or mark when they work on a timepiece. Does 'the foot of the westward oak' mean anything to you, Reverend? I think you will find your treasure buried there."

Mr Goselow, the professor of Greek and Latin, looked at Cork with unabashed admiration. "How perfectly Socratic, sir. My compliments."

"My compliments" indeed, for that's all our reward was to be. We were back at the Oar and Eagle the next evening, and I sat at the accounts dais glaring at him. "At least we could have claimed half of the jewels," I said. "Poor boys' scholarship, indeed."

"And why not? Old deJoonge's evil has done some good at last. Besides, possibly one of the indigent lads who will benefit from an education will become a doctor or lawyer and save you from sickness or me from the gallows. Come in, Tedderhorn. Good, you've brought the Knock. I've missed it."

I half-heartedly took my mug and sipped.

"Well, Oaks, have you figured it out yet?" Cork chaffed.

"Cloves," I said. "I'm sure of it."

"Good. Tedderhorn, hand the paper I gave you the other day to Oaks."

I read it and fumed:

Tedderhorn:
Add nothing to the Knock, but don't tell Oaks.

Cork

"This is . . . ah . . . dishonesty, foul play," I cried.

"Nonsense, my old son, it is deception, no more."

"And do you not consider deception dishonest?"

"Not when all the facts are in front of you. You had your sense of taste. I just misdirected you. Come, man, as Shakespeare says, 'would you pluck out the heart of my mystery?'"

I persevere.

# THE SCENT
# OF MURDER
# Theodore Mathieson

*From Captain Cork to Captain Cook. In 1960, Theodore Mathieson (b. 1913) published a volume called* The Great "Detectives" *which featured ten historical mysteries solved by famous characters from history starting with Alexander the Great and ending with Florence Nightingale. The stories are ingeniously researched selecting a theme wholly relevant to the character and creating a mystery that could so easily have happened. The following story was the first of them to be written. The series so fascinated Frederick Dannay (one-half of the Ellery Queen writing team) that he called it "one of the most ambitious literary projects ever envisioned."*

On the night of June 11, 1770, fourteen months after His Majesty's ship *Endeavour* had left England, and while she explored the waters three hundred miles off the coast of "New Holland," Captain James Cook was suddenly faced with a problem that he could not solve by quadrant or caliper.

It was two bells, most of the crew were below, and the captain slowly paced the afterdeck. He reached the starboard side, grasped the taffrail, and looked aloft to where the three masts of the sturdy sailing ship rose black against the tropical moonlight, when he heard a cry from the ladder.

"Captain, sir," a voice said shakily from the shadows.

"Come up, Blore," Cook said, recognizing the voice of the quartermaster of the watch.

"It's Prout, sir, the bosun's mate. He's dead. I just found him midship, hanging over the rail. There's a knife in his back. I haven't touched him, sir."

Cook hesitated a moment, looking down at the deep, concealing shadows on the main deck. This could be a trick. The men had been giving trouble, wanting to turn back after New Zealand, saying he'd gotten what the Admiralty had sent him for – the transit of Venus. It was true. On Tahiti three months ago he'd made the observation which, when combined with measurements made by scientists at other points on the globe, would determine for the first time in history the distance from the earth to the sun.

But now the men were homesick. The captain had been forced, after the outbreak of a drunken, resentful riot in the forecastle, to cut the ration of grog to a fourth. The men were in a sullen, threatening mood.

"Prout has been drinking, sir," Blore said, clucking his tongue. "Smells like he's been wallowing in the hogshead."

Cook made his decision. "Bring him here," he said sharply. "Get Hicks the cook to give you a hand. I see the light in his galley."

"Yes, sir, but – " Blore half turned away.

"But what?"

"I think it might be Hicks that did it, sir, after what happened between them this morning."

"Get Hicks to help you," Cook repeated.

Ship's surgeon Monkhouse, a mountain of a man, stood beside his stubborn-lipped captain as Blore and the cook, Hicks, lowered the body gently to the deck. It was still flexible and warm, although the bearded face of the bosun's mate had had time to smooth out, so that he looked peaceful and unconcerned over his sudden and violent end. Probably he'd not even caught sight of his assailant before he died, although it was doubtful if he'd been able to recognize him if he had.

"Grog must be coming out of his pores, sir," Monkhouse said. "Smell that."

"Ain't it something terrible?" Hicks, the wiry, whey-faced little cook said fervently. Fresh from the galley, his white apron gleamed in the moonlight.

At the captain's order Monkhouse leaned over and removed the knife from the dead man's back. He had a little difficulty, at which Blore made a choking sound and ran for the rail.

"An ordinary butcher's knife," the captain said. "Like one you use, Hicks, isn't it?"

"I wondered where it'd got to," the cook said, wetting his lips. "It's been gorn since last night."

The captain studied the little Cockney briefly, while the rigging creaked in the sway from the ocean swell.

"Come into the cabin, all of you," he said.

Inside the captain's cabin it was warm and close. Through the stern windows the moonlight could be seen coruscating upon the waves. The captain, a gaunt six-footer, lean of cheek and long of nose, stood for a moment in the stern alcove, seeming to tower over his men. Then he sat down at his writing desk and the others gathered round him, their faces white and tense in the light of the lantern swinging in brass gimbals over the desk. The captain's cat, Orleans, jumped on his master's lap and settled down undisturbed.

"You may sit down," the captain said, and as Blore entered belatedly, looking a sickly green, he admonished as an afterthought, "And *you* had better stay near the door." The captain swung around to the cook.

"What happened between you and Prout this morning?"

The unexpectedness of the question caused Hicks to gasp. Then his little black eyes narrowed and he slid them murderously toward Blore.

"I – don't quite know what you're gettin' at, Cap'n," Hicks said with a yellow-toothed smile. "Prout and I wasn't friends exactly, but – "

"I want to know what happened this morning."

"We had a little argument, that's all," Hicks mumbled.

"Perhaps I can tell you," Monkhouse the surgeon spoke up. "I went down to call on a patient during the noonday mess. Prout is – was – something of a bully. I think most of the men can tell you that. He was always making Hicks here take back his food and get him something else."

"Couldn't please 'im anyhow!" Hicks said venomously.

"It's gone on for six months, now, sir," Blore spoke up from the door. "Today Prout became pretty violent and sent food back twice. Said Cooky was the worst slob of a cook that'd ever sailed in His Majesty's service. Cooky got mad and swung the iron frying pan at Prout's head. Would have killed him if Prout hadn't jerked away. The frying pan made a gash in the table you could put your hand into."

"But I didn't kill him, did I?" Hicks protested in a shrill voice.

"You tried to," the captain said quietly. "And as for being a bad cook, I've had occasion to send certain dishes back myself, if you recall."

"I do me level best," Hicks whined. "That's all a bloke can do, beggin' your pardon, Cap'n."

"There's only one reason that makes me think you didn't do it," the captain said, looking at Hicks as one might look at a cockroach sitting on a tablecloth. "You hated Prout all right – that's clear to all of us. But I think you'd like to have had him suffer a little for bullying you these six months. The knife would have been too quick for you, I think."

The cook nodded quickly. "That it would," he said.

"Especially since if you had merely reported Prout, who has obviously broached the hogshead, he would have been strapped to the bowsprit and you could have seen him die slowly of hunger and exposure. That was the fate I ordered, as you all know, for anyone found tampering with the grog."

"Aye, 'e's 'ad it too easy, I'd say!" Cooky said, sniffing.

The surgeon stirred his heavy body and started to rise, then sat back again.

"There's still another one who might have done this," he said. "Although I – "

"No changing course now," the captain warned.

"It's young William Backus. First trip, has learned the ropes quickly. A likely lad . . . I hate to mention it, but in all fairness to Cooky here . . ."

"Backus wouldn't do it," Blore said quickly. "He's too nice a lad. Reads his Bible regular."

"But you think I did it!" Hicks cried shrilly, and the captain silenced him with a gesture. He turned back to the surgeon.

"But the lad had a grudge against Prout?"

"I'm afraid he did. The boy has his hammock next to Prout's. He'd try to sleep at night and Prout would push his foot against the lad's hammock. Prout didn't sleep well, so Will didn't get much sleep either. He tried to move away but Prout wouldn't let him. Finally the boy came to me, but I told him to fight it out for himself. He did fight it out, but Prout beat him almost to a pulp, and then went right on keeping him awake."

Blore said suddenly, "Prout was just asking to be killed, Captain! None of the men could get on with him."

"Except you," the surgeon said blandly. "I saw you and Prout together now and then. Very friendly, you seemed."

"I always try to see the other man's side of it," Blore said with a quiet dignity. "Besides, I recognized Prout for the bully he was, and never took anything from him. First week out from Plymouth I fought him, and laid him out flat on the deck. We got on together fine after that, but I didn't seek out his company."

The captain sighed. He knew it would not do to let the murder go unpunished among a crew whose temper was reaching a lawless pitch. He would have to sift and question, to find the murderer and make an example of him.

"Bring me Backus," he said to Blore.

Blore went out with a show of reluctance, and the captain had barely time to turn to Hicks, whom he was on the point of dismissing, when the quartermaster of the watch was back in the cabin, with his mouth hanging open, breathing heavily.

"Well, what is it?" the captain demanded.

"It's Prout, sir. We left him on the deck out there, but there's no trace of him. The body's gone, sir."

At the captain's order Monkhouse and Blore set about searching the ship unobtrusively for the corpse. From the heavy sprit to the boxy stern they looked, above and below deck, into the hollow cores of coils of hempen line, among the piles of uncut canvas, and between pyramids of oaken casks. They stumbled as noiselessly as they could manage over spars and blocks and pulleys and belaying pins. Breathing fetid air, they crawled on hands and knees in the forecastle beneath the hammocks of sleeping men. And at the end of two hours they concluded that the obvious solution had been the correct one: the body of the bosun's mate had been thrown over the side.

During the search Blore checked the spigot of the hogshead and found it still sealed, but another spigot, concealed by a bulkhead, had been thrust into the back of the cask. Prout had doubtless drunk his grog on the spot, not daring to carry it away in containers, for there was a quarter-filled mug in the shadow of a cask block. But for all his precautions the bosun's mate had overestimated his capacity, and if the murderer hadn't doomed him, his obvious condition would have.

Captain Cook found himself liking the boy Will Backus at once. He was tall, muscular and blond, about nineteen, red-cheeked and clear-eyed, although there were telltale dark circles under his eyes. He entered the captain's cabin with evident anxiety, but was self-possessed.

"Sit down, Backus," the captain said curtly. "I suppose Blore has told you what happened to Prout."

"Yes, sir."

"I understand you and he were not the best of friends."

The boy lowered his eyes and his lip trembled. "No, we were not, sir."

"Do you mind telling me why?"

Backus explained the trouble between him and the bosun's mate much as Monkhouse had done. When he had finished, the boy put his hand petitioningly on the captain's desk.

"Would you please believe me, sir," he said, "that although I had every reason to hate Mr Prout, I made every effort not to feel that way toward him."

"So I understand. You're a great reader of the Bible, Mr Blore tells me."

"Yes, sir. I promised my father I would read it and follow its precepts faithfully. I try to hate no man."

"But you'll agree that Prout made himself decidedly hateful to most of the men. And besides yourself, to the cook Hicks, particularly?"

"The Bible does not say that one should fail to recognize evil when he meets it. I believe Mr Prout was evil."

"And deserved to be murdered?"

"That would be God's decision, sir."

"And you would not think of being His instrument?"

The boy looked at the captain, paled, but did not answer.

"Answer my question."

"I believe, Captain Cook, that God often chooses His instruments to do – certain acts – on earth. But I swear to you, sir, that I did not kill Mr Prout."

Captain Cook reached for his pipe, filled it, and when he had it going well, he asked, "Did you know that Prout was soddenly drunk when he was killed?"

"Mr Blore did mention that, sir."

"And if you stepped up behind him to do him harm, and found him intoxicated, would you have reported him to your superior officer and have the ship's discipline punish him?"

"I cannot answer that, sir. I do not know."

"You do not know if it would satisfy God's justice to see Prout on the bowsprit, suffering day after day the pangs of starvation and thirst?"

"No, no!" the boy cried suddenly. "I could not want that. Nor would God want it."

Captain Cook pointed at the door of the cabin with the stem of his pipe.

"That will be all just now, Backus," he said.

The next morning the captain sat down wearily at his desk and took his journal from the drawer. With the sun warming his back, and the quill poised over the page, he sat staring at Orleans, curled upon his bunk.

There was so much more to be done, if the men could only understand. There were islands in these South Seas still unclaimed by Spain, Portugal, France or Holland. There were unknown waters to chart, and most important of all, there was the possibility of discovering a new continent for the glory of Britain.

He sighed and began writing: "After staying up half the night interrogating the men and officers, I have come to only one conclusion. Only two men have *suffered* sufficiently at Prout's hands to have murdered him – Backus and Hicks. The others have been able to handle Prout, and one of them, Blore, seemed even to be friendly with him. Blore is a problem. Although he has no apparent reason for murder, and got on well with Prout, still he was the only one of those who first knew of Prout's murder (Monkhouse, Hicks and myself) who was outside of the cabin long enough to have accomplished the removal of the body. Was he actually sick when the surgeon withdrew the knife, or was he pretending? The more I think about this, the more confusing it becomes. I shall keep Blore in mind, and for the moment add him to my list of possible criminals.

"As I see it, the answer to Prout's murder lies in how each one of these three men – Hicks, Backus, and Blore – would *actually* react if they knew that by merely reporting Prout's dereliction the bosun's mate would be condemned to a slow death. It is certain, I think, that men often are of two kinds – pain-givers and pain-savers. Prout was killed suddenly, quickly, while deeply intoxicated. Without question all three men knew of the penalty for broaching the hogshead. That means that whoever murdered Prout, although he knew he might have had much more satisfaction out of seeing Prout languish on the bow-sprit, preferred to kill him quickly and save him pain. The murderer, then, was a pain-saver. Now of these three men, who are the pain-savers and who are the pain-givers? Young Backus says that he is a pain-saver. Hicks is obviously a pain-giver. Blore, with his quiet ways and queasy stomach, would seem to be a pain-saver. Yet, how often does a man really know himself well enough to give an accurate description of his tendencies? *I cannot depend upon what these men say about themselves, or what they seem to me to be.*

"The only answer is to devise some sort of test and catch their reactions unexpectedly . . ."

The idea of the test came soon – as Cook watched his tabby, Orleans, playing with a pen that had fallen to the deck. The captain made his preparations, and on the evening following the murder he called Hicks into his cabin.

The cook had taken off his apron and slicked his hair in deference to the occasion. He stood smiling ingratiatingly in the doorway.

"Come in," the captain said affably. "I want you to feel at ease, Hicks. I'm not making any accusations. I just want to find out more about what happened last night, and I'd appreciate your help. Have a drink of brandy?"

Hicks lost his smile in bewilderment at this egalitarian treatment, but recovered sufficiently to bob his head at the invitation to imbibe.

As the captain carefully poured two brandies, a scratching from a wooden box set on the captain's desk attracted Hicks's attention.

"Orleans loves to play with a baby mouse now and then," Cook said casually. "And I enjoy watching the sport. You may look in."

Hicks nodded and peered down eagerly. Orleans held his young enemy lightly under his right paw.

"Of course, I believe in being fair about it," the captain said. "If the mouse manages to stay alive for the time it takes this hourglass to pour five minutes of its sand – to this mark – I let the mouse go."

"To plague the ship, Cap'n?"

"If he runs into you, of course, that's his misfortune. But he has earned his reprieve from me."

Hicks nodded noncommittally and continued avidly to watch Orleans and his prize. The captain sat down and began asking questions about the night before – perfunctory questions which had already been asked, but Hicks, with his attention divided, didn't seem to notice. Once or twice Orleans chased the little mouse from corner to corner with a commotion that threatened to upset the box, but the captain paid no attention, and continued his questioning. Hicks grew more and more excited.

"There, that makes it time," the captain said finally, turning the hourglass over.

"Oh, not yet, Cap'n!" Hicks said, pleading. "The cat hasn't begun to play proper yet."

"But the time is up."

"Please, Cap'n," Hicks said, his eyes on the box.

The captain waited deliberately, and a few seconds later Orleans pounced once more and a mortal squeal from the mouse told the story.

"There! 'e's damaged now, all right!" Hicks cried triumphantly.

"We waited too long," the captain sighed, and put the box upon the deck.

"Hicks is exactly what he appeared to be – a pain-giver," the captain wrote in his journal late that night. "And Backus didn't like the cat and mouse idea right from the start. He wouldn't even look, and I am convinced he was not shamming. He, too, was right about himself. Blore was the only one of the three who seemed to detect what I was about, and let me know it by his manner. He is an intelligent man, and I cannot be sure about his reactions. He looked on with little show of emotion, and when the time was up quietly agreed that I should terminate the struggle.

"I do not like what this leads me to surmise. It puts the boy Backus first in my suspicions, with Blore in the middle, and Hicks last. Unless

I can think of another plan of investigation, I'm afraid we shall not
uncover the truth about Prout's murder . . ."

The captain solved it the very next morning.

He sat at breakfast, looking through the stern windows at a huge
island looming up on the horizon like a great cloud. He could hear
the leadsman's chant as he sounded from the chains. "The existing
maps do not show an island here," the captain was thinking. "We
must investigate." Then his thought broke off like a thread. In the
middle of a bite he crashed his cup of tea into the saucer, rose, and
strode to the door of his cabin.

"Monkhouse!" he thundered at the surgeon who stood at the
rail outside. "Get those three up here – Backus, Hicks, and Blore.
Right away!"

Too startled for words, the surgeon nodded and made for the ladder
to the main deck. The captain withdrew to his cabin again, poured
three small drinks, and placed them in a row on the table.

Blore was the first to arrive, wiping his hands on a cloth; he had
been helping the botanists rearrange the specimens in their cabin.

"You called, Captain?" Blore asked mildly.

"All three of you, yes," the captain said grimly. "I think I have
discovered a way of revealing the criminal."

"Will he give up that easily, sir?"

"Two of you will help me hold him should he become violent," the
captain said, smiling.

Backus arrived, his hands still soapy from washing the companion-
way to the forecastle. His hair was tousled and his eyes wide with
excitement.

"I came right away, sir," he said eagerly.

"Yes. Give him your cloth, Blore, and let him wipe his hands free
of soap."

"Thank you, sir," Backus said, busy with the cloth.

And then Hicks came, not having bothered to remove his apron
this time, nor slick back his hair.

"At your service, Cap'n," he said easily, presuming on the friendliness the captain had shown him the night before.

The captain closed the door, then stood up before the three
of them.

"I wish you to drink with me – a little toast to the island we see
ahead. It is uncharted, and possibly uninhabited."

The captain handed the three glasses to the men.

"Do not drink until I give the word," he said sharply, and then
more slowly, "In a minute or two I think we shall find the criminal

who murdered Prout. And when we do, he will have the choice of swinging from the yardarm or of being marooned on that island."

"You know who it is?" It was Backus, his voice sounding high and young.

"Yes, I think I do, Backus. All I need now is proof."

"How do you propose to get it, Captain?" Blore asked.

Hicks said nothing; his look was almost uncomprehending.

"I shall answer your question after you drink my toast," said the captain. "But first, I should be considerably hurt if you do not consider the bouquet of this fine brandy." The captain raised the glass to his nose and sniffed, and the others did likewise.

"Now drink," he said, and swallowed the contents of his own glass quickly. When he looked at the others, two of them stood gazing at him wonderingly, their glasses still full in their hands. The third was spluttering, his eyes watering, his glass empty.

"Don't you like vinegar, Hicks?" the captain asked quietly. "*If you had been able to smell it when you sniffed, perhaps you wouldn't have drunk it.* The others didn't. You murdered Prout, didn't you? You would have let the ship's punishment take care of him the long and painful way if you could have smelled his drunkenness the other night; but since you couldn't, you killed him the quick, merciful way, which was quite unlike you."

"You don't know what you're talkin' abaht, Cap'n," Hicks said, his cheeks wet with tears drawn by the vinegar. "I was inside the cabin with you when the body was moved. The murderer did that, so I ain't the murderer."

"Yes, you are, Hicks," Backus said quietly. "I saw you do it. But because you'd been bullied the way I'd been bullied, I threw Prout overboard so you wouldn't be blamed for it. I thought I was justified, but it's been a terrible weight on my conscience. Now that God has let Captain Cook see the truth, I cannot hide it any longer."

"You little rat!" Hicks shrieked and rushed frantically toward Backus. Blore seized the little man by the collar and held him firmly, cuffing him until his protestations ceased.

"You burnt my breakfast once too often," the captain said. "Anyone who burns food as often as you, Hicks, must have a defective sense of smell. So you gave yourself away, you see."

Later, when Blore and Backus were gone and Hicks was safely locked in the hold, the captain said to the surgeon:

"We exchange one mystery for another, Monkhouse."

"How do you mean?" the surgeon asked.

"Where in the devil are we going to find another cook?"

# THE INN OF
# THE BLACK CROW
# William Hope Hodgson

*During the sixties and seventies the rediscovery of the works of William Hope Hodgson (1877–1918) raised him to almost cult status in the field of weird fiction. He was one of the most visionary writers of fantastic fiction in the first decades of this century in both the novel and short story forms. Indeed, his magnum opus,* The Night Land *(1912), set on a dying Earth millions of years in the future, is like nothing else ever written. All of his novels, especially* The House on the Borderland *(1908), are worth reading, as are many of his short stories, most of which reflect the horror of the sea that he knew so well. Although he is also known for his psychic detective stories collected in* Carnacki the Ghost-Finder *(1913), Hodgson's name is not immediately linked with detective fiction. But as he sought to make a living full-time writing in the years before the First World War, Hodgson began to churn out fiction in all genres, some of it highly original and some of it transparently imitative. I will give no prizes for the author Hodgson was copying here, but it is a creditable story nonetheless. This story has not been reprinted since its first appearance in* The Red Magazine *for October 1, 1915, and I am grateful to Jack Adrian for securing me a copy.*

*June 27th*   I cannot say that I care for the look of mine host. If he tippled more and talked more I should like him better; but he drinks not, neither does he speak sufficiently for ordinary civility.

I could think that he has no wish for my custom. Yet, if so, how does he expect to make a living, for I am paying two honest guineas a week for board and bed no better than the Yellow Swan at Dunnage does me for a guinea and a half. Yet that he knows me or suspects me of being more than I appear I cannot think, seeing that I have never been within a hundred miles of this desolated village of Erskine, where there is not even the sweet breath of the sea to blow the silence away, but everywhere the grey moors, slit by the lonesome mud-beset creeks, that I have few doubts see some strange doings at nights, and could, maybe, explain the strange crushed body of poor James Naynes, the exciseman, who had been found dead upon the moors six weeks gone; and concerning which I am here to discover secretly whether it was foul murder or not.

*June 30th* That I was right in my belief that Jalbrok, the landlord, is a rascal, I have now very good proof, and would shift my quarters, were it not that there is no other hostel this side of Bethansop, and that is fifteen weary miles by the road.

I cannot take a room in any of the hovels round here; for there could be no privacy for me, and I should not have the freedom of unquestioned movement that one pays for at all inns, along with one's bed and board. And here, having given out on arriving that I am from London town for my health, having a shortness of breath, and that I fish with a rod, like my old friend Walton – of whom no man hereabouts has ever heard – I have been let go my way as I pleased, with never a one of these grim Cornishmen to give me so much as a passing nod of the head; for to them I am a "foreigner," deserving, because of this stigma, a rock on my head, rather than a friendly word on my heart. However, in the little Dowe-Fleet river there are trout to make a man forget lonesomeness.

But though I am forced to stay here in the inn until my work is done, and my report prepared for the authorities, yet I am taking such care as I can in this way and that, and never do I venture a yard outside the inn without a brace of great flintlocks hidden under my coat.

Now, I have said I proved Jalbrok, the landlord of this inn of the Black Crow, a rascal. And so have I in two things; for this morning I caught him and his tapman netting the little Dowe-Fleet, and a great haul he had of fish, some that were three pounds weight and a hundred that were not more than fingerlings, and should never have left water.

I was so angry to see this spoiling of good, honest sport that I loosed out at Jalbrok with my tongue, as any fisherman might; but he told me to shut my mouth, and this I had to do, though with difficulty, and only by remembering that a man that suffers from a shortness of wind has no excuse to fight. So I made a virtue of the matter, and sat down suddenly on the bank, and panted pretty hard and spit a bit, and then lay on my side, as if I had a seizure. And a very good acting I made of it, I flattered myself, and glad that I had held my temper in, and so made them all see that I was a truly sick man.

Now, there the landlord left me, lying on my side, when he went away with all that great haul of good trout. And this was the second thing to prove the man a rascal, and liefer to be rid of me than to keep me, else he had not left me there, a sick man as he supposed. And I say and maintain that any man that will net a stream that may be fished with a feathered hook, and will also leave a sick man to recover or to die alone, all as may be, is a true rascal – and so I shall prove him yet.

*July 2nd (Night)*  I have thought that the landlord has something new on his mind lately, and the thing concerns me; for twice and again yesterday evening I caught him staring at me in a very queer fashion, so that I have taken more care than ever to be sure that no one can come at me during the night.

After dinner this evening I went down and sat a bit in the empty taproom, where I smoked my pipe and warmed my feet at the big log fire. The night had been coldish, in spite of the time of the year, for there is a desolate wind blowing over the great moorlands, and I could hear the big Erskine creek lapping on the taproom side of the house, for the inn is built quite near to the creek.

While I was smoking and staring into the fire, a big creekman came into the taproom and shouted for Jalbrok, the landlord, who came out of the back room in his slow, surly way.

"I'm clean out o' guzzle," the creekman said, in a dialect that was no more Cornish than mine. "I'll swop a good yaller angel for some o' that yaller sperrit o' yourn, Jal. An' that are a bad exchange wi'out robb'ry. He, he! Us that likes good likker likes it fresh from the sea, like a young cod. He, he!"

There is one of those farm-kitchen wind-screens, with a settle along it, that comes on one side the fireplace in the taproom, and neither Jalbrok nor the big creekman could see me where I sat, because the oak screen hid me, though I could look round it with the trouble of bending my neck.

Their talk interested me greatly, as may be thought, for it was plain that the man, whoever he might be, had punned on the gold angel, which is worth near half a guinea of honest English money; and what should a creekman be doing with such a coin, or to treat it so lightly, as if it were no more than a common groat? And afterwards to speak of liking the good liquor that comes fresh from the sea! It was plain enough what he meant.

I heard Jalbrok, the landlord, ringing the coin on the counter. And then I heard him saying it was thin gold; and that set the creekman angry.

"Gglag you for a scrape-bone!" he roared out, using a strange expression that was new to me. "Gglag you! You would sweat the oil off a topmast, you would! If you ain't easy, there's more nor one as ha' a knife into you ower your scrape-bone ways; and, maybe, us shall make you pay a good tune for French brandy one o' these days, gglag you!"

"Stow that!" said the landlord's voice. "That's no talk for this place wi' strangers round. I – "

He stopped, and there followed, maybe, thirty seconds of absolute silence. Then I heard someone tiptoeing a few steps over the floor, and I closed my eyes and let my pipe droop in my mouth, as if I were dosing. I heard the steps cease, and there was a sudden little letting out of a man's breath, and I knew that the landlord had found I was in the taproom with them.

The next thing I knew he had me by the shoulder, and shook me, so that my pipe dropped out of my mouth on to the stone floor.

"Here!" he roared out. "Wot you doin' in here!"

"Let go of my shoulder, confound your insolence," I said; and ripped my shoulder free from his fist with perhaps a little more strength than I should have shown him, seeing that I am a sick man to all in this part.

"Confound you!" I said again, for I was angry; but now I had my wits more about me. "Confound your putting your dirty hands on me. First you net the river and spoil my trout fishing, and now you must spoil the best nap I have had for three months."

As I made an end of this, I was aware that the big creekman was also staring round the oak wind-screen at me. And therewith it seemed a good thing to me to fall a-coughing and "howking," as we say in the North; and a better country I never want!

"Let un be, Jal. Let un be!" I heard the big creekman saying. "He ain't but a broken-winded man. There's none that need ha' fear o' that sort. He'll be growin' good grass before the winter. Come you, gglag you, an' gi'e me some guzzle, an' let me be goin'."

The landlord looked at me for nearly a minute without a word; then he turned and followed the creekman to the drinking counter. I heard a little further grumbled talk and argument about the angel being thin gold, but evidently they arranged it between them, for Jalbrok measured out some liquor, that was good French brandy by the smell of it, if ever I've smelt French brandy, and a little later the creekman left.

*July 5th*  Maybe I have kissed the inn wench a little heartily on occasions, but she made no sound objections, and it pleased me,

I fear, a little to hear Llan, the lanky, knock-kneed tapman and general help, rousting at the wench for allowing it. The lout has opinions of himself, I do venture to swear; for a more ungainly, water-eyed, shambling rascal never helped his master net a good trout stream before or since. And as on that occasion he showed a great pleasure, and roared in his high pitched crow at the way I lay on the bank and groaned and coughed, I take an equal great pleasure to kiss the maid, which I could think she is, whenever I chance to see him near.

And to see the oaf glare at me, and yet fear to attack even a sick man, makes me laugh to burst my buttons; but I make no error, for it is that kind of a bloodless animal that will put a knife between a man's shoulders when the chance offers.

*July 7th*  Now a good kiss, once in a way, may be a good thing all round, and this I discovered it to be, for the wench has taken a fancy to better my food, for which I am thankful; also, last night, she went further, for she whispered in my ear, as she served me my dinner, to keep my bedroom door barred o' nights; but when I would know why, she smiled, putting her finger to her lip, and gave me an old countryside proverb to the effect that a barred door let no corn out and no rats in. Which was a good enough hint for any man, and I repaid the wench in a way that seemed to please her well, nor did she say no to a half-guinea piece which I slipped into her broad fist.

Now, the room I sleep in is large, being about thirty feet long and, maybe, twenty wide, and has a good deal of old and bulky furniture in it, that makes it over-full of shadows at night for my liking.

The door of my room is of oak, very heavy and substantial, and without panels. There is a wooden snick-latch on it to enter by, and the door is made fast with a wooden bolt set in oak sockets, and pretty strong. There are two windows to the room, but these are barred, for which I have been glad many a time.

There are in the bedroom two great, heavy, oaken clothes-cupboards, two settees, a big table, two great wood beds, three lumbersome old chairs, and three linen-presses of ancient and blackened oak, in which the wench keeps not linen, but such various oddments as the autumn pickings of good hazel nuts, charcoal for the upstairs brazier, and in the third an oddment of spare feather pillows and some good down in a sack; and besides these, two gallon puggs – as they name the small kegs here – of French brandy, which I doubt not she has "nigged" from the cellars of mine host, and intends for a very welcome gift to some favoured swain, or, indeed, for all I know, to her own father, if she have one.

And simple she must be some ways, for she has never bothered to lock the press.

Well do I know all these matters by now, for I have a bothersome pilgrimage each night, first to open the great cupboards and look in, and then to shut and snick the big brass locks. And after that I look in the linen-chests, and smile at the two puggs of brandy, for the wench has found something of a warm place in my heart because of her honest friendliness to me. Then I peer under the two settees and the two beds; and so I am sure at last that the room holds nothing that might trouble me in my sleep.

The beds are simple, rustic, heavy-made affairs, cloddish and without canopies or even posts for the same, which makes them seem very rude and ugly to the eye. However, they please me well, for I have read in my time and once I saw the like – of bedsteads that had the canopy very great and solid and made to let down, like a press, upon the sleeper, to smother him in his sleep; and a devilish contrivance is such in those of our inns that are on the by-roads; and many a lone traveller has met a dreadful death, as I have proved in my business of a secret agent for the king. But there are few such tricks that I cannot discover in a moment, because of my training in all matters that deal with the ways of law-breakers, of which I am a loyal and sworn enemy.

But for me, at the Inn of the Black Crow, I have no great fear of any odd contrivance of death; nor of poison or drugging if I should be discovered, for there is a skill needed in such matters, and, moreover, the wench prepares my food and is my good friend; for it is always my way to have the women folk upon my side, and a good half of the battles of life are won if a man does this always. But what I have good cause to fear is lest the landlord, or any of the brute oafs of this lonesome moor, should wish to come at me in my sleep, and, maybe, hide in one of the great presses or the great cupboards to this end; and there you have my reasons for my nightly search of the room.

On this last night I paid a greater attention to all my precautions, and searched the big room very carefully, even to testing the wall behind the pictures, but found it of good moorland stone, like the four walls of the room.

The door, however, I made more secure by pushing one of the three linen-presses up against it, and so I feel pretty safe for the night.

Now, I had certainly a strong feeling that something might be in the wind, as the sailormen say, against me; and a vague uneasiness kept me from undressing for a time, so that, after I had finished making all secure for the night, I sat a good while in one of the chairs by the table and wrote up my report.

After a time I had a curious feeling that someone was looking in at me through the barred window to my left, and at last I got up and loosed the heavy curtains down over both it and the far one, for it was quite possible for anyone to have placed one of the short farm-ladders against the wall and come up to have a look in at me. Yet in my heart I did not really think this was so, and I tell of my action merely because it shows the way that I felt.

At last I said to myself that I had grown to fancying things because of the friendly warning that the wench had given me over my dinner; but even as I said it, and glanced about the heavy, shadowy room, I could not shake free from my feelings. I took my candle and slipped off my shoes, so that my steps should not be heard below; then I went again through my pilgrimage of the room. I opened the cupboards and presses, each in turn, and finally once more I looked under the beds and even under the table, but there was nothing, nor could there have been to my common-sense reasoning.

I determined to undress and go to bed, assuring myself that a good sleep would soon cure me, but at first I went to my trunk and unlocked it. I took from it my brace of pistols and my big knife, also my lantern, which had a cunning little cap over the face and a metal cowl above the chimney, so that, by means of the cap and the cowl, I can make the lantern dark and yet have a good light burning within ready for an instant use.

Then I drew out the wads from my pistols, and screwed out the bullets and the second wads, and poured out the powder. I tried the flints, and found them spark very bright and clean, and afterwards I reloaded the pistols with fresh powder, using a heavier charge, and putting into each twelve large buckshot as big as peas, and a wad on the top to hold them in.

When I had primed the two pistols, I reached down into my boot and drew out a small weapon that I am never without; and a finely made pistol it is, by Chamel, the gunsmith, near the Tower. I paid him six guineas for that one weapon, and well it has repaid me, for I have killed eleven men with it in four years that would otherwise have sent me early out of this life; and a better pistol no man ever had, nor, for the length of the barrel, a truer. I reloaded this likewise, but with a single bullet in the place of the buckshot slugs I had put into my heavier pistols.

I carried a chair close to the bedside, and on this chair I laid my three pistols and my knife. Then I lit my lantern, and shut the cap over the glass; after which I stood it with my weapons on the seat of the chair.

I took a good while to undress, what with the way I kept looking round me into the shadows, and wishing I had a dozen great candles, and again stopping to listen to the horrid moan of the moor wind blowing in through the crannies of the windows, and odd times the dismal sounding lap, lap of the big Erskine creek below.

When at last I climbed up into the great clumsy-made bed, I left the candle burning on the table, and lay a good while harking to the wind, that at one moment would cease, and leave the big, dark room silent and chill-seeming, and the next would whine and moan again in through the window crannies.

I fell asleep in the end, and had a pretty sound slumber. Then, suddenly, I was lying there awake in the bed, listening. The candle had burned itself out and the room was very, very dark, owing to my having drawn the curtains, which I never did before.

I lay quiet, trying to think why I had waked so sharply; and in the back of my brain I had a feeling that I had been wakened by some sound. Yet the room was most oppressive quiet, and not even was there the odd whine or moan of the wind through the window crannies, for now the wind had dropped away entirely.

Yet there were sounds below me in the big taproom, and I supposed that a company of the rough creek and moor men were drinking and jollying together beneath me, for as I lay and listened there came now and then the line of a rude song, or a shouted oath, or an indefinite babel of rough talk and argument, all as the mood served. And once, by the noise, there must have been something of a free fight, and a bench or two smashed, by the crash I heard of broken woodwork.

After a while there was a sudden quietness, in which the silence of the big chamber grew on me with a vague discomfort. Abruptly I heard a woman's voice raised in a clatter of words, and then there was a great shouting of hoarse voices, and a beating of mugs upon the benches, by the sounds.

I leaned up on my elbow in the bed and listened, for there was such a to-do, as we say, that I could not tell what to think.

As I leaned there and hearkened I heard the woman begin to scream, and she screamed, maybe, a dozen times, but whether in fear or anger or both I could not at once decide, only now I drew myself to the edge of the bed, meaning to open my lantern and have some light in the room. As I rolled on to the edge of the bed, and reached out my hand, the screaming died away, and there came instead, as I stiffened and harked, the sound of a woman crying somewhere in the house. And suddenly I comprehended, in some strange fashion of the spirit, that it was because of me – that some harm was to be done me, perhaps was even then coming.

I stretched out my hand swiftly and groped for the lantern; but my hand touched nothing, and I had a quick sickening and dreadful feeling that something was in the room with me, and had taken the chair away from the side of my bed, with all my weapons.

In the same moment that this thought flashed a dreadful and particular horror across my brain, I realized, with a sweet revulsion towards security, that I was reaching out upon the wrong side of the bed, for the room was so utter dark with the heavy curtains being across the windows.

I jumped to my feet upon the bed, and as I did so there sounded two sharp blows somewhere beneath me. I turned to stride quickly across, and as I did so the whole bed seemed to drop from under me, as I was in the very act of my stride. Something hugely great caught me savagely and brutally by my feet and ankles, and in the same instant there was a monstrous crash upon the floor of the bedroom that seemed to shake the inn. I pitched backwards, and struck my shoulder against the heavy timbers, but the dreadful grip upon my feet never ceased. I rose upright, using the muscles of my thighs and stomach to lift me; and when I was stood upright in the utter darkness I squatted quickly and felt at the thing which had me so horribly by the feet.

My feet seemed to be held between two edges that were padded, yet pressed so tight together that I could not force even my fist between them.

I stood up again and wrenched, very fierce and mad, to free my feet, but I could not manage it, and only seemed to twist and strain my ankles with the fight I made and the way I troubled to keep my balance.

I stopped a moment where I stood in the darkness on my trapped feet, and listened very intently. Yet there seemed everywhere a dreadful silence, and no sound in all the house, and I could not be sure whether I was still in the bedroom or fallen into some secret trap along with the bed when it fell from under me.

I reached up my hands over my head to see if I could touch anything above me, but I found nothing. Then I spread my arms out sideways to see whether I could touch any wall, but there was nothing within my reach.

All this time, while I was doing this, I said to myself that I *must* be still in the bedroom, for the taproom lay just below me; also, though the bed had fallen from under me, and I also had seemed to go down, yet I had not felt to have dropped far.

And then, in the midst of my fears and doubts and horrid bewilderment, I saw a faint little ray of light, no greater than the edge of a small knife, below me.

I squatted again upon my trapped feet, and reached out towards where I had seen the faint light; but now I could no longer see it. I moved my hands up and down, and from side to side, and suddenly I touched a beam of wood, seeming on a level with the thing which held my feet.

I gripped the beam and pulled and pushed at it, but it never moved; and therewith I put my weight on it and leaned more forward still; and so in an instant I touched a second beam.

I tried whether this second beam would hold me, and found it as firm and solid as the first. I put my weight on to it, using my left hand, and reached out my right hand, carrying myself forward, until suddenly I saw the light again, and had a slight feeling of heat not far below my face.

I put my hand towards the faint light and touched something. It was my own dark lantern. I could have cried out aloud with the joy of my discovery. I fumbled open the hinged cap that was shut over the glass, and instantly there was light upon everything near me.

A new amazement came to me as I discovered that I was yet in the bedroom, and the lamp was still upon the chair with my pistols, and that my feet had been trapped by the bed itself; for the two beams that I had felt were the supporting skeleton of one side of the heavy-made bedstead, and the mattress had shut up like a monstrous book; and what had been its middle part was now rested upon the floor of the bedroom, between the beams of its upholding framework, whilst the top edges had closed firmly upon my feet and ankles, so that I was held like a trapped rat. And a cunning and brutal machine of death the great bedstead was, and would have crushed the breath and the life out of my body in a moment had I been lying flat upon the mattress as a man does in sleep.

Now, as I regarded all this, with a fiercer and ever fiercer growing anger, I heard again the low sound of a woman weeping somewhere in the house, as if a door had been suddenly opened and let the sound come plain. Then it ceased, as if the door had been closed again.

Now, I saw that I must do two things. The one was to make no noise to show that I still lived, and the second was to free myself as speedily as I could. But first I snatched up my lamp and flashed it all round the big bedroom, and upon the door; but it was plain to me that there was no one gotten into the room, yet there might be a secret way in I now conceived, for how else should they come in to remove the dead if the door of the room were locked, just as I, indeed, had locked it before I made to sleep?

However, the first thing I shaped to do was to get free, and I caught up my knife from the chair and began to cut into the great box-mattress where the padding was nailed down solid with broad-headed clouts.

But all the time that I worked I harked very keen for any sound in the room that might show whether they were coming yet for my body. And I worked quick but quiet, so that I should make no noise, yet I smiled grim to myself to think how strange a corpse they should have to welcome them, and how lively a welcome!

And suddenly, as I worked, there came a faint creaking of wood from the far side of the big, dark room where stood one of the great clothes-cupboards. I stabbed my big knife into one of the edges of the closed mattress where it would be ready to my hand in the dark, and instantly closed the cover over my dark lantern and stood it by the knife. Then, in the darkness, I reached for my pistols from the chair seat, and the small one I stood by the knife, pushing the end of the barrel down between the mattress edges, so that its butt stood up handily for me to grip in the dark.

I caught up my two great pistols in my fists, and stared round me as I squatted, harking with a bitter eagerness, for it was sure enough that I must fight for my life, and, maybe, I should be found in the morning far out on the moor, like poor James Naynes was found. But of one thing I was determined, there should go two or three that night to heaven or to hell, and the choice I left with them, for it was no part of my business, but only to see that the earth was soundly rid of them.

Now there was a space of absolute silence, and then again I heard the creaking sound from the far end of the room. I stared hard that way, and then took a quick look round me, through the dark, to be sure that my ears had told me truly the direction of the sounds.

When I looked back again, there was a light inside the great cupboard, for I could see the glow of it around the edges of the door.

I knew now that there must be a hidden way into the bedroom, coming in through the back of the cupboard, which must be made to open; but I smiled a little to remember that I had locked the door, which had a very good and stout brass lock.

Yet I learned quickly enough that this was not likely to bother the men, for after I had heard them press upon the door, there was a low muttering of voices from within the cupboard, and then a sound of fumbling against the woodwork, and immediately there was a squeak of wood, and one end of the cupboard swung out like a door, and all that end of the bedroom was full of light from the lamp they had inside the cupboard.

In the moment when the end of the cupboard swung out there

came to me the sudden knowledge that I must not be seen until the murderers were all come into the room, otherwise they would immediately give back into the cupboard before I could kill them. And I should indeed be in a poor case if they fetched up a fowling-piece to shoot at me; for they could riddle me with swan-shot, or the like, by no more than firing round the edge of the great oak cupboard; and I tethered there by the feet and helpless as a sheep the moment I had fired off my pistols!

Now, all this reasoning went through my brain like a blaze of lightning for speed, and in the same moment I had glanced round me, for the light from the cupboard was sufficient to show those things that were near me. I saw that there was half of a coverlid draped out from between the two edges of the great trap, and I snatched at it, and had it over me in a trice, and was immediately crouched there silent upon the edge of the mattress, as if I were simply a heap of the bed-clothing that had not been caught in the trap.

I had no more than covered myself and crouched still, when I heard the men stepping into the room.

"It's sure got un proper!" I heard the voice of the knock-kneed Llan say.

And he crowed out one of his shrill, foolish laughs.

"There'll be less of these king's agents an' the like after this!" I heard Jalbrok's voice growl.

"Gglag the swine!" came a familiar voice. "I'll put my knife into un, to make sure. Why, blow me if he don't know enough to gaol us all."

"There'll be no need o' knives," said Jalbrok; "an if there is, it's me that does it. He's my lodger!"

"Share plunder alike! Share plunder alike!" said another voice from the cupboard, by the sound of it.

And then there was the noise of heavy feet approaching, and the sound of scuffling in the big cupboard, as if a number of the brutish crew were fighting to get their clumsy bodies into the room, all in a great haste to see how the death trap had worked.

In that instant, and when the men were no farther from the bed than five or six paces, I hove the covering clean off me, and stood up on my trapped feet, but keeping my two great pistols behind my back, for I had them all now at my mercy.

I think they thought in that first moment that I was a ghost by the howl of terror that some of them sent up to heaven. Such a brutish crew no man need have paused to shoot down; yet I did, for I wished to see what they would do now that I had discovered myself to them.

They had, all of them, their belt-knives in their hands, as if they had meant to thrust them into my dead body rather than let no blood. The landlord carried a lantern in one hand and a pig-sticker's knife, maybe two feet long from haft to point, in the other, and his eyes shone foully with the blood-lust such as you will see once in a lifetime in the red eyes of a mad swine.

So they had all of them stopped as I rose, and some had howled out, as I have told, in their sudden fear, thinking I was dead, and had risen in vengeance, as was seemly enough to their ignorant minds.

But now Jalbrok, the landlord, held his lantern higher, and drew the flat of his knife across his great thigh.

"Good-morning, mine host and kind friends all," I said gently. "Wherefore this rollicking visit? Am I invited to join you in jollying the small hours, or does Master Gglag, you with the open mouth there, desire my help in the landing of good liquor from the sea?"

"Slit him!" suddenly roared Jalbrok, with something like a pig's squeal in the note of his voice. "Slit him!"

And therewith he rushed straight at me with the pig-sticker, and the rest of that vile crew of murdering brutes after him. But I whipped my two great pistols from behind my back, and thrust them almost into their faces; and blood-hungry though they were, like wild beasts, they gave back like dogs from a whip, and the landlord with them.

"In the name of James Naynes, whom ye destroyed in this same room," I said quietly.

And I fired my right hand pistol at Jalbrok, and saw his face crumble, and he fell, carrying the lamp, and a man further back in the room tumbled headlong. The lamp had gone out when the landlord fell, and the room was full of a sound like the howling of frightened animals. There was a mad rush in the darkness for the great oak cupboard, and I loosed off again with my left-hand pistol into the midst of the noise; and immediately there were several screams, and a deeper pandemonium. I heard furniture thrown about madly, and some of the men seemed to have lost their bearings, for I heard the crash of broken glass as they blundered into the far window.

Then I had my lamp in my hands, and my third pistol. I opened the shutter, and shone the light upon the blundering louts; and as they got their bearings in the light there was a madder scramble than before to escape through the cupboard.

I did not shoot again, but let them escape, for I judged they had seen sufficient of me to suit their needs for that one night. And to prove that I was right, I heard them go tumbling away out of the front doorway at a run. And after that there was a great quietness throughout the inn.

I threw the light upon the men on the floor. Jalbrok and his murdering helpman appeared both to be dead, but there were three others who groaned, but were not greatly hurt, for when I called out to them to go before I shot them truly dead, they were all of them to their knees in a moment, and crept along the floor into the cupboard, and so out of my sight.

I had my feet free of the trap in less than the half of an hour, and went over to the men upon the floor, who were both as dead as they deserved to be.

Then I loaded my pistols, and, with one in each hand, I entered the cupboard, and found, as I had supposed, a ladder reared up within a big press that stands in the taproom from floor to ceiling, and the top of which is the floor of the cupboard in the bedroom. So that I was wrong when I thought, maybe, that there had been a false back to it.

I found the wench locked in a small pantry place where she slept, and when she saw me alive she first screamed, and then kissed me so heartily that I gave her a good honest guinea piece to cease; also because I was grateful to the lass for her regard for my safety.

Regarding the great machine in the bedroom, I made a close examination of this, and found that the hinged centre of the monstrously heavy mattress was supported upon a strut which went down into the taproom through the great central beam that held the ceiling up, and was kept in place by an oak peg, which passed through the beam and the supporting strut. It was when they went to knock the peg out that the wench screamed, and the two blows I heard beneath the bed were the blows of the hammer on the peg.

And so I have discovered, as I set out to do, the way in which poor James Naynes met his death, and my hands have been chosen to deal out a portion of the lawful vengeance which his murderers had earned.

But I have not yet finished with this district – not until I have rooted out, neck and crop, the ruthless and bloodthirsty band that do their lawless work in this lonesome part of the king's domain.

# THE SPIRIT OF THE '76
## Lillian de la Torre

*Within only a few days of the publication of* The Mammoth Book of Historical Whodunnits, *I was very saddened to learn of the death of Lillian de la Torre in September 1993 at the remarkable age of 91. For fifty years she had painstakingly (and all too infrequently) produced a series of clever stories in which Samuel Johnson resolved crimes and mysteries of his day, his investigations faithfully recorded by his equivalent of Dr Watson, James Boswell. The stories, all originally published in* Ellery Queen's Mystery Magazine, *have been collected in four volumes:* Dr Sam: Johnson, Detector *(1946),* The Detections of Dr Sam: Johnson *(1960),* The Return of Dr Sam: Johnson *(1985) and* The Exploits of Dr Sam: Johnson *(1987), with two subsequent stories remaining uncollected. Although spread over nearly fifty years the series totals only thirty-three stories, and now there will be no more.*

*Occasionally, Miss de la Torre would take liberties with history. Sam Johnson and Benjamin Franklin never met, but this story seeks to explore what might have happened had they done so. Apparently Franklin was rather bitter toward Johnson because of an anti-American pamphlet he had written,* Taxation No Tyranny, *in 1775. In December 1776, Franklin was at sea on his way to France, and it would not have taken much to have blown him off course to England. Here is a little of history revisited.*

"Free and equal!" growled Dr Sam: Johnson in high dudgeon. "All men, forsooth, created equal! What is to become of the proper order and subordination of society, if such frantick levelling doctrines are to prevail? Free and equal! Signed, John Hancock! Mark my words, sir, we shall yet see this fellow's head spiked above Temple Bar!"

"Is he sole authour of this independent declaration?" I wondered, for secretly I admired it.

"No, sir. This treasonous manifesto comes, I am told, from the pen of a planter named Jefferson, aided and abetted by Benjamin Franklin."

"Dr Franklin!" said I. "Now there's a head that would ill become Temple Bar. I dined in his company once, sir, some years since, and found him an agreeable companion, and moreover an ingenious contriver of devices to improve the lot of man, as his Pennsylvania fire place, his lightning rod, *et caetera*."

"I, too, Bozzy, have encountered the fellow. He was presiding at a meeting of benevolent gentlemen associated to provide education for the unfortunate Negroes of the New World. He then appeared to be a sincere friend to humanity, not at all addicted to republican phrenzy. Yet more's the pity, sir, he's a traitor to his King, and belongs on the scaffold with the rest of them!"

"Would you put him there?"

"Aye would I, and twenty such, let me but come in sight of them!"

"Which you are not like to do," I remarked. "They are safe on the other side of the water. Why should any of them put his head in the lion's mouth?"

"There you are out, sir, that same Franklin is now, they warn us, on the high seas, making for France – "

I doubted it not. Dr Johnson had recently made his pen useful to the Ministry, and his sources of information were many.

"– so that we may hope that a tempest will drive him upon our shores, or a man-o'-war catch him and bring him hither."

I hoped not; but I said no more. As to the dispute with our fellow subjects across the sea, Dr Johnson and I differed widely. Now that, with the Declaration of Independence, the breach had come, my friend was vehemently wishing success to our arms in putting down the insurgents; while, despite all, I wished them well, and desired they might all escape Jack Ketch.

This conversation took place in December of the year '76, in my philosophical friend's commodious dwelling in Bolt Court, Fleet Street. Tall, broad and bulky, in his full-skirted grey coat and broad stuff breeches, his little brown scratch-wig perched above his wide brow, he stood in the many-paned sash-window, looking down on the court. I felt once more a strong satisfaction that I, James Boswell, an advocate of North Britain thirty years his junior, was so often privileged to observe his proceedings as *detector* of crime and chicane. At that moment no problem engaged his massive intellect, unless the treason of America's rabid revolutionaries; but that situation was about to change.

As I stood at his shoulder looking down, a coach drew up with a jingle, and a lone woman descended, muffled in a dun-coloured capuchin. Another moment, and black Francis ushered her in to us. She burst into speech at once:

"Forgive my lack of ceremony, Dr Johnson. Your goodness is known so widely, I make bold to beg you – the child is stolen away, Dr Johnson! He's only seven, what am I to do?"

She choked back a sob. Dr Johnson took her slender hand and gently led her to the armed chair by the fire.

She was a small creature of a certain age, her soft face gently wrinkled, her grey hair pulled up in a plain pompadour above direct blue eyes now stained with tears.

"Be comforted, ma'am, we'll find him," said Dr Johnson reassuringly; "but you must tell me all you know of the matter."

"I will try. I am Mrs Stevenson – Margaret is my name. I dwell in Craven Street, Strand, and thence Benny has been spirited away."

"Your grandson, madam?"

"No, sir, but committed to my charge, and dearly loved."

"Perhaps he has wandered away?" I hazarded.

"No, sir, Benny was whipping his top before the door, when two men came by and carried him off. A servant saw from the window."

"Why did he not follow?"

"The wench is a she, and not over-bright. She formed the opinion that Benny was arrested by bailiffs, and knew not what was proper to do. I was from home, and only learned of the matter upon my return. What can they want of the boy? I have no money to buy him back."

"If he's to be bought back," remarked Dr Sam: Johnson, "we shall soon hear. Meanwhile, let us look over the ground in Craven Street."

In the modest dwelling in Craven Street, the wench Katty was stubborn, being what Dr Johnson is wont to denominate a "mule fool." She set her long jaw and stood to it. Master Benny was in the hands of the law. Time was wasted on her, before she remembered to say to her mistress:

"And, ma'am, there's a billet handed in for the gentleman – "

Mrs Stevenson seized it, scanned it, and extended it to my friend. At a sign, I moved to his elbow to share it with him.

Dear Doctor:

As you regard Benny, see that you present yourself at the Cat & Fiddle in Bow Street, this Day at five of the clock, & you shall hear further. Come alone. Fail us not, at Benny's Peril.

> I am, Sir,
> As you shall deal in this,
> Your Friend

Dr Johnson turned the missive in his strong, well-shaped fingers.

"Hm – paper of the best quality – a fair copying hand – this was never writ by a parcel of bum-bailiffs. Well, well, Mrs Stevenson, I'll present myself as directed, to hear further as they promise. There is not long to wait."

"O sir, you'll never go alone!"

"I must, at Benny's peril. But Boswell shall be handy, in case of trickery."

Thus it was that before five of the clock I was approaching the Cat & Fiddle, alert to detect the miscreants we had come to meet. As I neared the lighted doorway in the foggy darkness, my eye fell on a tall, burly figure in the shadow. At first I thought it was Dr Sam: Johnson himself in outlandish disguise, for the fellow was his replica in height and breadth. His powerful figure was enveloped in a vast coat of bull's hide, and a large fur cap was pulled down over his straggling grey locks. He wore a pair of cracked spectacles set in wire, and carried a porter's coil of rope. As I approached, he moved off, and I entered the Cat & Fiddle.

I was established on the fireside settle with a pint, when the door squeaked open, and a couple of rough-looking fellows made their appearance. Katty perhaps had not been so foolish, for sure enough they looked very like bum-bailiffs. Like bailiffs they took up their station on either side of the door. The potboy gave them a look, and discreetly vanished.

Another squeak, and Dr Sam: Johnson stood in the doorway. He was wrapped in his large dark grey greatcoat, and his cocked hat was firmly tied down by a knitted scarf.

From left and right the two fellows closed in and seized him.

"We arrest you," cried the smaller of the two triumphantly, "in the King's name!"

"Arrest me, ye boobies!" cried Dr Johnson. "What call have you to arrest me? Everyone knows me: I am Dr Johnson."

"O aye, Dr Johnson, Dr Brown, Dr Robinson, 'tis all one. We know you, Doctor, right enough, you must come along with us."

"I'll come with you to the magistrate in Bow Street, and no further," growled Dr Johnson.

"You're wanted elsewhere."

"What's the charge?"

The big one with the stupid face swelled up to proclaim it, but the ferret-nosed little one plucked his sleeve.

"Stubble your whids, Ned, 'ware rescue, we are not alone (jerking a gesture in my direction). There's a great price on this fellow's head. Do you want to share it?"

"Carry me before Sir John Fielding," insisted Dr Johnson. "We'll see if there's a price on my head!"

They hustled him off. I set down my pot and followed. It was but a step along Bow Street to the Publick Office. Beside the doorway a lighted lanthorn flickered. As we approached, the catchpolls began to edge their captive away from the light, when Dr Johnson with a powerful motion jerked suddenly from their grasp. Simultaniously the big pandour was pulled off his feet by the loop of a porter's rope.

Dr Johnson collared the ferrety one and dragged him inside, leaving Ned *hors de combat* on the pavement, and the doughty old porter vanished. Another moment, and the three of us stood in the publick room before the magistrate.

Sir John Fielding, the famous Blind Beak of Bow Street, sat quietly in the magistrate's chair, a large, handsome personage with venerable white locks and a fold of black silk over his sightless eyes. He turned his ear as we entered, and spoke in an edged voice:

"What, is it you, Greentree? There's no missing that effuvium of dirty linen and gin. What miscreants have you brought me?"

"I've taken up a traitor, sir, is wanted at the Ministry."

"Sir John," said Dr Johnson calmly, "the foolish fellow mistakes me for another."

Sir John, an old friend, knew the voice at once.

"Dr Johnson, your servant! And where is Mr Boswell? Not far away, I'll wager."

"Right here, Sir John, at your service."

Waiving courtesies, Dr Johnson at once adverted to the matter in hand.

"This Greentree," he said urgently, "baited me hither by stealing a child and sending this billet."

He began to read it out.

"I know nothing of your billet," muttered Greentree. "'Twas writ at the Ministry. I had only to nap the kid, which I did – arrest the Doctor when he broke cover, which I did – and fetch him to the Minister."

"What Doctor?"

"My Lord did not say."

"He gave you a warrant?"

"Well, no, sir, 'twas to be done in secret."

"Illegality upon illegality!" remarked Sir John. "Where is the child? Discover him, or you shall be the worse for it."

"In Water Lane," uttered the fellow grudgingly.

Instanter a posse of constables, with Greentree pinioned in their midst, conducted us to Water Lane. Our captive led us to a miserable hovel at the water's edge, where a slatternly harpy whined:

"Which I kept him secure as you bade me. He's locked in the loft that looks on the river. This way, gentlemen, you shall see he's safe enough."

The rusty key screeched in the lock, the door grated open. Dr Johnson started forward; but save for a small pair of buckled shoes, the room was empty. The cracked casement swung on one hinge. We looked out in dismay on the brown waters of Thames. Had the child been done away with in this lair?

Sir John's men took up the cursing woman, and bore her with Greentree off to the roundhouse, there to be sifted further. We were left to make our way back to Craven Street with news of our failure.

With heavy hearts we mounted the slope. I liked the neighbourhood ill. Fleet Ditch stank. Ragamuffins prowled or slept in doorways. Trulls loitered, and bullies swaggered. Once I thought I glimpsed the burly old porter with his rope, but then he was gone again in the darkness.

As the street rose, out of the foggy dark one more ragamuffin appeared. This one approached us confidently, a sandy-haired, solid-built little boy, shoeless and dripping wet. As we paused, he recited in a clear voice:

"Please, sir, my name is Benjamin Franklin Bache, I dwell at Craven Street in the Strand. My new Granny is Mrs Stevenson. Will you take me to her?"

"What, boy, did you say Benjamin Franklin?"

"He is my grandfather."

"Well, well, Bozzy, it appears there is more in this than meets the eye. Where is your grandfather, boy?"

"In Craven Street, sir."

"Then," said Dr Johnson, "in the King's name, on to Craven Street!"

We wrapped the shivering child in my waistcoat, and set a brisk pace. As he trotted along between us, he readily told what had befallen him.

"The men, they said they were officers of police, and I must come along. I didn't like them. I misliked the old witch too. I waited and waited for my grandfather to come. I was hungry and cold, and I went away from there."

"Went away! How?"

"Through the window, sir."

"In the *water*?" I ejaculated, dumfounded, since I cannot swim a stroak. "What, little boy, can you swim?"

"My grandfather," said the child with pride, "is the greatest swimmer in the world, and he taught me. 'Twas but a few stroaks to the nearest water stair."

"I can swim further than that," the small voice chattered on. "When the sloop was like to founder in the storm, my grandfather bade me fear nothing, we could swim for it. But the *Reprisal* made her way to shore at Hoy Cove, and as soon as the Westcombe men have put her to rights, we'll away to France."

"Will you so, my boy?" said Dr Johnson drily.

"Yes, indeed, sir. – I'm sleepy," he added with a prodigious yawn, and fell silent.

We arrived at Craven Street without further parley. Mrs Stevenson fell on the child with transport, but Dr Johnson held him fast.

"I claim the privilege," he said, "of restoring Dr Franklin's grandson to his arms myself."

Mrs Stevenson looked affrighted, but could not gainsay him. She ushered us to the two-pair-of-stairs parlour.

"Benny!" The sturdy old gentleman by the fire held out his arms, and the boy flew into them.

I stared. Gone were the bull's-hide coat and the porter's rope; but the fur cap and the spectacles remained to tell us that the old fellow who had dogged us on our errand was none other than Dr Franklin himself. I scanned the cheerful lined face. It was a face that had mellowed with the years, not handsome, but winning with its look of pleased surprise, as if perpetually astonished and gratified by the spectacle of the world in its infinite variety. The hazel eyes sparkled with a penetrating intelligence. Over the boy's tawny curls, the brilliant gaze turned to us.

"Dr Johnson, I believe?"

"Your servant, Dr Franklin."

"I am your debtor, sir," said Franklin stiffly, "little as I desire it. I regret that Margaret was so impulsive as to call upon your aid."

"Ben!" cried Mrs Stevenson softly, "we are much in Dr Johnson's debt for his efforts!"

"Dr Franklin knows," observed Dr Johnson, "for he trusted me so little. He dogged my every move in guise of a street porter."

"Trust?" exclaimed Franklin. "Why would I trust a man who wrote against us and counselled the Ministry to set upon us the Red Men and the Blacks?"

"You misread me, sir," said Johnson calmly. "True, I would give the Blacks their freedom, with means of sustenance and defence; from which, if memory serves, you yourself are not averse. And as to the raids of the Red Men, what else can you expect, if you renounce the protection of British arms?"

"The protection of British arms!" echoed Franklin bitterly. "It was British arms that shot down innocent people in the Boston Massacre!"

"We all deplore it, sir," conceded Johnson.

Franklin set down the boy from his lap.

"Make your bow, Benny, and go now with Granny."

The mannerly boy inclined solemnly to each of us, and left us. As Dr Franklin turned to us with an air of dismissal, a newcomer erupted into the room. From the tall form, the long dark face, the Satanick quirk of the black eyebrows, I recognized him with mixed emotions. It was Sir Francis Flashwood, he who raised the Devil in the caves under Hoy Head, whose witching daughter I had once thought to woo, whose Coven we had quelled at Westcombe in the '68 (all which I have set forth at large in my account of "The Westcombe Witch").

We had heard of that gentleman's doings since then, how with his close friend Benjamin Franklin he had "reformed" the Prayer Book – Satan rebuking sin? – how as Lord LeSpenser he had gone into politicks, acting as Postmaster General to such effect that he was now respectable, and the Westcombe Blacks were heard of no more.

Now he paid us not the slightest heed, but rushed to Franklin crying:

"Up, Ben, there's not a minute to waste! There's a plot against you at the Ministry. I have it on the surest advices. Since you are too elusive to be caught, they will lay hands on Benny, and so force you to come in, to who knows what fate – "

"Why, Francis," said Franklin calmly, "I thank you, but your warning is belated – "

"What, they have him?"

"No, no, dear friend, the attempt has been made, but it has been frustrated by Dr Johnson here."

For the first time my Lord's eyes focused upon us where we stood by the fire.

"Dr Johnson," he said wryly. "Yes, a notable frustrater. And Mr Boswell too. How do you, Sir Brimstone of Tophet?"

"Well, I thank you, sir," said I, grandly ignoring this allusion to my diabolical misadventures in the caves at Westcombe, "and how does your lovely daughter, Miss Fan?"

"Fan is wed to her cousin Talley. She lives in the West Country and raises a numerous progeny. But there's no time for gossip. Dr Franklin is in the gravest danger. O Ben, Ben, you might have been safe at Westcombe, why would you insist on coming up to London?"

"Money, business, and love," smiled Franklin, "what other human motives are there? To fetch the gold intended for the cause, to recover my papers, and to see once more my dear Mistress Margaret."

"Let us hope your recklessness will not cost you all three, and life besides. We must depart for Westcombe with all speed. My travelling coach stands waiting at the door, and the men of the Westcombe Blacks are a-horse and ready to escort us."

"A desperate set of men," remarked Dr Johnson. "I had thought them won over to the side of the law."

"Well, sir," Sir Francis smiled thinly, "not entirely, when my friend's life is at stake. For him they'll do their utmost. And you, Dr Johnson, what will you do for us? The issue now is greater than a few French bales. Will you keep silence?"

Johnson said nothing, and I struck in:

"You have *my* parole, sir. I wish the Americans only good."

"Then you may go, Mr Boswell."

"Not if Dr Johnson remains."

"He remains," said Sir Francis emphatically. "We cannot have him running to Lord North behind our backs."

"Tut, sir, I told you once, I am no catchpoll."

"And I believe you, Dr Johnson," said Franklin quietly.

"No, Ben, we cannot risk it. He shall go with us to Westcombe."

I started forward to protest, but Dr Johnson shook his head at me. I shrugged, and composed myself for the journey.

Now all was bustle. Papers were bagged, portmanteaus slammed shut, hampers filled with viands. Benny, dried off and warmly cloathed anew, was swathed in shawls and tucked in a corner of the travelling carriage, where he promptly fell asleep. In the hurly-burly, we might easily enough have slipped away, but Dr Johnson unaccountably sat on in smiling calm.

Soon we stood at the door bidding adieu. Franklin took little Margaret Stevenson warmly in his arms, and embraced her tenderly.

"Farewell once more, my dear, and once more, thanks for years together of sunshine without cloud. Let us be grateful to the storm which blew me hither and allowed us to meet for one more time; and if we never meet again, remember me."

We left her weeping in the doorway as we rolled off into the night. The dark-clad figures of the Westcombe Blacks closed in about us with silent hooves, and so we trotted briskly out of town and took the road towards the sea. No spies dogged us. The misadventure of Benny had clearly put the Ministry forces in disarray. If we could only get clear before they rallied!

It was a long way to go, to the harbour at Westcombe, where lay the *Reprisal*, refitted now and ready to slip her cable for France. The Westcombe Blacks had smoothed our way. Fresh horses awaited us at posting-houses, where we could refresh while the ostlers bustled, and the Westcombe men waited upon us – and watched us – attentively.

At first we rode together in stiff silence, which merged into sleep as exhausted nature claimed her due.

The day dawned sunny. We explored the contents of the hampers, and then sat back invigorated. The coach was new and commodious, smelling of leather and horseflesh and creaking lightly on easy springs. I regarded my companions. Sir Francis, clad in a bottle-green cloak with multiple capes, lounged in his corner, his watchful dark eyes fixed on Dr Johnson; who, for his part, sat complaisantly smiling with the pleasure he always derived from the swift motion of a carriage.

Dr Franklin in his snuff-coloured greatcoat wore neither wig nor hat, but that same fur cap, like a brown bee-hive, pulled down almost to his spectacles; through the round panes of which, he drank in the passing prospect. Next him sat small Benny, emerged from his cocoon. In the smiling quirk of his small upper lip and the brilliance of his eyes, the resemblance to his grandfather was strong.

It was impossible we should continue in sullen silence. My companions were men of wit and ingenuity, and had much to say to one another if it could but be brought out. And who should bring it out better than your humble servant, James Boswell? If I had been able to reconcile my stern friend to that devil Jack Wilkes – as I recently had done – it would go hard but I would bring Johnson and Franklin together.

Warmed by my breakfast glass, I first undertook to kindle the atmosphere with one of my own songs. I considered the bawdy strophes of "Gunter's Chain": Sir Francis would certainly relish it, and Dr Franklin with his almost-smiling mouth looked receptive. But I glanced at the lofty countenance of my moral mentor, and instead trolled out a stave of my ditty celebrating "Currant Jelly."

Franklin then reciprocated with a convivial drinking song of his own composition, writ, he said, some thirty years since, in praise of friendship and wine. His voice was husky, but true.

> "Then toss off your glasses and scorn the dull asses
>     Who missing the kernel still gnaw the shell.
> What's love, rule, or riches? Wise Solomon teaches
>     They're vanity, vanity, vanity still,
>         For honest souls know
>     Friend and a bottle still bear the bell."

"On this we can all agree," I exclaimed, "for Dr Johnson is wont to bid us, 'Keep your friendships in repair'."

"And in my country," replied Dr Franklin, "the Red Indians have a saying, 'Keep the chain of friendship bright'."

"What, has Benny no song to sing?" prompted Flashwood, smiling at the bright-eyed little boy.

At this Benny shrilled out a jolly jig tune entitled "Yankee Doodle."

> "Father and I went down to camp
>     Along with Cap'n Good'in,
> And there we saw the men and boys
>     As thick as hasty puddin'.
>         Yankee Doodle, keep it up,
>         Yankee Doodle Dandy,
>     Mind the musick and the step
>         And with the girls be handy!"

"With the girls!" repeated Dr Johnson, unable to repress a smile. "A precocious Yankee Dandy, Benny, indeed!"

Encouraged by my friend's smiling regard, Benny prattled on in his small high tones:

"I shall go to school in France," he told Dr Johnson proudly, "and when we have won the war – "

"Won, my boy?"

"Yes, sir, of course we shall win." The clear voice rang out. "We'll fight the redcoats on the beaches, in the streets, if need be in the wilderness: and thereto we have pledged our lives, our fortunes, and our sacred honour!"

"Why," said Dr Johnson, still smiling, "what an eloquent young rebel it is!"

"An eloquent young parrot," observed my Lord. "That last flourish, if memory serves, was writ by Thomas Jefferson of Virginia."

"With the assistance," added the American, "of Benjamin Franklin of Pennsylvania."

"And such," concluded Flashwood, "is the spirit of the '76!"

"Cant!" muttered Johnson, and I hastily turned the subject.

"Pray, Dr Franklin, what projects have you to the fore for the good of mankind?"

The smile that touched his lip deepened, and for a moment I thought he would say "Freedom!" Instead he replied civilly:

"Why, sir, I have newly made observations on the Gulf Stream, on the Aurora Borealis, and on further improvements in opticks."

"There, sir, I heartily wish you success," said Dr Johnson, "for my eyes serve me ill, and I have found no spectacles by which I can both read and view the world about me. I have wondered whether one might not be able to combine the two functions by joining two pieces of glass into one pane, the lower for reading, the upper for looking afar."

"Why, sir," replied Franklin, smiling, "not only can it be done, I have done it: as you may see by the spectacles I wear."

He took them off and handed them over. Johnson brought them up close to his near-sighted eyes and examined them attentively. I saw now that what I had hastily, in the half light of Bow Street, taken for cracks, were really the lines where two half circles joined.

"Ingenious!" said Dr Johnson, and put them to his eyes. After a moment he handed them back, shaking his head regretfully.

"They will not serve my turn."

"Of course not," said Franklin, "each double pane must be suited to the eye that wears it. Well, sir, when I come to France – if I am so fortunate – I purpose to set the lens-makers to work. If all goes well, you shall hear of this further."

Chatting thus of matters scientifick, we passed the rest of the morning in amity.

"You were right, Bozzy," said my friend in my ear at the next posting-house, "that's too well-furnished a head to let the Ministry have it to adorn Temple Bar!"

The sun was well past the meridian when with a sense of relief we rolled in to the village of Westcombe. There we turned in at the Admiral's Head, that our voyagers might recruit before going aboard the *Reprisal*. The master shipwright awaited us with the welcome news that she rode well and was ready for sea. His men at once carried off the baggage while we took a glass.

A sound of hooves thudding our way in hot haste broke our complacency, and a breathless youth flung into our presence.

"The redcoats, my Lord!" he cried. "We have been betrayed! Some one has given the word at Carnock Castle, and the troopers are riding this way to apprehend us. They cannot be ten minutes behind me!"

"Keep watch, Gannett!" commanded Sir Francis. "Up, Ben, we'll go by the caves. That way it is but two minutes to safety!"

I remembered the caves of Westcombe with their secret passage to the harbour, and took heart. But almost at once Gannett was back in the room, crying:

"They're coming, my Lord, they are at the top of the street. We are all trapped!"

Dr Sam: Johnson rose resolutely to his feet.

"Not yet. Give me a horse, and I'll draw them off."

"*You*, Dr Johnson," exclaimed Franklin, "you'll do so much for America?"

"Let us say I'll do it for Benny. Quickly, Doctor, here's a wig in exchange for your fur hat, and a grey coat for your brown one – "

The exchange was made, and most convincing it appeared, for the two tall, burly old men, tho' unlike in face, were of an age, and much alike in figure and bearing.

With the briefest of farewells we took horse in the inn yard; the gates were opened; we set spur and dashed into the street. Not a hundred yards away we perceived the redcoats trotting our way with a measured jingle of harness. Johnson wheeled his horse with a roar, and with incredulity I heard the words that he roared:

"Long live the United States of America!"

"Hold your fire!" cried the officer in the lead. "After him, for he's to be taken alive!"

In this coil it was well that in the '68 we had learned to know the ways of Westcombe. By a byway we left the town, and galloped away over the down.

Dr Johnson always said he rode harder at a fox-chace than anybody, and he rode harder now. Had I not been mounted on as swift a horse, and riding lighter in the saddle, I could not have kept pace with him. As it was, too soon our mounts were blown, and the soldiers cornered us in a fold of the hills.

"Benjamin Franklin," cried the lanky young officer, "I arrest you on a charge of high treason! And your accomplice too," he added with a jerk of his head towards me.

"Whither do you carry us?" I demanded.

"To London, sir, with all speed."

Johnson said nothing. The less he said, in his Litchfield accent, the less would our captors suspect trickery; and the longer we went unsuspected, the better the *Reprisal*'s chances of making good her escape to France. The soldiers closed in, and so we began the weary way back to London.

As we crossed the brow of the hill, we glimpsed the blue of the bay, and the schooner with all sails set standing out to sea for France. I sent a wordless wish after it: Success to your mission!

The return journey seemed interminable; but at last we entered London Town. Whither would our captors lead us now? Bow Street, Newgate Prison, the Tower? Had we seen the last of the sun?

Instead, the young lieutenant set our course for the fashionable end of the town, and drew rein before a handsome house in Grosvenor Square. Stiffly we dismounted and followed our guide within. Knocking, he flung wide a door, and announced with a flourish:

"My Lord, I have the honour to present – Dr Benjamin Franklin!"

A man with a star on his coat rose smiling from a marquetry writing table. By his florid face and prominent eyes, for one thunderstruck moment I thought him the King. Then I knew him for Lord North, the King's first Minister, about whose resemblance to his King courtiers talked behind their hands.

"My Lord!" Dr Johnson, who always prided himself on paying a nobleman the ceremony due him, removed the fur bee-hive and executed a stately bow. My Lord started, and peered close. The smile dissolved in a frown.

"What nonsense is this, Leftenant? This man is not Dr Franklin, but Dr Sam: Johnson, to whom I am indebted for political pamphleteering. By G-d, I am ill served by clodpates! Leave us, fellow! (The crestfallen soldier withdrew.) And you, Dr Johnson? What do you here in a rebel's coat? Have you turned your coat in earnest?"

Dr Johnson glowered. Tho' he upheld my Lord's politicks, he despised his person.

"I am no turncoat, my Lord," he replied sturdily. "I reprehend rebellion as much as ever I did. Yet when a man is to be secretly trepanned – and that man a benefactor of mankind – without colour of law, at the expense of a child, and for what clandestine purpose? Secret assassination, perhaps?"

"Not so!" cried North, stung, but Johnson swept on:

"Then I shall do what I can to save my country from such infamy.

If my company can protect, no matter how, my company shall be afforded."

"That explains," I cried, enlightened, "why you submitted – "

Johnson gave me a look which silenced me, and continued coolly:

"The Leftenant's mistake has given me much fatigue, my Lord; I beg leave to withdraw."

Would leave be granted? In a swift vision I again saw the Tower and the scaffold before me. Then my Lord smiled coldly.

"As you perceive, Dr Johnson, this transaction, were it known, would make my Ministry a byword and a laughing-stock. You have leave to depart; and see that you both hold your tongues."

"Yours to command, my Lord. But give me leave to tell you, after hours spent in company with the American and his grandson, I can prophesy the end. For determination, bravery and ingenuity, the Americans have never seen their match, and I fear your Lordship will find it difficult to prevail against the spirit of the '76!"

# PART IV
# Regency and Gaslight

# DEADLY WILL AND TESTAMENT
## Ron Burns

*Just as I was putting the final touches to the last volume, I came across a copy of* Roman Shadows *by Ron Burns, set in the Rome of 43 BC. I learned Burns had written another such novel,* Roman Nights, *set at the end of the second century AD, after the death of Marcus Aurelius, though I've still not been able to obtain a copy of that. Soon after, he surfaced with a new character and a new series.* The Mysterious Death of Meriwether Lewis *(1993) and* Enslaved *(1994) feature Harrison Hull, a confidant of Thomas Jefferson. When I contacted Ron Burns to see if he might contribute to this anthology he readily agreed and produced a new Harrison Hull story. Like the two novels, this story is based on actual events that happened in Richmond, Virginia, in the early years of the nineteenth century.*

I am crouching in the dark in a tiny upstairs closet of a little house in Richmond, Virginia. There are two loaded pistols on the floor beside me and a dagger in my belt.

It is my fourth night of this . . . waiting. And there is a growing shrillness to my thoughts – if thoughts can be shrill: I am the one who found the arsenic. I pointed the finger of guilt. So why do *I* have to hunker down in hiding? Indeed, I wonder morosely, why am I here at all?

An unexpected sound! Vague, off in the distance. Even so, my heart pounds and I listen, breathless. I wait until . . . Nothing. Nothing more. It is, I decide, only the breeze that's come up, or maybe just the house itself. I wipe the back of my hand across my forehead. It is hot in this closet, hot all over Richmond in fact – as always in the summer.

Richmond! That's where this nightmare started back in . . . God, is it nearly two months already? I'd planned to be here just a few days to attend a cousin's wedding. And it could have been that brief – I admit it. My family matters finished quickly, and it could be argued that what kept me was, strictly speaking, none of my business. But I've never been much for doing the predictable, especially when a friend was involved, or even a friend of a friend. In this case, a man named George Wythe was at the center of a series of events that would engulf us all.

Wythe had once been law tutor to President Jefferson and was one of the hallowed signers back in '76. There was even a little reception for him (the day before my relative's nuptials) to mark the thirtieth anniversary of the event, and I dropped by his house, which was just down the street, to pay my respects. Before that I'd met him only twice, but his rare blend of worldly wit and avuncular demeanor made him easy to admire and impossible to forget. So when trouble came I could hardly shrug it off. Indeed, taking a hand in the matter seemed unavoidable. Even inevitable.

What's that! I jump at another distant noise, probably a creaking step or floorboard. I reach for one of the pistols, but realize it is only Duval in his nightshirt heading for the water closet. As a precaution against even the chance of being overheard, I have ordered him not to talk to me after dark. But tonight, walking past, he hears my agitated breathing and stops just outside the closet door.

"You all right, Harry?" he asks very, very softly.

I tell him I am, and he shuffles away. And I cannot help smiling at the small irony of his unflappable obedience. For this is Duval's house, after all, his closet in which I hide these nights, waiting. It is also his work that has made this possible. For William Duval is a famous calligrapher and, incidentally, the designer of Jefferson's famous polygraph copying machines, as well as several of his writing desks.

Yes, I'm all right, I tell him. But I realize more and more that my nerves are feeling the strain, and once again my mind wanders to the troubles. They began when the Wythe household was stricken right after supper on the seventh of July, two days after the wedding. At first they thought it was cholera – what a joke! – though they'd set it right soon enough. The doctors voiced their doubts and the lawyer opened the will and then old Wythe regained consciousness and told us everything. And then it had seemed so simple – open and shut, as the lawyers like to say. Yet somehow it had all gone terribly wrong.

Besides Wythe, two others were afflicted: Wythe's Negro house-keeper, Lydia Broadnax, and a light-skinned Negro boy of fifteen, Michael Brown. Brown died within a few hours, while Wythe and

Broadnax remained unconscious for days, barely alive. The news swept the city – as I say, the rumor was cholera – and I walked over to Wythe's next morning to have a look. I met the doctors, who after a few tongue-tied moments conceded that there were "questions" even then about the diagnosis. I also met Duval who helped me in the search.

The houses – Wythe's and my cousin's – were on stately Kingman Avenue, a tree-lined street of handsome Virginia-style brickfronts, cultivated southern voices, chirping birds and the occasional clink of crystal in the soft summer breezes. It seemed, in other words, to be a place as far removed from mayhem and murder as any place could be.

Wythe's house in particular was filled with the mementos of a lifetime: scrolls from William and Mary College celebrating his legal abilities, a framed letter of thanks from Jefferson, a plaque from the governor of Virginia, and countless trophies, letters, awards from one town or another, merchants' groups, farmers' associations. Silhouettes of his late wife dotted each room and hallway, and assorted trinkets and bric-a-brac were everywhere. Finally, there was a portrait of Wythe himself in the front parlor that hardly did him justice. It captured well enough his imposing gray mutton chops, but turned his lively bright eyes flat and dull and replaced his engaging smile with pursed lips and a hard, taciturn jaw.

I searched through all this, with Duval beside me, finally uncovering the small bottle on the floor of an upstairs hall closet (not unlike the one I am in now, it suddenly occurs to me) tucked behind a formidable pile of old clothes, obscure papers and assorted other junk. I was certain what it was almost at once because though the container was well-corked traces had spilled down the sides and the aroma was unmistakeable. Duval knew, as well.

"Arsenic," he gasped, his skin suddenly snow-white.

We also found a sealed packet of documents in Wythe's study that were almost certainly his last will and testament. With the old man clinging to life just down the hall, Duval refused even to discuss tearing it open. I said little – I was hardly about to press for so radical a breach of custom (radical, even in my view). Still, Duval kept arguing, more with himself, I realized, than me – until finally at his most adamant he seemed to find a way around his dilemma.

"That's it, I'll get the lawyer," he said excitedly. "If these must be opened, he must be present."

And off he dashed to the offices of Wythe's attorney, Edmund Randolph, a mile or so away.

As I waited, still casually looking around, someone else came to the house, someone I'd never met before but whose name I'd already heard many times that day.

"Do I know you, sir?" George Sweney said. He'd walked in on me in Wythe's parlor and stared for an uncertain minute or two. I stared back at the look of pure spoiled brat snobbery on his face: eyes narrowed mischievously, mouth turned up just at the corners. It was a look I'd seen and dealt with all my life. Truth be told, I'd used it myself now and then. So I rather enjoyed it now, from Sweney, and my apparent amusement seemed to sap a little of the smugness from his face – even though I was the interloper, after all. For Sweney was Wythe's nephew and lived in this house.

"Yes, Harrison Hull, we met briefly the other day," I lied. "At your uncle's reception. A happier circumstance."

I put out my hand in greeting, but he just looked me up and down a while longer, too long really, then finally said, "O-o-o-o-o-h, yes," stretching that out too long, as well. Right from the start, it was Sweney's trouble: He was always overdoing things a bit. At last he shook my hand with nicely contrived reluctance, and it was all I could do to keep from laughing out loud.

Now *that* is a dangerous sound, I think with another jump. Like a window, probably downstairs someplace, being forced open. This time I really grab one of the pistols and snap to my feet. I listen but hear only my own pulse, breath. Whoever he is he's taking his time, moving carefully, that's for certain. But what else should I have expected? There's a lot at stake, after all, and he's worked a long time, come a long way to get this far. So he's in no hurry; he won't get clumsy or careless now. I listen and wait, but still the silence closes in. Is there a solitary prison cell somewhere this quiet? I wonder. Or perhaps the tomb of an ancient Pharaoh? Yet even now I cannot clear my mind of events leading to this moment.

"I heard of the illness here, I came to inquire after your uncle," I told George Sweney with as grim a face as I could manage. I said it partly to be polite, but also as a distraction to keep from laughing. "Terrible thing," I added.

"Terrible, yes," he said. The posturing manner was suddenly gone and his face wore a truly forlorn expression, and I recalled the story: that the childless Wythe had taken in the orphaned Sweney and raised him as his own; that the two were more like devoted father and son than mere uncle and nephew.

"I suppose you can be thankful you weren't stricken with the others," I said.

Sweney, who had turned away to fondle some trinket on the fireplace mantle, abruptly faced me. And just for an instant I caught a wildly angry flash in his eyes. I suppose that was thoughtless – what I said, I decided.

"Pardon me, my apologies, I meant nothing by it," I added hastily. I even bowed my head slightly, and just as quickly Sweney's anger vanished.

Just then Wythe's front door burst open and in came Duval, a bit breathless, with Edmund Randolph right behind.

"George? You all right? How are they? Any change? How's your uncle? Miz Lydia?" The lawyer's questions boomed like so many cannon shots, reducing poor Sweney to a kind of stuttering befuddlement.

"I . . . I don't know. The doctors aren't – "

Again, the door burst open, this time admitting the doctors, who now had with them an entourage of stretcher bearers and attendants. Through the window I could see an ambulance waiting in the street.

"What . . . what is this?" Sweney said. His eyes suddenly sparkled with anger again and his mouth curled up indignantly.

"We're here to check on our patients, of course," one of the doctors said. His voice was so sweetly soothing I felt a flush of embarrassment. Is he another who tends to overdo? I wondered. Or is it me, after all? Have I been schooled so well for so long in the subtleties, the so-called nuances, of human deportment that any demonstrable tone or expression leaves me fairly overcome with feelings of derision?

"Yes, yes, I know," Sweney began, "but what's all – "

"The nurse will stay behind. To care for – "

"I see, that's fine, but – "

"And the bearers are here for Michael Brown's body."

"Oh no, no, no," Sweney shouted at once. "That stays here, for proper burial out back."

The doctor shook his head implacably. "I have an order from the judge," he said, pulling a paper from his inside coat pocket. As he showed it to Sweney, I glimpsed the other doctor already leading the bearers upstairs.

Sweney stared at the paper, then passed it to Randolph who cleared his throat and nodded. "It's all legal, George," he said.

"We want to examine his remains, George," the doctor added.

Sweney seemed on the verge of another protest, but stopped short when Randolph put a calming hand on his shoulder. In a few minutes the physicians were gone and the ambulance rumbled off down Kingman Avenue.

"Why wasn't this on file in my office, George?" the lawyer suddenly demanded, waving yet another set of papers in Sweney's face.

The nephew opened and closed his mouth. Clearly, this wasn't one of his better days. "I don't . . . What . . . what is it?"

"It's your uncle's will, and it's not something that should be left lying around the house," Randolph grumbled.

The lawyer scratched his chin, while Sweney breathed heavily, seemed about to speak once or twice, but finally said nothing at all. All the while, Duval hadn't said a word – and for that matter neither had I.

"And who are you again?" Randolph said. Suddenly I was the dubious object of his attention, and – I couldn't help it – I actually gulped with nervous anticipation. "Oh yes, Duval told me. Hull, is it?"

"Harrison Hull, yes sir," I said.

"And just what brings you here, Mr Hull?"

I looked into his dark, dour eyes and a frown that bordered on the ferocious. He was an imposing man, even intimidating, who obviously knew he was and enjoyed the effect. So I would have feigned a stammer just to please him – even if I really hadn't been a little overwhelmed and quite honestly at a rare loss for words.

"It's . . . Actually, it's, uh, Captain Hull, Mr Randolph."

"State militia?"

"United States Army, Mr Randolph. In the past I've done some special assignments for my friend, Meriwether Lewis. And for the President, as well."

Randolph nodded slowly, and I swear I detected a microscopic flicker of a smile on his lips.

"Lewis? The explorer? Not back from the wilds yet, is he?"

"No, not yet, sir. Everyone's expecting word any time now." I paused, but he just widened his eyes and cocked his head. "In any case, when Mr Jefferson heard I was coming to Richmond he asked me to look in on Mr Wythe if I could. Naturally, when I learned he was ill . . ."

I let my words trail off with a gesture of upturned palms, and Randolph simply stared and rubbed his chin.

"Well, yes," he finally said, half under his breath. "As to this – " He seemed to study the will a moment. "Quite out of the question to open it now, of course, with Wythe still alive." He wheezed and muttered some more, then pulled out a cigar and lit up. "Still, certain . . . questions arise . . ." He mumbled and drew several long puffs. Then, abruptly, in a commanding tone: "Be at my office. All three of you. Ten o'clock tomorrow morning."

And with that he wheeled around and left the house at once.

It's mild to say the meeting was full of surprises. "First, let me tell you that I've spoken with the doctors and they say cholera definitely was *not* the cause of Michael Brown's death," Randolph said with quiet dignity.

"What then?" Sweney asked. But Randolph simply waved him off, then, with more of a flourish in his voice, fairly intoned: "What I am about to do is both extraordinary in itself and, for this very reason, entirely off the record." After a brief pause — obviously (to me) for dramatic effect, he unsealed Wythe's will and read the principal provisions. Quite simply, they named the housekeeper, Lydia Broadnax, heir to Wythe's house and substantial other properties, and Michael Brown heir to half of Wythe's bank stock. Sweney would inherit the other half.

The big shock was what wasn't said — what didn't need to be said. For the will in effect affirmed the long-standing secret, the secret that was never to be spoken of except in hushed tones in darkened corners. Now, upon Wythe's death, it would become public; it would be — that hated word — official: that Broadnax was Wythe's mistress, and had been for many years, and that Michael Brown was their illegitimate mulatto son. As if to add to the jolt, to invite even greater scandal, the will named no less than the President of the United States, Thomas Jefferson, executor in charge of young Brown's "maintenance, education and other benefit."

I'd known the secret, or known of it, but never gave it much thought, only half believed it. Now, taken aback by the inevitable publicity to come, my jaw fell and I gasped. But no one joined me: Duval's usually flat, open features revealed a tinge of smugness, as if to say that naturally he'd known it all along. Sweney, always a tad disdainful, even sneering, could not hide the anger, the rage, he felt.

"Goddam!" I heard Sweney mutter, but there was no time to discuss the point. Right then, one of Wythe's houseboys burst in: "Massa Wythe" had regained consciousness, he told us, and wanted to see us at once. As there were no horses or carriage at the ready, we madly dashed the mile and a half to Wythe's house — Randolph, Duval and I all moving as quickly as we could, arriving quite out of breath. It was only as we climbed the little front stoop and opened the door that I realized Sweney was lagging far behind.

Aging though still vigorous a few days before, Wythe now lay withered and trembling as he spoke in halting tones. "Poisoned," he whispered the moment we entered the room. "Arsenic." He stopped, apparently exhausted by the effort. Or was he just overcome? With anger, perhaps? Or remorse? "Like my own son," he said.

Just then, Sweney came in and that seemed to oddly invigorate him. "Sweney did it," he said, his voice suddenly firm and clear and unmistakeable. It was a condemnation of rare power, carrying, I believed, the clear sense of justice to come.

"He found out he had to share the estate," Wythe went on. "He's been so angry, making threats. I tried to calm him. I thought he'd let it go. But I guess he couldn't."

Another servant had gone for the doctors, and just then they came into the crowded bedroom. "Arsenic killed Michael Brown," one of them announced at once.

"Yes," Wythe answered, his voice weak again, but, it seemed to me, filled with relief – his accusations confirmed. "After supper. In the strawberries and coffee."

The doctors nodded. "Very likely," one said.

Then, for a moment it was as if a gloomy cloud had filled the room. Wythe lay back exhausted and the rest of us stood around, speechless. Helpless.

"How are the others?" Wythe finally asked. It was the question we'd been dreading.

Randolph looked at me and I looked at Duval, who finally stepped to the edge of the bed. "Lydia's still unconscious, George," he said, then paused. "Young Michael is dead."

A curious, animal-like noise rumbled from Wythe's throat – a noise, it seemed to me, of anger and resignation and inestimable sadness. "New will, Edmund," he said, very feebly, and Randolph swiftly pulled out pen and paper.

As Wythe dictated and the lawyer wrote, Duval and I hung back among the shadowy corners of the room. Almost unnoticed, Sweney had slipped out. Predictably, Wythe removed his nephew as his heir, leaving everything instead to Lydia Broadnax, should she survive.

Later, as we sat around the downstairs parlor together, it occurred to me that something was missing from the general flow of conversation. Something perhaps about Sweney's fate. Something about calling in the town marshals. After all, hadn't a boy been murdered? And wouldn't it be usual to have brought in the authorities by now? So why hasn't that been done? Could the niddling trace of a suspicion in the darkest recess of my mind be anywhere close to the truth? It made me sick even to consider the possibility; little did I know it was only a pale prelude.

The next morning, George Wythe, distinguished legal scholar, mentor to Thomas Jefferson and signer of the Declaration of Independence – thirty years before almost to the day, died of poisoning by arsenic at the hand of his nephew. Now the marshals were summoned at once, the formal charges made, and George Sweney was arrested for murder. Remarkably enough, within a few hours Lydia Broadnax seemed to rally from her coma. By early evening she regained consciousness, and the doctors pronounced her recovered. The next day, when she was strong enough, she confirmed Wythe's account of Sweney's actions, and the road to justice seemed swift, sure and undeniable.

The first inkling otherwise was not even that, but what seemed at the time to be a figment, a specter, looming only in my always-energetic imagination. It was what I took as, possibly, an unfriendly glance from one of Wythe's neighbors standing on her front porch across the street. Perhaps my eyesight is beginning to fail, I thought, for surely this amiable woman cannot be grimacing so nastily in my direction. But then when I said good afternoon to the neighbors right next door, that woman said, "Hmmph!" and the man shook his head dismally.

By then the newspapers had been trumpeting the story for days, and when I began reading them more closely I realized that the initial shock over Sweney's mere murders was quickly giving way to horror and outrage at the scandal of Wythe's miscegenation. Even so, I still felt that my imagination must be getting the best of me. After all, what could possibly outweigh these ghastly attacks by a beloved nephew on the very hand that had fed him for so long?

The day the trial opened Edmund Randolph unleashed his thunderbolt. At least for me that's what it was, though naturally nobody else in Richmond seemed to think much about it: that in Virginia Negroes could not testify against whites, so Lydia Broadnax would *not* be called to give her version of the events leading to the murders. What's more, Randolph said, the judge was considering a defense motion to deny admission of our versions of Wythe's deathbed denunciations on grounds that they were hearsay.

So it finally sank in. And over numerous brandies that evening I found myself asking just where had I been all these weeks? In what dream world had I been dwelling? Duval joined my commiserations at a local tavern, where talk predictably turned to the forthcoming trial. "Old Wythe been sticking it where it shouldn't be stuck, eh?" one man offered up. His companion snickered in reply, adding, "Too big an insult to let pass; poor Sweney did what he had to."

I started to turn toward them; I felt like killing them both. But Duval implored me otherwise and hurried me out. We finished our drinks in the solitary parlor of his little bachelor's bungalow.

"You know where I stand, Harrison," he said, and I did at that. He'd told me plainly enough, even showed me a copy of his letter to

Jefferson. "I share what must be your sorrow and grief over these terrible events," Duval had written, "and I will personally do all in my power to see that George Sweney is met with the full measure and power of the law."

"Harry to my friends," I told him over yet another round of drinks.

In the next few days, as the trial wore on, I scoured the neighborhood looking for any clue, any witness that might give credence to the truth. I even advertised, but all I got for my trouble was a rock through my cousin's front window and three letters telling me, variously, to "Leave town," "Drop dead," or "Prepare to die."

By the time I took the stand nine days later, the newspapers were in a virtual frenzy. "George Wythe's scandalous and utterly irrational behavior poses a grave insult to all freedom-loving Virginians," opined one editorial. "And while we cannot excuse murder in rebut, George Sweney's actions clearly bring to mind the label 'justifiable homicide.'"

My testimony was limited to a description of events leading up to my discovery of the container of arsenic. With the help of an unsuspecting prosecutor's laborious questions, I went through it all in meticulous detail. Then, with the court bored and half asleep, I shouted in defiance of the judge's earlier ruling: "Mr Wythe denounced his nephew on his deathbed. George Sweney murdered his uncle by poison."

It woke everybody up – that was certain. Otherwise, my efforts won me nothing save two days in jail for contempt. By the time I got out the all-white jury was ready to come back. It had taken them less than an hour to decide: George Sweney was not guilty.

And there was further insult to come. Two days later the charge of murdering Michael Brown was quashed without a trial, and the following week the courts even set aside Wythe's new will. Now Sweney was not only free but rich, for the judge awarded him Michael Brown's share of the estate as well as his own.

For a while, I seriously considered murdering Sweney. After all, I thought, in a place where justice is so unjust what else can one do save administer justice. And isn't that the way of the world? I could murder George Sweney, make good my escape, and chances are find that justice back in my home outside Philadelphia would adjudge me savior and hero. But if history is any guide it is only the very wicked (and now and then the very, very good) who can bring themselves to so single-mindedly and single-handedly impose justice upon the world. Clearly, I am neither sort of person.

So after a few more nights of rather morose drinking sessions with

Duval, and some with Edmund Randolph, I snapped out of it and understandably dispensed with outright murder as a possible course of action.

And then, exhausted, out of ideas, beaten down at last by such peculiar notions of right and wrong, I elaborately told my relatives goodbye, said my farewells to Duval and Randolph, made certain that a newspaper editor or two learned of my departure and left Richmond for good.

Or so it seemed.

In my hiding place in William Duval's closet I hear from somewhere downstairs the faint sound of a glass trinket tinkling; somewhere, another floorboard creaks. Down the hall Duval rustles edgily in his bedroom; obviously, he is no more asleep than I. Quiet down, William, I say to myself; stay calm. And mercifully he does; the noises from his room subside.

So, you ask, what am I doing here crouched in this closet? Did I leave Richmond or not? And if not, why not?

Well, it's simple enough, really: I left and then came back – snuck back, I should say, late that same night. And I've been back ever since, sleeping by day, keeping shy of the windows by night, eating sparingly, talking only when necessary, not talking at all after dark.

All the while Duval has kept me informed of certain events of importance. It seems that a few days after my return a messenger delivered a mysterious new set of documents to Edmund Randolph, and after checking up a bit the lawyer summoned Sweney and Duval to his office. He also called in a civil court judge of his acquaintance, one Phillip Lewiston, who had known George Wythe for many years. Randolph then explained to the three that from the markings on the outer envelope he had traced the documents back to a small transcription service.

"I personally spoke with the director of the service," Randolph said, "and he confirmed that an employee of his witnessed George Wythe writing these words at approximately seven o'clock on the morning of his death – actually about three hours before he died." The director, Randolph said, told him that this particular employee had since resigned his position and left Richmond. But he said the scribe had given him absolute assurances that Wythe himself had written the document. He said the employee later transcribed it into official form.

Randolph then unsealed the papers and showed them around, and all agreed the writing was Wythe's. Randolph also produced the professional transcription and read the essential parts: It was, as they had all suspected, a new will in which Wythe named "my old and trusted friend, William Duval, heir to all my property, my house, my bank stock, all my worldly possessions" – though with the provision that in the event of Duval's death, everything once again would revert to Sweney.

Sweney (Duval told me) sat through this literally open-mouthed, his eyes red with anger. "No," he kept saying, all the while shaking his head. But in the end Randolph declared the will genuine, and Judge Lewiston agreed.

"It's clearly his handwriting," the judge said, "and all the evidence shows plainly enough when it was written." Then, pausing to pick up the document, he declared, "There is no doubt that this is George Wythe's last will and testament."

Sweney stormed out and, from what Duval learned later, went straight to his own lawyer, who, after consulting Randolph, told his irate client that nothing could be done. Over the next ten days or so, Sweney was seen in half the saloons in Richmond, each time more drunk and angry. Neighbors reported him rampaging through his uncle's house late into the night, shouting curses and smashing up the place.

"Old fool," they heard him say more than once. "Nigger-loving, bastard-loving fool."

Then, a few nights ago, he grew quiet, and that was when I became alarmed. And now, loaded pistol in hand, I wait in Duval's upstairs hall closet.

And now, having waited so many nights, tonight I hear it plainly – the first creak at the bottom of the staircase. Then another. Then one more. Now I cannot hear my own breathing or the beat of my heart. Now I hear nothing in the world except this man on the stairs in the dark coming closer.

What drives men to such acts? I wonder. I have baited this silly trap, but he suspects nothing. He is blinded by his greed. And his hatred. He feels . . . victimized. I'm sure of it – that in his mind he's the one who's been put upon, swindled, deprived.

The groans on the stairs are much closer now, and then I hear him mount the last step and turn down the hall. The closet door is ajar, as it has been all along, and I see him walk past with graceful silence toward Duval's bedroom.

I stand up and slowly, quietly cock the pistol. But I wait till he is fully in the bedroom before I step into the hallway a few feet behind. The location of the doorway as he stands at the foot of Duval's bed keeps him fully in my line of fire, and I watch, his back to me, as he raises a knife above his head, ready to plunge it downward with all possible strength.

At last, my pistol aimed straight for him, I shout in a commanding tone, "Stop, thief!" as if I believe he is a burglar. But it is only to complete the ruse in case some lonely, late-night passerby should overhear us. "Stop," I say again, and for an instant he does stop, but he does not drop the knife. Still holding it above his head, he turns toward me, or starts to, but I do not let him turn entirely around. I do not wait; the waiting is over. I fire one round, and he drops instantly to the floor. I walk over to him with Duval behind me, kneel down and take a close look. It is George Sweney, all right, and I have killed him with one shot to the right temple.

Duval is trembling and ghostly pale, but I press the pistol into his hand. "Don't forget your promise, William," I say. I mean it as a joke, but he misunderstands.

"Yes, give you a few minutes before sounding the alarm," he says.

"Uh, yes, that, too," I answer with a feeble laugh. "But I mean about the money." It is my reminder, quite needless – as I say, a joke – to give all his "inheritance" to Lydia Broadnax.

He glares at me a moment, not sure what to make of it, then smiles thinly. He has relaxed a little, which is what I had intended. "Of course, Harry," he says. "I couldn't keep Wythe's money, you know that. So what choice do I have? It's either give it to Lydia, or . . . what? Maybe admit that I forged that last 'will' of George's? Maybe explain about you being here and about my brother-in-law owning that transcription service?"

I shake my head and laugh softly. "No, no," I say, and he laughs, too.

Then without another word, I slip out of the house, saddle a fast horse and leave Richmond.

And this time it is real. And for good.

# THE GOD OF
# THE HILLS
# Melville Davisson Post

*I must confess I have a passion for the Uncle Abner stories of Melville Davisson Post (1869–1930). Although they seem curiously dated and idiosyncratically American, they conjure up vivid images of a god-fearing but dangerously lawless rural landscape in early nineteenth-century Virginia. The original stories were published as* Uncle Abner, Master of Mysteries *in 1918. Ten years later Post returned to Uncle Abner and produced four more stories. These are much darker works. By then Post was in an increasing state of depression following the death of his wife and then of his father, to whom he was very close, and on whom Abner was probably based. These later stories, of which "The God of the Hills" was one, were not collected into book form until 1974 when the Aspen Press issued them as* The Methods of Uncle Abner. *To my knowledge these final stories have never been published in Britain.*

Abner used to say that one riding on a journey was in God's hand.

He never knew what lay before him; death standing in the road, invisible, as before the prophet; or a kingdom as in the case of Saul. One set out with his little intention, and found himself a factor in some large affair.

It is certain that my uncle had no idea of what he would come into when he rode on this early summer morning to Judge Bensen's house. It was some distance through the hills and he traveled early, with the dawn. He wished an hour with Bensen before the judge rode in to the county seat; for it was in the court term, and Bensen was the circuit judge.

It was a custom remaining in Virginia after the dominion of King George had passed.

The circuit judges were persons of property and distinction. They traveled on their circuits, holding their courts here and there about the country. There would be a group of counties in a circuit. And the county seat would take its name, not infrequently, from the fact that it was the domicile of these circuit courts. One finds the name remaining – Culpepper Court House, and the like.

Land was the evidence and insignia of distinction in Virginia.

One's importance was measured by his acres.

Every man who would command the attention of his fellows stood on an estate in lands. Judge Bensen lived some miles from the county seat. He had got a thousand acres from his father, and added to it. He had never married. He lived alone, with Negro servants, in their white-washed quarters, at some distance from his ancient house. His earnings and his salary from the state went to the purchase of new lands.

He had introduced the Hereford, and turning aside from the customs of the men about him, he bred young cattle, instead of fattening the beef bullock for the market. It happened then that Bensen's young cattle were not easily to be equaled. If one bought from him one got a drove of bullocks of one type, with no mongrel to be sold off to the little trader. Bensen had 200 young cattle – stockers, as they were called – for sale. And my uncle went, early, on this summer morning to see the drove: and to buy the cattle if he could, before Bensen set out for his court – on his horse with his legal papers in his saddle bags.

It was scarcely daylight when Abner descended into the long valley that extended north to the county seat, and in which lay the Bensen lands. At the foot of the hill where the road entered the valley he came on a man sitting his horse in the road. It was early, an hour before the sun, and there was a vague mist in this lowland.

The man and the horse looked gigantic.

Beyond them through an avenue of trees was the heavy outline of a house, still dark, from which the life within it had not yet awakened to the new day.

The whole earth was dry and the road bedded down with dust. My uncle was almost on the man before he knew him. It was Adam Bird, a traveling preacher of the hills, on his gray mare. The big old man was sitting motionless in his saddle looking up through the avenue of maples toward the shadowy house. He did not hear my uncle's horse in the soft dust until it was nearly on him. His hands lay on the pommel of his saddle and his face was lifted like one in some deep reflection.

He called out when he saw my uncle.

"Abner," he said, "do you see that house."

He did not pause for a reply from Abner nor for any formality of salutation. He went on, and directly, as though he merely uttered now aloud the thing that was passing in his mind.

"Caleb Greyhouse lived there until the devil took him. He married Virginia Lewis — for a woman when she is young will be a fool. She is long dead but she left a daughter that is a Lewis too. Not a Greyhouse, by the mercy of God! And now Abner," and he brought one of his big hands, clenched, down on the pommel of the saddle, "these accursed judges are going to dispossess her of her inheritance!"

My uncle knew what the man meant. It was common knowledge. Caleb Greyhouse had left a will written some years before, when the girl was young, leaving his estate, houses and lands, to his daughter, with a bequest to his brother who was to be the guardian and administrator of it. It had been written by Coleman Northcote, one of the best lawyers in Virginia, and so remained, until the girl had grown up. Then, when she had fallen in love, and wished to marry the son of a neighbor with whom Greyhouse had quarreled over a few acres of ridge land, the irascible old man had added a codicil to the will giving the whole estate to his brother, and no dollar and no acre to the girl.

The case was before the circuit court, now sitting, for the girl had got a sort of lawyer, and brought a suit.

But she had no money and no case.

Northcote had written the will only too accurately, with precise care for every technical detail. The codicil added by Greyhouse followed the form in Mayo's Guide. It was written and signed by the testator and contained no legal flaw. There seemed nothing that any court could do. Nevertheless, Bensen had called in a judge from a neighboring circuit to sit with him and decide the case. The case was before the judges. And it was the act of these judges and the case before them that moved the traveling preacher of the hills.

"Did Bensen decide the case?" replied my uncle.

"He did not," said Bird, "but the judge with him clamored to decide it and have it done, for he wished to go back to his circuit. Bensen delayed a little for he had a plan of his own about this thing. He said he would write an opinion and they would decide today. But it was an abominable pretension, Abner. They will dispossess the girl . . . unless the Lord God Almighty moves somewhere in this thing."

Again his big hand descended on the pommel of his saddle, as though he pounded the timber of a pulpit.

"And He will move in it! It is so written in The Book. If the widow and the orphan cry to me I will surely hear their cry."

He brought his big hand up and over his face and his voice descended into a lower note.

"She came to me and said, 'Uncle Adam, will you pray for me to win my case.' And I said I will not pray; for I will not supplicate the Lord God Almighty to do justice. I will call His attention to this wrong . . . And I stood up and cried to Him! And the word of the Lord came to me. And I saddled my horse, and rode down here and called Bensen out. He came shuffling with his little lawyer talk. It was the law. He had no discretion. He could not help the wrong of it. And besides I was in contempt of his court to talk with him about the case.

"In contempt of his court, Abner!"

And again the old man made his powerful dramatic gesture.

"I, the servant of God, in contempt of his court when I protested against a wrong! . . . I told Bensen that he was in contempt of God's court, and that if he went forward with this injustice Jehovah would include him in the damnation that followed after it."

He paused and looked my uncle in the face.

"For Bensen, Abner, is not guiltless in this thing. He will profit by it. He has coveted these lands as we all know and tried to purchase them. Old Caleb Greyhouse would not sell. But this brother will sell. And Bensen will get the lands he covets."

And again the old man returned to his dramatic vigor.

"And he shall not escape the damnation that followed Ahab the King of Samaria; because he takes the land he covets through the act of another.

"The writing of clerks and seals of courts shall not bring it to him guiltless, even as the writing of Jezebel and the sealing thereof did not bring the lands that he coveted to Ahab guiltless . . . I go now, Abner, as Elijah went to the King of Samaria! And if he say like that other, 'Hast thou found me, O mine enemy?' I will answer, I have found thee!"

He made a great sweeping gesture and turned his horse north in the valley. He rode as though he rode alone in the vague mist that lifted from the lowland and hung above the fields; a thin gray smoke screen spreading like a blanket.

The old man had not asked whither my uncle rode nor to what end.

He went like one on some tremendous mission, alone.

Abner followed. The circuit rider had brought a new element into this affair. A gain to Bensen at the end of it that my uncle had not considered. But now that the point was touched on he remembered. It was common knowledge that it was a covetous intent with Bensen to extend his lands; to add a field. He had endeavored to buy the Greyhouse tract. And it was the truth that while Caleb Greyhouse would not sell, this brother who took the estate under the written codicil would sell it to the last acre. He had sold all that he had received from his father as an inheritance except a few acres and a house on the highway near the Bensen residence.

There was a dissolute, a reckless strain in the man that was not in Caleb Greyhouse.

He wished to be a factor in political affairs, and lacking the confidence of the people he attached his fortunes to other men; and so he had got to be a sort of deputy about the courthouse, and a chimney-corner lawyer, with knowledge enough to thumb through the deed books searching for some defect in a title upon which he could bring a suit, or extort a blackmail.

He had a marked pride in this pretension.

In the suit before the judges, on the will, he appeared with much visible ostentation for himself. There was, as it happened, little peril to his case, for the girl, with no money to hire a competent attorney, had only a chimney-corner lawyer like himself. And so the case was one for judges to decide as it appeared, on its face, before them . . . Bensen would get the land. This Barnes Greyhouse, in funds, would try for the Assembly of Virginia. And with money he might win. There was here, as in every land, an element of the electorate that could be persuaded by a demagogue and a little money in the hand.

My uncle rode on after the old preacher, his big chestnut horse moving noiselessly in the deep dust.

But his heart was troubled.

The girl came up sharply outlined in his memory: fair-haired and slender, with the hope and the charm of the immortal morning. There was no reason why she should not go, in joy, to the youth that she loved.

He was of a better family and a better blood than Greyhouse.

Because that irascible old man had quarreled with the boy's father about some acres of stony land along a ridge line, everyone of the blood was damned. All were enemies, and endowed by that enmity with every vice.

Old Greyhouse would have no marriage with his enemy.

He fell into a fury of wild talk at the mere mention of it. And on a certain night, heated in that fury, he had written out the codicil that divested his daughter of his estate. It was not certain that at the bottom of the man he, in fact, wished to make that alienation.

In anger, affection is sometimes overridden.

Perhaps if he had had time, in illness, for reflection, he would have canceled it. Blood, as the old adage said, was thicker than water when death approached and one came to pass on the material things that one had gathered together in one's life.

But he had no such time.

Death came on him in the fields.

He had fallen, in harvest, at a stroke of sun. The farm hands carried him in. But he was already out of life. He lay for some hours in a coma, in his daughter's arms. Once, as the field hands told, he tried to stroke her hair and make known to her something that moved vaguely in his mind.

But he had had his hour, and he was granted no extension.

What he had written, he had written.

Death would not release his hand to cancel it.

It was the old eternal story.

Men acted in their anger to do wrong, as though they had a privilege of life; as though at their wish or need, in extremity, they would be granted a stay of execution until they could set their affairs in order and adjust any wrong they had accomplished.

The day was breaking.

The fog, extended through the valley, was lifting and parting into long streamers of white mist. The hills in the distance were sharp and clear in the morning light. In a short time the sun would appear. Already in the fields the cattle were at pasture.

My uncle had come up with the circuit rider.

And at once when the big chestnut emerged from the mist by his gray mare, the old man began to talk. He began, as before, with no introductory sentence.

"Abner," he said, "your father lived long in this land, and he did good in the sight of the Lord and not evil. And I can name a hundred men like him who have stood for righteousness. But in that company there is no Greyhouse. Old Caleb was the best. He was hard and mean but he was not a liar nor a thief. But this other, this Barnes Greyhouse, is the worst of an evil generation. His hands are full of evil. Did not little Benny Wilmoth, in despair, shoot himself in his house because this creature searching through the deed books found a defect in his title and brought a suit to dispossess him of his farm. It was a sort of murder, Abner!"

He thrust his clenched hand out.

"There was no law to hale Barnes Greyhouse into the court and hang him. But was he any less guilty for that lack? The hand of Virginia could not reach him. But, Abner, is he beyond God's hand? By little twists and turns a nimble man may slip away from the law. But he will not slip away from the vengeance of God."

His clenched hand made a great sweeping curve, as though it cleared a swathe before him.

"Abner," he said, "I will not be silent before this outrage. I will call Bensen to his door and warn him. I have seen it in a dream. He is a party to this wrong, and the Lord will make his house like the house of Jeroboam, the son of Nebat . . . and this Barnes Greyhouse!" He spread out the fingers of his extended arm as in the pronouncement of a curse. "As the dogs licked up the blood of Ahab in the pool of Samaria, shall the dogs lick up his blood! . . . for in shame, and in blackness, and in violence shall he go out of life!"

My uncle did not reply. This old man of the hills who stood for righteousness, like all who give themselves wholly to some principle of honor, had the dignity of the thing behind him. And he was not afraid. Neither courts nor judges could overawe him.

My uncle was in a deep reflection. He knew of this matter what was current gossip in the hills. But he did not know, until this morning, the sweeping terms in which Caleb Greyhouse, in his anger, had written out the codicil to this will. It would be, he had imagined, a sort of guardianship in the brother over the girl's estate until she came to a legal age, or some manner of trust. With such a writing there would be hope. But with a direct bequest in terms there would be no hope.

He was in a great perplexity and his mind turned from the mission on which he came.

It was broad day now with the sun beginning to appear.

They drew near to Bensen's house.

In the pasture by the road strolling down to water at the brook were the drove of young Hereford cattle. They were unequaled; as like in form and coloring as though they were all born of one mother, by some miracle of maternity on the same day of the year, and so reared and suckled. No cattleman of the hills could have passed that drove and not pulled up his horse to look it over, for in his mind's eye, after that, he would have carried the model for all other young cattle in the world.

And yet my uncle did not pull up his horse.

The two men passed in silence and, making a sharp turn in the road beside some oak trees, came to Bensen's house. They stopped in wonder. The house was open; the Negroes were hovering about as in a panic. Randolph's gig was before the door. He came out when they appeared.

"Abner," he said, "you are come, and I was about to send a Negro for you. Bensen is dead!

"You arrive also, Adam," he said, "as at a direction of God. It is the house of death that you have come to, and it is one of the duties of the preacher of the Gospels to minister to the dead. Come in."

"I will not come in," replied the old man. "But I will get down and sit before the door, for I did not come in peace."

But my uncle cried out astonished.

"Dead!" he echoed. "Bensen dead! What killed him?"

"Now, that," replied Randolph, "is the mystery that I was about sending after you to solve. Bensen was killed in the night as he sat here in his library at work among his books."

On the way in with Abner, Randolph explained the details of what had happened.

The circuit court was sitting.

The case over the will of Caleb Greyhouse was on the docket.

For some reason Bensen wished another judge to sit with him to decide the case and so had called in West from a neighboring circuit. There was no reason for this, Randolph said, for there was no ground on which to contest the will. Coleman Northcote had written it some years before. Northcote was the best chancery lawyer in Virginia, and he made no errors in a legal paper. The will was correctly drawn, signed by the testator, and witnessed as the law required.

Later, Caleb Greyhouse had added a codicil in his own hand-writing, on the blank sheet of the will. The codicil followed the form in Mayo's Guide and was signed, dated, and sealed in every feature, also as the law required.

Of course this attack on the will broke down at once.

There was no technical error in it.

The codicil added below the will on the same sheet of foolscap was also unassailable. It followed the legal form, was written by the testator in his own hand and signed by him.

It became thus, under the law of Virginia, a holograph will and required no witnesses.

West wanted to decide the case at once from the bench, so he could get back to his circuit. But Bensen said they would take it under advisement until morning.

That night all the Negroes about the place went to a frolic at the county seat.

They left the judge at work in his library, when they went out at dark.

In court time it was the custom of the judge to work late over his legal papers and so they had put new candles in the sticks on his table and lighted them before they left the house. They had been delayed in setting out, and as they left the house the judge had come to the door and directed them to stop on the way and ask Barnes Greyhouse to come and see him.

The man lived not farther than a quarter of a mile along the road.

They gave the message and saw him take his hat and cane and set out.

The frolic ran late. It was well toward dawn when the servants returned.

There was no light in Bensen's library or about the house and they naturally assumed that the judge had put out the lights and gone to bed.

In the morning when they came into the house they found the tragedy, and in terror sent for Randolph.

He found the library as the assassin had left it, for the Negroes had not gone in.

The judge had been killed as he sat before his table. He had been struck down from behind, apparently without warning. The assassin had used the poker from the fireplace. It was a terrific blow for it had crushed in the skull. The man had fallen sidewise under the table, for a second blow aimed at him had struck the table itself, leaving an indentation in the walnut wood.

The iron fire-poker lay on the floor behind the chair in which the judge had been sitting.

The deed had been done late, for the candles had burned down almost to the cup of the sticks before they had been extinguished. They had been snuffed out.

Randolph pointed out the iron poker, the mark on the walnut table, and the blood smear on the hardwood floor where the judge had fallen. Abner looked carefully about the room. And while he thus studied the situs of the crime, Randolph gave his opinion.

"This, Abner," he said, "will be the work of some vindictive convict. Our circuit judges are always in peril from these creatures when they come back from the penitentiary. I have seen them, when they were sentenced, scowl hard at the judges and mutter what they would do in revenge, when they should at length go free.

"This will be the work of such a creature. Bensen, in the counties of his circuit, will have sentenced all sorts of men for all sorts of felonies.

"But it is a peril of honor, Abner. And the one who dies from it dies in the service of his country, as though he died in battle before her enemies."

My uncle did not reply.

But there came a voice through the open door in answer.

The voice of the old circuit rider sitting in the sun.

"He did not die in honor, Randolph. Bensen died as a dog dieth!"

Randolph made a gesture as of one who dismisses the extravagances of a child with whom he will not contend. He got out some sheets of paper and sat down at a corner of the table to make a note of the details of the tragedy, accurately as he had found them on this morning.

Abner remained standing by the table, his big hand gathered about his chin, looking at the two tall candlesticks, with their bits of candles burned down to the cups.

New tallow candles had been put in on this night. These candles would burn long, almost from the dark till morning. They had been put in new on this night, and there was only a fragment left when the assassin had snuffed them out.

It was some time before my uncle moved, then he took up the snuffers and with the sharp point lifted the bits of candle out of the cups of the candlesticks.

But he did not otherwise disturb them.

He replaced them as they had been, put down the snuffers at their place, and went over to the far corner of the room.

There lying in the corner was a thing that he had noticed but upon which he had made no comment.

It was a small fragment of wood.

At first he had thought it a chip from the table broken off by the impact of the blow that had been directed at Bensen as he fell forward under it. But the table was walnut, and this fragment was some dark wood of a close texture. He did not take it up, nor disturb it where it lay in the corner, but he stooped over and studied it intently.

He arose, went over to the fireplace.

He took up the iron poker and turned it about in his hand.

There was a coating of ashes on the poker, extending from the point halfway to the handle, and over this toward the point was the blood of the man who had been murdered.

Abner put the poker down and remained for some moments by the hearth.

No fire had been lighted in it on this night. But there was a heap of wood ashes where former fires had burned.

Abner looked about him.

Randolph wrote sitting at a corner of the table with his back toward him. The old circuit rider was invisible beyond the open door; the Negroes had withdrawn in frightened groups beyond the house.

There was no one to question the thing he did – for he was not

yet ready to be questioned – and kneeling down on the brick hearth
he put his hand into the heap of ashes.

Then he withdrew his hand, smoothed the surface of the heap as
it had been, dusted the ashes from his hand, and rose.

He went around Randolph to the door and stepped out.

It was early in the morning.

No one had arrived, for the servants when they had found Bensen
dead had sent word only to Randolph, through the hills. And Abner
and old Adam had come by chance.

Abner did not pause.

He went on across the grassplot to the road. He stopped there and
looked carefully about.

Then he walked north in the dust of the road, in the direction of
the county seat. He went slowly, pausing now and then, and retracing
now and then a step. Finally he stopped, advanced, returned, and
stood still.

There was a little wood of scrub oak on his right hand, and a rail
fence. He crossed the fence and began to look about in this tangle of
scrub oak.

It was some time, perhaps half an hour, before he got back to
the house.

There was a haircloth sofa, facing toward a bookcase in a far corner
of the room. Abner went past Randolph to the sofa and leaning over
the back put down on it something that he had brought with him,
concealed under his long coat.

He returned to the table where Randolph sat before his sheets
of paper.

The man had been so taken up with what he wrote that he had
not marked my uncle's absence.

Abner put out his hand and took up, from beyond Randolph, a law
book with a cracked back. It was a volume of early legal reports.

The book fell open midway of the volume where the back was
cracked.

And when my uncle saw the page before him his face changed.

He read and his features hardened.

He was about to speak when the voice of a man entering from the
road stopped him.

It was Barnes Greyhouse.

He was a big man with a heavy brutal face laid over with a sort of
fawning geniality. He walked with a slight limp, for in some drunken
brawl, at an earlier time, he had been injured.

Randolph rose as the man came in; and my uncle turned about
toward the door.

But he did not move.

The man blurted out a jumble of greeting and amazed expletives at the tragedy.

"Good God!" he said. "Bensen murdered. Who could have killed him?"

My uncle did not reply.

But Randolph made a little gesture as of one who has penetrated to a meaning hidden from other men.

"It is the work of some convict that Bensen has sent to the penitentiary. Such creatures hold always a vindictive resentment against the judge; as though their punishment were his work."

"You are right, Randolph," said Greyhouse. "That's the explanation."

He uttered the words as though the conclusion could not be gainsaid, and was a pronouncement in finality. But there was a sort of eagerness in the voice and manner of the man.

My uncle spoke then.

"Greyhouse," he said, "you were here last night."

The man turned with a gesture of assent.

"Yes," he said, "early in the night. The Negroes passing said Bensen wished to see me, and I walked down. But I was here for a few moments only. The judge had sent for me to say that he and West would decide the case at once when they convened in the morning, and that I should come early into the court. I left the judge as I found him, sitting at his table there, and walked home. It was early: about dark."

"Were the candles lighted on Bensen's table?" inquired my uncle.

"Yes," replied the man, "just lighted, I think, as I came in; it was about dark."

"And the candles, Greyhouse; were they new tall candles, as the Negroes say?"

"Yes, Abner," he replied, "I can answer that. They were new tall candles for I noticed the flicker of the wick where the pointed ends had not yet caught up with the tallow."

Abner leaned over the table and took up Randolph's pencil.

"That is an important fact," he said, "for fragments only of these candles were burning in the sticks when the assassin snuffed them out after the murder. I think a note should be made of your observation to confirm what the Negroes say."

He put out his hand with the pencil in his fingers to write a line on Randolph's memorandum. But he bore too heavily and the point of the pencil broke. He turned toward Greyhouse with the pencil in his hand.

"Lend me your knife," he said.

The man took a penknife from his breeches and handed it to my uncle. Abner opened the knife and turned back to the table. But he did not sharpen the pencil. He put down the knife and pencil on the table and stood up.

My uncle looked hard at Greyhouse.

"You think Bensen was killed, late in the night, by some vindictive assassin who slipped in behind him. Is that your belief, Greyhouse?"

"Why, yes," he said, "that is the obvious conclusion. Here are the candles burned down to the cups and the bloody poker. It is indicated in these evidences. Bensen was murdered by some released convict who had a grudge against him, and slipping in behind killed him with the poker."

He was interrupted by a voice; a voice big and dominant that seemed to envelop and fill up the room.

"Bensen was not killed with the poker."

The three men turned as with a single motion of their bodies.

The old circuit rider was standing in the door. Greyhouse cried out at the words.

"How do you know that?"

The old circuit rider looked hard at the man.

"I know it," he answered, "as God knows it."

Then he closed his mouth and was silent.

It was my Uncle Abner that broke the silence.

"Adam is right," he said, "Bensen was not killed with the poker, nor in the time or manner that these evidences would indicate, for they are false and set up to mislead. There is blood on this poker. But there was no blood from the fracture of the skull that killed the judge and therefore there would be no blood on the implement with which the blow was dealt. There was hemorrhage only from the dead man's face where he lay under the table. But this poker was not there. It lay on the floor behind the chair. And consequently, it was made bloody by design."

He paused and turned toward the table.

"But this," he said, "was not the first thing that puzzled me. The first thing was the aspect of these candlesticks. If new tallow candles had burned down in them to the cups, the shafts of the sticks would have been fouled over with dripping grease. They were not so fouled. The shafts of the candlesticks were clean as you see them. How could that happen? The wicks of the bits of candles had been snuffed out. That was clear. But how could the candles have burned down to these bits, and there follow no drip of tallow?

"There was a reason. And I found that reason."

He took up the iron snuffers and with their sharp point lifted the bits of candles out of the cups of the sticks. The explanation was apparent. The candles had been cut off with a knife.

There was silence and he continued:

"What had become of the candles? I searched the room here. I found a certain thing but not the candles."

He made a gesture toward a distant corner, and went on.

"I looked again at the poker. It had a coating of wood ashes on it, as though it had been thrust into the heap yonder in the fireplace. Thrust in before it had been dipped into Bensen's blood, for the coating of ashes was underneath the blood . . . Then I found the candles."

He crossed the room with long strides, seized the poker, thrust it into the heap of ashes in the fireplace, and raked out the two long candles, cut off at their tips.

He put down the poker and stood up.

"The whole thing was clear now. Bensen had been killed early in the night when the candles were hardly lighted, and with some implement other than this poker; by one who had acted on a sudden determination to thus kill; and after the act endeavored to falsify events. He cut off the candles and snuffed them out. He made a hole in the ashes with the poker and concealed them and then, remembering that an implement must be found, had thought of the poker in his hand, and dipping it in the man's blood laid it on the floor behind the chair."

My uncle turned toward Greyhouse.

"Greyhouse," he said, "you are the one who came here early in the evening!"

The features of the man sagged and sweated. But there was a certain courage in him.

"Abner," he cried, "you go mad with your neat little conclusions. Why should I wish Bensen's death? I of all persons would wish his life; for today he and West would decide this will case in my favor."

Again the room reverberated with a voice that filled it. Again the old circuit rider spoke.

"Greyhouse," he said, "you are a liar! . . . I saw this thing in a dream; not all, but a fragment of it. I saw you and Bensen in this room, in anger. He beat a book, opened on the table, with his clenched hand and, from behind, you advanced on him, with something in your hand . . . not the poker, for it was setting against the chimney. You are a liar!"

The big accused creature wavered.

And Abner spoke, when the old man had ended.

"Yes, Greyhouse," he said, "you are a liar. I understand the whole thing to the end, although I have had no part in Adam's vision. That which was confused and hidden is now disclosed and clear. Bensen coveted these lands and he undertook to force you to a sale; a sale that would be a sort of dividing of the loot."

He crossed to the table and opened the volume of Virginia reports at the page where it fell apart from the broken back.

"Look!" he said. "Look, Randolph. Here on this page is the syllabus of a decision of the Supreme Court of Virginia, holding that a will and its codicil must be uniform to be valid. It cannot be half in one form and half in another. If the body of the will is written by someone other than the decedent and signed and witnessed, then the codicil must be so written and signed and witnessed.

"I understand it. I understand it clearly to the end . . . Bensen found this case last night and he sent for Barnes Greyhouse and held the case over him like a club to force a sale of these lands to him at some little price. He must take the price or Bensen would bring in the case today. And so they quarreled, and Bensen beat the book for emphasis, breaking the back under his clenched hand . . . And so Barnes Greyhouse killed him, knowing that West had no knowledge of this case and would decide in favor of the will, and the girl, with no money, could not take it to a higher court!"

There was utter silence. Then my uncle went on.

"Where is your cane, Greyhouse?"

The man did not reply, but his baggy face began to tremble.

"I will answer for you," continued Abner. "Listen, Greyhouse. I went over your track in the dust of the road. It was a clear track and beside it, also in the dust, was the round imprint of the ferrule of your cane. It was all along beside your tracks as you came here from your house, but on your return it was only to be seen beside your tracks for a certain distance. At the field of scrub oaks, on the right of the road, I could no longer find it. What did that mean, Greyhouse? It meant that at this point you had thrown the cane away . . . And why did you throw it away? Because you discovered, there, on your way from this murder, that the cane with which you had killed Bensen had suffered an injury that you might be called on to explain. Look, I will show you, for I found it in the scrub-oak wood by the roadside." He took up the cane from where it was hidden by the sofa and presented it to the man. It was a big heavy crook-handled cane of black wood like teak, and a split-off fragment at the turn of the crook was missing.

"Look at it, Greyhouse," he cried. "Look at it! A piece at the turn of the crook is missing, split off when the cane struck the table, under the powerful blow that you aimed at Bensen when he went down out of the chair. And that piece of it is yonder in the corner of the room."

He crossed with great strides, picked up the fragment of wood, and placed it on the crook of the cane.

"Look, Greyhouse, how the piece fits!"

He made a great gesture.

"There is other evidence against you. Why, sir, it cries like the blood of Abel . . . your knife, there on the table, has tallow on the blade where you cut the candles!"

Panic was on the trapped man and he bolted past my uncle through the open door.

But his foot tripped at the sill and he fell headlong outside, on the flag-paved path. His head struck a fragment of sharp curb and a thin trickle of blood flowed out. Then he got staggeringly to his feet to escape. But my uncle overtook him and the Negroes hurried up to help pin him down.

In the confusion as they drew near, the two hounds hovering about them paused and began to lick the blood where it had trickled on the curb.

The old circuit rider – sitting motionless in the sun, his white head uncovered, his big body, clothed in its rusty-colored homespun, filling up the chair – put out his hand and pointed to the thing.

It was the fulfilling of the prophecy.

As the dogs licked up the blood of Ahab in the pool of Samaria, so shall the dogs lick up his blood.

# THE ADMIRAL'S LADY
# Joan Aiken

*Joan Aiken (b. 1924) should need no introduction to most readers. She has been producing fantasy and horror stories for both children and adults for over forty years. She is probably most noted for her series about Dido Twite, set in a bleak alternative England where the Stuarts still rule. The series began with* The Wolves of Willoughby Chase *(1962) and ran through six volumes to* Dido and Pa *(1986). Her many stories of horror and dark suspense have appeared in over a dozen collections including* The Windscreen Weepers *(1969),* A Harp of Fishbones *(1972),* A Touch of Chill *(1979),* A Whisper in the Night *(1982) and* A Fit of Shivers *(1990). With this combination of dark mystery and twisted history you might think Joan Aiken would have written a historical mystery story before now. But not so. Here is her first: "The Admiral's Lady", written especially for this anthology.*

Having assisted for some seven hours at the accouchement of Her Grace the Duchess of Towcester (and a most unsuccessful business *that* was, rewarded after all the lady's pains and my own by no more than a five-pound female child with not the slightest similarity to either parent, but a fairly marked resemblance to Lord Derwentwater – and no more than a five-guinea fee for me, The Duke of Towcester being as penny-pinching a skinflint as ever wore ermine) I was not best pleased to find myself roused again from slumber only two hours later by a loud rat-tat at my door in Half Moon Street.

"Tell whoever it is to go to the devil!" I ordered my footman Joseph, but he reproved me.

"Oh, no, Mr Donovan, no indeed, sir, and ye can't do that –" Joe, like myself, hails from County Cork but, also like myself, has settled into London life as merrily as a mouse into Stilton – "Indeed we can't do that, sir, 'tis the Admiral himself, Admiral Crawford has sent for ye in the most express and vehement manner; Hobbs the coachman who waits at the door tells me 'tis desprit, desprit indeed, sir, or I wouldn't have made bold to rouse ye."

"Oh – very well – if it is the Admiral – I suppose I must bestir myself."

Admiral Sir Mark Crawford was one of my most regular and remunerative patients, a proclivity for a gormandizing and libidinous way of life, coupled with a gouty and choleric constitution rendering him liable to painful seizures of the most acute and agonizing nature at ever more frequent intervals.

"Well, at least the Admiral is no farther off than Hill Street," I mumbled, hastily re-tying my cravat, while Joseph packed the necessary vials of Urtica urents, colchicine, pulsatilla, and Ledum, besides a bag of ice to reduce inflammation, into my black medicine bag.

I had become the Admiral's regular practitioner after another summer evening some five years previously when, as I walked home through the dusk, a series of frantic yells issuing from an open window in Hill Street had impelled me to thrust my head through the casement and inquire if I could be of any use; which offer the Admiral's nephew, a friendly and well-mannered youth, then aged about sixteen or seventeen, had been only too glad to accept, his unfortunate relative being at that moment so distressed in his nether limbs that he sounded like a victim who was being broken on the wheel. This condition I was able to alleviate, and so gained the goodwill of the family. Even Lady Crawford, a female of a particularly glacial and repellent disposition, did not disdain, at times, to ask my advice on matters relating to her poodle Chowder, a fat, ill-conditioned beast with a nature closely resembling that of his mistress. Though it is true she had much to try her.

(The Admiral's lady being mistress of her own fortune, and that a handsome one amounting to over sixty thousand pounds invested in the Funds, must be considered a person of no small consequence in that family. But I digress.)

"Hey-day, coachman! Where are we going? This is not the way to Hill Street!" I exclaimed after a few minutes in the Admiral's barouche.

"Oo said anythink about 'Ill Street? It's Twit-nam *we're* bound for," retorted Hobbs the coachman. "An' a plaguey long way it is for my poor nags, what had to go round Richmond Park only this arternoon with Miss and her precious Ladyship."

"*Twickenham?* Oh, devil take it, if I'd known that was where Sir Mark expected me to go, I'd not have agreed to come, not though he was halfway through the portals of Dis."

"I dunno anything about Dis. But it ain't the Admiral, Mr

Donovan," Hobbs informed me. "He's all right and tight. 'Tis my lady. She's the one what's poorly. And precious poorly she *be*, by all accounts."

"Dear me, what can be amiss?"

I was surprised, for I had never known Lady Crawford to suffer from the least indisposition. Always upright, haughty, dressed in the impeccable height of the mode, she ignored her husband's cantrips, so far as was possible, and led a life of calm, balanced, acid elegance.

If I had understood that it was for *her* sake that I had been roused from my second slumber and obliged to proceed to Twickenham, I would have put up far more of a stand against losing the rest of my night's repose, for I could not believe there was anything seriously the matter with her. As it was, bowing to necessity, I contrived to slip into a doze between Hyde Park and Putney, while the horses wearily jogged on the second half of their twenty-mile journey.

Hitherto I had not been required to visit the Crawfords' cottage in Twickenham for the family had never, to my knowledge, passed a night there. The Admiral had bought the place some three years previously as a summer refuge. And possibly – I thought – as a refuge from his wife.

"It will make a neat little place enough," he declared, upon first acquiring it. "After I have cleared and opened the grounds to a greater degree, and improved the river frontage by means of a terrace or two, and given the building itself more of a picturesque and interesting aspect, by means of a few arches and a pair of gothic turrets, it will do well enough for passing agreeable summer afternoons."

But it seemed that the work was progressing very slowly.

"The truth of the matter is," Henry Crawford once explained to me, shrugging ruefully, "that my uncle seldom knows his mind for two days together. And, furthermore, since the Peace was declared, and Uncle retired from active service, he has not sufficient occupation elsewhere. So the cottage, where my aunt and sister were supposed to pass peaceful afternoons, is never anything but a perfect maelstrom of dirt and confusion, without a gravel path fit to walk on, or a bench to sit on. Uncle Mark is continually issuing contradictory sets of orders, has dismissed two architects, and my aunt is out of all patience with him. For my part, I am only thankful that I have my own estate in Norfolk where I may take refuge when the confusion becomes unbearable. But I pity my aunt and Mary. I do indeed."

For myself, I did not feel that too much sympathy need be expended upon Lady Crawford. She was never one to suffer in silence, and was at all times quite capable of expressing her dissatisfaction with her surroundings. As for Miss Mary Crawford, she moved in a different sphere from mine. Their own parents having died some twelve years before, the brother and sister had been brought up since then by the Admiral and his wife, an arrangement which had satisfied all parties. Henry and Mary were both young people of fortune, the brother with his estate in Norfolk, the sister with a handsome competence of her own. Both possessed of good looks, intelligence, and high spirits, the pair had many friends and, latterly, had passed less time with their uncle and aunt, more with fashionable acquaintances about Town. Miss Mary I knew principally as a well-gowned, bonneted, and parasol'd figure most often to be seen in an open carriage being driven briskly along Hill Street or through Berkeley Square.

I was not a little astonished, therefore, on arrival at Twickenham, the time being now near dawn, to find Miss Mary quite distracted, hair in dark dishevelled ringlets, beads of perspiration on her brow, her dress somewhat disordered, kneeling by the bedside of the suffering older lady, while the maidservant wrung frantic hands and Chowder the poodle howled dismally and ran unreproved about the room. This was a ground-floor chamber that had evidently been fitted up in haste as a sick-room with jugs of water, basins, a table covered by a towel, and some bunches of mint or lavender to give a pleasant odour.

"What appears to be the trouble?" was my inquiry, entering upon this scene.

"Ha, Donovan, there you are at *last*! Took long enough to make your way here!" declared the Admiral, hurrying towards me; and then remembered, I suppose, that it was his own coach that had fetched me. It did cross my mind then to wonder why Crawford had not sent for some medical practitioner who lived closer at hand; surely there must be several, now that Twickenham was becoming such a popular resort?

"Ar – hum – well, well – now you are here, what d'you make of her – hey?"

I could see that the lady upon the couch appeared to be suffering from some kind of seizure. The complexion of the face was greatly engorged, breath was taken only with the most frightful difficulty.

I applied ice to the feet, and called for hot mustard in water to plaster the spine and chest, besides a cold compress on the belly. I had planned to administer arsenicum album in water every quarter of an hour, but it proved impossible to make the patient swallow. The throat and windpipe were swollen and almost wholly closed up. I perceived with alarm that I might have to perform a tracheotomy.

"Can you give me the history of this malady, sir? When did it set in? Did the lady complain of any symptoms at an earlier stage?"

"Nothing wrong with her at dinner," stated the Admiral. "Was there, Mary?"

Miss Crawford shook her head.

"No, my aunt was quite herself earlier. We had come from Hill Street to spend the day and, after our excursion in Richmond Park the servants prepared a scratch repast of cold meat, fruit, and cake, of which my aunt partook; she did complain about the tea, served afterwards – she said that it was not hot enough – "

"Nor it was, hogwash," agreed her uncle. "How you females can maudle your innards with such stuff – if you were content to stick to port, now – "

"And then? Did Lady Crawford complain of any pains – nausea – faintness?"

"No, she merely said she wished to rest a little after tea. She retired with a book to this room, which we have been in the habit of using as a parlour. My uncle went to give orders to the architect, my brother and I decided to take a walk along the tow-path to Eel Pie Island. So we went our several ways – and when we came back we found my aunt as you see her now."

"There were servants in the house? She did not groan – call out – make any outcry?"

"No – or so Maule, her maid, asseverates – "

The hot water came, and I mixed a mustard plaster. But before I could apply it, the patient's face became even more congested, she had a last unsuccessful attempt at drawing breath, and finally expired.

"Dammit, she's gone!" quoth the Admiral, as the body writhed sharply, then came to its final quietus. "All that way for the horses to fetch you, and then you get here too late!"

"I deeply regret, sir – though, indeed, it was hardly my fault – "

The Admiral, to my considerable surprise, now burst out a-crying, and had to be led away by Mr Henry, whose own face was drawn and haggard. It was some months since I had seen him and I thought that he did not look well. I recalled hearing tales that he was in difficulties with gambling debts.

"Come, sir," he said to his uncle, not urgently. "Come, you will do better to rest a while – come, lie down and repose yourself in the conservatory."

They went off to a glass-walled room at the rear of the building.

"She was such a pretty gal – when she was a young thing –" blubbered Sir Mark.

Since there was nothing more to be done for Lady Crawford, I followed the two men and administered a soothing draught to the

Admiral, who soon nodded off to sleep on a wicker chaise-longue. I noticed that the conservatory, where he lay, was extremely dusty and littered with dead insects, bees. There must have been several hundred of them.

Henry Crawford looked about him in disgust and said, "This place is in a disgraceful state. Bartlett must clean it."

He opened the outer door, which led to what would some day be the garden – at present merely rough earth, piles of bricks and debris, builders' pails, and ladders – and shouted, "Bartlett? Where are you? Come here at once and bring a broom."

I was surprised that garden servants should be on the premises already, at such an early hour, but, consulting my watch, discovered that the time was after six. A young fellow soon arrived carrying a broom and, with a murmur of apology, began sweeping up the dead insects from the floor. I noticed that one of his legs was a wooden one.

"This should have been done yesterday, Bartlett," Henry said curtly. "You knew that my uncle was coming."

"Very sorry, sir, Mr Henry," the man answered softly, "but Sir Mark had given orders that the terrace was to be laid afore he come . . . We was hard at it all day yesterday – "

As he turned away with his pan full of dead bees I noticed that his hair was plaited in a naval pigtail.

"He was one of my uncle's seamen," Henry remarked, noticing my glance. "On board the *Thrush*. Discharged unfit, of course, after his leg was blown off at Trafalgar; he came to my uncle asking for work and was taken on as under-gardener."

"Very compassionate of the Admiral," said I.

Henry Crawford threw me a sharp look.

"It was indeed," he said. "For the man was of a somewhat questionable character. He had been flogged at the gangway with thirty strokes of the cat not long before the action in which he lost his leg."

"Indeed? For what offence?"

"He stole a piece of bread from the Midshipmen's Mess."

My brother Jack was a surgeon aboard a man o' war. He had told me about these floggings, which could reduce a man's back to raw pulp, or even kill the victim. And if there was a sea battle shortly afterward, what chance would he have to play his part or keep out of harm's way? He was lucky, I supposed, to have escaped with the loss of a leg. And all this for taking a piece of bread . . .

"Let us step out into the air," said Henry. "My sister has gone to try and make some order among the servants. I daresay they will bring

us a cup of coffee by and by. What happens now, Mr Donovan? Must
there be an inquest on my unfortunate Aunt?"

"I fear there must – and probably an autopsy as well. It is
considered needful, you know, in cases of such sudden and unexpected
fatality."

"That will upset my uncle very much."

Hardly more than the death itself, I thought. But that I did
not say.

After we had stared in silence for a while at the glum prospect of
sand-piles, timber, and builders' rubbish, Henry Crawford went back
into the house to hurry up some attempt at breakfast, and I walked
down through the confusion to a small rudimentary garden which
had been laid out beside the river. A brick terrace – brand-new,
presumably the one which had taken precedence over cleaning the
conservatory – flanked a few lumpy flower-beds where young roses,
lavender plants and rosemary cuttings had been set, not too long
ago, to judge from their drooping aspect.

"Those plants could do with a few cans of water," I suggested
to Bartlett, the pig-tailed young fellow, who was now hard at work
building a flight of rustic steps with logs of wood. He gave me a
harassed glance.

"I can't do everything at once, can I? Here, Jem, boy –" he called,
"water the roses, there's a good lad."

A small barefoot shrimp of a boy stumbled out of a hut which
I had supposed to be a toolshed, finishing off a crust of bread and
yawning as if he had just woken from sleep. He took a watering pot
and dipped some water from the river, which here ran brown, swift,
and silent, to pour over the neglected shrubs.

Returning from this errand he suddenly let out a sharp cry and
began to hobble, hopping on one foot.

"I've been stung! I've been stung!"

"Sit down and let us have a look," said I. He sat on the log-step
that his father was laying, and I inspected the bare and very dirty
foot. Sure enough, a bee clung to the hard sole. Fortunately I had
a pair of tweezers in my pocket, and was able to remove both the
bee and its sting, which had remained in the tiny wound.

"Come up to the house, and I will put some soda on the sting,
which will soon make it feel better," I told the child, who, snivelling,
accompanied me.

"I wish those pesky bees had never come here," he grumbled.
"Last week they all come down outer the sky like a big black cloud.
Dad were main pleased, for, he says, we can sell the honey to Missis
Propert for her sweeties – and owd Sir Mark, for a wonder, he don't

mind – he said as how they could stay – but that's the third time I been stung – "

"Do you live here, Jem?"

"Ay, in the hut, since Ma died in the work'us, and Dad came home from sea – Miss Maule, as looks after Miss Mary, is my Dad's cousin – "

Up at the cottage a hasty breakfast of coffee, bread, and cold ham had been assembled.

Little Jem, his wound treated, was pacified with a piece of ham wrapped in a slice of bread, and returned, limping, to his labours.

"Jem's mother, I fear, died in the workhouse while Bartlett was at sea," Mary Crawford told me, as she handed me a cup of coffee. "He was taken up by the Press Gang, you know. But after he lost his leg and was discharged he was able to reclaim the boy from the orphanage. He is a hard-working fellow and makes himself useful in many ways, as sailors often can. He even, it seems, has a knowledge of bees, and impounded in a straw skep the swarm that arrived here last week. A swarm of bees in June, you know, is worth a silver spoon!" She laughed, a delightful gurgle. "My poor Aunt was wholly opposed to the notion of bee-keeping and considered them a most noxious addition to this establishment. But my uncle was delighted – it gives him the feeling of a landowner with livestock." She laughed again. It seemed to me that she was recovering from her aunt's demise tolerably well.

Excusing myself I went off to locate and seek the assistance of a fellow medical practitioner who lived, I discovered, in Grotto Road, not very far away.

Events took their course, as events do, and must. An autopsy was held, and, to everybody's astonishment – except mine – a bee was discovered in Lady Crawford's gullet. She must somehow have started to swallow it, the bee had stung her, and the consequent swelling and inflammation of the throat and wind-passage had brought about her death by suffocation.

I myself inspected the oesophagus and windpipe, in the company of Dr Hugh Palliser and Sir Ormsby Murdoch, and, since both they and the Coroner were satisfied as to the cause, a verdict of Accidental Death was brought in.

"The unfortunate lady must, by chance, have accidentally allowed a bee to enter her mouth," solemnly pronounced Sir Ormsby. "It is a rare, but not a wholly unknown fatality. If a person should be, for instance, taking a bite from, say, a slice of bread-and-jam . . . and a bee suddenly alights upon the jam – as bees do – and is taken into the throat before the victim is aware . . ."

*Yes*, thought I, but we happen to know that Lady Crawford, very shortly before she died, had partaken of a substantial meal of cold chicken, angel cake, peaches, strawberries, and cream. So why – only half an hour later – would she succumb to a craving for bread-and-jam?

Nobody in the household has mentioned that she ate, or requested, anything of that nature?

Lady Crawford's will was read. I do not know if it caused any surprise. A portion to her niece, a portion to her nephew, an annuity to her maid Maule, the bulk of her fortune, as was proper, to her sorrowing husband.

I still felt uneasy, unsatisfied. To me, Lady Crawford seemed the last person in the world to be marked out for such a sudden and violent departure from life. Could her death have been *planned* – somehow intentionally brought about? But by whom? Who would have an interest in such a crime? The sailor, Bartlett? (For it had seemed a little singular to me that he should seek service in the home of a man who had been responsible for his flagellation and subsequent injury – unless he could find nothing else?)

But even if Bartlett bore a grudge against the Admiral and was bent on revenge, how would it be possible to introduce a bee into somebody's throat without their knowledge? I supposed, though, that Bartlett, if anybody, might have the skill and facility for such a deed, since I recalled that Mary Crawford said he had a knowledge of bees . . .

Some days went by while I pondered on the event and wondered where my duty lay. Ought I to investigate any further? Then a name let fall by little Jem floated up to the surface of my mind, providing another possible solution. A week or so after the poor lady's funeral, I made my way on foot to the Shepherds' Market, that nest of little streets that lies in a hollow just south of Berkeley Square. And, in a corner, in White Horse Mews, I found what I sought – Mrs Propert's Candy Corner. Here, in a tiny shop not much bigger than a grand piano, all kinds of juvenile delights were on offer: bulls' eyes, barley-sugar-walking-sticks, treacle candy, lollipops, Banbury cakes, lemon drops, and sugar plums. A warm scent of boiling sugar hung over the establishment.

"Where is Mrs Propert?" I inquired of the old dame who presided over all these delights. I remembered Mrs Propert as a fine, high-coloured female with sparkling blue eyes and gold ringlets – she was not unlike the figurehead on some noble ship.

"Why, she bain't here any more. Why? What d'ye want of her?" demanded the old lady.

"I wondered if you still kept those small candy sweetmeats that Mrs Propert used to make – Golden Bonbons, were they called? – a little shell, no bigger than my thumbnail, made of caramel, with a berry or some kind of filling inside?"

"No," snapped the old thing. "We ain't got them no more. They were Mrs Propert's specialty."

"How did she ever make them? Was it with a hard glaze that she moulded into little cups? And then she put in the filling and stuck the cups together?"

"I couldn't tell yer," brusquely replied the old lady. "They was her own special receipt. She never told no one else."

A girl in a mob cap with cherry ribbons had come from the rear of the shop with a tray of fondants.

"You talking about Auntie Chrissie's candies? Those ones she were so proud of? She'd never tell how she done 'em. The Admiral's lady were main fond of those," the girl told me. "Her maid, Miss Maule, used to come in for a pound of them every two-three days. Regular glutton for them, Lady Crawford was, by what Miss Maule did say. She'd scrunch down a whole bowlful of 'em after dinner, all by herself. If no one else was by."

"Oh, indeed?" said I. "Well – if they were as delicious as I remember – it seems very sad that the secret of making them has been lost."

"Oh well – maybe Auntie Chrissie will let it out to somebody by and by," said the mob-capped girl, carefully laying out her fondants on white confectioners' paper.

"Where is she now, then?" I inquired.

"Oh, she's gone to better herself!" said the girl, with a cheerful toss of her cherry ribbons. "Gone to housekeep for owd Admiral Crawford in Hill Street."

# THE EYE OF SHIVA
# Peter MacAlan

*Peter MacAlan is a pseudonym of Peter Berresford Ellis (b. 1943). When he isn't writing learned texts on Celtic history as Ellis, or producing fantasies or mysteries as Peter Tremayne, he is writing thrillers as Peter MacAlan. Somehow the MacAlan alias seemed appropriate for this story set in the days of the Indian Raj.*

The harsh monsoon winds were rattling fiercely at the closed shutters of the British Residency building. The Residency itself stood on an exposed hillock, a little way above the crumbling banks of the now turbulent Viswamitri River, as it frothed and plunged its way through the city of Baroda to empty into the broad Gulf of Khambhat. The building had been secured from the moaning wind and rain by the servants; the lamps were lit, and the male guests still lounged in the dining room, unperturbed by the rising noise of the storm outside.

The ladies had withdrawn, shepherded away by Lady Chetwynd Miller, the wife of the Resident, while the decanter of port began to pass sun-wise around the eight remaining men. The pungent odour of cigar smoke began to permeate the room.

"Well," demanded Royston, a professional big-game hunter, who was staying a few days in Baroda before pushing east to the Satpura mountains to hunt the large cats which stalked the ravines and darkened crevices there. "Well," he repeated, "I think the time has come to stop teasing us, your excellency. We all know that you brought us here to see it. So where is it?"

There was a murmur of enthusiastic assent from the others gathered before the remnants of the evening meal.

Lord Chetwynd Miller raised a hand and smiled broadly. He was a sprightly sixty year old; a man who had spent his life in the service of the British Government of India and who now occupied the post of Resident in the Gujarat state of Baroda. He had been Resident in Baroda ever since the overthrow of the previous despotic Gaekwar or ruler. Baroda was still ruled by native princes who acknowledged the suzerain authority of the British Government in India but who had independence in all internal matters affecting their principality.

Five years previously a new ruler, or Gaekwar, Savaji Rao III, had come to power. If the truth were known, he had deposed his predecessor with British advice and aid for the previous Gaekwar had not been approved of by the civil servants of Delhi. Indeed, he had the temerity to go so far as to murder the former Resident, Colonel Phayre. But the British Raj had not wanted it to appear as though they were interfering directly in the affairs of Baroda. The state was to remain independent of the British Government of India. Indeed, the secret of the success of the British Raj in India was not in its direct rule of that vast subcontinent, with its teeming masses, but in its persuasion of some 600 ruling princes to accept the British imperial suzerainty. Thus much of the government of India was in the hands of native hereditary princes who ruled half the land mass and one quarter of the population under the "approving" eye of the British Raj.

Baroda, since Savaji Rao III had taken power, was a peaceful city of beautiful buildings, of palaces, ornate gates, parks and avenues, standing as a great administrative centre at the edge of cotton rich plains and a thriving textile producing industry. A port with access to the major sea lanes and a railway centre with its steel railroads connecting it to all parts of the sub-continent.

After the establishment of the new regime in Baroda, the British Raj felt they needed a man who was able to keep firm control on British interests there. Lord Chetwynd Miller was chosen for he had been many years in service in India. Indeed, it was going to be his last appointment in India. He had already decided that the time had come for retirement. He was preparing for the return to his estates near Shrewsbury close to the Welsh border before the year was out.

"Come on, Chetwynd," urged Major Bill Foran, of the 8th Bombay Infantry, whose task it was to protect the interests of the British Residency and the community of British traders who lived in Baroda. He was an old friend of the Resident. "Enough of this game of cat and mouse. You are dying to show it to us just as much as we are dying to see it."

Lord Chetwynd Miller grinned. It was a boyish grin. He spread his hands in a deprecating gesture. It was true that he had been leading his guests on. He had invited them to see "The Eye of Shiva" and kept them waiting long enough.

He gazed around at them. Apart from Bill Foran, it could not be said that he really knew the other guests. It was one of those typical Residency dinner parties whereby it was his duty to dine with any British dignitaries passing through Baroda. Lieutenant Tompkins, his ADC, had compiled this evening's guest list.

Royston he knew by reputation. There was Father Cassian, a swarthy, secretive-looking Catholic priest who seemed totally unlike a missionary. He had learnt that Cassian was a man of many interests — not the least of which was an interest in Hindu religion and mythology. There was Sir Rupert Harvey. A bluff, arrogant man, handsome in a sort of dissolute way. He had just arrived in Baroda and seemed to dabble in various forms of business. Then there was the tall languid Scotsman, James Gregg. Silent, taciturn and a curious way of staring at one as if gazing right through them. He was, according to the list, a mining engineer. For a mere mining engineer, Tompkins had observed earlier, Gregg could afford to stay at the best hotel in Baroda and did not seem to lack money.

The last guest sat at the bottom of the table, slightly apart from the others. It was Lord Chetwynd Miller's solitary Indian guest, Inspector Ram Jayram, who, in spite of being a Bengali by birth, was employed by the Government of Baroda as its chief of detectives. Ram Jayram had a dry wit and a fund of fascinating stories which made him a welcome guest to pass away the tedium of many soirées. That evening, however, he had been invited especially. Word had come to Jayram's office that an attempt was going to be made to rob the Residency that night and Lord Chetwynd Miller had accepted Jayram's request that he attend as a dinner guest so that he might keep a close eye on events. It was Jayram who suggested to the Resident that the potential thief might be found among the guests themselves. A suggestion that the Resident utterly discounted.

But the news of the Resident's possession of the fabulous ruby — "The Eye of Shiva" — was the cause of much talk and speculation in the city. The Resident was not above such vanity that he did not want to display it to his guests on the one evening in which the ruby was his.

Lord Chetwynd Miller cleared his throat.

"Gentlemen . . .," he began hesitantly. "Gentlemen, you are right. I have kept you in suspense long enough. I have, indeed, invited you here, not only because I appreciate your company, but I want you to see the fabled 'Eye of Shiva' before it is taken on board the SS *Caledonia* tomorrow morning for transportation to London."

They sat back expectantly watching their host.

Lord Chetwynd Miller nodded to Tompkins, who clapped his hands as a signal.

The dining room door opened and Devi Bhadra, Chetwynd Miller's major-domo entered, pausing on the threshold to gaze inquiringly at the lieutenant.

"Bring it in now, Devi Bhadra," instructed the ADC.

Devi Bhadra bowed slightly, no more than a slight gesture of the head, and withdrew.

A moment later he returned carrying before him an ornate tray on which was a box of red Indian gold with tiny glass panels in it. Through these panels everyone could see clearly a white velvet cushion on which was balanced a large red stone.

There was a silence while Devi Bhadra solemnly placed it on the table in front of the Resident and then withdrew in silence.

As the door shut behind him, almost on a signal, the company leant towards the ornate box with gasps of surprise and envy at the perfection of the ruby which nestled tantalizingly on its cushion.

Father Cassian, who was nearest, pursed his lips and gave forth an unpriestly-like whistle.

"Amazing, my dear sir. Absolutely!"

James Gregg blinked, otherwise his stoic face showed no expression.

"So this is the famous 'Eye of Shiva', eh? I'll wager it has a whole history behind it?"

Royston snorted.

"Damned right, Gregg. Many a person has died for that little stone there."

"The stone, so it is said, is cursed."

They swung round to look at the quiet Bengali. Jayram was smiling slightly. He had approved the Resident's suggestion that if one of his guests was going to make an attempt on the jewel, it were better that the jewel be placed where everyone could see it so that such theft would be rendered virtually impossible.

"What d'you mean, eh?" snapped Sir Rupert Harvey irritably. It had become obvious during the evening that Harvey was one of those men who disliked mixing with "the natives" except on express matters of business. He was apparently not used to meeting Indians as his social equals and showed it.

It was Major Foran who answered.

"The Inspector," did he emphasize the Bengali's rank just a little? "The Inspector is absolutely right. There is a curse that goes with the stone, isn't that right, Chetwynd?"

Lord Chetwynd Miller grinned and spread his hands.

"Therein is the romance of the stone, my friends. Well, how can you have a famous stone without a history, or without a curse?"

"I believe I sense a story here," drawled Gregg, reaching for his brandy, sniffing it before sipping gently.

"Will you tell it, sir?" encouraged Royston.

Lord Chetwynd Miller's features bespoke that he would delight in nothing better than to tell them the story of his famous ruby – "The Eye of Shiva".

"You all know that the stone is going to London as a private gift from Savaji Rao III to Her Majesty? Yesterday the stone was officially handed into my safe-keeping as representative of Her Majesty. I have made the arrangements for it to be placed on the SS *Caledonia* tomorrow to be transported to London."

"We all read the *Times of India*," muttered Sir Rupert but his sarcasm was ignored.

"Quite so," Lord Chetwynd Miller said dryly. "The stone has a remarkable history. It constituted one of a pair of rubies which were the eyes of a statue of the Hindu god Shiva . . ."

"A god of reproduction," chimed in Father Cassian, almost to himself. "Both benign and terrible, the male generative force of Vedic religion."

"It is said," went on the Resident, "that the statue stood in the ancient temple of Vira-bhadra in Betul country. It was supposedly of gold, encrusted with jewels and its eyes were the two rubies. The story goes that during the suppression of the 'Mutiny', a soldier named Colonel Vickers was sent to Betul to punish those who had taken part. He had a reputation for ruthlessness. I think he was involved with the massacre at Allahabad . . ."

"What was that?" demanded Gregg. "I know nothing of the history here."

"Six thousand people regardless of sex or age were slaughtered at Allahabad by British troops as a reprisal," explained Father Cassian in a quiet tone.

"The extreme ferocity with which the uprising was suppressed was born of fear," explained Major Foran.

"Only way to treat damned rebels!" snapped Royston. "Hang a few and the people will soon fall into line, eh?"

"In that particular case," observed Royston, screwing his face up in distaste, "the Sepoys who had taken part in the insurrection were strapped against the muzzles of cannons and blown apart as a lesson to others."

"Military necessity," snapped Major Foran, irritated by the implied criticism.

The Resident paused a moment and continued.

"Well, it is said that Vickers sacked the temple of Vira-bhadra and took the rubies for himself while he ordered the rest of the statue melted down. This so enraged the local populace that they attacked Vickers and managed to reclaim the statue, taking it to a secret hiding place. Vickers was killed and the rubies vanished. Stories permeated afterwards that only one ruby was recovered by the guardians of the temple. A soldier managed to grab the other one from Vickers' dying hand. He, in his turn, was killed and the stone had a colourful history until it found its way into the hands of the Gaekwar of Baroda."

Inspector Ram Jayram coughed politely.

"It should be pointed out," he said slowly, "that the Gaekwar in question was not Savaji Rao III but the despot whom he overthrew a few years ago."

The Resident nodded agreement.

"The jewel was found in the Gaekwar's collection and Savaji Rao thought it would be a courteous gesture to send the jewel to Her Majesty as a token of his friendship."

Gregg sat staring at the red glistening stone with pursed lips.

"A history as bloody as it looks," he muttered. "The story is that all people who claimed ownership of the stone, who are not legitimate owners, meet with bad ends."

Sir Rupert chuckled cynically as he relit his cigar.

"Could be that Savaji Rao has thought of that and wants no part of the stone? Better to pass it on quickly before the curse bites!"

Lieutenant Tompkins flushed slightly, wondering whether Sir Rupert was implying some discourtesy to the Queen-Empress. He was youthful and this was his first appointment in India. It was all new to him and perplexing, especially the cynicism about Empire which he found prevalent among his fellow veteran colonials.

"The only curse, I am told, is that there are some Hindus who wish to return the stone to the statue," Father Cassian observed.

Sir Rupert turned to Inspector Jayram with a grin that was more a sneer.

"Is that so? Do you feel that the stone should belong back in the statue? You're a Hindu, aren't you?"

Jayram returned the gaze of the businessman and smiled politely.

"I am a Hindu, yes. Father Cassian refers to the wishes of a sect called the Vira-bhadra, whose temple the stone was taken from. They are worshippers of Shiva in his role of the wrathful avenger and herdsman of souls. For them he wears a necklace of skulls and a garland of snakes. He is the malevolent destroyer. I am not part of their sect."

Sir Rupert snorted as if in cynical disbelief.

"A Hindu is a Hindu," he sneered.

"Ah, so?" Inspector Jayram did not appear in the least put out by the obvious insult. "I presume that you are a Christian, Sir Rupert?"

"Of course!" snapped the man. "What has that to do with anything?"

"Then, doubtless, you pay allegiance to the Bishop of Rome as Holy Father of the Universal Church?"

"Of course not . . . I am an Anglican," growled Sir Rupert.

Jayram continued to smile blandly.

"But a Christian is a Christian. Is this not so, Sir Rupert?"

Sir Rupert reddened as Father Cassian exploded in laughter. "He has you there," he chuckled as his mirth subsided a little.

Jayram turned with an appreciative smile.

"I believe that it was one of your fourth-century saints and martyrs of Rome, Pelagius, who said that labels are devices for saving people the trouble of thinking. Pelagius was the great friend of Augustine of Hippo, wasn't he?"

Father Cassian smiled brightly and inclined his head.

"You have a wide knowledge, Inspector."

Sir Rupert growled angrily and was about to speak when Lord Chetwynd Miller interrupted. "It is true that the story of the curse emanated from the priests of the sect of Vira-bhadra, who continue to hunt for the stone."

Royston lit a fresh cheroot. He preferred them to cigars provided by their host.

"Well, it is an extraordinary stone. Would it be possible for me to handle it, your excellency?"

The Resident smiled indulgently.

"It will be the last chance. When it gets to London it will doubtless be locked away in the royal collection."

He took a small key from his waistcoat pocket and bent forward, turning the tiny lock which secured the box and raising the lid so that the stone sparkled brightly on its pale bed of velvet.

He reached forward and took out the stone with an exaggerated air of carelessness and handed it to the eager Royston. Royston held the stone up to the light between his thumb and forefinger and whistled appreciatively.

"I've seen a few stones in my time but this one is really awe inspiring. A perfect cut, too."

"You know something about these things, Royston?" inquired Sir Rupert, interested.

Royston shrugged.

"I don't wish to give the impression that I am an expert but I've traded a few stones in my time. My opinion is probably as good as the next man's."

He passed the ruby to Father Cassian who was seated next to him. The priest took the stone and held it to the light. His hand trembled slightly but he assumed a calm voice.

"It's nice," he conceded. "But the value, as I see it, is in the entire statue of the god. I place no value on solitary stones but only in an overall work of art, in man's endeavour to create something of beauty."

Sir Rupert snorted as an indication of his disagreement with this philosophy and reached out a hand.

Father Cassian hesitated still staring at the red stone.

At that moment there came the sound of an altercation outside. The abruptness of the noise caused everyone to pause. Lieutenant Tompkins sprang to his feet and strode to the door. As he opened it Lady Chetwynd Miller, a small but determined woman in her mid-fifties, stood framed in the doorway.

"Forgive me interrupting, gentlemen," she said with studied calm. Then looking towards her husband, she said quietly. "My dear, Devi Bhadra says the servants have caught a thief attempting to leave your study."

Lord Chetwynd Miller gave a startled glance towards Inspector Jayram, then rose and made his way to the door. Tompkins stood aside as the Resident laid a reassuring hand on Lady Chetwynd Miller's arm.

"Now then, dear, nothing to worry about. You go back to your ladies in the drawing room and we'll see to this."

Lady Chetwynd Miller seemed reluctant but smiled briefly at the company before withdrawing. The Resident said to his ADC: "Ask Devi Bhadra to bring the rascal here into the dining room."

He turned back with a thin smile towards Inspector Jayram.

"It seems as if your intelligence was right. We have a prisoner for you to take away, Inspector."

Jayram raised his hands in a curiously helpless gesture.

"This is technically British soil, excellency. But if you wish me to take charge . . .? Let us have a look at this man."

At that moment, Lieutenant Tompkins returned with Devi Bhadra together with a burly Sepoy from Foran's 8th Bombay Infantry. They frog-marched a man into the dining room. The man was thin, wearing a *dhoti*, a dirty loin cloth affected by Hindus, an equally dirty turban and a loose robe open at the front. He wore a cheap jewelled pendant around his neck hung on a leather thong.

The Resident went back to his seat and gazed up with a hardened scowl.

"Bring the man into the light and let us see him."

The man was young, handsome, but his face was disfigured in a sullen expression. His head hung forward. Devi Bhadra prodded the man forward so that the light from the lanterns reflected on his face.

"I have searched him thoroughly, sahib. He has no weapons."

"Do you speak English?" demanded Lord Chetwynd Miller.

The man did not reply.

The British Resident nodded to Devi Bhadra, who repeated the question in Gujarati, the language of the country. There was no response.

"Forgive me," Inspector Jayram interrupted. "I believe the man might respond to Hindi."

Devi Bhadra repeated his question but there was no reply.

"Looks like your guess was wrong," observed Royston.

Inspector Jayram rose leisurely and came to stand by the man. His eyes narrowed as he looked at the pendant. Then he broke into a staccato to which the captive jerked up his head and nodded sullenly. Jayram turned to the Resident with an apologetic smile.

"The man speaks a minor dialect called Munda. I have some knowledge of it. He is, therefore, from the Betul district."

"Betul?" The Resident's eyes widened as he caught the significance of the name.

Jayram indicated the pendant.

"He wears the symbol of the cult of Vira-bhadra."

"Does he? The beggar!" breathed Lord Chetwynd Miller.

"Well," drawled Gregg. "If he were after this little item, he was out of luck. We had it here with us."

He held up the ruby.

The captive saw it and gave a sharp intake of breath, moving as if to lunge forward but was held back by the powerful grip of Devi Bhadra and the Sepoy.

"So that's it?" snapped Major Foran. "The beggar was coming to steal the stone?"

"Or return it to its rightful owners," interposed Father Cassian calmly. "It depends on how you look at it."

"How did you catch him, Devi Bhadra?" asked Foran, ignoring the priest.

"One of the maids heard a noise in your study, sahib," said the man. "She called me and I went to see if anything was amiss. The safe was open and this man was climbing out of the window. I caught hold of him and yelled until a Sepoy outside came to help me."

"Was anything missing from the safe?"

"The man had nothing on him, sahib."

"So it was the stone that he was after?" concluded Gregg in some satisfaction. "Quite an evening's entertainment that you've provided, your excellency."

The captive burst into a torrent of words, with Jayram nodding from time to time as he tried to follow.

"The man says that the 'Eye of Shiva' was stolen and should be returned to the temple of Vira-bhadra. He is no thief but the right hand of his god seeking the return of his property."

The Resident sniffed.

"That's as maybe! To me he is a thief, who will be handed over to the Baroda authorities and punished. As Gregg said, it was lucky we were examining the stone while he was trying to open the safe."

Major Foran had been inspecting the stone, which he had taken from Gregg, and he now turned to the prisoner.

"Would you like to examine the prize that you missed?" he jeered.

They were unprepared for what happened next. Both the Sepoy and Devi Bhadra were momentarily distracted by the bright, shining object that Foran held out. Not so their prisoner. In the excitement of the moment, they had slackened their grip to the extent that the muscular young man seized his chance. With a great wrench, he had shaken free of his captors, grabbed the stone from the hand of the astonished major and bounded across the room as agilely as a mountain lion. Before anyone could recover from their surprise, he had flung himself against the shuttered windows.

The wood splintered open as the man crashed through onto the verandah outside.

The dinner company was momentarily immobile in surprise at the unexpected abruptness of the man's action.

A second passed. On the verandah outside, the Betulese jumped to his feet and began to run into the evening blackness and the driving rain.

It was the ADC, Lieutenant Tompkins, who first recovered from his surprise. He turned and seized the Sepoy's Lee Enfield rifle. Then he raised it to his shoulder. There was a crack of an explosion which brought the company to life.

Foran was through the door onto the verandah in a minute. Lord Chetwynd Miller was only a split second behind but he slipped and collided with Sir Rupert, who was just getting to his feet. The impact

was so hard that Sir Rupert was knocked to the floor. The Resident
went down on his knees beside him. Father Cassian was the first to
spring from his chair, with an expression of concern, to help them up.
The Resident was holding on to Cassian's arm when he slipped again
and, with a muttered expression of apology, climbed unsteadily to his
feet. By then it was all over.

The young man in the *dhoti* was lying sprawled face downwards.
There was a red, tell-tale stain on his white dirty robe which not
even the torrent of rain was dispersing. Foran had reached his side
and bent down, feeling for a pulse and then, with a sigh, he stood
up and shook his head.

He came back into the dining room, his dress uniform soaked by
the monsoon skies. As he did so, the dining room door burst open
and Lady Chetwynd Miller stood on the threshold again, the other
ladies of her party were crowding behind her.

The Resident turned and hurried to the door, using his body to
prevent the ladies spilling into the room.

"My dear, take your guests back into the drawing room. Immediately!" he snapped, as his wife began to open her mouth in protest.
"Please!" His unusually harsh voice caused her to blink and stare
at him in astonishment. He forced a smile and modulated his tone.
"Please," he said again. "We won't be long. Don't worry, none of
us have come to any harm."

He closed the door behind them and turned back, his face ashen.

"Well," drawled Foran, holding his hand palm outward and letting
the others see the bright glistening red stone which nestled there, "the
young beggar nearly got away with it."

The Resident smiled grimly and turned to his major-domo.

"Devi Bhadra, you and the Sepoy remove the body. I expect
Inspector Jayram will want to take charge now. Is that all right
with you, Foran?"

Major Foran, nominally in charge of the security of the Residency,
indicated his agreement and Devi Bhadra motioned the Sepoy to
follow him in the execution of their unpleasant task.

Lord Chetwynd Miller turned to his ADC and clapped him on the
shoulder. The young man had laid aside the Lee Enfield and was now
sitting on his chair, his face white, his hand shaking.

"Good shooting, Tompkins. Never saw better."

Foran was pouring the young officer a stiff brandy.

"Get that down you, lad," he ordered gruffly.

The young lieutenant stared up.

"Sorry," he muttered. "Never shot anyone before. Sorry." He took
a large gulp of his brandy and coughed.

"Did the right thing," confirmed the Resident. "Otherwise the beggar would have got clean away . . ."

He turned to Jayram and then frowned.

Inspector Jayram was gazing in fascination at the stone which Foran had set back in its box. He took it up with a frown passing over his brow.

"Excuse me, excellency," he muttered.

They watched him astounded as he reached for a knife on the table and, placing the stone on the top of the table, he drew the knife across it. It left a tiny white mark.

White-faced, Major Foran was the first to realize the meaning of the mark.

"A fake stone! It is not 'The Eye of Shiva'!"

Jayram nodded calmly. He was watching their faces carefully.

Sir Rupert was saying: "Was the stone genuine in the first place? I mean, did Savaji Rao give you the genuine article?"

"We have no reason to doubt it," Major Foran replied, but his tone was aghast.

Royston, who had taken the stone from where Jayram had left it on the table, was peering at it in disbelief.

"The stone was genuine when we started to examine it," he said quietly.

The Resident was frowning at him.

"What do you mean?"

"I mean . . ." Royston stared around thoughtfully, "I mean that this is not the stone that I held in my hand a few minutes ago."

"How can you be so sure?" demanded Gregg. "It looks exactly the same to me."

Royston held up the defaced stone to the light.

"See here . . . there is a shadow in this stone, a tiny black mark which indicates its flaw. The stone I held a few moments ago did not have such a mark. That I can swear to."

"Then where is the real stone?" demanded Father Cassian. "This stone is a clever imitation. It is worthless."

Major Foran was on his feet, taking the stone and peering at it with a red, almost apoplectic stare.

"An imitation, by George!"

The Resident was stunned.

"I bet that Hindu chappie had this fake to leave behind when he robbed the safe. The real one must still be on his body," Lieutenant Tompkins gasped.

"On his body or in the garden," grunted Foran. "By your leave, sir, I'll go and get Devi Bhadra to make a search."

"Yes, do that, Bill," instructed the Resident, quietly. He was obviously shocked. Foran disappeared to give the orders. There was a moment's silence and then Jayram spoke.

"Begging your pardon, excellency, you will not find the stone on the body of the dead priest."

Lord Chetwynd Miller's eyes widened as they sought the placid dark brown eyes of Jayram.

"I don't understand," he said slowly.

Jayram smiled patiently.

"The Betul priest did not steal the real ruby, your excellency. Only the fake. In fact, the real ruby has not left this room."

"You'd better explain that," Father Cassian suggested. "The ruby has been stolen. According to Lord Miller, the genuine stone was given into his custody. And according to Royston there, he was holding the genuine stone just before we heard Devi Bhadra capture that beggar. Then the Hindu priest was brought here into this room. He grabbed the stone from Foran and the real stone disappears. Only he could have had both fake and real stone."

Foran had come back through the shattered window of the dining room. Beyond they could see Devi Bhadra conducting a search of the lawn where the man had fallen.

"There is nothing on the dead man," Foran said in annoyance. "Devi Bhadra is examining the lawn now."

"According to Inspector Jayram here," interposed Gregg heavily, "it'll be a waste of time."

Foran raised an eyebrow.

"Jayram thinks the ruby never left this room," explained Father Cassian. "I think he believes the Hindu priest grabbed the fake when he tried to escape."

Jayram nodded smilingly.

"That is absolutely so," he confirmed.

The Resident's face was pinched.

"How did you know?" he demanded.

"Simple common sense, excellency," replied the Bengali policeman. "We have the stone here, the genuine stone. Then we hear the noise of the Betulese being captured as he makes an abortive attempt to steal the stone from your study – abortive because the stone is here with us. He is brought to this room and there he stands with his arms held between Devi Bhadra and the Sepoy. He makes a grab at what he thinks is the ruby and attempts to escape. He believes the stone genuine."

"Sounds reasonable enough," drawled Sir Rupert. "Except that you have no evidence that he was not carrying the fake stone on him to swap."

"But I do. Devi Bhadra searched the culprit thoroughly. He told us; he told us twice that he had done so and found nothing on the man. If the fake stone had been on the person of the priest of Vira-bhadra then his excellency's major-domo would have found it before he brought the priest here, into the dining room."

"What are you saying, Jayram? That old man Shiva worked some magic to get his sacred eye back?" grunted Gregg, cynically.

Jayram smiled thinly.

"No magic, Mister Gregg."

"Then what?"

"The logic is simple. We eight are sat at the table. The genuine stone is brought in. We begin to examine it. We are interrupted in our examination by the affair of the priest of Vira-bhadra. Then we find it is a faked stone. The answer is that someone seated at this table is the thief."

There was a sudden uproar.

Sir Rupert was on his feet bawling. "I am not going to be insulted by a . . . a . . ."

Jayram's face was bland.

"By a simple Bengali police inspector?" he supplied, helpfully. "As a matter of fact, I was not being insulting to you, Sir Rupert. My purpose is to recover the stone."

Lord Chetwynd Miller slumped back into his chair. He stared at Ram Jayram.

"How do you propose that?"

Jayram spread his hands and smiled.

"Since none of our party have left the room, with the exception of Major Foran," he bowed swiftly in the soldier's direction, "and he, I believe, is beyond reproach, the answer must be that the stone will still be on the person of the thief. Is this not logical, your excellency?"

Lord Chetwynd Miller thought a moment and then nodded, as though reluctant to concede the point.

"Good. Major Foran, will you have one of your Sepoys placed on the verandah and one at the door? No one is to leave now," Jayram asked.

Foran raised a cynical eyebrow.

"Are you sure that I'm not a suspect?"

"We are all suspects," replied Jayram, imperturbably. "But some more so than others."

Foran went to the door and called for his men, giving orders to station themselves as Jayram had instructed.

"Right," smiled Jayram. "We will now make a search, I think."

"Then we'll start with you," snapped Sir Rupert. "Of all the impertinent . . ."

Jayram held up a hand and the baronet fell silent.

"I have no objection to Major Foran searching my person," he smiled. "But, as a matter of fact, Sir Rupert, I was thinking of saving time by starting with you. You see, when there was the disturbance of the Betulese being brought in here, at that time you were the one holding the stone."

Royston whistled softly.

"That's right, by Jove! I held the genuine stone. Then I passed it on to Father Cassian and . . ."

The priest looked uncomfortable.

"I passed it on to Sir Rupert just as the commotion occurred."

Sir Rupert's face was working in rage.

"I'll not stand for this," he shouted. "A jumped-up punkah-wallah is not going to make me . . ."

Major Foran moved across to him with an angry look.

"Then I'll make you, if you object to obeying the Inspector's orders, Sir Rupert," he said quietly.

Sir Rupert stared at them and then with a gesture of resignation began to empty his pockets.

Jayram, still smiling, raised his hand.

"A moment, Sir Rupert. There may not be any need for this."

Inspector Foran hesitated and stared in surprise at the Bengali.

"I thought . . ." he began.

"The commotion started. Our attention was distracted. When our attention focused back on the jewel, who was holding it?"

They looked at one another.

Gregg stirred uncomfortably.

"I guess I was," he confessed.

Foran nodded agreement.

"I took the stone from him and that's when we discovered it was a fake."

Gregg rose to his feet and they all examined him with suspicion.

"You won't find anything on me," Gregg said with a faint smile. "Go ahead."

Jayram returned his smile broadly.

"I am sure we won't. You, Mister Gregg, did not take the stone from the hands of Sir Rupert, did you?"

Gregg shook his head and sat down abruptly.

"No. I took it from the box where Sir Rupert had replaced it. He put it back there when the Hindu priest was being questioned."

"Just so. The stone was genuine as it passed round the table until it reached Sir Rupert, who then replaced it in the box. Then Mister Gregg took the stone from the box and passed it round to the rest of us. It was then a fake one."

Sir Rupert was clenching and unclenching his hands spasmodically. Major Foran moved close to him.

"This is a damned outrage, I tell you," he growled. "I put the stone back where I found it."

"Exactly," Jayram said with emphasis. "*Where you found it.*"

They realized that he must have said something clever, or made some point which was obscure to them.

"If I may make a suggestion, Major," Jayram said quietly. "Have your Sepoys take Father Cassian into the study and hold him until I come. We will remain here."

The blood drained from Father Cassian's face as he stared at the little Bengali inspector. His mouth opened and closed like a fish for a few seconds. Everyone was staring at him with astonishment. If nothing else, Cassian's expression betrayed his guilt.

"That's a curious request," observed Foran, recovering quickly. "Are you sure that Father Cassian is the thief?"

"Will you indulge me? At the moment, let us say that Father Cassian is not all that he represents himself to be. Furthermore, at the precise moment of the disturbance, Cassian was holding the stone. Sir Rupert had asked him for it. Our attention was momentarily distracted by Lady Miller at the door. When I looked back, the stone had been replaced in its holder. Sir Rupert, seeing this, took up the stone, examined it and replaced it. The only time it could have been switched was when Cassian held it, before he replaced it in the casket."

Cassian half rose and then he slumped down. He smiled in resignation.

"If I knew the Bengali for 'it's a fair cop', I'd say it. How did you get on to me, Jayram?"

Jayram sighed: "I suspected that you were not a Catholic priest. I then made a pointed reference to Pelagius to test you. Any Catholic priest would know that Pelagius is not a saint and martyr of the fourth century. He was a philosopher who argued vehemently with Augustine of Hippo and was excommunicated from the Roman church as a heretic. You did not know this."

Cassian shrugged.

"I suppose we can't know everything," he grunted. "As I say, it's a fair . . ." He had reached a hand into his cassock. Then a surprised

look came over his features. He rummaged in his pocket and then
stared at Jayram.

"But . . ." he began.

Jayram jerked his head to Foran. Foran gave the necessary orders.
After the erstwhile "Father" Cassian had been removed, against a
background of stunned silence, Foran turned back to Jayram.

"Perhaps you would explain why you have had Cassian removed
to be searched. The search could easily have been done here."

"The reason," Jayram said imperturbably, "is that we will not find
the stone on him."

There was a chorus of surprise and protest.

"You mean, you know he is innocent?" gasped Foran.

"Oh no. I know he is guilty. When our attention was distracted
by the entrance of the captive, Father Cassian swapped the genuine
stone and placed the fake on the table for Sir Rupert to pick up later.
It was the perfect opportunity to switch the genuine stone for the
faked stone. Cassian is doubtless a professional jewel thief who came
to Baroda when he heard that Savaji Rao was going to present 'The
Eye of Shiva' to the Resident for transportation to England."

"You mean, Cassian was already prepared with an imitation
ruby?" demanded Royston.

"Just so. I doubt whether Cassian is his real name. But we
will see."

"But if he doesn't have the stone, what can we charge him with and,
moreover, who the hell has the genuine stone?" demanded Foran.

"Father Cassian can be charged with many things," Jayram
assured him. "Travelling on a fake passport, defrauding . . . I am
sure we will find many items to keep Father Cassian busy."

"But if he doesn't have the genuine 'Eye of Shiva' who the devil
has it?" repeated Lieutenant Tompkins.

Jayram gave a tired smile. "Would you mind placing the genuine
ruby on the table, your excellency?"

There was a gasp as he swung round to Lord Chetwynd Miller.

Lord Chetwynd Miller's face was sunken and pale. He stared up
at Jayram like a cornered animal, eyes wide and unblinking.

Everyone in the room had become immobile, frozen into a curious
theatrical tableau.

The Resident tried to speak and then it seemed his features began
to dissolve. He suddenly looked old and frail. To everyone's horror,
except for the placid Jayram, he reached into the pocket of his dinner
jacket and took out the rich red stone and silently placed it on the
table before him.

"How did you know?" he asked woodenly.

Ram Jayram shrugged eloquently.

"I think your action was one made on – how do you say – 'the spur of the moment'? The opportunity came when our prisoner tried to escape. You instinctively ran after him. You collided with Sir Rupert and both went down. Cassian went to your aid. He had his role as a priest to keep up. There was – how do you call it? – a mêlée? The jewel accidentally fell from Cassian's pocket unnoticed by him onto the floor. You saw it. You realized what had happened and staged a second fall across it, secreting it into your pocket. You were quick-witted. You have a reputation for quick reactions, excellency. It was an excellent manoeuvre."

Foran was staring at the Resident in disbelief. Tompkins, the ADC, was simply pale with shock.

"But why?" Foran stammered after a moment or two.

Lord Chetwynd Miller stared up at them with haunted eyes.

"Why?" The Resident repeated with a sharp bark of laughter.

"I have given my life to the British Government of India. A whole life's work. Back home my estates are heavily mortgaged and I have not been able to save a penny during all my years of service here. I was honest; too scrupulously honest. I refused to take part in any business deal which I thought unethical; any deal from which my position prohibited me. What's the result of years of honest dedication? A small pension that will barely sustain my wife and myself, let alone pay the mortgage of our estate. That together with a letter from the Viceroy commending my work and perhaps a few honours, baubles from Her Majesty that are so much worthless scrap metal. That is my reward for a lifetime of service."

Major Foran glanced at the imperturbable face of Jayram and bit his lip.

"So, you thought you saw a way of subsidizing your pension?" Jayram asked the Resident.

"I could have paid off my debts with it," confirmed the Resident. "It would have given us some security when we retired."

"But it was not yours," Sir Rupert Harvey observed in a shocked voice.

"Who did it belong to?" demanded the Resident, a tinge of anger in his voice. "Was it Savaji Rao's to give? Was it the Queen-Empress's to receive? Since Colonel Vickers stole it from the statue of Shiva in Betul it has simply been the property of thieves and only the property of the thief who could hold onto it."

"It was the property of our Queen-Empress," Lieutenant Tompkins said sternly. He was youthful, a simple young soldier who saw all things in black and white terms.

"She would have glanced at it and then let it be buried in the royal vaults for ever. No one would have known whether it was genuine or fake – they would merely have seen a pretty red stone. To me, it was life; comfort and a just reward for all I had done for her miserable empire!"

Lord Chetwynd Miller suddenly spread his arms helplessly and a sob racked his frail body. It was the first time that those gathered around the table realized that the Resident was merely a tired, old man.

"I have to tell my wife. Oh God, the shame will kill her."

They looked at his heaving shoulders with embarrassment.

"I don't know what to do," muttered Foran.

"A suggestion," interrupted Ram Jayram.

"What?"

"The stone was missing for a matter of a few minutes. It was not really stolen. What happened was a sudden impulse; an overpowering temptation which few men in the circumstances in which His Excellency found himself could have resisted. He saw the opportunity and took it."

Foran snorted.

"You sound like an advocate, Jayram," he said. "What are you saying?"

Jayram smiled softly.

"A policeman has to be many things, major. Let us look at it this way – the stone was placed in the safe keeping of the Resident by Savaji Rao. It is his responsibility until it is placed on the ship bound for England. Perhaps the Resident merely placed it in his pocket as a precaution when the thief was brought in. I suggest that you, Major Foran, now take charge of the genuine stone, on behalf of the Resident, and see that it goes safely aboard the SS *Caledonia* tomorrow. Lord Chetwynd Miller has only a few months before his retirement to England, so he will hardly be left in his position of trust much longer. He is a man who has already destroyed his honour in his own eyes, why make his dishonour public when it will gain nothing?"

Foran nodded agreement. "And Cassian must never be informed of how the stone was removed from him."

"Just so," Jayram agreed.

Sir Rupert Harvey rose with a thin-lipped look of begrudging approval at the Bengali.

"An excellent solution. That is a Christian solution. Forgiveness, eh?"

Ram Jayram grinned crookedly at the baronet.

"A Hindu solution," he corrected mildly. "We would agree that sometimes justice is a stronger mistress than merely the law."

# THE TRAIL OF THE BELLS
# Edward D. Hoch

*Over the last year I have been catching up on my reading of Edward Hoch's Ben Snow stories and have found them a most fascinating and infectious series. Hoch is the author of over seven hundred mystery stories, amongst them a fair number of historical mysteries. The most consistent series in that respect features Ben Snow, a gunman of the old Wild West, the stories spanning the years from 1887 into the twentieth century. Although not the first written, the following is the earliest setting of the Ben Snow stories.*

Ben Snow had been on the trail for two days before he found the dying man by the water hole. He drew his horse Oats up slowly, right hand resting on the butt of his pistol, aware that he might be riding into a trap. But then he saw the bloody bandage across the man's chest and recognized him as Tommy Gonzolas, the half-Mexican gunman who'd ridden with Poder since the beginning. His horse grazed on the sparse grass nearby.

Ben still approached slowly, even after he knew Gonzolas was dying. Although the desert terrain allowed little cover for a rifleman, he knew that Poder wouldn't be above the ruthlessness of baiting a trap with a dying man. "Are you armed?" he asked Gonzolas. "Throw me your gun."

The man barely lifted his head, and the hands that clutched at his chest made no movement toward the pistol that lay on the sand a foot away. Ben stepped quickly forward and kicked the weapon out of reach. Then he stooped to examine the wound.

"I'm dying," Gonzolas said quite clearly. He'd been wounded during the bank robbery back in Tosco, and the only reason Ben Snow had taken on the job of tracking Poder through the desert was the belief that the serious wound might slow down the fugitives. But

Poder had left the man to die beside a water hole with his gun and ridden on without him.

"Tell me about Poder," Ben asked the man. "Where's he headed? What does he look like without his mask?"

Gonzolas tried to laugh, but his mouth was filling with blood. "You'll never get Poder," he managed to gasp. "Nobody will."

"Come on, Gonzolas, he left you to die. You owe him nothing."

But it was too late. The Mexican's head lolled to one side and his eyes closed. For an instant it seemed he was dead. Then, as Ben started to straighten up, Gonzolas uttered his last words. "The bells," he said. "Listen for the bells and you will find Poder. Or Poder will find you."

Whether the words were meant to help or to lead Ben to his death, Ben didn't know. But the bells were the only lead he had, and after pausing long enough to bury Tommy Gonzolas at the water hole and unsaddle and set free his horse, he rode on in search of them.

It was the following day that he came upon the girl with the dead horse. She was dressed in denim pants and a man's shirt, but even from a distance there was no doubt about her sex. She held her head high and proud, with long dark hair hanging halfway down her back, and the rifle in her hands was warning enough that she was not to be tampered with. Still, with no towns or trails in sight, Ben felt an obligation to offer assistance. As he drew nearer, he was glad he had. The dead horse on the ground at her feet fitted closely the description of the pinto that Poder had ridden out of Tosco.

She lowered her rifle as he approached on horseback. "I thought at first it was him coming back," she said.

"Who? What happened here?"

"Masked man stole my horse."

Ben dismounted and went over to inspect the dead horse. It had been killed by a shot through the head at close range. "What did he look like?"

"I told you he was wearing a mask — a cloth bag that covered his head, with holes for his eyes. He was short, about my height, and he knew how to handle a gun."

"What are you doing out here alone?"

She started to raise the rifle again. "Who wants to know?"

Ben smiled, stepped up to the weapon, and pushed the barrel gently aside. "The man who stole your horse is known as Poder, and Poder never would have left you with a loaded rifle to shoot him in the back as he rode away. He took the bullets, didn't he?"

"You seem to know everything, Mr – "

"Snow. Ben Snow."

She seemed to relax a little, as if knowing his name made him more acceptable. "I'm Amy Forrest. My brother and I have a small ranch in the valley about forty miles from here. I was looking for strays – "

"In the desert?"

"Sometimes they come this far, especially the young ones that don't know any better. There are some water holes nearby."

"I saw one yesterday."

"Anyway, I heard a shot and rode over this way. When the man saw me coming, he pulled that hood over his head and drew a gun on me. Said his horse twisted a leg and he had to shoot it, and he was taking mine. He emptied the bullets out of my rifle, just as you guessed, and left me here. I wish I'd seen his face."

"If you had, you'd have been a dead woman. That masked man who calls himself Poder has never been seen by anyone. He's robbed banks and stagecoaches all over the New Mexico territory. Generally he doesn't even speak. A sidekick named Tommy Gonzolas did the talking for him. But Gonzolas is dead now."

"How come you know so much about him?"

"He killed a banker in Tosco a few days ago. I happened to be in town and they hired me to go after him – sort of a one-man posse."

"What makes you so good?"

He smiled at her. "They got some crazy notion I'm Billy the Kid."

"He's dead."

"Don't tell them. They're paying me well to bring back Poder, dead or alive."

"Does he have a first name?"

"He doesn't have any name, far as I know. *Poder* means 'power' in Spanish. It's just an alias he started using. Nobody knows a thing about him. Nobody but Gonzolas ever saw his face, and now he's dead."

"I guess I'm lucky to be alive. Can you get me back to my ranch? It's due north of here."

He stared out at the stark landscape, searching for a clue as to the direction Poder might have taken. "I don't know. I was figuring more on heading west. If you plot the locations of Poder's robberies on a map, they seem to be centered west of here. But my horse could carry us both as far as the next settlement and I could drop you there."

"Well, that's something."

He climbed into the saddle and helped her up behind him, surprised at her quick agility.

They'd barely started their trek when he thought he heard something far in the distance. Something that sounded like bells. "What's that?" he asked her.

She listened, cocking her head to the left. "You mean the bells? That's the mission at San Bernardino. It's only a few miles from here. Is that where you'll take me?"

"I think so," Ben decided. "Yes."

The mission came into view at the top of the next rise, and Ben judged it to be about five or six miles from the spot where Poder had stolen Amy Forrest's horse. He rode down the last dune slowly until he reached firmer ground, then urged his horse forward through the scattering of cactus and sagebrush. The mission itself sat in a small oasis and consisted of a white adobe church with a long, low building at the back. Amy explained that this was a monastery of the religious order that staffed the mission and raised what crops they could. "There are only a few priests. The rest are lay brothers who work in the fields. And there are Indians and Mexicans who have a sort of trading post outside the mission."

"You sound as if you know the place well," Ben said.

"I usually stop whenever I ride this way. Women aren't allowed into the monastery, of course, but I like the peacefulness of the church. It always seems cool there, even on a hot day."

He watched several dozen people emerging from the church. "What's going on?"

"It's Sunday morning. They've been to Mass."

"I forgot. Out here the days get to be the same."

"They have just the one Mass at ten o'clock, and that's the only time the bells ring all week. It's a wonder we heard them at all."

"Perhaps we were being called here," Ben murmured . . .

They dismounted near a paddock where the horses were kept and Amy ran to the railing. "That's King!" she pointed. "That's my horse!"

"The big brown one?"

"I'm certain of it!"

Ben spoke to an Indian standing nearby who seemed to be in charge of the paddock area.

"You there – what's your name?"

"Standing Elk. I am a Pueblo."

"All right, Standing Elk. Did you see who brought that big brown stallion in?"

"No. I do not know him." The Indian wore a suit of fringed buckskin, with a headband but no feathers. He was shorter than Ben and seemed younger.

"You saw no one ride in here about – how long ago, Amy?"

"An hour or so. He stole my horse an hour before you came along. Of course, he might have ridden faster than we did."

"I see no one," Standing Elk insisted.

"All right," Ben said. "Come on, Amy. We'll worry about your horse later."

A priest in Sunday vestments was standing outside the mission church, keeping carefully within the shadow cast by the mission's bell tower. He was young and fair-haired and Ben imagined his skin would burn quickly in the heat of the New Mexico desert.

"Good morning," he greeted Ben. "Welcome to the Mission of San Bernardino. And how are you today, Amy?"

"I'm fine now, Father. This is Ben Snow, Father Angeles."

The priest bowed his head in greeting and Ben noticed for the first time the cowl protruding from the back of his vestments. "I'm sorry you're late for Mass, Ben. We have only the one service here, at ten o'clock. There is also a weekday Mass every morning."

"Ben rescued me from the desert, Father. A gunman stole my horse."

"A gunman? Near here?"

"We think he rode this way, Father," Ben told him. "He's a killer and bank robber known as Poder."

"Power," the priest translated automatically. "I have not heard of him." He turned to Amy. "But, my dear child, you must be exhausted after such an experience – come inside and let Mrs Rodriguez tend to you."

Amy started to protest but Father Angeles insisted. Ben followed along until Amy had been delivered into the hands of a fat Mexican woman with a motherly look. Then he waited while the priest reverently shed his vestments and put them away.

"This is a lovely place to find in the middle of the desert," Ben said. "I don't know these parts as well as I should."

"Where are you from?" Father Angeles asked, brushing the sandy hair back from his forehead.

"The Midwest, originally. But I've been roaming for years now. I guess I don't really have a home." As they passed along a cloistered walkway leading to the monastery, he asked, "How many of you live here?"

"Father Reynolds, Father Canzas, and I. There are only five lay brothers at present, along with a few people to help us out.

Mrs Rodriguez cooks the meals, Luis rings the bells on Sunday, Standing Elk tends to the horses, and Pedro Valdez runs the trading post. The others are passers-by who stop to see us when they're in the neighborhood. Like Amy."

A monk with a boyish face came through the monastery door and Father Angeles stopped to introduce him. "Brother Abraham, this is Ben Snow, a traveler who has paused to rest with us."

Brother Abraham bowed slightly as the priest had done. "A pleasure to have you here. I hope your stay will be a pleasant one."

"I'm sure it will be," Ben told him and the monk continued on his way.

"Abraham," Ben said. "An Old Testament name."

"A presidential name," Father Angeles corrected. "The babies named after Lincoln have come of age now."

"Do you have any trouble with the Indians around here?"

"Nothing since Geronimo surrendered last September. The Apaches were a bother at times, but they seem at peace now. The Pueblos have always been our friends. Large numbers have converted to Christianity, though they cling tenaciously to their ancient rites."

He showed Ben through the monastery with its stark cell-like rooms. "It's almost like a prison," Ben observed.

"In a way, although the spirit is free. The lay brothers like Abraham toil in the fields, and often we're at their sides. One of us says Mass each morning, and generally all of the Indians and Mexicans at the trading post attend."

"A great many Mexicans," Ben observed.

"The border isn't that far from here."

"Do you know a man named Tommy Gonzolas? He would be half Mexican."

"I believe he's been here from time to time. Why do you ask? Are you searching for him?"

"I've already found him."

As they returned to the mission church, they passed beneath a large crucifix and Father Angeles crossed himself. "You wear your pistol like a gunfighter, Mr Snow. I hope no harm has come to Tommy Gonzolas."

"The harm had already been done when I found him, Father. I buried him out on the desert."

"May God have mercy on his soul."

"He was a bank robber and murderer, Father. He rode with the man called Poder, whom I've come to find."

"The person who stole Amy Forrest's horse."

"The same one."

"I know nothing of him."

"Was anyone away from the mission this week?"

"There is no way to tell. As I have said, they come and go. Standing Elk might know better than I do – he tends to the horses."

"Yes. I'll have to talk with him again."

"Join us for lunch first. Your questions will flow with more wisdom after a good meal."

The mission food was slight but tasty, and Mrs Rodriguez seemed to take special pride in cooking for them. Ben was only sorry Amy couldn't join them at the table, but the woman served her a special lunch in the kitchen. Only one of the five lay brothers was Mexican, and since he spoke no English Father Canzas conversed with him in Spanish. The third priest, Father Reynolds, had been a Civil War cavalry officer who'd come west to fight Indians and found God instead.

"I decided it was more important to save their souls than kill their bodies," he said. "But you would have been too young to remember the war."

"I was six when it ended," Ben said. "I'm twenty-eight now."

"You look older – or more mature, I should say. And riding in the sun has weathered your face."

Brother Abraham sat across the table from him, between Brother Franklin and Brother Rudolph. None of them were especially talkative but Abraham seemed the quietest. Ben wondered what his story was.

After lunch Father Canzas walked out to the trading post with Ben and introduced him to Pedro Valdez, a handsome moustached man who ran the place with a group of half-breed assistants. He joked with Father Canzas, and the fat priest seemed to enjoy what had obviously become a friendly ritual between them. "You are a friend of the Father's?" he asked Ben. "A new friend, surely, or he would have fattened you up to his size by now."

After more casual conversation Ben asked, "Do you know a half breed named Tommy Gonzolas who often comes here?"

"I know him, yes. I know many people."

"He died recently and I'm trying to get word to his close friends. He told me he had a friend at the mission here."

Valdez lit a thin Mexican cigarillo. "You were with him when he died?"

"I was, yes."

"I know nothing about it. He talked with the others, but had no special friends."

Ben remembered the dead horse. "Who around here might ride a pinto?"

"Mottled or spotted horses are common out here, where wild herds still roam and interbreed. Standing Elk must have a half dozen pintos in his corral right now."

Ben sighed. "I only want to give a message to the friend of Tommy Gonzolas. You're not much help."

"I know of no friend."

Father Canzas had drifted away, looking over some of the blankets and trinkets offered for sale by the Indians. It was a meager trade at best, Ben decided, with only a handful of people even knowing of the place's existence – the mission of San Bernardino was not exactly on the regular wagon routes. He wondered if its very remoteness was the reason Poder came here.

"I'm looking for a man named Poder," Ben said finally. "Do you know him?"

Valdez smiled and his eyes seemed to twinkle. "The people of Tosco have hired you to capture him. Yes, Mr Snow, the word has reached here already. An Indian told me just this morning that Billy the Kid was riding to capture Poder, or to kill him. But you're much too tall for Billy. He was short like me. And besides, he's dead. He's buried over in Fort Sumner, not far from here, where Pat Garrett dropped him with two bullets at his girl friend's house." Valdez studied the burning tip of his cigarillo. "Billy should have taken General Lew Wallace's offer of amnesty if he left the New Mexico territory. He met with Wallace, you know, but he refused the offer."

"Is there a message here for me?" Ben wondered. "Should I get out while I can, too?"

The Mexican shrugged. "Where do you think you might find Poder? Do you think it is fat Father Canzas who rides with the mask over his face? Or one of those Indian children playing in the dust? Do you really care?"

"I've come a long way."

"We have all come a long way, Mr Snow." Valdez turned away as a loud dispute erupted among the children. He shouted something at them in Spanish and they fell silent. Ben turned and headed toward the corral.

There were over twenty horses penned up, but no sign of Standing Elk. Perhaps, he, too, had gone to lunch. Ben wandered back toward the mission and noticed one of the monks hurrying along the cloister. His hood was up and there was no way of identifying him, but there was something about his movements that attracted Ben's attention. He was moving too fast, almost running.

Ben boosted himself over the low cloister wall and followed in the direction the monk had taken. He knew it led to the monastery itself, and as he stepped through the doorway he was aware he was entering forbidden territory. There was no Father Angeles with him now, giving him a tour.

The shadows were deep here, with only an occasional hint of the afternoon sun outside. He moved along the passageway, past the empty rooms where the lay brothers slept. Once he thought he heard a footstep behind him and whirled, his hand on his gun, but there was no one. He seemed to be alone in the building.

Then he rounded a corner and froze.

Straight ahead was a wooden partition, with spiraling bars like a grillwork. A man's arms extended between the bars and then hung down, as if he had been caught in the instant of escape.

It was the Indian, Standing Elk, and he was dead.

Father Reynolds was the first to arrive on the scene in response to Ben's shouts, and he administered the last rites to the dead man. "There's blood," he said as he finished.

"He's been stabbed."

Father Angeles arrived then, with Brother Franklin. "What's happened here?"

"Standing Elk has been murdered," Ben said. "I should have guessed it would happen."

"You can't blame yourself," Father Angeles said.

"My coming here was the cause of it. Poder killed him before he could tell me who rode here on Amy Forrest's horse."

"I cannot believe this person you seek is hiding here," Father Reynolds said.

"There's the evidence of it," Ben said, pointing to the body.

"If the body is here," Brother Franklin said, "does that mean one of us killed him?"

Ben shook his head. "If Standing Elk could enter this building, so could any other Indian or Mexican. Dressed in one of your robes with the hood up, who would know the difference?"

"There is no sheriff within a hundred miles," Father Angeles said. "What shall we do?"

"Bury him. I'll report it when I return to Tosco. You certainly can't leave the body above ground in this heat."

"We must have a funeral Mass," the priest said, rubbing his sandy hair. "But we have no method of embalming here. He must be buried soon."

*

The funeral Mass was held late that afternoon, with Father Angeles officiating. While the mission bells tolled mournfully, the people of the oasis filed into the church for the second time that day. Ben sat near the rear of the church with Amy Forrest, watching the ancient rituals. When the priest had finished, another Pueblo, Running Fox, came forward to add some beads and bracelets to the plain wooden coffin Pedro Valdez and his assistants had fashioned.

After it was over, after Ben and Amy had stood with the others in the little graveyard behind the mission, he studied the faces of the departing mourners. But if one was the face of Poder, there was no sign of it. Ben asked Father Canzas if he had a map of the territory. "There's one in our library," the fat priest answered.

He showed Ben and Amy to a book-filled room near the cloister and left them. On a map Ben measured the distance from the mission to the sites of Poder's crimes as well as he could remember them. As he worked, Brother Abraham came in to watch over his shoulder. "What are you doing?"

Ben glanced up from his task. "The man I seek, who probably murdered Standing Elk, committed a crime at each of these sites. All are within three days' ride of this mission."

The monk nodded silently, and after a time he left. Ben asked Amy, "Do you know anything about him? He seems a bit strange."

"Just that they say his parents were killed by Apaches when he was ten and he's been here ever since."

Ben returned to the map and she wandered over to the bookcases. "They have quite a library here. Melville, Victor Hugo, Dickens, Hawthorne. There's even a copy of *Ben Hur*, the novel by our territorial governor."

"I'm surprised they'd have Hugo. I heard once that the Church doesn't approve of his novels."

"I don't suppose anyone sees it but the priests and brothers. Most of the Indians and Mexicans probably don't read English."

"Do you think that's why Poder rarely speaks?" Ben asked. "Because his English is limited?"

"I had the same idea when you said this Gonzolas person usually did the talking. I wondered if it was because Poder's English was poor."

"But he talked to you when he stole your horse."

"Just a few words, and they were muffled by his mask."

"There is one other explanation of why he rarely spoke," Ben said quietly. It was something that had been hovering at the back of his mind all day. "Do you have your rifle handy?"

"I brought it into the kitchen when we arrived. It's probably still there."

"Let's go get it."

She seemed puzzled by his request but she went along with it. They found the rifle standing in a corner while Mrs Rodriguez worked on the evening meal. "We eat soon," she said. "Do not go far away."

"Just outside," Ben assured her.

They walked into the courtyard by the cloister and Ben pointed the weapon toward the sky. "I was saying there was one other explanation of why he rarely spoke. Poder could be a woman."

"I – "

"You might have been riding toward the mission when your horse twisted its leg. You had to shoot him, and when I happened along you feared I might recognize that pinto as Poder's. So you made up the story of his stealing your horse."

"Do you really believe that?"

"There's one way of testing it. If your story was false, then he didn't empty your rifle at all. It should still be loaded now." He squeezed the trigger.

There was a loud crack as the weapon fired toward the sky.

Amy Forrest stood her ground, staring at him. Neither of them moved for a full minute. Then she said, "I bought some cartridges from Valdez this afternoon and reloaded it. You can ask him if you don't believe me."

He lowered the rifle. "I believe you."

"Poder isn't a woman. It was a man's voice that spoke to me." She turned and went into the house.

Ben stood there for a moment, looking after her. Then he turned and walked out toward the trading post. There were few people around and he went to sit by himself in the shade of a large cactus, drawing letters in the sand.

Presently Father Angeles joined him. "I heard a shot," the priest said. "And I saw Amy. She's very upset."

"It's logical," Ben told him. "She killed Standing Elk not because he saw who rode into the corral this morning, but because he knew no one rode into the corral. He would know she lied."

"Logic is not always the same as truth," the priest said. "If Poder is really here, it is not that young woman."

Ben raised his eyes to stare at him. "You know the truth, don't you, Father? Poder has confessed to you."

"He has not, but of course I could not tell you even if he had."

His eyes strayed to the letters Ben had traced in the sand. "What is this?"

"*Poder* and *Pedro* have the same letters. One is an anagram of the other."

"So you have a new suspect in place of Amy."

"Is Valdez the only Pedro here?"

"Yes. But go slowly this time, Ben."

The priest left him as Mrs Rodriguez summoned them to dinner. But as Ben got to his feet and smoothed over the sand in front of him, he remembered one of the books in the mission library. His education was far from complete, but he had read the classics as a boy in the Midwest. Perhaps part of the answer was in that book.

A sudden movement among the cloisters caught his eye and he saw again the hurrying monk he'd been pursuing when he came upon Standing Elk's body. He broke into a run, intent on catching him this time. The man had been spying on him, and that could mean it was the one he sought.

"Stop!" Ben shouted as the cowled figure pulled open the door of the monastery. His fingers reached out, grasping the back of the hood and pulling it off just as the monk was about to disappear through the entrance. And as the figure turned around toward him, he saw what he'd hoped and feared.

There was no face. There was only a cloth mask with holes cut in it for the eyes.

"Poder! We meet at last!"

From beneath the folds of the cloak a pistol appeared. Ben grabbed it, wrestling at close quarters to keep it from pointing at him. There was a shot as a bullet tore past his head, and he relaxed his grip for just an instant. Too close to aim again, Poder swung the gun hard against Ben's temple.

Dazzling lights and a searing pain cut across his head and he felt himself falling. He clawed at the hooded face before him, managing to catch a finger in one of the eyeholes. As he went down, he pulled the mask with him, praying that with his dying breath he would at least see the face of his killer.

And then he saw it – the face of Poder.

It was the face of a man he had never seen before.

As his vision cleared and he returned to consciousness, Ben recognized Amy and Father Angeles kneeling by him. "Who was it?" Amy asked. "Who hit you?"

"Poder."

"Did you see his face?"

"Yes." He tried to stand up. His head hurt, but otherwise he seemed all right. His pistol was still in its holster. "I have to go after him."

"He'll kill you," Amy said.

"He didn't just now."

"We came running and frightened him away."

Ben leaned against the wall to steady himself and then took a few steps. He was all right. He could do it now. "You two stay here," he said.

"Do you know where he is?" Father Angeles asked.

"I know."

He left them and went to the church. Once inside, he found a ladder leading the way up and began climbing. He kept climbing until he reached the top of the bell tower, some fifty feet above the ground.

Poder was waiting for him, standing behind the two mission bells with his back to the sky.

"I knew you'd come up here," Ben said. "Luis is your name, isn't it? I remember Father Angeles telling me this morning, *'Luis rings the bells on Sunday.'* I thought I saw everyone at Standing Elk's funeral, but of course I didn't see you because you were ringing the bells then, too."

"You should have stayed away," Poder said. "You shouldn't have come up here."

"I was hired to bring you back."

"Gonzolas told you, didn't he? I was afraid someone might find him before he died, but I couldn't bring myself to kill him."

"He said to listen for the bells and I would find you. I didn't take it quite as literally as I should have. I thought he only meant you were here at the mission. But your mistake was in stealing Amy Forrest's horse."

"I had to take it."

"I know. Your time was running out. You must have had a moment of panic when your pinto twisted his leg and came up lame. But then you saw her, and took her horse. When I thought about it, I asked myself why. You were only five miles from the mission – certainly not a long walk for a man capable of robbing stagecoaches and banks. Why risk showing yourself, even masked, and then leaving the witness alive?"

"I have never killed a woman."

"But why risk it at all when you could have walked the distance in eighty or ninety minutes? Why – unless you had to be back at the mission for some Sunday morning duty? I asked myself what that duty might be. There was the Mass at ten o'clock, of course. Could

Poder be one of the mission's three priests? No, because they said Mass daily and Poder had been gone all week, riding three days to Tosco and three days back. He'd been away that long, or nearly that long, before. So he couldn't be a priest, nor one of the lay brothers who worked daily in the fields. Nor Mrs Rodriguez, who prepared all their meals. But the Indians and Mexicans came and went at will, and certainly wouldn't be missed on Sunday Mass. Only one person was free the rest of the week, to the best of my knowledge, but had Sunday morning duties – Luis, who rang the bells on Sunday. If those bells didn't ring at ten o'clock, people would ask where Luis was."

Poder shifted slightly and Ben saw the pistol in his hand. He stepped a bit to his right, putting the bells between them. "Draw!" Poder said. "The time for talking is over."

But Ben kept on talking. "I suppose it was the view from up here that did it to you. Looking down on all those little people can give a sense of power. Hugo's Hunchback of Notre Dame was a poor deformed creature until he looked down from his bell tower on the streets of Paris far below. It can make one feel like God up here – invincible, with the power to rob and kill. The mask and the silence were part of the image, adding to your legend."

"Draw, damn you!" Poder shouted, and fired his six-shooter. The bullet clanged off the bell, sending tremors through the air.

Ben drew his gun.

He stared down from the tower for a long time, watching the tiny figure on the ground, seeing Father Angeles and Amy running out to where it had landed. The priest knelt in the dust and prayed over Luis's body while Ben watched.

He could feel the power from up here, the power that Luis had felt, and finally he had to look away, toward the vastness of the desert horizon, until he felt small again.

# MURDERING
# MR BOODLE
## Amy Myers

*One of the enquiries I had after the publication of the first volume was
why I had not made any reference to the Auguste Didier stories by Amy
Myers. You may recall, in the bibliography at the end of that volume,
I had set a cut-off date of around 1870 for my survey of historical
mystery stories, mainly because after that date the volume of Sherlock
Holmes stories would have filled another entire book! But I probably
should have made reference to the many very excellent detective stories
set at the end of the nineteenth century. Some of the most eclectic
of these are the Auguste Didier stories. Didier is a cordon bleu
chef with a penchant for solving crimes. The novels, which began
in 1986 with* Murder in Pug's Parlour *and have now reached
their eighth volume, are written with a tongue-in-cheek humour and
a remarkable eye for parodying Victorian values. They are also very
clever crimes. So now, for the many fans of Auguste Didier, is his very
first short story.*

"Money? My dear Mr Didier!"
Gervase Budd was shocked. Checked in expansive mid-
flow, he was hurt beyond measure. The willow-patterned waistcoat
quivered with emotion, over the incline of Mr Budd's stomach. "My
partner, Mr Boodle, attends to such details."

Had he inadvertently transgressed some unwritten code by enquiring about financial terms, Auguste wondered, a code understood by
any gentleman who entered this sanctum but not by mere maître
chefs such as he? When he had been approached by this venerable
publishing firm he had been given to understand by Mr Budd that
had the sixteenth century been fortunate enough to produce Messrs
Boodle, Budd & Farthing, Mr William Shakespeare would have had
to look no further for a publisher who would have left the authorship
of his work in no doubt whatsoever, and moreover provided his widow

with considerably more financial reward than his second-best bed. On the threshold of the twentieth century, what better home could there be to immortalize Auguste's ten-volume magnum opus, *Dining with Didier?*

"Shall I be meeting Mr Boodle?" Auguste watched him carefully. There had been a certain heartiness in Mr Budd's tone which he was well accustomed to hearing in underchefs who assured him all was well with the entrées, when that was far from being the case.

"Ah, Mr Popple, come in, pray do," Gervase Budd boomed – in relief? – at the entry of a wild-eyed young man of about twenty years, with his hair artfully arranged as to suggest a life of constant debauchery lasting twice that number. "Mr Didier, may I present Mr Clarence Popple, our perspir – ah," Mr Budd mopped his brow with an ornamental red silk handkerchief – "*a*spiring poet."

"A poet can survive everything but a misprint," Clarence smirked.

"Ah yes, I recall dear Oscar did observe that once," murmured Mr Budd.

Clarence eyed him balefully. "Mr Budd is to do me the honour of publishing my thoughts on life."

"A wise decision." Auguste opted for diplomacy, while privately thinking this young man's thoughts would bear as much relevance to life as Francatelli's masterpieces to a soup kitchen.

Gervase Budd rose to his feet, his dark frock coat parting to either side of his paunch. "Shall we take a glass of port wine, gentlemen, while awaiting your fellow prospective authors?"

He flourished a cut glass decanter, much as Maskelyne and Devant might display their magical mysteries. Auguste's heart sank. He had a particular dislike of ruining his palate before the first great adventure of the day, namely luncheon, and regarded the glass that Mr Budd obviously believed contained the nectar of the gods without enthusiasm.

"I shall recite my ode to a golden carp," Clarence Popple announced.

At least he showed some appreciation of cuisine, Auguste thought tolerantly. The carp was the king of fish, a fish of remarkable powers and longevity. It was only as Clarence progressed it occurred to Auguste that he might possibly have misheard carp for harp.

"My muse she sings above . . ."

Auguste promptly lost interest, but Mr Budd smiled brightly throughout, though perhaps his eye had a glazed expression worthy of a dressed carp itself. It only sprang into life at the entry of a third author. Mr Budd however had not appeared bored so much as preoccupied, he thought: he seemed a distinctly worried man. Why?

"Ah, Miss Mellidew," Gervase greeted the new arrival.

Auguste rose to his feet, eager to meet the famous Queen of the Circulating Library, author of (among other delightful novels) *Cecilia's Sahara Sojourn* (3 vols, crown 8vo, illustrated boards, Heart & Whitestock, London, 1875), which had been devoured in enormous numbers by Mudie's Select Library, creating a market for every word penned by Millicent Mellidew thereafter. The three-decker novel might be waning in popularity but not if it had her name attached.

"Dear Miss Mellidew, or should I say Cecilia?"

Mr Budd's archness was wasted, for Miss Mellidew was clearly agitated at entering this masculine sanctum, though now considerably older than Cecilia.

"I am delighted to meet you, Miss Mellidew," Auguste said truthfully, as she nervously pushed back a lock of mousy hair which had escaped from beneath her old-fashioned ornate hat. The artificial robin that adorned it leered threateningly towards him, as if protesting that his nest had been jammed on to her head regardless of his comfort. "I of course know *Cecilia*. Dare we expect a sequel?"

Mr Budd beamed, taking this as a personal tribute to his acumen in persuading Miss Mellidew to change publishers.

"Oh!" Millicent Mellidew gasped breathlessly. "I do so value gentlemen readers." She smiled uncertainly. "But I fear Lambkin thought his Cecilia sadly changed."

In Auguste's opinion, any change to Simpering Cecilia could only be for the better, and years of feasting on Arab cuisine might well have taken their toll even on the magnificent physique of Sheikh Hamed the Shining One, known to his beloved Cecilia as Lambkin.

"Never." Gervase Budd assured the prize so nearly within his grasp. "The truly beautiful triumph over time."

Miss Mellidew looked her prospective publisher straight in the eye. "Provided they receive their just rewards," she whispered modestly. "What terms do you propose?"

Auguste almost applauded. Clarence showed no such restraint. "Bravo, Miss Mellidew," he declared enthusiastically.

Mr Budd was not dismayed. "Generous, dear lady, generous. You may be assured of that. Ah, you have arrived, General."

The meeting had been called for twelve o'clock, and it was now twelve-fifteen. No wonder it had taken so long to relieve Mafeking, Auguste thought irrepressibly, if this was the standard of organization.

"Naturally, I am an Army man, sir." General Eric Proudfoot-Padbury, a tall lean man of fifty-odd, with a fine moustache carefully curled for adorning commemorative china, glared at the assembled company.

"Will you take a glass of port, General?"

"Never touch the stuff. Brandy and soda."

Gloom spread once more over Mr Budd's jovial face, as he reluctantly opened a side cupboard, extracted a bottle, poured a small measure and firmly replaced it. The General snorted. "I trust the money flows more generously than your liquor, Budd. Me memoirs would be a major contribution to history, you told me. *Time Marches to a Drumbeat*", he told Miss Mellidew complacently. He did not bother with Clarence or Auguste. Poets were merely those unfit for soldierly service, and humble cooks, like batmen, did not rank. Armies might march on their stomachs but what went into them was of little importance.

"Naturally," Gervase Budd purred, sitting down, resting his hands proprietorially on his desk, in a vain attempt to imply all was well with himself, the company, its prospective authors and the entire world.

"Old Boodle still holding the purse strings, eh?"

Gervase Budd jumped. "You know of Mr Boodle?" There was a certain caution in his voice. "Indeed, yes, Boodle, Budd & Farthing are still fortunate enough to retain his services."

"Who is Mr Boodle?" Auguste enquired.

"Mr Boodle is *the* Mr Boodle," Mr Budd informed him reverently. "I myself am his junior." Mr Budd's girth and years made the word instantly inappropriate. "The original Budd was my father. I like to think of my little office as the temple to art, but we are ruled by the business acumen and wisdom of Mr Boodle."

"And Mr Farthing?" asked Millicent.

"Mr Farthing, dear man, retired from the business, having made his penny." Gervase Budd chuckled at his little joke, and stopped when nobody else did. "Mr Boodle also likes his merry jest." There was a touch of defiance in his voice. "When as a raw youth of twenty I entered these portals I was guided by the beneficent hand of Mr Boodle. That hand thankfully has been at the helm ever since."

"Then I shall look forward to discussing the details of a contract with Mr Boodle," Auguste told him firmly. Negotiating with publishers, after all, would be no different to dealing with butchers. The quality of meat supplied must determine the price.

"You may rest assured, Mr Didier, that here at Boodle, Budd &

Farthing, we acknowledge our duty to the future. The food of today nurtures England's gentlemen and mothers of tomorrow."

"Bravo," cried Miss Mellidew boldly, overcome with emotion. "I am glad you accord woman her rightful place. It is what I look for in a publisher. I do sometimes sense that lady novelists are not as highly regarded as they deserve. I trust you are not a disparager of womankind in any respect, Mr Budd?"

"I am not, dear lady," he assured her fervently. "Why, our own receptionist is a lady, Miss Violet Watkins. Doubtless you met her when you entered, together with our invaluable doorman, Mr Wallace."

"The bourgeoisie," declared Clarence languidly; he had obviously decided he had been excluded from the conversation long enough. "My poetry shall enrich their lives."

"It shall, it shall, Mr Popple," Budd assured him.

"I have entitled it *Poems for Posterity*."

"Ah." Mr Budd's face clouded over once more. "And might I enquire your proposed title, Miss Mellidew?"

"*Mildred's Missionary*."

"Ah." Gervase Budd looked even more dejected. "A story of passion and frustrated romance?" he enquired with no great hope.

"A priest torn between love and duty."

"My dear Miss Mellidew!" Tears of gratitude appeared in Mr Budd's eyes at this unexpected commercial break. "If I might suggest a change of title, however?"

"You may not."

"Me memoirs," the General shouted as Mr Budd showed no sign of interest in *Time Marches to a Drumbeat*, "centre on the reverse at Isandhlwana."

Mr Budd blenched in alarm. "I thought you were in command at Rorke's Drift," he cried, as sales prospects disintegrated before his eyes.

"Overrated," snarled his prospective author. "Now Isandhlwana, the Sudan . . ." He trumpeted on, as Budd regarded him with increasing dismay. The General seemed to have had a distressing tendency to be present at every reverse of the British army in recent times.

"And you, Mr Didier," Budd turned feverishly to Auguste. "May we hope for glimpses of food favoured by the famous, just a mention of the Prince of Wales, even Her Majesty Herself?"

"I regret we may not," Auguste returned amiably. "My professional code, you understand."

"Ah, but our advance – "

"How much *do* you pay in advances on royalties, Mr Budd?" Miss Mellidew asked. Auguste noted that timid though Miss Mellidew appeared a certain briskness entered her voice when money was mentioned.

"Ah. Mr Boodle has decreed a most democratic system," Mr Budd announced with nervous pride. "Here at Boodle, Budd & Farthing every author receives an identical advance in order that the well established may thus encourage our younger, less experienced authors."

Even as Auguste reflected on his own reaction to this somewhat startling concept (unknown to butchers), he saw Clarence Popple's languid look suddenly readjust to the possibility of receiving a sum far beyond most aspiring poets' expectations. Miss Mellidew, on the other hand, clearly had severe doubts about Mr Boodle's sanity, and the General looked decidedly frosty. Democracy was seldom practised in the British army.

"How much?" the latter demanded.

"Mr Boodle will – "

"How much?" Miss Mellidew's voice was suddenly strident.

Mr Budd recognized defeat. "Twenty-five pounds." He glanced round the stony faces, and cleared his throat. "I will speak to Mr Boodle – "

"I am far from sure I can agree to this," Miss Mellidew announced. "*Mildred's Missionary* deserves as much as Lambkin."

"Art, Miss Mellidew, is art. And there will, naturally, be royalties. On the 31s 6d edition, the 6s *and* the 2s editions," Mr Budd added ingratiatingly.

"I myself," Auguste decided to ally himself with the Missionary, "would expect an advance suitable to meet the considerable expense involved." Indeed his bachelor home life did not include the luxury of purchasing truffles for experimentation. The integrity of *Dining with Didier* must not be compromised by cutting back on quality.

"When shall we be meeting Mr Boodle?" the General asked grimly.

"Mr Boodle is a most reasonable – " Gervase stopped in mid unhappy flow. In the street below directly beneath his window a dull murmur of conversation had suddenly swelled into a vast commotion of shouting voices and banging on doors, unknown in this quiet London Georgian backwater. "What, I wonder, is that?"

Auguste crossed to the window and peered down into the street.

"There appears to be a large number of people attempting to gain entrance to your premises," he said with some interest. "I believe you should investigate, Mr Budd."

"No!" Gervase Budd's face was pale. "No doubt it is merely

a crowd eager to purchase *Steadfast's Last Stand*. A most popular recent publication. By Mr Arnold Hope." His voice trailed off as four prospective authors gazed at him unconvinced. "Our best selling author. At present," he added.

Clarence joined Auguste, all trace of languor vanished. "Wait till I tell Arnold about this," he grinned. "He'll dine me at the Ritz."

"*Steadfast's Last Stand* appears to appeal to ladies and gentlemen, both young and elderly," Auguste pointed out, observing both parasols and walking canes waving like military barley in the wind.

"They're demanding to see old Boodle," Clarence yelled in high glee, as Miss Mellidew elbowed her way in between him and Auguste.

"Mr Boodle?" Gervase Budd laughed lightly. "Dear me, how could I have forgotten? It's Mr Boodle's birthday," he announced triumphantly. "Doubtless these are his admirers bearing due tribute."

The General exerted his authority, pushing Auguste and Miss Mellidew aside at the very moment that some of the better aimed due tribute in the form of rotten fruit splattered on the window pane before him. He withdrew hastily. Behind them the door flew open and a terrified Miss Violet Watkins skidded to a halt at her employer's desk, distraught from her neat brown bun to the buttons quivering on her boots.

"I have been loyal, Mr Budd," she informed her employer, a choke in her voice. "I have been loyal for thirty years. But now our authors are insisting on seeing Mr Boodle immediately. They are causing an affray, Mr Budd. Mr Wallace cannot restrain them. Mr Boodle refuses to meet them since he is occupied on the yearly royalty accounts. But they are *abusive*, Mr Budd. What am I to do?"

Gervase Budd rose magnificently to his feet and the occasion.

"Mr Boodle must be protected at all costs. Kindly request Mr Simmonds of Printing, Mr Jones of Subscriptions, and Mr Catling of Reading to step to Mr Wallace's aid." The services of the red silk handkerchief were once more called upon.

"Oh . . ." Miss Watkins' wail would have done justice to Cecilia in mid-Sahara, as the noise intensified below.

"Lead on, Budd. We're behind you," the General announced, retirement at an end as new battle honours loomed in his sights.

"No!" Gervase's cry was heart-rending.

"Then allow me to go for you," Auguste offered immediately, hurrying to the door. Mr Budd however moved even quicker, forestalling the General, and somehow to his surprise Auguste found himself and Mr Budd outside the door, and the other three still inside. To Auguste's even greater surprise Mr Budd appeared

to be locking them in. He caught Auguste's stare of astonishment
and attempted nonchalance.

"For their own safety," he explained lightly. "I should not like
them to be mistaken for Mr Boodle."

"You mean the due tribute would reach the wrong person?"
Gervase looked blank.

"It is Mr Boodle's birthday," Auguste reminded him gravely,
having to shout now to be heard over the hubbub below. The
words "police", "the law", "immediate action" and "demand" could
be distinguished, amongst some far less polite.

"Bumps," gabbled Gervase wildly, following Auguste reluctantly
past the hallowed door and down towards mayhem. "They have come
to give Mr Boodle his birthday bumps." There was desperation in
his voice.

Below him on the staircase which wound its way up through the
four floors of Boodle House, Auguste could see Miss Watkins barring
the way as effectively as Horatius his bridge to Lars Porsena, her
arms outstretched against the tide. The advance rush of Mr Boodle's
admirers crossed the landing of the first floor and were checked as
they realized the strength of the defence.

"Mr Boodle is working," Miss Watkins shrieked. "On *your* royalty accounts. He must not be disturbed. The accounts will be
with you . . ." She hesitated for a moment, then proceeded firmly,
"*tomorrow*."

From the rear Auguste could see the stalwart form of Mr Wallace
already turning back the more faint-hearted of the mob, and the
apparently disorganized group first rumbled, then murmured, and
finally retreated piecemeal, beyond the hallowed portals of Boodle
House.

"It seems to me they lack organized union power," Auguste
observed. "Perhaps that might be my role?"

Mr Budd gave him a swift look of pure dislike. "Pray do not jest,
Mr Didier." His plump and highly agitated rear proceeded up the
staircase again. Hurrying in his wake, Auguste was beginning to
feel like the Lighthouse Keeper's Daughter in the old melodrama.
Certainly *Dining with Didier* was going to be a more adventurous
experience than he had hitherto realized, he decided, as he heard the
rumpus coming from behind the locked door of Mr Budd's office.

"Really, Mr Budd – " The door was opened to reveal a hysterical
Miss Mellidew. "I am a maiden lady. To lock me in with two strange
gentlemen is hardly the action one expects of one's prospective
publisher."

"I'm sure Mr Popple and the General are as gallant as Lambkin

– er – Sheikh Hamed the Shining One." Gervase Budd attempted to regain an urbane composure.

He failed. Miss Mellidew turned a cold eye on bohemian Clarence and the apoplectic General Proudfoot-Padbury. She turned an even colder one on Mr Budd.

"Lambkin was a true gentleman, I would remind you; he was almost *English*, educated at Oxford, fully conversant with Shakespeare and Keats, a former officer in the British army, and winner of the VC before returning to duty in his own land, his beloved desert."

"The dashed fellow had several wives. They don't allow that in the British army," snarled the General.

Miss Mellidew turned pink. "That, General, is what parted them. Lambkin, while loving Cecilia truly, passionately, eternally, was forced to marry for duty under Muslim law. He was the flower of chivalry to Cecilia however. And I am glad," she added pointedly, "that you have read my little book, General."

"My wife," the General trumpeted feebly, caught out. "I merely glanced at it. Thought it was Jorrocks."

"In life," intoned Clarence sanctimoniously, "one should experience all, read everything, and meet everyone."

"Including Boodle. *Now*," the General announced firmly.

"I must admit to a certain curiosity myself, Mr Budd," Auguste backed him up.

"Allow me first to introduce you to the rest of our devoted staff," Gervase Budd said hastily, beginning to regain composure. "I will then ascertain whether Mr Boodle might be persuaded to spare a few moments."

"Good of you," the General grunted.

"Publishing," Mr Budd continued forlornly, "is going through a very bad time. Trade has been quite devastated by these cheap sixpenny books. The death of the trade is at hand, I am reliably informed by Mr Jones of Subscriptions."

"Indeed? I understood that the new Net Book Agreement so vigorously requested by booksellers was proving the saviour of the trade," Auguste said mischievously.

"An improvement," Mr Budd conceded hastily, "but a drop in the ocean. We have a long way to go, Mr Didier, a very long way."

"Despite Arnold Hope's *Steadfast's Last Stand*?" Clarence asked innocently, winking at Auguste in a most unpoetic way. "I'm sure he'll be most distressed to hear of your pessimism."

"Ah, Mr Popple, of course you are a *close* friend of his. Naturally I did not mean to imply a lack of future for books of the quality of Mr Hope's."

"Romance will always find a market," Miss Mellidew reminded him sternly.

"As will food," Auguste contributed. Indeed the latter could claim precedence in his opinion.

"Miss Mellidew, if you will permit me to lead the way – " Gervase hastily put an end to this insubordinate talk of markets by prospective authors by bustling from the room. A casual hand flung open the door of the other office on this fourth floor of the tall narrow Boodle House. "The board room where Mr Boodle, the staff and I gather to discuss the running of the company. We pride ourselves on democracy."

It did not seem to be an overused room, to Auguste's eye. It was gloomy, overshadowed by the house opposite it, and its large table had a distinct film of dust. The portrait of Mr Budd Senior stared down at it in distaste, and his son hurriedly closed the door, descending the stairs to the third floor. Here was the hallowed door of Mr Boodle, according to its ornate nameplate. Or what Auguste could see of it, since Mr Budd was standing across the doorway, making it hard to squeeze past his stomach in the narrow passageway. Once Mr Boodle's privacy had been safely guaranteed, Gervase Budd led his flock downstairs and to one of the two offices on the second floor.

"Mr Simmonds, Printing," he shouted, throwing open the door.

He hardly needed to announce its role. The two tables were littered with photographs, rulers, piles of manuscript and compositor's proofs. A Remington typing machine adorned one table, a man with greying hair and moustache worked feverishly at the other. A monocled eye glanced briefly at them before returning to the work before him. "Crown octavo," he muttered cryptically. "Vellum, I must have vellum, Mr Budd. Nothing but the best for Boodle, Budd & Farthing authors."

"You shall have it, Mr Simmonds," his employer beamed. "May I present four new authors to you?"

Mr Simmonds inclined his head. "I trust you have all availed yourselves of the services of a lady typewriter?" he demanded in a high tremulous voice.

"My handwriting is excellent," Millicent Mellidew told him querulously. "I do not hold with such modern inventions."

"And I am a poet," Clarence said soulfully. "My pen is my poetry."

"My wife is my typewriter," the General boomed from the doorway where Mr Budd had kept them in order that the smooth running of Boodle, Budd & Farthing might not be interrupted. "All the Farthings are excellent at that sort of detail."

Mr Budd jumped. "Farthings?" he repeated cautiously. "My dear sir, did you mention the Farthing family?"

"I did, sir. My wife is William Farthing's sister."

Auguste had the distinct feeling from the General's moment of triumph (one of the few in his career) that he had been waiting for the opportunity to drop this in. Generals did not become generals by accident.

"Ah." Gervase rallied, rubbing his hands together with somewhat forced bonhomie. "How is dear Mr Farthing?"

"Dead. Without getting his money from Mr Boodle," the General said grimly.

"I am indeed sorry to hear of his demise," Gervase gabbled. "I had a high opinion of Mr Farthing, and so," he added unwisely, "did Mr Boodle."

"Then he can pay out what he owed him to his heirs."

On the whole the meeting with Mr Boodle bade fair to be spirited, Auguste thought with some amusement.

"I thought Mr Jones of Subscriptions and Trade next," Mr Budd announced brightly, not inviting disagreement, as he led the way slowly downstairs to the room beneath on the first floor.

"Moodie's have placed an excellent order for Mr Hope's next work." Mr Jones's dark hair and sideburns, almost disappearing into the tall white linen collar, were almost all that could be seen of him from their vantage point behind Mr Budd at the doorway; he was buried in ledgers and files that confirmed the age-old reputation and reliability of Boodle, Budd & Farthing.

"Splendid. And we are to be the proud publishers of Miss Mellidew's next novel."

"Delightful." Mr Jones appeared already to be writing up orders for it as he buried himself once more in his ledger. His demeanour suggested the sooner he returned to work the greater the sales. Miss Mellidew, Auguste noted, did not seem quite so enthusiastic at the prospect before her. He also noted one other interesting fact, his eye on Mr Jones's collar.

Mr Budd banged the door shut and beamed. "And now to return to the holy of holies. Reading." He almost tiptoed past the discreetly labelled Bathroom and up the staircase to the next floor once more, the room opposite Mr Simmonds'. He knocked, a courtesy he had not extended to the other staff.

"The muse must not be disturbed without warning," he whispered.

The muse answered readily enough in the guise of Mr Catling, the youngest of the three underlings, judging by his jaunty red hairstyle and moustache.

"I think I have a little gem here, Mr Budd." Mr Catling, it appeared, could no more be wrenched from his duty than his colleagues.

"Excellent, excellent. Mr Boodle will be delighted at the good news," Mr Budd beamed happily. "And that," he concluded with some relief, "completes the tour of our little kingdom with the exception of the stock cellars."

"What about Mr Boodle?" Miss Mellidew asked on Mildred's behalf.

"Luncheon first," Mr Budd told them firmly. "I had thought Romanos – " Clarence brightened with enthusiasm "– but I realized you would think the time more profitably spent discussing the finer details of publication."

"No," the General disagreed tersely.

"Shall we return to my office?" Mr Budd suggested loudly, apparently not having heard the General. "A sherry, and we could if you wish take a pie with it."

"Romanos," Clarence opted.

"I agree," Auguste said, beginning to enjoy himself hugely. "Surely the author of *Dining with Didier* should not be presented with a mere pie?"

Overcome by the prospect ahead, Gervase Budd temporarily neglected his duties as shepherd dog and it was not until they had reached his office that he realized that one of his flock was absent. His eyes glazed over in panic.

"Where is Miss Mellidew?" he shouted hysterically.

The General coughed in amazement, and Clarence sniggered.

"I think perhaps she has merely withdrawn for a few moments," Auguste soothed tactfully. "I am sure she will be with us shortly."

She was, but not in the state Gervase would have welcomed. The door burst open and Millicent almost fell inside.

"He's dead!" she shrieked. Auguste's reflexes stiffened.

"Dead. Dear lady, who's dead?" Gervase Budd squawked, paling slightly.

"Mr Boodle."

"How – where?" Auguste asked urgently, as Gervase Budd was speechless with shock.

"In his office. I opened his door to speak to him, and there he was. Dead."

"My dear Miss Mellidew." Gervase relaxed. "You must be mistaken. A trick of the light, no more. Mr Boodle is in perfect health."

"He is dead, Mr Budd." Her voice quivered, but held no uncertainty.

Auguste rose to his feet. "I suggest I investigate, Mr Budd."

"No, no. You obviously entered the wrong room, dear lady," Mr Budd protested.

"What does the room matter?" Auguste replied impatiently.

"It was Mr Boodle's room and he is *dead*," Millicent repeated adamantly, perhaps reflecting that Cecilia would have received rather better treatment than her creator, had she swooningly announced her discovery of a corpse.

"He can't be," Gervase replied complacently.

"I am going to see," Auguste repeated, walking to the door.

"No," shrieked Mr Budd, hurling his bulk across the room to prevent him.

"Are you mad, sir? Stand from our path," the General commanded. "Have you no concern for your partner's welfare?"

"No. I mean yes. But it can't be Mr Boodle," Gervase moaned.

"I demand you summon help." Hysteria was rapidly overtaking Miss Mellidew.

"There is no body."

"Kindly stand aside, Mr Budd," Auguste ordered. "If Miss Mellidew is mistaken I shall soon be able to confirm it."

"Mr Boodle can't be dead."

"Stand aside, Budd," the General commanded once more, with much the same effect as when he ordered the Boers to give up the siege of Ladysmith.

"I won't. He can't be dead."

"Why not?"

"Because he already is."

"Gibberish, man," snarled the General.

"Explain yourself, Mr Budd," Auguste asked quietly.

"There *is* no Mr Boodle," his late partner moaned. "Mr Boodle died twenty years ago."

"Are you out of your mind, sir?" the General exploded.

"Mr Boodle died in 1880."

"But – "

"What the deuce do you mean, sir?" The General saw no reason to wait for a mere woman's interjection.

Seeing no alternative, Gervase Budd crumpled, giving a fair unconscious imitation of Mr Jingle. "Mr Boodle – very fine man – certain trifling weaknesses – as we all have. Mr Arnold Hope discovered minor discrepancies – most unpleasant – blackmailed unfortunate Mr Boodle into publishing and advertising his books as great works. Succeeded – " he added gloomily. "Books sold – Boodle man of great integrity – driven beyond endurance to depart these

shores – with proceeds of autumn programme – lost them all – shot
himself – bad for Boodle, bad for Boodle, Budd & Farthing – why
tell anyone? So I let everyone continue to believe Mr Boodle still ran
the firm." Mr Budd looked round hopefully. "Brilliant idea."

"But – "

"I say – " This time it was Clarence who interrupted Miss
Mellidew. "Are you telling us all this yarn about Mr Boodle and
authors' royalties was balderdash?"

"But – "

"Bad time in publishing," Gervase said apologetically. "Seemed
best. Poor old Boodle. In his grave for twenty years."

"I am sorry to correct you," Miss Mellidew positively shrieked,
"but Mr Boodle's corpse is not in his grave; it is in his office and very
recently dead."

"It can't be, dear lady," Gervase beamed, much happier now all
was explained.

"I fear you are overlooking the point, Mr Budd, "Auguste intervened sharply. "Irrespective of Mr Boodle, Miss Mellidew claims to
have seen a corpse."

"I did, I did – "

"And I shall investigate now."

"By Jingo, I'm behind you, sir," the General bellowed.

"By Jingo, so am I," Clarence declared enthusiastically. Publishing
was obviously much more fun than writing sonnets in a garret.

Auguste wished he could share this youthful enthusiasm. Such
abilities as he had in detection hung like an albatross around his
neck. Alexis Soyer never had to contend with dead bodies while
writing his *Gastronomic Regenerator*, nor had Eliza Acton stumbled
across a corpse in her kitchen in the middle of *Modern Cookery*.
Mrs Marshall's cookery school was not spiced with sudden death,
or Brillat-Savarin interrupted in mid philosophical flow by the news
that he was to don a detective's hat. He tried to persuade himself that
Miss Mellidew was mistaken, that the man was merely stunned, but
as he put his hand to the hitherto inviolate knob of Mr Boodle's door
Auguste found his heart unaccountably fluttering. Life was seldom
as simple as that, and death even more rarely so.

Behind him breathed his seconds in command, the General and
Clarence, and lurking behind them the reluctant and ashen-faced
Mr Budd and Miss Mellidew. The room was still and quiet. Books
with heavy leather bindings stared gloomily from glass-fronted
bookcases, dark blue velvet curtains shielded Mr Boodle from too
close an inspection by the sun. A grandfather clock stood in one
corner, silent now, as if stopped never to go again when Mr Boodle

departed. On the floor the dark maroon carpet was alleviated by two skin rugs. Tiger-hunting not, presumably, having been a sport available to Mr Boodle, he had compromised with the skins of two bulldogs, heads and all, to guard their John Bull of British publishing.

Gervase Budd followed the direction of Auguste's eyes. "Mr Boodle's beloved Albert and Victoria," he explained faintly. "Mr Boodle was always one for a merry jest."

Auguste scarcely heard him. If there had been any doubt in his mind over Miss Mellidew's declaration, it had been dispelled. On the carpet by the fireplace was a portly elderly man, lying half on his side, half face down, and with a deep gash visible in his temple.

"I moved it," quavered Miss Mellidew. "I thought he was alive, you see. But there – there was no pulse." The memory overcame her, and she sank into a leather armchair. Auguste knelt over what he was already convinced was a corpse. Millicent Mellidew had been right. He stood up again, trembling slightly, wishing that men too had the privilege of sinking into chairs and being gently revived with smelling salts. Or preferably cognac.

"Miss Watkins" – seeing her with the redoubtable Wallace in the doorway – "pray make a telephone call to Scotland Yard and ask for Inspector Egbert Rose at my request, and the police doctor."

"Police?" shrieked Mr Budd.

"This is a sudden death," Auguste answered quietly.

"Accident. Think poor Boodle committed suicide by throwing himself on the corner of the fender, do you?" the General snorted disdainfully.

Auguste did not reply. Sometimes the albatross weighed heavier than at others. It probably *was* an accident he told himself firmly, fighting back the little niggle inside that had made him send for Egbert. There were tiny spots of blood on the shirt front that might, just might, have a different source than the wound on the temple.

Clarence had nervously come to stand at his side and looked down at the corpse. His eyes widened. His mouth fell open. "It's Arnold! It's not old Boodle at all." He ceased to be a "greenery-yallery, foot in the grave young man" and became the scared twenty-year-old he was inside. The General unceremoniously caught him as he fainted, and deposited him contemptuously in the adjoining chair to Miss Mellidew. With one cautious eye on the body, she waved her smelling salts under his nose and his revival was prompt if ungrateful.

"What did you do to him?" Clarence shouted at the unfortunate Mr Budd.

Gervase Budd shrank back. "Me?" he bleated. "I did nothing. Why should I cause harm to our favourite, beloved author? Our best-selling author," he added glumly, as the terrible truth began to strike home to him.

"He wasn't beloved by you, Budd. He was blackmailing you, he told me. He must have known about Boodle. That's why you've done for him. He was going to organize the protest this morning, unless you coughed up more royalties. Now I know why he wasn't there. Because he came to see you first."

Gervase regarded his budding poet with intense dislike.

"Is it true Arnold Hope was blackmailing you?" Auguste enquired gravely.

"Why else would I be publishing this dear boy's atrocious poems?" Gervase wailed.

Clarence fainted again, though an eye opened quickly at Auguste's next question. He had been delving deep in his memory of old scandals of which he had privileged knowledge from Egbert. "Didn't Hope leave England at much the same time as Oscar Wilde's trial, and on much the same issue?"

"Oh!"

"I beg your pardon, Miss Mellidew." Auguste turned instantly at her faint cry. "I forgot there was a lady present."

"If you mean was I his nancy, yes I was," Clarence shrieked. "I loved him. He loved me." Miss Mellidew's face turned an even sicklier hue.

"Dear Arnold's next work of art," Gervase remarked as if at random, "was to be entitled *My Nephew, My Friend*, a humorous book of recollections of travels on the Continent with his young friend Clarence, an ignorant and foolish young man whom he was able to instruct on the niceties of life. One might almost say the young man was to be held up to ridicule."

"It's not true," cried Clarence. "Arnold would never do such a thing. Our love is – was – too sacred."

"Sacred?" Miss Mellidew sat bolt upright, pink spots of anger in her pale cheeks. "How dare you profane the name of love, you – you – *criminal*." She burst into tears.

"Naturally *you* would say that," Clarence smirked.

There seemed to be remarkably little sympathy being shown for the late Arnold Hope, Auguste thought. Clarence was smug, Miss Mellidew self-righteous, and the General studiedly indifferent. Even the corpse of a stranger should arouse pity and shock, but here there seemed none. And if that were the case, it could only be because those present were thinking not of the corpse but of their own position. He decided not to pursue Clarence's comment for the moment, for he needed to reassess it in the light of his first reactions to his fellow prospective authors. Meanwhile he returned doggedly to fact. "If Mr Hope had been to see you, Mr Budd, what was he doing here, in Mr Boodle's room?"

"It was merely a social call he paid to me," Gervase gabbled, perceiving his drift and disliking it intensely.

"And then he came down here, fell over and died," Clarence jeered.

"I fear my port wine is a little on the strong side," Gervase Budd offered feebly. "No doubt it affected Mr Hope adversely. It is the best Oporto."

"Accident is highly probable," Auguste said diplomatically. "However since there is a slight possibility this unfortunate man did not die by accident, might I suggest we move downstairs, lock the front doors until the police arrive and ask all your staff to join us there."

"Ah. That may be difficult." Mr Budd looked sheepish.

"This poor fellow's dead, Budd. Surely you can afford to stop your staff working for a while?" the General roared. "Common decency, man."

"I think what Mr Budd means is that there is no staff," Auguste explained. "Is that not so?"

Gervase Budd nodded miserably.

"They *all* died twenty years ago?" squealed Miss Mellidew.

"Good God, you didn't murder the lot, did you?" snorted the General.

"They did not. I did not," Mr Budd replied with dignity.

"We saw them," Clarence pointed out.

"I rather think we saw the same man." Auguste glanced at Mr Budd who sulkily nodded. "Mr Simmonds, Mr Jones and Mr Catling were simply Mr Wallace in disguise, nimbly making use of the outside staircase provided for the event of fire, and climbing through windows." He had observed during their tour that while the hair and moustache changed colour, the three gentlemen all had a tiny ink blob in an identical position on their tall white linen collars.

"You run this whole show on your own?" the General demanded, astounded.

"No money for wages," Mr Budd explained miserably. "Publishing is going through a very bad time. Miss Watkins and Mr Wallace – most loyal." His voice trailed off, as he deemed this the appropriate moment to lead his band of increasingly unlikely additions to his future programme from Mr Boodle's desecrated office.

A quick examination after they left told Auguste no one had entered via Mr Boodle's window, which was firmly shut, and had

been these few years from the smell of the room. He forced himself
to look once more at the body, before leaving. In cookery one had to
select ingredients that complemented one another: in detection one
sought those that did not. Here were two such: the corpse and the
location.

Why had Arnold Hope come here? To meet Mr Boodle? Surely
Hope of all people must have been aware the room was untenanted.
Or had Gervase Budd fooled him too? Had there followed a quarrel
with Budd in this very room? And was it accident or murder? Did
his own fear of murder lead him to see it where it did not exist,
Auguste asked himself. Fortunately Egbert would shortly be here
to lift responsibility from him. Then conscience awoke. How often
had Egbert told him that the sight of sudden death often released
talkative tongues that later lost such agility. Now was the time to
lead and to listen. Later was the time for Egbert to judge.

The staff of Boodle, Budd & Farthing (Miss Watkins and Mr Wallace)
sat nervously on the edge of their chairs, unaccustomed to sitting in
the presence of authors, especially prospective ones – unlikely though
it now was that these four would be adding their lustre to the spring
programme.

"While we are waiting," Auguste began firmly, "we should establish our own arrival times, as well as Mr Hope's. What time was
his appointment with you, Mr Budd?" He invested just the correct
amount of authority in his tone.

"Eleven o'clock," Gervase supplied unhappily. "He was on time."

"Five minutes early," supplied Miss Watkins helpfully.

"You escorted him to Mr Budd's office, Miss Watkins?"

"Staffing arrangements did not permit." She avoided her employer's eyes in case he deduced a note of reproach.

"And what time did he leave, Mr Budd?"

"Shortly before you arrived," came the listless reply.

"And that was a quarter to twelve."

Miss Watkins nodded vigorously as if glad to help to exclude
Auguste from suspicion.

"I had a most friendly discussion with Mr Hope," Gervase
volunteered hopefully.

Clarence laughed in triumph. "That's not what he said." Revenge
was sweet, if ill-advised.

"*When* did he say that, Mr Popple?" Auguste asked mildly. Clarence
looked wildly around, as if pondering a further swoon.

"I meant darling Arnold was not *expecting* it to be a friendly
meeting."

"No. He was intending to tell the authors about Mr Boodle, wasn't he, if you refused to publish his next book on moral grounds?"

Sometimes guesswork succeeded, as Mr Budd's silence confirmed.

"And at what time did you arrive, Mr Popple?" Auguste switched attack.

"You should know. You were there."

"About ten minutes after you, Mr Didier," Mr Budd supplied, anxious to be helpful now the limelight had moved.

"I think not," declared Miss Watkins. "Mr Wallace, I distinctly remember this young man was here before Mr Didier. I thought he might *be* Mr Didier."

Auguste was not flattered. Messrs Wallace/Simmonds/Jones/Catling were in agreement, however. "As always you are correct, Miss Watkins."

"So where were you, Mr Popple?"

"In the closet," Clarence declared loudly. Miss Mellidew blushed at such bohemian frankness, then she looked puzzled.

"But – " She paused.

"Yes, Miss Mellidew?" Auguste prompted gently.

"Nothing." She pursed her lips.

"Please. It is necessary we should be frank, no matter the circumstances."

Millicent shut her eyes and whispered: "When I arrived, I visited the bathroom."

"And when was that?"

"She came in just after you," Miss Watkins supplied eagerly.

"Just a moment, madam." The General had been applying his thinking cap. "You went to the latrines after the tour round the house as well."

"Really, sir." Miss Mellidew looked ready to cry. "I am of a nervous disposition."

The General subsided, murmuring something about army manoeuvres and good training. Miss Mellidew stared into a future bleak with disgrace. So did Gervase Budd. At the very least he could expect Mildred's Missionary to escape unconverted.

"And you, General, arrived last. Just before twelve-fifteen, I recall."

"Before that," Wallace supplied gruffly.

"So where were you, sir?"

"Where do you blasted well think I was?" the General growled, caught out. "In the latrines."

Miss Mellidew bridled, her honour somewhat restored.

"So the intervals between your separate arrivals in the building

and your entries into Mr Budd's office, were all spent in ..."
Auguste hesitated. How could he put this delicately? He abandoned
the attempt. "All spent in the same closet on the first floor. Mr Popple
was there from, say, 11.40 to about 11.55, Miss Mellidew from 11.50
to somewhere close to 12.10, and the General from 12.05 to almost
12.15."

"You are indelicate, sir," Miss Mellidew gasped.

"Unusual, to say the least, since I presume none of you noticed
the others," Auguste continued regardless. "All of you in theory had
time to visit Mr Boodle's office, as did Mr Budd, since we only have
his word for it, as to when Arnold Hope left him." A bleat of protest
escaped the unhappy publisher. "Now Miss Watkins, Mr Wallace,
can you tell me where you were?"

They could. "Here," they said in unison. "Until the abusive mob
arrived." Miss Watkins added as a solo contribution.

"And then?"

"Mr Wallace restrained them while I came to see you, and
I restrained them on my return. I held them," she added in
modest pride.

"And after they had left?"

"I remained downstairs while Mr Wallace – " She broke off,
blushing.

"Carried out his amateur theatricals," the General barked.

Mr Wallace folded his arms, on behalf of Messrs Simmonds, Jones
and Catling.

"And you were here alone?"

"Yes." Miss Watkins suddenly realized her vulnerable position.
"But I would have been seen if I had come up to Mr Boodle's room,"
she cried in alarm.

"Calm yourself, Miss Watkins. We stood at the doorway to each
room. There is no way you could have passed us unseen."

"Wallace could," Clarence pointed out. "He could have gone up
to Mr Boodle's room and murdered poor Arnold before we opened
Mr Simmonds' door."

Mr Steven Wallace stood up. "I, young sir, was a soldier, a sergeant
in Her Majesty's Bloomin' Army, until injury to my health caused me
to abandon my profession. In the service of Boodle, Budd & Farthing
I have found contentment, even if it does involve jumping through
windows like a blasted clown, begging your pardon, ladies. But I
am forty-five years old and suchlike cavorting don't leave time for
running up stairs and murdering old gentlemen like Mr Boodle."

"But it wasn't Mr Boodle," Clarence wailed.

"Or anyone else," Mr Wallace amended. He sat down, the victor.

"It certainly seems unlikely," Auguste broke the silence that fell, "that Mr Wallace would have any reason to murder – unless for the good of Boodle, Budd & Farthing. I feel, however, that there may be less altruistic reasons for some of us here to have wished to murder Mr Hope – assuming that to be the terrible case. You for instance, Mr Popple. It is quite possible that you saw Mr Hope leaving Mr Budd's office, and went with him into Mr Boodle's room for a private talk, knowing it was empty."

"No, I didn't," yelled Clarence. "And even if I did, what of it? He loved me."

"Hah!" Mr Budd muttered.

"Yes, Mr Budd?" Auguste turned to him.

"Normally," Mr Budd continued virtuously, "I would never publish such cruel, nay obscene material, but Mr Hope, as you pointed out, Mr Popple, was threatening to tell my authors about poor Mr Boodle. Mr Hope mentioned to me that you knew the content of his novel: he had told you yesterday."

"Rubbish. You're lying. It wasn't me. It was *her*," Clarence shrieked.

Miss Mellidew paled. "Goodness gracious, young man, why should I wish to murder Mr Boodle, let alone Mr Hope, anymore than would the General here?"

"Me, madam? I could have you shot for less."

"That would hardly help," Auguste intervened firmly. "And you did have the opportunity to kill Mr Hope. Also, a reason."

"Never met the fellow in my life."

"Not Mr Hope. But you would have assumed you were addressing Mr Boodle. You had no idea that Boodle died twenty years ago."

"Dash it, sir," the General spluttered.

"Mr Boodle had hung on to Mr Farthing's portion of the business, I deduce, thus denying your wife her rights." The General scowled but did not refute it.

"It was *her*," Clarence shouted again. "Why don't you listen?"

"I discovered the body. How dare you take advantage of a maiden lady, young man." Miss Mellidew dissolved into tears.

"You announced it on your second absence, yes. But earlier you had had as much opportunity to go into Mr Boodle's room as the gentlemen,' said Auguste implacably.

"Why should I wish to kill Mr Boodle?" she sobbed. "I had come to find a new publisher. Why should I wish to quarrel with its accountant?"

"Not Mr Boodle." Auguste hesitated, then plunged, taking a gamble. An irritated robin, an interesting use of the past tense

where none was called for – trifling details in themselves, but now
assuming a vital relevance. "But perhaps you had a reason for killing
Arnold Hope."

"Of course she did, the old bat. How he laughed about her,"
Clarence jeered.

"I think," Auguste said gently, "you may have overheard a quarrel
between Mr Popple and Mr Hope while you were on your way up to
Mr Budd's office and recognized the voice. It was a quarrel that made
their relationship quite clear. You saw Mr Popple leaving, very upset,
and took your opportunity to speak your mind to Mr Hope."

"I am not a campaigner for moral purity, Mr Didier, whatever I
may or may not have overheard." Tears rolled down her face and Miss
Watkins solicitously produced a cambric handkerchief on behalf of
the sisterhood of women.

"Not even," Auguste asked, "if heroes turned out to have such
terrible feet of clay?"

"Oh." A gloved hand flew to her face.

"He was Lambkin, was he not, Sheikh Hamed, the Shining One,
and you were Cecilia?"

She drew herself up. "You may not believe it, but I was considered
a handsome girl."

"And the story of Cecilia is your own?"

"It is."

"And the four wives?"

"One wife only. In Balham, he told me. I believed it. But today I
overheard the truth. The Lambkin whose memory I had treasured
all these years was a degenerate. When Mr Popple left, I hurried in
to confront him." She paused, then continued, "He jeered at me, and
worse, he jeered at Cecilia, at the Shining One himself. He besmirched
my dearest child." She bowed her head.

"So you murdered him," Clarence shouted. "My Arnold. My
beloved."

"There is still Mildred, dear lady." Gervase rushed in, in case all
was not yet lost.

"No." Her head shot up. "It was an accident. I was standing by
Mr Boodle's desk. Lambkin was behind it. He said . . . he said he'd
give me a taste of what I'd been missing all these years. I realized he
was going to attack me, perhaps even kiss me. I could not bear it. I
took out my hatpin, the mainstay of a woman's defence, so Mama
instructed me. Keep away, I threatened, as he began to come round
the desk towards me.

"He saw, was startled and then it happened. I don't know *what*
happened though. There seemed to be a lot of noise and suddenly he

fell against me. I moved aside, he grunted and toppled over, hitting the corner of the fender. I realized the hatpin was still in my hand, and, terrified, knew it had entered him. But there was a wound on his head too. My sheikh was dead. I could feel no pulse. Such a predicament, Mr Didier. Even Mildred has never had to face such horror."

"Miss Watkins," Auguste said gently, as she heaved with sobs, "would you attend to Miss Mellidew." He ran quickly upstairs again. Who could doubt her story? But something was still curdling this hollandaise.

He stared round the late Mr Boodle's office, trying to keep his eyes from the body and from Albert and Victoria, whose eyes seemed to follow him everywhere. They mocked him, the room mocked him for he knew the answer was buried here.

If Miss Mellidew had been standing here – he gingerly took his place at the side of the body – and he *fell* towards her, was he already dead? If so, how? He looked up. Death could not have dropped from the ceiling, nor did the dogs' heads stand up sufficiently to cause Arnold Hope to fall against the hatpin quite so heavily.

He walked behind Mr Boodle's desk, imagining himself Arnold Hope. No, not Arnold Hope. He imagined himself Mr Boodle repelling demands from unreasonable authors, at the mercy of blackmailers like Hope.

*Mr Boodle was always one for a merry jest.*

The bulldog heads . . . in a flash he was mentally in his kitchen with the finest dish in all the land: the boar's head . . . stuffing it with the finest ingredients, bringing it back by art to simulate life.

He was Mr Boodle, a man beset by problems, but who liked a merry jest; his hands reached out, rather as Mr Budd's had done on his own desk. His fingers found two knobs as he stood up. He pressed, he pulled. Suddenly the air was full of growls, dog growls; as he rushed round the desk he was in time to see Albert's head rearing up, full of air, baring its teeth, a fearsome sight. Had he been Arnold Hope, startled, he might well have tripped over the monstrosity, tumbled headlong into Miss Mellidew's hatpin, the weight of his falling body knocking the air from Albert once again.

He was in a world of illusion, Auguste told himself, and like all illusions these would have a practical explanation. No doubt Egbert's men would find some kind of drum and catgut arrangement in the desk to produce the growls, and pistons or compressed air or gas pipes to control the air supply to Albert. Perhaps even a primitive electrical contact.

Even as he studied it, he heard banging at the door downstairs, movement and familiar voices. Egbert had arrived. By the time he reached the doorway, Egbert was already racing up the stairs. He looked up and saw Auguste waiting.

"Accident, Auguste?"

"Murder. There is motive, means and opportunity."

"Got the murderer for me, have you?"

"I believe so."

There was a faint cry from Miss Mellidew below, listening, terrified.

"Who is it?"

"A gentleman called Boodle. Mr Boodle."

# PART V
## Holmes and Beyond

# THE
# PHANTOM PISTOL
## Jack Adrian

*Jack Adrian (b. 1945) is a journalist and editor with an encyclopedic knowledge of genre fiction, particularly in the realms of mystery and the supernatural. As a novelist he has produced* The Blood of Dracula *(1977) as Jack Hamilton Teed, and probably more pseudonymous stories than you could shake a stick at. As an editor he has compiled several very worthy anthologies, including* The Art of the Impossible *(1990, with Robert Adey),* Detective Stories from the Strand *and* Strange Tales from the Strand *(both 1991) and* The Oxford Book of Historical Stories *(1994, with Michael Cox), as well as collections of lesser-known stories by Edgar Wallace, Dornford Yates, Sapper, E. F. Benson, A. M. Burrage, and Rafael Sabatini. His short fiction is less well known, so it is a pleasure to resurrect this "impossible crime" story set in a foggy London of 1912 and including that well-known solver of the impossible, Mr H. . . .*

O n this chill November night fog rolled up from the River Thames, a shifting, eddying blanket that insinuated itself inexorably through the grimy streets of central London. It pulsed like a living thing, moved by its own remorseless momentum – for there was no wind – great banks of it surging across the metropolis, soot and smoke from a hundred thousand chimneys adding to its murk. Within an hour from the moment the faint tendrils of a river mist had heralded its approach, the fog, like a dirty-ochre shroud, had entombed the city.

Here, in the heart of the metropolis, in High Holborn, the rattle of hansom cab wheels, the raucous coughs of the newfangled petrol-driven taxis, were muffled, the rumble of the crawling traffic stifled as it edged and lurched its way along, the dim yellow light of street lamps serving to obscure rather than illuminate. On the pavements, slick with slimy dew, hunched figures, only dimly discerned, almost wraithlike, groped and shuffled along through the gloom, an army of the newly blind, snuffling and hawking at the harsh, choking reek of soot and coalsmoke.

Yet only fifty yards away from the main thoroughfare, down a narrow side street that had not changed appreciably since Dr Johnson's day, sodium flares fizzed and roared, powerful electric globes thrust back the muddy haze. For only a few feet, to be sure, yet enough to reveal the tarnished gilt portico of the Empire Palace of Varieties, a large poster outside announcing in bold scarlet lettering, two inches high, that here, and only here, were to be witnessed the dazzling deeds of the Great Golconda – illusionist *extraordinaire*!

Inside the theatre the atmosphere was just as miasmal, but here the fog was a blend of pungent penny cigars and the richer reeks of Larangas, Partagas, Corona-Coronas, and Hoyos de Monterrey, for the astonishing variety and ingenuity of the Great Golconda's baffling feats of prestidigitation fascinated the rich as well as the poor.

The Great Golconda was something of a democrat. He had consistently refused to perform in the gilded palaces that lined the Haymarket and Shaftesbury Avenue, preferring the smaller halls of the outer circuit. Thus whenever and wherever he appeared, rich men, dukes, earls, high-born ladies, and even (it was whispered) members of the Royal Family were forced to make the unaccustomed trek away from the gilt and glitter of London's West End to less salubrious haunts, there to mix with the lower orders – not to mention enjoy the unusual experience of paying half the price for twice the amount of entertainment. For certainly the Great Golconda was a magician and illusionist of quite extraordinary ability. It was even rumoured that emissaries of Maskelyne and Devant – whose fame as illusionists was spread worldwide – had endeavoured to lure his secrets away with fabulous amounts of money and, when these offers were spurned, had even gone so far as to try for them by less scrupulous methods.

Whether or not this was true, the Great Golconda stubbornly performed on the stages of the tattier music halls, and all kinds and conditions and classes of men and women flocked to see him, and to cheer him.

But tonight was a special night. The Great Golconda was retiring from the stage. This was to be positively his final performance.

Unusually, the act started the show. Normally, the Great Golconda and his assistant Mephisto came on for the last half hour of the first house and the last half hour of the second. As an act, nothing could follow it.

Tonight, however, the audience – restless at the thought of having to sit through the somewhat dubious hors d'oeuvres of jugglers, low comedians, soubrettes, and "Come-into-the-garden-Maud" baritones before getting down to the main course – sat up in eager anticipation as the curtain rose at last to reveal a totally bare stage with a black backcloth, from the centre of which stared two enormous eyes woven in green and gold.

For several seconds there was utter silence, a total absence of movement – on the stage and off. Then the lights dimmed and the glowing figure of the Great Golconda himself could be seen – in black silk hat, long flowing cloak, arms folded across his chest – descending slowly from the darkness above the stage, apparently floating on air. Simultaneously, two more Golcondas, dressed exactly alike, marched towards the centre of the stage from both left and right wings. Just before they met, there was a flash of white light, a loud bang, a puff of red smoke, and all three figures seemed to merge.

And there, standing alone, smiling a mite maliciously, stood the Great Golconda. The audience roared.

From then on, for the next twenty minutes, wonders did not cease.

White horses cantered across the boards, to disappear in a dazzling firework display; doves, peacocks, birds-of-paradise soared and strutted, all, seemingly, appearing from a small Chinese lacquered cabinet on a rostrum; a girl in sequinned tights pirouetted in midair, had her head sawn off by the Great Golconda's assistant Mephisto, then, carrying her head beneath her arm, climbed a length of rope and slowly vanished, like the smile of the Cheshire Cat, about thirty feet above the ground.

Part of the performance was what appeared to be a running battle between the Great Golconda and his assistant Mephisto. Mephisto made it plain he wanted to do things his way but invariably, like the sorcerer's apprentice, failed, the Great Golconda smoothly but sensationally saving the trick – whatever trick it happened to be – at the very last moment. Penultimately, Mephisto became so incensed at the Great Golconda's successes that he knocked him down, crammed and locked him into a four-foot-high oak sherry cask, and then proceeded to batter and smash it to pieces with a long-handled axe.

Triumphantly, he turned to the audience, his chalk-white, clown-like face (its pallor accentuated by the skin-tight black costume he wore, leaving only his face, neck, and arms below the elbows bare) leering malevolently – to be greeted by gales of laughter as the Great Golconda himself suddenly appeared from the wings behind him to tap him on the shoulder.

At last the stage was cleared for the final act. Mephisto was to fire a revolver at the Great Golconda, who would catch the bullet between his teeth.

Members of the audience were invited up to the front of the stage to examine the .45 service revolver and six bullets and vouch for their authenticity. Among them was a stocky, moustachioed man in his late forties, in frock coat and bowler hat, who clearly, from the professional way he handled the gun – flicking open the chamber, extracting the bullets, testing them between his teeth – had more than a little knowledge of fire-arms. The Great Golconda noticed this.

"You sir!"

The stocky figure acknowledged this with an abrupt nod.

"You seem to know your way about a pistol, sir."

"I should do," admitted the man.

"May I enquire of your profession, sir?"

"You may. I'm a superintendent at Scotland Yard."

The Great Golconda was clearly delighted. Seen close up he was younger than the Scotland Yard man had supposed – perhaps in his mid-thirties. Something else he noted was the distinct resemblance between the Great Golconda and his assistant Mephisto, now standing to one side, his pasty white face impassive.

"And your name, sir?"

"Hopkins. Stanley Hopkins."

The Great Golconda bowed.

"A name that is not unknown to me from the newssheets, sir. Indeed, a name to be – ha-ha! – *conjured* with! And what is your professional opinion of the revolver, Superintendent?"

Still holding the bullets, Hopkins dry-fired the gun. The hammer fell with a loud "click", the chamber snapped round.

"Perfectly genuine."

"Pree-*cisely!*"

With a flourish of his cape, the Great Golconda handed the revolver to his assistant Mephisto and ushered the half dozen or so members of the audience off the stage.

The lights dimmed. Twin spots bathed the two men in two separate cones of light. They stood at the rear of the stage, against the black backcloth, about ten yards apart. All around them was utter darkness. From his seat Hopkins watched intently.

Mephisto, wearing black gloves now and holding the gun two-handed, raised his arms slowly into the air, high above his head. Hopkins, following the movement could only just see the revolver, which was now above the circle of radiance surrounding Mephisto – then light glittered along the barrel as the assistant brought his hands

back into the spotlight's glare and down, his arms held straight out.
The revolver pointed directly at the Great Golconda.

It seemed to Hopkins that the Great Golconda's expression – up
until then one of supercilious amusement – suddenly slipped. A look
of mild puzzlement appeared on his face.

Hopkins glanced at the right-hand side of the stage but could see
nothing but darkness. At that moment there was the oddly muted
crack of a shot, and Hopkins, his eyes already turning back to the
Great Golconda, saw the illusionist cry out and throw up his arms,
then fall to the floor.

There was a stunned silence.

Even from where he was sitting, the Scotland Yard man could
see plainly that around the Great Golconda's mouth were scarlet
splashes, where none had been before.

Then the screaming started.

Mr Robert Adey, the manager of the Empire Music Hall, looked as
though he was on the verge of an apoplexy. His face was red, his
mouth gaped, his mutton-chop whiskers quivered with emotion.

He stuttered, "It . . . it *couldn't* have happened!"

"But it did," Superintendent Stanley Hopkins said bluntly.

They were on the stage of the now-empty theatre. Even with
all the stagelights up and the crystal chandeliers blazing over the
auditorium, there was a desolate air about the place; shadows still
gathered thickly in the wings, and above, beams and struts and spars
could only just be glimpsed.

Since the shocking death of the Great Golconda – whose body now
lay under a rug where it had fallen – nearly an hour had elapsed.
During that time an extraordinary fact had emerged: although the
Great Golconda had been shot, his assistant Mephisto (now detained
in his dressing room) could not have shot him. Of that, there seemed
not a doubt.

And yet neither could anyone else.

Adey – with a slight West Midlands twang to his voice – gabbled,
"It . . . it's utterly inexplicable!"

"This is 1912," said a sharp voice behind him. "*Nothing* is
inexplicable."

Adey turned. The man who had spoken – a tall, thin, almost gaunt
individual of sixty or so, with a high forehead, dark hair shot with
gray, an aquiline nose, and eyes that seemed to pierce and probe
and dissect all that they looked upon – had accompanied Hopkins
up to the stage when the theatre had been cleared. Adey had no idea
who he was.

"A colleague?" he muttered to the Scotland Yard man.

"Just a friend," said Hopkins, "a very old friend. We're both interested in the impossible – why we're here tonight. The Great Golconda's illusions had certain . . ." he glanced at his friend ". . . points of interest."

"Although many, I fancy, were accomplished with the aid of certain kinematic devices," said the older man. "The girl in the sequinned tights, for example – a lifelike image only, I take it."

Adey nodded uneasily.

"Of course, I know very little about how he managed his tricks. Magicians are a close-mouthed bunch. This one in particular. He was adamant that during his act both wings should be blocked off, so no one – not even the stagehands – could see what he was doing. Always worried people were trying to pinch his tricks. Of course, he had to have some assistance in erecting certain items on stage, but all the preliminary construction work was done by him and his brother."

"Mephisto," said Hopkins.

"Yes. Their real name was Forbes-Sempill. Golconda was Rupert, Mephisto Ernest. They were twins – not identical. Rupert was the elder by fifteen minutes . . ." Adey's voice sank to a worried mumble. "That was half the trouble."

"The reason why the Great Golconda was retiring from the stage?" said the gaunt man. "The baronetcy, and the £200,000?"

Adey stared at him, open-mouthed.

"How the devil did you know that?"

"Ah," Hopkins said waggishly, "my friend here keeps his finger on the pulse of great events – don't you, Mr H?"

The older man permitted himself a thin smile.

"Now *you* tell us about the baronetcy, and all them sovs," said the Scotland Yard detective.

Adey shrugged his shoulders.

"Both Rupert and Ernest had a row with their family years ago. Left the ancestral home – somewhere in Scotland, I believe – never," he smiled faintly, "to darken its doors again. But their father's recently died, and Rupert succeeded to the title, estates, and money. It's as simple as that, although it wasn't generally known."

"I take it," said the gaunt old man, "that Ernest disliked his brother?"

"Ernest *hated* Rupert. Made no secret of the fact. One of the reasons their act went down so well – Ernest communicated that hatred to the audience. Rupert didn't object. Said it added spice to the performance. I don't see it myself, but it seemed to work."

"Doubtless the new Viennese school of mind analysis could explain that," said the older man dryly, "but for the time being I am far more interested in why Mephisto should for no apparent reason have donned black gloves to fire his revolver tonight."

"So he did," said Adey, in a surprised tone. "But how . . .?"

"This is not the first time we have seen the Great Golconda perform. As Mr Hopkins implied, his act was an unusual one, and I have always had an interest in the more sensational aspects of popular culture." The gaunt old man's eyes took on a faraway, introspective look. "On previous occasions Mephisto fired his revolver bare-handed. That he did not this time seems to me to be a matter of some significance."

"But the *weapon*, Mr H.!" said Hopkins, almost violently. "We now know what ought to have happened. The real revolver is shown to the audience. It's stone-cold genuine. But when Golconda hands the gun to Mephisto – flourishing his cloak and all – he's already substituted it for another gun – one that only fires blank shots. The real gun is now hidden in his cloak. Mephisto fires the fake gun at him and he pretends to catch the bullet, which is already in his mouth, between his teeth. Simple!"

"Except that this time he falls dead with a bullet in his head."

"*From a phantom pistol!*" exploded Hopkins. "The gun Mephisto held in his hands didn't fire that bullet – *couldn't* fire that bullet! The real gun was still in the folds of the Great Golconda's cloak – so that's out, too! He wasn't killed by someone firing from the wings, because the wings were blocked off! Nor through the backcloth, because there ain't no hole! Nor from above or from the audience, because the bullet went into his head in a straight line through his mouth!"

Here Adey broke in excitedly.

"It's as I said – inexplicable! Indeed, downright *impossible!*"

The gaunt old man shot him a darkly amused look.

"In my experience, Mr Adey, the more bizarre and impossible the occurrence, the less mysterious it will in the end prove to be."

"That's all very well, sir," said the manager a mite snappishly, "but facts are facts! The entire audience was watching Mephisto. When Golconda fell dead, all Mephisto did was drop the revolver he was holding and stand there gaping. Let's say for the sake of argument he had another weapon. What did he do with it? Damm it, sir, he didn't move an inch from where he was standing, nor did he make any violent gesture, as though to throw it away from him. We've searched the entire stage. We've even searched him – not that that was at all necessary because his costume's so skin-tight you couldn't hide a button on him without it bulging."

"Perhaps," said the older man slowly, "he didn't need to throw it away."

"Didn't need?" Adey's voice rose to an outraged squeak. "You'll be telling me next he popped it into his mouth and ate it!"

"By no means as outrageous a suggestion as you might imagine," said the gaunt old man sternly. He turned to the Scotland Yard detective. "You will recall, Hopkins, the case of the abominable Italian vendettist, Pronzini, who did just that."

Hopkins nodded sagely. The older man began to pace up and down the stage, gazing at the sable backcloth.

"Notice how black it is," he murmured, gesturing at the curtain. "How very black . . ." He swung around on Adey again. "Apart from the incident of the gloves, is there anything else to which you might wish to draw our attention?"

"Anything else?"

"Anything unusual."

Adey's honest face assumed a perplexed expression.

"Well . . . no, I don't believe so."

"The placing of the Great Golconda's act, for example?"

"Oh. Why, yes! Right at the beginning, you mean? That was unusual. They did have a bit of a barney about that. It was Mephisto's idea – begin the show and end it, he said. Golconda finally agreed."

"Nothing else?"

"Not that I can . . ."

"I noticed that tonight they both stood at the rear of the stage. Did they not normally stand at the front?"

"Well, yes. Now you come to . . ."

"You will forgive my saying so, Mr Adey," there was a touch of asperity in the old man's voice, "but your powers of observation are somewhat limited."

"You believe Mephisto killed Golconda?" said Hopkins.

"I am convinced of it."

"Then we'd better have a chat with him."

The older man smiled frostily.

"That will not be necessary. You have a stepladder?" he enquired of Adey. "Bring it on."

"Stepladder?" muttered Hopkins. "You think there's something up top?"

"Of course. There has to be. A second gun. Golconda was killed by a bullet. Bullets, for the most part, are shot from guns. Golconda's revolver was incapable of shooting anything, only of making a noise. Thus . . ."

The Scotland Yard man interrupted. "Ah. But. Wait on, Mr H. These two were masters of illusion, am I correct?"

"Certainly."

"But when you get right down to it, their illusions, like all illusions, are fake. Created. Constructed."

"To be sure."

"So this here Mephisto needn't have used a gun at all. He was a clever fellow. Could've built some kind of weapon that fired a bullet, and . . ." He stopped as a thought struck him. "Here, remember the to-do you once had with that tiger-potting colonel. Now *he* had a special shooter."

"Indeed, an air-gun constructed by a German mechanic, who, though blind, had a genius for invention." The old man smiled a skeletal smile. "But you miss the point entirely, my dear Hopkins. It matters not *what* the weapon is, but *where* it is. That is the nub of the problem. We have searched everywhere, eliminated everything, on this level. As we must inevitably strike out from our enquiry any suggestion of magic, the inexorable conclusion we must come to is that the weapon – whatever it is – must be above us."

Hopkins struck the palm of his hand with a clenched fist. "But it can't be! Mephisto stood stock-still the whole time. We *know* he didn't chuck anything into the air."

"As I remarked before, perhaps he did not need to . . ."

By this time the heavy wheeled ladder had been trundled on and heaved to the centre of the stage. A stagehand climbed into the darkness above.

"Merely look for anything that seems out of the ordinary," the old man directed.

In less than a minute the stagehand was calling out excitedly.

"Something here . . . wound round one of the spars on – why, it's elasticated cord!"

"Unwind it. Let it drop."

Seconds later a small object fell through the air, then bounced upwards again as the cord reached its nadir. The old man stretched up and caught it before it could fly out of reach. He turned to the watchers.

"What do you see?"

Hopkins frowned.

"Not a thing."

The old man opened his fingers.

"Come closer."

The Scotland Yard detective stepped forward, his expression turning to one of amazement. Gripped in the gaunt old man's hand – clearly seen against the white of his skin – was a miniature chamberless pistol, perhaps five inches long from grip to muzzle, painted entirely matt-black. The old man pressed at the bottom of the stock and the barrel slid forward, revealing a two-inch cavity.

"A Williamson derringer pistol, capable of firing one shot only – quite enough to kill a man," said the old man dryly. "Hand me the false pistol."

He held the blank-firing pistol in his left hand with the derringer gripped in his right, levelling both at an imaginary target. From the side all that could be seen was the massive bulk of the service revolver. Then he clicked the triggers of both guns and opened his right hand. The derringer, at the end of the taut elasticated cord – totally invisible against the black backcloth – flew upwards into the darkness above, whipping round and round the high spar to which it was attached.

Adey looked utterly at sea.

"But how did you . . . what made you . . .?" he babbled.

"When three singular variations in a set routine – the black gloves, the change of position not only of the act itself but of the two principals on the stage in that act – take place," said the old man a trifle testily, "one is tempted, to use the vernacular, to smell a rat. After that, it is a matter of simple deduction. The gift of observation – sadly lacking in the general populace – allied to intuition. Believe me, there is really no combination of events – however inexplicable on the surface – for which the wit of man cannot conceive an elucidation."

He began to pace up and down the stage again, his hands clasped firmly behind his back.

"Mephisto tied the derringer to the spar, letting it hang down just within reach of his outstretched arm. It could not be seen because he had painted it black and hung it close to the black curtain. In any case, the lighting was subdued. Even so, there was the risk of someone spotting it, so he persuaded his brother that their act should start the show. Came the climax of the performance. The two spotlights only lit up the area within their twin beams. Mephisto raised his arms, holding the false revolver, until his hands were just above the spotlight's glare. He had positioned himself perfectly – no doubt he rehearsed the entire sequence thoroughly – and the hanging derringer was now within inches of his right hand. If his hands had been bare, one might possibly have noticed that he was holding something else, but he took the precaution of wearing black gloves, thereby making assurance double sure. Grasping the derringer, he pulled it down on its elasticated thread, pressing it to the side of the much larger weapon, as his arms dropped to the levelled-off position. He was now holding not one, but *two* guns – one hidden from the audience's view and in any case virtually invisible. Except to the man at whom he was pointing them."

"Yes!" snapped Hopkins. "That's what made Golconda look surprised. I thought he'd seen something *behind* Mephisto."

"Mephisto then fired the derringer, releasing his grip on the gun, which shot up into the air. All eyes were on Golconda falling to the floor. The derringer wound itself round the spar to which its cord was attached. In the confusion afterwards, doubtless, Mephisto meant to get rid of the evidence. What he did not reckon on was the presence of a Scotland Yard detective who would immediately take charge of the proceedings and confine him to his dressing room. But in the meantime there was absolutely nothing to show that he had just murdered his brother in cold blood. It was as though," the old man finished, shrugging, "the Great Golconda had indeed been shot with a phantom pistol."

"And being next in line," said Hopkins, "Mephisto would've stepped into the baronetcy and all them lovely golden sovs. Nice work, Mr H. Nice work, indeed!"

# THE ADVENTURE OF THE FRIGHTENED GOVERNESS
## Basil Copper

*In 1929 the young August Derleth wrote to Sir Arthur Conan Doyle to enquire whether there would be any more stories featuring Sherlock Holmes. When Doyle replied that there would not, Derleth determined to write some himself, but to avoid any charge of plagiarism, he created his alternative Holmes and Watson, Solar Pons and Dr Lyndon Parker. Pons operated out of lodgings in Praed Street, London, and the stories are firmly set in the 1920s. Because they were contemporary with Derleth's original creation they are not classed as historical detective stories. However after Derleth's death, the Solar Pons stories were continued by British writer Basil Copper. Copper has been a prolific writer of American private-eye thrillers, with his long-running series featuring Los Angeles detective Mike Faraday. But he is also a noted writer of horror stories, and has blended the themes before in his wonderfully gothic mystery novels* Necropolis *(1977) and* The Black Death *(1991). Copper has now written six volumes of stories about Solar Pons and the wordage probably exceeds Derleth's. The stories are usually longer and more menacing, and are an even closer imitation of Holmes than Derleth's originals. In my previous volume some readers queried why I had drawn the line at the end of the last century and not included stories from the start of this century. Strictly speaking I did. My definition of a historical mystery had been a story set in the years before the author's birth. Well, most of the Pons stories are set in the early 1920s and as Basil Copper was not born until 1924 they just squeeze in. So we end with a rousing tribute to Sherlock Holmes.*

## I

"Wake up, Parker! It is six o'clock and we have pressing matters before us."

I struggled into consciousness to find the night-light on at the side of my bed and Solar Pons' aquiline features smiling down at me.

"Confound it, Pons!" I said irritably. "Six o'clock! In the morning?"

"It is certainly not evening, my dear fellow, or neither of us would have been abed."

I sat up, still only half-awake.

"Something serious has happened, then?"

Solar Pons nodded, his face assuming a grave expression.

"A matter of life and death, Parker. And as you have been such an assiduous chronicler of my little adventures over the past years, I thought you would not care to be left out, despite the inclement hour."

"You were perfectly correct, Pons," I said. "Just give me a few minutes to throw on some things and I will join you in the sitting-room."

Pons rubbed his thin hands briskly together with suppressed excitement.

"Excellent, Parker. I thought I knew my man. Mrs Johnson is making some tea."

And with which encouraging announcement he quitted the room.

It was a bitterly cold morning in early February and I wasted no time in dressing, turning over in my mind what the untimely visitor to our quarters at 7B Praed Street could want at such a dead hour.

I had no doubt there was a visitor with a strange or tragic story to tell or Pons would not have disturbed me so untimely, and as I knotted my tie and smoothed my tousled hair with the aid of the mirror, I found my sleepy mind sliding off at all sorts of weird tangents.

But when I gained our comfortable sitting-room, where the makings of a good fire were already beginning to flicker and glow, I was not prepared for the sight of the tall, slim, fair-haired girl sitting in Pons' own armchair in front of the hearth. The only indication of anything serious afoot was the paleness of our visitor's handsome features. She made as though to rise at my entrance but my companion waved her back.

"This is my old friend and colleague, Dr Lyndon Parker, Miss Helstone. I rely on him as on no other person and he is an invaluable helpmate."

There was such obvious sincerity in Pons' voice that I felt a flush

rising to my cheeks and I stammered out some suitable greeting as
the tall young woman gave me her cool hand.

"A bitterly cold morning, Miss Helstone."

"You may well be right, Dr Parker, but I must confess my mind
is so agitated that I have hardly noticed."

"Indeed?"

I looked at her closely. She did not seem ill but there was an
underlying tension beneath her carefully controlled manner which
told my trained eye there was something dreadfully wrong.

There was a measured tread upon the stair and the bright,
well-scrubbed features of our landlady, Mrs Johnson, appeared
round the door. She was laden with a tray containing tea things
and as I hastened to assist her I caught the fragrant aroma of hot,
buttered toast.

"I took the liberty of preparing something for the young lady to
sustain her on such a cold morning."

"Excellent, Mrs Johnson," said Pons, rubbing his thin hands. "As
usual, you are a model of thoughtfulness."

Our landlady said nothing but the faint flush on her cheeks showed
that the deserved praise had not gone unnoticed. She hastened to
pour out the tea and after handing a cup to Miss Helstone with a
sympathetic smile, quietly withdrew.

"Will you not draw closer to the fire, Miss Helstone?"

"I am perfectly comfortable here, Mr Pons."

"You have come from out of London, I see?"

"That is correct, Mr Pons."

Pons nodded, replacing his cup in the saucer with a faint clink in
the silence of the sitting-room.

"I see a good deal of mud on your boots which means you have
been walking on an unmade road."

"It is a fair stretch to the station, Mr Pons, and I was unable to
get transport at that time of the morning."

"Quite so, Miss Helstone. You are not more than an hour out of
town, I would surmise. Surrey, perhaps?"

Our client's surprise showed on her face as she took fastidious little
sips at the hot tea.

"That is correct, Mr Pons. Clitherington, a small village on the
Redhill line."

Solar Pons inclined his head and favoured me with a faint smile
as he bent forward in his armchair.

"That light, sandy soil is quite unmistakable, Parker. You no doubt
noticed, as did I, a distinctive sample on the seams of the young lady's
right boot."

I cleared my throat, caught unawares with a piece of toast halfway down.

"Now that you point it out, Pons, certainly."

"It is obviously something serious that brings you to us at this hour, Miss Helstone, and you have already told me it is a matter of life and death. You are equally obviously agitated beneath your calm manner. Please take your time. You are among friends."

The young woman drew in her breath with a long, shuddering sigh.

"That is good to know, Mr Pons. It has indeed been quite unbearable this last day or two. And affairs at the house . . ."

"You live there with your parents?" interrupted Pons.

The young woman paused and made an engaging little contraction of her mouth.

"I beg your pardon, Mr Pons. I am telling the story very badly. I am engaged as a governess at The Priory, Clitherington, the home of Mr Clinton Basden."

Solar Pons tented his thin fingers before him and gave our fair client his undivided attention.

"So far as I know, Miss Helstone, there is no train on the time-table which leaves a remote place like Clitherington at such an hour as 4.30 a.m."

Miss Helstone gave a faint smile, the first sign of returning normality she had evinced since I had entered the room.

"That is correct, Mr Pons. I came up on the milk train. There are always two carriages used mainly by railway staff and I found an empty compartment."

"So that the matter is one of the utmost gravity. Pray continue."

"My full name is Helen Jane Helstone, Mr Pons, and I come of a good family originally settled in the West Country. My parents were killed in a local uprising in India some years ago and after I had completed my schooling in England it became necessary to earn my living. I enjoy the company of children and so I became a governess with a view to entering a teacher-training college when I am a little older."

"What is your age now, Miss Helstone?"

"I am just turned twenty-one, Mr Pons."

Solar Pons nodded and looked thoughtfully at the girl, who had now recovered the colour in her cheeks. She looked even more handsome than before and I found the contemplation of her most engaging but turned again to the tea and toast, aware of Pons' glance on me.

"I give this information, Mr Pons, so that you shall know all of the salient circumstances."

"You are telling your story in an admirable manner, Miss Helstone."

"I had two positions, Mr Pons, one in Cornwall and another in Cumberland, which I held for several years, but I decided to move nearer to London and when I saw Mr Basden's advertisement in a daily newspaper, Surrey seemed ideal for my purposes and I hastened to answer his announcement."

"When was that, Miss Helstone?"

"A little over three months ago, Mr Pons."

Our visitor paused again and sipped at her tea; her face was thoughtful as though she were carefully contemplating her next words but my professional eye noted that her breathing was more regular and she was becoming calmer by the minute.

"There was something extremely strange about my engagement as governess, Mr Pons. I have often thought about it since."

"How was that, Miss Helstone?"

"For example, Mr Pons, it was extraordinarily well-paid, though the duties are somewhat unusual."

Pons nodded, narrowing his deep-set eyes.

"Pray be most explicit, Miss Helstone."

"Well, Mr Pons, I have no hesitation in telling you that the salary is some five hundred pounds a year, payable quarterly in advance."

Pons drew in his breath in surprise and I gazed at him open-mouthed.

"That is indeed princely for these times, Miss Helstone. I should imagine there would have been quite a few ladies in your position after the appointment."

"That is just it, Mr Pons. There were literally queues. I met some people on the train who were answering the advertisement. Apparently it had been running in the daily newspapers for more than a week."

"That is highly significant, Parker," put in Pons enigmatically and he again resumed his rapt study of Miss Helstone's face.

Our client went on breathlessly, as though some reserve had been breached by the confidence my friend inspired in her.

"My heart sank, Mr Pons, as you can well imagine, but as the train stopped at Clitherington, my spirits rose again. You see, I had heard one of the girls say that though the announcement had been running for some time, the prospective employers were very fastidious and no-one had yet been found to suit them."

"And as you already had experience of two similar appointments, you had high hopes?"

"Exactly, Mr Pons. But my spirits were dashed when we arrived at the house. A large car had been sent to the station to meet applicants and we were taken to a vast, gloomy mansion, set in an estate whose main entrance was locked and guarded by heavily-built men."

"An odd circumstance, Miss Helstone," said Pons, glancing quizzically at me.

"You may well say so, Mr Pons. But though the grounds, with their great clumps of rhododendron and pine plantations were gloomy and sombre indeed in that bleak December weather, the interior of the mansion was extremely luxurious and well appointed, evincing the most refined taste. It was evident that the prospective employer was a man of enormous wealth."

"And of fastidious nature if it took him so much time to select a governess for his children, Miss Helstone. How many were there, in fact?"

"Two, Mr Pons. A boy and a girl, aged nine and twelve respectively. But my heart sank again, when we were shown into a sumptuously furnished drawing-room to find between twenty and thirty young ladies already there."

"It sounds more like a theatrical producer's office, Pons," I could not resist observing.

Solar Pons gave me a faint smile and his eyes held a wry twinkle.

"Ah, there speaks the sybarite in you, Parker. The lover of night life, good wine and chorus girls."

"Heavens, Pons!" I stammered. "What will Miss Helstone think of me?"

"That you are a poor recipient of waggish remarks at your own expense, my dear fellow. But we digress."

Miss Helstone had smiled hesitantly at this little exchange, revealing two rows of dazzling white teeth.

"Well, there is a great deal of truth in Dr Parker's remark, Mr Pons," she said earnestly. "It did in truth look like a theatrical agency, though they are a good deal shabbier as a rule. But the most extraordinary thing was the proceedings. A hard-faced woman in black beckoned to the first girl as I sat down and she disappeared through the big double doors. In less than a minute she was back, with an angry shake of the head."

Miss Helstone put down her cup and leaned forward in her chair, regarding my companion with steady grey eyes.

"Mr Pons, five of the applicants went in and out of that room in five minutes and it was obvious by their angry expressions that none of them were suited. But even more extraordinary — and I learned this afterwards — each and every one was given a new five pound note for her trouble, a car to the station and a free railway ticket to London."

Solar Pons clapped his hands together with a little cracking noise in the silence of the sitting-room.

"Excellent, Parker!" said he. "This gets more intriguing by the minute, Miss Helstone. There is more, of course."

"Much more, Mr Pons. Of course, I got most intrigued as the minutes went by and the girls disappeared into the room. Those of us who were left moved up and fresh arrivals sat down behind us. Now and again there would be loud exclamations from behind the door and it was obvious as I got closer and closer to the double-doors guarded by the woman in black, that none of the girls had been found suitable by the mysterious advertiser. I did not, of course, at that stage, know the name of my employer, Mr Pons, as it was not given in the advertisement."

"I see. It was a box number?"

"Exactly, Mr Pons."

I got up at Pons' glance and re-filled the tea-cups for all of us.

"But I was within three places of the door before a girl came out with whom I had travelled down from London. She was angry and had a heavy flush on her cheeks. She came across to me and had time for a few words before the woman, who was letting in a new applicant, came back. She said she was not asked for references or even any questions. A tall, dark woman was sitting at a desk and she looked at someone obviously sitting behind a heavy screen who was concealed from the applicant. He must have had some method of observing the candidate but in every case the answer had been no, for the woman merely nodded and said that the interview was closed. My informant said she was merely asked her name, address and if it were true that she was an orphan. It was obvious that even these questions were a mere formality."

"An orphan, Miss Helstone?"

Solar Pons had narrowed his eyes and on his face was the alert expression I had noted so often when moments of great enterprise were afoot.

"Why, yes, Mr Pons. That was one of the stipulations of the advertisements. I have one here in my handbag. Another requirement was that applicants should be single or widows."

"Sounds most peculiar, Pons," I put in.

"Does it not, Parker?"

Solar Pons glanced at the newspaper cutting Miss Helstone had passed to him and read it with increasing interest.

"Just listen to this, Parker."

He smoothed out the cutting on the table in front of him and read as follows:

YOUNG GOVERNESS REQUIRED FOR TWO SMALL
CHILDREN IN HOME OF WEALTHY SURREY WID-
OWER. LARGE MANSION, CONGENIAL SURROUND-
INGS. DISCRETION ESSENTIAL, MANY ADVANTAGES.
SALARY £500 PER ANNUM. NO-ONE OVER THIRTY
NEED APPLY. REPLY INITIALLY IN WRITING AND
WITH TWO REFERENCES. THE POSITION IS FOR
THE BENEFIT OF ORPHANED YOUNG LADIES ONLY.
BOX 990.

Solar Pons frowned and looked at me quizzically.

"Extraordinary, is it not, Parker? I am obliged to you, Miss
Helstone. Despite my enthusiasm for bizarre cuttings, this is something I missed. There are a number of unusual points, Parker."

"Indeed, Pons. The orphan stipulation is strange, to say the
least."

"And tells us a great deal," said Solar Pons slyly. "Coupled with
the lavish inducements it indicates a certain line of thought. What
happened at your own interview, Miss Helstone?"

Our visitor put down her tea-cup and wiped her mouth fastidiously
with a small lace handkerchief, waving away my proffered plate
of toast.

"That was the most extraordinary thing of all, Mr Pons. Within
thirty minutes of my arrival at The Priory, thirty applicants had
passed through those doors and then it was my turn. It was a large,
though quite ordinary room, except for a circular window high up,
which made it a dark, shadowy place. There was a desk underneath
the window and a desk lamp alight on it, which threw the light
forward on to a chair placed in front of the desk.

"A dark-haired, pleasant-looking woman with a Central European
accent asked me to sit down and then put to me some perfunctory
questions. I naturally observed the large, heavy screen to the right of
the desk and was then startled to see, in an angled mirror placed so
as to favour my place on the chair, the reflections of a man's bearded
face, with eyes of burning intensity."

## II

There was another long pause which I employed in re-filling my
tea-cup. Miss Helstone leaned back in her chair and put out her
hands to the fire, which was now blazing cheerfully.

"Some signal must have passed between the two because the woman at the desk gave a relieved smile and, as though making the decision herself, informed me that the position was mine. She called me over to another table in the corner and asked me to sign a document. I just had time to see that this asserted that I was an orphan, specified my age and verified my references, before I heard a door close softly somewhere. I was sure that the man behind the screen had quitted the room, Mr Pons, and when we went back to the desk I could see that a chair placed behind the screen was empty."

Solar Pons rubbed his hands briskly.

"Admirable, Miss Helstone. This is distinctly promising. I may point out, by the way, that the document you signed has no legal standing whatsoever."

The girl smiled.

"I am glad to hear you say so, Mr Pons. But that is the least of my worries. You may imagine the consternation and dismay among the young ladies in the ante-room when they heard the position was filled. I was astonished when Mrs Dresden, the dark-haired woman, whom I then learned was the housekeeper, said I should start on my duties at once. But I prevailed upon her to let me return to my old employers to collect my luggage and to inform them of my new post, though even then they insisted on sending me by chauffeur-driven car in order to save time."

"You did not think this at all strange, Miss Helstone?"

"Strange indeed, Mr Pons, but the salary was so princely that I did not hesitate, I was so excited."

"So you left The Priory without seeing your future charges?"

"That is correct, Mr Pons. I was told the children were on holiday and would not be back until the following Monday.

"When I returned I was a little perturbed to see that the grounds were patrolled by similar men to those at the main gate and I realized then that I would not be free to get out and about as I had hoped and in the manner I had become used to in my other situations."

"You met this mysterious Mr Basden?"

"Almost at once on my return, Mr Pons. He was quite an ordinary little man, an Englishman obviously, and rather ill at ease, I thought, among the foreign-sounding employees among his retinue."

Solar Pons tented his fingers and stared at me sombrely.

"Does not that strike you as strange also, Parker?"

"Perhaps he had served in India, Pons?"

Solar Pons shook his head with a thin smile.

"I believe the young lady referred to Central Europeans, Parker."

"That is correct, Mr Pons. There were other extraordinary requirements in my new duties also. For example, I was asked by the housekeeper to leave my own clothes in my room. She supplied me with a new wardrobe. They were very expensive clothes, Mr Pons, but I had no objection, of course."

"Indeed," I put in.

"But then Mrs Dresden asked me to put my hair up in a different style and gave me expensive jewellery to wear. I was a little apprehensive in case I lost any but was told not to worry as Mr Basden was a very wealthy man. I was given the run of the magnificent house and was told I would be treated as a member of the family.

"I dined with Mr Basden that evening and my impression of him being ill at ease in his own house was reinforced. He said little and after two days at The Priory I knew very little more about the post than when I arrived. I noticed one other odd thing, also. I could go almost anywhere I liked in the house, but there was a wing stretching off the main landing. I was forbidden to go there by Mrs Dresden, as it was private.

"But I could not help seeing what went on, Mr Pons. There were disturbances in the night once and I have seen what looked like nurses with trays of medicine. One morning also I surprised a tall, dark man on the stairs, with a little black bag. He looked grave and I was convinced he was a doctor."

Solar Pons leaned forward and his deepset eyes stared steadily at the tall, fair girl.

"Just what do you think is in that wing, Miss Helstone?"

"Some sort of invalid, evidently, Mr Pons. I did not enquire, naturally."

Solar Pons leaned back again in his chair and half-closed his eyes.

"And you have not seen the bearded man again since that first accidental glimpse at the interview?"

"Not at all, Mr Pons. I had another shock when my two charges arrived. The children were attractive enough, but their voices were low and husky and I was told by Mrs Dresden they had colds. They seemed rather odd and sly and I was completely non-plussed when I found that neither spoke a word of English."

Solar Pons gave a low chuckle.

"Excellent, Miss Helstone."

The fair girl stared at my companion with very bright eyes.

"And what is more, Mr Pons, I am convinced their father cannot speak their language either!"

"Better and better, Parker."

Miss Helstone stared at my companion in astonishment.

"I do not follow you, Mr Pons."

"No matter, Miss Helstone. What was the next thing that happened in this extraordinary ménage?"

"Well, it was obvious, Mr Pons, that I could not begin to conduct any lessons. When I pointed this out to Mrs Dresden she said it was of no consequence as they had a tutor in their own tongue. I would be required for companionship; to take them on walks in the grounds; on motor-rides and to control their deportment."

"An unusual list of requirements and one which apparently commands a salary of five hundred pounds, Parker," said Pons, a dreamy expression on his face. "It gives one pause to think, does it not?"

"My words exactly, Pons."

"And when you hear that the walks were mostly conducted at night in the floodlit grounds of The Priory, you will begin to realize my perplexity, Mr Pons."

My companion's eyes had narrowed to mere slits and he leaned forward, an intent expression on his face.

"The grounds were floodlit, Miss Helstone? And the walks were how many times a week?"

"About three times on average, Mr Pons. Between ten o'clock and midnight."

"Unusual hours for small children, Parker."

"There is something wrong somewhere."

"For once you do not exaggerate, my dear fellow."

"The last three months have been strange ones for me, gentlemen," said our visitor, whose paleness had gone and whose natural vivacity had evidently returned, for her eyes were sparkling and her manner more animated.

"I took occasional meals with my employer; walked or drove with the children; read and played patience. I soon found that I was not allowed outside the gates alone, but I have learned that the art treasures in the house are so valuable that Mr Basden is scared of burglars. I myself think he is afraid that his employees will be approached by criminal elements, for he insists that if one goes outside, then one does not go alone."

"Another curious circumstance which gives one much food for thought," observed Solar Pons.

"This was the odd routine of my life until a few weeks ago," Miss Helstone continued. "The people in the house were kind to me and I was well treated, but I felt circumscribed; almost imprisoned. The sealed wing was still barred to me and medicines and medical staff were in evidence from time to time, but nothing was explained and I did not think it circumspect to ask. But there was another peculiar circumstance; my employer does not smoke, or at least I have never seen him do so, yet I have on several occasions smelt strong cigar smoke in the children's room when I go to collect them for their walks. On one occasion there was a half-smoked cigar end on the window sill and the little girl looked distinctly uneasy. I myself think that the bearded man had something to do with it."

Solar Pons looked searchingly at the girl.

"You think he may be the real father and not Mr Basden?"

Miss Helstone looked astonished.

"Those were my exact thoughts, Mr Pons! You see, there is no genuine resemblance to Mr Basden and the man with the beard had a foreign look."

"You may have stumbled on to something, Miss Helstone," Pons went on. "It is a most intriguing tangle that you have described. But you mentioned life and death?"

The girl swallowed once or twice and her eyes looked bleak.

"Twice in the past fortnight we have been accosted on our walks abroad, by strange, bearded men in a car. They spoke first to the children and then became very excited when I approached. I could swear they were all speaking the same language together. Yesterday a big black car tried to force ours off the road near Clitherington when we were out driving. Our chauffeur accelerated and drove back to the estate like a madman. We were all considerably shaken, I can tell you."

"Mr Basden was informed of this?"

"At once. He looked white and ill and came down to apologize to me immediately."

Solar Pons pulled once or twice at the lobe of his right ear and looked at me quizzically.

"Which brings us to the early hours of the morning, Miss Helstone."

"I was walking in the grounds with the children last night, Mr Pons. They sleep much during the day and their parent does not seem to mind their nocturnal habits. We had left the floodlit portion and followed the drive as it curved around. It was nearly midnight or a little after and we were about to turn back when there was a shot. It gave me such a shock, Mr Pons! The bullet glanced off a tree-trunk only a few feet from my head. I could hear guttural cries and I told the children to run."

"Highly commendable, Miss Helstone," I put in.

"Unfortunately, in their panic to escape they ran toward the voices," the girl went on. "Naturally, I had to go after them as they were my charges. We all got lost in the darkness, blundering about. I heard two more shots and then the same guttural voices I had heard from the men who had questioned the children on the road. I was so frightened, Mr Pons, that I hid. I must have been in the woods for hours.

"I found myself in an unfamiliar part of the grounds; it was dark and cold and I did not know what to do. I was in an absolute panic. I had abandoned my charges, you see, and I did not know what might have happened to them. I could not face Mr Basden. I found a small wicket-gate in the wall, which was unlocked; it may even have been used by the men to gain entrance to the grounds. Anyway, Mr Pons, to bring a long and exceedingly rambling story to an end, I ran from The Priory and caught the milk train. I had read your name in the newspapers some months ago as being the country's greatest private detective so here I am to put my destiny in your hands."

## III

Here our client paused and looked so appealingly at Pons that I could not forbear saying, "There, do not distress yourself further, little lady," while Pons himself looked at me disapprovingly.

"While deploring Parker's sentimental way of expressing it, I am in great sympathy with you, Miss Helstone. I have no hesitation in saying I will accept your case."

"Oh, thank you, Mr Pons."

Helen Helstone rose from her chair and shook Pons' hand warmly. Pons looked at me interrogatively.

"Are you free, Parker?"

"Certainly, Pons. I have only to telephone my locum."

"Excellent."

He turned back to Miss Helstone.

"We must make arrangements to get you back to The Priory as soon as possible, Miss Helstone."

"Go back?"

Dismay and apprehension showed on the girl's face.

"It is the only way. We all want to know what went on there and I must confess I have not been so intrigued for a long while. And Parker and I will be with you."

"How are we going to manage that, Pons?" I said. "Considering that the estate is so well guarded."

"Tut, Parker," said Pons severely. "We have found Miss Helstone upon the road in the early hours of the morning when we were driving through the district, brought her home with us and are now returning her to her employer. The man Basden will have to see us. If there are such strange goings-on at his estate he will deem it imperative to discover just exactly what the outside world knows."

"Of course, Pons. I follow you."

Pons turned to our visitor.

"Do you feel up to it, Miss Helstone?"

"If you gentlemen will accompany me, Mr Pons."

"That is settled, then."

The girl looked ruefully at her bedraggled coat and her muddied boots.

"If you will give me an hour or so, Mr Pons, I must get to the shops and purchase a few things."

"Certainly, Miss Helstone. If you will give me your parole?"

"I do not understand, Mr Pons."

"If you will promise to come back within the hour."

Our visitor flushed and glanced from Pons to me.

"Of course, gentlemen. I am over my fright now and am as anxious as you to know what is happening at Clitherington."

"Very well, then."

Pons looked at his watch.

"It is a quarter past eight now. Shall we say ten o'clock at latest."

"I will be here, Mr Pons."

When I returned from showing our visitor to the front door Pons was pacing up and down in front of the fireplace, furiously shovelling blue smoke from his pipe over his shoulder.

"This beats everything, Pons," I said. "I have never come across such an extraordinary story."

"Does it not, Parker? What do you make of it? Let us just have your views."

"Well, Pons," I said cautiously. "I hardly know where to begin. There is something curious, surely, about the high salary being paid to this young lady for her purely nominal duties."

"You have hit the crux of the matter, Parker. Inadvertently, perhaps, but part of the central mystery, certainly."

"Ah, I am improving then, Pons," I went on. "But I confess that I cannot see far into this tangle. The children who speak a different language from their father; the nocturnal habits of such young people; the invalid in the sealed wing; the heavily guarded estate; the floodlit promenades. And who is the bearded man who sat behind the screen?"

Solar Pons took the pipe from between his strong teeth and looked at me with piercing eyes.

"Who indeed, Parker? You have retained the salient points admirably and isolated the most important. You are at your most succinct, my dear fellow, and it is evident that my little lessons in the ratiocinative process have not been entirely lost."

"Let me have your views, Pons."

"It is foolish to theorize without sufficient data, Parker. But I see a few features which must resolve themselves with determined application. It is obvious why Miss Helstone was engaged but I would rather not speculate further at this stage."

"It is far from obvious to me, Pons," I said somewhat bitterly.

"Well, well, Parker, I am sure that if you employ your grey matter to good advantage, the solution will soon come to you."

And with that I had to be content until Pons returned from some mysterious errand of his own. I had just telephoned my locum when I heard his footstep upon the stair.

"I have hired a car, my dear fellow. If you will just step round to the garage in the next street and familiarize yourself with its controls, we will make our little expedition into the wilds of Surrey. Ah, here is Miss Helstone now."

Our client's step was light and she looked transformed as Mrs Johnson showed her into the sitting-room.

"I am quite ready now, Mr Pons."

Pons looked at her approvingly.

"Good, Miss Helstone. There are just a few preparations more. I have our plan of campaign mapped out. Parker, you will need your revolver."

"Revolver, Pons?"

"Certainly. I do not think the danger lies within the house. But the gentlemen who broke into the grounds appear to me to be an entirely different quantity altogether. Is there a tolerable inn in this village of Clitherington, Miss Helstone?"

"The Roebuck is very well spoken of, Mr Pons."

"Excellent. We shall make that our headquarters, Parker."

I fetched my revolver and packed it in my valise. When I returned from the garage with the car, Pons and Miss Helstone were at the door of 7B in conversation with Mrs Johnson, Pons well supplied with travelling rugs, for the day was a bitter one indeed. There was the usual tangle of traffic in town but I think I acquitted myself rather well, losing my way only once at a major junction, and we were soon well on the way to Surrey, the engine humming quietly while Pons and Miss Helstone, in the rear seats, conversed in low tones.

We arrived in the village of Clitherington about midday, smoke ascending in lazy spirals from the chimneys of the cluster of red-roofed houses which comprised the hamlet. As Miss Helstone had told us, The Roebuck was a comfortable, old-fashioned house with roaring fires and a friendly, well-trained staff. When we had deposited our baggage Pons, Miss Helstone and I repaired to the main lounge for a warming drink after our journey while Pons put the finishing touches to our strategy.

As we sat at a side table he looked sharply at a tall, cadaverous man in a frock-coat of sombre colour, who was just quitting the room.

"Memory, Parker," he said sharply. "Quite going. Once upon a time I should have been able to recall that man in a flash. A doctor, certainly. And a Harley Street man if I mistake not. You did not see him?"

I shook my head.

"I was attending to the inner man, Pons. Is the matter of any importance?"

Pons shook his head.

"Perhaps not, Parker, but the name is struggling to get out."

"Perhaps it will come later, Pons. In the meantime . . ."

"In the meantime we have much to do," he interrupted, draining his glass and getting to his feet. He smiled reassuringly at our companion.

"And now, Miss Helstone, to penetrate your den of mystery."

## IV

A drive of about twenty minutes over rough, unmade roads, the traces of which Pons had already noted on our visitor's boots, brought us up against a high brick wall which ran parallel to the highway for several hundred yards.

"That is the wall of the estate, Mr Pons," said our client in a low voice.

"Do not distress yourself, Miss Helstone," said Pons warmly. "I would not ask you to go inside again if I did not think it necessary.

And, as I have already pointed out, you are in no danger from the
occupants of The Priory unless I miss my guess. The shot came
from the men who broke into the grounds; therefore the peril is from
without."

Miss Helstone gave a relieved smile.

"Of course, Mr Pons. You are right. But what could those men
have wanted with me?"

"That is why we are here, Miss Helstone. Just pull over in front
of those gates, Parker."

It was indeed a sombre sight as we drew near; the sky was
lowering and dark and it was so cold that it seemed as though
it might snow at any minute. The road ran arrow-straight past
the high walls of the estate and two tall, gloomy iron gates with
a lodge set next to them framed a drive that was lost among dark
belts of trees.

I drew up at the entrance lodge and sounded the horn. Almost
at once a roughly dressed, dark man appeared, a sullen look upon
his face.

"Open the gates," I called above the noise of the engine. "Inform
your master that Miss Helstone is here."

As I spoke our client showed herself at the rear passenger window
and the big man's jaw dropped with surprise.

"One moment, sir. I must just inform the house," he said in a
marked foreign accent.

He shouted something and a second man whom I had not seen
set off at a run along the driveway and disappeared. I switched off
the motor and we waited for ten minutes. All this time Pons had
said nothing but I was aware of his comforting presence at my back.
The sentry at the gate – for that was his obvious function – stood
with arms folded behind the locked portals and stared impassively
in front of him.

Then there was the sound of running footsteps on the drive and
the second man re-appeared, close behind him a tall, dark woman
whom Miss Helstone immediately identified as Mrs Dresden, the
housekeeper. A short conversation followed, in a language with
which I was not conversant, and then the first man unlocked the
gates and drew them back. I drove through and Mrs Dresden, who
at once introduced herself, got into the rear of the car with Pons and
our client.

"My poor child!" she said, obviously moved, and embraced the
girl. "We thought something dreadful had happened to you."

"These gentlemen found me on the road and took me to their
London home," Miss Helstone explained. "I was exhausted and

incoherent, I am afraid. I explained the situation this morning and they kindly brought me back."

I was watching Mrs Dresden closely in the rear mirror as I negotiated the winding driveway and I saw her look sharply at Pons.

"That was very good of them, my dear. Mr Basden has been frantic with worry, I assure you. The children are quite safe."

"Thank God, Mrs Dresden. I have been so concerned. What will Mr Basden think? And what could those evil men have possibly wanted?"

The housekeeper faltered and I saw a look of indecision pass across her face.

"Do not trouble yourself further, Miss Helstone. Mr Basden will explain. He is waiting for you. And he will certainly want to thank these gentlemen."

I drove on for some way and then the estate road widened out into a gravel concourse. I was prepared for an imposing building but the fantastic folly which rose before us in the darkling winter morning was a Gothic monstrosity on the grand scale, with turrets like a French château and crenellated walls grafted on. All surrounded by sweeping banks of gloomy rhododendrons, interspersed here and there with groups of mournful statuary, which seemed to weep in the moist air.

I stopped the car before a massive flight of steps, at the top of which another bulky, anonymous-looking man waited to receive us. I felt somewhat apprehensive but Pons looked immensely at home as he descended from the vehicle and looked approvingly about him with keen, incisive glances.

"You have not exaggerated, Miss Helstone. The Priory is indeed a remarkable piece of architecture."

Our client said nothing but took Pons' arm timidly as he mounted the steps after the hurrying figure of the housekeeper. She paused at the imposing front entrance to the house.

"Whom shall I say, sir?"

"My name is Bassington," said Pons in clear, pleasant tones. "And this is my friend, Mr Tovey."

"A ridiculous name, Pons," I whispered as Mrs Dresden disappeared through the portals and we followed at a more leisurely pace.

"Perhaps, Parker, but it was all I could think of at the moment. It is not unpleasing, surely? The name of a distinguished musician came into my mind."

"As you wish, Pons," I said resignedly. "I only hope I can remember it."

We were being ushered into a vast hall floored with black and white tiles now and we waited while Mrs Dresden and our client hurried up the marble staircase to the upper floors.

I looked round curiously, only half aware of the bustle in the great house; it was evident that Miss Helstone's return had caused quite a stir and I could hear a man's voice raised in tones of relief. The mansion itself was magnificently appointed and all the strange circumstances of our client's story came back as I took in the details of our opulent surroundings.

We stood there for perhaps ten minutes, Pons silently observing the dark-coated men who scurried about the hall on furtive errands of their own, when a man came hurrying down the staircase. From his appearance and his timid air, I recognized the figure described so eloquently by Miss Helstone as Basden, the head of this strange household.

"Mr Bassington?" he said in a trembling voice. "I am indeed indebted to you for the rescue of our little Miss Helstone. I have been distraught with worry. Mr Tovey, is it? Do come into the drawing-room, gentlemen. Miss Helstone will join us once she has removed her hat and coat."

He led the way into a large, pine-panelled room in which an aromatic fire of logs burned in the marble Adam fireplace.

"Please be seated, gentlemen. May I offer you coffee or some stronger refreshment?"

"That is indeed good of you, Mr Basden," said Pons blandly. "But speaking for myself I require nothing."

I smilingly declined also and studied Basden closely while his conversation with Pons proceeded. He did indeed look furtive and ill at ease, and constantly glanced about him as if we were being observed, though we were quite alone in the room.

"And how are the children?"

Basden looked startled and then collected himself.

"Oh, quite well, Mr Bassington. They were merely frightened and ran back to the house. But I am not quite sure how you came across Miss Helstone . . ."

"We were on our way back to London in the early hours when we found the young lady bedraggled and half-conscious, lying by the side of the road. We got her into our car and as my companion is a doctor we thought it best to take her straight to my London house, where my wife made her comfortable overnight. In the morning, when she was sufficiently recovered, she told us her story and so we brought her immediately back."

Basden licked his lips.

"I see. As I have already indicated, that was extremely good of you both. If there is any way in which I could defray your expenses . . ."

Pons held up his hand with an imperious gesture.

"Say no more about it, Mr Basden. But they sound a dangerous gang of ruffians about your estate. Ought we not to call in the police?"

The expression of alarm that passed across Basden's features was so marked it was impossible to mistake, though he at once attempted to erase it.

"We have had a good deal of trouble with poachers, Mr Bassington," he said awkwardly. "My gamekeepers have dealt with the problem. We called the police, of course, but unfortunately the rogues got clean away without trace. The neighbourhood has been much plagued with the rascals."

"Oh, well, that would appear to dispose of the matter," said Pons with a disarming smile. "I am glad it was no worse. And now, if we could just say goodbye to our young companion, we will be on our way."

"Certainly, Mr Bassington. And a thousand thanks again for all your trouble."

We had just regained the hall when our client came hurrying down the stairs, the worry and strain of the past time still showing plainly on her face.

"Going so soon, gentlemen? I had hoped you would be staying to lunch."

"We have to get back to London immediately, Miss Helstone. But we leave you in safe hands, I'm sure."

Basden beamed in the background, one of the dark-coated men holding the hall-door ajar for us.

"You may rely on that, Mr Bassington."

Pons bent his head over Miss Helstone's finger-tips in a courteous gesture. I was close to him but even I had difficulty in making out the words he breathed to the girl.

"Have no fear, Miss Helstone. You are not in any danger. The doctor and I will be just outside the estate. Make sure you show yourself in the grounds tonight at about eight o'clock."

"Goodbye, gentlemen. And thank you."

There was relief on Miss Helstone's face as she and Basden said goodbye. The latter shook hands with us briefly and the two of them stood on the front steps watching us as we drove away. I had noticed previously that there were other cars in front of the house and Pons seemed to show great interest in a gleaming Rolls-Royce Silver Ghost which was parked near the steps. As soon as we had been passed through the entrance-gates by the guards and were rolling back toward Clitherington, Pons became less reticent.

"Well done, Parker. You played your part well. What did you think of The Priory?"

"Miss Helstone had not done it justice, Pons. But I judge it to be an elaborate façade."

"Excellent, Parker! You improve all the time. If Basden is master there I will devour my hat in the traditional manner. Just pull into the verge here like a good fellow, will you. I have a mind to engage in conversation with the owner of that Rolls-Royce when he comes out."

"But how do you know he is coming this way, Pons?" I protested.

Solar Pons chuckled, his face wreathed in aromatic blue smoke as he puffed at his pipe.

"Because, unless I am very much mistaken, the gentleman concerned is staying at the very same hostelry as ourselves. I assume that he would have remained at The Priory in order to let us get well clear."

"What on earth are you talking about, Pons?"

Pons vouchsafed no answer so I pulled the car up in a small lay-by at the end of the estate wall, where the road curved a little. We had not been sitting there more than ten minutes when Pons, who had been studying the road keenly in the rear mirror, which he had adjusted to suit himself, gave a brief exclamation.

"Ah, here is our man now. Just start the engine and slew the vehicle round to block the road, will you?"

I was startled but did as he bid and a few seconds later the big grey car glided up behind us and came to a halt with an imperious blaring of the horn. An irate figure at the wheel descended and I recognized the tall man in the frock coat whom Pons had pointed out in the bar of The Roebuck.

Pons bounded out of the passenger seat with great alacrity and beamed at the furious figure.

"Good morning, Sir Clifford. Sir Clifford Ayres, is it not? How goes your patient's health?"

The tall, cadaverous man's jaw dropped and he looked at Pons sharply, tiny spots of red etched on his white cheeks.

"How dare you block the road, sir? So far as I am concerned I do not know you. And I certainly do not discuss the private affairs of my patients with strangers."

"Come, Sir Clifford, you are remarkably obtuse for a Harley Street man. If you do not remember me, you must recall my distinguished colleague, Dr Parker?"

Sir Clifford made a little gobbling noise like a turkeycock and stepped forward with white features, as though he would have struck Pons.

"By God, sir, if this is a joke I do not like it. My presence here was confidential. If you are Press you will regret printing anything about me. I'll have you horsewhipped and thrown into prison. Clear the road or I will drive to the police immediately."

Pons chuckled and motioned to me to remove the car.

"Well, well, it does not suit your purpose to remember the Princes Gate reception last month, Sir Clifford. No matter. We shall meet again. Good day, sir."

And he politely tipped his hat to the apoplectic figure of Ayres at the wheel and watched him drive on in silence. He was laughing openly as he rejoined me.

"Sir Clifford is noted for his fiery temper and bad manners and he is running true to form today. Either he genuinely did not recognize me or it obviously suits his purpose to plead ignorance. But it merely strengthens my suspicions about his patient."

"What is all this about, Pons?" I said as we drove on. "I must confess the matter becomes more confusing by the minute."

"All in good time, my dear fellow. I must contact Brother Bancroft when we get back to the inn and then I must purchase a daily paper. We shall have a busy evening if I am not mistaken."

And with these cryptic utterances I had to be content for the time being. We lunched well at The Roebuck and though Pons was obviously on the lookout for Sir Clifford, the tall doctor did not put in an appearance. We were eating our dessert before Pons again broke silence.

"Come, Parker, I need your help. You are obviously more au fait than I with Sir Clifford. Just what is his forte?"

"In truth I have never met the man, Pons," I said. "Though you seemed to think he should know me. I do not move in such exalted circles. As a humble G.P. . . ."

"Tut, Parker, you are being too modest. My remark was merely meant to inform him that you were a fellow physician. We were introduced at the reception I spoke of but there were many people there; we were face to face for only a few seconds; and I relied on the traditional obtuseness of the medical profession and felt confident that he would not recall me."

"Come, Pons," I protested. "That is a definite slur."

Solar Pons chuckled with satisfaction.

"You are too easily ruffled, my dear fellow. You must practise indifference in such matters. But you have not answered my question."

"Sir Clifford? I know of his work, of course. He is one of the country's foremost specialists in heart disease and strokes."

"Indeed. I find that singularly interesting. This may not be so difficult as I had thought. If you will forgive me, I must telephone Bancroft. I will rejoin you for coffee in the lounge."

## V

"Now, Parker, let us just put a few things together. In addition to the other small points we have already discussed, we have an eminent Harley Street specialist staying in this small place and in attendance on someone within The Priory. Does not that suggest a fruitful line of enquiry?"

Solar Pons sat back in a comfortable leather chair in the coffee-room at The Roebuck and regarded me through a cloud of blue pipe-smoke. It was early evening and the place was quiet, only the occasional rumble of a cart or the higher register of a motor-vehicle penetrating the thick curtains.

"Certainly, Pons. The invalid in the sealed wing suffers from heart trouble."

"Elementary, Parker. But why?"

Pons' brows were knotted with thought and his piercing eyes were fixed upon a corner of the ceiling as he pulled reflectively at the lobe of his right ear.

"I do not follow the question, Pons."

"It is no matter, Parker. Things are becoming clearer and I should be able to arrive at some definite conclusion before the evening is out."

"You surprise me, Pons."

Solar Pons looked at me languidly, little sparks of humour dancing in his eyes.

"I have often heard you say so, Parker. I have spoken to Brother Bancroft and he has given me some interesting information on affairs in Eastern Europe."

"I should have thought this was hardly the time for it, Pons."

"Would you not? However, it is no matter. My thoughts were directed to the subject by the events of the last day's newspapers. Apparently things in Dresdania are not going too well. Her Highness is out of the country and there is a concerted effort to unseat the government in her absence. Bancroft is most concerned."

"I must confess I am completely bewildered by your line of thought, Pons."

"Perhaps this will clarify matters."

Pons handed me a bundle of newspapers, among them The Times and The Daily Telegraph. I perused them with mounting puzzlement. In each case Pons had heavily ringed or marked certain items in ink. I caught the large heading of The Daily Mail: PRINCE MIRKO APPEALS FOR CALM. Apparently things in the state Pons had mentioned were in serious disarray.

"I must admit that the Balkans has increasingly occupied the world's thoughts, Pons," I observed. "Matters are constantly in ferment there and it is certain that our own Foreign Office has a definite interest in maintaining peace in that area of the world. But I know little about such affairs . . ."

Solar Pons chuckled, holding his head on one side as he looked at me.

"Do you not see the connection, Parker? Oh, well, there is really no reason why you should. All will be made clear to you in due course. Now, you have your revolver handy, I trust?"

"It is in my valise in my room, Pons."

"Good. Just run along and fetch it, there's a good fellow. We may well have need of it before the night is out."

He paused and stared at me sombrely.

"Pray heaven we are in time, Parker. Either she is already dead or so ill that she cannot sign documents."

"Good Lord, Pons!" I cried. "If anything has happened to Miss Helstone through our neglect . . ."

To my astonishment Pons burst out laughing.

"Do not distress yourself, my dear fellow. I was not referring to Miss Helstone at all. You are on entirely the wrong tack."

He glanced at his watch.

"It is only just turned six o'clock. We have plenty of time. It is a fine night and we will walk, I think. As long as we are at the estate by eight we shall have ample room for manoeuvre."

It was a long and lonely walk, on a clear, moonlight night, though bitterly cold. As Pons and I, both heavily muffled, walked along the grass verge at the side of the road, with the wind whistling through the leafless branches of the trees which came down in thick belts of woodland close to the highway, I could not help reflecting on the anguish and terror which must have animated Miss Helstone when she ran along this same thoroughfare to catch the early morning train to bring her to Pons.

It wanted but a few minutes to eight when we arrived at the high wall of the estate belonging to The Priory. Pons' eyes were bright in the moonlight and his entire form seemed to radiate energy and determination.

"Now, Parker," he whispered, looking about him keenly. "We will just cast about for the side-gate Miss Helstone mentioned. I have a feeling that it may be in use again this evening."

"I do not see how we are to get in, Pons. Basden's people may be watching the entrance there."

"We shall have to risk that, Parker. And I daresay I can get over the wall at a pinch, with the aid of your sturdy shoulders. But come what may, we must get inside The Priory tonight."

I followed Pons as he stepped off the road and we skirted the wall for something like a quarter of a mile, beneath the dark boughs of overhanging trees.

"We must go carefully now," Pons breathed. "It cannot be far. I questioned Miss Helstone carefully about this gate and it should be somewhere here, according to her description."

As he spoke the moonlight shimmered on a gap in the wall; a few strides more brought us to the gate in question. I looked at Pons swiftly but he had already noted what I had seen. The portal was slightly ajar. I had my revolver out and we crept forward quietly. Pons bent to examine the chain and padlock.

"Our friends are already in the grounds," he whispered. "Cut through with a hacksaw. They must have made some noise. It is my opinion, Parker, that Basden's employers mean to bring the game to them. Which merely substantiates my conclusions."

"I wish I knew what on earth you were talking about, Pons," I murmured irritably.

Solar Pons smiled thinly.

"Just keep your revolver handy, friend Parker, and follow me."

He disappeared quietly through the small gate which pierced the massive wall and I followed him quickly, finding myself in almost total darkness, the shrubbery grew so thickly and so close to the boundary the other side.

But as we went farther in, treading carefully and taking care to see we made as little noise as possible, the trees fell away and soon we found ourselves near the estate road along which we had driven earlier in the day. There was a strange light in the sky ahead and as we rounded a bend, skirting the drive and keeping well into the thick undergrowth, the façade of The Priory suddenly sprang sharply into view, clear-etched in the flood-lights.

"The little charade seems to be successful," said Pons drily. "Now, just keep a sharp look-out, Parker. You are an excellent shot and I should not like the men who have preceded us through that wicket-gate to come upon us unaware."

I knelt by his side and looked round somewhat uneasily. We were well concealed here but through the fringe of leafless branches we had a good view of the house with its lawns and statuary. Even as we settled, the slim figure of Miss Helstone and two small children were descending the steps.

"Ah, they are early this evening, Parker," said Pons with satisfaction. "It seems that things are expected to happen. If I were you I should just throw off the safety-catch of your revolver, there's a good fellow."

I obeyed Pons's injunction, secretly puzzled at his remarks. Our client, after pausing initially at the foot of the steps, was now coming toward us across the grass, while the children shouted and ran in circles about her. Their shadows, caught by the glare of the floodlighting, cast long replicas before them across the lawn.

I was shifting my position when I was almost thrown off balance by my companion seizing my arm.

"There, Parker, there! We are just in time to avert tragedy."

I followed his pointing finger and saw the bushes move at the other side of the drive. Then I became fully aware of what his keen eyes had already discerned. A thin, dark man with a pointed beard, down on one knee, crouched over a black rectangle which glinted as he moved. Pons was up like a flash and running back down the verge, away from the figure in the bushes. I was only a yard away as we crossed the roadway behind him.

"Your bird, I think, Parker," Pons called as the bearded man turned. The flare of light was followed by the slap of the shot and I heard the bullet whistle somewhere through the bare branches. I was cool now and sighted the revolver carefully as I squeezed the trigger. The rifle went off in the air as the man dropped.

The night was suddenly full of cries and noise; heavy bodies blundered about the bushes. I saw Miss Helstone frozen in mid-stride, the two children running from her. I dropped to the gravel as more shots sounded. Then Pons was beside me and urging me up.

"We must get to the young lady, Parker."

A group of dark figures had debouched from the terrace and were running across the grass; I heard a whistle shrill. Miss Helstone's face was white as we drew near. But the children were before her. The little girl's face was twisted. I saw the knife glint and was astonished to see Pons fell her with a deft blow from the flat of his hand. The knife fell on the grass and I levelled my revolver at the little boy who was barking orders in a strange, guttural language.

He sullenly let the barrel of the pistol in his hand sag toward the ground.

"What does all this mean, Mr Pons?"

Helen Helstone's face was white, her eyes wide in astonishment.

"That the charade is over, Miss Helstone. You are quite safe now and have nothing to fear."

"I do not understand, Mr Pons. The children . . ."

Solar Pons smilingly shook his head and went to help the little girl up. She was quite unhurt and kicked him on the shin for his pains.

"Not children, but midgets, Miss Helstone," said Pons gravely. "Evidently to guard your safety. I will give the Prince that much, at any rate."

"What is all this, Pons?" I began when a sullen ring of dark figures closed in on us. Others appeared behind, bringing with them three roughly-dressed men with beards; one was wounded and had a blood-stained handkerchief clapped to his wrist. A tall man detached himself from the group which had come from the terrace. He had a commanding air and his eyes glittered.

"Drop that revolver!" he ordered me. "You will find it is a good deal easier to get in than to get out."

Solar Pons smiled pleasantly.

"On the contrary. I beg you not to be foolish. Just inform Prince Mirko that we are here and that we have averted a tragedy."

The big man's face was puzzled. His English was almost perfect but his sudden agitation made him stumble over the words as he replied.

"Who are you?"

"My name is Solar Pons. Just give the Prince my card, will you, and tell him that the British Foreign Office knows we are here and will hold him responsible for our safety and that of Miss Helstone."

The tall man stood in silence for a moment, studying the card Pons had given him, while the floodlights beat down their golden light on the melodramatic tableau on the broad lawn, turning the faces of ourselves and the guards into ashen masks.

"Very well, Mr Pons," the tall man said at last, lowering his pistol. "We will all go into the house."

# VI

"I think you owe me an explanation, Mr Pons."

The tall man with the quavering voice took a step forward and regarded Solar Pons with indignation. The big room with the opulent appointments seemed full of people; apart from ourselves there were a number of armed guards and the sullen captives. Only Solar Pons seemed supremely at ease as he stood, an elegant, spare figure, and regarded our host thoughtfully.

"On the contrary, Mr Basden, it is you who must explain yourself."

"I do not know what you mean."

"Oh, come, Mr Basden, if that is really your name. Shots, a murderous attack, threats, armed guards. To say nothing of the danger to Miss Helstone, a British subject. His Britannic Majesty's Government would not take kindly to a Balkan enclave within a friendly sovereign state."

Basden stepped back, his face turning white; he looked as if he were about to choke.

"Pray do not discompose yourself," said Solar Pons. "My guess is that you are an excellent actor, hired for the occasion, but a little out of your depth. Now, if you will kindly ask Prince Mirko to step out from behind that screen in the corner, we will proceed to hard facts."

Pons turned a mocking gaze toward the screen in question; now that he had directed my attention to it I could see a thin plume of blue smoke rising from behind it.

"How is Her Royal Highness's health this evening, Prince?"

There was an angry commotion and the screen was flung violently to the ground. A huge man with a thick beard stood before us, his eyes burning with rage.

"Why, that is the gentleman I glimpsed at my interview, Mr Pons!" said Miss Helstone in surprise.

"Allow me to present His Highness, Prince Mirko of Dresdania," said Pons. "Your real employer and the instigator of this elaborate farce."

Mirko had recovered himself.

"Hardly a farce, Mr Pons," said Mirko levelly, regarding Pons with a steady gaze from wide brown eyes. "You have unfortunately penetrated to the heart of Dresdania's secrets and you may find the price a high one to pay."

"I think not," said Solar Pons coolly. "My brother Bancroft holds an eminent position in the Foreign Office. If anything happens to us, troops will be here in short order."

He broke off and glanced at his watch.

"In fact, you have an hour to give me a satisfactory explanation of this affair."

There was an air of grudging admiration about Prince Mirko as he stared evenly at Pons.

"You do me a grave disservice, Mr Pons," he said quietly. "I wish you no harm and I have certainly done my best to protect Miss Helstone."

"After first putting her life at peril."

Mirko shrugged his massive shoulders.

"Politics, Mr Pons. Dresdania must come first with us. I implied no physical threat by my remark about paying a high price. Merely that the British Government will find the Balkans aflame if my efforts fail. Let us lay our cards on the table, shall we?"

"By all means," said Solar Pons equably. "Will you start or shall I?"

The Prince smiled grimly and led the way across to the far door. He said something in a foreign tongue to the big man who led the guards and they trooped from the room with their prisoners.

"We will be more comfortable in the library, Mr Pons. Will not you, the lady and the doctor sit down? Ah, I think you already know Sir Clifford Ayres."

The tall, sour figure of the Harley Street man uncoiled itself from an armchair and came down the room toward us. He held out his hand stiffly, embarrassment clear on his face.

"I must apologize for my earlier rudeness, Mr Pons, Dr Parker. I could not breach the code of professional conduct, as you well know. I did remember you from the reception, Mr Pons."

"Good of you to acknowledge it, Sir Clifford," said Pons smoothly, as we seated ourselves. "This is an unfortunate affair but events appear to have taken a turn for the better. How is the man Dr Parker shot?"

"Dead, Mr Pons," said the Prince.

He waved me down as I started to get up from my chair.

"You need not distress yourself, Dr Parker. Krenko was one of the most murderous scoundrels who ever walked in shoe-leather. You have done Dresdania a great service tonight, doctor, for which she cannot thank you enough."

I cleared my throat.

"Thank goodness for that, anyway, Pons. I should not like the thing to lie heavily on my conscience. And then there is the little matter of the police . . ."

Pons smiled.

"That is the least of our problems, Parker. You must just content yourself with knowing that you have saved Miss Helstone."

"At your instigation, Pons. I am completely baffled."

"And yet the matter was a fairly simple one, Parker, merely requiring the key. I am sure Prince Mirko will correct me if I am wrong, but it was obvious from the moment Miss Helstone consulted us that she was not required for duties as a governess; neither was she being paid five hundred pounds a year for her undoubted skills in that area."

"But for what, Pons?"

"For a masquerade, my dear fellow. For her remarkable resemblance to the Princess Sonia, the ruler of Dresdania. Everything pointed to it. And as soon as I saw the Princess's picture in the newspapers, the whole thing became clear. The interview with Mr Basden – he is an actor in your employ, is he not? – the man behind the screen who was making the selection; and the quite extraordinary way in which Miss Helstone alone from all the hundreds interviewed suddenly fitted the bill. She could not even speak the same language as her charges.

"But it was crystal-clear that the sole object of her employment was her unwitting impersonation of an absent person, even to changing her hair-style; wearing unaccustomed jewellery and expensive clothing; and to being seen late at night beneath the floodlighting outside this house. The whole thing smacked of the stage, Parker."

Prince Mirko gave a wry smile and studied the tip of his cigar.

"I can now see why Mr Pons is spoken of as England's greatest consulting detective," he observed to Sir Clifford.

Helen Helstone's eyes were wide as she turned toward Pons.

"Of course, Mr Pons. It is so simple when you put it like that. I had not thought of it."

"Exactly, Miss Helstone. And there was no reason why you should. But it is at least to the Prince's credit that while tethering you as a decoy he at least provided you with adequate bodyguards."

"It was a regrettable necessity," said Prince Mirko. "Dictated by the inexorable requirements of the State."

"And a most original method," said Pons reflectively. "They looked exactly like children. And they are potentially deadly."

He rubbed his shin with a slight grimace. Prince Mirko's smile broadened.

"They are the Zhdanov Twins, circus and music-hall performers. Boy and girl. They specialize in the personation of children and both are expert at ju-jitsu, knife and pistol. You were lucky they did not shoot you first and ask questions afterwards. We have several times used them in our secret service operations."

"But how could you know this, Pons?" I cried.

"It was a fairly rapid process to the trained mind, Parker. I soon

came to the conclusion they were midgets. The harshness of voice;
the fact that they stayed out so late at night, which no real children
would do; their peculiar actions when the attempt was made on Miss
Helstone's life."

His smile widened.

"You remember they ran toward the source of danger when Miss
Helstone's life was attempted. That was significant. To say nothing
of the male twin's cigar-smoking in their rooms. The lady suspected
that you were the parent in the case, Prince."

The bearded man bowed ironically to our client.

"That was most careless and I will see that the guilty party is
reprimanded."

"Your prisoners, Prince," put in Solar Pons sharply, as though
the idea had only just occurred to him. "No Dresdanian summary
justice on British soil."

"It shall be as you say, Mr Pons," said Prince Mirko. "In any
case, Dr Parker has despatched the principal viper. And with the
imprisonment of the others, the threat to Dresdania's internal politics
is entirely removed."

"If you would be kind enough to elucidate, Pons!" I said hotly.

"My dear fellow. Certainly. If you had taken the trouble to read
the newspapers properly this morning, they would have told you most
of the story about Dresdania's internal troubles. It is Princess Sonia,
is it not?"

Mirko nodded gravely.

"Her Royal Highness was in England incognito, on a short
holiday. She is only thirty-eight, as you know. To our alarm and
astonishment she had not been here more than three days when
she was laid low by a crippling stroke. That was some four months
ago. When she was well enough to be moved from a small, private
nursing home near Epsom, we brought her here to this mansion,
which belongs to the Dresdanian Embassy. Our own personnel
surrounded her and we had the world's finest medical attention
and nursing staff."

Here Sir Clifford bowed gratefully in acknowledgement of his
services.

Solar Pons turned his lean, alert face toward the Prince.

"And how is Her Royal Highness at this moment?"

"Much improved, I am glad to say. It was a freak condition, I
understand, and rare in one so young. I am assured by Sir Clifford
that she will make a complete recovery. She will be well enough to
sign State documents within the next few days."

"I am still not quite sure that I follow, Pons," I said.

"I see that you do not understand Balkan politics, doctor," said the Prince.

He held up his hand.

"And there is really no reason why you should. But Dresdania's internal stability is a vital element in the uneasy peace in that part of the world. Dissident elements have long been pledged to opposing the Throne and tearing it down. Vilest of them was Krenko; bombings, murder, political assassination and torture were only a few of the weapons he employed. As you know, the Princess is a widow and she has ruled as Regent, with me to guide her, on behalf of her son. He is now fourteen and of an age when he may soon be able to assume his responsibilities. Princess Sonia is anxious that he should do so, as the last decade has been a fearful strain. Indeed, it was probably this which precipitated the stroke. Her medical advisers prescribed complete rest and she came to England.

"But there was an attempted coup within a week of her arrival and unfortunately she was already ill. It was imperative for the country and for the sake of the young Crown Prince, who knows nothing of his mother's condition, that all should appear to be well."

"Hence the masquerade!" I put in.

I stared at Pons in admiration.

"And you saw all this at a glance?"

"Hardly, Parker. But it was not too difficult to arrive at the truth, once all the threads were in my hand."

Prince Mirko cast a regretful look at Miss Helstone.

"I must confess that I did not really think I would have much success with my ruse but I inserted the advertisement which Miss Helstone answered. I was in despair when I saw her at the interview but then realized what an astonishing likeness she had to the Princess."

Here he indicated a photograph in a heavy gilt frame which stood on a piano in one corner of the library.

"I determined to take a chance. It was a desperate act but the only card I had left to play. It was imperative that the Princess should be seen behaving normally. Hence the deception; the flood-lighting and the nightly promenades. We had heard that Krenko and a band of desperadoes had arrived in England. He would either make an attempt on the Princess's life, in which case we would be ready and try to eliminate him; or, he would merely report back to his political masters that the Princess was well and carrying out her normal duties. Either would have suited us, because there is no fear of a coup while the Princess is alive – she is so popular among the common people. All we wanted was to stabilize things until the Princess should be well enough to sign the Instrument of Succession on behalf of her son. But Krenko evaded our vigilance and made an attempt on her life; we knew he would try again."

"For which purpose you put on a visible show of guarding the estate, while deliberately leaving the side-gate vulnerable," said my companion. "And you required an orphan in case of any tragic developments."

"Exactly, Mr Pons. We had hoped that the presence of so distinguished a heart-specialist would pass unnoticed in the district – Sir Clifford insisted on staying at the inn where he could obtain his peculiarly English comforts – but we had not reckoned on your deductive genius."

"You are too kind, Prince Mirko."

Pons consulted his watch.

"I shall need to telephone Brother Bancroft, unless we wish the military to descend upon us."

Mirko nodded thoughtfully, the smoke from his cigar going up in heavy spirals to the library ceiling.

"It would be helpful if you would ask him for a responsible officer from Scotland Yard to attend to this affair, in conjunction with your Home Office and our Foreign Office, Mr Pons."

"Superintendent Stanley Heathfield is your man, Prince," said Solar Pons, with a conspiratorial nod which took in myself and Miss Helstone. "If you will just excuse me."

He paused by the door.

"It occurs to me, Prince Mirko, that Miss Helstone has been in considerable danger while under your roof. Now that her duties are prematurely ended, do you not think that some compensation is in order?"

"I had not overlooked that, Mr Pons," said Mirko gravely. "My Government's cheque for twenty thousand English pounds will be paid into any bank of her choice."

"Twenty thousand pounds!"

Helen Helstone's face was incredulous as she gazed from me to Pons.

"The labourer is worthy of his hire, my dear young lady," Solar Pons murmured.

"And it is cheap for the security of the state," Prince Mirko added.

"I hardly know what to say, Mr Pons."

"Take the money, Miss Helstone. I assume that Mr Basden has been well looked after?"

"You may rely upon it, Mr Pons," said Mirko gravely. "Though an admirable actor he is hardly ideal when called upon to play a part in which reality may intrude at any moment. His behaviour under stress has made him an unstable tool at times. And though we coached him carefully in the language he forgot even those few phrases when under pressure."

Solar Pons returned from telephoning within a few minutes, rubbing his thin hands together.

"Excellent! Superintendent Heathfield is running down with a party of selected officers just as soon as train and motor-car can bring him. In the meantime I think our work here is ended, Parker. No doubt you will wish to come with us, Miss Helstone?"

"If you will just give me a few minutes to pack, Mr Pons."

"Certainly. And I must emphasize that you must exercise the utmost discretion as to what you have heard in this room tonight."

"You have my word, Mr Pons."

Mirko looked on with admiration.

"Mr Pons, you should have been a diplomat."

"I leave all that to my brother, Prince Mirko," said my companion carelessly. "But I think that under the circumstances you would have done better to have taken our Foreign Office into your confidence."

"Perhaps, Mr Pons," said Prince Mirko, studiously examining the glowing red tip of his cigar.

Sir Clifford Ayres rose to his feet and stiffly shook hands.

"A rapid convalescence and a complete recovery to your patient, doctor. And my congratulations."

"Thank you. Good night, Mr Pons. Good night, doctor."

"Good night, Sir Clifford."

We waited in the hall as Miss Helen Helstone descended the stairs, her face still bearing traces of the excitement of the night and of her unexpected good fortune. Prince Mirko took the paper bearing her address and studied it beneath the chandelier in the hallway, his bearded face enigmatic.

"Dresdania is grateful, young lady."

He brushed her hand with his lips and bowed us out. The Princess's car was waiting outside and conveyed us back to the high road.

"A remarkable achievement, Pons," I said, as soon as we were driving back in the direction of Clitherington.

"A case not without its points of interest, my dear fellow," he said with tones of approbation.

He smiled across at our fair client.

"They do things a great deal differently in the Balkans, Parker, but by his own lights Mirko has not done badly by Miss Helstone. By the time she marries – and providing she has handled her funds wisely – she will be a well-propertied woman."

And he lit his pipe with considerable satisfaction.

Mike Ashley is a leading authority on horror, fantasy and science fiction. Since 1974 he has written and edited over thirty books, including *Weird Legacies*, *Souls in Metal*, *Mrs Gaskell's Tales of Mystery and Horror*, *Jewels of Wonder*, *Best of British SF* (2 vols.), *Who's Who in Horror and Fantasy Fiction*, and *The Mammoth Book of Short Horror Novels*, *Pendragon Chronicles* and *The Camelot Chronicles*.

He has also contributed widely to fantasy magazines and encyclopedias in Britain and America, including *Amazing Stories*, *Locus* and *Twilight Zone Magazine*.

# THE MAMMOTH BOOK OF
# HISTORICAL WHODUNNITS

*Also available*

The Mammoth Book of Classic Science Fiction – *Short Novels of the 1930s*

The Mammoth Book of Golden Age Science Fiction – *Short Novels of the 1940s*

The Mammoth Book of Vintage Science Fiction – *Short Novels of the 1950s*

The Mammoth Book of New Age Science Fiction – *Short Novels of the 1960s*

The Mammoth Book of Fantastic Science Fiction – *Short Novels of the 1970s*

The Mammoth Book of Modern Science Fiction

The Mammoth Book of Private Eye Stories

The Mammoth Book of Great Detective Stories

The Mammoth Book of Spy Thrillers

The Mammoth Book of True Murder

The Mammoth Book of True Crime

The Mammoth Book of True Crime 2

The Mammoth Book of Short Horror Novels

The Mammoth Book of True War Stories

The Mammoth Book of Modern War Stories

The Mammoth Book of the Western

The Mammoth Book of Ghost Stories

The Mammoth Book of Ghost Stories 2

The Mammoth Book of the Supernatural

The Mammoth Book of Astounding Puzzles

The Mammoth Book of Terror

The Mammoth Book of Vampires

The Mammoth Book of Killer Women

# The Mammoth Book of
# HISTORICAL
# WHODUNNITS

Edited by
Mike Ashley

Carroll and Graf Publishers Inc.
New York

Carroll & Graf Publishers, Inc.
260 Fifth Avenue
New York
NY 10001

First published in Great Britain 1993

First Carroll & Graf edition 1993

Introductory material and this arrangement copyright
© Mike Ashley 1993

ISBN 0–7867–0024–6

Printed and bound in Great Britain.

10 9 8 7 6 5

# Contents

## PART IV: HOLMES AND BEYOND

# Acknowledgements

There have been a number of people who have helped me in the compilation of this anthology. First and foremost I must thank Miss Edith Pargeter for kindly providing the foreword, and her own words of encouragement on the project. I must also thank Jack Adrian, a most learned expert on mystery and detective fiction, who suggested a number of stories to me, and provided me with copies of the lesser known ones. Likewise Peter Berresford Ellis who brought several other stories to my attention. My thanks to Michael Williams who provided me with his memories of Wallace Nichols. Finally my thanks to Robert Adey and Richard Dalby, both of whom took the great risk of loaning me copies of particularly rare volumes, and which I hope are now safely restored to them.

Acknowledgements are accorded to the following for the rights to reprint the stories in this anthology.

"Captain Nash and the Wroth Inheritance" © 1975 by Ragan Butler. Originally published by Harwood-Smart Publishing, Lewes. Reprinted by permission of the author.

"The Gentleman from Paris" © 1950 by John Dickson Carr. First appeared in *Ellery Queen's Mystery Magazine*, April 1950. Reprinted by permission of the agents for the author's estate, David Higham Associates (UK).

"Murder Lock'd In" © 1980 by Lillian de la Torre. First appeared in *Ellery Queen's Mystery Magazine*, December 1, 1980. Reprinted by permission of the author's agents, David Higham Associates (UK), and in the US by Harold Ober Associates.

"The Case of the Deptford Horror" © 1954 by Adrian Conan Doyle. Originally published in *The Exploits of Sherlock Holmes* (London: John Murray, 1954). Reprinted by permission of Richard Doyle for the author's estate.

"The Witch's Tale" © 1993 by Margaret Frazer. First printing, used by permission of the authors.

"A Sad and Bloody Hour" © 1965 by Joe Gores. First appeared in

*Ellery Queen's Mystery Magazine*, April 1965. Reprinted by permission of the author.

"The Confession of Brother Athelstan" © 1993 by Paul Harding. First printing, used by permission of the author.

"Murder in the Rue Royale" © 1967 by Michael Harrison. Originally published in *Ellery Queen's Mystery Magazine*, January 1968. Unable to trace the author's representative.

"The Golden Nugget Poker Game" © 1986 by Edward D. Hoch. Originally published in *Ellery Queen's Mystery Magazine*, March 1987.

"Five Rings in Reno" © 1976 by Edward D. Hoch [R. L. Stevens]. Originally published in *Ellery Queen's Mystery Magazine*, July 1976. Reprinted by permission of the author.

"Socrates Solves a Murder" © 1954 by Brèni James. Originally published in *Ellery Queen's Mystery Magazine*, October 1954. Unable to trace the author or the author's representative.

"Leonardo Da Vinci, Detective" © 1958 by Theodore Mathieson. Originally published in *Ellery Queen's Mystery Magazine*, January 1959. Reprinted by permission of the author.

"The Treasury Thefts" © 1950 by Wallace Nichols. Originally published as "The Case of the Empress's Jewels" in the *London Mystery Magazine*, April 1950, and as "The Treasury Thefts" in the *London Mystery Magazine*, June 1950. Unable to trace the author's representative.

"The Locked Tomb Mystery" © 1989 by Elizabeth Peters. First published in *Sisters in Crime*, edited by Marilyn Wallace, New York: Berkley Books, 1989. Reprinted by permission of the author's agent, David Grossman Literary Agency.

"Foreword" © 1993 by Ellis Peters. First printing, used by permission of the author.

"The Price of Light" © 1979 by Ellis Peters. Originally published in *Winter's Crimes 11*, edited by George Hardinge (London, Macmillan, 1979), and in the author's collection *A Rare Benedictine* (London, Headline Book Publishing PLC 1988). Reprinted by permission of the author and the author's publisher, Headline Book Publishing PLC.

"Father Hugh and the Deadly Scythe" © 1990 by Mary Monica

Pulver. Originally printed in *Alfred Hitchcock's Mystery Magazine*, 1990. Reprinted by permission of the author.

"The Christmas Masque" © 1976 by S.S. Rafferty. First appeared in *Ellery Queen's Mystery Magazine*, December 1976. Reprinted by permission of the author.

"A Byzantine Mystery" © 1993 by Mary Reed and Eric Mayer. First printing, used by permission of the author.

"Mightier Than the Sword" © 1993 by John Maddox Roberts. First printing, used by permission of the author.

"The High King's Sword" © 1993 by Peter Tremayne. First printing, used by permission of the authors.

"He Came With the Rain" © 1967 by Robert van Gulik. First published in *Judge Dee at Work* (London: William Heinemann, 1967). Reprinted by permission of Dr. Thomas M. van Gulik.

Every effort has been made to trace the owners of copyright material. The Editor would be pleased to hear from anyone if they believe there has been any inadvertent transgression of copyright, and also from anyone who can help trace the representatives of Michael Harrison, Brèni James and Wallace Nicols.

# Introduction
# THE CHRONICLES
# OF CRIME

This anthology is the first of a kind. It's the first to bring together a selection of stories featuring detectives from the entire history of the civilised world.

Stories about historical detectives are relatively new, though they are not as new as some may feel. To many, the historical detective field burst forth fully fledged with the Brother Cadfael novels of Ellis Peters. There is no doubt that Miss Peters's superbly developed works created a little niche of their own with the medieval mystery story, and that world has grown substantially in the last ten years. But the historical detective story has been around a while longer than that, though until Ellis Peters's creation, it lacked an identity.

So, what do I mean by the historical detective story. Quite simply it's the union of two much older literary fields – the historical fiction field with that of the detective story, but the emphasis has to be on the detective element, otherwise it is nothing more than a historical story containing some element of mystery. For the purposes of this anthology, and to give it some structure, I have been rather stringent in my definition of the historical detective story. Strictly speaking any detective story set in a period earlier than its composition would have to be regarded as historical. But I personally believe that any writer who can draw upon his direct personal memories of the past is still, in his own mind, writing a relatively contemporary work. I have thus been very restrictive and decided that a historical detective story should, at the very least, be set at a period before the author's birth, and to all intents and purposes that really means before the twentieth century.

I've made one exception to that self-imposed rule for a special reason that will be obvious when you encounter it. As you will see from the contents page, the stories I have selected range from as far back as 1400 BC, down through the years to the time of Sherlock Holmes. En route they pass through ancient Greece and Rome, the mystic Orient, the Middle Ages and Elizabethan period, to the Regency and Victorian periods. Over three thousand years of historical detection.

As an afterword I have reprinted a piece on the origins of detective work to show how it really developed. I've also assembled a checklist of novels and stories featuring historical detectives for further reading.

It's perhaps a little surprising that the fields of historical fiction and detective fiction didn't come together earlier than they did, but throughout the nineteenth century they kept to their own separate paths.

The detective story was created almost single-handedly by that tragic American genius Edgar Allan Poe, with his gruesome "The Murders in the Rue Morgue", published in *Graham's Magazine* for April 1841. It introduced the first detective in fiction, C. Auguste Dupin. Poe wrote two more stories featuring Dupin, "The Mystery of Marie Rogêt" (1842) and "The Purloined Letter" (1844). Since the settings for these stories were contemporary for Poe they could not qualify for this anthology, even though the stories are most certainly historic if not historical. However, a hundred-and-twenty years later the author Michael Harrison wrote a new series of stories about Dupin, and these of course do qualify. So I'm delighted to be able to include a story featuring the first ever fictional detective.

Dupin was a master of logical or ratiocinative deduction, a skill brought to the ultimate by the doyen of detection, Sherlock Holmes. Indeed, Dupin was one of a number of influences upon Arthur Conan Doyle in creating Holmes. I find it surprising that Doyle did not create a historical detective because Doyle preferred writing historical fiction and, in later years, came to resent the time he felt obliged to spend on creating new Holmes' stories. Quite why he never put the two together I do not know.

In researching for this anthology I tried to find if Doyle had written any story set in the past featuring someone using detective skills. A few of the Brigadier Gerard stories, set in the Napoleonic period, involve mysteries but no detection. With the assistance of Christopher and Barbara Roden of the Arthur Conan Doyle Society, the closest we could get was "The Silver Hatchet". This was written in 1883 but set in 1861 when Doyle was two years old, so it almost qualified. However, although the story does feature a police detective, he does very little detection.

I almost cheated! The Sherlock Holmes stories themselves are often set in periods earlier than their writing, as Watson dusts off another set of papers from his archives and recounts an ancient case. The earliest recorded investigation by Holmes is "The Gloria Scott", published in 1893 but set some twenty years earlier when Holmes was at college. But the story has a contemporary setting with Holmes relating to Watson his first case. It doesn't really qualify. Still, it's a good game working out the gap between the publication of a Holmes story and its setting. There are in fact a number of stories about Holmes by Doyle published well into the twentieth century but set in the 1880s and 90s, and the biggest span of years I could find is with "The Adventure of the Veiled Lodger" set in 1896 but not published until 1927.

However, I decided to remain pure to the cause. There have, in fact, been many stories written about Sherlock Holmes since Conan Doyle laid down his pen, including several by his son, Adrian. These have been unfairly overlooked, and since they are genuine historical detective stories, I have selected one of those for this volume.

The first author to write a story featuring a genuine historical detective was an American lawyer, Melville Davisson Post. In Uncle Abner, Post created a strong, upright, god-fearing man, in the early years of the nineteenth century, who had phenomenal powers of observation and deduction and at times equals Holmes in his perceptiveness. The first Uncle Abner story, "Angel of the Lord", was published in the *Saturday Evening Post* in 1911, and Post wrote another twenty or so over the next few years. "The Doomdorf Mystery", which is reprinted in this volume, remains to my mind the most ingenious.

Some may argue that there was an earlier historical detective in print, none other than the Scarlet Pimpernel, created by Baroness Orczy in 1905. There is no denying the popularity and influence of the character, but Sir Percy Blakeney, who masqueraded as the Pimpernel in the days of the French revolution, was really a secret agent and the purist in me does not regard a secret agent as a genuine detective.

In fact although the occasional short story appeared which could perhaps be shoe-horned into the historical detective *genre*, including some by the great author of swashbucklers, Rafael Sabatini, the Uncle Abner stories remained unique for almost thirty years. Then, in the forties, the American academic and mystery writer Lillian de la Torre, saw the wonderful opportunities presented by the British giant of letters, Dr Samuel Johnson, with his ready-made Watson, James Boswell. Starting in 1943 she began what has become the longest-running series of historical detective stories featuring the investigations of Dr Sam Johnson, Detector.

At about that same time, Agatha Christie became attracted to the possibilities of writing a detective novel set in ancient Egypt. It was in response to an idea suggested by an Egyptologist friend, Professor Stephen Glanville, to whom the book is dedicated. Up until that time no one had written an entire detective novel set in an historical period, let alone one so far back as 2000 BC.

It wasn't long though before another great writer of detective stories started to make the historical detective novel something of his own. John Dickson Carr, the master of the impossible crime, had toyed with historical mysteries for some years as short stories, but in 1950 he completed *The Bride of Newgate*. Set at the end of the Napoleonic era, the story is about Richard Darwent, imprisoned in Newgate and then pardoned for a crime he did not commit, who sets out to identify the real criminal. It is one of Carr's best novels, written when he was at the peak of his power. It was at the same time that he penned the story included in this anthology, "The Gentleman from Paris".

Carr wrote ten historical mystery novels. Some use as a device a modern-day character regressing in time, of which the best is *The Devil in Velvet* (1955), where a professor, following an apparent pact with the devil, has the chance to go back and solve a murder before it happens.

A genuine historical mystery was the subject of *The Daughter of Time* (1951) by Josephine Tey. Voted the favourite novel of all time by the Crime Writers Association, it is not technically an historical detective story. It features Tey's present-day detective, Alan Grant, who while laid up in hospital uses an acquaintance to help him research the deaths of the princes in the Tower. This was the same method used by Colin Dexter in his award-winning Inspector Morse novel, *The Wench is Dead*.

During the 1950s a number of authors turned to the historical detective form. Wallace Nichols, a poet and writer, began a long-running series about Sollius, the Slave Detective, in the *London Mystery Magazine*. His first case is reprinted here.

Robert van Gulik, one-time Dutch ambassador to Japan, had become fascinated by an eighteenth-century Chinese detective novel, *Dee Goong An*, which featured the cases of a real historical character, Dee Goong, a seventh-century Chinese magistrate. While on war duties in the Pacific, van Gulik translated the stories into English as *Dee Goong An: Three Murder Cases of Judge Dee* (1949). By then he had become so fascinated with this character that he continued to write about him for the next twenty years, producing a delightful series of novels and stories, one of which is reprinted here.

In America, Theodore Mathieson struck upon the idea of setting major historical characters difficult crimes to solve. The stories were collected together as *The Great Detectives* (1960), and showed the detective skills of Alexander the Great, Leonardo da Vinci, Captain Cook, even Florence Nightingale. Since several of these stories were set in the Middle Ages one might argue that Mathieson was the first to write a medieval mystery.

By the sixties and seventies there were a number of writers producing novels set in the nineteenth century. Leaving aside the many stories that feature Sherlock Holmes, there were a series of Victorian police procedurals, of which the best are Peter Lovesey's books about Sergeant Cribb, and there were several novels featuring the Bow Street Runners, such as those by Richard Falkirk and Jeremy Sturrock.

So, as we can see, by the time Brother Cadfael first tended his herb garden at Shrewsbury Abbey, the historical detective story had been gathering pace for some years. Yet, the stories had not been sown in especially fertile soil. Ellis Peters, on the other hand, if I may mix my metaphors, had struck a particularly rich vein. Here, for the first time, was an author skilled both in detective fiction and, under her real name of Edith Pargeter, equally skilled at historical fiction. She was thus able to blend the two genres seamlessly, along with immaculate characterisation and an ability to bring the past alive as no other had before.

A further boost came from the publication of *The Name of the Rose* (1980) by Umberto Eco, a superbly gothic detective novel set in a remote Italian monastery where Brother William seeks to solve a series of increasingly bizarre murders. Despite the gothic trappings the novel owes much to Sherlock Holmes. It is a fascinating puzzle and made an equally fascinating film, starring Sean Connery.

With the success of Brother Cadfael and *The Name of the Rose*, others have followed: the Brother Athelstan novels by Paul Harding, the Hugh Corbett books by Paul Doherty, the Matthew Stock stories by Leonard Tourney, the Nicholas Bracewell books by Edward Marston. These and many more are listed in the appendix.

In this anthology I have sought to include new stories by many of today's leading writers of historical whodunnits, as well as reprinting some of the classics of the field. I am also delighted that Ellis Peters has kindly provided a foreword for the collection. Since she opened up a whole new vein in mystery fiction, I can do no better than to hand over to her to declare this anthology open.

Mike Ashley
March 1993

# Foreword
# by Ellis Peters

I was not aware when I began my first novel featuring Brother
Cadfael that I was opening or developing a new area of fiction.
True, I had encountered hardly any previous historical mysteries,
though I can recall reading a few short stories, including one which
featured Aristotle as a detective. In general I avoid reading anything
that may overlap what I'm working on, in subject or period, to put
all influence out of the question.

In 1976 I was between books and passing the time while I thought
about the next one, and it happened that I dipped into the massive
*History of Shrewsbury* compiled by two nineteenth century clerics,
Owen and Blakeway; books I'd had since I was fifteen and knew
very well.

The story of the expedition from the Abbey to acquire a saint's
relics from Wales was familiar enough, but it suddenly occurred to
me that it would make a good plot for a murder mystery, and a novel
way of disposing of a body. So, *A Morbid Taste for Bones* was conceived
from the beginning as a murder mystery rather than an historical
novel. Its locations, Shrewsbury and North Wales, were laid down
by historical facts – historical, at least, according to the life of Saint
Winifred which Prior Robert Pennant afterwards wrote, concluding
it with the account of his own expedition into Wales to find and bring
her back. The book, by the way, is in the Bodleian if anyone cares to
pursue the study, though I have not seen it myself.

With so much recorded fact, I was not going to meddle too much
with the story, though I admit to a major departure from the actual
version of the result of the expedition. The whole process of working
fiction into fact without playing tricks with history appealed to me
strongly. The difficulties arising are half the attraction, like a cryptic
crossword puzzle.

I did not intend a series when I began. The first novel was
written as a one-off. But about a year later, after I had written another book, I became fascinated by King Stephen's siege
of Shrewsbury and as that happened only a short time after
the translation of St. Winifred, I could use the same cast of

characters. From then on the books took up a rhythm of their own.

Brother Cadfael did not emerge immediately. The cast of the novel was limited to the party of monks from Shrewsbury and the population of Gwytherin, so my protagonist had to be one of the Brothers: one with wider experience of life than an oblatus donated in infancy could have, so in middle life and with half a world behind him. He had to be one who spoke Welsh, a reason for including in the party a Brother of otherwise modest function. And so he started to emerge: elderly, travelled, humanely curious about his fellowmen, and Welsh. I hunted for a name unusual even in Wales, and found only two references to Cadfael in Lloyd's *History of Wales*, so I borrowed that name. And there he was.

All the greater magnates in the novels are real – the abbots, bishops, Welsh princes, even the Dublin Danish adventurers. There was an Abbot Radulfus as there was an Abbot Heribert before him, and Heribert was demoted just as related, by the Legatine Council that appointed Radulfus in his place. Prior Robert was real enough, as he proved by writing his book. Hugh Beringar is my own man. At that time FitzAlan was sheriff, but he fled when Stephen stormed Shrewsbury, and I can find no record of the man Stephen must have appointed in his place. So I was free to fill the vacancy and free to suppose that in time Gilbert Prestcote died and gave place to his equally imaginary deputy, Hugh Beringar.

The steady progression of the books has surprised me, and has led to an emphasis on season, weather and the religious sequence of the year; but as soon as I realized it, I recognised how appropriate it is, since we are concerned with the regular lives of a community. As a result I have been able to focus on the day-to-day detail of community life, and I believe it is that which has made the books so popular.

In the years since I began the Cadfael books I have not read many other historical mysteries, so I am fascinated by the wonderfully mixed bag of stories included in this anthology. I have also read Lindsey Davis's novels set in Vespasian's Rome, told in the colloquial style of a slightly seedy private eye, which I think absolutely first class. She brings Imperial Rome to life from the street angle, laundresses, thuggish trainee gladiators and all, and still presents us with a very likeable young protagonist.

Perhaps that is the secret of the successful historical detective story: the ability to include a human and likeable detective in a background that comes to life and becomes as real to today's readers as it was to the souls living all those centuries ago.

# PART I
# The Ancient World

# THE LOCKED TOMB MYSTERY
# Elizabeth Peters

*Elizabeth Peters (b. 1927) is ideally suited to open this anthology. Under her real name of Barbara Mertz she is a noted Egyptologist and has written a number of studies of ancient Egypt, including* Temples, Tombs and Hieroglyphs *(1964), which is the story of Egyptology. Under two pen names – Elizabeth Peters and Barbara Michaels – she has written a long line of mystery and detective novels. These include* The Curse of the Pharaohs *(1981), which introduced the Victorian archeologist, Amelia Peabody and her husband Radcliffe Emerson who, on their trips to Egypt, encounter any amount of bizarre crimes.*

*Elizabeth Peters has the following to say about our first fictional sleuth in the following story. "Amenhotep Sa Hapu was a real person who lived during the fourteenth century* BC. *Later generations worshipped him as a sage and scholar; he seems like a logical candidate for the role of ancient Egyptian detective."*

Senebtisi's funeral was the talk of southern Thebes. Of course, it could not compare with the burials of Great Ones and Pharaohs, whose Houses of Eternity were furnished with gold and fine linen and precious gems, but ours was not a quarter where nobles lived; our people were craftsmen and small merchants, able to afford a chamber-tomb and a coffin and a few spells to ward off the perils of the Western Road – no more than that. We had never seen anything like the burial of the old woman who had been our neighbor for so many years.

The night after the funeral, the customers of Nehi's tavern could talk of nothing else. I remember that evening well. For one thing, I had just won my first appointment as a temple scribe. I was looking forward to boasting a little, and perhaps paying for a round of beer, if my friends displayed proper appreciation of my good fortune. Three of the others were already at the tavern when I arrived, my linen shawl wrapped tight around me. The weather was cold even for winter, with a cruel, dry wind driving sand into every crevice of the body.

"Close the door quickly," said Senu, the carpenter. "What weather! I wonder if the Western journey will be like this – cold enough to freeze a man's bones."

This prompted a ribald comment from Rennefer, the weaver, concerning the effects of freezing on certain of Senebtisi's vital organs. "Not that anyone would notice the difference," he added. "There was never any warmth in the old hag. What sort of mother would take all her possessions to the next world and leave her only son penniless?"

"Is it true, then?" I asked, signaling Nehi to fetch the beer jar. "I have heard stories – "

"All true," said the potter, Baenre. "It is a pity you could not attend the burial, Wadjsen; it was magnificent!"

"You went?" I inquired. "That was good of you, since she ordered none of her funerary equipment from you."

Baenre is a scanty little man with thin hair and sharp bones. It is said that he is a domestic tyrant, and that his wife cowers when he comes roaring home from the tavern, but when he is with us, his voice is almost a whisper. "My rough kitchenware would not be good enough to hold the wine and fine oil she took to the tomb. Wadjsen, you should have seen the boxes and jars and baskets – dozens of them. They say she had a gold mask, like the ones worn by great nobles, and that all her ornaments were of solid gold."

"It is true," said Rennefer. "I know a man who knows one of the servants of Bakenmut, the goldsmith who made the ornaments."

"How is her son taking it?" I asked. I knew Minmose slightly; a shy, serious man, he followed his father's trade of stone carving. His mother had lived with him all his life, greedily scooping up his profits, though she had money of her own, inherited from her parents.

"Why, as you would expect," said Senu, shrugging. "Have you ever heard him speak harshly to anyone, much less his mother? She was an old she-goat who treated him like a boy who has not cut off the side lock; but with him it was always 'Yes, honored mother,' and 'As you say, honored mother.' She would not even allow him to take a wife."

"How will he live?"

"Oh, he has the shop and the business, such as it is. He is a hard worker; he will survive."

In the following months I heard occasional news of Minmose. Gossip said he must be doing well, for he had taken to spending his leisure time at a local house of prostitution – a pleasure he never had dared enjoy while his mother lived. Nefertiry, the loveliest and most expensive of the girls, was the object of his desire, and Rennefer remarked that the maiden must have a kind heart, for she could command higher prices than Minmose was able to pay. However, as time passed, I forgot Minmose and Senebtisi, and her rich burial. It was not until almost a year later that the matter was recalled to my attention.

The rumors began in the marketplace, at the end of the time of inundation, when the floodwater lay on the fields and the farmers were idle. They enjoy this time, but the police of the city do not; for idleness leads to crime, and one of the most popular crimes is tomb robbing. This goes on all the time in a small way, but when the Pharaoh is strong and stern, and the laws are strictly enforced, it is a very risky trade. A man stands to lose more than a hand or an ear if he is caught. He also risks damnation after he has entered his own tomb; but some men simply do not have proper respect for the gods.

The king, Nebmaatre (may he live forever!), was then in his prime, so there had been no tomb robbing for some time – or at least none had been detected. But, the rumors said, three men of west Thebes had been caught trying to sell ornaments such as are buried with the dead. The rumors turned out to be correct, for once. The men were questioned on the soles of their feet and confessed to the robbing of several tombs.

Naturally all those who had kin buried on the west bank – which included most of us – were alarmed by this news, and half the nervous matrons in our neighborhood went rushing across the river to make sure the family tombs were safe. I was not surprised to hear that that dutiful son Minmose had also felt obliged to make sure his mother had not been disturbed.

However, I was surprised at the news that greeted me when I paid my next visit to Nehi's tavern. The moment I entered, the others began to talk at once, each eager to be the first to tell the shocking facts.

"Robbed?" I repeated when I had sorted out the babble of voices. "Do you speak truly?"

"I do not know why you should doubt it," said Rennefer. "The richness of her burial was the talk of the city, was it not? Just what the tomb robbers like! They made a clean sweep of all the gold, and ripped the poor old hag's mummy to shreds."

At that point we were joined by another of the habitués, Merusir. He is a pompous, fat man who considers himself superior to the rest of us because he is Fifth Prophet of Amon. We put up with his patronizing ways because sometimes he knows court gossip. On that particular evening it was apparent that he was bursting with excitement. He listened with a supercilious sneer while we told him the sensational news. "I know, I know," he drawled. "I heard it much earlier – and with it, the other news which is known only to those in the confidence of the Palace."

He paused, ostensibly to empty his cup. Of course, we reacted as he had hoped we would, begging him to share the secret. Finally he condescended to inform us.

"Why, the amazing thing is not the robbery itself, but how it was done. The tomb entrance was untouched, the seals of the necropolis were unbroken. The tomb itself is entirely rock-cut, and there was not the slightest break in the walls or floor or ceiling. Yet when Minmose entered the burial chamber, he found the coffin open, the mummy mutilated, and the gold ornaments gone."

We stared at him, openmouthed.

"It is a most remarkable story," I said.

"Call me a liar if you like," said Merusir, who knows the language of polite insult as well as I do. "There was a witness – two, if you count Minmose himself. The sem-priest Wennefer was with him."

This silenced the critics. Wennefer was known to us all. There was not a man in southern Thebes with a higher reputation. Even Senebtisi had been fond of him, and she was not fond of many people. He had officiated at her funeral.

Pleased at the effect of his announcement, Merusir went on in his most pompous manner. "The king himself has taken an interest in the matter. He has called on Amenhotep Sa Hapu to investigate."

"Amenhotep?" I exclaimed. "But I know him well."

"You do?" Merusir's plump cheeks sagged like bladders punctured by a sharp knife.

Now, at that time Amenhotep's name was not in the mouth of everyone, though he had taken the first steps on that astonishing career that was to make him the intimate friend of Pharaoh. When I first met him, he had been a poor, insignificant priest at a local shrine. I had been sent to fetch him to the house where my master lay dead of a stab wound, presumably murdered. Amenhotep's fame had begun with that matter, for he had discovered the truth and saved an innocent man from execution. Since then he had handled several other cases, with equal success.

My exclamation had taken the wind out of Merusir's sails. He had hoped to impress us by telling us something we did not know. Instead it was I who enlightened the others about Amenhotep's triumphs. But when I finished, Rennefer shook his head.

"If this wise man is all you say, Wadjsen, it will be like inviting a lion to rid the house of mice. He will find there is a simple explanation. No doubt the thieves entered the burial chamber from above or from one side, tunneling through the rock. Minmose and Wennefer were too shocked to observe the hole in the wall, that is all."

We argued the matter for some time, growing more and more heated as the level of the beer in the jar dropped. It was a foolish argument, for none of us knew the facts; and to argue without knowledge is like trying to weave without thread.

This truth did not occur to me until the cool night breeze had cleared my head, when I was halfway home. I decided to pay Amenhotep a visit. The next time I went to the tavern, I would be the one to tell the latest news, and Merusir would be nothing!

Most of the honest householders had retired, but there were lamps burning in the street of the prostitutes, and in a few taverns. There was a light, as well, in one window of the house where Amenhotep lodged. Like the owl he resembled, with his beaky nose and large, close-set eyes, he preferred to work at night.

The window was on the ground floor, so I knocked on the wooden shutter, which of course was closed to keep out night demons. After a few moments the shutter opened, and the familiar nose appeared. I spoke my name, and Amenhotep went to open the door.

"Wadjsen! It has been a long time," he exclaimed. "Should I ask what brings you here, or shall I display my talents as a seer and tell you?"

"I suppose it requires no great talent," I replied. "The matter of Senebtisi's tomb is already the talk of the district."

"So I had assumed." He gestured me to sit down and hospitably indicated the wine jar that stood in the corner. I shook my head.

"I have already taken too much beer, at the tavern. I am sorry to disturb you so late – "

"I am always happy to see you, Wadjsen." His big dark eyes reflected the light of the lamp, so that they seemed to hold stars in their depths. "I have missed my assistant, who helped me to the truth in my first inquiry."

"I was of little help to you then," I said with a smile. "And in this case I am even more ignorant. The thing is a great mystery, known only to the gods."

"No, no!" He clapped his hands together, as was his habit when annoyed with the stupidity of his hearer. "There is no mystery. I know who robbed the tomb of Senebtisi. The only difficulty is to prove how it was done."

\*       \*       \*

At Amenhotep's suggestion I spent the night at his house so that I could accompany him when he set out next morning to find the proof he needed. I required little urging, for I was afire with curiosity. Though I pressed him, he would say no more, merely remarking piously, "'A man may fall to ruin because of his tongue; if a passing remark is hasty and it is repeated, thou wilt make enemies.'"

I could hardly dispute the wisdom of this adage, but the gleam in Amenhotep's bulging black eyes made me suspect he took a malicious pleasure in my bewilderment.

After our morning bread and beer we went to the temple of Khonsu, where the sem-priest Wennefer worked in the records office. He was copying accounts from pottery ostraca onto a papyrus that was stretched across his lap. All scribes develop bowed shoulders from bending over their writing; Wennefer was folded almost double, his face scant inches from the surface of the papyrus. When Amenhotep cleared his throat, the old man started, smearing the ink. He waved our apologies aside and cleaned the papyrus with a wad of lint.

"No harm was meant, no harm is done," he said in his breathy, chirping voice. "I have heard of you, Amenhotep Sa Hapu; it is an honor to meet you."

"I, too, have looked forward to meeting you, Wennefer. Alas that the occasion should be such a sad one."

Wennefer's smile faded. "Ah, the matter of Senebtisi's tomb. What a tragedy! At least the poor woman can now have a proper reburial. If Minmose had not insisted on opening the tomb, her *ba* would have gone hungry and thirsty through eternity."

"Then the tomb entrance really was sealed and undisturbed?" I asked skeptically.

"I examined it myself," Wennefer said. "Minmose had asked me to meet him after the day's work, and we arrived at the tomb as the sun was setting; but the light was still good. I conducted the funeral service for Senebtisi, you know. I had seen the doorway blocked and mortared and with my own hands had helped to press the seals of the necropolis onto the wet plaster. All was as I had left it that day a year ago."

"Yet Minmose insisted on opening the tomb?" Amenhotep asked.

"Why, we agreed it should be done," the old man said mildly. "As you know, robbers sometimes tunnel in from above or from one side, leaving the entrance undisturbed. Minmose had brought tools. He did most of the work himself, for these old hands of mine are better with a pen than a chisel. When the doorway was clear, Minmose lit a lamp and we entered. We were crossing the hall beyond the entrance corridor when Minmose let out a shriek. 'My mother, my mother,' he cried – oh, it was pitiful to hear! Then I saw it too. The thing – the thing on the floor . . .''

"You speak of the mummy, I presume," said Amenhotep. "The thieves had dragged it from the coffin out into the hall?"

"Where they despoiled it," Wennefer whispered. "The august body was ripped open from throat to groin, through the shroud and the wrappings and the flesh."

"Curious," Amenhotep muttered, as if to himself. "Tell me, Wennefer, what is the plan of the tomb?"

Wennefer rubbed his brush on the ink cake and began to draw on the back surface of one of the ostraca.

"It is a fine tomb, Amenhotep, entirely rock-cut. Beyond the entrance is a flight of stairs and a short corridor, thus leading to a hall broader than it is long, with two pillars. Beyond that, another short corridor; then the burial chamber. The august mummy lay here." And he inked in a neat circle at the beginning of the second corridor.

"Ha," said Amenhotep, studying the plan. "Yes, yes, I see. Go on, Wennefer. What did you do next?"

"I did nothing," the old man said simply. "Minmose's hand shook so violently that he dropped the lamp. Darkness closed in. I felt the presence of the demons who had defiled the dead. My tongue clove to the roof of my mouth and – "

"Dreadful," Amenhotep said. "But you were not far from the tomb entrance; you could find your way out?"

"Yes, yes, it was only a dozen paces; and by Amon, my friend, the sunset light has never appeared so sweet! I went at once to fetch the necropolis guards. When we returned to the tomb, Minmose had rekindled his lamp – "

"I thought you said the lamp was broken."

"Dropped, but fortunately not broken. Minmose had opened one of the jars of oil – Senebtisi had many such in the tomb, all of the finest quality – and had refilled the lamp. He had replaced the mummy in its coffin and was kneeling by it praying. Never was there so pious a son!"

"So then, I suppose, the guards searched the tomb."

"We all searched," Wennefer said. "The tomb chamber was in a dreadful state; boxes and baskets had been broken open and the contents strewn about. Every object of precious metal had been stolen, including the amulets on the body."

"What about the oil, the linen, and the other valuables?" Amenhotep asked.

"The oil and the wine were in large jars, impossible to move easily. About the other things I cannot say; everything was in such confusion — and I do not know what was there to begin with. Even Minmose was not certain; his mother had filled and sealed most of the boxes herself. But I know what was taken from the mummy, for I saw the golden amulets and ornaments placed on it when it was wrapped by the embalmers. I do not like to speak evil of anyone, but you know, Amenhotep, that the embalmers . . ."

"Yes," Amenhotep agreed with a sour face. "I myself watched the wrapping of my father; there is no other way to make certain the ornaments will go on the mummy instead of into the coffers of the embalmers. Minmose did not perform this service for his mother?"

"Of course he did. He asked me to share in the watch, and I was glad to agree. He is the most pious — "

"So I have heard," said Amenhotep. "Tell me again, Wennefer, of the condition of the mummy. You examined it?"

"It was my duty. Oh, Amenhotep, it was a sad sight! The shroud was still tied firmly around the body; the thieves had cut straight through it and through the bandages beneath, baring the body. The arm bones were broken, so roughly had the thieves dragged the heavy gold bracelets from them."

"And the mask?" I asked. "It was said that she had a mask of solid gold."

"It, too, was missing."

"Horrible," Amenhotep said. "Wennefer, we have kept you from your work long enough. Only one more question. How do you think the thieves entered the tomb?"

The old man's eyes fell. "Through me," he whispered.

I gave Amenhotep a startled look. He shook his head warningly.

"It was not your fault," he said, touching Wennefer's bowed shoulder.

"It was. I did my best, but I must have omitted some vital part of the ritual. How else could demons enter the tomb?"

"Oh, I see." Amenhotep stroked his chin. "Demons."

"It could have been nothing else. The seals on the door were intact, the mortar untouched. There was no break of the smallest size in the stone of the walls or ceiling or floor."

"But — " I began.

"And there is this. When the doorway was clear and the light entered, the dust lay undisturbed on the floor. The only marks on it were the strokes of the broom with which Minmose, according to custom, had swept the floor as he left the tomb after the funeral service."

"Amon preserve us," I exclaimed, feeling a chill run through me.

Amenhotep's eyes moved from Wennefer to me, then back to Wennefer. "That is conclusive," he murmured.

"Yes," Wennefer said with a groan. "And I am to blame – I, a priest who failed at his task."

"No," said Amenhotep. "You did not fail. Be of good cheer, my friend. There is another explanation."

Wennefer shook his head despondently. "Minmose said the same, but he was only being kind. Poor man! He was so overcome, he could scarcely walk. The guards had to take him by the arms to lead him from the tomb. I carried his tools. It was the least – "

"The tools," Amenhotep interrupted. "They were in a bag or a sack?"

"Why, no. He had only a chisel and a mallet. I carried them in my hand as he had done."

Amenhotep thanked him again, and we took our leave. As we crossed the courtyard I waited for him to speak, but he remained silent; and after a while I could contain myself no longer.

"Do you still believe you know who robbed the tomb?"

"Yes, yes, it is obvious."

"And it was not demons?"

Amenhotep blinked at me like an owl blinded by sunlight.

"Demons are a last resort."

He had the smug look of a man who thinks he has said something clever; but his remark smacked of heresy to me, and I looked at him doubtfully.

"Come, come," he snapped. "Senebtisi was a selfish, greedy old woman, and if there is justice in the next world, as our faith decrees, her path through the Underworld will not be easy. But why would diabolical powers play tricks with her mummy when they could torment her spirit? Demons have no need of gold."

"Well, but – "

"Your wits used not to be so dull. What do you think happened?"

"If it was not demons – "

"It was not."

"Then someone must have broken in."

"Very clever," said Amenhotep, grinning.

"I mean that there must be an opening, in the walls or the floor, that Wennefer failed to see."

"Wennefer, perhaps. The necropolis guards, no. The chambers of the tomb were cut out of solid rock. It would be impossible to disguise a break in such a surface, even if tomb robbers took the trouble to fill it in – which they never have been known to do."

"Then the thieves entered through the doorway and closed it again. A dishonest craftsman could make a copy of the necropolis seal . . ."

"Good." Amenhotep clapped me on the shoulder. "Now you are beginning to think. It is an ingenious idea, but it is wrong. Tomb robbers work in haste, for fear of the necropolis guards. They would not linger to replace stones and mortar and seals."

"Then I do not know how it was done."

"Ah, Wadjsen, you are dense! There is only one person who could have robbed the tomb."

"I thought of that," I said stiffly, hurt by his raillery. "Minmose was the last to leave the tomb and the first to reenter it. He had good reason to desire the gold his mother should have left to him. But, Amenhotep, he could not have robbed the mummy on either occasion; there was not time. You know the funeral ritual as well as I. When the priests and mourners leave the tomb, they leave together. If Minmose had lingered in the burial chamber, even for a few minutes, his delay would have been noted and remarked upon."

"That is quite true," said Amenhotep.

"Also," I went on, "the gold was heavy as well as bulky. Minmose could not have carried it away without someone noticing."

"Again you speak truly."

"Then unless Wennefer the priest is conspiring with Minmose – "

"That good, simple man? I am surprised at you, Wadjsen. Wennefer is as honest as the Lady of Truth herself."

"Demons – "

Amenhotep interrupted with the hoarse hooting sound that passed for a laugh with him. "Stop babbling of demons. There is one man besides myself who knows how Senebtisi's tomb was violated. Let us go and see him."

He quickened his pace, his sandals slapping in the dust. I followed, trying to think. His taunts were like weights that pulled my mind to its farthest limits. I began to get an inkling of truth, but I could not make sense of it. I said nothing, not even when we turned into the lane south of the temple that led to the house of Minmose.

There was no servant at the door. Minmose himself answered our summons. I greeted him and introduced Amenhotep.

Minmose lifted his hands in surprise. "You honor my house, Amenhotep. Enter and be seated."

Amenhotep shook his head. "I will not stay, Minmose. I came only to tell you who desecrated your mother's tomb."

"What?" Minmose gaped at him. "Already you know? But how? It is a great mystery, beyond – "

"You did it, Minmose."

Minmose turned a shade paler. But that was not out of the way; even the innocent might blanch at such an accusation.

"You are mad," he said. "Forgive me, you are my guest, but – "

"There is no other possible explanation," Amenhotep said. "You stole the gold when you entered the tomb two days ago."

"But, Amenhotep," I exclaimed. "Wennefer was with him, and Wennefer saw the mummy already robbed when – "

"Wennefer did not see the mummy," Amenhotep said. "The tomb was dark; the only light was that of a small lamp, which Minmose promptly dropped. Wennefer has poor sight. Did you not observe how he bent over his writing? He caught only a glimpse of a white shape, the size of a wrapped mummy, before the light went out. When next Wennefer saw the mummy, it was in the coffin, and his view of it then colored his confused memory of the first supposed sighting of it. Few people are good observers. They see what they expect to see."

"Then what did he see?" I demanded. Minmose might not have been there. Amenhotep avoided looking at him.

"A piece of linen in the rough shape of a human form, arranged on the floor by the last person who left the tomb. It would have taken him only a moment to do this before he snatched up the broom and swept himself out."

"So the tomb was sealed and closed," I exclaimed. "For almost a year he waited – "

"Until the next outbreak of tomb robbing. Minmose could assume this would happen sooner or later; it always does. He thought he was being clever by asking Wennefer to accompany him – a witness of irreproachable character who could testify that the tomb entrance was untouched. In fact, he was too careful to avoid being compromised; that would have made me doubt him, even if the logic of the facts had not pointed directly at him. Asking that same virtuous man to share his supervision of the mummy wrapping, lest he be suspected of connivance with the embalmers; feigning weakness so that the necropolis guards would have to support him, and thus be in a position to swear he could not have concealed the gold on his person. Only a guilty man would be so anxious to appear innocent. Yet there was reason for his precautions. Sometime in the near future, when that loving son Minmose discovers a store of gold hidden in the house, overlooked by his mother – the old do forget sometimes – then, since men have evil minds, it might be necessary for Minmose to prove beyond a shadow of a doubt that he could not have laid hands on his mother's burial equipment."

Minmose remained dumb, his eyes fixed on the ground. It was I who responded as he should have, questioning and objecting.

"But how did he remove the gold? The guards and Wennefer searched the tomb, so it was not hidden there, and there was not time for him to bury it outside."

"No, but there was ample time for him to do what had to be done in the burial chamber after Wennefer had tottered off to fetch the guards. He overturned boxes and baskets, opened the coffin, ripped through the mummy wrappings with his chisel, and took the gold. It would not take long, especially for one who knew exactly where each ornament had been placed."

Minmose's haggard face was as good as an admission of guilt. He did not look up or speak, even when Amenhotep put a hand on his shoulder.

"I pity you, Minmose," Amenhotep said gravely. "After years of devotion and self-denial, to see yourself deprived of your inheritance . . . And there was Nefertiry. You had been visiting her in secret, even before your mother died, had you not? Oh, Minmose, you should have remembered the words of the sage: "Do not go in to a woman who is a stranger; it is a great crime, worthy of death." She has brought you to your death, Minmose. You knew she would turn from you if your mother left you nothing."

Minmose's face was gray. "Will you denounce me, then? They will beat me to make me confess."

"Any man will confess when he is beaten," said Amenhotep, with a curl of his lip. "No, Minmose, I will not denounce you. The court of the vizier demands facts, not theories, and you have covered your tracks very neatly. But you will not escape justice. Nefertiry will consume your gold as the desert sands drink water, and then she will cast you off; and all the while Anubis, the Guide of the Dead, and Osiris, the Divine Judge, will be waiting for you. They will eat your heart, Minmose, and your spirit will hunger and thirst through all eternity. I think your punishment has already begun. Do you dream, Minmose? Did you see your mother's face last night, wrinkled and withered, her sunken eyes accusing you, as it looked when you tore the gold mask from it?"

A long shudder ran through Minmose's body. Even his hair seemed to shiver and rise. Amenhotep gestured to me. We went away, leaving Minmose staring after us with a face like death.

After we had gone a short distance, I said, "There is one more thing to tell, Amenhotep."

"There is much to tell." Amenhotep sighed deeply. "Of a good man turned evil; of two women who, in their different ways, drove him to crime; of the narrow line that separates the virtuous man from the sinner . . ."

"I do not speak of that. I do not wish to think of that. It makes me feel strange . . . The gold, Amenhotep – how did Minmose bear away the gold from his mother's burial?"

"He put it in the oil jar," said Amenhotep. "The one he opened to get fresh fuel for his lamp. Who would wonder if, in his agitation, he spilled a quantity of oil on the floor? He has certainly removed it by now. He has had ample opportunity, running back and forth with objects to be repaired or replaced."

"And the piece of linen he had put down to look like the mummy?"

"As you well know," Amenhotep replied, "the amount of linen used to wrap a mummy is prodigious. He could have crumpled that piece and thrown it in among the torn wrappings. But I think he did something else. It was a cool evening, in winter, and Minmose would have worn a linen mantle. He took the cloth out in the same way he had brought it in. Who would notice an extra fold of linen over a man's shoulders?

"I knew immediately that Minmose must be the guilty party, because he was the only one who had the opportunity, but I did not see how he had managed it until Wennefer showed me where the supposed mummy lay. There was no reason for a thief to drag it so far from the coffin and the burial chamber – but Minmose could not afford to have Wennefer catch even a glimpse of that room, which was then undisturbed. I realized then that what the old man had seen was not the mummy at all, but a substitute."

"Then Minmose will go unpunished."

"I said he would be punished. I spoke truly." Again Amenhotep sighed.

"You will not denounce him to Pharaoh?"

"I will tell my lord the truth. But he will not choose to act. There will be no need."

He said no more. But six weeks later Minmose's body was found floating in the river. He had taken to drinking heavily, and people said he drowned by accident. But I knew it was otherwise. Anubis and Osiris had eaten his heart, just as Amenhotep had said.

# THE THIEF VERSUS KING RHAMPSINITUS
## Herodotus

*Although all of the other stories in this volume date from the present century,
and many of them are new, this story is over 2,400 years old. And it is a
genuine historical mystery.*

*Herodotus, who lived between about 490 and 425 BC, has rightly been called
the father of history. Born at Halicarnassus, in Asia Minor, he travelled
throughout the Greek and Egyptian world, gathering facts and stories as he
went. He settled down around 440 BC and at that time wrote his* History.
*Herodotus did not always believe all he was told, but knew a good story when
he heard one. He thus recorded for posterity this story of the Egyptian pharaoh
Rhampsinitus, who is believed to equate to Rameses III, and who reigned seven
hundred years earlier, in the twelfth century BC.*

King Rhampsinitus was possessed, they said, of great riches in
silver – indeed to such an amount, that none of the princes,
his successors, surpassed or even equaled his wealth. For the better
custody of this money, he proposed to build a vast chamber of hewn
stone, one side of which was to form a part of the outer wall of his
palace. The builder, therefore, having designs upon the treasures,
contrived, as he was making the building, to insert in this wall a
stone, which could easily be removed from its place by two men,
or even one. So the chamber was finished, and the king's money
stored away in it.

Time passed, and the builder fell sick; when finding his end
approaching, he called for his two sons, and related to them
the contrivance he had made in the king's treasure-chamber,
telling them it was for their sakes he had done it, so that they
might always live in affluence. Then he gave them clear directions
concerning the mode of removing the stone, and communicated the
measurements, bidding them carefully keep the secret, whereby they
would be Comptrollers of the Royal Exchequer so long as they lived.

Then the father died, and the sons were not slow in setting to work; they went by night to the palace, found the stone in the wall of the building, and having removed it with ease, plundered the treasury of a round sum.

When the king next paid a visit to the apartment he was astonished to see that the money was sunk in some of the vessels wherein it was stored away. Whom to accuse, however, he knew not, as the seals were all perfect, and the fastenings of the room secure. Still each time that he repeated his visits, he found that more money was gone. The thieves in truth never stopped, but plundered the treasury ever more and more.

At last the king determined to have some traps made, and set near the vessels which contained his wealth. This was done, and when the thieves came, as usual, to the treasure chamber, and one of them entering through the aperture, made straight for the jars, suddenly he found himself caught in one of the traps. Perceiving that he was lost, he instantly called his brother, and telling him what had happened, entreated him to enter as quickly as possible and cut off his head, that when his body should be discovered it might not be recognized, which would have the effect of bringing ruin upon both. The other thief thought the advice good, and was persuaded to follow it; then, fitting the stone into its place, he went home, taking with him his brother's head.

When day dawned, the king came into the room, and marveled greatly to see the body of the thief in the trap without a head, while the building was still whole, and neither entrance nor exit was to be seen anywhere. In this perplexity he commanded the body of the dead man to be hung up outside the palace wall, and set a guard to watch it, with orders that if any persons were seen weeping or lamenting near the place, they should be seized and brought before him. When the mother heard of this exposure of the corpse of her son, she took it sorely to heart, and spoke to her surviving child, bidding him devise some plan or other to get back the body, and threatening that if he did not exert himself she would go herself to the king and denounce him as the robber.

The son said all he could to persuade her to let the matter rest, but in vain: she still continued to trouble him, until at last he yielded to her importunity, and contrived as follows: Filling some skins with wine, he loaded them on donkeys, which he drove before him till he came to the place where the guards were watching the dead body, when pulling two or three of the skins towards him, he untied some of the necks which dangled by the asses' sides. The wine poured freely out, whereupon he began to beat his head and shout with all his might, seeming not to know which of the donkeys he should turn to first.

When the guards saw the wine running, delighted to profit by the occasion, they rushed one and all into the road, each with some vessel or other, and caught the liquor as it was spilling. The driver pretended anger, and loaded them with abuse; whereon they did their best to pacify him, until at last he appeared to soften, and recover his good humor, drove his asses aside out of the road, and set to work to re-arrange their burthens; meanwhile, as he talked and chatted with the guards, one of them began to rally him, and make him laugh, whereupon he gave them one of the skins as a gift. They now made up their minds to sit down and have a drinking-bout where they were, so they begged him to remain and drink with them. Then the man let himself be persuaded, and stayed.

As the drinking went on, they grew very friendly together, so presently he gave them another skin, upon which they drank so copiously that they were all overcome with liquor, and growing drowsy, lay down, and fell asleep on the spot. The thief waited till it was the dead of the night, and then took down the body of his brother; after which, in mockery, he shaved off the right side of all the soldiers' beards, and so left them. Laying his brother's body upon the asses, he carried it home to his mother, having thus accomplished the thing that she had required of him.

When it came to the king's ears that the thief's body was stolen away, he was sorely vexed. Wishing, therefore, whatever it might cost, to catch the man who had contrived the trick, he had recourse (the priest said) to an expedient which I can scarcely credit. He announced that he would bestow his own daughter upon the man who would narrate to her the best story of the cleverest and wickedest thing done by himself. If anyone in reply told her the story of the thief, she was to lay hold of him, and not allow him to get away.

The daughter did as her father willed, whereon the thief, who was well aware of the king's motive, felt a desire to outdo him in craft and cunning. Accordingly he contrived the following plan: He procured the corpse of a man lately dead, and cutting off one of the arms at the shoulder, put it under his dress, and so went to the king's daughter. When she put the question to him as she had done to all the rest, he replied that the wickedest thing he had ever done was cutting off the head of his brother when he was caught in a trap in the king's treasury, and the cleverest was making the guards drunk and carrying off the body. As he spoke, the princess caught at him, but the thief took advantage of the darkness to hold out to her the hand of the corpse. Imagining it to be his own hand, she seized and held it fast; while the thief, leaving it in her grasp, made his escape by the door.

The king, when word was brought him of this fresh success, amazed at the sagacity and boldness of the man, sent messengers to all the towns in his dominions to proclaim a free pardon for the thief, and to promise him a rich reward, if he came and made himself known. The thief took the king at his word, and came boldly into his presence; whereupon Rhampsinitus, greatly admiring him, and looking on him as the most knowing of men, gave him his daughter in marriage. "The Egyptians," he said, "excelled all the rest of the world in wisdom, and this man excelled all other Egyptians."

# SOCRATES SOLVES A MURDER
## Brèni James

*Socrates was one of the greatest of Athenian philosophers whose religious attitudes found him at odds with the Greek establishment and led ultimately to his death. Ever questioning, ever seeking to banish ignorance, Socrates is an ideal choice as a detective.*

*He was portrayed in this role in two stories written by Brèni James in the 1950s. The one reprinted here was her first story, and won a special award in* Ellery Queen's Mystery Magazine's *annual competition. I am unable to tell you anything about her, other than that her real name was Mrs Brenie Pevehouse, under which name she published a third story in Ellery Queen's.*

Aristodemus was awakened towards daybreak by a crowing of cocks, and when he awoke, the others were either asleep, or had gone away; there remained only Socrates, Aristophanes, and Agathon . . . And first of all Aristophanes dropped off, then, when the day was already dawning, Agathon. Socrates, having laid them to sleep, rose to depart; Aristodemus, as his manner was, following him . . . to the Lyceum. – PLATO: Symposium (Jowett trans.)

Socrates strolled along barefoot, having left his sandals behind at Agathon's. Aristodemus, barefoot as always, ran on short legs to catch up with his friend.

Aristodemus: Here, Socrates; you left your sandals.

Socrates: You seem to be more interested in what I have forgotten, Aristodemus, than in what you ought to have learned.

Aristodemus: Well, it is true my attention wandered a bit, and I missed some of your discourse, but I agreed with your conclusions.

Socrates: My dear friend, your confidence is like that of a man who drinks from a goblet of vinegar because his host has recited a paean in praise of wine.

The philosopher, after this nettling remark, obliged his companion by stopping to put on the sandals; and they resumed their walk through the town, passing out of the two eastern gates. The sun was rising above Mount Pentelicus, and Hymettus glowed before them in shadows as purple as the thyme which bloomed on its slopes.

They were soon climbing the gentle rise which led them to the shrine of Apollo Lyceus. It was a small, graceful temple whose columns and caryatids had been hewn from sugarbright marble.

At the hilltop shrine they saw the fading wisps of smoke rising from its eastern altar. The priestess, her sacrifices completed, was mounting the stairs to enter the golden doors of her sanctuary. She was clothed in the flowing white robes of her office; her hair fell in a tumble of shimmering black coils about her shoulders; and a garland of laurel leaves dipped on her forehead. Her gray eyes were serene, and on her lips played a smile that was not gentle.

Socrates: What omens, Alecto?

Alecto: For some, good. For some, evil. The smoke drifted first to the west; but now, as you see, it hastens to the god.

Indeed, as she spoke, a gentle gust of wind rose from the slope before them and sent the smoke into the shrine.

Alecto withdrew, and the two men proceeded down the short path which led to the Lyceum itself and to their destination, the swimming pool.

It appeared at first that their only companion this morning would be the statue which stood beside the pool, a beautiful Eros that stood on tiptoe as if it were about to ascend on quivering wings over the water that shivered beneath it.

The statue was not large – scarcely five feet high even on its pedestal; but the delicacy of its limbs and the airy seeming-softness of its wings gave an illusion of soaring height. The right arm of the god was extended; in the waxing light it appeared to be traced with fine blue veins. The hand was palm upward; and the face, touched with a smile that was at once roguish and innocent, was also turned to the heavens.

When Socrates and Aristodemus came closer to the edge of the pool, they perceived for the first time a young man, kneeling before the statue in prayer. They could not distinguish his words, but he was apparently supplicating the god of love with urgency.

No sooner had they taken note of this unexpected presence than a concussion of strident voices exploded from the palaestra adjoining the pool, and a party of perhaps a dozen young men bounded into view. All laughing, they raced to the water's edge and leaped in one after another, with much splashing and gurgling.

Socrates led his companion to a marble bench a few yards from the pool, and bade him sit down.

"But," frowned Aristodemus, "I thought we came to swim. Surely you have not become afraid of cold water and morning air?"

"No," replied his friend, tugging at his paunch with laced fingers, "but I consider it prudent to discourse in a crowd, and swim in solitude."

Socrates turned from Aristodemus to watch the sleek young men at their play in the pool, and he listened with an indulgent smile on his satyr's face to their noisy banter.

Suddenly a piercing *Eee-Eee*, *Eee-EEE* screeched at the south end of the pool, where stood Eros and knelt the pious youth.

"A hawk!!" Socrates pointed to a shadow that sat on the fragile hand of Eros. The bird, not a large one, seemed a giant thing on so delicate a mount.

Its screams had not attracted the young men in the water. Their laughter was incongruous and horrible as the marble Eros swayed on its pedestal and then crashed to the ground at the pool's edge, sending the evil bird crying into the sun.

The two friends rushed to the assistance of the youth who, with only a glance at the bird, had remained at his prayers. The body of Eros was rubble; but its wings – which had seemed so tremulous, so poised for flight – had swept down like cleavers. One wing had cleanly severed the youth's head.

Socrates knelt beside the broken bodies, marble and flesh, the one glistening in crystalline fragments, the other twitching with the false life of the newly dead. He gently tossed a dark curl from the boy's pale forehead, and he looked into the vacant blue eyes for a long time before he drew down the lids.

Aristodemus, fairly dancing with excitement and fright, shouted, "Socrates, you know him? It is Tydeus, the Pythagorean. What a fool he was to try to bargain with Eros! The god has paid him justly!"

The philosopher rose slowly, murmuring, "Eros dispenses love, not justice." His eyes strayed over the rubble, now becoming tinted with the red of sunlight and the deeper red. A white cluster of fat clung to the shattered marble fingers of the god.

"The sacrifice," said Aristodemus, following his glance. "Tydeus was going to sacrifice that piece of lamb."

By this time the crowd of swimmers, glistening and shivering, had run to see what had happened. They chattered like birds, their voices pitched high by death.

"Someone must run to tell his friend Euchecrates," cried Aristodemus.

At this, the group fell silent. Socrates looked intently on each of the young men. "You are unwilling," he said mildly, "to tell a man of his friend's death?"

At last a youth spoke up: "We were all at dinner together last night, Tydeus and Euchecrates among us. Our symposiarch suggested that we discourse on the theme of Fidelity, for we all knew that Tydeus found it difficult to remain loyal to his friend Euchecrates. The symposiarch thought to twit him about it."

"But," broke in one of the others, "Tydeus immediately took up the topic and spoke as though he, not Euchecrates, were the victim of faithlessness!"

The first boy nodded. "It became a personal argument between them, then, instead of a discussion among friends. They began to rail at each other about gifts of money and gamecocks and I know not what. All manner of fine things, from what Tydeus said."

Socrates: Then these gifts were from our dead friend Tydeus to Euchecrates?

Youth: Yes, Socrates; and Tydeus was angry because Euchecrates had given them all away to someone else.

Socrates: To whom did Euchecrates give the gifts of Tydeus?

Once again silence fell, and the young men exchanged puzzled looks. But a bronzed athlete who had been standing outside the circle blurted out: "Even Tydeus didn't know who it was!"

Socrates: Why do you say that?

Athlete: I came here to the palaestra before any of the others, just at daybreak, and I met Tydeus on his way to the god. I recall that I asked him if he were going to swim, and he said, no, he was about to offer a prayer to Eros for a misdeed. Then I teased him about losing his gifts . . .

Socrates: And asked him who Euchecrates's admirer was?

Athlete: Yes, but Tydeus flew into a rage and began to say things in a distracted fashion about "that person," as he put it, "whoever it may be." I wanted to speculate with him on the identity, but Tydeus said he must hurry to Eros, for he wished to complete his prayer before the sun rose above the horizon.

Socrates: And he said nothing further? Well, then, will you now please go to Euchecrates's house and tell him what has befallen his friend Tydeus, and ask him to meet Socrates at the Shrine of Apollo Lyceus?

The bronzed youth agreed to do so, and Socrates took his companion Aristodemus by the arm, leading him back up the path to the shrine. "I shall return with water," he said, passing through the crowd, "that you who have touched the body may purify yourselves."

When they were out of the hearing of the young men, Aristodemus said in a low voice, "I know, Socrates, that you seek answers by the most devious questions; but I cannot discover what it is you attempt to glean from all that you have asked of those boys."

Socrates: I believe you said that the piece of fat which we saw in the rubble was sacrificial lamb?

Aristodemus: I would say so. And we saw Tydeus sacrificing, did we not?

Socrates: We saw him praying. Do you recall that the bronzed fellow told us that when first he saw Tydeus, he asked Tydeus if he were going to swim?

Aristodemus: Yes, I remember.

Socrates: And would it not be an exceedingly odd question to ask of a man who was carrying a sacrifice?

Aristodemus: That is true, Socrates; but what does it mean?

Socrates: You recall, too, that you spoke of Tydeus as a Pythagorean?

Aristodemus: Yes, I know that he was.

Socrates: Then perhaps you will also remember that, among Pythagoreans, it is a custom never to offer living sacrifice, or to kill any animal that does not harm man?

Aristodemus: I had forgotten, Socrates. And I see now that it could not have been possible that Tydeus intended to sacrifice.

Socrates: Yet we saw a piece of lamb, did we not? How else could we account for it, if it were not brought to be sacrificed?

Aristodemus: It seems unaccountable.

Socrates: Do you remember where you saw it?

Aristodemus: It was on the hand of Eros.

Socrates: And so, also, was the hawk. Does that not suggest another reason for the fat?

Aristodemus: Why, yes! It must have been placed on the hand as bait for the bird!

Socrates: Clearly, that is what was intended. And I think it must have been fastened there in some manner, for the hawk did not pick it up and fly off, but rather balanced himself on the fingertips and pulled at it until the statue was overbalanced.

The two had walked, in their preoccupation, to the very steps of the altar before the Shrine of Apollo Lyceus. The eastern doors of the marble sanctuary were still open, and they could see the god within, gold and ivory, gleaming softly now in the full morning light.

But at that moment they heard shouts from a footpath on their right, and they saw the bronzed athlete running toward them. He pulled up abruptly and panted heavily.

"He's dead, Socrates! Euchecrates is dead! I found him at Tydeus's house, in the doorway. He'd hanged himself from a porch beam!"

Socrates: Are you certain Euchecrates took his own life?

Athlete: Quite certain, Socrates. For he had scrawled a message on the wall, and I recognized his writing.

Socrates: What was his message?

Athlete: "Hide me in a secret place." Does not that mean he was ashamed?

Socrates: That is so.

"Who wishes to be hidden?" asked a woman's voice, and the three men turned to see Alecto, the priestess of the shrine, slowly and gracefully descending the marble steps.

Socrates: Euchecrates, who has killed himself, Alecto.

Alecto: It is indeed a dreadful thing to hear, Socrates.

Aristodemus: Oh, there is more! See where the statue has fallen? Tydeus lies dead beneath it.

Alecto: He must have displeased Eros mightily to have been felled by the god's own image?

Aristodemus: No, I think it fell because Euchecrates contrived that it should.

Alecto: How could it have been contrived, Aristodemus?

Socrates: Alecto, we came to ask you for some water which we will take to the Lyceum, for there are those of us who have not yet purified ourselves.

The priestess nodded and left. She returned in a few moments with a vessel of water.

Socrates: I should have asked also on behalf of this young man, so that he may take some to the place where he found Euchecrates.

Athlete: No, there is not need of that; for there was water there.

Socrates: Indeed? Then, Alecto, who preceded us with such a request?

Alecto: For water? Why, no one.

Socrates: Can purificatory water be simply drawn out of a well, or a pool, or any other ordinary source?

Alecto: No, of course it must be obtained from a priest or a priestess.

Socrates: And there is no other priest or priestess so close to the house of Tydeus, where Euchecrates lies?

Alecto: No, I am the closest.

Socrates: Then can we not assume the water was obtained here? Do you not recall such a request?

Alecto: Only that of Tydeus, several hours ago. I didn't know why he asked for water, but it would now seem to be for that reason.

Socrates: And we know also from this, do we not, Aristodemus, that Euchecrates was already dead when Tydeus went to pray to Eros? Tell me, Alecto, when Tydeus came for water, do you recall that he asked for anything else?

Alecto: I recall nothing else.

Socrates: Tydeus had told this young man that he could not stand and talk with him, since he wished to complete his prayers before the sun's rise. Does that not indicate that Tydeus knew beforehand that his prayers would be of some length?

Alecto: Yes, surely it does.

Socrates: And since he stayed to complete them even though the sun had already risen, and was not even distracted from his intentions by the presence and noise of the bird, what is the likely conclusion?

Aristodemus: I would say that he had a particular prayer to complete.

Socrates: Excellent. That would be my conclusion. Now, Alecto, do you think it likely that a young man still angry from a quarrel – indeed distraught – would sit down and compose a lengthy prayer?

Alecto: He would be more likely to pray spontaneously.

Socrates: But these things seem not to agree. The prayer, we may suppose, was planned beforehand; yet the young man was not prepared to plan the prayer. What may we surmise, then?

Alecto: That someone else composed the prayer for him?

Socrates: I believe so. And who would be likely to have done that?

Alecto: It would be someone expert in such matters, no doubt.

Socrates: Such as a priest or priestess?

Alecto: Yes, it must be so.

Socrates: And since Tydeus called, as you have said, upon yourself, Alecto, does it not seem inevitable that he asked you to compose his prayer?

Alecto: I am compelled to admit he did just that, Socrates.

Socrates: And one last matter: You were sacrificing lamb here at dawn?

Alecto: Yes, lamb and honey.

Socrates: And where is the fat of the lamb which you sacrificed this morning, Alecto? While Tydeus was within memorizing his prayer, did you not go down to the statue of Eros and affix some of the fat to that extended hand?

Alecto: You have a daemon advising you, Socrates!

Aristodemus: Oh, no, Alecto. It is as Cebes has said: Socrates can put a question to a person in such a way that only the true answer comes out! But, Alecto, how did Tydeus dare come to you?

Alecto: He did not know that it was to me his friend Euchecrates had given his gifts. But when Tydeus confessed to me that he had caused my lover's suicide, I could not but avenge the death!

The priestess turned her cold eyes proudly on Socrates. "I was named Alecto for good reason," she said with fierce triumph; "for like that divine Alecto, the Well-Wisher, I too found myself singled out by the gods to wreak vengeance!"

"But remember," cautioned Socrates quietly, "we call the divine Alecto the 'well-wisher' only to placate her. She is still one of the Furies. She still pursues the blood-guilty to death or madness. And think, Alecto: You are only mortal, and you have done murder."

Alecto's eyes widened with the sudden, horrible knowledge of her own fate.

The priestess wept then, and drew the heavy black coils of hair about her face like a shroud.

# MIGHTIER THAN THE SWORD
## John Maddox Roberts

*John Maddox Roberts (b. 1947) is the author of over twenty novels, most of them in the fantasy field, including a number featuring that mighty-thewed hero, Conan the Barbarian, created by Robert E. Howard. But Roberts also has a fascination for and an intense knowledge of the world of ancient Rome, and in a series of historical novels, starting with* SPQR *(1990), he has brought vividly to life the Roman world through the eyes of Decius Caecilius Metellus.*

*Roberts provides some further background:*

*"The advantage of writing about Decius Metellus is that he lived for a long time and had plenty of adventures. He was born around 93–91 BC. The stories are in the form of a memoir, written when he was a very old man, during the reign of Augustus. He has outlived most of his old enemies and rivals and is past caring what Augustus (whom he despises) does to him."*

*The first four novels take place early in Decius's career when he was a young and unimportant official. The present story, which was written specially for this anthology, jumps ahead a few years to 53 BC. The city is in utter turmoil. All three triumvirs are away from Italy and the gangs of Clodius, Milo and other politicians are staging daily riots in the streets. Decius is serving as a plebeian aedile and is trying to stay out of trouble by spending his days in the cellars of Rome – one of the tasks of his office is to inspect for building violations. But Decius can't go long without stumbling over a murder.*

T he wonderful thing about being *Aedile* is that you get to spend your days poking through every foul, dangerous, rat-infested, pestilential cellar in Rome. Building inspection is part of the job, and you can spend your whole year just prosecuting violations of the building codes, never mind putting on the Games and inspecting all the whorehouses, also part of the job. And I'd landed the office in a year when a plebeian couldn't be *Curule Aedile*. The *Curule* got to wear a purple border on his toga and sat around the markets all day in a folding chair, attended by a lictor and levying fines for

violations of the market laws. No, Marcus Aemilius Lepidus got that
job. Well, he never amounted to anything, so there is justice in the
world, after all. Mind you, he got to be Triumvir some years later,
but considering that the other two were Antony and Octavian, he
might as well have been something unpleasant adhering to the heel
of Octavian's sandal.

And the worst thing was, you didn't have to serve as *Aedile* to
stand for higher office! It was just that you had not a prayer of
being elected *Praetor* unless, as *Aedile*, you put on splendid Games
as a gift to the people. If you gave them enough chariot races, and
plays and pageants and public feasts and Campanian gladiators by
the hundred, then, when you stood for higher office, they would
remember you kindly. Of course the State only provided a pittance
for these Games, so you had to pay for them out of your own pocket,
bankrupting yourself and going into debt for years. That was what
being *Aedile* meant.

That was why I was in a bad mood when I found the body. It
wasn't as if bodies were exactly rare in Rome, especially that year.
It was one of the very worst years in the history of the City. The
election scandals of the previous year had been so terrible that our
two Consuls almost weren't allowed to assume office in January, and
the year got worse after that. My good friend, Titus Annius Milo,
politician and gang leader, was standing for Consul for the next
year, as was the equally disreputable Plautius Hypsaeus. Milo's
deadly enemy and mine, Publius Clodius Pulcher, was standing
for *Praetor*. Their mobs battled each other in the streets day and
night, and bodies were as common as dead pigeons in the Temple
of Jupiter.

But that was in the streets. Another plebeian *Aedile*, whose name
I no longer recall, had charge of keeping the streets clean. I resented
finding them in my nice, peaceful if malodorous cellars. And it wasn't
in one of the awful, disgusting tenement cellars, either, uninspected
for decades and awash with the filth of poverty and lax enforcement
of the hygienic laws.

Instead, it was in the clean, new basement of a town house just
built on the Aventine. I was down there inspecting because in Rome
honest building contractors are as common as volunteer miners in the
Sicilian sulphur pits. My slave Hermes preceded me with a lantern.
He was a fine, handsome, strapping young man by this time, and
very good at controlling his criminal tendencies. Unlike so many,
the basement smelled pleasantly of new-cut timber and the dry,
dusty scent of stone fresh from the quarry. There was another, less
pleasant smell beneath these, though.

Hermes stopped, a yellow puddle of light around his feet spilling over a shapeless form.

"There's a stiff here, Master."

"Oh, splendid. And I thought this was going to be my only agreeable task all day. I don't suppose it's just some old beggar, come down here to get out of the weather and died of natural causes?"

"Not unless there's beggars in the Senate, these days," Hermes said.

My scalp prickled. There were few things I hated worse than finding a high-ranking corpse. "Well, some of us are poor enough to qualify. Let's see who we have."

I squatted by the body while Hermes held the lantern near the face. Sure enough, the man wore a tunic with a senator's wide, purple stripe. He was middle-aged, bald and beak-nosed, none of which were distinctions of note. And he had had at least one enemy, who had stabbed him neatly through the heart. It was a tiny wound, and only a small amount of blood had emerged to form a palm-sized blot on his tunic, but it had done the job. Three thin streaks of blood made stripes paralleling the one that proclaimed his rank.

"Do you know him?" Hermes asked.

I shook my head. Despite all the exiles and purges by the Censors, there were still more than four hundred Senators, and I couldn't very well know all of them.

"Hermes, run to the Curia and fetch Junius the secretary. He knows every man in the Senate by sight. Then inform the *Praetor* Varus. He's holding court in the Basilica Aemilia today and by this hour he's dying for a break in the routine. Then go find Asklepiodes at the Statilian School."

"But that's across the river!" Hermes protested.

"You need the exercise. Hurry, now. I want Asklepiodes to have a look at him before the *Libitinarii* come to take him to the undertaker's."

He dashed off, leaving the lantern. I continued to study the body but it told me nothing. I sighed and scratched my head, wishing I had thought to bring along a skin of wine. Not yet half over, and it was one of the worst years of my life. And it had started out with such promise, too. The Big Three were out of Rome for a change: Caesar was gloriously slaughtering barbarians in Gaul, Crassus was doing exactly the opposite in Syria, and Pompey was sulking in Spain while his flunkies tried to harangue the Senate into making him Dictator. Their excuse this time was that only a Dictator could straighten out the disorder in the city.

It needed the straightening, although making a Dictator was a little drastic. My life wasn't worth a lead denarius after dark in my own city. The thought made me nervous, all alone with only a corpse for company. I was so deeply in debt from borrowing to support my office that I couldn't even afford a bodyguard. Milo would have lent me some thugs but the family wouldn't hear of it. People would think the Metelli were taking the Milo side in the great Clodius-Milo rivalry. Better to lose a Metellus of marginal value than endanger the family's vaunted neutrality.

After an hour or so Varus appeared, escorted by his lictors. Junius was close behind, his stylus tucked behind his ear, accompanied by a slave carrying a satchel full of wax tablets.

"Good afternoon, *Aedile*," Varus said. "So you've found a murder to brighten my day?"

"You didn't happen to bring any wine along, did you?" I said, without much hope.

"You haven't changed any, Metellus. Who do we have?" His lictors carried enough torches to light the place like noon in the Forum. The smoke started to get heavy, though.

Junius bent forward. "It's Aulus Cosconius. He doesn't attend the Senate more than three or four times a year. Big holdings in the City. This building is one of his, I think. Extensive lands in Tuscia as well." He held out a hand and his slave opened the leaves of a wooden tablet, the depressions on their inner sides filled with the finest beeswax, and slapped it into the waiting palm. Junius took his stylus from behind his ear and used its spatulate end to scrape off the words scratched on the wax lining. It was an elegant instrument of bronze inlaid with silver, befitting so important a scribe, as the high-grade wax befitted Senate business. With a dextrous twirl he reversed it and began to write with the pointed end. "You will wish to make a report to the Senate, *Praetor*?"

Varus shrugged. "What's to report? Another dead Senator. It's not like a visitation from Olympus, is it?"

Yes, the times were like that.

"I've sent for Asklepiodes," I said. "He may be able to tell something from the condition of the body."

"I doubt he'll be able to come up with much this time," Varus said, "but if you want, I'll appoint you to investigate. Make a note of it, Junius."

"Will you lend me a lictor?" I asked. "I'll need to summon people."

Varus pointed to one of his attendants and the man sighed. The days of cushy duty in the basilica were over. I said, "Go and inform

the family of the late Senator Auius Cosconius that they have just
been bereaved and that they can claim the body here. Junius should
be able to tell you where they live. Then go to the contractor who
built this place. His name is . . ." I opened one of my own wax
tablets. ". . . Manius Varro. He has a lumber yard by the Circus
Flaminius, next to the temple of Bellona. Tell him to call on me first
thing tomorrow morning, at my office in the Temple of Ceres."

The man handed his torch to a companion and conferred with
Junius, then he shouldered his *fasces* and marched importantly
away.

Asklepiodes arrived just as Junius and Varus were leaving, trailed
by two of his Egyptian slaves, who carried his implements and other
impedimenta. Hermes was with him, carrying a wineskin. I had
trained him well.

"Ah, Decius," the Greek said. "I can always count upon you to find
something interesting for me." He wore a look of bright anticipation.
Sometimes I wondered about Asklepiodes.

"Actually, this looks rather squalid, but the man was of some
importance and somebody left him in a building I was inspecting.
I don't like that sort of thing." Hermes handed me a full cup and
I drained it and handed it back.

Asklepiodes took the lantern and ran the pool of light swiftly over
the body, then paused to examine the wound. "He died within the
last day, I cannot be more precise than that, from the thrust of a
very thin-bladed weapon, its blade triangular in cross-section."

"A woman's dagger?" I asked. Prostitutes frequently concealed
such weapons in their hair, to protect themselves from violent
customers and sometimes to settle disputes with other prostitutes.

"Quite possibly. What's this?" He said something incomprehen-
sible to one of his slaves. The man reached into his voluminous pouch
and emerged with a long, bronze probe decorated with little golden
acanthus leaves and a stoppered bottle, rather plain. Asklepiodes
took the instrument and pried at the wound. It came away with an
ugly little glob of something no bigger than a dried pea. This the
Greek poked into the little bottle and restoppered it. He handed the
probe and the bottle to the slave, who replaced it in his pouch.

"It looks like dried blood to me," I said.

"Only on the surface. I'll take it to my surgery and study it in the
morning, when there is light."

"Do you think he was killed somewhere else and dragged down
here? That's not much blood for a skewered heart."

"No, with a wound like this most of the bleeding is internal, I
believe he died on this spot. His clothing is very little disarranged."

He poked at the feet. "See, the heels of his sandals are not scuffed, as usually happens when a body is dragged."

I was willing to take his word for it. As physician to the gladiators he had seen every possible wound to the human body, hundreds of times over. He left promising to send me a report the next day.

Minutes later the family arrived, along with the *Libitinarii* to perform the lustrations to purify the body. The dead man's son went through the pantomime of catching his last breath and shouted his name loudly, three times. Then the undertaker's men lifted the body and carried it away. The women set up an extravagant caterwauling. It wasn't a patch on the howling the professional mourners would raise at the funeral, but in the closed confines of the cellar it was sufficiently loud.

I approached the young man who had performed the final rites. "I am Decius Caecilius Metellius the Younger, plebeian *Aedile*. I found your father's body and I have been appointed investigator by the *Praetor* Varus. Would you come outside with me?"

"Quintus Cosconius," he said, identifying himself, "only son of Aulus." He was a dark, self-possessed young man. He didn't look terribly put out by the old man's passing: not an uncommon attitude in a man who has just found out that he has come into his inheritance. Something about the name ticked at my memory.

"Quintus Cosconius? Aren't you standing for the tribuneship for next year?"

"I'm not alone in that," he said. Indeed he wasn't. Tribune was the office to have, in those years. They got to introduce the laws that determined who got what in the big game of empire. Since the office was restricted to plebeians, Clodius, a patrician, had gone to the extremity of having himself adopted into a plebeian family just so he could serve as tribune.

"Did your father have enemies? Did any of the feuding demagogues have it in for him?" I was hoping he would implicate Clodius.

"No, in recent years he avoided the Senate. He had no stomach for a faction fight." I detected a faint sneer in his words.

"Who did he support?"

"Crassus, when he supported anyone. They had business dealings together." That made sense. Crassus held the largest properties in Rome. If you dealt in real estate, you probably dealt with Crassus.

"I take it you don't support Crassus yourself?"

He shrugged. "It's no secret. When I am Tribune I shall support Pompey. I've been saying that in the Forum since the start of the year. What has this to do with my father's murder?"

"Oh, politics has everything to do with murder, these days. The streets are littered with the bodies of those who picked the wrong side in the latest rivalries for office. But, since your father was a lukewarm member of the Crassus faction at best, it probably has no bearing upon his death."

"I should think not. What you need to do something about is the unchecked and unpunished violence in the City. It strikes me as ludicrous that our Senatorial authorities can pacify whole provinces but are helpless to make Rome a safe city." He looked as if a new thought had occurred to him. "Decius Caecilius Metellus the Younger? A friend of Milo's are you not?" It wasn't the first time that association had been held against me.

"Yes, but, like your father's political connections, it has no bearing here. If Milo should prove to be responsible, I shall hale him before the *Praetor* like any other malefactor."

"Rome needs a genuine police force!" he said, heatedly. "And laws with teeth!"

I was getting tired of this. "When did you last see your father?"

"Yesterday morning. He spoke to me in the Forum. He had been out of the City, touring his country estates – " I saw that look of satisfaction cross his face. They were *his* estates now. "– but he came back to inspect one of his town properties. This one, I think."

"He certainly seems to have ended up here. What plans did he have for this building?"

He shrugged again. "The usual, I suppose: Let out the ground floor to some well-to-do tenant and the upper floors to the less affluent. He owned many such properties." He smoothed a fold of his exceptionally white toga. "Will there be anything else?"

"Not at present. But I may wish to speak with you again."

"Anything for one on the service of the Senate and People of Rome," he said, none too warmly.

With the crowd gone, I went back to my inspection duties, giving them less than half of my attention. Much as I disliked the man's attitude, Quintus Cosconius had spoken nothing but the truth when he said that Rome needed a police force. Our ancient laws forbade the presence of armed soldiers within the sacred walls, and that extended to any citizen bearing arms in the City. From time to time someone would suggest forming a force of slave-police, on the old Athenian model, but that meant setting slaves in power over citizens, and that was unthinkable.

The trouble was that any force of armed men in the City would quickly become a private army for one of the political criminals who plagued the body politic in those days. In earlier times we had done well enough without police, because Romans were a mostly law-abiding people with a high respect for authority and civic order. Ever since the Gracchi, though, mob action had become the rule in Rome, and every aspiring politician curried favor with a criminal gang, to do his dirty work in return for protection in the courts.

The Republic was very sick and, despite my fondest hopes, there was to be no cure.

"You've been drinking," Julia said when I got home.

"It's been that sort of day." I told her about the dead Senator while we had dinner in the courtyard.

"You have no business investigating while you're in another office," she said. "Varus should appoint a *Iudex*."

"It may be years before a Court for Assassins is appointed to look into this year's murders. They're happening by the job lot. But this one occurred on my territory."

"You just like to snoop. And you're hoping to get something on Clodius."

"What will one more murder laid at his doorstep mean? No, for once, I doubt that Clodius had anything to do with it." Luckily for me, my Julia was a favourite niece of the great Caius Julius Caesar, darling of the Popular Assemblies. Clodius was Caesar's man and dared not move against me openly, and by this time he considered himself the veritable uncrowned king of Rome, dispensing largesse and commanding his troops in royal fashion. As such, sneaky, covert assassination was supposedly beneath his dignity. Supposedly.

At that time, there were two sorts of men contending for power: The Big Three were all that were left of the lot that had been trying to gain control of the whole Empire for decades. Then there were men like Clodius and Milo, who just wanted to rule the City itself. Since the great conquerors had to be away from the City for years at a time, all of them had men to look after their interests in Rome. Clodius represented Caesar. Milo had acted for Crassus, although he was also closely tied in with Cicero and the star of Crassus was rapidly fading, to wink out that summer, did we but know it at the time. Plautius Hypsaeus was with the Pompeian faction, and so it went.

"Tell me about it," Julia said, separating an orange into sections. She always believed her woman's intuition could greatly improve upon the performance of my plodding reasoning. Sometimes she was right, although I carefully refrained from telling her so.

"So you think a prostitute killed him?" she said when she had heard me out.

"I only said that was in keeping with the weapon. I have never known a man to use such a tool to rid himself of an enemy."

"Oh, yes. Men like sharp edges and lots of blood."

"Exactly. This little skewer bespeaks a finesse I am reluctant to credit to our forthright cutthroats."

"But if the man owned property all over the City, why take his hired companion to the cellar of an unfurnished house?"

"Good question," I allowed. "Of course, in such matters, some men have truly recondite tastes. Why, your own Uncle Caius Julius has been known to enjoy . . ."

"Spare me," she said, very clearly, considering that her teeth were clamped tightly together.

With my fellow *Aediles* I shared the warren of office space beneath the ancient Temple of Ceres. A man was waiting for me when I climbed the steps. "*Aedile* Metellus?" He was a short, bald man and he wore a worried look that furrowed his brow all the way back to the middle of his scalp. "I am Manius Varro, the builder."

"Ah, yes. You recently completed a townhouse property for Aulus Cosconius?"

"I did," he said, still worried. "And I used only the best . . ."

"You will be happy to learn that I found no violations of the code concerning materials or construction."

Relief washed over his face like a wave on a beach. "Oh. It's just about the body, then?" He shook his head ruefully, trying to look concerned. "Poor Aulus Cosconius. I'd done a fair amount of business for him over the years."

"Was there any dispute over your payment?"

He looked surprised that I should ask. "No. He paid in full for that job months ago. He'd been planning to put up a big tenement in the Subura, but he cancelled that a few days ago."

"Did he say why?"

"No, just that he didn't want to start anything big with uncertain times ahead. I thought he meant we might have a Dictator next year. You never can tell what that might mean."

"Very true," I said, my gaze wandering out over one of Rome's most spectacular views, the eye-stunning expanse of the Circus Maximus stretching out below us. To a native son of Rome, that view is immensely satisfying because it combines three of our passions: races, gambling and enormous, vulgar buildings. His gaze followed mine.

"Ah, *Aedile*, I take it you'll be organizing the races next month?"

"To the great distress of my purse, yes."

"Do you know who's driving in the first race?"

"Victor for the Reds, Androcles for the Greens, Philip for the Blues and Paris for the Whites." I could have reeled off the names of all sixteen horses they would be driving as well. I was good at that sort of thing.

"You Caecilians are Reds, aren't you?"

"Since Romulus," I told him, knowing what was coming.

"I support the Blues. Fifty sesterces on Philip in the first race, even money?" He undoubtedly knew the names of all the horses as well.

"The Sparrow has a sore forefoot," I said, naming the Red's near-side trace horse. "Give me three to two."

"Done!" he grinned. We took out the little tablets half the men in Rome carry around to record bets. With our styli we scratched our names and bets in each other's tablets. He walked away whistling and I felt better, too. Victor had assured me personally that the Sparrow's foot would be fine in plenty of time for the race. I flicked the accumulation of wax from the tip of my stylus, my mind going back to the condition of Cosconius's body.

I had dismissed Varro as a suspect in the murder. Building contractors as a class are swindlers rather than murderers and his manner was all wrong. But our little bet had set me on a promising mental trail. My borrowed lictor was sitting on the base of the statue of Proserpina that stood in front of the temple before the restorations commissioned by Maecaenas. He looked bored senseless. I summoned him.

"Let's go to the Forum." At that he brightened. Everything really interesting was happening in the Forum. In the Forum, lictors were respected as symbols of *imperium*. With him preceding me, we went down the hill and across the old Cattle Market and along the Tuscan Street to the Forum.

The place was thronged, as usual. It held an aura of barely-contained menace in that unruly year, but people still respected the symbol of the *fasces* and made way for the lictor. I made a slow circuit of the area, finding out who was there and, more importantly, who was not. To my great relief, neither Clodius nor Milo were around with their crowds of thugs. Among the candidates for the next year's offices I saw the young Quintus Cosconius. Unlike the others standing for the tribuneship in their specially whitened togas he wore a dingy, brown toga and he had not shaved his face nor combed his hair, all in token of mourning.

On the steps of the Basilica Opimia I found Cicero, surrounded as always by clients and friends. Ordinarily I would have waited upon his notice like everyone else, but my office and my lictor allowed me to approach him at once.

"Good morning, *Aedile*," he saluted, always punctilious in matters of office. He raised an eyebrow at sight of my lictor. "Does your office now carry *imperium*? I must have dozed off during the last Senate meeting."

"Good morning, Marcus Tullius, and no, I'm just carrying out an investigation for Varus. I would greatly appreciate your advice."

"Of course." We made that little half-turn that proclaimed that we were now in private conference and the others directed their attention elsewhere. "Is it the murder of Aulus Cosconius? Shocking business."

"Exactly. What were the man's political leanings, if any?"

"He was a dreadfully old-fashioned man, the sort who oppose almost anything unsanctioned by our remote ancestors. Like most of the men involved in City property trade, he supported Crassus. Before he left for Syria, Crassus told them all to fight Pompey's efforts to become Dictator. That's good advice, even coming from Crassus. I've spent months trying to convince the tribunes not to introduce legislation to that effect."

"What about next year's tribunes?" I asked.

"Next year's? I'm having trouble enough with the ones we have now."

"Even if Pompey isn't named Dictator, he's almost sure to be one of next year's Consuls. If the Tribunes for next year are all Pompey's men, he'll have near-dictatorial authority and the proconsular province of his choosing. He'll be able to take Syria from Crassus, or Gaul from Caesar, if he wants."

Cicero nodded. "That has always been Pompey's style — let someone else do all the fighting, then get the Tribunes to give him command in time for the kill." Now he looked sharply at me. "What are you getting at, Decius?"

"Be patient with me, Marcus Tullius. I have . . ." at that moment I saw a slave, one of Asklepiodes's silent Egyptian assistants, making his way toward me, holding a folded piece of papyrus, which he handed to me. I opened up the papyrus, read the single word it held, and grinned. "Marcus Tullius," I said, "if a man were standing for public office and were caught in some offense against the ancient laws — say, he carried arms within the boundaries set by Romulus — would it abnegate his candidacy?" My own solution to the law was to carry a *caestus*. The spiked boxing glove was, technically, sports equipment rather than a proper weapon.

"It's a commonly violated custom in these evil times, but if I were standing for office against that man I would prosecute him and tie him up in litigation so thoroughly that he would never take office."

"That is just what I needed to know. Marcus Tullius, if I might impose upon you further, could you meet with me this afternoon at the *ludus* of Statilius Taurus?"

Now he was thoroughly mystified, something I seldom managed to do to Cicero. "Well, my friend Balbus has been writing me from Africa for months to help him arrange the Games he will be giving when he returns. I could take care of that at the same time."

"Thank you, Marcus Tullius." I started to turn away.

"And, Decius?"

I turned back. "Yes?"

"Do be entertaining. That's a long walk."

"I promise it."

At the bottom of the steps I took the tablet thonged to the slave's belt and wrote on the wax with my stylus. "Take this to your master," I instructed. He nodded wordlessly and left. Asklepiodes's slaves could speak, but only in Egyptian, which in Rome was the same thing as being mute. Then I gave the lictor his orders.

"Go to Quintus Cosconius, the man in mourning dress over there with the candidates, and tell him that he is summoned to confer with me at the Statilian School in" – I glanced up at the angle of the sun – "three hours."

He ran off and I climbed the lower slope of the Capitoline along the Via Sacra to the Archive. I spoke with Calpurnius, the freedman in charge of estate titles, and he brought me a great stack of tablets and scrolls, bulky with thick waxen seals, recording the deeds of the late Aulus Cosconius. The one for the Aventine town house where I had discovered his body was a nice little wooden diptych with bronze hinges. Inside, one leaf bore writing done with a reed pen in black ink. The other had a circular recess that held the wax seal protecting it from damage.

"I'll just take this with me, if you don't mind," I said.

"But I do mind," Calpurnius said. "You have no subpoena from a *Praetor* demanding documents from this office." One always has to deal with such persons, on public duty. After much wrangling and talking with his superiors and swearing of sacred oaths upon the altars of the State, I got away with the wretched document, to be returned the next morning or forfeit my life.

Thus armed, I made my leisurely way toward the river and crossed the Aemilian Bridge into the Trans-Tiber district. There, among the river port facilities of Rome's newest district, was the *ludus* of Statilius

Taurus, where the best gladiators outside of Campania were trained. I conferred with Statilius for an hour or so, making arrangements for the Games that had already bankrupted me. Then Cicero arrived to do the same on behalf of his friend Balbus. He was accompanied by five or six clients, all men of distinction in their own right.

With our business concluded, we went out to the gallery that overlooked the training yard. It was an hour when only the fighters of the first rank were working out, while the tyros watched from the periphery. These men despised practice weapons, preferring to train with sharp steel. Their skill was amazing to see. Even Cicero, who had little liking for the public shows, was impressed.

Asklepiodes arrived as we were thus engaged, holding a folded garment. "This is the oddest task you have ever asked of me," he said, "but you always furnish amusement of the highest sort, so I expect to be amply rewarded." He handed me the thing.

"Excellent!" I said. "I was afraid the undertaker might have thrown it away."

"*Aedile*," Cicero said a bit testily. "I do hope this is leading somewhere. My time is not without value."

I saw a man in a dark toga come through the archway leading to the practice yard. "I promise not to disappoint you. Here's my man now."

Young Cosconius looked around, then saw me gesturing from the distinguished group on the gallery. He came up the stair, very stiff and dignified. He was surprised to see Cicero and his entourage, but he masked his perplexity with an expression of *gravitas* befitting one recently bereaved and seeking high office. He saluted Cicero, ex-Consul and the most important man currently residing in Rome.

"I am here on a matter of business," Cicero said. "I believe your business is with the *Aedile*."

"I apologize for summoning you here," I said. "I know that you must be preoccupied with your late father's obsequies." When I had last seen him, he had been busy grubbing votes.

"I trust you've made progress in finding my father's murderer," he said, coldly.

"I believe I have." I looked out over the men training in the yard below. "It's a chore, arranging for public Games. You'll find that out. I suppose you'll be exhibiting funeral games for your father?"

He shrugged. "He specified none in his will, which was read this morning. But I may do so when I hold the aedileship."

Confident little bastard, I thought. I pointed to a pair of men who were contending with sword and shield. One carried the big, oblong legionary shield and *gladius*, the other a small, round shield and curved shortsword.

"That's Celadus with the Thracian weapons," I said, referring to the latter. "Do you support the Big Shields or the Small Shields?"

"The Big Shields," he said.

"I've always liked the Small Shields," I told him. "Celadus fights Petraites from the School of Ampliatus at next month's Games." Petraites was a ranking Big Shield fighter of the time. I saw that special gleam come into his eye.

"Are you proposing a wager?"

"A hundred on Celadus, even money?" This was more than reasonable. Petraites had the greater reputation.

"Done," he said, taking out his tablet and stylus, handing the tablet to me. I gave him mine, then rummaged around in my tunic and toga.

"I've lost my stylus. Would you lend me yours?"

He handed it over. "Now, I believe you called me here concerning my father's murder."

"Oh, yes, I was coming to that, Quintus Cosconius, I charge you with the murder of your father, Senator Aulus Cosconius."

"You are insane!" he said, his dark face going suddenly pale, as well it might. Of the many cruel punishments on our law books, the one for parricide is one of the worst.

"That is a serious charge, *Aedile*," Cicero said. "Worse than poisoning, worse than treason, even worse than arson."

Cosconius pointed a finger at me. "Maybe you aren't mad. You are just covering up for another of your friend Milo's crimes."

"Asklepiodes pronounced that death was the result of a wound inflicted by a thin blade piercing the heart. He found a bit of foreign substance adhering to the wound, which he took to his surgery to study. I thought at first that the weapon was a bodkin such as prostitutes sometimes carry, but this morning it occurred to me that a writing stylus would serve as well, provided it was made of bronze." I held up the piece of paper Asklepiodes had sent me with its one word: "wax."

"This confirms it. Aulus Cosconius was stabbed through the heart with a stylus uncleaned by its owner since its last use. A bit of wax still adhered to its tip and was left on the wound."

Quintus Cosconius snorted. "What of it? Nearly every literate man in Rome carries a stylus!"

"Actually, I didn't really forget my own stylus today." I took it out. "You see, the common styli are round or quadrangular. Mine, for instance, is slightly oval in cross-section." Cicero and his friends drew out their own implements and showed them. All were as I had described. Cicero's was made of ivory, with a silver scraper.

"Yet Asklepiodes's examination indicated that the weapon used to kill Aulus Cosconius was triangular. You will note that young Quintus's implement is of that geometrical form, which is most rare among styli." I handed it to Cicero.

Then I shook out the tunic the dead man had been wearing. "Note the three parallel streaks of blood. That is where he wiped off the sides of the stylus."

"A coward's weapon," snorted one of Cicero's companions.

"But young Cosconius here is standing for office," I pointed out. "He couldn't afford to be caught bearing arms within the *pomerium*. But most Romans pack a stylus around. It isn't much of a weapon, but no one is going to survive having one thrust through his heart."

"Why should I do such a thing?" Cosconius demanded. You could smell the fear coming off him.

"Yesterday," I said, "you told me you didn't know what use your father intended for that town house. Here is the deed from the Archive." I took the diptych from a fold of my toga and opened it. "And here he states plainly that it is 'to serve as a residence for his only surviving son, Lucius.' He didn't bother showing you this deed or getting your seal on it because he was a very old-fashioned man, and by the ancient law of *patria potestas* you were a minor and could not legally own property while your father was alive. He took you to show you your new digs, and that is where you argued and you killed him."

Everyone glared at Cosconius, but by this time he had gained enough wisdom to keep his mouth shut.

"Killed the old man for his inheritance, did he?" Cicero said grimly.

I shook my head. "No, nobody gets killed over money these days. It's always politics. Aulus Cosconius was generous enough with his wealth, else why give his son a whole town house to himself? But he supported Crassus and Quintus here is Pompey's man. Aulus wouldn't stick his neck out for Crassus, but he could keep Pompey from getting another tame Tribune without risk, or so he thought."

I addressed Cosconius directly. "Sometime during the tour of that townhouse he told you that he forbade you to stand for Tribune. As *pater familias* it was his legal right to do so. Or perhaps he had told you before, and you waited until you were together in a lonely spot to kill him. The law admits of no distinction in such a case."

Cosconius started to get hold of himself, but Cicero deflated him instantly. "I shall prosecute personally, unless you wish to, Decius Caecilius."

"I shall be far too busy for the balance of this year."

Cosconius knew then he was a dead man. Cicero was the greatest prosecutor in the history of Roman jurisprudence, which was precisely why I had asked him there in the first place. He took few cases in those days, but a parricide in a senatorial family would be the splashiest trial of the year.

I summoned the owner of the school. "Statilius, lend me a few of your boys to escort this man to the basilica. I don't want him jumping into the river too soon."

Cosconius came out of his stupor. "Gladiators? You can't let scum like that lay hands on a free man!"

"You'll have worse company soon," Cicero promised him. Then, to me: "*Aedile*, do your duty." I nodded to my borrowed lictor. He walked up behind Quintus Cosconius and clapped a hand on his shoulder, intoning the old formula: "Come with me to the *Praetor*."

That's the good part about being *Aedile*: You get to arrest people.

These were the events of two days in the year 703 of the city of Rome, the consulship of Marcus Valerius Messalla Rufus and Cnaeus Domitius Calvinus.

# THE TREASURY THEFTS
# Wallace Nichols

*So far as I know Wallace Nichols (1888–1967) was the first writer to set a genuine detective story in ancient Rome. His stories about Sollius, the Slave detective, became extremely popular in the pages of the* **London Mystery Magazine,** *where over sixty of them ran between 1950 and 1968.*

*Michael Williams, a Cornish publisher and friend of Nichols for over thirty years called him "the most extraordinary man I have ever known." The author of over sixty books, Nichols was first and last a poet. His first book of poetry was published when he was sixteen. Born in Birmingham, he was for a while on the editorial staff of the* **Windsor Magazine** *and a reader at Ward Lock's before he moved to Cornwall for health reasons in 1934. In addition to his poetry and his detective stories he wrote historical novels and boys' adventures. He had known Churchill and Elgar, Dylan Thomas and Lawrence of Arabia. He spoke five modern languages and several ancient ones, including Egyptian and Babylonian. He had written his autobiography which sadly was never published and may well now be lost.*

*At least we can still savour the magic of his writing. His first two stories about Sollius are so intricately connected that I have run them together here as one full-length novella. This is the first time they have been reprinted in over forty years.*

## EPISODE I
## THE CASE OF THE EMPRESS'S JEWELS

Titius Sabinus the Senator found the Emperor in a dejected mood. Knowing Marcus Aurelius to be a philosopher, he set this down either to some unsolved problem of thought, or else to some domestic trouble which had broken into his usual calm of mind. He knew that rumour spoke of the Empress Faustina as being a very extravagant woman, and also of their son, the young Commodus, as being a stubborn, difficult youth to control. But Sabinus made a point of listening to rumour, especially to Roman rumour, with great cautiousness.

Gazing now at the Emperor's tired face, he began to wonder, with not a little unease, why he had been summoned so unexpectedly to the huge imperial palace on the Esquiline. As far as he knew, there was no public crisis of any kind upon which his advice might be required, nor, as he could see at a glance, had any other senator been summoned to the same audience. He was still more astonished when the Emperor, taking him aside at once, made a seemingly earnest enquiry about nothing of greater importance than a private occurrence in the Senator's household.

"Yes, sir, the thief was discovered," the Senator answered the Emperor, "and the money," he added, rubbing his hands, "was found also. I lost nothing — except my sleep for a few nights."

"It was, then, quite a large sum, Sabinus?"

"It was, sir. My steward from Sardinia had just come with the money from the sale of my lead mines there. He arrived late, and there was no time to deposit it in the bank before morning, and by morning — it had gone!"

"An unpleasant experience," commented the Emperor. "But you got it back — and found the culprit?"

"Both, sir, by the favour of the gods," replied Sabinus, and a rich man's satisfaction oozed from every syllable.

"Rumour has been busy with the affair," smiled Marcus Aurelius.

"Oh, rumour!" muttered Sabinus, and spread out his hands.

"I hope that for once," the Augustus went on, "rumour is true."

"Sir?"

"It is said that you owe the discovery both of the thief and the money's hiding-place to the cleverness of one of your slaves."

"That is so, Augustus," Sabinus answered, still surprised at the Emperor's apparently deep interest. "It is not the first time, either, that the wits of my good Sollius have served me well in the same way. But never before in so large a matter, but only in cases of petty pilfering at my house here in Rome or at one of my country villas."

"What did you say was his name?" asked Marcus Aurelius.

"Sollius, O Augustus."

"I understand, too," pursued the Emperor, "that he has been useful in uncovering thefts for one or two of your friends."

"I did not know," said Sabinus, unable longer to hide his astonishment at the course of the interview, "that the doings of one of my slaves had interested your august ear. I hope that he has not been meddling in public matters and joining a — conspiracy, sir!"

Marcus Aurelius laughed, and laid his hand familiarly on the other's shoulder.

"I only wanted your report of him," he said. "You see – "

The Emperor hesitated, and laughed again.

"You see," he concluded, "I wish to borrow him from you."

"Augustus!" cried Sabinus, and his mouth remained open.

"Listen, Sabinus," said Marcus Aurelius, and indicating an ivory chair to his guest, he took his seat on a small, gilded Greek couch nearby. "Listen, and I will explain. But what I am about to tell you," he went on in a voice suddenly vibrant with all the might of his august and sacred authority, "must be as secret as one of the old Mysteries until I release you myself from the obligation of silence."

"Why, of course, sir," answered Sabinus obsequiously, not a little flattered by the Emperor's personal confidence, for it was the first time in his life that he had been so honoured.

"It is like this," the Emperor continued. "The Treasury is being robbed."

"The gods forbid!" ejaculated Sabinus. "Who could do such a thing?"

"That is the problem," was the dry answer. "That is why I wish to borrow your cunning slave."

"Certainly, O Augustus, certainly; he is at your service, wholly at your service, of course! If I had known, I would myself have brought him with me – "

"Wait, wait, Sabinus," said Marcus Aurelius. "You go too quickly."

"Your pardon, sir!"

"The investigations of the Treasury officials," the Emperor went on gravely, "have discovered nothing. There are even no suspicions, and where there are no suspicions there can be no evidence. Probably, too, the whole matter touches someone highly placed. I have therefore to go very carefully. I must not make a mistake when I accuse – whomever I shall accuse. The whole affair, politically, could be very dangerous. It must be handled with more than secrecy, more than discretion: it must be handled wisely."

"Most truly spoken, sir!" hastily agreed the Senator.

"I must therefore test this slave of yours, Sabinus, before I permit him to touch an investigation so dangerous."

"You will find him wholly trustworthy."

"He is – a young man?"

"No, sir. He is a man in late middle life."

"So much the better. He is educated, I suppose?"

"He was the favourite slave of my uncle, from whom I inherited

**THE TREASURY THEFTS** **47**

him," replied Sabinus. "He was picked out, even as a youth, to be my uncle's reader – and my uncle was a great lover of philosophy and poetry, sir – and he had Sollius educated and well trained for that purpose."

"Excellent!" said the Emperor.

He considered a moment, frowning and stroking his beard, before saying anything further, and Sabinus looked at him expectantly. He thought that the master of the Roman world appeared less philosophical than usual, as if, indeed, he were seriously worried. He was pale, and his heavily lidded eyes lacked their usual lustre. Sabinus was about to venture a remark as to his slave's complete dependability when abruptly the Emperor took up the subject himself.

"These thefts," he said, "from the Treasury – for there have been more than one – are so delicate a matter that I would try your Sollius first, my good Sabinus, in something a little less serious before finally giving him so important and confidential a mission."

"Yes, Augustus, I fully understand," replied Sabinus, nodding.

"It happens that the occasion is unfortunately only too immediate – both in time and for my own peace of mind," went on Marcus Aurelius with a touch of awkwardness. "The Empress has lost some valuable jewels, and again everybody who has been employed to find them, or the stealer of them, has failed. Say nothing to your slave about the more serious matter; tell him merely that he is to help in seeking to discover the whereabouts of the Empress's lost jewels, and send him to me with a serious caution, Sabinus, as to his silence and discretion. I shall give him his instructions myself. Let him come about an hour after noon tomorrow, and ask for Alexias, my Greek freedman."

"You shall be obeyed, O Augustus," answered Titius Sabinus, and fussily took his leave.

Immediately on his return to his own house he sent for the slave named Sollius, and explained to him the great honour that was to be his in serving the Emperor himself, and then at great length, and without the slightest necessity, warned him to be thoroughly prudent and entirely secret.

"You are not to tell even *me* anything," he concluded, as if that was the final height and test of all perfect discretion.

Sollius the slave was a small man, but inclining to corpulency. His scanty hair was thin and greying, and he was more than beginning to go bald. He had a long, slightly fleshy nose with wide nostrils, and very dark, round eyes. He was cleanshaven, and walked with somewhat of a limp, for his left foot had been caught in a wolf-trap when he was a boy. He had a soft voice and a gentle manner. Always intensely neat as to his person, he went about his concerns and household duties with the candid gaze of an overgrown child. His fellow slaves regarded him without special friendliness, but not with enmity or suspicion; that is to say, he was one among them, but not exactly of them, except in the one undeniable fact of their common slavery. That they did not resent his aloofness, or call it the vanity of a favourite with their master, was a tribute to his natural goodness of heart, for he was as kindly a nurse in any case of their sickness as he was skilful as a prober into any matter of mystery.

He had, however, one friend in the son of a slave-girl who had died some years before, a youth now eighteen years old, and named Lucius. It was as though he had taken this youth under his special protection, and some of his fellow slaves would nudge each other when watching the elder man's kindness to the younger, and whisper together that they thought they knew why! Sollius had taught Lucius many scraps of his own knowledge. More than that, he had found him useful, since he had quick wits and a keen pair of eyes, in his various investigations of theft. He was a strong, healthy and athletic young man, and a general favourite in the Senator's household. Sollius had already determined in mind to use him as his assistant should he need help in what the Emperor might be going to ask him to do.

At the time appointed, Sollius had entered the great palace of the Roman Cæsars on the Esquiline Hill, and, evidently expected, was immediately escorted by a centurion of the Prætorians, the imperial bodyguard, into the presence of Alexias, the Emperor's principal and confidential freedman. He was a lean, dark Greek, with a cold, haughty manner, and he subjected the slave to a close, not to say jealous, scrutiny.

"How do you usually begin your enquiries?" he asked at once, as soon as the centurion had left them, and without wasting any words on greeting.

"By understanding the circumstances of the theft," quietly answered Sollius, and the modesty in his tone and manner was already mollifying the freedman's disapprobation of the slave's privileged employment. Alexias had been resolved to give him no unnecessary assistance, but found that his personality was disarming. He coughed, and a slight, involuntary smile touched his lips.

"I am to take you to the Augustus," he said without further preliminary, and at once led the way towards the Emperor's private apartments and into a small chamber filled with innumerable books and scrolls, but otherwise sparsely and most plainly furnished. It looked out on to a small marble portico from which gleaming steps led down into the vast palace gardens.

The Emperor was dictating to Alexander, his Greek secretary, as they entered, and indicating by a gesture that Alexias and Sollius were to stand quietly on the threshold, he continued pacing up and down and wording aloud a despatch to the commander of the Roman army on the Rhine. It was, Sollius soon decided, of no very great importance, and was more an injunction to be watchful rather than active; but the Emperor seemed to be taking unusual pains over the language in which he was clothing his commands. At moments, as he turned in his pacing, he would glance towards the slave of Titius Sabinus, so that by the time that his dictating was concluded he had already made a shrewd assessment of the man's character from the evidences of his features and manner. He was pleased to notice that instead of keeping his eyes respectfully, or timidly, on the ground, the slave had been regarding him with as much open interest as he himself had been regarding the slave.

"Come nearer," he said quietly and suddenly. "You are Sollius?"

"I am Sollius, Augustus."

"You are clever, I am told, in discovering thieves and lost property."

"I have been lucky, sir, and yet – yes! – I have an aptitude for such things."

Marcus Aurelius smiled. He was never one to appreciate the falsely modest when the simple truth could be spoken without vanity.

"The Empress," he said, "has lost a number of her jewels."

"When?" asked Sollius quickly.

The secretary and the freedman both stared. It was not usual for the Emperor to be challenged so abruptly – not even by a senator or a victorious general on leave.

Marcus Aurelius hesitated, and frowned thoughtfully. Sollius looked at him with eyes suddenly bright.

"Three days ago," said the Emperor, closing the slight pause with imperial decisiveness.

Sollius lowered his eyelids for a moment, and then, with an upward glance, he asked:

"Were they taken from her sleeping-chamber?"

"They were last seen in her sleeping-chamber," carefully replied the Emperor.

"Who saw them – last?"

"The Empress herself. She was choosing a ring from the casket containing them. They were there then."

"Was this at morning or at night?"

"It was about sunset. When the Empress retired to rest some hours later, and gave the ring to her attendant to put away, the casket was found empty."

"I should like to see the chamber, the empty casket and the waitingwoman."

"See to that, Alexias – and Sollius is to be admitted to me, without any delay, at all such times as he may wish," ordered the Emperor.

Alexias and Sollius bowed.

"Come," whispered the freedman, and when the Emperor's voice began dictating again they were already in the long, gilded and painted corridor.

"This way," whispered Alexias again. "Follow me."

A guard, another Prætorian, was on duty by a lofty, decorated door. Recognizing Alexias, he let them both pass.

The chamber of the Empress Faustina was spacious, beautifully proportioned and, in the eyes of Sollius at least, unbelievably luxurious. He stood in the doorway, marvelling. But, even while marvelling, he was darting his looks in all directions, and completing in his mind a picture which he knew would remain in his memory with great exactitude.

"This is Marcia," murmured Alexias, and a young, handsome woman came forward from the dressing-table, which she had been engaged in tidying at the moment of their entrance. "You are to answer all the questions which Sollius – this is Sollius, Marcia – will put to you," the freedman went on. "It is the Augustus's own command."

Marcia fixed Sollius with a clear and resentful gaze.

"I suppose you have already decided that I stole them," she burst out. "Not even the Empress thinks that, and I will not take it from a slave!"

"You yourself are a freedwoman?" asked Sollius with a smile.

"You mistake," she answered proudly. "I am the daughter of a freedman and a freedwoman, free on both sides, and I am a dutiful servant to the Roman Augusta."

"I do not doubt it," replied Sollius. "But tell me this: were you here when the Empress took the ring out of the casket? Oh, is that the same casket over there?"

She nodded, and he went across to the ornate, marble dressing-table. Its appointments were of gold, and the casket itself also was of gold. He stood staring down at it without touching it. Then, without turning, he repeated his previous question.

"I was, slave."

"Did you yourself see whether the casket was then filled with its jewels as usual?"

"I did, and it was, slave," said Marcia.

"Was the casket not kept locked?"

"It was always kept locked. It is only unlocked now because it is empty. Look!"

She moved to his side, and opened the casket by the mere insertion of a painted nail under its lid. It was certainly empty.

"Who entered this room between the time that the Empress took the ring out of this casket and the finding that the rest of the jewels had been stolen?" asked Sollius.

"Myself, twice," she answered. "None else, at least, had any right or proper occasion to enter."

Sollius rubbed his chin.

"Not even the Empress herself – and, perhaps, a friend with her?"

Marcia shook her head.

"The Empress was at a dinner party," she said. "Also," she went on, a trifle maliciously, as if she enjoyed making the problem still more difficult for the slave, "a guard, one of the Prætorians, stood in the corridor all the while."

"Was the guard changed during any part of the time?"

"He had but newly taken his post when the Empress left her chamber, and he had not been relieved," replied Marcia, "by the time of her return."

"Do you know this Prætorian personally?" asked Sollius sharply.

"No more," she answered with a faint, scornful smile, "than I know others of the Prætorians who take their turn of guard. He is not, though you seem to suspect so, my lover. I look higher, slave, than a soldier!"

"Is the same guard on duty now?"

"No, it is another man."

Sollius turned to Alexias.

"I should like to see that guard," he said.

"He shall be summoned," the freedman promised.

Sollius fixed his gaze once more upon Marcia, and eyed her for a moment or so in silence, but she did not fidget under his scrutiny, and returned it with the same proud scorn as before.

"Have you no guess, yourself, as to the thief?" he asked, and his voice was neither accusatory nor suspicious, but strangely compelling.

"None, O slave, I know nothing, and equally suspect nothing."

"Thank you," he answered, bowed courteously, and turned to go.

"I must see that guard as soon as possible," he said when he and Alexias were walking away down the corridor. "I should like also a list of the jewels. Judging from the size of the gold box from which they were taken, they were smallish in size and number."

"You shall have the list, Sollius," replied Alexias. "But I can tell you myself that they consisted of rings, ear-rings, bracelets and hair-adornments – but, though small and containable within a single casket, of great value. The Empress would not wear them if they were not," he added with a swift, sharp glance.

"That is true," answered Sollius gravely.

"What else do you wish to see, or do?" asked the freedman.

"I should like," replied Sollius, "to examine that part of the gardens which is outside the chamber that we have just left."

Alexias looked instantly dubious.

"That is a very private part of the gardens," he said. "I should have to obtain the permission of the Empress to take you there. She may be there herself at this hour – and no one may intrude upon her privacy."

"She is not there," answered Sollius confidently. "I saw no sign of her when I looked out over the gardens just now. Besides," he continued, drawing himself up into an attitude very unbecoming, thought Alexias, in a slave, "I have the Emperor's own commands to do as I wish – or have I not? You heard them from his own lips."

"He did not give you permission to intrude upon the privacy of the Augusta," said Alexias stubbornly. "I heard nothing about that. Be reasonable, Sollius."

"I *must* see that part of the gardens," insisted the slave of Sabinus. "Above all things it is important. Shall I go to the Augustus for his permission? He would, I am confident, give it to me."

"Come," answered the freedman brusquely. "I will take the risk!"

He led the other forth by secret passages into the air and the sunlight. Outside Faustina's apartments, below their position and the marble steps leading down from them into the scented luxury of the gardens themselves, Sollius became quickly busy, examining the grass, the shrubs, the nearest flower-beds, the gleaming steps, top to bottom, and, indeed, the whole vicinity. He was almost like a sniffing dog, thought Alexias disgustedly, for he could not see what good was being done by such actions, and he was annoyed, too, over having been forced to bring the slave into the imperial gardens at all. But the Emperor had a use for the fellow . . . he shrugged his shoulders, and stood watching while Sollius continued his investigations below the Empress's apartments.

"Do not be too long," whispered Alexias, staring nervously around. "The Empress could have us whipped for this – even *me*."

"I am ready now," said Sollius. "There is nothing to be seen – which is often as good, my friend, as to see everything! The two sides of a coin make but one piece of money after all, not two."

Alexias wrinkled his brows in the effort to understand such a puzzling remark, but what with his haste to leave the place where they were and his still doubtful opinion of the slave's qualities, he left the matter without comment, and hurried his companion back into the palace.

"What now?" he asked.

"I am going home," answered Sollius, "to think. I shall come again and ask for you early in the morning – and let that Prætorian be with you."

With a pleasant smile he begged the freedman to show him the nearest way out of the palace, for with its hundreds of confusing corridors and passages he felt bewildered, or so he said.

Alexias stared after him as he saw him forth, and wondered what would come of his enquiry. He had a sudden cold feeling about the heart, and turned away to his other duties with a deep sigh.

As soon as Sollius had returned to his master's house he sought out Lucius. He found him carrying in a huge basket of vegetables from the garden towards the kitchen.

"When you have taken those to the cook," he said, "I have need of you."

"But, Sollius, if the cook wants me to do more errands for him – "

"This is more important, far more important," Sollius answered. "It is on – ahem! – our master's business, and you can tell Tuphus the cook that for a little while you are as good as *my* slave."

Lucius looked at him enquiringly, and then suddenly a grin spread over his face.

"Good, Sollius! Oh, good!" he cried, and shouldering his basket once more, he went off into the kitchen. Almost immediately he was back again.

"Come," said Sollius, and he led the way along a dark passage which came out near the chariot-house and the stables.

Behind these lay a walled enclosure containing a round, stone pool filled with carp. It was a place where they could generally count upon being able to talk undisturbed. Standing beside the pool, and looking down among the dark, swimming forms without any expression upon his face, Sollius began to speak. He told his young companion everything. He knew that he could trust him, and that he would have to employ a helper in his new task, and also that there was nobody else, as he had already proved, with the right kind of aptitude for being his assistant.

"I suppose," said Lucius after he had listened carefully, "that either the waiting-woman – did you say she was named Marcia? – or the guard took them."

"I cannot answer about the guard," replied Sollius, "for I have not yet questioned him. But I am sure that Marcia had nothing to do with it, for I think that she is as puzzled as I am. I could see it in her eyes."

"And *are* you puzzled, Sollius?" asked Lucius seriously.

"I am," answered Sollius, and sighed. "The signs are so contradictory. I have even wondered whether there has been any theft at all!"

Lucius gaped at him.

"But would the Emperor himself have employed you to find out about it if – if there had *not* been anything stolen?" he asked.

"It could be possible: he might himself be deceived," said Sollius, musingly, still gazing down into the pool. "There are so many rumours," he muttered under his breath, "about the debts of the young Commodus – and his mother has always spoilt him."

"When you say that the signs are contradictory, what," asked Lucius, "do you mean?"

"I mean," Sollius replied, "that I saw no scratches about the small keyhole of the casket; that I saw no marks beneath the Empress's apartment; that Marcia was more puzzled than afraid, when I should have expected her to be more afraid than puzzled; and that I felt Alexias was, as it were, playing a part, as if he thought that my intrusion into the mystery was unnecessary, but that he dared not tell the Emperor so. All this," he added, spreading out his hands so that they made a shadow fall across the water and disturbed the otherwise sleepy carp, "makes me wonder if I am being – deliberately misled. But, Lucius, I must question that Prætorian who was on guard on the evening of the supposed theft before I make up my mind about that word 'supposed.'"

He sighed, and then was silent for a while, staring down into the pool at his feet. Suddenly he spoke again, and more briskly:

"There is something that I want you to do for me, Lucius."

"What is that, Sollius?" asked Lucius, and his eyes brightened.

"I want you to mingle with the slaves in the money-changers' quarters. Find out from gossip whether any jewels have been pledged for security yesterday or to-day, or sold for any large sum, or – any gossip about a sudden appearance of jewels in unusual places."

"I can do that, Sollius," replied Lucius eagerly.

"Meanwhile I shall see that Prætorian," mused Sollius. "But I doubt – I really doubt – if I shall learn much from him."

He shook his head dubiously, and led the way back to the kitchen quarters.

"Go on your errand at once," he whispered. "I will make it right with Tuphus – or our master will, if I fail. Is not the Emperor behind it?"

Lucius grinned, and sped away.

Early, as promised, Sollius hastened to the palace next morning, and asked for Alexias. He was taken to a small, bare room, somewhat away from the imperial apartments, and lit only by a pale, dusty light that filtered through a grating. It was like a guardroom, except that its appointments were domestic rather than military. He was left there alone for quite a long time, and was beginning to feel impatient, and even a little angry, when Alexias hurried in with a scared face.

"He has disappeared!" he whispered hollowly. "I went for him myself, but he was not in his quarters. He has disappeared," he repeated, "just as if he were a deserter. Nobody can understand it. Nobody!"

"Has the Emperor been told?" asked Sollius, plucking at his lips.

"It is not a nice report to make," answered Alexias, and gestured impotently.

Then his face brightened as he produced a scroll from somewhere about him.

"But I have the list of the missing jewels," he said.

Sollius brushed it aside, and the Emperor's freedman stared.

"But you asked for it?" he stammered.

"I know," said Sollius. "I may need it – or may not. But the disappearance of this Prætorian changes the order of my plans. The sooner he is found, whether alive or dead – "

"Dead?" cried Alexias in horror. "Do you think *that*?"

"I fear it," replied Sollius. "Have you seen the man's centurion?"

"He knows nothing."

"You mean that he *says* he knows nothing," answered Sollius. "Bring him here," he ordered abruptly.

The freedman drew himself up, but meeting Sollius's eye, he shrugged his shoulders.

"As you will," he said stiffly. "We have the Emperor's command to obey you."

He turned quickly, and left the slave once again alone. Sollius stood perfectly still, and closed his eyes. He did not open them until he heard the rustle of metal as the centurion was brought in by Alexias. Then he fixed the man with a deep stare.

"Your name?" he asked.

"Decius," answered the centurion sullenly.

He seemed to have come unwillingly and to resent any interrogation by a slave. He stood rigidly, one hand on the brazen hilt of his short stabbing-sword.

"What is the name of this missing soldier?" pursued Sollius.

"Constans."

"When did you last see him?"

"Last night – in a tavern."

"Was he drunk?"

"Constans had a strong head," answered Decius, and would have laughed if he had not remembered that his questioner was a slave. He stood more rigidly than ever.

"Did you leave him in the tavern, or did he come away with you?"

"I said I saw him last *in* a tavern – not going to it, nor coming from it," replied Decius.

"You did not part from him at the tavern door – in the street?"

"I left him with a girl on his knee," said Decius gruffly.

"Which tavern was it?"

"*The Two Cranes*, in the Subura," answered the centurion without hesitation.

Sollius rubbed his chin while he thought briefly.

"And you have no idea at all what has happened to him?" he asked.

"I know less about it than about the Emperor's philosophy," replied the still sullen centurion, yet with a fugitive touch of contemptuous humour, nevertheless, for he was beginning to thaw a little under the slave's quiet and assured manner.

"Has anybody been sent to that tavern to make enquiries?" asked Sollius.

"The tribune sent," was the answer.

"With no result?"

"With no result!"

"Did nobody there remember his leaving?"

"Nobody," answered Decius. "At least," he added, a little less surlily, "nobody was willing to admit to remembering anything."

"Ah-h!" breathed Sollius. "Has this tavern a good reputation?"

"It is in the Subura," answered the centurion with a meaning shrug.

"Even the worst district of Rome," said the slave, "can have one decent tavern in it!"

"Then your experience is different from mine," replied Decius, and this time he laughed outright.

He had a clear-cut, honest face, thought Sollius, looking at him with a newly probing gaze. Suddenly he made up his mind.

"Come, centurion, we will go there now, you and I, together."

"Softly, slave!" cried Decius. "Who are you to give me orders? I have answered your questions because Alexias told me to answer 'em, and Alexias is the Emperor's own servant. But this is another matter. What'll my tribune say? A soldier – and a Prætorian, mind you! – can only take orders from his own officers."

"That is all right," said Sollius quietly. "Alexias will tell you that in this matter my orders are as good as the Emperor's own."

"What, slave!" burst out Decius.

"Quietly," said Alexias, and touched the centurion's arm. "It is as he says. He has the Emperor's authority for what he is doing. Go with him. I will explain to your tribune."

"Castor and Pollux flay me!" cried Decius. "This is a pretty thing: a centurion of the Prætorians to take orders from a slave!"

Nevertheless, in spite of his bluster, for once it was so, and he and Sollius presently departed on their errand side by side, the upright, marching Prætorian, and the fattish, shuffling slave making a comical enough sight for those who passed by them in the narrow, tortuous and crowded streets.

The thoroughfares of Rome were inordinately dirty and noisy, and those who walked had a bad time of it, being continually pushed to the walls by the litters of the important or the wealthy, borne by running slaves, generally of huge stature, negroes or Cappadocians being the favourites for that kind of work. All Rome was dirty, tortuous, unsavoury and crowded, but no quarter was as bad in all those respects as the infamous Subura, the haunt and kennel of the worst elements of the population. Sollius knew it well, but he never entered it without the utmost distaste. The inns and hovels were little better than thieves' dens, and worse; every kind of rascality and vice was at home; it stank both physically and morally.

The centurion led the way down an evil-smelling byway between high walls that leant crookedly towards one another like two drunken men seeking to hold each other up, yet never managing to make actual contact in their swaying towards one another for support.

Though the day itself was bright, the byway was so dark that Sollius frequently stumbled over the uneven cobbles, slippery with all kinds of nauseous garbage.

The two had uttered no word during their journey. But it would have been difficult to have conversed amid such constant jostling and noise; and now, in that quieter spot, the centurion cleared his throat, spat and spoke:

"We are nearly there, O slave. The open doorway at the end, see?"

It was more like the entrance to a dark cave than the door of a supposedly inviting tavern, and was no advertisement of its pleasures. Indeed, thought Sollius, it needed courage to enter at all. At night it would be even more daunting to a timid man, though, no doubt, there would be a torch in the iron sconce at the side of the entrance.

"I'll see you come to no harm," grunted the centurion through the side of his mouth as if he had read his companion's thoughts.

He plunged into the darkest recesses of the alley with the familiarity of frequent experience, and was about to enter into the black mouth of the doorway when a man, rushing out as in a violent hurry, thrust him against the wall, and was gone before either he or Sollius could catch at him and hold him. They could hear his sandals slapping against the cobbles as he sped away down other thoroughfares, and then the noise was swallowed up in the greater noises round and about.

The centurion grunted angrily, and then entered the tavern without further hindrance. Sollius followed at his heels. It was lighter inside than the slave had expected, for two or three clay lamps were diffusing a pale light in an inner room. But the immediate entrance, a smaller room like a vestibule, was both dark and empty. The whole place smelt of rancid oil, sour wine, stale vegetables and fetid odours of every conceivable variety of dirt and corruption. Sollius sniffed audibly.

"You're too dainty!" muttered Decius as he led the way through towards the inner room.

But Sollius had not been savouring the unpleasant layers of dead air about him, but was trying to remember where he had smelt before the perfume which had come from the garments of the man who had rushed out past them. And then he knew. It had been in the bedchamber of the Empress. His mind suddenly grew wary. They should have stopped that running man!

He gave a swift glance about him as they entered the inner room. It had benches about the walls; winecasks at one end, in a kind of bricked, recessed tunnel, too small to be termed a cellar, yet serving something of the same purpose; and stools, some still lying where they had fallen the previous night, and others disposed about conveniently for those drinking. At the moment, however, only two occupants faced the centurion and Sollius as they entered, the tavern-keeper himself and a flute-boy, the latter very pale, puffed under the eyes, and drowsy. A flight of shallow stone steps led to an upper floor. They were festooned with cobwebs and covered with dust and dirt. The whole place seemed never to have been swept or cleaned since it had been built, perhaps over a hundred years before.

"What d'ye want?" asked the tavern-keeper, glowering through the dim light.

"You're to answer some questions," replied the centurion brusquely, "and mind you tell us no lies."

"I've been badgered with questions for hours," growled the other. "I know nothing. Your comrade strode out o' that doorway as well as he entered through it – or nearly as well," he added with a truculent leer. "I won't say as he wasn't drunk."

"Who helped him out?" asked Sollius.

"And who are *you* to be asking that or any other question?" demanded the tavern-keeper.

"I am his uncle," answered Sollius, lying glibly, "and his mother, my sister, lies dying. He must be fetched home. Cannot you help us at all?"

His voice was pitched just in the right key, neither wheedling nor exacting, but anxiously pleading. The centurion stared sidelong at him with a new appreciation of his parts.

"If I had nothing to tell a Prætorian officer," grunted the tavern-keeper, "am I like to have anything to tell a fat rascal like you who couldn't even pay me for a blind man's wink?"

"Even a blind man's wink," laughed Sollius, "might tell me what he had heard with his ears!"

"I heard nothing; I saw nothing; I know nothing," said the other, and his tone had finality. "D'ye think I'm such a fool as not to be able to sell any kind o' knowledge to a good bidder? Or not to save my skin if I had knowledge when a Prætorian officer came sniffing around with a meddling nose? I heard nothing; I saw nothing; I know nothing," he repeated, and spat without caring where.

"There was no brawl?" went on Sollius doggedly.

"There's always a brawl!" leered the other. "That's life: drink and brawling. Men are men in the Subura."

"There was a girl – " suggested Sollius.

"He had no money," answered the tavern-keeper shortly. "She wasn't on his knee long, I can tell you that. I don't allow it – when there's no money. But why this fuss over a missing soldier?" he asked with lowered brows, suspiciously. "What's he been doing? Threatening the life of the Emperor? Or teaching young Commodus evil manners? But any teacher o' such 'ud soon end by being the pupil o' that young lad, prince as he may be, and dainty brought up! I wonder his father lets him out of his eye. I'd keep him well watched, *I* would – or send him to one o' the frontiers to learn war."

"Peace, rascal!" cried the centurion. "D'ye want a whipping after I've made my report?"

"I'm only saying what everybody is saying," growled the tavern-keeper, and made a lewd gesture. "The Emperor is too good for such dogs. Good men don't see all as they ought to see, and there's a lot in Rome that needs looking at – though I hope it won't be in *my* time," he added with a salacious grin. "I've my living to get!"

Sollius could bear the fetid atmosphere no longer, and he was convinced by now that the tavern-keeper really knew nothing. He turned.

"Come," he said brusquely over his shoulder to the centurion. "There is nothing to learn here."

He stumbled out through the dark outer room and so to the alley outside. As soon as they were a little distance down this, he laid a hand on the centurion's arm, and whispered urgently:

"Go back, and fetch out that fluteboy!"

Decius stared, but seeing the expression on Sollius's face, he bit back the sarcastic retort which he had intended to make, turned smartly on his heel and re-entered the tavern. He was out again with the flute-boy before Sollius had reached the corner where the alley debouched into the crowded and wider way. The fluteboy appeared terrified. The centurion held him firmly by an arm.

"Come with us," said Sollius, and his voice was kindly. "We mean you no harm."

"What do you want?" stammered the boy. "I have done nothing. I'm a good boy. Everybody round here will give me a good name."

"Nobody round here could give anybody a good name!" answered Sollius a little primly. "Don't let go of him, centurion."

"Where are you taking me?" whimpered the boy.

"We can't talk in this noisy bustle," replied the slave, and he led the way, with the centurion still grasping the flute-boy by the arm, at his heels.

He did not lead them to the imperial palace, but to the house of Titius

Sabinus, his master. There he took them to the same walled enclosure behind the chariot-house where he had talked with Lucius.

"We can be private here," he said.

It was certainly very quiet, there by the carp-pool.

"Tell me," Sollius began, "who it was that hurriedly left as we entered the tavern where you play your flute."

The boy was shaking with fear, and could hardly stammer out: "He had b-been there all n-night."

"You have seen him in the tavern before?"

"Once or twice – lately. What are you w-wanting of me?"

"Only true answers to my questions," replied Sollius softly, "and then you can go back as quickly as you can run. Do you know his name?"

The flute-boy shook his head.

"He is a rich young man," he said, "but no one mentions his name."

"Have you seen him close – under the lamp? Does he wear a great deal of jewellery: rings and gold chains and so on?"

"He wouldn't in the Subura!" muttered the centurion. "Or not for long!"

"Answer me, flute-boy!"

"Not that I have seen. Myrtis says – "

"Who is Myrtis?"

"One of the girls in the house. I play for their dances."

"Go on."

"Myrtis says he is a gladiator. But – "

"Go on."

"I don't suppose she really knows. She is always telling lies."

At that moment Lucius joined them.

"I heard you had returned, Sollius," he said, "and Tuphus said you had come this way."

Sollius took his arm, and they walked to the other side of the carp-pool out of hearing of the others.

"What have you found out?" he asked in a lowered voice.

"Nothing, Sollius. No jewels in any quantity have been sold or pledged just lately."

"Not by – the Empress's son?"

Lucius started, and then looked scared.

"I did hear something about him," he whispered. "He is in great debt and seeking a loan."

Sollius rubbed his chin.

"Then no jewels have been – ahem! – abstracted for *his* benefit," he muttered in a muse, "so everything hangs upon finding that lost

Prætorian. Ah, you won't have heard about that," he added, and gave a brief account of his own researches that morning. "The flute-boy, after all, knows nothing. I am disappointed. I had expected more from him. I think it very likely that the man who brushed past us was a gladiator, as Myrtis says. Even his scentedness is a confirmation."

"A *scented* gladiator?" exclaimed Lucius. "But they are such tough men – they have to be!"

"Many of them," answered Sollius dryly, "are ladies' favourites. But that is a different matter."

He broke off with an impatient gesture, and led the way back to the centurion and the flute-boy.

"You can go," he said to the latter with a smile, and clapped him on the back. "Take him into the kitchen," he directed Lucius, "and wheedle Tuphus into giving him some aniseed cakes."

Lucius took the flute-boy away.

"A further question or two, my friend, and you can go, too," said Sollius to the centurion.

Decius mumbled under his breath, but appeared ready to answer, nevertheless.

"Had this missing Constans relatives in Rome?"

"A mother and an elder brother, a cobbler. Neither has heard of him. I was sent myself to find out."

Sollius frowned, and once more rubbed his chin.

"Had he any special interest in life outside his being a soldier?" he asked after pondering silently for a while.

"Drinking and girls: I know of naught else," answered the centurion bluntly and a little sourly.

"What was his character – as a soldier?"

"As a soldier? He wouldn't be one of *us*," said the centurion of the Prætorians proudly, "if he hadn't a good name and a clean tablet in records."

"Desertion has been hinted," suggested Sollius.

"No Prætorian ever deserts!" roundly asserted the other. "The pickings are too good!"

"I know you are the most privileged troops in the Empire," said Sollius placatingly. "But I am sure that you can tell me something that I ought to know – something that, perhaps, you don't realize that you know yourself. Think for a moment quietly. Look at the carp there as you think; their quiet swimming about will help to compose your mind. I have often found it useful in that way. And then speak the first thing about this Constans which enters your thoughts, no matter how trivial or how silly it may seem – just the first thing that enters your head, centurion."

Decius did as he was told, staring down at the carp in puckered concentration. Suddenly he began to laugh.

"What is it? What have you remembered?" cried Sollius eagerly.

"It was nothing, nothing at all," replied Decius, still laughing, "but it was funny at the time. We all laughed about it. Anyway, he got a gold piece from the Emperor for it, and the promise of a gardener's job when his service days are over. We've nicknamed him 'the gardener,' though I've never seen him dig in our camp garden all the while I've been stationed in Rome, and that is many years now, slave."

"Why did the Emperor give him a gold piece? Go on, go on!" urged Sollius impatiently.

"It was this way," answered the centurion leisurely, and laughing and smiling as he talked. "It was the Empress's birthday, and we were paraded in her honour. We had a rose issued to each of us, and we were ordered in the march past to throw our roses in a heap at her feet, each file in turn. Constans had had a thick night at a tavern, and had come on parade without breaking his fast, but with a bunch of radishes hid in his tunic to chew while standing at ease before the Augusta's arrival. We always have to parade hours before time! Well, somehow, after the roses had been issued to us and fastened in our helmets, Constans had the ill luck to drop his and lose it during a bit o' drill we were put through to fill out the time. It was a real bit of evil luck, for he would be on the outside of his file as it marched past the Emperor and Empress, and it would have been seen that he had nothing to throw on the heap. Had he been on the inside it might have passed unnoticed, though an officer *was* level with the rank behind. However, there it was, and without his rose he was in a fair sweat, I can tell you. When the time came, what else could he do but fling down his bunch o' radishes? Large 'uns, they were, too! Quite like prize ones! With luck, in such a shower o' roses, they'd not have been noticed. But Constans was never a lucky man. We often say he's the victim o' the evil eye! Anyhow, the Empress saw it. Sharp eyes, as well as beautiful ones, has the Empress! And she whispered to the Emperor. After the parade Constans was summoned to the Empress's footstool, and accused o' being disrespectful and unsoldierly. He was like to be whipped, but he always had a tongue in his head, had Constans, and the cheekiness of a British gooseboy. I have served in Britain, and know! Well, he got out of it. Said they were his own growing. Said he thought it more of a real homage to the Empress to give her something of his own, and not a mere flower provided by the Senate! The Emperor laughed, and the Empress – though I don't think that at first she had meant to be kind about it – took a look at the Emperor's face – and fetched up a smile. All was safely over – and then the Emperor made his promise to take Constans on as a gardener when his time of service should be up. And he no gardener at all! Laugh! That night the whole barracks was one roar! Well, that's all – and it can't have anything to do with his disappearance now. It was over a year ago."

"Thank you for telling me," said Sollius quietly. "Thank you, too, for taking me to *The Two Cranes*. I'd not like to go there alone. I think that is all I want of you."

"Then I'll go back to barracks," answered the centurion. "It's been better than drilling, anyway, even if it has been o' no use. If you want to know what *I* think, Constans is in the Tiber with some woman's husband's knife in him. Why there's such a fuss about him is what puzzles *me*."

He nodded, and marched away, whistling.

Lucius found Sollius still standing by the carp-pool.

"The flute-boy has gone," he said.

Sollius did not answer.

"Have you discovered anything?" asked Lucius after a pause.

Sollius sighed.

"I am not sure," he answered, and his face was grave and unhappy. "I do not like being – deceived. And I can see only deception, whichever way I look."

Lucius stared at him.

"I don't understand," he said.

"Neither do I," answered Sollius ruefully. "Is our master within?"

Lucius nodded.

Sollius went indoors, sought out the Senator his master, and put a single question.

"Why, yes," replied Sabinus. "It is about three miles out along the Appian Way. I have had the honour of visiting there myself. How are your investigations getting on?" he asked anxiously. "It was on my recommendation that the Emperor is employing you in this matter, and I should not like you to – fail," he whispered.

He looked at the slave questioningly, but Sollius did not respond in the confidential way that the Senator had expected.

"I have discovered hardly anything," murmured Sollius. "But a swallow can smell spring ahead before he begins flying home from Africa!"

Sabinus dismissed him almost irritably.

"I am going to the Augustus's palace, Lucius," announced Sollius in the early evening of the same day. "I wish to ask Alexias one more question."

The house of Sabinus stood in its own grounds, with extensive gardens, and the way from the house itself to the gates was long, winding and overshadowed by chestnut trees. It was growing dusk, and the sky was already filled with the first stars. Nearer the gates the trees were more crowded and the darkness more complete. Sollius strode on through the shadowy avenue in a deep muse. He was both sure and puzzled.

Something like a large corn-sack was suddenly and swiftly drawn over his head; his legs were knocked from under him; and then his hands were roped behind him, and his ankles were bound together at the same time. Evidently his assailants were two in number. And now, one taking his shoulders and the other his feet, he was carried away, half-smothered in the sack, he knew not whither.

He had not struggled with his captors, for he was not a man of violence. Except for being startled at first, he was not frightened. He was, in fact, intensely curious, eager to know what would happen next, for he knew that his abduction must have some connection with what he was investigating. He felt, too, that if they had been going to kill him they would have done so straightway.

They did not carry him very far, but transferred him to a vehicle of some sort, drawn either, he judged from the sounds, by a pair of horses or mules. Probably, he guessed from the creaking noise of four wooden wheels, it was some kind of a farmcart.

In this he was taken a considerable distance, but in what direction he had no means of telling. The cart was hooded, he judged, for all outside sounds seemed muffled – and by more than the sack over his head – even the voices of the driver and his companion. It was now quite dark, not only within the vehicle, but in the open air and the countryside through which they were passing. It must have been quite late at night when the cart suddenly stopped to the furious barking of watchdogs and the rattling of their chains in the kennels. He recognized the peculiar bark of one of them. It was, surely, a Gallic hound. Sabinus possessed one, which had been the gift of the Emperor himself. He was glad that none of the dogs was loose. To have him torn to pieces might be a good way to dispose of him with all the appearance of accident, and very unpleasant, indeed! But the longer he had thought – and he had had plenty of time for cogitation – the more sure he had become that no real violence was intended.

He was lifted out of the vehicle in the same manner that he had been lifted in, and carried into what seemed to be one of the outhouses of a farm. The corn-sack was taken from his head as he was laid against one of the mud walls, but neither his feet nor his hands were untied. A single clay lamp on the floor in one corner dimly lit the place. A number of spades and other agricultural implements were lying about, and he thought that his guess was probably correct, and that he was in an outbuilding of a farm, or perhaps of a country villa. He looked at the two men who had abducted him, and recognized neither; but he had not expected to recognize them. The dogs were still barking.

"Dost thou know why thou'st been brought here?" asked one of the men in a harsh, truculent voice.

"I think so," quietly answered Sollius, blinking in the light of the lamp which the other man had taken up and was now holding close to the prisoner's eyes. Sollius noticed that this second man was tall, lean and very straight of back.

"Thou'dst be a fool if not!" snarled the first man. "We have orders to tell thee to stop looking for the thief o' – thou knowest what as well as I do."

As he spoke he showed what he was holding in his hand: a short length of thin, knotted strangler's cord.

"Well, thou seest, slave? And understandest?"

The other man straightened himself, and laughed.

"Thou canst not escape," he said, and put down the lamp on a dusty tool-bench nearby.

Sollius looked at him.

"You, of course, are Constans," he said.

"Oho!" laughed the Prætorian, in no way disconcerted. "Thou'rt a sharp one!"

He seemed more good-humoured than his fellow, who was scowling, thought Sollius, in a very horrible manner. How far would they go in torturing him? He wondered if what he had come to guess could really be right! If it was, he could laugh at the proceedings; if not, he was in a most miserable and fearful position – and might never know the truth. To die without knowing all about the affair shook his equanimity in prospect more than the actual danger in which he stood.

It was Constans who finally menaced him with a woodcutter's axe, swinging it above his head, all his outward good-humour gone in a flash as his companion rasped out:

"A dead guesser can't guess – right. But it might save your life – to guess wrong."

"Dost hear, slave?" asked Constans, the axe still poised in air.

"What dost thou know?" demanded the other, fingering the knotted length of cord.

"Answer, slave!" said the Prætorian in a hissing whisper.

"I can tell what I know only to the Emperor," answered Sollius, and hoped that his voice sounded firm.

"Leave the Emperor out of this!" said the man with the strangler's cord.

"It is the Emperor's business," replied Sollius. "How, then, can I leave him out? I shall tell you nothing," he added with as much show of courage as he could imitate, and even then he did not know whether he had cause for his worst fears – or not. Well, he had to test it, the one way or the other. "You can kill me," he said huskily, "but you won't get a word out of me. And you must not be too sure," he added, blinking up at them, "that I have anything to tell."

"Anything or nothing, our orders are the same," said the man with the cord, and glanced at his companion.

Constans lowered the axe, and gave Sollius a nicely calculated blow with a chopping fist, and the slave knew no more.

When he came to himself, he found that he was lying near the gates of his master's house, with Lucius bending anxiously over him, and two others of his fellow slaves standing by. It was still night.

"What happened, Sollius?"

"That," replied Sollius ruefully, "is *my* question, not yours!"

"We heard a cry," said Lucius, "and found you unconscious on the ground here."

"It wasn't *my* cry," muttered Sollius.

"That is all we know."

"It was a signal – to fetch you out," whispered Sollius.

"Who attacked you?" asked one of the others.

"Help me up," murmured Sollius.

They led him into the slaves' quarters of the house, and attended to his bruises. He had more than one. He felt dizzy, and his head, neck and jaw ached most painfully. He was undressed and laid in his bed. Lucius watched over his uneasy slumbers until morning. It was not a long watch.

Sabinus, who had been informed of the "accident" to his favourite slave, came to see him with the first light.

"How did it happen, my good Sollius?" he asked.

Sollius answered with great care:

"I do not remember very much about it, lord. I was – thinking – and walking near the gates, and was suddenly attacked – and

I remember nothing more until I was found by Lucius and the others."

Sabinus rose from the stool on which he had been sitting, tiptoed to the door, and looked along the corridor outside the slaves' dormitory with exaggerated caution. Then he returned, and speaking in a whisper, said:

"You have discovered something, then, my good Sollius? The thief tried to silence you? Excellent! You must tell the Emperor to-day."

"Indeed, lord," replied Sollius weakly, "I had intended to ask for an audience to-day. I have not told you everything – but on second thoughts, lord, I will. I was more than just attacked," he went on, his voice gathering strength as he related the rest. "I was abducted, too."

Sabinus, after he had heard the whole of his slave's adventures, rubbed his hands.

"Excellent, Sollius, excellent!" he cried, beaming. "You are clearly on the right track. I am well pleased with you! I will myself accompany you to the Augustus."

Marcus Aurelius received them again in his small, plainly furnished, private chamber, filled with innumerable books and scrolls and scroll containers. There were just the four of them: the Emperor, Sabinus, Alexias and Sollius.

"You say," said the Emperor, a slight smile on the lips under his beard, "that you have discovered the thief of the Empress's jewels. This is quick work, Sabinus!"

The Senator, in a fluster of pleasure and self-satisfaction, bowed. He might have spoken had the Emperor given him the opportunity, but Marcus Aurelius, used to quelling the loquacity of senators, immediately addressed Sollius again:

"Have you the jewels?"

"No, sir," answered Sollius.

The Emperor frowned.

"But you know the thief?"

Sollius hesitated briefly, and then answered:

"If, O Augustus, I may set out what I take to be the circumstances, I think that you yourself will be able to name – the culprit."

"I shall be interested in every word you say," replied the Emperor. "Let me hear!"

"I have had many suspicions," Sollius began, "chasing one after the other like a dog after many hares. First, I suspected Marcia, the Augusta's waiting-woman, but there were no true signs pointing to her, and both she and Alexias seemed so genuinely puzzled – I had toyed with the idea of both of them being in league. I soon dismissed both from the case; but I had to consider them."

He glanced apologetically at the Emperor's Greek freedman, but received only a glare in response. He sighed, and went on:

"Have I your pardon, Augustus, for aught I may say? You have commanded me to tell you everything, yet if I do – "

He spread out his hands.

"Offence may come!" he whispered.

"I am no Caligula or Nero," replied Marcus Aurelius gravely. "Tell me everything you had in mind."

"Sir, I wondered whether the Empress herself might not have – secretly sold them."

"The Empress – sold them!" exclaimed Marcus Aurelius incredulously.

"For the money," pursued Sollius quietly.

"But the Empress," said Faustina's husband, "has no need of money."

"Perhaps," Sollius suggested in a lower tone, "to pay some debt of Prince Commodus."

The Emperor frowned.

"But I have just this morning paid his debts myself," he said in a voice of half-angry distaste.

"I am only relating my suspicions, O Augustus, in the order of their crossing my mind. I found out that I was certainly wrong in this one."

"Found out? How?" questioned the Emperor, very seriously.

"I had enquiries made in the quarter of the money-changers," the slave answered. "But no jewels had recently been offered for sale, or pledged, and Prince Commodus had been seeking a loan – before this morning, Augustus! – so no jewels had been sold for his benefit. And when the Prætorian was missing I was all the more certain of the Augusta's innocence. It was, in fact, the disappearance of the Prætorian which set me upon the right way. For, sir, a Prætorian does not 'disappear' – discipline in the Guards is too strong. But had he been murdered – because he knew something that it would be fatal to the thief for me to discover? Yet, had he been murdered, his body should have been found, probably near the tavern of *The Two Cranes* in the Subura. But it is clear that he left there, at least, safely. I decided that he had not been killed, but just – removed out of my way. That brought back into my mind the lack of evidence that there was concerning a theft at all."

He paused, and gave the Emperor a direct look.

"The jewels, after all," the Emperor quietly reminded him, "were missing from the Empress's casket."

"Precisely, sir: missing – from the casket. But 'stolen' is another word. I looked over the ground outside the Augusta's chamber, but saw no sign of any intruder. An intruder into that secret part of the imperial gardens would need wings to drop from Heaven: he could not go thither on his feet. It was the print of feet, and any other kind of visible disturbance, that I could not find. I decided against a thief entering from the gardens, O Augustus. And then the Prætorian was missing. At first, I did not understand that, and suspected, indeed, that he had been killed; but when I visited the tavern in the Subura where he had last been seen, I found no sign of anything like murder. I concluded that whatever had happened to him had taken place after he had left the tavern and not in the tavern itself. I saw a scented gladiator there – but suspected other matters, none relative to the missing man. But, sir, a scented gladiator is himself a cause for enquiry."

He gave the Emperor another deep glance, wondering the while how much, or how little, that august personage knew of the fearful rumours concerning his wife. He guessed that any clever woman could outwit that noble character, so philosophical in temper, so simple of heart. But Marcus Aurelius gave no sign of inward disturbance.

"Go on," was all he said.

The three listeners hung on the slave's every word, spellbound by what he was telling: Sabinus, smilingly proud of being his master; Alexias deeply puzzled and beginning to prick with unknown fears; the Emperor enigmatically calm.

"Then," continued Sollius, still fixing the Emperor with his gaze, "I was set upon. I expected to be slain out of hand. But I was not slain; I was abducted; I expected to be tortured to tell all that I knew, but I was not tortured, only threatened. Then I was knocked out skilfully – and returned where I was taken. There seemed no purpose in it unless it was to frighten me. I *was* frightened, of course. I am only an elderly slave, not a man of war or adventure. But when I came to no serious harm, I began to think again over all my scraps of evidence. One of the men who had abducted me was the missing Prætorian. Who could have employed *him*, except one whom he would obey without question? His companion, too, I recognized, though not at first: he is one of a troupe of actors. You, O Augustus, have shown him favour for his playing in Plautus."

"It does sound like a prank of Sicinius Malvus," said the Emperor with a smile.

"Then," pursued Sollius, "I recognized the kind of bark peculiar to a breed of hound among the many barkings at the farm to which they had taken me. It was the bark of a Gallic hound. There are few of them in Rome. My master has one, a gracious present from yourself, Augustus. Previously, as he will bear witness, I asked my master a question. He answered that a certain small, private villa and farm lay off the Appian Way about three miles out. I guessed that it was thither that I had been taken – and where else could the Prætorian have been so well hidden? When I came to myself, safely back at my master's gates, I knew the truth. It is that truth, sir, which I am waiting for you to command me to tell."

"Do you need my 'command' to tell it to me?" asked Marcus Aurelius, stroking his beard.

"I dare not tell it without, O Augustus," answered Sollius.

The Emperor rose, crossed the chamber to a recess containing some marble shelves upon which stood a number of circular, silver containers of scrolls and rolled books. Bringing one back with him, he returned to his former place, and tipped its contents on to a small, round, marble table in front of him. The missing jewels poured out in a glittering cascade of rainbow-coloured beauty.

"I took them with the Empress's permission," he said, smiling, "to make a test of your powers, Sollius, before I employed you in a more serious matter. I seem to have deceived you very ill! I hope that Malvus and Constans were not too rough with you. But I had to test your courage as well as your wits. I am satisfied. Sabinus, will you lend me this clever slave for as long as I need his quick brain?"

"Ah, Augustus," cried Sabinus, bowing and self-important – it might have been he who had unravelled the little mystery and not Sollius! – "all that I have is at your command."

"But I ask only for your Sollius," laughed the Emperor. "I have great need of him. If you will leave him behind you, Sabinus, I will tell him, now, at once, everything that is known about these thefts from the Treasury, and then he can set to work on a real mystery!"

## EPISODE II
## THE TREASURY THEFTS

The vaults under the ancient Temple of Saturn, which housed the imperial treasury at Rome, were vast, dark, and very like those of a prison. Sollius shuddered involuntarily as he was led down into

them, though he was there at the Emperor's command to investigate
the thefts which had so mysteriously been taking place, and though
he was in the company, and under the protection, of Alexias,
the Emperor's favourite freedman, and of Decius, a centurion of
the Prætorians, who had been assigned as his official bodyguard
during his enquiries. He had himself asked for Decius, whom he had
met when looking for the supposedly stolen jewels of the Empress
Faustina, and to whom he had taken a liking, though he was aware
that the man regarded him with a superior and only half-tolerant
contempt. Sollius sighed; to the centurion, he knew, he was only an
elderly slave. At the moment, however, the Emperor's commission
had given him a certain authority to which even the Prætorian would
have to bow – and the treasury officials no less.

Gennadius, the chief clerk to the treasury, was accompanying them, a middle-aged, burly man, though somewhat round-
shouldered from his avocation. He was of full citizenship, being the
son of a freedman, and an official and civil servant of long standing,
proud of his position, haughty and pompous to his inferiors, but
servile enough where servility might possibly advantage him.

Sollius and he had exchanged searching glances on their introduction by Alexias, and if the chief clerk had made less of the
slave than the slave of the chief clerk, that was only because the
men possessed different attributes. Each in his sphere was probably
equally clever, and that at least was spontaneously recognized by
both. Sollius had eyed the other a second time, while Gennadius
and Alexias had whispered for a moment or so apart, and he had
wondered whether behind the mask of departmental acquiescence
in the slave's investigations there had been any touch of personal
apprehension. But he had seen nothing in the man's face or manner
to suggest it.

Gennadius broke off his brief whispering with Alexias, and
turned more graciously to the slave detective than when he had
first greeted him.

"I hear much praise of you," he said "But the Emperor, I
suppose," he went on smilingly, "would not employ you in this
most important task if you were not the right man for it. Come!"

So saying, he had led the way down worn and winding steps into
the vast, underground passages. Decius the centurion was carrying
a torch, by the flaring light of which their descent was sufficiently
illuminated.

"Ask whatever you will," said Gennadius, "and I will answer
with truth."

He was still gracious towards the slave, and evidently filled with more curiosity than his habitual pompous pride could easily keep subdued.

They came to an iron grille which sealed off a huge section of the temple's vaults. Its inset gate was both locked and chained. This Gennadius importantly opened, and a stridence of harsh, unoiled metal echoed hollowly about; then, as soon as all had passed through, he relocked and rechained it with the same ceremony.

"We oil the lock and the hinges but rarely," he said, turning to Sollius. "It cannot, as you heard, be opened silently – and therefore not secretly. You approve of my simple precaution?"

Sollius bowed without speaking. His eyes were beginning to be busy. One fact he had already noted: the key to the gate was itself chained to the person of the chief clerk.

"Does the key ever leave your possession?" he asked abruptly. "Who has it when you sleep?"

Gennadius smiled complacently, and answered as though to a child. Many spoke to Sollius as though to a child – and repented of it afterwards.

"No one unlocks this gate but myself," he answered. "I have no deputy. At night the key hangs in my chamber on a nail at the head of my couch. It could not be reached without waking me."

("Unless," thought Sollius, "you were drugged in your drink at supper!")

"And when you go on leave?" he enquired aloud.

"Then I hand it to the Emperor himself, and he appoints a guardian for it. But I have not been on leave during the period of the thefts," replied Gennadius, as if pleased at being able to make the task of Sollius more and more difficult. "This way," he went on, and led them down a passage which dripped with moisture in both roof and walls. But the chamber into which finally they passed was itself dry enough and of considerable extent. It was, thought Sollius, like a great wine-cellar, with deep bins of bronze along three of its sides.

At one corner, within a small niche of dusty marble, stood a tutelary statuette in silver, but stained and tarnished from lack of proper care. It was a delicate work of art, and Sollius, in the lifted light of the torch, stared upon it with appreciation. He recognized it for a figure of the young, dead Verus, once the Emperor's much-loved colleague, though unworthy of his affection.

"It was set yonder a year ago," commented Gennadius, "by the Augustus in person. As a tutelary image," he added, with a slight cough, "it has brought us but little luck!"

"Why set it here?" asked Sollius curiously.

"Verus loved jewels, and came here often to inspect the hoard of

centuries. We never left him alone with them," added Gennadius
with a dry smile. "It seemed right to the Augustus to make his dead
spirit their guardian."

Sollius smiled, and lost interest.

"You can set the torch in the iron ring yonder," Gennadius
directed the centurion.

So disposed, the torch illuminated the whole chamber with vivid
crimson, and there being no draught, the flame burned with a
calm glow.

"It is from here," announced Gennadius, "that the money and
jewels are missing. But I must explain. This is not the section of the
treasury in which the current money for the business of the State is
stored; it is hardly ever entered by way of business, and is really a
kind of museum of money, though the value of what is stored here
transcends that of the current coin of the Empire. This section holds
the tribute of subject peoples for generations; some of it even from
the days of the Republic. It is all, of course, negotiable; especially
the naked gold and the raw silver. I mean, the thief could sell at a
great profit what he has stolen."

"How great," asked Sollius, "do you reckon the loss to the treasury
from these thefts?"

Gennadius mentioned a sum so large that Sollius could scarcely
believe his ears, but he had no doubt of the truth of the statement. A
smaller sum would not so seriously have perturbed the philosophic
Emperor, and that Marcus Aurelius was seriously perturbed had
been very plain both in the accents of his voice and in the
troubled weariness of his heavily lidded eyes when giving Sollius
his instructions.

"How many thefts have there been?"

"As far as we know: two."

"How were they discovered?"

"We take a periodic inventory," answered Gennadius. "Each of
these bronze containers is filled with either gold, silver or jewels.
You can see for yourself at a glance. Some of the jewels are of
fabulous value. The third container on the wall to your left, and
the seventh on the wall to your right, are empty. The others are
full and untouched. When I came down to make the inventory two
months ago, I saw at once that a container – that on your left –
which had held a most valuable collection of eastern jewellery, some
of it said to be part of the spoils brought back to Rome by Pompeius
the Great, was empty. That was the first that we knew of any theft,
and when it had taken place we had no means of knowing. The lock
seemed not to have been forced, nor the chain broken; everything at

the grille was as it should have been. We could none of us understand it. But the jewels certainly had vanished."

"And the second theft?" asked Sollius. "You said, I think, that there have been two thefts?"

"That is so," responded the chief clerk. "The very next day, on descending to superintend the fixing of a new chain and a new lock, so that if a key had been made to fit the old lock it should be found useless by the thief, I went again to examine the empty container. On looking round, I discovered, to my utter consternation, that a second container – that on your right – was empty, too. It had held bars of Parthian gold. Not one was left!"

"And the lock and the chain were again apparently undisturbed?" asked Sollius.

"There was not a sign of the iron grille having been forced in any way," answered Gennadius, throwing up his hands. "It is an incredible thing!"

"It is one matter to break through the grille," murmured Sollius thoughtfully, "and it is another to carry the stuff away. The gold, at least, would be heavy."

"Very heavy," agreed Gennadius. "But the jewels would be fairly easily borne off in a sack – at most in two sacks."

"More than one man would seem to be necessary for either operation," said Sollius, stroking his chin, and Gennadius nodded.

"Yet we have nobody whom we can even suspect," the chief clerk muttered in accents of despair. "My assistants are picked men; I would charge none of them. I trust them all."

"Have any been recently appointed?" enquired the slave.

"Not one. All are old and well-tried officials," was the answer. "Responsibility calls for honest men, and honesty here is the very condition of service. It must be."

"Are there any outside servants who should be considered more carefully? Some new doorkeeper, or porter?" Sollius asked.

"All are trusty men – most of them former gladiators," replied Gennadius, "and each is of long service. It is really a complete mystery," he sighed. "I have done my best to unravel it. But when nothing points in any way to a possible culprit, where can we begin? I do not wish to discourage you – the gods forbid! – but I have little hope of your succeeding where I, and Alexias here, have so completely failed. Still, Alexias says that you astonished the Augustus by your astuteness in another matter, so I shall watch you with – ahem! – interest, intense and immense interest, Sollius. That is your name?"

Sollius wasted no time in answering an unnecessary question, but went across to each of the two empty bronze coffers – for such they were – and examined them briefly in turn.

"There is nothing for me here," he said with a sigh. "The cleverest hunter cannot follow a spoor that does not exist."

"You give up – so soon?" asked Gennadius, his mouth agape.

"Not so," replied Sollius, smiling, "but I must begin elsewhere. You all began here – and got nowhere. Had there been a clue in these vaults you would, I am sure, have found it. The clues, therefore, are not to be found where the jewels and gold were stolen, but in some other place. It is that other place which I must find, and then work backwards to establish the means, and forwards to discover the user of the means, the thief. Perhaps I shall travel in a circle, and forwards and backwards will meet."

He turned away, and strode back towards the grille. The centurion took the torch from the ring, and moved behind him like a shadow which itself cast another shadow, and Alexias and Gennadius, after exchanging puzzled and slightly contemptuous glances, followed. Arrived at the grille, Sollius paused while Gennadius began the business of unlocking and unchaining. Suddenly the slave snatched the torch from the Prætorian, and held it high above his head. The roof of the vault sent back wisps of reek and smoke, while the bars of the grille seemed to run drippingly with fiery blood as Sollius slowly waved the torch searchingly about along the grille's iron face. Then, with a grunt, he returned the torch to Decius, and the gate being now open, stepped through into the passage beyond.

"Tell me," he said to Gennadius, who had stepped through before him, "what are the formalities by which a man may reach as far as this grille? To pass beyond has its special difficulty, as I have seen; but how easy is it for one to reach to this side of it, even if not through to the other side?"

The chief clerk gave him a shrewd, approving glance.

"The treasury office is above, in the temple. The only way down to these vaults is by the steps by which we descended and are now returning. They are perpetually guarded by soldiers at the top, as you saw when we passed through their watch. The door to these passages is never left for an instant. It would need a full cohort to force a way down. But – "

He paused, looked about him, took Sollius by the arm, and led him aside.

"It is said – it is but rumour – that there is a secret way down to other vaults from behind the altar of the temple itself," he whispered. "I speak not of my own knowledge. If such a way exists, it will be known only to the priest of Saturn. Peace! – do not interrupt. As I was about to explain: this secret way down would still not lead *behind* the grille. There is no other way in to the vaults of the treasury except through the grille. Every inch of the walls has been most carefully examined."

"Has the priest of Saturn been interrogated?" asked Sollius.

"By the Emperor himself – to no purpose. He knows nothing."

"You mean: he says that he knows nothing."

"I would take whatever he says to be true," answered Gennadius. "He is an elderly and most reputable person, learned, and of high family. I freely admit as much, though I dislike him – for his pride. We are not on speaking terms."

"How many priests are there in the college of Saturn?" enquired Sollius without comment.

"But three," replied the other. "It is a merely perfunctory tradition nowadays, and the sacrifices are few. The temple's function to-day is chiefly that of Rome's treasury. But it is never advisable to break entirely with even the superstition of the past, for who knows what magic truth may still linger in the ancient forms that swayed men's minds for so long? The prevalent Stoicism, however, seems slowly to be killing priesthood, and all augury and divination with it."

"I should like to see this priest of Saturn," said Sollius.

"Alexias shall conduct you to him," agreed Gennadius, "for, as I said, he and I are not on speaking terms. His chamber is behind the hangings at the temple's western end."

"Show me but the way," said Sollius firmly, "and I will intrude upon him unannounced."

The other stared at him. He could not forget that Sollius was a slave. Yet the slave had the Emperor's authority to do as he would! Gennadius shrugged his shoulders, and when they were back again in the temple itself, he pointed to where some rich hangings were draped between two archaic pillars.

"Behind, you will see a small door," he said, and stood and watched the slave pass on down the temple's full length.

"What a strange fellow!" he murmured to Alexias. "Is he really as clever as you say?"

"Not as *I* say," replied Alexias, a little waspishly, "but as the Emperor, my friend, wishes to think."

"But what think *you* of him, O Alexias? That is what I wish to know. I have faith in your judgement of men."

"He is certainly very astute," answered Alexias cautiously, "but he has never before had so difficult a matter to solve, and I hold back my praises, Gennadius, until he has finally deserved them."

"How wise! How philosophic!" murmured the chief clerk with

every accent of admiration, though inwardly condemning the
Emperor's freedman for an empty time-server, in which opinion,
as he really knew when less irritated, he was unjust.

Decius, meanwhile, had stood like a military statue until relieved
of his torch by an attendant. He then strode a few paces in the wake
of the man whom he was supposed to protect, and when he saw him
disappear behind the hangings he remained there on guard.

The chamber of the priest of Saturn was furnished in the outworn
fashion of the days of Augustus. It was bare and austere. The man
seated on a folding ivory stool, reading a roll of ancient manuscript,
was at least seventy years of age, thin, pale, and aristocratic, with
long, compressed lips, a hawklike nose, and piercing dark eyes.
Sollius had entered without ceremony, announcing his presence
merely by a cough.

"Who are you? What do you want?" demanded the priest of
Saturn, looking up in surprise and displeasure.

Sollius explained who he was, and produced his credentials, a
small tablet of wax impressed with the private imperial seal.

"I have already been questioned by the Augustus himself," was
the haughty answer, "and have nothing to tell you."

"There is, I understand, a secret way from this part of the temple
into the vaults below," persisted Sollius.

"That is well and widely rumoured," said the priest with a faint
smile of condescension, "but not how to find it. That is passed
on from priest to priest, and is known only to them. I cannot
divulge it."

Sollius gave him a long glance.

"But there *is* such a way?" he asked finally.

"There is," replied the other. "But it does not lead to that part of
the vaults which houses Rome's treasure," he went on. "I can tell
you that."

"When did you yourself descend to the vaults last?" pursued
Sollius.

"Many years ago," answered the priest of Saturn with a flash
of scornful amusement in his eyes. "I am an old man; the steps
downward are not easy for the aged; also, there is nothing there
except darkness, damp, and empty chambers and passages. In the
days of the Republic it was different. The Temple of Saturn had
then a more important life. But now – "

He spread out his hands in a gesture of resignation.

"Have you visited the treasury vaults?" he asked.

"I have visited them," replied Sollius precisely.

"Did you find any indication of how they were entered or forced?"

"I can answer only the Augustus as to that," said Sollius.

The priest of Saturn smiled thinly.

"You are quite right; I should not have asked. Did you see the silver statuette of Verus? It is a pity that so lovely a thing is so tarnished. Had *he* been alive, I should know, at least, who *loved* jewels and gold beyond most men – not, I mean, for their value in money, but for their beauty – and you might not have had to seek . . . farther. But, of course, he is dead."

"Yes, he is dead," agreed Sollius dully, and then added with a flash of humour, "I do not really suspect him."

The other laughed, and Sollius bowed, and adroitly withdrew before the conversation could be prolonged, as he felt it would have been, uselessly.

He found the others waiting for him where he had left them, the centurion still as though on guard, and Gennadius and Alexias conversing in whispers. At that end of the temple there was considerable activity of scribes, seated at desks in rows as in some great business of money-changing.

"What more would you see, O Sollius?" asked Gennadius, coming a pace or so forward to meet him. But his smile was false. Alexias, carefully watching so as to be able to report every detail to the Emperor, had taken no personal part whatever as yet in the investigation, and took no part now. He was an observer, not a participant, perhaps too jealous as a freedman to help a slave unnecessarily, yet not jealous enough – for, at bottom, he was a just man – wilfully to hinder, and he was waiting for the answer of Sollius with a certain studied mingling of indifference and curiosity.

"I have seen, I think, all that may be seen here," came the slave's words after a brief hesitation, and Alexias found that he had been holding his breath, but now he expended it in what was almost a sigh of relief. "I may come hither again tomorrow," Sollius went on. "But now I would return home to my master's house to think. Farewell!"

He departed without further courtesy, and left both the chief treasury clerk and the Emperor's freedman slightly outraged by his casual manners. Decius the centurion marched stolidly at his heels, and saw the slave safely to the house of Sabinus the senator, where, at the Emperor's command, he was to be billeted during the course of the investigations, and so be at hand when necessary, whether by day or by night.

"How did it go, Sollius?" asked young Lucius, the slave's usual confidant and sometimes his assistant.

Sollius related his morning's visit to the Temple of Saturn in close detail. The telling served not only to inform Lucius of everything, but likewise to arrange it all neatly within his own mind. They were pacing up and down in their favourite solitude, beside the small carp-pool behind the chariot-house.

"It is indeed a puzzle!" breathed Lucius. "How could anyone pass through that locked and chained grille?"

"Someone did," answered Sollius dryly. "Two, as I guess, were in it."

"Think you, then, that they stole the key? But, since it never leaves the person of this Gennadius, how?"

"The key was not stolen. The grille, Lucius, was never unlocked, nor unchained," said Sollius in a tone of certainty. "I am sure of all that."

Lucius gaped.

"But – " he began.

"I asked myself these two questions," Sollius broke in with a smile. "Was the gate of the grille opened? If it was not opened, is there another entrance? I think that the gate of the grille was *not* unlocked and unchained; but there is another entrance from the temple itself. The priest of Saturn did not deny it. But he did deny going down by the secret way for many years, and I believed him."

"But you said, Sollius," interjected Lucius, "that the secret way down does not come out *behind* the grille."

"That is so," returned Sollius placidly. "But the priest of Saturn made a slip. Did you not notice it, and see the implication?"

Lucius stared at his companion blankly.

"I have told you everything he said," pursued Sollius, and he gave the youth a sly, whimsical glance. "You do not see it?"

Lucius puckered his brows, and then shook his head.

"He asked me," said Sollius, "if I had seen the silver statuette of Verus. This, as I told you, is in the chamber behind the grille, and invisible from the grille because of the winding passages. Yet he had himself told me that he had not been in the vaults for many years – and again I say that I believe him. Moreover, this silver statuette had been placed in its marble niche but a year ago. How did he know that the statuette was – tarnished? Because he had been told so. He could not know it otherwise. Therefore, though he had not been in that treasury chamber himself, he has spoken to someone who *has* been there. It is that person whom I must discover."

"Might he not have heard it from Gennadius?" asked Lucius.

"They are not on speaking terms," replied Sollius. "I told you."

"Did you not ask him how he knew?"

"The time was not ripe. I shall ask him at the right moment, be assured!"

"He made a slip indeed!" said Lucius.

Sollius pursed his lips.

"I am not so sure, after all," he murmured. "Perhaps he was seeking to tell me something – by suggestion, I mean, rather than by statement. He has a very clever face. If I can, I would learn who it was who told him of the tarnished silver statuette by other methods than by direct questioning. I think it would be more – fruitful. Nor, I feel, would direct questioning succeed. His reticence has made that plain – and he was reticent even with the Augustus himself."

"How will you go about it, Sollius?" asked Lucius curiously.

"I shall not go about it," replied Sollius with a sly laugh. "*You* will!"

"I?" exclaimed Lucius, astonished and yet delighted, for he loved helping Sollius in his investigations, partly because of the excitement in doing so, but partly, too, because it took him away from his kitchen duties, for his position as a young slave in the house of Sabinus the senator was ordinarily that of one of the cook's menials, an occupation of much drudgery and little amusement.

"You," repeated Sollius. "Loiter outside the Temple of Saturn, and strike acquaintance with one of the porters. Any gossip about the old priest of Saturn – such as constant, or unusual, visitors to him of late – may kindle a little lamp in my brain. Go, Lucius, at once. I will explain to Tuphus the cook."

Lucius obeyed eagerly, and sped off like a stone from a Dacian sling.

Sollius remained by the carp-pool, pacing round and round in an unbroken muse. He admitted to himself that he was puzzled; the problem was like nothing that he had investigated before, and he did not know whether he was equal to its solution. But though a slave, he was a proud man, and he whipped his mind once more. He knew how entrance through the grille had been effected. He had not admitted that to Lucius, and certainly had not divulged it to either Gennadius or Alexias; he would keep it to himself for a while. He felt it was perhaps a dangerous thing to know, and assuredly a dangerous thing to blurt out until he had the whole matter plain in his mind and ready for laying before the Emperor.

His cogitations were abruptly broken by the running arrival of one of his fellow slaves.

"Our master wants you," the latter gasped out breathlessly. "You are to go to his private chamber at once."

Shaking himself free of his concentration, Sollius followed his summoner indoors, though more sedately than he had been fetched, and then proceeded alone through the cool, dark atrium to the inner chamber of Sabinus, his master and owner.

He paused on the threshold before entering, for he could hear many voices in a continual murmur of conversation. He was surprised and not a little annoyed. Surely Sabinus was not fool enough to waste the time of a man devoted to the Emperor's most secret business by exhibiting him as a curiosity to a pack of his idle friends? He knew only too well how garrulous Sabinus was, and how he was wont to boast over his slave's unusual aptitude for solving mysteries, but now that slave was more the Emperor's servant than his master's, and the senator should have recognized the position. With an impatient click of his tongue, Sollius entered, only to be brought to an amazed standstill as soon as his eye beheld the company whom his master was entertaining.

"Ah, there you are!" cried Sabinus, who obviously had been nervously on the look-out for him. "This is the fellow, Cæsar. Come hither, Sollius!"

A silence had fallen at the slave's appearance in the doorway, and every gaze was now fixed upon him as he moved forward to where his master stood beside a youth, who was dressed in the extreme of fashion, jewelled and scented – a dark, handsome, sullen youth, with lowering brows and a low forehead overhung by a crisply trimmed fringe. His hair, otherwise, was cut close to his head. Though he had not seen this young man before, Sollius knew immediately that it was the Emperor's son, already associated by his doting father in the imperial power, though but little over sixteen years of age and without any particular gifts except for the sports of the amphitheatre.

Sollius and Commodus took stock of one another as the former humbly approached: Commodus with more than a touch of insolence in his bearing, Sollius with a direct and piercing glance, such as the other was clearly unaccustomed to receive, and an unwilling flush suddenly stained the young Cæsar's cheeks. With an inward smile, the slave wondered whether the prince had ever been embarrassed by a human eye before – unless by his father's, and Marcus Aurelius was credited with a parental indulgence which was the very reverse of disciplinary.

"You are the slave Sollius?" asked Commodus in a husky voice that seemed only recently to have broken.

"Yes, Cæsar, this is my Sollius," put in Sabinus before his slave could reply.

"I have heard of you," went on Commodus without taking the

least notice of the senator and, in fact, almost turning his back upon his host. "You were very clever over my mother's jewels. I laughed for a whole hour! I am ready to like a man who has properly amused me."

Sollius bowed low.

"The most honourable Sabinus tells me that he has lent you again to my father," pursued Commodus.

Once more Sollius bowed. He could more easily feign humility in his limbs than in his eyes.

"Has he lost one of his precious philosophical treatises?" the prince asked with a laugh.

"If he has, Cæsar," replied Sollius quietly, "he has not employed *me* to find it."

The amusement died out of both voice and glance of the imperial youth, leaving only a tigerish glare and felinity in its place, as he demanded peremptorily what thing it was for which his father had employed him to look.

"After all, slave, I am half the Augustus," Commodus reminded him, "and I have a legitimate interest in what affects my father. Do you search for some thread of conspiracy against him – or against *me*?"

"No, Cæsar," answered Sollius.

Commodus waited as though in the sure expectation that the slave would say more, but being disappointed, frowned, and asked haughtily:

"What has he lost? Even my mother does not know!"

Sollius, on an impulse, knelt before the young man.

"Lord," he said, "the Augustus has laid secrecy upon me like a yoke upon the neck of a pair of ploughing oxen. I dare not tell you!"

"Not tell, not tell, Sollius," cried Sabinus irritably, "when the lord Commodus commands?"

Commodus himself had said nothing, but was standing motionless, biting his painted finger-nails.

"The Augustus commanded otherwise," said Sollius. "Not even to the lord Commodus can I tell anything."

Sabinus puffed out his cheeks in his annoyance at his promise to the young prince going unfulfilled.

"I like not this in you, Sollius," he muttered. "I might have you whipped for it."

The slave rose slowly to his feet.

"At the moment, master, I am the Emperor's; when I return as *your* slave, I will submit to your punishment," he said with dignity.

"There, there, Sollius," answered Sabinus, a little abashed, "I spoke hastily. The Emperor's commands must come first."

"It is a pity, slave," said one of the young courtiers standing about Commodus and who had accompanied him to the senator's house, "that you do not remember that even emperors are mortal, and that it is wise to anticipate the future. You seem as clever at losing as at finding!" he added with a malicious smile.

But it was not with his eyes that Sollius was really noticing him, but with his nose. He had savoured before the particular scent which hung about the young man's rich garments, and knew very well where: in the bedroom of the Empress Faustina when he had been investigating the supposed loss of her jewels; and, once again, a man so scented had brushed past him and Decius from the doorway of one of the lowest taverns in the Subura during the same investigation. Was he the same man? He had not seen his face then.

"Peace, Gaius," cried Commodus. "The slave has not offended me."

He gave Sollius, nevertheless, a suspicious and venomous look, and then with affected indolence turned away to his host. Sabinus made a curt sign of dismissal, and Sollius was only too glad to escape from the crowded chamber and from the curious eyes of those who had watched every imperial gesture and listened to each imperial word so as to adjust their own attitude to the notorious slave of Sabinus with the right obsequious agreement.

In the corridor Sollius met his master's household overseer, an Apulian freedman, for Sabinus was a widower.

"I did not hear that the Emperor's son had been invited to-day," said the slave, pausing as they passed one another.

"He was not," replied the other, and swore in Greek under his breath. "It has put us out, by Heracles, abominably! The accursed young man invited himself."

They separated, and Sollius went to his own quarters. It had been an interlude which had broken his concentration, and now, with an exasperated sigh, he endeavoured to immerse himself once again in his previous thoughts. Two new facts, moreover, had come teasingly into his mind, and he began trying to fit them into the pattern of his reasoning.

Lucius did not return until dusk. "I fear, Sollius," he reported disconsolately, "that I have only little things to tell you, and none of them, I think, likely to be useful."

"It is the adding up of the little things that makes the large things," said the older slave with a comfortable smile. "Set out your 'little things' in a row like stones on the top of a wall, and let us flick them away, or keep them, one by one."

"First," replied Lucius, "the priest of Saturn hardly ever leaves the temple; he lives like a hermit."

"Hardly ever leaves the temple, and lives like a hermit," repeated Sollius in a meditative echo.

"Then his three assistant priests," went on Lucius, "are, two of them, but so in name, and are present only at the annual sacrifice ordained by the State; each is a kind of relative of the Empress, and their connection with the rites of Saturn are perfunctory and official. Neither has entered the temple these six months."

"Neither has entered the temple these six months," echoed Sollius as before." And the third priest?" he asked.

"The third priest," Lucius replied, "is only a kind of servant who performs the daily offices about the place. It is really a temple no longer, but is given over to the business of the treasury; only the one end is still reserved to the god."

"As I saw," mused Sollius. "And now: what visitors has this priest of Saturn?"

"As few as a real hermit might have," said Lucius. "In fact, if the doorkeeper speaks true – and why should he not? – the only visitor he has had for many a long month is his nephew."

"His – nephew?" repeated Sollius.

"A young man – so said the doorkeeper – who has won some notoriety," Lucius went on, "as a gladiator. One or two of the young sprigs of fashion have ventured into the arena in competition with the professionals."

"Much to the Emperor's disgust," put in Sollius, "for his son is one of them. Did you learn this young man's name?"

"Rutilius Marcianus," said Lucius.

Sollius shook his head disappointedly.

"I do not know the name," he muttered. Then, after a pause, he added abruptly: "Has the lord Commodus ever visited this priest of Saturn?"

"I was not told so," Lucius answered, "and I think it would have been a sufficiently noteworthy occasion to have remained in the mind of that gossiping old doorkeeper!"

"Very like, very like," said Sollius. "Does this nephew of the priest of Saturn visit his uncle constantly, or only at long intervals?"

Lucius suddenly grinned.

"I have this for you," he said. "He has begun visiting his uncle only in the last few months. Until then nobody knew that the old priest had a nephew."

"All this may yet mean nothing," answered Sollius casually. "But I should like to see this young man – without his knowing either that I do see him or that I even wish to see him."

"Perhaps we could go to the arena," suggested Lucius, his eyes sparkling in anticipation. "He might be performing – "

"And might not," smiled Sollius, "and it would then be a waste of time. I must think of a better way."

But it was not through any thought or scheming of his own that the slave met with Rutilius Marcianus, and that in the very near future; in fact, on the next day, or, rather, the next night. He was summoned in the late evening by a messenger from the Temple of Saturn.

This messenger was a gigantic Cappadocian, the kind of man who usually was a litter-bearer. Sollius took him for one of the treasury porters.

"Do you come from Gennadius?" he asked.

The Cappadocian grinned, and nodded. He seemed a very pleasant kind of fellow, thought Sollius.

They set out for the temple at once, with the aroused centurion marching at Sollius's heels, lean, sinewy, upright and watchful, and as stiffly correct as if on parade in the Campus Martius. They reached their destination without delay, and Sollius was surprised and interested – and perhaps a little more interested than surprised – that the Cappadocian led him, not to the great bronze treasury doors themselves, but to a small, secret door in another part of the temple. This was opened at the first knocking upon it, and Sollius was beckoned inside by the man who had answered to the Cappadocian's knuckles. Sollius entered first, followed immediately by his Prætorian bodyguard, for whom the Cappadocian, with an alien politeness, made way. The door was then shut after them with silent precision.

A single lamp was burning in a niche. By its gleam Sollius saw that they were in a descending stone passage of considerable antiquity. But he was given no time for examining his surroundings at all closely.

"Go forward," whispered the Cappadocian.

After a few yards the passage turned abruptly at right angles and went on for some distance, still descending. This passage, too, was lit by a lamp in a niche. At the end was a small, bronze door, embossed with symbolic figures and green with damp and age. As the Cappadocian pushed it open with his huge hand, a metallic sigh seemed to echo along the passage. The door had been recently oiled, decided Sollius, but not quite well enough. Probably, however, the noise of its opening would not be heard in the temple, for clearly they were by now well underground.

The opened door led directly to an upward flight of ancient, worn, and uneven steps. The man who had opened the first door to them caught up the lamp from the niche in the passage, and led the way up. At the top a narrow aperture, hung with a heavy curtain, gave into a small chamber – the same chamber in which Sollius had had his interview with the priest of Saturn. A long, roundabout way, he reflected wryly, to bring him back to it! He was not surprised at finding himself there; he had suspected whither he was being taken; but he was somewhat more than surprised by the scene which immediately presented itself to his gaze, for the chamber was occupied by two men, both of whom he recognized on the instant, and one of them, the priest of Saturn himself, was leaning back in his chair as though asleep. But from more than one visible sign it was plain that it was no true sleep, but a drugged unconsciousness. The other occupant was the same scented young man who had been with the Emperor's son at the house of Sabinus on the previous day, and whom Sollius now certainly believed to be the man he had once encountered in one of the worst alleys of the Subura.

They were three to two, with the unconscious priest of Saturn between them.

"I expected you to bring him alone," said the scented young man to the Cappadocian.

"This fellow has the Emperor's orders to follow him everywhere he goes," was the sullen answer. "Could I order him away?"

"Stand by the door, Balbus!" commanded the scented young man, and he who had let them in moved a pace or so back and posted himself between the centurion and retreat. Decius fixed his eyes upon the slave, and wondered what his charge would do. As for himself, he had no fear. He was a trained soldier and was armed, and would confidently have taken on more than any such three at a time, unskilled men as they probably were. The Cappadocian, however, was of a terrible size ... The centurion fingered the heavy stabbing-sword at his belt: it was just as well for a man to be ready.

The scented young man turned to Sollius.

"You know me?" he asked.

"I recognize you," answered the slave. "You were at my master's yesterday."

"I am Gaius Rutilius Marcianus," the scented young man went on. "I am a practised gladiator," he added, his gaze falling for a moment on the centurion. "The priest of Saturn is my uncle," he

continued, turning back to Sollius. "No, he is not poisoned: have
no fears. He does but sleep – after a drink of wine containing – no
matter what. It will do him no harm. He will wonder a little at his
strange, sudden 'illness' – and will find his nephew most assiduous!
Well, slave, understand this: you are not the only person able to make
enquiries; I, too, have made some, and to-day I know for certain what
yesterday was only a guess: that you are thrusting your nose into the
thefts from the treasury. You need not, out of duty to the Augustus,
deny it," he concluded in a tone of menace.

"I do not deny it."

"You are not so clever as you think, or you would not have let
yourself be brought hither," sneered Marcianus.

"Perhaps I wished to be brought – wherever I might be taken,"
answered the slave, and their glances clashed.

"Shall I kill this scented fellow?" cried out the centurion.

"No, no; oh no!" answered Sollius in a tone of horror. "We wish
for no killing here."

"Who wishes for no killing?" asked Marcianus with a laugh. "You,
slave? Or is it I? There is little chance of our having the same wishes
about that! Silence is what we have brought you hither to have from
you, and there is no surer silence than death's."

The centurion drew his sword, but in the same instant the huge
Cappadocian twined an arm about the Prætorian's neck and held
him in a choking grip, while Balbus kicked his legs from under
him, and caught at his falling weapon. The conventionally trained
soldier is always at a disadvantage against irregulars who do not
play fair, that is to say, not in accordance with professional tactics.
Marcianus laughed once more, and then his eyes narrowed with
suspicious astonishment.

"You do not, slave, go on your knees for mercy?" he asked.

"Even a slave," replied Sollius, "can face death standing."

"But not here," said Marcianus. "Here your body would be found;
but I know of a place where it will never be found."

He moved swiftly and caught Sollius by the arm, and exerted force
to drag him towards a kind of apse in the wall to the right. To his
surprise, the slave did not resist, but docilely allowed himself to be
led whither his captor would.

"Bring the soldier after us," commanded Marcianus over his
shoulder, and he touched one of the bricks. The back of the
apse swung open, and some stone steps were seen to descend
into darkness. So that, thought Sollius, was the secret way down
into the vaults known to the priests of Saturn.

Marcianus, with his grasp still upon the slave's arm, paused at the top of the steps, and whistled a few sharp notes. There came an answering whistle from below, and gradually a pale light diffused itself about the bottom of the steps.

"Come," cried Marcianus brusquely, and he led Sollius down.

Behind them came the muffled noise of a sudden struggle, and Marcianus swore under his breath. He was about to turn back to see what was happening, though he could guess very well, when Sollius forestalled him by calling upward:

"Decius! Decius! You are to come quietly. It is my order, and my orders are the Emperor's! You know that. Come down quietly, Decius, and without protest."

In a sullen and contemptuous indignation the centurion allowed himself to be thrust down into the same underground passage of the vaults beneath the temple. The soft, diffused light which had dimly illuminated their descent was now seen to emanate from a lamp held high above the head of one dressed as a gladiator. The helmet, ornate and gleaming like gold in the lamplight, shadowed the face. With its fringe of metal teeth over eyes and nose, it was as good as a mask. The man turned as soon as they drew near, and led the way until they came to the grille.

Marcianus laughed, and struck the gate of the grille with his hand.

"Chained and locked," he said jeeringly. "And yet – someone – passed through. That is a puzzle, slave, for even *your* exalted wits."

"My wits," replied Sollius with a smile, "may not be exalted, but the entrance past this grille, at least, is no puzzle to them."

The other stared, and the lampbearer turned, and stared also.

"Your last boast, slave," mocked Marcianus, "is your most foolish."

Sollius spread out his hands in deprecation.

"It is no boast," he said.

"How, slave? You *know* the way in through this grille?"

"As well as – you," replied Sollius.

The lampbearer audibly caught his breath.

"What do you mean, wretch?" cried the scented but not all-effeminate Marcianus, and he gripped Sollius by the shoulder.

"I mean but this," Sollius answered. "That I know *how* the theft was worked."

"And by *whom*?" demanded Marcianus, and he began to shake the man in his grasp.

"Gently," said the centurion gruffly. "I am still here."

"But unarmed," the Cappadocian reminded him with a grin, and showed the Prætorian's sword which he had taken from Balbus.

"Answer me!" cried Marcianus, and his grip on the slave's shoulder cruelly tightened. "Do you know the *thief*?"

"No," said Sollius simply.

The other loosed him with a harsh laugh.

"I think you know nothing," he jeered. "But you are too cleverly nosy a fellow to be let live. Throttle him, Balbus!" he commanded. "Balbus," he laughed, "is a Samnite wrestler, and knows how to throttle a man, I can tell you!"

Balbus moved forward with a grim leer.

"Wait!" said the man holding the lamp.

Marcianus, Balbus and the Cappadocian stiffened where they stood.

"You have forgotten," went on the man with the lamp petulantly, "that I am here."

Marcianus raised his right arm in graceful salute, and was about to reply, when the other interrupted him:

"Before this fellow is killed – and I shall enjoy watching Balbus's strong thumbs! – I would learn what he knows. Slave, answer me: how is this grille to be passed through and not by its locked and chained door?"

Sollius caught his breath. It was barely perceptible, and he mastered himself at once. He did not think that his involuntary start had been noticed, and he answered as calmly as he could:

"Sir, will you lift your lamp higher – and nearer to the grille?"

The other moved a pace or two, and raised his lamp. Again Sollius caught his breath, but again checked himself, and went on as calmly as before:

"It needed two men. I knew that as soon as I was sure that the gate had not been opened by the – thieves. One man remained on this side of the grille; the other climbed through the upper part, stole what he would, passed it through to his companion, and then, with his help – without his help it would have been too difficult – climbed out again. That was how it was done."

"But that is folly," blustered Balbus. "There is not space enough between any of the bars, upper or lower, for a dog to be pushed through. How could a man, climb he ever so high, squeeze through the bars?"

"I will show you," answered Sollius. "Your – friend – has raised his lamp in *exactly* the right place! Look! Those three bars in the upper part of the grille beyond the crossbar have been sawn through, and replaced by being simply mortared together again. That was clever. They look so right, and so strong, still! I say again, it was clever. If the bars had been sawn in the lower part of the grille, that is to say, below the cross-bar, it might have been found out at any time, even by accident; but, having sawn them asunder in the upper half, there would be no occasion at all for them to be touched, even accidentally, for who, unnecessarily, would *climb* the grille? And who would examine them with any closeness – except an elderly slave who is too easily suspicious? Have I answered you?"

"Has the time come?" asked Balbus the Samnite, extending his hands with their fingers spread open.

"So we, Gaius there and I," pursued the man with the lamp, "are the thieves?"

Sollius nodded.

"Both of you sawed the bars and afterwards replaced them; you, I think – yes, you, certainly, for your lamp picked out the very place without hesitation – climbed in; and your confederate helped you to climb out again, and received the sacks with the jewels and the gold."

"Shall we deal with him?" cried the Cappadocian impatiently.

"Wait," commanded the other, and his voice, though strangely young in its tone, had authority. "What would you tell the Emperor, slave, if you lived to tell him anything?"

"That I had accomplished the task he set me," replied Sollius instantly.

"Could you, then, name the thieves? Though I am honoured, as you showed, by your suspicion," went on the young, authoritative, and now sarcastic voice, "you could not, I think, give *me* a name."

"If I am not to live to tell the Emperor anything," answered Sollius carefully, "does my knowledge matter?"

"That, at least," interjected the Cappadocian, "is a good, sensible remark! Balbus – "

At the sound of his name the Samnite wrestler edged nearer to his intended victim and again thrust out his hands with their fingers spread wide. The Cappadocian, leering in anticipation of a fine sight, and anxious not to miss a single instant of it, had grown careless. Decius saw his opportunity. He twisted aside, and in the same movement deftly wrenched his own sword from the other's grasp.

"Ha!" he cried in a loud voice. "Quick! Get behind me, slave!"

And he sent up a challenging roar as when in some battle in Mesopotamia a Roman legionary should invite a Persian "Immortal" to single combat. Sollius, however, did not accept his counsel to seek shelter behind him; instead, he set his back to the grille, and fixed his eyes on the man with the lamp.

The fight that followed between Decius and Marcianus, the Cappadocian, and the Samnite was as brief as it was savage. The centurion, who was no fool and knew well what he was about, raised as much clamour as he could, shouting, stamping and clashing steel against steel, for both the Samnite and the Cappadocian were armed with long knives. His armour protected him against any but the shrewdest thrust in the right place, and he was too skilled in his trade to lay himself open unwarily. He had not waited for their attack, but had taken the offensive right from the beginning, and very early in the proceedings had reduced his enemies to two – for the man with the lamp took no part in the struggle at all – by wounding the Samnite severely in the right arm. But almost immediately after he had thus lessened the odds, the event which he had expected, and for which his deliberate noisiness had played, came to pass, and the vaults were rushed by the guard which was on watch above at the ordinary entrance to them from the temple.

The fight was over at once, and the four contestants were roughly separated and impartially seized.

"Not *me*, asses!" spluttered Decius. "Do you not recognize me, Tribonius? Bid them take their hands off me!"

"What, you, old comrade!" cried the centurion of the watch. "What is all this about? It sounded as if old Hannibal's elephants were trampling about down here. What has been happening?"

"I am under the Emperor's own orders," replied the released Decius. "I am acting as a bodyguard – *his* bodyguard," he added, pointing to Sollius.

Tribonius stared at the slave fixedly.

"What is he doing at this grille?" he demanded, and his tone was both suspicious and truculent. "It is all very well, Decius, but I am in charge here, and I have a right to know what you are all up to. How did any of you get into these vaults? First tell me that. Not through *us*, anyway! Is there another way down? If so, it should have a sentry posted, and I must see to it."

Decius opened his mouth to reply, but Sollius forestalled him:

"That can wait," he said impatiently. "There is work to be done here in the Emperor's name."

He produced his tablet of authority. Tribonius took and examined it in amazement, stared at Sollius, and from Sollius to Decius.

"I told you," said the latter, who was beginning to enjoy the bewilderment of his fellow centurion and to appreciate his own favoured position beside the investigating slave, "I am his bodyguard, and he is on the Emperor's business. I am under his orders; and now *you* are, too!"

He laughed, and saluted Sollius in a half-mocking fashion, yet Sollius felt that the Prætorian's contempt for him, nevertheless, was rapidly thawing. Decius then summarily took the tablet from the still doubtful Tribonius, and gave it back to the slave with a wink and a flourish.

"It is always good to have a pass!" he said.

Sollius was again staring at the man with the lamp, the light of which was no longer necessary, since one of the soldiers was carrying a torch that blazed over a wide area. The whole grille was illuminated until it seemed like a huge spider's web iridescent with a bloody dew.

The man with the lamp remained still and silent. Suddenly he blew out his lamp, and let it fall. Being of clay, it flew into a dozen pieces on the stone floor, and the oil made a little puddle, redly gleaming in the flame of the torch. It might have been a pool of blood from some murdered man.

"I think that is enough," he said in a raised, overbearing tone, and he took his gladiator's helmet from his head. The two centurions and the soldiers at once gasped, stiffened and saluted. It was the Emperor's son. Sollius remained quietly at the grille, and he was smiling with a kind of sly passiveness.

Commodus took a pace or so forward.

"Take forth these men," he commanded, "and execute them without further delay. I charge them all with complicity in the thefts from Rome's treasure which this slave has been investigating at my father's order. I not only charge them, but myself bear witness against their deeds, and as Cæsar I now judge them."

The centurion of the treasury guard was obviously embarrassed, for there was no legality in the young Cæsar's command, and yet it was already widely known that the wrath of Commodus was more dangerous to awake than a sleeping tiger's. He looked at Decius, but found no help in his fellow centurion's expression; he then looked at Sollius, as if pleading for guidance.

"Did you not hear, centurion?" rasped Commodus.

"Cæsar – " said Sollius.

"What is it, slave?" cried Commodus, turning to him irritably. "I shall tell my father that you unearthed the plot and exposed the chief villain, Gaius Rutilius Marcianus yonder. By other ways I had come to the same conclusion – "

Marcianus started, opened his mouth to speak violently, but meeting the young prince's hard, level gaze, thought better of it and remained silent, and Commodus turned again to Sollius.

"You will not lose by this if you are circumspect," he went on, stressing his words. "What more can you wish? I shall speak well of you to the Augustus. If I did not, your master would be mulcted of a slave, I can tell you that! – but you can die more happily – and much older," he added, his eyes fierce, but his lips smiling.

"Cæsar," persisted Sollius, and he could not prevent his limbs from feeling as though made of water, "the Augustus has put this matter into my hands, and I must report to him before anyone can be condemned for his guilt. Your sacred father will then know how to punish."

Commodus stared at him.

"You address me as 'Cæsar'," he said, "but clearly have no idea what Cæsarship means!"

"Sir," answered Sollius, "under your permission, I am but seeking to obey the Augustus."

Commodus bit his underlip, but if he had flushed, the torchlight was too red for any addition to his cheeks to be noticeable.

"We are to hear," he burst out contemptuously, "a slave's suggestion, ha! Well, give it, give it! Let us hear this impertinent wisdom!"

"Have the three arrested, sir – even as they are already – and let my report be made to the Emperor this night – and in your presence, Cæsar – and everything will then be accomplished with speed and efficiency – except one thing," he added underbreath to himself.

"What is that you are murmuring?" demanded Commodus, frowning and glowering with suspicion.

"That even if we have found the culprits, Cæsar, we have not recovered what they stole," Sollius replied meekly. "But where it is hidden, no doubt, torture will get from them," he added, glancing sideways at Marcianus, who started, and turned impulsively to the Emperor's son, but his movement was immediately checked by the soldier at his side.

"Cæsar!" implored Marcianus. "You will not allow this – you cannot allow it! Why, you yourself, Cæsar – "

"Silence!" Commodus broke in shrilly. "All shall be thoroughly sifted; justice shall be done, Gaius! Centurion," he ordered, "take those two men to the Mamertine. You, Gaius, accompany me! I will be responsible for him," he said in a lower tone to Tribonius, "and will deliver him myself to the Emperor's will. You, slave, do as you suggested: go to my father at once. I shall meet you in his presence. Tell everything that you have seen here – and I will confirm it. Gaius, with *me*! Come!"

Taking Marcianus firmly by the arm, Commodus went up quickly into the temple above, and the commands which he had given to Tribonius were put into action at once and without question.

"We, Decius," said Sollius, "are for the Emperor's palace: let us get there as soon as we can."

Though the hour was considerably after midnight, Marcus Aurelius was reading and meditating still, and was at once accessible. Sollius was admitted to the Emperor's private study by Alexander, the Greek secretary, while Decius posted himself with the other guards in the gilded and painted corridor. Complete silence reigned in the vast palace, and only a single lamp was burning by the Emperor's marble writing-table. Alexias was not present.

"Well, Sollius?" asked the Augustus, turning to him somewhat wearily, and rubbing his tired, heavy eyes. "So you have something to report?"

Sollius was silent for a brief instant before replying. He had so great a veneration for the wise and benevolent Emperor that he hesitated to bring pain to his noble heart, and what he had to tell, he knew, would bring nothing but pain.

"Have no fears and no hesitations," said Marcus Aurelius, as if he had read the slave's doubtful thoughts. "Tell me everything. Should I have employed you if I had not desired the truth, the full truth?"

Carefully and completely the slave related what had taken place as far as the arrival of the treasury guard upon the clamour raised by Decius, but at that point in his narrative he paused, and glanced at the Emperor as though inviting question or comment. Marcus Aurelius had been listening with his head propped upon his hand as he leaned a little forward at the marble table, and when Sollius paused, had given a sigh.

"I know Marcianus," he breathed slowly. "He is a young man of parts and charm, and one of my son's – friends. Alas, that Rome's inner society should be touched in this unsavoury matter! But that is what I had feared, Sollius; yet I had to know and be certain. It was my duty to know and be certain. I can tell you now why I employed *you*. An official, or a courtier, would have been tempted to hide what implicated the man of rank; you, a slave, would have no such inhibition."

The imperial study was an inner chamber beyond a larger chamber, with two entrances, the one – that by which Sollius had been introduced – from the corridor, and the other through an archway from this larger chamber, into which the more private apartment could be thrown open, on occasions of council or reception, by the lifting of the hangings between. These, of a richly woven purple, were now drawn; but though Sollius had heard no sound, he was suddenly conscious that a listener was standing on the other side of these hangings in the large room beyond them, and he thought that he could very easily guess who that listener was.

Abruptly the Emperor asked the question which Sollius had been dreading:

"Who was the man in the gladiator's helmet? Did you see his face? Did you find out?"

Sollius knelt.

"It was the Cæsar!" he answered.

Marcus Aurelius started, and covered his face with his two hands.

"What was he doing beneath the temple?" he muttered. "Was he there to protect his friend from his wrong-doing? It must have been so. Was it, Sollius?" he asked earnestly, lowering his hands, and fixing the slave with a pleading scrutiny.

As Sollius looked up into the Emperor's face, he caught a slight movement in the folds of the purple hangings, as if a hand had been laid on them preparatory to someone's entrance, but as though, nevertheless, the man waiting still hesitated to make his appearance. But it was the Emperor's features which held the kneeling slave's deepest attention, and what he read in them struck him to the heart. That the master of the world, so constant and indefatigable in working for its well-being and happiness, should himself be so unhappy and so apprehensive of shame, and that his noble affections should be in such danger of that most horrible of disillusionments, the knowing his nearest and dearest to be unworthy of trust and even love: all this troubled Sollius in the depths of his soul. He could not add the final words which would reveal truth in its naked hideousness.

He rose, and keeping his eyes steadfastly away from the hangings, answered the Emperor's question with deliberate care.

"As I understood," he said in a clear voice, "the Cæsar had had his own suspicions of his friend, and had been playing a part to trap him. You employed *me*, O Emperor, to solve the mystery, but you owe your son a great deal of the evidence."

"You give me great comfort," sighed Marcus Aurelius.

As he spoke, the hangings were lifted, and Commodus made his entrance.

"My dear father," he said humbly, and went across and kissed the Emperor's cheek.

"My son," murmured Marcus Aurelius, and fleetingly laid a hand on the young man's scented garments with a briefly lingering, pathetic fondness.

"Has this good slave reported on our adventure of to-night?"

asked Commodus, glancing round at Sollius with a faint, satiric smile.

"Fully, as I think," returned his father. "I shall not forget his services."

"Nor I," murmured Commodus, lowering his gaze bashfully as he added: "Services to you and the Roman State are services to me also."

"There will, I am confident," said Sollius quietly, and not daring to glance even flickeringly at the young Cæsar, "be no more thefts from the imperial treasury."

"You have deserved well of Rome," answered Marcus Aurelius, smiling. "I shall tell Sabinus so, and your reward shall turn one slave into a rich man." He smiled again, and went on: "The Cappadocian and the Samnite strangler shall be tried in secret and, if found guilty, executed. What have you done with Marcianus, my son?" he asked. "You took him away with you, I understand, under your personal arrest."

"That is so, father," replied Commodus, and his meekness suddenly put on a mask of sadness and diffident unease. "I grieve to announce unwelcome news, but as I brought him through the streets – we were both cloaked against the common gaze of night-prowlers – he broke into a swerving run to escape. My Gaulish freedman was with me, and thinking that he was doing right, he threw his knife at once at the fugitive – the Gauls are very swift with the knife! – and it took Marcianus between the shoulders. It hurts me that Gaius should be immune from Rome's justice!"

"He is dead?" asked the Emperor.

"He is dead," answered Commodus, and turned and gave Sollius a direct look of arrogant complacency.

"Then I am foiled of magnanimity," said Marcus Aurelius with a sigh. "However, the mystery is cleared up, and the distressing matter closed. I am grateful to the gods. Do you think," he asked abruptly, speaking to his son, "that the stolen jewels and gold will be found at your dead friend's villa?"

"We can search it, father," replied Commodus gravely, "but I have no hopes of finding them. He was a clever man – always too clever for *me*, at any rate," he sighed.

"What say *you*, Sollius?" asked the Emperor.

Sollius gave a swift look at the Cæsar, and then answered:

"I do not think, sir, that any investigation into the whereabouts of the stolen treasure will ever succeed."

"Then you would not undertake it?"

"I would not undertake it with any hope, sir," answered the slave firmly.

"I see," muttered Marcus Aurelius, frowning a little, and then he rubbed his eyes more wearily than ever. "I see," he repeated. "Return to your master's house, Sollius, and tell him that I am well pleased with you. Where are you going, my son? Stay with me while I put away my tablets — "

The slave left the Augustus and the Cæsar together, and dismissing Decius to his barracks, since he no longer needed a bodyguard, he returned alone to the house of his master.

"But who did steal the treasure?" asked Lucius the next day, after Sollius had narrated all that had happened.

"If the lord Commodus had not lifted his lamp at exactly the right place in the grille where the thieves had broken in," answered Sollius, "I should not perhaps have known for a certainty that he himself was one of them, and I should have looked for the true accomplice of Marcianus — oh yes, he was the other of the two — in vain. I did little in this investigation, Lucius; they gave themselves away to me — probably out of the fear that I was really cleverer than I am!"

"Does the Emperor guess, think you?"

"I hope not," sighed Sollius. "Had you only seen his face you would have lied to him as I did."

"And the treasure *is* lost?" asked Lucius.

"Quite lost," said Sollius. "None of it will ever be seen in Rome again. No doubt, however, it will turn up in different thievish hands, dispersed in various parts of the Empire," he concluded, smiling at his own ironic thoughts, "and current coin will have taken its place — we know in whose private coffers. The arena, at least, and the fashionable gambling-houses will receive the final benefit of the criminal daring of a good man's son. It is the way of mankind under the indifference of the gods!"

In most of this Sollius was right, but not in everything. For instance, one portion of the treasure *was* seen again in Rome. For Sollius received a token of approval from the lord Commodus, a valuable and curiously barbaric jewel, which the slave was sure in his own mind had once formed part of the treasure brought as part of the tribute to the Roman people by the great Pompeius after his victorious campaigns against Mithridates of Pontus.

# A BYZANTINE MYSTERY
# Mary Reed and Eric Mayer

*Mary Reed is an ex-patriate Brit (or more appropriately an ex-pat Geordie) who moved to the United States in 1976. She had already made a name for herself in the small circle of British science-fiction fans for her delightful ramblings in the amateur magazines. In America she began to develop her writing in a variety of fields, with a special interest in food and the weather (a predictable British trait).*

*Her first published fiction was a detective story involving food, "Local Cuisine" (1987). Here, in collaboration with her husband Eric Mayer, who helped provide much of the plotline, Mary has written a story specially for this volume set in the volatile days of the Byzantine Empire.*

John the Eunuch, Lord Chamberlain to Emperor Justinian though he be, yet served a higher lord than his temporal ruler. Thus it was that, in the dog watches of a January morning which would normally be as dark as any other in Constantinople, were it not for the lurid glare of the Church of the Holy Wisdom of God burning to the ground, upon receiving an urgent summons to attend the emperor, he first finished the ceremonial meal being served beneath the starred ceiling of the Lord of Truth's underground sanctuary.

When John finally emerged, pulling his cloak closer against the chill of early morning air, he found a dark-robed and visibly shaken underling waiting by the entrance, torch in hand. Its guttering flames revealed a face know to John, although he had never seen it so pallid.

"Anatolius, what ails you?" he asked softly, thinking that to be summoned at this hour by the Emperor's private secretary meant there was more to be dealt with than household accounts or the ongoing riots. He said as much as they hurried along a flagstoned path crossing the grounds of the Great Palace. Out under a clear sky, the noise from the rioting was louder, drifting in huge gulps of incoherent rage over the palace walls as the wind shifted. Clouds of smoke could be seen blotting out patches of stars, and an occasional scream cut through the distant hubbub like a knife through a sacrificial bull. A few sparkling tracers marked the passage of windwhipped embers near the burnt-out gateway to the complex, heavily guarded by the Royal Bodyguard.

"The Emperor was contemplating flight," Anatolius confided, "but the Empress counseled him to stay."

"Well, between her and the guards, what does he want me for?" John was irritated. "Surely he doesn't expect me to wear a sword?"

"By Mithra!" his companion swore. "If he knew you were at a religious service with the city in an uproar, and blood fresh in the gutters . . ."

"Well, no doubt he's been doing a fair bit of praying himself."

"It's true that the Patriarch was here some time." They were approaching the doors of the Throne Room, which was standing open, and John, was surprised to see, unguarded. As they approached, Anatolius lowered his voice. "But then the Church is burning down, and the mob not yet crushed."

"Well, it's not too late to persuade Their Excellencies to leave for their country retreat, I suppose. Perhaps we could disguise them as Greens? Or Blues? Which do you think?"

Anatolius glared at him. Although the Emperor and Empress were commonly linked with the Blue faction, she had been born a Green, but since both factions were equally involved in the rampage of scattered destruction and pillage across the city, blame would be difficult to apportion – but, thought John as he stepped into the half-lit room, so would retribution. Behind him Anatolius' footsteps receded quickly, and, he thought sourly, thankfully into the distance.

Justinian, ever mindful of his position, occupied the great canopied throne, which John approached slowly, bowing his head to his earthly ruler.

The tall dark-haired man with arched brows, hooded eyes and a weak chin, spoke in a whisper. *And an odd thing, that*, John thought, *since they were alone*, as he bent his head respectfully to hear what had summoned him to this strange appointment.

"I have a special commision for you," the Emperor said, "of such delicacy that I cannot reveal it save but to you and the Empress." The chamberlain raised mental enquiring eyebrows while keeping a poker face. "The only other person who knows – as yet – is the Patriarch. But soon enough word will get out, and we must have the matter resolved by then." He paused. "It is a spiritual matter."

*Ah*, thought John. *No wonder the Patriarch is involved*. Like many followers of Mithra, he was amused by the similarities of the new – to them – religion, and his older, more spartan, cult. John found the encrusted palaces of the gentle god little to his taste, and thus the destruction of the Church of the Holy Wisdom, its smoldering ruins not far from where they stood, of little emotional consequence, unlike the deep blow it had been to Justinian, Although he, John, admittedly would have liked to have dealt harshly with the looters whom he had seen carrying out gem-encrusted reliquaries and beautifully painted icons, only to shatter them on the cobbles almost under the horrified nose of the stylite in the square – not so much because of outraged religious feelings, but because it offended his sense of order. What was it to him that an icon supposedly painted by St. Luke was regarded as protecting the city – not to mention the staff of Moses, or any number of other holy relics cared for by the white-togaed priests. Mere superstitious nonsense, in his opinion.

Justinian stood, pushing aside an ornate footstool with an impatient toe. "By God and all his angels, swear never to reveal what you will learn", he said hoarsely, descending from the dais and gripping John's arm tightly. The latter was reminded of King Midas's barber, who was given a secret to keep, but eventually unburdened himself to the reeds which whispered it abroad.

"Of course I swear," John said.

"I will rebuild the Church," Justinian said obliquely, in a distracted way, "and it will outdo Solomon. It will be a worthy home for all the relics which protect us, and of course, the city."

*How like Justinian to mention protection for himself first*, John thought contemptuously, for he did not suppose that the "us" was anything but the imperial us. He inclined his head respectfully as the Emperor spoke quickly and sibilantly in the shadowy hall.

"The Nubian is over six feet tall and has the strength of ten," protested Alexander, head charioteer of the Blue faction, picking his way over the rubble of a small wine shop toward a large barn. "And with all, clever with his hands. A fine carpenter and worker of wood, in fact right now repairing my best chariot, the one that nearly killed me by losing its axle last week." He turned his attention to his old friend John. "But he has the mind of a child. I doubt you'll get anything from him even if he understood you. His Greek is virtually nonexistent." His glance was curious, but he did not enquire in so many words what had brought John to visit, since he had appeared at the walnut door robed in officialdom from the red wool cloak to the golden wand of office.

John smiled thinly. "We'll see, Alexander."

"But what makes you think he can cast light on whatever it is?"

"My dear Alexander, even in a half-light of leaping flames and confusion, a man of his size stands out. He was seen on the spot. He may have . . . information." His tone was neutral but Alexander thanked Apollo *he* wasn't about to be interviewed. They entered the high-ceilinged building. Sitting at a workbench next to a wheel-less chariot, carving one of several pieces of wood with sure hands, was the slave under discussion. He glanced up as they entered, rising quickly to his feet. John looked at the young man before him. Tall and well proportioned, he noted, with symmetrical scars on his chest – tribal marks no doubt – he wore an ornate silver cross, a woodshaving-bedecked kilt and a disturbingly blank look.

"Mahmoud, I wish for you to answer the Lord Chamberlain's questions in all particulars, and truthfully, as a good servant should." The master spoke kindly and carefully as to the child to whom the giant had been compared. The man nodded, his eyes moving slowly to John as he spoke, then back to Alexander as he answered, as if it were the latter who was interrogating him. But he had nothing to tell, and indeed denied even being outside his master's enclosure during the riots, maintaining that he had been cowering in the barn during the entire night. Although he looked progressively more and more uneasy and upset, nothing changed his story, and, in the end, John told him to return to his work, gesturing Alexander to go outside. Sunshine washed the cobbles as they returned the way they had come.

"So," said his friend, "it seems he cannot assist."

"As you say, the mind of a child, although a faithful and certainly a talented one."

"He has given good service," Alexander replied, "and I would certainly be sorry to lose him if you're thinking of making an offer."

But lose him he did, because only four hours later, the body of the child-man was pulled out of the Bosphorus, as the barn burned down, taking with it his former master's best racing chariot.

John the Eunuch knelt long before the image of his lord, praying for divine help. The Emperor had given him but 24 hours to find the culprit, and he was no closer to solving the mystery. He had a feeling he might well find himself in the unenviable role of scapegoat, particularly since the Empress was just as likely to insist a Green such as himself was responsible – and had the power to make the allegation unchallenged truth. No, the prospects were not pleasant. His eye wandered over the sanctuary carvings, seeking inspiration as he formulated fantastic theories as to who the culprit could be. He was tired, and so was his mind, after interviewing several citizens seen, or supposedly seen (Constantinople being a city which thrived on intrigue and counterintrigue) abroad in the riots, pockets of which were still being put down by Imperial troops. How curious it would be if the culprit was not one of the street, but at a higher level of the hierarchy. *Why*, he thought with a thin smile that Alexander would recognize but shudder at, *what if it were the Empress herself?* It was said that she was devoted to Justinian, who upon marrying her had raised her from lowly ranks, but her back-stair intrigues were common enough knowledge, and her ambition endless.

His thoughts flowed on, from the highest to the lowest, or, in other words, the Nubian. How strange that he should have died so suddenly, so soon after he had seen him. Alexander had been angry about the loss of such valued property. John had replied he could only suspect suicide, or an accident, but now his thoughts began to take a different road. A slave might kill himself, although in his experience it was fairly uncommon. Accidents happened, of course, although this one was oddly timed. Yet who would want to kill a man like the Nubian? Unless, of course, he knew something he had not revealed. Or perhaps he thought he had been found guilty *in absentia*, and was terrified of the possibility of being taken away by the "gold stick man's" guards. Pillars of the community had a hard enough time establishing their innocence, particularly if they got on the wrong side of Empress Theodora. The vulgar irony of the thought prodded him into laughter, its chuckling echoes suddenly ceasing as John thought again, *Pillars of the community?* Pausing only to utter a quick prayer of thanks, he hurried out from the small room into late afternoon sunshine.

Riots may come, emperors may go, city buildings might burn all about him like red-tongued flowers from Hell, but the ancient stylite still stood 30 cubits above the Augusteum, wild eyed and half-naked, content to eat whatever was left by charity or a passing bird, standing aloft until his joints locked and his flesh mortified in more ways than one. There on his pillar, he communed with God and himself, always there, never descending, as much a part of the landscape as the Senate House or the statues on Zeuxippus' Baths – not that the stylite likely frequented the latter, John thought, wrinkling his nose a little as he ascended the ladder, to address the saintly occupant of the pillar, who had just received a pious gift of edibles.

"Bless you, my son," said the old man, through a mouthful of fish. John inclined his head in acknowledgement.

"O father," he began in a hoarse whisper, although there was little need to do so with the usual clamor from the street rising up about them, providing a cocoon of babbling sound which effectively masked their conversation. "I am here in the name of the Emperor, and wish to enquire of you certain things."

"Ask on, then, my son," the greybeard said, sunken eyes gentle under tangled brows, eyes much younger than the weatherbeaten face from which they peered. They were eyes, John hoped, which could, and had, seen far – and well.

"Tell me what you saw a night ago," he commanded.

The stylite smiled. "Ah, many things! It was as a vision, of hell on earth, with the flames of torment destroying all before them, and damned souls stalking the streets, crying for salvation, yet finding none." John hoped fervently that his informant would not, at this particular time, be seized with visions to recount. He was beginning to feel ludicrous, not to say precarious, as the wind from the Sea of Marmara plucked at his cloak. Furthermore, his sandals were increasingly insecure on the rungs. His informant bent kindly eyes upon him, fervent words a contrast to the gentleness of his gaze.

"It was as Orpheus must have experienced on his trip to Hades," the old man said. "Even to dark demons with treasures to tempt the faithful, stalking the pious in the shadows." John narrowed his eyes slightly. "Yes?" he prompted, wondering if he was barking up the wrong ladder. *Hell, demons, torment, indeed.* "Demons aside, did you see anything in the vicinity of the Church? It was certainly light enough."

"Yes, my son, I did. I saw the faithful remove all they could from the wicked conflagrations of the Devil blooming all over the city. Surely those pious souls were reserved a place in heaven because of their actions?"

John, noting to himself that while the stylite had excellent eyesight, he could not see too well, in that those whom he had characterized as pious souls saving religious treasures were actually looting the beautiful Church now in ruins to their left. A blindness which he shared, he felt, seeing, but not seeing. And time was growing short, darkness was creeping around the ramparts of the city. It would be another wet and cold night.

His informant wiped sticky fingers on his wild beard. "Yes, they stalk the night," he said, almost reading John's mind. "The demons, the demons . . ."

But more than that he was not prepared to say.

Justinian sat once more on the double throne on the dais below the domed roof, every inch an Emperor. He smiled kindly upon his Lord

Chamberlain, once more standing before him in the straight-backed stance of a man with good tidings.

"The results of your enquiries?" The tone was appropriately imperious.

John bowed. "Success, Excellency. The culprit was a simple-minded slave, now dead, who apparently saw his opportunity in the general unrest and took it. I have been able to recover . . . it."

Justinian beckoned him to the throne. "Bring it here!" he commanded, yet in a trembling voice. John obeyed, mounting gold-cloth covered stairs to three or four below the top, bowing low. Extending a thin, sunburnt hand, he placed into the Emperor's grasp a nondescript, slightly splintered piece of wood. John received it as his salvation, as indeed, John thought, he would consider it.

"This is from the True Cross itself," the Emperor said, eyes ablaze, "our most holy relic. You may go." John tactfully withdrew from the Great Hall, thankful to get away before the Emperor commanded further details of how he had found the relic in the teeming streets of Constantinople without being able to even reveal what he sought. He left the building, walking slowly along the winding path. A hundred yards away a burst of song issued from the Imperial Guard barracks. He smiled briefly. They served the Lord of Light in their own way. And, in his simple fashion, he served Him also.

For what was the Nubian but the dark demon with treasures (seen by the stylite emerging from the shadows) or rather with the gem-encrusted reliquary which had housed the holy relic for centuries? And why? Because he believed it would protect his master's chariot. Doubtless, the blasphemy of it would not enter his calculations, but enquiries from the Lord Chamberlain would certainly terrify him. Not to mention the possibility of retribution from the master he evidently loved. Thus it seemed likely he set the barn on fire and willed himself to destroy both evidence and himself. *A martyr to his religion,* John thought, standing in the shadows of a small pavilion in a garden which in a few months would bloom with all the flowers of the East. He could almost pity the slave, but had expected none from Justinian, if he had failed on his mission. Thus he had accordingly equipped himself with a piece of wood to replace the holy fragment, reasoning few had seen it, buried so long in its priceless reliquary, and those who might have would scarcely dare to contradict the Emperor. For what, after all, was in it but superstition? Still and all, if nothing else, the Blues would have no supernatural advantage now, thought John the Eunuch, servant of Mithra and supporter of the Greens, as he walked slowly home.

# HE CAME WITH THE RAIN
# Robert van Gulik

*Robert van Gulik (1910–1967) was a Dutch ambassador to Japan who became fascinated with the traditional tales about a seventh-century Chinese magistrate, Judge Dee. While on war duties, he translated the stories into English as* Dee Goong An: Three Murder Cases of Judge Dee *(1949). He then continued by writing new novels and stories about the character, starting with* The Chinese Bell Murders *(1958) and continuing through to* Poets and Murder *(1968).*

*"He Came With the Rain" is set early in Judge Dee's career, in the first year of his magistracy, and follows on from the events featured in* The Chinese Gold Murders *(1959), his earliest case, and* The Lacquer Screen *(1964).*

"This box won't do either!" Judge Dee's First Lady remarked disgustedly. "Look at the grey mould all along the seam of this blue dress!" She slammed the lid of the red-leather clothes-box shut, then turned to the Second Lady. "I've never known such a hot, damp summer. And the heavy downpour we had last night! I thought the rain would never stop. Give me a hand, will you?"

The judge, seated at the tea-table by the open window of the large bedroom, looked on while his two wives put the clothes-box on the floor, and went on to the third one in the pile. Miss Tsao, his First Lady's friend and companion, was drying robes on the brass brazier in the corner, draping them over the copper-wire cover above the glowing coals. The heat of the brazier, together with the steam curling up from the drying clothes, made the atmosphere of the room nearly unbearable, but the three women seemed unaware of it.

With a sigh he turned round and looked outside. From the bedroom here on the second floor of his residence one usually had a fine view of the curved roofs of the city, but now everything was shrouded in a thick leaden mist that blotted out all contours. The mist seemed to have entered his very blood, pulsating dully in his veins. Now he deeply regretted the unfortunate impulse that, on rising, had made

him ask for his grey summer robe. For that request had brought
his First Lady to inspect the four clothes-boxes, and finding mould
on the garments, she had at once summoned his Second and Miss
Tsao. Now the three were completely engrossed in their work, with
apparently no thought of morning tea, let alone breakfast. This was
their first experience of the dog-days in Peng-lai, for it was just
seven months since he had taken up his post of magistrate there.
He stretched his legs, for his knees and feet felt swollen and heavy.
Miss Tsao stooped and took a white dress from the brazier.

"This one is completely dry," she announced. As she reached up
to hang it on the clothes-rack, the judge noticed her slender, shapely
body. Suddenly he asked his First Lady sharply: "Can't you leave all
that to the maids?"

"Of course," his First replied over her shoulder. "But first I want
to see for myself whether there's any real damage. For heaven's sake,
take a look at this red robe, dear!" she went on to Miss Tsao. "The
mould has absolutely eaten into the fabric! And you always say this
dress looks so well on me!"

Judge Dee rose abruptly. The smell of perfume and stale cosmetics
mingling with the faint odour of damp clothes gave the hot room an
atmosphere of overwhelming femininity that suddenly jarred on his
taut nerves. "I'm just going out for a short walk," he said.

"Before you've even had your morning tea?" his First exclaimed.
But her eyes were on the discoloured patches on the red dress in
her hands.

"I'll be back for breakfast," the judge muttered. "Give me that blue
robe over there!" Miss Tsao helped the Second put the robe over his
shoulders and asked solicitously: "Isn't that dress a bit too heavy for
this hot weather?"

"It's dry at least," he said curtly. At the same time he realized with
dismay that Miss Tsao was perfectly right: the thick fabric clung to
his moist back like a coat of mail. He mumbled a greeting and went
downstairs.

He quickly walked down the semi-dark corridor leading to the
small back door of the tribunal compound. He was glad his old friend
and adviser Sergeant Hoong had not yet appeared. The sergeant
knew him so well that he would sense at once that he was in a bad
temper, and he would wonder what it was all about.

The judge opened the back door with his private key and slipped
out into the wet, deserted street. What was it all about, really? he
asked himself as he walked along through the dripping mist. Well,
these seven months on his first independent official post had been
disappointing, of course. The first few days had been exciting, and

then there had been the murder of Mrs. Ho, and the case at the fort. But thereafter there had been nothing but dreary office routine: forms to be filled out, papers to be filed, licences to be issued . . . In the capital he had also had much paperwork to do, but on important papers. Moreover, this district was not really his. The entire region from the river north was a strategic area, under the jurisdiction of the army. And the Korean quarter outside the East Gate had its own administration. He angrily kicked a stone, then cursed. What had looked like a loose boulder was in fact the top of a cobblestone, and he hurt his toe badly. He must take a decision about Miss Tsao. The night before, in the intimacy of their shared couch, his First Lady had again urged him to take Miss Tsao as his Third. She and his Second were fond of her, she had said, and Miss Tsao herself wanted nothing better. "Besides," his First had added with her customary frankness, "your Second is a fine woman but she hasn't had a higher education, and to have an intelligent, well-read girl like Miss Tsao around would make life much more interesting for all concerned." But what if Miss Tsao's willingness was motivated only by gratitude to him for getting her out of the terrible trouble she had been in? In a way it would be easier if he didn't like her so much. On the other hand, would it then be fair to marry a woman one didn't really like? As a magistrate he was entitled to as many as four wives, but personally he held the view that two wives ought to be sufficient unless both of them proved barren. It was all very difficult and confusing. He pulled his robe closer round him, for it had begun to rain.

He sighed with relief when he saw the broad steps leading up to the Temple of Confucius. The third floor of the west tower had been converted into a small tea-house. He would have his morning tea there, then walk back to the tribunal.

In the low-ceilinged, octagonal room a slovenly-dressed waiter was leaning on the counter, stirring the fire of the small tea-stove with iron tongs. Judge Dee noticed with satisfaction that the youngster didn't recognize him, for he was not in the mood to acknowledge bowing and scraping. He ordered a pot of tea and a dry towel and sat down at the bamboo table in front of the counter.

The waiter handed him a none-too-clean towel in a bamboo basket. "Just one moment please, sir. The water'll be boiling soon." As the judge rubbed his long beard dry with the towel, the waiter went on, "Since you are up and about so early, sir, you'll have heard already about the trouble out there." He pointed with his thumb at the open window, and as the judge shook his head, he continued with relish, "Last night a fellow was hacked to pieces in the old watchtower, out there in the marsh."

Judge Dee quickly put the towel down. "A murder? How do you know?"

"The grocery boy told me, sir. Came up here to deliver his stuff while I was scrubbing the floor. At dawn he had gone to the watchtower to collect duck eggs from that half-witted girl who lives up there, and he saw the mess. The girl was sitting crying in a corner. Rushing back to town, he warned the military police at the blockhouse, and the captain went to the old tower with a few of his men. Look, there they are!"

Judge Dee got up and went to the window. From this vantage-point he could see beyond the crenellated top of the city wall the vast green expanse of the marshlands overgrown with reeds, and further on to the north, in the misty distance, the grey water of the river. A hardened road went from the quay north of the city straight to the lonely tower of weather-beaten bricks in the middle of the marsh. A few soldiers with spiked helmets came marching down the road to the blockhouse halfway between the tower and the quay.

"Was the murdered man a soldier?" the judge asked quickly. Although the area north of the city came under the jurisdiction of the army, any crime involving civilians there had to be referred to the tribunal.

"Could be. That half-witted girl is deaf and dumb, but not too bad-looking. Could be a soldier went up the tower for a private conversation with her, if you get what I mean. Ha, the water is boiling!"

Judge Dee strained his eyes. Now two military policemen were riding from the blockhouse to the city, their horses splashing through the water that had submerged part of the raised road.

"Here's your tea, sir! Be careful, the cup is very hot. I'll put it here on the sill for you. No, come to think of it, the murdered man was no soldier. The grocery boy said he was an old merchant living near the North Gate – he knew him by sight. Well, the military police will catch the murderer soon enough. Plenty tough, they are!" He nudged the judge excitedly. "There you are! Didn't I tell you they're tough? See that fellow in chains they're dragging from the blockhouse? He's wearing a fisherman's brown jacket and trousers. Well, they'll take him to the fort now, and . . ."

"They'll do nothing of the sort!" the judge interrupted angrily. He hastily took a sip from the tea and scalded his mouth. He paid and rushed downstairs. A civilian murdered by another civilian, that was clearly a case for the tribunal! This was a splendid occasion to tell the military exactly where they got off! Once and for all.

All his apathy had dropped away from him. He rented a horse

from the blacksmith on the corner, jumped into the saddle and rode to the North Gate. The guards cast an astonished look at the dishevelled horseman with the wet house-cap sagging on his head. But then they recognized their magistrate and sprang to attention. The judge dismounted and motioned the corporal to follow him into the guardhouse beside the gate. "What is all this commotion out on the marsh?" he asked.

"A man was found murdered in the old tower, sir. The military police have arrested the murderer already; they are questioning him now in the blockhouse. I expect they'll come down to the quay presently."

Judge Dee sat down on the bamboo bench and handed the corporal a few coppers. "Tell one of your men to buy me two oilcakes!"

The oilcakes came fresh from the griddle of a street vendor and had an appetizing smell of garlic and onions, but the judge did not enjoy them, hungry though he was. The hot tea had burnt his tongue, and his mind was concerned with the abuse of power by the army authorities. He reflected ruefully that in the capital one didn't have such annoying problems to cope with: there, detailed rules fixed the exact extent of the authority of every official, high or low. As he was finishing his oilcakes, the corporal came in.

"The military police have now taken the prisoner to their watchpost on the quay, sir."

Judge Dee sprang up. "Follow me with four men!"

On the river quay a slight breeze was dispersing the mist. The judge's robe clung wetly to his shoulders. "Exactly the kind of weather for catching a bad cold," he muttered. A heavily armed sentry ushered him into the bare waiting-room of the watchpost.

In the back a tall man wearing the coat of mail and spiked helmet of the military police was sitting behind a roughly made wooden desk. He was filling out an official form with laborious, slow strokes of his writing-brush.

"I am Magistrate Dee," the judge began. "I demand to know . . ." He suddenly broke off. The captain had looked up. His face was marked by a terrible white scar running along his left cheek and across his mouth. His misshapen lips were half-concealed by a ragged moustache. Before the judge had recovered from this shock, the captain had risen. He saluted smartly and said in a clipped voice:

"Glad you came, sir. I have just finished my report to you." Pointing at the stretcher covered with a blanket on the floor in the corner, he added, "That's the dead body, and the murderer is in the back room there. You want him taken directly to the jail of the tribunal, I suppose?"

"Yes. Certainly," Judge Dee replied, rather lamely.

"Good." The captain folded the sheet he had been writing on and handed it to the judge. "Sit down, sir. If you have a moment to spare, I'd like to tell you myself about the case."

Judge Dee took the seat by the desk and motioned the captain to sit down too. Stroking his long beard, he said to himself that all this was turning out quite differently from what he had expected.

"Well," the captain began, "I know the marshland as well as the palm of my hand. That deaf-mute girl who lives in the tower is a harmless idiot, so when it was reported that a murdered man was lying up in her room, I thought at once of assault and robbery, and sent my men to search the marshland between the tower and the riverbank."

"Why especially that area?" the judge interrupted. "It could just as well have happened on the road, couldn't it? The murderer hiding the dead body later in the tower?"

"No, sir. Our blockhouse is located on the road halfway between the quay here and the old tower. From there my men keep an eye on the road all day long, as per orders. To prevent Korean spies from entering or leaving the city, you see. And they patrol that road at night. That road is the only means of crossing the marsh, by the way. It's tricky country, and anyone trying to cross it would risk getting into a swamp or quicksand and would drown. Now my men found the body was still warm, and we concluded he was killed a few hours before dawn. Since no one passed the blockhouse except the grocery boy, it follows that both the murdered man and the criminal came from the north. A pathway leads through the reeds from the tower to the riverbank, and a fellow familiar with the layout could slip by there without my men in the blockhouse spotting him." The captain stroked his moustache and added, "If he had succeeded in getting by our river patrols, that is."

"And your men caught the murderer by the waterside?"

"Yes, sir. They discovered a young fisherman, Wang San-lang his name is, hiding in his small boat among the rushes, directly north of the tower. He was trying to wash his trousers which were stained with blood. When my men hailed him, he pushed off and tried to paddle his boat into midstream. The archers shot a few string arrows into the hull, and before he knew where he was he was being hauled back to shore, boat and all. He disclaimed all knowledge of any dead man in the tower, maintained he was on his way there to bring the deaf-mute girl a large carp, and that he got the blood on his trousers while cleaning that carp. He was waiting for dawn to visit her. We searched him, and we found this in his belt."

The captain unwrapped a small paper package on his desk and showed the judge three shining silver pieces. "We identified the corpse by the visiting-cards we found on it." He shook the contents of a large envelope out on the table. Besides a package of cards there were two keys, some small change, and a pawn-ticket. Pointing at the ticket, the captain continued, "That scrap of paper was lying on the floor, close to the body. Must have dropped out of his jacket. The murdered man is the pawnbroker Choong, the owner of a large and well-known pawnshop, just inside the North Gate. A wealthy man. His hobby is fishing. My theory is that Choong met Wang somewhere on the quay last night and hired him to take him out in his boat for a night of fishing on the river. When they had got to the deserted area north of the tower, Wang lured the old man there under some pretext or other and killed him. He had planned to hide the body somewhere in the tower – the thing is half in ruins, you know, and the girl uses only the second storey – but she woke up and caught him in the act. So he just took the silver and left. This is only a theory, mind you, for the girl is worthless as a witness. My men tried to get something out of her, but she only scribbled down some incoherent nonsense about rain spirits and black goblins. Then she had a fit, began to laugh and to cry at the same time. A poor, harmless half-wit." He rose, walked over to the stretcher and lifted the blanket. "Here's the dead body."

Judge Dee bent over the lean shape, which was clad in a simple brown robe. The breast showed patches of clotted blood, and the sleeves were covered with dried mud. The face had a peaceful look, but it was very ugly: lantern-shaped, with a beaked nose that was slightly askew, and a thin-lipped, too large mouth. The head with its long, greying hair was bare.

"Not a very handsome gentleman," the captain remarked. "Though I should be the last to pass such a remark!" A spasm contorted his mutilated face. He raised the body's shoulders and showed the judge the large red stain on the back. "Killed by a knife thrust from behind that must have penetrated right into his heart. He was lying on his back on the floor, just inside the door of the girl's room." The captain let the upper part of the body drop. "Nasty fellow, that fisherman. After he had murdered Choong, he began to cut up his breast and belly. I say *after* he had killed him, for as you see those wounds in front haven't bled as much as one would expect. Oh yes, here's my last exhibit! Had nearly forgotten it!" He pulled out a drawer in the desk and unwrapped the oiled paper of an oblong package. Handing the judge a long thin knife, he said, "This was found in Wang's boat, sir. He says he uses it for cleaning his fish. There was no trace of blood on it. Why should there be? There was plenty of water around to wash it clean after he had got back to the boat! Well, that's about all, sir. I expect that Wang'll confess readily enough. I know that type of young hoodlum. They begin by stoutly denying everything, but after a thorough interrogation they break down and then they talk their mouths off. What are your orders, sir?"

"First I must inform the next of kin, and have them formally identify the body. Therefore, I . . ."

"I've attended to that, sir. Choong was a widower, and his two sons are living in the capital. The body was officially identified just now by Mr. Lin, the dead man's partner, who lived together with him."

"You and your men did an excellent job," the judge said. "Tell your men to transfer the prisoner and the dead body to the guards I brought with me." Rising, he added, "I am really most grateful for your swift and efficient action, captain. This being a civilian case, you only needed to report the murder to the tribunal and you could have left it at that. You went out of your way to help me and . . ."

The captain raised his hand in a deprecatory gesture and said in his strange dull voice, "It was a pleasure, sir. I happen to be one of Colonel Meng's men. We shall always do all we can to help you. All of us, always."

The spasm that distorted his misshapen face had to be a smile. Judge Dee walked back to the guardhouse at the North Gate. He had decided to question the prisoner there at once, then go to the scene of the crime. If he transferred the investigation to the tribunal, clues might get stale. It seemed a fairly straightforward case, but one never knew.

He sat down at the only table in the bare guardroom and settled down to a study of the captain's report. It contained little beyond what the captain had already told him. The victim's full name was Choong Fang, age fifty-six; the girl was called Oriole, twenty years of age, and the young fisherman was twenty-two. He took the visiting-cards and the pawn-ticket from his sleeve. The cards stated that Mr. Choong was a native of Shansi Province. The pawn-ticket was a tally, stamped with the large red stamp of Choong's pawnshop; it concerned four brocade robes pawned the day before by a Mrs. Pei for three silver pieces, to be redeemed in three months at a monthly interest of 5 per cent.

The corporal came in, followed by two guards carrying the stretcher.

"Put it down there in the corner," Judge Dee ordered. "Do you know about that deaf-mute girl who lives in the watchtower? The military police gave only her personal name – Oriole."

"Yes, sir, that's what she is called. She's an abandoned child. An old crone who used to sell fruit near the gate here brought her up and taught her to write a few dozen letters and a bit of sign language. When the old woman died two years ago, the girl went to live in the tower because the street urchins were always pestering her. She raises ducks there, and sells the eggs. People called her Oriole to make fun of her being dumb, and the nickname stuck."

"All right. Bring the prisoner before me."

The guards came back flanking a squat, sturdily built youngster. His tousled hair hung down over the corrugated brow of his swarthy, scowling face, and his brown jacket and trousers were clumsily patched in several places. His hands were chained behind his back, an extra loop of the thin chain encircling his thick, bare neck. The guards pressed him down on his knees in front of the judge.

Judge Dee observed the youngster in silence for a while, wondering what would be the best way to start the interrogation. There was only the patter of the rain outside, and the prisoner's heavy breathing. The judge took the three silver pieces from his sleeve.

"Where did you get these?"

The young fisherman muttered something in a broad dialect that the judge didn't quite understand. One of the guards kicked the prisoner and growled: "Speak louder!"

"It's my savings. For buying a real boat."

"When did you first meet Mr. Choong?"

The boy burst out in a string of obscene curses. The guard on his right stopped him by hitting him over his head with the flat of his sword. Wang shook his head, then said dully, "Only knew him by sight because he was often around on the quay." Suddenly he added viciously: "If I'd ever met him, I'd have killed the dirty swine, the crook . . ."

"Did Mr. Choong cheat when you pawned something in his shop?" Judge Dee asked quickly.

"Think I have anything to pawn?"

"Why call him a crook then?"

Wang looked up at the judge who thought he caught a sly glint in his small, bloodshot eyes. The youngster bent his head again and replied in a sullen voice: "Because all pawnbrokers are crooks."

"What did you do last night?"

"I told the soldiers already. Had a bowl of noodles at the stall on the quay, then went up river. After I had caught some good fish, I moored the boat on the bank north of the tower and had a nap. I'd planned to bring some fish to the tower at dawn, for Oriole."

Something in the way the boy pronounced the girl's name caught

Judge Dee's attention. He said slowly, "You deny having murdered the pawnbroker. Since, besides you, there was only the girl about, it follows it was she who killed him."

Suddenly Wang jumped up and went for the judge. He moved so quickly that the two guards only got hold of him just in time. He kicked them but got a blow on his head that made him fall down backwards, his chains clanking on the floorstones.

"You dog-official, you . . ." the youngster burst out, trying to scramble up. The corporal gave him a kick in the face that made his head slam back on the floor with a hard thud. He lay quite still, blood trickling from his torn mouth.

The judge got up and bent over the still figure. He had lost consciousness.

"Don't maltreat a prisoner unless you are ordered to," the judge told the corporal sternly. "Bring him round, and take him to the jail. Later I shall interrogate him formally, during the noon session. You'll take the dead body to the tribunal, corporal. Report to Sergeant Hoong and hand him this statement, drawn up by the captain of the military police. Tell the sergeant that I'll return to the tribunal as soon as I have questioned a few witnesses here." He cast a look at the window. It was still raining. "Get me a piece of oiled cloth!"

Before Judge Dee stepped outside he draped the oiled cloth over his head and shoulders, then jumped into the saddle of his hired horse. He rode along the quay and took the hardened road that led to the marshlands.

The mist had cleared a little and as he rode along he looked curiously at the deserted, green surface on either side of the road. Narrow gullies followed a winding course through the reeds, here and there broadening into large pools that gleamed dully in the grey light. A flight of small water birds suddenly flew up, with piercing cries that resounded eerily over the desolate marsh. He noticed that the water was subsiding after the torrential rain that had fallen in the night; the road was dry now, but the water had left large patches of duck-weed. When he was about to pass the blockhouse the sentry stopped him, but he let him go on as soon as the judge had shown him the identification document he carried in his boot.

The old watchtower was a clumsy, square building of five storeys, standing on a raised base of roughly hewn stone blocks. The shutters of the arched windows had gone and the roof of the top storey had caved in. Two big black crows sat perched on a broken beam.

As he came nearer he heard loud quacking. A few dozen ducks were huddling close together by the side of a muddy pool below the tower's base. When the judge dismounted and fastened the reins to a moss-covered stone pillar, the ducks began to splash around in the water, quacking indignantly.

The ground floor of the tower was just a dark, low vault, empty but for a heap of old broken furniture. A narrow, rickety flight of wooden stairs led up to the floor above. The judge climbed up, seeking support with his left hand from the wet, mould-covered wall, for the bannisters were gone.

When he stepped into the half-dark, bare room, something stirred among the rags piled up on the roughly made plank-bed under the arched window. Some raucous sounds came from under a soiled, patched quilt. A quick look around showed that the room only contained a rustic table with a cracked teapot, and a bamboo bench against the side wall. In the corner was a brick oven carrying a large pan; beside it stood a rattan basket filled to the brim with pieces of charcoal. A musty smell of mould and stale sweat hung in the air.

Suddenly the quilt was thrown to the floor. A half-naked girl with long, tousled hair jumped down from the plank-bed. After one look at the judge, she again made that strange, raucous sound and scuttled to the farthest corner. Then she dropped to her knees, trembling violently.

Judge Dee realized that he didn't present a very reassuring sight. He quickly pulled his identification document from his boot, unfolded it and walked up to the cowering girl, pointing with his forefinger at the large red stamp of the tribunal. Then he pointed at himself.

She apparently understood, for now she scrambled up and stared at him with large eyes that held an animal fear. She wore nothing but a tattered skirt, fastened to her waist with a piece of straw rope. She had a shapely, well-developed body and her skin was surprisingly white. Her round face was smeared with dirt but was not unattractive. Judge Dee pulled the bench up to the table and sat down. Feeling that some familiar gesture was needed to reassure the frightened girl, he took the teapot and drank from the spout, as farmers do.

The girl came up to the table, spat on the dirty top and drew in the spittle with her forefinger a few badly deformed characters. They read: "Wang did not kill him."

The judge nodded. He poured tea on the table-top, and motioned her to wipe it clean. She obediently went to the bed, took a rag and began to polish the table top with feverish haste. Judge Dee walked over to the stove and selected a few pieces of charcoal. Resuming his seat, he wrote with the charcoal on the table-top: "Who killed him?"

She shivered. She took the other piece of charcoal and wrote: "Bad black goblins." She pointed excitedly at the words, then scribbled quickly: "Bad goblins changed the good rain spirit."

"You saw the black goblins?" he wrote.

She shook her tousled head emphatically. She tapped with her forefinger repeatedly on the word "black", then she pointed at her closed eyes and shook her head again. The judge sighed. He wrote: "You know Mr. Choong?"

She looked perplexedly at his writing, her finger in her mouth. He realized that the complicated character indicating the surname Choong was unknown to her. He crossed it out and wrote "old man".

She again shook her head. With an expression of disgust she drew circles round the words "old man" and added: "Too much blood. Good rain spirit won't come any more. No silver for Wang's boat any more." Tears came trickling down her grubby cheeks as she wrote with a shaking hand: "Good rain spirit always sleep with me." She pointed at the plank-bed.

Judge Dee gave her a searching look. He knew that rain spirits played a prominent role in local folklore, so that it was only natural that they figured in the dreams and vagaries of this overdeveloped young girl. On the other hand, she had referred to silver. He wrote: "What does the rain spirit look like?"

Her round face lit up. With a broad smile she wrote in big, clumsy letters: "Tall. Handsome. Kind." She drew a circle round each of the three words, then threw the charcoal on the table and, hugging her bare breasts, began to giggle ecstatically.

The judge averted his gaze. When he turned to look at her again, she had let her hands drop and stood there staring straight ahead with wide eyes. Suddenly her expression changed again. With a quick gesture she pointed at the arched window, and made some strange sounds. He turned round. There was a faint colour in the leaden sky, the trace of a rainbow. She stared at it, in childish delight, her mouth half open. The judge took up the piece of charcoal for one final question: "When does the rain spirit come?"

She stared at the words for a long time, absentmindedly combing her long, greasy locks with her fingers. At last she bent over the table and wrote: "Black night and much rain." She put circles round the words "black" and "rain", then added: "He came with the rain."

All at once she put her hands to her face and began to sob convulsively. The sound mingled with the loud quacking of the ducks from below. Realizing that she couldn't hear the birds, he rose and laid his hand on her bare shoulder. When she looked up he was shocked by the wild, half-crazed gleam in her wide eyes. He quickly drew a duck on the table, and added the word "hunger". She clasped her hand to her mouth and ran to the oven. Judge Dee

scrutinized the large flagstones in front of the entrance. He saw there
a clean space on the dirty, dust-covered floor. Evidently it was there
that the dead man had lain, and the military police had swept up
the floor. He remembered ruefully his unkind thoughts about them.
Sounds of chopping made him turn round. The girl was cutting up
stale rice cakes on a primitive chopping board. The judge watched
with a worried frown her deft handling of the large kitchen knife.
Suddenly she drove the long, sharp point of the knife in the board,
then shook the chopped up rice cakes into the pan on the oven, giving
the judge a happy smile over her shoulder. He nodded at her and went
down the creaking stairs.

The rain had ceased, a thin mist was gathering over the marsh.
While untying the reins, he told the noisy ducks: "Don't worry, your
breakfast is under way!"

He made his horse go ahead at a sedate pace. The mist came
drifting in from the river. Strangely shaped clouds were floating over
the tall reeds, here and there dissolving in long writhing trailers that
resembled the tentacles of some monstrous water-animal. He wished
he knew more about the hoary, deeply rooted beliefs of the local
people. In many places people still venerated a river god or goddess,
and farmers and fishermen made sacrificial offerings to these at the
waterside. Evidently such things loomed large in the deaf-mute girl's
feeble mind, shifting continually from fact to fiction, and unable
to control the urges of her fullblown body. He drove his horse to
a gallop.

Back at the North Gate, he told the corporal to take him to the
pawnbroker's place. When they had arrived at the large, prosperous-
looking pawnshop the corporal explained that Choong's private
residence was located directly behind the shop and pointed at
the narrow alleyway that led to the main entrance. Judge Dee
told the corporal he could go back, and knocked on the black-
lacquered gate.

A lean man, neatly dressed in a brown gown with black sash and
borders, opened it. Bestowing a bewildered look on his wet, bearded
visitor, he said: "You want the shop, I suppose. I can take you, I was
just going there."

"I am the magistrate," Judge Dee told him impatiently. "I've just
come from the marsh. Had a look at the place where your partner
was murdered. Let's go inside, I want to hand over to you what was
found on the dead body."

Mr. Lin made a very low bow and conducted his distinguished
visitor to a small but comfortable side hall, furnished in conventional style with a few pieces of heavy blackwood furniture.

He ceremoniously led the judge to the broad bench at the back. While his host was telling the old manservant to bring tea and cakes, the judge looked curiously at the large aviary of copper wire on the wall table. About a dozen paddy birds were fluttering around inside.

"A hobby of my partner's," Mr. Lin said with an indulgent smile. "He was very fond of birds, always fed them himself."

With his neatly trimmed chin-beard and small, greying moustache Lin seemed at first sight just a typical middle-class shopkeeper. But a closer inspection revealed deep lines around his thin mouth, and large, sombre eyes that suggested a man with a definite personality. The judge set his cup down and formally expressed his sympathy with the firm's loss. Then he took the envelope from his sleeve and shook out the visiting-cards, the small cash, the pawn-ticket and the two keys. "That's all, Mr. Lin. Did your partner as a rule carry large sums of money on him?"

Lin silently looked the small pile over, stroking his chin-beard.

"No, sir. Since he retired from the firm two years ago, there was no need for him to carry much money about. But he certainly had more on him than just these few coppers when he went out last night."

"What time was that?"

"About eight, sir. After we had had dinner together here down-stairs. He wanted to take a walk along the quay, so he said."

"Did Mr. Choong often do that?"

"Oh yes, sir! He had always been a man of solitary habits, and after the demise of his wife two years ago, he went out for long walks nearly every other night and always by himself. He always had his meals served in his small library upstairs, although I live here in this same house, in the left wing. Last night, however, there was a matter of business to discuss and therefore he came down to have dinner with me."

"You have no family, Mr. Lin?"

"No, sir. Never had time to establish a household! My part-ner had the capital, but the actual business of the pawnshop he left largely to me. And after his retirement he hardly set foot in our shop."

"I see. To come back to last night. Did Mr. Choong say when he would be back?"

"No, sir. The servant had standing orders not to wait up for him. My partner was an enthusiastic fisherman, you see. If he thought it looked like good fishing weather on the quay, he would hire a boat and pass the night up river."

Judge Dee nodded slowly. "The military police will have told you that they arrested a young fisherman called Wang San-lang. Did your partner often hire his boat?"

"That I don't know, sir. There are scores of fishermen about on the quay, you see, and most of them are eager to make a few extra coppers. But if my partner rented Wang's boat, it doesn't astonish me that he ran into trouble, for Wang is a violent young ruffian. I know of him, because being a fisherman of sorts myself, I have often heard the others talk about him. Surly, uncompanionable youngster." He sighed. "I'd like to go out fishing as often as my partner did, only I haven't got that much time . . . Well, it's very kind of you to have brought these keys, sir. Lucky that Wang didn't take them and throw them away! The larger one is the key of my late partner's library, the other of the strongbox he has there for keeping important papers." He stretched out his hand to take the keys, but Judge Dee scooped them up and put them in his sleeve.

"Since I am here," he said, "I shall have a look at Mr. Choong's papers right now, Mr. Lin. This is a murder case, and until it is solved, all the victim's papers are temporarily at the disposal of the authorities for possible clues. Take me to the library, please."

"Certainly, sir." Lin took the judge up a broad staircase and pointed at the door at the end of the corridor. The judge unlocked it with the larger key.

"Thanks very much, Mr. Lin. I shall join you downstairs presently."

The judge stepped into the small room, locked the door behind him, then went to push the low, broad window wide open. The roofs of the neighbouring houses gleamed in the grey mist. He turned and sat down in the capacious armchair behind the rosewood writing-desk facing the window. After a casual look at the iron-bound strongbox on the floor beside his chair, he leaned back and pensively took stock of his surroundings. The small library was scrupulously clean and furnished with simple, old-fashioned taste. The spotless whitewashed walls were decorated with two good landscape scrolls, and the solid ebony wall table bore a slender vase of white porcelain, with a few wilting roses. Piles of books in brocade covers were neatly stacked on the shelves of the small bookcase of spotted bamboo.

Folding his arms, the judge wondered what connection there could be between this tastefully arranged library that seemed to belong to an elegant scholar rather than to a pawnbroker, and the bare, dark room in the half-ruined watchtower, breathing decay, sloth and the direst poverty. After a while he shook his head, bent and unlocked the strongbox. Its contents matched the methodical neatness of the room: bundles of documents, each bound up with green ribbon and provided with an inscribed label. He selected the bundles marked "private correspondence" and "accounts and receipts". The former contained a few important letters about capital investment and correspondence from his sons, mainly about their family affairs and asking Mr. Choong's advice and instructions. Leafing through the second bundle, Judge Dee's practised eye saw at once that the deceased had been leading a frugal, nearly austere life. Suddenly he frowned. He had found a pink receipt, bearing the stamp of a house of assignation. It was dated back a year and a half. He quickly went through the bundle and found half a dozen similar receipts, the last dated back six months. Apparently Mr. Choong had, after his wife's demise, hoped to find consolation in venal love, but had soon discovered that such hope was vain. With a sigh he opened the large envelope which he had taken from the bottom of the box. It was marked: "Last Will and Testament". It was dated one year before, and stated that all of Mr. Choong's landed property – which was considerable – was to go to his two sons, together with two-thirds of his capital. The remaining one-third, and the pawnshop, was bequeathed to Mr. Lin "in recognition of his long and loyal service to the firm".

The judge replaced the papers. He rose and went to inspect the bookcase. He discovered that except for two dog-eared dictionaries, all the books were collections of poetry, complete editions of the most representative lyrical poets of former times. He looked through one volume. Every difficult word had been annotated in red ink, in an unformed, rather clumsy hand. Nodding slowly, he replaced the volume. Yes, now he understood. Mr. Choong had been engaged in a trade that forbade all personal feeling, namely that of a pawnbroker. And his pronouncedly ugly face made tender attachments unlikely. Yet at heart he was a romantic, hankering after the higher things of life, but very self-conscious and shy about these yearnings. As a merchant he had of course only received an elementary education, so he tried laboriously to expand his literary knowledge, reading old poetry with a dictionary in this small library which he kept so carefully locked.

Judge Dee sat down again and took his folding fan from his sleeve. Fanning himself, he concentrated his thoughts on this unusual pawnbroker. The only glimpse the outer world got of the sensitive nature of this man was his love of birds, evinced by the paddy birds downstairs. At last the judge got up. About to put his fan back into his sleeve, he suddenly checked himself. He looked at the fan absentmindedly for a while, then laid it on the desk. After a last look at the room he went downstairs.

His host offered him another cup of tea but Judge Dee shook his head. Handing Lin the two keys, he said, "I have to go back to the tribunal now. I found nothing among your partner's papers suggesting that he had any enemies, so I think that this case is exactly what it seems, namely a case of murder for gain. To a poor man, three silver pieces are a fortune. Why are those birds fluttering about?" He went to the cage. "Aha, their water is dirty. You ought to tell the servant to change it, Mr. Lin."

Lin muttered something and clapped his hands. Judge Dee groped in his sleeve. "How careless of me!" he exclaimed. "I left my fan on the desk upstairs. Would you fetch it for me, Mr. Lin?"

Just as Lin was rushing to the staircase, the old manservant came in. When the judge had told him that the water in the reservoir of the birdcage ought to be changed daily, the old man said, shaking his head, "I told Mr. Lin so, but he wouldn't listen. Doesn't care for birds. My master now, he loved them, he . . ."

"Yes, Mr. Lin told me that last night he had an argument with your master about those birds."

"Well yes, sir, both of them got quite excited. What was it about, sir? I only caught a few words about birds when I brought the rice."

"It doesn't matter," the judge said quickly. He had heard Mr. Lin come downstairs. "Well, Mr. Lin, thanks for the tea. Come to the chancery in, say, one hour, with the most important documents relating to your late partner's assets. My senior clerk will help you fill out the official forms, and the registration of Mr. Choong's will."

Mr. Lin thanked the judge profusely and saw him respectfully to the door.

Judge Dee told the guards at the gate of the tribunal to return his rented horse to the blacksmith, and went straight to his private residence at the back of the chancery. The old housemaster informed him that Sergeant Hoong was waiting in his private office. The judge nodded. "Tell the bathroom attendant that I want to take a bath now."

In the black-tiled dressing-room adjoining the bath he quickly stripped off his robe, drenched with sweat and rain. He felt soiled, in body and in mind. The attendant sluiced him with cold water, and vigorously scrubbed his back. But it was only after the judge had been lying in the sunken pool in hot water for some time that he began to feel better. Thereafter he had the attendant massage his shoulders, and when he had been rubbed dry he put on a crisp clean robe of blue cotton, and placed a cap of thin black gauze on his head. In this attire he walked over to his women's quarters.

About to enter the garden room where his ladies usually passed the morning, he halted a moment, touched by the peaceful scene. His two wives, clad in flowered robes of thin silk, were sitting with Miss Tsao at the red-lacquered table in front of the open sliding doors. The walled-in rock garden outside, planted with ferns and tall, rustling bamboos, suggested refreshing coolness. This was his own private world, a clean haven of refuge from the outside world of cruel violence and repulsive decadence he had to deal with in his official life. Then and there he took the firm resolution that he would preserve his harmonious family life intact, always.

His First Lady put her embroidery frame down and quickly came to meet him. "We have been waiting with breakfast for you for nearly an hour!" she told him reproachfully.

"I am sorry. The fact is that there was some trouble at the North Gate and I had to attend to it at once. I must go to the chancery now, but I shall join you for the noon rice." She conducted him to the door. When she was making her bow he told her in a low voice, "By the way, I have decided to follow your advice in the matter we discussed last night. Please make the necessary arrangements."

With a pleased smile she bowed again, and the judge went down the corridor that led to the chancery.

He found Sergeant Hoong sitting in an armchair in the corner of his private office. His old adviser got up and wished him a good morning. Tapping the document in his hand, the sergeant said, "I was relieved when I got this report, Your Honour, for we were getting worried about your prolonged absence! I had the prisoner locked up in jail, and the dead body deposited in the mortuary. After I had viewed it with the coroner, Ma Joong and Chiao Tai, your two lieutenants, rode to the North Gate to see whether you needed any assistance."

Judge Dee had sat down behind his desk. He looked askance at the pile of dossiers. "Is there anything urgent among the incoming documents, Hoong?"

"No, sir. All those files concern routine administrative matters."

"Good. Then we shall devote the noon session to the murder of the pawnbroker Choong."

The sergeant nodded contentedly. "I saw from the captain's report, Your Honour, that it is a fairly simple case. And since we have the murder suspect safely under lock and key . . ."

The judge shook his head. "No, Hoong, I wouldn't call it a simple case, exactly. But thanks to the quick measures of the military police, and thanks to the lucky chance that brought me right into the middle of things, a definite pattern has emerged."

He clapped his hands. When the headman came inside and made

his bow the judge ordered him to bring the prisoner Wang before him. He went on to the sergeant, "I am perfectly aware, Hoong, that a judge is supposed to interrogate an accused only publicly, in court. But this is not a formal hearing. A general talk for my orientation, rather."

Sergeant Hoong looked doubtful, but the judge vouchsafed no further explanation, and began to leaf through the topmost file on his desk. He looked up when the headman brought Wang inside. The chains had been taken off him, but his swarthy face looked as surly as before. The headman pressed him down on his knees, then stood himself behind him, his heavy whip in his hands.

"Your presence is not required, Headman," Judge Dee told him curtly.

The headman cast a worried glance at Sergeant Hoong. "This is a violent ruffian, Your Honour," he began diffidently. "He might . . ."

"You heard me!" the judge snapped.

After the disconcerted headman had left, Judge Dee leaned back in his chair. He asked the young fisherman in a conversational tone, "How long have you been living on the waterfront, Wang?"

"Ever since I can remember," the boy muttered.

"It's a strange land," the judge said slowly to Sergeant Hoong. "When I was riding through the marsh this morning, I saw weirdly shaped clouds drifting about, and shreds of mist that looked like long arms reaching up out of the water, as if . . ."

The youngster had been listening intently. Now he interrupted quickly: "Better not speak of those things!"

"Yes, you know all about those things, Wang. On stormy nights, there must be more going on in the marshlands than we city-dwellers realize."

Wang nodded vigorously. "I've seen many things," he said in a low voice, "with my own eyes. They all come up from the water. Some can harm you, others help drowning people, sometimes. But it's better to keep away from them, anyway."

"Exactly! Yet you made bold to interfere, Wang. And see what has happened to you now! You were arrested, you were kicked and beaten, and now you are a prisoner accused of murder!"

"I told you I didn't kill him!"

"Yes. But did you know who or what killed him? Yet you stabbed him when he was dead. Several times."

"I saw red . . ." Wang muttered. "If I'd known sooner, I'd have cut his throat. For I know him by sight, the rat, the . . ."

"Hold your tongue!" Judge Dee interrupted him sharply. "You cut up a dead man, and that's a mean and cowardly thing to do!"

He continued, calmer, "However, since even in your blind rage you spared Oriole by refraining from an explanation, I am willing to forget what you did. How long have you been going with her?"

"Over a year. She's sweet, and she's clever too. Don't believe she's a half-wit! She can write more than a hundred characters. I can read only a dozen or so."

Judge Dee took the three silver pieces from his sleeve and laid them on the desk. "Take this silver, it belongs rightly to her and to you. Buy your boat and marry her. She needs you, Wang." The youngster snatched the silver and tucked it in his belt. The judge went on, "You'll have to go back to jail for a few hours, for I can't release you until you have been formally cleared of the murder charge. Then you'll be set free. Learn to control your temper, Wang!"

He clapped his hands. The headman came in at once. He had been waiting just outside the door, ready to rush inside at the first sign of trouble.

"Take the prisoner back to his cell, headman. Then fetch Mr. Lin. You'll find him in the chancery."

Sergeant Hoong had been listening with mounting astonishment. Now he asked with a perplexed look, "What were you talking about with that young fellow, Your Honour? I couldn't follow it at all. Are you really intending to let him go?"

Judge Dee rose and went to the window. Looking out at the dreary, wet courtyard, he said, "It's raining again! What was I talking about, Hoong? I was just checking whether Wang really believed all those weird superstitions. One of these days, Hoong, you might try to find in our chancery library a book on local folklore."

"But you don't believe all that nonsense, sir!"

"No, I don't. Not all of it, at least. But I feel I ought to read up on the subject, for it plays a large role in the daily life of the common people of our district. Pour me a cup of tea, will you?"

While the sergeant prepared the tea, Judge Dee resumed his seat and concentrated on the official documents on his desk. After he had drunk a second cup, there was a knock at the door. The headman ushered Mr. Lin inside, then discreetly withdrew.

"Sit down, Mr. Lin!" the judge addressed his guest affably. "I trust my senior clerk gave you the necessary instructions for the documents to be drawn up?"

"Yes, indeed, Your Honour. Right now we were checking the landed property with the register and . . ."

"According to the will drawn up a year ago," the judge cut in, "Mr. Choong bequeathed all the land to his two sons, together with two-thirds of his capital, as you know. One-third of the capital, and the pawnshop, he left to you. Are you planning to continue the business?"

"No, sir," Lin replied with his thin smile. "I have worked in that pawnshop for more than thirty years, from morning till night. I shall sell it, and live off the rent from my capital."

"Precisely. But suppose Mr. Choong had made a new will? Containing a new clause stipulating that you were to get only the shop?" As Lin's face went livid, he went on quickly, "It's a prosperous business, but it would take you four or five years to assemble enough capital to retire. And you are getting on in years, Mr. Lin."

"Impossible! How . . . how could he . . ." Lin stammered. Then he snapped, "Did you find a new will in his strongbox?"

Instead of answering the question, Judge Dee said coldly: "Your partner had a mistress, Mr. Lin. Her love came to mean more to him than anything else."

Lin jumped up. "Do you mean to say that the old fool willed his money to that deaf-mute slut?"

"Yes, you know all about that affair, Mr. Lin. Since last night, when your partner told you. You had a violent quarrel. No, don't try to deny it! Your manservant overheard what you said, and he will testify in court."

Lin sat down again. He wiped his moist face. Then he began, calmer now, "Yes, sir, I admit that I got very angry when my partner informed me last night that he loved that girl. He wanted to take her away to some distant place and marry her. I tried to make him see how utterly foolish that would be, but he told me to mind my own business and ran out of the house in a huff. I had no idea he would go to the tower. It's common knowledge that that young hoodlum Wang is carrying on with the half-wit. Wang surprised the two, and he murdered my partner. I apologize for not having mentioned these facts to you this morning, sir. I couldn't bring myself to compromise my late partner . . . And since you had arrested the murderer, everything would have come out anyway in court . . ." He shook his head. "I am partly to blame, sir. I should have gone after him last night, I should've . . ."

"But you did go after him, Mr. Lin," Judge Dee interrupted curtly. "You are a fisherman too, you know the marsh as well as your partner. Ordinarily one can't cross the marsh, but after a heavy rain the water rises, and an experienced boatman in a shallow skiff could paddle across by way of the swollen gullies and pools."

"Impossible! The road is patrolled by the military police all night!"

"A man crouching in a skiff could take cover behind the tall reeds,

Mr. Lin. Therefore your partner could only visit the tower on nights after a heavy rain. And therefore the poor half-witted girl took the visitor for a supernatural being, a rain spirit. For he came with the rain." He sighed. Suddenly he fixed Lin with his piercing eyes and said sternly, "When Mr. Choong told you about his plans last night, Lin, you saw all your long-cherished hopes of a life in ease and luxury go up into thin air. Therefore you followed Choong, and you murdered him in the tower by thrusting a knife into his back."

Lin raised his hands. "What a fantastic theory, sir! How do you propose to prove this slanderous accusation?"

"By Mrs. Pei's pawn-ticket, among other things. It was found by the military police on the scene of the crime. But Mr. Choong had completely retired from the business, as you told me yourself. Why then would he be carrying a pawn-ticket that had been issued that very day?" As Lin remained silent, Judge Dee went on, "You decided on the spur of the moment to murder Choong, and you rushed after him. It was the hour after the evening rice, so the shopkeepers in your neighbourhood were on the lookout for their evening custom when you passed. Also on the quay, where you took off in your small skiff, there were an unusual number of people about, because it looked like heavy rain was on its way." The glint of sudden panic in Lin's eyes was the last confirmation the judge had been waiting for. He concluded in an even voice, "If you confess now, Mr. Lin, sparing me the trouble of sifting out all the evidence of the eyewitnesses, I am prepared to add a plea for clemency to your death sentence, on the ground that it was unpremeditated murder."

Lin stared ahead with a vacant look. All at once his pale face became distorted by a spasm of rage. "The despicable old lecher!" he spat. "Made me sweat and slave all those years . . . and now he was going to throw all that good money away on a cheap, half-witted slut! The money I made for him . . ." He looked steadily at the judge as he added in a firm voice, "Yes, I killed him. He deserved it."

Judge Dee gave the sergeant a sign. While Hoong went to the door the judge told the pawnbroker, "I shall hear your full confession during the noon session."

They waited in silence till the sergeant came back with the headman and two constables. They put Lin in chains and led him away.

"A sordid case, sir," Sergeant Hoong remarked dejectedly.

The judge took a sip from his teacup and held it up to be refilled. "Pathetic, rather. I would even call Lin pathetic, Hoong, were it not for the fact that he made a determined effort to incriminate Wang."

"What was Wang's role in all this, sir? You didn't even ask him what he did this morning!"

"There was no need to, for what happened is as plain as a pikestaff. Oriole had told Wang that a rain spirit visited her at night and sometimes gave her money. Wang considered it a great honour that she had relations with a rain spirit. Remember that only half a century ago in many of the river districts in our Empire the people immolated every year a young boy or girl as a human sacrifice to the local river god – until the authorities stepped in. When Wang came to the tower this morning to bring Oriole her fish, he found in her room a dead man lying on his face on the floor. The crying Oriole gave him to understand that goblins had killed the rain spirit and changed him into an ugly old man. When Wang turned over the corpse and recognized the old man, he suddenly understood that he and Oriole had been deceived, and in a blind rage pulled his knife and stabbed the dead man. Then he realized that this was a murder case and he would be suspected. So he fled. The military police caught him while trying to wash his trousers which had become stained with Choong's blood."

Sergeant Hoong nodded. "How did you discover all this in only a few hours, sir?"

"At first I thought the captain's theory hit the nail on the head. The only point which worried me a bit was the long interval between the murder and the stabbing of the victim's breast. I didn't worry a bit about the pawn-ticket, for it is perfectly normal for a pawnbroker to carry a ticket about that he has made out that very same day. Then, when questioning Wang, it struck me that he called Choong a crook. That was a slip of the tongue, for Wang was determined to keep both Oriole and himself out of this, so as not to have to divulge that they had let themselves be fooled. While I was interviewing Oriole she stated that the 'goblins' had killed and *changed* her rain spirit. I didn't understand that at all. It was during my visit to Lin that at last I got on the right track. Lin was nervous and therefore garrulous, and told me at length about his partner taking no part at all in the business. I remembered the pawn-ticket found on the murder scene, and began to suspect Lin. But it was only after I had inspected the dead man's library and got a clear impression of his personality that I found the solution. I checked my theory by eliciting from the manservant the fact that Lin and Choong had quarrelled about Oriole the night before. The name Oriole meant of course nothing to the servant, but he told me they had a heated argument about birds. The rest was routine."

The judge put his cup down. "I have learned from this case how important it is to study carefully our ancient handbooks of detection, Hoong. There it is stated again and again that the first step of a murder investigation is to ascertain the character, daily life and habits of the victim. And in this case it was indeed the murdered man's personality that supplied the key."

Sergeant Hoong stroked his grey moustache with a pleased smile. "That girl and her young man were very lucky indeed in having you as the investigating magistrate, sir! For all the evidence pointed straight at Wang, and he would have been convicted and beheaded. For the girl is a deaf-mute, and Wang isn't much of a talker either!"

Judge Dee nodded. Leaning back in his chair, he said with a faint smile:

"That brings me to the main benefit I derived from this case, Hoong. A very personal and very important benefit. I must confess to you that early this morning I was feeling a bit low, and for a moment actually doubted whether this was after all the right career for me. I was a fool. This is a great, a magnificent office, Hoong! If only because it enables us to speak for those who can't speak for themselves."

# THE HIGH KING'S SWORD
## Peter Tremayne

*One of the pleasures of assembling this anthology is seeing the ancient world come alive through the eyes of keen observers of the day – and you can't get keener observers than the detectives featured here. When Peter Tremayne submitted his manuscript for the following story he explained that it was set in March 664. As the previous story was set in the year 663, we can see in the breadth of two stories two vastly differing cultures on opposite sides of the world, united by man's weakness for crime.*

*The following story features a new detective, Sister Fidelma. Tremayne has called her a "Dark Age Irish Perry Mason". Apart from being a religieuse, she is a dálaighe, or an advocate at the Brehon court. The background to the story is historically accurate. The Yellow Plague swept through Europe reaching Britain and Ireland in AD 664. The joint High Kings of Ireland, Blathmac and Diarmuid, died within days of each other in that year, and this provides the starting point for the story.*

*Peter Tremayne (b. 1943) is a well-known writer of fantasy and horror novels and stories and, under his real name of Peter Berresford Ellis, is a noted biographer and Celtic historian. He has already written several more stories about Sister Fidelma, including a full-length novel, so a new character is born.*

"God's curse is upon this land," sighed the Abbot Colmán, spiritual advisor to the Great Assembly of the chieftains of the five kingdoms of Ireland.

Walking at his side through the grounds of the resplendent palace of Tara, the seat of the High Kings of Ireland, was a tall woman, clad in the robes of a *religieuse*, her hands folded demurely before her. Even at a distance one could see that her costume did not seem to suit her for it scarcely hid the attractiveness of her youthful, well-proportioned figure. Rebellious strands of red hair crept from beneath her habit adding to the allure of her pale fresh face and piercing green eyes. Her cheeks dimpled and there was a scarcely concealed humour behind her enforced solemnity which hinted at a joy in living rather than being weighted down by the sombre pensiveness of religious life.

"When man blames God for cursing him, it is often to disguise the fact that he is responsible for his own problems," Sister Fidelma replied softly.

The Abbot, a thick-set and ruddy faced man in his mid-fifties, frowned and glanced at the young woman at his side. Was she rebuking him?

"Man is hardly responsible for the terrible Yellow Plague that has swept through this land," replied Colmán, his voice heavy with irritation. "Why, it is reported that one third of our population has been carried off by its venomousness. It has spared neither abbot, bishop nor lowly priest."

"Nor even High Kings," added Sister Fidelma, pointedly.

The official mourning for the brothers Blathmac and Diarmuid, joint High Kings of Ireland, who had died within days of each other from the terrors of the Yellow Plague, had ended only one week before.

"Surely, then, a curse of God?" repeated the Abbot, his jaw set firmly, waiting for Sister Fidelma to contradict him.

Wisely, she decided to remain silent. The Abbot was obviously in no mood to discuss the semantics of theology.

"It is because of these events that I have asked you to come to Tara," the Abbot went on, as he preceded her into the chapel of the Blessed Patrick, which had been built next to the High King's palace. Sister Fidelma followed the Abbot into the gloomy, incensed-sweetened atmosphere of the chapel, dropping to one knee and genuflecting to the altar before she followed him to the sacristy. He settled his stocky figure into a leather chair and motioned for her to be seated.

She settled herself and waited expectantly.

"I have sent for you, Sister Fidelma, because you are an advocate, a *dálaighe*, of the Brehon courts, and therefore knowledgeable in law."

Sister Fidelma contrived to shrug modestly while holding herself in repose.

"It is true that I have studied eight years with the Brehon Morann, may his soul rest in peace, and I am qualified to the level of *anruth*."

The Abbot pursed his lips. He had not yet recovered from his astonishment at his first meeting with this young woman who was

so highly qualified in law, and held a degree which demanded respect
from the highest in the land. She was only one step below an *ollamh*
who could even sit in the presence of the High King himself. The
Abbot felt awkward as he faced Sister Fidelma of Kildare. While
he was her superior in religious matters, he, too, had to defer to the
social standing and legal authority which she possessed as a *dálaighe*
of the Brehon Court of Ireland.

"I have been told of your qualification and standing, Sister
Fidelma. But, apart from your knowledge and authority, I have also
been told that you possess an unusual talent for solving puzzles."

"Whoever has told you that flatters me. I have helped to clarify
some problems. And what little talent I have in that direction is at
your service."

Sister Fidelma gazed with anticipation at the Abbot as he rubbed
his chin thoughtfully.

"For many years our country has enjoyed prosperity under the
joint High Kingship of Blathmac and Diarmuid. Therefore their
deaths, coming within days of one another, must be viewed as a
tragedy."

Sister Fidelma raised an eyebrow.

"Is there anything suspicious about their deaths? Is that why you
have asked me here?"

The Abbot shook his head hurriedly.

"No. Their deaths were but human submission to the fearsome
Yellow Plague which all dread and none can avoid once it has
marked them. It is God's will."

The Abbot seemed to pause waiting for some comment but, when
Sister Fidelma made none, he continued.

"No, Sister, there is nothing suspicious about the deaths of
Blathmac and Diarmuid. The problem arises with their successor
to the kingship."

Sister Fidelma frowned.

"But I thought that the Great Assembly had decided that
Sechnasach, the son of Blathmac, would become High King?"

"That was the decision of the provincial kings and chieftains of
Ireland," agreed the Abbot. "But Sechnasach has not yet been
inaugurated on the sacred Stone of Destiny." He hesitated. "Do
you know your Law of Kings?"

"In what respect?" Sister Fidelma countered, wondering where
the question was leading.

"That part relating to the seven proofs of a righteous king."

"The Law of the Brehons states that there are seven proofs of
the righteous king," recited Sister Fidelma dutifully. "That he be

approved by the Great Assembly. That he accept the Faith of the One True God. That he hold sacred the symbols of his office and swear fealty on them. That he rule by the Law of the Brehons and his judgement be firm and just and beyond reproach. That he promote the commonwealth of the people. That he must never command his warriors in an unjust war . . ."

The Abbot held up his hand and interrupted.

"Yes, yes. You know the law. The point is that Sechnasach cannot be inaugurated because the great sword of the Uí Néill, the 'Caladchalog', which was said to have been fashioned in the time of the ancient mist by the smith-god Gobhainn, has been stolen."

Sister Fidelma raised her head, lips slightly parted in surprise.

The ancient sword of the Uí Néill was one of the potent symbols of the High Kingship. Legend had it that it had been given by the smith-god to the hero Fergus Mac Roth in the time of the ancient ones, and then passed down to Niall of the Nine Hostages, whose descendants had become the Uí Néill kings of Ireland. For centuries now the High Kings had been chosen from either the sept of the northern Uí Néill or from the southern Uí Néill. The "Caladchalog", "the hard dinter", was a magical, mystical sword, by which the people recognized their righteous ruler. All High Kings had to swear fealty on it at their inauguration and carry it on all state occasions as the visible symbol of their authority and kingship.

The Abbot stuck out his lower lip.

"In these days, when our people go in fear from the ravages of the plague, they need comfort and distraction. If it was known throughout the land that the new High King could not produce his sword of office on which to swear his sacred oath of kingship then apprehension and terror would seize the people. It would be seen as an evil omen at the start of Sechnasach's rule. There would be chaos and panic. Our people cling fiercely to the ancient ways and traditions but, particularly at this time, they need solace and stability."

Sister Fidelma compressed her lips thoughtfully. What the Abbot said was certainly true. The people firmly believed in the symbolism which had been handed down to them from the mists of ancient times.

"If only people relied on their own abilities and not on symbols," the Abbot was continuing. "It is time for reform, both in secular as well as religious matters. We cling to too many of the pagan beliefs of our ancestors from the time before the Light of Our Saviour was brought to these shores."

"I see that you yourself believe in the reforms of Rome," Sister Fidelma observed shrewdly.

The Abbot did not conceal his momentary surprise.

"How so?"

Sister Fidelma smiled.

"I have done nothing clever, Abbot Colmán. It was an elementary observation. You wear the tonsure of St. Peter, the badge of Rome, and not that of St. John from whom our own Church takes its rule."

The corner of the Abbot's mouth drooped.

"I make no secret that I was in Rome for five years and came to respect Rome's reasons for the reforms. I feel it is my duty to advocate the usages of the Church of Rome among our people to replace our old rituals, symbolisms and traditions."

"We have to deal with people as they are and not as we would like them to be," observed Sister Fidelma.

"But we must endeavour to change them as well," replied the Abbot unctuously, "setting their feet on the truth path to God's grace."

"We will not quarrel over the reforms of Rome," replied Sister Fidelma quietly. "I will continue to be guided by the rule of the Holy Brigid of Kildare, where I took my vows. But tell me, for what purpose have I been summoned to Tara?"

The Abbot hesitated, as if wondering whether to pursue his theme of Rome's reforms. Then he sniffed to hide his irritation.

"We must find the missing sword before the High King's inauguration, which is tomorrow, if we wish to avoid civil strife in the five kingdoms of Ireland."

"From where was it stolen?"

"Here, from this very chapel. The sacred sword was placed with the *Lia Fáil*, the Stone of Destiny, under the altar. It was locked in a metal and wood chest. The only key was kept on the altar in full view. No one, so it was thought, would ever dare violate the sanctuary of the altar and chapel to steal its sacred treasures."

"Yet someone did?"

"Indeed they did. We have the culprit locked in a cell."

"And the culprit is . . .?"

"Ailill Flann Esa. He is the son of Donal, who was High King twenty years ago. Ailill sought the High Kingship in rivalry to his cousin, Sechnasach. It is obvious that, out of malice caused by the rejection of the Great Assembly, he seeks to discredit his cousin."

"What witnesses were there to his theft of the sword?"

"Three. He was found in the chapel alone at night by two guards of the royal palace, Congal and Erc. And I, myself, came to the chapel a few moments later."

Sister Fidelma regarded the Abbot with bewilderment.

"If he were found in the chapel in the act of stealing the sword, why was the sword not found with him?"

The Abbot sniffed impatiently.

"He had obviously hidden it just before he was discovered. Maybe he heard the guards coming and hid it."

"Has the chapel been searched?"

"Yes. Nothing has been found."

"So, from what you say, there were no witnesses to see Ailill Flann Esa actually take the sword?"

The Abbot smiled paternally.

"My dear sister, the chapel is secured at night. The deacon made a check last thing and saw everything was in order. The guards passing outside observed that the door was secure just after midnight, but twenty minutes later they passed it again and found it open. They saw the bolt had been smashed. The chapel door is usually bolted on the inside. That was when they saw Ailill at the altar. The altar table had been pushed aside, the chest was open and the sword gone. The facts seem obvious."

"Not yet so obvious, Abbot Colmán," Sister Fidelma replied thoughtfully.

"Obvious enough for Sechnasach to agree with me to have Ailill Flann Esa incarcerated immediately."

"And the motive, you would say, is simply one of malice?"

"Obvious again. Ailill wants to disrupt the inauguration of Sechnasach as High King. Perhaps he even imagines that he can promote civil war in the confusion and chaos, and, using the people's fears, on the production of the sacred sword from the place where he has hidden it, he thinks to overthrow Sechnasach and make himself High King. The people, in their dread of the Yellow Plague, are in the mood to be manipulated by their anxieties."

"If you have your culprit and motive, why send for me?" Sister Fidelma observed, a trace of irony in her voice. "And there are better qualified *dálaighe* and Brehons at the court of Tara, surely?"

"Yet none who have your reputation for solving such conundrums, Sister Fidelma."

"But the sword must still be in the chapel or within its vicinity."

"We have searched and it cannot be found. Time presses. I have been told that you have the talent to solve the mystery of where the sword has been hidden. I have heard how skilful you are in questioning suspects and extracting the truth from them. Ailill has, assuredly, hidden the sword nearby and we must find out where before the High King's inauguration."

Sister Fidelma pursed her lips and then shrugged.

"Show me the where the sword was kept and then I will question Ailill Flann Esa."

Ailill Flann Esa was in his mid-thirties; tall, brown-haired and full-bearded. He carried himself with the pride of the son of a former High King. His father had been Donal Mac Aed of the northern Uí Néill, who had once ruled from Tara twenty years before.

"I did not steal the sacred sword," he replied immediately Sister Fidelma identified her purpose.

"Then explain how you came to be in the chapel at such a time," she said, seating herself on the wooden bench that ran alongside the wall of the tenebrous grey stone cell in which he was imprisoned. Ailill hesitated and then seated himself on a stool before her. The stool, with a wooden bed and a table, comprised the other furnishings of the cell. Sister Fidelma knew that only Ailill's status gave him the luxury of these comforts and alleviated the dankness of the granite jail in which he was confined.

"I was passing the chapel . . ." began Ailill.

"Why?" interrupted Sister Fidelma. "It was after midnight, I believe?"

The man hesitated, frowning. He was apparently not used to people interrupting. Sister Fidelma hid a smile as she saw the struggle on his haughty features. It was clear he wished to respond in annoyance but realized that she was an *anruth* who had the power of the Brehon Court behind her. Yet he hesitated for a moment or two.

"I was on my way somewhere . . . to see someone."

"Where? Who?"

"That I cannot say."

She saw firmness in his pinched mouth, in the compressed lips. He would obviously say nothing further on that matter. She let it pass.

"Continue," she invited after a moment's pause.

"Well, I was passing the chapel, as I said, and I saw the door open. Usually, at that time of night, the door is closed and the bolt in place. I thought this strange, so I went in. Then I noticed that the altar had been pushed aside. I went forward. I could see that the chest, in which the sword of office was kept, had been opened . . ."

He faltered and ended with a shrug.

"And then?" prompted Sister Fidelma.

"That is all. The guards came in at that moment. Then the

Abbot appeared. I found myself accused of stealing the sword. Yet I did not."

"Are you saying that this is all you know about the matter?"

"That is all I know. I am accused but innocent. My only misdemeanour is that I am my father's son and presented a claim before the Great Assembly to succeed Blathmac and Diarmuid as High King. Although Sechnasach won the support of the Great Assembly for his claim, he has never forgiven me for challenging his succession. He is all the more ready to believe my guilt because of his hatred of me."

"And have you forgiven Sechnasach for his success before the Great Assembly?" Sister Fidelma asked sharply.

Ailill grimaced in suppressed annoyance.

"Do you think me a mean person, Sister? I abide by the law. But, in honesty, I will tell you that I think the Great Assembly has made a wrong choice. Sechnasach is a traditionalist at a time when our country needs reforms. We need reforms in our secular law and in our Church."

Sister Fidelma's eyes narrowed.

"You would support the reforms being urged upon us by the Roman Church? To change our dating of Easter, our ritual and manner of land-holding?"

"I would. I have never disguised it. And there are many who would support me. My cousin Cernach, the son of Diarmuid, for example. He is a more vehement advocate of Rome than I am."

"But you would admit that you have a strong motive in attempting to stop Sechnasach's inauguration?"

"Yes. I admit that my policies would be different to those of Sechnasach. But above all things I believe that once the Great Assembly chooses a High King, then all must abide by their decision. Unless the High King fails to abide by the law and fulfil its obligations, he is still High King. No one can challenge the choice of the Great Assembly."

Sister Fidelma gazed directly into Ailill's smouldering brown eyes.

"And did you steal the sword?"

Ailill sought to control the rage which the question apparently aroused.

"By the powers, I did not! I have told you all I know."

The warrior named Erc scuffed at the ground with his heel, and stirred uneasily.

"I am sure I cannot help you, Sister. I am a simple guardsman

and there is little to add beyond the fact that I, with my companion
Congal, found Ailill Flann Esa in the chapel standing before the
chest from which the sacred sword had been stolen. There is nothing
further I can add."

Sister Fidelma compressed her lips. She gazed around at the
curious faces of the other warriors who shared the dormitory of the
High King's bodyguard. The murky chamber, shared by a hundred
warriors when they were resting from their guard duties, stank of
spirits and body sweat which mixed into a bitter scent.

"Let me be the judge of that." She turned towards the door.
"Come, walk with me for a while in the fresh air, Erc. I would
have you answer some questions."

Reluctantly the burly warrior laid aside his shield and javelin and
followed the *religieuse* from the dormitory, accompanied by a chorus
of whispered comments and a few lewd jests from his comrades.

"I am told that you were guarding the chapel on the night the
theft occurred," Sister Fidelma said as soon as they were outside,
walking in the crystal early morning sunlight. "Is that correct?"

"Congal and I were the guards that night, but our duties were
merely to patrol the buildings of which the chapel is part. Usually
from midnight until dawn the doors of the chapel of the Blessed
Patrick are shut. The chapel contains many treasures and the Abbot
has ordered that the door be bolted at night."

"And what time did you arrive at your posts?"

"At midnight exactly, Sister. Our duties took us from the door of
the royal stables, fifty yards from the chapel, to the door of the great
refectory, a route which passes the chapel door."

"Tell me what happened that night."

"Congal and I took up our positions, as usual. We walked by the
chapel door. It seemed shut as usual. We turned at the door of the
great refectory from which point we followed a path which circum-
vents the buildings, so that our patrol follows a circular path."

"How long does it take to circumnavigate the buildings?"

"No more than half-an-hour."

"And how long would you be out of sight of the door of the
chapel?"

"Perhaps twenty minutes."

"Go on."

"It was on our second patrol, as I say, a half-hour later, that we
passed the door of the chapel. It was Congal who spotted that the
door was opened. We moved forward and then I saw that the door
had been forced. The wood was splintered around the bolt on the
inside of the door. We entered and saw Ailill Flann Esa standing

before the altar. The altar had been pushed back from the position where it covered the Stone of Destiny and the chest in which the sacred sword was kept had been opened."

"What was Ailill doing? Did he look flustered or short of breath?"

"No. He was calm enough. Just staring down at the open chest."

"Wasn't it dark in the chapel? How did you see so clearly?"

"Some candles were lit within the chapel and provided light enough."

"And then?"

"He saw our shadows and started, turning to us. At that point the Abbot came up behind us. He saw the sacrilege at once and pointed to the fact that the sword was gone."

"Did he question Ailill?"

"Oh, surely he did. He said the sword had gone and asked what Ailill had to say."

"And what did Ailill say?"

"He said that he had just arrived there."

"And what did you say?"

"I said that was impossible because we were patrolling outside and had the chapel door in sight for at least ten minutes from the royal stable doorway. Ailill must have been inside for that ten minutes at least."

"But it was night time. It must have been dark outside. How could you be sure that Ailill had not just entered the chapel before you, covered by the darkness?"

"Because the torches are lit in the grounds of the royal palace every night. It is the law of Tara. Where there is light, there is no treachery. Ailill must have been in the chapel, as I have said, for at least ten minutes. That is a long time."

"Yet even ten minutes does not seem time enough to open the chest, hide the sword, and repose oneself before you entered."

"Time enough, I'd say. For what else could be done with the sword but hide it?"

"And where is your companion, Congal? I would question him."

Erc looked troubled and genuflected with a degree of haste.

"God between me and evil, Sister. He has fallen sick with the Yellow Plague. He lies close to death now and maybe I will be next to succumb to the scourge."

Sister Fidelma bit her lip, then she shook her head and smiled reassuringly at Erc.

"Not necessarily so, Erc. Go to the apothecary. Ask that you be given an infusion of the leaves and flowers of the *centaurium vulgare*. It has a reputation for keeping the Yellow Plague at bay."

"What is that?" demanded the warrior, frowning at the unfamiliar Latin words.

"*Dréimire buí*," she translated to the Irish name of the herb. "The apothecary will know it. To drink of the mixture is supposedly a good preventative tonic. By drinking each day, you may avoid the scourge. Now go in peace, Erc. I have done with you for the meanwhile."

Sechnasach, lord of Midhe, and High King of Ireland, was a thin man, aged in his mid-thirties, with scowling features and dark hair. He sat slightly hunched forward on his chair, the epitome of gloom.

"Abbot Colmán reports that you have not yet discovered where Ailill has hidden the sword of state, Sister," he greeted brusquely as he gestured for Sister Fidelma to be seated. "May I remind you that the inauguration ceremony commences at noon tomorrow?"

The High King had agreed to meet her, at her own request, in one of the small audience chambers of the palace of Tara. It was a chamber with a high vaulted ceiling and hung with colourful tapestries. There was a crackling log fire in the great hearth at one end before which the High King sat in his ornate carved oak chair. Pieces of exquisite furniture, brought as gifts to the court from many parts of the world, were placed around the chamber with decorative ornaments in gold and silver and semi-precious jewels.

"That presupposes Ailill stole the sword," observed Sister Fidelma calmly as she sat before him. She observed strict protocol. Had she been trained to the degree of *ollamh* she could have sat in the High King's presence without waiting for permission. Indeed, the chief *ollamh* of Ireland, at the court of the High King, was so influential that even the High King was not allowed to speak at the Great Assembly before the chief *ollamh*. Sister Fidelma had never been in the presence of a High King before and her mind raced hastily over the correct rituals to be observed.

Sechnasach drew his brows together at her observation.

"You doubt it? But the facts given by Abbot Colmán are surely plain enough? If Ailill did not steal it, who then?"

Sister Fidelma raised a shoulder and let it fall.

"Before I comment further I would ask you some questions, Sechnasach of Tara."

The High King made a motion of his hand as though to invite her questions.

"Who would gain if you were prevented from assuming the High Kingship?"

Sechnasach grimaced with bitter amusement.

"Ailill, of course. For he stands as *tánaiste* by choice of the Great Assembly."

Whenever the Great Assembly elected a High King, they also elected a *tánaiste* or 'second'; an heir presumptive who would assume office should the High King become indisposed. Should the High King be killed or die suddenly then the Great Assembly would meet to confirm the *tánaiste* as High King but at no time were the five kingdoms left without a supreme potentate. Under the ancient Brehon Law of Ireland, only the most worthy were elected to kingship and there was no such concept of hereditary right by primogeniture such as practised in the lands of the Saxons or Franks.

"And no one else? There are no other claimants?"

"There are many claimants. My uncle Diarmuid's son, Cernach, for example, and Ailill's own brothers, Conall and Colcu. You must know of the conflict between the southern and northern Uí Néill? I am of the southern Uí Néill. Many of the northern Uí Neill would be glad to see me deposed."

"But none but Ailill stand as the obvious choice to gain by your fall?" pressed Sister Fidelma.

"None."

Compressing her lips, Sister Fidelma rose.

"That is all at this time, Sechnasach," she said.

The High King glanced at her in surprise at the abruptness of her questioning.

"You would give me no hope of finding the sacred sword before tomorrow?"

Sister Fidelma detected a pleading tone to his voice.

"There is always hope, Sechnasach. But if I have not solved this mystery by noon tomorrow, at the time of your inauguration, then we will see the resolution in the development of events. Events will solve the puzzle."

"Little hope of averting strife, then?"

"I do not know," Sister Fidelma admitted candidly.

She left the audience chamber and was moving down the corridor when a low soprano voice called to her by name from a darkened doorway. Sister Fidelma paused, turned and gazed at the dark figure of a girl.

"Come inside for a moment, Sister."

Sister Fidelma followed the figure through heavy drapes into a brightly lit chamber.

A young, dark haired girl in an exquisitely sewn gown of blue, bedecked in jewels, ushered her inside and pulled the drape across the door.

"I am Ornait, sister of Sechnasach," the girl said breathlessly.

Sister Fidelma bowed her head to the High King's sister.

"I am at your service, Ornait."

"I was listening behind the tapestries, just now," the girl said, blushing a little. "I heard what you were saying to my brother. You don't believe Ailill stole the sacred sword, do you?"

Sister Fidelma gazed into the girl's eager, pleading eyes, and smiled softly.

"And you do not want to believe it?" she asked with gentle emphasis.

The girl lowered her gaze, the redness of her cheeks, if anything, increasing.

"I know he could not have done this deed. He would not." She seized Sister Fidelma's hand. "I know that if anyone can prove him innocent of this sacrilege it will be you."

"Then you know then that I am an advocate in the Brehon Court?" asked Sister Fidelma, slightly embarrassed at the girl's emphatic belief in her ability.

"I have heard of your reputation from a sister of your order at Kildare."

"And the night Ailill was arrested in the chapel, he was on his way to see you? It was foolish of him not to tell me."

Ornait raised her small chin defiantly.

"We love each other!"

"But keep it a secret, even from your brother?"

"Until after my brother's inauguration as High King, it will remain a secret. When he feels more kindly disposed towards Ailill for standing against him before the Great Assembly, then we shall tell him."

"You do not think Ailill feels any resentment towards your brother, a resentment which might have motivated him to hide the sacred sword to discredit Sechnasach?"

"Ailill may not agree with my brother on many things but he agrees that the decision of the Great Assembly, under the Brehon Law, is sacred and binding," replied Ornait, firmly. "And he is not alone in that. My cousin, Cernach Mac Diarmuid, believes that he has a greater right to the High Kingship than Sechnasach. He dislikes my brother's attitude against any reform suggested by Rome. But Cernach does not come to the 'age of choice' for a while yet when he can legally challenge my brother to the High Kingship. Being too young to challenge for office, Cernach supported Ailill in his claim. It is no crime to be unsuccessful in the challenge for the High Kingship. Once the Great Assembly make the decision, there is an end to it. No, a thousand times – no! Ailill would not do this thing."

"Well, Sister?" The Abbot stared at Sister Fidelma with narrowed eyes.

"I have nothing to report at the moment, just another question to ask."

She had gone to see Abbot Colmán in his study in the abbey building behind the palace of Tara. The Abbot was seated behind a wooden table where he had been examining a colourful illuminated manuscript. He saw her eyes fall on the book and smiled complacently.

"This is the Gospel of John produced by our brothers at Clonmacnoise. A beautiful work which will be sent to our brothers at the Holy Island of Colmcille."

Sister Fidelma glanced briefly at the magnificently wrought handiwork. It was, indeed, beautiful but her thoughts were occupied elsewhere. She paused a moment before asking:

"If there were civil strife in the kingdom, and from it Ailill was made High King, would he depart from the traditional policies propounded by Sechnasach?"

The Abbot was taken off guard, his jaw dropping and his eyes rounding in surprise. Then he frowned and appeared to ponder the question for a moment.

"I would think the answer is in the affirmative," he answered at last.

"Particularly," went on Sister Fidelma, "would Ailill press the abbots and bishops to reform the Church?"

The Abbot scratched an ear.

"It is no secret that Ailill favours a rapprochement with the Church of Rome, believing its reforms to be correct. There are many of the Uí Néill house who do. Cernach Mac Diarmuid, for instance. He is a leading advocate among the laymen for such reforms. A bit of a hothead but influential. A youth who stands near the throne of Tara but doesn't reach the 'age of choice' for a month or so when he may take his place in the assemblies of the five kingdoms."

"But Sechnasach does not believe in reforms and would adhere strongly to the traditional rites and liturgy of our Church?"

"Undoubtedly."

"And, as one of the pro-Roman faction, you would favour Ailill's policies?"

The Abbot flushed with indignation.

"I would. But I make no secret of my position. And I hold

my beliefs under the law. My allegiance is to the High King as designated by that law. And while you have a special privilege as an advocate of the Brehon Court, may I remind you that I am abbot of Tara, father and superior to your order?"

Sister Fidelma made a gesture with her hand as if in apology.

"I am merely seeking facts, Abbot Colmán. And it is as *dálaighe* of the Brehon Court that I ask these questions, not as a Sister of Kildare."

"Then here is a fact. I denounced Ailill Flann Esa. If I had supported what he has done in order to overthrow Sechnasach simply because Ailill would bring the Church in Ireland in agreement with Rome, then I would not have been willing to point so quickly to Ailill's guilt. I could have persuaded the guards that someone else had carried out the deed."

"Indeed," affirmed Sister Fidelma. "If Ailill Flann Esa were guilty of this sacrilege then you would not profit."

"Exactly so," snapped the Abbot. "And Ailill is guilty."

"So it might seem."

Sister Fidelma turned to the door, paused and glanced back.

"One tiny point, to clarify matters. How is it that you came to be in the chapel at that exact time?"

The Abbot drew his brows together.

"I had left my *Psalter* in the sacristy," he replied irritably. "I went to retrieve it."

"Surely it would have been safe until morning? Why go out into the cold of night to the chapel?"

"I needed to look up a reference; besides I did not have to go out into the night . . ."

"No? How then did you get into the chapel?"

The Abbot sighed, in annoyance.

"There is a passage which leads from the abbey here into the chapel sacristy."

Sister Fidelma's eyes widened. She suddenly realized that she had been a fool. The fact had been staring her in the face all the time.

"Please show me this passage."

"I will get one of the brethren to show you. I am busy with the preparations for the inauguration."

Abbot Colmán reached forward and rang a silver bell which stood upon the table.

A moon-faced man clad in the brown robes of the order of the abbey entered almost immediately, arms folded in the copious sleeves of his habit. Even from a distance of a few feet, Sister Fidelma could smell the wild garlic on his breath, a pungent odour which caused her to wrinkle her nose in distaste.

"This is Brother Rogallach," the Abbot motioned with his hand. "Rogallach, I wish you to show Sister Fidelma the passage to the chapel." Then, turning to her, he raised his eyebrows in query. "Unless there is anything else . . .?"

"Nothing else, Colmán," Sister Fidelma replied quietly. "For the time being."

Brother Rogallach took a candle and lit it. He and Sister Fidelma were standing in one of the corridors of the abbey building. Rogallach moved towards a tapestry and drew it aside to reveal an entrance from which stone steps led downwards.

"This is the only entrance to the passage which leads to the chapel?" asked Sister Fidelma, trying to steel her features against his bad breath.

Brother Rogallach nodded. He stood slightly in awe of the young woman for it was already common gossip around the abbey as to her status and role.

"Who knows about it?" she pressed.

"Why, everyone in the abbey. When the weather is intemperate we use this method to attend worship in the chapel." The monk opened his mouth in an ingenuous smile, displaying broken and blackened teeth.

"Would anyone outside the abbey know about it?"

The monk grimaced eloquently.

"It is no secret, Sister. Anyone who has lived at Tara would know of it."

"So Ailill would know of its existence?"

Brother Rogallach gestured as if the answer were obvious.

"Lead on then, Brother Rogallach," Sister Fidelma instructed, thankful to push the monk ahead of her so that she was not bathed by the foul stench of his breathing.

The moon-faced monk turned and preceded her down the steps and through a musty but dry passage whose floor was laid with stone flags. It was a winding passage along which several small alcoves stood, most of them containing items of furniture. Sister Fidelma stopped at the first of them and asked Rogallach to light the alcove with his candle. She repeated this performance at each of the alcoves.

"They are deep enough for a person to hide in let alone to conceal a sword," she mused aloud. "Were they searched for the missing sword?"

The monk nodded eagerly drawing close so that Sister Fidelma took an involuntary step backward. "Of course. I was one of those called to assist in the search. Once the chapel was searched, it was obvious that the next place as a likely hiding place would be this passageway."

Nevertheless, Sister Fidelma caused Rogallach to halt at each alcove until she had examined it thoroughly by the light of his candle. At one alcove she frowned and reached for a piece of frayed cloth caught on a projecting section of wood. It was brightly coloured cloth, certainly not from the cheerless brown robes of a *religieux*, but more like the fragment of a richly woven cloak. It was the sort of cloth that a person in the position of wealth and power would have.

It took a little time to traverse the passage and to come up some steps behind a tapestry into the sacristy. From there Sister Fidelma moved into the chapel and across to the chapel door.

Something had been irritating her for some time about the affair. Now that she realized the existence of the passage, she knew what had been puzzling her.

"The chapel door is always bolted from the inside?" she asked.

"Yes," replied Rogallach.

"So if you wanted to enter the chapel, how would you do it?"

Rogallach smiled, emitting another unseen cloud of bitter scent to engulf her.

"Why, I would merely use the passage."

"Indeed, if you knew it was there," affirmed Sister Fidelma, thoughtfully.

"Well, only a stranger to Tara, such as yourself, would not know that."

"So if someone attempted to break into the chapel from the outside, they would obviously not know of the existence of the passage?"

Rogallach moved his head in an affirmative gesture.

Sister Fidelma stood at the door of the chapel and gazed down at the bolt, especially to where it had splintered from the wood and her eyes narrowed as she examined the scuff marks on the metal where it had obviously been hit with a piece of stone. Abruptly, she smiled broadly as she realized the significance of its breaking. She turned to Rogallach.

"Send the guard Erc to me."

Sechnasach, the High King, stared at Sister Fidelma with suspicion.

"I am told that you have summoned the Abbot Colmán, Aillil

Flann Esa, my sister Ornait and Cernach Mac Diarmuid to appear here. Why is this?"

Sister Fidelma stood, hands demurely folded before her, as she confronted Sechnasach.

"I did so because I have that right as a *dálaighe* of the Brehon courts and with the authority that I can now solve the mystery of the theft of your sword of state."

Sechnasach leaned forward in his chair excitedly. "You have found where Ailill has hidden it?"

"My eyes were blind for I should have seen the answer long ago," Sister Fidelma replied.

"Tell me where the sword is," demanded Sechnasach.

"In good time," Sister Fidelma answered calmly. "I need a further answer from you before I can reveal the answer to this puzzle. I have summoned Cernach, the son of your uncle Diarmuid, who was, with your father, joint High King."

"What has Cernach to do with this matter?"

"It is said that Cernach is a most vehement supporter of the reforms of the Church of Rome."

Sechnasach frowned, slightly puzzled.

"He has often argued with me that I should change my attitudes and support those abbots and bishops of Ireland who would alter our ways and adopt the rituals of Rome. But he is still a youth. Why, he does not achieve the 'age of choice' for a month or so and cannot even sit in council. He has no authority though he has some influence on the young members of our court."

Sister Fidelma nodded reflectively.

"This agrees with what I have heard. But I needed some confirmation. Now let the guards bring in Ailill and the others and I will tell you what has happened."

She stood silently before the High King while Ailill Flann Esa was brought in under guard, followed by the Abbot Colmán. Behind came a worried-looking Ornait, glancing with ill-concealed anxiety at her lover. After her came a puzzled-looking, dark-haired young man who was obviously Cernach Mac Diarmuid.

They stood in a semi-circle before the High King's chair. Sechnasach glanced towards Sister Fidelma, inclining his head to her as indication that she should start.

"We will firstly agree on one thing," began Sister Fidelma. "The sacred sword of the Uí Néill kings of Tara was stolen from the chapel of the Blessed Patrick. We will now also agree on the apparent motive. It was stolen to prevent the inauguration of Sechnasach as High King tomorrow . . . or to discredit him in the eyes of the people, to ferment civil disorder in the five kingdoms which might lead to Sechnasach being overthrown and someone else taking the throne."

She smiled briefly at Sechnasach.

"Are we agreed on that?"

"That much is obvious." It was Abbot Colmán who interrupted in annoyance. "In these dark times, it would only need such an omen as the loss of the sacred sword to create chaos and alarm within the kingdoms of Ireland. I have already said as much."

"And what purpose would this chaos and alarm, with the overthrow of Sechnasach, be put to?" queried Sister Fidelma. Before anyone could reply she went on. "It seems easy to see. Sechnasach is sworn to uphold the traditions of the kingdoms and of our Church. Rome claims authority over all the Churches but this claim has been disputed by the Churches of Ireland, Britain and Armorica as well as the Churches of the East. Rome wishes to change our rituals, our liturgy and the computations whereby we celebrate the *Cáisc* in remembrance of our Lord's death in Jerusalem. And there are some among us, even abbots and bishops, who support Rome and seek the abandoning of our traditions and a union with the Roman Church. So even among us we do not all speak with one voice. Is that not so, Ailill Flann Esa?"

Ailill scowled.

"As I have told you, I have never denied my views."

"Then let us agree entirely on the apparent inner motive for the theft of the sword. Destabilization of the High King and his replacement by someone who would reject the traditionalist ways and throw his support behind the reforms in line with Rome."

There was a silence. She had their full attention.

"Very well," went on Sister Fidelma. "This seems an obvious motive. But let us examine the facts of the theft. Two guards passed the door of the chapel in which the sword was kept shortly after midnight. The door was secured. But when they passed the chapel door twenty minutes later, they saw the door ajar with the bolt having been forced. Entering, they saw Ailill standing at the altar staring at the empty chest where the sword had been kept. Then the Abbot entered. He came into the chapel from the sacristy to which he had gained entrance from the passage which leads there from the abbey. He accused Ailill of stealing the sword and hiding it. The sword was not found in the chapel. If Ailill had stolen the sword, how had he time to hide it so well and cleverly? Even the ten minutes allowed him by the guards was not time enough. This is the first problem that struck my thoughts."

She paused and glanced towards Ornait, the sister of the High King.

"According to Ailill Flann Esa, he was walking by the chapel. He saw the door ajar and the bolt forced. He went inside out of curiosity and perceived the empty chest. That is his version of events."

"We know this is what he claims," snapped Sechnasach. "Have you something new to add?"

"Only to clarify," replied Fidelma unperturbed by the High King's agitation. "Ailill's reason to be passing the chapel at that hour was because he was on his way to meet with Ornait."

Ornait flushed. Sechnasach turned to stare at his sister, mouth slightly open.

"I regret that I cannot keep your secret, Ornait," Sister Fidelma said with a grimace. "But the truth must be told for much is in the balance."

Ornait raised her chin defiantly towards her brother.

"Well, Ornait? Why would Ailill meet with you in dead of night?" demanded the High King.

The girl pushed back her head defiantly.

"I love Ailill and he loves me. We wanted to tell you, but thought we would do so after your inauguration when you might look on us with more charity."

Sister Fidelma held up her hand as Sechnasach opened his mouth to respond in anger.

"Time enough to sort that matter later. Let us continue. If Ailill speaks the truth, then we must consider this. Someone knew of Ailill's appointment with Ornait. That person was waiting inside the chapel. Being a stranger to Tara, I had not realized that the chapel could be entered from within by means of a passageway. In this matter I was stupid. I should have known at once by the fact that the chapel doors bolted from *within*. The fact was staring me in the face. I should have realized that if the chapel was left bolted at night, then there must obviously be another means for the person who secured the bolt to make their exit."

"But everyone at Tara knows about that passage," pointed out Sechnasach.

"Indeed," smiled Sister Fidelma. "And it would be obvious that at some stage I would come to share that knowledge."

"The point is that the bolt on the door was forced," Abbot Colmán pointed out in a testy tone.

"Indeed. But not from the outside," replied Sister Fidelma. "Again my wits were not swift, otherwise I would have seen it immediately. When you force a bolted door, it is the metal on the door jamb, that which secures the bolt, that gets torn from its fixtures. But the bolt itself, on the chapel door, was the section which had been splintered away from its holdings."

She stood looking at their puzzled expressions for a moment.

"What happened was simple enough. The culprit had entered the chapel from the passage within. The culprit had taken the key, pushed back the altar, opened the chest. The sword had been removed and taken to a place of safety. Then the culprit had returned to arrange the scene. Ensuring that the guards were well beyond the door, the perpetrator opened it, took up a stone and smashed at the bolt. Instead of smashing away the metal catch on the door jamb, the bolt on the door was smashed. It was so obvious a clue that I nearly overlooked it. All I saw, at first, was a smashed bolt."

Ornait was smiling through her tears.

"I knew Ailill could not have done this deed. The real perpetrator did this deed for the purpose of making Ailill seem the guilty one. Your reputation as a solver of puzzles is well justified, Sister Fidelma."

Sister Fidelma responded with a slightly wan smile.

"It needed no act of genius to deduce that the evidence could only point to the fact the Ailill Flann Esa could not have stolen the sword in the manner claimed."

Ailill was frowning at Sister Fidelma.

"Then who is the guilty person?"

"Certain things seemed obvious. Who benefited from the deed?" Sister Fidelma continued, ignoring his question. "Abbot Colmán is a fierce adherent of Rome. He might benefit in this cause if Sechnasach was removed. And Abbot Colmán was in the right place at the right time. He had the opportunity to do this deed."

"This is outrageous!" snarled the Abbot. "I am accused unjustly. I am your superior, Fidelma of Kildare. I am the abbot of Tara and . . ."

Sister Fidelma grimaced. "I need not be reminded of your position in the Church, Abbot Colmán," she replied softly. "I also remind you that I speak here as an advocate of the Brehon Court and was invited here to act in this position by yourself."

Colmán, flushed and angry, hesitated and then said slowly:

"I make no secret of my adherence to the Rome order but to suggest that I would be party to such a plot . . ."

Sister Fidelma held up a hand and motioned him to silence.

"This is true enough. After all, Ailill would be Colmán's natural ally. If Colmán stole the sword, why would he attempt to put the blame onto Ailill and perhaps discredit those who advocated the cause of Rome? Surely, he would do his best to support Ailill so that when civil strife arose over the non-production of the sacred sword, Ailill, as *tánaiste*, the heir presumptive, would be in a position to immediately claim the throne of Sechnasach?"

"What are you saying?" asked Sechnasach trying to keep track of Sister Fidelma's reasoning.

Sister Fidelma turned to him, her blue eyes level, her tone unhurried.

"There is another factor in this tale of political intrigue. Cernach Mac Diarmuid. His name was mentioned to me several times as a fierce adherent of Rome."

The young man who had so far stood aloof and frowning, now started, his cheeks reddening. A hand dropped to his side as if seeking a weapon. But no one, save the High King's bodyguard, was allowed to carry a weapon in Tara's halls.

"What do you mean by this?"

"Cernach desired the throne of Tara. As son of one of the joint High Kings, he felt that it was his due. But moreover, he would benefit most if both Sechnasach and Ailill were discredited."

"Why . . .!" Cernach started forward, anger on his face. One of the warriors gripped the young man's arm so tightly that he winced. He turned and tried to shake off the grip but made no further aggressive move.

Sister Fidelma spoke to one of the guards.

"Is the warrior, Erc, outside?"

The guard moved to the door and called.

The burly warrior entered holding something wrapped in cloth. He glanced at Sister Fidelma and nodded briefly.

Sister Fidelma turned back to the High King.

"Sechnasach, I ordered this man, Erc, to search the chamber of Cernach."

Cernach's face was suddenly bloodless. His eyes were bright, staring at the object in Erc's hand.

"What did you find there, Erc?" asked Sister Fidelma quietly.

The warrior moved forward to the High King's seat, unwrapping the cloth as he did so. He held out the uncovered object. In his hands there was revealed a sword of rich gold and silver mountings, encrusted with a colourful display of jewels.

"The 'Caladchalo'!" gasped the High King. "The sword of state!"

"It's a lie! A lie!" cried Cernach, his lips trembling. "It was planted there. She must have planted it there!"

He threw out an accusing finger towards Sister Fidelma. Sister Fidelma simply ignored him.

"Where did you find this, Erc?"

The burly warrior licked his lips. It was clear he felt awkward in the presence of the High King.

"It was lying wrapped in cloth under the bed of Cernach, the son of Diarmuid," he replied, brusquely.

Everyone's eyes had fallen on the trembling young man.

"Was it easy to find, Erc?" asked Sister Fidelma.

The burly warrior managed a smile.

"Almost too easy."

"Almost too easy," repeated Sister Fidelma with a soft emphasis.

"Why did you do this deed, Cernach Mac Diarmuid?" thundered Sechnasach. "How could you behave so treacherously?"

"But Cernach did not do it."

Fidelma's quiet voice caused everyone to turn back to stare at her in astonishment.

"Who then, if not Cernach?" demanded the High King in bewilderment.

"The art of deduction is a science as intricate as any of the mysteries of the ancients," Sister Fidelma commented with a sigh. "In this matter I found myself dealing with a mind as complicated in thinking and as ruthless in its goal as any I have encountered. But then the stake was the High Kingship of Ireland."

She paused and gazed around at the people in the chamber, letting her eyes finally rest on Sechnasach.

"There has been one thing which has been troubling me from the start. Why I was called to Tara to investigate this matter? My poor reputation in law is scarcely known out of the boundaries of Holy Brigid's house at Kildare. In Tara, at the seat of the High Kings, there are many better qualified in law, many more able *dálaighe* of the Brehon Courts, many more renowned Brehons. The Abbot Colmán admitted that someone had told him about me for he did not know me. I have had a growing feeling that I was being somehow used. But why? For what purpose? By whom? It seemed so obvious that Ailill was demonstrably innocent of the crime. Why was it obvious?"

Ailill started, his eyes narrowing as he stared at her. Sister Fidelma continued oblivious of the tension in the chamber.

"Abbot Colmán summoned me hither. He had much to gain from this affair, as we have discussed. He also had the opportunity to carry out the crime."

"That's not true!" cried the Abbot.

Sister Fidelma turned and smiled at the ruddy-faced cleric.

"You are right, Colmán. And I have already conceded that fact. You did not do it."

"But the sword was found in Cernach's chamber," Sechnasach pointed out. "He must surely be guilty."

"Several times I was pointed towards Cernach as a vehement advocate of Roman reforms. A youthful hothead, was one description. Several times I was encouraged to think that the motive lay in replacing Sechnasach, a traditionalist, with someone who would encourage those reforms. And, obligingly, the sword was placed in Cernach's chamber by the real culprit, for us to find. To Cernach my footsteps were carefully pointed . . . But why Cernach? He was not even of the 'age of choice', so what could he gain?"

There was a silence as they waited tensely for her to continue.

"Abbot Colmán told me that Cernach was a supporter of Rome. So did Ailill and so did Ornait. But Ornait was the only one who told me that Cernach desired the throne, even though unable to do so by his age. Ornait also told me that he would be of age within a month."

Sister Fidelma suddenly wheeled round on the girl.

"Ornait was also the only person who knew of my reputation as a solver of mysteries. Ornait told the Abbot and encouraged him to send for me. Is this not so?"

She glanced back to Abbot Colmán who nodded in confusion.

Ornait had gone white, staring at Sister Fidelma.

"Are you saying that I stole the sword?" she whispered with ice in her voice.

"That's ridiculous!" cried Sechnasach. "Ornait is my sister."

"Nevertheless, the guilty ones are Ailill and Ornait," replied Sister Fidelma.

"But you have just demonstrated that Ailill was innocent of the crime," Sechnasach said in total bewilderment.

"No. I demonstrated that evidence was left for me in order that I would believe Ailill was innocent; that he could not have carried out the deed as it was claimed he had. When things are obvious, beware of them."

"But why would Ornait take part in this theft?" demanded the High King.

"Ornait conceived the plan. Its cunning was her own. It was carried out by Ailill and herself and no others."

"Explain."

"Ailill and Ornait entered the chapel that night in the normal way through the passage. They proceeded to carry out the plan. Ornait took the sword while Ailill broke the bolt, making sure of the obvious mistake. They relied on discovery by the two guards and Ailill waited for them. But, as always in such carefully laid plans, there comes the unexpected. As Ornait was proceeding back through the passage she saw the Abbot coming along it. He had left his *Psalter* in the sacristy and needed it. She pressed into an alcove and hid until he had gone by. When she left the alcove she tore her gown on some obstruction."

Sister Fidelma held out the small piece of frayed colourful cloth.

"But the rest of the plan worked perfectly. Ailill was imprisoned. The second part of the plan was now put into place. Ornait had been informed by a sister from my house at Kildare that I was a solver of mysteries. In fact, without undue modesty, I may say that Ornait's entire plan had been built around me. When the sword could not be found, she was able to persuade Abbot Colmán to send for me to investigate its mysterious disappearance. Colmán himself had never heard of me before Ornait dropped my name in his ear. He has just admitted this."

The Abbot was nodding in agreement as he strove to follow her argument.

"When I arrived, the contrived evidence led me immediately to believe Ailill Flann Esa was innocent, as it was supposed to do. It also led me to the chosen scapegoat, Cernach Mac Diarmuid. And in his chamber, scarcely concealed, was the sacred sword. It was all too easy for me. That ease made me suspicious. Both Ailill and Ornait were too free with Cernach's name. Then I saw the frayed cloth in the passage and I began to think."

"But if it was a simple plot to discredit me by the non-production of the sword," observed Sechnasach, "why such an elaborate plot? Why not simply steal the sword and hide it where it could not be so easily recovered?"

"That was the matter which caused the greatest puzzle. However, it became clear to me as I considered it. Ornait and Ailill had to be sure of your downfall. The loss of the sword would create alarm and dissension among the people. But it was not simply chaos that they wanted. They wanted your immediate downfall. They had to ensure that the Great Assembly would come to regret their decision and immediately proclaim for Ailill at the inauguration."

"How could they ensure that?" demanded Abbot Colmán. "The Great Assembly had already made their decision."

"A decision which could be overturned any time before the inauguration. After aspersions had been cast on Sechnasach's judgement, his ability to treat people fairly, the Great Assembly could change its support. By showing the Great Assembly that Sechnasach was capable of unjustly accusing one who had been his rival, this could be done. I am also sure that Sechnasach would be accused of personal enmity because of Ornait's love of Ailill. I was part of Ornait's plan to depose her brother and replace him with Ailill. I was to be invited to Tara for no other purpose but to demonstrate Ailill's innocence and Cernach's guilt. Doubt on Sechnasach's judgement would be a blemish on his ability for the High Kingship. Remember the Law of Kings, the law of the seven proofs of a righteous King? That his judgement be firm and just and beyond reproach. Once Sechnasach's decision to imprison Ailill was shown to have been unjust, Ailill, as *tánaiste*, would be acclaimed in his place with Ornait as his queen."

Sechnasach sat staring at his sister, reading the truth in her scowling features. If the veracity of Sister Fidelma's argument needed support, it could be found in the anger and hate written on the girl's features and that humiliation on Ailill's face.

"And this was done for no other reason than to seize the throne, for no other motive than power?" asked the High King incredulously. "It was not done because they wanted to reform the Church in line with Rome?"

"Not for Rome. Merely for power," Fidelma agreed. "For power most people would do anything."

# PART II
## The Middle Ages

# THE PRICE OF LIGHT
## Ellis Peters

*This anthology would not be complete without Brother Cadfael, the twelfth-century monk whose crime-solving abilities brought the medieval mystery to life.*

*Ellis Peters is the crime-writing persona of Edith Pargeter (b. 1913), in her own right a talented writer of historical novels. Her first book had been a short historical novel set in Roman times,* Hortensius, Friend of Nero *(1936), but the initial poor sales of her historical books caused her to turn to crime fiction. She first introduced her character of Inspector Felse in* Fallen Into the Pit *(1951); a later Felse novel,* Death and the Joyful Woman *(1961) won the Mystery Writers of America Edgar Award as the Year's Best Mystery Novel.*

*Brother Cadfael first appeared in* A Morbid Taste for Bones *and has now featured in nineteen novels and three short stories. The short story reprinted here is his earliest case as a monk. Although "A Light on the Road to Woodstock" is set earlier, Cadfael was still then a man of the world. "The Price of Light" takes place two years before* A Morbid Taste for Bones, *and reintroduces us to many of the familiar characters.*

Hamo FitzHamon of Lidyate held two fat manors in the north-eastern corner of the county, towards the border of Cheshire. Though a gross feeder, a heavy drinker, a self-indulgent lecher, a harsh landlord and a brutal master, he had reached the age of sixty in the best of health, and it came as a salutary shock to him when he was at last taken with a mild seizure, and for the first time in his life saw the next world yawning before him, and woke to the uneasy consciousness that it might see fit to treat him somewhat more austerely than this world had done. Though he repented none of them, he was aware of a whole register of acts in his past which heaven might construe as heavy sins. It began to seem to him a prudent precaution to acquire merit for his soul as quickly as possible. Also as cheaply, for he was a grasping and possessive man. A judicious gift to some holy house should secure the welfare of his soul. There was no need to go so far as endowing an abbey, or a new church of his own. The Benedictine abbey of Shrewsbury could put up a powerful assault of prayers on his behalf in return for a much more modest gift.

The thought of alms to the poor, however ostentatiously bestowed in the first place, did not recommend itself. Whatever was given would be soon consumed and forgotten, and a rag-tag of beggarly blessings from the indigent could carry very little weight, besides failing to confer a lasting lustre upon himself. No, he wanted something that would continue in daily use and daily respectful notice, a permanent reminder of his munificence and piety. He took his time about making his decision, and when he was satisfied of the best value he could get for the least expenditure, he sent his law-man to Shrewsbury to confer with abbot and prior, and conclude with due ceremony and many witnesses the charter that conveyed to the custodian of the altar of St. Mary, within the abbey church, one of his free tenant farmers, the rent to provide light for Our Lady's altar throughout the year. He promised also, for the proper displaying of his charity, the gift of a pair of fine silver candlesticks, which he himself would bring and see installed on the altar at the coming Christmas feast.

Abbot Heribert, who after a long life of repeated disillusionments still contrived to think the best of everybody, was moved to tears by this penitential generosity. Prior Robert, himself an aristocrat, refrained, out of Norman solidarity, from casting doubt upon Hamo's motive, but he elevated his eyebrows, all the same. Brother Cadfael, who knew only the public reputation of the donor, and was sceptical enough to suspend judgement until he encountered the source, said nothing, and waited to observe and decide for himself. Not that he expected much; he had been in the world fifty-five years, and learned to temper all his expectations, bad or good.

It was with mild and detached interest that he observed the arrival of the party from Lidyate, on the morning of Christmas Eve. A hard, cold Christmas it was proving to be, that year of 1135, all bitter black frost and grudging snow, thin and sharp as whips before a withering east wind. The weather had been vicious all the year, and the harvest a disaster. In the villages people shivered and starved, and Brother Oswald the almoner fretted and grieved the more that the alms he had to distribute were not enough to keep all those bodies and souls together. The sight of a cavalcade of three good riding horses, ridden by travellers richly wrapped up from the cold, and followed by two pack-ponies, brought all the wretched petitioners crowding and crying, holding out hands blue with frost. All they got out of it was a single perfunctory handful of small coin, and when they hampered his movements FitzHamon used his whip as a matter of course to clear the way. Rumour, thought Brother Cadfael, pausing on his way to the infirmary with his daily medicines for the sick, had probably not done Hamo FitzHamon any injustice.

Dismounting in the great court, the knight of Lidyate was seen to be a big, over-fleshed, top-heavy man with bushy hair and beard and eyebrows, all grey-streaked from their former black, and stiff and bristling as wire. He might well have been a very handsome man before indulgence purpled his face and pocked his skin and sank his sharp black eyes deep into flabby sacks of flesh. He looked more than his age, but still a man to be reckoned with.

The second horse carried his lady, pillion behind a groom. A small figure she made, even swathed almost to invisibility in her woollens and furs, and she rode snuggled comfortably against the groom's broad back, her arms hugging him round the waist. And a very well-looking young fellow he was, this groom, a strapping lad barely twenty years old, with round, ruddy cheeks and merry, guileless eyes, long in the legs, wide in the shoulders, everything a country youth should be, and attentive to his duties into the bargain, for he was down from the saddle in one lithe leap, and reaching up to take the lady by the waist, every bit as heartily as she had been clasping him a moment before, and lift her lightly down. Small, gloved hands rested on his shoulders a brief moment longer than was necessary. His respectful support of her continued until she was safe on the ground and sure of her footing; perhaps a few seconds more. Hamo FitzHamon was occupied with Prior Robert's ceremonious welcome, and the attentions of the hospitaller, who had made the best rooms of the guest-hall ready for him.

The third horse also carried two people, but the woman on the pillion did not wait for anyone to help her down, but slid quickly to the ground and hurried to help her mistress off with the great outer cloak in which she had travelled. A quiet, submissive young woman, perhaps in her middle twenties, perhaps older, in drab homespun, her hair hidden away under a coarse linen wimple. Her face was thin and pale, her skin dazzlingly fair, and her eyes, reserved and weary, were of a pale, clear blue, a fierce colour that ill suited their humility and resignation.

Lifting the heavy folds from her lady's shoulders, the maid showed a head the taller of the two, but drab indeed beside the bright little bird that emerged from the cloak. Lady FitzHamon came forth graciously smiling on the world in scarlet and brown, like a robin, and just as confidently. She had dark hair braided about a small, shapely head, soft, full cheeks flushed rosy by the chill air, and large dark eyes assured of their charm and power. She could not possibly

have been more than thirty, probably not so much. FitzHamon had
a grown son somewhere, with children of his own, and waiting some
said with little patience, for his inheritance. This girl must be a second
or a third wife, a good deal younger than her stepson, and a beauty, at
that. Hamo was secure enough and important enough to keep himself
supplied with wives as he wore them out. This one must have cost
him dear, for she had not the air of a poor but pretty relative sold
for a profitable alliance, rather she looked as if she knew her own
status very well indeed, and meant to have it acknowledged. She
would look well presiding over the high table at Lidyate, certainly,
which was probably the main consideration.

The groom behind whom the maid had ridden was an older man,
lean and wiry, with a face like the bole of a knotty oak. By the sardonic
patience of his eyes he had been in close and relatively favoured
attendance on FitzHamon for many years, knew the best and the
worst his moods could do, and was sure of his own ability to ride
the storms. Without a word he set about unloading the pack-horses,
and followed his lord to the guest-hall, while the young man took
FitzHamon's bridle, and led the horses away to the stables.

Cadfael watched the two women cross to the doorway, the lady
springy as a young hind, with bright eyes taking in everything around
her, the tall maid keeping always a pace behind, with long steps
curbed to keep her distance. Even thus, frustrated like a mewed
hawk, she had a graceful gait. Almost certainly of villein stock, like
the two grooms. Cadfael had long practice in distinguishing the free
from the unfree. Not that the free had any easy life, often they were
worse off than the villeins of their neighbourhood; there were plenty
of free men, this Christmas, gaunt and hungry, forced to hold out
begging hands among the throng round the gatehouse. Freedom, the
first ambition of every man, still could not fill the bellies of wives and
children in a bad season.

FitzHamon and his party appeared at Vespers in full glory to
see the candlesticks reverently installed upon the altar in the Lady
Chapel. Abbot, prior and brothers had no difficulty in sufficiently
admiring the gift, for they were indeed things of beauty, two fluted
stems ending in the twin cups of flowering lilies. Even the veins of
the leaves showed delicate and perfect as in the living plant. Brother
Oswald the almoner, himself a skilled silversmith when he had time to
exercise his craft, stood gazing at the new embellishments of the altar
with a face and mind curiously torn between rapture and regret, and
ventured to delay the donor for a moment, as he was being ushered
away to sup with Abbot Heribert in his lodging.

"My lord, these are of truly noble workmanship. I have some

knowledge of precious metals, and of the most notable craftsmen in these parts, but I never saw any work so true to the plant as this. A countryman's eye is here, but the hand of a court craftsman. May we know who made them?"

FitzHamon's marred face curdled into deeper purple, as if an unpardonable shadow had been cast upon his hour of self-congratulation. He said brusquely: "I commissioned them from a fellow in my own service. You would not know his name – a villein born, but he had some skill." And with that he swept on, avoiding further question, and wife and men-servants and maid trailed after him. Only the older groom, who seemed less in awe of his lord than anyone, perhaps by reason of having so often presided over the ceremony of carrying him dead drunk to his bed, turned back for a moment to pluck at brother Oswald's sleeve, and advise him in a confidential whisper: "You'll find him short to question on that head. The silversmith – Alard, his name was – cut and ran from his service last Christmas, and for all they hunted him as far as London, where the signs pointed, he's never been found. I'd let that matter lie, if I were you."

And with that he trotted away after his master, and left several thoughtful faces staring after him.

"Not a man to part willingly with any property of his," mused Brother Cadfael, "metal or man, but for a price, and a steep price at that."

"Brother, be ashamed!" reproved Brother Jerome at his elbow. "Has he not parted with these very treasures from pure charity?"

Cadfael refrained from elaborating on the profit FitzHamon expected for his benevolence. It was never worth arguing with Jerome, who in any case knew as well as anyone that the silver lilies and the rent of one farm were no free gift. But Brother Oswald said grievingly: "I wish he had directed his charity better. Surely these are beautiful things, a delight to the eyes, but well sold, they could have provided money enough to buy the means of keeping my poorest petitioners alive through the winter, some of whom will surely die for the want of them."

Brother Jerome was scandalized. "Has he not given them to Our Lady herself?" he lamented indignantly. "Beware of the sin of those apostles who cried out with the same complaint against the women who brought the pot of spikenard, and poured it over the Saviour's feet. Remember Our Lord's reproof to them, that they should let her alone, for she had done well!"

"Our Lord was acknowledging a well-meant impulse of devotion," said Brother Oswald with spirit. "He did not say it was well advised!

'She hath done what she could' is what he said. He never said that with a little thought she might not have done better. What use would it have been to wound the giver, after the thing was done? Spilled oil of spikenard could hardly be recovered."

His eyes dwelt with love and compunction upon the silver lilies, with their tall stems of wax and flame. For these remained, and to divert them to other use was still possible, or would have been possible if the donor had been a more approachable man. He had, after all, a right to dispose as he wished of his own property.

"It is sin," admonished Jerome sanctimoniously, "even to covet for other use, however worthy, that which has been given to Our Lady. The very thought is sin."

"If Our Lady could make her own will known," said Brother Cadfael drily, "we might learn which is the graver sin, and which the more acceptable sacrifice."

"Could any price be too high for the lighting of this holy altar?" demanded Jerome.

It was a good question, Cadfael thought, as they went to supper in the refectory. Ask Brother Jordan, for instance, the value of light. Jordan was old and frail, and gradually going blind. As yet he could distinguish shapes, but like shadows in a dream, though he knew his way about cloisters and precincts so well that his gathering darkness was no hindrance to his freedom of movement. But as every day the twilight closed in on him by a shade, so did his profound love of light grow daily more devoted, until he had forsaken other duties, and taken upon himself to tend all the lamps and candles on both altars, for the sake of being always irradiated by light, and sacred light, at that. As soon as Compline was over, this evening, he would be busy devoutly trimming the wicks of candle and lamp, to have the steady flames smokeless and immaculate for the Matins of Christmas Day. Doubtful if he would go to his bed at all until Matins and Lauds were over. The very old need little sleep, and sleep is itself a kind of darkness. But what Jordan treasured was the flame of light, and not the vessel holding it; and would not those splendid two-pound candles shine upon him just as well from plain wooden sconces?

Cadfael was in the warming-house with the rest of the brothers, about a quarter of an hour before Compline, when a lay brother from the guest-hall came enquiring for him.

"The lady asks if you'll speak with her. She's complaining of a bad head, and that she'll never be able to sleep. Brother Hospitaller recommended her to you for a remedy."

Cadfael went with him without comment, but with some curiosity, for at Vespers the Lady FitzHamon had looked in blooming health and sparkling spirits. Nor did she seem greatly changed when he met her in the hall, though she was still swathed in the cloak she had worn to cross the great court to and from the abbot's house, and had the hood so drawn that it shadowed her face. The silent maid hovered at her shoulder.

"You are Brother Cadfael? They tell me you are expert in herbs and medicines, and can certainly help me. I came early back from the lord abbot's supper, with such a headache, and have told my lord that I shall go early to bed. But I have such disturbed sleep, and with this pain how shall I be able to rest? Can you give me some draught that will ease me? They say you have a perfect apothecarium in your herb garden, and all your own work, growing, gathering, drying, brewing and all. There must be something there that can soothe pain and bring deep sleep."

Well, thought Cadfael, small blame to her if she sometimes sought a means to ward off her old husband's rough attentions for a night, especially for a festival night when he was likely to have drunk heavily. Nor was it Cadfael's business to question whether the petitioner really needed his remedies. A guest might ask for whatever the house afforded.

"I have a syrup of my own making," he said, "which may do you good service. I'll bring you a vial of it from my workshop store."

"May I come with you? I should like to see your workshop." She had forgotten to sound frail and tired, the voice could have been a curious child's. "As I already am cloaked and shod," she said winningly. "We just returned from the lord abbot's table."

"But should you not go in from the cold, madam? Though the snow's swept here in the court, it lies on some of the garden paths."

"A few minutes in the fresh air will help me," she said, "before trying to sleep. And it cannot be far."

It was not far. Once away from the subdued lights of the buildings they were aware of the stars, snapping like sparks from a cold fire, in a clear black sky just engendering a few tattered snow-clouds in the east. In the garden, between the pleached hedges, it seemed almost warm, as though the sleeping trees breathed tempered air as well as cutting off the bleak wind. The silence was profound. The herb garden was walled, and the wooden hut where Cadfael brewed and stored his medicines was sheltered from the worst of the cold. Once inside, and a small lamp kindled, Lady FitzHamon forgot her invalid role in wonder and delight, looking round her with bright, inquisitive eyes. The maid, submissive and still, scarcely turned her head, but her eyes ranged from left to right, and a faint colour touched life into her cheeks. The many faint, sweet scents made her nostrils quiver, and her lips curve just perceptibly with pleasure.

Curious as a cat, the lady probed into every sack and jar and box, peered at mortars and bottles, and asked a hundred questions in a breath.

"And this is necessary, these little dried needles? And in this great sack – is it grain?" She plunged her hands wrist-deep inside the neck of it, and the hut was filled with sweetness. "Lavender? Such a great harvest of it? Do you, then, prepare perfumes for us women?"

"Lavender has other good properties," said Cadfael. He was filling a small vial with a clear syrup he made from eastern poppies, a legacy of his crusading years. "It is helpful for all disorders that trouble the head and spirit, and its scent is calming. I'll give you a little pillow filled with that and other herbs, that shall help to bring you sleep. But this draught will ensure it. You may take all that I give you here, and get no harm, only a good night's rest."

She had been playing inquisitively with a pile of small clay dishes he kept by his work-bench, rough dishes in which the fine seeds sifted from fruiting plants could be spread to dry out; but she came at once to gaze eagerly at the modest vial he presented to her. "Is it enough? It takes much to give me sleep."

"This," he assured her patiently, "would bring sleep to a strong man. But it will not harm even a delicate lady like you."

She took it in her hand with a small, sleek smile of satisfaction. "Then I thank you indeed! I will make a gift – shall I? – to your almoner in requital. Elfgiva, you bring the little pillow. I shall breathe it all night long. It should sweeten dreams."

So her name was Elfgiva. A Norse name. She had Norse eyes, as he had already noted, blue as ice, and pale, fine skin worn finer and whiter by weariness. All this time she had noted everything that passed, motionless, and never said word. Was she older, or younger, than her lady? There was no guessing. The one was so clamant, and the other so still.

He put out his lamp and closed the door, and led them back to the great court just in time to take leave of them and still be prompt for Compline. Clearly the lady had no intention of attending. As for the lord, he was just being helped away from the abbot's lodging, his grooms supporting him one on either side, though as yet he was not gravely drunk. They headed for the guest-hall at an easy roll. No doubt only the hour of Compline had concluded the drawn-out supper, probably to the abbot's considerable relief. He was no drinker, and could have very little in common with Hamo FitzHamon. Apart, of course, from a deep devotion to the altar of St. Mary.

The lady and her maid had already vanished within the guest-hall. The younger groom carried in his free hand a large jug, full, to judge by the way he held it. The young wife could drain her draught and clutch her herbal pillow with confidence; the drinking was not yet at an end, and her sleep would be solitary and untroubled. Brother Cadfael went to Compline mildly sad, and obscurely comforted.

Only when service was ended, and the brothers on the way to their beds, did he remember that he had left his flask of poppy syrup unstoppered. Not that it would come to any harm in the frosty night, but his sense of fitness drove him to go and remedy the omission before he slept.

His sandalled feet, muffled in strips of woollen cloth for warmth and safety on his frozen paths, made his coming quite silent, and he was already reaching out a hand to the latch of the door, but not yet touching, when he was brought up short and still by the murmur of voices within. Soft, whispering, dreamy voices that made sounds less and more than speech, caresses rather than words, though once at least words surfaced for a moment. A man's voice, young, wary, saying: "But how if he *does* . . .?" And a woman's soft, suppressed laughter: "He'll sleep till morning, never fear!" And her words were suddenly hushed with kissing, and her laughter became huge, ecstatic sighs; the young man's breath heaving triumphantly, but still, a moment later, the note of fear again, half-enjoyed: "Still, you know him, he *may* . . ." And she, soothing: "Not for an hour, at least . . . then we'll go . . . it will grow cold here . . ."

That, at any rate, was true; small fear of them wishing to sleep out the night here, even two close-wrapped in one cloak on the bench-bed against the wooden wall. Brother Cadfael withdrew very circumspectly from the herb garden, and made his way back in chastened thought towards the dortoir. Now he knew who had swallowed that draught of his, and it was not the lady. In the pitcher of wine the young groom had been carrying? Enough for a strong man, even if he had not been drunk already. Meantime, no doubt, the body-servant was left to put his lord to bed, somewhere apart from the chamber where the lady lay supposedly nursing her indisposition and sleeping the sleep of the innocent. Ah, well, it was no business of Cadfael's, nor had he any intention of getting involved. He did not feel particularly censorious. Doubtful if she ever had any choice about marrying Hamo; and with this handsome boy for ever about them, to point the contrast . . . A brief experience of genuine passion, echoing old loves, pricked sharply through the years of his vocation. At least he knew what he was condoning. And who could help feeling some admiration for her opportunist daring, the quick wit that had procured the means, the alert eye that had seized on the most remote and adequate shelter available?

Cadfael went to bed, and slept without dreams, and rose at the Matin bell, some minutes before midnight. The procession of the brothers wound its way down the night stairs into the church, and into the soft, full glow of the lights before St. Mary's altar.

Withdrawn reverently some yards from the step of the altar, old Brother Jordan, who should long ago have been in his cell with the rest, knelt upright with clasped hands and ecstatic face, in which the great, veiled eyes stared full into the light he loved. When Prior Robert exclaimed in concern at finding him there on the stones, and laid a hand on his shoulder, he started as if out of a trance, and lifted to them a countenance itself all light.

"Oh, brothers, I have been so blessed! I have lived through a wonder . . . Praise God that ever it was granted to me! But bear with me, for I am forbidden to speak of it to any, for three days. On the third day from today I may speak . . .!"

"Look, brothers!" wailed Jerome suddenly, pointing, "Look at the altar!"

Every man present, except Jordan, who still serenely prayed and smiled, turned to gape where Jerome pointed. The tall candles stood secured by drops of their own wax in two small clay dishes, such as Cadfael used for sorting seeds. The two silver lilies were gone from the place of honour.

Through loss, disorder, consternation and suspicion, Prior Robert would still hold fast to the order of the day. Let Hamo FitzHamon sleep in happy ignorance till morning, still Matins and Lauds must be properly celebrated. Christmas was larger than all the giving and losing of silverware. Grimly he saw the services of the church observed, and despatched the brethren back to their beds until Prime, to sleep or lie wakeful and fearful, as they might. Nor would he allow any pestering of Brother Jerome by others, though possibly he did try in private to extort something more satisfactory from the old man. Clearly the theft, whether he knew anything about it or not, troubled Jordan not at all. To everything he said only: "I am enjoined to silence until midnight of the third day." And when they asked by whom? he smiled seraphically, and was silent.

It was Robert himself who broke the news to Hamo FitzHamon, in the morning, before Mass. The uproar, though vicious, was somewhat tempered by the after-effects of Cadfael's poppy draught, which dulled the edges of energy, if not of malice. His body-servant, the older groom Sweyn, was keeping well back out of reach, even with

Robert still present, and the lady sat somewhat apart, too, as though still frail and possibly a little out of temper. She exclaimed dutifully, and apparently sincerely, at the outrage done to her husband, and echoed his demand that the thief should be hunted down, and the candlesticks recovered. Prior Robert was just as zealous in the matter. No effort should be spared to regain the princely gift, of that they could be sure. He had already made certain of various circumstances which should limit the hunt. There had been a brief fall of snow after Compline, just enough to lay down a clean film of white on the ground. No single footprint had as yet marked this pure layer. He had only to look for himself at the paths leading from both parish doors of the church to see that no one had left by that way. The porter would swear that no one had passed the gatehouse; and on the one side of the abbey grounds not walled, the Meole brook was full and frozen, but the snow on both sides of it was virgin. Within the enclave, of course, tracks and cross-tracks were trodden out everywhere; but no one had left the enclave since Compline, when the candlesticks were still in their place.

"So the miscreant is still within the walls?" said Hamo, glinting vengefully. "So much the better! Then his booty is still here within, too, and if we have to turn all your abode doors out of dortoirs, we'll find it! It, and him!"

"We will search everywhere," agreed Robert, "and question every man. We are as deeply offended as your lordship at this blasphemous crime. You may yourself oversee the search, if you will."

So all that Christmas Day, alongside the solemn rejoicings in the church, an angry hunt raged about the precincts in full cry. It was not difficult for all the monks to account for their time to the last minute, their routine being so ordered that brother inevitably extricated brother from suspicion; and such as had special duties that took them out of the general view, like Cadfael in his visit to the herb garden, had all witnesses to vouch for them. The lay brothers ranged more freely, but tended to work in pairs, at least. The servants and the few guests protested their innocence, and if they had not, all of them, others willing to prove it, neither could Hamo prove the contrary. When it came to his own two grooms, there were several witnesses to testify that Sweyn had returned to his bed in the lofts of the stables as soon as he had put his lord to bed, and certainly empty-handed; and Sweyn, as Cadfael noted with interest, swore unblinkingly that young Madoc, who had come in an hour after him, had none the less returned with him, and spent that hour, at Sweyn's order, tending one of the pack-ponies, which showed signs of a cough, and that otherwise they had been together throughout.

A villein instinctively closing ranks with his kind against his lord? wondered Cadfael. Or does Sweyn know very well where that young man was last night, or at least what he was about, and is he intent on protecting him from a worse vengeance? No wonder Madoc looked a shade less merry and ruddy than usual this morning, though on the whole he kept his countenance very well, and refrained from even looking at the lady, while her tone to him was cool, sharp and distant.

Cadfael left them hard at it again after the miserable meal they made of dinner, and went into the church alone. While they were feverishly searching every corner for the candlesticks he had forborne from taking part, but now they were elsewhere he might find something of interest there. He would not be looking for anything so obvious as two large silver candlesticks. He made obeisance at the altar, and mounted the step to look closely at the burning candles. No one had paid any attention to the modest containers that had been substituted for Hamo's gift, and just as well, in the circumstances, that Cadfael's workshop was very little visited, or these little clay pots might have been recognized as coming from there. He moulded and baked them himself as he wanted them. He had no intention of condoning theft, but neither did he relish the idea of any creature, however sinful, falling into Hamo FitzHamon's mercies.

Something long and fine, a thread of silver-gold, was caught and coiled in the wax at the base of one candle. Carefully he detached candle from holder and unlaced from it a long, pale hair; to make sure of retaining it, he broke off the imprisoning disc of wax with it, and then hoisted and turned the candle to see if anything else was to be found under it. One tiny oval dot showed; with a fingernail he extracted a single seed of lavender. Left in the dish from beforetime? He thought not. The stacked pots were all empty. No, this had been brought here in the fold of a sleeve, most probably, and shaken out while the candle was being transferred.

The lady had plunged both hands with pleasure into the sack of lavender, and moved freely about his workshop investigating everything. It would have been easy to take two of these dishes unseen, and wrap them in a fold of her cloak. Even more plausible, she might have delegated the task to young Madoc, when they crept away from their assignation. Supposing, say, they had reached the desperate point of planning flight together, and needed funds to set them on their way to some safe refuge . . . yes, there were possibilities. In the meantime, the grain of lavender had given Cadfael another idea. And there was, of course, that long, fine hair, pale as flax, but brighter. The boy was fair. But so fair?

He went out through the frozen garden to his herbarium, shut himself securely into his workshop, and opened the sack of lavender, plunging both arms to the elbow and groping through the chill, smooth sweetness that parted and slid like grain. They were there, well down, his fingers traced the shape first of one, then a second. He sat down to consider what must be done.

Finding the lost valuables did not identify the thief. He could produce and restore them at once, but FitzHamon would certainly pursue the hunt vindictively until he found the culprit; and Cadfael had seen enough of him to know that it might cost life and all before this complainant was satisfied. He needed to know more before he would hand over any man to be done to death. Better not leave the things here, however. He doubted if they would ransack his hut, but they might. He rolled the candlesticks in a piece of sacking, and thrust them into the centre of the pleached hedge where it was thickest. The meagre, frozen snow had dropped with the brief sun. His arm went in to the shoulder, and when he withdrew it, the twigs sprang back and covered all, holding the package securely. Whoever had first hidden it would surely come by night to reclaim it, and show a human face at last.

It was well that he had moved it, for the searchers, driven by an increasingly angry Hamo, reached his hut before Vespers, examined everything within it, while he stood by to prevent actual damage to his medicines, and went away satisfied that what they were seeking was not there. They had not, in fact, been very thorough about the sack of lavender; the candlesticks might well have escaped notice even if he had left them there. It did not occur to anyone to tear the hedges apart, luckily. When they were gone, to probe all the fodder and grain in the barns, Cadfael restored the silver to its original place. Let the bait lie safe in the trap until the quarry came to claim it, as he surely would, once relieved of the fear that the hunters might find it first.

Cadfael kept watch that night. He had no difficulty in absenting himself from the dortoir, once everyone was in bed and asleep. His cell was by the night stairs, and the prior slept at the far end of the long room, and slept deeply. And bitter though the night air was, the sheltered hut was barely colder than his cell, and he kept blankets there for swathing some of his jars and bottles against frost. He took his little box with tinder and flint, and hid himself in the corner behind the door. It might be a wasted vigil; the thief, having survived one day, might think it politic to venture yet another before removing his spoils.

But it was not wasted. He reckoned it might be as late as ten o'clock when he heard a light hand at the door. Two hours before the bell would sound for Matins, almost two hours since the household had retired. Even the guest-hall should be silent and asleep by now; the hour was carefully chosen. Cadfael held his breath, and waited. The door swung open, a shadow stole past him, light steps felt their way unerringly to where the sack of lavender was propped against the wall. Equally silently Cadfael swung the door to again, and set his back against it. Only then did he strike a spark, and hold the blown flame to the wick of his little lamp.

She did not start or cry out, or try to rush past him and escape into the night. The attempt would not have succeeded, and she had had long practice in enduring what could not be cured. She stood facing him as the small flame steadied and burned taller, her face shadowed by the hood of her cloak, the candlesticks clasped possessively to her breast.

"Elfgiva!" said Brother Cadfael gently. And then: "Are you here for yourself, or for your mistress?" But he thought he knew the answer already. That frivolous young wife would never really leave her rich husband and easy life, however tedious and unpleasant Hamo's attentions might be, to risk everything with her penniless villein lover. She would only keep him to enjoy in secret whenever she felt it safe. Even when the old man died she would submit to marriage at an overlord's will to another equally distasteful. She was not the stuff of which heroines and adventurers are made. This was another kind of woman.

Cadfael went close, and lifted a hand gently to put back the hood from her head. She was tall, a hand's-breadth taller than he, and erect as one of the lilies she clasped. The net that had covered her hair was drawn off with the hood, and a great flood of silver-gold streamed about her in the dim light, framing the pale face and startling blue eyes. Norse hair! The Danes had left their seed as far south as Cheshire, and planted this tall flower among them. She was no longer plain, tired and resigned. In this dim but loving light she shone in austere beauty. Just so must Brother Jordan's veiled eyes have seen her.

"Now I see!" said Cadfael. "You came into the Lady Chapel, and shone upon our half-blind brother's darkness as you shine here. You are the visitation that brought him awe and bliss, and enjoined silence upon him for three days."

The voice he had scarcely heard speak a word until then, a voice level, low and beautiful, said: "I made no claim to be what I am not. It was he who mistook me. I did not refuse the gift."

"I understand. You had not thought to find anyone there, he took you by surprise as you took him. He took you for Our Lady herself, disposing as she saw fit of what had been given her. And you made him promise you three days' grace." The lady had plunged her hands into the sacks, yes, but Elfgiva had carried the pillow, and a grain or two had filtered through the muslin to betray her.

"Yes," she said, watching him with unwavering blue eyes.

"So in the end you had nothing against him making known how the candlesticks were stolen." It was not an accusation, he was pursuing his way to understanding.

But at once she said clearly: "I did not steal them. I took them. I will restore them − to their owner."

"Then you don't claim they are yours?"

"No," she said, "they are not mine. But neither are they FitzHamon's."

"Do you tell me," said Cadfael mildly, "that there has been no theft at all?"

"Oh, yes," said Elfgiva, and her pallor burned into a fierce brightness, and her voice vibrated like a harp-string. "Yes, there has been a theft, and a vile, cruel theft, too, but not here, not now. The theft was a year ago, when FitzHamon received these candlesticks from Alard who made them, his villein, like me. Do you know what the promised price was for these? Manumission for Alard, and marriage with me, what we had begged of him three years and more. Even in villeinage we would have married and been thankful. But he promised freedom! Free man makes free wife, and I was promised, too. But when he got the fine works he wanted then he refused the promised price. He laughed! I saw, I heard him! He kicked Alard away from him like a dog. So what was his due, and denied him, Alard took. He ran! On St. Stephen's Day he ran!"

"And left you behind?" said Cadfael gently.

"What chance had he to take me? Or even to bid me farewell? He was thrust out to manual labour on FitzHamon's other manor. When his chance came, he took it and fled. I was not sad! I rejoiced! Whether I live or die, whether he remembers or forgets me, he is free. No, but in two days more he will be free. For a year and a day he will have been working for his living in his own craft, in a charter borough, and after that he cannot be haled back into servitude, even if they find him."

"I do not think," said Brother Cadfael," "that he will have forgotten you! Now I see why our brother may speak after three days. It will be too late then to try to reclaim a runaway serf. And you hold that these exquisite things you are cradling belong by right to Alard who made them?"

"Surely," she said, "seeing he never was paid for them, they are still his."

"And you are setting out tonight to take them to him. Yes! As I heard it, they had some cause to pursue him towards London . . . indeed, into London, though they never found him. Have you had better word of him? *From* him?"

The pale face smiled. "Neither he nor I can read or write. And whom should he trust to carry word until his time is complete, and he is free? No, never any word."

"But Shrewsbury is also a charter borough, where the unfree may work their way to freedom in a year and a day. And sensible boroughs encourage the coming of good craftsmen, and will go far to hide and protect them. I know! So you think he may be here. And the trail towards London a false trail. True, why should he run so far, when there's help so near? But, daughter, what if you do not find him in Shrewsbury?"

"Then I will look for him elsewhere until I do. I can live as a runaway, too, I have skills, I can make my own way until I do get word of him. Shrewsbury can as well make room for a good seamstress as for a man's gifts, and someone in the silversmith's craft will know where to find a brother so talented as Alard. I shall find him!"

"And when you do? Oh, child, have you looked beyond that?"

"To the very end," said Elfgiva firmly. "If I find him and he no longer wants me, no longer thinks of me, if he is married and has put me out of his mind, then I will deliver him these things that belong to him, to do with as he pleases, and go my own way and make my own life as best I may without him. And wish well to him as long as I live."

Oh, no, small fear, she would not be easily forgotten, not in a year, not in many years. "And if he is utterly glad of you, and loves you still?"

"Then," she said, gravely smiling, "if he is of the same mind as I, I have made a vow to Our Lady, who lent me her semblance in the old man's eyes, that we will sell these candlesticks where they may fetch their proper price, and that price shall be delivered to your almoner to feed the hungry. And that will be our gift, Alard's and mine, though no one will ever know it."

"Our Lady will know it," said Cadfael, "and so shall I. Now, how were you planning to get out of this enclave and into Shrewsbury? Both our gates and the town gates are closed until morning."

She lifted eloquent shoulders. "The parish doors are not barred. And even if I leave tracks, will it matter, provided I find a safe hiding-place inside the town?"

"And wait in the cold of the night? You would freeze before morning. No, let me think. We can do better for you than that."

Her lips shaped: "*We?*" in silence, wondering, but quick to understand. She did not question his decisions, as he had not questioned hers. He thought he would long remember the slow, deepening smile, the glow of warmth mantling her cheeks. "You believe me!" she said.

"Every word! Here, give me the candlesticks, let me wrap them, and do you put up your hair again in net and hood. We've had no fresh snow since morning, the path to the parish door is well trodden, no one will know your tracks among the many. And, girl, when you come to the town end of the bridge there's a little house off to the left, under the wall, close to the town gate. Knock there and ask for shelter over the night till the gates open, and say that Brother Cadfael sent you. They know me, I doctored their son when he was sick. They'll give you a warm corner and a place to lie, for kindness' sake, and ask no questions, and answer none from others, either. And likely they'll know where to find the silversmiths of the town, to set you on your way."

She bound up her pale, bright hair and covered her head, wrapping the cloak about her, and was again the maidservant in homespun. She obeyed without question his every word, moved silently at his back round the great court by way of the shadows, halting when he halted, and so he brought her to the church, and let her out by the parish door into the public street, still a good hour before Matins. At the last moment she said, close at his shoulder within the half-open door. "I shall be grateful always. Some day I shall send you word."

"No need for words," said Brother Cadfael, "if you send me the sign I shall be waiting for. Go now, quickly, there's not a soul stirring."

She was gone, lightly and silently, flitting past the abbey gatehouse like a tall shadow, towards the bridge and the town. Cadfael closed the door softly, and went back up the night stairs to the dortoir, too late to sleep, but in good time to rise at the sound of the bell, and return in procession to celebrate Matins.

There was, of course, the resultant uproar to face next morning, and he could not afford to avoid it, there was too much at stake. Lady FitzHamon naturally expected her maid to be in attendance as soon as she opened her eyes, and raised a petulant outcry when there was no submissive shadow waiting to dress her and do her hair. Calling failed to summon and search to find Elfgiva, but it was an hour or more before it dawned on the lady that she had lost her accomplished maid for good. Furiously she made her own toilet, unassisted, and raged out to complain to her husband, who

had risen before her, and was waiting for her to accompany him
to Mass. At her angry declaration that Elfgiva was nowhere to be
found, and must have run away during the night, he first scoffed, for
why should a sane girl take herself off into a killing frost when she
had warmth and shelter and enough to eat where she was? Then he
made the inevitable connection, and let out a roar of rage.

"Gone, is she? And my candlesticks gone with her, I dare swear!
So it was *she*! The foul little thief! But I'll have her yet, I'll drag her
back, she shall not live to enjoy her ill-gotten gains . . ."

It seemed likely that the lady would heartily endorse all this;
her mouth was already open to echo him when Brother Cadfael,
brushing her sleeve close as the agitated brothers ringed the pair,
contrived to shake a few grains of lavender on to her wrist. Her
mouth closed abruptly. She gazed at the tiny things for the briefest
instant before she shook them off, she flashed an even briefer glance
at Brother Cadfael, caught his eye, and heard in a rapid whisper:
"Madam, softly! – proof of the maid's innocence is also proof of the
mistress's."

She was by no means a stupid woman. A second quick glance
confirmed what she had already grasped, that there was one man
here who had a weapon to hold over her at least as deadly as any
she could use against Elfgiva. She was also a woman of decision, and
wasted no time in bitterness once her course was chosen. The tone in
which she addressed her lord was almost as sharp as that in which
she had complained of Elfgiva's desertion.

"She your thief, indeed! That's folly, as you should very well know.
The girl is an ungrateful fool to leave me, but a thief she never has
been, and certainly is not this time. She can't possibly have taken
the candlesticks, you know well enough when they vanished, and you
know I was not well that night, and went early to bed. She was with
me until long after Brother Prior discovered the theft. I asked her
to stay with me until you came to bed. *As you never did!*" she ended
tartly. "You may remember!"

Hamo probably remembered very little of that night; certainly he
was in no position to gainsay what his wife so roundly declared.
He took out a little of his ill-temper on her, but she was not so
much in awe of him that she dared not reply in kind. Of course
she was certain of what she said! *She* had not drunk herself stupid
at the lord abbot's table, she had been nursing a bad head of
another kind, and even with Brother Cadfael's remedies she had
not slept until after midnight, and Elfgiva had then been still
beside her. Let him hunt a runaway maidservant, by all means,
the thankless hussy, but never call her a thief, for she was none.

Hunt her he did, though with less energy now it seemed clear he would not recapture his property with her. He sent his grooms and half the lay servants off in both directions to enquire if anyone had seen a solitary girl in a hurry; they were kept at it all day, but they returned empty-handed.

The party from Lidyate, less one member, left for home next day. Lady FitzHamon rode demurely behind young Madoc, her cheek against his broad shoulders; she even gave Brother Cadfael the flicker of a conspiratorial smile as the cavalcade rode out of the gates, and detached one arm from round Madoc's waist to wave as they reached the roadway. So Hamo was not present to hear when Brother Jordan, at last released from his vow, told how Our Lady had appeared to him in a vision of light, fair as an angel, and taken away with her the candlesticks that were hers to take and do with as she would, and how she had spoken to him, and enjoined on him his three days of silence. And if there were some among the listeners who wondered whether the fair woman had not been a more corporeal being, no one had the heart to say so to Jordan, whose vision was comfort and consolation for the fading of the light.

That was at Matins, at midnight of the day of St. Stephen's. Among the scattering of alms handed in at the gatehouse next morning for the beggars, there was a little basket that weighed surprisingly heavily. The porter could not remember who had brought it, taking it to be some offerings of food or old clothing, like all the rest; but when it was opened it sent Brother Oswald, almost incoherent with joy and wonder, running to Abbot Heribert to report what seemed to be a miracle. For the basket was full of gold coin, to the value of more than a hundred marks. Well used, it would ease all the worst needs of his poorest petitioners, until the weather relented.

"Surely," said Brother Oswald devoutly, "Our Lady has made her own will known. Is not this the sign we have hoped for?"

Certainly it was for Cadfael, and earlier than he had dared to hope for it. He had the message that needed no words. She had found him, and been welcomed with joy. Since midnight Alard the silversmith had been a free man, and free man makes free wife. Presented with such a woman as Elfgiva, he could give as gladly as she, for what was gold, what was silver, by comparison?

# THE CONFESSION OF BROTHER ATHELSTAN
# Paul Harding

*After Ellis Peters, Paul Harding is the most prolific writer of historical mystery novels. Harding is one of several pen names used by Paul C. Doherty, Headmaster of a school in Essex. As Doherty he has written a series of novels featuring the thirteenth-century clerk in Chancery, Hugh Corbett, who first appeared in* Satan in St. Mary's *(1986). As Michael Clynes he is the author of the Sir Roger Shallot series set at the time of Henry VIII, which started with* The White Rose Murders *(1991). Most recently, under the name C. L. Grace, he has signed a contract with an American publisher for a series about a woman physician/detective in fifteenth-century Canterbury.*

*Brother Athelstan first appeared in* The Nightingale Gallery *(1991), and three novels have followed. This is his first short story, specially written for this volume. Set in the summer of 1376 it features the wine-loving, corpulent Sir John Cranston, Coroner of London, and his amanuensis, Brother Athelstan, a Dominican monk and parish priest of St. Erconwald's in Southwark.*

I was reading Bartholomew the Englishman's *The Nature of Things* in which he describes the planet Saturn as cold as ice, dark as night and malignant as Satan. In an interesting after-thought he claims it governs the murderous intent of men; I wonder if Saturn governs my life. The death of my own brother in battle still plagues my dreams whilst Cranston and I deal with murder every week: men, violent in drink or overtaken by some ill humour, drawing sword, mace or club to hack and slash. Cranston says it's strange work for a priest, I remind him how the first crime mentioned in the Bible was one of murder – Cain plotting to slay his brother Abel and afterwards claiming he knew nothing about it. The first great mystery! Cain was discovered and he bore the mark which, I think, stains in varying hues all our souls. Again, I was reading John's gospel where Christ, arguing with the Pharisees, dismissed Satan as "An assassin from the start". An assassin! Someone who lurks in the shadows plotting violent death. Now most murders we witness are after the blood has been spilt and the body lies dead, but recently Cranston and I saw an evil, well-plotted murder carried out before our very eyes.

Spring had come, snapping winter's vice-like grip. The Thames, frozen from bank to bank, thawed and the waters flowed quickly, full of life. The rains loosened the soil and the sun rose higher and stronger. The crowds poured back into the London streets and, to mark the changing seasons, John of Gaunt, Duke of Lancaster, uncle of the young King and Regent, announced a great tournament to be held at Smithfield. Varlets, squires and men-at-arms poured into London. The streets were packed with men, helmeted and armoured. Great destriers, caparisoned in all the colours and awesome regalia of war, moved majestically along the roads. High in the saddle rode the knights and men of war resplendent in coloured surcoats, their slit-eyed helmets swinging from the saddlebow, their bannered lances carried before them by page or squire. To the crash of grating hooves, hordes of others followed, retainers, gaudy in the livery of great lords and the bright, French silks of the young gallants who swarmed into the city like butterflies returning under the warm sun and blue skies. They thronged the taverns, their coloured garments a sharp contrast to the dirty leather aprons of the blacksmiths and the short jerkins and caps of their apprentices. For days before the tournament London rejoiced. There were miracle plays, fairs, cock fights, dog battles and savage contests between wild hogs and mangy bears. Bonfires were lit in Cheapside and the Great Conduit ran with wine. Cranston and I saw it all, being very busy as men and women, drenched with drink, quarrelled and violently fought each other: a man was hacked to death for stealing ale, a woman, slashed from jaw to groin, was found floating in the Walbrook. Sometimes the assailants were found but usually all we got were blank glances and evasive replies. Cranston's temper, never the best, grew more abrupt.

"Brother," he announced at the end of one tiring day as we both squatted in the coolness of my parish church, sharing a bowl of watered ale. "Brother, we need a respite from this. The day after tomorrow, Thursday, the tournament begins at Smithfield. We should go."

I shook my head.

"No, Sir John, I thank you but I have had enough of war and violent death."

"Not this time," he answered quickly. "The first tournament is a game of great skill, a joust with blunted lances between two court favourites, Oliver Le Marche and Robert Woodville. No deaths there, Brother. They fight for the favour of Lady Isabella Lyons, a distant kinswoman of the King." He nudged me in the ribs and came closer. "My wife will come. You could always bring Benedicta."

I blushed not daring to ask how he knew about the widow woman. Cranston laughed. He was still bellowing when he got up and walked out of the church after making me agree I would think about it.

At early Mass the next morning I saw Benedicta with the other two members of my congregation kneeling at the entrance to the rood screen, her ivory face framed in its veil of black, luxurious curls. After Mass, as usual, she stayed to light a candle before the statue of the Virgin. Benedicta smiled as I approached, asking softly if I was well. I blurted out my invitation, her violet blue eyes rounded in surprise but she smiled and agreed so quickly I wondered if she too felt a kinship with me. God forgive me, I was in my own private heaven, so pleased I did not even bother to study the stars despite the sky being cloud-free and my mind unwilling to rest even for sleep. Instead I tossed and turned, hoping the boy I had sent, Girth the bricklayer's son, had delivered my acceptance at the coroner's house. I rose at dawn, said my Mass, pleased to see Benedicta kneeling there, her hair now braided, hidden under a wimple, a small basket by her side.

After Mass we talked and quietly walked to meet Cranston at the "Golden Pig", a comfortable tavern on the Southwark side of the river. The coroner's wife, small and pert, was cheerful as a little sparrow, accepting Benedicta as a long-lost sister. Cranston, with a flagon of wine down him already, was in good form, nudging me in the ribs and leering lecherously at Benedicta. We took a boat across the Thames not rowed, thank God, by one of my parishioners and made our way up Thames Street to the "Kirtle Tavern" which stands on the edge of Smithfield just under the vast forbidding walls of Newgate prison.

The day proved to be a fine one, the streets were hot and dusty so we welcomed the tavern's coolness. We sat in a corner watching the citizens of every class and station go noisily by, eager to get in a good place to watch the day's events. Merchants sweltering under beaver hats, their fat wives clothed in gaudy gowns, beggars, quacks, story tellers, hordes of apprentices and men from the guilds. I groaned and hid my face as a group of my parishioners, Black Hod, Crispin the carpenter, Ranulf the ratcatcher and Watle son of the dung-collector, passed the tavern door, roaring a filthy song at the tops of their voices. We waited until Cranston finished his refreshment and, with Benedicta so close beside me my heart kept skipping for joy, we walked out into the great area around Smithfield.

Three blackened, crow-pecked corpses still swung from the gibbet but the crowd ignored them. The food sellers were doing a roaring trade in spiced sausages whilst beside them water-sellers, great buckets slung around their necks, sold cooling drinks to soothe the mouths of those who chewed the hot, spicy meat. I watched and turned away, my gorge rising in my throat as I saw Ranulf the ratcatcher sidle up behind one of these water-sellers and quietly piss into one of the buckets.

Smithfield itself had been cleared for the joust; even the dung heaps and piles of ordure had been taken away. A vast open space had been cordoned off for the day. At one side was the royal enclosure with row after row of wooden seats all covered in purple or gold cloth. In the centre a huge canopy shielded the place where the King and his leading nobility would sit. The banners of John of Gaunt, resplendent with the gaudy device of the House of Lancaster, curled and waved lazily in the breeze. Marshals of the royal household resplendent in tabards, their white wands of office held high, stopped and directed us to our reserved seats. All around us the benches were quickly filling, ladies in silk gowns giggling and chattering, clutching velvet cushions to their bosoms as they simpered past the young men who stood eyeing them. These gallants, their hair long and curled, their bodies dripping in pearls and lace, proved to be raucous and strident. Cranston was merry but some of these young men were already far gone in their cups. I ignored the lustful glances directed at Benedicta, trying to curb the sparks of jealousy which flared in my own heart and, once we were seated, studied the tournament area. The field, a great grassy plain, was divided down the centre by a huge tilt barrier covered in a black and white checkered canvas. At each end of this barrier were two pavilions; one gold, the other blue. Already the contestants were preparing for the joust, around each pavilion scuttled pages and squires, armour glinted and dazzled in the sun. I stared at the jousting lances, great 14-foot-long ashpoles, each in its own case on a long wooden rack. I asked Cranston why there were so many.

"Oh, it's simple, Brother," he replied. "Each course run will use up one lance and, as this is a friendly combat, ten or twelve lances may be broken before an outright victory is won."

A bray of trumpets drowned his words, a shrill so angry the birds in the trees around Smithfield rose in noisy protesting flocks. The royal party had now arrived. I noticed John of Gaunt, Earl of Lancaster, a majestic, cruel face under his silver hair, with skin burnt dark brown from his campaigns in Castile; on either side of him, his brothers and a collection of young lords. In the centre with one of Gaunt's hands on his shoulder, stood a young boy, his face white as snow under a mop of gold hair, a silver chaplet on his head. Beside him a young lady, her red hair just visible under a lacey white veil, a real eye-catching beauty in her tawny samite dress. Again the shrill bray of trumpets sounded. Gaunt lifted his hand as if welcoming the plaudits of the crowd. There was some clapping from the claque of young courtiers around us but the London mob was stony silent and I remembered Cranston's mutterings about how the expensive tastes of the court, coupled with the military defeats against the French, had brought Gaunt and his party into disrepute.

"There's the King!" the coroner whispered to his wife though his voice carried for yards around us. "And beside him is Lady Isabella Lyons, the queen of the tournament."

I looked sideways at Benedicta and my heart lurched. She had turned slightly in her seat, staring coolly back at a young, dark-faced gallant, resplendent in red and white silks, who lounged in his seat with eyes for no one but my fair companion. Cranston, sharp enough under his bluff drunken exterior, caught my drift. He leaned over and tapped me on the arm.

"The joust is about to begin, Brother," he said. "Watch carefully, you may learn something."

Another shrill blast from the trumpets, banners were lowered, the noise of the crowd died away as the two contestants emerged and mounted their great destriers. Each donned a war helm, took a lance and rode gently into the middle of the field to stand on either side of the Master Herald. Slowly they advanced before the royal box, an awesome vision of grey steel armour and silken surcoats, all the more ominous for the silence, no sound except for the gentle screech of leather. Both knights had their visors raised; I glimpsed young faces, lined and scarred, eyes impatient for the contest to begin. They lowered their lances and saluted both the King and the object of their desires, who simpered back, hiding her face behind her hands. Then each knight turned away, riding back towards the pavilions, taking up their positions at either end of the tilt barrier. The Master Herald, a great, bald-headed man, dressed in the royal blue and gold tabard, raised himself in the stirrups and in a loud, booming voice announced the tournament, a joust with blunted lances.

"Any knight," he bellowed, glaring fiercely around, "who breaks the rules of the tournament or tarnishes the honour of chivalry, will be stripped of his arms, his shield reversed and covered in dust and he will be dismissed from the field."

"That's Sir Michael Lyons," Cranston whispered, nodding to the Master Herald, "father to our great beauty. They say he thoroughly enjoys his daughter being the object of desire of two redoubtable warriors."

Sir Michael bowed towards the young King who raised his hand as a sign for the joust to commence. The herald turned his horse and lifted his white baton of office. At either end of the field the two knights prepared, visors were lowered as their squires grasped the reins of the horses. Cranston burped, his wife cooed with embarrassment. A crash of trumpets, the crowd burst into loud cheering as both riders started advancing together, first at a walk then a quick trot. There was another short trumpet blast, the audience gave a long sigh which grew into a resounding cheer as both knights charged, shields up, lances lowered, the pennants at either end of the lance snapping up and down like the wings of some beautiful bird. The knights met in the centre with a resounding crash of lances against shields. Then they were past each other, back again to their squires, who brought up fresh lances, making sure they avoided the wicked, sharpened hooves of the now fiery destriers.

Benedicta smiled at me, clutching my arm tightly. I felt happy, free like a bird which whirls under the bluest of skies. Again the trumpets, the sound of hooves drumming on the packed earth, war-like and ominous. I heard the crowd gasp and I looked up. Woodville had begun his charge but he seemed out of control, swaying in the saddle as if he was drunk, his lance fell and his shield arm dropped, his posture was all askew but Le Marche did not stop. He came thundering down, lance lowered. Woodville tried to defend himself but, too late, his opponent hit him full in the chest. Woodville was lifted from the saddle, high in the air and crashed to earth like a bird brought down by sling shot. He lay in a crumpled heap, his splendid armour now defaced by blood and dirt. His gaudy plumage, shorn from the crest of his helmet, drifted like snowflakes on the breeze.

"Brave lance!" someone shouted, then silence.

Le Marche turned, his horse now prancing back as the Master Herald, followed by other marshals and squires, ran up to the fallen knight. They gathered round and the herald turned, hands extended, and shouted.

"He is dead! My Lord Woodville is dead!"

The crowd remained silent before bursting into a loud raucous chorus of boos and jeers. Mud, dirt and other offal were flung in the direction of Le Marche. The herald walked over and looked up at Le Marche.

"Your lance, my Lord, was pointed."

The booing and catcalls increased, a few rocks were thrown. John of Gaunt rose and gestured with his hand. A deafening blast of trumpets brought royal men-at-arms as if from nowhere, to throw a cordon of steel around the crowd. In the near distance, stripped of its armour, the corpse of Sir Robert Woodville was being carried away on a makeshift pallet. Meanwhile the Master Herald was conferring with John of Gaunt. The trumpets blared out again, the herald bellowed that, for this day at least, the tournament was finished. His message was greeted with a chorus of catcalls and jeers but the moment passed; the crowd began to break up and drift away to seek further amusements amongst the booths and stalls of the nearby fair.

I glanced across at the royal enclosure: the young King sat as if carved from wood, looking blankly over at the tournament field, where royal serjeants were now circling Le Marche, gesturing that he dismount and surrender his weapons. The knight shouted his innocence but obeyed their orders. Beside the King the young queen of the tournament sat disconsolate, head in hand. Cranston's wife muttered, "Oh, the pity! Oh, the pity!"

Benedicta clung close to me, her face white and drawn as if Woodville's death had reawakened memories in her own soul. Cranston, however, stood transfixed, rooted to the spot, his mouth open. He just stared across at the confusion around the tilt barrier.

"Sir John Cranston! Sir John Cranston!"

A young page, wearing the surcoat of the royal household, came weaving through the crowd.

"Sir John . . .!"

"Here!" I called.

The boy just dismissed me with a flicker of his girlish eyelashes.

"Here I am!" Cranston bellowed. "What is it, boy?"

"My Lord of Lancaster wishes to have words with you."

"I wonder," Cranston murmured. He glanced slyly at me. "Come on, Brother. Maude," he turned to his wife. "Look after Benedicta."

He waddled off with me in tow, pushing through the guards into the royal enclosure, the page skipping in front like a frisky puppy. Knight bannerets of the King's household stopped him but the pageboy, jumping up and down, screamed his orders so they let Cranston by. I stood outside the protective ring of steel watching Cranston bow at the foot of the steps and fall to one knee. John of Gaunt came down, laughing, tapped him on the shoulder and, raising him up, whispered into his ear, Cranston replied. Gaunt looked up and stared like a hungry cat back at me, his eyes yellow, hard and unblinking. He nodded, muttered something and Cranston backed away. Sir John said nothing until he had taken me further away from the royal enclosure.

"Brother," he muttered, "this is a right midden heap. Woodville was one of Gaunt's principal retainers and now my Lord wants the truth about his death."

Cranston narrowed his eyes and whispered out of the corner of his mouth.

"Gaunt thinks it's murder, Brother. So do I."

Oh, I could have laughed! Here we were on a glorious day, a festival, and murder had appeared as the poet says 'stalking across the green fields like the evil which walks at mid-day'. I now wished we had gone somewhere else – or was it me, was I a Jonah? Did murder and assassination always trail my footsteps? I looked up, clouds were beginning fitfully to block the sun, I gazed back over my shoulder. Cranston's wife was making herself comfortable on a bench whilst the gallant who had been eyeing Benedicta, had now moved down and was talking quietly with her. He was teasing her but Benedicta did not seem to mind. Cranston, however, pushing me by the elbow, hurried me on across to Woodville's tent.

Inside the pavilion retainers were already laying out and dressing the corpse of the dead knight, who would have looked as peaceful and composed as an effigy in a church, except for the awful ragged gash in his chest. Cranston looked around; the retainers he dismissed but went direct as an arrow to Eustace Howard, Woodville's principal squire in the recent deadly joust. Eustace, round-faced, with a scrub of ginger hair, fearful green eyes and a petulant mouth, was loud in condemnation of what had happened. He nervously fingered a rosary as Cranston questioned him. The squire was about to launch into a further litany of protest when Sir Michael Lyons, the Master Herald, swaggered into the tent. He was a magnificent fellow: a broad, rubicund face and a leonine head, his grey hair swept back over his forehead. His martial appearance was made all the more threatening by watery blue eyes and a long drooping moustache. Sir Michael greeted Cranston warmly but dismissed Eustace and myself with a look of disdain.

"Cranston," he rasped. "I know why you are here but I am Master Herald and chief steward of the tournament. Woodville," he nodded at the corpse, "was murdered."

"By whom, Sir Michael?"

"God's teeth, Cranston!" Lyons snarled. "By Le Marche of course. His lance should have been blunted but the pointed steel cap had been replaced. We have found two of his other lances similarly armed. If Woodville had not been killed on the second run course, it would have undoubtedly happened later."

"And does that make Le Marche a murderer?" Cranston asked.

Lyons stared at Cranston so hard his blue eyes seemed to pop out of his rubicund face whilst his white goatee beard bristled with anger.

"I mean," Cranston smiled, "Le Marche should have used a blunted lance but did not. I concede that but I cannot see how that makes him a murderer."

Howard bleated like a sheep whilst Lyons stroked his beard.

"Oh, come, Sir John!"

"Oh, come, Sir Michael!" Cranston mildly interrupted. "We are old soldiers. Let us not charge the first enemy in sight but, as Vegetius maintains in his manual of war, let us be patient. First, why should the noble Le Marche kill Woodville? Secondly, if he did, his method bordered on madness. He used a pointed lance, he must have known this would be discovered and the blame fall on him."

Cranston stared at the Master Herald.

"There is one other perplexing problem. Would you say Le Marche and Woodville were equally matched?"

"Yes," the Master Herald grunted.

"So," Cranston continued, "how did Le Marche, even with his lethal lance, know he would be successful? Remember history, Sir Michael, the great Richard the Lionheart was killed by a man with a broken crossbow and a frying pan to protect himself. Come, Sir Michael," he flattered soothingly, "you are an old warhorse like me, in battle nothing is predictable."

The Master Herald allowed himself a small smirk of self-satisfaction.

"As always, Sir John, you are correct." He took a deep breath and looked round the pavilion. "This morning," he continued, "I thought how fortunate I was, my beautiful Isabella, queen of the tournament, the lady love of the two greatest champions in the kingdom. Now both are gone. Sir Robert lies dead and Sir Oliver is disgraced. I thought one of them, for they were both poor men, would have won the one hundred pounds prize and my daughter's affection."

Cranston whistled.

"So great a prize!" he said.

"God's teeth!" Sir Michael snarled. "Now all is gone!"

He looked scathingly at Eustace, who surprisingly stood his ground.

"Do not blame me, Sir Michael!" he cried.

"Who said he was?" Cranston asked.

"Someone will pay," Sir Michael replied. "Something is rotten here."

He looked at me, for the first time bothering to acknowledge my presence.

"I inspected everything according to the rules of the tournament. Their horses, their armour."

"And their lances?" I added.

"Yes, each knight lays them out on the grass before they are taken and put in the racks." He shook his head. "Sir Oliver must have known the lance was tipped."

"We will see Sir Oliver," Cranston soothingly interrupted. "Come, Brother!"

"Pompous fool!" Cranston muttered after we had left the tent. "He is the reason Gaunt told me to intervene in this matter. A good warrior, Sir Michael," he added, "but a greedy climber. A courtier with great ambitions, without the talent to match. Mind you," he looked sideways at me, "we all have our failures, don't we, Brother?"

The sun had slipped behind a cloud, I felt tired and unable to deal with Sir John's teasing. The tournament field was now empty. All the glory was gone. The banners had lost their gloss and finery. The tilt barrier was damaged, the ground on either side pounded to a dust which whirled in small clouds as a cold breeze blew in. Only the pavilions remained, each ringed by men-at-arms and a few ostlers and grooms looking after the horses. I dare not look across at Benedicta and I cursed myself for being a love-lorn idiot but, I suppose, love makes fools of us all. I trailed along beside Cranston, through the ring of armed men into Le Marche's pavilion. The young knight, his blood-red hair cropped to a stubble, was calm enough in the circumstances. I was surprised how young he was, though his eyes wore that aged look you often see in men steeped in the blood of others. "Men of contrasts" I call these knights with their courtly ways, silken clothes and lust for killing and war. Sir Oliver gazed stonily at both of us before returning to glare at his squire who was polishing his armour with a greasy rag. The squire kept his back to us, head bowed and I gathered there had been harsh words between master and servant before we entered. Cranston waddled across, barking at the lazing men-at-arms to get out.

"You are Sir Oliver Le Marche?"

"Of course," Le Marche replied. "And you, because of your weight and wine-drenched breath, must be Sir John Cranston!"

"King's Coroner!" Cranston tartly retorted.

"Of course," Le Marche replied and swung slightly to one side to look at me. "And, of course, the faithful Brother Athelstan. That," he indicated with his hand towards the squire, "is my ever devoted servant Giles Le Strange." Le Marche stood up. "Now the courtesies are over, let's be blunt. I did not kill Woodville. I did not know my lance was tipped with a metal point. You know, Sir John, how easy it is to slip the metal point onto a blunted lance. Anyone could have done it."

Cranston pursed his lips.

"Yes, I do," he said. "So what did happen?"

Sir Oliver sighed.

"Well, you saw the racks beside my pavilion at the end of the tilt barrier? I ran the first course, the lance was shattered. I returned to my position and my squire gave me a fresh one. I did not know the lance was pointed. I believed all of them were blunted, the metal points taken off." He shrugged. "Anyway, it was not my fault."

"Then whose was it, Sir?" Cranston barked.

Le Marche squared his shoulders.

"I could say, ask Woodville. All I remember is cantering towards him. My horse broke into a gallop, I lowered my lance. Only then did I notice something wrong."

"What?"

"Woodville seemed to sway in his saddle, his shield lowered, his lance askew. I could not have stopped even if I had wanted to." Le Marche bit his lip. "My lance was aimed for his shield; when that dropped, I took him full on the chest."

He looked at me for pity.

"Even then I thought all would be well. Perhaps Woodville would be a little bruised, nothing else. I am as distressed as anyone that he is dead."

"Surely," I queried, "as you lowered your lance, you would have seen the metal point sheathed on the tip?"

Cranston guffawed.

"No, Brother." Le Marche smiled. "Remember, I was helmeted, my visor down and the first rule of a jouster is never to watch your lance but your opponent."

"Did you like Woodville?" I asked.

"No, I did not."

"Why?"

"He belonged to the faction of John of Gaunt, the King's uncle. I am a retainer of Gaunt's younger brother, Thomas of Gloucester. You know, as the whole kingdom does, there is little liking between the brothers and the same goes for their retainers. I am a loyal man. What Lord Thomas dislikes I dislike. He disliked Gaunt. He disliked Woodville and so do I!"

"Was there more?" I asked. "I mean, the lady?"

"Yes, there was more," Le Marche retorted bitterly. "Lady Isabella. I had asked for her hand in marriage but Gaunt refused because she is a royal ward. Woodville, too, had asked. She's a fair lady."

"And owns even fairer lands?" Cranston commented.

Le Marche's eyes snapped up.

"Yes, she owns lands. Woodville was a suitor, a rival for her hand. For that I could have killed him but in fair combat. I did not murder him in the tournament."

"And the prize," I queried, "you wanted that?"

"Of course," Le Marche retorted. "Now, if I am found guilty of foul play, I forfeit that as well as my honour!"

Cranston looked at the squire.

"And you, Giles. Surely you inspected the lances?"

The squire turned, a dour, whey-faced lad, though his eyes were anger-bright. If looks were arrows, Le Marche would have dropped dead on the spot.

"Why should I?" he answered, throwing the rag to the ground. "Yes, I put the lances in the rack but have you ever carried a lance, Sir John? You never think of looking at the tip, fourteen feet high, well over twice your height. The lances are in the rack, your master comes galloping back, you take one, you put it in his hand and the noble knight," his eyes flickered up to his master, "charges on for greater honour and the favour of his lady."

Le Marche smiled sourly at his squire's attempt to be sardonic.

"My squire, Giles," Le Marche interrupted, "does not like me and does not like tournaments. In fact, you've recently quarrelled with me, haven't you, Giles?" Le Marche looked at me. "Do you know, Brother, Giles here wants to be a priest. He wants to leave the military life, believes he is not fitted for it."

"Is that true, Giles?" I asked.

I looked at his thin face and large eyes. For all his bluster, the squire seemed a gentle man, more suited to study and prayer than hacking at his fellow man, be it on the tournament field or in the real, bloody business of war.

"Yes," the squire murmured. "I have a vocation, Brother, but I also have an indenture," he glared at his master, "with Sir Oliver Le Marche; it has another six months to run. When it is finished, so am I. I intend to return to my own village in Northampton, seek an audience with the bishop and ask to be ordained as a priest."

"Some people," I said slowly, "might say that you, Giles, disliked your master so much you were prepared to take your revenge by depicting him as a knight who cheated in a tournament. After all, two men touched those lances. You and your master. Or," I turned, ignoring the squire's look of fury, "they might say, Sir Oliver, that you hated Woodville so much, you thought it was worth killing him to win the hand of the fair Isabella."

"That's a lie!" the knight snapped, his hand falling to his belt where his sword should have been.

"Brother Athelstan," Cranston tactfully interrupted, "is not accusing either of you. He is just repeating what other people might say."

"Some people," I continued, "might even allege that it was a conspiracy between you, Sir Oliver and your squire, to kill Sir Robert Woodville. I am only repeating, Sir Oliver," I concluded, "what other people might say. Woodville was killed by your lance."

"My master is a knight banneret," the squire protested. "Yes, I dislike serving him but would a knight break his honour and would I, called to the priesthood, commit such a dreadful act?"

Cranston made a rude noise with his lips and looked around the tent. I knew what he was searching for. No drink can be hidden from Sir John for long and he'd glimpsed the earthenware jug full of coarse wine on a tray in the corner of the tent. He went across and picked it up. Le Marche sauntered over with a pewter cup he took from a chest.

"Sir John, you are thirsty? Be my guest."

Cranston filled the cup to the brim until it spilt over, the red wine dripping to the ground like drops of blood and, in one great gulp, drank and immediately refilled it. He looked at me and rolled his eyes heavenwards.

"So," he said expansively, "what we have here is one knight, you, Sir Oliver with an intense dislike for your opponent. A dislike which has its roots in the rivalry between both your royal masters as well as rivalry for the fair hand of Lady Isabella. Secondly, we have your squire, Giles, who has little love for you. Thirdly, the tournament is ready, the lances are inspected by Sir Michael earlier in the day though you, Sir Oliver, never touched a lance until you ran the first course."

Le Marche nodded, filled a wine cup and drank greedily from it.

"Yes," he said, smacking his lips as if he hadn't a care in the world. "That's how it was and, if any man believes, alleges or even thinks I am responsible for Woodville's death he should produce the proof before King's Bench or answer to me on the field of combat, and that includes you, Sir John, even though you are the King's Coroner. As for you, Brother," Le Marche grinned across at me, "you can say what you like. I am used to your type." He nodded to his squire. "I have him preaching to me every second of the waking day. However, I repeat, I did not kill Woodville."

"But someone did!"

We all turned as Sir Michael Lyons, the Master Herald, strode into the tent.

"I, too, am concerned, Sir Oliver, by what many people saw: as Woodville charged he lost control of his horse, his lance slipped, his shield went down. Now I have just examined his destrier, there is a cut on its hindquarters."

Le Marche's face went hard.

"So, it was the horse which jolted him."

"Yes and Eustace, Woodville's squire, must be the culprit. Just before the trumpet blast for the second charge, the squire would have held Woodville's horse by its bridle. The trumpet rang out, the horse gathered itself for the charge, Eustace stepped back and with a dagger concealed in his other hand, cut the horse as it burst forward."

The Master Herald paused.

"The rest you know." He nodded at the tent entrance behind him. "We have the squire outside. He claims he knows nothing of this."

I could see from Cranston's close face and hooded eyes, the way he cocked his head slightly to one side that he did not fully accept the Master Herald's story.

"Bring Eustace in!" the coroner snapped.

The Master Herald went back to the doorway of the tent and shouted. Two men-at-arms entered, the hapless Eustace struggling and squirming between them. His face was grey and drawn, his mouth sagging open in disbelief at the accusations which had been levelled against him. Cranston, without a word, refilled his wine cup and offered it to the squire.

"Drink, man," he murmured. "Gather your wits for God's sake! All that has happened is an allegation laid against you, no real proof."

"There is proof," the Master Herald interrupted. "Come outside!"

Cranston followed Lyons out. I trailed behind, quite bemused. (When Sir John exercises his authority, he is like a hunting dog; he seeks out his prey, not letting go, not giving up the scent, not even for a bucket of wine or a flagon of beer.) The unfortunate war horse, still coated in a white, sweaty foam but now unsaddled, stood waiting patiently; two pages either side of its head, held it quiet and docile. Sir Michael took Sir John to the left side of the horse where Eustace would have stood, one hand on his master's bridle. True enough, Sir Michael was right; along the sweat soaked hindquarters there was a long ugly cut; no casualty of the tournament; the horse had been deliberately gashed. Sir John studied this carefully, licked his lips, shook his head and went back inside.

"Sir Oliver," he said. "You knew Woodville?"

"Of course. I have admitted as much."

"He was a good jouster?"

Le Marche pursed his lips.

"Yes," he replied slowly. "Probably one of the best in the kingdom."

"So, did you expect to win today?" Sir John added.

Le Marche looked away.

"Sir Oliver," Cranston repeated, "I asked you an honest question! As one knight to another, did you expect to win today?"

Le Marche shook his head.

"No," he replied softly. "I expected to lose. Woodville was an excellent jouster and horseman."

"Do you think," Cranston persisted, "that if his horse was hurt as he gathered to charge, it would have alarmed him?"

Le Marche laughed drily.

"I doubt it. Sir Robert was an excellent horseman. Any knight has to face such a danger in battle whether it be an arrow, flaming torch or a man-at-arms springing up suddenly in ambuscade. Remember, Sir John, a knight does not control his horse with his hands but with his knees. If there had been such an accident or an attempt to damage the horse, I believe Sir Robert would have controlled it."

"But not," the Master Herald interrupted, "if he was not expecting it. Remember, Woodville was at full charge, lance lowered, shield up, suddenly his horse shies. I still believe," he pointed to where Eustace stood gibbering with fright, his moans peppered with pleas for mercy, "that he could have damaged the horse and for those few seconds Sir Robert lost his concentration."

Cranston pursed his lips and nodded. He turned to me.

"What do you think, Brother?"

I thought of Benedicta and Cranston's wife still being entertained by the ever so courteous gallant.

"I think, Sir John, we cannot stay here all day. There is a tavern nearby, 'The Swooping Eagle'. Perhaps, Sir Michael, you could have it cleared and we can use it to continue our questioning there. Sir John, if you would come with me?"

We walked out of the tent. Across the field the gallant was now a little closer to Benedicta. Lady Maude was gazing soulfully over the field as if she realized the young man was not interested in her and she now pined for the return of her corpulent, but ever-loving husband. Benedicta seemed absorbed. The young man was facing her, his hands in his lap only a few inches from hers, his face masked in concentration as he stared into her eyes. I had to control the sense of panic, remind myself that I was a priest, a monk ordained and given to God. I had taken a vow of celibacy and, although I may have a woman as a friend, I cannot lust, I cannot desire or covet any woman whether she be free or not. I steeled myself. I had to because I felt a growing rage at my condition. A deep longing to be with Benedicta. A sense of hurt that she could find someone else so attractive and entertaining. I knew my anger to be unfair and I remembered an old priest once saying how people think priests are different but we are just ordinary men, exercising an extraordinary office. I looked at Sir John, he just stared down at the ground. I knew what he was thinking, he was impatient with me, yet felt sorry.

"Sir John," I began, taking him by the arm and walking him over to the tilt barrier. "What you said back there, was it true, that a knight guides his horse with his legs rather than his hands?"

Sir John shrugged.

"Of course. Any man who has to fight on horseback knows that you cannot guide your horse in battle if your hands are engaged. That is why each knight forms a close relationship with his horse until his destrier senses every move, even the slightest touch of pressure, where to turn, when to stop, when to rear. Even I," he tapped his great stomach, "when younger, and a little slimmer, was an excellent horseman." Cranston coughed. "Le Marche was correct. Sir Robert was a fine jouster, his reputation was well known. I cannot understand how a horse, even if it panicked or reared, should throw him to such an extent that he would lower both lance and shield. Moreover, there is something else."

"What?" I asked.

Cranston closed his eyes.

"Let us put ourselves in Woodville's position. He is on a horse, he is in armour, his visor lowered, he carries shield and lance. He charges. His horse, stung to agony by a dagger prick, swerves and turns."

Cranston opened his eyes and looked at me.

"Yet Woodville could have reasserted himself, turned his horse away and avoided Le Marche's oncoming lance." He shook his head. "There must be something else. But, come, let us go back to our guests."

Inside the tent Sir Michael was issuing orders. Eustace stood with his hands bound behind his back like a convicted felon waiting to be taken to Tyburn. Cranston went up to him.

"Eustace," he barked. "Did you have any grievance against your lord?"

The squire shook his head, his eyes pleading for mercy.

"He was a good master?"

Eustace nodded.

"So why did you goad your master's horse with a dagger?"

"I did not!" the man screamed. "I did nothing of the sort. Yes, I had my hand on the horse but no dagger. I inflicted no injury."

Cranston turned to Giles.

"Do you two know each other?" he asked.

Eustace looked away. Now Giles became agitated, moving from one foot to another, the tent fell silent. The Master Herald who had been on the verge of leaving turned back.

"I asked you a question," Cranston repeated. "You see, it's quite simple. If Woodville was murdered, two people must have been involved. One at Le Marche's end, putting a point on the blunted lance, the other at Woodville's ready to wound the horse. What I am saying, gentlemen, is the only people who had access to both knights were their two squires. Perhaps," Cranston looked at the Master Herald triumphantly, "perhaps it is not one murderer, Sir Michael, but two. And so I ask you squires again, did you meet before the tournament?"

"No," Eustace murmured. "No, no, this is not fair, our words will be twisted."

Cranston ignored him and looked at Giles.

"You did meet, didn't you?"

The squire nodded.

"What about?"

Giles licked his lips.

"I had met Eustace before," he said. "Quite a few times. We know each other well. When great lords assemble in castles their servants are left to wander around, find food and lodgings. They are left to their own devices. When the royal party went to any castle, be it Sheen or Windsor, Eustace was there."

"Don't tell him!" Eustace yelled. "Whatever you say will be twisted!"

Cranston walked across and squeezed the young squire's mouth in his hand.

"You, sir," he said, "will keep quiet until my questions are answered. And you," he looked at Giles, "you will tell us the truth."

Giles chewed his lip, his eyes pleading with Cranston.

"Eustace has lost money," he began, "in many wagers. He is a gambler, be it dice, the toss of a penny, two flies crawling up a castle wall, two cocks fighting in a ring, bears against dogs, a hunt, a falcon swooping for a heron, you will find Eustace laying his wager."

Giles smiled.

"He is not very successful and usually loses. He came to me three days ago. He asked me who I thought would win the great tournament, his master or mine? He made enquiries about Sir Oliver's health, his horse, his armour, whether he had been practising and so on. Of course, I refused to answer even though he pleaded with me, telling me he had wagered on my master winning." Giles shrugged. "I told him nothing, nothing at all."

Cranston took his hand away from Eustace's mouth.

"Is that true, squire?"

Eustace, realizing the futility of further protests, nodded meekly.

"It's true," he muttered. "I owe money to the Lombards, to the merchants, to the bankers, to other squires. I thought Sir Oliver would win. I wagered heavily that he would."

"So," Le Marche interrupted, "you thought your own master would lose?"

"Yes, yes," Eustace mumbled, "he was nervous of you. He was infatuated with the Lady Isabella. His wits were not as keen." His voice rose. "But no bribes were given, no understandings reached. There was no conspiracy to harm Sir Robert!"

Cranston shrugged.

"Well, sir, it looks that way," he replied. He looked back towards Giles. "The King's serjeant-at-law may well argue that both of you put your heads together and plotted mischief. You, Giles, put a point on your master's lance; while you, Eustace, damaged your master's destrier so when the charge came it was faulted and led to an accident and Sir Robert's death. Perhaps you did not intend that, just a slight accident. Yet, if such a charge can be proved, both of you will hang at Tyburn."

Eustace now broke into tears, shaking his head. Giles just stood there as if carved out of wood, his face implacable.

"I am no murderer!" he hissed. "I do not like my master. I do not like the silly games he plays, either here or elsewhere. When my indenture is completed, before God, I will be pleased to go."

"But my accusation still stands," the coroner persisted. "It would have taken two men to plot Woodville's downfall in this tournament one putting a point on Le Marche's lance, the other damaging Sir Robert's horse. Gentlemen, you are both under arrest. When I have finished my questions, Brother Athelstan and I will return. If we find nothing new, we will order your immediate committal to Newgate prison or, if His Grace the Duke of Lancaster agrees, perhaps even to the Tower. As you know, Sir Robert was a member of the royal household: an attack on him will be construed as treason."

Sir John turned and nodded at the Master Herald.

"Sir Michael, we will join you in the tavern."

As we walked across the tournament field I thought about what Sir John had said.

"Do you really believe," I said, "that there was a conspiracy between the two squires to kill Woodville? That Eustace wanted his master to lose and brought Giles into it?"

"Of course," the coroner replied, "it's possible. There is little love lost between Le Marche and his squire and Eustace is heavily in debt. A good lawyer could prove it and send both of those young men to their deaths."

He stopped and, turning round, waved at his now disconsolate wife. I dare not look. I wanted to reassert myself, concentrate on the matter in hand. There was villainy here, mischief, a knight had been killed and two young men were now being accused. If the accusations were true they would die horrible deaths. Benedicta would have to wait and the problems she caused, perhaps resolved in confession or counselling by a brother monk.

"Sir John," I began, "accept my apologies for my mind being elsewhere but let us look at this afresh. Let's start from the beginning. You have seen Sir Robert Woodville's horse. What about the rest? The lances he used, his armour?"

Sir John nodded.

"A good place to start, Brother."

Cranston turned and yelled instructions to one of the serjeants-at-arms. He then took me by the arm and led me over to the tilt barrier. After a while the serjeant, with a few companions, brought across the dead knight's armour, horse harness as well as the remains of Le Marche's shattered lances. We scrutinized these, particularly the saddle, for any deliberate cut but we could find no faults. The same was true of the lances; those Woodville and Le Marche had used in the first course were broken. In the second joust, however, only Le Marche had shattered his lance, the unfortunate Woodville never had the opportunity to engage his enemy. Cranston showed how the pointed metal tip could be slid on as easily as a knife goes into a sheath. Finally, the armour; Sir John donned the dead knight's helmet and, his voice booming out from behind the visor, pronounced everything satisfactory.

"Sir John," I asked, "when a knight charges, how does he hold the lance?"

Cranston doffed the helmet and picked up Woodville's battered breastplate, the great death-dealing gash in its centre.

"Look," he explained, "years ago a knight would hold his lance under his right arm but" – he pointed to the lance rest on the right side of the breastplate – "nowadays the lance is couched in the rest which is fastened by rivets to the breastplate." He tapped the loose lance rest with his hand. "Or at least it should be. Woodville's, of course, must have been wrenched loose during the joust."

I examined this carefully, the lance rest had been riveted to the breastplate by two clasps. One of these must have broken free. I remembered Woodville swaying in the saddle at the beginning of the second charge. I turned and shouted across at the serjeant-at-arms.

"Is there an armourer here?"

"Yes, of course."

"Fetch him!"

The soldier scurried off. Sir John and I put the breastplate to one side and inspected everything else but we could find nothing unsound. At last the armourer came, lank and greasy, his face grimed with dirt and sweat. He was not too sure on his feet. The fellow must have thought that as the tournament was cancelled, he could spend the rest of the day swigging tankard after tankard of ale. Nevertheless, he had nimble fingers and, with the tools he carried in a small leather bag, he soon had the lance rest completely free. I looked at the breastplate carefully and I guessed the identity of the murderer, not by any evidence or proof but, as old Father Anselm would say, by the application of pure logic. Cranston watched me.

"What is it, Brother?" he grated. "You have found something new, haven't you?"

"Yes," I replied. "Yes, I have!"

I asked the armourer to stand well out of earshot and I gave my explanation. Cranston, at first, rejected it so I called over the armourer. He listened to what I said and his face paled. He stopped, reluctant to answer but Sir John took him by the wrist, squeezed it and the man stammered that I was probably correct. Sir John then called over the captain of the royal serjeants and told him to saddle Woodville's horse and bring it over. Once he had done this, I asked the serjeant to stand, holding the reins of the still exhausted horse in one hand, his dagger in the other. He, too, soon caught the drift of my questions and his ready answers faltered till he was reduced to a few stumbled words or phrases. Cranston ordered both to keep quiet and bring Woodville's breastplate and horse to the "Swooping Eagle". They followed us across the field, out through the noisy colourful fair, to the tavern where the Master Herald, together with the royal serjeants, now guarded both Sir Oliver Le Marche and the two squires in the huge taproom.

At my request Sir John cleared the room except for Giles, Eustace, Sir Oliver and, of course, the captain of the royal serjeants and the Master Herald. Cranston went up to Le Marche lounging in his chair, a wine cup in his hands. He still had that air of diffidence though he had distanced himself from his squire.

"Sir Oliver," he asked, "tell me, how did you prepare for this tournament? I mean, today."

The knight shrugged.

"I told you. I and members of my household, together with this creature," he nodded towards the squire, "brought my armour and lances down to the tournament field. My pavilion was set up, the Master Herald scrutinized the lances as they were lying on the ground before they were placed on the rack."

"I see. And your armour?"

"On its rest in my pavilion."

"And people could come in and out of there?"

"Of course. Lord John of Gaunt as well as other members of the court came in to see me."

I looked towards Eustace who had now regained some composure.

"And the same at the other end of the lists?" I asked.

He nodded.

"Of course. The same routine. Sir Robert's baggage was brought down in a cart and unloaded. I supervised the setting up of the pavilion, and the armour rest and placed Sir Robert's armour there. The Master Herald examined the lances, the horse and saddle." He shrugged. "The rest you know."

"And, of course," I said, "no knight wears his armour until he has to?"

Sir Oliver laughed.

"Of course, in this heat, you do not go strutting around in armour. After an hour like that you would be too exhausted to climb on your horse, never mind couch your lance! Why? What are you saying, Brother?"

"Captain," I turned to the serjeant-at-arms, "in the tavern yard, there's a cart with the lances from the tournament field, those not used. Get one out and stand with it!"

The fellow hurried off and, at my insistence, we followed soon after. The serjeant stood, rather embarrassed and ill at ease, the huge tilting lance alongside him; the butt on the cobbles and its tip towering above him, its pennant snapping in the early evening breeze.

"Captain," I asked, "is that lance capped or blunted?"

He shrugged.

"I cannot say, Brother. I pulled it from the cart by the handle."

"Well, look up, man!"

He tried to.

"What can you see?"

"Nothing," he mumbled. "It's too high and the pennant at the top obscures my view."

I turned.

"Sir Oliver? Sir John?"

Both narrowed their eyes, squinting up into the sky but neither could give a definite answer. I smiled and led them back into the taproom.

"Now, Sir John," I began, "had a theory that Woodville's death was caused by a conspiracy between the two squires. That was a logical deduction; someone at one end of the lists replaced the points on the lance and someone else damaged Woodville's horse. But now I put a new theory. I believe that the same person who put the point on the lance injured Woodville's horse and also ensured that the lance rest on his armour was deliberately weakened. When Woodville charged the second time the lance slipped and this caused Woodville's death."

The tent fell silent. I noticed Cranston had gone to block the exit.

"Now who could do this? Someone who had access to both pavilions. The only person who had that access," I turned to Sir Michael Lyons who had now lost his bluster as the blood faded from his rubicund face, "was you, Sir Michael Lyons, the Master Herald. I suggest this happened: Le Marche's lances were laid in a row on the ground. When you went to inspect them, you crouched down and quite simply placed metal points on three of the lances."

"That's preposterous!" the Master Herald interrupted. "Anyone could have seen the lances were pointed!"

"No, they wouldn't," I said. "They would only see the point if they were looking for it, our serjeant-at-arms has just proved that." I paused. "Now," I continued, "at the tournament, the lances were placed in the rack, in the same order as they were on the ground. The first lance was blunted, the next three pointed. However, everybody thought the lances had been examined. Now Giles here comes to take one. The lances are fourteen feet long, over twice a man's height." I looked at the squire. "He picked it up by the handle, and when the lance is in the air, who sees the point? He carries it to the rack and leaves it there. The next time he touches it he's hurrying in a frenetic haste; his master has already run a course and he needs a fresh lance. Giles runs up, takes the lance from its rack and gives it to his master. Sir Oliver also does not examine the top of the lance, towering some eleven feet above him in the air. He charges. Meanwhile, at the other end of the field Woodville is also waiting. His lance has no cutting edge, no pointed steel to break the armour. What he does not know is that the lance rest on his breastplate has been weakened by you, Sir Michael, when you went to inspect his armour."

"No!" Le Marche shouted out. "If the lance rest was broken, it was damaged when I struck him!"

"That's what Sir Michael would have liked us to think," Cranston added. "But the lance rest was untouched: it was not dented or even marked, it just swung loose on Woodville's breastplate."

Sir Michael, his face now wet with sweat, shook his head.

"This is foolishness!" he snapped. "The lance rest could have swung loose during the second charge or even the first."

"No, Sir Michael," Cranston replied. "This is what happened. Sir Robert ran the first course. He returned, took the second spear and couched it in his lance rest. He began his charge: the pressure of the couched lance pushed the rest, weakened in the first tourney, askew. Now, Sir Robert, a professional jouster, could cope with a wayward horse but not with a 14-foot ash pole which suddenly seemed to have a life of its own. For a few seconds Sir Robert panics: he drops his shield, the lance is askew, his horse, though troubled, still gallops forward, taking him on to the spearpoint of the charging Le Marche. Sir Robert falls dead off his horse, his armour dented and mauled, except for that death-dealing lance rest. Anyone else noticing it was loose would have put it down as a casualty of the tournament but, as has been said, the lance rest was unmarked."

Sir Michael just stared at me.

"You see, Sir Michael," I observed, "most murderers are caught because of evidence. They carry the bloody knife or take something from their victim's body or were the last person to hold the poisoned cup but the evidence against you is based on logic. You were the only person who had the right and the authority to visit Le Marche's pavilion and Woodville's. You alone had the right to touch both Le Marche's lances and Woodville's armour."

Sir Michael just shook his head wordlessly.

"Oh, yes," I insisted, "I believe you are guilty, Sir Michael. And who would blame you, the Master Herald, responsible for the laws and customs of the tournament? You would have investigated Woodville's death and placed the blame wherever you wanted, probably on one or both of these hapless squires. But my Lord of Gaunt summoned Sir John, you panicked and made your most dreadful mistake. Captain!" I turned to the serjeant-at-arms; "I understand Sir Robert's horse is here. Bring it over together with the saddle!"

The soldier hurried out. Cranston turned his back on Sir Michael and hummed a little ditty between clenched teeth. The two squires stood like statues, their eyes unblinking, mouths open, hands dangling by their sides. Poor lads! They could hardly believe what they were hearing – they, who only a few minutes earlier were facing the possibility of a dreadful death. I saw Sir Oliver take a step towards the Master Herald.

"Sir," Cranston grunted, "I would be grateful if you sat down and did not make a bad situation worse!"

The serjeant-at-arms returned, his face red with excitement, eager not to miss anything.

"Sir John!" he announced, "the horse is here!"

Cranston nodded and turned to the assembled company.

"Please," he said, "you will follow us."

Outside, Sir Robert's horse, cleaner and a little more refreshed, was waiting patiently in the cobbled yard, its great high-horned saddle on the ground nearby. Along its hindquarters still ran the red, wicked-looking gash Lyons had reported earlier . . .

"Now," Cranston beamed. "Eustace, stand where you would, if the horse was saddled and your master waiting to charge."

Eustace shambled up like a sleepwalker and listlessly held the reins. The horse whinnied affectionately and turned to nudge his hand. Eustace patted it on the neck, murmuring quietly for it to be still.

"Well, Eustace," Cranston said, "let us pretend that your left hand is now holding the reins of the horse and you wish to cut the horse where the scar now is."

Eustace's right hand went out.

"See!" Sir Michael shouted triumphantly. "He could have done it!"

"Now," Cranston continued smoothly, "please put Sir Robert's saddle on the horse."

The destrier moved excitedly, its iron hooves skittering on the uneven cobbles.

"Whoa, boy! Whoa!" Eustace whispered.

The serjeant-at-arms adjusted the saddle; first the blue caparisoned cloth, then the saddle itself, going gingerly under the horse's belly to tie straps and secure buckles.

"Good!" Cranston murmured. "Now, Eustace, pretend you have a knife. Try and cut the horse where the scar is."

The serjeant-at-arms gasped with astonishment. Eustace raised his hand, but half the scar was now hidden by the saddle and the saddle cloth. Sir Michael's mouth opened and closed as Cranston confronted him, pushing him roughly on the shoulder.

"I never believed the horse was cut before it charged," he said. "To do that Eustace would have had to cut him as he held the reins but the horse would have bucked immediately. Nor could he have cut the horse after he had released the reins and Sir Robert began to charge, that would have been very dangerous. The horse would undoubtedly have lashed back and a kick from an iron-shod hoof can be as lethal as a blow from a mace. Finally, however, Eustace could never have made that gash, as you have seen the hindquarters were covered by the saddle and its cloth, yet both of them are unmarked."

"Logic!" I quipped to the now sullen Sir Michael. "Once again, Master Herald, we have logic! The only time Sir Robert's horse could have been cut was after the joust when the saddle had been removed, and you did that. You panicked when Sir John was sent to investigate Woodville's death. You had to make certain one or both of those squires got the blame." I patted the horse. "You created your own evidence by cutting this poor horse and showing it to us. Only you could have done that: Sir Oliver and his squire had been detained in their pavilion, Eustace stayed by his master's corpse."

"Why?" Cranston rasped.

Sir Michael gazed back, eyes hard, face closed.

"Oh, I think I know," I said. "Sir Michael has a lovely daughter. It was nice to see her fought over by two stalwarts but Sir Michael, as you remarked earlier, Sir Oliver and Sir Robert were poor men. Why should your daughter and her lands go to men such as those?"

Sir Michael drew himself up.

"You have no jurisdiction over me, Sir John!" he snapped; "I keep my counsel to myself. I demand by the law and usages of this realm that I be tried by my peers in parliament!"

Suddenly both Cranston and myself were shoved violently aside. Sir Oliver pushed through, his face a mask of fury; before we could stop him, he spat full into the Master Herald's face and, with one gloved hand, struck him on the cheek before taking the gauntlet off and throwing it at the Master Herald's feet.

"Laws and usages!" Sir Oliver hissed. "I challenge you, Sir Michael Lyons, to a duel à l'outrance, to the death! And, if you are innocent of Sir Robert Woodville's death, you can prove it on my body."

Sir Michael moved his lips silently. He stared at Le Marche and, without demur, picked up the fallen gauntlet.

"I accept!" he replied.

Cranston strode across and knocked the gauntlet from his hand.

"You will stand trial!" the coroner declared. "God has already delivered you into the hands of the law. Why test His anger further?" Cranston turned and nodded at Le Marche. "You will arrest him. Have him conveyed to the Tower, let my Lord of Gaunt now decide."

Cranston picked up his belongings, stared around the assembled company who just stood like statues, their faces still full of surprise and shock at Cranston's revelations.

"Well?" Cranston barked.

Le Marche grasped Sir Michael's wrist. The two squires went to assist and Cranston left the taproom whilst I hastened behind.

"Sir John," I gasped, "why the hurry?"

The coroner didn't answer until we were out of the tavern yard.

"Sir John," I repeated. "Not even a pause for a bowl of claret or a jug of ale?"

Cranston stared back at the tavern. "I will not drink within earshot of that murdering bastard! Because of him, one good man was killed, another nearly lost his honour, and those two squires could have died at Tyburn!" Cranston's eyes narrowed as he stared at me. "You did well, monk."

"Friar," I corrected. "And don't thank me, my lord coroner, thank Queen Logic. Le Marche is too full of honour to do anything amiss. Oh, he likes killing people but according to the rules – whilst the squires? One's too feckless; and can a man who is seriously considering being a priest plot murder?"

Cranston grinned. "If you have met some of the priests I have, yes! But come back to Cheapside. The Lady Maude and Benedicta will be waiting for us in the 'Holy Lamb of God'!"

"Lady Maude may be," I muttered, "but Benedicta seemed more interested in that young courtier."

Cranston turned, his face solemn as a judge. "Tut! Tut! Tut!" he clicked. "Lust and envy in a friar?"

I just looked away.

"Brother!" Cranston was now grinning from ear to ear.

"What is it, Sir John?"

"Didn't I tell you? That young courtier is a friend of mine. I told him to look after Benedicta."

"But, Sir John, she seemed so attentive back." I coughed with embarrassment. "Not that I have any objection."

Cranston's smile became even more wicked.

"Oh, yes, and I told her that he was a friend who also was very lonely and would she talk to him during the tournament."

I grasped Sir John by his fat elbow. "What's the penalty for striking a coroner, Sir John?"

"A cup of claret but, if it's a priest, then it's two!"

# THE WITCH'S TALE
# Margaret Frazer

*Margaret Frazer is the pen name of the writing team of Mary Pulver Kuhfeld and Gail Bacon. Mary Pulver has another story in this anthology under her own name. Between them they have created the character of Sister Frevisse, a fifteenth-century nun at the priory of St. Frideswide's in Oxfordshire. She first appeared in* The Novice's Tale *(1992), followed by* The Servant's Tale *(1993) and* The Outlaw's Tale.

*The following story was inspired by a notice that Mary Pulver read years ago which said: "Roger, Reeve of Rattlesden, with the whole township of Rattlesden, took away from the coroner of the liberty of St. Edmund, Beatrice Cobb and Beatrice, daughter of said Beatrice, and Elias Scallard, indicted for and guilty of the death of William Cobbe, husband of said Beatrice, and thus prevented the coroner from doing his duty."*

*"I have always wondered," Mary commented, "what sort of fellow William Cobbe was that the whole town would collaborate in the freeing of his murderers."*

> *The gretteste clerkes been noght wisest men,*
> *As whilom to the wolf thus spak the mare.*
> Geoffrey Chaucer, The Reeve's Tale

The night's rain had given way to a softened sky streaked with thin clouds. The air was bright with spring, and the wind had a kindness that was not there yesterday. In the fields the early corn was a haze of green across the dark soil, and along the sheltered southward side of a hedgerow Margery found a dandelion's first yellow among the early grass. The young nettles and wild parsley were up, and in a few days would be far enough along to gather for salad, something fresh after the long winter's stint of dried peas and beans and not enough porridge.

Margery paused under a tree to smile over a cuckoo-pint, bold and blithe before the cuckoo itself was heard this spring. Farther along the hedge a chaffinch was challenging the world, sparrows were squabbling with more vigor than they had had for months, and a muted flash of red among the bare branches showed where a robin was about his business. As she should be about hers, she reminded herself.

She had set out early to glean sticks along the hedgerows but there was not much deadwood left so near the village by this end of winter; her sling of sacking was barely a quarter full, and all of it was wet and would need drying before it was any use. But she must go home. Jack would be coming for his dinner and then Dame Claire at the priory was expecting her.

Though she and Jack were among the village's several free souls and not villeins, Margery's one pride was that she worked with Dame Claire, St. Frideswide's infirmarian. They had met not long after Margery had married Jack and come to live in Priors Byfield. In the untended garden behind the cottage she had found a plant she could not identify despite the herb lore she had had from her mother and grandmother. With her curiosity stronger than her fear, she had gone hesitantly to ask at the nunnery gates if there were a nun who knew herbs. In a while a small woman neatly dressed and veiled in Benedictine black and white had come out to her and kindly looked at the cutting she had brought.

"Why, that's bastard agrimony," she had said. "In your garden? It must have seeded itself from ours. It's hardly common in this part of England and I've been nursing ours along. It's excellent for strengthening the lungs and to ease the spleen and against dropsy, you see."

"Oh, like marjoram. Wild marjoram, not sweet. Only better, I suppose?" Margery had said; and then had added regretfully, "I suppose you want it back?"

Dame Claire had regarded her with surprise. "I don't think so. We still have our own." She looked at the cutting more closely. "And yours seems to be doing very well. Tell me about your garden."

Margery had told her and then, drawn on by Dame Claire's questions, had told what she knew of herbs and finally, to her astonishment, had been asked if she would like to see the priory's infirmary garden. One thing had led on to another, that day and others; and with nothing in common between them except their love of herbs and using them to help and heal, she and Dame Claire had come to work together, Margery gathering wild-growing herbs for Dame Claire's use as well as her own and growing plants in her garden to share with the infirmarian, as Dame Claire shared her own herbs and the book-knowledge Margery had no way of having. And for both of them there was the pleasure of talking about work they both enjoyed, each with someone as knowledgeable as herself.

Now, this third spring of their friendship, the soil would soon be dry enough, God willing, for this year's planting. Margery and Dame Claire had appointed today to plan their gardens together, so that Dame Claire could ask the priory steward to bring back such cuttings as they needed when he went to Lady Day fair in Oxford.

But Margery had to hurry. Her husband Jack wanted both her and his dinner waiting for him when he came into the house at the end of the morning's work, and his displeasure was ugly when she failed him. She had left herself time enough this morning, she was sure, even allowing for her dawdling along the hedgerow; but as she let herself into her garden by the back gate from the field path she saw with a familiar sick feeling that Jack was standing in the cottage's back doorway, fists on his hips and a mean grin on his fleshy mouth. He was back early from hedging – Margery would have sworn he was early – and neither she nor his food was waiting and no excuse would make any difference to what he would do now.

Wearily, Margery set down her bundle on the bench beside the door and looked up at him. It was better to see it coming.

"Y'know better than to be late," he accused. "Y'know I've told you that."

"I can have your dinner on in hardly a moment." She said it without hope. Nothing would help now; nothing ever did.

"I don't want to wait!" Jack put his hand flat between her breasts and shoved her backward. He always began with shoving. "I shouldn't *have* to wait!"

Margery stumbled back. Jack came after her and she turned sideways, to make a smaller target, for all the good it would do her. He shoved her again, staggering her along the path, then caught her a heavy slap to the back of her head so that she pitched forward, her knees banging into the wooden edging of a garden bed, her hands sinking into the muddy soil. She scrambled to be clear of him long enough to regain her feet. So long as she was on her feet he only hit. Once she was down, he kicked. His fists left bruises, sometimes cuts. His feet were worse. There were places in her that still hurt from last time, three weeks ago. From experience she knew that if she kept on her feet until he tired, he did not kick her so long.

But her fear made her clumsy. He was yelling at her now, calling her things she had never been, never thought of being. A blow alongside of her head sent her stumbling to one side, into her herb bed among the straw and burlap meant to protect her best plants through the winter. She scrambled to be out of it but Jack came in after her, crushing his feet down on anything in his way.

Margery cried out as she had not for her own pain. "Stop

it! Leave my plants be!" Jack laughed and stomped one deliberately.

"Them and you both," he said, enjoying himself. "You'll learn to
do what you're told."

Margery fumbled in the pouch under her apron and, still
scrambling to keep beyond his reach and get out from among
her herbs, snatched out a small packet of folded cloth not so big
as the palm of her hand. She brandished it at him and screamed,
"You stop! You stop or I'll use this!"

For a wonder Jack did stop, staring at her in plain surprise. Then
he scoffed, "You've nothing there, y'daft woman!" and grabbed
for her.

Margery ducked from his reach, still holding out the packet. "It's
bits of you, Jack Wilkins!" she cried. "From when I cut your hair last
month and then when you trimmed your nails. Remember that? It's
bits of you in here and I've made a spell, Jack Wilkins, and you're
going to die for it if you don't leave me alone and get out of my
garden!"

"It's not me that's going to die!" he roared, and lurched for her.

After two days of sun the weather had turned back to low-trailing
clouds and rain. But it was a gentle, misting rain that promised
spring after winter's raw cold, and Dame Frevisse, leaving the guest
hall where everything was readied should the day bring guests to
St. Frideswide's, paused at the top of the stairs down into the
courtyard to look up and let the rain stroke across her face. Very
soon the cloister bell would call her into the church with the other
nuns for the afternoon's service of Vespers, and she would be able
to let go the necessities of her duties as the priory's hosteler to rise
into the pleasure of prayer.

But as she crossed the yard toward the cloister door, Master Naylor
overtook her. He was the priory's steward, a long-faced man who
kept to his duties and did them well but managed to talk with the
nuns he served, as little as possible. Bracing herself for something
she probably did not want to hear, Frevisse turned to him. "Master
Naylor?"

"I thought you'd best know before you went in to Vespers," he said,
with a respectful bow of his head. Master Naylor was ever particular
in his manners. "There's a man come in to say Master Montfort and
six of his men will be here by supper time."

Frevisse felt her mouth open in protest, then snapped it closed.
Among her least favorite people in the realm was Master Morys
Montfort, crowner for northern Oxfordshire. It was his duty to find

out what lay behind unexpected deaths within his jurisdiction, then to bring the malefactor – if any – to the sheriff's attention, and to see to it that whatever fines or confiscations were due King Henry VI were duly collected.

Frevisse had no quarrel with any of that, but Master Montfort had the regrettable tendency to prefer the least complicated solution to any problem and find his facts accordingly. He and Frevisse had long since struck a level of mutual hostility neither was inclined to abate. She was not happy to hear of his coming, and she said, "I trust he's just passing on his way to somewhere else? There's no one dead hereabouts that I've heard of."

Master Naylor shrugged. "It's Jack Wilkins in the village, the day before yesterday. They tolled the village bell for him but you were likely in church for Sext then."

"But why is Montfort coming? Is there doubt about the way this Wilkins died?"

"No doubt. His wife shook a charm at him and cast a spell, and he fell down dead. At least three of their neighbors saw it. I'd not have thought it of Margery," he added. "She's never been known to put her herbs to aught but good, that I've heard."

"*Margery*? Dame *Claire's* Margery?"

"That's her, the herbwife who visits here sometimes."

"Does Dame Claire know?"

"No more than you, I doubt. It was witchcraft and murder certain enough. Montfort will have it done a half hour after he's seen her and talked to her neighbors. He'll probably be on the road to Banbury with her before noon tomorrow and she'll be in the bishop's hands not long after that. I'd have reported it all to Domina Edith come week's end with the other village business." He seemed to think that was all the dealing there needed to be with the matter; Jack and Margery were not among the priory's villeins, and so not his responsibility. The lethal use of witchcraft wasn't usual; on the other hand, all herbwives used spells in their medicines, and it was but a small step to misuse them. He would not have mentioned it except he knew of Margery's link with Dame Claire.

The bell for Vespers began to ring. Frevisse said impatiently, "Where is she being kept?"

Master Naylor pointed through the gateway toward the outer yard. "She's in one of the sheds there. I've two of our men guarding her. She's gagged so it's all right; they're safe. There's nothing to be done."

"Dame Claire will want to see her after Vespers," Frevisse said.

"Please you, tell the guesthall servants for me that Montfort is coming. I have to go."

The Vespers she had expected to enjoy was instead a prolonged discomfort of impatience; and afterwards she had to wait until supper was finished and the nuns went out into the garden for recreation time – the one hour of the day their Benedictine rule allowed for idle talk – before she could tell Dame Claire what was to hand.

"*Margery*?" Dame Claire exclaimed in her deep voice. Disbelief arched her eyebrows high toward her veil. "Killed her husband with witchcraft? I very much doubt it. In fact I don't believe it at all! I want to see her."

That was easily done. Frevisse waited at the foot of the stairs to the prioress' parlor while Dame Claire went up to ask permission. Then they went together, out of the cloister and across the inner yard – Frevisse noting there were lights in the guesthall window so Montfort and his entourage must have arrived – through the gateway to the outer yard where a stable hand, surprised to see them outside the cloister, pointed to the shed at the end of the stables where the prisoner was being kept.

"I should have thought to bring a cloak for her, and something warm to eat," Dame Claire regretted as they went. "These spring nights are cold, and she must be desperate, poor thing."

As Master Naylor had said, two stolid stable men were keeping guard inside the shed door, and Margery was gagged and her hands bound at her waist. But a clay lamp set in the corner on the bare earth floor gave a comforting yellow glow to the rough boards of her prison, and by its light as they stood in the doorway – Dame Claire explaining to the guards that they were come with permission to talk with Margery – Frevisse saw that Margery had several blankets, a cloak, and a straw-stuffed pillow to make her a bed along the farther wall, and that beside it were a pot of ale and various plates with three different kinds of bread and parts of two cheeses. Frevisse knew that in such cases as Margery the nunnery provided a blanket and an occasional piece of bread. So who had done this much for Margery?

Margery herself had risen to her feet as the nuns entered. Despite her crime, she was much as Frevisse had remembered her, a middling sort of woman – of middling build, middling young, middling tall, with nothing particular about her, except – to judge by her eyes above the gag – that she was frightened. As well she should be.

Dame Claire finished with the men, and crossed the shed to her, Frevisse following. As Margery curtseyed, Dame Claire said, "Let me loose your hands so you can take off the gag. I've told them you won't do anything. We want to talk to you."

Dame Claire freed Margery's hands, and gratefully she unknotted the cloth behind her head. "Thank you, my lady," she said hoarsely.

"Have something to drink." Dame Claire indicated the ale kindly. "Have they let you eat?"

Margery nodded over the rim of the clay pot as she drank thirstily. When she had finished, she said, "They've been as kind as might be. And village folk have brought me things." She gestured at her bed and food and lamp. She was clearly tired as well as frightened, worn out by too many strange things happening to her. "But I hoped you'd come, so I could tell you why I didn't come t'other day when I said I would."

"I wondered what happened to you," Dame Claire answered. "But I never thought this."

Margery hung her head. "Nor did I."

"They say you killed your husband."

Margery nodded. "I did that."

"Margery, no!" Dame Claire protested.

"Jack came at me, the way he's done ever since we married whenever I've not done right. But this time we were in my garden and he was trampling my plants." It plainly mattered very much to her that Dame Claire understand. "I told him to stop but he didn't care, and I – lost my temper."

"You truly did kill him?" Dame Claire asked, still disbelieving it.

"Oh, yes. Sure as sure. I didn't know the spell would work that way but it did. Took him off afore he could hit me again, just like that."

"What – exactly – did you do?" Frevisse asked carefully. Murder, serious enough in itself, was worse for the murderer when done by witchcraft. Charms and spells were simply part of healing; every herbwife knew some. But if they were turned to evil, they became part of the Devil's work and a matter for the Church as well as lay law.

Margery looked at Frevisse with mingled shyness and guilt, and did not answer.

"Tell us, please," Dame Claire urged. "Dame Frevisse and I want to help you."

"There's no help for me!" Margery said in surprise. "I killed him."

"How?" Frevisse persisted.

Margery hung her head. She twisted her hands in her apron and, low-voiced with embarrassment, said, "I'd been saving bits of him this while. Hair, you know, and his nail cuttings."

"Margery! That's wicked!" Dame Claire exclaimed.

"I know it!" Margery said piteously. "But I was only going to make a small charm. When I'd money for the wax to make the figure. Not kill him, like, but weaken his arm so he couldn't hit me so hard. That's all I wanted to do. Just weaken him."

"But you hadn't made the figure yet?" Frevisse asked. Margery shook her head dumbly. Frevisse pressed, "What did you do then, that you think you killed him?"

"I had the – things in a little packet. I held it up and told him what it was and that he'd better stop what he was doing. That I'd made a charm and I'd kill him if he didn't stop."

"But you hadn't made a charm yet. You said so," said Dame Claire.

"That I hadn't. But I meant to. I really did." She looked anxiously from one nun to the other. "If I make confession and do penance before they hang me, I won't have to burn in hell, will I? Not if I'm truly penitent?"

"Surely not," Dame Claire reassured her.

"But if you didn't have the charm, what happened?" Frevisse asked.

Margery shuddered. "Jack kept hitting and shoving. I knew he'd near to kill me, once he had his hands on me, and I'd never have another chance to make a charm against him, not now he knew. I was that frighted, I grabbed the first words that came to me, thinking to scare him off with them. I didn't even think what they were. I just said them at him and shook the packet like I was ill-wishing him. I just wanted to keep him back from me, I swear that's all. Just hold him off as long as might be."

She broke off, closing her eyes at the memory.

"And then?" Dame Claire prompted.

Faintly, tears on her cheeks, Margery said, "He stopped. All rigid like I'd hit him with a board. He stared at me with his mouth open and then grabbed his chest, right in the center, and bent over double. He was gasping like he hurt, or couldn't catch his breath. Then he fell over. In the path, away from my herbs. He curled up and went on gasping and then – he stopped. He just stopped and was dead."

A little silence held them all. Frevisse was aware of the two men at her back, and knew that everything they were hearing would be told later all around the nunnery and village.

"Margery," Dame Claire said, "you can't wish a man dead. Or rather, you can wish it, but it won't happen, not that simply."

"But it did," Margery said.

And there would probably be no convincing anyone otherwise. But for Dame Claire's sake, Frevisse asked, "What was it you said to him? A spell?"

Margery nodded. "The one for – "

Master Naylor interrupted her with a firm rap on the door frame. He inclined his head respectfully to Frevisse and Dame Claire, and said, "The crowner wants to see her now."

"So late?" Dame Claire protested.

"He hopes to finish the matter tonight so he can be on his way at earliest tomorrow. He has other matters to see to," Master Naylor explained.

Matters more important than a village woman who was surely guilty, Frevisse thought. A woman who was the more inconvenient because she would have to be sent for examination before a bishop before she could be duly hanged.

"We'll come with her," said Dame Claire.

Master Montfort had been given the guesthall's best chamber, with its large bed and plain but sufficient furnishings. The shutters had been closed against the rainy dusk, the lamps lighted, and at a table against the farther wall his clerk was hunched over a parchment, quill in hand and inkwell ready.

The crowner himself stood by the brazier in the corner, his hands over its low warmth. He was short in the leg for the length of his body, and had begun to go fat in his middle, but to his own mind any shortcomings he might have – and he was not convinced that he had any – were amply compensated for by the dignity of his office; he no more than glanced over his shoulder as Master Naylor brought Margery in, then sharpened his look on Frevisse and Dame Claire following her. A flush spread up his florid face and over the curve of his balding head.

"You can stay, Naylor," he said. "But the rest of you may go." Belatedly, ungraciously, he added, "My ladies."

With eyes modestly downcast and her hands tucked up either sleeve of her habit, Frevisse said, "Thank you, but we'll stay. It would not be seemly that Margery be here unattended."

She had used that excuse in another matter with Master Montfort. He had lost the argument then, and apparently chose not to renew it now. His flush merely darkened to a deeper red as he said tersely, "Then stand to one side and don't interfere while I question her."

They did so. Master Montfort squared up in front of Margery and announced in his never subtle way, "I've questioned some several of your neighbors already and mean to see more of them before I'm to

bed tonight so you may as well tell what you have to tell straight out
and no avoiding it. Can you understand that?"

Margery did not lift her humbly bowed head. "Yes, m'lord."

"You killed your husband? Now, mind you, you were heard and
seen so there's no avoiding it."

Margery clearly had no thought of avoiding anything. While
the clerk's pen scratched busily at his parchment, recording her
words, she repeated what she had already told Frevisse and Dame
Claire. When she had finished, Master Montfort rocked back on
his heels, smiling grimly with great satisfaction. "Very well said,
and all agreeing with your neighbors' tales. I think there's no need
for more."

"Except," Dame Claire said briskly, knowing Master Montfort
would order her to silence if she gave him a chance, "I doubt her
husband died of anything more than apoplexy."

The crowner turned on her. In a tone intended to quell, he said,
"I beg your pardon, my lady?"

Dame Claire hesitated. Frevisse, more used to the crowner's bullying, said helpfully, "Apoplexy. It's a congestion of the blood – "

Master Montfort's tongue caught up with his indignation. "I know
what it is!"

Frevisse turned to Master Naylor. As steward of the priory's
properties he had far better knowledge of the villeins than she did.
"What sort of humor was this Jack Wilkins? Hot-tempered or not?"

"Hot enough it's a wonder he was in so little trouble as he was,"
Master Naylor said. "He knocked a tooth out of one of his neighbors
last week because he thought the man was laughing at him. The man
wasn't, being no fool, but Jack Wilkins in a temper didn't care about
particulars. It wasn't the first time he's made trouble with his temper.
And he was known to beat his wife."

"Choleric," said Dame Claire. "Easily given to temper. People of
that sort are very likely to be struck as Jack Wilkins was, especially
in the midst of one of their furies. He was beating his wife – "

"As he had every right to do!" Master Montfort declared.

As if musing on his own, Master Naylor said, "There's a feeling
in the village that he did it more often and worse than need
be."

But Dame Claire, refusing to leave her point, went on over his
words, "– and that's heavy work, no matter how you go about it.
Then she defied him, maybe even frightened him when she said her
spell – "

"And down he fell dead!" the crowner said, triumphant. "That's
what I'm saying. It was her doing and that's the end of it."

"What was the spell she said?" Frevisse interjected. "Has anyone asked her that?"

Master Montfort shot her an angry look; determined to assert himself, he swung back on Margery. "That was my next question, woman. What did you actually say to him? No, don't look at anyone while you say it! And say it slow so my clerk can write it down."

Eyes turned to the floor, voice trembling a little, Margery began to recite, "Come you forth and get you gone . . ."

If Master Montfort was expecting a roaring spell that named devils and summoned demons, he was disappointed. The clerk scratched away busily as Margery went through a short verse that was nevertheless quite apparently meant to call the spirit out of the body and cast it away. Part way through, Dame Claire looked startled.

In the pause after Margery finished speaking, the clerk's pen scritched on. Master Montfort, ever impatient, went to hover at his shoulder and, as soon as he had done, snatched the parchment away. While he read it over, Frevisse leaned toward Dame Claire, who whispered briefly but urgently in her ear. Before Frevisse could respond, Master Montfort demanded at Margery, "That's it? Just that?" Margery nodded. Master Montfort glared at his clerk and recited loudly, "Come you forth . . ."

The man's head jerked up to stare with near-sighted alarm at his master. The crowner went on through the spell unheeding either his clerk's dismay or Master Naylor's movement of protest. Margery opened her mouth to say something, but Frevisse silenced her with a shake of her head, while Dame Claire pressed a hand over her own mouth to keep quiet.

When Master Montfort had finished, a tense waiting held them all still, most especially the clerk. When nothing happened after an impatient minute, Master Montfort rounded on Margery. "How long is this supposed to take?"

Margery fumbled under his glare. "My husband – he – almost on the instant, sir. But – "

"Spare me your excuses. If it worked for you, why didn't it work for me? Because I didn't have clippings of his hair or what?"

Keeping her voice very neutral, Frevisse suggested, "According to Robert Mannying in his *Handling Sin*, a spell has no power if said by someone who doesn't believe in it. Margery uses herbs and spells to help the villagers. She believes in what she does. You don't. Do you believe in your charm, Margery? This one that you said at your husband?"

"Yes, but – "

"She's a witch," Master Montfort interrupted. "And whatever good you claim she's done, she's used a spell to kill a man this time, and her husband at that. Who knows what else she's tried." He rounded on Margery again and said in her face, "There's a question for you, woman. Have you ever used this spell before?"

Margery shrank away from him but answered, "Surely. Often and often. But – "

"God's blood!" Master Montfort exclaimed. "You *admit* you've murdered other men?"

"Margery!" Frevisse interposed, "*What* is the spell *for*?"

Driven by both of them, Margery cried out, "It's for opening the bowels!"

A great quiet deepened in the room. Margery looked anxiously from face to face. Frevisse and Dame Claire looked carefully at the floor. Red darkened and mounted over Master Montfort's countenance again. Master Naylor seemed to struggle against choking. The clerk ducked his head low over his parchment. Nervously Margery tried to explain. "I make a decoction with gill-go-on-the-ground, and say the spell over it while it's brewing, to make it stronger. It provokes urine, too, and . . . and . . ." She stopped, not understanding their reactions, then finished apologetically, "They were the first words that came into my head, that's all. I just wanted to fright Jack off me, and those were the first words that came. I didn't mean for them to kill him."

Master Montfort, trying to recover lost ground, strangled out, "But they did kill him, didn't they? That's the long and short of it, isn't it?"

Margery started to nod, but Frevisse put a stilling hand on her arm; and Dame Claire said, "It's a better judgement that her husband died not from her words but from his own choler, like many another man before him. It wasn't Margery but his temper that did for him at the last."

Master Montfort glared at her. "That's women's logic!" he snapped. "His wife warns him she has bits of him to use against him, and cries a spell in his face, and he drops down dead, and it's *his* fault? Where's the sense of that? No! She's admitted her guilt. She was seen doing it. There's no more questioning needed. Naylor, keep her until morning. Then I'll take her in charge."

The twilight had darkened to deep dusk but the rain had stopped as they came out of the guest hall. Master Naylor steadied Margery by her elbow as they went down the steps to the yard. No matter how much she had expected her fate, she seemed dazed by the crowner's pronouncement, and walked numbly where she was taken. Frevisse and Dame Claire followed with nothing to say, though Frevisse at least seethed with frustration at their helplessness and Montfort's stupidity. Even the acknowledgement of the *possibility* of doubt from him would have been something.

Margery's two guards were waiting at the foot of the steps in the spread of light from the lantern hung by the guest hall door. They stood aside, then followed as the silent group made their way around the rain-puddles among the cobbles to the gateway to the outer yard. Beyond it was the mud and deeper darkness of the outer yard where the lamplight showing around the ill-fitted door of Margery's prison shed was the only brightness. Busy with her feet and anger, Frevisse did not see the knot of people there until one of them swung the shed door open to give them more light, and Master Naylor said in surprise, "Tom, what brings you out? And the rest of you?"

Frevisse could see now that there were seven of them, four women and three men, all from the village. The women curtseyed quickly to her, Dame Claire, and Master Naylor as they came forward to Margery. Crooning to her like mothers over a hurt child, they enveloped her with their kindness; and one of them, with an arm around her waist, soothed, "There now, Margery-girl, we can see it didn't go well. You come in-by. We've something warm for you to eat." Together they drew her into the shed, leaving the men to front the priory-folk.

Tom, the village reeve and apparently their leader in this, ducked his head to her and Dame Claire, and again to Master Naylor before he said, "She's to go then? No help for it?"

"No help for it," Master Naylor agreed. "The crowner means to take her with him when he goes in the morning."

The men nodded as if they had expected no less. But Tom said, "It makes no difference that there's not a body in the village but's glad to have Jack gone? He was a terror and no mistake and she didn't do more than many of us have wanted to."

"I can't argue that, but it changes nothing," Master Naylor said. "Margery goes with the crowner in the morning, and be taken before the bishop for what she's done."

"She didn't do anything!" Dame Claire said with the impatience she had had to curb in Master Montfort's presence.

Frevisse agreed. "This Jack died from his own temper, not from Margery's silly words!"

"It was apoplexy," said Dame Claire. "People who indulge in ill temper the way Jack Wilkins did are like to die the way Jack Wilkins did."

"If you say so, m'lady," Tom said in a respectful voice. "But Margery cried something out at him, and Jack went down better than a poled ox. God keep his soul," he added as an after-thought, and everyone crossed themselves. Jack Wilkins was unburied yet; best to say the right things for he would make a wicked ghost.

"It wasn't even a spell to kill a man. Margery says so herself."

"Well, that's all right then," Tom said agreeably. "And a comfort to Margery to know it wasn't her doing that killed Jack, no matter what the crowner says. But what we've come for is to ask if some of us can stand Margery's guard tonight, for friendship's sake, like, before she goes."

Dim with distance and the mist-heavy dusk, the bell began to call to Compline, the nuns' last prayers before bed. Frevisse laid a hand on Dame Claire's arm, drawing her away. Master Naylor could handle this matter. There was nothing more for the two of them to do here. Better they go to pray for Margery's soul. And Jack Wilkins', she thought belatedly.

Watery sunshine was laying thin shadows across the cloister walk next morning as Frevisse went from chapter meeting toward her duties. She expected Master Montfort and his men and Margery would be gone by now, ridden away at first light; and she regretted there had been nothing that could be done to convince anyone but herself and Dame Claire that Margery had not killed her lout of a husband with her poor little spell and desperation. But even Margery had believed it, and would do penance for it as if her guilt were real, and go to her death for it.

Frevisse was distracted from her anger as she neared the door into the courtyard by the noise of Master Montfort's raised voice, the words unclear but his passion plain. She glanced again at the morning shadows. He was supposed to be miles on his way by this time. She opened the door from the cloister to the courtyard.

Usually empty except for a passing servant and the doves around the well, the yard was half full of villagers crowded to the foot of the guest hall steps. Master Montfort stood above them there, dressed for riding and in a rage.

"You're still saying there's no trace of her?" he ranted. Frevisse stopped where she was with a sudden hopeful lift of her spirits. "You've been searching the wretched place since dawn! My men have scoured the fields for miles! *Someone* has to know where she is! Or if she's truly bolted, we have to set the hounds to her trail!"

Even from where she was, Frevisse could see the sullen set of every villein's shoulders. But it was clear that the main thrust of his words

was at Master Naylor, standing straight-backed at the head of the
villeins, deliberately between them and the crowner's rage. With a
hard-edged patience that told Frevisse he had been over this already
more than once, he answered in his strong, carrying voice, "We have
no hounds to set to her trail. This is a priory of nuns. They're not
monks; they don't ride to hunt here."

Standing close behind the steward, Tom the reeve growled so
everyone could hear, "And where she went, you wouldn't care to
follow!"

Master Montfort pointed at him, furious. "You! You're one of the
fools who slept when you were supposed to be guarding her! Dreaming your way to perdition while she walks off free as you please! What
do you mean, 'where she went'? Hai, man, what do you mean?"

"I mean it wasn't a natural sleep we had last night!" Tom answered
loudly enough to send his words to the outer yard, to Master
Montfort's entourage and a number of priory servants clustered
just beyond the gateway. Frevisse saw them stir as he spoke. "Aye,
it wasn't a natural sleep and there's not one of us will say it was. We
fell to sleep all at once and together, between one word and another.
That's not natural! No more than Jack Wilkins falling down dead
was natural. We're lucky it was only sleep she did to us! That's what
I say! And anybody who tried to follow her is asking for what happens
to him!"

Behind and around him the other villeins glanced at each other
and nodded. One of the bolder men even spoke up, "Tom has the
right of it!"

A woman – Frevisse thought she was one of four who had come to
Margery last night – said shrilly, "You can't ask any decent man to
follow where she's gone!"

Master Montfort pointed at her. "You know where she's gone? You
admit you know?"

"I can make a fair guess!" the woman flung back. "Flown off to her
master the devil, very like, and you'll find no hound to go that trail!"

"Flown off?" Master Montfort raged. "*Flown* off? I'm supposed
to believe that? Naylor, most of these folk are the priory's villeins!
Warn them there's penalties for lying to the king's crowner and
hiding murderers. She's around here somewhere!"

"If she is, we haven't found her yet for all our searching," Master
Naylor said back. "Twice through the village is enough for one day,
and there's no sign where she might have gone across country. As you
say, these are our villeins and I can say I've never known them given
to such lying as this. Maybe they've the right of it. You said yourself
last night she was a witch, and now she seems to have proved it!"

Master Montfort stared at him, speechless with rage.

"What we say," shouted another of the men, "is you're welcome to come search us house to house yourself, you being so much smarter than the rest of us. But if you find her, you'd better hope she doesn't treat you like she did her husband!"

There was general angry laughter among all the villeins at that; and some from beyond the gateway. For just a moment Master Montfort lost the stride of his anger, paused by the man's words. Then he gathered himself together and rounded on Master Naylor. With a scorn that he meant to be withering, he said, "I've greater matters to see to than hunting down some petty village witch. She was in your charge, Naylor, and the loss is to you, not to me. There'll be an amercement to pay for losing the king's prisoner, and be assured I'll see the priory is charged it to the full!"

"I'm assured you will," Master Naylor returned tersely, his scorn stronger than Master Montfort's.

For a balanced moment he and the crowner held each other's eyes. Then Master Naylor gestured sharply for the villeins to move back from the foot of the steps. Crowding among themselves, they gave ground. Master Montfort's mouth opened, then closed, and with great, stiff dignity he descended, passed in front of them to his horse being held for him beyond the gateway, and mounted. He glared around at them one final time and, for good measure, across the courtyard at Frevisse still standing in the doorway, then jerked his horse around and went.

No one moved or spoke until the splash and clatter of his going, and his entourage after him, were well away. And even then the response among them all seemed no more than a long in-drawn breath and a slow release of tension. Heads turned to one another, and Frevisse saw smiles, but no one spoke. There were a few chuckles but no more as they all drifted out of the gateway, some of them nodding to Master Naylor as they passed him. He nodded back, and did not speak either; and when they were gone, he stayed where he was, waiting for Frevisse to come to him.

She did, because there in the open courtyard they could most easily talk without chance of being overheard so long as they kept their voices low. "Master Naylor," she said as she approached him.

He inclined his head to her. "Dame Frevisse."

"I take it from what I heard that Margery Wilkins escaped in the night?"

"It seems her guards and the friends who came to keep her company slept. When they awoke this dawn, she was gone."

"And cannot be found?"

"We've searched the village twice this morning, and Master Montfort's men have hunted the near countryside."

"They think she used her witch-powers to escape?"

"So it would seem. What other explanation is there?"

"I can think of several," Frevisse said dryly.

Master Naylor's expression did not change. "Just as you and Dame Claire could think of some other reason for Jack Wilkins' death besides his wife's words striking him down."

"And the fine to the priory for your carelessness in losing your witch?"

"It was villeins who had the watch of her and lost her. I mean to make an amercement on the village to help meet the fine our crowner will surely bring against the priory."

"Won't there be protest over that?"

"Villeins always protest over paying anything. But in this I think there'll be less arguing than in most. She's their witch. Let them pay for her. Dear-bought is held more dear."

"They still truly believe she killed her husband?" Frevisse asked. "Despite what we told them last night, they still believe she's a witch with that much power?"

"What else can they believe?" the steward asked quietly in return. "They saw her do it."

"What do you believe?" Frevisse asked, unable to tell from his neutral expression and voice.

Instead of an answer to that, Master Naylor said, "I think a straw-filled loft is not an uncomfortable place to be for a week and more this time of year. And that by the time summer comes there'll be a new herb-wife in the village, maybe even with the same first name but someone's widowed sister from somewhere else, freeborn like Margery was and no questions asked."

"And after all, witchcraft in itself is no crime or sin," Frevisse said. "The wrong lies in the use it's put to."

"And all the village knows Margery has ever used her skills for good, except this one time, if you judge what she did was ill. All her neighbors judge it wasn't," Master Naylor said solemnly.

"They mean to keep her even if it costs them?" Frevisse asked.

"They know she's a good woman. And now that they're certain she has power, she's not someone they want to lose."

"Or to cross," Frevisse said.

Master Naylor came as near to a smile as he ever came, but only said, "There'll likely be no trouble with anyone beating her ever again."

# FATHER HUGH AND THE DEADLY SCYTHE
## Mary Monica Pulver

*When not writing with Gail Bacon as Margaret Frazer, Mary Pulver Kuhfeld has written a number of crime novels and stories under her maiden name. She is perhaps best known for her series about police sergeant Peter Brichter, a dashing detective with a Porsche to match. She has written five novels featuring his adventures, starting with* Knight Fall.

*The following is her first story about Father Hugh of Paddington, a rather individualistic fifteenth-century priest who is determined to root sin out from his parishioners, no matter how he does it.*

The man's death was no accident. That was clear from the first report, given by an ashen-faced Austin, our steward's assistant. Austin had been on his way to Deerfield Village to remind our reeve that tomorrow the women were required in the meadow to rake the hay the men cut today, when he saw the body.

"Still warm he was," gasped Austin, wiping his broad face with his hand, "but with all the blood drained out of him, his arm off at the elbow and his throat open to heaven like a mouth screaming for vengeance."

Austin, for all his low birth, had a taste for a fancy turn of speech, acquired from our steward, the indispensable John Freemantle.

"Where is John?" I asked.

"Gone to Banbury, to buy that ambling mare Will Frazee has for sale," said Sister Harley.

"Oh, that's right." In my excitement I had forgotten. "Where does the body lie?"

"In the ditch along the fallow field."

"Has the hue and cry been raised?"

"Yes, Madame. There's blood all along the edge of the fallow field where I found him, great smears, like he was a beast of the forest, chased down – " Austin stopped, goggling at the memory, wiped

again at his sweating face, then staggered and would have fallen if
Sister Harley had not pushed a stool under him as he went down.
We were in my quarters in the cloister, where Austin had come with
the horrible news.

"You're sure it's Frick Cotter lying dead?" I asked.

"Oh, yes, madam," muttered Austin, wiping his wet hand on his
heavy mat of auburn hair. "There's no mistaking that nose."

Frick was a familiar figure in the village. He owned no strips
in the three big fields around it, and his cottage was one of the
humblest. He kept body and soul together by means honest and
less so, hiring himself out for odd jobs, growing peas and beans in
the tiny garden behind his cottage, collecting and selling wood from
the forest, poaching the occasional rabbit or stealing an egg.

But his main occupation was gossip. For all they talk about
women's tongues going on wheels, there was none so quick to sniff
out a tale or spread it to every ear as Frick. And as if to advertise
his failing, he was the owner of the biggest nose in Oxfordshire.

"Still, poor old Frick," sighed Sister Harley, handing Austin a
drink of wine – in my good silver chalice, I noticed, but I said
nothing. Harley had seen Austin's need and taken the first cup at
hand, which was fine; Austin was a good man.

Sister Harley touched a long, slender finger to her long, slender
nose. "I wonder what story he told to bring this on himself?"

"What do you mean?"

"Murder, of course."

"Surely it was a robbery," I objected. "After all, he was out of the
village and on the high road."

"Rob old Frick?" said Harley. "Of what? He's one of the poorest
men for miles around!"

"But a highway robber, a stranger to these parts, might not know
that," I said.

"You had only to look at Frick to know he was very poor," said
Harley. "No, it was someone driven to fury by Frick's tongue."

"I'm not so sure," said Austin, "it wasn't a knife did this, but
something bigger. A sword, maybe."

"Sword?" Sister Harley turned her aristocratic face to Austin. "But
no one in the village has a sword."

"Nor the ordinary robber," added Austin. "By the cut, the blade
was fresh and keen, not some chipped castoff a robber might carry.
This blade would be swung from a noble hand."

An ugly silence fell in the room. England in these unhappy times
needed a strong man to lead her, but our Henry VI was made of
straw. Local bullies rose and everywhere defied the helpless law. Our

local bully was Lord Ranulf Fitzralph. Rich and with friends at court, he took what he wanted and none dared gainsay him. From what we all knew of him, it was not beyond reason that he might amuse himself by killing a villein.

"But this means he's gone too far at last," I said. "Sister Harley, send word that I want to see John Freemantle the instant he returns. We will send him to the Sheriff and then with a letter to the bishop." For Ranulf could defy the Sheriff, defy even the King; but no man would dare defy the Church. And this was Church business; Frick Cotter was, like every villein in Deerfield Village, the property of Deerfield Abbey. By killing him, Lord Ranulf now found himself at the mercy of not just me, as abbess, or even the bishop, but the Church itself, Vicar of Christ on earth.

It was two hours later that the abbey Mass priest, Father Hugh of Paddington, asked to see me. He is a small, brown fellow, rather common, but he knows the ways of the village, and said he had some information about Frick Cotter to impart.

"My lady," he said from his humble kneeling position, "I am most distressed to report that Frick Cotter was murdered by someone in the village."

"Nay, Father Hugh; Austin reports the wounds on the body would indicate a sword killed him. We need to raise our eyes to Sir Ranulf to find the doer of this wickedness."

Father Hugh rose – the floor of my quarters is tile, nearly as hard as stone, so I require no one to remain kneeling long. "Ah, I wish it were that easy. But I have seen men done to death by the sword, and a closer look at Frick's body tells a different tale."

I recalled that he had in truth seen men injured in battle, while Austin had not. I asked, "What weapon do you think did this, if not a sword?"

"A billhook, perhaps. But I think it was more likely a scythe."

The workers in the meadow today had been cutting hay with their scythes. I had heard some of them whistling merrily as they departed along the road home about half an hour before Austin left for the village – to find Frick's body, freshly killed.

"But surely not," I said. "No one of our own villeins could do a murder." Especially when I had my heart so firmly settled on at last ridding the area of Lord Ranulf. "Who among them would do such a thing?"

"I believe, my lady, that old Frick's gossiping ways may have caught up with him."

I stared at him. "Then you know who it was?"

"No, no, not yet. But it appears Frick was not such a gossip as we thought. That is, for a price, he would not tell all that he knew."

"What do you mean?"

"I mean, he would go to someone whose secret he had discovered, and say that for two cabbages, or a loaf of bread, or a chicken, he would not tell anyone that this someone had feigned sickness to get out of his boonwork plowing in the abbey fields."

"Who feigned sickness?" I demanded.

"No one, Madame," replied Hugh, not covering in time the smile tweaking his mouth; "I but used that as an example. But I have learned two secrets Frick knew about, and that the owners of the secrets were angry with him. It's near Vespers now, too late to continue my search. But with your leave, I will go back in the morning and see what more there is to learn about Frick's little enterprise."

"You think it was one of these two who killed Frick, to keep their secret from being told?"

"Perhaps. Or perhaps it was another, whose secret I don't as yet know."

"But if you can't discover all the secrets, how will you know who did this wicked thing?"

"Madame, I shall trust God to show me the truth."

I said very well and dismissed him, thinking Father Hugh an unlikely sort of vehicle for trusting in. He is popular among our villeins, who find him more approachable than their own priest, but that's because he is shabby, clumsy and unlearned, just like them.

The next day Father Hugh came to me about mid-afternoon with a report. I summoned Sister Mildred, in charge of lay labor, and Sister Harley, my chaplain, to hear it with me.

"I feel there are but three men who might have done this deed," said Father Hugh. "One is Jack Strong. He's the fellow who claimed a bit of waste near the forest and fenced it and has been raising parsnips in it this year. And enriching the soil with the bones and other scraps of the deer he and his son Will have been poaching."

"Jack Strong has been poaching deer?" said Sister Harley, surprised.

"Yes, of course he has," I interjected. "Sister Mildred told me about it months ago. He's only taken three in the past two years, and for all the hunting King Henry does, he'll not miss those few. Though if Jack takes another before winter, I'll have to warn him I know about it. Go on, Master Hugh."

"The second is Tiffany Dickins."

Sister Mildred said, "He's father to Christopher, Madame, who ran away right after Michaelmas last year." Villeins may buy their freedom if they can save the money, or they may run away to a city, where, if they manage to survive a year and a day, they gain the status of citizen, making them free.

Christopher had taken this second choice, and was but two months from his year-day, if he had not by now starved to death, or fallen victim to one of the diseases that infest the cities, or gone to another manor and accepted anew the burden of villeinage for a bit of land and something to eat.

"Have you news of Christopher?" asked Harley.

Father Hugh nodded. "Christopher slips home to visit his family every so often. He was here just last Sunday."

"Why the fool!" I said, because should anyone catch him outside the city, he would forfeit the time he spent there, and must begin again. We could have sent men searching after him, but Christopher was a lazy lout and it would be a waste to send good labor to go after bad – and he would just have run again at first chance. "He ran to Oxford, I believe?"

"Yes," nodded Father Hugh. "But he's finding it difficult to make a living. He comes home to be fed and to court Hob's daughter Megan."

"Does he now!" said Sister Mildred. "We'll have to put a stop to that. It's all very well for him to run off, but I'll not have him trying to steal away Megan!"

I agreed; the girl was a talented weaver and a hard worker, a credit to her family. "Besides, she's only thirteen." I frowned. "You don't think it was Christopher who set upon Frick?"

"No, Christopher left Deerfield Sunday evening. But someone saw Frick speaking to Chris' father this morning as he was coming out to the meadow with his scythe, and said Tiffany walked off with a face like a thundercloud. It may be that Frick saw Christopher during his last visit and offered to keep the news from us, for a price."

"That wicked old eavesdropper; I wish God had struck him blind for a Peeping Tom!" said Mildred.

"Yes, a blind snoop is much less dangerous than a sighted one," said Sister Harley. "And if God had struck, perhaps no mortal would have put his soul in danger by killing him. And then Frick, living his allotted days, might have gone to judgement from his bed, with a priest to shrive him, instead of leaping into eternity with his sins hot and smoking on him. God have mercy on us all, though His ways are ever mysterious." And we all crossed ourselves and hoped to die peacefully in our beds, properly shriven.

"I begin to see that my policy of keeping silent about transgressions among our villeins is not a wise practice," I remarked. "Who is your third suspect, Master Hugh?"

"Evan Harmony. He's been . . . er, delving Toby's wife. Or so Frick hinted to someone."

"Oh, my," I said. Toby, the village blacksmith, was typical of the breed, large and strong, but Toby came also equipped with a violent temper. Evan Harmony wasn't small or frail, but he was no match for our blacksmith. Killing Frick Cotter might seem the obvious way to keep him from telling our blacksmith Evan had made a cuckold of him.

"Perhaps we should look at the blacksmith himself," I said. "If Frick went to Toby with his tale, Toby might have killed him to keep the news from spreading. Or, if Toby didn't believe him, he might not take kindly to someone telling such tales about his wife."

But Father Hugh shook his head. "No, Toby is the sort who uses his hands, or, at worst, reaches for his hammer. A scythe is an awkward weapon for someone not used to it. I think, madam, ladies, our murderer is Tiffany, Jack or Evan, one."

"So which is it?" asked Mildred.

Father Hugh lifted his shoulders. "I don't know," he said simply. "They came home separately and no one saw them along the road. Jack has a bloodstained tunic in his house, but he says it's from the deer he poached – and there's almost half a deer hanging from the rafters in that shed behind his house. Tiffany has a brand new haft on his scythe, but he says he cracked it yesterday in the field and came home a little early to replace it. There are three witnesses who say he left the meadow early, but none of them noticed a cracked haft. Evan knocked Frick down after Mass last Sunday and said if he ever caught him alone he'd kill him. Half the village saw and heard it – some cheered. Frick was not a popular person."

"But you don't know who actually did it?" I asked.

"No, my lady. And I can't think of a way of finding out."

There the matter stood, and would stand, we thought. Then, late in the afternoon, Father Hugh sent word he would like me to come to the stables, as he was about to accuse the murderer.

"Did he say who it is?" I said, rising.

"Nay, madame," said Austin. "He's put on his best robe and carrying the good processional cross, and talks as if he's expecting a sign from heaven. And he's sure enough that he'll get one that he's sent for a beadle to detain the guilty party for your judgement."

Concerned because I do not like anyone, most especially a priest, to trifle with miracles – there is such a thing as getting more than you ask for – and angry with my little priest for rousing my concern, I left the cloister and went into the inner courtyard, where I saw Sister Harley just coming out of the guesthouse. I gestured at her to accompany me. We went out the double wooden doors that led to the big outer yard, with its barns, sheds, and smell of animal muck. The sunlight fell slantwise from a still brazen sky, and the air was hot and motionless. Good haying weather, Sister Mildred would have declared.

She was there, part of a small gathering by the stables, which also included our swineherd, a shepherd, a girl from the kitchen with a bowl of scraps for the chickens, a few others. I made note of their faces, for I would scold them later as idlers, if Sister Mildred did not.

The three suspected villeins were standing beside the beadle with an air of being in custody. Jack Strong, the poacher, was a tallish man, with broad shoulders and a lot of shaggy brown hair. Tiffany of the runaway son was also strongly built, if not so tall, and there was a lot of gray in his dark hair and beard. Young Evan, as befits an adulterous lover, was handsome, with fair hair, a red mouth, and eyes as gray as glass.

The beadle turned at our approach and reported gravely, "Father Hugh assures me one of these three is the guilty one. He asked that they bring their scythes, which I made them do, but all three have been carefully cleaned."

"Yes, all scythes are cleaned after use," said Father Hugh from behind, making me start. I hadn't heard him come up. "They are cleaned and sharpened and put away dry against the next use." He was, as reported, in his best new habit, and dwarfed by the height of the processional cross he carried, which ought not to leave the cloister, especially to be dragged in the dirt of a barnyard.

"For a townsman you know a lot about farm tools," remarked Sister Harley.

"The villeins of Deerfield village are my people, too," replied Father Hugh. "I spend a certain amount of time in their company, and naturally I learn something of their ways. Even the wicked ones. Where are the scythes?"

"Over there by the stable door," replied the beadle.

"Father Hugh squinted against the lowering sun, spied the scythes, and went for a closer look, not noticing the puddle of filth he was walking through, nor how the tail of his good habit dragged in it. Then he looked at the three villeins and ordered, "Each one of you will go and stand beside his scythe!"

The villeins looked at the beadle, who nodded curtly, and each walked across the yard to stand beside his tool, facing Father Hugh and the rest of us. The beadle, frowning officiously, moved closer, but I stayed where I was with Sisters Harley and Mildred. As abbess

I would have to punish the guilty one, but this inquest was man's business.

The ungainly weapons – for so the scythes appeared to me now – leaned against the wall in a row, each very like the other.

Father Hugh began pacing up and down the line, throwing each villein a sharp glance. "When God first made the world," he said, in that measured tone he uses when beginning a sermon, "He chose Adam and Eve to be His stewards on earth. They were his creatures, who swore Him fealty. But then!" The little monk whirled and gestured sharply. "Came the *devil* – " he growled the word – "and he tempted Eve, who foreswore her oath! She went to Adam, who wickedly abjured his on her advice. And therefore all the earth came under the devil's dominion, until our Lord Jesu came and bought it back with His blood, alleluia!" If there is one thing Father Hugh can do well, it is preach. His sermons are as racy as any friar's. He raised a small hand in affected horror. "Yet, O yet, there are those who would still break the oath sworn for them at baptism, and take livery and maintenance of – Beelzebub." He drew out the name with a hiss, and a little tremor ran through us all. "There is among you," he said, turning and pointing a small finger at the villeins, "one who serves *not* God but the devil! Who is so puffed up with PRIDE and ANGER he cannot – *even now that I know who he is* – repent and confess his sin!"

This made an uneasy stir among the trio, but none opened his mouth, even in protest.

"Do you know what Beelzebub means?" asked Father Hugh, and even I shook my head. "*Lord of the Flies*. The filthy fly, engendered in filth, drawn to filth all its life, a true blazon for the livery of its filthy lord, Beelzebub." His voice dropped on that last word and we all leaned forward a little to hear what he would say next.

"And here, in worship of their master, and in witness to the devil's human servant, the flies gather . . . on the weapon used to take the life of Frick Cotter!" Father Hugh pointed suddenly at the third scythe, the one belonging to Jack Strong, deer poacher.

Jack stared at his tool, then kicked at it until it fell, sending the flies in all directions. "Nay, see?" he cried. "Them flies gather where they wist, then go off and gather some'eres else. Thee cannot be blamin' me for where the flies land!"

"Perhaps," said Father Hugh, but as one who knows otherwise, "it is as you say. Very well, all of you, wave the flies off, send them a good distance. Then we'll watch where they gather again."

The villeins set to with a will, shouted and kicked at the dusk and muck of the yard, flapping their tunics at the air, clearing a wide space around themselves and the scythes. Jack worked hardest,

which is only natural, but even he was satisfied at last, and they came
back and stood each in front of his scythe again. Now even I came
closer to watch, because it seemed to me Jack Strong was perfectly
right; flies gather here, then there, then are gone, all to no purpose
or understanding, unless there is a heap of filth to draw them.

But silence had scarce fallen when they were back, thicker than
ever, clustering all along the sharp blade of Jack's scythe, especially
near where it fastened to the handle. Their numbers were so great
they made a buzz as loud as if from bees.

The other two men stared and crossed themselves, backing off to
leave Jack by himself in front of the damning blade. Jack swung at
the flies again, but half-heartedly, and watched them collect as swiftly
as before. He swallowed, then said, as if continuing a statement, "He
says he seen me with the deer, and wanted half to keep his mouth
shut. Half! He couldn't eat half a deer, not if he sat in his cottage
all day and night stuffing himself; it'd spoil before he ate a quarter of
it. And anyway there wasn't a half left; I'd only a half to start with,
bein' I'd gone shares with – " Jack stopped, wiped his mouth. "With
someone else." His angry gaze moved to me. "We be not horses or
oxen, Mistress; we can't live on grass and roots, like!" And continued,
to Father Hugh, "With all the work of my own strips in the fields to
do, and the bidreaps and boon work for yon nuns, and trying to keep
up that little patch we claimed from the waste, my family needs meat.
Frick don't – *didn't* need it, not the way he lays idle, and I told him so. I
offered to share other of my harvest with him. But he laughs and wipes
that nose of his and 'e says, 'Jack, bring half of that deer to me after
dark tonight, or I tell what I know.' And I was so angry I just swung
at him without thinkin', forgettin' like I was carryin' that scythe, and he
flings up his arm and the blade takes it off like it was a stem of grass. I
couldn't say who was the more surprised, him or me. But I'd started it
then, and though he run I had to ketch him, and finish it, and so I did;
and went home as if nothing had happened, and cleaned the blade with
grass and dirt and washed it best I could and put it away. I meant to
take it off the haft and put it in the fire tonight to rid it of the last of
the blood – " He did stop then and pointed at Father Hugh.

"You an' your Beelzebub! St. Mary, what a load of old codswallop!
It was blood, that's all; it came like a fountain out of his arm, and his
leg when I brought him down after I ketched him up, and, and – I'm
surprised there was any left to come out of his throat, though it did,
like a river in flood. It clings, does blood, and fills into cracks, like.
And it draws flies; anyone who's ever been to a butcherin' knows that.
So you can take your Beelzebub and hang him – " He drew breath in
a ragged sob. "Just like they'll do to me."

# LEONARDO DA VINCI, DETECTIVE
## Theodore Mathieson

*Theodore Mathieson (b. 1913) turned to writing in 1955 after fifteen years as an English teacher in the public high schools of California. After he had started to sell regularly to* Ellery Queen's Mystery Magazine, *he turned to an ambitious project of writing a series of stories each featuring a famous character from history faced with a puzzling crime to solve. The series began with "Captain Cook, Detective" (1958) and ran on through a dozen stories.*

*The remarkable achievement of the series is that the crime and background in each story is directly related to its main character, using their own particular skills and abilities and linked very firmly to the world and beliefs about him. This required a considerable amount of research, for the series spanned the years from Alexander the Great to Florence Nightingale. The following story is one of the most ingenious, with its step-by-step unravelling of a seemingly impossible crime.*

On a fine late-spring afternoon in 1516, Leonardo da Vinci sat peacefully in the rose-embowered garden behind his mansion near Amboise, with a sketching pad upon his lap, drawing a golden oriole which fluttered occasionally within the confines of a large aviary. Although the Italian master was over sixty now, white-bearded and slightly stooped, the hand that had painted *The Last Supper* and *Mona Lisa* had lost none of its deftness, nor his eyes their keen brilliance. All around rose the gentle, sunwarmed hills of central France, and the bees hummed in the chaparral.

His young servant Jacques stepped hesitantly from the terrace to confront him, then spoke softly.

"Maître, a gentleman from Amboise. He demands to see you."

Leonardo nodded kindly, but before the boy could turn to deliver the message, a tall, sturdy black-haired figure with a thick beard strode across the terrace.

"Ah, Monsieur Blanchard," Leonardo said sympathetically. "You shatter the sylvan peace with your distress. Sit down and observe the golden oriole with me. I do not care to take the bird into captivity like this, but the oriole is most difficult to sketch in its natural habitat – "

"You mistake me, Monsieur," the man said. "I am not Monsieur Blanchard."

"Have my eyes lost their skill?" Leonardo said, blinking up at him. "Indeed, they must have, for you are not the King's minister after all!"

"I am Baron de Marigny, at your service. The Queen is most anxious that you come to Amboise at once."

"The Queen!" Leonardo looked surprised. His Majesty, Francis I, of the House of Valois, favored him. He had invited Leonardo to live in France, had given him this house, opened the castle at Amboise to him, and often sought his company. But the Queen! The regal French beauty had never liked him and had not dissembled from the first.

"How can my humble services be of value to the Queen?" Leonardo asked, temporizing.

"She gave me explicit orders to discuss nothing. At the same time – " Marigny's eyes shifted uneasily to the flutterings of the oriole. "His Majesty was not in favor of her calling you at all."

"But he permitted her to do so?"

"Yes. The Queen's whims are not easily discouraged."

"Then I shall come at once," Leonardo said, moving toward the terrace. "Ever to investigate, to *know* – especially when it is a Queen's whim. Jacques, my cloak!"

The coach carrying Leonardo and the Baron jolted along the narrow, poplar-lined road to within a hundred meters of the gray, rounded contours of the castle, and then debouched into a green open field to the west toward gently rising hills, perhaps a kilometer distant.

"We approach the amphitheater?" Leonardo asked.

"That is where it happened," Marigny said absently. Then his lips thinned and tightened. "They are waiting for you there. They will explain everything."

The coach drew up in a cloud of dust at the entrance of the amphitheater, which lay to the south. Here Francis, passionately fond of tournaments, masquerades, and amusements of all kinds, provided outdoor entertainment for himself, his court, and his guests. Colored flags fluttered from tall masts, announcing the afternoon's gala entertainment, already concluded, and nearly everyone had now departed except a small group sitting beneath a striped canopy inside a circle of soldiers. Leonardo recognized the King and Queen and their retinue.

The minister Blanchard approached Leonardo, his arms out-stretched, his pale face smudged with perspiration and dust.

"This is terrible, Monsieur da Vinci. Monsieur Laurier has been stabbed in the chest and lies dead within the amphitheater. Her Majesty wishes you investigate this crime and demands to see you at once."

Leonardo nodded and strode like a noble patriarch to the others sitting beneath the awning. Arriving before the royal pair, Leonardo bowed deeply.

The King, handsome in his large-nosed way, acknowledged the greeting wearily, but his eyes were alert and watchful.

"Before the Queen speaks to you, Leonardo, let me say that I did not wish to disturb you. She is upset and may say things that are personal and uncomplimentary, but I ask you to make allowances. A friend of ours, Philip Laurier, lies dead out on that field. Murdered."

"A foul, most flaunting deed!" the Queen broke in, her voice strident with emotion.

The King raised his hand imperiously. "Let me acquaint Leonardo with the facts. Today we had a fine demonstration of marching formations done by special troops from the Netherlands, from Spain, and from Scotland."

"Is it not the Scottish warriors who wear the skirts?" Leonardo asked curiously.

"Kilts, Monsieur," corrected the minister Blanchard, cracking his knuckles.

"Kilts and tartans," said Francis, "a brilliant uniform of red and green and yellow which, I should imagine, would make these barbarians easy to shoot at."

"These and other colors are set in squares and stripes, Monsieur – a distinctive pattern which differs from clan to clan, from terrain to terrain," said Blanchard.

"Blanchard knows more about it than I do," said the King tolerantly. "He went to Scotland to make the arrangements for their coming."

"*Monsieur Laurier is dead,*" chanted the Queen.

The King looked annoyed. "What happened," he said, "was that when the exhibition closed with the Scottish clan parading and playing their weird instruments – "

"Bagpipes," said the minister.

"Then the Queen and I and the others here left the field and returned to the castle. We had just descended from the coach when word came that Philip had been killed upon the field, and we returned here at once."

"*Tell him how he died*," said the Queen.

A look passed between Francis and his wife — hers of acute suspicion, his of impenetrable aloofness.

"Come, Leonardo — and all of you," said the King deliberately, rising and leading the way toward the amphitheater. "You must see how it was."

Leonardo saw how Marigny, his former coach companion, walked close beside the Queen, who paid no attention to him; she appeared to be sleepwalking. Then the King gave a quick sign to Marigny, and the latter came at once to his sire's side, like a hound trained to heel.

"Philip is — was — a promising young nobleman from the south," the King continued as they walked. "He went far in the last year, since he came to court. It was his office at these outdoor affairs to represent the King's power at the close, after all the spectators had gone. He would approach the center of the field, blow a trumpet as a signal to the guards mounted along the hills, and remain in possession of the field until the soldiers had closed formation and retired."

The King and Leonardo, followed by the others, passed through a pair of marble portals into a wide corridor cut from the hills, and entered a dell, the floor of which was covered with thick, springy turf. Elliptical in shape, with only the one entrance, the vale was perhaps two hundred feet long, and fifty at the widest point, close to the midsection. From the arena's level floor the sides sloped gently upward, the reddish earth neatly landscaped with low-lying shrubs — cotoneasters, pyracanths — no one of them high enough to conceal a man. Creepers partially covered the ground, and flat round stones were laid here and there so that one might mount to the hilltop without stepping upon the earth.

At a glance Leonardo could see that no one but himself and the royal party were within the amphitheater — they, and the figure lying motionless upon the greensward close to the center of the field. At the sight of the inert body the Queen gave a cry of dismay.

"It was your order, my dear, that he should remain there," the King said.

"Let me speak now — "

"In a moment, my dear! Let us tarry here. Today, after almost everyone had left, Laurier approached the center of the field. The guards all had their backs to the arena, as is a fixed rule, so they did not see anything. The last three people to leave the arena were Count and Countess Angerville and their daughter."

The King turned to a distinguished-looking middle-aged couple and a beautiful blond girl.

"Tell them what you saw, Angerville," the King said.

"I turned first," Angerville said in a firm, resolute tone. "Philip had just started to raise the trumpet to his lips. We walked on for several seconds and were just about *here*, and then when no sound came, I looked back, my wife and daughter looking back too. Philip seemed to stagger forward – away from us – dropping his trumpet. He turned slightly and we caught the glint of the knife-hilt as he fell. The knife could not have been thrown from the hilltop by any of the guardsmen!"

"They are too distant," the King said, "and the angle is too oblique for accuracy. The knife could only have been thrown by someone standing at the level of the arena floor!"

"*But how could that be?*" cried the girl with the blond hair.

Angerville took his daughter's hand in his. "It is impossible – and yet it happened," he said simply. "My wife and I and our daughter looked all about the arena from where we stood. There is no place of concealment. See there? Even the tiers of marble benches are set flush in the hillside and offer no hiding place. I swear it, *there was nobody within the arena but ourselves!*"

"But you did not mind that Laurier was killed, did you, Angerville?" said the Queen bitterly.

Angerville paled and the King raised his hand, but he could hold the Queen in check no longer.

"You knew your daughter was in love with Monsieur Laurier, and you were afraid they might marry!" the Queen went on. "Oh, the entire court knew about it."

"Your Majesty – " Angerville protested.

"Oh, I don't say you did it, Angerville. You wouldn't have dared. But I cannot stand your hypocritical *concern* – "

She turned and faced Leonardo, her dark beauty wild with passion.

"Monsieur da Vinci – "

"Careful now, my dear," Francis said resignedly. "Leonardo might take offense at your words and return to Italy, and we should be the poorer for it."

The Queen's lips curled in scorn. "Always Francis says to me, until I am weary: 'No other man has ever been born who knows as much as Leonardo da Vinci. Artist, inventor, engineer, mathematician, musician, philosopher – all these and more. He sees everything, he knows everything.' Well, Monsieur, I have not been willing to share my husband's views. I spent my girlhood in Valladolid, where Italian accomplishment is not held in too high regard. I cannot help my feelings."

Leonardo tilted his head in quick sympathy, tinged with satire.

"A friend – of ours – lies dead there." The Queen closed her eyes. "So far as we can see, no one was at his side nor anywhere around to kill him – yet he was stabbed. His Majesty and I shall remain outside the arena until the sun sets. That is in perhaps a little over an hour. We shall answer willingly any and all questions you may ask. If in that time 'the greatest mind in all Europe' can discover who killed Monsieur Laurier, I shall be ready to agree with my husband's opinion of da Vinci's skill!"

In the moment of intense silence that followed the Queen's outburst, Leonardo was aware of the long shadows of the late afternoon, of a cloud of midges, and of the lazy flappings of the festive banners. A hysterical woman had flung down a challenge which the others were waiting to see if he would accept. He needn't accept, of course; he could go back to his peaceful garden and sketch golden orioles, but not for long. A frustrated Queen would leave her husband no peace, and Leonardo felt a return to Florence now would be an anticlimax to his life.

"Very well, Your Highness," he said finally. "I prefer death to lassitude. And I never tire of serving others."

He turned then, and with the minister Blanchard at his heels walked toward the silent figure in the center of the field . . .

Before his death, three years later, Leonardo da Vinci told Francis how and why he set out to work as he did that fateful afternoon.

"When I was a boy in Vinci," the Italian master said, "my closest village playmates told me that a mark made upon the trunk of a tree grew higher from the ground with each year's growth of that tree. First I made sure they *believed* what they said; if they were lying, it would be needless to investigate. When I soon found that even the adults of the village believed this true, I went into the woods, notched a healthy young tree with a fleur de lis, and measured it from the ground. I returned each year for three years and measured again, and found that what everyone said was *not* true. A mark upon the trunk of a tree remains at the same height for the life of the tree, because a tree grows vertically from the crown, while its trunk increases only in girth!" . . .

First, then, that afternoon, Leonardo called Countess Angerville and her daughter to him.

"Are you as certain as your husband, Madame, that there was no one within the arena at the time Laurier was killed?"

"Yes, Monsieur," the woman said without hesitation, and her gray eyes were honest and steadfast.

"And you, Mademoiselle?"

The girl nodded, though she seemed under a spell.

"What did you do when you saw Laurier fall to the ground?" he asked the Countess.

"My husband ran forward to look at him, warning us to stay where we were. Then he ran back and told us to follow him, so that we might tell the others what had happened."

"He forgot the soldiers who stood circling the tops of the hills?"

"I suppose he did, Monsieur."

"Then all three of you ran out of the arena leaving Laurier upon the ground?"

"Yes."

Leonardo turned to the girl. "Is it true, Mademoiselle, as the Queen suggests, that you and Monsieur Laurier wished to marry?"

"No, no!" She seemed to come suddenly alive. "I – I loved him, yes, but – he did not wish to marry me. I know this because there was someone else – "

Her mother laid a warning hand upon the girl's arm, and she fell silent. Leonardo did not press the question. He could guess who her rival was.

"Would it be possible," Leonardo addressed both the mother and the girl, "that Laurier might have conceived this as a way of dramatically committing suicide?"

"No, no," the Countess assured him vehemently. "Philip was ambitious, alive to his very fingertips. The whole world was before him."

Leonardo examined the sprawled body before he had it removed from the field, and withdrew the knife from Laurier's chest, where it had been embedded to the dudgeon. It was a plain hunting knife, razor-sharp, with a yellow bone handle.

The Italian then had minister Blanchard order the soldiers to bring a thick plank into the arena and set it upright – in the exact spot Laurier had occupied. The soldiers obeyed with alacrity.

"Now who is proficient in the art of hurling the knife?" Leonardo asked Blanchard.

"I am," the minister announced quietly. Leonardo was surprised: such a skill appeared at odds with the man's self-effacement.

"And anyone else in the party?"

"It is a common skill here in France," the minister said, shrugging. "Baron de Marigny is my equal, and even the barbarian, Bruce Stewart, the leader of the Scottish troops, has vied successfully with us."

"Ask those two to come here at once," Leonardo said.

Marigny arrived with a gloomy countenance and stood sulkily by as they waited for Stewart, who at last marched vigorously into the arena, resplendent in his brilliant tartan.

"Ach, mon, the laddies tell me you want me to throw the knife," Stewart said, smiling. He was a ruddy-faced Scot with heavy jaws and craggy brows, and he looked as if all of life was a laughing matter. "I'd be muckle pleased to know my competitor."

Leonardo stationed Marigny on the floor of the arena, about fifteen paces from the board, Blanchard halfway up the east side, cautioning him to stand only upon the flat stones amid the creepers; he placed Stewart at the top of the hill, between two guards, whose discipline apparently was so stern that not one had turned to look at the proceedings below. And they had been standing there all afternoon.

Leonardo used the bone-handled hunting knife in the test. Marigny threw first and embedded the knife so deeply in the board that it took two soldiers to pull it out. But first Leonardo studied the angle of the penetration. Blanchard threw second and again Leonardo studied the angle. Stewart made four tries, missing the board altogether thrice, and succeeding only on his fourth try.

"The sun was in my eyes," said the Scot, his face almost as red as his tartan.

"But it was not only the sun," Leonardo told Francis. "It was the distance which made it unfeasible, too, and I consoled him. You were right, Your Highness. The murderer had stood on a level with his victim or slightly above – not as high as I placed Blanchard – for the blade had entered Laurier's chest at only a slight angle, and not acute as it would have been if the knife had been thrown from higher up."

So now Leonardo knew that in spite of three witnesses who claimed the arena was empty, *the murderer was there all the time!* But where?

He had a hint of the truth, but only a hint, and his time was now half used up. He had Blanchard order six soldiers to search carefully the west side of the arena for sign of footprints, for he knew the murderer would not handicap his aim by permitting the sun to shine in his eyes. In the meantime, while the soldiers searched, he detained Stewart and spoke with him.

"When you left the field with your detachment, Monsieur Stewart," he said, "you returned at once to the castle?"

"Aye, marching all the way and cutting tricks. The laddies were in fine form."

"And was any man absent from your group?"

"Not a one. All sixteen of them, acting as one man!" he said proudly.

Leonardo sat down upon one of the marble benches and sighed.

Momentarily he wished he were back in his garden making one of his numerous sketches of the golden oriole. Why should the oriole keep coming into his mind? Da Vinci listened a moment to the silence of his unconscious, for which he had a great reverence, and then said:

"Tell me, Monsieur Stewart, have you enjoyed your sojourn in France?"

"I have, aye. But many of the laddies are homesick and will be glad to leave. It's the country here, you know. Most of Scotland is very bleak and rocky, but there are parts of Appin, where we Stewarts roam, which are like this earth here – gentle and wooded and covered with brush. It reminds the laddies of home."

"Footprints, footprints!" one of the soldiers cried from a quarter way up the western side.

Leonardo hastened up to him and saw two fresh imprints of a shoe beside a stepping stone, both of the right foot. Doubtless someone – the murderer? – had missed his footing, perhaps in the excitement of a quick escape.

The soldiers found no other print on the entire western slope.

"At once," Leonardo cried to Blanchard, "get those guards down from the hill – those five!" He pointed to the men who guarded the major portion of the western side. "Monsieur Stewart, would you accompany him, please?"

The Scotsman nodded willingly and set off climbing beside the King's minister. Halfway up, the minister sat down and rested, and instantly Leonardo took a small drawing pad and crayon from his cloak and in a few deft lines portrayed Blanchard seated, clearly indicating his dejection and fatigue.

"Why do you draw only Blanchard?" Baron de Marigny said querulously, looking over Leonardo's shoulder.

"I draw what I see," the artist replied, putting his pad quickly away and swinging around to face the Baron. "Where were you when this tragedy occurred?"

"I was at the castle," said Marigny, scowling. "I was not feeling well, and I stayed the afternoon in my chamber."

"And yet when the Queen reached the castle on her return from the day's event, she sent you to fetch me, knowing you were ill?"

"I was feeling better. I met them as they arrived, and when Her Majesty received the news of Laurier's death – "

"And what was His Majesty's reaction?"

"He didn't want her to send for you. I told you." Marigny's face grew suffused with anger. "But she was insistent."

The five guardsmen from the hill watch arrived now and lined up for Leonardo's interrogation. Time was growing short. The sun had dipped behind the western hill and the arena lay in blue shadow. One by one Leonardo took a guardsman aside and said, conspiratorially:

"You and I know who slipped by you twice over the hill, don't we, Monsieur?"

Out of five poker faces it was Leonardo's good fortune to find one which mirrored every thought process. The guard denied joint knowledge with Leonardo, of course, but at least the Italian now knew that if one was lying, so in all probability were the other four.

Leonardo was now sure of the solution to the mystery – so sure that he walked out of the arena, the minister Blanchard and Stewart trailing behind him. Marigny remained where he was.

At His Majesty's pavilion the Queen called out, "Your time is about up, da Vinci!"

Many in the group eyed him with suspicion and hostility. Leonardo bowed and said, "One moment, Your Highness." He turned to Count Angerville who stood surveying him calmly from beside the King.

"Where were you seated during the performance?" he asked.

Angerville looked taken aback. "Why, beside His Majesty, on his left."

Francis nodded, frowning. "Angerville was on my left, and Blanchard on my right."

"And did His Majesty speak with you during the presentation?"

Angerville appeared to think hard for a moment. "Only once, I believe."

"And what did he say?"

"Come, come, Leonardo," the King said testily. "Where is this leading us?"

"Perhaps to the truth, Your Highness. What did His Majesty say to you, Count Angerville?"

"He said – " Angerville colored, and looked abashed at the women present. "His Majesty asked me if I thought the Scotsmen wore anything *under* their skirts!"

There was a ripple of laughter in the party, and some of the tenseness and hostility relaxed. Only the King glared fiercely at Leonardo.

"Are you trying to make sport of me?" he demanded.

"God forbid, Your Highness," Leonardo said humbly. Out of the corner of his eye he could see the Queen fidgeting, preparing to quell his questions.

"And where, Your Highness," he said, addressing the Queen, "were you sitting?"

"On a bench on the opposite side of the field, where the women always sit!"

And then, to the surprise of the entire party, Leonardo da Vinci sank down on one knee, bowed his head, and said:

"I confess I do not deserve a higher evaluation in Her Majesty's eyes than I already possess. I have failed to discover how Monsieur Laurier was murdered by an invisible assassin. Moreover, were I given a year, or two years, I do not believe I could solve this mystery. In extenuation, I will say that I am an old man and perhaps my powers of observation have waned. I beg now to be excused."

After a moment the Queen nodded. Leonardo rose, and while the King and his party watched in frozen silence, he walked slowly, almost falteringly, to the coach that had brought him.

But Leonardo da Vinci, in addition to his other accomplishments, was also a fine actor.

Next morning he was sitting in his garden as usual, calmly and confidently making another sketch of the golden oriole when Jacques announced the arrival of the King.

Francis waved Leonardo back to his chair, then sat down on a bench beside him.

"Leonardo," he said at once, "I wish to thank you for what you did for me yesterday. I shall not soon forget it. Now do not pretend further with me. You know who murdered Laurier, and how the miracle was accomplished."

Leonardo said nothing, but watched the King steadily, as if he awaited further word.

"There are times," the monarch said, lowering his eyes, "when it is politically expedient to remove a dangerous subject. Your own countryman Machiavelli has said this. Laurier was a traitor, bargaining in secrets with a foreign power."

Leonardo nodded, knowing the real reason why Laurier had died; the Queen had made that plain for all to see. The King's subterfuge was pathetic, but Leonardo's acceptance of it made it possible for the two men to talk freely about the crime.

"Tell me now what you know, Leonardo."

"I know you had him killed, Sire. When I realized the man whom you chose to commit the murder both entered and escaped from the arena with the complicity of the guardsmen, I knew they had their orders *only from you*. If the cause of the murder had been a simple, spontaneous grudge, and committed, say, by one of the Scottish soldiers or by Stewart himself, there could have been no such collusion."

Francis nodded approvingly. "And you know the man whom I picked?"

"The men," Leonardo corrected gravely. "One to commit the deed, the other to replace him by your side. When I learned that you asked Angerville a question about the Scottish dress, I knew the man on the *other* side of you was not Blanchard. Blanchard, who had been to Scotland, was familiar with all these details, and if he'd been at your other side you'd have directed your question to him. Therefore, the man on the other side of you was someone who superficially resembled Blanchard – Baron de Marigny who looks so much like Blanchard that I mistook him for the minister when he came here to fetch me yesterday. It must have been a shock to him when I addressed him thus. He took pains to make himself up to resemble Blanchard even more, in order to deceive Her Majesty, who sat facing you on the other side of the field."

"Ah, yes," the King said quickly. "Her Majesty liked Laurier – I did not wish to hurt her."

"Of course. And now as to how it was done – "

"I thought my plan would amaze and perplex!" cried the King. "And yet you perceived the truth. You must tell me your methods."

Leonardo pointed toward the aviary.

"By the help of the golden oriole, there, who started a train of thought. I mentioned to Marigny yesterday how the oriole was hard to sketch in his natural habitat, which is among the green and yellow of the woods. His plumage blends into the background of sun-shot leaves in a protective coloration, making him virtually invisible. It is the same with the uniforms of soldiers, which are designed in many cases to help throw a cloak of invisibility about the soldier. It is common knowledge. The brilliant tartan of the Scottish warrior does this, paradoxically. The terrain within the arena, with its red earth and green shrubbery is much like the country of Appin, where the Stewarts live and fight. Stewart himself told me this. And when he climbed up the slope on the shadowed side of the arena with Blanchard, and they rested a moment, I was moved to make a quick sketch of Blanchard, partly *because Blanchard was all I saw*. He appeared to be sitting alone, unless one focused one's eyes especially to detect Stewart beside him . . . Curiously, was it not Blanchard who suggested to you this means of achieving invisibility?"

The King nodded.

"As I reconstructed it," Leonardo went on, "Laurier stood in the center of the field, waiting for the last spectator to leave. He must have seen Blanchard come over the hill and wondered at it. Perhaps it delayed his putting the trumpet to his lips. Blanchard threw the knife at the defenseless soldier, and when the Angervilles turned and saw Laurier clutching his throat, Blanchard must have already crouched upon the side of the hill, with a borrowed tartan concealing him. The sun was still up, and his was the shadowed part of the hill, so he must have been virtually invisible. Then when the Angervilles ran from the arena to fetch help, Blanchard completed his escape."

Suddenly Francis seemed to lose interest.

"Thank you, thank you, Leonardo, you have explained it all with wondrous accuracy. And now I must go – I am needed at Amboise. I shall visit you again shortly."

The King was hastening across the sunny garden when Leonardo stopped him with a final question.

"And what about Monsieur Blanchard? He is to be rewarded for his pains?"

The King whirled around, open-mouthed. Then, as a look of faint concern appeared, he shrugged.

"Poor man, Blanchard," he said. "Her Majesty must have learned he did it, too. They found him by the castle pond this morning, with a hunting knife in his chest. A pity, too, for it was a fine reward I promised him!"

And with that the King disappeared behind a hedgerow, and Leonardo da Vinci, citizen of the world, contemporary of Machiavelli, sat peacefully down to sketching the elusive golden oriole, almost invisible in the sun-brilliant foliage.

# A SAD AND
# BLOODY HOUR
## Joe Gores

*Joe Gores (b. 1931) has excellent credentials for writing detective stories. For twelve years he was a private detective in San Francisco. He has written ten novels and over a hundred short stories and has been a three-time winner of the Mystery Writers of America Edgar Award. He has also written for cinema and television. His TV work includes scripts for* Columbo, Kojak, Magnum *and* Remington Steele.

*It may not take you too long to work out who the mystery detective is in the following story, but once you've done that you may discover there is much more of a challenge for you in identifying the sources of the 396 quotes which are turned into dialogue in the story. The events are those which, four centuries on, inspired Anthony Burgess to write* A Dead Man in Deptford *(1993).*

Perhaps it was unscanned self-love, concern for the first heir of my wit's invention, that brought me back to London from the safety of Dover where The Admiral's Men were presenting Marlowe's *Tragical History of Doctor Faustus*. It was a grisly visit, for elevenhundred a week were dying of the plague. This scourge of God had carried away few of my acquaintance save poor Kit, but his loss was heavy: our friendship had been much deeper than mere feigning.

I finished my business with Dick Field and in the afternoon returned to my rented room on Bishopsgate near Crosby Hall. When I ascended the dank ill-lit staircase to my chamber I found a lady waiting me within. As she turned from a window I saw she was not Puritan Agnes come to see her player husband, but a pretty bit of virginity with a small voice as befits a woman.

"Thank God I found you before your return to the provinces!"

Her words, and the depths of her steady blue eyes, made me realize that she was only about five years younger than my twenty-nine. With her bodice laces daringly loosened to display her bright red stomacher beneath, and wearing no hat or gloves, she might have been a common drab: but never had I seen a bawdy woman with so much character in her face. As if reading my thought she drew herself up.

"I am Anne Page, daughter to Master Thomas Page and until recently maid to Mistress Audry, wife of Squire Thomas Walsingham of Scadbury Park, Chislehurst."

All things seemed that day conspired to remind me of poor Marlowe, for Walsingham had been his patron since Cambridge.

"Then you knew Kit?"

"Knew him?" She turned away as if seeking his swarthy face in the unshuttered window. "With his beard cut short like a Spaniard's, full of strange oaths and quick to quarrel for his honour! Knew him?" She turned back to me suddenly. "Were you truly his friend? By all the gods at once, I need a man to imitate the tiger!"

"I am young and raw, Mistress Page, but believe me: sorrow bites more lightly those who mock it."

"Say rage, rather! Oh, were I a man my sword should end it!" Her eyes flashed as if seeing more devils than hell could hold. "Didn't you know that last May when Tom Kyd was arrested, he deposed that Kit had done the heretical writings found in his room?"

"The players were scattered by the closing of the theatres."

"On the strength of Kyd's testimony a warrant was issued; Kit was staying at Scadbury Park to avoid the plague, so Squire Thomas put up bail. But then a second indictment was brought, this time before the Privy Council by the informer Richard Baines. On May twenty-ninth I was listening outside the library door when the Squire accused Kit of compromising those in high places whose friendship he had taken."

I shook my head sorrowfully. "And the next day he died!"

"Died!" Her laugh was scornful. "When he left the library, Kit told me that two of Squire Thomas's creatures, Ingram Frizer and Nicholas Skeres, would meet him at a Deptford tavern to help him flee the country. I begged him be careful but ever he sought the bubble reputation, even in the cannon's mouth; and so he now lies in St. Nicholas churchyard. And so I wish I were with him, in heaven or in hell?"

"But why do you say cannon's mouth? His death was – "

"Murder! Murder most foul and unnatural, arranged beneath the guise of friendship and bought with gold from Walsingham's coffers! Kit was stabbed to death that afternoon in Eleanor Bull's tavern!"

I shivered, and heard a spy in every creaking floor-board; it is ever dangerous for baser natures to come between the mighty and their designs, and Squire Thomas's late cousin Sir Francis, had, as

Secretary of State, crushed the Babington Conspiracy against the Queen.

"But what proof could you have? You were not there to see it."

"Do I need proof that Rob Poley, back from the Hague only that morning, was despatched to the tavern two hours before Kit's end? Proof that Squire Thomas, learning that I had been listening outside the library door, discharged me without reference so I have become . . ." She broke off, pallid cheeks aflame, then plunged on: "Oh, player, had you the motive and cue for passion that I have! I beg you, go to Deptford, ferret out what happened! If it was murder, then I'll do bitterness such as the day will fear to look upon!"

She admitted she was a discharged serving wench with a grievance against Walsingham; yet her form, conjoined with the cause she preached, might have made a stone capable. I heard my own voice saying staunchly: "To-morrow I'll go to Deptford to learn the truth of it."

"Oh, God bless you!" Swift as a stoat she darted to the door; her eyes glowed darkly back at me from the folds of her mantle. "Tomorrow night and each night thereafter until we meet . . . Paul's Walk."

She was gone. I ran after her but St. Mary's Axe was empty. Down Bishopsgate the spires of St. Helen's Church were sheathed in gold.

Kit Marlowe murdered by his patron Thomas Walsingham! It could not be. And yet . . . I determined to seek Dick Quiney and his advice.

The doors wore red plague crosses and the shops were shuttered as I turned into Candlewick towards the imposing bulk of St. Paul's. In Carter Lane the householders were lighting their horn lanterns; beyond Tom Creed's house was The Bell where I hoped to find Dick Quiney. Though he's now a High Bailiff in Warwickshire, his mercer's business often calls him to London. I hoped that I would find him now in the City.

The Bell's front woodwork was grotesquely carved and painted with red and blue gargoyles, and a sign worth £40 creaked over the walk on a wrought-iron bracket: it bore a bell and no other mark besides, but good wine needs no bush to herald it. Through the leaded casement windows came the tapster's cry, "Score at the bar!" When I asked the drawer, a paunchy man with nothing on his crown between him and heaven, if Dick Quiney were staying there, he gestured up the broad oak stairway.

"In the Dolphin Chamber, master."

The room faced the inner court on the second floor. When I thrust

open the door, Dick, with an oath, sprang for the scabbarded rapier
hung over the back of his chair: forcible entry to another's chamber
has been often used for hired murder. But then he laughed.

"Johannus Factotem! I feared my hour had come. How do you,
lad?"

"As an indifferent child of earth."

"What makes the handsome well-shaped player brave the plague
– oho! September twenty-second tomorrow!" He laughed again, a
wee quick wiry man in green hose and brown unpadded doublet.
"The upstart crow, beautified with their feathers, will give them all
a purge."

"'Let base conceited wits admire vile things, fair Phoebus lead me
to the Muses' springs'," I quoted. "You ought to recognize Ovid –
we read him in the grammar long ago. As for the translation, I had
it from Kit last spring."

"Still harping on Marlowe, lad? We all owe God a death."

"What reports have you had of the cause of his?"

"Surely it was the plague. Gabriel Harvey's 'Gorgon' says – "

"That's now disputed." Over meat I recounted all. "I fear
Walsingham, but if I should be fattening the region's kites with
his – "

"Would you number sands and drink oceans dry? In justice – "

"– none of us should see salvation. Not justice, friendship: forgotten, it stings sharper than the winter wind."

"Pah! Marlowe was hasty as fire and deaf as the sea in his rages.
You'd do him no disservice to leave his bones lie." Then he shrugged.
"But as you say, use men as they deserve and who would escape the
whipping? So you'll off to Deptford, seeking truth."

"I will. If you could go to Harrison's White Greyhound – "

"I'll oversee your interests." He clapped me on the back. "Give
tomorrow to gaunt ghosts the grave's inherited, to-night there's excellent *theologicum* and humming ale made with fat standing Thames
water."

I could find no boats at Paul's Pier; and at Queenhithe, the
watermen's gathering place of late years, were boats but no pilots.
As I started for the Red Knight, a boy hailed me from the dock.

"John Taylor, boatman's apprentice, at your service." Barely
thirteen, he had an honest open face, curly brown hair, and sharp
eyes. "Do you travel to escape the plague?"

I sat down on the embroidered cushions in the stern of his boat.
"No, I'm a journeyman to grief. Westward ho – to Deptford, lad."

The ebbing tide carried us towards the stone arches of London
Bridge, sliding us beneath her covered arcade and crowded houses

like an eel from the hand. As we passed the Tower the boy spoke suddenly.

"Weren't you a player in *The True Tragedy of Richard, Duke of York*, at The Theatre last year?"

"You know much of the stage for one so young," I grunted. Yet I was pleased that he had recognized me, for all men seek fame.

The bells of St. Saviour's on the Surrey Side were pealing eight far behind us when Deptford docks came into view around a bend in the river, crowded with the polyglot shipping of all nations. A sailor with one eye directed me to St. Nicholas Church, the mean stone chapel not far from the docks where Anne Page had said Kit was buried.

The rector was a stubby white-haired man, soberly dressed as befits the clergy, with his spectacles on his nose and his hose hanging on shrunken shanks.

"Give you God's blessings, sir." His piping voice would have been drowned in the Sunday coughings of his congregation. "Even as the holy Stephen gave soft words to those heathens who were stoning him."

"Let's talk of graves and worms and epitaphs. I want to see your register of burials for the present year."

"Here are many graved in the hollow ground, as was holy Lawrence after that naughty man Valerian broiled him on a slow grid." He squeaked and gibbered like the Roman dead upon the death of Caesar, but finally laid out the great leather-covered volume I desired. "Seek only that which concerns you: sin not with the eyes. Consider Lucy of Syracuse; when complimented by a noble on her beautiful eyes, she did tear them out and hand them to him so that she might avoid immodest pride."

"I search for only one name – that of Christopher Marlowe."

"Marlowe? Why, a very devil, that man, a player and – "

"Churlish priest! Kit will be singing when you lie howling! And why have you written only: *First June, 1593, Christopher Marlowe slain by Francis Archer*. No word of his monument or epitaph."

The old cleric, ruffled by my words, chirped like a magpie. "His bones lie tombless, with no rememberance over them."

"But he had high friends! Why, after a violent death, was he given such an unworthy burial?"

"Squire Walsingham himself so ordered." Animosity faded from his whizzled walnut face in the hope of vicarious scandal. "Surely his death was a simple tavern brawl? It was so accepted by William Danby, Coroner to the Royal Household, who held the inquest since Her Gracious Highness was lying at Kew."

"The Queen's Coroner would not be corrupt," I said brusquely. But could he be misled? "Now take me to Kit's grave."

In an unmarked oblong of sunken earth in the churchyard, under a plane tree, was Kit, safely stowed with flowers growing from his eyes. I felt the salt tears trickling down my own face.

"Even as St. Nicholas once restored to life through God's grace three boys who had been pickled in a salting-rub for bacon, so may we gather honey from the weed and make a moral of this devil Marlowe. The dead are as but pictures – and only children fear painted devils – but Marlowe was so evil that God struck him down in the midst of sin."

"Pah!" I burst out angrily, dashing away my unmanly tears. "Your preaching leaves an evil taste like easel! Speak only from the pulpit, father – play the fool only in your own house."

"My Father's House! In His House are many mansions, but none – "

I left his querulous anger behind to search for Eleanor Bull's tavern. Walsingham might have ordered just such a hurried obscure funeral if Kit had died of the plague; but then why had the burial record shown him slain by Francis Archer? And why had Anne Page given me Ingram Frizer as Kit's killer? Had her tale been more matter and less art than it had seemed? Perhaps Eleanor Bull would have the answers.

Playbills were tattered on the notice-post beside the door and Dame Eleanor would have made a good comic character upon the stage herself: a round-faced jolly woman with a bawdy tongue and a nose that had been thrust into more than one tankard of stout, by its color. She wore a fine scarlet robe with a white hood.

"Give you good morrow, sir."

"Good morrow, dame. Would you join me in a cup of wine?"

"By your leave, right gladly, sir." She preceded me up the narrow stairs, panting her remarks over her shoulder in beery lack of breath. "I get few ... phew ... other than seafarers here. Rough lot they be, much ... phew ... given to profanity." She opened a door, dug me slyly in the ribs as I passed. "La! If I but lodge a lonely gentlewoman or two who live honestly by their needlework, straightway it's claimed I keep a bawdy house!"

I laughed and ordered a pint of white wine each. It was a pleasant chamber overlooking an enclosed garden; the ceiling was oak and a couch was pushed back against the cheap arras showing Richard Crookback and Catesby on Bosworth Field. A fireplace pierced one wall.

"Tell me, mistress: did a man named Christopher Marlowe meet an untimely end in your house some months ago?"

"You knew Marlowe, in truth?" She regarded me shrewdly. "For all his abusing of God's patience and the King's English with quaint curses, he was a man women'd run through fire for. Lord, Lord, master, he was ever a wanton! I'll never laugh as I did in that man's company."

I kept my voice casual. "A brawl over a wench, wasn't it? And the fellow who killed him – Francis Archer?"

"La!" She jingled the keys on her silver-embroidered sash. "You must have seen the decayed cleric of St. Nicholas Church – he can scarce root the garden with his shaking fingers, let alone write right a stranger's name. Ingram Frizer was the man who shuffled Kit off."

"I would be pleased to hear an account of it."

"Heaven forgive him and all of us, I say; he died in this very room, on that very couch. God's blood, I don't know what he was doing in such company, as Nick Skeres is a cutpurse and Frizer a swindler for all his pious talk; but all three were living at Scadbury Park and once spied together for the Privy Council. Rob Poley, another of the same, arrived on a spent horse in the afternoon, and two hours later the fight started. By the time I had run up here, Kit was already flat upon the couch, stabbed through the skull above the right eye."

"Wasn't Frizer charged when the guard arrived?"

"Right speedily: but the others backed his story that Kit, who was lying drunk upon the couch, had attacked him through an argument over the score. Frizer was watching Skeres and Poley at backgammon, when Kit suddenly leaped up cursing, seized Frizer's own knife from its shoulder sheath, and started stabbing him in the face. Frizer got free, they scuffled, Kit fell on the knife." She shrugged. "The inquest was the first of June; by the twenty-eighth Frizer'd been pardoned by the Queen and was back at Scadbury Park in the Squire's pay."

I sat down on the couch, muscles crawling. Kit had been as strong and agile as myself from the tumbling and fencing at which all players excel; and even in a drunken rage would the creator of haughty Tamburlaine and proud Faustus stab from behind? *The room seemed to darken; four dim figures strained in the dusk, Kit's arms jerked back, feet thrust cunningly between his, a cry – silence –* murder.

I looked up at Eleanor Bull. "Do you believe their story?"

"I'll not put my finger in the fire." But then her gaze faltered; her thumb ring glinted as she clutched the arras. She turned suddenly, face distorted. "La! I'll speak of it though hell itself forbid me! It was I who saw him fumble at his doublet, and smile upon his fingers, and cry out 'God! God! God!' It was I who felt his legs and found them cold as any stone. And it is I who now declare that here was cruel murder done!"

Her words brought me to my feet. "Then I'm for Scadbury Park to pluck this bloody villain's beard and blow it in his face!"

She cast her bulk before me, arms outstretched. "Oh, master, that sword which clanks so bravely against your flank will be poor steel against the viper you seek to rouse. These other swashers – la! Three such antics together don't make a man. Skeres is white-livered and red-faced; Frizer has a killing tongue and a quiet sword; and Poley's few good words match as few good deeds. But Squire Thomas! Cross him to learn that one may smile and smile and be a viilain."

"I'm committed to one with true cause for weeping. Go I must."

"Then take one of my horses – and my prayers with you."

After a few miles of gently rolling downs whose nestled farmers' cots reminded me of my own Warwickshire, I came to Chislehurst. Beyond a mile of forest was Manor Park Road curving gently up through open orchards to the moated main house of Scadbury Manor, a sprawling tile-roofed timber building over two-hundred years old.

I was led through the vast unceiled central hall to the library, which was furnished in chestnut panels. His books showed the Squire's deep interest in the arts: Holinshed's *Chronicles*; Halle's *Union*; Plutarch's *Lives*; Sir Philip Sydney's *Arcadia*, chief flower of English letters. These were bound in leather and set on the shelves with their gilt-edged leaves facing out to show the gold clasps and jewelled studs. On the other shelves were rolled and piled manuscripts – *Diana Enamorada*, *Menaechmi* – which I was examining when a low melancholy voice addressed me from the doorway.

"Who asks for Walsingham with Marlowe's name also on his lips?"

He looked the knight that he so ardently sought to be, elegant as a bridegroom and trimly dressed in silken doublet, velvet hose, and scarlet cloak. His voice was like his thrice-gilt rapier in its velvet scabbard: silk with steel beneath. Lengthened by a pointed beard and framed in coiling hair, his face had the cruel features of a Titus or a Caesar: Roman nose, pale appraising eyes, well-shaped disdainful lips. A face to attract and repel in an instant.

"A poor player who begs true detail of Marlowe's quick end."

He advanced leisurely into the room, giving his snuff-box to his nose. "Your clothes make your rude birth and ruder profession obvious. I knew Marlowe slightly and sponsored his serious work

– not the plays, of course. But why ask me about his death when the plague – "

"I had it from An – from a mutual friend that he was slain, not by plague, but in a Deptford tavern brawl by your man Ingram Frizer."

"Did you now? And this gossip – the trollop Anne Page?"

"No," I retorted quickly, "Tom Kyd in Newgate Gaol."

He sneered and rang a small silver bell. "A quick eye and open ear such as yours often make gaol smell of home; and your tongue runs so roundly that it may soon run your head from your irreverent shoulders. But perhaps even the meanly born can honour friendship."

The man who entered was easily recognized as Nicholas Skeres: he was indeed beet-nosed and capon-bellied, and when he learned of my errand he advanced bellowing as if I would melt like suet in the sun.

"Why, you nosey mummer, Kit was a bawcock and a heart of gold! Why, were he among us now, I'd kiss his dirty toe, I would; for well I loved the lovely bully." He laughed coarsely. "Of course now he's at supper with the worms; but here's Frizer to set you right."

Ingram Frizer had a churchwarden's face but the eye of a man who sleeps little at night. His mouth was an O and his eyes were to heaven, and he aped the cleric's true piety as ill as the odious prattler replacing the well-graced actor upon the stage.

"Poor Marlowe," he intoned unctuously. "He left this life as one who had been studied in his death. Here am I, watching backgammon; there is Kit, upon the couch. He leaps up, seizes my knife – " He moved, and the deadly blade whose hilt was visible over his left shoulder darted out like a serpent's tongue to slash the dancing dustmotes. "He strikes me twice in the face, I pull loose, we grapple, he slips . . . sheathed in his brain. I pluck away the steel, kiss the gash yawning so bloodily on his brow. He smiles a last brave time, takes my hand in feeble grip – but his soul is fled to the Eternal Father."

"Satisfied now, Mars of malcontents?"

"Just one more question, Squire." As my profession is counterfeit emotion, my tone matched Frizer's for buttery sorrow. "Then I will take my leave."

"Nothing will I more readily give you."

"Why did Poley, fresh from the Hague as from the seacoasts of Bohemia, come hurriedly that day to Dame Eleanor's tavern?"

"Question my actions, player, and you'll yield the crows a pudding!" Poley advanced from the shadows; huge, silent-moving, dark and sensual of face, his eyes falcon-fierce and his nose bent aside as if seeking the smell of death. His arms were thick and his chest a brine-barrel beneath his stained leather doublet.

Squire Thomas's sad disdainful smile fluttered beneath his new-reaped moustache like a dove about the cote. "He was just come from Holland. Where better than a tavern to wash away the dust of travel?"

"What of Baines's indictment of Kit that was sure to embarrass you and the others of Raleigh's Circle if it came to court? You had learned of it only the night before; this had nothing to do with Poley's despatch to the tavern on that day?"

His face went ashen, his lips bloodless; his pale eyes flashed and his voice shook with suppressed rage. "Divine my downfall, you little better thing than earth, and you may find yourself beneath it!" With an effort he controlled his emotion. "Apes and actors, they say, should have their brains removed and given to the dog for a New Year's gift."

He held up a detaining hand. "Soft, you – a word or two before you go. I have done the state some service and they know it. Beware! You said Tom Kyd gave you the news of Marlowe's death, then prattled details only Anne Page could have told you. No murder have I done – yet she spreads her scandals. Seek her out in secret and you will feel that the very cobbles beneath your feet do prate to me your whereabouts."

Such a man bestrides my narrow world like a Colossus; yet was he more fully man than I?

"You despise me for my birth, Walsingham; yet nature cannot choose its origin. Blood will have blood if blood has been let, and murder will out for all your saying."

But I didn't feel safe until good English oak was between us.

Ten had struck before I arrived, in defiance of Squire Thomas, at St. Paul's Cathedral Church. During the hours of worship the shrill cries of the hawkers and the shouts of the roistering Paul's Men compete among the arches with the chants of the choir; but then only my boots echoed upon the stones of Paul's Walk, the great central nave.

I loosened my sword, for one may as easily have his throat cut in the church as elsewhere. When a slight figure in homespun darted from behind a pillar, I recognized Anne Page's eyes glowing beneath the coarse grey mantle just before my steel cleared the sheath.

"You come most carefully upon your hour, player. Tell me, quickly, what did you learn?" Present fears forgotten, we patrolled the nave in measured steps. When I had finished she cried: "Oh, smiling damned villain! From this time shall my thoughts be only bloody!"

I cautioned: "Squire Thomas said that he had done no murder."

"Then you're a fool, or coward! On May eighteenth Walsingham sent Poley to find Kit a place to hide in Holland from the warrant brought by Kyd's deposition. But Baines's charge of blasphemy was too serious – Walsingham feared he would be compromised by helping Kit defy it. More, he determined on murder to prevent the public disclosures of Kit's trial." Her voice writhed in its own venom like a stricken serpent. "Oh, player, I would lay the dust with showers of that man's blood. But hold – enough! My quarrel is yours no further."

"I'll not leave you, Anne," I declared passionately.

"You must. Had I met you before Kit – " Her fingers brushed my lips in sexless caress, and regret laid its vague wings across her face. "Too late! Hell has breathed contagion on me; I am fit only to drink hot blood."

I shook my head and declared flatly: "I will walk with you, Anne; take you through the dark night to your home."

Outside the Cathedral it was cold and the air bit shrewdly. Rank river fog, driven by the eager nipping wind, obscured all about us. Noxious plague odours assailed us, and from the muffling smoke came the clop-clop of hoofs as a death cart rattled about its grisly business, the cartmen leaping down with iron tongs to drag the sprawled and sightless corpses from the slops and urine of the gutters.

Through the swirling fog of Dowgate Hill I could see the cobbler's house where last year Rob Greene was lost in death's dateless night. Here Anne broke in upon my reverie.

"Now surely twelve has struck – the moon is down, and it goes down at twelve. It's the witching time of night; in my soul shriek owls where mounting larks should sing. And now I must leave you."

"Now? Here? Surely not here, Anne?"

For we had arrived at Cold Harbour, where criminals impudently mock our English courts and the filthy tenements breed every vice.

"Yes, here," she whispered. "Here night cloaks me from my own sight while my body buys me sustenance to nurse revenge; and here I live only in hope of one day taking Walsingham about some act with no salvation in it, so his heels may kick to heaven while his soul is plunged to deepest hell."

She led me down a narrow alley where rats scuttled unseen and my boots slithered in foul mud; suddenly a man was silhouetted before us, naked steel glittering in his right hand.

"Back – this way!" I warned.

Too late! Behind were two more figures. Light glinted off bared swords, a spur chinked stone. I felt so unmanned with terror of my sins that I could not even draw my sword – for thus conscience makes cowards of us all. But then one of the men called out.

"Stand aside – we seek only the woman."

But I recognized the voice; and with recognition came anger.

"Booted and spurred, Rob Poley?" When I cried his name Anne gasped. "You three have ridden hard from Scadbury Park this night."

"You know us, player? Then by these hands you *both* shall die!"

"If hell and Satan hold their promises." My sword hissed out like a basking serpent from beneath its stone, barely in time to turn his darting steel. "Aha, boy!" I cried, "Say you so?"

But as he gave way before me Anne Page flashed by, dagger high.

"Murderer! Your deeds stink above the earth with carrion men!"

His outthrust rapier passed through her body, showed me half its length behind. She fell heavily sideways. Before his weapon was free I might have struck, but I was slow, for never before had I raised my blade in anger. Then it was too late. He put a ruthless foot against her neck, and jerked free.

"Stand on distance!" he bellowed at Skeres and Frizer. "Make him open his guard. He must not live!"

But by then my youthful blood was roused, and like all players I am expert in the fence. I turned Skeres's blade, shouting: "Now, while your purple hands reek and smoke." I lunged, skewered his dancing shadow in the throat so sparks flew from the stone behind his head, and jerked free. "I know these passes . . . these staccadoes . . ."

My dagger turned Frizer's sword, I covered, thrust, parried, thrust again, my arm longer by three feet of tempered steel. ". . . they're common on the stage . . . here . . . here . . . the heart!"

Frizer reeled drunkenly away, arms crossed over his punctured chest; but what of Poley? Fire lanced my arm and my rapier clattered from my nerveless grasp. Fingers like Hanse sausages closed about my windpipe. I felt myself thrust back so his long sword could reach me.

"Say you so now?" His voice was a snarl of triumph. "Are you there, truepenny?"

My head whirled giddily for lack of blood. In an instant his steel would – but then my dagger touched his belly. "How now!" I cried. "Dead for a ducat, dead!"

With my last despairing strength I ripped the two-edged cutter up through his guts, sprawled over his twitching corpse.

Silence. Moisture dripping from overhanging eaves, hot blood staining my fingers. A rat rustling in the gutter. The turning world turning on, aeons passing. Yet I lay silent in the drifting smoke. Then from beyond eternity a weak voice called me back to life.

"Player – my gashes cry for help – " Somehow I crawled to her, cradled her weakly lolling head against my shoulder. Her voice was small, so very small. "The churchyard yawns below me. I'll trade the world for a little grave, a little, little grave, an obscure grave . . ."

My salt tears gave benediction to her death-ravaged face; her body now was lead within the angle of my arm. "Anne!" I cried. "Anne! Oh, God! God forgive us all!"

"Let not this night be the whetstone of your sword." Her heart fluttered briefly within the frail cage of her body; her whispers touched my ear in failing cadence. "Let your heart be blunted. This death is – a joy unmixed with – sorrow."

No more. I lowered her gently to the waiting earth, struggled erect. My breath still rasped and rattled in my throat; dark walls weaved, receded, shifted; lantern bright above Cold Harbour Stairs, stone slimy beneath my vagrant gory fingers, cold Thames below, whispering its litany *she is dead she is dead she is.*

Falling. Nothing else besides.

Movement aroused me. I lay on the cushions of a waterman's boat, river fog upon my face. Peering forward I saw a familiar figure.

"Lad, how did I come here?"

John Taylor turned anxious eyes on me. "I found you at the foot of Cold Harbour Stairs." He indicated my sword at my feet. "Your blood upon the cobbles led to this – and one that was a woman. But rest her soul, she's dead. Two others were there also, one with his wizand slit, the other drawn like a bull in the flesh shambles."

I thrust my arm into the clear Thames water, found the wound only a painful furrow in the flesh. Frizer had escaped. Anne was dead. I needed time – time to think.

"The Falcon, lad. I'll see what physic the tavern accords."

I gave the boy my silver and went through the entrance, narrow and thick-walled from pre-Tudor days, to the tap-room. Here I was met by a blast of light and noise. I kept my arm against my side to mask the blood. A jolly group was gathered by the bar.

A cup of wine that's brisk and fine
And drink unto the leman mine:
And a merry heart lives long-a.

"Before God, an excellent song!"

"An English song," laughed the singer. "Indeed, we English are most potent in our potting. I'll drink your Dane dead drunk; I'll overthrow your German; and I'll give your Hollander a vomit before the next bottle's filled!"

But this was Will Sly, the red-faced jolly comedian I'd left in Dover! At sight of me he threw his arms wide.

"Out upon it, old carrion! You can't have heard: The Admiral's Men have been disbanded! By William the Conqueror who came before Richard III, Will Sly finds himself in the good Falcon with bad companions swilling worse ale." He suited actions to words, then leaned closer and lowered his voice as he wiped the foam from his moustache. "But you look pale, lad; and your tankard's dry. Ho! Drawer!"

"Anon, sir."

I had barely drawn him aside with my story when a blustery voice broke in. "Players in the corner? Then some man's reputation's due for a fall. In faith, it's better to have a bad epitaph than the players' ill report while alive. But let me tell you what I'm about."

"Why, two yards at least, Tom Lucy," laughed Will Sly.

Lucy was from Charlecote, a few miles from my home – a trying man with severe eyes and beard of formal cut, and the brains of a pecking sparrow.

"Perhaps two yards around the waist, Will Sly, but now I'm about thrift, not waste."

He was always full of wise saws and modern instances, so I cut in curtly: "We'll join you at the bar presently, Master Lucy."

After he had turned about I went on; soon Will Sly's face was as long as his cloak. When I told of the meeting with Anne in St. Paul's he burst out bitterly: "Fool! What if you were seen with this Anne Page? If – "

"Anne Page?" said Lucy to me. "I wondered at the name of the doxy you walked beside on Dowgate Hill hard upon mid-night, player."

Will Sly matched his name. "Then you've been seeing double, Tom Lucy; he's matched me pot for pot these four hours past."

"I'm not deceived in her," said Lucy. "In the Bankside Stews her eyes have met mine boldly, like any honest woman's."

"Then the sun shone on a dunghill!" I burst out.

"Now vultures gripe your guts, player!" Lucy clapped hand to sword dramatically. "This'll make you skip like any rat!" When I stiffened he laughed loudly. "What? A tiger wrapped in a player's hide – or merely a kitten crying mew?"

Will Sly drew me away with a hasty hand. "Make nothing of it, lad – bluster must serve him for wit. He lives but for his porridge and fat bull-beef. But never before have I seen you foam up so, like sour beer, at any man. Is this my honest lad, my free and open nature – " He broke off abruptly, eyes wide at the blood upon his fingers.

"They set upon us in Cold Harbour. I left them stiff."

"How many? All? Dead? Why, you hell-kite, you!"

"There were three – Frizer lived, I think. Man, they made love to that employment! They're not near my conscience."

He shook his head. "Until tonight I'd have thought you incapable of taking offence at any man – nothing deeper in you than a smooth and ready wit. But yonder fat fool may yet breed you unnatural troubles."

"Just keep him from me," I said. "My blood is up."

But Lucy stopped me at the door, still not plumbing my mood.

"Hold, puppy! When a man mouths me as you have done, why, I'll fight with him until my eyelids no longer wag!"

Then he winked broadly at the company, waiting for me to turn away as is my wont. But suddenly I found myself with my rapier in hand, and saw, through the red mists, Lucy's mouth working like a netted luce's.

"Softly, master player!" He backed off rapidly. "I only jested. Er – I hold it fit that we should shake hands and part. You as your desires point you and me – why, I'll go pray."

I saw that he would pass it off as a joke, so I thrust away my sword and ignored his hand to stride from the place with Will Sly behind.

"Why so hot to-night, lad? The rightly great stir only with great argument. When honour's at stake find a quarrel in a straw – "

"Before my eyes they killed her!" I burst out. "Killed Anne!"

"No!" His homely face crinkled in honest sympathy; he turned away. "And you had begun to feel something more for her than pity?"

"I know not, but she and Kit cannot lie unavenged. What is a man if all he does is feed and sleep?"

"A beast, nothing more. And yet, lad, two carrion men crying for burial also shout to me of vengeance taken."

"But Walsingham – "

"Leave him to heaven. Look: he said no murder had he done. Are you God, to judge him false? They might have struck for private reasons, or for hire other than his. Can you be sure they didn't?"

We were at the verge of the river. I could smell the mud and osiers. Across the broad reach of gliding water a few firefly lanterns winked on the London side, for the mist had lifted; from downstream came the creak and grumble of the old bridge in the flood-tide.

*Could* I be sure of Walsingham's guilt? If killing is once started, where did it end?

The calm gliding river had begun to calm my own troubled spirit. My nature was not bloody, my trade was not revenge. Kit had died as he had lived, in violence; but his death, perhaps, had shown me the way to even greater things than he had done: plumb man's nature to its depths, transfigure with creative light the pain and sorrow and suffering of the human spirit – yes! White hairs to a quiet grave mean not always failure, nor does a life thrown away upon a gesture mean success. Perhaps in all of this my mettle had been hardened.

Perhaps . . .

Will Sly spoke as if divining my thoughts: "Forget these sad and bloody hours, lad; the night is long indeed which never finds a day. In these bones of mine I know the world yet shall hear of you. Don't toss your life away upon revenge, as the tapster tosses off his pot of ale, for one day the mass of men will come to honour and revere your name – the name of William Shakespeare."

# PART III
# Regency and Gaslight

# THE CHRISTMAS MASQUE
## S. S. Rafferty

*S. S. Rafferty is the pen name of former reporter and advertising executive, Jack J. Hurley (b. 1930). He has been the author of scores of short stories in the mystery magazines but has only published one book,* Fatal Flourishes *(1979), which features the adventures of Captain Cork in colonial America.*

*The series started in 1974, in the years leading up to the American bicentennial celebrations, when Rafferty determined to write a detective mystery set in each of the original thirteen states. As continuity between these stories he used businessman Captain Cork, who delights in "social puzzles", and who is accompanied everywhere by his associate, Oaks, who serves as his Watson in recording his cases. The series spans forty years from the earliest case, "The Rhode Island Lights", to the grand finale, "The Pennsylvania Thimblerig", set at the outset of the War of Independence. The following tantalizing crime is set in the year 1754.*

As much as I prefer the steady ways of New England, I have to agree with Captain Jeremy Cork that the Puritans certainly know how to avoid a good time. They just ignore it. That's why every 23rd of December we come to the New York colony from our home base in Connecticut to celebrate the midwinter holidays.

I am often critical of my employer's inattention to his many business enterprises and his preoccupation with the solution of crime – but I give him credit for the way he keeps Christmas. That is, as long as I can stop him from keeping it clear into February.

In our travels about these colonies, I have witnessed many merry parties, from the lush gentility of the Carolinas to the roughshod ribaldry of the New Hampshire tree line; but nothing can match the excitement of the Port of New York. The place teems with prosperous men who ply their fortunes in furs, potash, naval timber, and other prime goods. And the populace is drawn from every-where: Sephardim from Brazil, Huguenots from France, visitors from

London, expatriates from Naples, Irishmen running to or from something. I once counted 18 different languages being spoken here.

And so it was in the Christmas week of 1754 that we took our usual rooms at Marshall's in John Street, a few steps from the Histrionic Academy, and let the yuletide roll over us. Cork's celebrity opens many doors to us, and there was the expected flood of invitations for one frivolity after another.

I was seated at a small work table in our rooms on December 23, attempting to arrange our social obligations into a reasonable program. My primary task was to sort out those invitations which begged our presence on Christmas Eve itself, for that would be our highpoint. Little did I realize that a knock on our door would not only decide the issue, but plunge us into one of the most bizarre of those damnable social puzzles Cork so thoroughly enjoys.

The messenger was a small lad, no more than seven or eight, and he was bundled against the elements from head to toe. Before I could open the envelope to see if an immediate reply was required, the child was gone.

I was opening the message when Cork walked in from the inner bedchamber. Marshall's is one of the few places on earth with doorways high enough to accommodate his six-foot-six frame.

"I take the liberty," I said. "It's addressed to us both."

"On fine French linen paper, I see."

"Well, well," I said, reading the fine handscript. "This is quite an honour."

"From the quality of the paper and the fact that you are 'honoured' just to read the message, I assume the reader is rich, money being the primer for your respect, Oaks."

That is not absolutely true. I find nothing wrong with poverty; however, it is a condition I do not wish to experience. In fact, as Cork's financial yeoman, it is my sworn duty to keep it from our door sill. The invitation was from none other than Dame Ilsa van Schooner, asking us to take part in her famous Christmas Eve Masque at her great house on the Broad Way. Considering that we had already been invited to such questionable activities as a cockfight, a party at a doss house, a drinking duel at Cosgrove's, and an evening of sport at the Gentlemen's Club, I was indeed honoured to hear from a leader of New York quality.

Cork was glancing at the invitation when I discovered a smaller piece of paper still in the envelope.

"This is odd," I said, reading it:

van Schooner Haus
22 December

Dear Sirs:

I implore you to accept the enclosed, for I need you very much to investigate a situation of some calamity for us. I shall make myself known at the Masque.

It was unsigned. I passed it to the Captain, who studied it for a moment and then picked up the invitation again.

"I'm afraid your being honoured is misplaced, my old son," he said. "The invitation was written by a skilled hand, possibly an Ephrata penman, hired for such work. But our names have been fitted in by a less skilled writer. The author of the note has by some means invited us without the hostess' knowledge. Our *sub rosa* bidder must be in some dire difficulty, for she does not dare risk discovery by signing her name."

"Her?"

"No doubt about it. The hand is feminine and written in haste. I thought it odd that a mere boy should deliver this. It is usually the task of a footman, who would wait for a reply. This is truly intriguing – an impending calamity stalking the wealthy home in which she lives."

"How can you be sure of that, sir?"

"I can only surmise. She had access to the invitations and she says 'calamity for us,' which implies her family. Hello." He looked up suddenly as the door opened and a serving girl entered with a tray, followed by a man in royal red. "Sweet Jerusalem!" Cork got to his feet. "Major Tell in the flesh! Sally, my girl, you had better have Marshall send up extra Apple Knock and oysters. Tell, it is prophetic that you should appear just as a new puzzle emerges."

Prophetic indeed. Major Philip Tell is a King's agent-at-large, and he invariably embroiled us in some case of skulduggery whenever he was in our purlieu. But I bode him no ill this time, for he had nothing to do with the affair. In fact, his vast knowledge of the colonial scene might prove helpful.

"Well, lads," Tell said, taking off his *rogueloure* and tossing his heavy cloak onto a chair. "I knew Christmas would bring you to New York. You look fit, Captain, and I see Oaks is still at his account books."

When Cork told him of our invitation and the curious accompanying note, the officer gave a low whistle. "The van Schooners, no less! Well, we shall share the festivities, for I am also a guest at the affair. The note is a little disturbing, however. Dame Ilsa is the mistress of a large fortune and extensive land holdings, which could be the spark for foul play."

"You think she sent the note?" I asked.

"Nonsense," Cork interjected. "She would not have had to purloin her own invitation. What can you tell us of the household, Major?"

I don't know if Tell's fund of knowledge is part of his duties or his general nosiness, but he certainly keeps his ear to the ground. No gossip-monger could hold a candle to him.

"The family fortune was founded by her grandfather, Nils van der Malin – patroon holdings up the Hudson, pearl potash, naval stores, that sort of old money. Under Charles the Second's Duke of York grant, Nils was rewarded for his support with a baronetcy. The title fell in the distaff side to Dame Ilsa's mother, old Gretchen van der Malin. She was a terror of a woman, who wore men's riding clothes and ran her estates with an iron first and a riding crop. She had a young man of the Orange peerage brought over as consort, and they produced Ilsa. The current Dame is more genteel than her mother was, but just as stern and autocratic. She, in turn, married a van Schooner – Gustave, I believe, a soldier of some distinction in the Lowland campaigns. He died of drink after fathering two daughters, Gretchen and her younger sister, Wilda."

"The line is certainly Amazonite and breeds true," Cork said with a chuckle. "Not a climate I would relish, although strong women have their fascination."

"Breeds true is correct, Captain. The husbands were little more than sire stallions; good blood but ruined by idleness."

This last, about being "ruined by idleness," was ignored by Cork, but I marked it, as well he knew.

"Young Gretchen," Tell went on, "is also true to her namesake. A beauty, but cold as a steel blade, and as well honed. They say she is a dead shot and an adept horsewoman."

"You have obviously been to the van Schooner haus, as our correspondent calls it."

"Oh, yes, on several occasions. It is truly a place to behold."

"No doubt, Major." Cork poured a glass of Apple Knock. "Who else lives there besides the servants?"

"The younger daughter Wilda, of course, and the Dame's spinster sister, Hetta van der Malin, and an ancient older brother of the dead husband – the brother is named Kaarl. I have only seen him once, but I am told he was quite the wastrel in his day, and suffers from the afflictions of such a life."

"Mmm," Cork murmured, offering the glass to Tell. "I change my original Amazonite observation to that of Queen Bee. Well, someone in that house feels in need of help, but we shall have to wait until to-morrow night to find out why."

"Or who," I said.

"That," Cork said, "is the heart of the mystery."

The snow started falling soon after dinner that night and kept falling into the dawn. By noon of the 24th, the wind had drifted nature's white blanket into knee-high banks. When it finally stopped in the late afternoon, New York was well covered under a blotchy sky. The inclemency, however, did not deter attendance at the van Schooner Ball.

I had seen the van Schooner home from the road many times, and always marveled at its striking architecture, which is in the Palladio style. The main section is a three-storey structure, and it is flanked by one-storey wings at both sides.

The lights and music emanating from the north wing clearly marked it a ballroom of immense size. The front entrance to the main house had a large raised enclosure which people in these parts call a stoop. The interior was as rich and well appointed as any manse I have ever seen. The main hall was a gallery of statuary of the Greek and Roman cast, collected, I assumed, when the family took the mandatory Grand Tour.

Our outer clothes were taken at the main door, and we were escorted through a sculptured archway across a large salon towards the ballroom proper. We had purposely come late to avoid the reception line and any possible discovery by Dame van Schooner. We need not have bothered. There were more than 200 people there, making individual acquaintance impossible. Not that some of the guests were without celebrity. The Royal Governor was in attendance, and I saw General Seaton and Solomon deSilva, the fur king, talking with Reeves, the shipping giant.

It was difficult to determine the identity of the majority of the people, for most wore masks, although not all, including Cork and myself. Tell fluttered off on his social duties, and Cork fell to conversation with a man named Downs, who had recently returned from Spanish America and shared common friends there with the Captain.

I helped myself to some hot punch and leaned back to take in the spectacle. It would be hard to say whether the men or the women were the more lushly bedizened. The males were adorned in the latest fashion with those large, and, to my mind, cumbersome rolled coat cuffs. The materials of their plumage were a dazzling mixture of gold and silver stuffs, bold brocades, and gaudy flowered velvets. The women, not to be outdone by their peacocks, were visions in fan-hooped gowns of silks and satins and fine damask. Each woman's *tête-de-moutin* back curls swung gaily as her partner spun her around the dance floor to madcap tunes such as "Roger de Coverly," played with spirit by a seven-piece ensemble. To the right of the ballroom entrance was a long table with three different punch bowls dispensing cheer.

The table was laden with all manner of great hams, glistening roast goose, assorted tidbit meats and sweets of unimaginable variety. Frothy syllabub was cupped up for the ladies by liveried footmen, while the gentlemen had their choice of Madeira, rum, champagne, or Holland gin, the last served in small crystal thimbles which were embedded and cooled in a silver bowl mounded with snow.

"This is most lavish," I said to Cork when he disengaged himself from conversation with Downs. "It's a good example of what diligent attention to industry can produce."

"Whose industry, Oaks? Wealth has nothing more to do with industry than privilege has with merit. Our hostess over there does not appear to have ever perspired in her life."

He was true to the mark in his observation, for Dame van Schooner, who stood chatting with the Governor near the buffet, was indeed as cold as fine-cut crystal. Her well-formed face was sternly beautiful, almost arrogantly defying anyone to marvel at its handsomeness and still maintain normal breathing.

"She *is* a fine figure of a woman, Captain, and, I might add, a widow."

He gave me a bored look and said, "A man would die of frostbite in her bedchamber. Ah, Major Tell, congratulations! You are a master at the jig!"

"It's a fantastical do, but good for the liver, I'm told. Has the mysterious sender of your invitation made herself known to you?"

"Not as yet. Is that young lady now talking with the Dame one of her daughters?"

"Both of them are daughters. The one lifting her mask is Gretchen, and, I might add, the catch of the year. I am told she has been elected Queen of the Bal, and will be crowned this evening."

The girl was the image of her mother. Her sister, however, must have followed the paternal line.

"The younger one is Wilda," Tell went on, "a dark pigeon in her own right, but Gretchen is the catch."

"Catch, you say." I winked at Cork. "Perhaps *her* bedchamber would be warmer?"

"You'll find no purchase there, gentlemen," Tell told us. "Along with being crowned Queen, her betrothal to Brock van Loon will probably be announced this evening."

"Hand-picked by her mother, no doubt?" Cork asked.

"Everything is hand-picked by the Dame. Van Loon is a stout fellow, although a bit of a tailor's dummy. Family is well landed across the river in Brueckelen. Say, they're playing "The Green Cockade," Captain. Let me introduce you to Miss Borden, one of our finest steppers."

I watched them walk over to a comely piece of frippery and then Cork and the young lady stepped onto the dance floor. "The Green Cockade" is one of Cork's favourite tunes, and he dances it with gusto.

I drifted over to the serving table and took another cup of punch, watching all the time for some sign from our mysterious "hostess," whoever she was. I mused that the calamity mentioned in the note might well have been pure hyperbole, for I could not see how any misfortune could befall this wealthy, joyous home.

With Cork off on the dance floor, Tell returned to my side and offered to find a dance partner for me. I declined, not being the most nimble of men, but did accept his bid to introduce me to a lovely young woman named Lydia Daws-Smith. The surname declared her to be the offspring of a very prominent family in the fur trade, and her breeding showed through a delightfully pretty face and pert figure. We were discussing the weather when I noticed four footmen carrying what appeared to be a closed sedan chair into the hall and through a door at the rear.

"My word, is a Sultan among the assemblage?" I asked my companion.

"The sedan chair?" She giggled from behind her fan. "No, Mr. Oaks, no Sultan. It's our Queen's throne. Gretchen will be transported into the hall at the stroke of midnight, and the Governor will proclaim her our New Year's Sovereign." She stopped for a moment, the smile gone. "Then she will step forward to our acclaim and, of course, mandatory idolatry."

"I take it you do not like Gretchen very much, Miss Daws-Smith."

"On the contrary, sir. She is one of my best friends. Now you will have to excuse me, for I see Gretchen is getting ready for the crowning, and I must help her."

I watched the young girl as she followed Gretchen to the rear of the hall where they entered a portal and closed the door behind them. Seconds later, Lydia Daws-Smith came back into the main hall and spoke with the Dame, who then went through the rear door.

Cork had finished his dance and rejoined me. "This exercise may be good for the liver," he said, "but it plays hell with my thirst. Shall we get some refills?"

We walked back to the buffet table to slake his thirst, if that were ever possible. From the corner of my eye I caught sight of the Dame re-entering the hall from the rear door. She crossed over to the Governor and was about to speak to him when the orchestra struck up another tune. She seemed angry at the intrusion into what was obviously to have been the beginning of the coronation. But the Dame was ladylike and self-contained until the dancing was over. She then took a deep breath and nervously adjusted the neckline of her dress, which was shamefully bare from the bodice to the neck.

"Looks like the coronation is about to begin," Major Tell said, coming up to us. "I'll need a cup for the toast."

We were joking at the far end of the table when a tremendous crash sounded. We turned to see a distraught Wilda van Schooner looking down at the punch bowl she had just dropped. The punch had splashed down her beautiful velvet dress, leaving her drenched and mortified.

"Oh-oh," Tell said under his breath. "Now we'll hear some fireworks from Dame van Schooner."

True to his prediction, the Dame sailed across the floor and gave biting instructions to the footmen to bring mops and pails. A woman, who Tell told me in a whisper was Hetta van der Malin, the Dame's sister, came out of the crowd of tittering guests to cover her niece's embarrassment.

"She was only trying to help, Ilsa," the aunt said as she dabbed the girl's dress with a handkerchief.

The Dame glared at them. "You'd better help her change, Hetta, if she is going to attend the coronation."

The aunt and niece quickly left the ballroom and the Dame whirled her skirts and returned to the Governor's side. I overheard her say her apologies to him and then she added, "My children don't seem to know what servants are for. Well, shall we begin?"

At a wave of her hand, the orchestra struck up the "Grenadier's March," and six young stalwarts lined up in two ranks before the Governor. At his command, the lads did a left turn and marched off towards the rear portal in the distinctive long step of the regiment whose music they had borrowed for the occasion.

They disappeared into the room where Gretchen waited for transport, and within seconds they returned, bearing the ornate screened sedan chair. "Aah's" filled the room over the beauty and pageantry of the piece. I shot a glance at Dame van Schooner and noted that she was beaming proudly at the impeccably executed production.

When the sedan chair had been placed before the Governor, he stepped forward, took the curtain drawstrings, and said, "Ladies and gentlemen, I give you our New Year's Queen."

The curtains were pulled open and there she sat in majesty. More "aah's" from the ladies until there was a screech and then another and, suddenly, pandemonium. Gretchen van Schooner sat on her portable throne, still beautiful, but horribly dead with a French bayonet through her chest.

"My Lord!" Major Tell gasped and started forward toward the sedan chair. Cork touched his arm.

"You can do no good there. The rear room, man, that's where the answer lies. Come, Oaks." He moved quickly through the crowd and I followed like a setter's tail on point. When we reached the door, Cork turned to Tell.

"Major, use your authority to guard this door. Let no one enter." He motioned me inside and closed the door behind us.

It was a small room, furnished in a masculine manner. Game trophies and the heads of local beasts protruded from the walls and were surrounded by a symmetrical display of weaponry such as daggers, blunderbusses, and swords.

"Our killer had not far to look for his instrument of death," Cork said, pointing to an empty spot on the wall about three feet from the fireplace and six feet up from the floor. "Move with care, Oaks, lest we disturb some piece of evidence."

I quickly looked around the rest of the chamber. There was a door in the south wall and a small window some ten feet to the left of it.

"The window!" I cried. "The killer must have come in – "

"I'm afraid not, Oaks," Cork said, after examining it. "The snow on the sill and panes is undisturbed. Besides, the floor in here is dry. Come, let's open the other door."

He drew it open to reveal a short narrow passage that was dimly lit with one sconced candle and had another door at its end. I started toward it and found my way blocked by Cork's outthrust arm.

"Have a care, Oaks," he said. "Don't confound a trail with your own spore. Fetch a candelabrum from the table for more light."

I did so, and to my amazement he got down on his hands and knees and inched forward along the passageway. I, too, assumed this stance and we crept along like a brace of hounds.

The polished planked floor proved dry and bare of dust until we were in front of the outer door. There, just inside the portal, was a pool of liquid.

"My Lord, it is blood!" I said.

"Mostly water from melted snow."

"But, Captain, there is a red stain to it."

"Yes," he said. "Bloody snow and yet the bayonet in that woman's breast was driven with such force that no blood escaped from her body."

Cork got to his feet and lifted the door latch, opening the passageway to pale white moonlight which reflected off the granules of snow. He carefully looked at the doorstoop and then out into the yard.

"Damnation," he muttered, "it looks as if an army tramped through here."

Before us, the snow was a mass of furrows and upheavals with no one set of footprints discernible.

"Probably the servants coming and going from the wood yard down by the gate," I said, as we stepped out into the cold. At the opposite end of the house, in the left wing, was another door, obviously leading to the kitchen, for a clatter of plates and pots could be heard within the snug and frosty windowpanes. I turned to Cork and found myself alone. He was at the end of the yard opening a slatted gate in the rear garden wall.

"What ho, Captain," I called ahead, as I went to meet him.

"The place abounds in footprints," he snarled in frustration.

"Then the killer has escaped us," I muttered. "Now we have the whole population of this teeming port to consider."

He turned slowly, the moonlight glistening off his barba, his eyes taking on a sardonic glint. "For the moment, Oaks, for the moment. Besides, footprints are like empty boots. In the long run we would have had to fill them."

I started to answer when a voice called from our backs, at the passage doorway. It was Major Tell.

"Hello, is that you there, Cork? Have you caught the dastard?"

"Some gall," I said to the Captain. "As if we could pull the murderer out of our sleeves like a magician."

"Not yet, Major," Cork shouted and then turned to me. "Your powers of simile are improving, Oaks."

"Well," I said, with a bit of a splutter. "Do you think magic is involved?"

"No, you ass. Sleight of hand! The quick flick that the eye does not see nor the mind inscribe. We'll have to use our instincts on this one."

He strode off towards the house and I followed. I have seen him rely on instinct over hard evidence only two times in our years together, and in both cases, although he was successful, the things he uncovered were too gruesome to imagine.

The shock that had descended on the van Schooner manse at midnight still lingered three hours later when the fires in the great fireplaces were reduced to embers, the shocked guests had been questioned, and all but the key witnesses had been sent homeward. Cork, after consultation with the Royal Governor, had been given a free hand in the investigation, with Major Tell stirred in to keep the manner of things official.

Much to my surprise, the Captain didn't embark on a flurry of questions of all concerned, but rather drew up a large baronial chair to the ballroom hearth and brooded into its sinking glow.

"Two squads of cavalry are in the neighbourhood," Major Tell said. "If any stranger were in the vicinity, he must have been seen."

"You can discount a stranger, Major," Cork said, still gazing into the embers.

"How so?"

"Merely a surmise, but with stout legs to it. If a stranger came to kill, he would have brought a weapon with him. No, the murderer knew the contents of the den's walls. He also seems to have known the coronation schedule."

"The window," I interjected. "He could have spied the bayonet, and when the coast was clear, entered and struck."

"Except for the singular fact that the snow on the ground in front of the window is undisturbed."

"Well, obviously someone entered by the back passage," Tell said. "We have the pool of water and the blood."

"Then where are the wet footprints into the den, Major?"

"Boots!" I shouted louder than I meant to. "He took off his boots and then donned them again on leaving."

"Good thinking, Oaks," Tell complimented me. "And in the process, his bloody hands left a trace in the puddle."

"And what, pray, was the motive?" Cork asked. "Nothing of value was taken that we can determine. No, we will look within this house for an answer."

Tell was appalled. "Captain Cork, I must remind you that this is the home of a powerful woman, and she was hostess to-night to the cream of New York society. Have a care how you cast aspersions."

"The killer had best have a care, Major. For a moment, let us consider some *facts*. Mistress Gretchen went into the den to prepare for her coronation with the aid of – ah – "

"Lydia Daws-Smith," I supplied.

"So we have one person who saw her before she died. Then these six society bucks who were to transport her entered, and among their company was Brock van Loon, her affianced. Seven people involved between the time we all saw her enter the den and the time she was carried out dead."

"Eight," I said, and then could have bit my tongue.

"Who else?" Cork demanded.

"The Dame herself. I saw her enter after Miss Daws-Smith came out."

"That is highly irresponsible, Oaks," Tell admonished.

"And interesting," Cork said. "Thank you, Oaks, you have put some yeast into it with your observation."

"You're not suggesting that the Dame killed her own daughter!"

"Major," Cork said, "she-animals have been known to eat their young when they are endangered. But enough of this conjecture. Let us get down to rocks and hard places. We will have to take it step by step. First, let us have a go at the footmen who carried the chair into the den before Gretchen entered."

They were summoned, and the senior man, a portly fellow named Trask, spoke for the lot.

"No, sir," he answered Cork's question. "I am sure no one was lurking in the room when we entered. There is no place to hide."

"And the passage to the back door?"

"Empty, sir. You see, the door leading to the passage was open and I went over to close it against any draughts coming into the den. There was no one in the den, sir, I can swear to it."

"Is the outside door normally kept locked?"

"Oh, yes, sir. Leastways, it's supposed to be. It was locked earlier this afternoon when I made my rounds, preparing for the festivities."

"Tell me, Trask," Cork asked, "do you consider yourself a good servant, loyal to your mistress' household?"

The man's chubby face looked almost silly with its beaming pride. "Twenty-two years in this house, sir, from kitchen boy to head footman, and every day of it in the Dame's service."

"Very commendable, Trask, but you are most extravagant with tapers."

"Sir?" Trask looked surprised.

"If the backyard door was locked, why did you leave a candle burning in the passageway? Since no one could come in from the outside, no light would be needed as a guide. Certainly anyone entering from the den would carry his own."

"But, Captain," the footman protested, "I left no light in the passageway. When I was closing the inner door, I held a candela-brum in my hand, and could see clear to the other end. There was no candle lit."

"My apologies, Trask. Thank you, that will be all."

When the footmen had left, I said, "Yet we found a lit candle out there right after the murder. The killer must have left it in his haste."

Cork merely shrugged. Then he said, "So we go a little further. Major, I would like to see Miss Daws-Smith next."

Despite the circumstances, I was looking forward to seeing the comely Miss Daws-Smith once more. However, she was not alone when she entered, and her escort made it clear by his protective manner that her beauty was his property alone. She sat down in a straight-backed chair opposite Cork, nervously fingering the fan in her lap. Brock van Loon took a stance behind her.

"I prefer to speak to this young lady alone," Cork said.

"I am aware of your reputation, Captain Cork," van Loon said defensively, "and I do not intend to have Lydia drawn into this."

"Young man, she *is* in it, and from your obvious concern for her, I'd say you are, too."

"It is more than concern, sir. I love Lydia and she loves me."

"Brock," the girl said, turning to him.

"I don't care, Lydia. I don't care what my father says and I don't care what the Dame thinks."

"That's a rather anti-climactic statement, young man. Since your betrothed is dead, you are free of that commitment."

"You see, Brock? Now he suspects that we had something to do with Gretchen's death. I swear, Captain, we had no hand in it."

"Possibly not as cohorts. Was Gretchen in love with this fellow?"

"No. I doubt Gretchen could love any man. She was like her mother, and was doing her bidding as far as a marriage went. The van Schooner women devour males. Brock knows what would have become of him. He saw what happened to Gretchen's father."

"Gustave van Schooner," Brock said, "died a worthless drunkard locked away on one of the family estates up the Hudson. He had been a valiant soldier, I am told, and yet, once married to the Dame, he was reduced to a captured stallion."

"Quite poetic," Cork said. "Now, my dear, can you tell me what happened when you and Gretchen entered the den this evening?"

The girl stopped toying with the fan and sent her left hand to her shoulder where Brock had placed his. "There's nothing to tell, really. We went into the den together and I asked her if she wanted a cup of syllabub. She said no."

"What was her demeanour? Was she excited?"

"About being the Queen? Mercy, no. She saw that as her due. Gretchen was not one to show emotion." She stopped suddenly in thought and then said, "But now that I think back, she was fidgety. She walked over to the fireplace and tapped on the mantel with her fingers. Then she turned and said, 'Tell the Dame I'm ready,' which was strange, because she never called her mother that."

"Was she being sarcastic?"

"No, Captain, more a poutiness, I went and gave Dame van Schooner the message. That was the last I saw of Gretchen." Her eyes started to moisten. "The shock is just wearing off, I suppose. She was spoiled and autocratic, but Gretchen was a good friend."

"Hardly, Miss Daws-Smith. She had appropriated your lover."

"No. She knew nothing of how I felt towards Brock. We were all children together, you see – Gretchen, Wilda, Brock, and I. When you grow up that way, you don't always know childish affection from romantic love. I admit that when plans were being made for the betrothal, love for Brock burned in me, but I hid it, Captain, I hid it well. Then, earlier this evening, Brock told me how he felt, and I was both elated and miserable. I decided that both Brock and I would go to the Dame tomorrow. Gretchen knew nothing of our love."

"And you, sir," Cork said to Brock, "you made no mention of your change of heart to Gretchen?"

The fellow bowed his head. "Not in so many words. This has been coming on me for weeks, this feeling I have for Lydia. Just now as you were talking to her, I wondered – God, how terrible! – if Gretchen could have committed suicide out of despair."

"Oh, Brock!" Lydia was aghast at his words.

"Come," Cork commanded sharply, "this affair is burdensome enough without the added baggage of melodrama. Use your obvious good sense, Miss Daws-Smith. Is it likely that this spoiled and haughty woman would take her own life? Over a man?"

Lydia raised her head and looked straight at Cork. "No. No, of course not. It's ridiculous."

"Now, Mr. van Loon, when you entered the den with the others in the escort party to bring in the sedan chair, were the curtains pulled shut?"

"Yes, they were."

"And no one spoke to its occupant?"

"No, we didn't."

"Strange, isn't it? Such a festive occasion, and yet no one spoke?"

"We were in a hurry to get her out to where the Governor was waiting. Wait, someone did say, 'Hang on, Gretchen' when we lifted the chair. I don't remember who said it, though."

"You heard no sound from inside the chair? No groan or murmur?"

"No, sir, not a sound."

"Well thank you for your candour. Oh, yes, Miss Daws-Smith, when you left Gretchen, was she still standing by the fire?"

"Yes, Captain."

"Was her mask on or off?"

She frowned. "Why, she had it on. What a queer question!"

"It's a queer case, young lady."

The great clock in the center hall had just tolled three when Cork finished talking with the other five young men who had carried the murdered girl in the sedan chair. They all corroborated Brock's version. All were ignorant of any expression of love between Brock and Lydia, and they were unanimous in their relief that Brock, and not one of them, had been Gretchen's intended. As one young man named Langley put it, "At least Brock has an inheritance of his own, and would not have been dependent on his wife and mother-in-law."

"Dependent?" Cork queried. "Would he not assume her estate under law?"

"No, sir, not in this house," Langley explained. "I am told it's a kind of morganatic arrangement and a tradition with the old van der Malin line. I have little income, so Gretchen would have been no bargain for me. Not that I am up to the Dame's standards."

When Langley had left, Trask the footman entered to tell us that rooms had been prepared for us at the Major's request. Cork thanked him and said, "I know the hour is late, but is your mistress available?"

He told us he would see, and showed us to a small sitting-room off the main upstairs hall. It was a tight and cosy chamber with a newly-stirred hearth and the accoutrements of womankind – a small velvet couch with tiny pillows, a secretaire in the corner, buckbaskets of knitting and mending.

Unusual, however, was the portrait of the Dame herself that hung on a wall over the secretaire. It was certainly not the work of a local limner, for the controlled hand of a master painter showed through. Each line was carefully laid down, each colour blended one with the other, to produce a perfect likeness of the Dame. She was dressed in a gown almost as beautiful as the one she had worn this evening. At her throat was a remarkable diamond necklace which, despite the two dimensions of the portrait, was lifelike in its cool, blue-white lustre.

Cork was drawn to the portrait and even lifted a candle to study it more closely. I joined him and was about to tell him to be careful of the flame when a voice from behind startled me.

"There are additional candles if you need more light."

We both turned to find Wilda van Schooner standing in the doorway. She looked twice her seventeen years with the obvious woe she carried inside her. Her puffed eyes betrayed the tears of grief that had recently welled there.

"Forgive my curiosity, Miss van Schooner," Cork said, turning back to the portrait. "Inquisitiveness and a passion for details are my afflictions. This work was done in Europe, of course?"

"No, sir, here in New York; although Jan der Trogue is from the continent. He is – was – to have painted all of us eventually." She broke off into thought and then rejoined us. "My mother is with my sister, gentlemen, and is not available. She insists on seeing to Gretchen herself."

"That is most admirable." Cork bid her to seat herself, and she did so. She did not have her sister's or her mother's colouring, nor their chiselled beauty, but there was something strangely attractive about this tall dark-haired girl.

"I understand, Captain, that you are here to help us discover the fiend who did this thing, but you will have to bear with my mother's grief."

"To be sure. And what can you tell me, Miss Wilda?"

"I wish I could offer some clew, but my sister and I were not close – we did not exchange confidences."

"Was she in love with Brock van Loon?"

"Love!" she cried, and then did a strange thing. She giggled almost uncontrollably for a few seconds. "That's no word to use in this house, Captain."

"Wilda, my dear," a female voice said from the open door. "I think you are too upset to make much sense to-night. Perhaps in the morning, gentlemen?"

The speaker was the girls' aunt, Hetta van der Malin, and we rose as she entered.

"Forgive our intrusion into your sitting room, Ma'am," Cork said with a bow. "Perhaps you are right. Miss Wilda looks exhausted."

"I agree, Captain Cork," the aunt said, and she put her arm around the girl and ushered her out the door.

"Pray," Cork interrupted, "could *you* spare us some time in your niece's stead?"

Her smile went faint, but it was a smile all the same. "How did you know this was *my* room, Captain? Oh, of course, Trask must have – "

"On the contrary, my eyes told me. Your older sister does not fit the image of a woman surrounded by knitting and mending and pert pillowcases."

"No, she doesn't. The den is Ilsa's sitting room. Our mother raised her that way. She is quite a capable person, you know."

"So it would seem. Miss Hetta, may I ask why you invited us here this evening?"

I was as caught off guard as she was.

"Whatever put that notion into your head? My sister dispatched the invitations herself."

"Precisely! That's why you had to purloin one and fill in our names yourself. Come, dear woman, the sample of your hand on the letters on your secretaire matches the hand that penned the unsigned note I received."

"You have looked through my things!"

"I snoop when forced to. Pretence will fail you, Ma'am, for the young lad who delivered this invitation will undoubtedly be found and will identify you. Come now, you wrote to invite me here and now you deny it. I will have an answer."

"Captain Cork," I cautioned him, for the woman was quivering.

"Yes, I sent it." Her voice was tiny and hollow. "But it had nothing to do with this horrible murder. It was trivial compared to it, and it is senseless to bring it up now. Please believe me, Captain. It was foolish of me."

"You said 'calamity' in your note, and now we have a murder done. Is that not the extreme of calamity?"

"Yes, of course it is. I used too strong a word in my note. I would gladly have told you about it after the coronation. But now it would just muddle things. I can't."

"Then, my dear woman, I must dig it out. Must I play the ferret while you play the mute?" His voice was getting sterner. I know how good an actor he is, but was he acting?

"Do you know what a colligation is, Madam?"

She shook her head.

"It is the orderly bringing together of isolated facts. Yet you blunt my efforts; half facts can lead to half truths. Do you want a half truth?" He paused and then spat it out. "Your sister may have killed her older daughter!"

"That is unbearable!" she cried.

"A surmise based on a half truth. She was the last person to see Gretchen alive, if the Daws-Smith girl is to be believed. And why not believe her? If Lydia had killed Gretchen, would she then send the mother into the room to her corpse? Take the honour guard who were to carry the sedan chair: if Gretchen were alive when her mother left her, could one of those young men have killed her in the presence of five witnesses?"

"Anyone could have come in from the outside." Miss Hetta's voice was frantic.

"Nonsense. The evidence is against it."

"Why would Ilsa want to kill her own flesh and blood? It is unthinkable!"

"And yet people will think it, rest assured. The whole ugly affair can be whitewashed and pinned to some mysterious assailant who stalked in the night season, but people will think it just the same, Madam."

She remained silent now, and I could feel Cork's mind turn from one tactic to another, searching for leverage. He got to his feet and walked over to the portrait.

"So in the face of silence, I must turn the ferret loose in my mind. Take, for example, the question of this necklace."

"The van der Malin Chain," she said, looking up at the portrait. "What about it?"

"If the painter was accurate, it seems of great worth, both in pounds sterling and family prestige. Its very name proclaims it an heirloom."

"It is. It has been in our family for generations."

"Do you wear it at times?"

"No, of course not. It is my sister's property."

"Your estates are not commingled?"

"Our family holds with primogeniture."

"I do not. Exclusive rights to a first born make a fetish of nature's caprice. But that is philosophy, and beyond a ferret. Where is the necklace, Madam?"

"Why, in my sister's strong box, I assume. This is most confusing, Captain Cork."

I could have added my vote to that. I have seen Cork search for answers with hopscratch questions, but this display seemed futile.

"It is I who am confused, Madam. I am muddled by many things in this case. Why, for instance, didn't your sister wear this necklace to the year's most important social function? She thought enough of it to have it painted in a portrait for posterity."

"Our minds sometimes work that way, Captain. Perhaps it didn't suit her costume."

Cork turned from the picture as if he had had enough of it. "I am told there is an Uncle Kaarl in this household, yet he was not in attendance at the Bal to-night. Did he not suit the occasion?"

"You are most rude, sir. Kaarl is an ill man, confined to his bed for several years." She got to her feet. "I am very tired, gentlemen."

"I, too, grow weary, Madam. One last question. Your late niece was irritable this evening, I am told. Did something particular happen recently to cause that demeanour?"

"No. What would she have to sulk about? She was the centre of attraction. I really must retire now. Good night."

When the rustle of her skirts had faded down the silent hallway, I said, "Well, Captain, we've certainly had a turn around the mulberry bush."

He gave me that smirk-a-mouth of his. "Some day, Oaks, you will learn to read between the lines where women are concerned. I am sure you thought me a bully for mistreating her, but it was necessary, and it worked."

"Worked?"

"To a fair degree. I started on her with several assumptions. Some have more weight now, others are discounted. Don't look so perplexed. I am sure that Hetta's note to us did not concern Gretchen directly. She did not fear for the girl's life in this calamity she now chooses to keep secret."

"How is that?"

"Use your common sense, man. If she had suspected an attempt on her niece's life, would she stand mute? No, she would screech her accusations to the sky. Her seeking outside aid from us must have been for another problem. Yes, Trask?"

I hadn't seen the footman in the shadows, nor had I any idea how long he had been there.

"Beg pard, Captain Cork, but Major Tell has retired to his room and would like to see you when you have a moment."

"Thank you, Trask. Is your mistress available to us now?"

"Her maid tells me she is abed, sir."

"A shame. Maybe you can help me, Trask. My friend and I were wondering why the Dame's picture hangs in this small room. I say it was executed in such a large size to hang in a larger room. Mr. Oaks, however, says it was meant for Miss Hetta's room as an expression of love between the two sisters."

"Well, there is an affection between them, sirs, but the fact is that the portrait hung in the Grand Salon until the Dame ordered it destroyed."

"When was this, Trask?"

"Two days ago. 'Trask,' she said to me, 'take that abomination out and burn it.' Strange, she did like it originally, then, just like that, she hated it. Of course, Miss Hetta wouldn't let me burn it, so we spirited it in here, where the Dame never comes."

"Ha, you see I was right, Oaks. Thanks for settling the argument, Trask. Where is Major Tell's room?"

"Right next to yours, if you'll follow me, gentlemen."

Tell's chamber was at the back of the house where we found him sitting in the unlighted room, looking out at the moonlit yard.

"Nothing yet, Major?" Cork asked, walking to the window to join him.

"Not a sign or a shadow. I have men hiding at the front and down there near the garden gate and over to the left by the stable. Do you really expect him to make a move?"

"Conjecture costs us nothing, although I have more information now."

Although the room was bathed in moonlight, as usual I was in the dark. "Would either of you gentlemen mind telling me what this is all about? *Who* is coming?"

"Going would be more like it," the Major said.

"Going – ah, I see! The killer hid himself in the house somewhere and you expect him to make a break for it when everyone is bedded down. But where could he have hidden? Your men searched the den and passageway for secret panels, did they not?"

"Ask your employer," Tell said. "I am only following his orders – hold on, Cork, look down by the passage door."

I looked over Cork's shoulder to catch a glimpse of a cloaked figure in a cockade, moving among the shadows towards the stable.

"Our mounts are ready, Major?" Tell nodded. "Excellent. Let us be off."

As I followed them downstairs, I remarked on my own puzzlement. "Why are we going to *follow* this scoundrel? Why not stop him and unmask him?"

"Because I know who our mysterious figure is, Oaks. It is the destination that is the heart of the matter," Cork said as we hurried into the ballroom and back to the den door.

Once inside, I saw that Tell had placed our greatcoats in readiness and we bustled into them. Cork walked over to the weapon wall and looked at two empty hooks.

"A brace of pistols are gone. Our shadow is armed, as expected," he said.

"I'll take this one," I said, reaching for a ball-shot handgun.

"No need, Oaks," Cork said. "We are not the targets. Come, fellows, we want to be mounted and ready."

The night was cold as we waited behind a small knoll 20 yards down from the stable yard. Suddenly the doors of the stable burst open and a black stallion charged into the moonlight, bearing its rider to the south. "Now keep a small distance, but do not lose sight for a second," Cork commanded, and spurred his horse forward.

We followed through the drifts for ten minutes and saw our quarry turn into a small alley. When we reached the spot, we found the lathered mount tied to a stairway which went up the side of the building to a door on the second-storey landing. With Cork in the lead, we went up the cold stairs and assembled ourselves in front of the door. "Now!" Cork whispered, and we butted our shoulders against the wood panelling and fell into the room.

Our cloaked figure had a terrified man at gunpoint. The victim was a man in his forties, coiled into a corner. I was about to rush the person with the pistols when the tricornered hat turned to reveal the chiselled face and cold blue eyes of Dame Ilsa van Schooner.

"Drop the pistols, Madam, you are only compounding your problem," Cork said firmly.

"He murdered my child!"

"I swear, Dame Ilsa!" The man grovelled before her. His voice was foreign in inflection. "Please, you must hear me out. Yes, I am scum, but I am not a murderer."

Cork walked forward and put his hands over the pistol barrels. For a split second, the Dame looked up at him and her stern face went soft. "He's going to pay," she said.

"Yes, but not for your daughter's death."

"But only he could have – " She caught herself up in a flash of thought. Her lips quivered and she released the pistol butts into Cork's control. He took her by the arm and guided her to a chair.

The tension was broken, and I took my first look about. It was a large and comfortable bachelor's room. Then I saw the work area at the far end – with an easel, palettes, and paint pots.

"The painter! He's Jan der Trogue, the one who painted the portrait."

"You know about the painting?" the Dame said with surprise.

I started to tell her about seeing it in her sister's sitting-room, but never got it out. Der Trogue had grabbed the pistol that Cork had stupidly left on the table and pointed it at us as he edged towards the open door. "Stay where you are," he warned. "I owe you my life, sir." He bowed to Cork. "But it is not fitting to die at a woman's hands."

"Nor a hangman's," Cork said. "For you will surely go to the gallows for your other crime."

"Not this man, my fine fellow. Now stay where you are and no one will get hurt." He whirled out onto the landing and started to race down the stairs. Cork walked to the door. To my surprise, he had the other pistol in his hand. He stepped out onto the snowy landing.

"Defend yourself!" Cork cried. Then, after a tense moment, Cork

took careful aim and fired. I grimaced as I heard der Trogue's body
tumbling down the rest of the stairs.

Cork came back into the room with the smoking pistol in his hand.
"Be sure your report says 'fleeing arrest,' Major," he said, shutting
the door.

"Escape from what? You said he didn't kill the girl! This is most
confusing and, to say the least, irregular!"

"Precisely put, Major. Confusing from the start and irregular for
a finish. But first to the irregularity. What we say, see, and do here
to-night stays with us alone." He turned to the Dame. "We will
have to search the room. Will you help, since you have been here
before?"

"Yes." She got up and started to open drawers and cupboards.
She turned to us and held out a black felt bag which Cork opened.

"Gentlemen, I give you the van der Malin Chain, and quite
exquisite it is."

"So he did steal it," I said.

"In a manner of speaking, Oaks, yes. But, Madam, should
we not also find what you were so willing to pay a king's ransom for?"

"Perhaps it is on the easel. I only saw the miniature."

Cork took the drape from the easel and revealed a portrait of a
nude woman reposing on a couch.

"It's Gretchen!" I gasped. "Was that der Trogue's game? Blackmail?"

"Yes, Mr. Oaks, it was," the Dame said. "I knew it was not an
artist's trick of painting one head on another's body. That strawberry
mark on the thigh was Gretchen's. How did you know of its existence,
Captain? I told no one, not even my sister."

"Your actions helped tell me. You ordered your own portrait
burned two days ago, the same day your sister sent me a note and
an invitation to the Masque."

"A note?"

"Portending calamity," I added.

"Oh, the fool. She must have learned about my failure to raise
enough cash to meet that fiend's demands."

"Your sudden disdain for a fine portrait betrayed your disgust with
the artist, not with the art. Then Wilda told us that you had planned
to have your daughters painted by the same man and, considering
the time elapsed since your portrait was finished, I assumed that
Gretchen's had been started."

"It was, and he seduced her. She confessed it to me after I saw the
miniature he brought to me."

"Why did you not demand its delivery when you gave him the necklace to-night?"

"I never said I gave it to him to-night."

"But you did. You went into the den, not to see your daughter, but to meet der Trogue at the outside passage door. You lit a taper there, and he examined his booty at the entryway, and then left, probably promising to turn over that scandalous painting when he had verified that the necklace was not an imitation."

"Captain, you sound as if you were there."

The clews were. In the puddle just inside the door, there was a red substance. Oaks believed it was blood. It was a natural assumption, but when the question of your anger with a painter came to light, I considered what my eyes now confirm. Painters are sloppy fellows; look at this floor. Besides, blood is rarely magenta. It was paint, red paint from his boot soles. Then, Madam, your part of the bargain completed, you returned to the den. Your daughter was still by the fire."

"Yes."

"And you returned to the ballroom."

"Yes, leaving my soiled child to be murdered! He came back and killed her!"

"No, Dame van Schooner, he did not, although that is the way it will be recorded officially. The report will show that you entered the den and presented the van der Malin Chain to your daughter to wear on her night of triumph. My observation of the paint in the puddle will stand as the deduction that led us to der Trogue. We will say he gained entry into the house, killed your daughter, and took the necklace. And was later killed resisting capture."

"But he *did* kill her!" the Dame insisted. "He had to be the one! She was alive when I left her. No one else entered the room until the honour guard went for her."

Cork took both her hands.

"Dame van Schooner, I have twisted truth beyond reason for your sake to-night, but now you must face the hard truth. Der Trogue was a scoundrel, but he had no reason to kill Gretchen. What would he gain? And how could he get back in without leaving snow tracks? Gretchen's executioner was in the den all the time – when Lydia was there, when you were. I think in your heart you know the answer – if you have the courage to face it."

To watch her face was to see ice melt. Her eyes, her cold, diamond-blue eyes watered. "I can. But must it be said – here?"

"Yes."

"Wilda. Oh, my God, Wilda."

"Yes, Wilda. You have a great burden to bear, my dear lady."

Her tears came freely now. "The curse of the van Schooners," she cried. "Her father was insane, and his brother Kaarl lives in his lunatic's attic. My mother thought she was infusing quality by our union."

"Thus your stern exterior and addiction to purifying the blood-line with good stock."

"Yes, I have been the man in our family far too long. I have had to be hard. I thank you for your consideration, Captain. Wilda will have to be put away, of course. Poor child, I saw the van Schooner blood curse in her years ago, but I never thought it would come to this." The last was a sob. Then she took a deep breath. "I think I am needed at home." She rose. Thank you again, Captain. Will you destroy that?" She pointed to the portrait.

"Rest assured."

As he opened the door for her, she turned back with the breaking dawn framing her. "I wish it was I who had invited you to the Bal. I saw you dancing and wondered who you were. You are quite tall."

"Not too tall to bow, Madam," Cork said, and all six-foot-six of him bent down and kissed her cheek. She left us with an escort from the detachment of soldiers that had followed our trail.

The room was quiet for a moment before Major Tell exploded. "Confound it, Cork, what the deuce is this? I am to falsify records to show der Trogue was a thief and a murderer and yet you say it was Wilda who killed her sister. What's your proof, man?"

Cork walked over to the painting and smashed it on a chair back. "You deserve particulars, both of you. I said that Wilda was in the den all the time. Your natural query is how did she get there unseen? Well, we all saw her. She was carried in – in the curtained sedan chair. In her twisted mind, she hated her sister, who would inherit everything by her mother's design. One does not put a great fortune into a madwoman's hands."

"Very well," Tell said, "I can see her entry. How the deuce did she get out?"

"Incipient madness sometimes makes the mind clever, Major. She stayed in the sedan chair until her mother had left, then presented herself to Gretchen."

"And killed her," I interjected. "But she was back in the ballroom before the honour guard went in to get her sister."

"There is the nub of it, Oaks. She left the den by the back passage, crossed the yard, and re-entered the house by the kitchen in the far wing. Who would take any notice of a daughter of the house in a room filled with bustling cooks and servants coming and going with vittles for the buffet?"

"But she would have gotten her skirts wet in the snow," I started to object. "Of course! The spilled punch bowl! It drenched her!"

Cork smiled broadly. "Yes, my lad. She entered the kitchen, scooped up the punch bowl, carried it into the ballroom, and then deliberately dropped it."

"Well," Tell grumped, "she may be sprung in the mind, but she understands the theory of tactical diversion."

"Self-preservation is the last instinct to go, Major."

"Yes, I believe you are right, Cork, but how are we to explain all this and still shield the Dame's secret?"

Cork looked dead at me. "You, Oaks, have given us the answer."

"I? Oh, when I said the killer took off his boots to avoid tracks in the den? You rejected that out of hand when I mentioned it."

"I rejected it as a probability, not a possibility. Anything is possible, but not everything is probable. Is it probable that a killer bent on not leaving tracks would take off his boots *inside* the entry where they would leave a puddle? No, I couldn't accept it, but I'm sure the general public will."

The major looked disturbed. "I can appreciate your desire to protect the Dame," he said, "but to *suppress* evidence – "

"Calm yourself, Major, we are just balancing the books of human nature. I have saved the Crown the time and expense of trying and executing an extortionist. God knows how many victims he has fleeced by his artistic trickery over the years. And we have prevented the Dame from the commission of a homicide that any jury, I think, would have found justifiable. Let it stand as it is, Major, it is a neater package. The Dame has had enough tragedy in her life."

The last of his words were soft and low-toned, and I watched as he stared into the flames. By jing, could it possibly be that this gallivanting, sunburnt American had fallen in love? But I quickly dismissed the thought. We are fated to our roles, we two – he, the unbroken stallion frolicking from pasture to pasture, and I, the frantic ostler following with an empty halter, hoping some day to put the beast to work. I persist.

# MURDER LOCK'D IN
# Lillian de la Torre

*Lillian de la Torre (b. 1902) is the grande-dame of American mystery fiction. A literary scholar of some note, all of her books feature real people and events, thoroughly researched and brought to life. Her most famous re-creation has been Dr. Sam: Johnson, the renowned British lexicographer, who had a ready-made Watson in the shape of his diarist, James Boswell. Starting in 1943, Lillian de la Torre began a series of stories featuring Johnson, which has run for over forty years. If anyone is responsible for the shaping of the historical detective story, it is Miss de la Torre. Two collections of stories have been published,* Dr. Sam: Johnson, Detector *(1946) and* The Detections of Dr. Sam Johnson *(1960). The following story did not appear in either collection, and records the first meeting of the two literary greats in 1763.*

"*M*urder! Murder lock'd in!"
        With these horrifying words began my first experience of the *detective* genius of the great Dr. Sam: Johnson, him who – but let us proceed in order.

The '63 was to me a memorable year; for in it I had the happiness to obtain the acquaintance of that extraordinary man. Though then but a raw Scotch lad of two-and-twenty, I had already read the WORKS OF JOHNSON with delight and instruction, and imbibed therefrom the highest reverence for their author. Coming up to London in that year, I came with the firm resolution to win my way into his friendship.

On Monday, the 16th of May, I was sitting in the back-parlour of Tom Davies, book-seller and sometime actor, when the man I sought to meet came unexpectedly into the shop. Glimpsing him through the glass-door, Davies in sepulchral tone announced his approach as of Hamlet's ghost: "Look, my Lord, it comes!"

I scrambled to my feet as the great man entered, his tall, burly form clad in mulberry stuff of full-skirted antique cut, a large bushy greyish wig surmounting his strong-cut features of classical mould.

"I present Mr. Boswell – " began Davies. If he intended to add "from Scotland," I cut him off.

"Don't tell him where I come from!" I cried, having heard of the great man's prejudice against Scots.

"From Scotland!" cried Davies roguishly.

"Mr. Johnson," said I – for not yet had he become "Doctor" Johnson, though as such I shall always think of him – "Mr. Johnson, I do indeed come from Scotland, but I cannot help it."

"That, sir, I find," quipped Johnson with a smile, "is what a great many of your countrymen cannot help!"

This jest, I knew, was aimed at the hordes of place-seekers who "could not help coming from" Scotland to seek their fortunes in London when Scottish Lord Bute became first minister to the new King; but it put me out of countenance.

"Don't be uneasy," Davies whispered me at parting, "I can see he likes you very well!"

Thus encouraged, I made bold to wait upon the philosopher the very next Sunday, in his chambers in the Temple, where the benchers of the law hold sway. I strode along Fleet Street, clad in my best; my new bloom-coloured coat, so I flattered myself, setting off my neat form and dark, sharp-cut features. As I walked along, I savoured in anticipation this, my first encounter with the lion in his den, surrounded by his learned volumes and the tools of his trade.

But it was not yet to be, for as I turned under the arch into Inner Temple Lane, I encountered the philosopher issuing from his doorway in full Sunday panoply. His mulberry coat was well brushed, his full-bottom wig was new-powdered, he wore a clean linen neckcloth and ruffles to his wrists.

"Welcome, Mr. Boswell," said he cordially, "you are welcome to the Temple. As you see, I am just now going forth. Will you not walk along with me? I go to wait on Mistress Lennon the poetess, who dwells here in the Temple, but a step across the gardens, in Bayfield Court. Come, I will present you at her levee."

"With all my heart, sir," said I, pleased to go among the wits, and in such company.

But as it turned out, I never did present myself at the literary levee, for as we came to Bayfield Court, a knot of people buzzing about the door caught us up in their concerns.

"Well met, Mr. Johnson," called a voice, "we have need of your counsel. We have sent for the watch, but he does not come, the sluggard."

"The watch? What's amiss, ma'am?"

A babble of voices answered him. Every charwoman known to Bayfield Court, it seemed, seethed in a swarm before the entry.

"Old Mrs. Duncom – locked in, and hears no knock – here's Mrs. Taffety come to dine – "

A dozen hands pushed forward an agitated lady in a capuchin.

"Invited, Mr. Johnson, two o'clock the hour, and Mrs. Duncom don't answer. I fear the old maid is ill and the young maid is gone to fetch the surgeon, and Mrs. Duncom you know has not the use of her limbs."

"We must rouse her. Come, Mrs. Taffety, I'll make myself heard, I warrant."

The whole feminine contingent, abandoning hope of the watch, escorted us up the stair. As we mounted, I took stock of our posse. The benchers of the law, their employers, were off on their Sunday occasions, but the servitors were present in force. I saw an Irish wench with red hair and a turned-up nose, flanked close by a couple of lanky, ill-conditioned lads, probably sculls to the benchers and certainly admirers to the wench. A dark wiry little gypsy of a woman with alert black eyes boosted along a sturdy motherly soul addressed by all as Aunt Moll. Sukey and Win and Juggy, twittering to each other, followed after.

Arrived at the attick landing, Dr. Johnson raised his voice and called upon Mrs. Duncom in rolling stentorian tones. Mrs. Taffety seconded him, invoking the maids in a thin screech: "Betty! Annet!" Dead silence answered them.

"Then we must break in the door," said Dr. Johnson.

Indeed he looked abundantly capable of effecting such a feat single-handed; but at that moment a stumble of feet upon the stair proclaimed the arrival of the watch. "Hold!" cried that worthy. "None of your assault and battery, for I'll undertake to spring the lock."

"Will you so?" said Dr. Johnson, eyeing him thoughtfully.

The watch was no Bow Street constable, but one of the Temple guardians, a stubby old man in a seedy fustian coat, girded with a broad leather belt from which depended his short sword and his truncheon of office.

The women regarded him admiringly as he stepped forward, full of self-importance, and made play with a kind of skewer which he thrust into the lock.

Nothing happened.

After considerable probing and coaxing the man was fain to desist.

"'Tis plain, sir," he covered his failure, "that the door is bolted from within."

"Bolted!" cried Mrs. Taffety. "Of course 'tis bolted! Mistress

Duncom ever barred herself in like a fortress, for she kept a fortune in broad pieces under her bed in a silver tankard, and so she went ever in fear of robbers."

"How came you to know of this fortune, ma'am?" demanded Dr. Johnson.

"Why, sir, the whole world knew, 'twas no secret."

"It ought to have been. Well, fortress or no, it appears we must break in."

"Hold, sir!" cried the black-eyed charwoman. "You'll affright the old lady into fits. I know a better way."

"Name it, then, ma'am."

"My master Grisley's chambers, you must know, sir, lie on the other side of the court – "

"Ah, Mr. Grisley!" murmured Aunt Moll. "Pity he's not to the fore, he'd set us right, I warrant, he's that fond of Annet!"

"Mr. Grisley is from home. But I have the key. Now if I get out at his dormer, I'll make my way easily round the parapet, and so get in at Mrs. Duncom's casement and find out what's amiss."

"Well thought on, Mistress Oliver," approved the watch, "for the benchers of the Temple would take it ill, was we to go banging in doors."

"And how if the casement be bolted and barred, as surely it will be?"

"Then, Mrs. Taffety, I must make shift. Wait here. I'll not be long."

Waiting on the landing, we fell silent, listening for we knew not what. When it came, it startled us – a crash, and the tinkle of falling glass.

"Alack, has she fallen?"

"Not so, ma'am, she has made shift. Now she's within, soon she'll shoot the great bolt and admit us."

We waited at the door in suspense. After an interminable minute, the lock turned, and we heard someone wrenching at the bolt. It stuck; then with a shriek it grated grudgingly back, and the heavy door swung slowly in.

On the threshold stood Mrs. Oliver, rigid and staring. Her lips moved, but no sound came.

"In God's name, what is it?" cried Mrs. Taffety in alarm.

Mrs. Oliver found a hoarse whisper:

"Murder!" she gasped. "Murder lock'd in!"

Her eyes rolled up in her head, her knees gave way, and she collapsed in a huddle in the doorway.

"Let me, sirs." The motherly female stepped forward. "When Katty's in her fits, I know how to deal."

Leaving her to deal, the rest of us pressed in, Dr. Johnson, myself, the watch, and the fluttering women. The Irish girl was with us, but her swains, the sculls, I noted, had vanished.

What a sight met our eyes! The young maid's pallet was made up in the passage, by the inner door as if to guard it, and there lay Annet in her blood. She had fought for her life, for blood was everywhere, but repeated blows of an axe or hammer had broke her head and quelled her forever.

In the inner room old Mrs. Duncom lay strangled. The noose was still around her neck. In the other bed old Betty had suffered the same fate. Of the silver tankard there was no trace.

"Murder and robbery! We must send for the Bow Street men!" I cried.

"Not in my bailiwick!" growled the Temple watchman. "*I* am the law in Bayfield Court!"

"So he is, Mr. Boswell," assented Dr. Johnson. "Well, well, if we put our minds to it, we may make shift to unravel this dreadful riddle for ourselves – three women dead in an apartment locked and barred!"

Cold air touched me, and a shudder shook me. The icy air was no ghostly miasma, I soon saw, but a chill spring breeze from the casement, where the small old-fashioned panes nearest the bolt had been shattered when entrance was effected.

"The window was bolted, I told you so!" cried Mrs. Taffety. "Every bolt set! The Devil is in it!"

"The Devil – the Devil!" the charwomen took up the chorus.

"Y'are foolish females!" said the watch stoutly. "Look you, Mr. Johnson, I'll undertake to shew you how 'twas done."

"I thank you, my man – "

"Jonas Mudge, sir, at your service."

"I thank you, honest Mudge, pray instruct me, for I am ever happy to be instructed."

"Then behold, sir! I take this string – " It came out of his capacious pocket with a conjurer's flourish at which the females gaped. "Now pray step this way, sir (leading us to the outer door). Now mark me! I loop my string around the knob of the bolt – I step outside, pray follow – "

On the outside landing Mistress Katty Oliver was sitting propped against the wall with closed eyes, and her friend was assiduously fanning her. They paid us no mind. Lowering his tone, Mudge continued his lecture:

"I bring the two ends of the string with me – I close the door. Now I will pull on both ends of the string, which will shoot the bolt – and so I shall have only to pull away the string by one end, the door is bolted, and I stand outside. As thus – "

As he spoke, he pulled on the two ends of the string. Nothing happened. The unwieldly bolt stuck, and no force applied to the string could budge it.

"An old trick, not always to be relied upon," smiled Dr. Johnson. "I thank you, sir, for demonstrating how this strange feat was *not* accomplished!"

As Mudge stood there looking foolish, there was a clatter on the stair, and three gentlemen arrived on the run. The benchers had come back from Commons. Dr. Johnson knew them all, the red-faced one, the exquisite one, the melancholy one, and greeted each in turn.

"What, Mr. Kerry, Mr. Geegan, Mr. Grisley, you come in an unhappy time."

"Your servant, Mr. Johnson, what's amiss?"

Mistress Oliver was on her feet, her hand on his arm.

"Don't go in, Mr. Grisley, for God's sake don't go in. Come away, I'll fetch you a tot, come away."

"Alack, sirs, murder's amiss!" I blurted.

The two young benchers were through the door in an instant, and the melancholy Grisley shook off his maid's hand and followed. When his eye lit on Annet's bloody brow, he cried aloud.

"Cover her face! For God's sake cover her face!"

Quick hands drew up the crimsoned bed-cloathes, and so we found the hammer. Dr. Johnson's shapely strong fingers handled it gingerly, bringing it close to his near-sighted eyes.

"An ordinary hammer. What can it tell us?"

"Perhaps much, for I perceive there's an initial burned in the wood of the handle," said I, feeling pleased with myself. "A G, sir, if I mistake not."

"A G. Yours, Mr. Geegan?"

The exquisite youth jibbed in alarm.

"Not mine, Divil a whit, no, sir, not mine!"

"Mr. Grisley?"

"I cannot look on it, do not ask me. Kat will know."

The little dark woman took his hand and spoke soothingly to him.

"I think, sir, 'tis the one you lent to Mr. Kerry some days since."

"To me!" cried the ruddy-faced bencher. "You lie, you trull!"

"I don't lie," said the woman angrily. "Don't you remember, you sent your charwoman for it, I gave it to Biddy to knock in some nails?" In a sudden silence, all eyes turned to the red-haired girl.

"No, sir, I never!" she cried in alarm.

"Go off, you trull!" bawled the alarmed Kerry. "I dismiss you! So you may e'en fetch your bundle and be off with you!"

"Nay, sir, not so fast, she must remain!" remonstrated the watch.

"Not in my chambers, the d—d trull! She may take up her bundle outside my door, and be d—d to her!"

I perceived that Mr. Kerry had come from Commons not a little pot-valiant, and thought it good riddance when he stamped off.

Biddy gave us one scared look, and followed him. Young Geegan seemed minded to go along, but was prevented by the arrival of Mudge's mate of the watch. Leather-belted, truncheon in hand, flat and expressionless of face, there he stood, filling the doorway and saying nothing. It gave us a sinister feeling of being under guard in that chamber of death. Mrs. Taffety fell to sobbing, and the women to comforting her. Dr. Johnson was probing the chimneys, neither deterred nor assisted by the blank-faced watchman, when suddenly Mr. Kerry was back again, redder than ever, hauling a reluctant Biddy by the wrist, and in his free hand brandishing a silver tankard.

"'Tis Mrs. Duncom's!" cried Mrs. Taffety.

"Hid in Biddy's bundle! I knew it, the trull!"

The wretched Biddy began to snivel.

"I had it for a gift," she wept. "I did not know murder was in it!"

Dr. Johnson took her in hand: "Who gave it you?"

"My f-friends."

"What friends?"

Biddy was loath to say, but the philosopher prevailed by sheer moral force, and Biddy confessed:

"The Sander brothers. Scouts to the benchers. Them that's gone off."

"They shall be found. And what did you do for them?"

"I – " The girl's resistance was broken. "I kept watch on the stair."

Then it came with a rush: "When Annet went in the evening
for some wine to make the old lady's nightly posset, she left
the door on the jar as was her wont, that she might come in
again without disturbing old Betty; and knowing it would be
so, Matt Sander, that's the puny one, he slips in and hides
under the bed. When all is still, he lets in his brother, and I
keep watch on the stair, and they come out with the tankard of
broad pieces – " The wretched girl began to bawl. "They swore
to me they had done no murder, only bound and gagged the folk
for safety's sake."

"And when they came out," pursued Dr. Johnson, "they shot the
bolt from outside. How did they do that?"

"I know not what you mean, sir. They pulled the door to, 'tis a
spring lock, I heard it snick shut, and so we came away and shared
out in the archway below."

"Which of them carried the hammer?"

"Neither, sir, for what would they need a hammer?"

Then realization flooded her, and she bawled louder, looking
wildly about for a refuge. Suddenly, defiantly, Mr. Geegan stepped
forward and took her in his arms.

"So, Mr. Johnson," said watchman Mudge smugly, "our problem
is solved, we had no need of Bow Street! You come along of me,
Mistress Biddy. Nay, let go, sir." Mr. Geegan reluctantly obeyed.
"Pray, Mr. Johnson, do you remain here, I'll fetch the crowner to
sit on the bodies."

"Do so, good friend. I'll desire all those present – " his eye took in
the three benchers and the huddling women "– to bear me company
till he comes. Bucket will stand by to keep order. Come, friends, we
shall sit more at our ease in the dining room. After you, ma'am.
After you, sir."

They went without demur, all save Grisley. In the passage, by
Annet's still form on her pallet, he balked. "Shall she lie alone?" he
cried piteously. "I'll stay by her while I may."

"And I by you," said Kat Oliver.

Her master sank to the hallway bench, wringing his hands and
crying: "O Annet, Annet, why did you not admit me? I might have
saved you!"

"Come, sir," soothed his maid, "be easy, you could do nothing."

We left them fallen silent on the bench. Instead of following the
others into the dining room, Dr. Johnson led me back into the
inner chamber, where two bodies lay coldly blown upon from the
broken window panes.

*Johnson* There's more in this, Mr. Boswell, than meets the eye.

*Boswell* Did not the Sanders do it?

*Johnson* And got out through a door locked and barred, and left it so? Biddy saw no hocussing of the lock, and I question whether they knew how to do it.

*Boswell* Mudge knew how. Were they in it together? I ask myself, sir, what is this guardian of the Temple peace, that carries a picklock in his pocket, and knows how to shoot a bolt from without? I smell Newgate on him.

*Johnson* You may be right, sir. They are a queer lot, the Temple watch. But this one is no wizard, he could neither, in the event, pick the lock nor shoot the bolt.

*Boswell* Then how was it done? This seems an impossible crime.

*Johnson* 'Twas all too possible, sir, for it happened.

*Boswell* The women are right, the Devil did it.

*Johnson* A devil did it indeed, but in human form.

*Boswell* One who got in through bolts and bars, and got out again leaving all locked and barred behind him?

*Johnson* There was a way in, for someone got in, and a way out too, that's plain to a demonstration. We must find it.

*Boswell* I am at a loss, sir. Where must we look?

*Johnson* We must look where all answers are found, sir, in our own heads. Perpend, sir. Murder in a locked dwelling, and no murderer there to take – 'tis a pretty mystery, and this one the more complex because it is triple. Let us consider the problem at large. Many answers are possible.

*Boswell* (ruefully) In *my* head, sir, I don't find even one.

*Johnson* Well, sir, here's one: Perhaps there is no murderer there to take, because there is no murder, only accident that looks like murder.

*Boswell* Two old women simultaneously strangle themselves by accident, while the young one accidentally falls afoul of a hammer? Come, sir, this is to stretch coincidence and multiply impossibilities!

*Johnson* Granted, Mr. Boswell. Then is it perhaps double murder and suicide behind bolted doors?

*Boswell* Suicide by the hammer? Unheard of!

*Johnson* And nigh on impossible. Well, then, sir, was the tragedy engineered from without, and no murderer ever entered at all?

*Boswell* The nooses were tightened and the hammer wielded, by someone on the wrong side of the door? This is witchcraft and sorcery, nothing less.

*Johnson* Then suppose there is no murder, the victim is only stunned or stupefied, until the person who breaks in commits it?

*Boswell Three* murders, sir, and the third a noisy one, all in the one minute while we listened at the door? Come, sir, these conjectures are ingenious, but none fits this case.

*Johnson* Then there must be a way in, and a way out. Think, Mr. Boswell: all is not so locked and sealed, but holes exist.

*Boswell* I have it! The keyhole!

*Johnson* A keyhole that not even a picklock could penetrate? Think again, sir. What else?

*Boswell* Nay, I know not, sir. There is no scuttle to the roof.

*Johnson* There is not, sir.

*Boswell* And the chimneys are narrow, and stuffed with soot undisturbed.

*Johnson* So we saw. Not the chimneys. Good. We progress.

*Boswell* How, progress?

*Johnson* When one has eliminated all impossibilities, then what remains, however improbable, must be the truth.

*Boswell* What truth?

*Johnson* Nay, sir, I have yet to test it. Come with me.

In the passage-way Annet lay still under the reddened blankets. Grisley and his maid sat as still on the settle, he with his face in his hands, she at his shoulder regarding him with a countenance full of concern. A blackened old chair with high back stood opposite. Dr. Johnson ensconced himself therein like some judge on the bench, and I took my stand by him like a bailiff.

"Mistress Oliver," he began, "pray assist our deliberations."

"As best I can, sir," she answered readily.

Grisley did not stir.

"Then tell us, in your airy peregrination, in what condition did you find Mrs. Duncom's casement window?"

"Bolted fast, sir, I was forced to break the glass that I might reach in and turn the catch."

"I know, we heard it shatter. You broke the glass and reached in. With both hands?"

"Certainly not, sir, I held on with the other hand."

"Then why did you break two panes?"

"I don't know. For greater assurance – "

"Nonsense! I put it to you, my girl, *you found the window broken.*"

"Then why would I break it again?"

"Because you knew at once who had been there before you, and thought only to shield him. So you broke the second pane, that we might hear the crash of glass, and think you had been forced to break in. The broken window would else tell us that the murderer came from Mr. Grisley's casement."

"He never!" cried the woman, on her feet before her master as if to shield him. "Would he kill Annet, that he lusted after?"

"Would he not, if she resisted him? These violent passions have violent ends. No, no. I pity him, but justice must be done. Think, Mistress Oliver, this is the man that slunk around the parapet at dead of night, a hammer in his pocket. With it he breaks a pane, turns the bolt, and enters. The two helpless old women fall victim to his string, lest they hinder his intent. When Annet resists him, in his fury he batters her to death, and so flees as he came. May such a creature live?"

This harangue slowly penetrated the mind of the unhappy Grisley, and he rose to his feet.

"Bucket!" called Dr. Johnson sharply. The watchman appeared. "Take him in!"

"No! No!" cried the woman. "He is innocent!"

"Who will believe it?" countered Johnson. "No, ma'am, he'll hang for it, and justly too. Did you ever see a man hanged, Mr. Boswell? It is a shocking sight to see a man struggling as he strangles in a string, his face suffused, his limbs convulsed, for long horrible minutes. Well, he has earned it. Take him, Bucket."

As Bucket collared the unresisting Grisley, we found we had a fury on our hands. With nails and teeth Kat Oliver fell upon Dr. Johnson. I had her off in a trice; but I could not have held her had not Bucket come to my aid.

"I thank you, Mr. Boswell," said Dr. Johnson, settling his neckcloth and staunching his cheek, "your address has saved me a mauling. A woman's a lioness in defence of what she loves."

"In my belief she's mad," said I angrily, as the wiry little woman wrenched against our pinioning arms.

"That may also be true. A thin line divides great love and madness. Give over, ma'am, let justice take its course. So, that's better – let her go, Mr. Boswell. As to Mr. Grisley, Bucket, to Newgate with him, and lock him in the condemned cell."

"You shan't! You shan't!" sobbed Kat Oliver wildly. "It was I that killed them, it was I, it was I!"

"You, ma'am? A likely story! Why would you do such a thing?"

"Why would I destroy that prim little bitch, that was destroying him? For his sake, gladly. Yet I never meant to use the hammer, that I carried only to break the glass – "

"But," I objected, "Biddy had the hammer!"

"You are deceived, Mr. Boswell. To disclaim the hammer, this woman did not scruple to lie. Well, then, Mrs. Oliver, if not to use the hammer, what was your intent?"

The little woman's eyes looked inward, and she spoke with a kind of horrid relish:

"When I knew the people lay bound and gagged – "

"How did you know?"

"I heard the talk on the landing. I could not sleep for thinking of – I could not sleep, and the boys were drunk and loud. I opened the door and listened. I saw my opportunity. How I entered you know. The old women I finished neatly, with their own curtain cords. The young one – "

"Yes, the young one?"

"The young one I reserved for a more dreadful fate. It was I who shot the front-door bolt, intending to leave her locked in with murder, and see her hanged for it."

"Who could think she did it, when she lay bound?" I demanded.

"Of course I did away with the bonds," said the woman contemptuously.

"Yet you killed her, how was that to your purpose?"

"I meant only to stun her, but she got loose and fought me. I saw red. I killed her. Then I returned as I came."

"And when the people became alarmed and would break in," Dr. Johnson supplied, "you saw it must be you, and no one else, to break the window and effect an entrance there, lest the broken window be observed by others, pointing directly at the folk from Mr. Grisley's."

She made no answer, but turned to her master.

"I did it for you, Edward."

With a blind gesture, Grisley turned away.

"All for nothing, then."

Dining together the next day at the Mitre, we naturally turned our talk to the exciting hours we had spent in Bayfield Court the day before.

*Boswell* Were you not surprised, sir, when Katty Oliver confessed her guilt?

*Johnson* Not at all, sir, I knew it all along. What did she care if the door was battered in? Only the strongest of motives would suffice to set her on that precarious circuit she traversed. She must have known what would be found at the end of it. Nay, more, how did she know it was an easy way around the parapet, if she had not traversed it before?

*Boswell* Yet how eloquently you depicted the unhappy Grisley's crime and his imminent fate.

*Johnson* Thus I put her to the torture, for I could see how much he meant to her; and when I turned the screw with talk of the horrors of hanging, she confessed to save him, as I foresaw she would.

*Boswell* What will become of her? Surely she'll hang?

*Johnson* In the ordinary course, sir, yes. But I had the curiosity to inquire this morning, and by what I learn, she will not hang. It appears that, as Aunt Moll said, she was ever subject to fits, no doubt she committed her terrible crimes in an unnatural phrenzy. Well, sir, when she saw the cells last night she fell into a dead catalepsy and was carried insensible to Bedlam, where 'tis clear she belongs.

*Boswell* And Biddy, what of her?

*Johnson* The Sander brothers, that delivered over the old women bound to be murdered, have made good their escape, leaving Biddy to pay for their crime.

*Boswell* This seems unfair, sir.

*Johnson* Why, sir, receiving of stolen goods is a hanging offence, Miss Biddy cannot complain. But the Temple watchmen are not incorruptible, and the Temple watch-house is not impregnable. Moreover, Mr. Geegan, the son of an Irish Peer, has well-lined pockets. In short, sir, he has spirited away Miss Biddy, who knows whither. And so ends the affair of murder lock'd in.

*Boswell* (boldly) Which I hope I may one day narrate at large when, as I mean to do, I record for posterity the exploits of *Sam: Johnson, detector*!

## AUTHOR'S COMMENT

The hardest thing about writing this story was making it probable. I suppose this is because it actually happened. Real events don't necessarily bother about probability.

It happened, and I tell it as it happened, except of course for the intervention of Dr. Sam: Johnson. The solution is my own. In actual fact the Irish girl was hanged, which seems hard for only keeping watch and accepting a silver tankard; but such was justice in those inhuman days.

In analyzing the "locked-room mystery" and its possible solutions, with singular prescience, Dr. Johnson seems to have anticipated

John Dickson Carr's "locked-room lecture" in THE THREE COFFINS; though the solution that detector Sam: Johnson arrives at is not among those considered by Carr.

The classic "string trick" for bolting a door from outside, here explained by the watchman, was actually demonstrated at the Irish girl's trial, when they brought the door into open court and performed the trick upon it to the amazement of all beholders. You may read all about it in George Borrow's CELEBRATED TRIALS, II, 536–571.

# CAPTAIN NASH AND THE WROTH INHERITANCE
# Raymond Butler

*A trained chef, market researcher and language teacher, Raymond Ragan Butler has written over a hundred radio plays and further stage and television plays, including scripts for a soap opera.* Captain Nash and the Wroth Inheritance *(1975) was his first full-length novel, and a fascinating attempt at establishing the world's first private detective. There is a sequel,* Captain Nash and the Honour of England *(1977).*

## AN INTRODUCTION

When I first began to investigate crime in England, the profession of detection did not exist. The Parish Constable, the Informer, the Bow Street Runner – these were the only agents of the Law. Yet England was a lawless place in those days.

It was in 1771 (in my thirtieth year) that I first conceived the idea of a scientific system of detection and, like all original ideas, it was received with no great degree of enthusiasm. With the exception of my cousin Scrope, who was employed in the Commissioners' Office, I was largely ignored by the Authorities.

As a result, I was forced to work in a private capacity – that is, outside the protection of the Law. I became a "Private Detective", the first in modern Europe, I believe.

*An advertisement in* The Daily Courant, *July 5th, 1771*
*A Gentleman of considerable abilities is able to provide a service for the gathering of information and the detection of crimes. If any have suffered the attentions of thieves and miscreants and are not happy with the Law's performance, let them come to me and I shall restore their*

*property and apprehend the villains. My original scientific approach to
the art of detection ensures the success of my endeavours. Those who come
to me are assured that investigations will be made with all honour and
secrecy imaginable.*

*For further particulars inquire of Captain George Nash, late of His
Majesty's 5th Regiment of Dragoons, at Mr Trygwell, Bookseller, Greek
Court, Soho.*

# I

For my first case, I took the one which looked to be the most
intriguing and which promised the most reward financially, for the
Wroth family was one of the richest in England.

Accordingly, I presented myself, as requested, at Stukeley Hall
upon the following Thursday. I had taken some trouble with
my appearance, realizing that since my new profession would
seem dubious even to my employers, I would have to make a
good impression from the first. I wore a plain green coat, which
although no longer in the fashion still had a certain style. My
waistcoat, though faded in places, looked bravely enough from
the front; and my breeches, though they were as unfashionable
as my coat, showed off my legs to great advantage. My buckled
shoes were low-at-heel, but I have always worked on the principle
that most people look keenest at one's neck, so I wore my best lawn
cloth. I left my hair unpowdered, though wig-style, and I buckled
on my sword, to let the Dowager Lady Wroth see that she had to
deal with a gentleman.

At all events, my appearance seemed to pass muster with the
servants. As I rode up to the porte-cochere a lurking groom came
forward, touched his forelock civilly enough and led my roan away
to the stables. The ancient retainer who admitted me to the house
did so without a hint of that insolence he would have used had he
been more certain of my true station in life. He merely regarded me
with the same hauteur he would have turned upon a Duke. After
crossing a cavernous hall, he showed me into a reception room.

"If you will wait in here, Sir, her ladyship will be free directly."
The door gently sighed to behind him.

I looked about me with interest. Considering the legend of their
wealth, I was somewhat disappointed with their display of it. This
room was ponderously magnificent in its weighty "Roman" way, with
a tastelessly painted ceiling and a tiled floor. It was furnished in the
style of the Second George, opulent but demodé. The woodwork was

profusely carved and ornamented, looking absurd yet brave against the dank austerity of the gloomy walls.

Stukeley itself was a dilapidated relic of the Thirteenth Century, a moated grange built upon the ruins of an old castle. To my eye, it seemed almost unfit for civilized living. Most of the building was well on the way to ruin again and I could see from the exterior that only a few rooms remained habitable. Apparently this was one of them. I found it odd that the family refused to spend their vast wealth on the property. Their neglect seemed almost wilful.

I was drawn to the window by the clash of steel upon steel and the shrill cries of what I, at first, took to be a peacock. I looked through the window.

A fine lawn ran down to the river; green, smooth, and quite deserted. Somewhere behind a mossy wall sword rang on sword and the peacock's cries became almost intolerable.

Then the duellists came into sight and my mouth fell open in blank astonishment. Two young women danced onto the lawn, fencing furiously. They were dressed in the height of French fashion, that is, with too much rigging and wearing monstrous hooped skirts, with ruching and pleating much in evidence. Their hair was greased, powdered, curled and dressed high over enormous cushions and surmounted by imitation fruits, flowers and ships. The size of fashionable heads in those days was notoriously vast, but these were grotesquely so.

They moved like ships in full sail. It was hard to imagine they were made in God's image, for He that made them would never have recognized them with their plumes, their silken vizards, their ruffs like sails, and the feathers in their hats like two flags in their tops to tell which way the wind blew. They looked almost deformed, capering about upon the green lawn.

When the initial shock had faded, I found myself admiring the dexterity with which they handled the foils. Despite their towering plumes and the stiff, unmanageable brocade of their gowns, they moved like professional duellists.

They danced upon the lawn like two creatures in some fable and all the while they fenced, the smaller of the two kept up an amazing clamour. It was as if she had some raucous and frightful bird locked up in her rib-cage. It was she I had mistaken for a peacock!

I looked on in amazement.

Although I have seen many professional women fight (including the great Mary Brindle of New England), I had never seen action to equal this. The smaller woman lunged and thrust at the taller with

dangerously bold strokes, which her opponent parried with ease.
But it was no formal display of technique – their blades clashed
and slithered and threw out sparks in grim earnest.

Suddenly the tall girl slipped as her foot caught in the hem of her
gown. She lurched, and made a frantic effort to recover her balance,
but failed and fell to the ground in a wild flurry of petticoats. As
she fell, the sword flew out of her hand in a great flashing arc. The
smaller woman now towered over her, her sword drawn back so that
it pointed downwards towards the unprotected breast. Laughing, she
seemed to be considering whether or no to plunge her sword into the
inert body beneath her. She pricked the bodice maliciously, looking
for the softest spot.

I held my breath.

With a quick twist of her body, the fallen girl jerked aside – and
the other, startled, lunged. The point of the sword passed within
an inch of her side, tearing the fabric of her gown. It penetrated
the smooth grass and remained quivering there.

Shrieking with hysterical laughter, the small girl threw herself
upon the other, grasped her with both hands by the throat and
strove to throttle her!

The other girl, laughing almost as hysterically, seized her wrists
and endeavoured to tear them apart. But her tormentor clung to her
neck, forcing her nails into the flesh until even I could see the blood
begin to fleck her hands. Although the battle seemed to be in largely
high-spirits, I thought there must be some danger of their doing each
other an injury. I wondered why nobody ran out to call this strange
affair to a halt.

Then I noticed that I was not the only observer. Close by the corner
of the wall, a young man stood watching this display. He watched
them with an intolerant eye, but seemed little inclined to interfere.
I received a strong impression that this was no new sight to him.

Squirming, kicking, and striking at her attacker's face, the fallen
girl fought desperately to wrench herself free. But she seemed
quite helpless beneath the power of the diminutive tornado that
bestraddled her. Until, suddenly, this tornado appeared to blow
itself out. With a long, agonized cry, she shuddered down the entire
length of her body, her grip relaxed, and she collapsed inert upon
the other girl's body.

Nobody moved. The girl pinned beneath her fought for her
breath. She seemed almost too exhausted to push the still, small
form aside.

With slow, deliberate strides, the young man walked over to the
prostrate pair and casually, even a little disdainfully, he shoved the

girls apart with one delicately arched foot. He then gave the taller girl his hand and hauled her unceremoniously to her feet.

Upright and stationary, she presented a curiously awkward figure. With bad grace, she thanked the young man and, kneeling by the inert figure on the grass, turned her over to face the light. As she did so, she raised a hand to her own head and pulled off her hat.

To my utter astonishment, the architectural wig came away with it, revealing the features of a singularly handsome young man. My amazement grew even greater as he stood up and proceeded to undress upon the lawn.

I gaped as he undid the pointed bodice of his gown and stripped off plumes, brocade and lace. Three petticoats were removed and thrown aside and I saw that he was, in truth, a lean and sinewy young stripling wearing only his breeches beneath the finery. He must have been mortifyingly hot under it all!

Stripped of his encumbrances, he turned his attention to his partner. He took a phial from the phlegmatic on-looker and waved it under her nose. She stirred indolently and sat up suddenly.

She was helped to her feet and she, too, began to disrobe. Off came the wig and the plumes, the gown was torn impatiently from her body, and the tout ensemble dropped to the feet of a cherubic young fellow dressed, like his friend, in nothing but his breeches.

I found myself staring curiously at the ladies' brocade shoes which still adorned their feet. In some odd way I had found this last metamorphosis less unnerving than the first – not simply because I was the less astonished, but because the soft young figure in masculine dress and feminine shoes, though unmistakably a man, had a body that more approached the feminine in its roundness and softness. He was a very young man, no more than seventeen years, I should have said.

All memory of their maniacal duel seemed forgotten between them. Laughing, they threw their arms around each other and teetered away across the lawn in their absurd shoes. They disappeared behind the same wall from which they had so sensationally appeared.

The third young man drifted away in another direction. Even at this distance I could see there had been no love lost between them.

So engrossed had I been in this curious performance, that I had failed to hear the door open behind me. The manservant now coughed discreetly. I turned, feeling strangely as though I had been caught rattling the family skeletons. The servant regarded me with a bright and noncommittal eye. I presumed he had seen the two upon the lawn, but he stared at me impassively.

"Her ladyship is ready to receive you, Sir," he said.

## II

I followed the manservant through the roof-high hall. It was stone-flagged and draughty, with a faintly medieval smell to it. Although the air outside was breathless, a faint wind murmured in the baronial fireplace and the sun had abandoned the attempt to penetrate the mullioned windows. The ceiling and walls were lost in a gloom of shadows, and history lay thick upon the air. I could almost see the ghostly generations of tenants assembled before the high table.

As we climbed the staircase, I examined the family portraits lining the walls. They were a more direct link with the ghostly past. It gave me an odd feeling to think that once, on this same ground, they had walked, but now all were gone like shadows at midday, one generation following another.

Another strange thought occurred to me as we passed the portraits. They were arranged in chronological order, but reaching backwards in time. They ended with the first Lord Wroth (circa 1489) and I could not but fail to notice that, as the family history rolled back into obscurity, the distinctive features of the Wroth clan faded into obliteration. But for the last four generations, at least, the painted faces had betrayed considerable inbreeding. The grandfather of the present Lord Wroth, for example, had a very mad look – a look of almost fatal softness – which no amount of painterly skill had been able to conceal. He was, I recollected suddenly, the husband of the Dowager Lady Wroth, to whom I was now about to be introduced.

The servant knocked briskly on a massive door and a high, querulous voice bade us enter. I was shown into a room the servant called the "solar".

After the gloom of the hall, this room seemed vibrant with light. It gleamed in the burnished woodwork, it sparkled warmly on the brass fireirons, it flashed out from the many mirrors in the room, and it coruscated among the facets of the chandeliers and lustres. The sunlight gave to the room a feeling of splendid unruliness. There was something pleasurably sluttish about it, as though it were unable to control its behaviour after the rigours of the hall. Among the sober furnishings, the sun was *gay*.

And all this gaiety seemed gathered into the person of the mistress of the house. The Dowager Lady Wroth was the most splendidly illuminated creature that I had ever seen. At first glance she seemed to be composed almost entirely of diamonds – they glittered from her ears, her throat, her wrists and her fingers. Her white hair shone with a bluish sheen, her skin had the gleam of coral, and her tabby[1] gown was the colour of daffodils.

With a shock, I realized that this exuberantly youthful figure must be touching her eightieth year. My second thought was that she was monstrous overdressed for a simple country morning. It seemed that fifty years of living among the gentry had not dampened the essentially theatrical spirit of the one-time actress, Sarah Laverstitch.

I, too, had been the object of as close a scrutiny. Her brilliantly undimmed eyes had been evaluating me point by point. She approved of what she saw, apparently, for she smiled and invited me to sit on a sofa of truly regal proportions. Her teeth were startlingly grey in her rosy face, and I now saw that her cheeks were very finely enamelled. I had a strong suspicion that beneath the flattering wig she was as bald as a magistrate.

She came directly to business. If I could satisfy her as to my credentials, she would be interested in using my services.

I presented her with my references and, after a careful reading of them, she asked how soon I would be free to act for her.

"I am at your service now, my lady," I said.

She looked surprised. "You are at liberty?"

I laughed and said frankly: "Business is not yet brisk, Lady Wroth. I have been advertising my services since April, but the public have not, so far, responded as I could have wished. There is still some suspicion of my calling among folk generally."

She nodded sympathetically. "It is understandable, Captain. The public are suspicious both of advertisements and thief-takers. Advertisements are largely unfulfilled promises, and thief-takers are often as rascally as the rogues they take!"

Having shot this barb, she looked slyly at me to see if it had struck home.

"I don't describe myself as a thief-taker, Lady Wroth," I said. "I am more interested in the gathering of information and the detection of crimes. I call myself a detective."

The word was unknown to her, as, indeed, it was still unknown to many.

"A detective?" she asked.

"From the Latin, Ma'am. *Detegere*, to uncover," I explained, and outlined my scientific methods.

"A detective," she said, seemingly impressed with my summary. "Well, that is an original calling."

[1]Watered silk.

"Not entirely original," I said, smiling. "There were detectives of a kind in ancient Egypt. Is not the story of Rhampsinitus, as told by Herodotus, a sort of detective-story?" She returned my smile uncomprehendingly. "But I think it safe to say that I am the only one in existence today."

"You are not attached to the Bow Street Police?" she asked.

"No, my lady. I prefer to work independently. I am a private gentleman. A Private Detective, if you wish."

"Good!" she said, and I noticed a distinct note of relief in her voice. "My commission calls for a man of independent spirit."

"You prefer not to use the Bow Street Police?" I asked, emphasizing the word "police" deliberately, and looking to see how she received it. Even at this early stage in my career, I knew that my employers would be largely comprised of those who would be too embarrassed to use the regular channels of the law.

She looked briefly away and replied shortly: "I think this is not a suitable business for them."

"You think they are not competent?"

"I think they are not *suitable*," she said briskly. "For one thing, I doubt if they would even consider the matter. I am not, as yet, certain that any crime has been committed. Unless you count sheer human folly to be a crime."

I waited for her to explain the matter further. She tapped the arm of her chair with her tortoise-shell fan, and said decisively: "I had better start from the beginning."

"I'd be obliged to your ladyship."

She paused, then shook herself, flashing fire from every facet. She reached for a small brocade bag, and extracted from it a sheaf of papers tied with a frivolous looking ribbon. She held them out to me.

"Read them!" she commanded.

I walked over to her chair and took them from her. The diamonds on her wrists and fingers shivered slightly, and I saw that she was trying valiantly to control a fit of trembling.

The papers were addressed to the Dowager Lady Wroth at Stukeley, Hertfordshire. The writing was neat and clerkly. The first paper was headed "At the Sign of the Anodyne Necklace" and was signed "Asclepius (Doctor)" followed by a string of meaningless and, I suspected, largely fictitious medical degrees. It read, simply, "For Services Rendered".

The other papers, seven in all, were signed receipts. The signature at the foot of each one was large, ill-formed and boorish. With difficulty, I deciphered the name "Wroth".

Lord Wroth had promised to pay the sum of 480 guineas for "Value Received".

My eyebrows rose slightly at the nature of the "Value Received".

| | |
|---|---|
| *Imprimis*, for use of the Royall Chymicall Washball, and for Ridding the Skin of all Deformities | 28 gns |
| *Item*, to use of application to Cure a Stammer | 28 gns |
| *Item*, to preserving Eyes | 28 gns |
| *Item*, to clearing away Phlegm, Rheum and Foul Humours from Breast, Stomach and Lungs | 28 gns |
| *Item*, to Removal of a Ringworm | 10 gns |
| *Item*, to Removal of Pimples | 10 gns |
| *Item*, to enticing of a Lengthy, Hairy and Voracious Worm, conjured from His Lordship's gut | 28 gns |

And more amazing than this:

| | |
|---|---|
| *Item*, to stimulation of His Lordship's Growth in various parts of His Person | 120 gns |

And even more amazing still:

| | |
|---|---|
| *Item*, to curing His Lordship of the Hideous Crime of Self-Pollution | 200 gns |
| | 480 gns |

I looked up. Lady Wroth stared at me with her hard, gemlike eyes. I could scarcely keep the amazement out of my own.

"Well, Sir? What do you think?"

"It seems your grandson suffers from singular ill-health, Ma'am," I said.

Her Ladyship snorted with disgust.

"Tcha! My grandson is in the most blatant good health. This is a brazen humbug! He has got into the hands of this quack. We live in an age of magnificent quacks, Captain Nash. They have cut short more lives with their pills and elixirs than were ever killed off by the plague!"

I waited for her to recover her temper. I was also waiting for her to come more to the point. There was more to it, I was sure, than these bizarre but basically harmless receipts.

"Do you know this 'Asclepius' fellow?" she asked tentatively. She toyed with her fan – a veritable weapon in her hands. It weaved, twisted, snapped shut and opened again. Her fan was the real sign-manual to her emotions, for her face told me nothing.

"I have heard tell of him, Ma'am," I replied. "I think he is far removed from the 'blameless Physician' of Greek legend."

"He is a magnificent quack, Sir!" she exploded. "A self-created doctor. These so-called medical receipts are not worth the paper they are written on."

"But the signature is genuine?"

She paused, then admitted scornfully: "There's not a doubt of it. Only my grandson could manage so illiterate a flourish!"

"Yet you wish to fight this claim on you?"

She positively winced.

"How can I, Sir? There's nothing here I can fight. Wroth could have used such services."

"But a court might question their legality, Lady Wroth," I said quietly.

"Yes, but . . ." She faltered. ". . . There's more."

She proffered me a further sheet of paper.

I read it thoughtfully. It was a cleverly constructed letter. Every word had been carefully chosen to mean precisely nothing if challenged in a court of law. Yet the overall tone was threatening.

These present receipts were the lesser part of his lordship's debt to the Doctor, the writer said. As his lordship was still not yet in possession of his fortune, the writer hoped that her ladyship would honour the debt. There were, however, three more receipts still in the Doctor's possession, for services of a rather more serious nature. These services were highly intimate and in view of the Doctor's sacred oath, would remain *arcanum*. Her ladyship could be assured that the Doctor had no wish to embarrass such an eminent family as the Wroths by publishing indelicate details, and the Doctor remained confident that her ladyship would oblige . . . etc. . . . etc. The value of these receipts amounted to . . . 3000 guineas!

"Well, Sir?" Lady Wroth asked, as I looked up from the paper. "What does his lordship say about them?"

She snorted again. "He refuses to discuss it, though he admits to receiving some services. What do you suggest I do?"

"I would buy the receipts," I said without hesitation.

She looked surprised and ruffled. Clearly, that was not the answer she expected to hear from me. Her diamonds glittered angrily as she slapped her fan against the arm of her chair.

"You would advise that?" she said sharply.

"Unless you wish to be embarrassed publicly," I said. "It's possible that this is merely some kind of gammon, my lady, but it's possible that these receipts are for genuine services."

"Genuine! I tell you my grandson is in perfect health!"

I said reasonably: "There are many ailments a healthy young man can fall prey to, Lady Wroth; some of a most embarrassing nature."

"To a hair, Sir!" she snorted. "Onanism, for example! The Hideous Crime of Self-Pollution!"

The fan fluttered like an outraged dove.

". . . Or worse," I said carefully.

She considered the possibilities.

"I can think of nothing worse than the pox, Sir. And a young man getting cured of the pox is hardly a matter for blackguarding me."

The truth was out.

"Why should you think these receipts blackguard you, my lady?" I asked.

She looked away and moved uncomfortably.

"My grandson is a singular fellow, Sir," she said.

I had a quick vision of the two young women on the lawn. Suddenly enlightened, I asked: "Does his lordship often duel *en travesti?*"

She smiled grimly.

"You saw them?"

"I saw two young men fencing on the lawn. I did not know them by sight."

"My grandson was the smaller of the two." She grimaced with distaste. "The other is his friend, Mr d'Urfey. A led captain, I believe.[1] Wroth is very proud of his skill with the members. They delight in creating difficulties for themselves. I have seen them fight in all kinds of fantasticals: masks, sacks, with their arms manacled, their hands tied behind their backs, suits of armour . . . blindfold, even. This female rig-out is a favourite device."

"They are both exceptional duellists," I said with genuine admiration.

She looked away, uncomfortably flushed.

I asked delicately: "*Why* do you think these receipts will blackguard you, Lady Wroth?"

Her hands fretted away at the fan. Her voice, when it came, was a mere croak.

"Because it has happened before, Sir!"

She took a deep breath before she continued.

"Six months ago I paid off a low trollop called Dewfly."

She paused.

"Why, Ma'am?"

---

[1] A professional duellist.

"She said she could incriminate my grandson in . . . in some unsavouriness," she finished lamely.

"And was this true, do you think?"

"It could have been. My grandson is rogue-wild." A look of almost superstitious dread came into her eyes. "Young people of quality are so very vicious in these times."

"So you paid this woman off."

"Yes."

"And what exactly do you want of me, Lady Wroth?"

"I want you to rid me of this new menace."

"How?"

"In any way you can . . . legally, of course."

"I see . . ." I said. But, to be honest, I didn't.

"Do you think you can?" she asked anxiously.

"Without buying these receipts for any price, do you mean?"

"I would prefer not to . . . but if I must! . . . There must be no scandal, you see. I have hopes of my grandson making a brilliant match. A girl of good family with £20,000 a year. Nothing must interfere with my plans."

"Then don't you think it would be wiser to settle this man's debt?"

She stood up, shivering with anger. The patina of the great lady cracked slightly, and she swore juicily – an oath from her playhouse days.

"I will not be rooked, Sir! I paid this Dewfly creature because once paid she had no further claim on me. But with a rogue of this sort – " she tapped the papers violently – "there will be no end to it! He'd suck me dry!"

She moved to a porcelain desk and opened a drawer. Taking a money bag from the drawer, she turned to me again.

"What are your charges, Captain Nash?"

I quoted a figure which she promptly reduced by a sixth.

I repeated my figure and for a few moments we argued busily. But eventually she agreed on my price and seemed the better pleased that I had stuck to my word.

She counted out a number of coins and put them in my hand.

"I'll leave the matter entirely to you. Find out what you can about this Asclepius. When you have some ammunition I can use against this – this *Paphlagonian*, come to me and I shall settle with you completely."

I bowed my acceptance. She rang a handbell and almost immediately the door opened and the old manservant looked into the room.

"Captain Nash is ready to leave now, Chives," she said. She inclined her head towards me graciously and bid me good-day. I bowed to her and the interview was over. We left the room.

Chives, it seemed, now had my social measure. Instead of conducting me back through the great hall to the front door, he turned down a mean looking stairway and led me along a grimy passage, past several pantries and a buttery.

We came into the stable yard. My roan waited patiently by the mounting-block. The forelock-touching groom was nowhere to be seen. He too, it seemed, had quickly learned of the "gentleman's" true status.

I unhitched the reins from the post and prepared to mount.

A lordly voice hailed me from the stables.

## III

The voice was crisp and arrogant. It matched the man's profile perfectly. A haughty nose, sculptured cheeks, and a strong, pugnacious chin, which suggested stubbornness rather than strength of character. The eyes, when he turned them upon me, were of a curious fawn colour.

It was the indolent young observer of the fencing match. There was nothing indolent about him now. He marched purposefully towards my horse and took a firm hold of the bridle.

"I want to speak to you," he said curtly.

"I am at your service, Sir," I replied civilly.

The young man bowed in a stiff, unamiable way.

"My name is Wroth, Sir," he said. "Oliver Wroth. I am his lordship's cousin."

"My name is Nash," I began.

"Yes! Yes!" Wroth said abruptly. I know who you are. Moreover, I know *what* you are. You are a Bow Street Man, though you describe yourself in some new-fangled way."

"I work privately, Mr Wroth," I said. "I am a private gentleman." I stressed the last word slightly. Young Wroth's eyebrows rose superciliously.

"You are a Bow Street Man," he said stubbornly. "Or else you are one of Flowery's men.[1] If you are one of Flowery's rogues, you have no place here."

"I am a private individual," I explained patiently. "It is true

[1] Flowery: a notorious thief-taker, subsequently hanged for perverting the course of justice.

that I am licensed as an auxiliary to the Bow Street Police, but I am responsible only to the Mansion House. My occupation is somewhat in the nature of an experiment, Mr Wroth. I am hoping to prove to the authorities that there is scope for a detective force in England. My cousin Scrope Bentham is the Principal Secretary to the Commissioners' Office."

My explanation, and the mention of my well-placed relation, did nothing to mollify young Wroth. If anything, he grew sharper. Plainly, he regarded me as a meddling eccentric. The structure of society was very clearly defined in his mind. Judges, he knew, were gentlemen; lawyers less so. The Bar was a road to wealth and nobility, but any man lower than an attorney was beneath contempt, a battener on the misfortunes of others. That a man who called himself a gentleman should occupy himself with crime was clearly unthinkable to Lord Wroth's cousin.

These thoughts showed plainly enough on his face, but behind this outright hostility, I felt the suggestion of a separate unease.

I soon learned of it. Wroth seemed a man incapable of masking his thoughts.

"What did my grandmother want with you?" he asked bluntly.

"That, Sir, is your grandmother's business," I replied as bluntly.

"On the contrary, I think it is very much my business," he exploded, adding bitterly: "She is my cousin, the damned whore, and we will not have her back."

I said nothing. His light-coloured eyes searched my face for a sign of confirmation. I stared back at him noncommittally.

His face worked furiously.

"Lady Wroth wants you to find and bring her back?" he asked. "Is that it?"

"I can't discuss her ladyship's business with any man, Sir," I said.

"I've just told you, fellow, that it *is* my business," Wroth cried.

I spoke very courteously.

"No, Mr Wroth, you're quite wrong on that point. Her ladyship told me nothing of your cousin. Or of yourself even."

Wroth's brows drew together in a bitter black line.

"Then what?"

I swung myself up into the saddle.

"Is it my cousin Lord Wroth?"

Without answering, I took a firm hold of the reins.

"Is he in trouble again?"

I settled my feet into the stirrups.

"Is my cousin in disgrace?"

"I have told you, Mr Wroth, that I cannot betray her ladyship's confidence." I tipped my hat, clamped it upon my head, and bade him good-day.

I trotted out of the stable yard. I could feel that bright gaze following me until I turned the corner by the coachyard gate.

Once beyond the porter's lodge and out onto the open road, I spurred my horse into a gallop.

Wishing to travel at all speed back to London, I kept to the main road. But straight lines were not a prominent feature of the Wroth landscape; the main road was little more than a bridle path winding through the rich cornfields and meadows, and today was market day. Sheep and cattle, geese and turkeys, were all being driven to town, as they went, and I was reduced to moving at a snail's pace, fuming and cursing.

I was practically at a standstill, trying to extricate from a seethe of greasy sheep, when I heard the brisk tattoo of hooves coming up fast behind me. The furious pace never faltered for an instant, livestock notwithstanding. Blood-curdling shouts rent the air. I turned to see who could be so careless of the beasts. Two whooping riders charged through scattering all before them.

The sheep parted miraculously, like the waves of a fleecy sea, and the young Lord Wroth rode heavily to my side, his horse steaming. A moment later he was joined by d'Urfey.

His lordship spat out a particularly nasty oath and grabbed hold of my reins to halt my horse – an unnecessary move, as it happened, for we were once more trapped by a flowing tide of sheep.

I sat quietly, looking into his lordship's blazing grey eyes. The pale, delicate face was suffused with rage, the head thrown back, his dishevelled hair streaming out behind him. He sat astride his big bay stallion with the sinister grace of an Arabian tribesman.

"My cousin tells me you're here to spy on me," he cried, his voice cutting through the demented bleating of the sheep.

"Then your cousin tells you wrong, my lord," I said evenly, trying to retrieve possession of my reins.

Wroth refused to surrender them and slapped at my hands with the stock of his whip.

"He tells me that you're some sort of Runner. A constable, or an informer. Well, I'm here to tell you, Sir, that I won't tolerate your kind on my land. We are quite feudal here. We have our own methods of dealing with trespassers."

After a short struggle I managed to recapture the reins from him.

"It seems that you have been misinformed on all counts, my lord," I said. "I'm neither an informer nor a trespasser. I came here at your grandmother's invitation, and she has entrusted me with certain business."

He looked at me for a moment with uncertainty, and exchanged a brief, puzzled, questioning glance with d'Urfey. That handsome youth observed me moodily, a restless hand gripping the hilt of his sheathed sword.

"What business?" Wroth asked at last.

"That is your grandmother's affair, Sir," I replied.

Wroth flushed and jerked his head back. His smooth, pretty face turned amazingly ugly of a second.

"Wroth family business is *my* business, Sir. I am the *head* of my family, by God!"

The hand resting lightly on his sword tightened. The knuckles showed whitely. D'Urfey's hand also gripped his sword more purposefully.

The swarming sheep had thinned out slightly. With a gentle pressure of my knees, I urged my roan forward. A gaggle of geese waddled around Wroth's horse, causing it to rear a little, its ears flattening. His master was forced to fall back a yard or so and I took advantage of the incident to move off.

"Is it concerning me that she called you in?" Wroth shouted after me.

I rode on in silence, but I eased my sword out of its scabbard. I thought it very possible that I might have to defend myself, his lordship looked mad enough for any mischief. In his mind there was rather more sail than ballast!

With a rush, he came up behind me, forcing my roan into the hedgerow and cutting off the road before me.

"I asked you – is it me?" he hissed.

"And I have told you, my lord, that I am not at liberty to say."

For a moment we stared each other out. Then Wroth's eyes tilted crazily. D'Urfey had silently manoeuvred himself into position behind my roan. They were about to do me some injury. A furtive signal passed between them, which I rightly interpreted before they could move against me.

With a stabbing flash, I had my sword in my hand, at the ready. It described an undeviating arc in the air and hovered – the point vibrating – a half an inch from his lordship's throat.

Wroth stared at it, bemused.

D'Urfey had drawn his own sword. Now he looked at it foolishly.

"If you will tell your friend to return his sword to its scabbard, my lord," I said easily, "I shall continue on my way."

Wroth frowned, but did as he was asked.

"And now, if you will fall back, Sir, I shall be free to go," I said, my sword held steadily before me.

Wroth paused.

"One moment," he said.

I waited. The young lord regarded me coldly. He sat astride his horse, as rigid as death.

"I think I know why you visited my grandmother," he said huskily, his voice scarcely more than a thread in the clear air. "If you're so inclined, you can do her a great service."

He smiled. A rather crooked, nasty smile. I waited in silence.

"Tell her not to interfere," he said, with sudden passion. "Advise her to pay the man without delay. Otherwise . . ."

He paused. For so fragile a youth, he possessed an amazing quality of menace.

"Otherwise it will be the worse for . . . us."

## IV

I lay upon the splendiferously unplatonic breasts of my mistress, who was known to her world as Clarety-faced Jane. This lady, a trollop by nature, was perhaps my greatest asset in my new-found trade, for Clarety is impeccably informed about London life at all levels. It is understandable enough, perhaps. When a woman spends most of her working life with both feet planted firmly in the air, it is easy enough to keep an ear to the ground. Clarety is adept at her work. She is a complete treasury of secrets, though it is not impossible to unlock her breast if one knows the trick of it.

"Tell me about Asclepius," I asked her, as we rested between the pleasing motion.

"Who, sweet?" she murmured drowsily.

"Doctor Asclepius."

"Oh, him."

I stroked her soft round belly with a hard round coin. She palmed it from me in a nonchalant manner and it disappeared beneath her pillow.

"Cunning Murrell, you mean," she said, with some distaste. "That elevated rogue."

"Cunning Murrell?" I asked. "Why do you call that?"

"Because that's his name. He's just a common or garden 'cunning' man," she said contemptuously. "He travelled the road for years in Wessex. He was famous there as a wise man."

"A wise man?"

"It's not difficult to gain a reputation for wisdom in Wessex," she said scornfully. "Anyway, he prospered there, and grew ambitious seemingly. He moved to town."

"And has he prospered here?"

She laughed shortly.

"The rich and fashionable often find it dull to listen to doctor's advice," she said. "And deadly, indeed, to act upon it. Particularly when they're advised to fast or give up their pleasures. They prefer to go to a man like Murrell with his pills and his potions. But he began in a very low fashion, entertaining the mob with his magic tools."

"Oh? What tools?"

"Well, he has a magic glass that he claims can see through a brick wall!"

"Amazing!"

"Oh, truly!" she scoffed. "A truly amazing instrument. It gained the rogue much fame among the simple country folk."

"But it hasn't impressed the sophisticated London folk?"

She laughed.

"Oh, he don't use tricks like that here," she said. "A man I know got to look at this wonder. He soon robbed it of its mystery."

"What was it?"

"Nothing but a simple arrangement of mirrors in a wooden case. He said a schoolboy could have made it with a little patience and the ruins of a straining-glass. But he does have another instrument, which is far more strange."

"And what's that?"

"It's nothing more than a piece of round dull copper. But he says that by its aid he can tell a true man from a liar. For the liar might stare at it till his eyes are sore, yet he'll never see anything in it but his own self. But if you're a virtuous man, an honest man, then you can see something in it. Something of which Murrell has the secret, something which you must declare to him as proof and test of his truth. But of what that something is, nobody can tell a word, for it seems that nobody has ever seen it!" She laughed uproariously. "But belief in it is as wide as Wessex, and it's served its turn well for him, for it laid the ground-work for his fortune."

She laughed again, causing her breasts to bobble against my arm.

"It's a great time for quackery," she said. "But he has the vantage on most Empirics for sheer effrontery."

She dismissed Murrell and his nonsense by adopting a most indecent posture, and for fully twenty minutes no more was said of a sensible nature.

Despite her opprobrious nickname, my mistress is a greatly desirable woman, tall and graceful in her person, more of a fine woman than a pretty one, but with good teeth, soft lips, sweet breath and an expressive eye. She has a bosom, full, firm and white, a good understanding without being a wit, but cheerful and lively. She is humane and tender, and feels delight where she most wishes to give it. I am a well and strong-backed man, and the time passed agreeably.

After an hour or so of playful toying, cajolery and bribery, I had learned rather more about the former wise man of Wessex.

Asclepius was, indeed, the reincarnation of that Paphlagonian impostor, Alexander, of the Second Century A.D.. Like that ancient charlatan, he had adopted the name of the Greek God of Health, and also many of his practices. By means of the most childish tricks, he had managed to convince an incredible number of credulous people that the God had been reborn in the form of a serpent, with the name of Glycon. Rumour had it that he carried out his treatments whilst draped with this large, tame serpent, which wore a human head. He had a number of other strange practices and, apparently, an answer to all life's ills. His establishment was equipped with almost everything that is necessary for life. If a man had pains in his head, colic in his bowels, or spots on his clothes, the Doctor had the proper cure or remedy. If he wanted anything for his body or his mind, the Doctor's house was the place to look for it. The Doctor could recover a strayed wife, a stolen horse, or a lost memory. He had cured the consumption, the dropsy, gout, scurvy, the King's Evil, and hypochondriac winds. All was done, it seems, by the use of one miraculous cure – no bleeding, no physic. He had, he said, been taught his trade by an Eastern Magus.

"And when he runs out of real sicknesses to cure, he invents his own," Clarety said. "He's invented Moonpall, the Marthambles, Hockogrockle and the Strong Fives."

"Very wise," I said. "If you invent an illness, it is easy enough to invent a cure for it."

She grew serious.

"There is something about him, though. The girls here swear by his 'telling'."

"Oh? Does he deal in the supernatural also?"

Like most women of her type, my mistress is careless of life but terrorized by the thought of "the Beyond". She would not jest about this aspect of the Doctor's activities. It took a great deal of by-play, a small stream of honeyed phrases, and five more coins, before she told me of the Doctor's acquaintance with the occult sciences. He had a familiar, it seems, an oracle who would answer questions put to him. And in illustration of his necromantic skill, he would erect pyramids of numbers, Solomon's key – what the vulgar call the Cabbala – by which he could extract answers at will; either clear, ambiguous or unfathomably mysterious.

I began to see the true nature of the Doctor's practice. When gullible folk seek such answers to their problems, they as often as not give away far more than they receive. The three outstanding receipts on sale to Lady Wroth would contain a great deal more poison than had ever been taken from his lordship's body.

Thus, armed with a little knowledge, I went to confront the Doctor. By dint of gentle bullying, I could, I felt sure, persuade him to part with the embarrassing records of Lord Wroth's follies or vices or worse.

## V

It proved easy enough to find the Doctor's establishment, for the route was well advertised. The posts of houses and the corners of streets were plastered over with his bills and papers urging the public to go to him for remedies. The advertisements had a fine flourish to them, and he had a gallimaufry of cures.

INFALLIBLE Preventative Pills against The Plague.
NEVER-FAILING Preservatives against The Infection.
SOVEREIGN Cordials against the Corruption of the Air.
EXACT Regulations for the Conduct of the Body in the Case of Infection.
UNFAILING Anti-Pestilential Pills.
The ONLY True Plague-Water.
The ROYAL Antidote against all Kinds of Infection, and such a MIRACULOUS beautifying Liquid that it will Restore the Bloom of 15 to a Lady of 50.

They were such a number that I lost count. He even offered to advise the poor for nothing. Which advice, I had no doubt, would be to buy the Doctor's physic.

All of them were to be had only at the Sign of the "Anodyne Necklace", at the East End of Barnard's Row by the School.

Barnard's Row was a grey-faced, respectable looking street, behind the tall, rambling façade of the Bars. The sign of the "Anodyne Necklace" hung before the most solidly built house in that solidly built street. Plainly, business was thriving, which scarcely surprised me in view of Clarety's information. The public are always ready to throw their money away on physics, charms, philtres, exorcisms, incantations and amulets. It is indeed a golden age of quackery and one remedy is as fatal as another!

I opened the door and entered beneath the swinging sign. A bell jangled, but the room was empty.

To walk into this unusual, strange looking shop, was to be transported to another world entirely. Here in profusion were all the varied ingredients of the cure-pedlar. It was a dark, magical cavern rather than a shop.

There were big pails of pickled entrails and buckets of what I took to be black, salted eggs; they could as easily have been a beast's parts marinading in a preservative. Counters and shelves were laden with jars of brightly coloured powders and packets of black and forbidding dried stuffs. Some of the jars were labelled with such exotic information as that they contained: "Snail's Water", "Oil of Earthworms", "Roast Slugs", "Viper's Fat", and even "Live Lice" – for swallowing, Clarety had informed me.

It was like a witch-woman's pantry. There were dried cuttlefish, dried mushrooms, dried shoots, dried nuts, dried stalks, and from the ceiling there hung the stomachs of dried fish. In one corner there were some curious live reptiles in a glass-box, so ugly-looking that they would have frightened Old Nick himself. From the walls there hung the implements of his trade: a bristling armoury of fierce looking knives, scissors and choppers. The shop could have armed an uprising. It was a place of potent atmosphere and it stank dreadfully.

I stood in the midst of all this strangeness for a moment or two before I called out "Shop!" The eyes of dead fish and live reptiles stared at me unwinkingly. I had an eerie feeling that, somewhere out of sight, more nightmarish eyes were watching me.

I thumped with my cane on the floor. At the rear of the shop a door opened and a bizarre figure emerged from the shadows.

He was a singularly unattractive young fellow of about middle height, thick-set and muscular, with a truculent expression and an aggressive jaw. His hair was of a bright and forbidding red, his eyebrows drawn like a portcullis over small and bloodshot eyes. But his most distinguishing feature was the pair of white buck-teeth which protruded from his upper lip and gleamed with absolute savagery when he smiled. There hung about him an odd, perverse aroma, and he was clad in what seemed to be an archaic livery.

"Can I help you, Sir?"

The voice was low and silky, surprisingly beautiful. A voice well-used to putting the prospective customer at his ease.

I decided straightway to use the brash approach.

"I wish to see Mr. Murrell," I said.

The young man's smile stayed fixed, but gleamed obscenely.

"Mr. Murrell, Sir? You must have the wrong address."

"No, this is the right address. I refer to the old wise man of Wessex, 'Cunning' Murrell."

The smile had faded now, only the red eyes gleamed.

"We have no Mr. Murrell here, Sir," he said bleakly.

"The Doctor, then," I said impatiently. "Asclepius. The 'Blameless Physician'."

The red eyes peered at me ferociously beneath the rufous brows, but his voice remained as smooth as silk tabby.

"Asclepius sees nobody without an appointment, Sir. Is there anything that I can do for you?"

"I doubt it. My business is with your master. Tell him I am come to settle a debt."

The young man's fears were now thoroughly aroused. He examined me closely, computing to make up his mind concerning me. He almost sniffed at me, scenting trouble. At length he said:

"I am empowered to settle accounts, Sir."

"It is not in your power to settle this account," I said. "My business is with your master."

He hesitated. He was now appraising me quite frankly, measuring my physical strength against his own. He decided that I might prove too much for his weight.

"My master is not here," he said stubbornly.

"Then I shall wait."

"He won't be here until very late, if at all today."

"Then I shall make myself comfortable." I settled myself upon a small gilt gesso chair, tipping it back against the low wooden counter.

The red-eyed man observed me sourly for a moment. Then he turned on his heel and faded back into the shadows, the bright red hair doused like a candle in the general murk. I waited for the next pass. Once more, I felt the numerous eyes fixed upon me.

The servant reappeared a moment later. His eyes held my own, his chin was thrust out pugnaciously. He had obviously received instructions. I tensed myself, expecting him to try to hustle me from the shop.

But he said patiently: "If you will state your business, Sir, I'll settle it for you."

"My business is with your master," I repeated.

"My master is not here," he said, as stolidly.

"Then I shall wait."

"He will not be here today."

I crossed my legs, balancing my back against the counter carefully.

"Then tell me where I may find him," I said.

"My master never receives outside of here."

His small red eyes were on my sword, swinging negligently at my side. His foot was placed so that, should the opportunity arise, one quick flip of his leg would send my chair spinning. I eased myself out of the chair, yawning.

It seemed final. If the old impostor refused to see me, I had no means at my disposal of forcing him to do so, short of tackling this brutish young servant physically. I had decided beforehand that the best way to deal with Murrell was to approach him directly and try to browbeat him into relinquishing the receipts. But I could see no purpose in forcing myself on him bodily, thus raising his defences immediately. The situation required some subtlety. Besides, for all I knew, there was a back way out of the premises, and it is impossible for one man to lay siege to a house with several exits. And, in the main, it might not be a bad thing to leave the Doctor sweating a little.

I smiled at the young man affably enough.

"I'll call tomorrow," I said. "At what time will the Doctor receive me?"

The servant hesitated. He said truculently: "He'll be busy tomorrow. Why can't you state your business plainly, and be done?"

"I'll call tomorrow," I said, trying to mix pleasantry and menace in my manner.

His troubled eyes never left me until I myself had left the shop.

I was convinced that the Doctor was still in the shop and so I decided to lay in wait for him.

I quickly spied-out the area. First of all, I made sure that Murrell could not escape me by way of a rear exit. With businesses like Murrell's, there has always to be a backdoor.

The only rear access to the house seemed to be a narrow passage between the houses. I walked quickly down it and found myself in a broad court, surrounded by a high wall.

Satisfied that the Doctor could only leave by one of two exits, I returned to the street, keeping well out of sight of the shop-window.

Like Murrell, I had a trick or two of my own. I, too, possessed a glass, that if it could not see through a brick wall, at least it could look round corners. It was my own invention, a small, round mirror, smoked in order not to reflect the sun's rays, and angled on a telescopic stick. A primitive device, yet with it I could stand out of sight of my suspects and still keep them under observation.

I took my place behind a mews' wall and focused my mirror on the shop.

For two hours I remained stationed there and nothing of any importance happened at all. A few callers came to the "Anodyne Necklace", but not a great press of people, by any means. They almost all entered self-consciously, if not furtively, and they all left carrying small parcels. The Doctor's customers seemed to consist largely of middle-aged women and decrepit old men.

But nobody came out who had not gone in and I began to feel that I was, perhaps, playing a wrong hand.

Within the space of this two hours, the weather had changed dramatically. Warring thunder clouds came up out of the west, and by mid-afternoon the sky was as cold and lowering as a moorland bog.

I thought of abandoning the siege.

Then, at five o'clock, there was a sudden flurry of activity outside the shop. A sedan chair carried by two scrawny looking chairmen came to a stop before the door. The door opened, the red-haired man peeked out, looking left and right. His head disappeared, and a moment later a man and a woman came down the steps.

They were an eccentric pair. The man was an old, dun-coloured man, as dry and precise as arithmetic, hollow-faced, scant of hair, long-nosed, short of chin, and possessed of a most uncivil leer. He climbed into the chair and the chairmen closed the door on him.

The woman who followed him out was a most extraordinary creature. I had never seen her like. She was a strong-looking black woman, as ugly and misshapen as her master, wall-eyed and bandy-legged. It was impossible to tell her age, so marked was her face with the pox and the Evil. She walked with a curious sideways roll, for all the world like a sailor on shore-leave, but this may have been due to the way she was encumbered. On her head towered an enormous turban, topped with a package, which she held secure with one hand. She was saddled like a mule, with a harness of parcels, two small baskets like donkey panniers at her hips, and a bag slung from her shoulders.

The men heaved the chair from the ground and set off at a steady pace, the black woman following like some fantastic pack-horse.

I trailed behind at a discreet distance.

They plunged into a maze of twisting streets and stinking alleys that led towards Cripplegate. The road was pitted with holes filled with last week's rain-water, and everyday's filth. The kennels were running with sweepings and dung.

I walked along, keeping one eye on the chair and one eye out for the natural hazards of the street, and I held a scented sachet to my nostrils, for the stink grew appalling. I kept as close to the walls as I could, as a protection from any slops thrown from the windows, though this grew increasingly more difficult as we penetrated deeper into the slums, for even the walls themselves were plastered with excrescences.

Stepping out from a particularly gruesome protuberance, I was almost bowled over by two horsemen who came careening around the corner. Stepping back into the safety of the wall, I was accosted by a huge young savage who stopped me from proceeding further. We almost came to blows over who would "take the wall".

In the end, I half-drew my sword and the hulking lad stepped aside with a mouthful of coarse abuse.

By the time I reached the end of the street, the sedan chair had vanished into the thick air.

## VI

I searched the surrounding streets rapidly, but without success. I felt vastly discouraged. They had vanished like water down a drain, though leaving less trace. I spent over an hour trying to track down the sedan chair, asking questions of a quantity of people.

But people in this part of the world had little inclination to impart information, even for money. Indeed, people in this part of the world hardly seemed to be of the human race. Every creature I spoke to was as surly as a butcher's dog.

My temper was fairly kindled at my folly. All my walking about in the clammy heat had been totally unnecessary. I should have played the game with more finesse, smoothed my way into Murrell's presence and only then turned upon him. I had made a tactical error in alerting him to his danger. I saw that now. There seemed nothing else for it but to give up for the day.

Two horses dashed out of a side street, showering me with small stones and dry mud. I looked up angrily and then stood staring after them, gawping.

Lord Wroth and d'Urfey sped down the street, endangering the lives of several unwary pedestrians.

I turned my attention eagerly to the street from which they had so precipitously emerged. It proved to be a blind alley of even more sinister an appearance than the rest of the neighbourhood. The buildings to either side had derelict, windowless walls of blackened brick, so tall they cast a permanent shadow across the street.

I walked to the end of the alley. The structure facing me was as featureless as the others. A wall, bare of doors or windows. The only gate was boarded up and had not been opened for months or even years.

I stood there, feeling baffled. I was as sure as certain that the horses had turned out of this street and, indeed, my nose told me pungently that horses had used the area. Physical proof of it lay on the cobblestones. But it seemed impossible that Wroth and his comrade had been visiting in this street. Perhaps the house they had visited stood near by? Perhaps they had only stabled their horses here temporarily?

I walked down the alley once more, and stood looking at the gate. It had a monstrously derelict air about it. I lowered my eyes to stare at the cobbles immediately before it. Stooping, I picked up between my thumb and forefinger a small amount of grey ash. Somebody, only moments before, had emptied the bowl of his pipe here. I then noticed faint silvery scratches on the cobbles. A horse – or two horses – had stood before this gate, their shoes striking restlessly upon the ground.

Why had they been waiting by this particular gate? I looked at it again. It was about a foot and a half above my height. I reached up and grasping the rim of it raised myself to peer over it.

I found myself looking into a narrow yard and at the back part of a tall and crooked house. It leaned perilously towards me, grim and menacing, its windows blank with dust. There appeared, at first, to be no entrance to the building, and then I saw that steps led down to a deep-cut area in which was set a narrow door.

The yard was strewn with rubbish and thick with dirt. Even from my place above the gate I could see the faint trace of footsteps leading across it. They began about a yard away with a deep scuffed mark where a body had landed after jumping, and the returning footsteps stopped by a large box set immediately below the gate.

Almost without stopping to think, I climbed over the gate. I dropped into the grey dust of the yard. There was a narrow, dismal passage at the side of the house which led into what appeared to be a tunnel. I entered it cautiously and was at once plunged into a sable gloom, lit only by the faint light forcing its way through the dingy fanlight of a door at its far end. Dust swirled in my nostrils, and I could feel them beginning to swell. It was a damp, dispiriting place, with a curiously threatening air to it. I walked slowly and carefully, half expecting to be ambushed at every step. With my sword drawn, I opened the door cautiously. It groaned like a soul in purgatory . . .

I was amazed to find myself in a pleasant and expansive courtyard, elegantly paved and set about with vines and jessamine. A screen wall surrounded the courtyard, broken in the centre by an impressive iron-grille gate. The gate was guarded by two stone lions, fiercely rampant, yet with expressions of unshakeable piety. I stepped into the court and turned to look at the house.

It was a middling sort of house, a square rose-bricked edifice. The contrast between its frontage and its rear was remarkable. The façade was charming, strong and placid, with no frippery. The shutters were painted a gay yellow and the large front door had both a canopy and a fanlight.

For a moment, I believed that I had made another mistake. But no, the sedan chair rested in a corner of the courtyard, cooled by the shade of a fragrant tree.

This, I saw, was the house I was looking for. But how had Murrell got here from that warren of dirty lanes behind me? No doubt I could find that out when I faced him. I walked up the broad steps and pulled at the bell-rope.

The bell pealed deep inside the house and I waited for the echoes to die away before I pulled the rope again.

I waited two minutes more and then set the bell a-jangling. There was no response.

After twenty minutes of futile bell-pulling and frustrating door-knocking, it seemed obvious that either the house was deserted, the occupants were deaf or I was going to be ignored. Once again, I had a strange feeling of being watched. I felt that even the lions had their pious gaze upon me.

I tried to peer into the ground floor windows, but I could see nothing; the heavy curtains were drawn tightly against the evening light.

I turned away from the house and decided to leave by the front gate. It was, of course, locked.

For a moment, I was lost for action. It must, I knew, be obvious to whoever was inside (if anybody was) that I, too, had entered through the back-premises, and this must have greatly alarmed them.

And forewarned them. For I would have to return by that direction. I felt a proper annoyance at my lack of thought. Indeed, I seemed to have taken no thought in this matter so far! It was apparent to me now, from the assistant's unusual behaviour in the shop, that the Doctor was the type of man to have any number of enemies of a greater or a lesser sort. It was also apparent from the Doctor's subsequent behaviour that he was a sly and nasty individual who would deal with his enemies in a sly and nasty manner. No doubt, at this very moment, some thoroughbred bruiser lurked below, waiting for my hesitant steps. The criminality is audacious and brutal, I am a brave enough man, but I don't believe in courting ill-fortune. I had no intention of returning through that treacherous black tunnel.

Without further ado, I set one foot on a lion's backside, put the other foot on its kingly head and, making sure that the street was empty, heaved myself over the wall. I dropped down on the other side to find myself in a broad street.

"What street is this?" I foolishly asked a passer-by.

"Why, Paradise Close, to be sure," the surprised man replied.

I pointed at the house I had just left.

"What house is that?" I asked.

He looked affronted.

"Why that, Sir, is the notorious Temple of Health!" and chuntering furiously, he hurried away.

Dr. Godbold's notorious Temple of Health. What had "Cunning" Murrell, alias Dr. Asclepius, to do with that hot-bed of quacksalvery?

And how had the wise man managed to transport himself from the squalid streets of St. Giles' to this ample and respectable close? By magic? More likely by sleight of mind. He certainly hadn't entered by the back-gate through the mucky yard. I had followed the track of only one man through it; and, besides, the sedan chair would never have passed through the narrow confines of the tunnel.

How, then? Was there a third entrance to the house? I decided to try to trace one, should it be so. I would have to accost the slippery fellow in the street if he continued to refuse to meet me. And if the man made use of secret entrances and exits, as seemed likely, it would be as well to know.

The Doctor, I could see, was going to be the devil to catch.

## VII

I had walked around the house three times and had come to the conclusion that the chair had travelled from the street where I had lost it by way of an intricate maze of stinking alleys and ill-lit wynds. It was the only possible way that I could trace, and not very satisfactory, but I was now convinced that there were no secret entrances or exits.

I returned to Paradise Close and settled down to waiting. It was growing dark and a faint gleam of candle-light showed between the curtains. I tried the gate once again and found it locked. I saw no point in vaulting over the wall to hammer on the door. In this uncertain light, I couldn't be sure of the welcome I'd receive.

I found a convenient waiting-place, about five houses away from the Temple, sharing an alcove with a battered Venus. She was a most formidable lady with a monstrously ostentatious bosom, and I felt rather relieved that she was cast in bronze.

The rainclouds swelled and the watery night gathered in, the sun bidding a tearful farewell to the West.

An hour passed and the broad street became deserted. An hour more and it was dark, hot and heavy – the prelude to a storm.

A light showed at the door of the Temple. There were coarse voices raised in anger, and the scrape of steel on a wall. The Doctor, it appeared, was about to take to the streets once more. And this time, his servants were to be armed.

The gate opened and the chairmen jogged into view. A link-boy preceded them, the flame of his torch smoking steadily in the still air. The chair was followed by the Negress, saddled as before with numerous parcels. The chairmen each carried a short sword.

The small procession disappeared into the murky streets. I followed from close enough behind, the link-boy's torch leading me steadily onwards.

They had travelled for about half an hour when the storm broke. What happened then was too confusing for me to understand from a distance. The rain fell in a sudden sheet, and it was either the rain that quenched the light, or else the boy deliberately plunged it into the mud. With a terrified cry, he fled.

Cursing heartily, the chairmen dropped the sedan, and scrabbled in the mud for the torch. One man struck his tinder in an attempt to make some light for the search. A peal of thunder shook the sky and lightning streaked above the black houses.

What happened next occurred with inexpressible speed.

A group of men came running from behind the houses. They were armed with cudgels and cutlasses, and they were yelling like savages. They encircled the sedan and tried to wrench open the door. The chairmen turned and ran, without waiting to defend their master. Only the Negress tried valiantly to ward off the swarm of men, but she was sadly hampered by her harness. She fought like a demon, straddled between the bars of the chair, but a well-placed blow from a cudgel knocked her roughly to one side and she fell over, rolling about the street like a tortoise turned upon its back, trying desperately to rise. Even whilst lying helpless on the ground, she managed to take hold of a stout leg to try to throw a man on his back.

Inside the sedan, the terrified old man kept a desperate hold on the door, but his efforts were futile. With a crack of splintering glass, a sword broke through the window and, plunging into his breast, pinned him firmly against the back of the cabinet. Then the sword was drawn smartly out again and the old man slumped against the window, the shattered glass tinkling to the ground.

The men ran off into the darkness.

I ran to the sedan chair. The Negress had managed to pull herself to her knees, moaning and chattering to herself in some outlandish tongue.

I pulled open the door and reached inside. Blood ran over my hand and the old man groaned horribly. For a moment, I thought that he still lived, but blood gurgled throatily from his lips and he died with a dreadful rattle even as I pressed against his chest. I quickly searched his pockets, only to find them empty.

The Negress came up behind me, hissing fiercely. I turned in time to catch the arm that plunged towards me wielding a wicked looking dagger. I deflected the blow, pushing her heavily to one side. She fell against the sedan chair, which toppled over and fell with an ear-splitting crash to the ground, the momentum of the fall taking her with it. High above the street a few shutters were opened and lights showed at the windows. The citizenry were beginning to take a tentative interest in the affair.

I wasted no more time, but ran off in the same direction that the ruffians had taken. I stopped at the corner of the street, faced with three different directions. Of the murderers, there was no sign.

## VIII

I walked quickly away from the area. When the Negress revived, she would no doubt rouse the neighbourhood and the night-watch would take care of the corpse. I saw no point in implicating myself in Murrell's death.

As I walked through the mean streets, my mind was busy with various conjectures. Who had killed the old man? Was it a purely fortuitous incident? Violence and death were only too common in these streets at night, the Great Unwashed are infinitely more dangerous than any savage tribe. Murrell was, quite possibly, simply an ordinary casualty.

Or was it deliberately designed? Had he been the victim of a plot? The old charlatan must have made many enemies in his career. No doubt Lady Wroth was not the only wealthy aristocrat to be challenged with such a demand. Ours is a licentious age. The possibilities of evildoing are limitless, and Murrell was a man to profit by them. It seemed more than likely that some poor catspaw, harassed beyond endurance, had decided to rid himself of a money-sucking leech. It is an easy enough business to hire an assassin, some men would do the task for the price of a gin, and this matter had a designed look to it. The way the link-boy had doused the light and fled at the precise spot where the bravoes had lain in wait suggested a collusion. Unless the butchers had been following? Then again, the chairmen had put up no fight at all, the Negress had shown more spirit. It could be that they had thought the battle too unequal, but the fact that they had fled in silence with no cries of help, or for the watch, seemed to point to their implication in a plot. It would be interesting to know if they were in the Doctor's service or whether they were casually employed. If they were professional chairmen, then it was the more likely that they had been procured by assassins. It is easy enough to bribe a chairman, they are frequently in the pay of thieves and cut-throats and they will often lead their hirers into a trap, only to run and leave them to be murdered, raped or robbed. Yet Murrell must have trusted them to have had them carry him through the streets at night? He must have known of his danger, or else why arm his men?

The more I thought on it, the more obvious it became that the affair had been managed in some way. The clearest evidence of this was that Murrell alone had been slain by the assassins. And they had not stopped to plunder him. That surely pointed to a planned attempt to silence him. Well, there would be many a timorous soul glad to have him silenced.

How was Wroth involved in tonight's doings? He knew of Murrell's second house and the obscure ways to reach it. He had preferred to call upon the old charlatan in secret. Why had he gone there? To threaten the old man? To warn him? He seemed wondrously concerned to let his grandmother squander his own inheritance to stop the wise man's mouth. What was the secret of Murrell's hold over him? It must be grave to bring him rushing up to town in such a funk. Had he gone to Murrell to take the receipts by main force? And had he failed in his first attempt?

The thought pulled me up short. Had Wroth been implicated in the murder? Having failed to secure the papers at that afternoon's interview, had he arranged to take them by violence tonight?

I shrugged the thought away. Even the foolhardy Lord Wroth would know that Murrell was unlikely to carry such valuables on his person. They would be safely locked away in some chest.

Locked away! The implication struck me like a blow. Whoever had killed the old man had lifted the lid of a Pandora's Box. The nasty contents would scandalize London to its very core!

Once Murrell's death was known, his house would be investigated by the Bow Street Police. Whatever evidence he had against Wroth would become public property. God knows what others would suffer also. Rather than silencing Murrell, they had done the reverse. If a dead man could talk, the old Cunning-man would shout from the rooftops.

Confronted with this fact, I saw that I had two alternatives, both of them equally obnoxious to me. My commission had been to secure the papers by any means legally possible. To fail to do so would part me from a very powerful patroness. It might even put an end to my career at its outset. Yet in order to secure them I would have to place myself in an even more invidious position. Breaking and entering, however justifiable the reason, would not do me any good service with the authorities, should I be discovered.

It was a fine point of morality. Yet, somehow, I must get hold of those receipts.

Two hours later, I had raided the shop in Barnard's Row. I had searched the place from cellar to attic, to no avail. What papers I found were straightforward accounts and bills of lading, quite innocent of double meaning. Either others had forestalled me, or else Murrell kept his secret papers in a less accessible locality. The latter seemed more likely. He was far too wily a rogue to leave such a treasure unburied.

I decided to investigate the house in Paradise Close.

I raised my head above the rim of the gate. The back of the house leaned towards me, as forbidding as God and as silent.

Carefully I eased myself over the gate and dropped softly into the dust of the yard. I moved cautiously towards the house.

I looked at the lower windows and at once ruled them out as a means of entry. Beyond the grimy glass they were either boarded up or covered by an iron grille. I turned my attention to the basement. It was pitch-black at the bottom of the steps, but covered. I risked a light, and struck my tinder. It was a strong looking door and had not been used for an age or more. Cobwebs glittered from the corners and the disturbed dust gleamed all around me. After a brief examination, I realized that nothing short of a battering ram wielded by a dozen men would have any effect on it.

I walked back into the yard and looked up at the house. The overhanging eaves loomed above me. My eye was caught by a protruding object, a water-spout in the form of a gargoyle. If I could climb on to it, it would give me a foot-hold from which I could reach the upper windows.

I looked about the yard and came upon the box that Wroth had used to climb the gate. I heaved it on to my shoulders and carried it back to the house. Placing it beneath the window, I mounted it and stretching my arms upwards towards the gargoyle, I grabbed the spout with ease. Slowly I pulled myself up.

Five strenuous minutes later, I was precariously balanced upon the ugly stone head and my eyes were on a level with the window. I saw with relief that it was a simple affair of plain glass set in a flimsy wooden frame, fastened by an iron catch. I took out my jack knife and inserted it beneath the fastening. Rust flaked from it beneath my pressure and, with a faint squeal, I forced the clasp upwards.

I opened the window and pulled myself over the sill. In a moment I was standing in a room bare of furniture, save for a deal table and three rickety chairs. It was a mournful place, the whitewashed walls were peeling and yellow, the ceiling blackened with decades of dirt.

I creaked across the floorboards and stood behind the shabby door. There was no sound beyond it. My entrance had gone unremarked. I opened the door as quietly as I could, but the hinges still screeched slightly. I looked into a long and narrow corridor, as bare as the room behind me. Pools of water gleamed on the boards in the light of a dusty dormer window. Obviously, the back of the house was little used.

Slowly and carefully I edged my way along the corridor feeling my way with every tread. My steps seemed to creak with devastating effect in the eerie stillness of an empty house.

I came to the end door which was more solidly built. I waited a moment, listening hard for a sign of life beyond it. There was an absolute silence. I turned the handle and pulled the door back inch by careful inch.

A weird blue light filled my eyes. It blazed from a brazier, intense and fierce, and yet soft and lambent. I had never seen a light to equal it. It was a strange mixture of radiance and mystery.

Lesser lights shone in odd corners of the room. One in particular attracted my attention. It was a monstrous lamp that stood on what appeared to be a black marble altar. It was lewdly designed in the shape of a bat, with an erect member.

The lamps illuminated the strangest room that I had ever seen. It can only be described as "Dionysiac" – an orgiastic display of a wild and dissolute character. Over the entire length of the gaudily painted ceiling, naked men ravished naked women in a bewildering variety of postures. Seen from below, it was an outlandish sight; these couples seemed to be copulating in mid-air, and their freedom of movement enabled them to indulge in the most amazing amatory acrobatics.

The murals on the walls were more prosaic, not to say more basic, though the models here, too, were supple in the extreme. The murals were poor copies of the indecent paintings from ancient Roman frescoes. All the known positions of sexual gratification were illustrated, and when human partners were exhausted, the animal kingdom took over, along with creatures from the ancient world: sileni, pans, satyrs and centaurs. But the females were always female, if not more than female.

Along the sides of the room were arranged richly upholstered couches, and several statues stood about the room, all of them highly indecent. There were a number of Egyptian gods, including the god Min, with his proudly displayed phallus. Among the Greek entries were several metamorphoses of Zeus and a bronze Hermes holding a staff carved with a phallic symbol with the tip painted red. Rome was represented by a squatting Cloacina, the Goddess of the Sewer, befouling her own shrine.

An oriental odour perfumed the air, and by the brazier a number of jars were placed. They were filled with "magical" herbs, waiting to be burned: belladonna, hemlock, henbane, verbena, mandrake. All of them powerful narcotics.

In a large glass case were the prostitute's stock-in-trade for the relief of carnal desire – whips, ropes, high boots and oddly constructed instruments whose exact purpose escaped me, but whose meaning was plain enough.

The room was a shrine of sexual abnormality. Apart from curing his patients of their ills, and foretelling their futures, it seemed that Murell also catered for their lusts. That is, *if* he had any connection with the Temple. Clarety had told me nothing of it and if he had an interest here, she would surely know of it.

Against one wall stood the centrepiece of the whole ensemble. A great bed, an extravagance of crimson silks and glass pillars, perfumed with essences; a bed designed for pleasure, a bed dedicated to the cult of Aphrodite. It was large enough to accommodate at least ten people and, no doubt, often had. Beneath the gleaming canopy hung a mirror, contrived to reflect the transports on the mattress below. I never saw such a bed in my life before. It could have come from the Grand Turk's Seraglio.

I realized that I was looking at the most famous bed in London. Dr. Godbold's Celestial Bed, designed for "the Propagation of Beings Rational and Far Stronger and More Beautiful in Mental as well as Bodily Endowments than the Present Puny, Feeble and Nonsensical Race of Christians. No One exists Frigid enough to Resist the Influence of the Pleasure of Those Transports which this Enchanting Place inspires."

This was the notorious bed, guaranteed to restore the impaired constitutions of emaciated youths and debilitated old men, warranted to revive any constitutions that were not absolutely mouldered away. I had heard that some jaded voluptuaries had paid upwards of £500 for the privilege of fornicating on this bed. Two great lords swore that their heirs had been sired in it when all other means had failed. I tested its resilience; it seemed filled with the most springy hair, but behaved much as any ordinary mattress would.

. . . Dr. Nathaniel Godbold. What was his connection with Murrell? Or was it yet another alias? Was this Temple the real core of his blackguarding activities? This room would prove more fertile when it came to extracting secrets from his customers than the shop in Barnard's Row. Men are at their most vulnerable when taken either in drink or in lust, and under the influence of this sense-saturating room what would they not reveal?

Yes, I felt sure that this house was the centre of the web. I moved to the door and opened it cautiously. With a shock, I started back.

In the hall a figure stood with one finger to his lips, as if bidding me to be silent. Both frozen, we outstared each other.

Then I laughed softly to myself. The figure was a statue. Hippocrates himself. The lamplight flickering on his face had made him seem lifelike.

I walked down a broad corridor, frugally lit by candles in sconces. I opened five doors leading into various rooms, all comfortably furnished, but eerie in the unsteady light of the candles.

In one room, resplendently furnished in marble, another statue of the Goddess Cloacina squatted on a marble pedestal. This, I realized, was the famed Temple of Ease, devoted to those suppliants who suffered from digestive ailments. Again the variously ambiguous instruments were in evidence.

I left the room, and walked down the corridor. A wide staircase descended to the ground floor which was shrouded in darkness. By the head of the stairs stood a heavy, mahogany door. I tried the handle gently. The door remained solidly barred against me.

A few minutes with the blade of my knife, and the door swung open smoothly. The shuttered room was stiflingly dark; a dim assembly of shapes. I struck my tinder.

My eye was caught immediately by the iron strong-box. It stood upon a solid desk.

Naturally, it was locked. It took five minutes of concentrated effort to force the lock, and my heart sank with disappointment at the result. The box contained nothing but a leather-bound book with a faulty clasp. The same neat and clerkly hand that had addressed the letter to Lady Wroth had written a jumble of meaningless phrases and figures in this book. I saw that the book was an elaborate code in the Cant Language, the thieves' dialect. The first thing I could make sense of was a name, "Charles Winstanley" coupled with the date of 18th March 1769 and a place, "Caper's Gardens".[1] My mind turned this information over, and I was suddenly alerted. Had there not been a notorious scandal at Caper's Gardens concerning a certain young rakehell by that name?

I put the notebook in my pocket, thinking that I could probably break this code since I am fairly conversant with the Cant. I searched the rest of the room to no purpose, and descending the stairs, turned my attention to the lower floor.

The hall of this Temple was a testament to Godbold's (or Murrell's) cures. It was ornamented with crutches, walking sticks, ear-trumpets, eye-glasses, trusses and so on, all discarded by grateful patients. Had he been of the Catholic persuasion, the good doctor might have qualified for sainthood.

A bare half hour later, I let myself out by the way I had entered. The rooms below had proved to be conventional reception rooms that gave up no secrets, for they had no secrets to keep.

## IX

I was taking my morning chocolate at the "Black Cat" Coffee-House in Greek Court, and searching diligently through the *Gazette* to see

---

[1] A pleasure-garden after the fashion of Vauxhall.

what news there was of last night's doings. There was none, which
scarcely surprised me, since murder and violent theft are rife in those
streets. The people of St. Giles' have a rat's eye view of life, are more
fearsome than any brute beast, and nearly as ignorant. The crime
would have to be of a very sensational quality for it to be registered
in print.

In this instance, I would do better with my ears than with
my eyes. I set myself to listen in the neighbouring taverns and
coffee-houses.

But not a murmur reached me of Murrell's death. Not even my
mistress mentioned it, though her working day is spiced with news of
vice and crime. If Clarety-faced Jane has no knowledge of an event,
then it has not usually taken place. But no detail of Murrell's death
had come to her, nobody had breathed a word of it. This silence
intrigued me almost as much as the mystery of his death. It was as
if all the world had compacted to treat his murder with the greatest
possible secrecy.

Not wishing to display my own association with the affair, I made
my enquiries indirectly. It is always best to question Clarety when
she is lost in heat, for then her mind is only triflingly occupied
with the questions and her answers fall from her lips involuntarily.
Accordingly, I set myself to thoroughly arouse her that morning.
When she threw her arms around me warmly, I embraced her as
warmly. As she wound her arms around my neck with passion, I
took her legs with equal force and passed them round my waist.
I met her kisses and murmurs of pleasure with just as strong an
amorous toying and sucked her tongue as readily as she sucked
mine. By the time I loosed her drawstrings and got into her, she
was purring with delight and in a good frame of mind to pass on
any information to hand. But she knew nothing of Murrell, though
I pumped her mind as thoroughly as her body.

I left her scratching herself erotically with a silver piece.

On reflection, I decided to walk back into the filthy maze of
St. Giles'. I might, I thought, be better rewarded in the low drinking
dens of that quarter. Information, of a sort, is always to be bought
in such places, if one can cut through their barbarous jargon.

Turning into the stinking alley of Jay Row, I saw a crowd gathered
by an open well. The shrill sound of their conversation rattled against
the walls of the houses, making the street hum like a gigantic beehive.
A woman howled fanatically, another screamed, men's voices were
raised in a righteous anger. I almost hesitated to linger there long
enough to find out what disturbed their peace. For the London mob
is a thing to be avoided at all times, even the king dare not stand in

its way once it is aroused. And this seething mass of dirty humanity was thoroughly aroused. I began to skirt around it gingerly, feeling my way among the mud and filth of the street. The crowd stank so badly that it was all I could do not to raise my wipe[1] to my nose in plain self-defence. Had I done so, they would have set about me at once. Delicacy, in that area, is a red rag to a bull. And they were in a very ugly turn of mind.

Two enormous men appeared to be pulling some object from the well. As I passed by, the crowd fell back slightly and the men dumped their burden on the ground.

It was a dead man. The mob howled with fury.

"Christ a'mighty," said a voice close-by. "'Tis bad enough with mice, rats and tabbies in the warter – but this dirty, buttocking bastard!"

"'ow the 'ell did 'e get in the supply?" asked another.

"This was the best warter in St. Giles'," wailed a woman. "Now we gotta drink it an' 'e's warshed 'is scabby feet in it."

The mob roared agreement. A woman kicked the sodden body.

I found myself staring at the dead man. His eyes stared back into mine, without light or sense. The head was bent at a peculiar angle to his body as if it had been struck a heavy blow. He looked like some large, pathetic doll thrown casually away by a thoughtless child. The eyes gleamed dully, and a trickle of water ran from the gaping mouth. A knife protruded from the base of his neck. There was no blood, that had been washed away; the water of the well was crimsoned, as I could see in a bucket that had been drawn up. The corpse's skin was a bluish white from some hours' immersion in the well.

A few hours before, he had been young, lithe, very handsome, and *dangerous*.

I was looking at the mortal remains of Lord Wroth's duelling partner. Tom d'Urfey had lost his last fight. His body was already stiffening obscenely in the morning air.

"What happened?" I asked my vociferous neighbour.

A dozen outraged voices clamoured to enlighten me.

"He fell in the well!"

"Dirty maggot!"

"Pushed more like!"

"'e's broke 'is neck, I'd say!"

"Been down there for 'ours, the block, cloggin' the warter."

"We couldn't understand it. Warter just dried up."

"Like a drought it was."

[1]Handkerchief.

"A visitation more like!"

"Garn! Got his dessarts, I'd say."

A lively argument ensued as to how the dead man had found his way into the well. Under cover of it, I leaned forward to get a closer look at the body.

I could see at once that he had not bruised himself by falling. The blow had been delivered by a sharp, clean rap from a heavy instrument. It had been performed by somebody who knew what they were doing. A skull-cracking cudgel wielder. Also, he had not drowned. There was not enough water in him for that.

For whatever reason, young d'Urfey had been killed with cold deliberation rather than in a hot-blooded brawl. Concussed and then knifed. And by a dabster in the art.


# X


The following morning, I again read the *Gazette* from the first to the last page, hoping to find some reference to Murrell's death, but there was no mention of it. On the other hand, young d'Urfey's untimely end had been immortalized in five well-turned paragraphs, no less – no doubt because of his eccentric burial place. When murder is a daily commonplace, it is only the unusual detail that will titillate the public's jaded palate.

But, apart from the natural sense of outrage (only a thoroughly unsociable murderer would poison the water supply in this manner), the journal was parlously short of any real information. There was nothing to identify the body, he had neither money nor papers upon him when finally he was handed over to the Bow Street Office and, as a pauper, he was to be thrown into the common grave.

His murder was simply one more unanswerable crime in the calendar of daily violence.

I decided to pay another visit to Murrell's shop, and an hour later I faced his uncivil assistant. The red eyes gleamed more ferociously than ever, and his hair stood up as though brushed backwards by some unseen hand. His smile, though resolute, was skeletal.

"Is your master ready to meet me now?" I asked.

He looked over my shoulder towards the door, almost as if he expected the ghost of his master to waft into the room. His manner, though uncouth, was distinctly more polite than it had been yesterday.

"No, Sir. He is not here. If you will tell me your business, he has empowered me to act for him."

"And I have been instructed to deal only with your master."

"He is not here," he repeated, much subdued.

"Then where may I find him, man?" I snapped impatiently. "This business could have been settled twenty-four hours ago. Twenty-four hours would have made all the difference."

A look of blind panic swept over his foxy face. His Adam's-apple ran up and down his skinny throat until I thought it must surely pop out of his flapping mouth. With a great effort, he set himself to answer me. His voice was like that of a broken bell.

"He is not here. He is not in London . . . You must come again."

"Tomorrow?" I asked ironically.

"Tomorrow," he repeated vacantly.

I stared at him severely. "Where," I wondered, "will you be tomorrow?"

Tipping my hat to him, I turned and left the shop.

It was time to take up my position behind the wall again. I did so, and adjusted my spy-glass.

My patience was soon rewarded on this occasion. From the back access to the shop emerged the strapping Negress, garlanded much as she had been upon the previous night. But today she was pulling a small handcart which was packed tight with boxes. Behind her walked the red-haired assistant, wearing a small-sword and, I suspected from the bulge in his pocket, sporting a loaded pistol.

I allowed them to gain the full length of the street before I emerged from my hiding place. For the rest of our journey together, I kept a street length respectably between us, for I had no desire to confront the Negress again. And as for her fiery attendant, he looked too jittery altogether to be entrusted with fire-arms.

Following them through the rank warrens of St. Giles' proved to be more difficult than one would expect. Apart from the natural hazards of walking through such streets in the darkling light, there was always the possibility of running blindly into them round each crazy twist and bend. Indeed, this almost happened on at least two occasions, the nervous assistant having loitered behind the Negress, obviously fearful of being followed.

I felt relieved when they had left the hideous tangle of St. Giles' and Soho behind them, and we turned into the more spacious quarters of Mayfair, though shadowing them here presented a new hazard, for in the long wide walks I was the more exposed. Trying valiantly to keep them in sight, I began to hang back, hugging the walls. And in the shady reaches of Newick Square, I lost sight of them entirely. I walked along all four sides of the leafy square, looking into the great mews on each side of it, but with no success at first. Then, on the southern side, towards Green Park, I looked into a mews and saw the handcart leaning against a hitching post. I walked under the archway, keeping a watchful eye on the windows. Fortunately, the walls to either side were largely blank-faced.

The yard was empty, as was the handcart. A few wisps of straw stirred limply on the bottom planks. A few wisps of the same straw led me directly to the back door of No. 12, Newick Square. The door was closed, the studs of which looked at the world dead-eyed.

I retraced my steps into the street and stood looking at the even more imposing front door of No. 12, Newick Square, wondering moodily what sort of house it was and what manner of people lived there. Nobody at all respectable, I eventually decided. But somebody with an imposing income – or remarkable wits.

## XI

As I reached the door to my chambers, a familiar voice hailed me. It was as crisp, cool and arrogant in my quarters as it had been in his own stable yard. The eyes were as hard and bright above the proud nose, but his manner was a touch more conciliatory. He bowed almost politely.

"I should like to talk to you, if you are at liberty," he said.

I bowed in reply and waited. Mr. Oliver Wroth was obviously experiencing the greatest embarrassment in seeking me out. Wroth was the sort of man who can define a gentleman as dispassionately as one can define a kipper. He could claim coat-armour, I could claim nothing – not even a decent trade. I watched him writhe for a moment or two. He had no clear idea of how to treat me.

I unlocked my door at last, and allowed him to precede me into my rooms. He seemed impressed by my spartan taste in furnishings (the pure result of my impecunious state). He looked about with interest at my spoils and trophies, the mementos of my travels and adventures, that lay dotted about the room.

"You aren't, I take it, a man of any great property," he said bluntly.

I waved a hand about the room and said airily: "You see before you the full extent of my fortune."

He was amazed at my candour and at my raillery.

"Do you hope to make money from your trade?" he asked at length.

"If there is any to be made."

He looked at me carefully, as if weighing up my chances.

"I should think you could make opportunities," he said guard-edly.

He waited for me to make a reply. I disobliged him. After a moment he went on uneasily: "I've been trying to reach you for the last six hours. You're a hard man to track down."

"I have that talent," I said drily and waited again.

He seemed to have fallen into a profound mood.

"Has something happened?" I asked eventually.

"Happened?"

"I gather your cousin's friend is now your cousin's late friend," I said bluntly.

He looked up, startled.

"D'Urfey?"

"Yes."

"He's dead?"

"Yes."

He gnawed at his nether lip for a while and he then seemed to shrug the matter away.

"Well, he's no great loss to the world," he said. "No doubt he met a just end."

"A poetic end, at least. Face down in a public well."

He gazed at me in blank astonishment, but he seemed to be startled rather than shocked.

"A public sewer would have been more fitting," he said savagely, and sat down. "But, no matter for that. I came to see you on other business."

I waited again. At last he said, putting his hand against his wallet suggestively: "Is it quite impossible for you to tell me why my grandmother sent for you?"

"Quite impossible."

"Was it about my cousin Wroth?" he persisted. He appeared not to have heard my reply, but all the same his hand moved the wallet until it showed above his pocket.

"I am not at liberty to say, Mr. Wroth," I said, somewhat severely. ". . . For any price."

He looked at me closely, read my face aright, and his hand fell away from his pocket. He seemed obscurely pleased at my attitude.

After a moment's thought, he reached into his greatcoat pocket and pulled out a bulky envelope. As he handed it to me, I discerned a slight tremor in his hand.

"Read that," he said. "Then tell me if it is why you were hired by my grandmother."

I opened the envelope. It was addressed to Mr. Oliver Wroth in the same neat hand that had written to his grandmother. I drew out a sheet of paper which was unsigned. It proved to be a copy only of another receipt for "services rendered" to Lord Wroth. They proved to be highly original services, and prodigiously obscene. The original of this receipt had been signed by Lord Wroth, an enclosed note explained.

I raised my eyes from the paper and looked into the impassive face of young Wroth. The light eyes glittered faintly, otherwise the handsome face was immaculately composed.

"How much do they demand?" I asked.

"There's more, apparently," he said between his teeth.

"But how much do they ask?"

"£20,000. For all the receipts together. We have to pay them by Saturday or they will publish the details. Once they do, my cousin is finished in society. His chances of making a tolerable match are nil."

"The demand came with this letter?"

Wroth smiled unpleasantly. "Yes."

"You have the letter?"

His smile grew even more unpleasant.

"No. The messenger allowed me to read it, then took it back with him."

"What kind of a man was this messenger?"

"A heavily armed man," he answered wryly.

"Did he have bright red hair and eyes like poker-ends?"

"No. He was a grey-faced man."

"What did he say exactly?"

"Very little. He just delivered the letter. I rather think he knew nothing of the matter himself."

"So there's no proof of demand," I said.

"None at all. Deuced clever, really."

"And there's nothing more to it than this?" I asked sharply.

The question took him by surprise. A look almost of alarm flashed through his eyes and his mouth tightened perceptibly.

"Is this not sufficient?" he asked bitterly. "You know English society. Let a thing be rumoured and it can be passed over. A man can even acquire a kind of clandestine fame. But let it once become public property and a man is as good as dead. My cousin Wroth, at the moment, passes for a brainless young eccentric like a good many of his kind. Many young men of today lack the resources which can lead to a cure imposed by self-discipline – " He gestured towards the paper with distaste. "But once that nastiness becomes common knowledge, there's not a good family in England will be on nodding terms with us, let alone marry into us."

"Where is his lordship now?"

"At home."

"Where was he last night?"

"Last night? Why, at home."

"All the night?"

"To my knowledge. I was myself in London."

"In London?"

"At the Italian Opera House. I went to hear Catiani sing. She has a damned fine voice," he added appreciatively.

"She keeps it in a damned fine chest," I said.

He looked complacent. "It's not too difficult to open, either, if you have the right key," he said modestly. I gathered that he had already tampered with the lock.

"And d'Urfey?" I asked.

"What of him?"

"Isn't he generally inseparable from your cousin?"

I let the implication stand, letting it brew a little. He scarcely seemed to notice.

"Generally," he said. "But not last night, it seems." I tapped the paper.

"Do you intend paying this?"

"If I can lay my hands upon the money."

"Is that possible?"

"Not impossible."

"Your grandmother will no doubt – "

"No!" he said sharply. "She's not to be bothered by it. I can raise the colour elsewhere."

"Oh?"

"I can borrow it. From the Jews, perhaps. From friends."

"Why not go to the Bow Street Police?" I asked reasonably.

"I can't," he said simply. "I have to protect grandmama," and added, as an afterthought: "and my cousin."

I gestured towards the paper again. "But if this is all there is to it – in a matter of this sort, they would say neither muff nor mum – "

"No!"

There was a strained pause. When he spoke, it was with difficulty.

"I can't. Word would get about in the way it does. The scandal would kill grandmama, and ruin us all."

He raised his head arrogantly, his pride mastering his conscience.

I could not shake off a belief that there was something more behind his refusal. Nauseating as this receipt was, I felt there was a worse matter on his mind.

I said as much.

He flushed hotly.

"There's nothing worse. What could there be that's worse than . . . that!" He flicked the paper from my hand and ground his foot upon it angrily.

Suddenly he looked at me in an almost beseeching manner. Strain and anxiety showed plainly in his face. Only pride kept him from complete supplication.

"Can you help me? It's what I came for."

"I might be able to," I said cautiously.


# XII

The Temple of Health stood aloof from the activity of the Close, like a ship pulled high on a beach, away from the invading waves. The windows looked as empty as the house behind it.

The house *was* empty, I knew that well enough, for I had kept it under observation for the last twenty-four hours. Like the shop in Barnard's Row, it had been abandoned with scant ceremony, its occupants fled God knew whither.

Having kept such a close watch on it without a sign of life, I had almost decided to abandon it. But an odd demon of obstinacy kept me at my post. Although I felt that the house had revealed all the secrets it held, I believed that patience would still reward me. For one thing, I was sure that the book I had taken from the strong-box was a key to the mystery. When this key was found to be missing, others would come seeking it. They would naturally come here to this house. So I continued my vigil.

I wondered if they would have understood the book better than I did. So far, my own attempts to break the code had been lamentably unsuccessful. Apart from one or two unimportant details, the book was all Greek to me – except, of course, that I speak a passable Greek.

Daylight was fading and I was on the point of turning away, when a slight movement in an attic window caught my eye. For a moment I wondered if I had imagined it but, as I looked more closely at the window, I saw that a shutter was, indeed, a trifle ajar. At my last inspection it had been fast tight.

Within five minutes I was over the wall, through the passage, and climbing through the back upstairs window. It had been conveniently opened for me by a visitor who had left his tracks clear away from the alley wall.

Padding soft as a cat through the upper rooms, I gained the front stairs. I stood, listening hard, straining for a sound from above or below.

An almost imperceptible creak from the landing above alerted me. I edged back into a recess, my hand easing my sword from its scabbard.

A leg appeared on the bend of the stairs, feeling for the tread. It was an elegant, well-turned, almost delicate leg. A second after, the torso appeared and a moment later I was looking into the smooth face of the young Lord Wroth. In the obscure light, it was truly amazing how much menace was packed into that slight frame. The face, with its fresh, translucent skin, looked at the same time to be old and drawn. The eyes were drained of feeling. He had, I felt, undergone some great emotional crisis in these past few hours.

Like myself, his hand was on the hilt of his sword, yet for some reason he neglected to draw it as I stepped out of the alcove, my sword at the ready.

I gave him a slight bow.

He stared at me with a curious, blind stare. I could swear that he hardly saw me and certainly did not know me.

"What are you doing here, my lord?"

He continued to stare at me, apparently trying to fix me into his scheme of things.

"Do you remember me, my lord?"

He swallowed, frowned, and then nodded. The eyes began to come alive. He flushed painfully and the mad glitter swept through his eyes, and was gone as quickly. His eyes were then as blank as before.

"What are you doing here, my lord?" I asked again, patiently.

"What are you doing here?" he countered vacantly. His fingers began to fret at the hilt of his sword, yet he made no move to withdraw it . . . for the moment.

He was obviously never going to answer me. He behaved like a man whose mainspring had broken. I felt it time to administer a shock.

"Who killed him, my lord?"

"Killed?" he echoed. The word hung like dust in the air.

"Who killed Tom d'Urfey?"

The eyes tilted suddenly and his whole body twitched convulsively. The sword rattled from its scabbard and then scraped along the wall as it dropped to his side. His body sagged dejectedly.

"I don't know," he said dully and sighed deeply.

It was time to administer a second shock.

"Perhaps it was the magician?"

His head reared back and his eyes rolled wildly. For a moment it looked as if he was going to jump over my head and flee. He shrank back against the wall.

"Asclepius," I said. "Alias 'Cunning' Murrell."

He looked over my shoulder fearfully. I half wondered if he expected to see Murrell's mutilated body materialize before him. Then his eyes seemed to clear, the superstitious awe faded, and he looked at me contemptuously, but with a greater awareness in his eyes, almost an interest.

"But then," I said gently, "the good Doctor could hardly have come back from the dead to avenge himself, could he? Despite his powers."

He was regarding me with a definite interest now.

"So it must have been somebody else who murdered your friend," I said.

He breathed out slowly.

"Yes," he whispered. ". . . Yes."

"Why did you come here, my lord?" I asked again.

The interest in his eyes faded. Once more he repeated my own question. This time, however, I got a distinct impression that he was addressing himself.

With a shock I realized that he *was* addressing himself. He had no clear idea of his purpose there.

"Were you looking for something?"

He frowned.

"What did you hope to find here?"

The frown deepened.

I nodded towards the upper regions. "You didn't find it there?"

". . . Not there," he said slowly.

"Down below, perhaps?"

He looked at the lower stairs as though he had never seen them before. Since quite a lot of his pleasuring must have been done between these walls, his lack of comprehension now was highly disconcerting, almost unnerving.

Like a sleepwalker, he began to descend the stairs, a foundling strayed, the sword trailing behind him like a discarded plaything. He seemed to have forgotten my presence. I followed a few paces behind, to see where his steps would lead him, to discover what part of the house would revive his memory.

The trailing sword looked harmless enough in his loose grasp but, remembering his dexterity on the lawn, I kept a tight grip on my own weapon.

It was an eerie experience to walk through those lewd rooms behind this once favoured customer, who responded in no way to what he saw. With his fair, almost angelic face, he looked like a scrubbed, country innocent, a Christian choirboy who had wandered, by chance, into some heathen temple.

Walking thuswise, we reached the reception hall. By this time, the last of the daylight had drained from the sky. The hall was a gloomy cavern of marble and porphyry.

Wroth stood in the hall, at a total loss. He looked around him in a dazed sort of way. Nothing stirred in his eyes.

Then he stiffened suddenly and I stiffened with him. He had heard the faint whine of the iron gate as it swung open. Feet paused before the steps, then climbed them steadily. A key turning in the lock and a streak of dirty twilight swept along the floor as the door fell open.

But long before the door was fully wide, I had pushed Wroth into the safety of a small alcove. I leaned forward slightly, trying to see who had entered. Young Wroth leaned limply against my arm. I could feel him trembling, and his breath was short and shallow. It must, I felt, quickly betray us. I put a hand over his mouth. He struggled for a while, the whites of his eyes alarmingly prominent. Then he seemed to relax, his breathing loosened and I myself breathed more freely. He was not, I realized, in any way afraid. He was, rather, monstrously excited.

Not that my fears for our position were immediately justified. Whoever had entered showed no interest in our hiding place. He had walked purposefully in the direction of the back premises where he struck a tinder and lit a candle. His head disappeared below stairs and a moment later I heard a succession of doors open and shut in the cellars.

There were a few minutes of strained and agonizing silence. Then from below came a muffled oath and a heavy object crashed to the ground. At once, the man came running up the stairs as if the Devil and all his fiends were in pursuit of him. The front door swung open and crashed thunderously behind him.

The reverberations echoed for a few seconds, to be followed by an uncanny silence. Young Wroth gasped like a man surfacing from deep water. He shook himself like a dog. For the first time I saw a real sign of intelligence in his eyes.

"Pelham," he said hoarsely. The name shot out of him like a cork from a bottle.

Pelham? The Pelham? The notorious Sir Harry Pelham?

"Pelham?" I asked.

"'Gambling' Pelham."

The Pelham. Sir Harry Pelham. What was his connection with this house? I knew he owned a gambling-hell and was reputed to own shares in Mother Wells' brothel, but what was his relationship to Godbold (or Murrell)? A very close one, by what I could judge. He had moved around this house with great familiarity.

I turned to Wroth to question him further, but his eyes were glazed over once again and he had retreated into his own private world.

I decided to investigate below stairs. But what to do with Wroth? I thought it best not to leave his lordship to his own devices. I would be safer with him under my eye. If he came to his "senses", I might well be his next duelling partner. Taking him by his sword arm, I led him to the head of the cellar steps. He came along as docile as a child. In my own sword hand I carried the candlestick, hastily thrown down by Sir Harry in his flight.

We began to descend the stairs . . .

The first room that we came to was the kitchen, a vast place cluttered with the paraphernalia of a well-run establishment. My candle reflected a forest of gleaming copper and dull pewter. There was nothing untoward in its appearance, all was exactly as I had last seen it.

Passing along a short corridor, we came to another door and behind this, I remembered, lay a small office. This, too, was as I had last seen it, save in one particular.

Beyond the office lay yet another room – a room that had not been in evidence at my last visit.

A panel was drawn back in the wall, giving access to a sort of priest-hole. It looked to be no larger than a handsome tomb. Which is what it now was. Sepulchral candles glimmered beyond the wainscot. A rank, stale smell mingled with the headier scent of incense.

I felt Wroth's arm tense beneath my hand and his knuckles whitened on his sword-hilt. My own hand circled his arm in a tight grip as I waited for his next move.

Nothing happened, save that he went limp again. Like a man in a dream he moved forward, under the gentle pressure of my hand. The candlelight flickered as we bent to pass into the secret chamber, then it steadied, and the light magnified with a startling brilliance as the rays were reflected from the innumerable silver and copper ornaments that decked the room. For a moment we were dazzled, then our astonished eyes took in the full, garish horror of the scene.

Gaudy coloured idols stood upon pedestals, surrounded by flowers of a monstrous vulgarity. Strings of glass beads, winking baubles and cheap rosaries were hung from a number of gold crucifixes. A Virgin, with a face as black as midnight, exposed her breasts to an infant Jesus of equal darkness. In one corner stood an enormous wooden cross, surmounted by a black tricorn hat. A skull with brilliants in its eye-sockets grinned at us from beneath it.

It was a foul, obscene, and heathen funeral chamber, and it produced a strong impression on my mind. What effect it had on young Wroth's less regulated senses can only be imagined. His arm trembled like an aspen beneath my fingers.

The centrepiece of these gaudy trappings sat enthroned in a chair. "Cunning" Murrell, his ghastly, lifeless eyes staring beneath his magician's hat, sat waxen-faced, dressed in a robe covered in strange hieroglyphics, his body in a state of rapid decomposition.

The heat of the candles and the rancid odour of the corpse filled the room to turn your stomach.

It was clear now why Murrell's murder had not been reported. In the eyes of his servant, the poor, half-savage Negress, her master had not died. He sat here, among her baubles, awaiting resurrection!

The same thought must instantly have occurred to Lord Wroth. With a weird, echoing howl he tore himself from my grasp and fled up the stairs.


# XIII

It was time to pay a call upon the house in Newick Square, which I now knew belonged to Sir Harry Pelham.

I stood before the imposing door and pulled the bell-rope. A proud and saucy-looking footman opened it to me.

"Sir?" he asked insolently.

"I wish to see Sir Harry Pelham."

"Many do, Sir," he said squarely. "What name shall I give?"

"My name is Nash. Captain Nash."

"And what business may I state, Captain?"

"My business."

"Sir?" The impudent eyes rose superciliously. He sneered at me openly. He was a good man at a door. It began to close imperceptibly. I recognized that he had all the qualifications necessary for a footman.

He had, no doubt, turned away twelve duns that morning. He knew his duty to his master – to lie for him, pimp for him, and allow nobody to cheat him but himself.

"Sir Harry is not receiving today," he said, gazing unseeingly somewhere above my head.

Casually I scratched my nose with a small shiner. His eyes travelled slowly down my face. The movement of the door was halted fractionally.

"My master is not receiving today," he repeated, his gaze fixed upon the coin.

"Will he be at home all day?" I asked.

"He'll be walking out to his club within the hour," he said. With a startling rapidity, the coin disappeared beneath the lace cuff of his sleeve and the door was shut firmly in my face.

I set myself to wait.

Surely enough, the door opened some forty minutes later and the tall, bull-headed figure of Sir Harry Pelham walked down the steps. He strode purposefully in the direction of St. James' and I marched after him as resolutely.

Sir Harry Pelham was a most notorious rake with a scandalous past. He had always sported a reputation. As a student at Cambridge he had drunk the most beer, sworn the deepest oaths, sang the noisiest songs, and fought the most duels. He had honoured all his friends by the most liberal levies on their purses. After expulsion from his college he came to London, where he speedily got rid of the remnants of a small fortune. A sad scamp as a youth, he had grown into a full-blown rogue in manhood. In order to raise supplies, he had to betake himself to such resources as a nimble wit presented to a not over-scrupulous conscience. Detected in false play, kicked out of one gambling-hell after another, until finding them all too hot to hold him, he had taken to arranging card-parties which, despite (or because of) his extreme reputation, were doing very well. He was the perfect rake; he would die of fast women, slow horses, crooked cards and straight drink – but he would die in his own good time.

I caught up with him as he turned into Green Park.

"Sir Harry!"

He looked at me enquiringly. A man with a mortal aversion to bailiffs and constables, he regarded me for a moment as if I had crept from beneath a stone. Then realizing that I was not an agent of the law, the heavy brown eyes regarded me with a sort of dull impassivity. All the same, his hand tightened on his walking-stick, his "oaken towel", his "knocking-down argument", as he called it.

"Sir?"

I bowed.

"What is your business with me, Sir?"

"Murrell's business," I replied.

There was not a flicker of light in that turgid brown stare.

"Murrell?" he drawled. His voice had the easy, insolent quality that can make the most commonplace statement sound like an epigram and this was largely the basis for his reputation as a wit.

"'Cunning' Murrell," I said. "Or Dr. Asclepius, if you prefer that name."

"The 'Paphlagonian'?" he asked lazily, a slight interest stirring in his eyes and his hand encircling his stick with a tighter grip. "What have I to do with his business?"

I smiled at him confidingly.

"You have his business stacked away in your cellars, Sir," I said. "Unfortunately, as you must know by now, you lack the key to it. I have the code-book."

A gleam like a small cinder began to glow in the treacly eyes. A slow and dangerous anger.

"Shall we take a turn about the park, Sir Harry?"

His mind was made up on the instant. Perhaps I was too great a challenge to his gambling instinct. With a slight ironic bow, he indicated a path leading towards a leafy arbour.

We paced together slowly down the path. Not a word was exchanged until we reached the comparative seclusion of the trees.

"Well, Sir?" he drawled.

I waited whilst a nursemaid and her charges passed beyond our hearing. He grew restive.

"Patience is not one of my virtues, Sir," he said.

"Neither is caution, Sir," I replied coolly.

His eyebrows rose.

"The little cavalcade that brought the goods to your back door, Sir Harry," I explained reproachfully. "A veritable circus. I'm surprised that half the children in London weren't on their backs."

Sir Harry sighed dolefully.

"Time would not allow for a more finished performance," he said heavily. "What do you want? You said that you possessed the code-book."

"And you have the provisions," I said. "The patents and the medicines."

My ploy was to confuse him as to my motives. He would not, I felt, do business if he thought it honest.

"The patents! The medicines!" he snapped. "Quackery. Sugar and water! That is what I have invested in."

"Is it all quite useless?" I asked.

The cinders in his eyes now glowed like coals.

"Water cannot be turned into wine, Sir, without a worker of miracles!" he said shortly.

"But there's money to be made from his gulls – once you can read the code."

A dull flush crept into his face.

"There are famous names in that book, Sir Harry," I went on, gently insistent. "The whole world would be interested in the disclosure of their vices."

The stick shook slightly in his hand.

"There is a treasure house between its covers," I said.

A look of the purest anguish showed in his dark eyes.

"Of course," I told him, almost affectionately, "such an enterprise would require a considerable power of organization behind it, if it is to run smoothly. It needs a man confident of his position in society to guide it properly. A man well-used to catering for the whims and fancies of the great and noble."

"True," he agreed, and spat contemptuously. "Murrell was an incompetent, a man without style." His eyes ran over me like a horse-coper sizing up the season's stock. "Do you fancy your chances in this line of work, Mr. er . . .?"

"Nash," I said. "Captain Nash."

"Well, Captain? Do you?"

I shrugged nonchalantly. "I could hardly do less justice to the trade than Murrell did," I replied. "And I'd know where the danger lies."

"The danger?"

"I'd know who my enemies were, Sir Harry."

"And Murrell didn't?"

"He was singularly careless. He should never have entrusted himself to a sedan chair so late at night and in such an area."

Genuine surprise showed in Pelham's eyes. For a brief moment I exacted a look of wary admiration from him.

"How did you know that?" he asked.

"I was there, Sir. I saw it all."

He was puzzled by me. He mused silently for a moment, his large hand massaging the head of his broad-stick.

"He must have received an urgent summons to bring him into those streets at that hour," I said suggestively.

A strange smile played about his lips, but it did not linger.

"Are you saying that I was responsible for his death, Sir?" he asked.

"I am saying that you could be made to seem so."

He raised the stick and struck the ground with a snapping blow.

"You take risks, Sir," he said softly.

"I am merely saying that the charge could be laid at your door, Sir Harry. You would have a hard time proving that you aren't connected with him."

He shrugged wearily.

"Why should I want to rid myself of a partner in a lucrative venture?" he said.

"In order to make the venture more lucrative – for yourself, perhaps?" I suggested.

"Pah! As I said before, miracles need a miraculous hand. Murrell was the magician."

"Murrell was a box of tricks, Sir Harry. No more than that. A sham is what Murrell was, Sir. Such tricks can be taught to any avid learner."

He considered it.

"What do you want from me?" he asked at last.

"Little enough," I said. "I want the Wroth papers."

"The Wroth papers?"

"The receipts signed by Lord Wroth. In return for which you may have the code-book and my silence."

He frowned. "And if I don't have the papers?"

"I think you have them, Sir."

He smiled wryly.

"And if I were to assure you, Sir, that I don't?"

He laughed without amusement, then answered my unspoken question.

"The old rapscallion! I fear our magician may have had more partners than we bargained for."

He laughed aloud – an alarming sound. If a tiger could laugh, he would make a sound like that.

We walked into a clearing and Pelham's laughter turned to a choked gurgle. He fell heavily against a tree, his stout walking-stick breaking beneath him.

A knife had whistled through the green air, catching him in the shoulder a little below his neck.

# XIV

He was not greatly injured, but he was bleeding profusely and swearing like a duchess in labour. The knife lay on the ground where he had flung it. He was trying to stem the flow of blood with a silk handkerchief. He looked up, his face working savagely.

"After him!" he spat. "I'm not dead – nor even dying. After him! Get after him, man!"

He spoke to me much as he would to a hound. I ran across the clearing without another thought, in full cry.

There was no sign of his assailant but a few broken twigs and some leaves swept aside by a cloak. And a small leather pouch. I picked it up and put it in my pocket, then pressed through the trees to where the park spread out in the afternoon sun.

It was a calm enough scene, a typical English park, with the greensward and the red deer grazing. Towards the lake a few people sauntered along the walks.

I skirted the clump of trees in which the would-be assassin had lurked. There was no sign of him. Nothing disturbed the utter stillness of the leafy thicket but the twittering of birds. I made my way cautiously back to Pelham.

He had struggled to his feet and was leaning languidly against the tree which had broken his fall. His hands clutching the material to his wound were soaked with blood.

I took off my neckcloth and attended to his wound as efficiently as I could. He looked at me, his eyes as dull as molasses.

"Did you see him?"

"Him?" I asked.

"Wroth." he answered thickly.

"Wroth!"

His mouth twitched bitterly. "Did you not see him?"

I shook my head.

"Naturally not," he said sarcastically. "You are their man."

I looked at him closely.

"Did *you* see him, Sir Harry?" I asked. ". . . Truly."

His eyes flickered sideways.

"I thought I did. It seemed like."

"Did he wear a bandana?" I asked abruptly.

He looked up from examining the still welling blood, his eyes puzzled.

"A bandana?"

"Yes."

"What do you mean, man?"

"I found this in the wood opposite," I said, and showed him the leather pouch.

"So?"

I turned it over. On the reverse side was an embossed design. A strange device, a barbaric device. I picked up the knife; emblazoned on the cheap gilt hilt was the same design.

His eyelids twitched nervously, for a moment the whites of his eyes gleamed fiercely then, once again, they dulled over. I knew that he had recognized the symbol, it had been prominently displayed in Murrell's funeral chamber.

"So?" he asked again.

"You've never seen this device before?"

He shook his head slowly.

"And yet Murrell was your partner?"

"Is it his?"

"Did you never remark his cabbalistic designs?" I asked. "You must have seen it on the cloth that covered his corpse."

This time I had struck home. The breath whistled out of his body.

"His corpse?"

"You saw it laid out in the Temple of Health."

His eyes met my own. A look of superstitious awe passed over his face.

"Are you ubiquitous?" he asked, at length.

"I was there."

He gestured towards the pouch.

"And this?"

"This held that knife."

His lips twisted ferociously.

"Has Murrell returned from the dead then? To cut down a man who never harmed him?"

"Not Murrell, no. But his slave, possibly."

"His slave?"

"Servant, then."

"The black woman?"

"Yes."

He looked incredulous.

"She thinks I killed her master?"

"It would seem so," I said.

He staggered and shivered violently. I thought he was about to fall and reached out a hand to steady him.

"You'd better get me home," he said.

The impudent footman let us into the house, his face an amusing mixture of concern at his master's condition and surprise at seeing me in attendance. I sent out for a surgeon at once, and saw Pelham stripped and put to his bed. The wound was in his flesh only, but it could have been dangerous had it gone a bare half an inch deeper or higher.

Pelham lay on his crimson damask bed. So far not a murmur of complaint had passed his lips, though he swore roundly and often at the covey of servants who crowded in and out of the vast room. He had forbidden them to send for the Bow Street Men, insisting that it was no more than a common street brawl he had been involved in and not worth the inconvenience of calling in the Law. His servants, who knew their master, were willing enough to give way to him in this.

I stood by a classical fireplace in the elegant Adam room, musing deeply whilst all this activity surged around me. I was trying to create some pattern from the events that had occurred. But nothing emerged with any clarity.

I was mostly concerned with the most recent incident. Why did Pelham think he had seen Wroth in the clearing? Had he seen him truly? If so, why was Wroth there? Had he thrown the knife? The possibility had to be admitted. It was even possible that the knife was his, a gift from Murrell; it was the sort of toy that he'd appreciate. Perhaps Murrell had breathed some magic incantation over it, rendering it as accurate as Achilles' immortal weapon? That was the sort of preposterous flummery to impress his lordship.

I looked at the knife, which lay upon a Pembroke table, its blade encrusted with dried blood. Yes, it was more than possible that Wroth had hurled it; remembering his murderous skill with the foils, this deadly toy seemed a likely weapon for him to use.

But then again, remembering his skill, it seemed more like that he would directly have challenged Pelham to a mad, fanatical duel if he had any quarrel with him. This method of despatch seemed altogether too sinister, too stealthy, for such an impetuous person.

An image of Lord Wroth as he had stood beside me in the Temple came into my mind. He had been curiously reluctant to take his sword from its scabbard, though it had been halfdragged from there. All the mad, murderous rage in him seemed to have died. Could it be that without d'Urfey to jack him up, he had no taste for the game? Lady Wroth had called d'Urfey a "led captain" – could it be that he had allowed young Wroth to seem a better man with a sword than he was in truth? It would have been in his favour to flatter his lordship. And Wroth was not perhaps too mad to realize that he was no match for a stronger man without his friend's support. No match for a man of Pelham's talents, anyway.

In which case, he might well resort to stealthier tricks. But his shot had gone wide of the mark and that fact bothered me if I had to consider him as a suspect. For Wroth had shown he had a good eye for a mark and this knife had been intended for Pelham's exposed neck.

Pelham's neck! The knife that had killed d'Urfey had protruded from the base of his neck, though he had been an unresisting victim when the blow was struck. Was it possible that whoever had killed d'Urfey had killed him in an identical way to Wroth's plans for Pelham? Could it have been a purely fortuitous coincidence? But no, it seemed too close.

Pelham had been mistaken when he thought he saw young Wroth. Unless, of course, the boy believed Pelham responsible for d'Urfey's death and had planned an identical end for the baronet? It had the right, gory, poetical touch to it.

But . . . I turned the pouch over in my hand. The device glittered in the sunlight . . . What of the Negress? This pouch seemed to link her with the crime more fittingly than Wroth. To kill a man by a knife thrown in stealth seemed a more primitive method of despatch than an Englishman would use in a London park. And the knife was obviously connected with Murrell. It had a barbaric feeling about it. It looked to be a ceremonial sort of knife. Such a killing, to a woman like that, would be more in the nature of a ceremony than a plain act of revenge.

But why should she seek to murder Pelham who was her master's friend? And if she had dealt in this way with Pelham, then she must have dealt with d'Urfey in a like manner? Save that one had been unsuccessful, the two means of despatch were the same, and two unconnected murders in the same manner would be stretching coincidence beyond the bounds of probability.

But surely there could be no connection between the murdered youth and the luckily escaped Pelham?

Which brought my thoughts back to Wroth.

Wroth! A sudden thrill passed down my spine. Why had such an important fact escaped my notice before?

Pelham had made no mention of *Lord* Wroth. Or even *young* Wroth. He had simply said "Wroth". Could he have meant the cousin? Could it have been Oliver Wroth that he had thought he saw?

There was a commotion from the servants as the surgeon prepared to leave. I went forward and stood by the footpost of the bed, waiting to put my question to Sir Harry. As the surgeon turned away, he laid an admonishing finger to his lips, as if to say: "No more excitation today, please."

"I have given Sir Harry a draught," he said, self-importantly. "He should sleep quite soundly now."

Pelham already slept extremely soundly.

# XV

I spent the rest of the day in deep thought, equally divided between the pros and cons of the business and the wrongs and the rights of it.

My mood was an uneasy one, for it was growing increasingly apparent to me that I could not continue to act contrary to the Law in this affair for much longer. I ought, at the very least, to report my finding to the Bow Street Office. Two men, both closely connected with this case, had been done to death, and one more had come near to death. That was a matter for the official authorities of the Law, and could I, at this stage of my new career, afford to ignore it?

On the other hand, I had an employer to protect and a living to earn. How could I go to the police with my story, relevant in all its details, without involving her? I had been granted a licence to act as an auxiliary to the police, but how could I count upon future patronage if I were to deliver my employers into the hands of those they most sought to avoid?

No, before I approached the police, or even my cousin Scrope in the Commissioners' Office, I must be able to present them with sufficient evidence to enable them to carry out their duties, yet without involving my employer. (The extortionary aspect had to be suppressed, at least as far as the names of the parties were concerned.)

My spirits sank beneath the weight of this legal incubus. How could I disassociate the Wroth family from these crimes? They were too deeply implicated, if not at the very centre of the matter. How could I possibly keep the two killings separate, and Lady Wroth's name out of both of them, without sacrificing myself in the process?

At five o'clock in the afternoon with the shadows creeping over my worn carpet, I was not exactly in an optimistic frame of mind.

But at six thirty that same evening, I felt slightly improved in my condition.

The door bell rang and I answered it to find Pelham's saucy footman standing on the step. He regarded me with considerably less contempt than he had shown at his own door.

"Yes?" I asked.

He had a message for me from Sir Harry. Could I return with him at once?

"On what business?" I asked tersely.

"Sir Harry's business," he answered jauntily.

"Touché," I said. "One moment."

I left him on the step whilst I returned to my rooms to dress for the street. When I set out with him ten minutes later, my sword hung at my side and I carried the extra protection of a light pistol.

Sir Harry was, apparently, fully conscious and in a hurry to see me. He had very considerately sent his carriage. I took my seat in its elegant interior and the footman hoisted himself aloft beside the coachman. Fifteen minutes later I was being ushered into Pelham's bedroom. Sir Harry eyed me sourly. He was in full possession of his faculties and, but for the bandage showing at his throat, seemed in remarkably good health.

He held out a massive hand.

"I have to thank 'ee, Captain Nash," he said.

"I did nothing, Sir," I replied.

A glimmer of sardonic amusement showed deep in his glutinous eyes. "I have to be assured yet on that point," he said with a wry twist to his mouth.

"Sir?"

"How do I know that I don't have you to thank for leading me into an ambush?" he asked. "I don't know 'ee from Adam, man."

"You know my name, Sir," I said. "And it was you that chose the path we took."

"And it was you that suggested a walk in the park."

There was a nasty pause. He regarded me keenly. If eyes can boil, then Pelham's did.

"You have only my word for it, Sir Harry," I said. "But if I had sought your death, why should I have brought you back to safety? It is not in my interest to do away with such an important connection as yourself."

A look of baffled impatience came into his face.

"Who are you, man? And what's your interest in this business?"

I thought hard for a moment. Would it be best, at this stage, to declare my real interest, or should I continue with my deception? If Pelham had been in league with Murrell then he would know about the Wroth papers and if there was money to be made out of the situation, I could scarcely expect him to ally himself to my cause. On the other hand, I held the code-book, without which he could not act further. If he would not vouchsafe me their return, I had the means to cut him off from a much larger fortune. He was not the man to lose a mackerel for the sake of a sprat.

Perhaps I could bargain with him?

I decided on candour.

"It's as I told you in the park, Sir. I'm interested only in the Wroth receipts."

His eyebrows rose superciliously.

"I am employed by Lady Wroth to obtain certain embarrassing papers concerning her grandson – "

"Which grandson?" he asked sharply.

"The young Lord Wroth."

He frowned. The brown, syrupy eyes looked cunning.

"Oh?"

"These papers were held by Murrell," I said. "Once I am able to place them in her ladyship's hands, my interest in this business is at an end."

He mused on this for a while.

"If Murrell died on account of these papers, they were undoubtedly worth a fortune," he said, at length, flashing a calculating look at me. "And you presumably want them for nothing?"

"No. I am prepared to pay a price."

"How much?"

"I don't know the exact amount . . . yet."

He looked at me in astonishment.

"What do you mean, Sir?"

"I am prepared to exchange the code-book for the papers."

He laughed into his pillows, seemingly diverted by some thought. He recovered himself eventually and said:

"Well, Sir! We shall see about that!" He reached for the bell. I stopped his hand as it touched.

"One moment, Sir Harry."

He looked up at me.

"Yes?"

"You said this afternoon that your assailant was Wroth."

"Yes."

"Did you see him?"

His hand stroked the bell thoughtfully.

"Or did you only imagine that you had?" I asked.

The heavy eyes looked up at me from beneath weary lids.

"Why should I imagine it?"

"If you expected an attack from that quarter," I said with meaning.

A startled gleam showed in his eyes. He looked at me with respect.

"And why should I expect an attack from that quarter?" he asked softly.

"You would know the answer to that, Sir Harry. If you were truly Murrell's partner . . ."

He snuffled into his pillows again, convulsed with silent laughter.

"Ah!" he said. "You thought I meant *that* Wroth."

His shoulders shaking, he rang the bell before I could question him further.

A manservant opened the door.

"Captain Nash is ready to leave now, Griddle," Pelham said.

"And my offer, Sir Harry?" I asked.

He laughed shortly. "Well, Captain, if I had the papers in question, I'd undoubtedly trade them with you," he said. "But, unfortunately, I don't have them, you see."

He bowed from the bed, his shoulders still shaking weakly. I wondered at the nature of the joke. It must be an uncommonly strong one.

Pelham had no intention of enlightening me, it seemed. He dismissed me with an airy wave of the hand. I turned and left the room, his unconfined laughter following me clear out into the hall.

I had to forgo the luxury of the carriage on my return journey, since the offer was denied me. As I walked back to my rooms, I pondered this new development. Why should Pelham think that Oliver Wroth was his assailant? What reason could he have to revenge himself upon Sir Harry? Did Wroth believe that Pelham owned the receipts? Or was there yet another reason? Prior to calling on me at my rooms, young Wroth's main preoccupation appeared to have been the disappearance of his female cousin.

I stopped with my hand upon the door-knob of my room.

His female cousin. The cousin who had so mysteriously disappeared. Was Pelham in some way involved in her disappearance. Was her disappearance in any way connected with the receipts? It might pay looking into. In the meantime, a sound night's sleep would do me no great harm.

I opened the door and stood astonished on the threshold. My rooms looked as though a horde of ruffians had passed through them. Drawers were opened, cupboards unlocked, curtains torn from their rods, upholstery slashed. Even the stuffing in my mattress oozed upon the bed.

I now knew why Sir Harry had found the joke so amusing. The interview with him had been a meaningless rigmarole, empty talk merely. His sole purpose in sending for me had been to make sure that I was out of my rooms when his men came to ransack them.

But the jest was on him. The code-book was not even on the premises. It was safely tucked away elsewhere.

## XVI

Clarety shifted comfortably and spread her legs. She took the coin
I gave her and idly stroked herself with it between her breasts, over
her smooth white belly and between her thighs. Clarety has a lewd
way with hard cash.

"Catherine Wroth?" she said. "Why, her disappearance was no
secret. All the world knew of it at the time."

"I never heard of it."

"You could not have been in England then. It was a great scandal
in its day. Every coffee-house in London hummed with it."

"What happened?"

"God Himself can tell you, I can't. It remains a mystery."

"But what did folk say had happened?"

"A multitude of things. Most of them the wildest fancies, I've
no doubt on it! – facts being in such short supply. But there's one
element they all did suppose that's remained evergreen."

"What?"

"They were all of the opinion that she's Pelham's mistress, though
her manner of becoming so is open to doubt and rumour ran its full
gamut. Some said she ran away of her own free will, some that she
had been forced into joining him, and others that she had been
coarsely abducted. But all agree that she's now kept by him – in
close seclusion, somewhere deep in the heart of the country."

"How do they think she was forced?"

"He blackguarded her."

"How?"

Clarety shrugged.

"Nobody knows," she said.

"But they think she is his mistress now?"

"Oh yes. Why else should she live with him – in the depths of the
country? Miles away from civilized folk!"

She shuddered at this doleful prospect, her glorious breasts
quivering.

Her performance with the coin had had its usual effect upon me.
I was once again ready for the sport. My questions ceased while
we kissed and toyed. Her hair, which she had let down about her
body, crackled beneath her as we rode upon the bed. It was a very
paradise of pleasure and in a short while I got into her and abated
my passion.

Then, pleasantly sated, all my questions answered (and all my
small change taken), I left the house and walked home, pondering
on all she had told me.

Pelham was intimately connected with the Wroth family by two separate scandals, it appeared. I wondered if they could be in any way connected? What could he know of their family history that could both force Miss Wroth into compromising her honour and also feed Murrell's demands? And, if either of the Wroths had attempted to kill him in Green Park yesterday, were they trying to settle two separate scores, or were the two situations dependent on each other?

I kept my mind busy with these conjectures whilst I waited for Pelham to contact me again with regard to the codebook. One thing puzzled me especially. If Pelham had seduced Miss Wroth, why had he not gone on to wed her? She was in every way a prospect – young, beautiful, well-born, and tolerably wealthy in her own right. For a man in Pelham's position it seemed strange that he should neglect such an opportunity to increase his fortune. Nothing stood in his way, as far as one could see. He was a bachelor of equal station in life, and even owned his own parson! Yet he had not tied her to him in a legal way.

Another puzzling aspect of the case was the business of Miss Wroth's horse. For Miss Wroth, like any other redblooded English girl, was passionately fond of her horse Zubaydah. Yet on the day that she had disappeared, she had ridden off from the Hall on her beloved mare and Zubaydah had been found grazing peacefully some ten miles distant to the west of Stukeley. There had been no signs of foul play, or of an accident. The saddle was intact, the horse was calm, unsweated and unmarked. Why she had left this valuable and well-loved animal behind was another mystery. The mare had years of good riding in her still.

Another fact, which I had discovered, was perhaps less surprising. Miss Wroth had taken her jewel-box with her, an heirloom inherited from her mother. At least, it was never seen after her strange departure. The value of the jewellery was not inconsiderable but, oddly enough, she had made no further claim on her fortune. So, whatever Pelham's reasons for seducing the girl away from her family, money had been no great object.

There was, I found, no absolute proof in the rumour that Miss Wroth lived with Pelham, either in captivity or at liberty. Her name had been linked with his during a London season and that was the only basis for it. With a reputation such as Pelham sported, it was natural to suppose that he had, in some way, enticed her away from respectability. But she could, in truth, simply have disappeared of her own free will.

Another disturbing certainty was that the Wroth family had made no *official* enquiry into her disappearance, which suggested, to my mind, that they knew where she was at least, and even tolerated her situation. That is, in public. For whatever reason, and I largely suspected pride, the Wroths had decided to ignore her disaffection. And Oliver Wroth had feared (or pretended to fear?) that I was hired to bring her home!

All this led to one very important point – a point that was becoming increasingly apparent to me. There was considerably more behind this business of the receipts than I had been told. The receipts were only a lure. Had Lady Wroth met Murrell's demands, she would have found herself faced with a larger demand for his suppression of a more criminal exposure – more incriminating even than the nastiness I had read in the paper brought to me by Oliver Wroth. And she, too, I was convinced knew of this, or else why take such trouble?

If there was an unspeakable skeleton in the Wroth closet, who better to rattle it than a man like Pelham? If it was true that the grand-daughter was his mistress, then he could undoubtedly have learned of this secret.

Miss Wroth might well repay investigation. If she was alive, she must have left a trace of her existence somewhere. If she was living with Pelham however remotely, she could be flushed out. If she was alone and independent, then she must have left a trail from Stukeley to wherever she now resided – a bed slept in, a meal taken, a jewel sold or pawned.

The Wroth affair was at a standstill. To search in another direction might reawaken those tell-tale echoes which, returning to one's ears, guide one like a bat to the light of reality.

It seemed logical to begin my search at Stukeley. Besides, I owed my employer a report on my progress.


# XVII

I followed Chives' magisterial back up the oaken staircase, examining the family portraits more carefully than before.

I paused before the portraits of Lord Wroth and Mr. Oliver. To the left of the latter, a faint discoloration on the wall showed where another picture might possibly have hung. The remaining two pictures had been slightly rearranged to cover the omission. Miss Wroth, I surmised, had been banished from the gallery.

Chives, aware that I was no longer immediately behind him, had turned at the door of the "solar".

"Did the lady carry away her own portrait, Chives?" I asked.

He stared at me with his Olympian eyes.

"Her ladyship is waiting, Sir," he said reprovingly, and opened the door. I passed through into that sparkling room. Her ladyship waited for me in her great chair, more resplendent than ever, a veritable sunburst of diamonds. A large cap worn over monstrous high hair, crossed beneath her chin and was tied at the back of her neck. She wore a morning gown of dazzling hue.

I bowed and she replied with a gracious inclination of her extraordinary head.

The door closed softly behind us and she asked impatiently: "Well, Captain Nash? Do you have the receipts?"

"No, my lady," I said. "Nor do I know who has."

She snapped her fan viciously on the side of her chair, her eyes glittering frostily.

"Sir?"

I explained the situation carefully. She listened with a growing rancour.

"Well, Sir," she said, as I finished the tale, "stinking fish don't grow any fresher for lying idle."

She glared at me, seeming almost to accuse me of negligence in the matter; suggesting almost that I was in some way to blame for what had happened.

"I was not asked to protect Murrell's life, Ma'am," I admonished her gently. "Nor d'Urfey's."

She laughed abruptly, without merriment, showing her startlingly grey teeth.

"And what do you deduce from all this, Sir? What do you 'detect'?" she asked sharply.

I regarded her steadily. "I deduce, Ma'am, that Murrell was murdered by someone with an interest in his demise. There are innumerable people interested in that condition. At a guess, I'd say about half London society."

"And what of d'Urfey's death?" she asked less severely. "Is it connected, do you think?"

"There seems to be a tenuous sort of link, Lady Wroth. It seems likely."

"Likely, Sir!" she spluttered. "No more than that?"

"Very likely, if you wish."

"No, Sir," she exclaimed passionately. "I do *not* wish it!"

She sat very still for a while, then busied herself with her handkerchief, snuff-box, patch-box, perfume-bottle and headscratcher in turn. She returned to fretting away with her fan, and at length said wearily: "If d'Urfey was involved, then my rascal of a grandson must be involved also."

"Not necessarily, Ma'am," I said evenly. "D'Urfey could have been about his own business."

"His own business?"

Her diamonds sparkled as her hand shook, and I had a sudden flash of inspiration. His own business, indeed. I had a vision of d'Urfey, the dear friend, the boon companion, the sharer of boyish confidences. Could he have been the prime mover in all this? If there were any skeletons to be rattled in the Wroth cupboard, he would be privy to them all. He, d'Urfey, the privileged guest. He could well have been the link with Murrell – and, if his purpose had been served, then, like Murrell, he could have been disposed of.

But in the same way as Pelham? With a knife through his throat? There was a break in my vision, the divine afflatus reascended.

"What are you thinking, Captain Nash?" Lady Wroth asked, looking at me curiously.

Without taking thought, I answered: "If only you would be honest with me, Ma'am!"

She bridled. "Sir?"

"Your ladyship may not be aware that I have twice suppressed information regarding two crimes . . . temporarily. I did it to serve *your* interests. If only you could have more confidence in me."

Her manner relented somewhat. But, all the same, her eyes pierced through me sharply, as she said: "I have told you all I know."

"Not entirely, Ma'am," I answered.

She blinked at my impertinence, but controlled herself. She made the picture of a perfect great lady dealing with an insolent menial.

"For example, Sir?" she asked.

"Where is your grand-daughter, Miss Catherine Wroth?"

An astonished pause. She lost control of herself – her acting days were far behind her. She gaped and spluttered.

"What has that to do with anything, Sir?"

I came to the point.

"Lady Wroth, your grand-daughter disappeared, turning her back on a grand fortune and her place in society. She went in haste and there must have been a reason for it. Rumour has it that she lives with Sir Harry Pelham, and we know that he has some unsavoury connection with Murrell's business. I think there is more to the receipts than is written on them. Murrell had some knowledge of a secret and scandalous nature concerning your family, which he was willing to sell. Somebody must have provided Murrell with that information and I think it may well have been – "

I was going to say Pelham, but she interrupted me with a cry.

"No, Sir! That is a monstrous suggestion. She could no more have passed such information to that – "

She caught herself short, with a furious look for me.

"So she is with Pelham?" I said.

"That, Sir, is none of your business. She has done what she has done, and that is between herself and her Creator. But I know that she is not in any way connected with this business."

"She lives with Pelham and he is connected to it," I said stubbornly.

"Enough, Sir!" she cried, and rose. I was about to be dismissed both from the room and probably from the enquiry.

She hesitated. The façade of the grande dame crumbled and a troubled old lady peered anxiously out at me from behind the elaborate framework.

I spoke gently. "I apologize if I have offended you, Lady Wroth," I said. "But you must admit that you have been less than frank with me."

"I have told you all you need to know, Captain Nash," she replied. "You were commissioned to deal with the receipts only, Sir," adding viciously: "Which you have failed so to do!"

She rang her bell imperiously.

"Not quite yet, Ma'am," I said distinctly.

She looked up in surprise, the bell tinkled to a foolish halt. Her mouth twisted with contempt.

"Are you saying that you can still get them for me?"

"Yes."

She frowned at me.

"How, Sir?"

"I still have an important piece to bargain with, my lady," I said. "The code-book. Pelham will need it soon. He wants it badly enough now – so much so that he is willing to storm my rooms to get it."

She caught her breath.

"Do you think Pelham has the receipts?" She looked almost fearful.

"If he hasn't, I think he knows where he can lay a hold to them," I smiled. "Do you still wish me to act for you?"

"Providing that you can do so without involving innocent people," she said grimly.

The door opened. Chives awaited his instructions. Lady Wroth looked from me to him and back again.

She made up her mind.

"Bring a dish of tea, Chives," she ordered. "Captain Nash is staying for a while longer."

She sat down and beckoned me to resume my seat.

Chives closed the door. Lady Wroth began to tell me about her grand-daughter, Miss Catherine.

And an hour later I rode away from Stukeley, not much the wiser for her confidences. Her ladyship had spoken quite freely, but without imparting the least information. She knew where the girl was, she was in no peril, either physical or moral, and she was not in the least entangled in this sad business.

She would say no more than that. But what she said was highly emphatic. Her grand-daughter was an honest, decent girl that the world traduced. She had her own reasons for behaving as she had and, however wrong-headed she might be, she had behaved with all possible honour. But, in any case, it was none of society's business. It was none of my business.

And with regard to my business, she asked, how soon did I think I should be able to procure the receipts and have finished with the whole squalid affair?

Ah, when indeed? I wondered, as I turned into my street. It depended entirely upon how the action fell from this point on.

But some new development was about to commence, it seemed. For the past four miles, I had been aware of being followed. Obviously I had been tracked all the way from the Hall.

A grey man on a grey mare was trying his best to merge into the grey day, but not altogether succeeding.

And not entirely wishing to succeed, perhaps.

## XVIII

I sat in my rooms waiting for the knocker to rattle or for the bell to jangle, but both objects refused to oblige me. Pelham seemed in no hurry to contact me again. Either he had lost interest in the code-book or else he was experiencing some difficulty in unearthing the receipts.

It seemed scarcely possible that he had lost interest, so the latter solution seemed the more likely. If this was so, I realized that I myself would experience some difficulty in obtaining the receipts. Both Murrell's rufous-haired assistant and the uncomely Negress appeared to have vanished into the limbo of the netherworld and, although I had set my Seven Dials contacts on to trying to discover their lair, I had, so far, received no encouraging news from that quarter.

My best chance remained with Pelham. I had put a man to watch his house in Newick Square. This fellow, Droop by name, was an old and experienced hand at keeping watch. He was to send for me at the slightest sign of any activity and report on all Sir Harry's visitors. To date, he had reported nothing of note, only the comings and goings of tradesmen, nothing at all suspicious, though with a man of Pelham's stamp, nothing could ever seem wholly innocent. But I kept him at his post because I felt sure that if I was to be led in a new direction, Pelham would lay the scent for me.

As I finished my supper, the bell rang. I opened the door to find a ragged-arsed urchin grinning up at me.

"Capting Nash?" he piped.

"Yes, boy."

"Droop says yo're to come, yore 'onour."

He held out a grimy hand into which I fed a coin. With a nod and a wink, he ran off into the night.

Five minutes later I followed him.

At some point I became aware of the man in grey, drifting like a moth from shadow to shadow behind me. He looked to be the greyest man I ever saw, in the uncertain light, grey from head to boots. Even his face seemed to be a subtle shade of grey.

I kept to the main thoroughfares and as much in the light as possible. At that time of the evening, the streets were reasonably crowded with folk taking the air. People flowed and eddied around me. As I walked purposefully towards Newick Square, my pursuer kept up an even pace behind me. When, for the space of a few minutes, I passed through a patch of darkness empty of people, I speeded my steps slightly, expecting the man to make some move, tensing myself for a sudden lethal rush from behind.

But nothing happened. The man kept a discreet distance and I arrived in Newick Square without incident. Droop was waiting for me. He emerged from behind the plinth of a statue, where he had been lurking.

"What is it?" I asked.

"Copper-top," he replied. "He went into the house by the back way about a half an hour ago."

I looked at Pelham's house. Almost all the rooms were ablaze with light, a prodigious waste. One would have thought he was at home to the world instead of being confined to his room.

Had Murrell's apprentice brought the receipts at last? If so, Pelham would soon be in contact with me to arrange for their delivery.

We stood half-hidden behind the plinth and waited. A terrace away, my pursuer waited in his turn. I was dimly aware of his grey shape hovering behind a house corner.

"Don't look around," said Droop hoarsely, "but we're a-being hobserved."

I chuckled. Very little escaped Droop's baleful eye.

"He followed me here," I said.

"Shall I run 'im orf?"

"No. When we leave, I may want you to follow him."

"Foller him follerin' you, d'you mean?"

"Yes."

Droop laughed softly. The notion of a mouser[1] following a mouser amused him greatly.

We waited ten minutes more. Nothing happened to disturb our solitude. The street emptied of people. A carriage passed along the cobbles, its wheels rattling quietly over the straw. A sedan stopped before a neighbouring house and a rouged, patched and powdered old nobleman was carried off to his evening's entertainments.

Presumably all the inhabitants of Newick Square were away for the evening, for their houses were lighted modestly. Only Pelham's house was lit up, as for a ball. The lights streamed from every window, except one. This room I judged to be his bedroom: it was a black oblong and a curious, almost sinister, contrast to the rest of the house.

At one point, I thought I heard a cry wrung from behind the unlighted window.

"Did you hear anything, Droop"? I asked.

"Wot?"

"A cry of some kind."

"Naw."

Droop's ears were foxy-sharp. I must have imagined it, I thought.

The minutes crawled past.

But at last there was a sudden stir of activity from the house. The saucy footman poked his head from behind the great door, looking up and down the street. Droop and I ducked quickly behind our refuge. The door closed.

Five minutes later, a clumsy carriage trundled from Pelham's mews. Creaking heavily, it passed us, turning in the direction of Piccadilly.

I made up my mind in an instant. "Follow that fellow yonder,"

[1]Tracker.

I ordered Droop, and I nodded back towards the grey man, still skulking behind his corner.

I ran swiftly and silently after the carriage. As it paused for a moment before plunging into the busy traffic of Piccadilly, I jumped lightly onto the back axle-tree and settled myself on the perch between the wheels. The carriage dipped a trifle beneath my weight, but as it jolted forward at the instant of my stepping upon it, I trusted my presence to go unnoticed.

Once beyond the Knightsbridge toll-gate and out onto the open road, the carriage covered ground quickly. Indeed, for such an ungainly vehicle, I was amazed at the turn of speed whipped up by the coachman.

An hour or more passed. We were in the country now, somewhere close to the village of Hammersmith. The coach turned towards the river. A breeze sprang up and the leather braces that I clung to grew clammy in the damp night air.

The coach turned off the high road onto a grassy track. I was bumped mightily as we rattled along without decreasing speed. The coachman was in a mortal hurry.

We came to rest at the entrance to a field. There was neither a house nor a hovel in sight. The winking lights of Hammersmith shone a mile beyond. A dismal miasma rose from the river, gleaming ghostly a few yards away. I huddled deeper below the body of the carriage.

The coachman climbed down and opened the gate into the field. He was a hulking fellow, even when he stripped off his greatcoat. He opened the carriage door and reached inside. Breathing stertorously, he dragged some object along the floor and, with a grunting heave, slung it over his shoulder. From my vantage point beneath the carriage, I saw him stride away across the field towards the river, a white, shrouded shape draped across his back.

The horses whickered gently as I slipped from my hiding place. I walked through the gate and, slipping through a gap in the hedge, I followed the staggering coachman down the length of the field. As he dropped the bundle on the marshy ground by the river's edge, I sought shelter behind a leafy tree.

The man did not trouble to look around. He was confident that he was unobserved. Without ceremony, he stripped the white cloth away from the black shape and, taking a deep breath, lifted it up high above his shoulders and hurled it with great force into the river.

It fell with a dull splash and a small wavelet washed up the reedy bank. The coachman waited only long enough to make sure that his burden was far enough out to catch the current of the tide when it drained away towards the sea. Satisfied, he picked up the white cloth and turned away from the river. In a moment he was halfway across the field, the cloth glimmering in the weird light.

I looked towards the river. A dim shape floated just beneath the surface of the water some four yards out. The current had already caught it and was tugging it downstream, a hump-backed object like some obscene fish.

Suddenly the dark mass changed direction. It began to drift in towards the bank. Greatly excited, I walked along the river's edge, keeping myself parallel to the floating hump. A tooth of land projected some five yards distant and I saw that the black mass would be washed ashore upon it. I ran forward snatching at a broken branch with which to haul it in.

Two minutes later I was looking at the Thames-soaked body of Murrell's singular assistant. His hands and feet were lightly bound with twine, his eyes gazed up at me with lightless horror, the strange teeth protruding in a grim rictus – a parody of a grimace.

I struck a light and leaned over the body. His wet shirt had been torn on a floating spar and where the flesh showed I could see faint blue markings. He had obviously been tortured. My ears had not deceived me.

Had he been tortured to death? He appeared to have met his death by some blunt instrument. A dark bruise stood out against the pallor of his skin. I fingered his head, peering closely at the bruise, moved the head around with both hands and felt at his ribs. I lifted the lax hand and examined the fingernails. I let the hand fall. He had died of a broken neck. Already the body was beginning to stiffen in the chill night air.

## XIX

The bell jangled through my sleep, cutting into a soft and pleasant dream. I descended the stairs, more asleep than awake. It had been three o'clock in the morning before I had trudged wearily up my stairs to bed.

I opened the door and snapped suddenly into full awareness. I could not have been more abruptly awakened had somebody dowsed me with freezing water.

The grey man stood upon my steps, greyer than ever in the bright morning light.

"Captain Nash?" he enquired in a grey voice, a wraith of a voice, as solid as a river mist.

"I think you know me, Sir," I said half-severely, half-amused.

He blushed, if that is the word to describe it, for a darkish hue crept under his grey cheeks.

"I should like to speak to you privately, Captain," he said quite meekly.

I examined him keenly. He looked harmless enough in the daylight. Out of the shadows, shorn of all mystery, he presented a rather nondescript, even a pathetic figure.

He carried no arms about him, of that I was sure. I thought it safe enough to admit him.

He sat in my room like a shrivelled elephant. His skin sagged about him like a hide, grey and leathery, with all the lines running downwards in the most depressing way.

"My name is Smith," he said in his whispery voice. "'Coffin' Smith," he emphasized. The epithet conveyed distinction.

I bowed. He flushed again, as if common politeness were in some obscure way an insult to him. He was, I could see, a man well-used to snubs.

He licked his lips nervously and looked about the room. Thinking to put him at his ease, for I feared that he would never get started until I had reassured him, I offered him a pinch of snuff. A man generally gains confidence from the use of trifling properties, such little actions give a release from tension.

He flushed, or "greyed", even deeper and took the snuffbox from me awkwardly. He took the snuff between his fingers with a very gauche air and, with a most unfashionable sniff-sniff, inhaled the powder. After a prodigious sneeze, he said, "God amercy!" and then sat looking as awkward, miserable and grey as ever.

"I'm a mate o' Betty's," he said, and waited. I was obviously expected to know who Betty was, and as I was in ignorance, I thought it best to hold to an enigmatic silence. I could see it greatly impressed him.

"Betty is a good woman," he said and paused again.

"I don't doubt that," I answered evenly.

He darkened again. He seemed to find some critical note in my innocent comment.

"That old bastard used her ill," he said.

I waited a full minute for him to continue, but he only said: "She's a good woman", and flashed me a swift, pugnacious look, as though he expected me to challenge him on this occasion.

"And what does Betty want with me?" I asked, feeling that I must get his story launched before he ran out of confidence altogether.

He hawed and hemmed and sneezed fiercely again.

"She wants to do business with you," he said at last.

"Oh?" I said carefully.

He wiped his nose with a greasy clout.[1]

"Is that why you have been haunting me for the last twenty-four hours?" I asked.

He looked away unhappily, for all the world as if I had caught him with his hand in my purse.

"She wants to do business," he said again.

"What kind of business?" I barked, suddenly losing my patience.

He blinked.

"You can trust her," he then said maddeningly. "For all that she's black outside."

Light dawned in a great blinding flash. Murrell's packhorse. The uncomely Negress. Here was her emissary.

"She has the receipts?" I asked.

"She knows where they are," he said.

"Can she get them for me?"

He shook his head.

"No, Captain. But you can."

"I can? How?"

"She'll tell you that. For one hundred guineas."

There was something wrong with this proposition. I pondered it for a moment, then I saw what it was. The price they asked was far too low. One hundred guineas for receipts valued in thousands. Why was she prepared to sell so cheap?

He looked towards me anxiously.

"Are you interested?"

"Is it only the information I shall buy?"

He nodded. "Aye. But it's the only way you'll get them back. You'd never find them in a hundred years without Betty's help."

"Are you sure?"

He looked puzzled by my question.

"What do you mean, Sir?"

"Is she the only one who knows their whereabouts?"

"There's nobody else," he replied stoutly.

I thought of the bruised and tortured body of the redhaired assistant. If he had had knowledge of the receipts, it seemed unlikely that the secret had died with him. I could not imagine that fiercely grinning mouth had remained silent under the pressure of such pain. Pelham must also know by now. In which case, the code-book was still my best lever. And cheaper, too.

[1]Handkerchief.

"There's more to these receipts than you think," Smith said sharply. His grey face looked suddenly deeply cunning.

"Oh?"

"You'll be paying for that, too."

"You must need the money badly to think of selling so cheap," I said.

He moved against the chair-back uncomfortably.

"We need to move away," he said.

Pelham. They were afraid of Pelham.

"The climate here won't suit your mort,"[1] I said, pleasantly.

"Will you buy?" he asked.

"I'd need to know more before I do."

"It's Betty's business," he said. "I'm just her Mercury."

"And when can we strike hands?" I asked.

"Come down to my flash[2] tonight," he said. "Roach's Landings, that's where I hang out."

"No," I said. "You must come here."

I had a vision of my reception at Roach's Landings. A quick blow behind the ear and eternal darkness for George Nash. Did they take me for a gawney?[3]

He shifted from buttock to buttock.

"She won't stir out," he said. "Not 'til we're ready to ship away."

"She must be greatly feared," I said. "Doesn't she trust to her own magic?"

A look of baffled resentment crept into his face, a closed expression to his eye. I decided not to probe any further into his extraordinary relationship with the black savage. I wondered briefly whether Murrell had received a decent interment yet. Presumably the poor creature had now abandoned hope of his return from the dead, for she obviously no longer felt herself protected by his magic.

"Will you come?" Smith asked.

I weighed up the alternatives. Until Pelham made a move, this ill-assorted couple were my chief lead to the receipts. It would be better to trust them – up to a point.

"I'll go to Roach's Landings for the information," I said. "But you must come here for the money."

He paused for only a moment and then nodded his agreement. If I had expected an angry reaction to my proposal, I was to be

---

[1] Woman. A near-harlot.
[2] Flash-crib: lodging house.
[3] A fool.

disappointed. He accepted my terms stoically. "Coffin" Smith was well-used to toeing other people's lines. He had danced all his life to other people's tunes.

"We'd better go now," he said.

Roach's Landings was arrived at through a snake of stinking streets. It was a place of ruined houses and collapsing walls. Most of the buildings seemed to have foundered in the mud and the rest looked as though a cough would bring them down. The only reassuring constituents of this dismal scene were the sun shining on the waters of the Thames and the boats, those alluring symbols of escape, their masts springing like a bizarre forest behind the chimney stacks. It was a most sinister area, amid warehouses and workshops, surrounded by the huge ramps of the dock walls. Strident voices shattered the air around us and soot stuck to my skin in the oppressive heat. Smith threaded his way through the twisting, dirty alleys with the sureness of long acquaintance. In this part of the world he was entirely confident.

I was far from feeling confident myself. We had passed at least half a dozen gallows, the corpses polishing the King's irons.[1] But there seemed little likelihood that the people we saw were much moved by such grisly warnings. They eyed one with speculative glances and I walked with half my mind to my exposed back. The inhabitants of Roach's Landings were scarcely human. They were treated by their superiors as hardly more than wild beasts, and with good reason. Officers of the Law paraded here in groups of five and then only in daylight. I almost wished that I had dressed with less care that morning.

I kept a ready hand to my sword and felt a mixture of relief and anxiety as we turned in to an alarmingly dark hallway, stinking of cats and piss. A dozen eyes followed us as we mounted the broken stairs. The walls were sweating and peeling, and the air was redolent of damp and despair.

As we reached the head of the stairs, Smith struck a tinder. The air had grown fouler the higher we rose and the only light came from the cracks in the roof, through which the winter rains had seeped.

He knocked on a door in a secret signal. There was no answer. He waited a moment, then repeated the signal.

Again, a still, uncanny silence. Smith caught his breath in a muffled gasp. Something soft and furry brushed against my ankles. There was

---

[1] Hanging in chains inside iron cages. To preserve them for as long as possible, as a warning to evil-doers.

no sound but a faint whisper from behind the wainscot and a dull murmur from far below in the street.

Smith called out her name.

There was no reply. Before I could stop him, Smith had put a shoulder to the door and burst into the room.

He stopped abruptly, aghast at the sight that met his eyes. A cry broke from him, hoarse, pathetic, broken. I would never have supposed such an explicit sound could issue from that grey mouth.

The hot little room was a shambles. The rickety chairs and cheap wooden table lay splintered and broken, shards of crockery lay where they had been hurled. The greasy walls were splattered with blood and bloodied skin curled in the dust of the floor. The most fearful battle had taken place here and the loser lay where she had fallen upon the filthy bed. The Negress, almost naked, lolled across the bloodsoaked pallet. Her eyes had rolled wildly back into her head, her enormous shining legs were cut in notches and other terrible wounds flowered like obscene roses on her breasts and stomach.

It was a cruel and diabolic scene, a mad scene out of Bedlam. She had been put to the sword with a vengeance and must have suffered beyond agony.

Smith stood by the bed. After a deathly pause, he covered the grotesque body with a sheet. In the midst of this reeling, drunken nastiness he looked, of a sudden, immensely composed, almost sedate. When he turned to look at me, his eyes were dry and as lifeless as the corpse.

He began to swear quietly. A string of the most trenchant obscenities dropped from his mouth in his hoarse, grey voice.

## XX

I passed a day in immeasurable gloom, only relieved by a deadly sleepiness, which passed leaving me with the naked prospect of absolute failure. Betty was dead and with her death all my chances of receiving the correct information may well have died also. The outlines of the case seemed like the outlines of a lost boat slowly being buried by the tide.

Betty had known where the receipts were to be got. Pelham may or may not know. If he hadn't known, had he been responsible for the frightful butchery in that squalid room? In which case, had he learned of their whereabouts?

I thought it hardly likely. Looking at that grim body on the bed, looking at the condition of the room, I could scarcely believe that any woman who could fight so hard would disclose her knowledge easily.

I could not shake off the feeling that her secret had died with her.

Pelham must be still as ignorant as I myself.

But more prepared to help himself! Three men had died, and one woman. I knew that he had killed the assistant. If one death could be laid at his door, why not all? It was possible, even logical. And if he was prepared to go to such lengths to secure the receipts, what lengths would he not go to in order to take the code-book?

And yet, so far, I had remained unmolested.

Another thought nagged at my mind. For all Pelham's debauched and tarnished reputation, he had never been noted for savagery. Whenever I thought of the scene in that dismal room, it was the maniacal quality of it that disturbed me most. It accorded ill, somehow, with what I knew of Pelham's methods. It didn't have his grain.

On the other hand, I remembered the body of the redhaired man, the lacerations, the engraved terror on the ghastly, grinning face. Pelham was either losing his finesse, or else he was beginning to employ some vicious skips.[1]

My own situation had become extremely vulnerable. I would have to keep a sharp eye out for danger. The codebook was still my greatest asset, but Pelham, it now appeared, was not the man to sit and bargain when he could obtain his will by shorter means.

In the midst of suchlike cogitations, the bell rang and I opened the door to Pelham's saucy footman. Sir Harry desired to see me urgently, the man said. I was to go at once, the coach stood at my door.

"You may tell your master," I said, "that nothing will induce me to walk into his house. If he has anything whatever to discuss with me, he must come to do it here."

The footman looked very surprised. Then he turned on his heel and went to confer with the coachman, the same hulking fellow who had carried me unknowingly to Hammersmith. I stood watching.

Then the footman hoisted himself aboard, and the coach rattled away into the night.

An hour later the bell jangled again. I lay aside my book and went to answer the door. I opened it to find Pelham standing on the step. He leaned heavily upon his walking-stick. Behind him loomed the enormous figure of the coachman.

[1]Skip-kennel: footmen.

Pelham bowed in his negligent, ironical way and produced a small and elegant snuff-box from his pocket. He took a pinch with a delicate air and raised it to his nostrils.

"Well, Sir, here I am," he said pleasantly enough.

I bowed and, stepping slightly aside, opened the door a trifle wider.

With a swift, upward motion, Pelham flung the contents of the snuff-box in my face. A stinging powder flew into my eyes, which began to swell immediately, smarting most horribly. I started back, half-blinded, the edge of the door still in my hand.

I tried to close the door, but Pelham's foot was against it, blocking its movement.

Out of the stinging cloud of darkness, I was dimly aware of the huge bulk of the coachman lunging forward. The door cracked back against the wall as he thrust it out of my hand. I felt two enormous arms encircle me and I was lifted bodily from the doorway and carried, coughing and sneezing, to the coach.

He bundled me without ceremony into its dressed leather interior.

Pelham was back in his elegant bed, looking as if he had never left it. The footman fussed about him, settling his pillows and straightening his counterpane. He left a full glass of light-coloured liquid on the night table by his master's side and left the room. The gigantic coachman stood behind me.

I was sitting in a mahogany Chippendale chair, my arms securely tied. My eyes still itched abominably from the powder. It burned in my nostrils and my mouth was very dry.

Pelham took a deep swig of the amber liquid. He smiled at me as I ran my tongue involuntarily over my stinging lips. It was a slow, wide smile, quite without malice.

"I'm sorry you felt you had to refuse my invitation, Captain," he said conversationally, for all the world as if we were seated at some evening party. "But I'm glad you saw fit to come along in the end."

"How could I refuse such a gracious request?" I replied, mustering as much ease as I could in the circumstances. I did not feel at all at ease. The silent bear of a man loomed behind me, smelling of leather and horse sweat.

"Why did you refuse?" Pelham asked curiously.

I nodded my head towards my bound hands. It seemed answer enough.

Pelham took another draught from the glass. I watched the liquid

tilt into his mouth and my own seemed drier than summer dust.
He caught me licking my lips again and raised his glass in a
mocking salute.

"My cure-all," he said smiling.

"One of Murrell's prescriptions, I've no doubt," I murmured. He
laughed obligingly.

"Good God, man, I'd no more have drunk one of his remedies
than I would drink piss," he said. "Murrell was a cheap rogue."

I raised an eyebrow. He looked up at that moment and saw the
disbelieving expression on my face. He laughed again.

"A cheap rogue," he repeated. "And a fool."

He lay back on his pillows, gazing ruminatively into the yellow
fluid in the glass. His treacle-brown eyes looked fathomless as
he asked:

"Where is the code-book?"

I took a deep breath.

"Where are the receipts?" I countered.

Pelham nodded almost imperceptibly. The greasy giant behind me
leaned forward slightly and I felt a slight pressure on my shoulder.

Sir Harry yawned.

"I hope you will be reasonable about this, Nash," he said. "I
detest unnecessary violence and I despise unnecessary heroics."

The giant's huge hands massaged my shoulders gently.

"We made a bargain, Sir Harry," I said.

"Unfortunately, it's a bargain I can't keep," he drawled, adding
insolently: "I give you my word on it."

"And if I insist on your keeping to our agreement?"

The coachman must have been the bastard son of Sally Mapp,[1]
only his profession was to throw a man's bones out of joint, not to
set them. The fingers digging into my neck seemed to separate each
muscle. The pain, though brief, was excruciating. For a minute or
two the world went black.

"You are not in a position to insist," Pelham said reasonably. "I
must point out that an injury to one's neck is more serious than to
any other part of the body. A fracture may cause paralysis, or if
Jemmy here should tear your spinal cord . . ." He left the rest to
my imagination.

The fingers went to work in earnest now. A light danced before
my eyes like a malevolent firefly. Pain shot from my neck in every
direction, only to be gathered up again in a tight knot under the
giant's probing fingers. I gritted my teeth and began to sweat.

[1] A famous bone-setter of the period.

CAPTAIN NASH AND THE WROTH INHERITANCE

The torture ceased as Pelham spoke once more.

"Would you believe me, Nash, if I told you that these receipts you are so anxious to find, don't – and never did – exist?"

The fingers relaxed their hold and the red mist in front of my eyes cleared slightly. I looked over towards the bed, which seemed to be floating in a slight haze.

Pelham smiled his slow smile. Again, there seemed to be no harm in it.

"Do you tell me this out of real knowledge, Sir Harry?" I asked. "Or have you exhausted all the possibilities of finding them?"

He frowned, not following my drift for a moment. The implications of what I had said appeared to strike him unexpectedly. His eyes glowed hot as coals. He nodded towards the coachman, with an altogether different expression on his face.

The coachman stepped forward, but this time I was ready for him. I rolled from beneath the plaguily teasing fingers, flexed my knees and sprang upright, carrying the chair with me like some absurd extension of my backside. As I turned in a tight circle, I aimed the chair legs at the man's crotch in a vicious, stabbing motion. With a howl of rage and pain he clutched at his culls and as he did so, I whirled the body of the chair towards his lowered head. I felt like a terrier baiting a bull. But, caught off balance, the bull fell heavily, striking his head against a heavy mahogany dresser. He grunted and then lay still. My wrists felt as if they were clean broken in two and I was still vexatiously imprisoned in the chair.

I turned my attention to the bed. Pelham lay half-stupefied, half-amused at my performance. Suddenly aroused to his vulnerability, be made a belated move towards the bellrope hanging by his bed. With a clumsy stride, I fell against his outstretched hand and pushed him back upon his pillows aiming for his wounded neck. He grimaced with pain as I caught his shoulder, but the effort caused me almost as much agony. I stood panting from my exertions, looking down at him. I must have cut a weird figure, bruised and dishevelled, the chair sticking out behind me.

Pelham lay pale and exhausted on his pillows. He looked almost as if he expected a blow of some kind and had my hands been free, I no doubt would have obliged him.

As it was, my efforts, painful though they had been, had made some effect. The bonds that secured my hands to the chair had loosened, tearing the skin sorely. Now, after a few painful twists of my wrists I had one hand free. I worked upon the other hand, keeping an eye always on Pelham, and very shortly the chair dropped to the floor with a thud.

All this time Pelham lay with his eyes closed, as white as wax. I picked up his drink and took a deep draught of it. The pale liquid ran smoothly enough down my throat, though it hardly slaked the itching dust in my mouth. Then, a small fire was lit in my bowels.

Pelham opened one eye and regarded me speculatively. I looked across the room and found what I most needed at that moment. A brace of duelling pistols lay in their inlaid case upon a tallboy. I lifted a pistol from its nest and, weighing it carefully, walked over to the recumbent body of the coachman, lying like a small mountain of clothes where he had fallen. A pool of blood had formed about a deep cut on his head. He lay as stiff as death in a curiously twisted position, one hand still curving protectively about his parts. I hoped that by now his culls had swollen to an inconvenient size. For a moment I thought I had killed the man. Then he snored suddenly.

I walked back to the bed. Pelham eyed the pistol quizzically.

"Well Sir?" he asked.

"I thank you for your invitation, Sir Harry, but I find that I cannot stay after all."

"A pity," he said wryly. "And how do you plan to leave?"

"Oh, I have a safe-conduct," I answered, and waved the pistol at him encouragingly.

He laughed his pleasant laugh.

"Fortune favours the reckless," he said. "If you have luck on your side you have no need of brains."

On the night table by his side lay a pair of scissors.

I reached up and cut off the silk of the bell-rope, leaving a portion well out of Pelham's reach.

He looked up at me, lazily amused.

"Are you still in the market for the code-book?" he drawled.

"Are the receipts for sale after all?" I asked, binding the silk sash around his arms.

I moved towards the door.

"There are no receipts that I know of," Pelham said quietly. "But if they do exist I'm prepared to pay hard for them. How much do you hope to earn from serving Lady Wroth?"

I told him.

"I will pay you a dozen times more."

I paused on my way to the door. Something in his tone stopped me – a new and unaccountable note of honesty.

He saw my hesitation and said more urgently: "And you may be assured that any such receipts will never be used against his lordship."

I turned towards him. The syrup-coloured eyes were amazingly alert. He looked almost sincere.

"You seem very certain of it," I said.

He smiled a weary smile that barely moved the muscles of his mouth.

"As you said, I've exhausted the possibilities. I'm now convinced that they don't exist."

I looked at him more closely. His expression seemed stripped of all pretences. He gazed at me with an appearance of infinite weariness.

Was what he said true? How could it be? Had three men and one woman died for something that had never existed? A lethal chimera? It seemed impossible.

"You don't believe me?" he asked.

I shrugged. A doubt still lingered.

"If I were to believe you now," I said, "what a fool I shall look when I have delivered the code-book and you go back to blackguarding the Wroth family."

He gestured impatiently.

"I've already told you they won't be troubled," he said.

"My business is to protect my patroness," I answered.

"And mine is to protect my children," he replied to that. "My children," he emphasized tartly and, looking at me with the most intense expression in his eyes, he added slowly and clearly:

"Your protection of Lady Wroth and my protection of my own children amounts to the same thing."

I gazed back at him in blank astonishment.

"As a father, I suffer from a belated sense of duty," he said meditatively. "But I have a sense of duty, nevertheless. My wish to protect Lady Wroth's grandchildren is as great as her own. The only difference in our situation is that they are *not* her grandchildren – and they *are* my flesh and blood."

I continued to gape at him, deprived of speech.

"You may know that Kitty Wroth is reputed to live with me. Well, it's true enough – she does. In some style at my estate in Shropshire. She is the mistress of my house. But not *my* mistress." He smiled wryly as my jaw continued to hang in frank disbelief. "Kitty is my natural daughter. I had her by Lavinia Wroth, as I did young Charlie."

I blinked.

"Kitty was told of this by her mother before she died last year. Being a creature of honour and some spirit, she found she couldn't endure to live on as a Wroth. She said she was my responsibility and that I would have to answer for my actions. She came to me with nothing but her mother's jewellery and the clothes she stood up in," he added with some pride. "She wouldn't even condescend to bring her adored mare."

"But Lady Wroth?" I stammered stupidly.

"She refuses to acknowledge the truth. Always has, and will till she dies. Call it what you wish, an old woman's pride comes closest to it, I suppose. A demned curious sort of pride that refuses to believe that the son she bore was as sterile as a harem-eunuch. Perhaps it's not so hard to understand, though. She prided herself on bringing fresh, healthy blood into the Wroth stock. I don't know what miracle she performed on her husband, but she managed to sire two sons. And old Thomas Wroth was as incapable of breeding as the last Spanish Hapsburg. Stukeley has been 'Fumbler's Hall' these two generations past . . ."

I thought of the lost, silly face of Lord Wroth's grandfather and conceded that Pelham might have a point at that.

"I can't imagine what humiliations the old woman endured in trying to breed from old Thomas, but she managed to foal twice. It explains why she refuses to believe that her own sons weren't breeders, though. She won't let her eyes tell her the truth. You've only to see my Kitty to know the truth of it. She has the Pelham eyes."

His own brown, turgid eyes stared resolutely into mine.

"And his lordship?" I asked. Pelham frowned.

"He favours his mother. In every way but his nature."

"And does Lord Wroth know of his true parentage?"

A strange, brooding, crafty look came into Pelham's face.

"Who knows what his lordship knows?" he said.

Who indeed, I wondered. What man in his right senses would forfeit the Wroth fortune and a title of great quality to acknowledge himself the bastard son of a worthless rake like Pelham?

I looked up to find Sir Harry watching me with a theorizing look in his eye. He lowered his gaze.

"What kind of father would I be to ask my son to give up a great position in life?" he asked with a wry smile. A look of almost benign amusement crept into his face. "But you can see, Nash, that I have no great wish to harm him."

"None at all, Sir Harry . . . If what you say is true," I answered.

A flicker of annoyance showed in his eyes.

"If you need further confirmation, Nash, my daughter can supply it."

"But you said she was in Shropshire," I said.

"God's ballock, man! Shropshire is not the end of the world. She can be reached."

There was a brief and nasty silence. I tried to sort out a number of conflicting questions. Pelham looked at me keenly. I wondered what ideas were running through his head. He said softly:

"You must be assured that I have done all I can to trace the receipts. You must take my word for it that they don't exist. And I will pay you well for the code-book."

A sudden vision entered my mind. I had a picture of two young men dressed in absurd female finery, dancing upon a mint-green lawn, sword clashing upon sword. At the corner of the wall stood a silent observer. A young man with a cool profile, looking on in contempt.

"Tell me, Sir Harry," I asked. "Does young Mr. Oliver know about your part in his cousin's conception?"

He was momentarily startled.

"What?"

"Does he also know the true story, Sir?"

"It is possible that he knows about my daughter, yes."

"And Lord Wroth? Is he aware of *his* true parentage?"

He looked reluctant. "I suppose so, yes."

"And tell me, Sir Harry," I asked carefully. "Is Mr. Oliver also a love-child?"

"Why, Sir," Pelham replied levelly, "from what I hear, Mr. Oliver is the result of a triumvirate. At least three gentlemen share the honour of his begetting."

There was a long pause while we out-stared each other. I was trying to discover whether he had lied to me and he was trying to ascertain whether I had believed him. It was a deadlock.

In the corner the felled coachman groaned and stirred. Pelham looked towards him expectantly, but the hope faded from his eyes when he saw that the man could be of no service to him yet awhile.

It was time for me to go. I moved to the door.

"Where are you going?" Pelham called after me.

"Why, Sir Harry, to corroborate your extraordinary story, to be sure," I answered.

I walked through the door and pulled it fast behind me, locking it and pocketing the key. There was nobody on the landing or in the hall. With the pistol cocked I walked quickly down the stairs and out into the street.

## XXI

Riding out to Stukeley, I fitted the pieces of the puzzle together as well as I was able. By the time I had reached the great gates to the avenue, I had made some sense of it all despite conflicting evidence. That is, if I were to give credence to Pelham's version of the truth. If I could believe him, the story would run this way:

Sir Harry had fathered both Lord Wroth and his sister Kitty. Young Charles had inherited not the Wroth family inbreeding, but the Pelham wildness. As a natural result of his follies, he had fallen into the manipulative hands of Murrell, who had accidentally discovered the secret of his birth. Knowing that the Dowager Lady Wroth had ambitious plans for her grandson's future, he had decided to capitalize on his discovery. But, being the devious rogue that he was, he had first sounded out his prospective victim. Hence the bogus approach, hinting at unspeakable secrets. The receipts, obnoxious as they were, were not in themselves to be feared. A young man's extravagances, however bad they may seem, would be overlooked by any ambitious family wishing to marry into the landed aristocracy. But if there was a possible doubt of the heir's legitimate right to the title and property, that would be another matter. It would be a secret worth paying out good money to keep undisclosed. If there was a smattering of truth in such a rumour, Lady Wroth would pay to cover the artificial scandal in order to protect her family from the larger threat of the real one.

But Lady Wroth was an obstinate woman and no fool. She had seen the receipts as a test and realized that if she played Murrell's game, she would be playing it to the death. So she had hired me, not to retrieve the receipts but to supply her with enough information to silence Murrell by a counterthreat to his liberty.

Murrell's brutish end had changed the situation only in that a single threat had sprouted a hydra-head. If he had been killed in order to silence him, his murderers had overlooked one important fact – Murrell had accomplices. Others were willing enough to carry on his work.

Yet I could only think that Murrell *had* been silenced. And who had undertaken the task? The list of possible assassins was an impressive one, to judge by the names that featured in the code-book. But out of all his numerous gulls and catspaws, I must concentrate my attention on those most closely connected to my end of this business.

Which led me to another point. If Murrell had not died simply to stop his tongue, then he must have been eliminated for other reasons. If this was so, then there was only one possible suspect – Pelham. I could not see either the red-topped youth nor black Betty with her grey-faced gallant engineering his death in order to inherit his business. Such an enterprise required style and Pelham was the only man for the game. The apprentice had definitely died at his instigation, if not by his own hand. And the poor black woman also?

It seemed possible. They both stood between Pelham and the realization of his plans, if they knew of the whereabouts of the receipts. For Pelham must hold the receipts in order to gain the code-book. And by his own admission, Pelham had exhausted the possibilities of retrieving the papers.

But d'Urfey? How had d'Urfey died?

I could not fit d'Urfey's death into the general scheme. If he had died because he, too, was an accomplice, whose accomplice had he been? I thought it very likely that the young Adonis had played some vital part in the affair, for he seemed the type of man to profit by being well-placed. I thought it likely that he had revealed Wroth's true parentage to Murrell, I thought it more than probable that he had gone to the old charlatan with the proposition to blackguard the dowager in the first instance. And had Pelham, whilst ridding himself of a superfluous partner, also rid himself of the originator?

But that required that Pelham knew of Murrell's discovery and was a party to the plot. Yet I was fairly convinced that, until I had enlightened him, he had had no knowledge of Murrell's involvement with young Wroth. There could be no doubting the concern in his eyes when I had informed him of it.

Unless, of course, he was an actor of genius and his tale had been a fantastication from beginning to end.

I jogged along, trying to slot together the pieces of such information as I had. It seemed to me that I had two separate strands which, taken singly, made some vague kind of pattern, but which, when I tried to weave them together, refused to create a satisfactory whole.

My first theory was that Murrell had been removed by Pelham, the intention being to rid himself of an encumbrance. When I had confounded Sir Harry by appropriating the all-important code-book, he had put the miserable assistants to death in his efforts to find the missing papers. This was my favourite theory, for the last two murders, I felt sure, could be linked directly to Pelham.

But this also left d'Urfey's death unaccounted for; likewise the fact that the attempt on Pelham's own life had some similarity to d'Urfey's.

My second theory was that Lord Wroth and d'Urfey had engineered Murrell's death between them, if they had not actually taken part in the bloody brawl. It seemed the uncomplicated way that a lad like his lordship would deal with a threat to his "honour". The black savage had murdered d'Urfey in revenge, after her own fashion. Then, still being uncertain of the true identity of her master's executioner, she had made a similar attempt on Pelham's life. If she had planned further retribution on Lord Wroth, she had been baulked of her satisfaction by her own violent end.

All this, as I say, made some kind of pattern in my mind, but there were too many inexplicable knots in the weave, too many rough ends. The single strands would not thread together.

That is, if I took Pelham at his word.

If I ignored his tale, of course, the pattern was quite different and made more appeal. Pelham himself was the black, villainous thread throughout. Everything that had happened could be laid to his hand. He had murdered Murrell, the apprentice, the Negress, and possibly d'Urfey. The attack on his own life had been carried out by the black woman and he had tried to confound me by implicating Oliver Wroth.

Which made me think of Oliver Wroth. What, if anything, had he to do with the business? His sole concern, he had suggested, was the protection of his grandmother.

Why had he tried to make me abandon the search for his cousin Kitty? If Pelham's story was true and Lord Wroth was not the legitimate heir, Oliver had more right to the succession. And if Oliver knew this extraordinary story, he would be a rare man indeed not to seek to profit by it. And yet he had tried to dissuade me from finding Miss Kitty, and she was the one who might settle the title on his shoulders.

If only I could disentangle the facts from the fiction in Pelham's story! If only I could ask for the Wroth version of his extraordinary tale.

But how could I approach Lady Wroth on such an indelicate mission? She had hired me to return the receipts, not to uncover a potential cesspit. Was it not enough that I had to go to her saying that no such receipts existed, without insulting her family into the bargain?

I had not worked out the answer to this by the time I was admitted to the house.


## XXII


In the event, my anxiety proved unnecessary, for I was not allowed to see her ladyship. Instead, I was left to brood downstairs for above half an hour. When the door opened, it was Mr. Oliver who came into the room.

He inclined his head by a bare fraction. The unamiable stiffness had returned to his bearing. He advanced towards a table and taking a purse from his pocket he counted out a number of coins.

"This was the price agreed upon for your services, Captain Nash. If you will give me an account of your expenses, we shall conclude this business."

"*We* shall, Sir?" I said, taken with some surprise.

"My grandmother is indisposed. This affair has caused her considerable hardship. She asks me to thank you on her behalf and to settle your account."

"But, Sir," I protested. "My business is not yet at an end."

The curious light-coloured eyes were, of a sudden, as dull as stones.

"I assure you that it is, Captain. We have no further need of you."

"I have not yet – "

"This business is finished!" he said violently. "The receipts were delivered here last night."

"Delivered?" I was stunned. I had come to report the possibility that no such papers existed.

"How?" I asked.

"They were simply delivered," he repeated grimly. "That is all you need to know, I think."

"Indeed, Mr. Wroth," I said sharply. "I think not, Sir."

His eyebrows rose superciliously.

"Really?"

"No, Sir. I have some rights in this matter. It may not have occurred to you, Mr. Wroth, but I have compromised my reputation to some extent in trying to secure the receipts. I feel I have a right to know how they were returned to you and by whom."

He looked down at the purse on the table, his fawn-coloured eyes veiled. When he spoke, it was politely, almost gently.

"I acknowledge that you may feel you have some rights, Captain Nash, and if you have compromised your reputation on our behalf, I thank you." The veil lifted slightly and his eyes flashed like the tips of arrows. "Though the less said about 'compromise' the better, for all our sakes."

He looked at me directly. The expression in his eyes was plain enough. By protecting their name, I would be protecting my own.

"On the contrary, Mr. Wroth," I answered, meeting the challenge. "It is my duty to make a report, of sorts, to the Mansion House."

He blinked.

"Concerning our business?"

"Concerning four deaths, Mr. Wroth. All of which *could* be connected with the receipts."

"You have no proof of that!" he said harshly.

"Do you think not?" I said, and paused. His eyes met mine searchingly, then they shifted away.

"I have not been entirely idle," I went on. "But since I must protect my reputation and as I have obviously forfeited your family's confidence . . ."

He picked up the purse and extracted more coins. He regarded me steadily as he laid out six pieces on the tabletop.

"Captain Nash, if I were to give you my word that none of these deaths are the responsibility of my family, would you . . . could you consider making your report to the Mansion House without involving our name?"

He moved the coins towards me suggestively.

"I don't see how I can, Mr. Wroth, in all conscience."

The hand moving the coins fell abruptly away.

"Do you connect the deaths with my family?" he asked coldly.

"Murrell was blackguarding you, Sir. He died. His assistants died too. Very violent deaths. As for d'Urfey, he was your cousin's closest companion."

"But we are not involved, except fortuitously."

I remained silent. He regarded me bitterly. Then the arrogant façade crumbled and the beseeching, almost supplicating look that I had seen on his face before came into it again.

"My grandmother is dying," he said quietly. "I would like her to die in peace."

"And ignorance?" I asked.

His head jerked back.

"Ignorance?"

I stood the bluff.

"Mr. Wroth, how much do you know of your antecedents?"

He flushed. I saw that I had struck home. Suddenly I was convinced that Pelham had told me the truth.

I had a brief and wild revelation. Oliver Wroth *knew* that he was the rightful heir (if one disregarded Pelham's malicious insinuations about his own conception). Knowing this, one could only guess at the disorder of his feelings. His grandmother's wilful refusal to recognize his true status must goad him beyond endurance. The realization that he could never prove his claim and the thought of losing both title and fortune to a worthless bastard must be almost more than he could bear. He was a young man with a cool head and a strong stomach, that was plain to see. Had he sought a desperate remedy for his wrongs? Knowing that he had no legal means of coming at his inheritance, had he sought to gain something of his own fortune by stealth?

Without fully grasping the extent of his motives, I felt strongly that he *had* been a prime mover in all this. The idea was fantastic, but no less possible for all that.

I observed him very closely as I said: "Sir Harry Pelham says that there are no receipts, Mr. Wroth. He also says that Lord Wroth is his natural son and Miss Kitty his natural daughter. If that is so, I am addressing the real Lord Wroth."

He flushed again and when he replied his voice seemed curiously sealed-off.

"Pelham lies in both cases, Sir. My cousin is who the world thinks he is and the receipts were delivered into our hands last night. This affair is over."

He scooped up the money. All at once he seemed to have regained his composure. He regarded me with the old, crisp arrogance.

"If you will state your expenses, Captain Nash, we shall draw a line under your account. As for your dealings with the Mansion House, you may tell them what you will. If you incriminate my family unnecessarily in the deaths you mentioned we shall, of course, take measures."

The fawny eyes glared at me. Generations of privileged and haughty ancestors looked out from behind them.

"I shall do all I can to protect my grandmother while she lives," he said quietly. "When she is gone, I shall come into my own."

My revelation turned slightly arsy-varsey. I had misjudged him. He was not the man to blackguard his own kin. I now saw why he wished to protect his cousin Kitty. She would be his most valuable witness when he came to claim his rights by Law. And she would undoubtedly be safer under Pelham's protection.

Under the bright pressure of those eyes, I glanced away.

There came an urgent knocking on the door and almost before Wroth could call out the door opened and Chives entered with undignified haste. He was oddly flustered for so impassive a man. I would not have imagined that his careful face could betray so much passion.

"What is it, Chives?"

It took some time before Chives could make himself understood, so great was the extent of his outrage.

"It's the master, Mr. Oliver! His lordship! He's been taken!"

"Taken? Taken where? By whom?"

With shaking hands, the old servant proffered a letter sealed with a rusty pin.

"We found this on Knottersmole Common, Sir. His Lordship was out there all morning shooting pigeon. I sent to remind him that dinner would be early today — and Grimes came back with this. It had been nailed to a tree by the lake. His lordship's gone, Sir. There's no doubt of it. We've searched everywhere."

Wroth looked up from the sheet of paper. I saw that on the outside in roughly printed red block-capitals were the words: "LADY WROTH. IN ALL HAIST." The paper looked to have been handled by a number of none too cleanly fingers.

"My cousin has been kidnapped," Wroth said. He handed the paper to me.

The letter read: "IF YOO WONT TO SEE LORD WROTH ALIV AGEN, FOLOW OUR COMANDS TO THE LETER. GETT HOLDE OF 5000 GNS. LD WROTH WILL SEE HIS MANI AFFTER YOO GIV UP THE RIJE. DO NOT TRY AND BAMBOOZ UZ OR CAKLE TO THE RUNNERS. NEETHER RAMP UZ ELS HIS LDSHIP WILL DYE AND THE OLDE LADIE WILL MAK A NEWE WILL.

"WEE WIL GIV YOO 2 DAYS TO GET THE RIJE. PLAIS THE GNS IN A BOKS AND WAYT FOR MOR TIDINGS."

"I don't understand half that jargon," Wroth said, his eyes bleak.

"Just thieves' cant, Mr. Wroth," I answered and could not forbear adding: "The writer seems anxious that you should not offend her ladyship."

His eyebrows rose in the familiar way. "Sir?"

"The letter seems to be directed more towards you, Sir, than her ladyship. Despite the fact that it's addressed to her. It is as though they feared that you might neglect to pay out, Mr. Wroth, unless you are reminded that her ladyship ultimately holds the purse-strings."

The tawny eyes glittered. He snatched the paper from my hand and snapped: "I will remind you, Sir, that our business is at an end. Chives, show the Captain to his horse."

He bowed and walked stiffly from the room.

Chives coughed discreetly from behind a diplomatic hand.

"Her ladyship wishes to see you, Captain," he said.

As we climbed the gloomy stairs, I had an inner conviction that I was about to be replaced in my former capacity; and a nagging conviction, also, that I already knew the answer to the case.

The clue, I felt sure, lay in the composition of the kidnapper's message. The thieves' vocabulary struck a false note somewhere. It was too literary in tone, while the spelling and the grammar were altogether too much contrived!

There was no lack of eyewitnesses to the kidnapping, though their versions of what had happened left more holes in the evidence than otherwise.

A stolid farmhand, working in a field adjoining the common, said he had seen a man who resembled his lordship in build and colouring, enter a black phaeton in company with an older man. He described this man as wearing a grey coat and kneebreeches. His lordship had not seemed to object to being carried off.

A drayman passing the east entrance to Stukeley (the nearest gate to the common) had seen a black and silver *chaise* standing beneath a clump of trees. But he had not seen his lordship or his kidnapper enter the carriage. Another witness (a milkmaid) said a *gig* had been driven away by a fellow wearing a beaver hat and a grey coat.

It would seem that Lord Wroth, who in my estimation was not by nature a quiet lad, had gone quite docilely with his kidnappers. Although he carried a fowling-piece, he had yet been constrained to leave the woods without a struggle. The elderly gamekeeper who had accompanied him to flush the birds had gone for half a mile before becoming aware that the birds that took to the sky at his coming were returning, unshot at, to the trees. Needless to say, he had seen nothing of his master's disappearance.

The crime appeared to have been planned in advance. The black and silver carriage had been seen in the vicinity on many days prior to the abduction, and for a number of nights, dogs in neighbouring kennels had been disturbed by prowlers. Or so willing witnesses hastened to tell me.

Among the eyewitness accounts that I collected, two completely contradictory ones stood out.

A servant at a house in the village said that at three o'clock on the day of the kidnapping, she had seen the black carriage pass by with two men in the back who appeared to be struggling with each other.

Against this was the story of the toll-keeper who, at the same time, had seen a black phaeton going in the *opposite* direction – that is, towards London. There were two men inside, one at the reins and the other partially concealed by a blanket. The driver had flung a handful of coppers in the toll-keeper's face and had cried out that his passenger was "taken sick with the buboes". The carriage had sped with uncommon speed towards London, which had scarcely surprised the toll-keeper, considering the patient's alarming disorder.

In all these conflicting statements only two facts remained constant. Firstly, the carriage, though variously described as a phaeton, a chaise, or a gig, was always black. Secondly, and a detail that I found more rewarding, in all the descriptions the kidnapper was described as being dressed in grey.

When the toll-keeper added the information that the driver's voice was curiously hoarse – as "thick as cheesecloth" was the way he put it – I felt that I was a long way on to retrieving his lordship and my reputation.

I knew only one grey man with a very hoarse voice who could have an interest in abducting Lord Wroth. Yet I feared that he might have little interest in returning the boy to his "mani" alive!

## XXIII

Roach's Landings stank as menacingly as ever in the glaring noonday heat. Wizened brats sailed their boats and fished in the foul gutter as I made my way through a herd of swine snuffling at the piled refuse in the unpaved street.

I climbed the greasy stairs, leaving behind the stench of rotting vegetables corrupting the air and exchanged it for the equally foul stuff that passed for ventilation in the grey man's lodgings.

Just as I placed my foot upon the last flight, I hesitated. The dull murmur of voices drifted down the stairs. I could detect the hoarse tones of the grey man and another strong, harsh voice.

As daintily as a dancing master, I passed up the remaining stairs and tripped like a peewit across the dusty boards to an alcove set at an angle to the grey man's attic. A filthy cloth hung from a rod, giving some protection. Swiftly I eased myself into the narrow confine of the alcove and arranged the frowzy cloth to hide me from any who should mount the stair.

I set my ear to the wall.

The harsh voice seemed to explode in my ear. He could not have been a foot away beyond the wall.

"You ain't very bright, 'Coffin'," he said. "Not at the best of times! I reckon the blackie bedevilled your wits. You should never have got caught up in the likes of this."

The grey man swore hoarsely. "Pike off."

"Where are the papers?" the harsh voice demanded.

Smith's bravery was only temporary. A note of pleading crept into the grey tones as he said patiently: "I've told yer – over and over. They're where they always was – with Himself."

The harsh man spat.

"It's true," Smith whined.

"My master wants them receipts. And I'm to take them back with me. Remember what overtook Betty."

The crude menace in the voice brought an image into my mind. The mad carnage made of that poor black woman with her flowering wounds.

The warning must have affected Smith likewise. I had to strain to hear his cringing reply.

"That game's finished. We been fleeced. We all been fleeced. *He's* made gawneys of us all."

"Stow that tale, Smith, or I'll tap your claret."

A note of desperate sincerity crept into the grey man's tone, so urgent that his wraith-like voice almost acquired substance.

"Hang me, if it's not true."

The other man laughed coarsely. "Hanging's too quick a death!"

Countless cracks of light showed through the diseased plaster. I applied my eye to the largest one and squinted through it.

The grey man, stared back at me disconsolately. For a moment it threw me into a confusion. He seemed so close and his scrutiny was so intent upon me that I imagined he must have seen the glimmer of my eye between the crack. Then I saw more clearly that his gaze was fixed upon a spot a little to my left, which meant that his interrogator stood behind the door.

The grey man's face seemed greyer than ever. His grey shape seemed to reject the light. His eyes, as I could see, stared with desperate hatred at a point some four feet above the ground. I wondered whether the object of his loathing was a knife, a pistol, or a sword.

Whatever it was, I resolved to come to his aid and for that purpose edged towards the door. A hearty shove would easily burst the flimsy wood and the force of my entry would throw the man off balance – if he remained behind the door. Smith and I could settle the resulting argument between us. At all events, I must save the grey man. He was my only hope of finding young Wroth.

What happened next occurred with such dazzling speed that I was taken completely off-guard. The fact that it took place out of sight confused me further. In shifting my position I must have disclosed my presence in some way, though I thought I had moved as lightly as a Ratcliffe fog.

Smith's unwelcome guest must have turned slightly, momentarily distracted by the sound and, quick as a cat, the grey man had attacked. I heard his breath whistle with the effort of it and I felt the wall shake as a weighty body fell against it. Immediately after, there was the deafening roar of a pistol shot reverberating among the rafters, followed by an uncanny silence.

A muffled oath, a groan. Somebody stirred. Sword in hand, I kicked at the door. It flew open and struck against an object lying behind it.

The gargantuan body of Pelham's coachman lay humped against the wall with the life fast ebbing out of him. His hands clutched weakly at his neck from which hung a knife like a bright red barb. My face was the last thing he saw on earth. He snarled feebly, the blood bubbling from his mouth as he died.

The grey man, too, was sinking to his knees, his hands slipping loosely over the bed on which the Negress had met such a terrifying end. I caught him as he dropped face forwards and turned him to the light. Blood soaked my hand.

Unaccountably he was not mortally wounded. The bullet had torn through his right arm only, leaving it a shattered mass of blood, flesh and bone-splinters. He would never again throw a knife with such devastating effect, but he would live to mount the scaffold.

His eyes were beginning to glaze. They seemed suddenly to shrink and to retreat inwards. His skin was the colour of congealed gravy. He fainted in my arms, spotting my linen liberally with his blood.

I patched him up, inexpertly using the bed linen to stem the flowing blood. I am no surgeon, but I did my best for him. For all his grey exterior he was as sound as a horse, and like a horse could have been bled of two quarts. He had survived enough in his lifetime – the pox at least to judge by the condition of his skin – and he would live to contract gaol fever. When I had finished with his arm, I filled his mouth with brandy; he choked slightly, his eyes opened resentfully and were filled with a dull sort of recognition.

"Where's Lord Wroth, 'Coffin'?" I asked.

His lips twisted with a weak defiance. "Pike off," he whispered.

I poked gently at his arm. A wave of nausea flushed the grey face. He swore again, though not so bravely. I reached for his broken arm. He whimpered in anticipation of the pain. My outstretched finger menaced his well-being as I asked again: "Where is Lord Wroth?"

There was no more fight left in him, but he still strove to make a profit from his situation. There is truly no honour among thieves! The informer is the principal support of the law. If one does one's crime with a confederate, and if one has little faith in him, it is always soothing to know that one can run off to the Justice, save one's own neck by telling the whole tale, and perhaps receive a substantial reward in addition.

In his half-fevered state, Smith strove to make such a bargain. My hovering finger brought him up against the reality of his situation. I was in no position – and no mood – to strike a bargain. He howled like a dog before fainting away.

"Where is Lord Wroth, and who is 'Himself'?" I asked, as he recovered consciousness.

He told me then. He told me all. A madder tale I never heard in my life before.


# XXIV

I skirted the edge of the common, making my way towards a coppice. As I reached the first line of trees, I saw a familiar figure ahead of me, flitting noiselessly from tree to tree, intent upon God knows what game.

The figure disappeared into the wood.

There was a dazzle of wings as a covey of birds rose, startled by the report of a gun. The shot had sounded away to my left and I turned in that direction. Silently I plunged between the saplings and forged ahead in the direction of the shot.

A cry rang out through the woods. The cry of some strange demented bird.

I broke into a run, crashing through the trees like a wild boar. Branches flailed at my arms and whipped my back as I pushed through the dense thickets. With a gasp, I braked short at the edge of the trees. A thin branch caught my cheek as I fell into the clearing. I stared, amazed.

"My lord!"

Lord Wroth stood drooping against a tree, his pale face contorted. The fowling-piece he had carried lay where it had fallen in the bracken.

His lordship twisted towards me, his face a livid white.

"Help me!"

Half fainting with pain, he pointed down to where one elegant ankle lay caught in the fierce embrace of a fearsome looking mantrap. He had run into it unsuspecting.

It was an odd mistake for a man to make on his own land, but then Lord Wroth was not on familiar ground. Slope Manor was a good many miles from Stukeley, a remote and unconsidered possession, little used by his family, and a perfect place from which to manage a kidnapping!

Despite her condition, her ladyship had sent for me, demanding to
be told all. She lay back upon her pillows, her face the colour of
cheap tallow.

I lay the receipts upon the bedcover, Oliver Wroth having allowed
me this privilege. She plucked at them merely, regarding them with
icy eyes. The Dowager Lady Wroth looked her great age. I gave her,
at best, five more months of life.

"Well, Sir," she said gruffly. "I suppose you are to be congratulated
on a successful *detection*."

I bowed my thanks for the reluctant compliment.

A sound escaped her. I could not tell whether she sobbed
or spat.

"Tell me what you know, Captain Nash."

I glanced at Oliver Wroth, who stood by the bed's canopy. He
frowned slightly and shook his head. Her ladyship, looking up, caught
the gesture.

"I will be told!" she snapped. "And I will have the truth. It was
I who paid for your services, was it not? I want the truth."

Oliver shrugged, and gave his unwilling assent.

So I began from the beginning. I first explained about my
attempts to break the code of Murrell's book and what my efforts
had revealed.

"You learned something from the book?" she asked.

"Yes, my lady. I subsequently learned something very important.
I learned that neither your name nor his lordship's figured among
the many distinguished names in it."

"And what did that tell you, Sir?"

"It told me that Murrell was double-dealing his partner Pelham.
For you may be sure that Sir Harry would not have countenanced
exposing his lordship to scandal."

That brought a muddy flush to her worn cheeks.

"Sir?"

"Rightly or wrongly, Pelham believes himself to be the father of
Miss Kitty and Lord Wroth."

She waved away the suggestion with the ghost of a theatrical
gesture. But it was a theatrical gesture, empty as air.

"Though, of course," I continued as she lay back, "Murrell *was*
double-dealing Sir Harry, and no doubt Sir Harry knew it in some
fashion. But he didn't murder the old man. I know this to be true,
for Pelham knew nothing of Lord Wroth's involvement and he
was genuinely shocked by the old charlatan's death. Moreover,
he was dependent upon him. I ruled him out quite early on

with regard to that death. Murrell was murdered by his other partner."

"Pelham's other partner?" Lady Wroth asked with a sharp drawn breath. Her old eyes flashed fearfully towards her grandson. That young man was staring gloomily out of the window, as if he would penetrate the depths of the clouds with his naked eye.

"No Ma'am, Murrell's. Murrell was not the man to manage such a business on his own," I said. "He had not the style. Nor, in this particular case, the required knowledge. That knowledge could only have come from a peculiarly placed confidant."

"D'Urfey?"

"Yes, young d'Urfey, though even he was not acting on his own account. He was also in partnership."

Her diamond eyes widened in a chilling gleam, and again she looked towards Oliver Wroth.

". . . Who, Sir?"

But she did not need to ask. She knew the answer in her heart.

"Lord Wroth, Madam."

She half rose in a feeble attempt at protest, but the effort was too great for her and the gesture again too empty. She fell back, her fingers plucking at the counterpane.

"What makes you suppose that?"

"It is no supposition, Lady Wroth. It is a deducible fact. I can give you evidence of it. And as you yourself said, his lordship is rogue-wild. He is heavily in debt and still years away from his inheritance. He needed money and you denied him. So, he was offered a way out of his difficulties."

"Offered a way?"

She seemed to be grasping at this straw of comfort.

"It was d'Urfey's idea originally, Ma'am. It was he who put his lordship up to it."

"But he was killed, and the demands still came!"

"That is why I had to rule him out as being the sole candidate. He simply set the scheme in motion. And afterwards with Murrell dead and both his servants murdered and the receipts still not found, I had to admit that there was yet another partner."

"Pelham," she said stubbornly. "Why could it not be Pelham?"

"Pelham was still looking for the receipts as late as three days ago," I said gently. "He sent his man for them. So, with all the obvious suspects removed, there remained only the one."

She would not allow me to name the one.

"When Mr. Oliver told me the receipts had been mysteriously

returned, but would not say by whom, my suspicions were confirmed. I knew it could only be – "

Again, a gesture stopped me from speaking the name aloud.

From his place by the window, Oliver spoke.

"I discovered them in Charlie's room," he said harshly.

With a dazzle of diamonds, the old lady swept the offensive papers from the bed.

"So you see," I said reasonably, "I could scarcely return property which was already beneath your roof."

She turned away, her expression hidden by the lace edge of her pillow.

"When you hired me to retrieve the receipts," I went on, "I think Lord Wroth took fright. He was afraid that you would discover his complicity in the matter. Accordingly, he tried to warn me off. When I refused to be intimidated, he made a mad dash up to town and tried to put a stop to the whole affair. But Murrell was a greedy fellow and he, in turn, I think, refused to be dissuaded. So d'Urfey arranged for his . . . removal."

"D'Urfey?" she asked dully, her face still hidden.

I spared her what I thought to be the absolute truth, and detected a grateful look in her grandson's eye.

"Your grandson was here at Stukeley on that night."

She didn't move. I had no idea from the unyielding way in which she lay, whether I had been believed or not.

"The black woman, Betty, must have recognized d'Urfey in some manner. In her primitive fashion, she saw her duty to her master. D'Urfey was left to poison a well. Similarly, she felt an obligation to try to eliminate Pelham, since he also could easily have had a motive for assassinating Murrell."

"And my grandson? Why was he not murdered if she knew him to be in partnership with d'Urfey?"

"It is a miracle that he was not, Ma'am. The black woman had a protector of sorts. A man called Smith. For a time I thought he believed that Lord Wroth had revenged himself upon the Negress."

Her head reared sharply from the pillow. She could not frame the question on her lips.

"It was Pelham's coachman, my lady," I reassured her happily. "He was seeking information."

She sank back upon her pillows, sucking what comfort she could from my words.

"And the kidnapping?"

"That was partly Smith's notion . . . but largely your grandson's."

She huddled deeper beneath the bedclothes, shivering slightly.

"Why?" Her voice cracked. She sounded infinitely old, tired, and broken.

"The business with the receipts had failed and Lord Wroth's debts were still unpaid. He grew desperate, and he had only one acquaintance left in St. Giles': the grey man, Smith. *He* was equally desperate. He had every encouragement to leave the country, but lacked the wherewithal. Your grandson sought him out to try to raise the rhino, and between them they concocted the scheme."

There was a silence. Oliver continued to stare out of the window, and her ladyship lay like an effigy in her ponderous bed.

"And are you happy with your piece of detection?" she asked at last.

I bowed for lack of an answer.

The old fingers scrabbled angrily at the counterpane. Her yellowish face appeared suddenly to disintegrate into a hundred ugly lines. Pain and humiliation were stamped funereally behind her eyes. She raised herself upon an elbow and stared accusingly, her voice flailed me like a thin, worn lash.

"Why, Sir! I don't believe a word of it!" she cried. "I think you are completely wrong! You are a rash amateur, Sir, and have no business to meddle! You are nothing but a *raw beginner!*"

She sank back upon her pillows and dismissed me with a limp wave of her hand. She was spent. Dulled forever.

I bowed slightly, having no words. Oliver came and took me gently by the arm. Quietly, politely even, he led me from the room.

"I thank you, Captain Nash," he said gravely.

"*You* thank me, Sir?"

"For not seeking to defend yourself to my grandmother."

"I saw no point, Sir."

"No," he mused sadly, "she is not open to reason and is in no condition to judge."

"To judge what, Sir?"

"Your performance, Captain."

I smiled at his oblique compliment, knowing I would receive no other kind.

"Why, Sir," I replied, "as to that, I must agree with your grandmother. I *am* a raw beginner and what else can I be but a sort of amateur? Mine is scarcely yet a profession!"

## EPILOGUE

So ended my first investigation. Jogging back to town, I contemplated my future. Although I had brought the Wroth affair to an end, I had not done so without damage to myself, having made two very powerful enemies in Sir Harry Pelham and Lord Wroth. True, I had gained the respect of young Oliver, but I did not yet know whether he would gain the Wroth inheritance. (It so turned out that he did not after all try to claim his rights, possibly because to level a charge of bastardy at his cousin would raise doubts about his own birth and bring the whole family into disrepute. A family in the elevated social position of the Wroths would avoid an open scandal at all costs, as I had seen. Lord Wroth grew from a wild youth to a wilder man, married his heiress and sired fourteen children on her before dying in 1835 of gout and old age.)

But to return to the present affair: I was much concerned as to how I was to explain my involvement in the deaths of five people. I would have to take this problem to my cousin Scrope in the Commissioner's Office.

Scrope relieved my fears by putting the situation into some perspective: a young rake had murdered an old charlatan and been slain in turn by a half-savage. She had been done to death by Sir Harry's sadistic coachman, who had come to a bad end himself. His slayer, "Coffin" Smith, had died of gaol fever two days after his committal. Thus the various assailants were all conveniently dead, and death being beyond the Law, the Law would therefore remain silent on the subject.

"But what of the Cunning-man's assistant?" I asked. "He was murdered in Pelham's house."

"Aye, in Pelham's *house*," my cousin answered. "But what proof have you that it was at Pelham's hand? Pelham was confined to his sick-bed at the time."

I remembered my own ordeal whilst Pelham lay in his sick-bed.

"But he may have ordered his death."

"Aye, he *may* have. But it would be his word against yours. And should you lose the suit . . ."

He had no need to elaborate further. Pelham was a potent enough enemy under the present circumstances and there would be little purpose in provoking him further. Though the thought of an unproved murder rankled.

"I seem not to have come out of this too well," I said.

My cousin clapped me on the shoulder encouragingly.

"Not so! Not so, George! You have done middling-well. Fielding's

Runners could not have done better given the strange nature of the Wroth affair."

"But *I* feel that I should have done better. Fielding's men lack science."

"Why, man!" he cried. "What chance have you under the present system? We live in a state of legal anarchy. Would you try to overturn the Constitution at one blow? It has taken Fielding twenty years to show that crime can be suppressed without serious damage to that mythological entity. He has rid us of street gangs and cleared the roads of highwaymen, but is his work fully appreciated? Bones-a-me, if it is! Yet change is coming, cousin! Change is coming! There will be a place for your scientific detection yet. Take heart, George."

He clapped me on the back once more, and misquoted the Bard at me:

"Thus far thy fortune keeps an upward course,
And thou art graced with wreaths of victory."

"Well," thought I wryly. "Not a wreath perhaps, on this proceeding, but a chaplet certainly."

My cousin Scrope, caught in the poetic vein, poured out a bumper of Canary and, with further recourse to the Bard, offered this health.

"All the gods go with you! Upon your sword
sit laurel victory! And smooth success
be strew'd before your feet!"

# THE DOOMDORF MYSTERY
## Melville Davisson Post

*Post (1871–1930), was an American attorney in the final years of the last century before turning to writing full-time. His first book,* The Strange Schemes of Randolph Mason *(1896), featured a rather unorthodox lawyer who often bent the law in the defence of his clients. The character later reformed, and the collection,* The Corrector of Destinies *(1908), is regarded as one of the cornerstones of American crime fiction. In creating Uncle Abner, though, Post made a bold move forward. It was the first fictional character to be set in an historical period and who used detective methods. Abner was a country squire in Virginia, in the early days of the nineteenth century. He was an intensely righteous, God-fearing man and a keen observer of human nature, and brought the skills of detection to a peak rivalled only by Sherlock Holmes. Surprisingly the stories never really caught on in Britain, but in America they remain highly respected. Ellery Queen regarded them as "second only to Poe's* Tales *among all the books of detective short stories written by American authors", calling them the "crème du crime". The story reprinted here originally appeared in the* Saturday Evening Post *for 18 July 1914, and is one of the most intriguing of the whole series.*

The pioneer was not the only man in the great mountains behind Virginia. Strange aliens drifted in after the Colonial wars. All foreign armies are sprinkled with a cockle of adventurers that take root and remain. They were with Braddock and La Salle, and they rode north out of Mexico after her many empires went to pieces.

I think Doomdorf crossed the seas with Iturbide when that ill-starred adventurer returned to be shot against a wall; but there was no Southern blood in him. He came from some European race remote and barbaric. The evidences were all about him. He was a huge figure of a man, with a black spade beard, broad, thick hands, and square, flat fingers.

He had found a wedge of land between the Crown's grant to Daniel

Davisson and a Washington survey. It was an uncovered triangle not worth the running of the lines; and so, no doubt, was left out, a sheer rock standing up out of the river for a base, and a peak of the mountain rising northward behind it for an apex.

Doomdorf squatted on the rock. He must have brought a belt of gold pieces when he took to his horse, for he hired old Robert Steuart's slaves and built a stone house on the rock, and he brought the furnishings overland from a frigate in the Chesapeake; and then in the handfuls of earth, wherever a root would hold, he planted the mountain behind his house with peach trees. The gold gave out; but the devil is fertile in resources. Doomdorf built a log still and turned the first fruits of the garden into a hell-brew. The idle and the vicious came with their stone jugs, and violence and riot flowed out.

The government of Virginia was remote and its arm short and feeble; but the men who held the lands west of the mountains against the savages under grants from George, and after that held them against George himself, were efficient and expeditious. They had long patience, but when that failed they went up from their fields and drove the thing before them out of the land, like a scourge of God.

There came a day, then, when my Uncle Abner and Squire Randolph rode through the gap of the mountains to have the thing out with Doomdorf. The work of this brew, which had the odors of Eden and the impulses of the devil in it, could be borne no longer. The drunken Negroes had shot old Duncan's cattle and burned his haystacks, and the land was on its feet.

They rode alone, but they were worth an army of little men. Randolph was vain and pompous and given over to extravagance of words, but he was a gentleman beneath it, and fear was an alien and a stranger to him. And Abner was the right hand of the land.

It was a day in early summer and the sun lay hot. They crossed through the broken spine of the mountains and trailed along the river in the shade of the great chestnut trees. The road was only a path and the horses went one before the other. It left the river when the rock began to rise and, making a detour through the grove of peach trees, reached the house on the mountain side. Randolph and Abner got down, unsaddled their horses and turned them out to graze, for their business with Doomdorf would not be over in an hour. Then they took a steep path that brought them out on the mountain side of the house.

A man sat on a big red-roan horse in the paved court before the door. He was a gaunt old man. He sat bare-headed, the palms of his hands resting on the pommel of his saddle, his chin sunk in his black stock, his face in retrospection, the wind moving gently his great shock of voluminous white hair. Under him the huge red horse stood with his legs spread out like a horse of stone.

There was no sound. The door to the house was closed; insects moved in the sun; a shadow crept out from the motionless figure, and swarms of yellow butterflies maneuvered like an army.

Abner and Randolph stopped. They knew the tragic figure – a circuit rider of the hills who preached the invective of Isaiah as though he were the mouthpiece of a militant and avenging overlord; as though the government of Virginia were the awful theocracy of the Book of Kings. The horse was dripping with sweat and the man bore the dust and the evidences of a journey on him.

"Bronson," said Abner, "where is Doomdorf?"

The old man lifted his head and looked down at Abner over the pommel of the saddle.

"'Surely,'" he said, "'he covereth his feet in his summer chamber.'"

Abner went over and knocked on the closed door, and presently the white, frightened face of a woman looked out at him. She was a little, faded woman, with fair hair, a broad foreign face, but with the delicate evidences of gentle blood.

Abner repeated his question.

"Where is Doomdorf?"

"Oh, sir," she answered with a queer lisping accent, "he went to lie down in his south room after his midday meal, as his custom is; and I went to the orchard to gather any fruit that might be ripened." She hesitated and her voice lisped into a whisper: "He is not come out and I cannot wake him."

The two men followed her through the hall and up the stairway to the door.

"It is always bolted," she said, "when he goes to lie down." And she knocked feebly with the tips of her fingers.

There was no answer and Randolph rattled the doorknob.

"Come out, Doomdorf!" he called in his big, bellowing voice.

There was only silence and the echoes of the words among the rafters. Then Randolph set his shoulder to the door and burst it open.

They went in. The room was flooded with sun from the tall south windows. Doomdorf lay on a couch in a little offset of the room, a great scarlet patch on his bosom and a pool of scarlet on the floor.

The woman stood for a moment staring; then she cried out:

"At last I have killed him!" And she ran like a frightened hare.

The two men closed the door and went over to the couch.

Doomdorf had been shot to death. There was a great ragged hole in his waistcoat. They began to look about for the weapon with which the deed had been accomplished, and in a moment found it – a fowling piece lying in two dogwood forks against the wall. The gun had just been fired; there was a freshly exploded paper cap under the hammer.

There was little else in the room – a loom-woven rag carpet on the floor; wooden shutters flung back from the windows; a great oak table, and on it a big, round, glass water bottle, filled to its glass stopper with raw liquor from the still. The stuff was limpid and clear as spring water; and, but for its pungent odor, one would have taken it for God's brew instead of Doomdorf's. The sun lay on it and against the wall where hung the weapon that had ejected the dead man out of life.

"Abner," said Randolf, "this is murder! The woman took that gun down from the wall and shot Doomdorf while he slept."

Abner was standing by the table, his fingers round his chin.

"Randolph," he replied, "what brought Bronson here?"

"The same outrages that brought us," said Randolph. "The mad old circuit rider has been preaching a crusade against Doomdorf far and wide in the hills."

Abner answered, without taking his fingers from about his chin:

"You think this woman killed Doomdorf? Well, let us go and ask Bronson who killed him."

They closed the door, leaving the dead man on his couch, and went down into the court.

The old circuit rider had put away his horse and got an ax. He had taken off his coat and pushed his shirtsleeves up over his long elbows. He was on his way to the still to destroy the barrels of liquor. He stopped when the two men came out, and Abner called to him.

"Bronson," he said, "who killed Doomdorf?"

"I killed him," replied the old man, and went on toward the still.

Randolph swore under his breath. "By the Almighty," he said, "everybody couldn't kill him!"

"Who can tell how many had a hand in it?" replied Abner.

"Two have confessed!" cried Randolph. "Was there perhaps a third? Did you kill him, Abner? And I too? Man, the thing is impossible!"

"The impossible," replied Abner, "looks here like the truth. Come with me, Randolph, and I will show you a thing more impossible than this."

They returned through the house and up the stairs to the room. Abner closed the door behind them.

"Look at this bolt," he said; "it is on the inside and not connected with the lock. How did the one who killed Doomdorf get into this room, since the door was bolted?"

"Through the windows," replied Randolph.

There were but two windows, facing the south, through which the sun entered. Abner led Randolph to them.

"Look!" he said. "The wall of the house is plumb with the sheer face of the rock. It is a hundred feet to the river and the rock is as smooth as a sheet of glass. But that is not all. Look at these window frames; they are cemented into their casement with dust and they are bound along their edges with cobwebs. These windows have not been opened. How did the assassin enter?"

"The answer is evident," said Randolph: "The one who killed Doomdorf hid in the room until he was asleep; then he shot him and went out."

"The explanation is excellent but for one thing," replied Abner: "How did the assassin bolt the door behind him on the inside of this room after he had gone out?"

Randolph flung out his arms with a hopeless gesture.

"Who knows?" he cried. "Maybe Doomdorf killed himself."

Abner laughed.

"And after firing a handful of shot into his heart he got up and put the gun back carefully into the forks against the wall!"

"Well," cried Randolph, "there is one open road out of this mystery. Bronson and this woman say they killed Doomdorf, and if they killed him they surely know how they did it. Let us go down and ask them."

"In the law court," replied Abner, "that procedure would be considered sound sense; but we are in God's court and things are managed there in a somewhat stranger way. Before we go let us find out, if we can, at what hour it was that Doomdorf died."

He went over and took a big silver watch out of the dead man's pocket. It was broken by a shot and the hands lay at one hour after noon. He stood for a moment fingering his chin.

"At one o'clock," he said. "Bronson, I think, was on the road to this place, and the woman was on the mountain among the peach trees."

Randolph threw back his shoulders.

"Why waste time in a speculation about it, Abner?" he said. "We know who did this thing. Let us go and get the story of it out of their own mouths. Doomdorf died by the hands of either Bronson or this woman."

"I could better believe it," replied Abner, "but for the running of a certain awful law."

"What law?" said Randolph. "Is it a statute of Virginia?"

"It is a statute," replied Abner, "of an authority somewhat higher. Mark the language of it: 'He that killeth with the sword must be killed with the sword.'"

He came over and took Randolph by the arm.

"Must! Randolph, did you mark particularly the word 'must'? It is a mandatory law. There is no room in it for the vicissitudes of chance or fortune. There is no way round that word. Thus, we reap what we sow and nothing else; thus, we receive what we give and nothing else. It is the weapon in our own hands that finally destroys us. You are looking at it now." And he turned him about so that the table and the weapon and the dead man were before him. "'He that killeth with the sword must be killed with the sword.' And now," he said, "let us go and try the method of the law courts. Your faith is in the wisdom of their ways."

They found the old circuit rider at work in the still, staving in Doomdorf's liquor casks, splitting the oak heads with his ax.

"Bronson," said Randolph, "how did you kill Doomdorf?"

The old man stopped and stood leaning on his ax.

"I killed him," replied the old man, "as Elijah killed the captains of Ahaziah and their fifties. But not by the hand of any man did I pray the Lord God to destroy Doomdorf, but with fire from heaven to destroy him."

He stood up and extended his arms.

"His hands were full of blood," he said. "With his abomination from these groves of Baal he stirred up the people to contention, to strife and murder. The widow and the orphan cried to heaven against him. 'I will surely hear their cry,' is the promise written in the Book. The land was weary of him; and I prayed the Lord God to destroy him with fire from heaven, as he destroyed the Princes of Gomorrah in their palaces!"

Randolph made a gesture as of one who dismisses the impossible, but Abner's face took on a deep, strange look.

"With fire from heaven!" he repeated slowly to himself. Then he asked a question. "A little while ago," he said, "when we came, I asked you where Doomdorf was, and you answered me in the language of the third chapter of the Book of Judges. Why did you answer me like that, Bronson? – 'Surely he covereth his feet in his summer chamber.'"

"The woman told me that he had not come down from the room where he had gone up to sleep," replied the old man, "and that the door was locked. And then I knew that he was dead in his summer chamber like Eglon, King of Moab."

He extended his arm toward the south.

"I came here from the Great Valley," he said, "to cut down these groves of Baal and to empty out this abomination; but I did not know that the Lord had heard my prayer and visited His wrath on Doomdorf until I was come up into these mountains to his door. When the woman spoke I knew it." And he went away to his horse, leaving the ax among the ruined barrels.

Randolph interrupted.

"Come, Abner," he said; "this is wasted time. Bronson did not kill Doomdorf."

Abner answered slowly in his deep, level voice:

"Do you realize, Randolph, how Doomdorf died?"

"Not by fire from heaven, at any rate," said Randolph.

"Randolph," replied Abner, "are you sure?"

"Abner," cried Randolph, "you are pleased to jest, but I am in deadly earnest. A crime has been done here against the state. I am an officer of justice and I propose to discover the assassin if I can."

He walked away toward the house and Abner followed, his hands behind him and his great shoulders thrown loosely forward, with a grim smile about his mouth.

"It is no use to talk with the mad old preacher," Randolph went on. "Let him empty out the liquor and ride away. I won't issue a warrant against him. Prayer may be a handy implement to do a murder with, Abner, but it is not a deadly weapon under the statutes of Virginia. Doomdorf was dead when old Bronson got here with his Scriptural jargon. This woman killed Doomdorf. I shall put her to an inquisition."

"As you like," replied Abner. "Your faith remains in the methods of the law courts."

"Do you know of any better methods?" said Randolph.

"Perhaps," replied Abner, "when you have finished."

Night had entered the valley. The two men went into the house and set about preparing the corpse for burial. They got candles, and made a coffin, and put Doomdorf in it, and straightened out his limbs, and folded his arms across his shot-out heart. Then they set the coffin on benches in the hall.

They kindled a fire in the dining room and sat down before it, with the door open and the red firelight shining through on the dead man's narrow, everlasting house. The woman had put some cold meat, a golden cheese and a loaf on the table. They did not see her, but they heard her moving about the house; and finally, on the gravel court outside, her step and the whinny of a horse. Then she came in, dressed as for a journey. Randolph sprang up.

"Where are you going?" he said.

"To the sea and a ship," replied the woman. Then she indicated the hall with a gesture. "He is dead and I am free."

There was a sudden illumination in her face. Randolph took a step toward her. His voice was big and harsh.

"Who killed Doomdorf?" he cried.

"I killed him," replied the woman. "It was fair!"

"Fair!" echoed the justice. "What do you mean by that?"

The woman shrugged her shoulders and put out her hands with a foreign gesture.

"I remember an old, old man sitting against a sunny wall, and a little girl, and one who came and talked a long time with the old man, while the little girl plucked yellow flowers out of the grass and put them into her hair. Then finally the stranger gave the old man a gold chain and took the little girl away." She flung out her hands. "Oh, it was fair to kill him!" She looked up with a queer, pathetic smile.

"The old man will be gone by now," she said; "but I shall perhaps find the wall there, with the sun on it, and the yellow flowers in the grass. And now, may I go?"

It is a law of the story-teller's art that he does not tell a story. It is the listener who tells it. The story-teller does but provide him with the stimuli.

Randolph got up and walked about the floor. He was a justice of the peace in a day when that office was filled only by the landed gentry, after the English fashion; and the obligations of the law were strong on him. If he should take liberties with the letter of it, how could the weak and the evil be made to hold it in respect? Here was this woman before him a confessed assassin. Could he let her go?

Abner sat unmoving by the hearth, his elbow on the arm of his chair, his palm propping up his jaw, his face clouded in deep lines. Randolph was consumed with vanity and the weakness of ostentation, but he shouldered his duties for himself. Presently he stopped and looked at the woman, wan, faded like some prisoner of legend escaped out of fabled dungeons into the sun.

The firelight flickered past her to the box on the benches in the hall, and the vast, inscrutable justice of heaven entered and overcame him.

"Yes," he said. "Go! There is no jury in Virginia that would hold a woman for shooting a beast like that." And he thrust out his arm, with the fingers extended toward the dead man.

The woman made a little awkward curtsy.

"I thank you, sir." Then she hesitated and lisped, "But I have not shoot him."

"Not shoot him!" cried Randolph. "Why, the man's heart is riddled!"

"Yes, sir," she said simply, like a child. "I kill him, but have not shoot him."

Randolph took two long strides toward the woman.

"Not shoot him!" he repeated. "How then, in the name of heaven, did you kill Doomdorf?" And his big voice filled the empty places of the room.

"I will show you, sir," she said.

She turned and went away into the house. Presently she returned with something folded up in a linen towel. She put it on the table between the loaf of bread and the yellow cheese.

Randolph stood over the table, and the woman's deft fingers undid the towel from round its deadly contents; and presently the thing lay there uncovered.

It was a little crude model of a human figure done in wax with a needle thrust through the bosom.

Randolph stood up with a great intake of the breath.

"Magic! By the eternal!"

"Yes, sir," the woman explained, in her voice and manner of a child. "I have try to kill him many times – oh, very many times! – with witch words which I have remember; but always they fail. Then, at last, I make him in wax, and I put a needle through his heart; and I kill him very quickly."

It was as clear as daylight, even to Randolph, that the woman was innocent. Her little harmless magic was the pathetic effort of a child to kill a dragon. He hesitated a moment before he spoke, and then he decided like the gentleman he was. If it helped the child to believe that her enchanted straw had slain the monster – well, he would let her believe it.

"And now, sir, may I go?"

Randolph looked at the woman in a sort of wonder.

"Are you not afraid," he said, "of the night and the mountains, and the long road?"

"Oh no, sir," she replied simply. "The good God will be everywhere now."

It was an awful commentary on the dead man – that this strange half-child believed that all the evil in the world had gone out with him; that now that he was dead, the sunlight of heaven would fill every nook and corner.

It was not a faith that either of the two men wished to shatter, and they let her go. It would be daylight presently and the road through the mountains to the Chesapeake was open.

Randolph came back to the fireside after he had helped her into the saddle, and sat down. He tapped on the hearth for some time idly with the iron poker; and then finally he spoke.

"This is the strangest thing that ever happened," he said. "Here's a mad old preacher who thinks that he killed Doomdorf with fire from Heaven, like Elijah the Tishbite; and here is a simple child of a woman who thinks she killed him with a piece of magic of the Middle Ages — each as innocent of his death as I am. And, yet, by the eternal, the beast is dead!"

He drummed on the hearth with the poker, lifting it up and letting it drop through the hollow of his fingers.

"Somebody shot Doomdorf. But who? And how did he get into and out of that shut-up room? The assassin that killed Doomdorf must have gotten into the room to kill him. Now, how did he get in?" He spoke as to himself; but my uncle sitting across the hearth replied:

"Through the window."

"Through the window!" echoed Randolph. "Why, man, you yourself showed me that the window had not been opened, and the precipice below it a fly could hardly climb. Do you tell me now that the window was opened?"

"No," said Abner, "it was never opened."

Randolph got on his feet.

"Abner," he cried, "are you saying that the one who killed Doomdorf climbed the sheer wall and got in through a closed window, without disturbing the dust or the cobwebs on the window frame?"

My uncle looked Randolph in the face.

"The murderer of Doomdorf did even more," he said. "That assassin not only climbed the face of that precipice and got in through the closed window, but he shot Doomdorf to death and got out again through the closed window without leaving a single track or trace behind, and without disturbing a grain of dust or a thread of a cobweb."

Randolph swore a great oath.

"The thing is impossible!" he cried. "Men are not killed today in Virginia by black art or a curse of God."

"By black art, no," replied Abner; "but by the curse of God, yes. I think they are."

Randolph drove his clenched right hand into the palm of his left.

"By the eternal!" he cried. "I would like to see the assassin who could do a murder like this, whether he be an imp from the pit or an angel out of Heaven."

"Very well," replied Abner, undisturbed. "When he comes back tomorrow I will show you the assassin who killed Doomdorf."

When day broke they dug a grave and buried the dead man against the mountain among his peach trees. It was noon when that work was ended. Abner threw down his spade and looked up at the sun.

"Randolph," he said, "let us go and lay an ambush for this assassin. He is on the way here."

And it was a strange ambush that he laid. When they were come again into the chamber where Doomdorf died he bolted the door; then he loaded the fowling piece and put it carefully back on its rack against the wall. After that he did another curious thing: He took the blood-stained coat, which they had stripped off the dead man when they had prepared his body for the earth, put a pillow in it and laid it on the couch precisely where Doomdorf had slept. And while he did these things Randolph stood in wonder and Abner talked:

"Look you, Randolph . . . We will trick the murderer . . . We will catch him in the act."

Then he went over and took the puzzled justice by the arm.

"Watch!" he said. "The assassin is coming along the wall!"

But Randolph heard nothing, saw nothing. Only the sun entered. Abner's hand tightened on his arm.

"It is here! Look!" And he pointed to the wall.

Randolph, following the extended finger, saw a tiny brilliant disk of light moving slowly up the wall toward the lock of the fowling piece. Abner's hand became a vise and his voice rang as over metal.

"'He that killeth with the sword must be killed with the sword.' It is the water bottle, full of Doomdorf's liquid, focusing the sun . . . And look, Randolph, how Bronson's prayer was answered!"

The tiny disk of light traveled on the plate of the lock.

"It is fire from heaven!"

The words rang above the roar of the fowling piece, and Randolph saw the dead man's coat leap up on the couch, riddled by the shot. The gun, in its natural position on the rack, pointed to the couch standing at the end of the chamber, beyond the offset of the wall, and the focused sun had exploded the percussion cap.

Randolph made a great gesture, with his arm extended.

"It is a world," he said, "filled with the mysterious joinder of accident!"

"It is a world," replied Abner, "filled with the mysterious justice of God!"

# MURDER IN THE
# RUE ROYALE
## Michael Harrison

*Michael Harrison (1907–1991) was a writer in a variety of fields, but his passion was for mystery fiction, and particularly the world of Sherlock Holmes. He was regarded as one of the foremost Holmesian scholars.*

*The son of a lawyer and nephew of an architect, Michael sought to follow in his uncle's footsteps and studied architecture, but turned to writing and journalism when his first novel,* Weep for Lycidas *(1934), proved a success. Over the next fifty years he wrote over fifty books under his own name and several pseudonyms. Perhaps his most popular was his attempt at an autobiography by Holmes, called* I, Sherlock Holmes *(1977).*

*Harrison did not confine his research to the world of Holmes, but also explored Holmes's fictional predecessor, August Dupin, created by Edgar Allan Poe. He wrote a series of stories in the late 1960s for* Ellery Queen's Mystery Magazine. *A selection were published in America as* The Exploits of Chevalier Dupin *(1968), and then expanded for British publication as* Murder in the Rue Royale *(1972), and it is the title story which is reprinted here.*

*Harrison's Dupin reflects perhaps rather more of Holmes than the Poe original, but the stories are fascinating in themselves and provide us with an opportunity to revisit the world of the first ever fictional detective.*

The murder of Monsieur Cuvillier-Millot, the eminent banker, in his bedroom in the Rue Royale, caused what the newspapers are always pleased to call "a profound sensation." Even in a capital city which, as our friend G— would assure you, has the oldest and most efficient police in the world, crimes are still numerous, and murders not unknown.

Yet the *bizarre* character of this particular crime gave it, as it were, a *permanence* in the public consciousness which prevented its passing out of the public memory within the traditional period of nine days. All murder is, to a greater or lesser degree, a problem for those who are not killed; but this murder of Monsieur Cuvillier-Millot posed problems over and above those customarily inseparable from the violent taking of another's life.

For instance, how, in this case, did the murderer make his escape, from a window on the second floor, literally within seconds of his having fired the one shot which killed the well-known banker? Moreover, how had the assassin made his escape with such miraculous speed that those who forced open the door of the bedroom never caught a glimpse of him?

There were other puzzling features, of course, but these two questions were universally held to be the crucial ones compared with which all others were trifling. One might almost have dismissed the idea that there had been a murderer at all, save that there was a very real corpse in evidence, lying in Monsieur Cuvillier-Millot's four-poster bed, and that the bullet-wound in the back of the corpse's neck could hardly have been self-inflicted. (Were it even possible to suppose that, where then was the pistol which the deceased must have fired in the act of *felo-de-se?*)

The more one reflected upon the many puzzling features of this extraordinary crime, the more puzzling it appeared. The police, though promising a "speedy arrest," within twenty-four hours, as is usual in all cases where the murderer – or, at least, a promising suspect – is not safely lodged in the *Dépôt de la Préfecture de Police*, were obviously baffled. They could scarcely hunt for a suspect among the known burglars of Paris – nothing had been taken from the bedroom of Monsieur Cuvillier-Millot; and though it might have been argued that the thief (supposing the assassin to have been a thief) had been scared off before he had time to rob the banker, surely he had time to snatch up the valuables in plain sight – diamond ring, Bréguet watch and guard, diamond scarf-pin, and a liberally-stuffed pocketbook – which were lying on a dressing-table near the bed.

Then, as to motive, the only person – apart from a hypothetical burglar – who could conceivably have had an interest in the death of the banker was his nephew and presumed heir, who lived with Monsieur Cuvillier-Millot and who, indeed, had played a leading part in the events immediately preceding the discovery of his uncle's dead body. The deceased banker, a widower whose only son had been killed in the Algerian fighting, had sent to London for his sole nephew, the son of a Cuvillier-Millot who had fled to England during the Terror of '93, and, save for fleeting visits to his far wealthier brother in Paris, had never returned to the land of his birth. Gaspard Cuvillier-Millot, heir to the immense fortune of his murdered uncle, had attended one of those English schools which, removing to France after the Reformation, had returned to England more than two centuries later because of the troubles into which the Revolution of 1789 had plunged France.

Following a few terms at Oxford, young Monsieur Gaspard accepted a clerkship in the renowned banking-house of Herries, Farquhar & Co., of St. James's Street, London – a move not uncalculated, one felt, to bring him to the sympathetic notice of his prosperous Parisian uncle. In the London banking-house, whose circular and transferable exchange-notes have made it famous and influential throughout Europe, Monsieur Gaspard served with diligence, until the death of his cousin in a skirmish at Tlemcen brought him to Paris, to take the place of that son whom the banker had lost in military action.

So much of the history of this fortunate young man we owed to G—, the Prefect of the Parisian Police, who called on us just after breakfast two days after the murder which had set all Paris by the ears. Now, on this sunless Spring morning of the year 183–, G— sat in our little back library, or book-closet, *au troisième*, No. 33, Rue Dunôt, Faubourg St. Germain, sipped at his hot chocolate, and gave, generally, the impression of a man at his wits' end.

"When a banker is murdered," said G—, harshly peremptory in tone, as he always was when baffled and filled with anxiety for his reputation and his lucrative appointment under Government, "it involves a good deal more than merely his family. The repercussions on the Bourses of all the capitals of Europe – well, you understand me perfectly, I am sure, my dear Chevalier?"

"Yes, yes, I understand well," replied Dupin, stifling a yawn, for we had sat up late the night before. "Monsieur Cuvillier-Millot had just floated a loan for Brazil of eight million gold francs, another for New Granada of two million, another for Turkey of twenty million, and was about to raise one for Spain of thirty millions, to provide the Iberian Peninsula with a railroad system. Yes, I read the newspapers, too."

"You will know, then," said G—, in no wise abashed by my friend's curt manner, "that we are also too near to the social unrest of 1830 and 1832 not to feel alarmed when something – anything – casts doubt upon the stability of the *régime* under which we live. Two French Revolutions in less than fifty years are enough – but there are always Radical newspapers and irresponsible demagogues to raise the cry of corruption whenever something happens in the world of banking."

"I am well aware of this," said Dupin, reaching out for the heavy pewter tobacco-jar in which he kept his favorite Latakia. "As I am well aware," he added, beginning to fill his meerschaum pipe, "that you have come to ask my assistance in this matter because your own methods have not produced the hoped-for results. Very well, then: tell me what your own methods have yielded thus far."

"Very little, I am afraid," said G— candidly. "We have ascertained the cause of death – that goes without saying – "

"Indeed!" observed Dupin, though with a strong hint of sarcasm in his intonation. He puffed furiously at his pipe, so that it was almost as if from within a cloud that we heard his voice ask, with a deceptive mildness, "And what, pray, was the cause of Monsieur Cuvillier-Millot's death?"

"Why, it was in all the newspapers – "

"I am not concerned with what the newspapers print, or with what I read in their columns. I am asking *you*. What was the cause of the banker's death?"

"Why, a pistol-shot fired into the base of the skull."

"You have recovered the ball?"

"No."

"Why not?"

"Well now, Dupin, why should we have probed for the ball? It was evident beyond doubt what had killed the banker."

"You mean, by that remark, that the usual *sequelæ* of a pistol-shot were present – powder-burns around the wound, blackening of the skin around the point of entry of the ball, and so on?"

"Precisely," replied G—, with a little grimace of self-satisfaction and self-congratulation.

"There has been no *post-mortem* examination of the cadaver?"

"*Que diable*, Dupin! Of course not. Where the cause of death is so self-evident, why on earth should we offend both the living and the dead by anatomizing the corpse? I tell you, the man died of a bullet-wound in the top of his spinal column, immediately under the cerebellum – *here!*" And suiting the action to the word, G— bent his head forward and placed the index finger of his right hand on the spot indicated, a half-inch or so above the upper edge of his tall, starched neckcloth. "In such a place, a bullet-wound is, as you well know, inevitably fatal."

"In such a confoundedly difficult place against which to place the muzzle of a pistol, common justice would hardly deny the assassin the reward of a fatal assault. But tell me, my dear G—, what was the eminent victim doing all this time that the assassin was getting behind him? Was the shot in the back of the neck accidentally aimed there? Was the wound the result of a *ricochet*? Or – stay!! – was the victim perhaps asleep at the time?"

"No," said G—, with a vigorous shake of his head, "that is

impossible. It was the noise of voices raised in some altercation which brought the members of the household – I should say, rather, the *other* members of the household – hurrying toward the door of Monsieur Cuvillier-Millot's bedroom – only, of course, to find it locked, so that the door had to be forced. It was while they were standing outside, debating what to do, that the fatal shot was heard. The door was then attacked vigorously by a couple of footmen – well-built farmer lads from Normandy – and broken open. Their master was lying on his bed – a corpse – and the assassin was nowhere to be seen."

"And the window, you say, was open?"

"With the dimity curtains blowing in – the heavy drapes had been pulled back. On entering the room of death, some hurried to see what might be done for the victim, others ran to the window. But, scan the surrounding courtyards and streets as they would, they saw no sign of anyone who might have escaped from the bedroom, after having murdered their master. And that, Dupin, is what makes the whole affair so very mysterious."

"What, precisely, makes this affair so very mysterious? Are you referring to the fact that, on looking through an open window, no one was seen? I find that possibly the least mysterious fact of all. Now," as he saw that G— was about to protest, "let us consider this matter of the fatal shot, as you call it – "

"As *I* call it!"

"As you call it. Whatever you and your colleagues may have surmised, it is still to be proven that the fatal shot was heard – or, rather that what was heard was the fatal shot."

"But a shot *was* heard. We have a dozen witnesses to depose to that fact."

"Possibly. Possibly not. A dozen witnesses may be as wrong as one. Suppose now that *you* tell *me* what it was these twelve witnesses claim to have heard?"

"Well, let us begin somewhat farther back. I shall briefly mention that it is Monsieur Gaspard's custom to rise earlier than the time at which his uncle stirs, so that he may be downstairs at his desk a few minutes before the bank opens for business at 8:30 A.M. He does not – at least customarily – look in on his uncle, who is called by his valet at half-past seven, with a tray of chocolate and rolls and a morning newspaper.

"However, as Monsieur Gaspard walked along the corridor on his way to the bathroom – yes, there is a modern bathroom, fitted with all the latest conveniences, even to a patent English contrivance for heating water by gas – on his way to this bathroom, I say, of which he takes good advantage judging by his fastidious appearance, Monsieur

Gaspard passed the door of his uncle's bedroom. The door, though of solid mahogany, is not particularly thick, and sounds within the room may be heard by anyone in the corridor. Monsieur Gaspard tells me that he has often heard his uncle's snores as he passed the door.

"Now – to-day is Thursday, so that all this would have happened on Tuesday last – on Tuesday, then, something much out of the ordinary occurred. Monsieur Gaspard rose – I forgot to tell you that no servant calls him; he is awakened by a small alarum-clock which stands on his bed-side table – Monsieur Gaspard rose as usual, donned his *robe de chambre*, went out into the corridor, and walked along in the direction of the bathroom."

"All precisely as usual?"

"All precisely as usual. But – certainly not as usual – were the sounds coming through the door of his uncle's bedroom – sounds of angry voices, of reproaches, of threats, of I don't-know-what. Monsieur Gaspard stopped at once; he has a natural delicacy in such matters, and hardly relished the thought of listening at his uncle's door – "

"Or of being detected in the act of doing so? No matter. Pray proceed with your narrative, which I find most interesting."

"At any rate, as Monsieur Gaspard listened, he became aware that the altercation sounded as though it were approaching a climax. He could distinguish no words, but it was clear that two men were angry, and one was menacing the other.

"Monsieur Gaspard became alarmed, and ran rather to get advice than to get help. He hurried down stairs, and poured out his story to the old *suisse*, who has been with the household since before the first Revolution."

"You have taken this man's evidence, of course?"

"Yes – and the evidence of all who were in a position to be witnesses. Well, to proceed: the *suisse* expressed the view that all should repair, with the utmost despatch, to the bed-room, and there call out – in case Monsieur Cuvillier-Millot required assistance in repelling anyone who was threatening him."

"One moment, please! Why did not Monsieur Gaspard open the door of his uncle's bedroom, and just walk in?"

"He says that he had a nervousness as regards his uncle. The banker was rather a martinet, a domestic tyrant. I can well believe that the nephew may have hesitated to expose himself to the shame of an embarrassing situation. In any case, as was proved later, the door was locked."

"Yes, but he cannot say whether or not the bedroom-door was

locked when he passed it – or, say, when he halted to listen to the stranger menacing his uncle."

"No, he cannot say. I put the question to him, but he could not answer it, one way or the other."

"Hem! So, merely observing that this precious Monsieur Gaspard strikes me as rather a poltroon, let us go on. The *suisse* had no sooner been asked his advice by this far too fastidious nephew than the domestic called for the footmen, and, probably accompanied now by the other servants, led the party to the door of their master's bedroom. Or – stay! – did Monsieur Gaspard, shamed into at least the affectation of resolution, lead the way? Ah, he did lead! Good! And what did the *suisse* and all the domestics have to tell you of the quality of the voices heard through the strong but thin door?"

"Well now, here we strike a formidable difficulty. I had hoped that we might have some evidence which would help us to trace the assassin through someone's recognition of his voice."

"But now there was only silence? The voices had ceased?"

"Just so."

"The banker was dead – and the assassin had fled through the window?"

"Impossible! Just as Monsieur Gaspard and the footmen were readying themselves to break open the door – I mentioned, did I not, that Monsieur Gaspard tried the handle and found the door locked? – just as they had come to the decision to break down the door – "

"One moment, please! *Why* had they come to this serious decision? Did they not first call out and ask Monsieur Cuvillier-Millot if aught were wrong? Ah, you forgot to mention that? Pray continue."

"You were right to remind me of what I had overlooked. It is true that when the group arrived outside the door, Monsieur Gaspard called out, several times, 'Uncle, is anything the matter?' – or words to that effect. But there was no answer; and, at a sign from Monsieur Gaspard, the footmen then advanced to throw themselves against the door. At that moment the shot was heard – just one shot; very clear, though not, as the witnesses say, very loud."

"But unmistakably a shot? On which, with commendable courage – for the man with the firearm might have been waiting inside the bedroom for *them* – the footmen hurled themselves against the door, the lock broke, the door opened, and they fell headlong into the room, to see what you have already described to me – nothing. Now, a most important point. After the shot had been fired, did anyone hear the footsteps of the assassin as he ran across the room to the window? Did anyone hear the window opened?"

"No. The reason is easy to comprehend. On hearing the shot, the female domestics, led by the cook, set up such a cry of shock and terror that an army might have tramped across the room and gone unheard."

"So! And though but one person – Monsieur Gaspard – can testify that voices were raised in quarrel, many can testify that a shot was fired immediately before the door was broken down?"

"All, in fact, who were present. Not only did they hear the report of the firearm, they entered a room full of smoke, to say nothing of the characteristic odor of gunpowder."

"We must recover the ball – if it still be in the dead man's head. Is it?"

"Is it still in the dead man's head? Yes, there is but one wound – that of entry. Evidently the ball did not penetrate with sufficient force to pass through the skull."

"Do you not find that fact remarkable?" Dupin asked.

"How so? It merely means that the charge was a light one; the muscles at the back of the head are very thick and tough – I have known many cases where they have stopped a ball."

"Perhaps. But have you known them to stop a ball fired against the skin? No matter, all these points will be resolved later. What I should like you first to do is to cause a police surgeon to probe for the bullet, and – having found it – to remove it without damaging it in any way. Can this be done?"

G— looked dubious. "The family's friends will not approve. The dead banker is even now lying in state in his drawing-room. But – yes, of course, Dupin, you shall have the bullet. Why do you wish it?"

"I desire to know the type of firearm from which it came."

Dupin and I were present when the two surgeons attached to the Prefecture of Police carried out the *post-mortem* examination of the deceased banker. The formal permission of the dead man's nearest relative – in this case, Monsieur Gaspard – had to be obtained; but, though the young man began to voice objections, G— soon silenced them by representing the necessity of the autopsy in the interests of justice.

The cadaver was decently carried into a small room adjoining the drawing-room, and here the surgeons prepared to extract the ball in whose nature Dupin had evinced so keen an interest.

The corpse had, of course, been washed, and made presentable by those cosmetic arts in which our modern morticians excel.

Having expressed a wish to examine the body – but more particularly the head – before the surgeons cut into it with their scalpels and bistouries, Dupin went carefully over the entire anatomy with a strong magnifying glass. Rising from the most minute inspection of the wound in the neck, Dupin asked G— if the witnesses who had first discovered the body had noticed the characteristic blackening of a gunshot wound.

"Yes, without doubt. It is not present now, I see, but the undertaker's woman would have washed the burnt powder off."

"So thoroughly? The skin, too, does not appear to have been scorched at all. *Diable*, this is a most singular wound to have been caused by a pistol-ball! Monsieur le Préfet, a word with you, please."

Dupin led the Prefect to the far corner of the room, out of hearing of the surgeons, and said, "Unless this household is very different from other households, the washing will be done on a Monday. Today is Thursday. Let an *agent* be instructed to impound all the dirty linen at present awaiting the week's wash. What shall he look for? Well, in the first place, a particularly dirty handkerchief."

No more would Dupin say on this point; and when G—, after having issued the requisite instructions, came back to the room, Dupin took him by the arm and called his attention to the wound, handing over his powerful magnifying glass so that G— might see what my friend had already noticed.

"Observe," said Dupin, "the curious reddening, in perfectly circular form, which rims the wound. This is *not* the customary scorching which occurs with gunshot wounds, but something altogether different. Another point: has either of you gentlemen" – addressing himself to the surgeons – "ever known of a case where, the weapon being brought sufficiently close to the body to cause scorching, there was not some serious derangement of the skin, caused by the escape of gases into the wound opened by the ball? No, gentlemen, and neither have I. Monsieur G— suggested that the curious nature of this wound might be due to the assassin's having used only a small charge of powder – for what reason, I cannot suggest. It may be so. But now, let us proceed."

"To open the cranium, sir?" the elder of the two surgeons asked, a scalpel in his hand.

"Not yet, sir. First, I should like the stomach evacuated. We have with us, I take it, a stomach-pump?"

A stomach-pump having been produced the contents of the dead man's stomach were soon transferred to a covered dish, and to this disagreeable material, Dupin, to whom, in the interests of justice, nothing proved an obstacle, gave his minute attention. Indeed, it was with an air of noticeable triumph that he turned to us, and said, "I am astonished that we did not smell it on the man's breath! What, Monsieur G— ! You, with your sharp scent! Yes, gentlemen – laudanum, and in a very copious draught. Of one thing we may be sure, our dead banker was not very coherent at half-past seven on Tuesday morning, no matter what Monsieur Gaspard heard through the closed door.

"Did the dead man's physician prescribe laudanum? No matter, we shall find out. And now, before you cut, gentlemen, may I beg of you *very carefully* to probe the wound, and tell me exactly how far beneath the surface the ball is lying?"

Watched by a puzzled G— and (I confess it) by a no more enlightened me, the senior surgeon introduced a fine but strong wire probe into the wound, and pushed it gently forward until, encountering an unyielding surface, he assumed that the ball had been reached. Noting the length of wire which had entered the wound before reaching the ball, Dupin quickly translated this length, by means of a pocket rule, into terms of centimetres.

"Just over seven-and-a-half centimetres – three inches" – for, in those days, the old measurements were more commonly employed than the new. "Now, gentlemen, cut, if you please – and I beg of you not to damage the ball in any way."

After a few minutes of the surgeons' grisly labors a leaden ball was placed in Dupin's hand. He examined it with his powerful glass, and uttered a small cry of satisfaction before proffering both ball and glass to G—.

"What do you see, Monsieur le Préfet?"

"How very – how *excessively* – odd!" said G—, staring at the ball resting on his thick palm. "It is – how *very* curious! I see what appears to be a set of teeth-marks in a small circle. Dupin, how do you explain this? Could the firing of the pistol have marked the lead of the ball in this most unusual way?"

Dupin did not answer. Taking back the ball from G—, he dropped it into a pocket of his waistcoat, and said briskly. "The body can now be restored to a seemly appearance, and taken back for its lying-in-state. Monsieur G—, I should be infinitely obliged by a sight of the dead man's sleeping chamber, and, in particular, of the cupboard in which he kept his medicines."

"We walked up stairs, having dismissed the servants who, out of well-trained habit, sought to accompany us. Dupin carefully surveyed the room in which Monsieur Cuvillier-Millot had died.

One had the impression, in watching my friend at work, that those eyes of his observed everything – what was of importance, and what was not – and took away a complete record of visual, auditory, and tactile impressions (not forgetting, of course, the olfactory), to be analyzed and indexed at leisure, over his favorite pipe, in the peace of our little book-closet in the Rue Dunôt.

As we walked across the room to the small dressing-room adjoining, in which it was to be presumed that Monsieur Cuvillier-Millot had kept his medicines, Dupin said idly, "You will already have made some inquiries relative to the character and standing of Monsieur Gaspard? I venture to suggest that you have uncovered some scandalous information?"

"Indeed. I can hardly believe he would have continued in his uncle's favor had the news of his extravagances and debts come to the ears of the worthy banker. What is more, he was – is, I suppose one should say – being strongly pressed for settlement. There is an expensive young person with whom he has contracted one of those alliances generally as costly as they are irregular. However, he may now whistle at his creditors, with all the banker's millions in his pocket. A happy accident – for him, I mean – that the assassin should have put a fortune in his way."

"I see," said Dupin, opening the medicine-chest, which stood on a side-table, "that the late Monsieur Cuvillier-Millot was obviously not a valetudinarian. There is no medicine here that one would not find in most if not all households. Indeed, there is much absent that one might expect to find. Flowers of sulphur. I take this blood-purifier myself. So, I imagine, do most people. Chlorate of potash. Excellent as a throat-gargle. But did Monsieur Cuvillier-Millot suffer from sore throats?

"I can find out. But I suggest that, as he sang in the choir of La Madeleine – yes, he did; does that surprise you? – he had a constant use for chlorate of potash. What else? No laudanum. Well, I hardly expected it. But we shall find it somewhere in the house."

We walked to the window through which the assassin had made his miraculous escape. We opened the casements and leaned out. It was difficult indeed to see how the man could have escaped at all, let alone so quickly that no one had even seen him. I expressed my opinion, and G— concurred.

"When I shall have explained that to you," Dupin said, with a smile, "you will be in possession of all the facts in this extraordinary case. Now I have seen what I need to see. With your permission, Monsieur le Préfet, I shall borrow this iron door-stop."

"Door-stop? But why should you wish to borrow that?"

"When you call at our house this afternoon at five o'clock, precisely, you shall find out why. May I call your attention to this splendid clock on the mantel-shelf? Yes, by Bréguet, of course.

I wonder if, with all this upset, the servant entrusted with the duty has remembered to wind it? Now, where is the key? Ah, yes, here it is – in its proper place behind the clock."

Dupin held it up for the attention of our perfectly mystified eyes. It was an ordinary steel clock-key, of the fashion of some fifty years or more earlier, but of a type which is still favored by the horologists of Paris. A short tube, which fitted into a hole in the clock's face, was attached to a little crank-handle, with a polished wooden knob.

Dupin took out his pocket-glass and most minutely examined this commonplace article of domestic use. "Indeed, someone is to be felicitated on the care with which even the clock-key has been wiped. Still, I have a use for this, and I shall also borrow it, if I may."

"You may borrow what you like, Dupin," said G— in a surly tone. "Your whimsicalities are quite beyond my poor powers of comprehension. But I'm not so sure the servants haven't been upset by all this to-do – in spite of what you say. For instance, that door-stop that you propose to borrow: I take it that you didn't notice that it was not standing by the door, but had been moved to the fire-place – within the steel-fender?"

"Ah!" said Dupin, with a pleased expression, "so you *did* notice that! Bravo! Did you also notice another trivial proof of the servants' unusual neglect – this?"

"What is it?" said G—, coming closer, to peer at the object which my friend was holding between two fingers. "Ah, yes. What is it? A short length of black pack-thread? Is it important? Where did you find it?"

"It may be important. And I found it caught in the handle of the bell-pull just to the side of the fire-place."

At Dupin's request I did not accompany him back to our house, but made my way idly in the direction of the river. I walked down the Rue Royale, crossed the Rue St. Honoré, and, finding myself in the Place de la Concorde, obeyed a whim and paid my ten sous to enter the Navalorama, a spectacle I had never seen before.

This ingenious naval panorama, at the entrance of the Champs Elysées, exhibits a truly convincing representation of some of the most famous battles of history, from Salamis to Navarino, with the vessels and the water in motion, and the guns firing most realistically. So full of interest did I find this panorama – one of the many in Paris – that the time passed quickly, and I had to hail a *fiacre* in order to keep my appointment with Dupin and G— in the Faubourg St. Germain.

The clock in the belfry of St. Germain-des-Prés was just striking five as I entered the vestibule of our house, where I was greeted by Hyacinthe with the intelligence that G— had already arrived – a supererogatory piece of news, since I had seen G—'s spanking English tilbury in our courtyard; and that Monsieur le Chevalier awaited me in the drawing room.

"Bravo!" said Dupin sarcastically, as I entered the drawingroom. "You are learning the English idea of punctuality – which is to be so punctiliously on time as to give the impression of being late! However, since we are now all present, let us go upstairs to our little back library. I am sorry, Monsieur G—, to put you under the necessity of climbing another pair of stairs, but I have something above well worth your seeing. Pray follow me, please."

Obviously in obedience to some instructions given to him while I was absent, Hyacinthe did not accompany us; and, with Dupin leading the way, we came at last to our favorite room on the third floor. The door, as usual, was closed.

Dupin placed his hand on the door-knob, but, no sooner had he done so than a loud report, as of a pistol's discharge, sounded from within the room.

Dupin flung wide the door, and shouted, "The assassin! After him!!"

The window was open – the muslin curtains billowing in the breeze from without and the draught of the opened door from within. Dupin literally hurled himself across the room, to lean half out of the casement, pointing his finger downward, and gesticulating wildly. We crowded after him, thrust ourselves to each side of him, to catch a glance of – what?

"He has vanished!" said Dupin, with a comical expression of disgust. "He must have – no, he cannot have hooked his finger nails into the cracks in the brickwork – yes, I have it! – he must have escaped in one of Mr. Green's balloons. Quick, G—, look up, to see if you can catch a sight of the miscreant disappearing into the clouds!"

G— threw himself into a *fauteuil* with an angry exclamation.

"*Peste!*" he said. "Is this another of your jokes, Dupin? It *is* a joke, of course?"

"If so," replied my friend, with a severe expression, "it is a joke which has cost Monsieur Cuvillier-Millot his life. It was upon certain evidence of eyes, ears, and noses that a theory has been built up of an assassin, striking when Monsieur Gaspard – the man who stood most to gain by the dead banker's decease – was in full sight of a dozen trustworthy witnesses. *He* did not fire the shot. Oh, no! How could he have done so, when the shot was fired on the other side of a locked door?

"But tell me, Monsieur le Préfet, did *you* not hear a shot? Do *you* not smell the burnt gunpowder? Did you not see an open window, and jump instantly to the conclusion – placed so cunningly by *me* into *your* head – that there *must* have been someone who had fired the shot, and that someone *must* have escaped through the window, since he was not visible within the room?

"However, now it is different, is it not? A moment's reflection showed you the impossibility of someone's having escaped through a window so far above the ground, and with no tree or other means by which a man, however agile, could have got away so rapidly. You asked me if this were a joke? It is not a joke. Had you asked me, was this a trick, I should have answered – yes."

"You imply," said G— thoughtfully, "that Monsieur Gaspard is the murderer whom we seek?"

"Monsieur Gaspard," said Dupin decisively, "is without doubt the murderer. He had the motive, the means, and the opportunity, as I propose to demonstrate – though you will have to trick him, as he has tricked you, to extract from him the admission of guilt that you need. Did you find, in the dirty linen, a very dirty handkerchief?"

"Yes. I have it here." G— took a packet from the tails of his coat and handed it to Dupin, who opened it eagerly, examined it, and then put his nose to it.

"Excellent! This is mere lamp-black, since it smells of burnt spermaceti, such as is consumed in lamps, and not of burnt gunpowder. Monsieur Gaspard almost deserved to succeed in his diabolical plan, he was so clever. He used, for the planned killing of his uncle, only such things as were to be found in the house. No traceable purchases of arsenic for him! Lamp-black from an ordinary lamp, to smear around the wound! No, not a single substance or object which was not readily to hand in the mansion."

"But how in heaven's name did he shoot his uncle!" G— cried. Dupin smiled.

"He did not shoot his uncle. *Monsieur Cuvillier-Millot was not shot.* Look at this small piece of plaster-of-Paris: it is a cast of the ball extracted from the dead man's skull."

G— took it, and examined it.

"Why, yes, here are the indentations – the ring of indentations – that I noticed on the ball when it was first extracted by the surgeons. Now this cast shows the indentations as small teeth, sticking up. *Peste!* what does that ring of teeth remind me of?"

"Of *this*, I suggest," said Dupin, producing the clock-key, and indicating the ratchet at the end of the small tube.

"Dupin, what are you suggesting?"

"You will find," said Dupin calmly, "that Monsieur Gaspard, though he did not enter his uncle's room in the morning, did take in his evening cup of spiced wine. On the evening before the discovery of the murder the wine was even more heavily spiced – with laudanum. If the dead man did not use laudanum, you will find it somewhere in the house.

"Then, at some time in the early morning – but not too early – Monsieur Gaspard entered his uncle's bedroom, took a ball, turned the drugged man until he was face downward, and tapped the ball, using a hammer doubtless muffled in cloth, into the unconscious uncle's brain, with the end of the clock-key. This end is about three inches long – and only to that extent was the ball driven into the head; though that was enough to cause death. He wiped the key – there will be blood as well as lamp-black on the handkerchief – and replaced the key behind the clock. He then set up an ingenious device to trick the domestics a few hours later; then, after opening the window, he left the room and locked the door.

"At his customary time of rising he ran downstairs to report the angry voices within his uncle's room – though, of course, poor Monsieur Cuvillier-Millot had then been dead some two hours or so.

"Monsieur Gaspard, having collected all the servants as witnesses, then approached the door. The witnesses will testify that a shot was heard, and the door was then forced open.

"In strict truth, the shot was heard *as* Monsieur Gaspard put his hand on the door-knob; for all he did was to put his finger under the black pack-thread which had been passed *through* the key-hole and *over* the handle of the bell-pull to the side of the fire-place, and which held – by a quick-release hitch such as sailors or horsemen use – this iron door-stop I borrowed, and that you may now return to the house in the Rue Royale.

"The door-stop, released by the quick-release hitch, fell straight down into the steel-fender which surrounds the fireplace. But – and take careful note of this – it fell on to a mixture of two very ordinary substances, to be found in the medicine-chests in most homes: chlorate of potash and flowers of sulphur, a mixture so highly explosive that it takes but a light blow to detonate it."

"*Diable*! Of course!"

"The bang – the smell of sulphur – the open window – who would not have sworn, on twenty Bibles, that he had heard a shot fired, and been just too late to spy the assassin, detected almost – but not quite – *in flagrante delicto*?

"By the way, with his commendable proclivity for using only

the tools to hand, Monsieur Gaspard will have cast himself a ball with the bullet-mould to be found in the case of pistols kept in the library, or gunroom if there is one. Examination under a microscope will establish the origin of the ball taken from the dead banker's head."

G— coughed.

"Dupin ... excuse me, but since you have helped me thus far, tell me: how shall I bring the fact of his guilt home to this most ingenious ruffian?"

Dupin smiled, and reached for the tobacco-jar.

"Well, my dear G—, you might begin by re-staging the charade with which I startled and annoyed you a few minutes ago. Even Monsieur Gaspard's aplomb might be so shaken to hear *another* pistol-shot in his dead uncle's bedroom that you might well obtain his confession . . ."

It was so. Three months later, despite the advocacy of those Solons of the French Bar whom Monsieur Gaspard retained to defend him, a melancholy procession set out one morning for a certain space within the Barrière de St. Jacques, and here a dastardly assassin paid the ultimate penalty.

# THE GENTLEMAN FROM PARIS
## John Dickson Carr

*This story is another tribute to Edgar Allan Poe and is written by the world's master of the impossible crime. Whether writing under his own name or as Carter Dickson, Carr (1906–1977) produced time and again a masterful series of locked-room mysteries, of which the following is a fine example. Carr was one of the pioneers of the historical detective novel, the best being* The Bride of Newgate *(1950) and* The Devil in Velvet *(1955), though he remains best known for his series of novels about Dr. Gideon Fell, a rather overweight and pompous detective who nevertheless had a talent for solving the impossible.* The Hollow Man *(1935) contains a chapter where Carr provides the definitive lecture on locked-room mysteries, a study which has yet to be bettered.*

Carlton House Hotel
Broadway, New York
14 April 1849

M y dear brother:
Were my hand more steady, Maurice, or my soul less agitated, I should have written to you before this. *All is safe:* so much I tell you at once. For the rest, I seek sleep in vain; and this is not merely because I find myself a stranger and a foreigner in New York. Listen and judge.

We discussed, I think, the humiliation that a Frenchman must go to England ere he could take passage in a reliable ship for America. The *Britannia* steam-packet departed from Liverpool on the second of the month, and arrived here on the seventeenth. Do not smile, I implore you, when I tell you that my first visit on American soil was to Platt's Saloon, under Wallack's Theater.

Great God, that voyage!

On my stomach I could hold not even champagne. For one of my height and breadth I was as weak as a child.

"Be good enough," I said to a fur-capped coachman, when I had struggled through the horde of Irish immigrants, "to drive me to some fashionable place of refreshment."

The coachman had no difficulty in understanding my English, which pleased me. And how extraordinary are these "saloons"!

The saloon of M. Platt was loud with the thump of hammers cracking ice, which is delivered in large blocks. Though the hand-colored gas globes, and the rose paintings on the front of the bar-counter, were as fine as we could see at the Three Provincial Brothers in Paris, yet I confess that the place did not smell so agreeably. A number of gentlemen, wearing hats perhaps a trifle taller than is fashionable at home, lounged at the bar-counter and shouted. I attracted no attention until I called for a sherry cobbler.

One of the "bartenders," as they are called in New York, gave me a sharp glance as he prepared the glass.

"Just arrived from the Old Country, I bet?" he said in no unfriendly tone.

Though it seemed strange to hear France mentioned in this way, I smiled and bowed assent.

"Italian, maybe?" said he.

This bartender, of course, could not know how deadly was the insult.

"Sir," I replied, "I am a Frenchman."

And now in truth he was pleased! His fat face opened and smiled like a distorted, gold-toothed flower.

"Is that so, now!" he exclaimed. "And what might your name be? Unless" – and here his face darkened with that sudden defensiveness and suspicion which, for no reason I can discern, will often strike into American hearts – "unless," said he, "you don't want to give it?"

"Not at all," I assured him earnestly. "I am Armand de Lafayette, at your service."

My dear brother, what an extraordinary effect!

It was silence. All sounds, even the faint whistling of the gas jets, seemed to die away in that stone-flagged room. Every man along the line of the bar was looking at me. I was conscious only of faces, mostly with whiskers under the chin instead of down the cheekbones, turned on me in basilisk stare.

"Well, well, well!" almost sneered the bartender. "You wouldn't be no relation of the *Marquis* de Lafayette, would you?"

It was my turn to be astonished. Though our father has always forbidden us to mention the name of our late uncle, due to his republican sympathies, yet I knew he occupied small place in the history of France and it puzzled me to comprehend how these people had heard of him.

"The late Marquis de Lafayette," I was obliged to admit, "was my uncle."

"You better be careful, young feller," suddenly yelled a grimy little man with a pistol buckled under his long coat. "We don't like being diddled, we don't."

"Sir," I replied, taking my bundle of papers from my pocket and whacking them down on the bar-counter, "have the goodness to examine my credentials. Should you still doubt my identity, we can then debate the matter in any way which pleases you."

"This is furrin writing," shouted the bartender. "*I* can't read it!"

And then – how sweet was the musical sound on my ear! – I heard a voice addressing me in my own language.

"Perhaps, sir," said the voice, in excellent French and with great stateliness, "I may be able to render you some small service."

The newcomer, a slight man of dark complexion, drawn up under an old shabby cloak of military cut, stood a little way behind me. If I had met him on the boulevards, I might not have found him very prepossessing. He had a wild and wandering eye, with an even wilder shimmer of brandy. He was not very steady on his feet. And yet, Maurice, his manner! It was such that I instinctively raised my hat, and the stranger very gravely did the same.

"And to whom," said I, "have I the honor . . .?"

"I am Thaddeus Perley, sir, at your service."

"Another furriner!" said the grimy little man, in disgust.

"I am indeed a foreigner!" said M. Perley in English, with an accent like a knife. "A foreigner to this dram shop. A foreigner to this neighborhood. A foreigner to – " Here he paused, and his eyes acquired an almost frightening blaze of loathing. "Yet I never heard that the reading of French was so very singular an accomplishment."

Imperiously – and yet, it seemed to me, with a certain shrinking nervousness – M. Perley came closer and lifted the bundle of papers.

"Doubtless," he said loftily, "I should not be credited were I to translate these. But here," and he scanned several of the papers, "is a letter of introduction in English. It is addressed to President Zachary Taylor from the American minister at Paris."

Again, my brother, what an enormous silence! It was interrupted by a cry from the bartender, who had snatched the documents from M. Perley.

"Boys, this is no diddle," said he. "This gent is the real thing!"

"He ain't!" thundered the little grimy man, with incredulity.

"He is!" said the bartender. "I'll be a son of a roe (*i.e., biche*) if he ain't!"

Well, Maurice, you and I have seen how Paris mobs can change. Americans are even more emotional. In the wink of an eye hostility became frantic affection. My back was slapped, my hand wrung, my person jammed against the bar by a crowd fighting to order me more refreshment.

The name of Lafayette, again and again, rose like a holy diapason. In vain I asked why this should be so. They appeared to think I was joking, and roared with laughter. I thought of M. Thaddeus Perley, as one who could supply an explanation.

But in the first rush toward me M. Perley had been flung backward. He fell sprawling in some wet stains of tobacco juice on the floor, and now I could not see him at all. For myself, I was weak from lack of food. A full beaker of whisky, which I was obliged to drink because all eyes were on me, made my head reel. Yet I felt compelled to raise my voice above the clamor.

"Gentlemen," I implored them, "will you hear me?"

"Silence for Lafayette!" said a big but very old man, with faded red whiskers. He had tears in his eyes, and he had been humming a catch called "Yankee Doodle." "Silence for Lafayette!"

"Believe me," said I, "I am full of gratitude for your hospitality. But I have business in New York, business of immediate and desperate urgency. If you will allow me to pay my reckoning . . ."

"Your money's no good here, monseer," said the bartender. "You're going to get liquored-up good and proper."

"But I have no wish, believe me, to become liquored up! It might well endanger my mission! In effect, I wish to go!"

"Wait a minute," said the little grimy man, with a cunning look. "What *is* this here business?"

You, Maurice, have called me quixotic. I deny this. You have also called me imprudent. Perhaps you are right; but what choice was left to me?

"Has any gentleman here," I asked, "heard of Mme Thevenet? Mme Thevenet, who lives at Number 23 Thomas Street, near Hudson Street?"

I had not, of course, expected an affirmative reply. Yet, in addition to one or two sniggers at mention of the street, several nodded their heads.

"Old miser woman?" asked a sportif character, who wore checkered trousers.

"I regret, sir, that you correctly describe her. Mme Thevenet is very rich. And I have come here," cried I, "to put right a damnable injustice!"

Struggle as I might, I could not free myself.

"How's that?" asked half a dozen.

"Mme Thevenet's daughter, Mlle Claudine, lives in the worst of poverty at Paris. Madame herself has been brought here, under some spell, by a devil of a woman calling herself . . . Gentlemen, I implore you!"

"And I bet you," cried the little grimy man with the pistol, "you're sweet on this daughter what's-her-name?" He seemed delighted. "Ain't you, now?"

How, I ask of all Providence, could these people have surprised my secret? Yet I felt obliged to tell the truth.

"I will not conceal from you," I said, "that I have in truth a high regard for Mlle Claudine. But this lady, believe me, is engaged to a friend of mine, an officer of artillery."

"Then what do you get out of it? Eh?" asked the grimy little man, with another cunning look.

The question puzzled me. I could not reply. But the bartender with the gold teeth leaned over.

"If you want to see the old Frenchie alive, monseer," said he, "you'd better git." *(Sic,* Maurice.) "I hearn tell she had a stroke this morning."

But a dozen voices clamored to keep me there, though this last intelligence sent me into despair. Then up rose the big and very old man with the faded whiskers: indeed, I had never realized how old, because he seemed so hale.

"Which of you was with Washington?" said he, suddenly taking hold of the fierce little man's neckcloth, and speaking with contempt. "Make way for the nephew of Lafayette!"

They cheered me then, Maurice. They hurried me to the door, they begged me to return, they promised they would await me. One glance I sought — nor can I say why — for M. Thaddeus Perley. He was sitting at a table by a pillar, under an open gas jet; his face whiter than ever, still wiping stains of tobacco juice from his cloak.

Never have I seen a more mournful prospect than Thomas Street, when my cab set me down there. Perhaps it was my state of mind; for if Mme Thevenet had died without a sou left to her daughter: you conceive it?

The houses of Thomas Street were faced with dingy yellow brick, and a muddy sky hung over the chimney pots. It had been warm all day, yet I found my spirit intolerably oppressed. Though heaven knows our Parisian streets are dirty enough, we do not allow pigs in

them. Except for these, nothing moved in the forsaken street save
a blind street musician, with his dog and an instrument called a
banjo; but even he was silent too.

For some minutes, it seemed to me, I plied the knocker at Number
23, with hideous noise. Nothing stirred. Finally, one part of the door
swung open a little, as for an eye. Whereupon I heard the shifting
of a floor bolt, and both doors were swung open.

Need I say that facing me stood the woman whom we have agreed
to call Mlle Jezebel?

She said to me: "And then, M. Armand?"

"Mme Thevenet!" cried I. "She is still alive?"

"She is alive," replied my companion, looking up at me from under
the lids of her greenish eyes. "But she is completely paralyzed."

I have never denied, Maurice, that Mlle Jezebel has a certain
attractiveness. She is not old or even middle aged. Were it not that
her complexion is as muddy as was the sky above us then, she would
have been pretty.

"And as for Claudine," I said to her, "the daughter of madame – "

"You have come too late, M. Armand."

And well I remember that at this moment there rose up, in the
mournful street outside, the tinkle of the banjo played by the street
musician. It moved closer, playing a popular catch whose words run
something thus:

> Oh, I come from Alabama
>    With my banjo on my knee;
> I depart for Louisiana
>    My Susannah for to see.

Across the lips of mademoiselle flashed a smile of peculiar quality,
like a razor cut before the blood comes.

"Gold," she whispered. "Ninety thousand persons, one hears, have
gone to seek it. Go to California, M. Armand. It is the only place you
will find gold."

This tune, they say, is a merry tune. It did not seem so, as the
dreary twanging faded away. Mlle Jezebel, with her muddy blonde
hair parted in the middle and drawn over her ears after the best
fashion, faced me implacably. Her greenish eyes were wide open.
Her old brown taffeta dress, full at the bust, narrow at the waist,
rustled its wide skirts as she glided a step forward.

"Have the kindness," I said, "to stand aside. I wish to enter."

Hitherto in my life I had seen her docile and meek.

"You are no relative," she said. "I will not allow you to enter."

"In that case, I regret, I must."

"If you had ever spoken one kind word to *me*," whispered mademoiselle, looking up from under her eyelids, and with her breast heaving, "one gesture of love – that is to say, of affection – you might have shared five million francs."

"Stand aside, I say!"

"As it is, you prefer a doll-faced consumptive at Paris. So be it!"

I was raging, Maurice; I confess it; yet I drew myself up with coldness.

"You refer, perhaps, to Claudine Thevenet?"

"And to whom else?"

"I might remind you, mademoiselle, that the lady is pledged to my good friend Lieutenant Delage. I have forgotten her."

"Have you?" asked our Jezebel, with her eyes on my face and a strange hungry look in them. Mlle Jezebel added, with more pleasure: "Well, she will die. Unless you can solve a mystery."

"A mystery?"

"I should not have said mystery, M. Armand. Because it is impossible of all solution. It is an Act of God!"

Up to this time the glass-fronted doors of the vestibule had stood open behind her, against a darkness of closed shutters in the house. There breathed out of it an odor of unswept carpets, a sourness of stale living. Someone was approaching, carrying a lighted candle.

"Who speaks?" called a man's voice; shaky, but as French as Mlle Jezebel's. "Who speaks concerning an Act of God?"

I stepped across the threshold. Mademoiselle, who never left my side, immediately closed and locked the front doors. As the candle glimmer moved still closer in gloom, I could have shouted for joy to see the man whom (as I correctly guessed) I had come to meet.

"You are M. Duroc, the lawyer!" I said. "You are my brother's friend!"

M. Duroc held the candle higher, to inspect me.

He was a big, heavy man who seemed to sag in all his flesh. In compensation for his bald head, the grayish-brown mustache flowed down and parted into two hairy fans of beard on either side of his chin. He looked at me through oval gold-rimmed spectacles; in a friendly way, but yet frightened. His voice was deep and gruff, clipping the syllables, despite his fright.

"And you" – *clip-clip*; the candle holder trembled – "you are Armand de Lafayette. I had expected you by the steam packet today. Well! You are here. On a fool's errand, I regret."

"But why?" (And I shouted at him, Maurice.)

I looked at mademoiselle, who was faintly smiling.

"M. Duroc!" I protested. "You wrote to my brother. You said you had persuaded madame to repent of her harshness toward her daughter!"

"Was that your duty?" asked the Jezebel, looking full at M. Duroc with her greenish eyes. "Was that your right?"

"I am a man of law," said M. Duroc. The deep monosyllables rapped, in ghostly bursts, through his parted beard. He was perspiring. "I am correct. Very correct! And yet – "

"Who nursed her?" asked the Jezebel. "Who soothed her, fed her, wore her filthy clothes, calmed her tempers and endured her interminable abuse? *I* did!"

And yet, all the time she was speaking, this woman kept sidling and sidling against me, brushing my side, as though she would make sure of my presence there.

"Well!" said the lawyer. "It matters little now! This mystery . . ."

You may well believe that all these cryptic remarks, as well as reference to a mystery or an Act of God, had driven me almost frantic. I demanded to know what he meant.

"Last night," said M. Duroc, "a certain article disappeared."

"Well, well?"

"It disappeared," said M. Duroc, drawn up like a grenadier. "But it could not conceivably have disappeared. I myself swear this! Our only suggestions as to how it might have disappeared are a toy rabbit and a barometer."

"Sir," I said, "I do not wish to be discourteous. But – "

"Am I mad, you ask?"

I bowed. If any man can manage at once to look sagging and uncertain, yet stately and dignified, M. Duroc managed it then. And dignity won, I think.

"Sir," he replied, gesturing the candle toward the rear of the house, "Mme Thevenet lies there in her bed. She is paralyzed. She can move only her eyes or partially the lips, without speech. Do you wish to see her?"

"If I am permitted."

"Yes. That would be correct. Accompany me."

And I saw the poor old woman, Maurice. Call her harridan if you like. It was a square room of good size, whose shutters had remained closed and locked for years. Can one smell rust? In that room, with faded green wallpaper, I felt I could.

One solitary candle did little more than dispel shadow. It burned atop the mantelpiece well opposite the foot of the bed; and a shaggy man, whom I afterward learned to be a police officer, sat in a green-upholstered armchair by an unlighted coal fire in the fireplace grate, picking his teeth with a knife.

"If you please, Dr. Harding!" M. Duroc called softly in English.

The long and lean American doctor, who had been bending over the bed so as to conceal from our sight the head and shoulders of Madame Thevenet, turned round. But his cadaverous body – in such fashion were madame's head and shoulders propped up against pillows – his cadaverous body, I say, still concealed her face.

"Has there been any change?" persisted M. Duroc in English.

"There has been no change," replied the dark-complexioned Dr. Harding, "except for the worse."

"Do you want her to be moved?"

"There has never been any necessity," said the physician, picking up his beaver hat from the bed. He spoke dryly. "However, if you want to learn anything more about the toy rabbit or the barometer, I should hurry. The lady will die in a matter of hours, probably less."

And he stood to one side.

It was a heavy bed with four posts and a canopy. The bed curtains, of some dullish-green material, were closely drawn on every side except the long side by which we saw Madame Thevenet in profile. Lean as a post, rigid, the strings of her cotton nightcap tightly tied under her chin, Madame Thevenet lay propped up there. But one eye rolled towards us, and it rolled horribly.

Up to this time the woman we call the Jezebel had said little. She chose this moment again to come brushing against my side. Her greenish eyes, lids half-closed, shone in the light of M. Duroc's candle. What she whispered was: "You don't really hate me, do you?"

Maurice, I make a pause here.

Since I wrote the sentence, I put down my pen, and pressed my hands over my eyes, and once more I thought. But let me try again.

I spent just two hours in the bedroom of Madame Thevenet. At the end of the time – oh, you shall hear why! – I rushed out of that bedroom, and out of Number 23 Thomas Street, like the maniac I was.

The streets were full of people, of carriages, of omnibuses, at early evening. Knowing no place of refuge save the saloon from which I had come, I gave its address to a cabdriver. Since still I had swallowed no food, I may have been lightheaded. Yet I wished to pour out my heart to the friends who had bidden me return there. And where were they now?

A new group, all new, lounged against the bar-counter under brighter gaslight and brighter paint. Of all those who smote me on the back and cheered, none remained save the ancient giant who had implied friendship with General Washington. *He*, alas, lay helplessly drunk with his head near a sawdust spitting box. Nevertheless I was so moved that I took the liberty of thrusting a handful of bank notes into his pocket. He alone remained.

Wait, there was another!

I do not believe he had remained there because of me. Yet M. Thaddeus Perley, still sitting alone at the little table by the pillar, with the open gas jet above, stared vacantly at the empty glass in his hand.

He had named himself a foreigner; he was probably French. That was as well. For, as I lurched against the table, I was befuddled and all English had fled my wits.

"Sir," said I, "will you permit a madman to share your table?"

M. Perley gave a great start, as though roused out of thought. He was now sober: this I saw. Indeed, his shiver and haggard face were due to lack of stimulant rather than too much of it.

"Sir," he stammered, getting to his feet, "I shall be – I shall be honored by your company." Automatically he opened his mouth to call for a waiter; his hand went to his pocket; he stopped.

"No, no, no!" said I. "If you insist, M. Perley, you may pay for the second bottle. The first is mine. I am sick at heart, and I would speak with a gentleman."

At these last words M. Perley's whole expression changed. He sat down, and gave me a grave courtly nod. His eyes, which were his most expressive feature, studied my face and my disarray.

"You are ill, M. de Lafayette," he said. "Have you so soon come to grief in this – this *civilized* country?"

"I have come to grief, yes. But not through civilization or the lack of it." And I banged my fist on the table. "I have come to grief, M. Perley, through miracles or magic. I have come to grief with a problem which no man's ingenuity can solve!"

M. Perley looked at me in a strange way. But someone had brought a bottle of brandy, with its accessories. M. Perley's trembling hand slopped a generous allowance into my glass, and an even more generous one into his own.

"That is very curious," he remarked, eying the glass. "A murder, was it?"

"No. But a valuable document has disappeared. The most thorough search by the police cannot find it."

Touch him anywhere, and he flinched. M. Perley, for some extraordinary reason, appeared to think I was mocking him.

"A document, you say?" His laugh was a trifle unearthly. "Come, now. Was it by any chance – a letter?"

"No, no! It was a will. Three large sheets of parchment, of the size you call foolscap. Listen!"

And as M. Perley added water to his brandy and gulped down about a third of it, I leaned across the table.

"Mme Thevenet, of whom you may have heard me speak in this café, was an invalid. But (until the early hours of this morning) she was not bedridden. She could move, and walk about her room, and so on. She had been lured away from Paris and her family by a green-eyed woman named the Jezebel.

"But a kindly lawyer of this city, M. Duroc, believed that madame suffered and had a bad conscience about her own daughter. Last night, despite the Jezebel, he persuaded madame at last to sign a will leaving all her money to this daughter.

"And the daughter, Claudine, is in mortal need of it! From my brother and myself, who have more than enough, she will not accept a sou. Her affianced, Lieutenant Delage, is as poor as she. But, unless she leaves France for Switzerland, she will die. I will not conceal from you that Claudine suffers from that dread disease we politely call consumption."

M. Perley stopped with his glass again halfway to his mouth.

He believed me now; I sensed it. Yet under the dark hair, tumbled on his forehead, his face had gone as white as his neat, mended shirt frill.

"So very little a thing is money!" he whispered. "So very little a thing!"

And he lifted the glass and drained it.

"You do not think I am mocking you, sir?"

"No, no!" says M. Perley, shading his eyes with one hand. "I knew myself of one such case. She is dead. Pray continue."

"Last night, I repeat, Mme Thevenet changed her mind. When M. Duroc paid his weekly evening visit with the news that I should arrive today, madame fairly chattered with eagerness and a kind of terror. Death was approaching, she said; she had a presentiment."

As I spoke, Maurice, there returned to me the image of that shadowy, arsenic-green bedroom in the shuttered house; and what M. Duroc had told me.

"Madame," I continued, "cried out to M. Duroc that he must bolt the bedroom door. She feared the Jezebel, who lurked but said nothing. M. Duroc drew up to her bedside a portable writing desk,

with two good candles. For a long time madame spoke, pouring
out contrition, self-abasement, the story of an unhappy marriage,
all of which M. Duroc (sweating with embarrassment) was obliged
to write down until it covered three large parchment sheets.

"But it was done, M. Perley!

"The will, in effect, left everything to her daughter, Claudine. It
revoked a previous will by which all had been left (and this can be
done in French law, as we both know) to Jezebel of the muddy
complexion and the muddy yellow hair.

"Well, then! . . ."

"M. Duroc sallies out into the street, where he finds two sober
fellows who come in. Madame signs the will, M. Duroc sands it,
and the two men from the street affix their signatures as witnesses.
Then *they* are gone. M. Duroc folds the will lengthways, and prepares
to put it into his carpetbag. Now, M. Perley, mark what follows!

"'No, no, no!' cries madame, with the shadow of her peaked
nightcap wagging on the locked shutters beyond. 'I wish to keep
it – for this one night!'

"'For this one night, madame?' asks M. Duroc.

"'I wish to press it against my heart,' says Mme Thevenet. 'I
wish to read it once, twice, a thousand times! M. Duroc, what
time is it?'

"Whereupon he takes out his gold repeater, and opens it. To his
astonishment it is one o'clock in the morning. Yet he touches the
spring of the repeater, and its pulse beat rings one.

"'M. Duroc,' pleads Mme Thevenet, 'remain here with me for the
rest of the night!'

"'Madame!' cried M. Duroc, shocked to the very fans of his beard.
'That would not be correct.'

"'Yes, you are right,' says madame. And never, swears the lawyer,
has he seen her less bleary of eye, more alive with wit and cunning,
more the great lady of ruin, than there in that green and shadowy
and foul-smelling room.

"Yet this very fact puts her in more and more terror of the Jezebel,
who is never seen. She points to M. Duroc's carpetbag.

"'I think you have much work to do, dear sir?'

"M. Duroc groaned. 'The Good Lord knows that I have!'

"'Outside the only door of this room,' says madame, 'there is a
small dressing room. Set up your writing desk beside the door there,
so that no one may enter without your knowledge. Do your work
there; you shall have a lamp or many candles. Do it,' shrieks madame,
'for the sake of Claudine and for the sake of an old friendship!'

"Very naturally, M. Duroc hesitated.

"'*She* will be hovering,' pleads Mme Thevenet, pressing the will against her breast. '*This* I shall read and read and read, and sanctify with my tears. If I find I am falling asleep,' and here the old lady looked cunning, 'I shall hide it. But no matter! Even *she* cannot penetrate through locked shutters and a guarded door.'

"Well, in fine, the lawyer at length yielded.

"He set up his writing desk against the very doorpost outside that door. When he last saw madame, before closing the door, he saw her in profile with the green bed curtains drawn except on that side, propped up with a tall candle burning on a table at her right hand.

"Ah, that night! I think I see M. Duroc at his writing desk, as he has told me, in an airless dressing room where no clock ticked. I see him, at times, removing his oval spectacles to press his smarting eyes. I see him returning to his legal papers, while his pen scratched through the wicked hours of the night.

"He heard nothing, or virtually nothing, until five o'clock in the morning. Then, which turned him cold and flabby, he heard a cry which he describes as being like that of a deaf-mute.

"The communicating door had not been bolted on Mme Thevenet's side, in case she needed help. M. Duroc rushed into the other room.

"On the table, at madame's right hand, the tall candle had burned down to a flattish mass of wax over which still hovered a faint bluish flame. Madame herself lay rigid in her peaked nightcap. That revival of spirit last night, or remorse in her bitter heart, had brought on the last paralysis. Though M. Duroc tried to question her, she could move only her eyes.

"Then M. Duroc noticed that the will, which she had clutched as a doomed religious might clutch a crucifix, was not in her hand or on the bed.

"'Where is the will?' he shouted at her, as though she were deaf too. 'Where is the will?'

"Mme Thevenet's eyes fixed on him. Then they moved down, and looked steadily at a trumpery toy – a rabbit, perhaps four inches high, made of pink velours or the like – which lay on the bed. Again she looked at M. Duroc, as though to emphasize this. Then her eyes rolled, this time with dreadful effort, toward a large barometer, shaped like a warming pan, which hung on the wall beside the door. Three times she did this before the bluish candle flame flickered and went out."

And I, Armand de Lafayette, paused here in my recital to M. Perley.

Again I became aware that I was seated in a garish saloon, swilling brandy, amid loud talk that beat the air. There was a thumping noise from the theater above our heads, and faint strains of music.

"The will," I said, "was not stolen. Not even the Jezebel could have melted through locked shutters or a guarded door. The will was not hidden, because no inch of the room remains unsearched. *Yet the will is gone!*"

I threw a glance across the table at M. Perley.

To me, I am sure, the brandy had given strength and steadied my nerves. With M. Perley I was not so sure. He was a little flushed. That slightly wild look, which I had observed before, had crept up especially into one eye, giving his whole face a somewhat lopsided appearance. Yet all his self-confidence had returned. He gave me a little crooked smile.

I struck the table.

"Do you honor me with your attention, M. Perley?"

"What song the Syrens sang," he said to me, "or what name Achilles assumed when he hid himself among women, although puzzling questions, are not beyond *all* conjecture."

"They are beyond *my* conjecture!" I cried. "And so is this!"

M. Perley extended his hand, spread the fingers, and examined them as one who owns the universe.

"It is some little time," he remarked, "since I have concerned myself with these trifles." His eyes retreated into a dream. "Yet I have given some trifling aid, in the past, to the Prefect of the Parisian police."

"You are a Frenchman! I knew it! And the police!" Seeing his lofty look, I added: "As an amateur, understood?"

"Understood!" Then his delicate hand — it would be unjust to call it clawlike — shot across the table and fastened on my arm. The strange eyes burned toward my face. "A little more detail!" he pleaded humbly. "A little more, I beg of you! This woman, for instance, you call the Jezebel?"

"It was she who met me at the house."

"And then?"

I described for him my meeting with the Jezebel, with M. Duroc, and our entrance to the sickroom, where the shaggy police officer sat in the armchair and the saturnine doctor faced us from beside the bed.

"This woman," I exclaimed, with the room vividly before my eyes as I described it, "seems to have conceived for me (forgive me) a kind of passion. No doubt it was due to some idle compliments I once paid her at Paris.

"As I have explained, the Jezebel is *not* unattractive, even if she would only (again forgive me) wash her hair. Nevertheless, when once more she brushed my side and whispered, 'You don't really hate me, do you?' I felt little less than horror. It seemed to me that in some fashion I was responsible for the whole tragedy.

"While we stood beside the bed, M. Duroc the lawyer poured out the story I have recounted. There lay the poor paralytic, and confirmed it with her eyes. The toy rabbit, a detestable pink color, lay in its same position on the bed. Behind me, hung against the wall by the door, was the large barometer.

"Apparently for my benefit, Mme Thevenet again went through her dumb show with imploring eyes. She would look at the rabbit; next (as M. Duroc had not mentioned), she would roll her eyes all round her, for some desperate yet impenetrable reason, before fixing her gaze on the barometer.

"It meant . . . what?

"The lawyer spoke then. 'More light!' gulped out M. Duroc. 'If you must have closed shutters and windows, then let us at least have more light!'

"The Jezebel glided out to fetch candles. During M. Duroc's explanation he had several times mentioned my name. At first mention of it the shaggy police officer jumped and put away his clasp knife. He beckoned to the physician, Dr. Harding, who went over for a whispered conference.

"Whereupon the police officer sprang up.

"'Mr. Lafayette!' And he swung my hand pompously. 'If I'd known it was you, Mr. Lafayette, I wouldn't 'a' sat there like a bump on a log.'

"'You are an officer of police, sir,' said I. 'Can *you* think of no explanation?'

"He shook his head.

"'These people are Frenchies, Mr. Lafayette, and you're an American,' he said, with *somewhat* conspicuous lack of logic. '*If* they're telling the truth – '

"'Let us assume that!'

"'I can't tell you where the old lady's will is,' he stated positively. 'But I can tell you where it ain't. It ain't hidden in this room!'

"'But surely . . .!' I began in despair.

"At this moment the Jezebel, her brown taffeta dress rustling, glided back into the room with a handful of candles and a tin box of the new-style lucifer matches. She lighted several candles, sticking them on any surface in their own grease.

"There were one or two fine pieces of furniture; but the mottled-marble tops were chipped and stained, the gilt sides cracked. There were a few mirrors, creating mimic spectral life. I saw a little more clearly the faded green paper of the walls, and what I perceived to be the partly open door of a cupboard. The floor was of bare boards.

"All this while I was conscious of two pairs of eyes: the imploring gaze of Mme Thevenet, and the amorous gaze of the Jezebel. One or the other I could have endured, but both together seemed to suffocate me.

"'Mr. Duroc here,' said the shaggy police officer, clapping the distressed advocate on the shoulder, 'sent a messenger in a cab at half-past five this morning. And what time did we get here? I ask you and I tell you! Six o'clock!'

"Then he shook his finger at me, in a kind of pride and fury of efficiency.

"'Why, Mr. Lafayette, there's been fourteen men at this room from six this morning until just before you got here!'

"'To search for Mme Thevenet's will, you mean?'

"The shaggy man nodded portentously, and folded his arms.

"'Floor's solid.' He stamped on the bare boards. 'Walls and ceiling? Nary a inch missed. We reckon we're remarkable smart; and we are.'

"'But Mme Thevenet,' I persisted, 'was not a complete invalid until this morning. She could move about. If she became afraid of – the name of the Jezebel choked me – 'if she became afraid, and *did* hide the will . . .'

"'Where'd she hide it? Tell me!'

"'In the furniture, then?'

"'Cabinetmakers in, Mr. Lafayette. No secret compartments.'

"'In one of the mirrors?'

"'Took the backs of 'em off. No will hid there.'

"'Up the chimney!' I cried.

"'Sent a chimney-sweep up there,' replied my companion in a ruminating way. Each time I guessed, he would leer at me in friendly and complacent challenge. 'Ye-es, I reckon we're pretty smart. But we didn't find no will.'

"The pink rabbit also seemed to leer from the bed. I saw madame's eyes. Once again, as a desperate mind will fasten on trifles, I observed the strings of the nightcap beneath her scrawny chin. But I looked again at the toy rabbit.

"'Has it occurred to you,' I said triumphantly, 'to examine the bed and bedstead of Mme Thevenet herself?'

"My shaggy friend went to her bedside.

"'Poor old woman,' he said. He spoke as though she were already a corpse. Then he turned round. 'We lifted her out, just as gentle as a newborn babe (didn't we, ma'am?). No hollow bedposts! Nothing in the canopy! Nothing in the frame or the feather beds or the curtains or the bedclothes!'

"Suddenly the shaggy police officer became angry, as though he wished to be rid of the whole matter.

"'And it ain't in the toy rabbit,' he said, 'because you can see we slit it up, if you look close. And it ain't in that barometer there. It just – ain't here.'

"There was a silence as heavy as the dusty, hot air of this room.

"'It is here,' murmured M. Duroc in his gruff voice. 'It must be here!'

"The Jezebel stood there meekly, with downcast eyes.

"And I, in my turn, confess that *I* lost my head. I stalked over to the barometer, and tapped it. Its needle, which already indicated, 'Rain; cold,' moved still further toward that point.

"I was not insane enough to hit it with my fist. But I crawled on the floor, in search of a secret hiding place. I felt along the wall. The police officer – who kept repeating that nobody must touch anything and he would take no responsibility until he went off duty at something o'clock – the police officer I ignored.

"What at length gave me pause was the cupboard, already thoroughly searched. In the cupboard hung a few withered dresses and gowns, as though they had shriveled with Mme Thevenet's body. But on the shelf of the cupboard . . .

"On the shelf stood a great number of perfume bottles: even today, I fear, many of our countrymen think perfume a substitute for water and soap; and the state of madame's hands would have confirmed this. *But*, on the shelf, were a few dusty novels. There was a crumpled and begrimed copy of yesterday's New York *Sun*. This newspaper did not contain a will; but it did contain a black beetle, which ran out across my hand.

"In a disgust past describing, I flung down the beetle and stamped on it. I closed the cupboard door, acknowledging defeat. Mme Thevenet's will was gone. And at the same second, in that dim green room – still badly lighted, with only a few more candles – two voices cried out.

"One was my own voice:

"'*In God's name, where is it?*'

"The other was the deep voice of M. Duroc:

"'*Look at that woman! She knows!*'

"And he meant the Jezebel.

"M. Duroc, with his beard fans atremble, was pointing to a mirror; a little blurred, as these mirrors were. Our Jezebel had been looking into the mirror, her back turned to us. Now she dodged, as at a stone thrown.

"With good poise our Jezebel writhed this movement into a curtsy, turning to face us. But not before I also had seen that smile – like a razor cut before the blood comes – as well as full knowledge, mocking knowledge, shining out of wide-open eyes in the mirror.

"'You spoke to me, M. Duroc?' She murmured the reply, also in French.

"'Listen to me!' the lawyer said formally. 'This will is *not* missing. It is in this room. You were not here last night. Something has made you guess. You know where it is.'

"'Are you unable to find it?' asked the Jezebel in surprise.

"'Stand back, young man!' M. Duroc said to me. 'I ask you something, mademoiselle, in the name of justice.'

"'Ask!' said the Jezebel.

"'If Claudine Thevenet inherits the money to which she is entitled, you will be well paid; yes, overpaid! You know Claudine. You know that!'

"'I know it.'

"'But if the new will be *not* found,' said M. Duroc, again waving me back, 'then you inherit everything. And Claudine will die. For it will be assumed – '

"'Yes!' said the Jezebel, with one hand pressed against her breast. 'You yourself, M. Duroc, testify that all night a candle was burning at madame's bedside. Well! The poor woman, whom *I* loved and cherished, repented of her ingratitude toward me. She burned this new will at the candle flame; she crushed its ashes to powder and blew them away!'

"'Is that true?' cried M. Duroc.

"'They will assume it,' smiled the Jezebel, 'as you say.' She looked at me. 'And for you, M. Armand!'

"She glided closer. I can only say that I saw her eyes uncovered; or, if you wish to put it so, her soul and flesh together.

"'I would give you everything on earth,' she said. 'I will not give you the doll face in Paris.'

"'Listen to me!' I said to her, so agitated that I seized her shoulders. 'You are out of your senses! You cannot give Claudine to me! She will marry another man!'

"'And do you think that matters to me,' asked the Jezebel, with her green eyes full on mine, 'as long as you still love her?'

"There was a small crash as someone dropped a knife on the floor.

"We three, I think, had completely forgotten that we were not alone. There were two spectators, although they did not comprehend our speech.

"The saturnine Dr. Harding now occupied the green armchair. His long thin legs, in tight black trousers with strap under the boot instep, were crossed and looked spidery; his high beaver hat glimmered on his head. The police officer, who was picking his teeth with a knife when I first saw him, had now dropped the knife when he tried to trim his nails.

"But both men sensed the atmosphere. Both were alert, feeling out with the tentacles of their nerves. The police officer shouted at me.

"'What's this gabble?' he said. 'What's a-gitting into your head?'

"Grotesquely, it was that word 'head' which gave me my inspiration.

"'The nightcap!' I exclaimed in English.

"'What nightcap?'

"For the nightcap of Mme Thevenet had a peak; it was large; it was tightly tied under the chin; it might well conceal a flat-pressed document which – but you understand. The police officer, dull-witted as he appeared, grasped the meaning in a flash. And how I wished I had never spoken! For the fellow meant well, but he was not gentle.

"As I raced round the curtained sides of the bed, the police officer was holding a candle in one hand and tearing off madame's nightcap with the other. He found no will there, no document at all; only straggly wisps of hair on a skull grown old before its time.

"Mme Thevenet had been a great lady, once. It must have been the last humiliation. Two tears overflowed her eyes and ran down her cheeks. She lay propped up there in a nearly sitting position; but something seemed to wrench inside her.

"And she closed her eyes forever. And the Jezebel laughed.

"That is the end of my story. That is why I rushed out of the house like a madman. The will has vanished as though by magic; or is it still there by magic? In any case, you find me at this table: grubby and disheveled and much ashamed."

For a little time after I had finished my narrative to M. Perley in the saloon it seemed to me that the bar-counter was a trifle quieter. But a faint stamping continued from the theater above our heads. Then all was hushed, until a chorus rose to a tinkle of many banjos.

> Oh, I come from Alabama
> With my banjo on my knee;
> I depart for Louisiana . . .

Enough! The song soon died away, and M. Thaddeus Perley did not even hear it.

M. Perley sat looking downward into an empty glass, so that I could not see his face.

"Sir," he remarked almost bitterly, "you are a man of good heart. I am glad to be of service in a problem so trifling as this."

"*Trifling!*"

His voice was a little husky, but not slurred. His hand slowly turned the glass round and round.

"Will you permit two questions?" asked M. Perley.

"Two questions? Ten thousand!"

"More than two will be unnecessary." Still M. Perley did not look up. "This toy rabbit, of which so much was made: I would know its exact position on the bed?"

"It was almost at the foot of the bed, and about the middle in a crossways direction."

"Ah, so I had imagined. Were the three sheets of parchment, forming the will, written upon two sides or upon only one?"

"I had not told you, M. Perley. But M. Duroc said: upon one side only."

M. Perley raised his head.

His face was now flushed and distorted with drink, his eye grown wild. In his cups he was as proud as Satan, and as disdainful of others' intelligence; yet he spoke with dignity, and with careful clearness.

"It is ironic, M. de Lafayette, that I should tell you how to lay your hand on the missing will and the elusive money; since, upon my word, I have never been able to perform a like service for myself." And he smiled, as at some secret joke. "Perhaps," he added, "it is the very simplicity of the thing which puts you at fault."

I could only look at him in bewilderment.

"Perhaps the mystery is a little *too* plain! A little *too* self-evident!"

"You mock me, sir! I will not . . ."

"Take me as I am," said M. Perley, whacking the foot of the glass on the table, "or leave me. Besides," here his wandering eye encountered a list of steam sailings pasted against the wall, "I – I leave tomorrow by the *Parnassus* for England, and then for France."

"I meant no offence, M. Perley! If you have knowledge, speak!"

"Mme Thevenet," he said, carefully pouring himself some more brandy, "hid the will in the middle of the night. Does it puzzle you that she took such precautions to hide the will? But the element of the outré must always betray itself. The Jezebel *must not* find that will! Yet Mme Thevenet trusted nobody – not even the worthy physician who attended her. If madame were to die of a stroke, the police would be there and must soon, she was sure, discover her simple device. Even if she were paralyzed, it would ensure the presence of other persons in the room to act as unwitting guards.

"Your cardinal error," M. Perley continued dispassionately, "was one of ratiocination. You tell me that Mme Thevenet, to give you a hint, looked fixedly at some point near the foot of the bed. Why do you assume that she was looking at the toy rabbit?"

"Because," I replied hotly, "the toy rabbit was the only object she could have looked at!"

"Pardon me; but it was *not*. You several times informed me that the bed curtains were closely drawn together on three sides. They were drawn on all but the 'long' side toward the door. Therefore the ideal reasoner, without having seen the room, may safely say that the curtains were drawn together at the foot of the bed?"

"Yes, true!"

"After looking fixedly at this point represented by the toy, Mme Thevenet then 'rolls her eyes all round her' – in your phrase. May we assume that she wishes the curtains to be drawn back, so that she may see something *beyond* the bed?"

"It is – possible, yes!"

"It is more than possible, as I shall demonstrate. Let us direct our attention, briefly, to the incongruous phenomenon of the barometer on another wall. The barometer indicates, 'Rain; cold.'"

Here M. Perley's thin shoulders drew together under the old military cloak.

"Well," he said, "the cold is on its way. Yet this day, for April, has been warm outside and indoors, oppressively hot?"

"Yes! Of course!"

"You yourself," continued M. Perley, inspecting his fingernails, "told me what was directly opposite the foot of the bed. Let us suppose that the bed curtains are drawn open. Mme Thevenet, in her nearly seated position, is looking *downward*. What would she have seen?"

"The fireplace!" I cried. "The grate of the fireplace!"

"Already we have a link with the weather. And what, as you have specifically informed me, was in the grate of the fireplace?"

"An unlighted coal fire!"

"Exactly. And what is essential for the composition of such a fire? We need coal; we need wood; but primarily and above all, we need . . ."

"*Paper*!" I cried.

"In the cupboard of that room," said M. Perley, with his disdainful little smile, "was a very crumpled and begrimed (mark that; not

dusty) copy of *yesterday's* New York Sun. To light fires is the
most common, and indeed the best, use for our daily press. That
copy had been used to build yesterday's fire. But something else,
during the night, was substituted for it. You yourself remarked the
extraordinarily dirty state of Mme Thevenet's hands."

M. Perley swallowed the brandy, and his flush deepened.

"Sir," he said loudly, "you will find the will crumpled up, with
ends most obviously protruding, under the coal and wood in the
fireplace grate. Even had anyone taken the fire to pieces, he would
have found only what appeared to be dirty blank paper, written
side undermost, which could never be a valuable will. It was too
self-evident to be seen. – Now go!"

"Go?" I echoed stupidly.

M. Perley rose from his chair.

"Go, I say!" he shouted, with an even wilder eye. "The Jezebel
could not light that fire. It was too warm, for one thing; and all
day there were police officers with instructions that an outsider must
touch nothing. But now? *Mme Thevenet kept warning you that the fire must
not be lighted, or the will would be destroyed!*"

"Will you await me here?" I called over my shoulder.

"Yes, yes! And perhaps there will be peace for the wretched girl
with – with the lung trouble."

Even as I ran out of the door I saw him, grotesque and pitiful,
slump across the table. Hope, rising and surging, seemed to sweep
me along like the crack of the cabman's whip. But when I reached
my destination, hope receded.

The shaggy police officer was just descending the front steps.

"None of us coming back here, Mr. Lafayette!" he called cheerily.
"Old Mrs. What's-her-name went and burned that will at a candle
last night. – Here, what's o'clock?"

The front door was unlocked. I raced through that dark house,
and burst into the rear bedroom.

The corpse still lay in the big, gloomy bed. Every candle had
flickered almost down to its socket. The police officer's clasp knife,
forgotten since he had dropped it, still lay on bare boards. But the
Jezebel was there.

She knelt on the hearth, with the tin box of lucifer matches she
had brought there earlier. The match spurted, a bluish fire; I saw
her eagerness; she held the match to the grate.

"A lucifer," I said, "in the hand of a Jezebel!"

And I struck her away from the grate, so that she reeled against
a chair and fell. Large coals, small coals rattled down in puffs of
dust as I plunged my hands into the unlighted fire. Little sticks,

sawed sticks; and I found it there: crumpled parchment sheets, but incontestably madame's will.

"M. Duroc!" I called. "M. Duroc!"

You and I, my brother Maurice, have fought the Citizen-King with bayonets as we now fight the upstart Bonapartist; we need not be ashamed of tears. I confess, then, that the tears overran my eyes and blinded me. I scarcely saw M. Duroc as he hurried into the room.

Certainly I did not see the Jezebel stealthily pick up the police officer's knife. I noticed nothing at all until she flew at me, and stabbed me in the back.

Peace, my brother: I have assured you all is well. At that time, faith, I was not much conscious of any hurt. I bade M. Duroc, who was trembling, to wrench out the knife; I borrowed his roomy greatcoat to hide the blood; I must hurry, hurry, hurry back to that little table under the gas jet.

I planned it all on my way back. M. Perley, apparently a stranger in this country, disliked it and was evidently very poor even in France. But *we* are not precisely paupers. Even with his intense pride, he could not refuse (for such a service) a sum which would comfort him for the rest of his life.

Back I plunged into the saloon, and hurried down it. Then I stopped. The little round table by the pillar, under the flaring gas jet, was empty.

How long I stood there I cannot tell. The back of my shirt, which at first had seemed full of blood, now stuck to the borrowed greatcoat. All of a sudden I caught sight of the fat-faced bartender with the gold teeth, who had been on service that afternoon and had returned now. As a mark of respect, he came out from behind the bar-counter to greet me.

"Where is the gentleman who was sitting at that table?"

I pointed to it. My voice, in truth, must have sounded so hoarse and strange that he mistook it for anger.

"Don't you worry about that, monseer!" said he reassuringly. "*That's* been tended to! We threw the drunken tramp out of here!"

"You threw . . ."

"Right bang in the gutter. Had to crawl along in it before he could stand up." My bartender's face was pleased and vicious. "Ordered a bottle of best brandy, and couldn't pay for it." The face changed again. "Goddelmighty, monseer, what's wrong?"

"*I* ordered that brandy."

"*He* didn't say so, when the waiter brought me over. Just looked me up and down, crazy-like, and said a gentleman would give his I.O.U. Gentleman!"

"M. Perley," I said, restraining an impulse to kill that bartender, "is a friend of mine. He departs for France early tomorrow morning. Where is his hotel? Where can I find him?"

"Perley!" sneered my companion. "That ain't even his real name, I hearn tell. Gits high-and-mighty ideas from upper Broadway. But his real name's on the I.O.U."

A surge of hope, once more, almost blinded me. "Did you keep that I.O.U.?"

"Yes, I kepp it," growled the bartender, fishing in his pocket. "God knows why, but I kepp it."

And at last, Maurice, I triumphed!

True, I collapsed from my wound; and the fever would not let me remember that I must be at the dock when the *Parnassus* steam packet departed from New York next morning. I must remain here, shut up in a hotel room and unable to sleep at night, until I can take ship for home. But where I failed, you can succeed. He was to leave on the morrow by the *Parnassus* for England, and then for France – so he told me. You can find him – in six months at the most. In six months, I give you my word, he will be out of misery for ever!

"*I.O.U.*," reads the little slip, "*for one bottle of your best brandy, forty-five cents. Signed: Edgar A. Poe.*"

I remain, Maurice,
Your affectionate brother,
Armand

# THE GOLDEN NUGGET POKER GAME
## Edward D. Hoch

*Edward Hoch (b. 1930), has written a few novels, but is best known as a short-story writer and must be one of the most prolific writers of crime and mystery short fiction of all time, with over seven hundred stories published since his first in 1955. Despite this prodigious output Hoch can still bring a verve and originality to each new story. Hoch's diversity is maintained by the many series characters he has created, amongst them Simon Ark, Captain Leopold, Nick Velvet and Jeffrey Rand. His stories related by Dr. Sam Hawthorne are technically historical mysteries, as Hawthorne, a New England country doctor, recounts cases from his youth in the 1920s and 30s. But more appropriate for this volume are the stories featuring western gunman Ben Snow. The series spans the years 1881 to 1905 and ranges throughout the wild west and as far north as the Yukon, in western Canada, the setting for the following story.*

B en Snow reached for the freshly dealt cards and picked them up carefully. It wasn't the sort of game where one made quick moves that could be misconstrued. Glancing around at the other five players, he decided he had never seen a more unsavory group of men in one place, and that included Dodge City at its worst.

The poker game in the back room at the Golden Nugget had been going on, some said, since the saloon opened the previous summer in one of the wooden shacks that had gone up almost overnight along the main street in Dawson. The saloon was well named because in that summer of '98 gold nuggets were as acceptable a currency as silver dollars in the bars and sporting houses of the Yukon Territory. Most places had small scales for weighing and evaluating nuggets on the spot.

Ben Snow hadn't traveled north to prospect for gold. He'd come as something of a paid bodyguard to a prospector named Race Johnson, who knew a great deal about panning for gold but very little about gunfighting. Even at the age of 38, Ben's reputation with

a six-shooter was as firm as ever. People rarely mistook him for Billy
the Kid as they had in his younger days, but they still came to him
when there was need of a keen mind and a fast gun.

The journey north with Race Johnson had begun in the early
spring, a full year after the first wave of the gold rush started.
They'd sailed from San Francisco on a tramp steamer jammed to
the gunwales with gold-seekers, following the inside channel through
the Alaska islands to Skagaway. From there it was a back-breaking
journey north to Dawson, starting with a rocky portage over the
Chilkoot Pass for which they hired Indians to assist them.

Already some of their fellow passengers were turning back, their
meager funds exhausted. After the portage of twenty-five miles,
Johnson and Ben had to hire a boat for the journey across Lake
Linderman to the headwaters of the Yukon River. Dawson was still
more than two hundred miles downriver and it wasn't a pleasant
voyage. Ben would have preferred a bucking horse to the rapids
they encountered.

It was June when they finally reached Dawson, steering the boat
between the occasional ice floes that were a reminder of the hard
winter too recently departed. They had camped along the way in
abandoned cabins or on the boat itself, seeing fewer and fewer
people the farther north they went. That was why the first sight
of Dawson itself came as something of a shock. It was a city of tents
and shacks, its population mushroomed in a year's time to nearly fifty
thousand people. Its muddy main street was lined with saloons like
the Golden Nugget, in which the prospectors ate and drank, bought
their provisions, and spent a few hours with hard-eyed sporting
ladies. Most saloons even rented rooms by the week or month.

A gold nugget – and more often gold dust – was the common currency, and there were professional gamblers like those
at the Golden Nugget to grab as much of it as they could.
What was left in the prospectors' pockets usually went for supplies, in an economy where a plate of ham and eggs could
cost $3.50.

Although dance-hall girls frequented the saloons, the Northwest
Mounted Police did their best to keep the prostitutes across the river
in an area variously called Louse Town or Paradise Alley. It was
reached by a rope bridge not far from the point where the Klondike
River branched off from the Yukon. A better bridge for wagons and
horses was a mile upriver.

Race and Ben quickly learned of two important events which
had occurred during their eight-week journey. On April 25th the
United States Congress had declared war on Spain. And of more

immediate importance, on June 13th the Yukon Territory had joined the Canadian Confederation.

It was Sam Wellman, owner of the Golden Nugget, who explained the importance of this action to them. "This place is like the end of the world, and until now we were our own law. With this Confederation business, the Mounted Police have more power. They're corralling prostitutes and even arresting some of the gamblers. Dawson will never be the same."

"Even a town at the end of the world has to have laws," Ben pointed out.

Sam Wellman was a big man who liked to make his own laws. He pointed angrily.

"I've had a poker game going in the back room ever since I opened a year ago. They gonna tell me to close it down?"

Race Johnson had his own rules as well. "Look here, Sam – if these Mounties are anything like the cops back home, a few dollars or some gold dust will have them looking the other way."

Wellman was inclined to agree. "But you get all sorts. There's a Sergeant Baxter in charge here and I haven't quite figured him out. If I offered him a little money he might take it. Or he might lock me up for attempted bribery. When I figure out which, I'll know what to do."

Sam Wellman rarely sat in on his never-ending poker game. Ben didn't, either, at first. But it soon became obvious that there was little point in accompanying Johnson to the creek every day. Dawson's diversions were limited to women, booze, and cards, and after considering those possibilities Ben started sitting in on the game.

The prospectors who gambled were mostly the newcomers, those who hadn't yet made the acquaintance of the professional cardsharps like Yancy Booth who made their living off them. Of the five men grouped around the table with Ben the first evening in early July, he had to admit Yancy was the most respectable in appearance, with a string tie and black coat that would have made a banker proud. Still, after a few days of poker with him, Ben knew him to be totally ruthless. After he wiped out a tough-looking prospector named Grogan, winning everything the man possessed and reducing him to actual tears, Ben decided he'd had enough for the night.

As he left the table, a bar girl named Tess approached him. "Want to try your luck at my place, Mister?"

"Where would that be?" Ben sat down on a bar stool.

"Across the river in Paradise Alley."

"I don't trust that bridge."

She laughed and slapped his knee. "I'll carry you across."

"Have a drink with me and I'll think about it."

"Fair enough. Give me a whiskey, Pete."

The bartender's name was Pete Waters and Ben knew he kept a shotgun behind the bar. He wondered if it had ever been used.

"Here you are," Pete said, sliding the whiskey down to Tess.

"How long you been here?" Ben asked the girl. She was prettier than some of the others, with dark hair that framed a soft, inquisitive face.

"I came up last August. It's been almost a year."

"How are the winters here?"

"Cold, but not as snowy as you'd expect. We only had about fifty inches of snow all this winter. I'm used to more than that back in the States. But you can get a frost here in late August, and they last till early June. Summer's nice – usually in the sixties like today – but it's too short."

"You like it here at the Nugget?"

She shrugged. "Sam's good to me. All the bars got their own girls and most don't like outsiders floating around. I been watching you. How come you're not out panning for gold with the rest of them?" she asked.

"I'm here with Race Johnson. You might say I'm his traveling companion," Ben explained.

That brought a short, sharp laugh from Tess. "Bodyguard, you mean. Or hired gunfighter. How's he doing?"

"He brought in a small nugget yesterday."

"He should go farther up the Klondike, toward Bonanza Creek. That's where the first gold was found two summers ago. There are lots of little cabins up there he could use."

"He might do that, but then I'd have to go with him. I prefer staying in Dawson if I can, at least for now."

She took that as an opening to renew her invitation. "Sure you don't want to come over to Paradise Alley with me? If you're gonna stay in Dawson for the winter you'll need a warm place when the temperature hits twenty below."

"That's all the persuasion I needed," Ben said.

She grinned, happy with her conquest. "You can buy a bottle of whiskey from Pete to bring along if you want."

"Sounds like a fine idea."

There was still plenty of daylight left in the long northern summer and Ben followed her across the rope bridge without difficulty. Paradise Alley was composed of a number of wooden shacks built close together.

Several young women called out to Tess as they arrived and one came to meet them.

"Tess, we're having a whiskey party for the boys on Sunday afternoon. You gonna be in on it?"

"Sure, why not? Mary, this here's Ben Snow. He's only been in Dawson a few weeks."

Mary was a plain young woman in her early twenties, running a bit to fat. "Hi, Ben. Welcome to Dawson. Is this your first visit to Paradise?"

"The first time I could face the trip across that bridge."

"Now that you know the way, come to the party on Sunday."

"I will," Ben promised.

He brought Race Johnson with him on Sunday afternoon, and they discovered that a whiskey party in Paradise Alley was something like a tea party back home. The sporting ladies were dressed in their finest duds, complete with straw hats, sailor caps, and a variety of other headgear. Tables had been arranged outside the shacks, and glasses and whiskey bottles were much in evidence. A few of the ladies held pets, little puppies or a cat, and one had a half grown Eskimo husky.

The past few days had been good ones for Johnson. He'd ended the week with a handful of gold nuggets that would bring several thousand dollars. Ben decided he'd have to stick closer to him if he meant to earn his pay. This was especially true at the Sunday whiskey party, which attracted the sort of motley crowd usually found around the poker table at the Golden Nugget. When Ben came upon Yancy Booth sipping whiskey with Tess's friend Mary he even felt compelled to ask, "Who's at the poker game this afternoon?"

Yancy gave an unamused laugh. "When I left, Pete Waters was sittin' in with that crybaby Grogan and a couple of strangers."

"Where'd Grogan get the money? I thought you wiped him out the other night."

"Who knows? He probably panned some gold dust out of the river."

Toward evening, the party started growing boisterous. Race Johnson had gone into a shack with one of the girls and Ben figured he had to stay to see him safely back to their room at the Golden Nugget.

Unfortunately, the noise attracted a pair of Mounted Police, who rode up on horseback. The older of the two wore sergeant's stripes and Ben guessed correctly that he was the Sergeant Baxter he'd been hearing about.

"You there!" the Mountie shouted, getting down from his horse and motioning to Ben. "I don't think I've seen you before – what's your name?"

"Ben Snow."

"I'm Sergeant Baxter. Where are you from?"

"The States. San Francisco, most recently."

"When did you arrive?"

"Third week in June."

The sergeant took out a notebook. "Let me have your gun."

"I – "

"Let me have it – I'm not in the habit of asking twice!"

Baxter's weathered face was one that meant business, and he had another Mountie backing him up. Ben shrugged and handed over his revolver.

The sergeant checked to see that it was fully loaded, then made a note of the serial number and Ben's name. "What's that for?" Ben asked.

"My own private gun-registration system. With this many people around, all carrying weapons, I need some way to keep the peace. This helps a little." He handed the six-shooter back. "Carrying anything else? A boot Derringer, maybe?"

"No."

"All right. Keep your nose clean, Mr. Snow, and you won't have any trouble from me."

Baxter walked away, leading his horse, no doubt seeking other unfamiliar faces.

Ben found Race Johnson just coming out of the shack. "Good party," Race commented with a grin. "A nice way to relax on a Sunday."

"I got stopped by that Mountie – Baxter."

"I heard he's been around. They patrol up the river, too. I guess no one can complain. It's a pretty open town."

Ben sometimes thought it was the lure of adventure, of open gambling and sex, that brought Johnson north as much as the promise of gold. He'd told Ben once that he came from a wealthy family. It was Ben's mention of the endless poker game at the Golden Nugget that finally drew Race in as a participant. His gold-hunting luck continued good by day, and perhaps he thought some of it would rub off on the evening game. Ben sat in with him on Tuesday and Wednesday of that week, watching him draw reasonably good cards and win a few nuggets and some cash from the other players.

On Thursday, the stakes went up with the appearance of Yancy Booth for the first time that week. No one knew exactly where he'd been since Sunday's party. Some said he'd fallen in love with one of the girls in Paradise Alley, but no one took that too seriously. In any event he was back, and his presence was immediately reflected in the amount of money riding on each pot. Race and Ben were in the game that night, along with Grogan and the bartender, Pete Waters. Tess wasn't around, but her friend Mary perched on a bar stool to watch. And even Sam Wellman came out of his office a couple of times when the table became especially noisy – or quiet – with excitement.

Race started out in a bad mood, having himself had a run-in with Sergeant Baxter. But he got over it when he was dealt three aces and won a fair-sized pot. The action continued like that for a couple of hours. Ben noticed that Yancy was losing heavily, but didn't think much of it until the man's mood started turning sour. He began slamming his hand on the table and tossing his cards haphazardly. Ben hadn't seen this side of him before, and it hardly seemed in keeping with his reputation as a professional gambler.

Once at the end of a hand, he came close to accusing Race of having cheated and Ben tensed for possible trouble. But Wellman was standing nearby and managed to quiet him.

"If one of you goes for a gun, you're both outa here – and I mean it. I'm not gonna have the Mounties close me up at the peak of the summer business."

Yancy calmed down until Grogan made the mistake of laughing gleefully when he bluffed him out with a pair of fives. The gambler's eyes hardened to slits and his hand twitched toward his coat, but then he seemed to relax and gain control of himself. That was why Ben was taken off guard a few hands later when Yancy suddenly sprang to his feet.

"That's the last time you deal yourself an ace from the bottom of the deck!" he shouted at Race, and in a flash he pulled a small Derringer from beneath his coat.

Ben moved fast, but Race was faster. His six-shooter was in his hand and firing before Ben could draw. Yancy Booth spun to one side like a dancer and went down. Mary started screaming from her bar stool and Sam Wellman ran out of his office, gun drawn.

Ben sat there feeling like a fool. He'd traveled to the end of the world as the bodyguard for a man who was a faster draw than he was.

Sam Wellman and Pete Waters quickly carried the body away, but Sergeant Baxter and another Mountie arrived on the scene and took Race into custody. Grogan and Ben were told they'd be needed as witnesses.

"That means don't try to leave town," Baxter explained. "There's noplace you can run to around here."

Wellman told Ben that Race would be held in the local jail until a traveling judge – a circuit rider – arrived the following week for the arraignment. The trial would follow soon after, and if he was found guilty Race would be sent down to the larger jail at Whitehorse to serve his sentence.

Ben visited his employer in jail the following morning. "I should have shot him, not you. That's what you were paying me for."

"Hell, don't let it worry you," Race said. "It's a clear case of self-defense. Once the judge hears the testimony, he'll toss it out of court."

"I hope so," Ben said, but he didn't feel half as confident as Race. This was a strange part of the world, and the people up here were no friends of theirs.

The day was cloudy, with a chill in the air to add to his depression. He left the jail and decided a visit to Tess might cheer him up. Crossing the rope bridge to Paradise Alley, he could see little activity among the shacks. The men had gone out to pan for gold and the women were sleeping late.

Tess heard his knocking and came to the door, wrapping a fuzzy pink robe around her. "Come on in," she said.

"Sorry to wake you up."

She yawned. "I had a late night. Want some breakfast?"

"What are you making?"

"Bacon and eggs."

"Sounds good to me."

He watched her start a fire in the wood stove. They talked about the weather, and then Tess said, "I hear Yancy got himself killed again last night."

"Again?"

Her back was to him as she started to fry the bacon and eggs in a large iron pan. "I don't know. Forget it."

"Tell me. You must have meant something by it."

"No, it's just that the same thing happened last fall, about a month after I got here. Yancy got into a fight with a guy at Sam's poker game and the guy shot him. Killed him, so the story went at the time. But it was all hushed up and the fellow who did it got spirited out of town. A couple of weeks later Yancy reappeared, good as new. He told me it had only been a flesh wound and he'd just been hiding out till things blew over."

"I never heard of a *victim* hiding out. Did you see the shooting?"

"No."

"Who did?"

"Most of them have moved on, I think. No, one's still here – that fellow Grogan. I'm pretty sure he was in on the game."

"How about Sam Wellman and Pete Waters?"

"Well, sure. I think Pete was working that night."

"Thanks," he said, getting to his feet.

"Don't you want your bacon and eggs?"

"Another time. Thanks, Tess."

He found Grogan down along a shallow part of the river, panning for gold dust in an area that must have been tried by every miner in Dawson. "How's your luck?" Ben called to the shaggy-haired man.

"Found myself a little dust. Not worth mentioning. Guess I'll have to move upriver."

"If you've got a minute, I'd like to ask you about Yancy Booth."

Grogan was immediately on guard. "What about him? He's dead. That's all I know."

"I hear tell something like this happened before. Everyone thought he was dead and he staged an amazing resurrection."

"I wouldn't know about that."

"You were there when it happened, Grogan. You saw the whole thing."

"I don't know. I got a bad memory."

"What do you owe to any of them? I saw Yancy beat you out of every cent you had in the world last week."

"That was last week."

Ben took a small nugget of gold from his pocket. It was one that Race Johnson had given him as his pay so far. "How about if I break off half of this for you? It'll get you started again and you can tell everyone you panned it out of the river."

Grogan glanced around to make sure no one was watching them. "Yeah. I could tell you about it," he agreed in a voice that was almost a whisper.

Ben picked up Grogan's small hammer and carefully placed the nugget against a rock before hitting it. The split was irregular and he gave Grogan the smaller half. The shaggy man didn't complain. "Now start talking."

"They set it up to fleece this guy who was new to Dawson. Yancy pretended to be shot and they carried him out."

"Sam Wellman was in on it?"

"I don't know. But Pete Waters was. He helped carry the body out. They got some money out of the mark and sent him on his way. Then when it was safe, Yancy turned up alive."

"If the mark shot him, how come he lived?"

Grogan shrugged.

"It was a trick of some sort. I don't know how they worked it."

"All right. Thanks."

"You won't say I told you?"

"Don't worry, Grogan."

He hadn't told Ben much more than Tess had, except for his implication of the bartender. Still, the confirmation of her story was worth the portion of the nugget he'd paid Grogan. His next stop was the jail, where he found Sergeant Baxter laboriously filling out a stack of government forms.

"The job is getting to be all paperwork," he grumbled. "What can I do for you today, Mr. Snow?"

"You have a good memory for names."

Baxter smiled. "It's my business."

"I came about the shooting of Yancy Booth."

"Yes, Race Johnson is a friend of yours, isn't he? You've been here to see him."

"I'm trying to free him."

"Don't try too hard or I'll have you in the next cell."

"I understand Yancy was shot last fall, same as this, only he didn't really die. I was thinking maybe he didn't die this time, either."

Baxter got to his feet and buttoned the collar of his red uniform jacket. "Let's go see. He's over in the icehouse."

He led Ben out the back door of the jail and across a narrow street, adjusting his hat as they went. "I've never been here," Ben said.

Sergeant Baxter unlocked the door of a building on the river bank. "They cut up ice from the river during the winter and store it here for use in the summer, just like in the big cities. I find it makes a good morgue for unclaimed bodies."

"Booth had no family?"

"None that I know of." Baxter led the way past piles of ice blocks covered with a light coating of sawdust. The temperature must have been twenty degrees cooler than outside. "If no one claims him by next week, we'll bury him in potter's field."

They stopped before a rough wooden coffin and the sergeant lifted the lid.

"Look for yourself."

It was Yancy Booth and he'd never be any deader. The naked body was partly wrapped in a winding sheet, but Ben could see the twin wounds near the heart from Race's bullets. "He's dead, all right," Ben agreed. "Are those powder burns around the wounds?"

"Not really. More a powder residue. Black powder leaves a slight residue up to about six feet away. I'd guess these shots were fired from a distance of around four feet."

"That's about right," Ben agreed. "It was a clear case of self-defense."

"The courts will rule on that."

"And Race stays in jail till they do?"

"That's right," the Mountie told him, stepping aside to let Ben precede him out of the icehouse. "I'm not in the habit of turning gunmen loose to do more shooting."

Ben left the jail without seeing Race again. His hope of discovering Yancy was still alive had been dashed. There seemed to be no hope left unless Grogan was right about the bartender's involvement. It wasn't much of a lead, but it was the only one Ben had.

He searched all afternoon for Pete Waters without finding him. Mary said she thought he'd gone prospecting with some of the others up along the Klondike River. That could mean anything. They might decide to camp out overnight or for a month.

Back at the Golden Nugget, the poker game was still in progress. It would take more than a shooting to end it. Sam Wellman was sitting in, dealing a hand of stud to three strangers. "Is Pete working tonight?" Ben asked him.

"He's supposed to, but I haven't seen him. If he doesn't show up soon, I'll have to take over myself."

It was getting dark when Ben decided to call on Tess over in Paradise Alley. There was nothing to be gained by waiting any longer for Waters.

He'd started across the rope bridge in the dusk when a voice called out behind him.

"Snow! Ben Snow!"

Ben turned and saw a shadowy figure barely visible at the end of the bridge.

"Who is it?" he called back.

"Pete Waters – I hear you been lookin' for me!"

"That's right, I have!" Ben started back toward shore, the bridge swaying a bit underfoot.

"Well, you found me – or I found you!"

There was the sudden flare and boom of a shotgun. Ben felt the rope railing come loose in his hand as the spray of buckshot parted its strands. He was drawing his gun when the second barrel discharged and he went off the bridge, still clutching the loose rope railing.

By some miracle, the rope swung him back toward shore, and when his feet hit the water he was almost to dry land. He fell forward onto the river bank, trying not to reveal his location in the darkness. Some twenty feet above him, he heard Waters break open the shotgun to reload it.

Suddenly there was a shout from the opposite shore. "Ben! Ben, are you hurt?"

He recognized Tess's voice calling out of the darkness, but he dared not reveal his position by answering her. She had seen him crossing in the dusk, seen him falling, and now she was hoping he was alive. The bridge above him hung at an awkward angle without one of its rope supports, and outlined against the night sky he saw her venture out a few feet, still calling his name.

Ben heard the shotgun snapped shut and cocked. He scrambled up on the river bank, shouting, "Go back, Tess! It's Waters and he has a shotgun!"

The bartender fired down at his voice and Ben heard the chatter of buckshot striking the rocks around him. He realized suddenly that his arm was bleeding, either from the first shot or the fall.

"Ben!" Tess yelled again.

The bartender's shotgun boomed, but this time there was the crack of a pistol at almost the same instant. Ben saw Waters stagger onto the bridge and fall, his body caught by the rope support as the shotgun slipped from his grip to splash into the river below.

"You can come up now!" Sergeant Baxter shouted down to Ben. "It's all over!"

An hour later, when Ben's flesh wounds had been tended to by Tess and Mary, he sat in Sam Wellman's office at the Golden Nugget and tried to explain what had happened. Wellman and the girls were there, along with Sergeant Baxter, who'd promised to free Race Johnson if Ben convinced him of his innocence. Ben called Grogan in from the poker game to bolster his case, and the man repeated what he'd told Ben.

"Why didn't you come forward with this before?" Sergeant Baxter wanted to know.

"Because I was afraid of Waters and Yancy. If they're both dead, they can't hurt me now."

"You claim the two of them were extorting money from prospectors by pretending Yancy was dead?"

"That's right. Yancy wore a metal pan full of sawdust under his shirt. Pete Waters doctored the bullets somehow, removing some of their powder, so when they were fired at Yancy's chest they just thudded into the sawdust. Yancy pretended to be dead and the mark got arrested. Then, when he paid Waters enough money, Yancy staged an amazing recovery."

"That's what happened last fall," Wellman admitted. "But I never connected it with this week's shooting."

"I hear they pulled the same trick in Whitehorse before they came here," Grogan said.

But Baxter shook his head.

"That doesn't change the fact that this time Yancy was really killed, and by two bullets fired into his chest by Race Johnson. You saw the body yourself, Snow."

"Yes, I did," Ben admitted. "But what I saw convinced me of Race's innocence."

"How come?"

"Remember the residue of black powder around the wounds? It was consistent with the distance between Race and Yancy at the time of the shooting, but it was all wrong for another reason. The powder residue would have been on Yancy's shirt or coat, not on his bare skin. He was shot later, after he'd removed both his shirt and the metal pan that protected him. And that means Race didn't do it."

"Wait a minute," Sergeant Baxter said, holding up his hand as everyone started talking at once. "You're saying Yancy was alive, only pretending to be shot, when Sam here and Waters carried him out?"

"Exactly. He was killed later."

"But why?"

"A falling-out among thieves, I suppose. What safer time to kill Yancy than when everyone thought he was already dead?"

"All right," Baxter agreed. "You've convinced me. If Pete Waters killed Yancy, your friend should go free. Yancy obviously incited Johnson to shoot him as part of the plot."

"Exactly," Ben said. "But I didn't say Waters killed Yancy."

"What? Then who did?"

"Someone had to tamper with the bullets in Race's gun so they wouldn't fire a full charge. Not only that, but whoever it was had to do the same with my gun. I was Race's bodyguard. When Yancy drew his gun, this person couldn't know whether Race or I would shoot first."

"You're saying Waters couldn't have tampered with your gun?"

"Yes. Only you could have done that, Sergeant, when you checked the serial number. You pretended to check the cartridges, too, but with a little sleight of hand you were actually substituting half loaded bullets that wouldn't penetrate the metal pan under Yancy's shirt. You were there when he took it off, and you're

EDWARD D. HOCH

the one who killed him, just as you killed Pete Waters later so he wouldn't talk."

Baxter was smiling as he drew his pistol. "I've heard enough from you. Want to try drawing against me?"

"Not with these bullets," Ben said.

The rest were frozen in position, watching the gun in the Mountie's hand. It was Tess who moved first. She picked up a whiskey bottle and brought it down on Baxter's head.

The next day, when Race Johnson had been released from jail, Ben suggested it was time for them to move on. "We've given our sworn statement and that should be enough. But if you stay around Dawson, someone's going to decide you should testify at Baxter's trial."

"What about the gold? There's lots more around."

"Maybe we should head over to the Alaska Territory," Ben said. "I'd just as soon stay clear of Baxter's Mountie friends. They might not like our giving them a bad name."

Race still had some questions about the set-up. "But with Yancy really dead, how could Baxter hope to shake me down for my gold?"

"Probably by offering you a chance to escape. He'd have shot you, of course, after he got your gold. I guess he figured he couldn't resurrect Yancy twice in the same town, but by killing him and then shooting Pete Waters he figured he'd removed all the potential evidence against himself. I should have suspected him sooner than I did. Naturally, he would have examined the body and seen the metal pan under Yancy's shirt. He had to be part of the scheme."

Race glanced sadly down the main street of Dawson. "I was getting to like this place. How soon do we have to leave?"

"Maybe we can stay over a day or two," Ben decided. "I did promise the girls I'd try to help them repair their bridge."

# PART IV
## Holmes and Beyond

# THE CASE OF THE DEPTFORD HORROR
## Adrian Conan Doyle

*It wasn't possible to put together a volume such as this and exclude the most famous fictional detective of all time, Sherlock Holmes. The Holmes stories by Arthur Conan Doyle are not historical detective stories in their own right, even though some of them are set several decades before their date of publication. But since Doyle's death scores of writers have turned their hand to keeping the great detective alive.*

*For this volume, I wanted to include something special, and also saw the appeal of keeping it in the family. Despite the world-wide popularity of the Holmes stories, many fans seem to have forgotten that Conan Doyle's son, Adrian, turned his hand to several sequels. Adrian Conan Doyle (1910–1970) was Doyle's youngest son. He frequently travelled with his father and became dedicated to his memory. After the Second World War Adrian arranged for John Dickson Carr to work on his father's biography. Carr and Adrian became friends and in 1952 the two determined to write up some of the missing cases, those that Watson refers to in his narratives but never published. Although they began plotting the stories together Carr fell ill and Adrian completed the series. The twelve stories were published as* The Exploits of Sherlock Holmes *(1954).*

*The following story "The Adventure of the Deptford Horror," picks up the tantalizing reference in "The Adventure of Black Peter" (1904) to the case of "Wilson the notorious canary-trainer". I also feel the story owes a little to one of the most famous Holmes adventures, "The Speckled Band".*

I have remarked elsewhere that my friend, Sherlock Holmes, like all great artists, lived for his art's sake and, save in the case of the Duke of Holderness, I have seldom known him claim any substantial reward.

However powerful or wealthy the client, he would refuse to undertake any problem that lacked appeal to his sympathies, while he would devote his most intense energies to the affairs of some humble person whose case contained those singular and remarkable qualities which struck a responsive chord in his imagination.

On glancing through my notes for that memorable year '95, I find recorded the details of a case which may be taken as a typical instance of this disinterested and even altruistic attitude of mind which placed the rendering of a kindly service above that of material reward. I refer, of course, to the dreadful affair of the canaries and the soot-marks on the ceiling.

It was early June that my friend completed his investigations into the sudden death of Cardinal Tosca, an inquiry which he had undertaken at the special request of the Pope. The case had demanded the most exacting work on Holmes's part and, as I had feared at the time, the aftermath had left him in a highly nervous and restless state that caused me some concern both as his friend and his medical adviser.

One rainy night towards the end of the same month I persuaded him to dine with me at Frascatti's, and thereafter we had gone on to the Café Royal for our coffee and liqueurs. As I had hoped, the bustle of the great room with its red plush seats and stately palms bathed in the glow of numerous crystal chandeliers drew him out of his introspective mood, and as he leaned back on our sofa, his fingers playing with the stem of his glass, I noted with satisfaction a gleam of interest in those keen grey eyes as he studied the somewhat bohemian clientele that thronged the tables and alcoves.

I was in the act of replying to some remark when Holmes nodded suddenly in the direction of the door.

"Lestrade," said he. "What can he be doing here?"

Glancing over my shoulder, I saw the lean, rat-faced figure of the Scotland Yard man standing in the entrance, his dark eyes roving slowly around the room.

"He may be seeking you," I remarked. "Probably on some urgent case."

"Hardly, Watson. His wet boots show that he has walked. If there was urgency he would have taken a cab. But here he comes."

The police agent had caught sight of us and, at Holmes's gesture, he pushed his way through the throng and drew up a chair to the table.

"Only a routine check," said he, in reply to my friend's query. "But duty's duty, Mr. Holmes, and I can tell you that I've netted some strange fish before now in these respectable places. While you are comfortably dreaming up your theories in Baker Street, we poor devils at Scotland Yard are doing the practical work. No thanks to us from popes and kings but a bad hour on the Superintendent's carpet if we fail."

"Tut," smiled Holmes good-humouredly. "Your superiors must surely hold you in some esteem since I solved the Ronald Adair murder, the Bruce-Partington theft, the – "

"Quite so, quite so," interrupted Lestrade hurriedly. "And now," he added, with a heavy wink at me, "I have something for you."

"Of course, a young woman who starts at shadows may be more in Dr. Watson's line."

"Really, Lestrade," I protested warmly, "I cannot approve your – "

"One moment, Watson. Let us hear the facts."

"Well, Mr. Holmes, they are absurd enough," continued Lestrade, "and I would not waste your time were it not that I have known you to do a kindness or two before now and your word of advice may in this instance prevent a young woman from acting foolishly. Now, here's the position.

"Down Deptford way, along the edge of the river, there are some of the worst slums in the East End of London but, right in the middle of them, you can still find some fine old houses which were once the homes of wealthy merchants centuries ago. One of these tumbledown mansions has been occupied by a family named Wilson for the past hundred years and more. I understand that they were originally in the china trade and when that went to the dogs a generation back, they got out in time and remained on in the old home. The recent household consisted of Horatio Wilson and his wife, with one son and a daughter, and Horatio's younger brother Theobold who had gone to live with them on his return from foreign parts.

"Some three years ago, the body of Horatio Wilson was hooked out of the river. He had been drowned and, as he was known to have been a hard-drinking man, it was generally accepted that he had missed his step in the fog and fallen into the water. A year later his wife, who suffered from a weak heart, died from a heart attack. We know this to be the case, because the doctor made a very careful examination following the statements of a police constable and a night watchman employed on a Thames barge."

"Statements to what effect?" interposed Holmes.

"Well, there was talk of some noise rising apparently from the old Wilson house. But the nights are often foggy along Thames-side and the men were probably misled. The constable described the sound as a dreadful yell that froze the blood in his veins. If I had him in my division, I'd teach him that such words should never pass the lips of an officer of the law."

"What time was this?"

"Ten o'clock at night, the hour of the old lady's death. It's merely a coincidence, for there is no doubt that she died of heart."

"Go on."

Lestrade consulted his notebook for a moment. "I've been digging up the facts," he continued. "On the night of May 17 last the daughter went to a magic-lantern entertainment accompanied by a woman servant. On her return she found her brother, Phineas Wilson, dead in his arm-chair. He had inherited a bad heart and insomnia from his mother. This time there were no rumours of shrieks and yells, but owing to the expression on the dead man's face the local doctor called in the police surgeon to assist in the examination. It was heart all right, and our man confirmed that this can sometimes cause a distortion of the features that will convey an impression of stark terror."

"That is perfectly true," I remarked.

"Now, it seems that the daughter Janet has become so over-wrought that, according to her uncle, she proposes to sell up the property and go abroad," went on Lestrade. "Her feelings are, I suppose, natural. Death has been busy with the Wilson family."

"And what of this uncle? Theobold, I think you said his name was."

"Well, I fancy that you will find him on your doorstep to-morrow morning. He came to me at the Yard in the hope that the official police could put his niece's fears at rest and persuade her to take a more reasonable view. As we are engaged on more important affairs than calming hysterical young women I advised him to call on you."

"Indeed! Well, it is natural enough that he should resent the unnecessary loss of what is probably a snug corner."

"There is no resentment, Mr. Holmes. Wilson seems to be genuinely attached to his niece and concerned only for her future." Lestrade paused, while a grin spread over his foxy face. "He is not a very worldly person, is Mr. Theobold, and though I've met some queer trades in my time his beats the band. The man trains canaries."

"It is an established profession."

"Is it?" There was an irrating smugness in Lestrade's manner as he rose to his feet and reached for his hat. "It is quite evident that you do not suffer from insomnia, Mr. Holmes," said he, "or you would know that birds trained by Theobold Wilson are different from other canaries. Good night, gentlemen."

"What on earth does the fellow mean?" I asked, as the police agent threaded his way towards the door.

"Merely that he knows something that we do not," replied Holmes drily. "But, as conjecture is as profitless as it is misleading to the analytical mind, let us wait until to-morrow. I can say, however, that I do not propose to waste my time over a matter that appears to fall more properly within the province of the local vicar."

To my friend's relief, the morning brought no visitor. But when, on my return from an urgent case to which I had been summoned shortly after lunch, I entered our sitting-room, I found that our spare chair was occupied by a bespectacled middle-aged man. As he rose to his feet, I observed that he was of an exceeding thinness and that his face, which was scholarly and even austere in expression, was seamed with countless wrinkles and of that dull parchment-yellow that comes from years under a tropic sun.

"Ah, Watson, you have arrived just in time," said Holmes. "This is Mr. Theobold Wilson about whom Lestrade spoke to us last night."

Our visitor wrung my hand warmly. "Your name is, of course, well known to me, Dr. Watson," he cried. "Indeed, if Mr. Sherlock Holmes will pardon me for saying so, it is largely thanks to you that we are aware of his genius. As a medical man doubtless well versed in the handling of nervous cases, your presence should have a most beneficial effect upon my unhappy niece."

Holmes caught my eye resignedly. "I have promised Mr. Wilson to accompany him to Deptford, Watson," said he, "for it would seem that the young lady is determined to leave her home to-morrow. But I must repeat again, Mr. Wilson, that I fail to see in what way my presence can affect the matter."

"You are over-modest, Mr. Holmes. When I appealed to the official police, I had hoped that they might convince Janet that, terrible though our family losses have been in the past three years, nevertheless they lay in natural causes and that there is no reason why she should flee from her home. I had the impression," he added, with a chuckle, "that the inspector was somewhat chagrined at my ready acceptance of his own suggestion that I should invoke your assistance."

"I shall certainly remember my small debt to Lestrade," replied Holmes drily as he rose to his feet. "Perhaps, Watson, you would ask Mrs. Hudson to whistle a four-wheeler and Mr. Wilson can clarify certain points to my mind as we drive to Deptford."

It was one of those grey brooding summer days when London is at its worst and, as we rattled over Blackfriars Bridge, I noted that wreaths of mist were rising from the river like the poisonous vapours of some hot jungle swamp. The more spacious streets of the

West End had given place to the great commercial thoroughfares, resounding with the stamp and clatter of the drayhorses, and these in turn merged at last into a maze of dingy streets that, following the curve of the river, grew more and more wretched in their squalor the nearer we approached to that labyrinth of tidal basins and dark evil-smelling lanes that were once the ancient cradle of England's sea-trade and of an empire's wealth. I could see that Holmes was listless and bored to a point of irritation and I did my best, therefore, to engage our companion in conversation.

"I understand that you are an expert on canaries," I remarked.

Theobold Wilson's eyes, behind their powerful spectacles, lit with the glow of the enthusiast. "A mere student, sir, but with thirty years of practical research," he cried. "Can it be that you too? No? A pity! The study, breeding and training of the Fringilla Canaria is a task worthy of a man's lifetime. You would not credit the ignorance, Dr. Watson, that prevails on this subject even in the most enlightened circles. When I read my paper on the crossing of the Madeira and the Canary Island strains to the British Ornithological Society I was appalled at the puerility of the ensuing questions."

"Inspector Lestrade hinted at some special characteristic in your training of these little songsters."

"Songsters, sir! A thrush is a songster. The Fringilla is the supreme ear of nature, possessing a unique power of imitation which can be trained for the benefit and edification of the human race. But the inspector was correct," he went on more calmly, "in that I have put my birds to a special effect. They are trained to sing by night in artificial light."

"Surely a somewhat singular pursuit."

"I like to think that it is a kindly one. My birds are trained for the benefit of those who suffer from insomnia and I have clients in all parts of the country. Their tuneful song helps to while away the long night hours and the dowsing of the lamplight terminates the concert."

"It seems to me that Lestrade was right," I observed. "Yours is indeed an unique profession."

During our conversation Holmes, who had idly picked up our companion's heavy stick, had been examining it with some attention.

"I understand that you returned to England some three years ago," he observed.

"I did."

"From Cuba, I perceive."

Theobold Wilson started and for an instant I seemed to catch a gleam of something like wariness in the swift glance that he shot at Holmes.

"That is so," he said. "But how did you know?"

"Your stick is cut from Cuban ebony. There is no mistaking that greenish tint and the exceptionally high polish."

"It might have been bought in London since my return from, say, Africa."

"No, it has been yours for some years." Holmes lifted the stick to the carriage window and tilted it so that the daylight shone upon the handle. "You will perceive," he went on, "that there is a slight but regular scraping that has worn through the polish along the left side of the handle, just where the ring finger of a left-handed man would close upon the grip. Ebony is among the toughest of woods and it would require considerable time to cause such wear and a ring of some harder metal than gold. You are left-handed, Mr. Wilson, and wear a silver ring on your middle-finger."

"Dear me, how simple. I thought for the moment that you had done something clever. As it happens, I was in the sugar trade in Cuba and brought my old stick back with me. But here we are at the house and, if you can put my silly niece's fears at rest as quickly as you can deduce my past, I shall be your debtor, Mr. Sherlock Holmes."

On descending from our four-wheeler, we found ourselves in a lane of mean slatternly houses sloping, so far as I could judge from the yellow mist that was already creeping up the lower end, to the river's edge. At one side was a high wall of crumbling brickwork pierced by an iron gate through which we caught a glimpse of a substantial mansion lying in its own garden.

"The old house has known better days," said our companion, as we followed him through the gate and up the path. "It was built in the year that Peter the Great came to live in Scales Court, whose ruined park can be seen from the upper windows."

Usually I am not unduly affected by my surroundings, but I must confess that I was aware of a feeling of depression at the melancholy spectacle that lay before us. The house, though of dignified and even imposing proportions, was faced with blotched, weather-stained plaster which had fallen away in places to disclose the ancient brickwork that lay beneath, while a tangled mass of ivy covering one wall had sent its long tendrils across the high-peaked roof to wreathe itself around the chimney stacks.

The garden was an overgrown wilderness, and the air of the whole place reeked with the damp musty smell of the river.

Theobold Wilson led us through a small hall into a comfortably furnished drawing-room. A young woman with auburn hair and a freckled face, who was sorting through some papers at a writing-desk, sprang to her feet at our entrance.

"Here are Mr. Sherlock Holmes and Dr. Watson," announced our companion. "This is my niece, Janet, whose interests you are here to protect against her own unreasonable conduct."

The young lady faced us bravely enough, though I noted a twitch and tremor of the lips that spoke of a high nervous tension. "I am leaving to-morrow, uncle," she cried, "and nothing that these gentlemen can say will alter my decision. Here, there is only sorrow and fear – above all, fear!"

"Fear of what?"

The girl passed her hand over her eyes. "I – I cannot explain. I hate the shadows and the funny little noises."

"You have inherited both money and property, Janet," said Mr. Wilson earnestly. "Will you, because of shadows, desert the roof of your fathers? Be reasonable."

"We are here only to serve you, young lady," said Holmes with some gentleness, "and to try to put your fears at rest. It is often so in life that we injure our own best interests by precipitate action."

"You will laugh at a woman's intuitions, sir."

"By no means. They are often the signposts of Providence. Understand clearly that you will go or stay as you see fit. But perhaps, as I am here, it might relieve your mind to show me over the house."

"An admirable suggestion!" cried Theobold Wilson cheerily. "Come, Janet, we will soon dispose of your shadows and noises."

In a little procession we trooped from one over-furnished room to another on the ground floor.

"I will take you to the bedrooms," said Miss Wilson as we paused at last before the staircase.

"Are there no cellars in a house of this antiquity?"

"There is one cellar, Mr. Holmes, but it is little used save for the storage of wood and some of uncle's old nest-boxes. This way, please."

It was a gloomy, stone-built chamber in which we found ourselves. A stack of wood was piled against one wall and a pot-bellied Dutch stove, its iron pipe running through the ceiling, filled the far corner. Through a glazed door reached by a line of steps and opening into the garden, a dim light filtered down upon the flagstones. Holmes sniffed the air keenly, and I was myself aware of an increased mustiness from the nearby river.

"Like most Thames-side houses, you must be plagued by rats," he remarked.

"We used to be. But, since uncle came here, he has got rid of them."

"Quite so. Dear me," he continued, peering down at the floor. "What busy little fellows!"

Following his gaze, I saw that his attention had been drawn by a few garden ants scurrying across the floor from beneath the edge of the stove and up the steps leading to the garden door. "It is as well for us, Watson," he chuckled, pointing with his stick at the tiny particles with which they were encumbered, "that we are not under the necessity of lugging along our dinners thrice our own size. It is a lesson in patience." He lapsed into silence, staring thoughtfully at the floor. "A lesson," he repeated slowly.

Mr. Wilson's thin lips tightened. "What foolery is this," he exclaimed. "The ants are there because the servants would throw garbage in the stove to save themselves the trouble of going to the dustbin."

"And so you put a lock on the lid."

"We did. If you wish, I can fetch the key. No? Then, if you are finished, let me take you to the bedrooms."

"Perhaps I may see the room where your brother died," requested Holmes as we reached the top floor.

"It is here," replied Miss Wilson, throwing open the door.

It was a large chamber furnished with some taste and even luxury and lit by two deeply recessed windows flanking another pot-bellied stove decorated with yellow tiles to harmonize with the tone of the room. A pair of birdcages hung from the stove pipe.

"Where does that side-door lead?" asked my friend.

"It communicates with my room, which was formerly used by my mother," she answered.

For a few minutes, Holmes prowled around listlessly.

"I perceive that your brother was addicted to night-reading," he remarked.

"Yes. He suffered from sleeplessness. But how – "

"Tut, the pile of the carpet on the right of the armchair is thick with traces of candlewax. But, hullo! What have we here?"

Holmes had halted near the window and was staring intently at the upper wall. Then, mounting the sill, he stretched out an arm and, touching the plaster lightly here and there, sniffed at his finger-tips. There was a puzzled frown on his face as he clambered down and commenced to circle slowly around the room, his eyes fixed upon the ceiling.

"Most singular," he muttered.

"Is anything wrong, Mr. Holmes?" faltered Miss Wilson.

"I am merely interested to account for these odd whorls and lines across the upper wall and plaster."

"It must be those dratted cockroaches dragging the dust all over the place," exclaimed Wilson apologetically. "I've told you before, Janet, that you would be better employed in supervising the servants' work. But what now, Mr. Holmes?"

My friend, who had crossed to the side-door and glanced within, now closed it again and strolled across to the window.

"My visit has been a useless one," said he, "and, as I see that the fog is rising, I fear that we must take our leave. These are, I suppose, your famous canaries?" he added, pointing to the cages above the stove.

"A mere sample. But come this way."

Wilson led us along the passage and threw open a door.

"There!" said he.

Obviously it was his own bedroom and yet unlike any bedroom that I had entered in all my professional career. From floor to ceiling it was festooned with scores of cages and the little golden-coated singers within filled the air with their sweet warbling and trilling.

"Daylight or lamplight, it's all the same to them. Here, Carrie, Carrie!" He whistled a few liquid notes which I seemed to recognize. The bird took them up into a lovely cadency of song.

"A skylark!" I cried.

"Precisely. As I said before, the Fringilla if properly trained are the supreme imitators."

"I confess that I do not recognize that song," I remarked, as one of the birds broke into a low rising whistle ending in a curious tremolo.

Mr. Wilson threw a towel over the cage. "It is the song of a tropic night-bird," he said shortly, "and, as I have the foolish pride to prefer my birds to sing the songs of the day while it is day, we will punish Peperino by putting him in darkness."

"I am surprised that you prefer an open fireplace here to a stove," observed Holmes. "There must be a considerable draught."

"I have not noticed one. Dear me, the fog is indeed increasing. I am afraid, Mr. Holmes, that you have a bad journey before you."

"Then we must be on our way."

As we descended the stairs and paused in the hall, while Theobold Wilson fetched our hats, Sherlock Holmes leaned over towards our young companion.

"I would remind you, Miss Wilson, of what I said earlier about a woman's intuition," he said quietly. "There are occasions when the truth can be sensed more easily than it can be seen. Good night."

A moment later we were feeling our way down the garden path to where the lights of our waiting four-wheeler shone dimly through the rising fog.

My companion was sunk in thought as we rumbled westward through the mean streets whose squalor was the more aggressive under the garish light of the gas-lamps that flared and whistled outside the numerous public houses. The night promised to be a bad one, and already through the yellow vapour thickening and writhing above the pavements the occasional wayfarer was nothing more than a vague hurrying shadow.

"I could have wished, my dear fellow," I remarked, "that you had been spared the need to uselessly waste your energies, which are already sufficiently depleted."

"Well, well, Watson. I fancied that the affairs of the Wilson family would prove no concern of ours. And yet – " he sank back, absorbed for a moment in his own thoughts – "and yet it is wrong, wrong, all wrong!" I heard him mutter under his breath.

"I observed nothing of a sinister nature."

"Nor I. But every danger bell in my head is jangling its warning. Why a fireplace, Watson, why a fire-place? I take it that you noticed that the pipe from the cellar connected with the stoves in the other bedrooms?"

"In one bedroom."

"No. There was the same arrangement in the adjoining room, where the mother died."

"I see nothing in this save an old-fashioned system of heating flues."

"And what of the marks on the ceiling?"

"You mean the whorls of dust."

"I mean the whorls of soot."

"Soot! Surely you are mistaken, Holmes."

"I touched them, smelt them, examined them. They were speckles and lines of wood-soot."

"Well, there is probably some perfectly natural explanation."

For a time we sat in silence. Our cab had reached the beginnings of the City and I was gazing out of the window, my fingers drumming idly on the half-lowered pane, which was already befogged with moisture, when my thoughts were recalled by a sharp ejaculation from my companion. He was staring fixedly over my shoulder.

"The glass," he muttered.

Over the clouded surface there now lay an intricate tracery of whorls and lines where my fingers had wandered aimlessly.

Holmes clapped his hand to his brow and, throwing open the other window, he shouted an order to the cabby. The vehicle turned in its tracks and, with the driver lashing at his horse, we clattered away into the thickening gloom.

"Ah, Watson, Watson, true it is that none are so blind as those who will not see!" quoted Holmes bitterly, sinking back into his corner. "All the facts were there, staring me in the face, and yet logic failed to respond."

"What facts?"

"There are nine. Four alone should have sufficed. Here is a man from Cuba, who not only trains canaries in a singular manner but knows the calls of tropical nightbirds and keeps a fireplace in his bedroom. There is devilry here, Watson. Stop, cabby, stop!"

We were passing a junction of two busy thoroughfares, with the golden balls of a pawnshop glimmering above a street lamp. Holmes sprang out. But after a few minutes he was back again and we recommenced our journey.

"It is fortunate that we are still in the City," he chuckled, "for I fancy that the East End pawnshops are unlikely to run to golf-clubs."

"Good heavens –!" I began, only to lapse into silence while I stared down at the heavy niblick which he had thrust into my hand. The first shadows of some vague and monstrous horror seemed to rise up and creep over my mind.

"We are too early," exclaimed Holmes, consulting his watch. "A sandwich and a glass of whisky at the first public house will not come amiss."

The clock on St. Nicholas Church was striking ten when we found ourselves once again in that evil-smelling garden. Through the mist, the dark gloom of the house was broken by a single feeble light in an upper window. "It is Miss Wilson's room," said Holmes. "Let us hope that this handful of gravel will rouse her without alarming the household."

An instant later, there came the sound of an opening window.

"Who is there?" demanded a tremulous voice.

"It is Sherlock Holmes," my friend called back softly. "I must speak with you at once, Miss Wilson. Is there a side-door?"

"There is one in the wall to your left. But what has happened?"

"Pray descend immediately. Not a word to your uncle."

We felt our way along the wall and reached the door just as it opened to disclose Miss Wilson. She was in her dressing-gown, her hair tumbled about her shoulders and, as her startled eyes peered at us across the light of the candle in her hand, the shadows danced and trembled on the wall behind her.

"What is it, Mr. Holmes?" she gasped.

"All will be well, if you carry out my instructions," my friend replied quietly. "Where is your uncle?"

"He is in his room."

"Good. While Dr. Watson and I occupy your room, you will move into your late brother's bedchamber. If you value your life," he added solemnly, "you will not attempt to leave it."

"You frighten me!" she whimpered.

"Rest assured that we will take care of you. And now, two final questions before you retire. Has your uncle visited you this evening?"

"Yes. He brought Peperino and put him with the other birds in the cage in my room. He said that as it was my last night at home I should have the best entertainment that he had the power to give me."

"Ha! Quite so. Your last night. Tell me, Miss Wilson, do you suffer at all from the same malady as your mother and brother?"

"A weak heart? I must confess it, yes."

"Well, we will accompany you quietly upstairs where you will retire to the adjoining room. Come, Watson."

Guided by the light of Janet Wilson's candle, we mounted silently to the floor above and thence into the bedchamber which Holmes had previously examined. While we waited for our companion to collect her things from the adjoining room, Holmes strolled across and, lifting the edge of the cloths which now covered the two birdcages, peered in at the tiny sleeping occupants.

"The evil of man is as inventive as it is immeasurable," said he, and I noticed that his face was very stern.

On Miss Wilson's return, having seen that she was safely ensconced for the night, I followed Holmes into the room which she had lately occupied. It was a small chamber but comfortably furnished and lit by a heavy silver oil-lamp. Immediately above a tiled Dutch stove there hung a cage containing three canaries which, momentarily ceasing their song, cocked their little golden heads at our approach.

"I think, Watson, that it would be as well to relax for half an hour," whispered Holmes as we sank into our chairs. "So kindly put out the light."

"But, my dear fellow, if there is any danger it would be an act of madness!" I protested.

"There is no danger in the darkness."

"Would it not be better," I said severely, "that you were frank with me? You have made it obvious that the birds are being put to some evil purpose, but what is this danger that exists only in the lamplight?"

"I have my own ideas on that matter, Watson, but it is better that we should wait and see. I would draw your attention, however, to the hinged lid of the stokehole on the top of the stove."

"It appears to be a perfectly normal fitting."

"Just so. But is there not some significance in the fact that the stokehole of an iron stove should be fitted with a tin lid?"

"Great heavens, Holmes!" I cried, as the light of understanding burst upon me. "You mean that this man Wilson has used the interconnecting pipes from the stove in the cellar to those in the bedrooms to disseminate some deadly poison to wipe out his own kith and kin and thus obtain the property. It is for that reason that he has a fireplace in his own bedroom. I see it all."

"Well, you are not far wrong, Watson, though I fancy that Master Theobold is rather more subtle than you suppose. He possesses the two qualities vital to the successful murderer – ruthlessness and imagination. But now, dowse the light like a good fellow and for a while let us relax. If my reading of the problem is correct, our nerves may be tested to their limit before we see to-morrow's dawn."

I lay back in the darkness and, drawing some comfort from the thought that ever since the affair with Colonel Sebastian Moran I had carried my revolver in my pocket, I sought in my mind for some explanation that would account for the warning contained in Holmes's words. But I must have been wearier than I had imagined. My thoughts grew more and more confused and finally I dozed off.

It was a touch upon my arm that awoke me. The lamp had been relit and my friend was bending over me, his long black shadow thrown upon the ceiling.

"Sorry to disturb you, Watson," he whispered. "But duty calls."

"What do you wish me to do?"

"Sit still and listen. Peperino is singing."

It was a vigil that I shall long remember. Holmes had tilted the lampshade, so that the light fell on the opposite wall broken by the window and the great tiled stove with its hanging birdcage. The fog had thickened and the rays from the lamp, filtering through the window glass, lost themselves in luminous clouds that swirled and boiled against the panes.

My mind darkened by a premonition of evil, I would have found our surroundings melancholy enough without that eerie sound that was rising and falling from the canary cage. It was a kind of whistling beginning with a low throaty warble and slowly ascending to a single chord that rang through the room like the note of a great wineglass, a sound so mesmeric in its repetition that almost imperceptibly the present seemed to melt away and my imagination to reach out beyond those fog-bound windows into the dark lush depth of some exotic jungle.

I had lost all count of time, and it was only the stillness following the sudden cessation of the bird's song that brought me back to reality. I glanced across the room and, in an instant, my heart gave one great throb and then seemed to stop beating altogether.

The lid of the stove was slowly rising.

My friends will agree that I am neither a nervous nor an impressionable man, but I must confess that, as I sat there gripping the sides of my chair and glaring at the dreadful thing that was gradually clambering into view, my limbs momentarily refused their functions.

The lid had tilted back an inch or more, and through the gap thus created a writhing mass of yellow stick-like objects was clawing and scrabbling for a hold. And then, in a flash, it was out and standing motionless upon the surface of the stove.

Though I have always viewed with horror the bird-eating tarantulas of South America, they shrank into insignificance when compared with the loathsome creature that faced us now across that lamplit room. It was bigger in its spread than a large dinner-plate, with a hard, smooth, yellow body surrounded by legs that, rising high above it, conveyed a fearful impression that the thing was crouching for its spring. It was absolutely hairless save for tufts of stiff bristles around the leg-joints, and above the glint of its great poison mandibles clusters of beady eyes shone in the light with a baleful red iridescence.

"Don't move, Watson," whispered Holmes, and there was a note of horror in his voice that I had never heard before.

The sound roused the creature for, in a single lightning bound, it sprang from the stove to the top of the birdcage and, reaching the wall, whizzed round the room and over the ceiling with a dreadful febrile swiftness that the eye could scarcely follow.

Holmes flung himself forward like a man possessed.

"Kill it! Smash it!" he yelled hoarsely, raining blow after blow with his golf-club at the blurred shape racing across the walls.

Dust from broken plaster choked the air, and a table crashed over as I flung myself to the ground when the great spider cleared the room in a single leap and turned at bay. Holmes bounded across me, swinging his club. "Keep where you are!" he shouted, and even as his voice rang through the room the thud ... thud ... thud of the blows was broken by a horrible squelching sound. For an instant the creature hung there, and then, slipping slowly down, it lay like a mess of smashed eggs with three thin bony legs still twitching and plucking at the floor.

"Thank God that it missed you when it sprang!" I gasped, scrambling to my feet.

He made no reply, and glancing up I caught a glimpse of his face reflected in a wall mirror. He looked pale and strained, and there was a curious rigidity in his expression.

"I am afraid it's up to you, Watson," he said quietly. "It has a mate."

I spun round to be greeted by a spectacle that I shall remember for the rest of my days. Sherlock Holmes was standing perfectly still within two feet of the stove and on top of it, reared up on its back legs, its loathsome body shuddering for the spring, stood another monstrous spider.

I knew instinctively that any sudden movement would merely precipitate the creature's leap and so, carefully drawing my revolver from my pocket, I fired point-blank.

Through the powder-smoke, I saw the thing shrink into itself and then, toppling slowly backward, it fell through the open lid of the stove. There was a rasping, slithering sound rapidly fading away into silence.

"It's fallen down the pipe," I cried, conscious that my hands were now shaking under a strong reaction. "Are you all right, Holmes?"

He looked at me and there was a singular light in his eye.

"Thanks to you, my dear fellow!" he said soberly. "If I had moved, then – but what is that?"

A door had slammed below and, in an instant later, we caught the swift patter of feet upon the gravel path.

"After him!" cried Holmes, springing for the door. "Your shot warned him that the game was up. He must not escape!"

But fate decreed otherwise. Though we rushed down the stairs and out into the fog, Theobold Wilson had too much start on us and the advantage of knowing the terrain. For a while, we followed the faint sound of his running footsteps down the empty lanes towards the river, but at length these died away in the distance.

"It is no good, Watson. We have lost our man," panted Holmes. "This is where the official police may be of use. But listen! Surely that was a cry?"

"I thought I heard something."

"Well, it is hopeless to look further in the fog. Let us return and comfort this poor girl with the assurance that her troubles are now at an end."

"They were nightmare creatures, Holmes," I exclaimed, as we retraced our steps towards the house, "and of some unknown species."

"I think not, Watson," said he. "It was the Galeodes spider, the horror of the Cuban forests. It is perhaps fortunate for the rest of the world that it is found nowhere else. The creature is nocturnal in its habits and, unless my memory belies me, it possesses the power to actually break the spine of smaller creatures with a single blow of its mandibles. You will recall that Miss Janet mentioned that the rats had vanished since her uncle's return. Doubtless Wilson brought the brutes back with him," he went on, "and then conceived the idea of training certain of his canaries to imitate the song of some Cuban night-bird upon which the Galeodes fed. The marks on the ceiling were caused, of course, by the soot adhering to the spiders' legs after they had scrambled up the flues. It is fortunate, perhaps, for the consulting detective that the duster of the average housemaid seldom strays beyond the height of a mantelpiece.

"Indeed, I can discover no excuse for my lamentable slowness in solving this case, for the facts were before me from the first and the whole affair was elementary in its construction.

"And yet, to give Theobold Wilson his dues, one must recognize his almost diabolical cleverness. Once these horrors were installed in the stove in the cellar, what more simple than to arrange two ordinary flues communicating with the bedrooms above. By hanging the cages over the stoves, the flues would themselves act as a magnifier to the bird's song and guided by their predatory instinct the creatures would invariably ascend whichever pipe led to it. Having devised some means of luring them back again to their nest, they represented a comparatively safe way of getting rid of those who stood between himself and the property."

"Then its bite is deadly?" I interposed.

"To a person in weak health, probably so. But there lies the devilish cunning of the scheme, Watson. It was the sight of the thing rather than its bite, poisonous though it may be, on which he relied to kill his victim. Can you imagine the effect upon an elderly woman, and later upon her son, both suffering from insomnia and heart disease, when in the midst of a bird's seemingly innocent song this appalling spectacle arose from the top of the stove? We have sampled it ourselves, though we are healthy men. It killed them as surely as a bullet through their hearts."

"There is one thing I cannot understand, Holmes. Why did he appeal to Scotland Yard?"

"Because he is a man of iron nerve. His niece was instinctively frightened and, finding that she was adamant in her intention of leaving, he planned to kill her at once and by the same method.

"Once done, who should dare to point the finger of suspicion at Master Theobold? Had he not appealed to Scotland Yard, and even invoked the aid of Mr. Sherlock Holmes himself to satisfy one and all? The girl had died of a heart attack like the others, and her uncle would have been the reciprocant of general condolences.

"Remember the padlocked cover of the stove in the cellar and admire the cold nerve that offered to fetch the key. It was bluff, of course, for he would have discovered that he had 'lost' it. Had we persisted and forced that lock, I prefer not to think of what we would have found clinging around our collars."

Theobold Wilson was never heard of again. But it is perhaps suggestive that, some two days later, a man's body was fished out of the Thames. The corpse was mutilated beyond recognition, probably by a ship's propeller, and the police searched his pockets in vain for means of identification. They contained nothing, however, save for a small notebook filled with jottings on the brooding period of the *Fringilla Canaria*.

"It is the wise man who keeps bees," remarked Sherlock Holmes when he read the report. "You know where you are with them and at least they do not attempt to represent themselves as something that they are not."

From *"Black Peter"* (THE RETURN OF SHERLOCK HOLMES).
  *"In the memorable year '95, a curious and incongruous succession of cases had engaged his attention ranging from . . . the sudden death of Cardinal Tosca down to the arrest of Wilson the notorious canary-trainer,\* which removed a plague-spot from the East End of London."*

---

\* *In the Wilson case, Holmes did not actually arrest Wilson, as Wilson was drowned. This was a typical Watson error in his hurried reference to the case.*

# FIVE RINGS IN RENO
# R. L. Stevens

*Stevens is one of the pen names of the prolific Edward D. Hoch whom we have
already encountered in this anthology. I could think of no better way to close
this volume than to include a story in which Conan Doyle himself features as a
detective. For that reason I made the one exception to my rule of stories being
set in the nineteenth century or earlier. The following is set in 1910, and brings
our historical detectives into the modern era.*

*In his excellent biography,* The Life of Sir Arthur Conan Doyle, *John
Dickson Carr tells us that Doyle was invited to act as referee for the
heavyweight championship fight between Jack Johnson and Jim Jeffries in
Reno, Nevada, on July 4, 1910. Doyle tentatively accepted, with great pleasure,
but changed his mind a week later and sent his regrets.*

*Now what if Doyle had gone to Reno . . .?*

Arthur Conan Doyle stepped off the train at the Reno depot looking
a bit bewildered. After traveling across an ocean and a continent to
reach the small city near the foot of the Sierra Nevada mountains,
he had at least expected someone would be there to meet him and
take his bags.

"Sir Arthur!" a voice called suddenly, and he turned to see a slim
blond young man striding toward him. "Didn't expect the train to
be on time. They never are!"

"These are my bags," Doyle said, indicating two well-traveled
Gladstones. "You would be Mr. Summons?"

"Charlie Summons, at your service, Sir Arthur."

"The title I value most is that of 'Doctor,' if you don't mind."

"Oh – certainly, Dr. Doyle! This way, please."

"Somehow I expected Reno would be larger."

Charlie Summons turned with a trace of apology. "Well, it's not
London, Sir – Dr. Doyle – but we like to think of ourselves as the
biggest little city in the west. And this fight is really goin' to put us
on the map!"

"It's certainly a lengthy journey by train," Doyle remarked. "I've written occasionally about the American west, but this is my first personal view of it. When I visited the States in '94 I never came further west than Chicago and Milwaukee."

"I read what you wrote about the Mormons of Utah in *A Study in Scarlet*. Could have sworn you'd actually been there!"

Doyle smiled at the compliment. "I read a great deal about your country before coming here."

They had reached the street outside the depot, and Summons was loading the bags into the back seat of an elegant black motorcar with polished brass trim. "This is a 1908 Packard," Summons explained. "You don't see many cars out west yet, but we have a few of 'em available for special visitors like yourself."

"It is quite a handsome vehicle," Doyle conceded, climbing up into the passenger's seat. "I suppose the motorcar is the coming thing in London too, though I do hate to see them replacing the hansom cabs."

Charlie Summons cranked the engine and then jumped in as the car coughed into life. "Times are changing, Dr. Doyle. Last month a biplane took off from a street in Washington right next to the White House."

"I'll remain on the ground, thank you," Doyle said with a smile.

"We've got you a fine room at the Reno Hotel. Everyone important is staying there. There's another writer too – Jack London. He's covering the fight for the San Francisco *Chronicle* and the New York *Herald*."

Doyle's face lit up. "I'll be interested in meeting Jack London. Some people have detected minor evidences of us in each other's stories. When I toured America last time I met Rudyard Kipling in Vermont and we became good friends."

Summons pulled the car up in front of the hotel. "Oh, oh! There's Monica Malone – that means trouble!"

Doyle found himself mildly amused by the man. "And what trouble might such a comely young woman offer?"

"She read how you helped solve that mystery in England a few years back, and she imagines you're Sherlock Holmes himself. She'll be wanting your help."

"Holmes! Is that name going to haunt me here too?"

But he climbed down from the car and went to meet the young lady. "Dr. Conan Doyle?" she asked. "I must speak with you on a most urgent matter."

"Nothing is so urgent right now as the fight that will take place in two days. I am not here in my capacity as an author – or as a doctor – but as a referee." Though he was 51 years old and only recently married to his charming second wife, Doyle still had an eye for a beautiful woman. Miss Malone's cameo face reminded him of a girl he had known long ago, during his university days.

"I realize I'm intruding on your time," she said apologetically, "but if you could only listen to my story – "

"My dear young lady, I have only just arrived in your city. I have important meetings with the principals in this prizefight, and you understand I must attend to that business first. But should you chance to be in the neighborhood early this evening, I will try to find time to speak with you."

"That's most kind," she said.

Then, before Doyle could say more, he was whisked away by Charlie Summons. "We're running a bit late, Dr. Doyle. They're waiting for us."

Summons settled him into a front room with windows overlooking South Virginia Street. The hotel was crowded with guests, and even in the halls Doyle was aware of money changing hands. Obviously the fight was attracting a great deal of betting interest.

After a half hour in which Doyle unpacked and washed up, Summons escorted him to a first-floor meeting room where a number of men were awaiting him. Doyle's first impression was that the sporting classes were much the same in America as in England. Colonel Raff Grayson, who seemed to be one of the fight's promoters, could easily have acted a role in Doyle's prizefighting drama, *The House of Temperley*, which was playing at London's Adelphi Theatre.

"So good of you to make the journey, Dr. Doyle," he said, rising to shake hands. "The problems of selecting a referee acceptable to both sides in this fight has been immense. The color question – black versus white – has raised needless tensions on all sides. Frankly, you were the only person acceptable to both managers."

Doyle bowed slightly. "I consider that a sincere compliment, especially since I know so little of American boxing."

"The rules are much the same as in your British sport," Colonel Grayson assured him. "The Marquis of Queensberry is well known here. But our main problem was finding a referee whom both sides trusted. As you know, Jeffries has come out of retirement to win back his heavyweight title from this black man, Jack Johnson. Feelings are running high, and there is even talk of race riots in some American cities."

"All seems peaceful here," Doyle observed.

"Don't be deceived. A man was knifed to death near the depot two nights ago – a reporter out here to cover the fight. His killer has not yet been found."

"I know enough about the American west," Doyle said, "to realize that the price of human life is not high out here. A wrong word spoken during a poker game, I understand, can lead to a stabbing or shooting."

Grayson exchanged glances with the other men, whom he had not yet introduced. "Come, Dr. Doyle, we feel ourselves far more civilized than that! The west of 1910 is far removed from the west of 1890."

"Perhaps," Doyle admitted. "Even passing through New York I read of a recent diamond robbery and killing. Crime is certainly not confined to the western states."

"In any event, precautions have been taken for Monday's fight. As one of the promoters I can assure you the crowd will be under complete control."

A large man of indeterminate middle age spoke up. "I was a fighter myself, Dr. Doyle. I know what it's like to stand in the center of a ring and hear the crowd shouting for blood after an unpopular decision."

The Colonel made the belated introductions. "This is Nevada Wade, Dr. Conan Doyle."

Doyle smiled. "Sounds like a cowboy's name."

"Cowboys and boxers aren't much different," Wade agreed. "I was a heavyweight contender in my fighting days, but I never had a crack at the championship."

He looked like a man who could still hold his own in the prize ring, and Doyle wondered why he had retired. From the looks of the large diamond ring on his little finger he might well have come into money. "When will I see the site of Monday's battle?" Doyle asked, shifting his attention back to the Colonel.

"We'll go out to the fairgrounds tomorrow morning. The ring and the seating are already in place, but the workmen are still adding the finishing touches." He looked up at the ornate wall clock. "Only forty-eight hours to fight time, Dr. Doyle. Less than that, really."

He made an effort to introduce the others in the room – backers and managers and promoters – but Doyle found himself quickly engaged in more conversation with Nevada Wade. "I understand there's a new Sherlock Holmes play in the Strand this summer."

Doyle nodded. "*The Speckled Band* opened last month, and it's been quite successful."

"One of my favorite stories – the one with the snake."

Americans never failed to amaze him. This man with a cowboy's name and callused fists had actually read his stories! "That is the one. We tried using a real snake on stage – nonpoisonous, of course – but it didn't work out. Now we have an ingeniously jointed dummy manipulated with black thread like a puppet. It is most effective."

"I should like to see the play sometime," Wade said.

"Perhaps we will have an American production."

Charlie Summons appeared at Doyle's side and whispered, "If you want to scram out of here, I'll help you."

"Scram – ?"

"On the weekend of a big fight this crowd'll be drinking all night. I already told the Colonel you needed to rest after your long trip out here."

"Thank you," Doyle said, and he was genuinely grateful.

He ate with Summons in the hotel restaurant, listening to the slim young man's tales of Reno's sporting life. At one point he asked, "Just what is your connection with Colonel Grayson?"

"Oh, the Colonel pays me. I run errands for him – things like that."

Doyle had earlier noticed the bulge under the other man's coat, and now he commented upon it. "Are you his bodyguard too?"

"What? Oh, you mean the gun? This is still the west, Dr. Doyle. You'll find a good many men carrying weapons."

"Interesting."

"I guess they don't carry guns in London."

"No, not in London. Not even our police-officers."

Charlie Summons took a sip of the wine Doyle had ordered with the meal. "Say, this isn't bad."

"My tastes run more to French than to California wines, I'm afraid. But as you say, it isn't bad." He was beginning to like the young man for some reason, perhaps because he was so typically American.

"You going to see Monica Malone?" Summons asked suddenly.

"Who?"

"The girl outside the hotel when you arrived."

"I'd completely forgotten about her."

"She'll prob'ly come around tonight to see you."

As Doyle was to discover within the hour, the young man's prediction proved accurate. He had barely left Summons and started up to his room when Monica Malone intercepted him. She clutched a folded newspaper in one hand, and as she spoke there were tears in her eyes. "I must see you, Dr. Doyle. You said you would talk with me."

"And I will. But I can hardly invite you up to my room.

Let us sit in that corner of the lobby where we won't be disturbed."

She followed him to a red plush sofa partly hidden by a tall fern in an ornate jardinière. "Thank you so much, Dr. Doyle. These last days have been a nightmare for me."

He sat down beside her. "I assume you are referring to the brutal murder of your fiancé near the railway station two nights ago."

"Someone has told you who I am!"

"No, not really, Miss Malone. But I noticed your agitated state, and the fact that you are carrying a copy of yesterday's newspaper folded so that an account of the killing is visible. You also wear an engagement ring, which you twist nervously with your fingers, as if you were considering removing it. The conclusion seems a likely one."

"You sound like Sherlock Holmes himself!"

"Please!" He held up a hand to silence her. "I pretend no special powers to solve this mystery. But tell me what happened."

"Tom – my fiancé, Tom Andrews – came out here last month to cover preparations for the fight. He was a reporter for *Ring & Turf*, an eastern sporting weekly. I arrived yesterday to join him and discovered he'd been murdered."

"I understand the fight has touched off some scattered violence because of the racial aspects."

"No one would have killed Tom for that reason – he was completely fair to both men! They'd more likely have stabbed Jack London – he's been wondering aloud about the Negro having a yellow streak."

"What about one of the other reporters? Had your fiancé been on bad terms with any of them?"

She shook her head, fighting back the tears, and he wanted to comfort her somehow. To give her a few moments to compose herself, he took the folded newspaper from her hand and read the brief account of the murder. There had been no witnesses, and the young reporter's wallet was found intact. So robbery could not have been the motive. The fatal stabbing near the railroad station must have had another cause.

"Could he have gone there to meet someone arriving by train?" Doyle asked.

"But who? I wasn't due until yesterday and he knew that."

"Still, a great many persons are arriving daily for the fight. He might have gone to meet one of them."

"I think he knew he might be killed, Dr. Doyle."

"Why do you say that?"

"He left a message for me at his hotel. Just a brief note – I have it here." She opened her purse and produced an envelope with a folded piece of paper inside.

Doyle read it aloud. "'*Dearest Monica: If anything should happen to me before you arrive, remember the fifth day of Christmas. All my love, Tom.*'" He studied the note with a deepening frown. "The fifth day of Christmas? What could that mean?"

"That's why I want your help, Dr. Doyle – I don't know! I tried to talk with the police about it, but they paid no attention. They're too busy keeping things calm before Monday's fight."

He continued to study the note, the only message from a man he'd never known, a man now dead. "Did you know Tom last Christmas?"

"Certainly. He gave me this ring then."

Doyle was instantly alert. "Just one ring?"

"Of course. Why do you ask?"

"In the old carol, *The Twelve Days of Christmas*, there is a line that goes, '*The fifth day of Christmas, my true love sent to me five gold rings.*'"

"Of course! We always sang that at Christmas-time! Tom was sending me a message about five gold rings. But what rings?"

"I don't know," Doyle admitted.

"Engagement rings?"

"One other possibility presents itself. This weekend in Reno the word *ring* has another meaning."

"A prizefighting ring!"

"Perhaps." He folded the note and returned it to its envelope. "He left this at the hotel for you?"

"Yes, at the desk."

"Let me keep it for a time. Something might occur to me."

"Thank you, Dr. Doyle. If you can find the person who killed Tom – "

"We won't go quite that far yet." He rose. "Please excuse me now. I have had a tiring train trip, and I am anxious to get some sleep."

"I'll look for you tomorrow."

He smiled at her. "Tomorrow I must go to the fairgrounds to inspect the scene of the action and meet the participants. But I will try to help you in any way that I can."

"Thank you, Mr. Holmes – I mean, Dr. Doyle."

He watched as she crossed the lobby to the street, and then went up to his room. Once more that confounded Sherlock Holmes had intruded on his life.

On Sunday morning he walked down to the Reno railway station using the newspaper account of the tragedy to seek out the scene of the crime. He thought that he had found it, and was bending to examine a stain on the sidewalk, when a familiar voice hailed him.

"Dr. Conan Doyle! What brings you out this early?"

It was Colonel Raff Grayson, just alighting from his motorcar. He seemed to be alone. "Good morning, Colonel. I'm just exploring a bit of your city."

"Nothing to see down at the depot. But if you'll wait while I pick up some freight I'll drive you out to the fairgrounds."

His freight proved to be a wooden cage of pheasants, which Doyle helped him carry to the back seat of the motorcar. "Will you be having a pheasant shoot after the fight?" he asked the Colonel.

"No, just a pheasant roast. These birds are only two to three pounds each, but at two servings a bird I have enough here for ten of us. I figure my wife and me, Nevada Wade and his lady, both fighters and their women, yourself, and Mr. Jack London. I hope you'll be able to join us."

"I'd be pleased," Doyle said, "though I don't know whether Mr. Johnson and Mr. Jeffries will feel up to roast pheasant after fighting fifteen rounds."

Colonel Grayson smiled. "Oh, I think Jeffries will finish the black boy much quicker than that. Just off the record, of course."

Doyle was silent, avoiding any hint of favoritism on the day before he was to referee the event. He waited until they were on the road, heading for the fairgrounds, before he spoke. "Did you know the reporter who was murdered the other night?"

Colonel Grayson turned to smile at him. "The old detective instinct getting you, Dr. Doyle? I didn't know him, but Charlie Summons had played cards with him a few times these past weeks. Charlie says he was a nice fellow."

"Who do you think stabbed him?"

"The fight is attracting a certain criminal element to Reno, Dr. Doyle. It's unfortunate but true."

The Reno fairgrounds was at the northeast edge of the city. Today, under a warm July sun, it was a beehive of activity. Motorcars and wagons were parked everywhere in a haphazard fashion, while workers climbed over the grandstand putting the finishing touches on the seats and refreshment stands.

As they approached after parking the automobile, Charlie Summons hurried forward to meet them. "You'd better come quick, Colonel! Johnson and Jeffries are both here, and I'm afraid they'll start fighting a day early!"

They found the two heavyweights at the center of a growing circle of partisan supporters. Jack Johnson, his gleaming black head catching the noonday sun, was taunting the grizzly Jim Jeffries. Johnson never lost his smile, not even when one of the crowd called out, "What about the yellow streak, Johnson?"

"I will show you tomorrow who has the yellow streak." And still smiling he turned his back on Jeffries.

Colonel Grayson quickly interrupted to introduce the fighters to Conan Doyle. Jim Jeffries shook his hand vigorously. "I been reading those Sherlock Holmes stories – he's a great one, he is!"

And Johnson was no less enthusiastic. Doyle was amazed they would welcome an Englishman so warmly to referee their fight. He was really beginning to enjoy himself for the first time since his arrival when Nevada Wade approached with a short, light-haired man in his mid-thirties. At the sight of them Jack Johnson stalked away.

"Dr. Arthur Conan Doyle, this here's a great admirer of yours – Mr. Jack London."

London shook Doyle's hand with as much vigor as Jeffries had. "A pleasure to meet you, Dr. Doyle – or Sir Arthur."

"Dr. Doyle suits me fine. I read your book *The People of the Abyss* with a great deal of interest, Mr. London."

"I wrote it while living in London for some months in 1901. My funds had run out and I actually lived with those poor East End people." London smiled. "Later I rented a room in the home of a London detective. It wasn't 221B Baker Street, though."

"I should hope not," Doyle replied with a chuckle. Summons and the Colonel went off to unload the pheasants, while Nevada Wade continued to stroll with the two authors. Doyle was anxious to see the ring itself, and to get the feel of the place. When they reached it he went up the steps and climbed between the ropes, closely followed by London.

"There is nothing quite so invigorating as the prize ring," the American said. "I've been here ten days writing up the training camps and the fight preliminaries."

Doyle bent to examine London's eye. "As a physician skilled in such matters, I could not help noticing the fading after-effects of a black eye. Have you been engaging in some fisticuffs yourself, Mr. London?"

"That happened two weeks ago, in an Oakland bar. It was in all the papers, I'm afraid. A drunken brawl, they called it."

"Was it?"

London sighed, gazing out at the empty rows of seats, and changed the subject. "My wife gave birth to a daughter on June 19th. The baby only lived three days."

"I am sorry," Doyle said.

Nevada Wade joined them in the ring, "Which of you chaps has published the most?" he asked, flashing his diamond ring.

Doyle laughed. "Oh, Mr. London is far ahead of me. How many books is it now?"

"Twenty-four," London answered almost mechanically. "Though I hardly have your fame."

"Tell me something," Doyle pursued. "In *The People of the Abyss* you showed a real compassion for the poor and downtrodden of London's East End. Yet your writings thus far about the fight have shown a decided racist slant. How do you explain this seeming contradiction?"

Jack London shrugged. "I am what I am, Dr. Doyle. And we will see tomorrow who the better fighter is."

"Jeffries can't come back," Nevada Wade said. "Once they've retired they never come back."

"We'll see." London gave a slight bow in Doyle's direction. "Until tomorrow."

Doyle watched the younger writer climb out of the ring, then turned to Wade. "An odd sort of chap – a real contradiction."

"He's had some hard times, Dr. Doyle."

"He mentioned his daughter's death."

"That's only part of it."

Doyle was reminded of the other death in recent days, and of the message Tom Andrews had left for Monica. "Tell me, Mr. Wade, is this the only prize ring brought in for the fight?"

"Brought in?" Wade didn't grasp the question.

"I mean, are there any other boxing rings in Reno?"

"Well, sure." He removed his western hat and scratched at his balding head. "The Athletic Club has one, and the Boxing Club. And right now each of the two training camps has a ring."

"Counting this one, that would make five in all."

"Well, I guess so," Nevada Wade conceded. "What about it?"

Doyle shrugged. "Now, tell me about yourself. You say you boxed professionally?"

"That was a good many years ago, but the sport was my life then."

"Why did you give it up?"

"In the west a man has to live the best way he can. Some gamblers wanted me to take a dive and when I won instead, they broke my hands. I decided it was better to be a gambler than a fighter.'

"Are you betting on tomorrow's fight?"

"Sure thing."

"Which way?"

"Like I said, Jeffries can't come back. If there's to be a Great White Hope, it isn't Jim Jeffries."

"Which side is the Colonel on?"

"The other side,". Wade answered with a dry chuckle. "He's always on the other side."

Doyle stood for a moment in the center of the ring, turning first one way, then the other, imagining himself as he would be the following day. He touched his mustache, smoothing the ends with their long waxed points. "They say Johnson is something of a clown in the ring, constantly taunting his opponent."

"He play-acts a lot, it's true," Wade agreed. "But it'll be a Jeffries crowd here tomorrow."

"It should be an interesting fight."

Doyle dined again that evening with Charlie Summons, finding himself increasingly taken with the little man. But before they'd had time to relax over coffee and cigars, Monica Malone rushed up to the table. "Dr. Doyle, I must see you! Will you be long?" I've been looking everywhere for you."

Doyle excused himself and followed her out to the hotel lobby. "What agitates you so, my dear girl?"

"I didn't want to speak in front of that man."

"Summons? He was a friend of your fiancé."

"I doubt that," she said. "But what I have to tell you is that I recognized someone Tom did know – a man named Draco. He's connected with the rackets back east. Tom wrote an exposé about him – how he doped a race horse."

"Giving him a motive for wanting to kill your fiancé. Where can I find this man?"

"I just saw him entering a bar down the block."

"Did he recognize you?"

"I don't think so. He wouldn't remember me."

Doyle made his regrets to Charlie Summons and set off down the block to the bar Monica had indicated. She pointed out a tall, dark-haired man lounging against a corner of the bar, and Doyle approached him.

"Mr. Draco, I presume?"

The face that turned to him was scarred and ugly. It was plain to see how Monica had recognized him so easily. Doyle remembered Jack London's black eye from the barroom brawl, and prayed the writer would never end up like this. "What do you want?" Draco asked.

"Just to talk. My name is Arthur Conan Doyle."

The name obviously meant nothing to the man. "You a Limey?"

"I'm from England, yes. I am over here to referee the fight tomorrow."

"Yeah?" This interested him.

"I believe you know a man named Tom Andrews."

Draco muttered an obscenity.

"He was murdered here in Reno three nights ago. Did you know that?"

"If I'd been in town I'd of done the job myself."

"But you weren't in town?"

"Just got in today. Come for the fight."

Doyle was inclined to believe the man. Besides, his statement could be easily checked. "I have been told you drug race horses. Wouldn't think of trying your skill on a prizefighter, would you?"

"Not a chance! Listen, I'll tell you about your friend Tom Andrews, in case you still think he's some sorta saint." The man stepped a bit closer, and Doyle could smell gin on his breath. "Sure, I doped a horse or two in my day. Andrews found out about it and wrote his story. But he didn't turn it in to his editor right away. Oh, no. He came to me first and showed it to me. Said he'd tear it up if I'd give him five thousand dollars."

"Interesting. What did you do?"

"Told him I wouldn't be blackmailed and kicked his butt outa my office." He smiled at the memory. "I didn't have no five grand anyhow."

"So he printed the article?"

"Damned right! Ruined my racing career."

"What are you doing now?"

"Picking up a buck any way I can."

"Do five rings mean anything to you? Five rings in Reno?"

Draco looked blank. "Not a thing."

Doyle put down money for another gin and left the man there. In the street, fighting to keep her place on the crowded sidewalk, Monica was waiting. "What did you find out?" she demanded.

"Nothing. Draco only just arrived in Reno."

"So he says!"

"Let me escort you back to your hotel, Miss Malone. The city is growing more crowded by the hour, and the streets may not be safe for a young woman."

"I can take care of myself."

"I am sure you can. But the person who killed Tom might find it very easy to knife you in a crowd. Your inquiries could be worrying him."

She paled at his words. "Perhaps you're right."

"Come along."

"I was foolish to think of you as Sherlock Holmes. There's nothing you can do for me or Tom."

"I never pretended to be Holmes," he insisted. But was it true? Five gold rings . . .

He started humming it to himself as they walked. *Seven swans a-swimming, six geese a-laying, five gold rings, four colly birds, three French hens, two turtle doves, and a partridge in a pear tree.*

Ahead of them a boy set off a string of firecrackers in the gutter. It was the eve of America's Independence Day, an odd time to be humming Christmas carols to oneself.

Five gold rings . . .

"You're right," he told her at the door of the hotel. "I'm not Holmes."

She turned to gaze into his eyes. "I only wish that you were."

The morning dawned warm and sunny. There would be a shirtsleeve crowd at the fight in a few hours. Doyle hoped the decision would be clean-cut. Any uncertainty as to the outcome could only carry over into the streets of Reno.

Charlie Summons called for him promptly at nine, escorting him out to the motorcar. "Beautiful day for it, Dr. Doyle."

"That it is, Charlie."

"The Colonel has a tent up on the fairgrounds, for his celebration dinner afterwards."

"Too bad you're not included on the guest list."

Charlie snickered. "Colonel Grayson said he might include me, if one of the fighters doesn't feel up to eating."

Though the fight was still some hours off, people were already streaming into the grandstand. Many carried picnic lunches and bottles of beverage. And the crackle of fireworks had become almost constant. "Is this how they celebrate your Fourth of July?" Doyle asked.

"You'll get used to the noise," Summons assured him.

In the striped tent set off beyond the parking lot they found Colonel Raff Grayson making last-minute preparations. "I will have chefs to prepare dinner after the main event," he told Doyle. "By that time I'm sure you'll have worked up an appetite."

Doyle nodded.

Nevada Wade came in with a young woman clinging to his arm. "The press is searching for you, Dr. Doyle. They want an interview with Sherlock Holmes!"

"I'm not – " Doyle began, then fell silent. What difference did it make? He could be Sherlock Holmes if they wanted him to be.

Outside, heading toward the press tent, he came upon Monica Malone. "Here for the fight?" he asked.

"I'm here to settle with Tom's killer."

"What?"

"One of the reporters told me Tom was on Draco's trail. He was sure Draco was heading for Reno to close some sort of crooked deal. I have a gun in this handbag, Dr. Doyle, and when I see Draco – "

"My dear, don't even talk such foolishness!" He grasped at the purse, feeling the metallic weight of it. "I'd better take that."

He slipped the small weapon out of the purse and dropped it in his pocket.

"That won't stop me," she insisted. "If you can't do anything, I will!"

The crowd was thickening around them. Spectators mingled with souvenir vendors, and at that moment Doyle's eyes were caught by a gold American eagle on the cover of an Independence Day program. "Birds," he muttered to himself.

"What did you say?" Monica asked.

"Of course! They were all birds! I remember now!"

"What are you talking about?"

The excitement welled within him. "Hurry, woman! Find some police-officers and bring them to Colonel Grayson's tent!"

Then he was on his way. The first person he saw as he burst into the tent was Draco. The ugly man turned from his task, surprised at the sudden intrusion. "You again!"

And then Colonel Grayson came forward. "Can I be of service, Dr. Doyle?"

"On the contrary, Colonel. I came to assist you in dressing those birds for dinner."

Grayson shot a glance at the table behind him. "You needn't concern yourself – "

Doyle felt the hardness of Monica Malone's gun in his pocket, and he drew it out. "Just stand there, both of you. Police-officers will be here soon enough."

"Police? For what?"

"To arrest you for murder, Colonel. You killed Tom Andrews when he tried to blackmail you."

"That's insane!"

"Is it? Andrews was killed near the railway station, because that is where he found you awaiting your delivery. Just as I found you yesterday morning. He left a message for Monica Malone, telling her to remember the fifth day of Christmas. In the old carol the fifth day's gift was five gold rings. Not wedding rings, or prize rings. I finally remembered something I read long ago. In the carol the gifts of the first seven days are all birds. The five gold rings referred to five ring-necked pheasants – like those on the table behind you. I didn't count the birds at the station yesterday, but I remembered you had enough to feed ten guests, at two servings per bird. Therefore, five birds – five ring-necked pheasants."

Grayson started to move then, but Monica lifted the tent flap and entered with the police. "What's all this?" one detective asked. "Aren't you Arthur Conan Doyle?"

Doyle handed over his weapon and picked up a carving knife instead. "If you'll cover the Colonel, we'll see what's in these five birds."

He slit them open, one after another, and carefully extracted a number of small hard objects. "Wash them off and you will find they are diamonds – no doubt from that New York robbery a few weeks back. Colonel Grayson was acting as a fence for the loot, and probably planning to resell it to Draco here. Somehow Andrews found out about Draco's involvement and tried to blackmail the Colonel. That's when he was killed. I should have known those birds were valuable. Grayson sent Charlie Summons to meet me at the station, but he went himself – and alone – to pick up a heavy cage of pheasants."

But how did you know there were jewels in the birds?" Monica asked.

Arthur Conan Doyle smiled. "The diamonds? Well, you see Sherlock Holmes once solved a case in which a carbuncle was hidden inside a Christmas goose. But come, it is almost fight time and I must be in the ring."

*Jack Johnson stopped Jim Jeffries in the fifteenth round, thus retaining the heavyweight championship of the world. And Jack London wrote, "Jeff today disposed of one question. He could not come back. Johnson, in turn, answered another question. He has not the yellow streak."*

*His article made no mention of Sir Arthur Conan Doyle.*

# AFTERWORD: OLD-TIME DETECTION
## Arthur Griffiths

*The following article appeared in the April 1902 issue of* Cassell's Magazine, *and I thought it might be of interest to readers in showing the historical development of the real-life detective. Arthur Griffiths (1838–1908), was a renowned army officer who rose to the rank of major. Noted for his discipline he entered the prison service in 1870, first as deputy-governor at Chatham and later as one of Her Majesty's Inspectors of Prisons, a post he held until 1896. He retired from the army in 1875 and turned to writing and editing in his spare time. His early novels, starting with* The Queen's Shilling (1873) *drew upon his experiences in the Crimean War, but he later turned to a series of popular detective thrillers, and a number of sensational tales of prison life, including the very popular* Criminals I Have Known (1895). *He was one of the noted experts of his day on the history and development of the police service.*

The modern detective, whether of fact or fiction, had no exact prototype in the past. The constable was an officer of the law attached to a particular locality, but except to raise the hue-and-cry, take up the criminal when he was caught, he exercised few of the functions of the police officer. A century ago there were a round dozen of Bow Street runners whose services might be engaged by private parties, but they cannot be said to have been remarkable for astuteness. The ingenious piecing together of clues, and the following up of light and baffling scent, was the work, generally, of the lawyers engaged by the parties aggrieved.

One of the earliest cases on record of this clever detection of a great fraud was the upsetting of the claim made in 1684 by a certain Lady Ivy to a large property in Shadwell. The contention was over seven acres which her ladyship, who was the widow of Sir Thomas Ivy, claimed on the strength of deeds drawn, or purporting to be drawn, in the 2 and 3 Philip and Mary, or 1555–6, and which gave her ancestors the land. The case was tried before the "famous," or rather infamous, Judge Jeffreys, and it was proved to the satisfaction of the jury that the deeds were forged. It had been discovered that the style and titles of the king and queen as they appeared in the deed were not those used by them at that date. In the preambles of Acts of Parliament in 1555–6, Philip and Mary were styled "King and Queen of Naples, princes of Spain and Sicily," not as in the deed, "King and Queen of Spain and both the Sicilies." Again, in the deed Burgundy was put before Milan as a dukedom; in the Acts of Parliament it was just the reverse. The style did in effect come in later, but the person drawing the deeds could not prophesy that, and as a fair inference it was urged that the deeds were a forgery. Other evidence was adduced to show that Lady Ivy had forged other deeds, and it was so held by Judge Jeffreys. "If you produce deeds in such a time when, say you, such titles were used, and they were not so used, that sheweth your deeds are counterfeit and forged and not true deeds. And there is *Digitus Dei*, the finger of God, in it, that though the design be deep laid and the contrivance sculk, yet truth and justice will appear at one time or other."

Accordingly, my Lady Ivy lost her verdict, and an information for forgery was laid against her, but with what result does not appear.

Fifty years later, a painstaking lawyer in Berkshire was able to unravel another case of fraud which must have eluded the imperfect police of the day. It was an artful attempt to claim restitution from a certain locality for a highway robbery which had never occurred.

Upon the 24th March, 1847, one Thomas Chandler, an attorney's clerk, was travelling on foot along the high road between London and Reading. Having passed through Maidenhead thicket and in the neighbourhood of Hare Hatch, some thirty miles out, he was set upon by three men, bargees, who robbed him of all he possessed – his watch and cash, the latter amounting to £960, all in bank-notes. After the robbery, they bound him and threw him into a pit by the side of the road. He lay there some three hours, till long after dark, being unable to obtain release from his miserable situation – although the road was much frequented, and he heard many carriages and people passing along. At length he got out of the pit unaided and, still bound hand and foot, jumped rather than walked for half a mile up hill, calling out lustily for anyone to set him loose. The first passer-by was a gentleman who gave him a wide berth; then a shepherd came and cut his bonds, and at his entreaty guided him to the constable or tything man of the Hundred of Sunning, in the County of Berks.

Here he set forth in writing the evil that had happened him, with a full and minute description of the thieves, and at the same time gave notice that he would in due course sue the Hundred for the amount under the statutes. All the formalities being observed, process was duly served on the High Constable of Sunning, and the people of the Hundred, alarmed at the demand which, if insisted upon, would be the "utter ruin of many poor families," engaged a certain attorney, Edward Wise, of Wokingham, to defend them.

Mr. Wise had all the qualities of a good detective; he was ingenious, yet patient; cleverly piecing together the facts he soon picked up about Chandler. Some of these seemed at the very outset much against him. That a man should tramp along the road with nearly £1,000 in his pocket was quite extraordinary; again, that he should not escape from the pit till after dark, and that his bonds should have been no better than tape, a length of which was found on the spot where he was untied. He seemed, moreover, to be very little concerned by his great loss after he had given the written notices to the constable, concerning which he was strangely well informed, with all the statutes at his fingers' ends as though studied beforehand, and he ordered a hot supper and a bowl at the Hare and Hounds in Hare Hatch, where he kept it up till late in the night. Nor was he in any hurry to return to town and stop payment of the notes at the banks, but started late and rode leisurely to London.

It was easy enough to trace him there. He had given his address in the notices, and was found to be the clerk of Mr. Hill, an attorney in Clifford's Inn. It now appeared that Chandler had negotiated a mortgage for a client of his master's upon certain lands in the neighbourhood of Devizes for £500, much more, as it was proved, than their value. An old mortgage was to be paid off in favour of the new, and Chandler had set off on the day stated to complete the transaction, carrying with him the £500 and the balance of £460, supposed to be his own property, but how obtained was never known. His movements on the days previous were also verified. He had dined with the mortgagee, when the deed was executed and the money handed over in notes. These notes were mostly for small sums, making up too bulky a parcel to be comfortably carried under his garters (the safest place for them, as he thought), and he had twice changed a portion – £440 at the Bank of England for two notes, and again at "Sir Richard Hoare's shop" for three notes, two of £100 and one of £200. With the whole of his money he then started to walk ninety miles in twenty-four hours, for he was expected next day at Devizes to release the mortgage.

Mr. Hill had kept a list of the notes made out in Chandler's handwriting, which Chandler got back, in order, as he said, to stop payment of them at the banks. His real object was to alter the numbers of three notes from Hoares', which he wished to cash and use, and he effected this by having a fresh list made out in which these notes were given new and false numbers. Thus the notes with the real numbers would not be stopped on presentation. He did it cleverly, changing 102 to 112, 195 to 159, 196 to 190, variations so slight as to pass unnoticed by Mr. Hill when the list (as copied) was returned to him. These three notes were cashed and eventually traced back to Chandler. Further, it was clearly proved that he had got those notes at Hoares' in exchange for the £400 note, for that note presently came back to Hoares' through a gentleman who had received it in part payment for a captain's commission of Dragoons, and it was then seen that it had been originally received from Chandler.

While Mr. Wise was engaged in these inquiries, the trial of Chandler's case against the Hundred came on at Abingdon assizes in June, and a verdict was given in his favour for £975, chiefly because Mr. Hill was associated with the mortgage, and he was held a person of good repute. But a point of law was reserved, for Chandler had omitted to give a full description of the notes as required by statute when advertising his loss.

But now Chandler disappeared. He thought the point of law would go against him, that the mortgagee would press for the return of the £500 which he had recovered from the Hundred, that his master Mr. Hill had now strong doubts of his good faith. The first proved to be the case; on argument of the point of law, the Abingdon verdict was set aside. There was good cause for his other fears. News now came of the great bulk of the other notes, which reached the Bank from Amsterdam through brokers named Solomons, who had bought them from one "John Smith," a person answering to the description of Chandler, who, in signing the receipt, "wrote his name as if it had been wrote with a skewer." The indefatigable Mr. Wise presently found that Chandler had been in Holland with a trader named Casson, and then found Casson himself.

Mr. Hill was in indirect communication with Chandler, writing letters to him by name "at Easton, in Suffolk, to be left for him at the 'Crown' at Ardley, near Colchester, in Essex." Thither Mr. Wise followed him accompanied by the mortgagee, Mr. Winter, and the "Holland trader," Mr. Casson, who was ready to identify Chandler. They reached the "Crown" at Ardley, and actually saw a letter "stuck behind the plates of the dresser" awaiting Chandler, who rode in once a fortnight from a distance, for "his mare seemed always to be very hard rid." There was nothing known of a place called Easton, but Aston and Assington were both suggested to the eastward, and in search of them Mr. Wise with his friends rode through Ipswich as far as Southwold, and there found Easton, a place washed by the sea, and "being thus pretty sure of going no further eastward." But the scent was false, and although a young man was run into, whom they proposed to arrest with the assistance of "three fellows from the Keys who appeared to be smugglers, for they were pretty much maimed and scarred," the person was clearly not Chandler. So finding "we had been running the wrong hare, we trailed very coolly all the way back to Ipswich."

Travelling homeward, they halted a night at Colchester, and called at an inn – the "Three Crowns" or the "Three Cups" – where Chandler had been seen a few months before. Here, as a fact, after over-running their game near four-score miles, "they got to the very form – yet even there lost their hare." This inn was kept at that very time by Chandler in partnership with his brother-in-law Smart, who naturally would not betray him, although he was in the house when asked for.

For this, Chandler thought Colchester "a very improper place for him to continue long in"; there were writs out against him in Essex, Suffolk, and Norfolk; so he sold off his goods and moved to another inn at Coventry, where he set up at the "Sign of the Golden Dragon" under the name of John Smith. Now still fearing arrest, he thought to buy off Winter, the mortgagee, by repaying him something, and sent him £130. But Winter was bitter against him, and writs were taken out for Warwickshire. Chandler had in some way secured the protection of Lord Willoughby de Broke; he had also made friends with the constables of Coventry, and it was not easy to compass his arrest. But at last he was taken, and lodged in the town gaol. Two years had been occupied in this pertinacious pursuit, and Mr. Wise was greatly complimented upon his zeal and presented with a handsome testimonial.

Chandler, who was supposed to have planned the whole affair with the idea of becoming possessed of a considerable sum in ready money, was found guilty of perjury, and was sentenced to be put in the pillory next market-day at Reading from twelve to one and afterwards to be transported for seven years.

A curious feature in the trial was the identification of Chandler as John Smith by Casson, who told how at Amsterdam he (Chandler) had received payment for his bills partly in silver, £150 worth of ducats and Spanish pistoles, which broke down both his pockets so that the witness had to get a rice sack and hire a wheel-barrow to convey the coin to the Delft "scout," where it was deposited in a chest and so conveyed to England.

As the years ran on, it was claimed for the officers of Bow Street that they effected many captures, and the names of such men as

Vickery, Lavender, Sayer, Donaldson, and Townshend are still remembered for their skill. None of them did better, however, than a certain Mr. Denovan, a Scotch officer of great intelligence and unwearied patience who was employed by the Paisley Union Bank to defend it against the extraordinary pretensions of a man who had robbed it and yet sued it for the restoration of property which was clearly the Bank's and not his. For the first and probably only time known in this country, an acknowledged thief was seen contending with people in open court for property he had stolen from them.

The hero of this strange episode was one Mackcoull, a hardened criminal who had entered the Royal Navy to escape arrest, had served with credit but on discharge in 1785 had relapsed, returning to evil courses, and he is said to have eclipsed all his former companions in iniquity. He was proficient in every line, had been "pugilist, horse-racer, cockfighter, gambler, swindler, and pickpocket, choosing churches as his favourite hunting-ground." His self-possession was so great that he was commonly called the "Heathen Philosopher" by his associates. Bank burglary now promised to be a more profitable business than any, and he started in it well equipped with the best implements and well-chosen confederates.

His robbery of the Paisley Union Bank in Glasgow was cleverly planned and boldly executed. He was assisted by two men, French and Huffey White – the latter a convict at the hulks whose escape Mackcoull had compassed on purpose. They broke in one Sunday night, July 14th, 1811, with keys carefully fitted long in advance, and soon ransacked the safe and drawers, securing in gold and notes something like £20,000. Of course they left Glasgow, travelling full speed in a post-chaise and four first to Edinburgh, and then *via* Edinburgh, Haddington, Newcastle, southward to London. In the division of the spoil, which now took place, Mackcoull contrived to keep the lion's share. White was apprehended, and to save his life a certain sum was surrendered to the Bank, but some of the money seems to have stuck to the fingers of a Bow Street officer, Sayer, who had negotiated between Mackcoull and the Bank. Mackcoull himself had retained about £8,000.

In 1812, after a supposed visit to the West Indies, he reappeared in London, where he was arrested for breach of faith with the Bank and sent to Glasgow for trial. He got off by a promise of further restitution, and because the Bank was unable at that time to prove his complicity in the burglary. An agent, who had handed over £1,000 on his account, was then sued by Mackcoull for acting without proper authority, and was obliged to refund a great part of the money. Nothing could exceed his effrontery. He traded openly as a bill broker for Scotland under the names of James Martin, buying the bills with the stolen notes and having sometimes as much as £2,000 on deposit in another bank. At last he was arrested, and a quantity of notes and drafts were seized with him. He was presently discharged, but they were impounded, and by-and-by he began a suit to recover "his property," the proceeds really of his theft from the Bank. His demeanour in court was most impudent. Crowds filled the court when he gave his evidence, which he did with great effrontery, posing always as an innocent and much injured man.

It was incumbent upon the Bank to end this disgraceful parody of legal proceedings; either they must prove Mackcoull's guilt or lose their action – an action brought, it must be remembered, by a public depredator against a respectable banking company for trying to keep back part of the property of which he had robbed them. In this difficulty they appealed to Mr. Denovan, and sent him to collect evidence showing that Mackcoull was implicated in the original robbery in 1811.

Denovan left Edinburgh on the 8th January, 1820, meaning to follow the exact route of the fugitives to the south. All along the road he came upon traces of them in the "post-books" or in the memory of inn-keepers, waiters, and ostlers. He passed through Dunbar, Berwick, and Belford, pausing at the latter place to hunt up a certain George Johnson, who was said to be able to identify Mackcoull. Johnson had been a waiter at the "Talbot" Inn, Darlington, in 1811, but was now gone, where, his parents (who lived in Belford) could not say. "Observing, however, that there was a church behind the inn," writes Mr. Denovan, "a thought struck me I might hear something in the churchyard on Sunday morning," and he was rewarded with the address of Thomas Johnson, a brother of George's, "a pedlar or travelling merchant." "I immediately set forth in a post-chaise and found Thomas Johnson, who gave me news of George." He was still alive, and was a waiter either at the "Bay Horse" in Leeds or somewhere in Tadcaster, or at a small inn at Spittal-on-the-Moor, in Westmoreland, but his father-in-law, Thomas Cockburn of York, would certainly know.

Pushing on, Denovan heard of his men at Alnwick. A barber there had shaved them. "I was anxious to see the barber, but found he had put an end to his existence some years, ago." At Morpeth, the inn at which they had stopped was shut up. At Newcastle, the posting-book was lost, and, when found in the bar of the "Crown and Thistle," was "so mutilated as to be useless." But at the "Queen's Head," Durham, there was an entry: "Chaise and four to Darlington – Will and Will." The second "Will" was still alive – an ancient postboy who remembered Mackoull as the oldest – a stiff, red-faced man," the usual description given of him. The landlady here, Mrs. Jane Escott, remembered three men arriving in a chaise, who said they were pushing on to London with a quantity of Scotch banknotes. At the "Talbot" Inn, Darlington, where George Johnson lived, the scent failed till Denovan at another inn, the "King's Head," ascertained that the landlord remembered three fugitives coming from Durham, and that he had observed that three such queer-looking chaps should be posting it.

At Northallerton there was evidence; that of Scotch notes changed and at York news of George Johnson, who was found at last at a fish hawker's in Tadcaster. Johnson's evidence was most valuable, and he willingly agreed to give it in court at Edinburgh. He had seen men at Dunbar, the oldest, "a stiff stout man with a red face seemed to take the management and paid the post-boys their hire." He had offered a £20 Scotch note in payment for two pints of sherry and some biscuits, but there was not change enough in the house, and White was asked for smaller money, when he took out his pocket-book stuffed full of bank-notes, all too large, so the first note was changed by Johnson at the Darlington Bank. Johnson ws sure he would know the stiff man again, amongst a hundred others, in any dress.

There was nothing more now till the "White Hart," Welwyn, where the fugitives took the light post coach. At Welwyn, too, they had sent off a portmanteau to an address, and this portmanteau was afterwards recovered with the address in Mackcoull's hand, the other two being unable to write. At Welwyn Mr. Denovan heard of one Cunington who had been a waiter at the inn in 1811, but left in 1813 for London, who was said to know something of the matter. The search for this Cunington was the next task, and Mr. Denovan pushed on to London hoping to find him there. "In company with a private friend, I went up and down Holborn, from house to house, inquiring for him at every baker's, grocer's, or public house," but heard nothing. The same at the coaching offices, until at last a guard who knew Cunington said he was in Brighton. But the man had left Brighton, first for Horsham, then for Margate, and then back to London, where Mr. Denovan ran him down at last as a patient in the Middlesex Hospital.

Cunington was quite as important a witness as Johnson. He declared he would know Mackcoull among a thousand. He had seen the three men counting over notes at the "White Hart";

Mackcoull did not seem to be a proper companion for the two; he took the lead and was the only one who used pen, ink, and paper. Cunington expressed his willingness to go to Edinburgh if his health permitted.

Since Denovan's arrival in London he had received but little assistance at Bow Street. The runners were irritated at the way the case had been managed. One of them, Sayer, who had been concerned in the restitution, flatly refused to have anything to do with the business or to go to Edinburgh to give evidence. This was presently explained by another runner, the famous Townshend, who hinted that Sayer's hands were not clean, and that he was on very friendly terms with Mackcoull's wife, a lady of very questionable character, who was living in comfort on some of her husband's ill-gotten gains. Indeed, Sayer's conduct had caused a serious quarrel between him and his colleagues, Lavender, Vickery, and Harry Adkins, because he had deceived and forestalled them. Denovan was, however, on intimate terms with Lavender, another famous runner, whom he persuaded to assist, and through him he came upon the portmanteau sent from Welwyn, which had been seized at the time of Huffey White's arrest. Huffey had been taken in the house of one Scottock, a blacksmith in the Tottenham Court Road, also the portmanteau, and a box of skeleton keys. The portmanteau contained a great many papers and notes damaging to Mackcoull, and in the box were house-breaking implements, punches, files, and various "dubs" and "skrews," as well as two handkerchiefs of fawn colour with a broad border, such as the three thieves often wore when in their lodgings in Glasgow, immediately before the robbery.

How Mr. Denovan found and won over Mr. Scottock is the chief feather in his cap. His success astonished even the oldest officers in Bow Street. Scottock was the friend and associate of burglars constantly engaged in manufacturing implements for them. He had long been a friend of Mackcoull's, and had made many tools for him, those especially for the robbery of the Paisley Union Bank, a coup prepared long beforehand. The first set of keys supplied had really been tried on the Bank locks and found useless, so that Scottock furnished others and sent them down by mail. These also were ineffective, as the Bank had "simple old-fashioned locks," and Mackcoull came back from Glasgow, bringing with him "a wooden model of the key-hole and pike of the locks," which enabled Scottock to complete the job easily. "I wonder," said Scottock to Mr. Denovan, "that the Bank could have trusted so much money under such very simple things." Scottock would not allow any of this evidence to be set down in writing, but he agreed to go down to Edinburgh and give it in Court, swearing also to receiving the portmanteau addressed in the handwriting of Mackcoull.

Denovan's greatest triumph was with Mrs. Mackcoull. She kept a house furnished in an elegant manner, but was not a very reputable person. "She was extremely shy at first, and as if by chance, but to show me she was prepared for anything, she lifted one of the cushions on her settee, displaying a pair of horse pistols that lay below," on which he produced a down-barrelled pistol and a card bearing the address "at the public office, Bow Street." Then she gave him her hand, and "we understood each other." But still she was very reticent, acting, as Mr. Denovan believed, under the advice of Sayer, her friend, the Bow Street Runner. She was afraid she would be called upon to make restitution of that part of the booty that had gone her way. Denovan strongly suspected that she had received a large sum from her husband, and had refused to give it back to him – "the real cause of their misunderstanding," which was indeed so serious that he had no great difficulty in persuading her also to give evidence at Edinburgh.

Such was the result of an inquiry that scarcely occupied a month. It was so complete that the celebrated Lord Cockburn, who was at that time counsel for the Bank, declared "nothing could exceed Denovan's skill, and that the investigation had the great merit of being amply sustained by evidence in all its important parts." When the trial of the cause came on in February, and Denovan appeared in Court with all the principal witnesses, Johnson, Cunington, Scottock, and Mr. Mackcoull, the defendant – it was only a civil suit – he was unable to conceal his emotion, and fainted away.

Next month Mackcoull was arraigned on the criminal charge, and after trial was found guilty and sentenced to death. But he cheated the gallows. Even before the verdict was given his changed demeanour was noticed in Court; he frequently muttered, ground his teeth, or looked around with a vacant stare. Afterwards he broke down utterly, and although reprieved, his mind gave way.

# Appendix
# THE CHRONICLERS
# OF CRIME
## The forerunners of
## Sherlock Holmes

The following traces the adventures of fictional detectives from 2000 BC to 1870, nearly four thousand years of detection. It's by no means exhaustive but I believe it covers the majority of novels and stories. I'd like to hear from anyone who knows of any significant omissions. I have excluded stories which are more historical crime than detection, particularly those from the Victorian period. I have also drawn the completion date at 1870, as thereafter the "modern" detective/police novel takes over, and the number of Sherlock Holmes stories would fill a book of their own.

### Ancient Egypt

Agatha Christie, *Death Comes as the End* (1941), *c*2000 BC.
As death follows death the survivors in an Egyptian family try to identify the murderer.
Elizabeth Peters, "The Locked Tomb Mystery" (1989), *c*1400 BC.
Amenhotep Sa Hapu, a venerated Egyptian sage and scholar, investigates a robbed tomb. Reprinted in this anthology.
Anton Gill, *City of the Horizon* (1991), 1361 BC.
In the days after the death of the reformist pharaoh Akhenaten, Huy the Scribe, jobless and fearing for his life, finds himself becoming the world's first private investigator. Followed by *City of Dreams* (1993) and *City of the Dead*.

## Ancient Greece

Brèni James, "Socrates Solves a Murder" (1954), *c*400 BC.
One of two short stories where Socrates uses his powers of deduction to solve two murders. The first is reprinted in this anthology. The second is "Socrates Solves Another Murder" (1955).

Theodore Mathieson, "Alexander the Great, Detective" (1959), 323 BC.
One of Mathieson's stories in *The Great Detectives* (1960) featuring famous historical characters solving crimes.

## Ancient Rome

John Maddox Roberts, *SPQR* (1990), 70 BC onwards.
First in a series featuring Decius Caecilius Metellus, a Roman official and a member of a noble Roman family, who lived through the most turbulent period of Roman history. The series continues with *The Catiline Conspiracy* (1991), *The Sacrilege* (1992) *The Temple of the Muses* (1992), and *Saturnalia*, plus the new short story, "Mightier Than the Sword", in this anthology.

Ron Burns, *Roman Nights* (1991), 43 BC onwards.
Features the young Roman senator Gaius Livinius Severus who finds himself engulfed in danger and intrigue in the turbulent days after the death of Julius Caesar. Sequel is *Roman Shadows* (1992).

Edward D. Hoch, "The Three Travelers" (1976), 4 BC.
In which the Three Wise Men on their way to the birth of the Messiah, find they have to investigate the theft of one of their precious gifts.

Anthony Price, "The Boudica Killing" (1979), AD 60.
Features the old and grizzled soldier Gaius Celer whose battle-weary knowledge allows him to resolve a murder in ancient Britain. An earlier story by Price, "A Green Boy" (1973), also features Celer but is set some years later, about AD 77.

Lindsey Davis, *The Silver Pigs* (1989), AD 70.
Set in the days after the death of Nero, this is the first of the novels about Marcus Didius Falco, who finds himself embroiled in a plot against the new emperor Vespasian. The investigation takes him to ancient Britain. The sequels are *Shadows in Bronze* (1990), *Venus in Copper* (1991) *The Iron Hand of Mars* (1992), and *Poseidon's Gold* (1993).

Barbara Hambly, *The Quirinal Hill Affair* (1983), AD 116.

What starts with a kidnap, leads young Marcus Silanus deeper and deeper into the Roman underworld. Reprinted in paperback as *Search the Seven Hills* (1987).

Wallace Nichols, "The Case of the Empress's Jewels" (1950), AD *c*174.
The first of sixty-one stories about Sollius, the Slave Detective, which ran in the *London Mystery Magazine*, concluding with "The Two Musicians" (1968). Reprinted in this anthology.

## The Dark Ages

Phyllis Ann Karr, *The Idylls of the Queen* (1982), AD *c*500.
Combines murder and fantasy in the days of King Arthur, as Sir Kay investigates the murder of Sir Patrise.

Peter Tremayne, "Murder in Repose" (1993), AD 664 onward.
The first of the stories about Sister Fidelma of which the second, "The High King's Sword" is included in this anthology.

## The Mystic East

Robert Van Gulik, *The Chinese Gold Murders* (1959), AD 663.
In reading order, the first of the stories about Judge Dee, a real-life Chinese magistrate who lived from 630–700. Van Gulik wrote fifteen other books about Judge Dee. In sequence they run, *The Lacquer Screen* (1964), *The Chinese Lake Murders* (1960), *The Haunted Monastery* (1963), *The Monkey and the Tiger* (1965), *The Chinese Bell Murders* (1958), *The Chinese Nail Murders* (1961), *The Chinese Maze Murders* (1962), *The Emperor's Pearl* (1963), *The Red Pavilion* (1964), *The Willow Pattern* (1965), *Murder in Canton* (1966), *The Phantom of the Temple* (1966), *Necklace and Calabash* (1967) and *Poets and Murder* (1968). The stories in *Judge Dee at Work* (1967) interweave throughout the novels.

Theodore Mathieson, "Omar Khayyam, Detective" (1960), *c*1100.
Another of Mathieson's stories in *The Great Detectives* (1960).

## The Middle Ages

Ellis Peters, "A Light on the Road to Woodstock" (1985), 1120.
The earliest chronological setting of the stories about Brother Cadfael, of which the second, "The Price of Light", is included

THE CHRONICLERS OF CRIME

in this volume. Cadfael's world is an England split by the civil war
between King Stephen and Queen Matilda. The novels, starting
with *A Morbid Taste for Bones* (1977), begin in the year 1137. The
series continues with *One Corpse Too Many* (1979), *Monk's-Head*
(1980), *Saint Peter's Fair* (1981), *The Leper of Saint Giles* (1981),
*The Virgin in the Ice* (1982), "The Eye Witness" (1981), *The
Sanctuary Sparrow* (1983), *The Devil's Novice* (1983), *Dead Man's
Ransom* (1984), *The Pilgrim of Hate* (1984), *An Excellent Mystery*
(1985), *The Raven in the Foregate* (1986), *The Rose Rent* (1986), *The
Hermit of Eyton Forest* (1987), *The Confession of Brother Halvin* (1988),
*The Heretic's Apprentice* (1989), *The Potter's Field* (1989), *The Summer
of the Danes* (1991) and *The Holy Thief* (1992).

P. C. Doherty, *Satan in St. Mary's* (1986), 1284.
The first of the novels featuring Hugh Corbett, a clerk to the King's
Bench in the latter part of the reign of Edward I. After this
case, in which he investigates the death of a goldsmith and
murderer found hanged inside a locked church, Corbett rises
to the position of Edward's master spy. The series continues
with *Crown in Darkness* (1988), *Spy in Chancery* (1988), *The Angel
of Death* (1989), *The Prince of Darkness* (1992) and *Murder Wears a
Cowl* (1992).

Umberto Eco, *The Name of the Rose* (1980), 1323.
A highly atmospheric, gothic novel about the investigations of
Brother William into deaths in a remote Italian monastery.

P. C. Doherty, *The Death of a King* (1985), 1344.
Follows the undercover investigations of Edmund Beche, a clerk
at the royal chancery, into the death of King Edward II.

Paul Harding, *The Nightingale Gallery* (1991), 1376.
Introduces Brother Athelstan, parish priest of St Erconwald's, in
Southwark, and assistant to Sir John Cranston, Coroner of the
City of London. The series concentrates on impossible crimes in
a disgustingly real London. Later novels are *The House of the Red
Slayer* (1992), *Murder Most Holy* (1992) and *The Anger of God* (1993).
The first Athelstan short story is included in this anthology.

Margaret Frazer, *The Novice's Tale* (1992), 1431.
Set in the priory of St. Frideswide, in Oxfordshire, during the
infancy of King Henry VI. Introduces Sister Frevisse, hosteler of
the priory who sets out to solve the bizarre death of the unwelcome
Lady Ermentrude. Later novels are *The Servant's Tale* (1993) and
*The Outlaw's Tale*. The first Sister Frevisse short story is included
in this anthology.

Mary Monica Pulver, "Father Hugh and the Deadly Scythe"
(1990), 1450s.

The first of the stories about Father Hugh, priest of Deerfield
Village in Oxfordshire. The story is reprinted in this anthology.
Sequel is "Father Hugh and the Miller's Devil" (1990).
P. C. Doherty, *The Fate of the Princes* (1990), 1483–1487.
An investigation into the death of the princes in the tower by
Francis Lovell, a close ally of Richard III. The death of the
princes is one of history's most famous mysteries. A modern-day
novel about their disappearance is *The Daughter of Time* (1951) by
Josephine Tey. One set a few years after the period, in 1536, is
*A Trail of Blood* (1970), by Jeremy Potter, where Brother Thomas
of Croyland Abbey is asked to solve the matter once and for all.
Elizabeth Eyre, *Death of a Duchess* (1991), 1490s.
Labelled "an Italian Renaissance whodunnit", it introduces
Sigismondo, a man from nowhere, who is employed by the Duke of
Rocca to find a kidnapped girl, but soon finds himself investigating
a murder. Sequels are *Curtains for the Cardinal* (1992) and *Poison for
the Prince* (1993).
Theodore Mathieson, "Leonardo da Vinci, Detective" (1959), 1516.
Another of Mathieson's stories in *The Great Detectives* (1960)
featuring famous historical characters. This one is reprinted in
this anthology. Set in the same period (1520), with the first
detective in the New World, is "Hernando Cortez, Detective"
(1959).


## The Tudors and Stuarts


Michael Clynes, *The White Rose Murders* (1991), 1517.
The first novel featuring the memoirs of Sir Roger Shallot, Justice
of the Peace, who, following the battle of Flodden, finds himself
investigating the death of a physician, poisoned in a locked and
guarded chamber in the Tower of London. The second novel is
*The Poisoned Chalice* (1992).
J. F. Peirce, "The Double Death of Nell Quigley" (1973), 1585.
The first of a series featuring the investigations of Will Shakespeare,
Detective. The stories ran in *Ellery Queen's Mystery Magazine* from
1973–5 and have not been reprinted in book form. Another story
with Shakespeare as detective is "A Sad and Bloody Hour" by
Joe Gores (1965), reprinted in this anthology.
Edward Marston, *The Queen's Head* (1988), 1588.
The Elizabethan stage is the background for this series about the
investigations of Nicholas Bracewell, agent of the troupe of players,

Lord Westfield's Men. The murder of an actor is just the start of a series of investigations following in the wake of the execution of Mary, Queen of Scots. Later novels are *The Merry Devils* (1989), *The Trip to Jerusalem* (1989), *The Nine Giants* (1991) and *The Mad Courtesan* (1992).

Theodore Mathieson, "Galileo, Detective" (1961), 1520.

Another of Mathieson's stories about the Great Detectives, but one not included in the book. In this story Galileo's unpopularity in Italy forces him to undertake his experiment of falling bodies at the Leaning Tower of Pisa. Two more falling bodies force him to turn detective.

Leonard Tourney, *The Players' Boy is Dead* (1982), 1601.

The Elizabethan stage is also the background for the first novel featuring Matthew Stock, clothier and constable in the county of Essex. Stock, a man who hates fuss and attention, soon finds himself having to solve a murder amongst a troupe of travelling players. Later novels are *Low Treason* (1983), *Familiar Spirits* (1984), *The Bartholomew Fair Murders* (1986), *Old Saxon Blood* (1988) and *Knaves Templar* (1991).

Theodore Mathieson, "Don Miguel de Cervantes, Detective" (1959), 1605.

Another of Mathieson's stories in *The Great Detectives* (1960), this one featuring the author of *Don Quixote*.

John Dickson Carr, *Devil's Kinsmere* (1934), 1670.

A narrator in 1815 tells the story of his grandfather, Roderick Kinsmere, and the murder of a man in a tavern against a wider background of court intrigue. This novel was rewritten in 1964 as *Most Secret*.

John Dickson Carr, *The Devil in Velvet* (1951), 1675.

One of Carr's novels where a person from the modern day is whisked back in time and so is able to bring twentieth-century perceptions to the thinking of the day. Despite that mechanism, this is one of Carr's best novels. A Cambridge professor goes back in time to solve a murder that is about to happen.

## The Eighteenth Century

Theodore Mathieson, "Daniel Defoe, Detective" (1959), 1719.

Another of Mathieson's stories in *The Great Detectives* (1960), this one featuring the author of *Robinson Crusoe*.

S.S. Rafferty, *Fatal Flourishes* (1979), 1730s–1770s.

A series of stories which feature Captain Cork, a businessman

and entrepreneur in the American colonies who has a fascination
for "social puzzles". The stories span a period of forty years and
travel around each of the original thirteen states. "The Christmas
Masque", from the middle period, is reprinted in this anthology.

Robert Lee Hall, *Benjamin Franklin Takes the Case* (1990), 1757.
Written as the recently discovered chronicles of Nicolas Handy
who, in 1795, set down his adventures with Benjamin Franklin
during his days in England. The sequel is *Benjamin Franklin and
a Case of Christmas Murder* (1991).

Lillian de la Torre, *Dr. Sam: Johnson, Detector* (1946), 1763–1783.
The longest-running series of historical detective stories, written
over a period of forty years. The series started with "Dr. Sam
Johnson: Detector" in *Ellery Queen's Mystery Magazine* in 1943.
More stories are collected in *The Detections of Dr. Sam: Johnson*
(1960). The story in which Johnson and Boswell first met,
"Murder Lock'd In", is included in this anthology.

Theodore Mathieson, "Captain Cook, Detective" (1958), 1770 and
"Dan'l Boone, Detective" (1960), 1777.
Two more stories from Mathieson's *The Great Detectives* (1960).

Ragan Butler, *Captain Nash and the Wroth Inheritance* (1975), 1771–1772.
Novel of Britain's first private detective, reprinted in full in
this anthology. Sequel is *Captain Nash and the Honour of England*
(1977).

Charles Sheffield, *Erasmus Magister* (1982), 1777 onwards.
A collection of three novellas featuring the fantastic investigations
of Erasmus Darwin.

David Donachie, *The Devil's Own Luck* (1991), 1792.
A nautical detective: Harry Ludlow, a privateer, tries to solve a
murder aboard ship of which his own brother stands accused. The
second novel is *The Dying Trade* (1993).

John Dickson Carr, *Fear is the Same* (1956), 1795.
Another of Carr's novels where a person from the modern day is
whisked back in time, this time to the days just after the French
revolution.

J. G. Jeffreys, *The Thieftaker* (1972), 1798.
Jeremy Sturrock of the Bow Street Runners (under whose name
the books were published in England) finds himself involved with
highway robbery in the first novel, but is soon involved in crime on
the international scene in the Napoleonic era. The first novel was
entitled *The Village of Rogues* for British publication. Later novels
are *A Wicked Way to Die* (1973), *The Wilful Lady* (1975), *A Conspiracy
of Poisons* (1977), *Suicide Most Foul* (1981), *Captain Bolton's Corpse*
(1982) and *The Pangersbourne Murders* (1983).

## The early Nineteenth Century

John Dickson Carr, *Captain Cut-Throat* (1955), 1805.

Set at the time of the Napoleonic wars. British agent Alan Hepburn gets involved in a series of murders of sentries in the French army whose bodies are left with a message signed by Captain Cut-Throat.

Melville Davisson Post, *Uncle Abner, Master of Mysteries* (1918), 1800s.

Seventeen stories, of which the first published was "Angel of the Lord" (1911), featuring the powerful deductive work of a god-fearing country squire in Virginia – the first genuinely historical detective in fiction. This book along with other previously uncollected stories was later published as *The Complete Uncle Abner* (1977). In 1979 John F. Suter began a new series of Uncle Abner stories in *Ellery Queen's Mystery Magazine* starting with "The Oldest Law". One of Post's stories is reprinted in this anthology.

John Dickson Carr, *The Bride of Newgate* (1950), 1815.

Richard Darwent, sentenced to death for a murder he did not commit, is reprieved at the last moment, and begins his hunt for the real murderer.

Richard Falkirk, *Blackstone* (1972), 1820s.

Edmund Blackstone, a Bow Street Runner, finds himself moving in exalted circles. In this first novel he has to protect the infant Princess Victoria from a threat of kidnapping. Later novels are *Blackstone on Broadway* (1972), *Blackstone's Fancy* (1973), *Beau Blackstone* (1973), and *Blackstone and the Scourge of Europe* (1974), in which he is despatched to St. Helena to investigate the security of the island-prison of Napoleon.

John Dickson Carr, *Fire, Burn!* (1957), 1829.

Detective-Inspector John Cheviot suddenly finds himself back in the year 1929 helping Robert Peel establish the police force, only to find himself accused of murder.

Michael Harrison, *The Exploits of the Chevalier Dupin* (1968), 1830s–1840s.

Starting in 1965, Michael Harrison wrote a new series of stories featuring Edgar Allan Poe's trail-breaking detective C. Auguste Dupin. The expanded British edition was published as *Murder in the Rue Royale* (1972). The title story is reprinted in this anthology, as is John Dickson Carr's "The Gentleman from Paris" (1950), which features Poe as one of the main characters.

Theodore Mathieson, "Florence Nightingale, Detective" (1960), 1854 and "Alexander Dumas, Detective" (1961), 1840s.

The first is included in Mathieson's *The Great Detectives* (1960), but the second has only appeared in magazine form.

John Dickson Carr, *The Hungry Goblin* (1972), 1869.

One of Carr's best historical novels featuring Wilkie Collins as the detective. A more recent novel featuring both Wilkie Collins and Charles Dickens as detectives is *The Detective and Mr. Dickens* by William J. Palmer (1990), set in 1851.

And there we conclude our survey. Stories set from the 1870s on become increasingly "modern", featuring either an established police force (as in the novels of Anne Perry, H. R. F. Keating, John Buxton Hilton and Julian Symons), or well-known historical characters (as in the works of Peter Lovesey and Donald Thomas), or Sherlock Holmes and his many associated characters, as in the works of Michael Harding, Glen Petrie, M. J. Trow and many more.